Bayard Taylor (January 11, 1825 – December 19, 1878) was an American poet, literary critic, translator, travel author, and diplomat. Taylor was born on January 11, 1825, in Kennett Square in Chester County, Pennsylvania. He was the fourth son, the first to survive to maturity, of the Quaker couple, Joseph and Rebecca (née Way) Taylor. His father was a wealthy farmer. Bayard received his early instruction in an academy at West Chester, Pennsylvania, and later at nearby Unionville. At the age of seventeen, he was apprenticed to a printer in West Chester. The influential critic and editor Rufus Wilmot Griswold encouraged him to write poetry. The volume that resulted, Ximena, or the Battle of the Sierra Morena, and other Poems, was published in 1844 and dedicated to Griswold. Using the money from his poetry and an advance for travel articles, he visited parts of England, France, Germany and Italy, making largely pedestrian tours for almost two years. He sent accounts of his travels to the Tribune, The Saturday Evening Post, and The United States Gazette. (Source: Wikipedia)

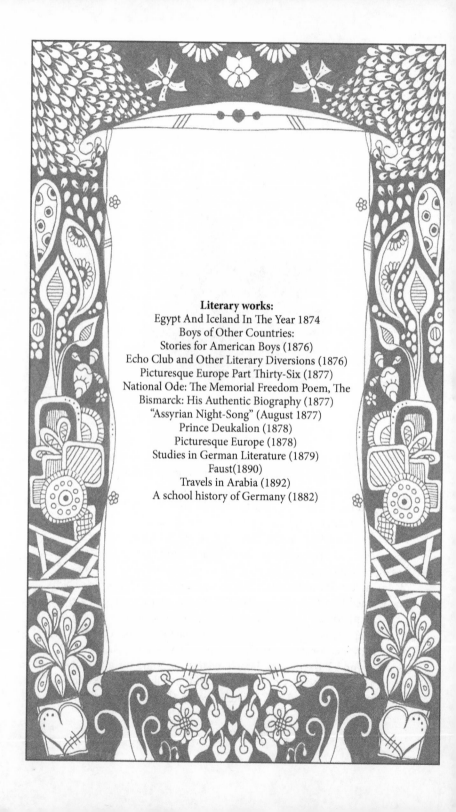

Literary works:
Egypt And Iceland In The Year 1874
Boys of Other Countries:
Stories for American Boys (1876)
Echo Club and Other Literary Diversions (1876)
Picturesque Europe Part Thirty-Six (1877)
National Ode: The Memorial Freedom Poem, The
Bismarck: His Authentic Biography (1877)
"Assyrian Night-Song" (August 1877)
Prince Deukalion (1878)
Picturesque Europe (1878)
Studies in German Literature (1879)
Faust(1890)
Travels in Arabia (1892)
A school history of Germany (1882)

THRONE CLASSICS

Northern Travel
Summer and Winter Pictures of Sweden, Denmark, and Lapland,

Views A-foot
&
Joseph and His Friend
A Story of Pennsylvania

BAYARD TAYLOR

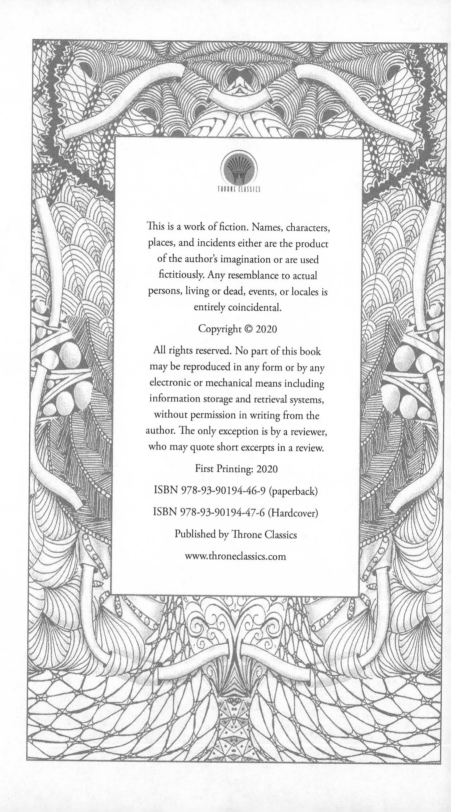

First Printing: 2020

ISBN 978-93-90194-46-9 (paperback)

ISBN 978-93-90194-47-6 (Hardcover)

Published by Throne Classics

www.throneclassics.com

Contents

Northern Travel
Summer and Winter Pictures of
Sweden, Denmark, and Lapland,

Views A-foot
&
Joseph and His Friend
A Story of Pennsylvania

NORTHERN TRAVEL: SUMMER AND WINTER PICTURES OF SWEDEN, DENMARK, AND LAPLAND

PREFACE.

This book requires no further words of introduction than those with which I have prefaced former volumes—that my object in travel is neither scientific, statistical, nor politico-economical; but simply artistic, pictorial,—if possible, panoramic. I have attempted to draw, with a hand which, I hope, has acquired a little steadiness from long practice, the people and the scenery of Northern Europe, to colour my sketches with the tints of the originals, and to invest each one with its native and characteristic atmosphere. In order to do this, I have adopted, as in other countries, a simple rule: to live, as near as possible, the life of the people among whom I travel. The history of Sweden and Norway, their forms of Government, commerce, productive industry, political condition, geology, botany, and agriculture, can be found in other works, and I have only touched upon such subjects where it was necessary to give completeness to my pictures. I have endeavoured to give photographs, instead of diagrams, or tables of figures; and desire only that the untravelled reader, who is interested in the countries I visit, may find that he is able to see them by the aid of my eyes.

BAYARD TAYLOR.

London: November, 1857.

CHAPTER I. A WINTER VOYAGE ON THE BALTIC.

We went on board the little iron Swedish propeller, Carl Johan, at Lübeck, on the morning of December 1, A.D. 1856, having previously taken our passage for Stockholm. What was our dismay, after climbing over hills of freight on deck, and creeping down a narrow companion-way, to find the cabin stowed full of bales of wool and barrels of butter. There was a little pantry adjoining it, with a friendly stewardess therein, who, in answer to my inquiries, assured us that we would probably be placed in a hut. After further search, I found the captain, who was superintending the loading of more freight, and who also stated that he would put us into a hut. "Let me see the hut, then," I demanded, and we were a little relieved when we found it to be a state-room, containing two of the narrowest of bunks. There was another hut opposite, occupied by two more passengers, all that the steamer could carry and all we had, except a short deck-passenger, who disappeared at the commencement of the voyage, and was not seen again until its close.

The day was clear and cold, the low hills around Lübeck were covered with snow, and the Trave was already frozen over. We left at noon, slowly breaking our way down the narrow and winding river, which gradually widened and became clearer of ice as we approached the Baltic. When we reached Travemünde it was snowing fast, and a murky chaos beyond the sandy bar concealed the Baltic. The town is a long row of houses fronting the water. There were few inhabitants to be seen, for the bathing guests had long since flown, and all watering places have a funereal air after the season is over. Our fellow-passenger, a jovial Pole, insisted on going ashore to drink a last glass of Bavarian beer before leaving Germany; but the beverage had been so rarely called for that it had grown sharp and sour, and we hurried back unsatisfied.

A space about six feet square had been cleared out among the butter-kegs in the cabin, and we sat down to dinner by candle-light, at three o'clock. Swedish customs already appeared, in a preliminary decanter of lemon-colored brandy, a thimbleful of which was taken with a piece of bread and sausage, before the soup appeared. The taste of the liquor was sweet, unctuous and not agreeable. Our party consisted of the captain, the chief officer, who was his brother-in-law, the Pole, who was a second-cousin of Kosciusko, and had a name consisting of eight consonants and two vowels, a grave young Swede with a fresh Norse complexion, and our two selves. The steward, Hildebrand, and the silent stewardess, Marie, were our attendants and purveyors. The ship's officers were rather slow and opaque, and the Swede sublimely self-possessed and indifferent; but the Pole, who had been condemned to death at Cracow, and afterwards invented cheap gas, was one of the jolliest fellows alive. His German was full of funny mistakes, but he rattled away with as much assurance as if it had been his native tongue. Before dinner was over, we were all perfectly well acquainted with each other.

Night had already set in on the Baltic; nothing was to be seen but snow; the deck was heaped with freight; the storm blew in our teeth; and the steamer, deeply laden, moved slowly and labouriously; so we stretched ourselves on the narrow bunks in our hut, and preserved a delicate regard for our equilibrium, even in sleep. In the morning the steep cliffs of Möen, a Danish island, were visible on our left. We looked for Rügen, the last stronghold of the worship of Odin in the Middle Ages, but a raw mist rolled down upon the sea, and left us advancing blindly as before. The wind was strong and cold, blowing the vapory water-smoke in long trails across the surface of the waves. It was not long, however, before some dim white gleams through the mist were pointed out as the shores of Sweden, and the Carl Johan slackened her speed to a snail's pace, snuffing at headland after headland, like a dog off the scent, in order to find her way into Ystad.

A lift of the fog favored us at last, and we ran into the little harbor. I walked the contracted hurricane deck at three o'clock, with the sunset already flushing the west, looked on the town and land, and thought of my friend Dr. Kane. The mercury had fallen to 16°, a foot of snow covered the house-roofs, the low, undulating hills all wore the same monotonous no-color, and the yellow-haired people on the pier were buttoned up close, mittened and fur-capped. The captain telegraphed to Calmar, our next port, and received an answer that the sound was full of ice and the harbor frozen up. A custom-house officer, who took supper with us on board, informed us of the loss of the steam-ship Umeå, which was cut through by the ice near Sundsvall, and sunk, drowning fifteen persons—a pleasant prospect for our further voyage—and the Pole would have willingly landed at Ystad if he could have found a conveyance to get beyond it. We had twelve tons of coal to take on board, and the work proceeded so slowly that we caught another snow-storm so thick and blinding that we dared not venture out of the harbor.

On the third morning, nevertheless, we were again at sea, having passed Bornholm, and were heading for the southern end of the Island of Oland. About noon, as we were sitting huddled around the cabin stove, the steamer suddenly stopped. There was a hurried movement of feet overhead—a cry—and we rushed on deck. One of the sailors was in the act of throwing overboard a life buoy. "It is the Pole!" was our first exclamation. "No, no," said Hildebrand, with a distressed face, "it is the cabin-boy"—a sprightly, handsome fellow of fourteen. There he was struggling in the icy water, looking toward the steamer, which was every moment more distant. Two men were in the little boat, which had just been run down from the davits, but it seemed an eternity until their oars were shipped, and they pulled away on their errand of life or death. We urged the mate to put the steamer about, but he passively refused. The boy still swam, but the boat was not yet half-way, and headed too much to the left. There was no tiller, and the men could only guess at their course. We guided them by signs, watching the boy's head, now a mere speck, seen at intervals under the lowering sky. He struggled gallantly; the boat drew nearer, and one of the men stood up and looked around. We watched with breathless suspense for the reappearance of the brave young swimmer, but we watched in vain. Poor boy! who can know what was the agony of those ten minutes, while the icy waves gradually benumbed and dragged down the young life that struggled with such desperate energy to keep its place in the world! The men sat down and rowed back, bringing only his cap, which they had found floating on the sea. "Ah!" said Hildebrand, with tears in his eyes, "I did not want to take him this voyage, but his mother begged me so hard that I could not refuse, and this is the end!"

We had a melancholy party in the cabin that afternoon. The painful impression made by this catastrophe was heightened by the knowledge that it might have been prevented. The steamer amidships was filled up to her rail with coal, and the boy was thrown overboard by a sudden lurch while walking upon it. Immediately afterwards, lines were rove along the stanchions, to prevent the same thing happening again. The few feet of deck upon which we could walk were slippery with ice, and we kept below, smoking gloomily and saying little. Another violent snow-storm came on from the north, but in the afternoon we caught sight of some rocks off Carlscrona, and made the light on Oland in the evening. The wind had been blowing so freshly that our captain suspected Calmar Sound might be clear, and determined to try the passage. We felt our way slowly through the intricate sandbanks, in the midst of fog and snow, until after midnight, when only six miles from Calmar, we were stopped by fields of drift ice, and had to put back again.

The fourth morning dawned cold and splendidly clear. When I went on deck we were rounding the southern point of Oland, through long belts of floating ice. The low chalk cliffs were covered with snow, and looked bleak and desolate enough. The wind now came out of the west, enabling us to carry the foresail, so that we made eight or nine knots, in spite of our overloaded condition. Braisted and I walked the deck all day, enjoying the keen wind and clear, faint sunshine of the North. In the afternoon, however, it blew half a gale, with flurries of mingled rain and snow. The sea rose, and the steamer, lumbered as she was, could not be steered on her course, but had to be "conned," to keep off the strain. The hatches were closed, and an occasional sea broke over the bows. We sat below in the dark huts; the Pole, leaning against the bulkhead, silently awaiting his fate, as he afterwards confessed. I had faith enough in the timidity of our captain, not to feel the least alarm—and, true enough, two hours had not elapsed before we lay-to under the lee of the northern end of Oland. The Pole then sat down, bathed from head to foot in a cold sweat, and would have landed immediately, had it been possible. The Swede was as inexpressive as ever, with the same half-smile on his fair, serious face.

I was glad to find that our captain did not intend to lose the wind, but would start again in an hour or two. We had a quieter night than could have been anticipated, followed by a brilliant morning. Such good progress had been made that at sunrise the lighthouse on the rocks of Landsort was visible, and the jagged masses of that archipelago of cloven isles which extends all the way to Torneå, began to stud the sea. The water became smoother as we ran into the sound between Landsort and the outer isles. A long line of bleak, black rocks, crusted with snow, stretched before us. Beside the lighthouse, at their southern extremity, there were two red frame-houses, and a telegraph station. A boat, manned by eight hardy sailors, came off with a pilot, who informed us that Stockholm was closed with ice, and that the other steamers had been obliged to stop at the little port of Dalarö, thirty miles distant. So for Dalarö we headed, threading the channels of the scattering islands, which gradually became higher and more picturesque, with clumps of dark fir crowning their snowy slopes. The midday sun hung low on the horizon, throwing a pale yellow light over the wild northern scenery; but there was life in the cold air, and I did not ask for summer.

We passed the deserted fortress of Dalarö, a square stone structure, which has long since outlived its purpose, on the summit of a rock in the sound. Behind it, opened a quiet bay, held in a projecting arm of the mainland, near the extremity of which appeared our port—a village of about fifty houses, scattered along the abrupt shore. The dark-red buildings stood out distinctly against the white background; two steamers and half a dozen sailing crafts were moored below them; about as many individuals were moving quietly about, and for all the life and animation we could see, we might have been in Kamtchatka.

As our voyage terminated here, our first business was to find means of getting to Stockholm by land. Our fellow-passengers proposed that we should join company, and engage five horses and three sleds for ourselves and luggage. The Swede willingly undertook to negotiate for us, and set about the work with his usual impassive semi-cheerfulness. The landlord of the only inn in the place promised to have everything ready by six o'clock the next morning, and our captain, who was to go on the same evening, took notices of our wants, to be served at the two intervening post-stations on the road. We then visited the custom-house, a cabin about ten feet square, and asked to have our luggage examined. "No," answered the official, "we have no authority to examine anything; you must wait until we send to Stockholm." This was at least a new experience. We were greatly vexed and annoyed, but at length, by dint of explanations and entreaties, prevailed upon the man to attempt an examination. Our trunks were brought ashore, and if ever a man did his duty conscientiously, it was this same Swedish official. Every article was taken out and separately inspected, with an honest patience which I could not but admire. Nothing was found contraband, however; we had the pleasure of repacking, and were then pulled back to the Carl Johan in a profuse sweat, despite the intense cold.

CHAPTER II. STOCKHOLM.—PREPARATIONS FOR THE NORTH.

On the following morning we arose at five, went ashore in the darkness, and after waiting an hour, succeeded in getting our teams together. The horses were small, but spirited, the sleds rudely put together, but strong, and not uncomfortable, and the drivers, peasants of the neighborhood, patient, and good-humoured. Climbing the steep bank, we were out of the village in two minutes, crossed an open common, and entered the forests of fir and pine. The sleighing was superb, and our little nags carried us merrily along, at the usual travelling rate of one Swedish mile (nearly seven English) per hour. Enveloped from head to foot in our fur robes, we did not feel the sharp air, and in comparing our sensations, decided that the temperature was about 20°. What was our surprise, on reaching the post-station, at learning that it was actually 2° below zero!

Slowly, almost imperceptibly, the darkness decreased, but the morning was cloudy, and there was little appearance of daybreak before nine o'clock. In the early twilight we were startled by the appearance of a ball of meteoric fire, nearly as large as the moon, and of a soft white lustre, which moved in a horizontal line from east to west, and disappeared without a sound. I was charmed by the forest scenery through which we passed. The pine, spruce, and fir trees, of the greatest variety of form, were completely coated with frozen snow, and stood as immovable as forests of bronze incrusted with silver. The delicate twigs of the weeping birch resembled sprays of crystal, of a thousand airy and exquisite patterns. There was no wind, except in the open glades between the woods, where the frozen lakes spread out like meadow intervals. As we approached the first station there were signs of cultivation—fields inclosed with stake fences, low red houses, low barns, and scanty patches of garden land. We occasionally met peasants with their sleds—hardy, red-faced fellows, and women solid enough to outweigh their bulk in pig-iron.

The post-station was a cottage in the little hamlet of Berga. We drove into the yard, and while sleds and horses were being changed, partook of some boiled milk and tough rye-bread, the only things to be had, but both good of their kind. The travellers' room was carpeted and comfortable, and the people seemed poor only because of their few wants. Our new sleds were worse than the former, and so were our horses, but we came to the second station in time, and found we must make still another arrangement. The luggage was sent ahead on a large sled, while each pair of us, seated in a one horse cutter, followed after it, driving ourselves. Swedish horses are stopped by a whistle, and encouraged by a smacking of the lips, which I found impossible to learn at once, and they considerately gave us no whips. We had now a broad, beaten road, and the many teams we met and passed gave evidence of our approach to Stockholm. The country, too, gently undulating all the way, was more thickly settled, and appeared to be under tolerable cultivation.

About one in the afternoon, we climbed a rising slope, and from its brow looked down upon Stockholm. The sky was dark-gray and lowering; the hills were covered with snow, and the roofs of the city resembled a multitude of tents, out of which rose half a dozen dark spires. On either side were arms of the Mälar Lake—white, frozen plains. Snow was already in the air, and presently we looked through a screen of heavy flakes on the dark, weird, wintry picture. The impression was perfect of its kind, and I shall not soon forget it.

We had passed through the southern suburb, and were descending to the lake, when one of our shafts snapped off. Resigning the cutter to the charge of a stout maiden, who acted as postillion, Braisted and I climbed upon the luggage, and in this wise, shaggy with snowy fur, passed through the city, before the House of Nobles and the King's Palace, and over the Northern Bridge, and around the northern suburb, and I know not where else, to the great astonishment of everybody we met, until our stupid driver found out where he was to go. Then we took leave of the Pole, who had engaged horses to Norrköping, and looked utterly disconsolate at parting; but the grave Swede showed his kind heart at last, for—neglecting his home, from which he had been absent seven years—he accompanied us to an hotel, engaged rooms, and saw us safely housed.

We remained in Stockholm a week, engaged in making preparations for our journey to the North. During this time we were very comfortably quartered in Kahn's Hotel, the only one in the capital where one can get both rooms and meals. The weather changed so entirely, as completely to destroy our first impressions, and make the North, which we were seeking, once more as distant as when we left Germany. The day after our arrival a thaw set in, which cleared away every particle of snow and ice, opened the harbor, freed the Mälar Lake, and gave the white hills around the city their autumnal colors of brown and dark-green. A dense fog obscured the brief daylight, the air was close, damp, and oppressive, everybody coughed and snuffled, and the air-tight rooms, so comfortable in cold weather, became insufferable. My blood stagnated, my spirits descended as the mercury rose, and I grew all impatience to have zero and a beaten snow-track again.

We had more difficulty in preparing for this journey than I anticipated—not so much in the way of procuring the necessary articles, as the necessary information on the subject. I was not able to find a man who had made the journey in winter, or who could tell me what to expect, and what to do. The mention of my plan excited very general surprise, but the people were too polished and courteous to say outright that I was a fool, though I don't doubt that many of them thought so. Even the maps are only minute enough for the traveller as far as Torneå, and the only special maps of Lapland I could get dated from 1803. The Government, it is true, has commenced the publication of a very admirable map of the kingdom, in provinces, but these do not as yet extend beyond Jemteland, about Lat. 63° north. Neither is there any work to be had, except some botanical and geological publications, which of course contain but little practical information. The English and German Handbooks for Sweden are next to useless, north of Stockholm. The principal assurances were, that we should suffer greatly from cold, that we should take along a supply of provisions, for nothing was to be had, and that we must expect to endure hardships and privations of all kinds. This prospect was not at all alarming, for I remembered that I had heard much worse accounts of Ethiopia while making similar preparations in Cairo, and have learned that all such bugbears cease to exist when they are boldly faced.

Our outfit, therefore, was restricted to some coffee, sugar, salt, gunpowder, lucifer-matches, lead, shot and slugs, four bottles of cognac for cases of extremity, a sword, a butcher-knife, hammer, screw-driver, nails, rope and twine, all contained in a box about eighteen inches square. A single valise held our stock of clothing, books, writing and drawing materials, and each of us carried, in addition, a double-barrelled musket. We made negotiations for the purchase of a handsome Norrland sleigh (numbers of which come to Stockholm, at this season, laden with wild-fowl), but the thaw prevented our making a bargain. The preparation of the requisite funds, however, was a work of some time. In this I was assisted by Mr. Moström, an excellent valet-de-place, whom I hereby recommend to all travellers. When, after three or four days' labour and diplomacy, he brought me the money, I thought I had suddenly come in possession of an immense fortune. There were hundreds of bank-notes, and thousands of silver pieces of all sizes—Swedish paper, silver and copper, Norwegian notes and dollars, Danish marks, and Russian gold, roubles and copecks. The value belied the quantity, and the vast pile melted away so fast that I was soon relieved of my pleasant delusion.

Our equipment should have been made in Germany, for, singularly enough, Stockholm is not half so well provided with furs and articles of winter clothing as Hamburg or Leipsic. Besides, everything is about fifty per cent dearer here. We were already provided with ample fur robes, I with one of gray bear-skin, and Braisted with yellow fox. To these we added caps of sea-otter, mittens of dog-skin, lined with the fur of the Arctic hare, knitted devil's caps, woollen sashes of great length for winding around the body, and, after long search, leather Russian boots lined with sheepskin and reaching half-way up the thigh. When rigged out in this costume, my diameter was about equal to half my height, and I found locomotion rather cumbrous; while Braisted, whose stature is some seven inches shorter, waddled along like an animated cotton-bale.

Everything being at last arranged, so far as our limited information made it possible, for a two months' journey, we engaged places in a diligence which runs as far as Gefle, 120 miles north of Stockholm. There we hoped to find snow and a colder climate. One of my first steps had been to engage a Swedish teacher, and by dint of taking double lessons every day, I flattered myself that I had made sufficient progress in the language to travel without an interpreter—the most inconvenient and expensive of persons. To be sure, a week is very little for a new language, but to one who speaks English and German, Swedish is already half acquired.

CHAPTER III. FIRST EXPERIENCES OF NORTHERN TRAVEL.

The diligence was a compact little vehicle, carrying four persons, but we two were so burdened with our guns, sword, money-bag, field-glass, over-boots and two-fathom-long sashes, that we found the space allotted to us small enough. We started at eight o'clock, and had not gone a hundred yards before we discovered that the most important part of our outfit—the maps—had been left behind. It was too late to return, and we were obliged to content ourselves with the hope of supplying them at Upsala or Gefle.

We rolled by twilight through the Northern suburb. The morning was sharp and cold, and the roads, which had been muddy and cut up the day before, were frozen terribly hard and rough. Our fellow-passengers were two Swedes, an unprepossessing young fellow who spoke a few words of English, and a silent old gentleman; we did not derive much advantage from their society, and I busied myself with observing the country through which we passed. A mile or two, past handsome country-seats and some cemeteries, brought us into the region of forests. The pines were tall and picturesque in their forms, and the grassy meadows between them, entirely clear of snow, were wonderfully green for the season. During the first stage we passed some inlets of the Baltic, highly picturesque with their irregular wooded shores. They had all been frozen over during the night. We were surprised to see, on a southern hill-side, four peasants at work ploughing. How they got their shares through the frozen sod, unless the soil was remarkably dry and sandy, was more than I could imagine. We noticed occasionally a large manor-house, with its dependent out-buildings, and its avenue of clipped beeches or lindens, looking grand and luxurious in the midst of the cold dark fields. Here and there were patches of wheat, which the early snow had kept green, and the grass in the damp hollows was still bright, yet it was the 15th of December, and we were almost in lat. 60° N.

The houses were mostly one-story wooden cottages, of a dull red color, with red roofs. In connection with the black-green of the pine and fir woods they gave the country a singularly sombre aspect. There was little variation in the scenery all the way to Upsala. In some places, the soil appeared to be rich and under good cultivation; here the red villages were more frequent, and squat church-towers showed themselves in the distance. In other places, we had but the rough hills, or rather knobs of gray gneiss, whose masses were covered with yellow moss, and the straggling fir forests. We met but few country teams on the road; nobody was to be seen about the houses, and the land seemed to be asleep or desolated. Even at noon, when the sun came out fairly, he was low on the horizon, and gave but an eclipsed light, which was more cheerless than complete darkness.

The sun set about three o'clock, but we had a long, splendid twilight, a flush of orange, rose and amber-green, worthy of a Mediterranean heaven. Two hours afterwards, the lights of Upsala appeared, and we drove under the imposing front of the old palace, through clean streets, over the Upsala River, and finally stopped at the door of a courtyard. Here we were instantly hailed by some young fellows, who inquired if we did not want rooms. The place did not appear to be an inn, but as the silent old gentleman got out and went in, I judged it best to follow his example, and the diligence drove off with our baggage. We were right, after all: a rosy, handsome, good-humored landlady appeared, promised to furnish us with beds and a supper, to wake us betimes, and give us coffee before leaving.

The old gentleman kindly put on his coat and accompanied us to a bookstore on the public square, where I found Akrell's map of Northern Sweden, and thus partially replaced our loss. He sat awhile in our room trying to converse, but I made little headway. On learning that we were bound for Torneå, he asked: "Are you going to buy lumber?" "No," I answered; "we are merely going to see the country." He laughed long and heartily at such an absurd idea, got up in a hurry, and went to bed without saying another word. We had a supper of various kinds of sausage, tough rye bread, and a bowl of milk, followed by excellent beds—a thing which you are sure to find everywhere in Sweden.

We drove off again at half-past six in the morning moon light, with a temperature of zero. Two or three miles from the town we passed the mounds of old Upsala, the graves of Odin, Thor and Freja, rising boldly against the first glimmerings of daylight. The landscape was broad, dark and silent, the woods and fields confusedly blended together, and only the sepulchres of the ancient gods broke the level line of the horizon. I could readily have believed in them at that hour.

Passing over the broad rich plain of Upsala, we entered a gently undulating country, richer and better cultivated than the district we had traversed the previous day. It was splendidly wooded with thick fir forests, floored with bright green moss. Some of the views toward the north and west were really fine from their extent, though seen in the faded light and long shadows of the low northern sun. In the afternoon, we passed a large white church, with four little towers at the corners, standing in the midst of a village of low red stables, in which the country people shelter their horses while attending service. There must have been fifty or sixty of these buildings, arranged in regular streets. In most of the Swedish country churches, the belfry stands apart, a squat, square tower, painted red, with a black upper story, and is sometimes larger than the church itself. The houses of the peasants are veritable western shanties, except in color and compactness. No wind finds a cranny to enter, and the roofs of thick thatch, kept down by long, horizontal poles, have an air of warmth and comfort. The stables are banked with earth up to the hay-loft, and the cattle enter their subterranean stalls through sloping doorways like those of the Egyptian tombs.

Notwithstanding we made good progress through the day, it was dark long before we reached the bridge over the Dal Elv, and of the famous cascades we saw only a sloping white glimmer, between dark masses of forest, and heard the noise of the broken waters. At Elfkarleby we were allowed twenty minutes for dinner—boiled salmon and beefsteak, both bad. I slept after this, until aroused by the old Swede, as we entered Gefle. We drove across a broad bridge, looked over vessels frozen into the inlet of the Gulf, passed a large public square, and entered the yard of the diligence office. A boy in waiting conducted us to a private house, where furnished rooms were to be had, and here we obtained tea, comfortable beds, and the attendance of a rosy servant-girl, who spoke intelligible Swedish.

My first care the next morning, was to engage horses and send off my förbud papers. We were now to travel by "skjuts" (pronounced shoos), or post, taking new horses at each station on the road. The förbud tickets are simply orders for horses to be ready at an appointed time, and are sent in advance to all the stations on the road, either by mail or by a special messenger. Without this precaution, I was told, we might be subjected to considerable delay. This mode of travelling is peculiar to Sweden and Norway. It has been in existence for three or four centuries, and though gradually improved and systematized with the lapse of time, it is still sufficiently complex and inconvenient to a traveller coming from the railroad world.

Professor Retzius had referred me to the botanist Hartman, in case of need, but I determined to commence by helping myself. I had a little difficulty at first: the people are unused to speaking with foreigners, and if you ask them to talk slowly, they invariably rattle away twice as fast as before. I went into a variety shop on the public square, and asked where I could engage horses for Sundsvall. After making myself understood, as I supposed, the clerk handed me some new bridles. By dint of blundering, I gradually circumscribed the range of my inquiries, and finally came to a focus at the right place. Having ordered horses at six the next morning, and despatched the förbud tickets by the afternoon's mail, I felt that I had made a good beginning, and we set out to make the tour of Gefle.

This is a town of eight or ten thousand inhabitants, with a considerable shipping interest, and a naval school. It is a pretty place, well built, and with a neat, substantial air. The houses are mostly two stories high, white, and with spacious courts in the rear. The country around is low but rolling, and finely clothed with dark forests of fir and pine. It was a superb day—gloriously clear, with a south wind, bracing, and not too cold, and a soft, pale lustre from the cloudless sun. But such a day! Sunrise melting into sunset without a noon—a long morning twilight, a low, slant sun, shining on the housetops for an hour or so, and the evening twilight at three in the afternoon. Nothing seemed real in this strange, dying light—nothing but my ignorance of Swedish, whenever I tried to talk.

In the afternoon, we called on the Magister Hartman, whom we found poring over his plants. He spoke English tolerably, and having made a journey through Lapland from Torneå to the Lyngen Fjord, was able to give us some information about the country. He encouraged us in the belief that we should find the journey more rapid and easy in winter than in summer. He said the Swedes feared the North and few of them ever made a winter journey thither, but nothing could stop the Americans and the English from going anywhere. He also comforted us with the assurance that we should find snow only six Swedish (forty English) miles further north. Lat. 60° 35' N., the 17th of December, and no snow yet! In the streets, we met an organ-grinder playing the Marseillaise. There was no mistaking the jet-black hair, the golden complexion and the brilliant eyes of the player, "Siete Italiano?" I asked. "Sicuro!" he answered, joyously: "e lei anche?" "Ah," he said, in answer to my questions, "io non amo questo paese; è freddo ed oscuro; non si gagna niente—ma in Italia si vive." My friend Ziegler had already assured me: "One should see the North, but not after the South." Well, we shall see; but I confess that twenty degrees below zero would have chilled me less than the sight of that Italian.

We were at the inn punctually at six in the morning, but our horses were not ready. The hållkarl, or ostler, after hearing my remonstrances, went on splitting wood, and, as I did not know enough of Swedish to scold with any profit, I was obliged to remain wrathful and silent. He insisted on my writing something (I could not understand what) in the post-book, so I copied the affidavit of a preceding traveller and signed my name to it, which seemed to answer the purpose. After more than half an hour, two rough two-wheeled carts were gotten ready, and the farmers to whom they belonged, packed themselves and our luggage into one, leaving us to drive the other. We mounted, rolled ourselves in our furs, thrust our feet into the hay, and rattled out of Gefle in the frosty moonlight. Such was our first experience of travelling by skjuts.

The road went northward, into dark forests, over the same undulating, yet monotonous country as before. The ground was rough and hard, and our progress slow, so that we did not reach the end of the first station (10 miles) until nine o'clock. As we drove into the post-house, three other travellers, who had the start of us, and consequently the first right to horses, drove away. I was dismayed to find that my förbud had not been received, but the ostler informed me that by paying twelve skillings extra I could have horses at once. While the new carts were getting ready, the postman, wrapped in wolf-skin, and with a face reddened by the wind, came up, and handed out my förbud ticket. Such was our first experience of förbud.

On the next station, the peasant who was ahead with our luggage left the main road and took a rough track through the woods. Presently we came to a large inlet of the Bothnian gulf, frozen solid from shore to shore, and upon this we boldly struck out. The ice was nearly a foot thick, and as solid as marble. So we drove for at least four miles, and finally came to land on the opposite side, near a sawmill. At the next post-house we found our predecessors just setting off again in sleds; the landlord informed us that he had only received my förbud an hour previous, and, according to law was allowed three hours to get ready his second instalment of horses, the first being exhausted. There was no help for it: we therefore comforted ourselves with breakfast. At one o'clock we set out again in low Norrland sleds, but there was little snow at first, and we were obliged to walk the first few miles. The station was a long one (twenty English miles), and our horses not the most promising. Coming upon solid snow at last, we travelled rather more swiftly, but with more risk. The sleds, although so low, rest upon narrow runners, and the shafts are attached by a hook, upon which they turn in all directions, so that the sled sways from side to side, entirely independent of them. In going off the main road to get a little more snow on a side track, I discovered this fact by overturning the sled, and pitching Braisted and myself out on our heads. There were lakes on either side, and we made many miles on the hard ice, which split with a dull sound under us. Long after dark, we reached the next station, Stråtjära, and found our horses in readiness. We started again, by the gleam of a flashing aurora, going through forests and fields in the uncertain light, blindly following our leader, Braisted and I driving by turns, and already much fatigued. After a long time, we descended a steep hill, to the Ljusne River. The water foamed and thundered under the bridge, and I could barely see that it fell in a series of rapids over the rocks.

At Mo Myskie, which we reached at eight o'clock, our horses had been ready four hours, which gave us a dollar banco väntapenningar (waiting money) to pay. The landlord, a sturdy, jolly fellow, with grizzly hair and a prosperous abdomen, asked if we were French, and I addressed him in that language. He answered in English on finding that we were Americans. On his saying that he had learned English in Tripoli, I addressed him in Arabic. His eyes flashed, he burst into a roaring laugh of the profoundest delight, and at once answered in the majestic gutturals of the Orient. "Allah akhbar!" he cried; "I have been waiting twenty years for some one to speak to me in Arabic, and you are the first!" He afterwards changed to Italian, which he spoke perfectly well, and preferred to any foreign language. We were detained half an hour by his delight, and went off forgetting to pay for a bottle of beer, the price of which I sent back by the skjutsbonde, or postillion.

This skjutsbonde was a stupid fellow, who took us a long, circuitous road, in order to save time. We hurried along in the darkness, constantly crying out "Kör på!" (Drive on!) and narrowly missing a hundred overturns. It was eleven at night before we reached the inn at Kungsgården, where, fortunately, the people were awake, and the pleasant old landlady soon had our horses ready. We had yet sixteen English miles to Bro, our lodging-place, where we should have arrived by eight o'clock. I hardly know how to describe the journey. We were half asleep, tired out, nearly frozen, (mercury below zero) and dashed along at haphazard, through vast dark forests, up hill and down, following the sleepy boy who drove ahead with our baggage. A dozen times the sled, swaying from side to side like a pendulum, tilted, hung in suspense a second, and then righted itself again. The boy fell back on the hay and slept, until Braisted, creeping up behind, startled him with terrific yells in his ears. Away then dashed the horse, down steep declivities, across open, cultivated valleys, and into the woods again. After midnight the moon rose, and the cold was intenser than ever. The boy having fallen asleep again, the horse took advantage of it to run off at full speed, we following at the same rate, sometimes losing sight of him and uncertain of our way, until, after a chase of a few miles, we found the boy getting his reins out from under the runners. Finally, after two in the morning, we reached Bro.

Here we had ordered a warm room, beds and supper, by förbud, but found neither. A sleepy, stupid girl, who had just got up to wait on a captain who had arrived before us and was going on, told us there was nothing to be had. "We must eat, if we have to eat you," I said, savagely, for we were chilled through and fierce with hunger; but I might as well have tried to hurry the Venus de Medici. At last we got some cold sausage, a fire, and two couches, on which we lay down without undressing, and slept. I had scarcely closed my eyes, it seemed, when the girl, who was to call us at half-past five o'clock, came into the room. "Is it half-past five?" I asked. "Oh, yes," she coolly answered, "it's much more." We were obliged to hurry off at once to avoid paying so much waiting money.

At sunrise we passed Hudiksvall, a pretty town at the head of a deep bay, in which several vessels were frozen up for the winter. There were some handsome country houses in the vicinity, better cultivation, more taste in building, and a few apple and cherry orchards. The mercury was still at zero, but we suffered less from the cold than the day previous, and began to enjoy our mode of travel. The horses were ready at all the stations on our arrival, and we were not delayed in changing. There was now plenty of snow, and the roads were splendid—the country undulating, with beautiful, deep valleys, separated by high, wooded hills, and rising to bold ridges in the interior. The houses were larger and better than we had yet seen—so were the people—and there was a general air of progress and well-doing. In fact, both country and population improved in appearance as we went northward.

The night set in very dark and cold, threatening snow. We had an elephant of a horse, which kicked up his heels and frisked like an awkward bull-pup, dashed down the hills like an avalanche, and carried us forward at a rapid rate. We coiled ourselves up in the hay, kept warm, and trusted our safety to Providence, for it was impossible to see the road, and we could barely distinguish the other sled, a dark speck before us. The old horse soon exhausted his enthusiasm. Braisted lost the whip, and the zealous boy ahead stopped every now and then to hurry us on. The aurora gleamed but faintly through the clouds; we were nearly overcome with sleep and fatigue, but took turns in arousing and amusing each other. The sled vibrated continually from side to side, and finally went over, spilling ourselves and our guns into a snow-bank. The horse stopped and waited for us, and then went on until the shafts came off. Toward ten o'clock, the lights of Sundsvall appeared, and we soon afterwards drove into the yard of the inn, having made one hundred and fifty-five miles in two days. We were wretchedly tired, and hungry as bears, but found room in an adjoining house, and succeeded in getting a supper of reindeer steak. I fell asleep in my chair, before my pipe was half-finished, and awoke the next morning to a sense of real fatigue. I had had enough of travelling by förbud.

CHAPTER IV. A SLEIGH RIDE THROUGH NORRLAND.

Sundsvall is a pretty little town of two or three thousand inhabitants, situated at the head of a broad and magnificent bay. It is the eastern terminus of the only post-road across the mountains to Trondhjem (Drontheim) in Norway, which passes through the extensive province of Jemteland. It is, consequently, a lively and bustling place, and has a considerable coasting trade. The day after our arrival was market-day, and hundreds of the Norrlanders thronged the streets and public square. They were all fresh, strong, coarse, honest, healthy people—the men with long yellow hair, large noses and blue eyes, the women with the rosiest of checks and the fullest development of body and limb. Many of the latter wore basques or jackets of sheepskin with the wool inside, striped petticoats and bright red stockings. The men were dressed in shaggy sheepskin coats, or garments of reindeer skin, with the hair outward. There was a vast collection of low Norrland sleds, laden with butter, cheese, hay, and wild game, and drawn by the rough and tough little horses of the country. Here was still plenty of life and animation, although we were already so far north that the sun did not shine upon Sundsvall the whole day, being hidden by a low hill to the south. The snowy ridges on the north, however, wore a bright roseate blush from his rays, from ten until two.

We called upon a merchant of the place, to whom I had a letter of introduction. He was almost the only man I met before undertaking the journey, who encouraged me to push on. "The people in Stockholm," said he, "know nothing about Northern Sweden." He advised me to give up travelling by förbud, to purchase a couple of sleds, and take our chance of finding horses: we would have no trouble in making from forty to fifty English miles per day. On returning to the inn, I made the landlord understand what we wanted, but could not understand him in return. At this juncture came in a handsome fellow; with a cosmopolitan air, whom Braisted recognised, by certain invisible signs, as the mate of a ship, and who explained the matter in very good English. I purchased two plain but light and strongly made sleds for 50 rigs (about $14), which seemed very cheap, but I afterwards learned that I paid much more than the current price.

On repacking our effects, we found that everything liquid was frozen—
even a camphorated mixture, which had been carefully wrapped in flannel.
The cold, therefore, must have been much more severe than we supposed.
Our supplies, also, were considerably damaged—the lantern broken, a
powder-flask cracked, and the salt, shot, nails, wadding, &c., mixed together
in beautiful confusion. Everything was stowed in one of the sleds, which was
driven by the postilion; the other contained only our two selves. We were off
the next morning, as the first streaks of dawn appeared in the sky. The roads
about Sundsvall were very much cut up, and even before getting out of the
town we were pitched over head and ears into a snow-bank.

We climbed slowly up and darted headlong down the ridges which
descend from the west toward the Bothnian Gulf, dividing its tributary rivers;
and toward sunrise, came to a broad bay, completely frozen over and turned
into a snowy plain. With some difficulty the skjutsbonde made me understand
that a shorter road led across the ice to the second post-station, Fjäl, avoiding
one change of horses. The way was rough enough at first, over heaped blocks
of ice, but became smoother where the wind had full sweep, and had cleared
the water before it froze. Our road was marked out by a double row of young
fir-trees, planted in the ice. The bay was completely land-locked, embraced
by a bold sweep of wooded hills, with rich, populous valleys between. Before
us, three or four miles across, lay the little port of Wifsta-warf, where several
vessels—among them a ship of three or four hundred tuns—were frozen in for
the winter. We crossed, ascended a long hill, and drove on through fir woods
to Fjäl, a little hamlet with a large inn. Here we got breakfast; and though
it may be in bad taste to speak of what one eats, the breakfast was in such
good taste that I cannot pass over it without lingering to enjoy, in memory,
its wonderful aroma. Besides, if it be true, as some shockingly gross persons
assert, that the belly is a more important district of the human economy
than the brain, a good meal deserves chronicling no less than an exalted
impression. Certain it is, that strong digestive are to be preferred to strong
thinking powers—better live unknown than die of dyspepsia. This was our
first country meal in Norrland, of whose fare the Stockholmers have a horror,

yet that stately capital never furnished a better. We had beefsteak and onions, delicious blood-puddings, the tenderest of pancakes (no omelette soufflée could be more fragile), with ruby raspberry jam, and a bottle of genuine English porter. If you think the bill of fare too heavy and solid, take a drive of fifteen miles in the regions of Zero, and then let your delicate stomach decide.

In a picturesque dell near Fjäl we crossed the rapid Indal River, which comes down from the mountains of Norway. The country was wild and broken, with occasional superb views over frozen arms of the Gulf, and the deep rich valleys stretching inland. Leaving Hernösand, the capital of the province, a few miles to our right, we kept the main northern road, slowly advancing from station to station with old and tired horses. There was a snow-storm in the afternoon, after which the sky came out splendidly clear, and gorgeous with the long northern twilight. In the silence of the hour and the deepening shadows of the forest through which we drove, it was startling to hear, all at once the sound of voices singing a solemn hymn. My first idea was, that some of those fanatical Dissenters of Norrland who meet, as once the Scotch Covenanters, among the hills, were having a refreshing winter meeting in the woods; but on proceeding further we found that the choristers were a company of peasants returning from market with their empty sleds.

It was already dark at four o'clock, and our last horses were so slow that the postilion, a handsome, lively boy, whose pride was a little touched by my remonstrances, failed, in spite of all his efforts, to bring us to the station before seven. We stopped at Weda, on the Angermann River, the largest stream in Northern Sweden. Angermannland, the country which it drains, is said to be a very wild and beautiful region, where some traces of the old, original Asiatic type which peopled Scandinavia are yet to be traced in the features of its secluded population. At Weda, we found excellent quarters. A neat, quiet, old-fashioned little servant-girl, of twelve or fourteen, took charge of us, and attended to all our wants with the greatest assiduity. We had a good supper, a small but neat room, clean beds, and coffee in the morning, beside a plentiful provision for breakfast on the way, for a sum equal to seventy-five cents.

We left at half-past seven, the waning moon hanging on the horizon, and the first almost imperceptible signs of the morning twilight in the east.

The Angermann River which is here a mile broad, was frozen, and our road led directly across its surface. The wind blew down it, across the snow-covered ice, making our faces tingle with premonitory signs of freezing, as the mercury was a little below zero. My hands were chilled inside the fur mittens, and I was obliged to rub my nose frequently, to prevent it from being nipped. The day was raw and chilly, and the temperature rose very little, although the hills occasionally sheltered us from the wind. The scenery, also, grew darker and wilder as we advanced. The fir-trees were shorter and stunted, and of a dark greenish-brown, which at a little distance appeared completely black. Nothing could exceed the bleak, inhospitable character of these landscapes. The inlets of the Bothnian Gulf were hard, snow-covered plains, inclosed by bold, rugged headlands, covered with ink-black forests. The more distant ridges faded into a dull indigo hue, flecked with patches of ghastly white, under the lowering, sullen, short-lived daylight.

Our road was much rougher than hitherto. We climbed long ridges, only to descend by as steep declivities on the northern side, to cross the bed of an inland stream, and then ascend again. The valleys, however, were inhabited and apparently well cultivated, for the houses were large and comfortable, and the people had a thrifty, prosperous and satisfied air. Beside the farmhouses were immense racks, twenty feet high, for the purpose of drying flax and grain, and at the stations the people offered for sale very fine and beautiful linen of their own manufacture. This is the staple production of Norrland, where the short summers are frequently insufficient to mature the grain crops. The inns were all comfortable buildings, with very fair accommodations for travellers. We had bad luck with horses this day, however, two or three travellers having been in advance and had the pick. On one stage our baggage-sled was driven by a poike of not more than ten years old—a darling fellow, with a face as round, fresh and sweet as a damask rose, the bluest of eyes, and a cloud of silky golden hair. His successor was a tall, lazy lout, who stopped so frequently to talk with the drivers of sleds behind us, that we lost all patience, drove past and pushed ahead in the darkness, trusting our horse to find the way. His horse followed, leaving him in the lurch, and we gave him a long-winded chase astern before we allowed him to overtake us. This so exasperated him that we had no trouble the rest of the way. Mem.—If you wish to travel with

40

speed, make your postilion angry.

At Hörnäs they gave us a supper of ale and cold pig's feet, admirable beds, and were only deficient in the matter of water for washing. We awoke with headaches, on account of gas from the tight Russian stove. The temperature, at starting, was 22° below zero—colder than either of us had ever before known. We were a little curious, at first, to know how we should endure it, but, to our delight, found ourselves quite warm and comfortable. The air was still, dry, and delicious to inhale. My nose occasionally required friction, and my beard and moustache became a solid mass of ice, frozen together so that I could scarcely open my mouth, and firmly fastened to my fur collar. We travelled forty-nine miles, and were twelve hours on the way, yet felt no inconvenience from the temperature.

By this time it was almost wholly a journey by night, dawn and twilight, for full day there was none. The sun rose at ten and set at two. We skimmed along, over the black, fir-clothed hills, and across the pleasant little valleys, in the long, gray, slowly-gathering daybreak: then, heavy snow-clouds hid half the brief day, and the long, long, dusky evening glow settled into night. The sleighing was superb, the snow pure as ivory, hard as marble, and beautifully crisp and smooth. Our sleds glided over it without effort, the runners making music as they flew. With every day the country grew wilder, blacker and more rugged, with no change in the general character of the scenery. In the afternoon we passed the frontier of Norrland, and entered the province of West Bothnia. There are fewer horses at the stations, as we go north, but also fewer travellers, and we were not often detained. Thus far, we had no difficulty: my scanty stock of Swedish went a great way, and I began to understand with more facility, even the broad Norrland dialect.

The people of this region are noble specimens of the physical man— tall, broad-shouldered, large-limbed, ruddy and powerful; and they are mated with women who, I venture to say, do not even suspect the existence of a nervous system. The natural consequences of such health are: morality and honesty—to say nothing of the quantities of rosy and robust children which bless every household. If health and virtue cannot secure happiness, nothing can, and these Norrlanders appear to be a thoroughly happy and contented race. We had occasional reason to complain of their slowness; but, then, why should they be fast? It is rather we who should moderate our speed. Braisted, however, did not accept such a philosophy. "Charles XII. was the boy to manage the Swedes," said he to me one day; "he always kept them in a hurry."

We reached Lefwar, our resting-place for the night, in good condition, notwithstanding the 22° below, and felt much colder in the house, after stripping off our furs, than out of doors with them on. They gave us a supper consisting of smörgås ("butter-goose"—the Swedish prelude to a meal, consisting usually of bread, butter, pickled anchovies, and caviar flavored with garlic), sausages, potatoes, and milk, and made for us sumptuous beds of the snowiest and sweetest linen. When we rose next morning it was snowing. About an inch had fallen during the night, and the mercury had risen to 6° below zero. We drove along in the dusky half-twilight toward Angesjö, over low, broad hills, covered with forests of stunted birch and fir. The scenery continued the same, and there is no use in repeating the description, except to say that the land became more cold and barren, and there seemed to be few things cultivated except flax, barley and potatoes. Still the same ridges sweeping down to the Gulf, on one hand, the same frozen bays and inlets on the other, and villages at intervals of eight or ten miles, each with its great solid church, low red belfry and deserted encampment of red frame stables. Before reaching the second station, we looked from a wooded height over the open expanse of the Gulf,—a plain of snow-covered ice, stretching eastward as far as the eye could reach.

The day gradually became still and cold, until the temperature reached -22° again, and we became comfortable in the same proportion. The afternoon twilight, splendid with its hues of amber, rose and saffron, died away so gradually, that it seemed scarcely to fade at all, lighting our path for at least three hours after sunset. Our postilions were all boys—ruddy, hardy young fellows of fourteen or fifteen, who drove well and sang incessantly, in spite of the cold. They talked much with us, but to little purpose, as I found it very difficult to understand the humming dialect they spoke. Each, as he received his drickpenningar (drink-money, or gratuity), at the end of the station, expressed his thanks by shaking hands with us. This is a universal custom throughout the north of Sweden: it is a part of the simple, natural habits of the people; and though it seemed rather odd at first to be shaking hands with everybody, from the landlord down to the cook and the ostler, we soon came to take it as a matter of course. The frank, unaffected way in which the hand was offered, oftener made the custom a pleasant one.

At Stocksjö we decided to push on to a station beyond Umeå, called Innertafle, and took our horses accordingly. The direct road, however, was unused on account of the drifts, so we went around through Umeå, after all. We had nearly a Swedish mile, and it was just dark when we descended to the Umeå River, across whose solid surface we drove, and up a steep bank into the town. We stopped a few moments in the little public square, which was crowded with people, many of whom had already commenced their Christmas sprees. The shops were lighted, and the little town looked very gay and lively. Passing through, we kept down the left bank of the river for a little distance, and then struck into the woods. It was night by this time; all at once the boy stopped, mounted a snow-bank, whirled around three or four times, and said something to me which I could not understand. "What's the matter?" I asked; "is not this the road to Innertafle?" "I don't know—I think not," he said. "Don't you know the way, then?" I asked again. "No!" he yelled in reply, whirled around several times more, and then drove on. Presently we overtook a pedestrian, to whom he turned for advice, and who willingly acted as guide for the sake of a ride. Away we went again, but the snow was so spotless that it was impossible to see the track. Braisted and I ran upon a snow-bank, were overturned and dragged some little distance, but we righted ourselves again, and soon afterwards reached our destination.

In the little inn the guests' room lay behind the large family kitchen, through which we were obliged to pass. We were seized with a shivering fit on stripping off our furs, and it seemed scarcely possible to get warm again. This was followed by such intense drowsiness that we were obliged to lie down and sleep an hour before supper. After the cold weather set in, we were attacked with this drowsy fit every day, toward evening, and were obliged to take turns in arousing and stimulating each other. This we generally accomplished by singing "From Greenland's icy mountains," and other appropriate melodies.

At Innertafle we were attended by a tall landlady, a staid, quiet, almost grim person, who paid most deliberate heed to our wants. After a delay of more than two hours, she furnished us with a supper consisting of some kind of fresh fish, with a sauce composed of milk, sugar and onions, followed by gryngröt, a warm mush of mixed rice and barley, eaten with milk. Such was our fare on Christmas eve; but hunger is the best sauce, and our dishes were plentifully seasoned with it.

CHAPTER V. PROGRESS NORTHWARDS.—A STORM.

We arose betimes on Christmas morn, but the grim and deliberate landlady detained us an hour in preparing our coffee. I was in the yard about five minutes, wearing only my cloth overcoat and no gloves, and found the air truly sharp and nipping, but not painfully severe. Presently, Braisted came running in with the thermometer, exclaiming, with a yell of triumph, "Thirty, by Jupiter!" (30° of Reaumur, equal to 35-1/2° below zero of Fahrenheit.) We were delighted with this sign of our approach to the Arctic circle.

The horses were at last ready; we muffled up carefully, and set out. The dawn was just streaking the East, the sky was crystal-clear, and not a breath of air stirring. My beard was soon a solid mass of ice, from the moisture of my breath, and my nose required constant friction. The day previous, the ice which had gathered on my fur collar lay against my face so long that the flesh began to freeze over my cheek-bones, and thereafter I was obliged to be particularly cautious. As it grew lighter, we were surprised to find that our postilion was a girl. She had a heavy sheepskin over her knees, a muff for her hands, and a shawl around her head, leaving only the eyes visible. Thus accoutred, she drove on merrily, and, except that the red of her cheeks became scarlet and purple, showed no signs of the weather. As we approached Sörmjöle, the first station, we again had a broad view of the frozen Bothnian Gulf, over which hovered a low cloud of white ice-smoke. Looking down into the snowy valley of Sörmjöle, we saw the straight pillars of smoke rising from the houses high into the air, not spreading, but gradually breaking off into solid masses which sank again and filled the hollow, almost concealing the houses. Only the white, handsome church, with its tall spire, seated on a mound, rose above this pale blue film and shone softly in the growing flush of day.

We ordered horses at once, after drinking a bowl of hot milk, flavored with cinnamon. This is the favourite winter drink of the people, sometimes with the addition of brandy. But the finkel, or common brandy of Sweden, is a detestable beverage, resembling a mixture of turpentine, train oil, and bad molasses, and we took the milk unmixed, which admirably assisted in keeping up the animal heat. The mercury by this time had fallen to 38° below zero. We were surprised and delighted to find that we stood the cold so easily, and prided ourselves not a little on our powers of endurance. Our feet gradually became benumbed, but, by walking up the hills, we prevented the circulation from coming to a stand-still.

The cold, however, played some grotesque pranks with us. My beard, moustache, cap, and fur collar were soon one undivided lump of ice. Our eyelashes became snow-white and heavy with frost, and it required constant motion to keep them from freezing together. We saw everything through visors barred with ivory. Our eyebrows and hair were as hoary as those of an octogenarian, and our cheeks a mixture of crimson and orange, so that we were scarcely recognizable by each other. Every one we met had snow-white locks, no matter how youthful the face, and, whatever was the colour of our horses at starting, we always drove milk-white steeds at the close of the post. The irritation of our nostrils occasioned the greatest inconvenience, and as the handkerchiefs froze instantly, it soon became a matter of pain and difficulty to use them. You might as well attempt to blow your nose with a poplar chip. We could not bare our hands a minute, without feeling an iron grasp of cold which seemed to squeeze the flesh like a vice, and turn the very blood to ice. In other respects we were warm and jolly, and I have rarely been in higher spirits. The air was exquisitely sweet and pure, and I could open my mouth (as far as its icy grating permitted) and inhale full draughts into the lungs with a delicious sensation of refreshment and exhilaration. I had not expected to find such freedom of respiration in so low a temperature. Some descriptions of severe cold in Canada and Siberia, which I have read, state that at such times the air occasions a tingling, smarting sensation in the throat and lungs, but I experienced nothing of the kind.

This was arctic travel at last. By Odin, it was glorious! The smooth, firm road, crisp and pure as alabaster, over which our sleigh-runners talked with the rippling, musical murmur of summer brooks; the sparkling, breathless firmament; the gorgeous rosy flush of morning, slowly deepening until the orange disc of the sun cut the horizon; the golden blaze of the tops of the bronze firs; the glittering of the glassy birches; the long, dreary sweep of the landscape; the icy nectar of the perfect air; the tingling of the roused blood in every vein, all alert to guard the outposts of life against the besieging cold— it was superb! The natives themselves spoke of the cold as being unusually severe, and we congratulated ourselves all the more on our easy endurance of it. Had we judged only by our own sensations we should not have believed the temperature to be nearly so low.

The sun rose a little after ten, and I have never seen anything finer than the spectacle which we then saw for the first time, but which was afterwards almost daily repeated—the illumination of the forests and snow-fields in his level orange beams, for even at midday he was not more than eight degrees above the horizon. The tops of the trees, only, were touched: still and solid as iron, and covered with sparkling frost-crystals, their trunks were changed to blazing gold, and their foliage to a fiery orange-brown. The delicate purple sprays of the birch, coated with ice, glittered like wands of topaz and amethyst, and the slopes of virgin snow, stretching towards the sun, shone with the fairest saffron gleams. There is nothing equal to this in the South—nothing so transcendently rich, dazzling, and glorious. Italian dawns and twilights cannot surpass those we saw every day, not, like the former, fading rapidly into the ashen hues of dusk, but lingering for hour after hour with scarce a decrease of splendour. Strange that Nature should repeat these lovely aerial effects in such widely different zones and seasons. I thought to find in the winter landscapes of the far North a sublimity of death and desolation—a wild, dark, dreary, monotony of expression—but I had, in reality, the constant enjoyment of the rarest, the tenderest, the most enchanting beauty.

The people one meets along the road harmonise with these unexpected impressions. They are clear eyed and rosy as the morning, straight and strong as the fir saplings in their forests, and simple, honest, and unsophisticated beyond any class of men I have ever seen. They are no milksops either. Under the serenity of those blue eyes and smooth, fair faces, burns the old Berserker rage, not easily kindled, but terrible as the lightning when once loosed. "I would like to take all the young men north of Sundsvall," says Braisted, "put

them into Kansas, tell them her history, and then let them act for themselves."
"The cold in clime are cold in blood," sings Byron, but they are only cold
through superior self-control and freedom from perverted passions. Better is
the assertion of Tennyson:

> "That bright, and fierce, and fickle is the South,
>
> And dark, and true, and tender is the North."

There are tender hearts in the breasts of these northern men and women,
albeit they are as undemonstrative as the English—or we Americans, for that
matter. It is exhilarating to see such people—whose digestion is sound, whose
nerves are tough as whipcord, whose blood runs in a strong full stream, whose
impulses are perfectly natural, who are good without knowing it, and who are
happy without trying to be so. Where shall we find such among our restless
communities at home?

We made two Swedish miles by noon, and then took a breakfast of fried
reindeer meat and pancakes, of which we ate enormously, to keep up a good
supply of fuel. Braisted and I consumed about a pound of butter between us.
Shriek not, young ladies, at our vulgar appetites—you who sip a spoonful
of ice-cream, or trifle with a diminutive meringue, in company, but make
amends on cold ham and pickles in the pantry, after you go home—I shall
tell the truth, though it disgust you. This intense cold begets a necessity for
fat, and with the necessity comes the taste—a wise provision of Nature! The
consciousness now dawned upon me that I might be able to relish train-oil
and tallow-candles before we had done with Lapland.

I had tough work at each station to get my head out of my wrappings,
which were united with my beard and hair in one solid lump. The cold
increased instead of diminishing, and by the time we reached Gumboda, at
dusk, it was 40° below zero. Here we found a company of Finns travelling
southward, who had engaged five horses, obliging us to wait a couple of hours.
We had already made forty miles, and were satisfied with our performance,
so we stopped for the night. When the thermometer was brought in, the
mercury was frozen, and on unmuffling I found the end of my nose seared as
if with a hot iron. The inn was capital; we had a warm carpeted room, beds

of clean, lavendered linen, and all civilised appliances. In the evening we sat down to a Christmas dinner of sausages, potatoes, pancakes, raspberry jam, and a bottle of Barclay and Perkin's best porter, in which we drank the health of all dear relatives and friends in the two hemispheres. And this was in West Bothnia, where we had been told in Stockholm that we should starve! At bedtime, Braisted took out the thermometer again, and soon brought it in with the mercury frozen below all the numbers on the scale.

In the morning, the landlord came in and questioned us, in order to satisfy his curiosity. He took us for Norwegians, and was quite surprised to find out our real character. We had also been taken for Finns, Russians and Danes, since leaving Stockholm. "I suppose you intend to buy lumber?" said the landlord. "No," said I, "we travel merely for the pleasure of it." "Ja so-o-o!" he exclaimed, in a tone of the greatest surprise and incredulity. He asked if it was necessary that we should travel in such cold weather, and seemed reluctant to let us go. The mercury showed 25° below zero when we started, but the sky was cloudy, with a raw wind from the north-west. We did not feel the same hard, griping cold as the day previous, but a more penetrating chill. The same character of scenery continued, but with a more bleak and barren aspect, and the population became more scanty. The cloudy sky took away what little green there was in the fir-trees, and they gloomed as black as Styx on either side of our road. The air was terribly raw and biting as it blew across the hollows and open plains. I did not cover my face, but kept up such a lively friction on my nose, to prevent it from freezing, that in the evening I found the skin quite worn away.

At Daglösten, the third station, we stopped an hour for breakfast. It was a poverty-stricken place, and we could only get some fish-roes and salt meat. The people were all half-idiots, even to the postilion who drove us. We had some daylight for the fourth station, did the fifth by twilight, and the sixth in darkness. The cold (-30°) was so keen that our postilions made good time, and we reached Sunnanå on the Skellefteå River, 52 miles, soon after six o'clock. Here we were lodged in a large, barn-like room, so cold that we were obliged to put on our overcoats and sit against the stove. I began to be troubled with a pain in my jaw, from an unsound tooth—the commencement of a martyrdom from which I suffered for many days afterwards. The existence of nerves in one's teeth has always seemed to me a superfluous provision of Nature, and I should have been well satisfied if she had omitted them in my case.

The handmaiden called us soon after five o'clock, and brought us coffee while we were still in bed. This is the general custom here in the North, and is another point of contact with the South. The sky was overcast, with raw violent wind—mercury 18° below zero. We felt the cold very keenly; much more so than on Christmas day. The wind blew full in our teeth, and penetrated even beneath our furs. On setting out, we crossed the Skellefteå River by a wooden bridge, beyond which we saw, rising duskily in the uncertain twilight, a beautiful dome and lantern, crowning a white temple, built in the form of a Greek cross. It was the parish church of Skellefteå. Who could have expected to find such an edifice, here, on the borders of Lapland? The village about it contains many large and handsome houses. This is one of the principal points of trade and intercourse between the coast and the interior.

The weather became worse as we advanced, traversing the low, broad hills, through wastes of dark pine forests. The wind cut like a sharp sword in passing the hollows, and the drifting snow began to fill the tracks. We were full two hours in making the ten miles to Frostkage, and the day seemed scarcely nearer at hand. The leaden, lowering sky gave out no light, the forests were black and cold, the snow a dusky grey—such horribly dismal scenery I have rarely beheld. We warmed ourselves as well as we could, and started anew, having for postilions two rosy boys, who sang the whole way and played all sorts of mad antics with each other to keep from freezing. At the next station we drank large quantities of hot milk, flavored with butter, sugar and cinnamon, and then pushed on, with another chubby hop-o'-my-thumb as guide and driver. The storm grew worse and worse: the wind blew fiercely over the low hills, loaded with particles of snow, as fine as the point of a needle and as hard as crystal, which struck full on our eyeballs and stung them so that we could scarcely see. I had great difficulty in keeping my face from freezing, and my companion found his cheek touched.

By the time we reached Abyn, it blew a hurricane, and we were compelled to stop. It was already dusk, and our cosy little room was doubly pleasant by contrast with the wild weather outside. Our cheerful landlady, with her fresh complexion and splendid teeth, was very kind and attentive, and I got on very well in conversation, notwithstanding her broad dialect. She was much astonished at my asking for a bucket of cold water, for bathing. "Why," said she, "I always thought that if a person put his feet into cold water, in winter, he would die immediately." However, she supplied it, and was a little surprised to find me none the worse in the morning. I passed a terrible night from the pain in my face, and was little comforted, on rising, by the assurance that much snow had fallen. The mercury had risen to zero, and the wind still blew, although not so furiously as on the previous day. We therefore determined to set out, and try to reach Piteå. The landlady's son, a tall young Viking, with yellow locks hanging on his shoulders, acted as postilion, and took the lead. We started at nine, and found it heavy enough at first. It was barely light enough to see our way, and we floundered slowly along through deep drifts for a mile, when we met the snow-plows, after which our road became easier. These plows are wooden frames, shaped somewhat like the bow of a ship—in fact, I have seen very fair clipper models among them— about fifteen feet long by ten feet wide at the base, and so light that, if the snow is not too deep, one horse can manage them. The farmers along the road are obliged to turn out at six o'clock in the morning whenever the snow falls or drifts, and open a passage for travellers. Thus, in spite of the rigorous winter, communication is never interrupted, and the snow-road, at last, from frequent plowing, becomes the finest sleighing track in the world.

The wind blew so violently, however, that the furrows were soon filled up, and even the track of the baggage-sled, fifty yards in advance, was covered. There was one hollow where the drifts of loose snow were five or six feet deep, and here we were obliged to get out and struggle across, sinking to our loins at every step. It is astonishing how soon one becomes hardened to the cold. Although the mercury stood at zero, with a violent storm, we rode with our faces fully exposed, frost-bites and all, and even drove with bare hands, without the least discomfort. But of the scenery we saw this day, I can give no description. There was nothing but long drifts and waves of spotless snow, some dim, dark, spectral fir-trees on either hand, and beyond that a wild chaos of storm. The snow came fast and blinding, beating full in our teeth. It was impossible to see; the fine particles so stung our eyeballs, that we could not look ahead. My eyelashes were loaded with snow, which immediately turned to ice and froze the lids together, unless I kept them in constant motion. The storm hummed and buzzed through the black forests; we were all alone on the road, or even the pious Swedes would not turn out to church on such a day. It was terribly sublime and desolate, and I enjoyed it amazingly. We kept warm, although there was a crust of ice a quarter of an inch thick on our cheeks, and the ice in our beards prevented us from opening our mouths. At one o'clock, we reached the second station, Gefre, unrecognisable by our nearest friends. Our eyelashes were weighed down with heavy fringes of frozen snow, there were icicles an inch long hanging to the eaves of our moustaches, and the handkerchiefs which wrapped our faces were frozen fast to the flesh. The skin was rather improved by this treatment, but it took us a great while to thaw out.

At Gefre, we got some salt meat and hot milk, and then started on our long stage of fifteen miles to Piteå. The wind had moderated somewhat, but the snow still fell fast and thick. We were again blinded and frozen up more firmly than ever, cheeks and all, so that our eyes and lips were the only features to be seen. After plunging along for more than two hours through dreary woods, we came upon the estuary of the Piteå River, where our course was marked out by young fir-trees, planted in the ice. The world became a blank; there was snow around, above and below, and but for these marks a man might have driven at random until he froze. For three miles or more, we rode over the solid gulf, and then took the woods on the opposite shore. The way seemed almost endless. Our feet grew painfully cold, our eyes smarted from the beating of the fine snow, and my swollen jaw tortured me incessantly. Finally lights appeared ahead through the darkness, but another half hour elapsed before we saw houses on both sides of us. There was a street, at last, then a large mansion, and to our great joy the skjutsbonde turned into the courtyard of an inn.

CHAPTER VI. JOURNEY FROM PITEÅ TO HAPARANDA.

My jaw was so painful on reaching Piteå, that I tossed about in torment the whole night, utterly unable to sleep. The long northern night seemed as if it would never come to an end, and I arose in the morning much more fatigued and exhausted than when I lay down. It was 6° below zero, and the storm still blowing, but the cold seemed to relieve my face a little, and so we set out. The roads were heavy, but a little broken, and still led over hills and through interminable forests of mingled fir and pine, in the dark, imperfect day. I took but little note of the scenery, but was so drowsy and overcome, that Braisted at last filled the long baggage-sled with hay, and sat at the rear, so that I could lie stretched out, with my head upon his lap. Here, in spite of the cold and wind, I lay in a warm, stupid half-sleep.

It was dark when we reached Ersnäs, whence we had twelve miles to Old Luleå, with tired horses, heavy roads, and a lazy driver. I lay down again, dozed as usual, and tried to forget my torments. So passed three hours; the night had long set in, with a clear sky, 13° below zero, and a sharp wind blowing. All at once an exclamation from Braisted aroused me. I opened my eyes, as I lay in his lap, looked upward, and saw a narrow belt or scarf of silver fire stretching directly across the zenith, with its loose, frayed ends slowly swaying to and fro down the slopes of the sky. Presently it began to waver, bending back and forth, sometimes slowly, sometimes with a quick, springing motion, as if testing its elasticity. Now it took the shape of a bow, now undulated into Hogarth's line of beauty, brightening and fading in its sinuous motion, and finally formed a shepherd's crook, the end of which suddenly began to separate and fall off, as if driven by a strong wind, until the whole belt shot away in long, drifting lines of fiery snow. It then gathered again into a dozen dancing fragments, which alternately advanced and retreated, shot hither and thither, against and across each other, blazed out in yellow and rosy gleams or paled again, playing a thousand fantastic pranks, as if guided by some wild whim.

We lay silent, with upturned faces, watching this wonderful spectacle.

Suddenly, the scattered lights ran together, as by a common impulse, joined their bright ends, twisted them through each other, and fell in a broad, luminous curtain straight downward through the air until its fringed hem swung apparently but a few yards over our heads. This phenomenon was so unexpected and startling, that for a moment I thought our faces would be touched by the skirts of the glorious auroral drapery. It did not follow the spheric curve of the firmament, but hung plumb from the zenith, falling, apparently, millions of leagues through the air, its folds gathered together among the stars and its embroidery of flame sweeping the earth and shedding a pale, unearthly radiance over the wastes of snow. A moment afterwards and it was again drawn up, parted, waved its flambeaux and shot its lances hither and thither, advancing and retreating as before. Anything so strange, so capricious, so wonderful, so gloriously beautiful, I scarcely hope to see again.

By this time we came upon the broad Luleå River, and were half an hour traversing its frozen surface, still watching the snow above us, which gradually became fainter and less active. Finally we reached the opposite shore, drove up a long slope, through a large village of stables, and past the imposing church of Old Luleå to the inn. It was now nearly eight o'clock, very cold, and I was thoroughly exhausted. But the inn was already full of travellers, and there was no place to lay our heads. The landlord, a sublimely indifferent Swede, coolly advised us to go on to Persö, ten miles distant. I told him I had not slept for two nights, but he merely shrugged his shoulders, repeated his advice, and offered to furnish horses at once, to get us off. It was a long, cold, dreary ride, and I was in a state of semi-consciousness the whole time. We reached Persö about eleven, found the house full of travellers, but procured two small beds in a small room with another man in it, and went to sleep without supper. I was so thoroughly worn out that I got about three hours' rest, in spite of my pain.

We took coffee in bed at seven, and started for Rånbyn, on the Rånea River. The day was lowering, temperature 8-1/2° below zero. The country was low, slightly undulating with occasional wide views to the north, over the inlets of the gulf, and vast wide tracts of forest. The settlements were still as frequent as ever, but there was little apparent cultivation, except flax. Rånbyn is a large village, with a stately church. The people were putting up booths for a fair (a fair in the open air, in lat. 65° N., with the mercury freezing!), which explained the increased travel on the road. We kept on to Hvitå for breakfast, thus getting north of the latitude of Torneå; thence our road turned eastward at right angles around the head of the Bothnian Gulf. Much snow had fallen, but the road had been ploughed, and we had a tolerable track, except when passing sleds, which sometimes gave us an overturn.

We now had uninterrupted forest scenery between the stations—and such scenery! It is almost impossible to paint the glory of those winter forests. Every tree, laden with the purest snow, resembles a Gothic fountain of bronze, covered with frozen spray, through which only suggestive glimpses of its delicate tracery can be obtained. From every rise we looked over thousands of such mimic fountains, shooting, low or high, from their pavements of ivory and alabaster. It was an enchanted wilderness—white, silent, gleaming, and filled with inexhaustible forms of beauty. To what shall I liken those glimpses under the boughs, into the depths of the forest, where the snow destroyed all perspective, and brought the remotest fairy nooks and coverts, too lovely and fragile to seem cold, into the glittering foreground? "Wonderful! Glorious!" I could only exclaim, in breathless admiration. Once, by the roadside, we saw an Arctic ptarmigan, as white as the snow, with ruby eyes that sparkled like jewels as he moved slowly and silently along, not frightened in the least.

The sun set a little after one o'clock, and we pushed on to reach the Kalix River the same evening. At the last station we got a boy postilion and two lazy horses, and were three hours and a half on the road, with a temperature of 20° below zero. My feet became like ice, which increased the pain in my face, and I began to feel faint and sick with so much suffering and loss of rest. The boy aggravated us so much by his laziness, that Braisted ran ahead and cuffed his ears, after which he made better speed. After a drive through interminable woods, we came upon the banks of the Kalix, which were steep and fringed with splendid firs. Then came the village of Månsbyn, where, thank Heaven, we got something to eat, a warm room, and a bed.

While we were at supper, two travellers arrived, one of whom, a well-made, richly-dressed young fellow, was ushered into our room. He was a bruk-patron (iron-master), so the servant informed us, and from his superfine broad-cloth, rings, and the immense anchor-chain which attached him to his watch, appeared to be doing a thriving business. He had the Norse bloom on his face, a dignified nose, and English whiskers flanking his smoothly-shaven chin. His air was flushed and happy; he was not exactly drunk, but comfortably within that gay and cheerful vestibule beyond which lies the chamber of horrors. He listened to our conversation for some time, and finally addressed me in imperfect English. This led to mutual communications, and a declaration of our character, and object in travel—nothing of which would he believe. "Nobody can possibly come here for pleasure," said he; "I know better; you have a secret political mission." Our amusement at this only strengthened him in his suspicions. Nevertheless he called for a bottle of port wine, which, when it came, turned out to be bad Malaga, and insisted on drinking a welcome. "You are in latitude 66° north," said he; "on the Kalix, where no American has ever been before, and I shall call my friend to give a skål to your country. We have been to the church, where my friend is stationed."

With that he went out, and soon returned with a short, stout, broad faced, large-headed man of forty or thereabouts. His manner was perfectly well-bred and self-possessed, and I took him to be a clergyman, especially as the iron-master addressed him as "Brother Horton." "Now," said he, "welcome to 66° north, and prosperity to free America! Are you for Buchanan or Fremont?" Brother Horton kept a watchful eye upon his young friend, but cheerfully joined in the sentiment. I gave in return: "Skål to Sweden and the Swedish people," and hoped to get rid of our jolly acquaintance; but he was not to be shaken off. "You don't know me," he said; "and I don't know you—but you are something more than you seem to be: you are a political character." Just then Braisted came in with the thermometer, and announced 24° of cold (Reaumur). "Thousand devils!" exclaimed Brother Horton (and now I was convinced that he was not a clergyman), "what a thermometer! How cold it makes the weather! Would you part with it if I were to give you money in return?" I declined, stating that it was impossible for us to procure so cold a thermometer in the north, and we wanted to have as low a temperature as could be obtained.

56

This seemed to puzzle the iron-master, who studied awhile upon it, and then returned to the subject of my political mission. "I suppose you speak French," said he; "it is necessary in diplomacy. I can speak it also"—which he began to do, in a bungling way. I answered in the same language, but he soon gave up the attempt and tried German. I changed also, and, finding that he had exhausted his philology, of which he was rather proud, especially as Brother Horton knew nothing but Swedish, determined to have a little fun. "Of course you know Italian," said I; "it is more musical than German," and forthwith addressed him in that language. He reluctantly confessed his ignorance. "Oh, well," I continued, "Spanish is equally agreeable to me;" and took up that tongue before he could reply. His face grew more and more blank and bewildered. "The Oriental languages are doubtless familiar to you;" I persisted, "I have had no practice in Arabic for some time," and overwhelmed him with Egyptian salutations. I then tried him with Hindustanee, which exhausted my stock, but concluded by giving him the choice of Malay, Tartar, or Thibetan. "Come, come," said Brother Horton, taking his arm as he stood staring and perplexed—"the horses are ready." With some difficulty he was persuaded to leave, after shaking hands with us, and exclaiming, many times, "You are a very seldom man!"

When we awoke, the temperature had risen to 2° above zero, with a tremendous snow-storm blowing. As we were preparing to set out, a covered sled drove in from the north, with two Swedish naval officers, whose vessel had been frozen in at Cronstadt, and who had been obliged to return home through Finland, up the eastern coast of the Bothnian Gulf. The captain, who spoke excellent English, informed me that they were in about the same latitude as we, on Christmas day, on the opposite side of the gulf, and had experienced the same degree of cold. Both of them had their noses severely frozen. We were two hours and a half in travelling to the first station, seven miles, as the snow was falling in blinding quantities, and the road was not yet ploughed out. All the pedestrians we met were on runners, but even with their snow skates, five feet long, they sank deep enough to make their progress very slow and toilsome.

By the time we reached Näsby my face was very much swollen and inflamed, and as it was impossible to make the next stage by daylight, we wisely determined to stop there. The wind blew a hurricane, the hard snow-crystals lashed the windows and made a gray chaos of all out-of-doors, but we had a warm, cosy, carpeted room within, a capital dinner in the afternoon, and a bottle of genuine London porter with our evening pipe. So we passed the last day of A. D. 1856, grateful to God for all the blessings which the year had brought us, and for the comfort and shelter we enjoyed, in that Polar wilderness of storm and snow.

On New Year's morning it blew less, and the temperature was comparatively mild, so, although the road was very heavy, we started again. Näsby is the last Swedish station, the Finnish frontier, which is an abrupt separation of races and tongues, being at the north-western corner of the Bothnian Gulf. In spite of the constant intercourse which now exists between Norrland and the narrow strip of Finnish soil which remains to Sweden, there has been no perceptible assimilation of the two races. At Näsby, all is pure Swedish; at Sängis, twelve miles distant, everything is Finnish. The blue eyes and fair hair, the lengthened oval of the face, and slim, straight form disappear. You see, instead, square faces, dark eyes, low foreheads, and something of an Oriental fire and warmth in the movements. The language is totally dissimilar, and even the costume, though of the same general fashion, presents many noticeable points of difference. The women wear handkerchiefs of some bright color bound over the forehead and under the chin, very similar to those worn by the Armenian women in Asia Minor. On first coming among them, the Finns impressed me as a less frank and open hearted, but more original and picturesque, race than the Swedes. It is exceedingly curious and interesting to find such a flavour of the Orient on the borders of the Frigid Zone.

The roads were very bad, and our drivers and horses provokingly slow, but we determined to push on to Haparanda the same night. I needed rest and medical aid, my jaw by this time being so swollen that I had great difficulty in eating—a state of things which threatened to diminish my supply of fuel, and render me sensitive to the cold. We reached Nickala, the last station, at seven o'clock. Beyond this, the road was frightfully deep in places. We could scarcely make any headway, and were frequently overturned headlong into the drifts. The driver was a Finn, who did not understand a word of Swedish, and all our urging was of no avail. We went on and on, in the moonlight, over arms of the gulf, through forests, and then over ice again—a flat, monotonous country, with the same dull features repeated again and again. At half-past nine, a large white church announced our approach to Haparanda, and soon afterwards we drove up to the inn, which was full of New-Year carousers. The landlord gave us quarters in the same room with an old Norrlander, who was very drunk, and annoyed us not a little until we got into bed and pretended to sleep. It was pretence nearly the whole night, on my part, for my torture was still kept up. The next morning I called upon Dr. Wretholm, the physician of the place,—not without some misgivings,—but his prescription of a poultice of mallow leaves, a sudorific and an opiate, restored my confidence, and I cheerfully resigned myself to a rest of two or three days, before proceeding further northward.

CHAPTER VII. CROSSING THE ARCTIC CIRCLE.

I was obliged to remain three days in Haparanda, applying poultices, gargles, and liniments, according to the doctor's instructions. As my Swedish was scarcely sufficient for the comprehension of prescriptions, or medical technicalities in general, a written programme of my treatment was furnished to Fredrika, the servant-maid, who was properly impressed with the responsibility thereby devolving upon her. Fredrika, no doubt, thought that my life was in her hands, and nothing could exceed the energy with which she undertook its preservation. Punctually to the minute appeared the prescribed application, and, if she perceived or suspected any dereliction on my part, it was sure to be reported to the doctor at his next visit. I had the taste of camomile and mallows in my mouth from morning till night; the skin of my jaw blistered under the scorching of ammonia; but the final result was, that I was cured, as the doctor and Fredrika had determined.

This good-hearted girl was a genuine specimen of the Northern Swedish female. Of medium height, plump, but not stout, with a rather slender waist and expansive hips, and a foot which stepped firmly and nimbly at the same time, she was as cheerful a body as one could wish to see. Her hair was of that silky blonde so common in Sweden; her eyes a clear, pale blue, her nose straight and well formed, her cheeks of the delicate pink of a wild-rose leaf, and her teeth so white, regular and perfect that I am sure they would make her fortune in America. Always cheerful, kind and active, she had, nevertheless, a hard life of it: she was alike cook, chambermaid, and hostler, and had a cross mistress to boot. She made our fires in the morning darkness, and brought us our early coffee while we yet lay in bed, in accordance with the luxurious habits of the Arctic zone. Then, until the last drunken guest was silent, towards midnight, there was no respite from labour. Although suffering from a distressing cough, she had the out-door as well as the in-door duties to discharge, and we saw her in a sheepskin jacket harnessing horses, in a temperature 30° below zero. The reward of such a service was possibly about eight American dollars a year. When, on leaving, I gave her about as much as one of our hotel servants would expect for answering a question, the poor girl was overwhelmed with gratitude, and even the stern landlady was so impressed by my generosity that she insisted on lending us a sheepskin for our feet, saying we were "good men."

There is something exceedingly primitive and unsophisticated in the manners of these Northern people—a straight-forward honesty, which takes the honesty of others for granted—a latent kindness and good-will which may at first be overlooked, because it is not demonstrative, and a total unconsciousness of what is called, in highly civilised circles, "propriety." The very freedom of manners which, in some countries, might denote laxity of morals, is here the evident stamp of their purity. The thought has often recurred to me—which is the most truly pure and virginal nature, the fastidious American girl, who blushes at the sight of a pair of boots outside a gentleman's bedroom door, and who requires that certain unoffending parts of the body and articles of clothing should be designated by delicately circumlocutious terms, or the simple-minded Swedish women, who come into our bedrooms with coffee, and make our fires while we get up and dress, coming and going during all the various stages of the toilet, with the frankest unconsciousness of impropriety? This is modesty in its healthy and natural development, not in those morbid forms which suggest an imagination ever on the alert for prurient images. Nothing has confirmed my impression of the virtue of the Northern Swedes more than this fact, and I have rarely felt more respect for woman or more faith in the inherent purity of her nature.

We had snug quarters in Haparanda, and our detention was therefore by no means irksome. A large room, carpeted, protected from the outer cold by double windows, and heated by an immense Russian stove, was allotted to us. We had two beds, one of which became a broad sofa during the day, a backgammon table, the ordinary appliances for washing, and, besides a number of engravings on the walls, our window commanded a full view of Torneå, and the ice-track across the river, where hundreds of persons daily passed to and fro. The eastern window showed us the Arctic dawn, growing and brightening through its wonderful gradations of color, for four hours, when the pale orange sun appeared above the distant houses, to slide along their roofs for two hours, and then dip again. We had plentiful meals, consisting mostly of reindeer meat, with a sauce of Swedish cranberries, potatoes, which had been frozen, but were still palatable, salmon roes, soft bread in addition to the black shingles of fladbröd, English porter, and excellent Umeå beer. In fact, in no country inn of the United States could we have been more comfortable. For the best which the place afforded, during four days, with a small provision for the journey, we paid about seven dollars.

The day before our departure, I endeavored to obtain some information concerning the road to Lapland, but was disappointed. The landlord ascertained that there were skjuts, or relays of post-horses, as far as Muonioniska, 210 English miles, but beyond this I could only learn that the people were all Finnish, spoke no Swedish, were miserably poor, and could give us nothing to eat. I was told that a certain official personage at the apothecary's shop spoke German, and hastened thither; but the official, a dark-eyed, olive-faced Finn, could not understand my first question. The people even seemed entirely ignorant of the geography of the country beyond Upper Torneå, or Matarengi, forty miles off. The doctor's wife, a buxom, motherly lady, who seemed to feel quite an interest in our undertaking, and was as kind and obliging as such women always are, procured for us a supply of fladbröd made of rye, and delightfully crisp and hard—and this was the substance of our preparations. Reindeer mittens were not to be found, nor a reindeer skin to cover our feet, so we relied, as before, on plenty of hay and my Scotch plaid. We might, perhaps, have had better success in Torneå, but I knew no one there who would be likely to assist us, and we did not even visit the old place. We had taken the precaution of getting the Russian visé, together with a small stock of roubles, at Stockholm, but found that it was quite unnecessary. No passport is required for entering Torneå, or travelling on the Russian side of the frontier.

Trusting to luck, which is about the best plan after all, we started from Haparanda at noon, on the 5th of January. The day was magnificent, the sky cloudless, and resplendent as polished steel, and the mercury 31° below zero. The sun, scarcely more than the breadth of his disc above the horizon, shed a faint orange light over the broad, level snow-plains, and the bluish-white hemisphere of the Bothnian Gulf, visible beyond Torneå. The air was perfectly still, and exquisitely cold and bracing, despite the sharp grip it took upon my nose and ears. These Arctic days, short as they are, have a majesty of their own—a splendor, subdued though it be; a breadth and permanence of hue, imparted alike to the sky and to the snowy earth, as if tinted glass was held before your eyes. I find myself at a loss how to describe these effects, or the impression they produce upon the traveller's mood. Certainly, it is the very reverse of that depression which accompanies the Polar night, and which even the absence of any real daylight might be considered sufficient to produce.

Our road was well beaten, but narrow, and we had great difficulty in passing the many hay and wood teams which met us, on account of the depth of the loose snow on either side. We had several violent overturns at such times, one of which occasioned us the loss of our beloved pipe—a loss which rendered Braisted disconsolate for the rest of the day. We had but one between us, and the bereavement was not slight. Soon after leaving Haparanda, we passed a small white obelisk, with the words "Russian Frontier" upon it. The town of Torneå, across the frozen river, looked really imposing, with the sharp roof and tall spire of its old church rising above the line of low red buildings. Campbell, I remember, says,

"Cold as the rocks on Torneo's hoary brow,"

with the same disregard of geography which makes him grow palm trees along the Susquehanna River. There was Torneå; but I looked in vain for the "hoary brow." Not a hill within sight, nor a rock within a circuit of ten miles, but one unvarying level, like the western shore of the Adriatic, formed by the deposits of the rivers and the retrocession of the sea.

Our road led up the left bank of the river, both sides of which were studded with neat little villages. The country was well cleared and cultivated, and appeared so populous and flourishing that I could scarcely realise in what part of the world we were. The sun set at a quarter past one, but for two hours the whole southern heaven was superb in its hues of rose and orange. The sheepskin lent us by our landlady kept our feet warm, and we only felt the cold in our faces; my nose, especially, which, having lost a coat of skin, was very fresh and tender, requiring unusual care. At three o'clock, when we reached Kuckula, the first station, the northern sky was one broad flush of the purest violet, melting into lilac at the zenith, where it met the fiery skirts of sunset.

We refreshed ourselves with hot milk, and pushed ahead, with better horses. At four o'clock it was bright moonlight, with the stillest air. We got on bravely over the level, beaten road, and in two hours reached Korpikylä, a large new inn, where we found very tolerable accommodations. Our beds were heaps of reindeer skins; a frightfully ugly Finnish girl, who knew a few words of Swedish, prepared us a supper of tough meat, potatoes, and ale. Everything was now pure Finnish, and the first question of the girl, "Hvarifrån kommar du?" (Where dost thou come from?) showed an ignorance of the commonest Swedish form of address. She awoke us with a cup of coffee in the morning, and negotiated for us the purchase of a reindeer skin, which we procured for something less than a dollar. The hus-bonde (house-peasant, as the landlord is called here) made no charge for our entertainment, but said we might give what we pleased. I offered, at a venture, a sum equal to about fifty cents, whereupon he sent the girl to say that he thanked us most heartily.

The next day was a day to be remembered: such a glory of twilight splendors for six full hours was beyond all the charms of daylight in any zone. We started at seven, with a temperature of 20° below zero, still keeping up the left bank of the Torneå. The country now rose into bold hills, and the features of the scenery became broad and majestic. The northern sky was again pure violet, and a pale red tinge from the dawn rested on the tops of the snowy hills. The prevailing color of the sky slowly brightened into lilac, then into pink, then rose color, which again gave way to a flood of splendid orange when the sun appeared. Every change of color affected the tone of the landscape. The woods, so wrapped in snow that not a single green needle was to be seen, took by turns the hues of the sky, and seemed to give out, rather than to reflect, the opalescent lustre of the morning. The sunshine brightened instead of dispelling these effects. At noon the sun's disc was not more than 1° above the horizon, throwing a level golden light on the hills. The north, before us, was as blue as the Mediterranean, and the vault of heaven, overhead, canopied us with pink. Every object was glorified and transfigured in the magic glow.

At the first station we got some hot milk, with raw salmon, shingle bread and frozen butter. Our horses were good, and we drove merrily along, up the frozen Torneå. The roads were filled with people going to church, probably to celebrate some religious anniversary. Fresh ruddy faces had they, firm features, strong frames and resolute carriage, but the most of them were positively ugly, and, by contrast with the frank Swedes, their expression was furtive and sinister. Near Päckilä we passed a fine old church of red brick, with a very handsome belfry. At Niemis we changed horses in ten minutes, and hastened on up the bed of the Torneå to Matarengi, where we should reach the Arctic Circle. The hills rose higher, with fine sweeping outlines, and the river was still half a mile broad—a plain of solid snow, with the track marked out by bushes. We kept a sharp look-out for the mountain of Avasaxa, one of the stations of Celsius, Maupertius, and the French Academicians, who came here in 1736, to make observations determining the exact form of the earth. Through this mountain, it is said, the Arctic Circle passes, though our maps were neither sufficiently minute nor correct to determine the point. We took it for granted, however, as a mile one way or the other could make but little difference; and as Matarengi lies due west of Avasaxa, across the river, we decided to stop there and take dinner on the Arctic Circle.

The increase of villages on both banks, with the appearance of a large church, denoted our approach to Matarengi, and we saw at once that the tall, gently-rounded, isolated hill opposite, now blazing with golden snow, could be none other than Avasaxa. Here we were, at last, entering the Arctic Zone, in the dead of winter—the realization of a dream which had often flashed across my mind, when lounging under the tropical palms; so natural is it for one extreme to suggest the opposite. I took our bearings with a compass-ring, as we drove forward, and as the summit of Avasaxa bore due east we both gave a shout which startled our postilion and notably quickened the gait of our horses. It was impossible to toss our caps, for they were not only tied upon our heads, but frozen fast to our beards. So here we were at last, in the true dominions of Winter. A mild ruler he had been to us, thus far, but he proved a despot before we were done with him.

Soon afterwards, we drove into the inn at Matarengi, which was full of country people, who had come to attend church. The landlord, a sallow, watery-eyed Finn, who knew a few words of Swedish, gave us a room in an adjoining house, and furnished a dinner of boiled fish and barley mush, to which was added a bottle labelled "Dry Madeira," brought from Haparanda for the occasion. At a shop adjoining, Braisted found a serviceable pipe, so that nothing was wanting to complete our jubilee. We swallowed the memory of all who were dear to us, in the dubious beverage, inaugurated our Arctic pipe, which we proposed to take home as a souvenir of the place, and set forward in the most cheery mood.

Our road now crossed the river and kept up the Russian side to a place with the charming name of Torakankorwa. The afternoon twilight was even more wonderful than that of the forenoon. There were broad bands of purple, pure crimson, and intense yellow, all fusing together into fiery orange at the south, while the north became a semi-vault of pink, then lilac, and then the softest violet. The dazzling Arctic hills participated in this play of colors, which did not fade, as in the South, but stayed, and stayed, as if God wished to compensate by this twilight glory for the loss of the day. Nothing in Italy, nothing in the Tropics, equals the magnificence of the Polar skies. The twilight gave place to a moonlight scarcely less brilliant. Our road was hardly broken, leading through deep snow, sometimes on the river, sometimes through close little glens, hedged in with firs drooping with snow—fairy Arctic solitudes, white, silent and mysterious.

By seven o'clock we reached a station called Juoxengi. The place was wholly Finnish, and the landlord, who did not understand a word of Swedish, endeavoured to make us go on to the next station. We pointed to the beds and quietly carried in our baggage. I made the usual signs for eating, which speedily procured us a pail of sour milk, bread and butter, and two immense tin drinking horns of sweet milk. The people seemed a little afraid of us, and kept away. Our postilion was a silly fellow, who could not understand whether his money was correct. In the course of our stenographic conversation, I learned that "cax" signified two. When I gave him his drink-money he said "ketox!" and on going out the door, "hüweste!"—so that I at least discovered the Finnish for "Thank you!" and "Good-bye!" This, however, was not sufficient to order horses the next morning. We were likewise in a state of delightful uncertainty as to our future progress, but this very uncertainty gave a zest to our situation, and it would have been difficult to find two jollier men with frozen noses.

CHAPTER VIII. ADVENTURES AMONG THE FINNS.

We drank so much milk (for want of more solid food) at Juoxengi, that in spite of sound sleep under our sheepskin blankets, we both awoke with headaches in the morning. The Finnish landlord gave me to understand, by holding up his fore-finger, and pronouncing the word "üx," that I was to pay one rigsdaler (about 26 cents), for our entertainment, and was overcome with grateful surprise when I added a trifle more. We got underway by six o'clock, when the night was just at its darkest, and it was next to impossible to discern any track on the spotless snow. Trusting to good luck to escape overturning, we followed in the wake of the skjutsbonde, who had mounted our baggage sled upon one of the country sledges, and rode perched upon his lofty seat. Our horses were tolerable, but we had eighteen miles to Pello, the next station, which we reached about ten o'clock.

Our road was mostly upon the Torneå River, sometimes taking to the woods on either side, to cut off bends. The morn was hours in dawning, with the same splendid transitions of colour. The forests were indescribable in their silence, whiteness, and wonderful variety of snowy adornment. The weeping birches leaned over the road, and formed white fringed arches; the firs wore mantles of ermine, and ruffs and tippets of the softest swan's down. Snow, wind, and frost had worked the most marvellous transformations in the forms of the forest. Here were kneeling nuns, with their arms hanging listlessly by their sides, and the white cowls falling over their faces; there lay a warrior's helmet; lace curtains, torn and ragged, hung from the points of little Gothic spires; caverns, lined with sparry incrustations, silver palm-leaves, doors, loop-holes, arches and arcades were thrown together in a fantastic confusion and mingled with the more decided forms of the larger trees, which, even, were trees but in form, so completely were they wrapped in their dazzling disguise. It was an enchanted land, where you hardly dared to breathe, lest a breath might break the spell.

There was still little change in the features of the country, except that it became wilder and more rugged, and the settlements poorer and further apart. There were low hills on either side, wildernesses of birch and fir, and floors of level snow over the rivers and marshes. On approaching Pello, we saw our first reindeer, standing beside a hut. He was a large, handsome animal; his master, who wore a fur dress, we of course set down for a Lapp. At the inn a skinny old hag, who knew a dozen words of Swedish, got us some bread, milk, and raw frozen salmon, which, with the aid of a great deal of butter, sufficed us for a meal. Our next stage was to Kardis, sixteen miles, which we made in four hours. While in the midst of a forest on the Swedish side, we fell in with a herd of reindeer, attended by half-a-dozen Lapps. They came tramping along through the snow, about fifty in number, including a dozen which ran loose. The others were harnessed to pulks, the canoe-shaped reindeer sledges, many of which were filled with stores and baggage. The Lapps were rather good-looking young fellows, with a bright, coppery, orange complexion, and were by no means so ill-favoured, short, and stunted as I had imagined. One of them was, indeed, really handsome, with his laughing eyes, sparkling teeth, and a slender, black moustache.

We were obliged to wait a quarter-of-an-hour while the herd passed, and then took to the river again. The effect of sunset on the snow was marvellous— the spotless mounds and drifts, far and near, being stained with soft rose colour, until they resembled nothing so much as heaps of strawberry ice. At Kardis the people sent for an interpreter, who was a young man, entirely blind. He helped us to get our horses, although we were detained an hour, as only one horse is kept in readiness at these stations, and the neighbourhood must be scoured to procure another. I employed the time in learning a few Finnish words—the whole travelling-stock, in fact, on which I made the journey to Muonioniska. That the reader may see how few words of a strange language will enable him to travel, as well as to give a sample of Finnish, I herewith copy my whole vocabulary:

one	üx
two	cax
three	kolma

four	nelia
five	viis
six	oos
seven	settima
eight	kahexa
nine	öhexa
ten	kiumene
a half	puoli
horses	hevorste
immediately	varsin
ready	walmis
drive on!	ayò perli!
how much?	guinga palia
a mile	peligorma
bread	leba
meat	liha
milk	maito
butter	voy
fire	valkär
a bed	sängu (Swedish)
good	hüva
bad	páhá

We kept on our way up the river, in the brilliant afternoon moonlight. The horses were slow; so were the two skjutsbonder, to whom I cried in vain: "Ayò perli!" Braisted with difficulty restrained his inclination to cuff their ears. Hour after hour went by, and we grew more and more hungry, wrathful and impatient. About eight o'clock they stopped below a house on the Russian side, pitched some hay to the horses, climbed the bank, and summoned us to follow. We made our way with some difficulty through the snow, and entered the hut, which proved to be the abode of a cooper—at least the occupant, a rough, shaggy, dirty Orson of a fellow, was seated upon the floor, making a tub, by the light of the fire. The joists overhead were piled with seasoned wood, and long bundles of thin, dry fir, which is used for torches during the winter darkness. There was neither chair nor table in the hut; but a low bench ran around the walls, and a rough bedstead was built against one corner. Two buckets of sour milk, with a wooden ladle, stood beside the door. This beverage appears to be generally used by the Finns for quenching thirst, instead of water. Our postilions were sitting silently upon the bench, and we followed their example, lit our pipes, and puffed away, while the cooper, after the first glance, went on with his work; and the other members of his family, clustered together in the dusky corner behind the fireplace, were equally silent. Half an hour passed, and the spirit moved no one to open his mouth. I judged at last that the horses had been baited sufficiently, silently showed my watch to the postilions, who, with ourselves, got up and went away without a word having been said to mar the quaint drollery of the incident.

While at Haparanda, we had been recommended to stop at Kingis Bruk, at the junction of the Torneå and Muonio. "There," we were told, "you can get everything you want: there is a fine house, good beds, and plenty to eat and drink." Our blind interpreter at Kardis repeated this advice. "Don't go on to Kexisvara;" (the next station) said he, "stop at Kengis, where everything is good." Toward Kengis, then, this oasis in the arctic desolation, our souls yearned. We drove on until ten o'clock in the brilliant moonlight and mild, delicious air—for the temperature had actually risen to 25° above zero!—before a break in the hills announced the junction of the two rivers. There was a large house on the top of a hill on our left, and, to our great joy, the postilions drove directly up to it. "Is this Kengis?" I asked, but their answers I could not understand, and they had already unharnessed their horses.

There was a light in the house, and we caught a glimpse of a woman's face at the window, as we drove up. But the light was immediately extinguished, and everything became silent. I knocked at the door, which was partly open, but no one came. I then pushed: a heavy log of wood, which was leaning against it from the inside, fell with a noise which reverberated through the house. I waited awhile, and then, groping my way along a passage to the door of the room which had been lighted, knocked loudly. After a little delay, the door was opened by a young man, who ushered me into a warm, comfortable room, and then quietly stared at me, as if to ask what I wanted. "We are travellers and strangers," said I, "and wish to stop for the night." "This is not an inn," he answered; "it is the residence of the patron of the iron works." I may here remark that it is the general custom in Sweden, in remote districts, for travellers to call without ceremony upon the parson, magistrate, or any other prominent man in a village, and claim his hospitality. In spite of this doubtful reception, considering that our horses were already stabled and the station three or four miles further, I remarked again: "But perhaps we may be allowed to remain here until morning?" "I will ask," he replied, left the room, and soon returned with an affirmative answer.

We had a large, handsomely furnished room, with a sofa and curtained bed, into which we tumbled as soon as the servant-girl, in compliance with a hint of mine, had brought up some bread, milk, and cheese. We had a cup of coffee in the morning, and were preparing to leave when the patron appeared. He was a short, stout, intelligent Swede, who greeted us courteously, and after a little conversation, urged us to stay until after breakfast. We were too hungry to need much persuasion, and indeed the table set with tjäde, or capercailie (one of the finest game birds in the world), potatoes, cranberries, and whipped cream, accompanied with excellent Umeå ale, and concluded with coffee, surpassed anything we had sat down to for many a day. The patron gave me considerable information about the country, and quieted a little anxiety I was beginning to feel, by assuring me that we should find post-horses all the way to Muonioniska, still ninety-five miles distant. He informed me that we had already got beyond the daylight, as the sun had not yet risen at Kengis. This, however, was in consequence of a hill to the southward, as we afterwards found that the sun was again above the horizon.

We laid in fuel enough to last us through the day, and then took leave of our host, who invited us to visit him on our return. Crossing the Torneå, an hour's drive over the hills brought us to the village of Kexisvara, where we were obliged to wait some time for our horses. At the inn there was a well forty feet deep, with the longest sweep-pole I ever saw. The landlady and her two sisters were pleasant bodies, and sociably inclined, if we could have talked to them. They were all spinning tow, their wheels purring like pleased lionesses. The sun's disc came in sight at a quarter past eleven, and at noon his lower limb just touched the horizon. The sky was of a splendid saffron hue, which changed into a burning brassy yellow.

Our horses promised little for speed when we set out, and their harness being ill adapted to our sleds increased the difficulty. Instead of hames there were wide wooden yokes, the ends of which passed through mortices in the ends of the shafts, and were fastened with pins, while, as there was no belly-bands, the yokes rose on going down hill, bringing our sleds upon the horses' heels. The Finnish sleds have excessively long shafts, in order to prevent this. Our road all day was upon the Muonio River, the main branch of the Torneå, and the boundary between Sweden and Russia, above the junction. There had been a violent wind during the night, and the track was completely filled up. The Torneå and Muonio are both very swift rivers, abounding in dangerous rapids, but during the winter, rapids and all, they are solid as granite from their sources to the Bothnian Gulf. We plunged along slowly, hour after hour, more than half the time clinging to one side or the other, to prevent our sled from overturning—and yet it upset at least a dozen times during the day. The scenery was without change: low, black fir forests on either hand, with the decorative snow blown off them; no villages, or signs of life, except the deserted huts of the wood-cutters, nor did we meet but one sled during the whole day. Here and there, on the banks, were sharp, canoe-like boats, twenty or thirty feet long, turned bottom upward. The sky was overcast, shutting out the glorious coloring of the past days. The sun set before one o'clock, and the dull twilight deepened apace into night. Nothing could be more cheerless and dismal: we smoked and talked a little, with much silence between, and I began to think that one more such day would disgust me with the Arctic Zone.

It was four o'clock, and our horses were beginning to stagger, when we reached a little village called Jokijalka, on the Russian side. The postilion stopped at a house, or rather a quadrangle of huts, which he made me comprehend was an inn, adding that it was 4 polàn and 3 belikor (a fearfully unintelligible distance!) to the next one. We entered, and found promise

73

enough in the thin, sallow, sandy-haired, and most obsequious landlord, and a whole herd of rosy children, to decide us to stop. We were ushered into the milk-room, which was warm and carpeted, and had a single narrow bed. I employed my vocabulary with good effect, the quick-witted children helping me out, and in due time we got a supper of fried mutton, bread, butter, and hot milk. The children came in every few minutes to stare at our writing, an operation which they probably never saw before. They would stand in silent curiosity for half an hour at a time, then suddenly rush out, and enjoy a relief of shouts and laughter on the outside. Since leaving Matarengi we had been regarded at all the stations with much wonder, not always unmixed with mistrust. Whether this was simply a manifestation of the dislike which the Finns have for the Swedes, for whom they probably took us, or of other suspicions on their part, we could not decide.

After a time one of the neighbors, who had been sent for on account of his knowing a very few words of Swedish, was ushered into the room. Through him I ordered horses, and ascertained that the next station, Kihlangi, was three and a half Swedish miles distant, but there was a place on the Russian side, one mile off, where we could change horses. We had finished writing, and were sitting by the stove, consulting how we should arrange the bed so as to avoid contact with the dirty coverlet, when the man returned and told us we must go into another house. We crossed the yard to the opposite building, where, to our great surprise, we were ushered into a warm room, with two good beds, which had clean though coarse sheets, a table, looking-glass, and a bit of carpet on the floor. The whole male household congregated to see us take possession and ascertain whether our wants were supplied. I slept luxuriously until awakened by the sound of our landlord bringing in wood to light the fire. He no sooner saw that my eyes were open than he snatched off his cap and threw it upon the floor, moving about with as much awe and silence as if it were the Emperor's bedroom. His daughter brought us excellent coffee betimes. We washed our faces with our tumblers of drinking water, and got under way by half-past six.

The temperature had changed again in the night, being 28° below zero, but the sky was clear and the morning moonlight superb. By this time we were so far north that the moon did not set at all, but wheeled around the sky, sinking to within eight degrees of the horizon at noonday. Our road led across the river, past the church of Kolare, and through a stretch of the Swedish forests back to the river again. To our great surprise, the wind had not blown here, the snow still hung heavy on the trees, and the road was well beaten. At the Russian post-house we found only a woman with the usual troop of children, the eldest of whom, a boy of sixteen, was splitting fir to make torches. I called out "hevorste!" (horses), to which he made a deliberate answer, and went on with his work. After some consultation with the old woman, a younger boy was sent off somewhere, and we sat down to await the result. I called for meat, milk, bread, and butter, which procured us in course of time a pitcher of cold milk, some bread made of ground barley straw, horribly hard and tough, and a lump of sour frozen butter. There was some putrid fish in a wooden bowl, on which the family had breakfasted, while an immense pot of sour milk, butter, broken bread, and straw meal, hanging over the fire, contained their dinner. This was testimony enough to the accounts we had heard in Stockholm, of the year's famine in Finland; and we seemed likely to participate in it.

I chewed the straw bread vigorously for an hour, and succeeded in swallowing enough to fill my stomach, though not enough to satisfy my hunger. The younger children occupied themselves in peeling off the soft inner bark of the fir, which they ate ravenously. They were handsome, fair-skinned youngsters, but not so rosy and beautiful as those of the Norrland Swedes. We were obliged to wait more than two hours before the horses arrived, thus losing a large part of our daylight. The postilions fastened our sleds behind their own large sledges, with flat runners, which got through the snow more easily than ours. We lay down in the sledge, stretched ourselves at full length upon a bed of hay, covered our feet with the deerskin, and set off. We had gone about a Swedish mile when the postilions stopped to feed the horses before a house on the Russian side. There was nobody within, but some coals among the ashes on the hearth showed that it had been used, apparently, as a place of rest and shelter. A tall, powerful Finn, who was travelling alone, was there, smoking his pipe. We all sat down and did likewise, in the bare, dark hut. There were the three Finns, in complete dresses of reindeer skin, and ourselves, swaddled from head to foot, with only a small segment of scarlet face visible between our frosted furs and icy beards. It was a true Arctic picture, as seen by the pale dawn which glimmered on the wastes of snow outside.

We had a poor horse, which soon showed signs of breaking down, especially when we again entered a belt of country where the wind had blown, the trees were clear, and the track filled up. At half-past eleven we saw the light of the sun on the tops of the hills, and at noon about half his disc was visible. The cold was intense; my hands became so stiff and benumbed that I had great difficulty in preventing them from freezing, and my companion's feet almost lost all feeling. It was well for us that we were frequently obliged to walk, to aid the horse. The country was a wilderness of mournful and dismal scenery—low hills and woods, stripped bare of snow, the dark firs hung with black, crape-like moss, alternating with morasses. Our Finnish postilions were pleasant, cheerful fellows, who insisted on our riding when there was the least prospect of a road. Near a solitary hut (the only one on the road) we met a man driving a reindeer. After this we lost all signs of our way, except the almost obliterated track of his pulk. The snow was deeper than ever, and our horses were ready to drop at every step. We had been five hours on the road; the driver said Kihlangi was "üx verst" distant, and at three, finally, we arrived. We appreciated rather better what we had endured when we found that the temperature was 44° below zero.

I at once ordered horses, and a strapping young fellow was sent off in a bad humor to get them. We found it impossible, however, to procure milk or anything to eat, and as the cold was not to be borne else, we were obliged to resort to a bottle of cognac and our Haparanda bread. The old woman sat by the fire smoking, and gave not the least attention to our demands. I paid our postilions in Norwegian orts, which they laid upon a chair and counted, with the assistance of the whole family. After the reckoning was finished they asked me what the value of each piece was, which gave rise to a second general computation. There was, apparently, more than they had expected, for they both made me a formal address of thanks, and took my hand. Seeing that I had produced a good effect I repeated my demand for milk. The old woman refused, but the men interfered in my behalf; she went out and presently returned with a bowl full, which she heated for us. By this time our horses had arrived, and one of our new postilions prepared himself for the journey, by stripping to the loins and putting on a clean shirt. He was splendidly built, with clean, firm muscle, a white glossy skin, and no superfluity of flesh. He then donned a reindeer of pösk, leggings and boots, and we started again.

It was nearly five o'clock, and superb moonlight. This time they mounted our sleds upon their own sledges, so that we rode much higher than usual. Our way lay up the Muonio River: the track was entirely snowed up, and we had to break a new one, guided by the fir-trees stuck in the ice. The snow was full three feet deep, and whenever the sledge got a little off the old road, the runners cut in so that we could scarcely move. The milk and cognac had warmed us tolerably, and we did not suffer much from the intense cold. My nose, however, had been rubbed raw, and I was obliged to tie a handkerchief across my face to protect it.

While journeying along in this way, the sledge suddenly tilted over, and we were flung head foremost into the snow. Our drivers righted the sledge, we shook ourselves and got in again, but had not gone ten yards before the same thing happened again. This was no joke on such a night, but we took it good-humouredly, to the relief of the Finns, who seemed to expect a scolding. Very soon we went over a third time, and then a fourth, after which they kept near us and held on when there was any danger. I became very drowsy, and struggled with all my force to keep awake, for sleeping was too hazardous. Braisted kept his senses about him by singing, for our encouragement, the mariner's hymn:—

"Fear not, but trust in Providence,

Wherever thou may'st be."

Thus hour after hour passed away. Fortunately we had good, strong horses, which walked fast and steadily. The scenery was always the same— low, wooded hills on either side of the winding, snowy plain of the river. We had made up our minds not to reach Parkajoki before midnight, but at half-past ten our track left the river, mounted the Swedish bank, and very soon brought us to a quadrangle of low huts, having the appearance of an inn. I could scarcely believe my eyes when we stopped before the door. "Is this Parkajoki?" I asked. "Ja!" answered the postilion. Braisted and I sprang out instantly, hugged each other in delight, and rushed into the warm inn. The thermometer still showed -44°, and we prided ourselves a little on having travelled for seventeen hours in such a cold with so little food to keep up our animal heat. The landlord, a young man, with a bristly beard of three weeks' growth, showed us into the milk room, where there was a bed of reindeer skins. His wife brought us some fresh hay, a quilt and a sheepskin coverlet, and we soon forgot both our hunger and our frozen blood.

In the morning coffee was brought to us, and as nothing else was to be had, we drank four cups apiece. The landlord asked half a rigs (13 cents) for our entertainment, and was overcome with gratitude when I gave him double the sum. We had the same sledges as the previous night, but new postilions and excellent horses. The temperature had risen to 5° below zero, with a cloudy sky and a light snow falling. We got off at eight o'clock, found a track partly broken, and went on at a merry trot up the river. We took sometimes one bank and sometimes the other, until, after passing the rapid of Eyanpaika (which was frozen solid, although large masses of transparent ice lay piled like rocks on either side), we kept the Swedish bank. We were in excellent spirits, in the hope of reaching Muonioniska before dark, but the steady trot of our horses brought us out of the woods by noon, and we saw before us the long, scattering village, a mile or two distant, across the river. To our left, on a gentle slope, stood a red, two-story building, surrounded by out-houses, with a few humbler habitations in its vicinity. This was Muoniovara, on the Swedish side—the end of our Finnish journey.

CHAPTER IX. LIFE IN LAPLAND.

As we drove up to the red two-story house, a short man with dark whiskers and a commercial air came forward to meet us. I accosted him in Swedish, asking him whether the house was an inn. He replied in the negative, adding that the only inn was in Muonioniska, on the Russian side, a mile or more distant. I then asked for the residence of Mr. Wolley, the English naturalist, whose name had been mentioned to me by Prof. Retzius and the botanist Hartman. He thereupon called to some one across the court, and presently appeared a tall, slender man dressed in the universal gray suit which travelling Englishmen wear, from the Equator to the Poles. He came up with extended hand, on hearing his own language; a few words sufficed for explanation, and he devoted himself to our interests with the cordiality of an old acquaintance. He lived with the Swede, Herr Forström, who was the merchant of the place; but the wife of the latter had just been confined, and there was no room in his house. Mr. Wolley proposed at first to send to the inn in Muonioniska, and engage a room, but afterwards arranged with a Norsk carpenter, who lived on the hill above, to give us quarters in his house, so that we might be near enough to take our meals together. Nothing could have suited us better. We took possession at once, and then descended the hill to a dinner—I had ventured to hint at our famished condition—of capercailie, cranberries, soft bread, whipped cream, and a glass of genuine port.

Warmed and comforted by such luxurious fare, we climbed the hill to the carpenter's house, in the dreary Arctic twilight, in the most cheerful and contented frame of mind. Was this, indeed, Lapland? Did we, indeed, stand already in the dark heart of the polar Winter? Yes; there was no doubt of it. The imagination could scarcely conceive a more desolate picture than that upon which we gazed—the plain of sombre snow, beyond which the black huts of the village were faintly discernible, the stunted woods and bleak hills, which night and the raw snow clouds had half obscured, and yonder fur-clad figure gliding silently along beside his reindeer. Yet, even here, where Man seemed to have settled out of pure spite against Nature, were comfort and hospitality and kindness. We entered the carpenter's house, lit our candles and pipes, and sat down to enjoy at ease the unusual feeling of shelter and of home. The building was of squared fir-logs, with black moss stuffed in the crevices, making it very warm and substantial. Our room contained a loom, two tables, two beds with linen of voluptuous softness and cleanness, an iron stove (the first we had seen in Sweden), and the usual washing apparatus, besides a piece of carpet on the floor. What more could any man desire? The carpenter, Herr Knoblock, spoke some German; his son, Ludwig, Mr. Wolley's servant, also looked after our needs; and the daughter, a fair, blooming girl of about nineteen, brought us coffee before we were out of bed, and kept our fire in order. Why, Lapland was a very Sybaris in comparison with what I had expected.

Mr. Wolley proposed to us another luxury, in the shape of a vapour-bath, as Herr Forström had one of those bathing-houses which are universal in Finland. It was a little wooden building without windows. A Finnish servant-girl who had been for some time engaged in getting it in readiness, opened the door for us. The interior was very hot and moist, like an Oriental bathing-hall. In the centre was a pile of hot stones, covered with birch boughs, the leaves of which gave out an agreeable smell, and a large tub of water. The floor was strewn with straw, and under the roof was a platform extending across one end of the building. This was covered with soft hay, and reached by means of a ladder, for the purpose of getting the full effect of the steam. Some stools, and a bench for our clothes, completed the arrangements. There was also in one corner a pitcher of water, standing in a little heap of snow to keep it cool.

The servant-girl came in after us, and Mr. W. quietly proceeded to undress, informing us that the girl was bathing-master, and would do the usual scrubbing and shampooing. This, it seems, is the general practice in Finland, and is but another example of the unembarrassed habits of the people in this part of the world. The poorer families go into their bathing-rooms together—father, mother, and children—and take turns in polishing each other's backs. It would have been ridiculous to have shown any hesitation under the circumstances—in fact, an indignity to the honest simple-hearted, virtuous girl—and so we deliberately undressed also. When at last we stood, like our first parents in Paradise, "naked and not ashamed," she handed us bunches of birch-twigs with the leaves on, the use of which was suggested by the leaf of sculpture. We mounted to the platform and lay down upon our backs, whereupon she increased the temperature by throwing water upon the hot stones, until the heat was rather oppressive, and we began to sweat profusely. She then took up a bunch of birch-twigs which had been dipped in hot water, and switched us smartly from head to foot. When we had become thoroughly parboiled and lax, we descended to the floor, seated ourselves upon the stools, and were scrubbed with soap as thoroughly as propriety permitted. The girl was an admirable bather, the result of long practice in the business. She finished by pouring hot water over us, and then drying us with warm towels. The Finns frequently go out and roll in the snow during the progress of the bath. I ventured so far as to go out and stand a few seconds in the open air. The mercury was at zero, and the effect of the cold on my heated skin was delightfully refreshing.

I dressed in a violent perspiration, and then ran across to Herr Forström's house, where tea was already waiting for us. Here we found the länsman or magistrate of the Russian district opposite, a Herr Bràxen, who was decorated with the order of Stanislaus for his services in Finland during the recent war. He was a tall, dark-haired man, with a restless light in his deep-set eyes, and a gentleman in his demeanor. He entered into our plans with interest, and the evening was spent in consultation concerning them. Finally, it was decided that Herr Forström should send a messenger up the river to Palajoki (forty miles off), to engage Lapps and reindeer to take us across the mountains to Kautokeino, in Norway. As the messenger would be absent three or four days, we had a comfortable prospect of rest before us, and I went to bed with a light heart, to wake to the sixth birthday I have passed in strange lands.

In the morning, I went with Mr. Wolley to call upon a Finn, one of whose children was suffering from inflamed eyes, or snowthalmia, as it might be called. The family were prolific, as usual—children of all sizes, with a regular gradation of a year between. The father, a short, shock-headed fellow, sat in one corner; the mother, who, like nine-tenths of all the matrons we had seen between Lapland and Stockholm, gave promise of additional humanity, greeted us with a comical, dipping courtesy—a sudden relaxing and stiffening again of the muscles of the knees—which might be introduced as a novelty into our fashionable circles. The boy's eyes were terribly blood-shot, and the lids swollen, but a solution of nitrate of silver, which Mr. W. applied, relieved him greatly in the course of a day or two. We took occasion to visit the stable, where half a dozen cows lay in darkness, in their warm stalls, on one side, with two bulls and some sheep on the other. There was a fire in one corner, over which hung a great kettle filled with a mixture of boiled hay and reindeer moss. Upon this they are fed, while the sheep must content themselves with bunches of birch, willow and aspen twigs, gathered with the leaves on. The hay is strong and coarse, but nourishing, and the reindeer moss, a delicate white lichen, contains a glutinous ingredient, which probably increases the secretion of milk. The stable, as well as Forström's, which we afterwards inspected, was kept in good order. It was floored, with a gutter past each row of stalls, to carry off the manure. The cows were handsome white animals, in very good condition.

Mr. Wolley sent for his reindeer in the course of the morning, in order to give us a lesson in driving. After lunch, accordingly, we prepared ourselves for the new sensation. I put on a poesk of reindeer skin, and my fur-lined Russian boots. Ludwig took a pulk also, to assist us in case of need. These pulks are shaped very much like a canoe; they are about five feet long, one foot deep, and eighteen inches wide, with a sharp bow and a square stern. You sit upright against the stern-board, with your legs stretched out in the bottom. The deer's harness consists only of a collar of reindeer skin around the neck, with a rope at the bottom, which passes under the belly, between the legs, and is fastened to the bow of the pulk. He is driven by a single rein, attached to the base of the left horn, and passing over the back to the right hand of the driver, who thrusts his thumb into a loop at the end, and takes several turns around his wrist. The rein is held rather slack, in order that it may be thrown over to the right side when it slips to the left, which it is very apt to do.

I seated myself, took proper hold of the rein, and awaited the signal to start. My deer was a strong, swift animal, who had just shed his horns. Ludwig set off first; my deer gave a startling leap, dashed around the corner of the house, and made down the hill. I tried to catch the breath which had been jerked out of me, and to keep my balance, as the pulk, swaying from side to side, bounced over the snow. It was too late; a swift presentiment of the catastrophe flashed across my mind, but I was powerless to avert it. In another second I found myself rolling in the loose snow, with the pulk bottom upward beside me. The deer, who was attached to my arm, was standing still, facing me, with an expression of stupid surprise (but no sympathy) on his face. I got up, shook myself, righted the pulk, and commenced again. Off we went, like the wind, down the hill, the snow flying in my face and blinding me. My pulk made tremendous leaps, bounding from side to side, until, the whirlwind suddenly subsiding, I found myself off the road, deep overhead in the snow, choked and blinded, and with small snow-drifts in my pockets, sleeves and bosom. My beard and eyebrows became instantly a white, solid mass, and my face began to tingle from its snow-bath; but, on looking back, I saw as white a beard suddenly emerge from a drift, followed by the stout body of Braisted, who was gathering himself up after his third shipwreck.

We took a fresh start, I narrowly missing another overturn, as we descended the slope below the house, but on reaching the level of the Muonio, I found no difficulty in keeping my balance, and began to enjoy the exercise. My deer struck out, passed the others, and soon I was alone on the track. In the grey Arctic twilight, gliding noiselessly and swiftly over the snow, with the low huts of Muonioniska dimly seen in the distance before me, I had my first true experience of Lapland travelling. It was delightfully novel and exhilarating; I thought of "Afraja," and the song of "Kulnasatz, my reindeer!" and Bryant's "Arctic Lover," and whatever else there is of Polar poetry, urged my deer with shouts, and never once looked behind me until I had climbed the opposite shore and reached the village. My companions were then nowhere to be seen. I waited some time before they arrived, Braisted's deer having become fractious and run back with him to the house. His crimson face shone out from its white frame of icy hair as he shouted to me, "There is nothing equal to this, except riding behind a right whale when he drives to windward, with every man trimming the boat, and the spray flying over your bows!"

We now turned northward through the village, flying around many sharp corners, but this I found comparatively easy work. But for the snow I had taken in, which now began to melt, I got on finely in spite of the falling flakes, which beat in our faces. Von Buch, in his journey through Lapland in 1807, speaks of Muonioniska as "a village with an inn where they have silver spoons." We stopped at a house which Mr. Wolley stated was the very building, but it proved to be a more recent structure on the site of the old inn. The people looked at us with curiosity on hearing we were Americans. They had heard the name of America, but did not seem to know exactly where it was. On leaving the house, we had to descend the steep bank of the river. I put out my feet to steady the pulk, and thereby ploughed a cataract of fine snow into my face, completely blinding me. The pulk gave a flying leap from the steepest pitch, flung me out, and the deer, eager to make for home, dragged me by the arm for about twenty yards before I could arrest him. This was the worst upset of all, and far from pleasant, although the temperature was only zero. I reached home again without further mishap, flushed, excited, soaked with melted snow, and confident of my ability to drive reindeer with a little more practice.

During the first three days, the weather was raw, dark, and lowering, with a temperature varying from 9° above to 13° below zero. On the morning of the 14th, however, the sky finally cleared, with a cold south wind, and we saw, for the first time, the range of snowy mountains in the east. The view from our hill, before so dismally bleak and dark, became broad and beautiful, now that there was a little light to see it by. Beyond the snowy floor of the lake and the river Muonio stretched the scattering huts of Muonioniska, with the church overlooking them, and the round, white peak of Ollastyntre rising above his belt of black woods to the south. Further to the east extended alternate streaks of dark forest and frozen marsh for eighteen miles, to the foot of the mountain range of Palastyntre, which stood like a line of colossal snow-drifts against the soft violet sky, their sides touched by the rosily-golden beams of the invisible sun. This and the valley of the Torneå, at Avasaxa, are two of the finest views in Lapland.

I employed part of my time in making some sketches of characteristic faces. Mr. Wolley, finding that I wished to procure good types of the Finns and Lapps, kindly assisted me—his residence of three years in Muoniovara enabling him to know who were the most marked and peculiar personages. Ludwig was despatched to procure an old fellow by the name of Niemi, a Finn, who promised to comply with my wishes; but his ignorance made him suspicious, and it was necessary to send again. "I know what travellers are," said he, "and what a habit they have of getting people's skulls to carry home with them. Even if they are arrested for it, they are so rich, they always buy over the judges. Who knows but they might try to kill me for the sake of my skull?" After much persuasion, he was finally induced to come, and, seeing that Ludwig supposed he was still afraid, he said, with great energy: "I have made up my mind to go, even if a shower of knives should fall from heaven!" He was seventy-three years old, though he did not appear to be over sixty— his hair being thick and black, his frame erect and sturdy, and his colour crimson rather than pale. His eyebrows were jet-black and bushy, his eyes large and deep set, his nose strong and prominent, and the corners of his long mouth drawn down in a settled curve, expressing a melancholy grimness. The high cheek-bones, square brow, and muscular jaw belonged to the true Finnish type. He held perfectly still while I drew, scarcely moving a muscle of his face, and I succeeded in getting a portrait which everybody recognised.

I gave him a piece of money, with which he was greatly delighted; and, after a cup of coffee, in Herr Knoblock's kitchen, he went home quite proud and satisfied. "They do not at all look like dangerous persons," said he to the carpenter; "perhaps they do not collect skulls. I wish they spoke our language, that I might ask them how people live in their country. America is a very large, wild place. I know all about it, and the discovery of it. I was not there myself at the time, but Jenis Lampi, who lives in Kittila, was one of the crew of the ship, and he told me how it happened. Jenis Lampi said they were going to throw the captain overboard, but he persuaded them to give him three days, and on the third day they found it. Now I should like to know whether these people, who come from that country, have laws as we have, and whether they live as comfortably." So saying, Isaaki Anderinpoika Niemi departed.

No sooner had he gone than the old Lapp woman, Elsa, who had been sent for, drove up in her pulk, behind a fast reindeer. She was in complete Lapp costume—a blue cloth gown with wide sleeves, trimmed with scarlet, and a curious pear-shaped cap of the same material, upon her head. She sat upon the floor, on a deerskin, and employed herself in twisting reindeer sinews, which she rolled upon her cheek with the palm of her hand, while I was sketching her. It was already dark, and I was obliged to work by candle light, but I succeeded in catching the half-insane, witch-like expression of her face. When I took the candle to examine her features more closely, she cried out, "Look at me, O son of man!" She said that I had great powers, and was capable of doing everything, since I had come so far, and could make an image of her upon paper. She asked whether we were married, saying we could hardly travel so much if we were; yet she thought it much better to be married and stay at home. I gave her a rigsdaler, which she took with joyful surprise, saying, "What! am I to get my coffee and tobacco, and be paid too? Thanks, O son of man, for your great goodness!" She chuckled very much over the drawing, saying that the dress was exactly right.

In the afternoon we took another reindeer drive to Muonioniska, paying a visit to Pastor Fali, the clergyman whom we had met at Forström's. This time I succeeded very well, making the trip without a single overturn, though with several mishaps. Mr. Wolley lost the way, and we drove about at random for some time. My deer became restive, and whirled me around in the snow, filling my pulk. It was so dark that we could scarcely see, and, without knowing the ground, one could not tell where the ups and down were. The pastor received us courteously, treated us to coffee and pipes, and conversed with us for some time. He had not, as he said, a Swedish tongue, and I found it difficult to understand him. On our way back, Braisted's and Ludwig's deers ran together with mine, and, while going at full speed, B.'s jumped into my pulk. I tried in vain either to stop or drive on faster; he trampled me so violently that I was obliged to throw myself out to escape his hoofs. Fortunately the animals are not heavy enough to do any serious harm. We reached Forström's in season for a dinner of fat reindeer steak, cranberries, and a confect of the Arctic raspberry.

After an absence of three days Salomon, the messenger who had been

86

sent up the river to engage reindeer for us, returned, having gone sixty miles before he could procure them. He engaged seven, which arrived the next evening, in the charge of a tall, handsome Finn, who was to be our conductor. We had, in the meantime, supplied ourselves with reindeer poesks, such as the Lapps wear,—our own furs being impracticable for pulk travelling— reindeer mittens, and boas of squirrel tails strung on reindeer sinews. The carpenter's second son, Anton, a lad of fifteen, was engaged to accompany us as an interpreter.

CHAPTER X. A REINDEER JOURNEY ACROSS LAPLAND.

We left Muoniovara at noon on the 15th, fully prepared for a three days' journey across the wilds of Lapland. We were about to traverse the barren, elevated table-land, which divides the waters of the Bothnian Gulf from those of the Northern Ocean,—a dreary, unfriendly region, inhabited only by a few wandering Lapps. Even without the prevalence of famine, we should have had difficulty in procuring food from them, so we supplied ourselves with a saddle of reindeer, six loaves of rye bread, sugar, and a can of coffee. The carpenter lent us a cup and saucer, and Anton, who felt all the responsibility of a boy who is employed for the first time, stowed everything away nicely in the broad baggage pulk. We found it impossible to procure Lapp leggings and shoes at Muoniovara, but our Russian boots proved an admirable substitute. The poesk of reindeer skin is the warmest covering for the body which could be devised. It is drawn over the head like a shirt, fitting closely around the neck and wrists, where it is generally trimmed with ermine, and reaching half-way below the knee. A thick woollen sash, wrapped first around the neck, the ends then twisted together down to the waist, where they are passed tightly around the body and tied in front, not only increases the warmth and convenience of the garment, but gives it a highly picturesque air. Our sea-otter caps, turned down so as to cover the ears and forehead, were fastened upon our heads with crimson handkerchiefs, and our boas, of black and red squirrel tails, passed thrice around the neck, reached to the tips of our noses. Over our dog-skin mittens we drew gauntlets of reindeer skin, with which it was difficult to pick up or take hold of anything; but as the deer's rein is twisted around one's wrist, their clumsiness does not interfere with the facility of driving. It would seem impossible for even Arctic cold to penetrate through such defences—and yet it did.

Herr Forström prepared us for the journey by a good breakfast of reindeer's marrow, a justly celebrated Lapland delicacy, and we set out with a splendidly clear sky and a cold of 12° below zero. The Muonio valley was superb, towards sunrise, with a pale, creamy, saffron light on the snow, the forests on the tops of the hills burning like jagged masses of rough opal, and the distant range of Palastyntre bathed in pink light, with pure sapphire shadows on its northern slopes. These Arctic illuminations are transcendent; nothing can equal them, and neither pen nor pencil can describe them. We passed through Muonioniska, and kept up the Russian side, over an undulating, wooded country. The road was quite good, but my deer, in spite of his size and apparent strength, was a lazy beast, and gave me much trouble. I was obliged to get out of the pulk frequently and punch him in the flanks, taking my chance to tumble in headlong as he sprang forward again. I soon became disgusted with reindeer travelling, especially when, after we had been on the road two hours and it was nearly dark, we reached Upper Muonioniska, only eight miles. We there took the river again, and made better progress to Kyrkessuando, the first station, where we stopped an hour to feed the deer. Here there was a very good little inn, with a bed for travellers.

We had seven reindeer, two of which ran loose, so that we could change occasionally on the road. I insisted on changing mine at once, and received in return a smaller animal, which made up in spirit what he lacked in strength. Our conductor was a tall, handsome Finn, with blue eyes and a bright, rosy complexion. His name was Isaac, but he was better known by his nickname of Pitka Isaaki, or Long Isaac. He was a slow, good-humoured, prudent, careful fellow, and probably served our purpose as well as anybody we could have found. Anton, however, who made his first journey with us, was invaluable. His father had some misgivings on account of his timidity, but he was so ambitious to give satisfaction that we found him forward enough.

I have already described the country through which we passed, as it was merely a continuation of the scenery below Muonioniska—low, wooded hills, white plains, and everywhere snow, snow, snow, silence and death. The cold increased to 33° below zero, obliging me to bury my nose in my boa and to keep up a vigorous exercise of my toes to prevent them from freezing, as it is impossible to cover one's boots in a pulk. The night was calm, clear, and starry; but after an hour a bank of auroral light gradually arose in the north, and formed a broad arch, which threw its lustre over the snow and lighted up our path. Almost stationary at first, a restless motion after a time agitated the gleaming bow; it shot out broad streamers of yellow fire, gathered them in and launched them forth again, like the hammer of Thor, which always returned to his hand, after striking the blow for which it had been hurled. The most wonderful appearance, however, was an immense square curtain, which fell from all the central part of the arch. The celestial scene-shifters were rather clumsy, for they allowed one end to fall lower than the other, so that it over-lapped and doubled back upon itself in a broad fold. Here it hung for probably half an hour, slowly swinging to and fro, as if moved by a gentle wind. What new spectacle was in secret preparation behind it we did not learn, for it was hauled up so bunglingly that the whole arch broke and fell in, leaving merely a pile of luminous ruins under the Polar Star.

Hungry and nearly frozen, we reached Palajoki at half-past nine, and were at once ushered into the guests' room, a little hut separated from the main building. Here, barring an inch of ice on the windows and numerous windy cracks in the floor, we felt a little comfort before an immense fire kindled in the open chimney. Our provisions were already adamantine; the meat was transformed into red Finland granite, and the bread into mica-slate. Anton and the old Finnish landlady, the mother of many sons, immediately commenced the work of thawing and cooking, while I, by the light of fir torches, took the portrait of a dark-haired, black-eyed, olive-skinned, big-nosed, thick-lipped youth, who gave his name as Eric Johan Sombasi. When our meal of meat, bread, and coffee had been despatched, the old woman made a bed of reindeer skins for us in one corner, covered with a coarse sheet, a quilt, and a sheepskin blanket. She then took her station near the door, where several of the sons were already standing, and all appeared to be waiting in silent curiosity to see us retire. We undressed with genuine Finnish freedom of manner, deliberately enough for them to understand the peculiarities of our apparel, and they never took their eyes from us until we were stowed away for the night in our warm nest.

It was snowing and blowing when we arose. Long Isaac had gone to the woods after the reindeer, and we employed the delay in making a breakfast off the leavings of our supper. Crossing the Muonio at starting, we entered the Russian territory and drove up the bed of the Palajok, a tributary stream which comes down from the north. The sky became clearer as the dawn increased; the road was tolerably broken, and we sped merrily along the windings of the river, under its tall banks fringed with fir trees, which, loaded with snow, shone brilliantly white against the rosy sky. The temperature was 8° below zero, which felt unpleasantly warm, by contrast with the previous evening.

After a time we left the river and entered a rolling upland—alternate thickets of fir and birch, and wastes of frozen marsh, where our path was almost obliterated. After more than two hours' travel we came upon a large lake, at the further end of which, on the southern side of a hill, was the little hamlet of Suontajärvi. Here we stopped to bait the deer, Braisted's and mine being nearly fagged out. We entered one of the huts, where a pleasant woman was taking charge of a year-old baby. There was no fire on the hearth, and the wind whistled through the open cracks of the floor. Long Isaac and the woman saluted each other by placing their right arms around each other's waists, which is the universal manner of greeting in Finland. They only shake hands as a token of thanks for a favour.

We started again at noon, taking our way across a wilderness of lakes and snow-covered marshes, dotted with stunted birch-thickets. The road had entirely disappeared, but Eric of Palajoki, who accompanied us as an extra guide, went ahead with a strong reindeer and piloted us. The sagacity with which these animals find the track under a smooth covering of loose snow, is wonderful. They follow it by the feet, of course, but with the utmost ease and rapidity, often while going at full speed. I was struck by the sinuous, mazy character of our course, even where the ground was level, and could only account for it by the supposition that the first track over the light snow had followed the smoothest and firmest ridges of the marshes. Our progress was now slow and toilsome, and it was not long before my deer gave up entirely. Long Isaac, seeing that a change must be made, finally decided to give me a wild, powerful animal, which he had not yet ventured to intrust to either of us.

The deer was harnessed to my pulk, the rein carefully secured around my wrist, and Long Isaac let go his hold. A wicked toss of the antlers and a prodigious jump followed, and the animal rushed full tilt upon Braisted, who was next before me, striking him violently upon the back. The more I endeavored to rein him in, the more he plunged and tore, now dashing against the led deer, now hurling me over the baggage pulk, and now leaping off the track into bottomless beds of loose snow. Long Isaac at last shouted to me to go ahead and follow Eric, who was about half a mile in advance. A few furious plunges carried me past our little caravan, with my pulk full of snow, and my face likewise. Now, lowering his neck and thrusting out his head, with open mouth and glaring eyes, the deer set off at the top of his speed.

Away I went, like a lance shot out from the auroral armoury; the pulk slid over the snow with the swiftness of a fish through the water; a torrent of snow-spray poured into my lap and showered against my face, until I was completely blinded. Eric was overtaken so quickly that he had no time to give me the track, and as I was not in a condition to see or hear anything, the deer, with the stupidity of his race, sprang directly upon him, trampled him down, and dragged me and my pulk over him. We came to a stand in the deep snow, while Eric shook himself and started again. My deer now turned and made for the caravan, but I succeeded in pulling his head around, when he charged a second time upon Eric, who threw himself out of his pulk to escape. My strength was fast giving way, when we came to a ridge of deep, loose snow, in which the animals sank above their bellies, and up which they could hardly drag us. My deer was so exhausted when we reached the top, that I had no further difficulty in controlling him.

Before us stretched a trackless plain, bounded by a low mountain ridge. Eric set off at a fast trot, winding hither and thither, as his deer followed the invisible path. I kept close behind him, white as a Polar bear, but glowing like a volcano under my furs. The temperature was 10° below zero, and I could have wished it ten degrees colder. My deer, although his first savage strength was spent, was still full of spirit, and I began to enjoy this mode of travel. We soon entered the hills, which were covered with thickets of frozen birch, with here and there a tall Scotch fir, completely robed in snow. The sun, which had showed about half his disc at noon, was now dipping under the horizon, and a pure orange glow lighted up the dazzling masses of the crystal woods. All was silver-clear, far and near, shining, as if by its own light, with an indescribable radiance. We had struck upon a well-beaten track on entering the hills, and flew swiftly along through this silent splendour, this jewelled solitude, under the crimson and violet mode of the sky. Here was true Northern romance; here was poetry beyond all the Sagas and Eddas that ever were written.

We passed three Lapps, with heavy hay-sleds, drawn by a reindeer apiece, and after a time issued from the woods upon a range of hills entirely bare and white. Before us was the miserable hamlet of Lappajärvi, on the western side of the barren mountain of Lippavara, which is the highest in this part of Lapland, having an altitude of 1900 feet above the sea. I have rarely seen anything quite so bleak and God-forsaken as this village. A few low black huts, in a desert of snow—that was all. We drove up to a sort of station-house, where an old, white-headed Finn received me kindly, beat the snow off my poesk with a birch broom, and hung my boa near the fire to dry. There was a wild, fierce-looking Lapp in the room, who spoke some Norwegian, and at once asked who and what I was. His head was covered with a mop of bright brown hair, his eyes were dark blue and gleamed like polished steel, and the flushed crimson of his face was set off by the strong bristles of a beard of three weeks growth. There was something savage and ferocious in his air, as he sat with his clenched fists planted upon his knees, and a heavy knife in a wooden scabbard hanging from his belt. When our caravan arrived I transferred him to my sketch-book. He gave me his name as Ole Olsen Thore, and I found he was a character well known throughout the country.

Long Isaac proposed waiting until midnight, for moon-rise, as it was already dark, and there was no track beyond Lippajärvi. This seemed prudent, and we therefore, with the old woman's help, set about boiling our meat, thawing bread, and making coffee. It was necessary to eat even beyond what appetite demanded, on account of the long distances between the stations. Drowsiness followed repletion, as a matter of course, and they gave us a bed of skins in an inner-room. Here, however, some other members of the family were gathered around the fire, and kept up an incessant chattering, while a young married couple, who lay in one corner, bestowed their endearments on each other, so that we had but little benefit of our rest. At midnight all was ready, and we set out. Long Isaac had engaged a guide, and procured fresh deer in place of those which were fatigued. There was a thick fog, which the moon scarcely brightened, but the temperature had risen to zero, and was as mild as a May morning. For the first time in many days our beards did not freeze.

We pursued our way in complete silence. Our little caravan, in single file, presented a strange, shadowy, mysterious appearance as it followed the winding path, dimly seen through the mist, first on this side and then on that; not a sound being heard, except the crunching of one's own pulk over the snow. My reindeer and myself seemed to be the only living things, and we were pursuing the phantoms of other travellers and other deer, who had long ago perished in the wilderness. It was impossible to see more than a hundred yards; some short, stunted birches, in their spectral coating of snow, grew along the low ridges of the deep, loose snow, which separated the marshes, but nothing else interrupted the monotony of the endless grey ocean, through which we went floundering, apparently at haphazard. How our guides found the way was beyond my comprehension, for I could discover no distinguishable landmarks. After two hours or more we struck upon a cluster of huts called Palajärvi, seven miles from Lippajärvi, which proved that we were on the right track.

The fog now became thicker than ever. We were upon the water-shed between the Bothnian Gulf and the Northern Ocean, about 1400 feet above the sea. The birches became mere shrubs, dotting the low mounds which here and there arose out of the ocean of snow. The pulks all ran in the same track and made a single furrow, so that our gunwales were generally below the sea-level. The snow was packed so tight, however, that we rarely shipped any. Two hours passed, and I was at length roused from a half-sleep by the evidence of our having lost the way. Long Isaac and the guide stopped and consulted every few minutes, striking sometimes in one direction and sometimes in another, but without any result. We ran over ridges of heavy, hard tussocks, blown bare of snow, which pitched our pulks right and left, just as I have bumped over the coral reefs of Loo-Choo in a ship's cutter. Then followed deep beds of snow-drifts, which tasked the utmost strength of our deer, low birch thickets and hard ridges again, over which we plunged in the wildest

94

way possible.

After wandering about for a considerable time, we suddenly heard the barking of a dog at some distance on our left. Following the welcome sound, we reached a scrubby ridge, where we were saluted with a whole chorus of dogs, and soon saw the dark cone of a Lapp tent. Long Isaac aroused the inmates, and the shrill cry of a baby proclaimed that there was life and love, even here. Presently a clumsy form, enveloped in skins, waddled out, and entered into conversation with our men. I proposed at once to engage a Lapp to guide us as far as Eitajärvi, which they informed us was two Norwegian (fourteen English) miles farther. The man agreed, but must first go off to the woods for his deer, which would detain us two hours. He put on his snow-skates and started, and I set about turning the delay to profit by making acquaintance with the inmates of the tents. We had now reached the middle of the village; the lean, wolfish dogs were yelling on all sides, and the people began to bestir themselves. Streams of sparks issued from the open tops of the tents, and very soon we stood as if in the midst of a group of volcanic cones.

The Lapps readily gave us permission to enter. We lifted the hanging door of reindeer hide, crept in, stumbling over a confused mixture of dogs and deerskins, until we found room to sit down. Two middle-aged women, dressed in poesks, like the men, were kindling a fire between some large stones in the centre, but the air inside was still as cold as outside. The damp birch sticks gave out a thick smoke, which almost stifled us, and for half an hour we could scarcely see or breathe. The women did not appear to be incommoded in the least, but I noticed that their eyes were considerably inflamed. After a time our company was increased by the arrival of two stout, ruddy girls of about seventeen, and a child of two years old, which already wore a complete reindeer costume. They were all very friendly and hospitable in their demeanour towards us, for conversation was scarcely possible. The interior of the tent was hung with choice bits of deer's hide, from the inside of the flanks and shoulders, designed, apparently, for mittens. Long Isaac at once commenced bargaining for some of them, which he finally purchased. The money was deposited in a rather heavy bag of coin, which one of the women drew forth from under a pile of skins. Our caps and Russian boots excited their curiosity, and they examined them with the greatest minuteness.

These women were neither remarkably small nor remarkably ugly, as the Lapps are generally represented. The ground-tone of their complexion was rather tawny, to be sure, but there was a glowing red on their cheeks, and their eyes were a dark bluish-grey. Their voices were agreeable, and the language (a branch of the Finnish) had none of that barbaric harshness common to the tongues of nomadic tribes. These favorable features, nevertheless, were far from reconciling me to the idea of a trial of Lapp life. When I saw the filth, the poverty, and discomfort in which they lived, I decided that the present experience was all-sufficient. Roasting on one side and freezing on the other, with smarting eyes and asphyxiated lungs, I soon forgot whatever there was of the picturesque in my situation, and thought only of the return of our Lapp guide. The women at last cleared away several dogs, and made room for us to lie down—a more tolerable position, in our case; though how a whole family, with innumerable dogs, stow themselves in the compass of a circle eight feet in diameter, still remains a mystery.

The Lapp returned with his reindeer within the allotted time, and we took our leave of the encampment. A strong south wind had arisen, but did not dissipate the fog, and for two hours we had a renewal of our past experiences, in thumping over hard ridges and ploughing through seas of snow. Our track was singularly devious, sometimes doubling directly back upon itself without any apparent cause. At last, when a faint presentiment of dawn began to glimmer through the fog, the Lapp halted and announced that he had lost the way. Bidding us remain where we were, he struck off into the snow and was soon lost to sight. Scarcely a quarter of an hour had elapsed, however, before we heard his cries at a considerable distance. Following, as we best could, across a plain nearly a mile in diameter, we found him at last in a narrow dell between two hills. The ground now sloped rapidly northward, and I saw that we had crossed the water-shed, and that the plain behind us must be the lake Jedeckejaure, which, according to Von Buch, is 1370 feet above the sea.

On emerging from the dell we found a gentle slope before us, covered with hard ice, down which our pulks flew like the wind. This brought us to another lake, followed by a similar slope, and so we descended the icy terraces, until, in a little more than an hour, some covered haystacks gave evidence of human habitation, and we drew up at the huts of Eitajärvi, in Norway. An old man, who had been watching our approach, immediately climbed upon the roof and removed a board from the chimney, after which he ushered us into a bare, cold room, and kindled a roaring fire on the hearth. Anton unpacked our provisions, and our hunger was so desperate, after fasting for twenty hours, that we could scarcely wait for the bread to thaw and the coffee to boil. We set out again at noon, down the frozen bed of a stream which drains the lakes, but had not proceeded far before both deers and pulks began to break through the ice, probably on account of springs under it. After being almost swamped, we managed to get up the steep snow-bank and took to the plain again, making our own road over ridge and through hollow. The caravan was soon stopped, that the pulks might be turned bottom upwards and the ice scraped off, which, like the barnacles on a ship's hull, impeded their progress through the snow. The broad plain we were traversing stretched away to the north without a break or spot of color to relieve its ghastly whiteness; but toward the south-west, where the sunset of an unrisen sun spread its roseate glow through the mist, arose some low mounds, covered with drooping birches, which shone against the soft, mellow splendor, like sprays of silver embroidered on rose-colored satin.

Our course, for about fifteen miles, lay alternately upon the stream (where the ice was sufficiently strong) and the wild plain. Two or three Lapp tents on the bank exhibited the usual amount of children and dogs, but we did not think it worth while to extend the circle of our acquaintance in that direction. At five o'clock, after it had long been dark, we reached half a dozen huts called Siepe, two Norwegian miles from Kautokeino. Long Isaac wished to stop here for the night, but we resolutely set ourselves against him. The principal hut was filthy, crowded with Lapps, and filled with a disagreeable smell from the warm, wet poesks hanging on the rafters. In one corner lay the carcases of two deer-calves which had been killed by wolves. A long bench, a table, and a rude frame covered with deerskins, and serving as a bed, comprised all the furniture. The usual buckets of sour milk, with wooden ladles, stood by the door. No one appeared to have any particular occupation, if we except the host's wife, who was engaged with an infant in reindeer breeches. We smoked and deliberated while the deers ate their balls of moss, and the result was, that a stout yellow-haired Lapp youngster was engaged to pilot us to Kautokeino.

Siepe stands on a steep bank, down which our track led to the stream again. As the caravan set off, my deer, which had behaved very well through the day, suddenly became fractious, sprang off the track, whirled himself around on his hind legs, as if on a pivot, and turned the pulk completely over, burying me in the snow. Now, I had come from Muoniovara, more than a hundred miles, without being once overturned, and was ambitious to make the whole journey with equal success. I therefore picked myself up, highly disconcerted, and started afresh. The very same thing happened a second and a third time, and I don't think I shall be considered unreasonable for becoming furiously angry. I should certainly have committed cervicide had any weapon been at hand. I seized the animal by the horns, shook, cuffed, and kicked him, but all to no purpose. Long Isaac, who was passing in his pulk, made some remark, which Anton, with all the gravity and conscientiousness of his new position of interpreter, immediately translated.

"Long Isaac says," he shouted, "that the deer will go well enough, if you knew how to drive him." "Long Isaac may go to the devil!" was, I am sorry to say, my profane reply, which Anton at once translated to him.

Seating myself in the pulk again, I gave the deer the rein, and for a time kept him to the top of his speed, following the Lapp, who drove rapidly down the windings of the stream. It was quite dark, but our road was now somewhat broken, and for three hours our caravan swiftly and silently sped on its way. Then, some scattered lights appeared in the distance; our tired deers leaped forward with fresher spirit, and soon brought us to the low wooden huts of Kautokeino. We had travelled upwards of sixty miles since leaving Lippajärvi, breaking our own road through deep snow for a great part of the way. During this time our deers had not been changed. I cannot but respect the provoking animals after such a feat.

CHAPTER XI. KAUTOKEINO.—A DAY WITHOUT A SUN.

While in Dresden, my friend Ziegler had transferred to me a letter of introduction from Herr Berger, a merchant of Hammerfest, to his housekeeper in Kautokeino. Such a transfer might be considered a great stretch of etiquette in those enlightened regions of the world where hospitality requires certificates of character; but, in a benighted country like Lapland, there was no danger of very fine distinctions being drawn, and Ziegler judged that the house which was to have been placed at his disposal had he made the journey, would as readily open its doors to me. At Muoniovara, I learned that Berger himself was now in Kautokeino, so that I needed only to present him with his own letter. We arrived so late, however, that I directed Long Isaac to take us to the inn until morning. He seemed reluctant to do this, and I could not fathom the reason of his hesitation, until I had entered the hovel to which we were conducted. A single room, filled with smoke from a fire of damp birch sticks, was crammed with Lapps of all sizes, and of both sexes. There was scarcely room to spread a deerskin on the floor while the smell exhaled from their greasy garments and their unwashed bodies was absolutely stifling. I have travelled too much to be particularly nice in my choice of lodgings, but in this instance I instantly retreated, determined to lie on the snow, under my overturned pulk, rather than pass the night among such bed-fellows.

We drove on for a short distance, and drew up before a large, substantial log-house, which Long Isaac informed me was the residence of the Länsman, or magistrate of the district. I knocked at the door, and inquired of the Norwegian servant girl who opened it, where Herr Berger lived. Presently appeared a stout, ruddy gentleman—no less than Herr Berger himself—who addressed me in fluent English. A few words sufficed to explain everything, and in ten minutes our effects were deposited in the guest's room of the Länsman's house, and ourselves, stripped of our Polar hides, were seated on a sofa, in a warm, carpeted room, with a bountiful supper-table before us. Blessed be civilisation! was my inward ejaculation. Blessed be that yearning for comfort in Man, which has led to the invention of beds, of sofas, and easy chairs: which has suggested cleanliness of body and of habitation, and which has developed the noble art of cooking! The dreary and perilous wastes over which we had passed were forgotten. With hearts warmed in both senses, and stomachs which reacted gratefully upon our hearts, we sank that night into a paradise of snowy linen, which sent a consciousness of pleasure even into the oblivion of sleep.

The Länsman, Herr Lie, a tall handsome man of twenty-three, was a native of Altengaard, and spoke tolerable English. With him and Herr Berger, we found a third person, a theological student, stationed at Kautokeino to learn the Lapp tongue. Pastor Hvoslef, the clergyman, was the only other Norwegian resident. The village, separated from the Northern Ocean, by the barren, uninhabited ranges of the Kiölen Mountains, and from the Finnish settlements on the Muonio by the swampy table-lands we had traversed, is one of the wildest and most forlorn places in all Lapland. Occupying, as it does, the centre of a large district, over which the Lapps range with their reindeer herds during the summer, it is nevertheless a place of some importance, both for trade and for the education, organization, and proper control of the barely-reclaimed inhabitants. A church was first built here by Charles XI. of Sweden, in 1660, although, in the course of subsequent boundary adjustments, the district was made over to Norway. Half a century afterwards, some families of Finns settled here; but they appear to have gradually mixed with the Lapps, so that there is little of the pure blood of either race to be found at present. I should here remark that throughout Norwegian Lapland the Lapps are universally called Finns, and the Finns, Quäns. As the change of names, however, might occasion some confusion, I shall adhere to the more correct Swedish manner of designating them, which I have used hitherto.

Kautokeino is situated in a shallow valley, or rather basin, opening towards the north-east, whither its river flows to join the Alten. Although only 835 feet above the sea, and consequently below the limits of the birch and the fir in this latitude, the country has been stripped entirely bare for miles around, and nothing but the scattering groups of low, dark huts, breaks the snowy monotony. It is with great difficulty that vegetables of any kind can be raised. Potatoes have once or twice been made to yield eight-fold, but they are generally killed by the early autumn frosts before maturity. On the southern bank of the river, the ground remains frozen the whole year round, at a depth of only nine feet. The country furnishes nothing except reindeer meat, milk, and cheese. Grain, and other supplies of all kinds, must be hauled up from the Alten Fjord, a distance of 112 miles. The carriage is usually performed in winter, when, of course, everything reaches its destination in a frozen state. The potatoes are as hard as quartz pebbles, sugar and salt become stony masses, and even wine assumes a solid form. In this state they are kept until wanted for use, rapidly thawed, and immediately consumed, whereby their flavour is but little impaired. The potatoes, cabbage, and preserved berries on the Länsman's table were almost as fresh as if they had never been frozen.

Formerly, the place was almost entirely deserted during the summer months, and the resident missionary and Länsman returned to Alten until the Lapps came back to their winter huts; but, for some years past, the stationary population has increased, and the church is kept open the whole year. Winter, however, is the season when the Lapps are found at home, and when their life and habits are most characteristic and interesting. The population of Kautokeino is then, perhaps, about 800; in summer it is scarcely one-tenth of this number. Many of the families—especially those of mixed Finnish blood—live in wooden huts, with the luxury of a fireplace and chimney, and a window or two; but the greater part of them burrow in low habitations of earth, which resemble large mole hills raised in the crust of the soil. Half snowed over and blended with the natural inequalities of the earth, one would never imagine, but for the smoke here and there issuing from holes, that human beings existed below. On both sides of the stream are rows of storehouses, wherein the Lapps deposit their supplies and household articles during their summer wanderings. These structures are raised upon birch posts, each capped with a smooth, horizontal board, in order to prevent the rats and mice from effecting an entrance. The church is built upon a slight eminence to the south, with its low red belfry standing apart, as in Sweden, in a small grove of birches, which have been spared for a summer ornament to the sanctuary.

We awoke at eight o'clock to find a clear twilight and a cold of 10°

101

below zero. Our stay at Muoniovara had given the sun time to increase his altitude somewhat, and I had some doubts whether we should succeed in beholding a day of the Polar winter. The Länsman, however, encouraged us by the assurance that the sun had not yet risen upon his residence, though nearly six weeks had elapsed since his disappearance, but that his return was now looked for every day, since he had already begun to shine upon the northern hills. By ten o'clock it was light enough to read; the southern sky was a broad sea of golden orange, dotted with a few crimson cloud-islands, and we set ourselves to watch with some anxiety the gradual approach of the exiled god. But for this circumstance, and two other drawbacks, I should have gone to church to witness the Lapps at their religious exercises. Pastor Hvoslef was ill, and the service consisted only of the reading of some prayers by the Lapp schoolmaster; added to which, the church is never warmed, even in the coldest days of winter. One cause of this may, perhaps, be the dread of an accidental conflagration; but the main reason is, the inconvenience which would arise from the thawing out of so many antiquated reindeer garments, and the effluvia given out by the warmed bodies within them. Consequently, the temperature inside the church is about the same as outside, and the frozen moisture of the worshippers' breath forms a frosty cloud so dense as sometimes to hide the clergyman from the view of his congregation. Pastor Hvoslef informed me that he had frequently preached in a temperature of 35° below zero. "At such times," said he, "the very words seem to freeze as they issue from my lips, and fall upon the heads of my hearers like a shower of snow." "But," I ventured to remark, "our souls are controlled to such a degree by the condition of our bodies, that I should doubt whether any true devotional spirit could exist at such a time. Might not even religion itself be frozen?" "Yes," he answered, "there is no doubt that all the better feelings either disappear, or become very faint, when the mercury begins to freeze." The pastor himself was at that time suffering the penalty of indulging a spirit of reverence which for a long time led him to officiate with uncovered head.

The sky increased in brightness as we watched. The orange flushed into rose, and the pale white hills looked even more ghastly against the bar of glowing carmine which fringed the horizon. A few long purple streaks of cloud hung over the sun's place, and higher up in the vault floated some

102

loose masses, tinged with fiery crimson on their lower edges. About half-past eleven, a pencil of bright red light shot up—a signal which the sun uplifted to herald his coming. As it slowly moved westward along the hills, increasing in height and brilliancy until it became a long tongue of flame, playing against the streaks of cloud we were apprehensive that the near disc would rise to view. When the Länsman's clock pointed to twelve, its base had become so bright as to shine almost like the sun itself; but after a few breathless moments the unwelcome glow began to fade. We took its bearing with a compass, and after making allowance for the variation (which is here very slight) were convinced that it was really past meridian, and the radiance, which was that of morning a few minutes before, belonged to the splendours of evening now. The colours of the firmament began to change in reverse order, and the dawn, which had almost ripened to sunrise, now withered away to night without a sunset. We had at last seen a day without a sun.

The snowy hills to the north, it is true, were tinged with a flood of rosy flame, and the very next day would probably bring down the tide-mark of sunshine to the tops of the houses. One day, however, was enough to satisfy me. You, my heroic friend,[A] may paint with true pencil, and still truer pen, the dreary solemnity of the long Arctic night: but, greatly as I enjoy your incomparable pictures, much as I honour your courage and your endurance, you shall never tempt me to share in the experience. The South is a cup which one may drink to inebriation; but one taste from the icy goblet of the North is enough to allay curiosity and quench all further desire. Yet the contrast between these two extremes came home to me vividly but once during this journey. A traveller's mind must never stray too far from the things about him, and long habit has enabled me to throw myself entirely into the conditions and circumstances of each separate phase of my wandering life, thereby preserving distinct the sensations and experiences of each, and preventing all later confusion in the memory. But one day, at Muoniovara, as I sat before the fire in the afternoon darkness, there flashed across my mind a vision of cloudless Egypt—trees rustling in the hot wind, yellow mountain-walls rising beyond the emerald plain of the Nile, the white pencils of minarets in the distance, the creamy odour of bean-blossoms in the air—a world of glorious vitality, where Death seemed an unaccountable accident. Here, Life existed

103

only on sufferance, and all Nature frowned with a robber's demand to give it up. I flung my pipe across the room and very soon, behind a fast reindeer, drove away from the disturbing reminiscence.

I went across the valley to the schoolmaster's house to make a sketch of Kautokeino, but the frost was so thick on the windows that I was obliged to take a chair in the open air and work with bare hands. I soon learned the value of rapidity in such an employment. We spent the afternoon in the Länsman's parlor, occasionally interrupted by the visits of Lapps, who, having heard of our arrival, were very curious to behold the first Americans who ever reached this part of the world. They came into the room with the most perfect freedom, saluted the Länsman, and then turned to stare at us until they were satisfied, when they retired to give place to others who were waiting outside. We were obliged to hold quite a levee during the whole evening. They had all heard of America, but knew very little else about it, and many of them questioned us, through Herr Berger, concerning our religion and laws. The fact of the three Norwegian residents being able to converse with us astonished them greatly. The Lapps of Kautokeino have hitherto exalted themselves over the Lapps of Karasjok and Karessuando, because the Länsman, Berger, and Pastor Hvoslef could speak with English and French travellers in their own language, while the merchants and pastors of the latter places are acquainted only with Norwegian and Swedish; and now their pride received a vast accession. "How is it possible?" said they to Herr Berger, "these men come from the other side of the world, and you talk with them as fast in their own language as if you had never spoken any other!" The schoolmaster, Lars Kaino, a one-armed fellow, with a more than ordinary share of acuteness and intelligence, came to request that I would take his portrait, offering to pay me for my trouble. I agreed to do it gratuitously, on condition that I should keep it myself, and that he should bring his wife to be included in the sketch.

He assented, with some sacrifice of vanity, and came around the next morning, in his holiday suit of blue cloth, trimmed with scarlet and yellow binding. His wife, a short woman of about twenty-five, with a face as flat and round as a platter, but a remarkably fair complexion, accompanied him, though with evident reluctance, and sat with eyes modestly cast down while

104

I sketched her features. The circumstance of my giving Lars half a dollar at the close of the sitting was immediately spread through Kautokeino, and before night all the Lapps of the place were ambitious to undergo the same operation. Indeed, the report reached the neighboring villages, and a Hammerfest merchant, who came in the following morning from a distance of seven miles, obtained a guide at less than the usual price, through the anxiety of the latter to arrive in time to have his portrait taken. The shortness of the imperfect daylight, however, obliged me to decline further offers, especially as there were few Lapps of pure, unmixed blood among my visitors.

Kautokeino was the northern limit of my winter journey. I proposed visiting Altengaard in the summer, on my way to the North Cape, and there is nothing in the barren tract between the two places to repay the excursion. I had already seen enough of the Lapps to undeceive me in regard to previously-formed opinions respecting them, and to take away the desire for a more intimate acquaintance. In features, as in language, they resemble the Finns sufficiently to indicate an ethnological relationship. I could distinguish little, if any, trace of the Mongolian blood in them. They are fatter, fairer, and altogether handsomer than the nomadic offshoots of that race, and resemble the Esquimaux (to whom they have been compared) in nothing but their rude, filthy manner of life. Von Buch ascribes the difference in stature and physical stamina between them and the Finns to the use of the vapor bath by the latter and the aversion to water of the former. They are a race of Northern gipsies, and it is the restless blood of this class rather than any want of natural capacity which retards their civilisation. Although the whole race has been converted to Christianity, and education is universal among them—no Lapp being permitted to marry until he can read—they have but in too many respects substituted one form of superstition for another. The spread of temperance among them, however, has produced excellent results, and, in point of morality, they are fully up to the prevailing standard in Sweden and Norway. The practice, formerly imputed to them, of sharing their connubial rights with the guests who visited them, is wholly extinct,—if it ever existed. Theft is the most usual offence, but crimes of a more heinous character are rare.

Whatever was picturesque in the Lapps has departed with their paganism.

No wizards now ply their trade of selling favorable winds to the Norwegian coasters, or mutter their incantations to discover the concealed grottoes of silver in the Kiölen mountains. It is in vain, therefore, for the romantic traveller to seek in them the materials for weird stories and wild adventures. They are frightfully pious and commonplace. Their conversion has destroyed what little of barbaric poetry there might have been in their composition, and, instead of chanting to the spirits of the winds, and clouds, and mountains, they have become furious ranters, who frequently claim to be possessed by the Holy Ghost. As human beings, the change, incomplete as it is, is nevertheless to their endless profit; but as objects of interest to the traveller, it has been to their detriment. It would be far more picturesque to describe a sabaoth of Lapland witches than a prayer-meeting of shouting converts, yet no friend of his race could help rejoicing to see the latter substituted for the former. In proportion, therefore, as the Lapps have become enlightened (like all other savage tribes), they have become less interesting. Retaining nearly all that is repulsive in their habits of life, they have lost the only peculiarities which could persuade one to endure the inconveniences of a closer acquaintance.

I have said that the conversion of the Lapps was in some respects the substitution of one form of superstition for another. A tragic exemplification of this fact, which produced the greatest excitement throughout the North, took place in Kautokeino four years ago. Through the preaching of Lestadius and other fanatical missionaries, a spiritual epidemic, manifesting itself in the form of visions, trances, and angelic possessions, broke out among the Lapps. It infected the whole country, and gave rise to numerous disturbances and difficulties in Kautokeino. It was no unusual thing for one of the congregation to arise during church service, declare that he was inspired by the Holy Ghost, and call upon those present to listen to his revelations. The former Länsman arrested the most prominent of the offenders, and punished them with fine and imprisonment. This begat feelings of hatred on the part of the fanatics, which soon ripened into a conspiracy. The plot was matured during the summer months, when the Lapps descended towards the Norwegian coast with their herds of reindeer.

I have the account of what followed from the lips of Pastor Hvoslef, who was then stationed here, and was also one of the victims of their resentment. Early one morning in October, when the inhabitants were returning from their summer wanderings, he was startled by the appearance of the resident merchant's wife, who rushed into his house in a frantic state, declaring that her husband was murdered. He fancied that the woman was bewildered by some sudden fright, and, in order to quiet her, walked over to the merchant's house. Here he found the unfortunate man lying dead upon the floor, while a band of about thirty Lapps, headed by the principal fanatics, were forcing the house of the Länsman, whom they immediately dispatched with their knives and clubs. They then seized the pastor and his wife, beat them severely with birch-sticks, and threatened them with death unless they would acknowledge the divine mission of the so-called prophets.

The greater part of the day passed in uncertainty and terror, but towards evening appeared a crowd of friendly Lapps from the neighbouring villages, who, after having received information, through fugitives, of what had happened, armed themselves and marched to the rescue. A fight ensued, in which the conspirators were beaten, and the prisoners delivered out of their hands. The friendly Lapps, unable to take charge of all the criminals, and fearful lest some of them might escape during the night, adopted the alternative of beating every one of them so thoroughly that they were all found the next morning in the same places where they had been left the evening before. They were tried at Alten, the two ringleaders executed, and a number of the others sent to the penitentiary at Christiania. This summary justice put a stop to all open and violent manifestations of religious frenzy, but it still exists to some extent, though only indulged in secret.

We paid a visit to Pastor Hvoslef on Monday, and had the pleasure of his company to dinner in the evening. He is a Christian gentleman in the best sense of the term, and though we differed in matters of belief, I was deeply impressed with his piety and sincerity. Madame Hvoslef and two rosy little Arctic blossoms shared his exile—for this is nothing less than an exile to a man of cultivation and intellectual tastes. In his house I saw—the last thing one would have expected to find in the heart of Lapland—a piano. Madame Hvoslef, who is an accomplished performer, sat down to it, and gave us the barcarole from Massaniello. While in the midst of a maze of wild Norwegian melodies, I saw the Pastor whisper something in her ear. At once, to our infinite amazement, she boldly struck up "Yankee Doodle!" Something like an American war-whoop began to issue from Braisted's mouth, but was smothered in time to prevent an alarm. "How on earth did that air get into Lapland!" I asked. "I heard Ole Bull play it at Christiania," said Madame Hvoslef, "and learned it from memory afterwards."

The weather changed greatly after our arrival. From 23° below zero on Sunday evening, it rose to 8-1/2° above, on Monday night, with a furious hurricane of snow from the north. We sent for our deer from the hills early on Tuesday morning, in order to start on our return to Muoniovara. The Lapps, however, have an Oriental disregard of time, and as there was no chance of our getting off before noon, we improved part of the delay in visiting the native schools and some of the earthen huts, or, rather, dens, in which most of the inhabitants live. There were two schools, each containing about twenty scholars—fat, greasy youngsters, swaddled in reindeer skins, with blue eyes, light brown or yellow hair, and tawny red cheeks, wherever the original colour could be discerned. As the rooms were rather warm, the odour of Lapp childhood was not quite as fresh as a cowslip, and we did not tarry long among them.

Approaching the side of a pile of dirt covered with snow, we pushed one after another, against a small square door, hung at such a slant that it closed of itself, and entered an ante-den used as a store-room. Another similar door ushered us into the house, a rude, vaulted space, framed with poles, sticks and reindeer hides, and covered compactly with earth, except a narrow opening in the top to let out the smoke from a fire kindled in the centre. Pieces of reindeer hide, dried flesh, bags of fat, and other articles, hung from the frame and dangled against our heads as we entered. The den was not more than five feet high by about eight feet in diameter. The owner, a jolly, good-humoured Lapp, gave me a low wooden stool, while his wife, with a pipe in her mouth, squatted down on the hide which served for a bed and looked at me with amiable curiosity. I contemplated them for a while with my eyes full of tears (the smoke being very thick,) until finally both eyes and nose could endure no more, and I sought the open air again.

FOOTNOTES:

[A] This was written in Lapland; and at the same time my friend Dr. Elisha Kent Kane, of immortal memory, lay upon his death-bed, in Havana. I retain the words, which I then supposed would meet his eye, that I may add my own tribute of sorrow for the untimely death of one of the truest, bravest, and noblest-hearted men I ever knew.

CHAPTER XII. THE RETURN TO MUONIOVARA.

While at Kautokeino I completed my Lapp outfit by purchasing a scarlet cap, stuffed with eider down, a pair of bœllinger, or reindeer leggings, and the komager, or broad, boat-shaped shoes, filled with dry soft hay, and tightly bound around the ankles, which are worn by everybody in Lapland. Attired in these garments, I made a very passable Lapp, barring a few superfluous inches of stature, and at once realized the prudence of conforming in one's costume to the native habits. After the first feeling of awkwardness is over, nothing can be better adapted to the Polar Winter than the Lapp dress. I walked about at first with the sensation of having each foot in the middle of a large feather bed, but my blood preserved its natural warmth even after sitting for hours in an open pulk. The bœllinger, fastened around the thighs by drawing-strings of reindeer sinew, are so covered by the poesk that one becomes, for all practical purposes, a biped reindeer, and may wallow in the snow as much as he likes without the possibility of a particle getting through his hide.

The temperature was, nevertheless, singularly mild when we set out on our return. There had been a violent storm of wind and snow the previous night, after which the mercury rose to 16° above zero. We waited until noon before our reindeers could be collected, and then set off, with the kind farewell wishes of the four Norwegian inhabitants of the place. I confess to a feeling of relief when we turned our faces southward, and commenced our return to daylight. We had at last seen the Polar night, the day without a sunrise; we had driven our reindeer under the arches of the aurora borealis; we had learned enough of the Lapps to convince us that further acquaintance would be of little profit; and it now seemed time to attempt an escape from the limbo of Death into which we had ventured. Our faces had already begun to look pale and faded from three weeks of alternate darkness and twilight, but the novelty of our life preserved us from any feeling of depression and prevented any perceptible effect upon our bodily health, such as would assuredly have followed a protracted experience of the Arctic Winter. Every day now would bring us further over the steep northern shoulder of the Earth, and nearer to that great heart of life in the south, where her blood pulsates with eternal warmth. Already there was a perceptible increase of the sun's altitude, and at noonday a thin upper slice of his disc was visible for about half an hour.

By Herr Berger's advice, we engaged as guide to Lippajärvi, a Lapp, who had formerly acted as postman, and professed to be able to find his way in the dark. The wind had blown so violently that it was probable we should have to break our own road for the whole distance. Leaving Kautokeino, we travelled up the valley of a frozen stream, towards desolate ranges of hills, or rather shelves of the table-land, running north-east and south-west. They were spotted with patches of stunted birch, hardly rising above the snow. Our deer were recruited, and we made very good progress while the twilight lasted. At some Lapp tents, where we stopped to make inquiries about the ice, I was much amused by the appearance of a group of children, who strikingly resembled bear-cubs standing on their hind legs. They were coated with reindeer hide from head to foot, with only a little full-moon of tawny red face visible.

We stopped at Siepe an hour to bait the deer. The single wooden hut was crowded with Lapps, one of whom, apparently the owner, spoke a little Norwegian. He knew who we were, and asked me many questions about America. He was most anxious to know what was our religion, and what course the Government took with regard to different sects. He seemed a little surprised, and not less pleased, to hear that all varieties of belief were tolerated, and that no one sect possessed any peculiar privileges over another. (It is only very recently that dissenters from the Orthodox Church have been allowed to erect houses of worship in Norway.) While we were speaking on these matters, an old woman, kneeling near us, was muttering prayers to herself, wringing her hands, sobbing, and giving other evidences of violent religious excitement. This appeared to be a common occurrence, as none of the Lapps took the slightest notice of it. I have no doubt that much of that hallucination which led to the murders at Kautokeino still exists among the people, kept alive by secret indulgence. Those missionaries have much to answer for who have planted the seeds of spiritual disease among this ignorant and impressible race.

The night was cold and splendidly clear. We were obliged to leave the river on account of rotten ice, and took to the open plains, where our deers sank to their bellies in the loose snow. The leading animals became fractious, and we were obliged to stop every few minutes, until their paroxysms subsided. I could not perceive that the Lapps themselves exercised much more control over them than we, who were new to the business. The domesticated reindeer still retains his wild instincts, and never fails to protest against the necessity of labour. The most docile will fly from the track, plunge, face about and refuse to draw, when you least expect it. They are possessed by an incorrigible stupidity. Their sagacity applies only to their animal wants, and they seem almost totally deficient in memory. They never become attached to men, and the only sign of recognition they show, is sometimes to allow certain persons to catch them more easily than others. In point of speed they are not equal to the horse, and an hour's run generally exhausts them. When one considers their size, however, their strength and power of endurance seem marvellous. Herr Berger informed me that he had driven a reindeer from Alten to Kautokeino, 112 miles, in twenty-six hours, and from the latter place to Muoniovara in thirty. I was also struck by the remarkable adaptation of the animal to its uses. Its hoof resembles that of the camel, being formed for snow, as the latter for sand. It is broad, cloven and flexible, the separate divisions spreading out so as to present a resisting surface when the foot is set down, and falling together when it is lifted. Thus in snow where a horse would founder in the space of a hundred yards, the deer easily works his way, mile after mile, drawing the sliding, canoe-like pulk, burdened with his master's weight, after him.

The Lapps generally treat their animals with the greatest patience and forbearance, but otherwise do not exhibit any particular attachment for them. They are indebted to them for food, clothing, habitation and conveyance, and their very existence may therefore almost be said to depend on that of their herds. It is surprising, however, what a number of deer are requisite for the support of a family. Von Buch says that a Lapp who has a hundred deer is poor, and will be finally driven to descend to the coast, and take to fishing. The does are never made to labour, but are kept in the woods for milking and breeding. Their milk is rich and nourishing, but less agreeable to the taste than that of the cow. The cheese made from it is strong and not particularly palatable. It yields an oil which is the sovereign specific for frozen flesh. The male deer used for draft are always castrated, which operation the old Lapp women perform by slowly chewing the glands between their teeth until they are reduced to a pulp, without wounding the hide.

During this journey I had ample opportunity of familiarising myself with reindeer travel. It is picturesque enough at the outset, but when the novelty of the thing is worn off nothing is left but a continual drain upon one's patience. Nothing can exceed the coolness with which your deer jumps off the track, slackens his tow-rope, turns around and looks you in the face, as much as to say: "What are you going to do about it?" The simplicity and stupidity of his countenance seem to you to be admirably feigned, and unless you are an old hand you are inevitably provoked. This is particularly pleasant on the marshy table-lands of Lapland, where, if he takes a notion to bolt with you, your pulk bounces over the hard tussocks, sheers sideways down the sudden pitches, or swamps itself in beds of loose snow. Harness a frisky sturgeon to a "dug-out," in a rough sea, and you will have some idea of this method of travelling. While I acknowledge the Providential disposition of things which has given the reindeer to the Lapp, I cannot avoid thanking Heaven that I am not a Lapp, and that I shall never travel again with reindeer.

The aberrations of our deer obliged us to take a very sinuous course. Sometimes we headed north, and sometimes south, and the way seemed so long that I mistrusted the quality of our guide; but at last a light shone ahead. It was the hut of Eitajärvi. A lot of pulks lay in front of it, and the old Finn stood already with a fir torch, waiting to light us in. On arriving, Anton was greeted by his sister Caroline, who had come thus far from Muoniovara, on her way to visit some relatives at Altengaard. She was in company with some Finns, who had left Lippajärvi the day previous, but losing their way in the storm, had wandered about for twenty-four hours, exposed to its full violence. Think of an American girl of eighteen sitting in an open pulk, with the thermometer at zero, a furious wind and blinding snow beating upon her, and neither rest nor food for a day! There are few who would survive twelve hours, yet Caroline was as fresh, lively, and cheerful as ever, and immediately set about cooking our supper. We found a fire in the cold guest's room, the place swept and cleaned, and a good bed of deerskins in one corner. The temperature had sunk to 12° below zero, and the wind blew through wide cracks in the floor, but between the fire and the reciprocal warmth of our bodies we secured a comfortable sleep—a thing of the first consequence in such a climate.

Our deer started well in the morning, and the Lapp guide knew his way perfectly. The wind had blown so strongly that the track was cleared rather than filled, and we slipped up the long slopes at a rapid rate. I recognised the narrow valley where we first struck the northern streams, and the snowy plain beyond, where our first Lapp guide lost his way. By this time it was beginning to grow lighter, showing us the dreary wastes of table-land which we had before crossed in the fog. North of us was a plain of unbroken snow, extending to a level line on the horizon, where it met the dark violet sky. Were the colour changed, it would have perfectly represented the sandy plateaus of the Nubian Desert, in so many particulars does the extreme North imitate the extreme South. But the sun, which never deserts the desert, had not yet returned to these solitudes. Far, far away, on the edge of the sky, a dull red glimmer showed where he moved. Not the table-land of Pamir, in Thibet, the cradle of the Oxus and the Indus, but this lower Lapland terrace, is entitled to the designation of the "Roof of the World." We were on the summit, creeping along her mountain rafters, and looking southward, off her shelving eaves, to catch a glimpse of the light playing on her majestic front. Here, for once, we seemed to look down on the horizon, and I thought of Europe and the Tropics as lying below. Our journey northward had been an ascent but now the world's steep sloped downward before us into sunshine and warmer air. In ascending the Andes or the Himalayas, you pass through all climates and belts of vegetation between the Equator and the Pole, and so a journey due north, beyond the circle of the sun, simply reverses the phenomenon, and impresses one like the ascent of a mountain on the grandest possible scale.

In two hours from the time we left Eitajärvi we reached the Lapp encampment. The herds of deer had been driven in from the woods, and were

114

clustered among the birch bushes around the tents. We had some difficulty in getting our own deer past them, until the Lapps came to our assistance. We made no halt, but pushed on, through deeper snows than before, over the desolate plain. As far as Palajärvi we ran with our gunwales below the snow-level, while the foremost pulks were frequently swamped under the white waves that broke over them. We passed through a picturesque gorge between two hills about 500 feet high, and beyond it came upon wide lakes covered deep with snow, under which there was a tolerable track, which the leading deer was able to find with his feet. Beyond these lakes there was a ridge, which we had no sooner crossed than a dismally grand prospect opened before us. We overlooked a valley-basin, marked with belts of stunted birch, and stretching away for several miles to the foot of a bleak snowy mountain, which I at once recognised as Lippavara. After rounding its western point and turning southward again, we were rejoiced with the sight of some fir trees, from which the snow had been shaken, brightening even with their gloomy green the white monotony of the Lapland wilderness. It was like a sudden gleam of sunshine.

We reached Lippajärvi at twelve, having made twenty-eight miles of hard travel in five hours. Here we stopped two hours to cook a meal and change our deer, and then pushed on to reach Palajoki the same night. We drove through the birch woods, no longer glorious as before, for the snow had been shaken off, and there was no sunset light to transfigure them. Still on, ploughing through deep seas in the gathering darkness, over marshy plains, all with a slant southward, draining into the Muonio, until we reached the birchen ridge of Suontajärvi, with its beautiful firs rising here and there, silent and immovable. Even the trees have no voices in the North, let the wind blow as it will. There is nothing to be heard but the sharp whistle of the dry snow— the same dreary music which accompanies the African simoom. The night was very dark, and we began to grow exceedingly tired of sitting flat in our pulks. I looked sharp for the Palajok Elv, the high fir-fringed banks of which I remembered, for they denoted our approach to the Muonio; but it was long, long before we descended from the marshes upon the winding road of snow-covered ice. In vain I shifted my aching legs and worked my benumbed hands, looking out ahead for the embouchure of the river. Braisted and I encouraged each other, whenever we were near enough to hear, by the reminder that we had only one more day with reindeer. After a long time spent in this way, the high banks flattened, level snows and woods succeeded, and we sailed into the port of Palajoki.

The old Finnish lady curtsied very deeply as she recognised us, and hastened to cook our coffee and reindeer, and to make us a good bed with sheets. On our former visit the old lady and her sons had watched us undress and get into bed, but on this occasion three buxom daughters, of ages ranging from sixteen to twenty-two, appeared about the time for retiring, and stationed themselves in a row near the door, where they watched us with silent curiosity. As we had shown no hesitation in the first case, we determined to be equally courageous now, and commenced removing our garments with great deliberation, allowing them every opportunity of inspecting their fashion and the manner of wearing them. The work thus proceeded in mutual silence until we were nearly ready for repose, when Braisted, by pulling off a stocking and displaying a muscular calf, suddenly alarmed the youngest, who darted to the door and rushed out. The second caught the panic, and followed, and the third and oldest was therefore obliged to do likewise, though with evident reluctance. I was greatly amused at such an unsophisticated display of curiosity. The perfect composure of the girls, and the steadiness with which they watched us, showed that they were quite unconscious of having committed any impropriety.

The morning was clear and cold. Our deer had strayed so far into the woods that we did not get under way before the forenoon twilight commenced. We expected to find a broken road down the Muonio, but a heavy snow had fallen the day previous, and the track was completely filled. Long Isaac found so much difficulty in taking the lead, his deer constantly bolting from the path, that Anton finally relieved him, and by standing upright in the pulk and thumping the deer's flanks, succeeded in keeping up the animal's spirits and forcing a way. It was slow work, however, and the sun, rolling his whole disc above the horizon, announced midday before we reached Kyrkessuando. As we drove up to the little inn, we were boisterously welcomed by Häl, Herr Forström's brown wolf-dog, who had strayed thus far from home. Our deer were beginning to give out, and we were very anxious to reach Muoniovara in time for dinner, so we only waited long enough to give the animals a feed of moss and procure some hot milk for ourselves.

The snow-storm, which had moved over a narrow belt of country, had not extended below this place, and the road was consequently well broken. We urged our deer into a fast trot, and slid down the icy floor of the Muonio, past hills whose snows flashed scarlet and rose-orange in the long splendour of sunset. Hunger and the fatigue which our journey was producing at last, made us extremely sensitive to the cold, though it was not more than 20° below zero. My blood became so chilled, that I was apprehensive the extremities would freeze, and the most vigorous motion of the muscles barely sufficed to keep at bay the numbness which attacked them. At dusk we drove through Upper Muonioniska, and our impatience kept the reindeers so well in motion that before five o'clock (although long after dark,) we were climbing the well-known slope to Herr Forström's house at Muoniovara. Here we found the merchant, not yet departed to the Lapp fair at Karessuando, and Mr. Wolley, who welcomed us with the cordiality of an old friend. Our snug room at the carpenter's was already warmed and set in order, and after our reindeer drive of 250 miles through the wildest parts of Lapland, we felt a home-like sense of happiness and comfort in smoking our pipes before the familiar iron stove.

The trip to Kautokeino embraced about all I saw of Lapp life during the winter journey. The romance of the tribe, as I have already said, has totally departed with their conversion, while their habits of life scarcely improved in the least, are sufficiently repulsive to prevent any closer experience than I have had, unless the gain were greater. Mr. Wolley, who had been three years in Lapland, also informed me that the superstitious and picturesque traditions of the people have almost wholly disappeared, and the coarse mysticism and rant which they have engrafted upon their imperfect Christianity does not differ materially from the same excrescence in more civilised races. They have not even (the better for them, it is true) any characteristic and picturesque vices—but have become, certainly to their own great advantage, a pious, fanatical, moral, ignorant and commonplace people. I have described them exactly as I found them, and as they have been described to me by those who knew them well. The readers of "Afraja" may be a little disappointed with the picture, as I confess I have been (in an artistic sense, only) with the reality; but the Lapps have lost many vices with their poetic diablerie, and nobody has a right to complain.

It is a pity that many traits which are really characteristic and interesting in a people cannot be mentioned on account of that morbid prudery so prevalent in our day, which insults the unconscious innocence of nature. Oh, that one could imitate the honest unreserve of the old travellers—the conscientiousness which insisted on telling not only the truth, but the whole truth! This is scarcely possible, now; but at the same time I have not been willing to emasculate my accounts of the tribes of men to the extent perhaps required by our ultra-conventionalism, and must insist, now and then, on being allowed a little Flemish fidelity to nature. In the description of races, as in the biography of individuals, the most important half of life is generally omitted.

CHAPTER XIII. ABOUT THE FINNS.

We remained but another day in Muoniovara, after our return from Kautokeino, and this was devoted to preparations for the return journey to Haparanda. My first intention had been to make an excursion across the country to the iron mountains of Gellivara, thence to Quickjock, at the foot of the Northern Alp, Sulitelma, "Queen of Snows," and so southward through the heart of Swedish Lappmark; but I found that such a journey would be attended with much difficulty and delay. In the first place, there were no broken roads at this season, except on the routes of inland trade; much of the intermediate country is a wilderness, where one must camp many nights in the snow; food was very scarce, the Lapps having hardly enough for their own necessities, and the delays at every place where guides and reindeer must be changed, would have prolonged the journey far beyond the time which I had allotted to the North. I began to doubt, also, whether one would be sufficiently repaid for the great fatigue and danger which such a trip would have involved. There is no sensation of which one wearies sooner than disgust; and, much as I enjoy a degree of barbarism in milder climates, I suspected that a long companionship with Lapps in a polar winter would be a little too much for me. So I turned my face toward Stockholm, heartily glad that I had made the journey, yet not dissatisfied that I was looking forward to its termination.

Before setting out on our return, I shall devote a few pages to the Finns. For the principal facts concerning them, I am mostly indebted to Mr. Wolley, whose acquaintance with the language, and residence of three years in Lapland, have made him perfectly familiar with the race. As I have already remarked, they are a more picturesque people than the Swedes, with stronger lights and shades of character, more ardent temperaments, and a more deeply-rooted national feeling. They seem to be rather clannish and exclusive, in fact, disliking both Swedes and Russians, and rarely intermarrying with them. The sharply-defined boundaries of language and race, at the head of the Bothnian Gulf, are a striking evidence of this. Like their distant relatives, the Hungarian

Magyars, they retain many distinct traces of their remote Asiatic origin. It is partly owing to this fact, and partly to that curious approach of extremes which we observe in nature no less than in humanity, that all suggestive traits of resemblance in these regions point to the Orient rather than to Europe.

I have already described the physical characteristics of the Finns, and have nothing to add, except that I found the same type everywhere, even among the mixed-blooded Quäns of Kautokeino—high cheek-bones, square, strong jaws, full yet firm lips, low, broad foreheads, dark eyes and hair, and a deeper, warmer red on the cheeks than on those of the rosy Swedes. The average height is, perhaps, not quite equal to that of the latter race, but in physical vigor I can see no inferiority, and there are among them many men of splendid stature, strength, and proportion. Von Buch ascribes the marked difference of stature between the Finns and the Lapps, both living under precisely the same influences of climate, to the more cleanly habits of the former and their constant use of the vapor-bath; but I have always found that blood and descent, even where the variation from the primitive stock is but slight, are more potent than climate or custom. The Finns have been so long christianised and civilised (according to the European idea of civilisation), that whatever peculiar characteristic they retain must be looked for mainly in those habits which illustrate their mental and moral natures. In their domestic life, they correspond in most particulars to the Swedes of the same class.

They are passionate, and therefore prone to excesses—imaginative, and therefore, owing to their scanty education, superstitious. Thus the religious element, especially the fantastic aberrations thereof engendered by Lestadius and other missionaries, while it has tended greatly to repress the vice, has in the same proportion increased the weakness. Drunkenness, formerly so prevalent as to be the curse of Lapland, is now exceedingly rare, and so are the crimes for which it is responsible. The most flagrant case which has occurred in the neighborhood of Muoniovara for some years past, was that of a woman who attempted to poison her father-in-law by mixing the scrapings of lucifer matches with his coffee, in order to get rid of the burden of supporting him. Although the evidence was very convincing, the matter was hushed up, in order to avoid a scandal upon the Church, the woman being a steadfast member. In regard to drunkenness, I have heard it stated that, while it was formerly no unusual thing for a Finn to be frozen to death in this condition, the same catastrophe never befell a Lapp, owing to his mechanical habit of keeping his arms and feet in motion—a habit which he preserves even while utterly stupefied and unconscious.

A singular spiritual epidemic ran through Polar Finland three or four years ago, contemporary with the religious excitement in Norwegian Lapland, and partly occasioned by the same reckless men. It consisted of sobbings, strong nervous convulsions, and occasional attacks of that state of semi-consciousness called trance, the subjects of which were looked upon as having been possessed by the Spirit, and transported to the other world, where visions like those of John on Patmos, were revealed to them. The missionaries, instead of repressing this unhealthy delusion, rather encouraged it, and even went so far as to publish as supernatural revelations, the senseless ravings of these poor deluded people. The epidemic spread until there was scarcely a family some member of which was not affected by it, and even yet it has not wholly subsided. The fit would come upon the infected persons at any time, no matter where they were, or how employed. It usually commenced with a convulsive catching of the breath, which increased in violence, accompanied by sobbing, and sometimes by cries or groans, until the victim was either exhausted or fell into a trance, which lasted some hours. The persons who were affected were always treated with the greatest respect during the attack no one ventured to smile, no matter how absurd a form the visitation might take. The principle of abstinence from strong drinks was promulgated about the same time, and much of the temperance of the Finns and Lapps is undoubtedly owing the impression made upon their natures by these phenomena.

The same epidemic has often prevailed in the United States, England and Germany. The barking and dancing mania which visited Kentucky thirty or forty years ago, and the performances of the "Holy Rollers," were even more ludicrous and unnatural. Such appearances are a puzzle alike to the physiologist and the philosopher; their frequency shows that they are based on some weak spot in human nature; and in proportion as we pity the victims we have a right to condemn those who sow the seeds of the pestilence. True religion is never spasmodic; it is calm as the existence of God. I know of nothing more shocking than such attempts to substitute rockets and blue lights for Heaven's eternal sunshine.

So far as regards their moral character, the Finns have as little cause for reproach as any other people. We found them as universally honest and honourable in their dealings as the Northern Swedes, who are not surpassed in the world in this respect. Yet their countenances express more cunning and reserve, and the virtue may be partly a negative one, resulting from that indolence which characterises the frigid and the torrid zone. Thus, also, notwithstanding physical signs which denote more ardent animal passions than their neighbors, they are equally chaste, and have as high a standard of sexual purity. Illegitimate births are quite rare, and are looked upon as a lasting shame and disgrace to both parties. The practice of "bundling" which, until recently, was very common among Finnish lovers, very seldom led to such results, and their marriage speedily removed the dishonour. Their manners, socially, in this respect, are curiously contradictory. Thus, while both sexes freely mingle in the bath, in a state of nature, while the women unhesitatingly scrub, rub and dry their husbands, brothers or male friends, while the salutation for both sexes is an embrace with the right arm, a kiss is considered grossly immodest and improper. A Finnish woman expressed the greatest astonishment and horror, at hearing from Mr. Wolley that it was a very common thing in England for a husband and wife to kiss each other. "If my husband were to attempt such a thing," said she, "I would beat him about the ears so that he would feel it for a week." Yet in conversation they are very plain and unreserved, though by no means gross. They acknowledge that such things as generation, gestation and parturition exist, and it may be that this very absence of mystery tends to keep chaste so excitable and imaginative a race.

Notwithstanding their superstition, their love of poetry, and the wild, rich, musical character of their language, there is a singular absence of legendary lore in this part of Finland. Perhaps this is owing to the fact that their ancestors have emigrated hither, principally within the last two centuries, from the early home of the race—Tavastland, the shores of the

Pajana Lake, and the Gulf of Finland. It is a difficult matter to preserve family traditions among them, or even any extended genealogical record, from the circumstance that a Finn takes his name, not only from his father's surname, but from his residence. Thus, Isaaki takes the name of "Anderinpoika" from his father Anderi, and adds "Niemi," the local name of his habitation. His son Nils will be called Nils Isakipoika, with the addition of the name of his residence, wherever that may be; and his family name will be changed as often as his house. There may be a dozen different names in the course of one generation, and the list soon becomes too complicated and confused for an uneducated memory. It is no wonder, therefore, that the Finn knows very little except about what happened during his own life, or, at best, his father's. I never heard the Kalewala spoken of, and doubt very much whether it is known to the natives of this region. The only songs we heard, north of Haparanda, were hymns—devout, but dismal. There must be ballads and household songs yet alive, but the recent spiritual fever has silenced them for the time.

I was at first a little surprised to find the natives of the North so slow, indolent and improvident. We have an idea that a cold climate is bracing and stimulating—ergo, the further north you go, the more active and energetic you will find the people. But the touch of ice is like that of fire. The tropics relax, the pole benumbs, and the practical result is the same in both cases. In the long, long winter, when there are but four hours of twilight to twenty of darkness—when the cows are housed, the wood cut, the hay gathered, the barley bran and fir bark stowed away for bread, and the summer's catch of fish salted—what can a man do, when his load of wood or hay is hauled home, but eat, gossip and sleep? To bed at nine, and out of it at eight in the morning, smoking and dozing between the slow performance of his few daily duties, he becomes at last as listless and dull as a hibernating bear. In the summer he has perpetual daylight, and need not hurry. Besides, why should he give himself special trouble to produce an unusually large crop of flax or barley, when a single night may make his labours utterly profitless? Even in midsummer the blighting frost may fall: nature seems to take a cruel pleasure in thwarting him: he is fortunate only through chance; and thus a sort of Arab fatalism and acquiescence in whatever happens, takes possession of him.

His improvidence is also to be ascribed to the same cause. Such fearful famine and suffering as existed in Finland and Lapland during the winter of 1856-7 might no doubt have been partially prevented, but no human power could have wholly forestalled it.

The polar zone was never designed for the abode of man. In the pre-Adamite times, when England was covered with palm-forests, and elephants ranged through Siberia, things may have been widely different, and the human race then (if there was any) may have planted vineyards on these frozen hills and lived in bamboo huts. But since the geological émeutes and revolutions, and the establishment of the terrestrial régime, I cannot for the life of me see whatever induced beings endowed with human reason, to transplant themselves hither and here take root, while such vast spaces lie waste and useless in more genial climes. A man may be pardoned for remaining where the providences of birth and education have thrown him, but I cannot excuse the first colonists for inflicting such a home upon centuries of descendants. Compare even their physical life—the pure animal satisfaction in existence, for that is not a trifling matter after all—with that of the Nubians, or the Malays, or the Polynesians! It is the difference between a poor hare, hunted and worried year after year by hounds and visions of hounds and the familiar, confiding wren, happiest of creatures, because secure of protection everywhere. Oh that the circle of the ecliptic would coincide with that of the equator! That the sun would shine from pole to pole for evermore, and all lands be habitable and hospitable, and the Saharan sands (according to Fourier) be converted into bowers of the Hesperides, and the bitter salt of the ocean brine (vide the same author) become delicious champagne punch, wherein it would be pleasure to drown! But I am afraid that mankind is not yet fit for such a millennium.

Meanwhile it is truly comforting to find that even here, where men live under such discouraging circumstances that one would charitably forgive them the possession of many vices, they are, according to their light, fully as true, and honest, and pure, as the inhabitants of the most favoured countries in the world. Love for each other, trust in each other, faith in God, are all vital among them; and their shortcomings are so few and so easily accounted for,

124

that one must respect them and feel that his faith in man is not lessened in knowing them. You who spend your lives at home can never know how much good there is in the world. In rude unrefined races, evil naturally rises to the surface, and one can discern the character of the stream beneath its scum. It is only in the highest civilisation where the outside is goodly to the eye, too often concealing an interior foul to the core.

But I have no time to moralise on these matters. My duty is that of a chronicler; and if I perform that conscientiously, the lessons which my observations suggest will need no pointing out. I cannot close this chapter, however, without confessing my obligations to Mr. Wolley, whose thorough knowledge of the Lapps and Finns enabled me to test the truth of my own impressions, and to mature opinions which I should otherwise, from my own short experience, have hesitated in stating. Mr. Wolley, with that pluck and persistence of English character which Emerson so much admires, had made himself master of all that Lapland can furnish to the traveller, but intended remaining another year for scientific purposes. If he gives to the world—as I hope and trust he will—the result of this long and patient inquiry and investigation, we shall have at last a standard authority for this little-known corner of Europe. We were also indebted to Mr. Wolley for much personal kindness, which I take pleasure in acknowledging in the only way he cannot prevent.

CHAPTER XIV. EXPERIENCES OF ARCTIC WEATHER.

We bade a final adieu to Muoniovara on the afternoon of the 24th of January, leaving Mr. Wolley to wait for June and the birds in that dismal seclusion. Instead of resuming skjuts, we engaged horses as far as Kengis from Herr Forström and a neighbouring Finn, with a couple of shock-headed natives as postillions. Our sleds were mounted upon two rough Finnish sledges, the only advantage of which was to make harder work for the horses—but the people would have it so. The sun was down, but a long, long twilight succeeded, with some faint show of a zodiacal light. There was a tolerable track on the river, but our Finns walked their horses the whole way, and we were nearly seven hours in making Parkajoki. The air was very sharp; my nose, feet and hands kept me busily employed, and I began to fear that I was becoming unusually sensitive to cold, for the thermometer indicated but 15° below zero when we started. At Parkajoki, however, my doubts were removed and my sensations explained, on finding that the temperature had fallen to 44° below.

We slept warmly and well on our old bed of reindeer skins, in one corner of the milk-room. When Braisted, who rose first, opened the door, a thick white mist burst in and rolled heavily along the floor. I went out, attired only in my shirt and drawers, to have a look at the weather. I found the air very still and keen, though not painfully cold—but I was still full of the warmth of sleep. The mercury, however, had sunk into the very bulb of the thermometer, and was frozen so solid that I held it in the full glare of the fire for about a minute and a half before it thawed sufficiently to mount. The temperature was probably 50° below zero, if not more—greater than any we had yet experienced. But it was six o'clock, and we must travel. Fortifying ourselves with coffee and a little meat, and relying for defence in case of extremity on a bottle of powerful rum with which we had supplied ourselves, we muffled up with more than usual care, and started for Kihlangi.

We devoted ourselves entirely to keeping warm, and during the ride of six hours suffered very little except from the gradual diminution of our bodily temperature. It was a dreary journey, following the course of the Muonio between black, snow-laden forests. The sun rose to a height of seven or eight degrees at meridian; when we came over the same road, on our way north, he only showed half his disc. At Kihlangi the people recognised us, and were as well disposed as their stupidity would allow. The old woman cooked part of our reindeer joint, which, with half a dozen cups of strong coffee, brought back a comfortable warmth to our extremities. There were still twenty-four miles to be traversed; the horses were already exhausted, and the temperature only rose to -42° at midday, after which it fell again. We had a terrible journey. Step by step the horses slowly pulled us through the snow, every hour seeming lengthened to a day, as we worked our benumbed fingers and toes until the muscles were almost powerless, and yet it was dangerous to cease. Gradually the blood grew colder in the main channels; insidious chills succeeded, followed by a drowsy torpor, like that which is produced by a heavy dose of opium, until we were fain to have recourse to the rum, a horrid, vitriolic beverage, which burned our throats and stomachs like melted lead, yet gave us a temporary relief.

We almost despaired of reaching Jokijalka, on finding, about ten o'clock at night, that our postillions had taken us to the village of Kolare, and stopped before a large log house, where they seemed to think we would spend the night. Everybody had gone to bed, we knew not where we were, and had set our hearts upon the comfortable guest's room at Jokijalka. It was impossible to make the fellows understand me, but they saw that we were angry, and after a short consultation passed on. We again entered the snowy woods, which were dimly lighted up by an aurora behind us—a strange, mysterious, ghastly illumination, like the phosphorescent glow of a putrefying world. We were desperately cold, our very blood freezing in our veins, and our limbs numb and torpid. To keep entirely awake was impossible. We talked incessantly, making random answers, as continual fleeting dreams crossed the current of our consciousness. A heavy thump on the back was pardoned by him who received it, and a punch between the eyes would have been thankfully accepted had it been necessary.

At last, at last, Kolare church on the river bank came in sight; we crossed to the Russian side, and drove into the yard of the inn. It was nearly midnight, 47° below zero, and we had been for seventeen hours exposed to such a temperature. Everybody had long been asleep. Locks and bolts are unknown, however, so we rushed into the family room, lit fir splinters, and inspected the faces of the sleeping group until we found the landlord, who arose and kindled a fresh fire in the milk-room. They made us coffee and a small bed, saying that the guest's room was too cold, which indeed it was, being little less than the outside temperature. On opening the door in the morning, the cold air rushed in as thick and white as steam. We had a little meat cooked, but could not eat enough, at such an early hour, to supply much fuel. As for taking anything with us for refreshment on the road, it was out of the question. One of our Finns turned back to Muoniovara with the laziest horse, and we got another from our Russian landlord. But it was a long, long journey to the next station (twenty miles), and the continuance of the extreme cold began to tell upon us. This part of the road was very heavy, as on the journey up—seemingly a belt of exposed country where the snow drifts more than elsewhere.

At Kexisvara we found two of the three pleasant women, who cooked our last fragment of reindeer meat, and sent off for horses to Kardis. We here parted with our other Finn, very glad to get rid of his horse, and take a fresh start. We had no difficulty now in making our way with the people, as they all recognised us and remembered our overpayments; besides which, I had enlarged my Finnish vocabulary at Muoniovara. Our horses were better, our sledges lighter and we were not long in reaching the iron-works at Kengis, which we passed at dusk. I should willingly have called upon the hospitable bruk-patron, but we were in too great a hurry to get out of the frigid zone. We were warmed by our meal, and sang lustily as we slid down the Torneå, finding its dreary, sparsely-settled banks cheerful and smiling by contrast with the frightful solitudes we had left. After some hours the postillion stopped before a house on the Swedish bank to hay his horses. We went up and found a single inhabitant, a man who was splitting fir for torches, but the conversation was limited to alternate puffs from our pipes. There was a fine aurora behind us—a low arch of white fire, with streamers radiating outward, shifting and dancing along its curve.

It was nearly ten o'clock before we reached Kardis, half unconscious from the cold. Our horse ran into the wrong place, and we lost sight of the baggage-sled, our only guide in the darkness. We could no longer trust the animal's instinct, but had to depend on our own, which is perhaps truer: at least, I have often found in myself traces of that blind, unreasoning faculty which guides the bee and the bird, and have never been deceived in trusting to it. We found the inn, and carried a cloud of frozen vapor into the kitchen with us, as we opened the door. The graceful wreaths of ice-smoke rolled before our feet, as before those of ascending saints in the old pictures, but ourselves, hair from head to foot, except two pairs of eyes, which looked out through icy loop-holes, resembled the reverse of saints. I told the landlord in Finnish that we wanted to sleep—"mia tarvi nuku á." He pointed to a bed in the corner, out of which rose a sick girl, of about seventeen, very pale, and evidently suffering. They placed some benches near the fire, removed the bedding, and disposed her as comfortably as the place permitted. We got some hot milk and hard bread, threw some reindeer skins on the vacant truck, and lay down, but not to sleep much. The room was so close and warm, and the dozen persons in it so alternately snoring and restless, that our rest was continually disturbed. We, therefore, rose early and aroused the lazy natives.

The cold was still at 47° below zero. The roads were so much better, however, that we descended again to our own runners, and our lively horses trotted rapidly down the Torneå. The signs of settlement and comparative civilisation which now increased with every mile were really cheering. Part of our way lay through the Swedish woods and over the intervening morasses, where the firs were hung with weepers of black-green moss, and stood solid and silent in their mantles of snow, lighted with a magnificent golden flush at sunrise. The morning was icy-clear and dazzling. There was not the least warmth in the sun's rays, but it was pleasant to see him with a white face once more. We could still stare at him without winking, but the reflection from the jewelled snow pained our eyes. The cold was so keen that we were obliged to keep our faces buried between our caps and boas, leaving only the smallest possible vacancy for the eyes. This was exceedingly disagreeable, on account of the moisture from the breath, which kept the squirrel tails constantly wet and sticky. Nevertheless, the cold penetrated through the little aperture; my eyes and forehead were like marble, the eyeballs like lumps of ice, sending a sharp pang of cold backward into the brain. I realised distinctly how a statue must feel.

Beyond Pello, where we stopped to "fire up," our road lay mostly on the Russian side. While crossing the Torneå at sunset, we met a drove of seventy or eighty reindeer, in charge of a dozen Lapps, who were bringing a cargo from Haparanda. We were obliged to turn off the road and wait until they had passed. The landlord at Juoxengi, who was quite drunk, hailed us with a shout and a laugh, and began talking about Kautokeino. We had some difficulty in getting rid of his conversation, and his importunities for us to stay all night. This was the place where they tried to make us leave, on the way up. I replied to the landlord's torrent of Finnish with some choice specimens of Kentucky oratory, which seemed to make but little impression on him. He gave us excellent horses, however, and we sped away again, by the light of another brilliant auroral arch.

Our long exposure to the extreme cold, coupled as it was with lack of rest and nourishment, now began to tell upon us. Our temperature fell so low that we again had recourse to the rum, which alone, I verily believe, prevented us from freezing bodily. One is locked in the iron embrace of the polar air, until the very life seems to be squeezed out of him. I huddled myself in my poesk, worked my fingers and toes, buried my nose in the damp, frozen fur, and laboured like a Hercules to keep myself awake and alive—but almost in vain. Braisted and I kept watch over each other, or attempted it, for about the only consciousness either of us had was that of the peril of falling asleep. We talked of anything and everything, sang, thumped each other, but the very next minute would catch ourselves falling over the side of the sled. A thousand dreams worried my brain and mixed themselves with my talk; and the absurdities thus created helped to arouse me. Speaking of seeing some wolves in the woods of California, I gravely continued: "I took out my sword, sharpened it on the grindstone and dared him to come on," when a punch in the ribs stopped me. Another time, while talking of hippopotami in the White Nile, I said: "If you want any skins, you must go to the Hudson's Bay Company. They have a depôt of them on Vancouver's Island." Braisted gave me much trouble, by assuring me in the most natural wide-awake voice that he was not in the least sleepy, when the reins had dropped from his hands and his head rocked on his shoulder. I could never be certain whether he was asleep or awake. Our only plan was not to let the conversation flag a minute.

At Torakankorwa we changed horses without delay, and hurried on to Matarengi. On turning out of the road to avoid a hay-sled, we were whirled completely over. There was no fun in this, at such a time. I fell head foremost into deep snow, getting a lump in my right eye, which completely blinded me for a time. My forehead, eyebrows, and the bridge of my nose were insufferably painful. On reaching Matarengi I found my nose frozen through, and considerably swollen. The people were in bed, but we went into the kitchen, where a dozen or more were stowed about, and called for the landlord. Three young girls, who were in bed in one corner, rose and dressed themselves in our presence without the least hesitation, boiled some milk, and gave us bread and butter. We had a single small bed, which kept us warm by obliging us to lie close. Sometime in the night, two Swedes arrived, who blustered about and made so much noise, that Braisted finally silenced them by threats of personal violence, delivered in very good English.

In the morning the mercury froze, after showing 49° below zero. The cold was by this time rather alarming, especially after our experiences of the previous day. The air was hazy with the fine, frozen atoms of moisture, a raw wind blew from the north, the sky was like steel which has been breathed upon—in short, the cold was visible to the naked eye. We warmed our gloves and boots, and swathed our heads so completely that not a feature was to be seen. I had a little loophole between my cap and boa, but it was soon filled up with frost from my breath, and helped to keep in the warmth. The road was hard and smooth as marble. We had good horses, and leaving Avasaxa and the polar circle behind us, we sped down the solid bed of the Torneå to Niemis. On the second stage we began to freeze for want of food. The air was really terrible; nobody ventured out of doors who could stay in the house. The smoke was white and dense, like steam; the wind was a blast from the Norseman's hell, and the touch of it on your face almost made you scream. Nothing can be more severe—flaying, branding with a hot iron, cutting with a dull knife, &c., may be something like it, but no worse.

The sun rose through the frozen air a little after nine, and mounted quite high at noon. At Päckilä we procured some hot milk and smoked reindeer, tolerable horses and a stout boy of fourteen to drive our baggage-sled. Every one we met had a face either frozen, or about to freeze. Such a succession of countenances, fiery red, purple, blue, black almost, with white frost spots, and surrounded with rings of icy hair and fur, I never saw before. We thanked God again and again that our faces were turned southward, and that the deadly wind was blowing on our backs. When we reached Korpikilä, our boy's face, though solid and greasy as a bag of lard, was badly frozen. His nose was quite white and swollen, as if blistered by fire, and there were frozen blotches on both cheeks. The landlord rubbed the parts instantly with rum, and performed the same operation on our noses.

On this day, for the first time in more than a month, we saw daylight, and I cannot describe how cheering was the effect of those pure, white, brilliant rays, in spite of the iron landscape they illumined. It was no longer the setting light of the level Arctic sun; not the twilight gleams of shifting colour, beautiful, but dim; not the faded, mock daylight which sometimes glimmered for a half-hour at noon; but the true white, full, golden day, which we had almost forgotten. So nearly, indeed, that I did not for some time suspect the cause of the unusual whiteness and brightness. Its effect upon the trees was superb. The twigs of the birch and the needles of the fir were coated with crystal, and sparkled like jets of jewels spouted up from the immaculate snow. The clumps of birches can be compared to nothing but frozen fountains—frozen in full action, with their showery sheaves of spray arrested before they fell. It was a wonderful, a fairy world we beheld—too beautiful to be lifeless, but every face we met reminded us the more that this was the chill beauty of Death—of dead Nature. Death was in the sparkling air, in the jewelled trees, in the spotless snow. Take off your mitten, and his hand will grasp yours like a vice; uncover your mouth, and your frozen lips will soon acknowledge his kiss.

Even while I looked the same icy chills were running through my blood, precursors of that drowsy torpor which I was so anxious to avoid. But no; it

132

would come, and I dozed until both hands became so stiff that it was barely possible to restore their powers of motion and feeling. It was not quite dark when we reached Kuckula, the last station, but thence to Haparanda our horses were old and lazy, and our postillion was a little boy, whose weak voice had no effect. Braisted kept his hands warm in jerking and urging, but I sat and froze. Village after village was passed, but we looked in vain for the lights of Torneå. We were thoroughly exhausted with our five days' battle against the dreadful cold, when at last a row of lights gleamed across the river, and we drove up to the inn. The landlord met us with just the same words as on the first visit, and, strange enough, put us into the same room, where the same old Norrland merchant was again quartered in the same stage of tipsiness. The kind Fredrika did not recognise us in our Lapp dresses, until I had unrobed, when she cried out in joyful surprise, "Why, you were here before!"

We had been so completely chilled that it was a long time before any perceptible warmth returned. But a generous meal, with a bottle of what was called "gammal scherry" (though the Devil and his servants, the manufacturers of chemical wines, only knew what it was), started the flagging circulation. We then went to bed, tingling and stinging in every nerve from the departing cold. Every one complained of the severity of the weather, which, we were told, had not been equalled for many years past. But such a bed, and such a rest as I had! Lying between clean sheets, with my feet buried in soft fur, I wallowed in a flood of downy, delicious sensations until sunrise. In the morning we ventured to wash our faces and brush our teeth for the first time in five days, put on clean shirts, and felt once more like responsible beings. The natives never wash when the weather is so cold, and cautioned us against it. The wind had fallen but the mercury again froze at 47° below zero. Nevertheless, we went out after breakfast to call upon Dr. Wretholm, and walk over the Torneå.

The old Doctor was overjoyed to see us again. "Ah!" said he, "it is a good fortune that you have got back alive. When the weather was so cold, I thought of you, travelling over the Norwegian fjeller, and thought you must certainly be frozen to death." His wife was no less cordial in her welcome. They brought us ale and Swedish punch, with reindeer cheese for our frozen noses, and insisted on having their horse put into the sled to take us over to Torneå and bring us back to dinner. The doctor's boy drove us, facing the wind with our faces exposed, at -42°, but one night's rest and good food enabled us to bear it without inconvenience. Torneå is a plain Swedish town, more compactly built than Haparanda, yet scarcely larger. The old church is rather picturesque, and there were some tolerable houses, which appeared to be government buildings, but the only things particularly Russian which we noticed were a Cossack sentry, whose purple face showed that he was nearly frozen, and a guide-post with "150 versts to Uleaborg" upon it. On returning to the Doctor's we found a meal ready, with a capital salad of frozen salmon, bouillon, ale, and coffee. The family were reading the Swedish translation of "Dred" in the Aftonblad, and were interested in hearing some account of Mrs. Beecher Stowe. We had a most agreeable and interesting visit to these kind, simple-hearted people.

I made a sunset sketch of Torneå. I proposed also to draw Fredrika, but she at once refused, in great alarm. "Not for anything in the world," said she, "would I have it done!" What superstitious fears possessed her I could not discover. We made arrangements to start for Kalix the next day, on our way to Stockholm. The extreme temperature still continued. The air was hazy with the frozen moisture—the smoke froze in solid masses—the snow was brittle and hard as metal—iron stuck like glue—in short, none of the signs of an Arctic winter were wanting. Nevertheless, we trusted to the day's rest and fatter fare on the road for strength to continue the battle.

CHAPTER XV. INCIDENTS OF THE RETURN JOURNEY.

We left Haparanda on the 30th of January. After six days of true Arctic weather—severer than any registered by De Haven's expedition, during a winter in the polar ice—the temperature rose suddenly to 26° below zero. We were happy and jolly at getting fairly started for Stockholm at last, and having such mild (!) weather to travel in. The difference in our sensations was remarkable. We could boldly bare our faces and look about us; our feet kept warm and glowing, and we felt no more the hazardous chill and torpor of the preceding days. On the second stage the winter road crossed an arm of the Bothnian Gulf. The path was well marked out with fir-trees—a pretty avenue, four or five miles in length, over the broad, white plain. On the way we saw an eruption of the ice, which had been violently thrown up by the confined air. Masses three feet thick and solid as granite were burst asunder and piled atop of each other.

We travelled too fast this day for the proper enjoyment of the wonderful scenery on the road. I thought I had exhausted my admiration of these winter forests—but no, miracles will never cease. Such fountains, candelabra, Gothic pinnacles, tufts of plumes, colossal sprays of coral, and the embodiments of the fairy pencillings of frost on window panes, wrought in crystal and silver, are beyond the power of pen or pencil. It was a wilderness of beauty; we knew not where to look, nor which forms to choose, in the dazzling confusion. Silent and all unmoved by the wind they stood, sharp and brittle as of virgin ore—not trees of earth, but the glorified forests of All-Father Odin's paradise, the celestial city of Asgaard. No living forms of vegetation are so lovely. Tropical palms, the tree-ferns of Penang, the lotus of Indian rivers, the feathery bamboo, the arrowy areca—what are they beside these marvellous growths of winter, these shining sprays of pearl, ivory and opal, gleaming in the soft orange light of the Arctic sun?

At Sängis we met a handsome young fellow with a moustache, who proved to be the Länsman of Kalix. I was surprised to find that he knew all about us. He wondered at our coming here north, when we might stay at home thought once would be enough for us, and had himself been no further than Stockholm. I recognised our approach to Näsby by the barrels set in the snow—an ingenious plan of marking the road in places where the snow drifts, as the wind creates a whirl or eddy around them. We were glad to see Näsby and its two-story inn once more. The pleasant little handmaiden smiled all over her face when she saw us again. Näsby is a crack place: the horses were ready at once, and fine creatures they were, taking us up the Kalix to Månsbyn, eight miles in one hour. The road was hard as a rock and smooth as a table, from much ploughing and rolling.

The next day was dark and lowering, threatening snow, with a raw wind from the north-west, and an average temperature of 15° below zero. We turned the north-western corner of the Bothnian Gulf in the afternoon, and pushed on to Old Luleå by supper-time. At Persö, on the journey north, I had forgotten my cigar-case, an old, familiar friend of some years' standing, and was overjoyed to find that the servant-girl had carefully preserved it, thinking I might return some day. We drove through the streets of empty stables and past the massive church of Old Luleå, to the inn, where we had before met the surly landlord. There he was again, and the house was full, as the first time. However we obtained the promise of a bed in the large room, and meanwhile walked up and down to keep ourselves warm. The guests' rooms were filled with gentlemen of the neighborhood, smoking and carousing. After an hour had passed, a tall, handsome, strong fellow came out of the rooms, and informed us that as we were strangers he would give up the room to us and seek lodgings elsewhere. He had drunk just enough to be mellow and happy, and insisted on delaying his own supper to let us eat first. Who should come along at this juncture but the young fellow we had seen in company with Brother Horton at Månsbyn, who hailed us with: "Thank you for the last time!" With him was a very gentlemanly man who spoke English. They were both accompanied by ladies, and were returning from the ball of Piteå. The guests all treated us with great courtesy and respect, and the landlord retired and showed his surly face no more. Our first friend informed me that he had been born and brought up in the neighborhood, but could not recollect such a severe winter.

136

As we descended upon the Luleå River in the morning we met ten sleighs coming from the ball. The horses were all in requisition at the various stations, but an extra supply had been provided, and we were not detained anywhere. The Norrland sleds are so long that a man may place his baggage in the front part and lie down at full length behind it. A high back shields the traveller from the wind, and upon a step in the rear stands the driver, with a pair of reins as long as a main-top-bowline, in order to reach the horse, who is at the opposite end of a very long pair of shafts. In these sleds one may travel with much comfort, and less danger of overturning, though not so great speed as in the short, light, open frames we bought in Sundsvall. The latter are seldom seen so far north, and were a frequent object of curiosity to the peasants at the stations. There is also a sled with a body something like a Hansom cab, entirely closed, with a window in front, but they are heavy, easily overturned, and only fit for luxurious travellers.

We approached Piteå at sunset. The view over the broad embouchure of the river, studded with islands, was quite picturesque, and the town itself, scattered along the shore and over the slopes of the hills made a fair appearance. It reminded me somewhat of a small New-England country town, with its square frame houses and an occasional garden. Here I was rejoiced by the sight of a cherry-tree, the most northern fruit-tree which I saw. On our way up, we thought Piteå, at night and in a snow-storm, next door to the North Pole. Now, coming from the north, seeing its snowy hills and house-roofs rosy with the glow of sunset, it was warm and southern by contrast. The four principal towns of West and North Bothnia are thus characterised in an old verse of Swedish doggerel: Umeå, the fine; Piteå, the needle-making; Luleå, the lazy; and in Torneå, everybody gets drunk.

We took some refreshment, pushed on and reached Abyn between nine and ten o'clock, having travelled seventy miles since morning. The sleighing was superb. How I longed for a dashing American cutter, with a span of fast horses, a dozen strings of bells and an ebony driver! Such a turnout would rather astonish the northern solitudes, and the slow, quaint northern population. The next day we had a temperature of 2° above zero, with snow falling, but succeeded in reaching Skellefteå for breakfast. For the last two or three miles we travelled along a hill-side overlooking a broad, beautiful valley, cleared and divided into cultivated fields, and thickly sprinkled with villages and farm-houses. Skellefteå itself made an imposing appearance, as the lofty dome of its Grecian church came in sight around the shoulder of the hill. We took the wrong road, and in turning about split one of our shafts, but Braisted served it with some spare rope, using the hatchet-handle as a marlingspike, so that it held stoutly all the rest of the way to Stockholm.

We went on to Burea that night, and the next day to Djekneboda, sixty miles farther. The temperature fluctuated about the region of zero, with a heavy sky and light snow-falls. As we proceeded southward the forests became larger, and the trees began to show a dark green foliage where the wind had blown away the snow, which was refreshing to see, after the black or dark indigo hue they wear farther north. On the 4th of February, at noon, we passed through Umeå, and congratulated ourselves on getting below the southern limit of the Lapland climate. There is nothing to say about these towns; they are mere villages with less than a thousand inhabitants each, and no peculiar interest, either local or historical, attaching to any of them. We have slept in Luleå, and Piteå, and dined in Umeå,—and further my journal saith not.

The 5th, however, was a day to be noticed. We started from Angersjö, with a violent snow storm blowing in our teeth—thermometer at zero. Our road entered the hilly country of Norrland, where we found green forests, beautiful little dells, pleasant valleys, and ash and beech intermingled with the monotonous but graceful purple birch. We were overwhelmed with gusts of fine snow shaken from the trees as we passed. Blinding white clouds swept the road, and once again we heard the howl of the wind among boughs that were free to toss. At Afwa, which we reached at one o'clock, we found a pale, weak, sickly young Swede, with faded moustaches, who had decided to remain there until next day. This circumstance induced us to go on, but after we had waited half an hour and were preparing to start, the weather being now ten times worse than before, he announced his resolution to start also. He had drunk four large glasses of milk and two cups of coffee during the half hour.

We went ahead, breaking through drifts of loose snow which overtopped our sleds, and lashed by the furious wind, which drove full in our faces. There were two or three plows at work but we had no benefit from them, so long as we were not directly in their wake. Up and down went our way, over dark hills and through valleys wild with the storm, and ending in chaos as they opened toward the Bothnian Gulf. Hour after hour passed by, the storm still increased, and the snow beat in our eyes so that we were completely blinded. It was impossible to keep them open, and yet the moment we shut them the lashes began to freeze together. I had a heavy weight of ice on my lids, and long icicles depending from every corner of my beard. Yet our frozen noses appeared to be much improved by the exposure, and began to give promise of healing without leaving a red blotch as a lasting record of what they had endured. We finally gave up all attempts to see or to guide the horse, but plunged along at random through the chaos, until the postillion piloted our baggage-sled into the inn-yard of Onska, and our horse followed it. The Swede was close upon our heels, but I engaged a separate room, so that we were freed from the depressing influence of his company. He may have been the best fellow in the world, so far as his heart was concerned, but was too weak in the knees to be an agreeable associate. There was no more stiffness of fibre in him than in a wet towel, and I would as soon wear a damp shirt as live in the same room with such a man. After all, it is not strange that one prefers nerve and energy, even when they are dashed with a flavour of vice, to the negative virtues of a character too weak and insipid to be tempted.

Our inn, in this little Norrland village, was about as comfortable and as elegant as three-fourths of the hotels in Stockholm. The rooms were well furnished; none of the usual appliances were wanting; the attendance was all that could be desired; the fare good and abundant, and the charges less than half of what would be demanded in the capital. Yet Stockholm, small as it is, claims to be for Sweden what Paris is to France, and its inhabitants look with an eye of compassion on those of the provinces. Norrland, in spite of its long winter, has a bracing, healthy climate, and had it not been for letters from home, facilities for studying Swedish, occasional recreation and the other attractions of a capital, I should have preferred waiting in some of those wild valleys for the spring to open. The people, notwithstanding their seclusion

139

from the world, have a brighter and more intelligent look than the peasants of Uppland, and were there a liberal system of common school education in Sweden, the raw material here might be worked up into products alike honourable and useful to the country.

The Norrlanders seem to me to possess an indolent, almost phlegmatic temperament, and yet there are few who do not show a latent capacity for exertion. The latter trait, perhaps, is the true core and substance of their nature; the former is an overgrowth resulting from habits and circumstances. Like the peasants, or rather small farmers, further north, they are exposed to the risk of seeing their summer's labours rendered fruitless by a single night of frost. Such a catastrophe, which no amount of industry and foresight can prevent, recurring frequently (perhaps once in three years on an average), makes them indifferent, if not reckless; while that patience and cheerfulness which is an integral part of the Scandinavian as of the Saxon character, renders them contented and unrepining under such repeated disappointments. There is the stuff here for a noble people, although nature and a long course of neglect and misrule have done their best to destroy it.

The Norrlanders live simply, perhaps frugally, but there seems to be little real destitution among them. We saw sometimes in front of a church, a representation of a beggar with his hat in his hand, under which was an iron box, with an appeal to travellers to drop something in for the poor of the parish; but of actual beggars we found none. The houses, although small, are warm and substantial, mostly with double windows, and a little vestibule in front of the door, to create an intermediate temperature between the outer and inner air. The beds, even in many of the inns, are in the family room, but during the day are either converted into sofas or narrow frames which occupy but little space. At night, the bedstead is drawn out to the required breadth, single or double, as may be desired. The family room is always covered with a strong home-made rag carpet, the walls generally hung with colored prints and lithographs, illustrating religion or royalty, and as many greenhouse plants as the owner can afford to decorate the windows. I have seen, even beyond Umeå, some fine specimens of cactus, pelargonium, calla, and other exotics. It is singular that, with the universal passion of the Swedes for flowers and for music, they have produced no distinguished painters or composers—but, indeed, a Linnæus.

We spent the evening cosily in the stately inn's best room, with its white curtains, polished floor, and beds of sumptuous linen. The great clipper-plows were out early in the morning, to cut a path through the drifts of the storm, but it was nearly noon before the road was sufficiently cleared to enable us to travel. The temperature, by contrast with what we had so recently endured, seemed almost tropical—actually 25° above zero, with a soft, southern breeze, and patches of brilliant blue sky between the parting clouds. Our deliverance from the Arctic cold was complete.

CHAPTER XVI. CONCLUSION OF THE ARCTIC TRIP.

On leaving Onska, we experienced considerable delay on account of the storm. The roads were drifted to such an extent that even the ploughs could not be passed through in many places, and the peasants were obliged to work with their broad wooden spades. The sky, however, was wholly clear and of a pure daylight blue, such as we had not seen for two months. The sun rode high in the firmament, like a strong healthy sun again, with some warmth in his beams as they struck our faces, and the air was all mildness and balm. It was heavenly, after our Arctic life. The country, too, boldly undulating, with fir-forested hills, green and warm in the sunshine, and wild, picturesque valleys sunk between, shining in their covering of snow, charmed us completely. Again we saw the soft blue of the distant ranges as they melted away behind each other, suggesting space, and light, and warmth. Give me daylight and sunshine, after all! Our Arctic trip seems like a long, long night full of splendid dreams, but yet night and not day.

On the road, we bought a quantity of the linen handkerchiefs of the country, at prices varying from twenty-five to forty cents a piece, according to the size and quality. The bedding, in all the inns, was of home-made linen, and I do not recollect an instance where it was not brought out, fresh and sweet from the press, for us. In this, as in all other household arrangements, the people are very tidy and cleanly, though a little deficient as regards their own persons. Their clothing, however, is of a healthy substantial character, and the women consult comfort rather than ornament. Many of them wear cloth pantaloons under their petticoats, which, therefore, they are able to gather under their arms in wading through snow-drifts. I did not see a low-necked dress or a thin shoe north of Stockholm.

"The damsel who trips at daybreak

Is shod like a mountaineer."

Yet a sensible man would sooner take such a damsel to wife than any delicate Cinderella of the ball-room. I protest I lose all patience when I think of the habits of our American women, especially our country girls. If ever the Saxon race does deteriorate on our side of the Atlantic, as some ethnologists anticipate, it will be wholly their fault.

We stopped for the night at Hörnäs, and had a charming ride the next day among the hills and along the inlets of the Gulf. The same bold, picturesque scenery, which had appeared so dark and forbidding to us on our way north, now, under the spring-like sky, cheered and inspired us. At the station of Docksta, we found the peasant girls scrubbing the outer steps, barefooted. At night, we occupied our old quarters at Weda, on the Angermann river. The next morning the temperature was 25° above zero, and at noon rose to 39°. It was delightful to travel once more with cap-lappets turned up, fur collar turned down, face and neck free, and hands bare. On our second stage we had an overgrown, insolent boy for postillion, who persisted in driving slow, and refused to let us pass him. He finally became impertinent, whereupon Braisted ran forward and turned his horse out of the road, so that I could drive past. The boy then seized my horse by the head; B. pitched him into a snow-bank, and we took the lead. We had not gone far before we took the road to Hernösand, through mistake, and afterwards kept it through spite, thus adding about seven miles to our day's journey. A stretch of magnificent dark-green forests brought us to a narrow strait which separates the island of Hernösand from the main land. The ice was already softening, and the upper layer repeatedly broke through under us.

Hernösand is a pretty town, of about 2000 inhabitants, with a considerable commerce. It is also the capital of the most northern bishopric of Sweden. The church, on an eminence above the town, is, next to that of Skellefteå, the finest we saw in the north. We took a walk while breakfast was preparing, and in the space of twenty minutes saw all there was to be seen. By leaving the regular road, however, we had incurred a delay of two hours, which did not add to our amiability. Therefore, when the postillion, furiously angry now as well as insolent, came in to threaten us with legal prosecution in case we did not pay him heavy damages for what he called an assault, I cut the discussion short by driving him out of the room, and that was the last we saw of him. We reached Fjäl as the moon rose,—a globe of silver fire in a perfect violet sky. Two merry boys, who sang and shouted the whole way, drove us like the wind around the bay to Wifsta. The moonlight was as bright as the Arctic noonday, and the snowy landscape flashed and glittered under its resplendent shower. From the last hill we saw Sundsvall, which lay beneath us, with its wintry roofs, like a city of ivory and crystal, shining for us with the fairy promise of a warm supper and a good bed.

On the 9th, we drove along the shores of the magnificent bay of Sundsvall. Six vessels lay frozen in, at a considerable distance from the town. Near the southern extremity of the bay, we passed the village of Svartvik, which, the postillion informed us, is all owned by one person, who carries on ship-building. The appearance of the place justified his statements. The labourers' houses were mostly new, all built on precisely the same model, and with an unusual air of comfort and neatness. In the centre of the village stood a handsome white church, with a clock tower, and near it the parsonage and school-house. At the foot of the slope were the yards, where several vessels were on the stocks, and a number of sturdy workmen busy at their several tasks. There was an air of "associated labour" and the "model lodging-house" about the whole place, which was truly refreshing to behold, except a touch of barren utilitarianism in the cutting away of the graceful firs left from the forest, and thus depriving the houses of all shade and ornament. We met many wood-teams, hauling knees and spars, and were sorely troubled to get out of their way. Beyond the bay, the hills of Norrland ceased, sinking into those broad monotonous undulations which extend nearly all the way to Stockholm. Gardens with thriving fruit-trees now began to be more frequent, giving evidence of a climate where man has a right to live. I doubt whether it was ever meant that the human race should settle in any zone so frigid that fruit cannot ripen.

Thenceforth we had the roughest roads which were ever made upon a foundation of snow. The increase in travel and in the temperature of the air, and most of all, the short, loosely-attached sleds used to support the ship-timber, had worn them into a succession of holes, channels, and troughs, in and out of which we thumped from morning till night. On going down hill, the violent shocks frequently threw our runners completely into the air, and the wrench was so great that it was a miracle how the sled escaped fracture. All the joints, it is true, began to work apart, and the ash shafts bent in the most ticklish way; but the rough little conveyance which had already done us such hard service held out gallantly to the end. We reached Mo Myskie on the second night after leaving Sundsvall, and I was greeted with "Salaam aleikoom, ya Sidi!" from the jolly old Tripolitan landlord. There was an unusual amount of travel northward on the following day, and we were detained at every station, so that it was nearly midnight before we reached the extortionate inn at Gefle. The morning dawned with a snow-storm, but we were within 120 miles of Stockholm, and drove in the teeth of it to Elfkarleby. The renowned cascades of the Dal were by no means what I expected, but it was at least a satisfaction to see living water, after the silent rivers and fettered rapids of the North.

The snow was now getting rapidly thinner. So scant was it on the exposed Upsala plain that we fully expected being obliged to leave our sleds on the way. Even before reaching Upsala, our postillions chose the less-travelled field-roads whenever they led in the same direction, and beyond that town we were charged additional post-money for the circuits we were obliged to make to keep our runners on the snow. On the evening of the 13th we reached Rotebro, only fourteen miles from Stockholm, and the next morning, in splendid sunshine, drove past Haga park and palace, into the North-Gate, down the long Drottning-gatan, and up to Kahn's Hotel, where we presented our sleds to the valet-de-place, pulled off our heavy boots, threw aside our furs for the remainder of the winter, and sat down to read the pile of letters and papers which Herr Kahn brought us. It was precisely two months since our departure in December, and in that time we had performed a journey of 2200 miles, 250 of which were by reindeer, and nearly 500 inside of the Arctic Circle. Our frozen noses had peeled off, and the new skin showed no signs of the damage they had sustained—so that we had come out of the fight not only without a scar, but with a marked increase of robust vitality.

I must confess, however, that, interesting as was the journey, and happily as we endured its exposures, I should not wish to make it again. It

145

is well to see the North, even after the South; but, as there is no one who visits the tropics without longing ever after to return again, so, I imagine, there is no one who, having once seen a winter inside the Arctic Circle, would ever wish to see another. In spite of the warm, gorgeous, and ever-changing play of colour hovering over the path of the unseen sun, in spite of the dazzling auroral dances and the magical transfiguration of the forests, the absence of true daylight and of all signs of warmth and life exercises at last a depressing influence on the spirits. The snow, so beautiful while the sunrise setting illumination lasts, wears a ghastly monotony at all other times, and the air, so exhilarating, even at the lowest temperature, becomes an enemy to be kept out, when you know its terrible power to benumb and destroy. To the native of a warmer zone, this presence of an unseen destructive force in nature weighs like a nightmare upon the mind. The inhabitants of the North also seem to undergo a species of hibernation, as well as the animals. Nearly half their time is passed in sleep; they are silent in comparison with the natives of the other parts of the world; there is little exuberant gaiety and cheerfulness, but patience, indifference, apathy almost. Aspects of nature which appear to be hostile to man, often develop and bring into play his best energies, but there are others which depress and paralyse his powers. I am convinced that the extreme North, like the Tropics, is unfavourable to the best mental and physical condition of the human race. The proper zone of man lies between 30° and 55° North.

To one who has not an unusual capacity to enjoy the experiences of varied travel, I should not recommend such a journey. With me, the realization of a long-cherished desire, the sense of novelty, the opportunity for contrasting extremes, and the interest with which the people inspired me, far outweighed all inconveniences and privations. In fact, I was not fully aware of the gloom and cold in which I had lived until we returned far enough southward to enjoy eight hours of sunshine, and a temperature above the freezing point. It was a second birth into a living world. Although we had experienced little positive suffering from the intense cold, except on the return from Muoniovara to Haparanda, our bodies had already accommodated themselves to a low temperature, and the sudden transition to 30° above zero came upon us like the warmth of June. My friend, Dr. Kane, once described to me the comfort he felt when the mercury rose to 7° below zero, making it pleasant to be on deck. The circumstance was then incomprehensible to me, but is now quite plain. I can also the better realise the terrible sufferings of himself and his men, exposed to a storm in a temperature of -47°, when the same degree of cold, with a very light wind, turned my own blood to ice.

Most of our physical sensations are relative, and the mere enumeration of so many degrees of heat or cold gives no idea of their effect upon the system. I should have frozen at home in a temperature which I found very comfortable in Lapland, with my solid diet of meat and butter, and my garments of reindeer. The following is a correct scale of the physical effect of cold, calculated for the latitude of 65° to 70° North:

15° above zero—Unpleasantly warm.

Zero—Mild and agreeable.

10° below zero—Pleasantly fresh and bracing.

20° below zero—Sharp, but not severely cold. Keep your fingers and toes in motion, and rub your nose occasionally.

30° below zero—Very cold; take particular care of your nose and extremities: eat the fattest food, and plenty of it 40° below—Intensely cold; keep awake at all hazards, muffle up to the eyes, and test your circulation frequently, that it may not stop somewhere before you know it.

50° below—A struggle for life.

* We kept a record of the temperature from the time we left Sundsvall (Dec. 21) until our return to Stockholm. As a matter of interest, I subjoin it, changing the degrees from Reaumur to Fahrenheit. We tested the thermometer repeatedly on the way, and found it very generally reliable, although in extremely low temperature it showed from one to two degrees more than a spirit thermometer. The observations were taken at from 9 to 8 A. M., 12 to 2 P. M., and 7 to 11 P. M., whenever it was possible.

	Morning.	Noon.	Evening.
December 21	+ 6	--	zero.
December 22	+ 6	--	- 3
December 23	-22	-29	-22
December 24	- 6	-22	-22
December 25	-35	-38	mer. frozen.
December 26	-30	-24	-31
December 27 (storm)	-18	-18	-18
December 28 (storm)	zero.	zero.	zero.
December 29	- 6	-13	-13
December 30	- 6	-13	-22
December 31 (storm)	- 3	+ 9	+ 9
January 1, 1857	+ 3	+ 3	+ 3
January 2	- 6	- 6	- 6
January 3	-30	-22	-22
January 4	-18	--	-22
January 5	-31	-30	-33
January 6	-20	- 4	zero.
January 7	+ 4	+18	+25
January 8	+18	--	-11
January 9	-28	-44	-44
January 10 (storm)	- 5	--	- 2
January 11 (storm)	- 2	zero.	- 5
January 12 (storm)	- 5	- 4	- 4
January 13 (storm)	+ 5	+ 5	+ 5
January 14	- 6	-13	- 64
January 15	- 8	-13	-33
January 16	- 9	-10	-11
January 17 (fog)	zero.	zero.	zero.

January 18	-10	-18	-23
January 19 (storm)	- 3	- 3	- 9
January 20	+20	--	+ 6
January 21	- 4	zero.	zero.
January 22	+ 2	- 6	-13
January 23	-13	- 3	-13
January 24	-15	-22	-44
January 25 mer. froz.	-50?	-42	mer. frozen
January 26	-45	-35	-39
January 27 frozen	-47?	-45	-35
January 28 frozen	-49?	-47	-44
January 29	-47?	-43	-43
January 30	-27	-11	-35
January 31	-17	-16	- 7
February 1	zero.	- 9	-13
February 2	+ 2	+ 6	zero
February 3	zero.	zero.	zero.
February 4	- 9	zero.	- 3
February 5 (storm)	+ 3	+ 3	+ 3
February 6	+25	+25	+18
February 7	+14	+18	+25
February 8	+25	+39	+22
February 9	+ 5	+22	+16
February 10	+25	+37	+37
February 11	+34	+34	+32
February 12	+32	+37	+23
February 13	+16	+30	+21
February 14	+25	+30	+25

CHAPTER XVII. LIFE IN STOCKHOLM.

The Swedes are proud of Stockholm, and justly so. No European capital, except Constantinople, can boast such picturesque beauty of position, and none whatever affords so great a range of shifting yet ever lovely aspects. Travellers are fond of calling it, in the imitative nomenclature of commonplace, the "Venice of the North"—but it is no Venice. It is not that swan of the Adriatic, singing her death-song in the purple sunset, but a northern eaglet, nested on the islands and rocky shores of the pale green Mälar lake. The Stad, or city proper, occupies three islands, which lie in the mouth of the narrow strait, by which the waters of the lake, after having come a hundred miles from the westward, and washed in their course the shores of thirteen hundred islands, pour themselves into the outer archipelago which is claimed by the Baltic Sea. On the largest of these islands, according to tradition, Agne, King of Sweden, was strangled with his own golden chain, by the Finnish princess Skiolfa, whom he had taken prisoner. This was sixteen hundred years ago, and a thousand years later, Birger Jarl, on the same spot, built the stronghold which was the seed out of which Stockholm has grown.

This island, and the adjoining Riddarholm, or Island of the Knights, contain all the ancient historic landmarks of the city, and nearly all of its most remarkable buildings. The towers of the Storkyrka and the Riddarholm's Church lift themselves high into the air; the dark red mass of the Riddarhus, or House of Nobles, and the white turrets and quadrangles of the penitentiary are conspicuous among the old white, tile-roofed blocks of houses; while, rising above the whole, the most prominent object in every view of Stockholm, is the Slot, or Royal Palace. This is one of the noblest royal residences in Europe. Standing on an immense basement terrace of granite, its grand quadrangle of between three and four hundred feet square, with wings (resembling, in general design, the Pitti Palace at Florence), is elevated quite above the rest of the city, which it crowns as with a mural diadem. The chaste and simple majesty of this edifice, and its admirable proportions, are a perpetual gratification to the eye, which is always drawn to it, as a central point, and thereby prevented from dwelling on whatever inharmonious or unsightly features there may be in the general view.

Splendid bridges of granite connect the island with the northern and southern suburbs, each of which is much greater in extent than the city proper. The palace fronts directly upon the Norrbro, or Northern Bridge, the great thoroughfare of Stockholm, which leads to the Square of Gustavus Adolphus, flanked on either side by the palace of the Crown Prince and the Opera House. The northern suburb is the fashionable quarter, containing all the newest streets and the handsomest private residences. The ground rises gradually from the water, and as very little attention is paid to grading, the streets follow the undulations of the low hills over which they spread, rising to the windmills on the outer heights and sinking into the hollows between. The southern suburb, however, is a single long hill, up the steep side of which the houses climb, row after row, until they reach the Church of St. Catherine, which crowns the very summit. In front of the city (that is eastward, and toward the Baltic), lie two other islands, connected by bridges with the northern suburb. Still beyond is the Djurgård, or Deer-Park, a singularly picturesque island, nearly the whole of which is occupied by a public park, and the summer villas of the wealthy Stockholmers. Its natural advantages are superior to those of any other park in Europe. Even in April, when there was scarcely a sign of spring, its cliffs of grey rock, its rolling lawns of brown grass, and its venerable oaks, with their iron trunks and gnarled, contorted boughs, with blue glimpses of ice-free water on all sides, attracted hundreds of visitors daily.

The streets of Stockholm are, with but two or three exceptions, narrow and badly paved. The municipal regulations in regard to them appear to be sadly deficient. They are quite as filthy as those of New-York, and the American reader will therefore have some idea of their horrid condition. A few trottoirs have been recently introduced, but even in the Drottning-gatan, the principal street, they are barely wide enough for two persons to walk abreast. The pavements are rough, slippery, and dangerous both to man and beast. I have no doubt that the great number of cripples in Stockholm is owing to this cause. On the other hand, the houses are models of solidity and stability. They are all of stone, or brick stuccoed over, with staircases of stone or iron, wood being prohibited by law, and roofs of copper, slate or tiles. In fact, the Swedes have singularly luxurious ideas concerning roofs, spending much more money upon them, proportionately, than on the house itself. You even see wooden shanties with copper roofs, got up regardless of expense. The houses are well lighted (which is quite necessary in the dark streets), and supplied with double windows against the cold. The air-tight Russian stove is universal. It has the advantage of keeping up sufficient warmth with a very small supply of fuel, but at the expense of ventilation. I find nothing yet equal to the old-fashioned fireplace in this respect, though I must confess I prefer the Russian stove to our hot-air furnaces. Carpets are very common in Sweden, and thus the dwellings have an air of warmth and comfort which is not found in Germany and other parts of the Continent. The arrangements for sleeping and washing are tolerable, though scanty, as compared with England, but the cleanliness of Swedish houses makes amends for many deficiencies.

The manner of living in Stockholm, nevertheless, is not very agreeable to the stranger. There is no hotel, except Kahn's, where one can obtain both beds and meals. The practice is to hire rooms, generally with the privilege of having your coffee in the morning, and to get your meals at a restaurant, of which there are many, tolerably cheap and not particularly good. Even Davison's, the best and most fashionable, has but an ordinary cuisine. Rooms are quite dear—particularly during our sojourn, when the Diet was in session and the city crowded with country visitors—and the inclusive expenses of living were equal to Berlin and greater than in Paris. I found that it cost just about as much to be stationary here, as to travel with post-horses in the Northern provinces. The Swedes generally have a cup of coffee on getting out of bed, or before, a substantial breakfast at nine, dinner at three, and tea in the evening. The wealthier families dine an hour or two later, but the crowds at the restaurants indicate the prevailing time. Dinner, and frequently breakfast, is prefaced with a smörgås (butter-goose), consisting of anchovies, pickled herrings, cheese and brandy. Soup which is generally sweet, comes in the middle and sometimes at the end of dinner, and the universal dessert is preserved fruit covered with whipped cream. I have had occasion to notice the fondness of the Swedes for sugar, which some persons seem to apply to almost every dish, except fish and oysters. I have often seen them season crab soup with powdered sugar. A favourite dish is raw salmon, buried in the earth until it is quite sodden—a great delicacy, they say, but I have not yet been hungry enough to eat it. Meat, which is abundant, is rarely properly cooked, and game, of which Sweden has a great variety, is injured by being swamped in sauces. He must be very fastidious, however, who cannot live passably well in Stockholm, especially if he has frequent invitations to dine with private families, many of whom have very excellent cooks.

My Swedish friends all said, "You should see Stockholm in summer! You have passed the worst part of the whole year among us, and you leave just when our fine days begin." I needed no assurance, however, of the summer charm of the place. In those long, golden evenings, which give place to an unfading twilight, when the birch is a network of silver and green, and the meadows are sown with the bright wild flowers of the North, those labyrinths of land and water must be truly enchanting. But were the glories of the Northern Summer increased tenfold, I could not make my home where such a price must be paid for them. From the time of our arrival, in February, until towards the close of April, the weather was of that kind which aggravates one to the loss of all patience. We had dull, raw, cloudy skies, a penetrating, unnerving, and depressing atmosphere, mud under foot, alternating with slushy snow,—in short, everything that is disagreeable in winter, without its brisk and bracing qualities. I found this season much more difficult to endure than all the cold of Lapland, and in spite of pleasant society and the charms of rest after a fatiguing journey, our sojourn in Stockholm was for a time sufficiently tedious.

At first, we lived a rather secluded life in our rooms in the Beridarebansgatan, in the northern suburb, devoting ourselves principally to gymnastics and the study of the Swedish language,—both of which can be prosecuted to more advantage in Stockholm than anywhere else. For, among the distinguished men of Sweden may be reckoned Ling, the inventor of what may be termed anatomical gymnastics. His system not only aims at reducing to a science the muscular development of the body, but, by means of both active and passive movements, at reaching the seat of disease and stimulating

153

the various organs to healthy action. In the former of these objects, Ling has certainly succeeded; there is no other system of muscular training that will bear comparison with his; and if he has to some extent failed in the latter, it is because, with the enthusiasm of a man possessed by a new discovery, he claimed too much. His successor, Prof. Branting, possesses equal enthusiasm, and his faith in gymnastics, as a panacea for all human infirmities, is most unbounded. The institution under his charge is supported by Government, and, in addition to the officers of the army and navy, who are obliged to make a complete gymnastic course, is largely attended by invalids of all ages and classes.

Neither of us required the system as a medical application. I wished to increase the girth of my chest, somewhat diminished by a sedentary life, and Braisted needed a safety-valve for his surplus strength. However, the professor, by dint of much questioning, ascertained that one of us was sometimes afflicted with cold feet, and the other with headaches, and thereupon clapped us both upon the sick list. On entering the hall, on the first morning of our attendance, a piece of paper containing the movements prescribed for our individual cases, was stuck in our bosoms. On inspecting the lists, we found we had ten movements apiece, and no two of them alike. What they were we could only dimly guess from such cabalistic terms as "Stödgångst," "Krhalfligg," "Simhäng," or "Högstrgrsitt." The hall, about eighty feet in length by thirty in height, was furnished with the usual appliances for gymnastic exercises. Some fifty or sixty patients were present, part of whom were walking up and down the middle passage with an air of great solemnity, while the others, gathered in various little groups on either side, appeared to be undergoing uncouth forms of torture. There was no voluntary exercise, if I except an old gentleman in a black velvet coat, who repeatedly suspended himself by the hands, head downwards, and who died of apoplexy not long afterwards; every one was being exercised upon. Here, a lathy young man, bent sideways over a spar, was struggling, with a very red face, to right himself, while a stout teacher held him down; there, a corpulent gentleman, in the hands of five robust assistants, was having his body violently revolved upon the base of his hip joints, as if they were trying to unscrew him from his legs; and yonder again, an individual, suspended by his arms from a cross-bar, had his feet held up and his legs stretched apart by another, while a third pounded vigorously with closed fists upon his seat of honour. Now and then a prolonged yell, accompanied with all sorts of burlesque variations, issued from the throats of the assembly. The object of this was at first not clear to me, but I afterwards discovered that the full use of the lungs was considered by Ling a very important part of the exercises. Altogether, it was a peculiar scene, and not without a marked grotesque character.

On exhibiting my matsedel, or "bill of fare," to the first teacher who happened to be disengaged, I received my first movement, which consisted in being held with my back against a post, while I turned my body from side to side against strong resistance, employing the muscles of the chest only. I was then told to walk for five minutes before taking the second movement. It is unnecessary to recapitulate the various contortions I was made to perform; suffice it to say, that I felt very sore after them, which Professor Branting considered a promising sign, and that, at the end of a month, I was taken off the sick list and put among the friskas, or healthy patients, to whom more and severer movements, in part active, are allotted. This department was under the special charge of Baron Vegesach, an admirable teacher, and withal a master of fencing with the bayonet, a branch of defensive art which the Swedes have the honour of originating. The drill of the young officers in bayonet exercise was one of the finest things of the kind I ever saw. I prospered so well under the Baron's tuition, that at the end of the second month I was able to climb a smooth mast, to run up ropes with my hands, and to perform various other previous impossibilities, while my chest had increased an inch and a half in circumference, the addition being solid muscle.

During the time of my attendance I could not help but notice the effect of the discipline upon the other patients, especially the children. The weak and listless gradually straightened themselves; the pale and sallow took colour and lively expression; the crippled and paralytic recovered the use of their limbs; in short, all, with the exception of two or three hypochondriacs, exhibited a very marked improvement. The cheerfulness and geniality which pervaded the company, and of which Professor Branting himself was the best example, no doubt assisted the cure. All, both teachers and pupils, met on a platform of the most absolute equality, and willingly took turns in lending a hand wherever it was needed. I have had my feet held up by a foreign ambassador, while a pair of Swedish counts applied the proper degree of resistance to the muscles of my arms and shoulders. The result of my observation and experience was, that Ling's system of physical education is undoubtedly the best in the world, and that, as a remedial agent in all cases of congenital weakness or deformity, as well as in those diseases which arise from a deranged circulation, its value can scarcely be over-estimated. It may even afford indirect assistance in more serious organic diseases, but I do not believe that it is of much service in those cases where chemical agencies are generally employed. Professor Branting, however, asserts that it is a specific for all diseases whatsoever, including consumption, malignant fevers, and venereal affections. One thing at least is certain—that in an age when physical training is most needed and most neglected, this system deserves to be introduced into every civilised country, as an indispensable branch in the education of youth.

I found the Swedish language as easy to read as it is difficult to speak correctly. The simplicity of its structure, which differs but slightly from English, accounts for the former quality, while the peculiar use of the definite article as a terminal syllable, attached to the noun, is a great impediment to fluent speaking. The passive form of the verb also requires much practice before it becomes familiar, and the mode of address in conversation is awkward and inconvenient beyond measure. The word you, or its correspondent, is never used, except in speaking to inferiors; wherever it occurs in other languages, the title of the person addressed must be repeated; as, for example: "How is the Herr Justizråd? I called at the Herr Justizråd's house this morning, but the Herr Justizråd was not at home." Some of the more progressive Swedes are endeavouring to do away with this absurdity, by substituting the second person plural, ni, which is already used in literature, but even they only dare to use it in their own private circle. The Swedes, especially in Stockholm, speak with a peculiar drawl and singing accent, exactly similar to that which is often heard in Scotland. It is very inferior to the natural, musical rhythm of Spanish, to which, in its vocalisation, Swedish has a great resemblance. Except Finnish, which is music itself, it is the most melodious of northern languages, and the mellow flow of its poetry is often scarcely surpassed by the

Italian. The infinitive verb always ends in a, and the language is full of soft, gliding iambics, which give a peculiar grace to its poetry.

It is rather singular that the Swedish prose, in point of finish and elegance, is far behind the Swedish poetry. One cause of this may be, that it is scarcely more than fifty years since the prose writers of the country began to use their native language. The works of Linnæus, Swedenborg, and other authors of the past century must now be translated into Swedish. Besides, there are two prose dialects—a conversational and a declamatory, the latter being much more artificial and involved than the former. All public addresses, as well as prose documents of a weighty or serious character, must be spoken or written in this pompous and antiquated style, owing to which, naturally, the country is almost destitute of orators. But the poets,—especially men of the sparkling fancy of Bellman, or the rich lyrical inspiration of Tegner, are not to be fettered by such conventionalities; and they have given the verse of Sweden an ease, and grace, and elegance, which one vainly seeks in its prose. In Stockholm, the French taste, so visible in the manners of the people, has also affected the language, and a number of French words and forms of expression, which have filtered through society, from the higher to the lower classes, are now in general use. The spelling, however, is made to conform to Swedish pronunciation, and one is amused at finding on placards such words as "trottoar," "salong," and "paviljong."

No country is richer in song-literature than Sweden. The popular songs and ballads of the different provinces, wedded to airs as original and characteristic as the words, number many hundreds. There are few Swedes who cannot sing, and I doubt whether any country in Europe would be able to furnish so many fine voices. Yet the taste for what is foreign and unaccustomed rules, and the minstrels of the cafes and the Djurgård are almost without exception German. Latterly, two or three bands of native singers have been formed, who give concerts devoted entirely to the country melodies of Sweden; and I believe they have been tolerably successful.

In these studies, relieved occasionally by rambles over the hills, whenever there was an hour's sunshine, and by occasional evenings with Swedish, English, and American friends, we passed the months of March and April, waiting for the tardy spring. Of the shifting and picturesque views which Stockholm presents to the stranger's eye, from whatever point he beholds her, we never wearied; but we began at last to tire of our ice-olation, and to look forward to the reopening of the Gotha Canal, as a means of escape. Day after day it was a new satisfaction to behold the majestic palace crowning the island-city and looking far and wide over the frozen lakes; the tall, slender spire of the Riddarholm, soaring above the ashes of Charles XII. and Gustavus Adolphus, was always a welcome sight; but we had seen enough of the hideous statues which ornament the public squares, (Charles XII. not among them, and the imbecile Charles XIII. occupying the best place); we grew tired of the monotonous perambulators on the Forrbro, and the tameness and sameness of Stockholm life in winter: and therefore hailed the lengthening days which heralded our deliverance.

As to the sights of the capital, are they not described in the guide-books? The champion of the Reformation lies in his chapel, under a cloud of his captured banners: opposite to him, the magnificent madman of the North, with hundreds of Polish and Russian ensigns rustling above his heads. In the royal armory you see the sword and the bloody shirt of the one, the bullet-pierced hat and cloak of the other, still coated with the mud of the trench at Fredrickshall. There are robes and weapons of the other Carls and Gustavs, but the splendour of Swedish history is embodied in these two names, and in that of Gustavus Vasa, who lies entombed in the old cathedral at Upsala. When I had grasped their swords, and the sabre of Czar Peter, captured at Narva, I felt that there were no other relics in Sweden which could make my heart throb a beat the faster.

CHAPTER XVIII. MANNERS AND MORALS OF STOCKHOLM.

As a people, the Swedes are very hospitable, and particularly so toward foreigners. There is perhaps no country in Europe where travellers are treated with so much kindness and allowed so many social privileges. This is fortunate, as the conventionalities of the country are more rigid than the laws of the Medes and Persians. Nothing excites greater scandal than an infraction of the numberless little formalities with which the descendants of the honest, spontaneous, impulsive old Scandinavians have, somehow or other, allowed themselves to be fettered, and were not all possible allowance made for the stranger, he would have but a dismal time of it. Notwithstanding these habits have become a second nature, they are still a false nature, and give a painfully stiff and constrained air to society. The Swedes pride themselves on being the politest people in Europe. Voltaire called them the "Frenchmen of the North," and they are greatly flattered by the epithet. But how much better, to call themselves Swedes?—to preserve the fine, manly characteristics of their ancient stock, rather than imitate a people so alien to them in blood, in character, and in antecedents. Those meaningless social courtesies which sit well enough upon the gay, volatile, mercurial Frenchman, seem absurd affectations when practiced by the tall, grave, sedate Scandinavian. The intelligent Swedes feel this, but they are powerless to make headway against the influence of a court which was wholly French, even before Bernadotte's time. "We are a race of apes," said one of them to me bitterly. Gustavus III. was thoroughly French in his tastes, but the ruin of Swedish nationality in Stockholm was already commenced when he ascended the throne.

Stockholm manners, at present, are a curious mixture of English and French, the latter element, of course, being predominant. In costume, the gentlemen are English, with exaggeration. Nowhere are to be seen such enormously tall and stiff black chimney-pots (misnamed hats), nowhere such straight-cut overcoats, descending to the very heels. You might stick all the men you see into pasteboard cards, like a row of pins, so precisely are they clothed upon the same model. But when you meet one of these grim, funereal figures, he pulls off his hat with a politeness which is more than French; he keeps it off, perhaps, while he is speaking; you shake hands and accept his invitation to enter his house. After you are within, he greets you a second time with the same ceremonies, as if you had then first met; he says, "Tak for sist!" (equivalent to; "thank you for the pleasure of your company the last time we met!") and, after your visit is over, you part with equal formality. At dinner the guests stand gravely around the table with clasped hands, before sitting down. This is repeated on rising, after which they bow to each other and shake hands with the host and hostess. Formerly they used to say "I thank you for the meal," a custom still retained in Denmark and Norway. Not long ago the guests were obliged to make a subsequent visit of ceremony to thank the host for his entertainment, and he was obliged to invite them all to a second dinner, in consequence thereof; so that giving one dinner always involved giving two. Fortunately the obligation was cancelled by the second, or the visits and dinners might have gone on alternately, ad infinitum.

At dinners and evening parties, white gloves and white cravats are invariably worn, and generally white vests. The same custom is observed at funerals, even the drivers of the hearse and carriages being furnished with resplendent white gloves for the occasion. I have a horror of white cravats, and took advantage of the traveller's privilege to wear a black one. I never could understand why, in England, where the boundaries of caste are so distinctly marked, a gentleman's full dress should be his servant's livery. The chimney-pots are no protection to the head in raw or very cold weather, and it required no little courage in me to appear in fur or felt. "I wish I could wear such a comfortable hat," said a Swede to me; "but I dare not; you are a traveller, and it is permitted; but a Swede would lose his position in society, if he were to do so." Another gentleman informed me that his own sisters refused to appear in the streets with him, because he wore a cap. A former English Consul greatly shocked the people by carrying home his own marketing. A few gentlemen have independence enough to set aside, in their own houses, some of the more disagreeable features of this conventionalism, and the success of two or three, who held weekly soirees through the winter, on a more free and unrestrained plan, may in the end restore somewhat of naturalness and spontaneity to the society of Stockholm.

160

The continual taking off of your hat to everybody you know, is a great annoyance to many strangers. A lift of the hat, as in Germany, is not sufficient. You must remove it entirely, and hold it in the air a second or two before you replace it. King Oscar once said to an acquaintance of mine, who was commiserating him for being obliged to keep his hat off, the whole length of the Drottning-gatan, in a violent snow-storm: "You are quite right; it was exceedingly disagreeable, and I could not help wishing that instead of being king of Sweden, I were king of Thibet, where, according to Huc, the polite salutation is simply to stick out your tongue." The consideration extended to foreigners is, I am told, quite withdrawn after they become residents; so that, as an Englishman informed me, Stockholm is much more pleasant the first year than the second. The principle, on the whole, is about the same as governs English, and most American society, only in Sweden its tyranny is more severely felt, on account of the French imitations which have been engrafted upon it.

I do not wish to be understood as saying a word in censure of that genial courtesy which is characteristic of the Swedes, not less of the bonder, or country farmers, than of the nobility. They are by nature a courteous people, and if, throughout the country, something of the primness and formality of ancient manners has been preserved, it the rather serves to give a quaint and picturesque grace to society. The affectation of French manners applies principally to the capital, which, both in manners and morals, can by no means be taken as a standard for the whole country. The Swedes are neither licentious, nor extravagantly over-mannered: the Stockholmers are both. During the whole of our journey to Lapland, we were invariably treated with a courtesy which bordered on kindness, and had abundant opportunities of noticing the general amenity which exists in the intercourse even of the poorest classes. The only really rude people we saw, were travelling traders, especially those from the capital, who thought to add to their importance by a little swaggering.

I recollect hearing of but a single instance in which the usual world-wide rules of hospitality were grossly violated. This occurred to an English traveller, who spent some time in the interior of the country. While taking tea one evening with a prominent family of the province, he happened to make use of his thumb and fore-finger in helping himself to a lump of sugar. The mistress of the house immediately sent out the servant, who reappeared after a short time with another sugar-bowl, filled with fresh lumps. Noticing this, the traveller, in order to ascertain whether his harmless deviation from Swedish customs had really contaminated the whole sugar-bowl, sweetened his second cup in the same manner. The result was precisely the same: the servant was again sent out, and again returned with a fresh supply. The traveller, thereupon, coolly walked to the stove, opened the door, and threw in his cup, saucer, and tea-spoon, affecting to take it for granted that they never could be used again.

Speaking of King Oscar reminds me that I should not fail to say a word about this liberal and enlightened monarch. There is probably no king in Europe at present, who possesses such extensive acquirements, or is animated by a more genuine desire for the good of his kingdom. The slow progress which Sweden has made in introducing needful reforms is owing to the conservative spirit of the nobility and the priesthood, who possess half the legislative power. I do not believe there is a greater enemy to progress than an established church. Oscar is deservedly popular throughout Sweden, and I wish I could believe that his successor will exhibit equal intelligence and liberality. During my stay I saw all the members of the Royal Family frequently, and once had an informal self-presentation to the whole of them. I was descending the stairway of Kahn's Hotel one afternoon, when a tall, black-bearded, Frenchy gentleman coming up, brushed so close to me in the narrow passage that he received the full benefit of a cloud of smoke which I was ejaculating. It was the Crown Prince, as a servant whispered to me, but as my cigar was genuine Havana, and he is said to be a connoisseur of the article, there was no harm done. As I reached the street door a dragoon dashed up, preceding the carriages containing the Royal Family, who were coming to view Professor Enslen's panoramas. First, the Crown Princess, with her children; she bowed gracefully in answer to my greeting. The Princess Eugenia, a lady of twenty-seven, or thereabouts, with a thoroughly cheerful and amiable face, came next and nodded, smiling. With her was the Queen, a daughter of Eugene Beauharnais, a handsome woman for her years, with the dark hair and eyes of her grandmother, Josephine. King Oscar followed, at the head of a company of officers and nobles, among whom was his second son, Prince Oscar, the handsomest young man in Stockholm. He wore his Admiral's uniform, and made me a naval salute as he passed. The King is about medium height, with a symmetrical head, a bold, finely-cut nose, keen, intelligent eyes, and a heavy grey moustache. There was something gallant, dashing, and manly in his air, despite his fifty-seven years. He gave me the impression of an honest, energetic and thoroughly accomplished man; and this is the character he bears throughout Sweden, except with a small class, who charge him with being insincere, and too much under the influence of the Queen, against whom, however, they can find no charge, except that of her Catholicism.

I was sorry to notice, not only in Stockholm, but more or less throughout Sweden, a spirit of detraction in regard to everything Swedish. Whenever I mentioned with admiration the name of a distinguished Swede, I was almost always sure to hear, in return, some disparaging remark, or a story to his disadvantage. Yet, singularly enough, the Swedes are rather sensitive to foreign criticism, seeming to reserve for themselves the privilege of being censorious. No amount of renown, nor even the sanctity which death gives to genius, can prevent a certain class of them from exhibiting the vices and weaknesses of their countrymen. Much the severest things which I heard said about Sweden, were said by Swedes themselves, and I was frequently obliged to rely upon my own contrary impressions, to protect me from the chance of being persuaded to paint things worse than they really are.

Just before leaving Stockholm I made application, through the Hon. Mr. Schroeder, our Minister Resident, and Baron Lagerheim, for the privilege of an interview with the king. A few days previously, however, he had been attacked with that illness which has obliged him to withdraw from the labours of government, and was advised by his physicians to receive no one. He sent me a very kind message, with an invitation to renew my request as soon as his health should be restored. Gentlemen who had opportunities of knowing the fact, assured me that his health broke down under an accumulation of labour and anxiety, in his endeavours to bring the question of religious liberty before the Diet—a measure in which he had to contend with the united influence of the clergy, the House of Peasants, whom the clergy rule to a great extent, and a portion of the House of Nobles. It is not often that a king is in advance of the general sentiment of his people, and in losing the services of Oscar, I fear that Sweden has lost her best man. The Crown Prince, now Prince Regent, is said to be amiably weak in his character, rather reactionary in his views, and very ambitious of military glory. At least, that is the average of the various opinions which I heard expressed concerning him.

After speaking of the manners of Stockholm, I must not close this chapter without saying a few words about its morals. It has been called the most licentious city in Europe, and, I have no doubt, with the most perfect justice. Vienna may surpass it in the amount of conjugal infidelity, but certainly not in general incontinence. Very nearly half the registered births are illegitimate, to say nothing of the illegitimate children born in wedlock. Of the servant-girls, shop-girls, and seamstresses in the city, it is very safe to say that scarcely ten out of a hundred are chaste, while, as rakish young Swedes have coolly informed me, many girls of respectable parentage, belonging to the middle class, are not much better. The men, of course, are much worse than the women, and even in Paris one sees fewer physical signs of excessive debauchery. Here, the number of broken-down young men, and blear-eyed, hoary sinners, is astonishing. I have never been in any place where licentiousness was so open and avowed—and yet, where the slang of a sham morality was so prevalent. There are no houses of prostitution in Stockholm, and the city would be scandalised at the idea of allowing such a thing. A few years ago two were established and the fact was no sooner known than a virtuous mob arose and violently pulled them down! At the restaurants, young blades order their dinners of the female waiters, with an arm around their waists, while the old men place their hands unblushingly upon their bosoms. All the baths in Stockholm are attended by women (generally middle-aged and hideous, I must confess), who perform the usual scrubbing and shampooing with the greatest nonchalance. One does not wonder when he is told of young men who have passed safely through the ordeals of Berlin and Paris, and have come at last to Stockholm to be ruined.[B]

It is but fair to say that the Swedes account for the large proportion of illegitimate births, by stating that many unfortunate females come up from the country to hide their shame in the capital, which is no doubt true. Everything that I have said has been derived from residents of Stockholm, who, proud as they are, and sensitive, cannot conceal this glaring depravity. The population of Stockholm, as is proved by statistics, has only been increased during the last fifty years by immigration from the country, the number of deaths among the inhabitants exceeding the births by several hundreds every year. I was once speaking with a Swede about these facts, which he seemed inclined to doubt. "But," said I, "they are derived from your own statistics." "Well," he answered, with a naïve attempt to find some compensating good, "you must at least admit that the Swedish statistics are as exact as any in the world!"

Drunkenness is a leading vice among the Swedes, as we had daily evidence. Six years ago the consumption of brandy throughout the kingdom was nine gallons for every man, woman, and child annually; but it has decreased considerably since then, mainly through the manufacture of beer and porter. "Bajerskt öl" (Bavarian beer) is now to be had everywhere, and is rapidly becoming the favourite drink of the people. Sweden and the United States will in the end establish the fact that lager beer is more efficacious in preventing intemperance than any amount of prohibitory law. Brandy-drinking is still, nevertheless, one of the greatest curses of Sweden. It is no unusual thing to see boys of twelve or fourteen take their glass of fiery finkel before dinner. The celebrated Swedish punch, made of arrack, wine, and sugar, is a universal evening drink, and one of the most insidious ever invented, despite its agreeable flavor. There is a movement in favor of total abstinence, but it seems to have made but little progress, except as it is connected with some of the new religious ideas, which are now preached throughout the country.

I have rarely witnessed a sadder example of ruin, than one evening in a Stockholm café. A tall, distinguished-looking man of about forty, in an advanced state of drunkenness, was seated at a table opposite to us. He looked at me awhile, apparently endeavoring to keep hold of some thought with which his mind was occupied. Rising at last he staggered across the room, stood before me, and repeated the words of Bellman:

"Så vandra våra stora män'

Från ljuset ned til skuggan."[C]

A wild, despairing laugh followed the lines, and he turned away, but came back again and again to repeat them. He was a nobleman of excellent family, a man of great intellectual attainments, who, a few years ago, was considered one of the most promising young men in Sweden. I saw him frequently afterwards, and always in the same condition, but he never accosted me again. The Swedes say the same thing of Bellman himself, and of Tegner, and many others, with how much justice I care not to know, for a man's faults are to be accounted for to God, and not to a gossiping public.

FOOTNOTES:

[B] The substance of the foregoing paragraph was contained in a letter published in The New-York Tribune during my travels in the North, and which was afterwards translated and commented upon by the Swedish papers. The latter charged me with having drawn too dark a picture and I therefore took some pains to test my statements, both by means of the Government statistics, and the views of my Swedish friends. I see no reason to change my first impression: had I accepted all that was told me by natives of the capital, I should have made the picture much darker. The question is simply whether there is much difference between the general adoption of illicit connections, or the existence of open prostitution. The latter is almost unknown; the former is almost universal, the supply being kept up by the miserable rates of wages paid to female servants and seamstresses. The former get, on an average, fifty rigsdaler ($13) per year, out of which they must clothe themselves: few of the latter can make one rigsdaler a day. These connections are also encouraged by the fact, that marriage legitimates all the children previously born. In fact, during the time of my visit to Stockholm, a measure was proposed in the House of Clergy, securing to bastards the same right of inheritance, as to legitimate children. Such measures, however just they may be so far as the innocent offspring of a guilty connection are concerned, have a direct tendency to impair the sanctity of marriage, and consequently the general standard of morality.

This, the most vital of all the social problems, is strangely neglected. The diseases and excesses which it engenders are far more devastating than those which spring from any other vice, and yet no philanthropist is bold enough to look the question in the face. The virtuous shrink from it, the vicious don't care about it, the godly simply condemn, and the ungodly indulge—and so the world rolls on, and hundreds of thousands go down annually to utter ruin. It is useless to attempt the extirpation of a vice which is inherent in the very nature of man, and the alternative of either utterly ignoring, or of attempting to check and regulate it, is a question of the most vital importance to the whole human race.

[C] "Thus our great men wander from the light down into the shades."

CHAPTER XIX. JOURNEY TO GOTTENBURG AND COPENHAGEN.

I never knew a more sudden transition from winter to summer than we experienced on the journey southward from Stockholm. When we left that city on the evening of the 6th of May, there were no signs of spring except a few early violets and anemones on the sheltered southern banks in Haga Park; the grass was still brown and dead, the trees bare, and the air keen; but the harbour was free from ice and the canal open, and our winter isolation was therefore at an end. A little circulation entered into the languid veins of society; steamers from Germany began to arrive; fresh faces appeared in the streets, and less formal costumes—merchants and bagmen only, it is true, but people of a more dashing and genial air. We were evidently, as the Swedes said, leaving Stockholm just as it began to be pleasant and lively.

The steamer left the Riddarholm pier at midnight, and took her way westward up the Mälar Lake to Södertelje. The boats which ply on the Gotha canal are small, but neat and comfortable. The price of a passage to Gottenburg, a distance of 370 miles, is about $8.50. This, however, does not include meals, which are furnished at a fixed price, amounting to $6 more. The time occupied by the voyage varies from two and a half to four days. In the night we passed through the lock at Södertelje, where St. Olaf, when a heathen Viking, cut a channel for his ships into the long Baltic estuary which here closely approaches the lake, and in the morning found ourselves running down the eastern shore of Sweden, under the shelter of its fringe of jagged rocky islets. Towards noon we left the Baltic, and steamed up the long, narrow Bay of Söderköping, passing, on the way, the magnificent ruins of Stegeborg Castle, the first mediæval relic I had seen in Sweden. Its square massive walls, and tall round tower of grey stone, differed in no respect from those of contemporary ruins in Germany.

Before reaching Söderköping, we entered the canal, a very complete and substantial work of the kind, about eighty feet in breadth, but much more crooked than would seem to be actually necessary. For this reason the boats make but moderate speed, averaging not more than six or seven miles an hour, exclusive of the detention at the locks. The country is undulating, and neither rich nor populous before reaching the beautiful Roxen Lake, beyond which we entered upon a charming district. Here the canal rises, by eleven successive locks, to the rich uplands separating the Roxen from the Wetter, a gently rolling plain, chequered, so far as the eye could reach, with green squares of springing wheat and the dark mould of the newly ploughed barley fields. While the boat was passing the locks, we walked forward to a curious old church, called Vreta Kloster. The building dates from the year 1128, and contains the tombs of three Swedish kings, together with that of the Count Douglas, who fled hither from Scotland in the time of Cromwell. The Douglas estate is in this neighbourhood, and is, I believe, still in the possession of the family. The church must at one time have presented a fine, venerable appearance: but all its dark rich colouring and gilding are now buried under a thick coat of white-wash.

We had already a prophecy of the long summer days of the North, in the perpetual twilight which lingered in the sky, moving around from sunset to sunrise. During the second night we crossed the Wetter Lake, which I did not see; for when I came on deck we were already on the Viken, the most beautiful sheet of water between Stockholm and Gottenburg. Its irregular shores, covered with forests of fir and birch, thrust out long narrow headlands which divide it into deep bays, studded with wild wooded islands. But the scenery was still that of winter, except in the absence of ice and snow. We had not made much southing, but we expected to find the western side of Sweden much warmer than the eastern. The highest part of the canal, more than 300 feet above the sea, was now passed, however, and as we descended the long barren hills towards the Wener Lake I found a few early wild flowers in the woods. In the afternoon we came upon the Wener, the third lake in Europe, being one hundred miles in extent by about fifty in breadth. To the west, it spread away to a level line against the sky; but, as I looked southward, I perceived two opposite promontories, with scattered islands between, dividing the body of water into almost equal portions. The scenery of the Wener has great resemblance to that of the northern portion of Lake Michigan. Further down on the eastern shore, the hill of Kinnekulle, the highest land in Southern Sweden, rises to the height of nearly a thousand feet above the water, with a graceful and very gradual sweep; but otherwise the scenery is rather tame, and, I suspect, depends for most of its beauty upon the summer foliage.

There were two or three intelligent and agreeable passengers on board, who showed a more than usual knowledge of America and her institutions. The captain, however, as we walked the deck together, betrayed the same general impression which prevails throughout the Continent (Germany in particular), that we are a thoroughly material people, having little taste for or appreciation of anything which is not practical and distinctly utilitarian. Nothing can be further from the truth; yet I have the greatest difficulty in making people comprehend that a true feeling for science, art, and literature can co-exist with our great practical genius. There is more intellectual activity in the Free States than in any other part of the world, a more general cultivation, and, taking the collective population, I venture to say, a more enlightened taste. Nowhere are greater sums spent for books and works of art, or for the promotion of scientific objects. Yet this cry of "Materialism" has become the cant and slang of European talk concerning America, and is obtruded so frequently and so offensively that I have sometimes been inclined to doubt whether the good breeding of Continental society has not been too highly rated.

While on the steamer, I heard an interesting story of a Swedish nobleman, who is at present attempting a practical protest against the absurd and fossilised ideas by which his class is governed. The nobility of Sweden are as proud as they are poor, and, as the father's title is inherited by each of his sons, the country is overrun with Counts and Barons, who, repudiating any means of support that is not somehow connected with the service of the government, live in a continual state of debt and dilapidation. Count R——, however, has sense enough to know that honest labour is always honourable, and has brought up his eldest son to earn his living by the work of his own hands. For the past three years, the latter has been in the United States, working as a day-labourer on farms and on Western railroads. His experiences, I learn, have not been agreeable, but he is a young man of too much spirit and courage to give up the attempt, and has hitherto refused to listen to the entreaties of his family, that he shall come home and take charge of one of his father's estates. The second son is now a clerk in a mercantile house in Gottenburg, while the Count has given his daughter in marriage to a radical and untitled editor, whose acquaintance I was afterwards so fortunate as to make, and who confirmed the entire truth of the story.

We were to pass the locks at Trollhätta in the middle of the night, but I determined to visit the celebrated falls of the Gotha River, even at such a time, and gave orders that we should be called. The stupid boy, however, woke up the wrong passenger, and the last locks were reached before the mistake was discovered. By sunrise we had reached Lilla Edet, on the Gotha River, where the buds were swelling on the early trees, and the grass, in sunny places, showed a little sprouting greenness. We shot rapidly down the swift brown stream, between brown, bald, stony hills, whose forests have all been stripped off to feed the hostile camp-fires of past centuries. Bits of bottom land, held in the curves of the river, looked rich and promising, and where the hills fell back a little, there were groves and country-houses—but the scenery, in general, was bleak and unfriendly, until we drew near Gottenburg. Two round, detached forts, built according to Vauban's ideas (which the Swedes say he stole from Sweden, where they were already in practice) announced our approach, and before noon we were alongside the pier. Here, to my great surprise, a Custom-house officer appeared and asked us to open our trunks. "But we came by the canal from Stockholm!" "That makes no difference," he replied; "your luggage must be examined." I then appealed to the captain, who stated that, in consequence of the steamer's being obliged to enter the Baltic waters for two or three hours between Södertelje and Söderköping, the law took it for granted that we might have boarded some foreign vessel during that time and procured contraband goods. In other words, though sailing in a narrow sound, between the Swedish islands and the Swedish coast, we had virtually been in a foreign country! It would scarcely be believed that this sagacious law is of quite recent enactment.

We remained until the next morning in Gottenburg. This is, in every respect, a more energetic and wide-awake place than Stockholm. It has not the same unrivalled beauty of position, but is more liberally laid out and kept in better order. Although the population is only about 40,000, its commerce is much greater than that of the capital, and so are, proportionately, its wealth and public spirit. The Magister Hedlund, a very intelligent and accomplished gentleman, to whom I had a letter from Mügge, the novelist, took me up the valley a distance of five or six miles, to a very picturesque village among the hills, which is fast growing into a manufacturing town. Large cotton, woollen and paper mills bestride a strong stream, which has such a fall that it leaps from one mill-wheel to another for the distance of nearly half a mile. On our return, we visited a number of wells hollowed in the rocky strata of the hills, to which the country people have given the name of "The Giant's Pots." A clergyman of the neighbourhood, even, has written a pamphlet to prove that they were the work of the antediluvian giants, who excavated them for the purpose of mixing dough for their loaves of bread and batter for their puddings. They are simply those holes which a pebble grinds in a softer rock, under the rotary action of a current of water, but on an immense scale, some of them being ten feet in diameter, by fifteen or eighteen in depth. At Herr Hedlund's house, I met a number of gentlemen, whose courtesy and intelligence gave me a very favourable impression of the society of the place.

The next morning, at five o'clock, the steamer Viken, from Christiania, arrived, and we took passage for Copenhagen. After issuing from the Skärgaard, or rocky archipelago which protects the approach to Gottenburg from the sea, we made a direct course to Elsinore, down the Swedish coast, but too distant to observe more than its general outline. This part of Sweden, however—the province of Halland—is very rough and stony, and not until after passing the Sound does one see the fertile hills and vales of Scania. The Cattegat was as smooth as an inland sea, and our voyage could not have been pleasanter. In the afternoon Zealand rose blue from the wave, and the increase in the number of small sailing craft denoted our approach to the Sound. The opposite shores drew nearer to each other, and finally the spires of Helsingborg, on the Swedish shore, and the square mass of Kronborg Castle, under the guns of which the Sound dues have been so long demanded, appeared in sight. In spite of its bare, wintry aspect, the panorama was charming. The picturesque Gothic buttresses and gables of Kronborg rose

172

above the zigzag of its turfed outworks; beyond were the houses and gardens of Helsingör (Elsinore)—while on the glassy breast of the Sound a fleet of merchant vessels lay at anchor, and beyond, the fields and towns of Sweden gleamed in the light of the setting sun. Yet here, again, I must find fault with Campbell, splendid lyrist as he is. We should have been sailing

"By thy *wild and stormy steep,*

Elsinore!"

only that the level shore, with its fair gardens and groves wouldn't admit the possibility of such a thing. The music of the line remains the same, but you must not read it on the spot.

There was a beautiful American clipper at anchor off the Castle. "There," said a Danish passenger to me, "is one of the ships which have taken from us the sovereignty of the Sound." "I am very glad of it," I replied; "and I can only wonder why the maritime nations of Europe have so long submitted to such an imposition." "I am glad, also," said he, "that the question has at last been settled, and our privilege given up—and I believe we are all, even the Government itself, entirely satisfied with the arrangement." I heard the same opinion afterwards expressed in Copenhagen, and felt gratified, as an American, to hear the result attributed to the initiative taken by our Government; but I also remembered the Camden and Amboy Railroad Company, and could not help wishing that the same principle might be applied at home. We have a Denmark, lying between New-York and Philadelphia, and I have often paid sand dues for crossing her territory.

At dusk, we landed under the battlements of Copenhagen. "Are you travellers or merchants?" asked the Custom-house officers. "Travellers," we replied. "Then," was the answer, "there is no necessity for examining your trunks," and we were politely ushered out at the opposite door, and drove without further hindrance to a hotel. A gentleman from Stockholm had said to me: "When you get to Copenhagen, you will find yourself in Europe:" and I was at once struck with the truth of his remark. Although Copenhagen is by no means a commercial city—scarcely more so than Stockholm—its streets are gay, brilliant and bustling, and have an air of life and joyousness which contrasts strikingly with the gravity of the latter capital. From without, it makes very little impression, being built on a low, level ground, and surrounded by high earthen fortifications, but its interior is full of quaint and attractive points. There is already a strong admixture of the German element in the population, softening by its warmth and frankness the Scandinavian reserve. In their fondness for out-door recreation, the Danes quite equal the Viennese, and their Summer-garden of Tivoli is one of the largest and liveliest in all Europe. In costume, there is such a thing as individuality; in manners, somewhat of independence. The Danish nature appears to be more pliant and flexible than the Swedish, but I cannot judge whether the charge of inconstancy and dissimulation, which I have heard brought against it, is just. With regard to morals, Copenhagen is said to be an improvement upon Stockholm.

During our short stay of three days, we saw the principal sights of the place. The first, and one of the pleasantest to me, was the park of Rosenborg Palace, with its fresh, green turf, starred with dandelions, and its grand avenues of chestnuts and lindens, just starting into leaf. On the 11th of May, we found spring at last, after six months of uninterrupted winter. I don't much enjoy going the round of a new city, attended by a valet-de-place, and performing the programme laid down by a guide-book, nor is it an agreeable task to describe such things in catalogue style; so I shall merely say that the most interesting things in Copenhagen are the Museum of Northern Antiquities, the Historical Collections in Rosenborg Palace, Thorwaldsen's Museum, and the Church of our Lady, containing the great sculptor's statues of Christ and the Apostles. We have seen very good casts of the latter in New-York, but one must visit the Museum erected by the Danish people, which is also Thorwaldsen's mausoleum, to learn the number, variety and beauty of his works. Here are the casts of between three and four hundred statues, busts and bas reliefs, with a number in marble. No artist has ever had so noble a monument.

On the day after my arrival, I sent a note to Hans Christian Andersen, reminding him of the greeting which he had once sent me through a mutual friend, and asking him to appoint an hour for me to call upon him. The same afternoon, as I was sitting in my room, the door quietly opened, and a tall, loosely-jointed figure entered. He wore a neat evening dress of black, with a white cravat; his head was thrown back, and his plain, irregular features wore an expression of the greatest cheerfulness and kindly humour. I recognised him at once, and forgetting that we had never met—so much did he seem like an old, familiar acquaintance—cried out "Andersen!" and jumped up to greet him. "Ah," said he stretching out both his hands, "here you are! Now I should have been vexed if you had gone through Copenhagen and I had not known it." He sat down, and I had a delightful hour's chat with him. One sees the man so plainly in his works, that his readers may almost be said to know him personally. He is thoroughly simple and natural, and those who call him egotistical forget that his egotism is only a naïve and unthinking sincerity, like that of a child. In fact, he is the youngest man for his years that I ever knew. "When I was sixteen," said he, "I used to think to myself, 'when I am twenty-four, then will I be old indeed'—but now I am fifty-two, and I have just the same feeling of youth as at twenty." He was greatly delighted when Braisted, who was in the room with me, spoke of having read his "Improvisatore" in the Sandwich Islands. "Why, is it possible?" he exclaimed: "when I hear of my books going so far around the earth, I sometimes wonder if it can be really true that I have written them." He explained to me the plot of his new novel, "To Be, or Not To Be," and ended by presenting me with the illustrated edition of his stories. "Now, don't forget me," said he, with a delightful entreaty in his, voice, as he rose to leave, "for we shall meet again. Were it not for sea-sickness, I should see you in America; and who knows but I may come, in spite of it?" God bless you, Andersen! I said, in my thoughts. It is so cheering to meet a man whose very weaknesses are made attractive through the perfect candour of his nature!

Goldschmidt, the author of "The Jew," whose acquaintance I made, is himself a Jew, and a man of great earnestness and enthusiasm. He is the editor of the "North and South," a monthly periodical, and had just completed, as he informed me, a second romance, which was soon to be published. Like most of the authors and editors in Northern Europe, he is well acquainted with American literature.

Professor Rafn, the distinguished archæologist of Northern lore, is still as active as ever, notwithstanding he is well advanced in years. After going up an innumerable number of steps, I found him at the very top of a high old building in the Kronprinzensgade, in a study crammed with old Norsk and Icelandic volumes. He is a slender old man, with a thin face, and high, narrow head, clear grey eyes, and a hale red on his cheeks. The dust of antiquity does not lie very heavily on his grey locks; his enthusiasm for his studies is of that fresh and lively character which mellows the whole nature of the man. I admired and enjoyed it, when, after being fairly started on his favourite topic, he opened one of his own splendid folios, and read me some ringing stanzas of Icelandic poetry. He spoke much of Mr. Marsh, our former minister to Turkey, whose proficiency in the northern languages he considered very remarkable.

CHAPTER XX. RETURN TO THE NORTH.—CHRISTIANIA.

I was obliged to visit both Germany and England, before returning to spend the summer in Norway. As neither of those countries comes within the scope of the present work, I shall spare the reader a recapitulation of my travels for six weeks after leaving Copenhagen. Midsummer's Day was ten days past before I was ready to resume the journey, and there was no time to be lost, if I wished to see the midnight sun from the cliffs of the North Cape. I therefore took the most direct route, from London, by the way of Hull, whence a steamer was to sail on the 3rd of July for Christiania.

We chose one of the steamers of the English line, to our subsequent regret, as the Norwegian vessels are preferable, in most respects. I went on board on Friday evening, and on asking for my berth, was taken into a small state-room, containing ten. "Oh, there's only seven gentleman goin' in here, this time," said the steward, noticing my look of dismay, "and then you can sleep on a sofa in the saloon, if you like it better." On referring to the steamer's framed certificate, I found that she was 250 tons' burden, and constructed to carry 171 cabin and 230 deck passengers! The state-room for ten passengers had a single wash-basin, but I believe we had as many as four small towels, which was a source of congratulation. "What a jolly nice boat it is!" I heard one of the English passengers exclaim. The steward, who stood up for the dignity of the vessel, said: "Oh, you'll find it very pleasant; we 'ave only twenty passengers, and we once 'ad heighty-four."

In the morning we were upon the North Sea, rolling with a short, nauseating motion, under a dismal, rainy sky. "It always rains when you leave Hull," said the mate, "and it always rains when you come back to it." I divided my time between sea sickness and Charles Reade's novel of "Never too Late to Mend," a cheery companion under such circumstances. The purposed rowdyism of the man's style shows a little too plainly, but his language is so racy and muscular, his characters so fairly and sharply drawn, that one must not be censorious. Towards evening I remembered that it was the Fourth, and so procured a specific for sea-sickness, with which Braisted and I, sitting alone on the main hatch, in the rain, privately remembered our Fatherland. There was on board an American sea-captain, of Norwegian birth, as I afterwards found, who would gladly have joined us. The other passengers were three Norwegians, three fossil Englishmen, two snobbish do., and some jolly, good-natured, free-and-easy youths, bound to Norway, with dogs, guns, rods, fishing tackle, and oil-cloth overalls.

We had a fair wind and smooth sea, but the most favourable circumstances could not get more than eight knots an hour out of our steamer. After forty-eight hours, however, the coast of Norway came in sight—a fringe of scattered rocks, behind which rose bleak hills, enveloped in mist and rain. Our captain, who had been running on this route some years, did not know where we were, and was for putting to sea again, but one of the Norwegian passengers offered his services as pilot and soon brought us to the fjord of Christiansand. We first passed through a Skärgaard—archipelago, or "garden of rocks," as it is picturesquely termed in Norsk—and then between hills of dark-red rock, covered by a sprinkling of fir-trees, to a sheltered and tranquil harbour, upon which lay the little town. By this time the rain came down, not in drops, but in separate threads or streams, as if the nozzle of an immense watering-pot had been held over us. After three months of drouth, which had burned up the soil and entirely ruined the hay-crops, it was now raining for the first time in Southern Norway. The young Englishmen bravely put on their waterproofs and set out to visit the town in the midst of the deluge; but as it contains no sight of special interest, I made up my mind that, like Constantinople, it was more attractive from without than within, and remained on board. An amphitheatre of rugged hills surrounds the place, broken only by a charming little valley, which stretches off to the westward.

The fishermen brought us some fresh mackerel for our breakfast. They are not more than half the size of ours, and of a brighter green along the back; their flavour, however, is delicious. With these mackerels, four salmons, a custom-house officer, and a Norwegian parson, we set off at noon for Christiania. The coast was visible, but at a considerable distance, all day. Fleeting gleams of sunshine sometimes showed the broken inland ranges of mountains with jagged saw-tooth peaks shooting up here and there. When night came there was no darkness, but a strong golden gleam, whereby one could read until after ten o'clock. We reached the mouth of Christiania Fjord a little after midnight, and most of the passengers arose to view the scenery. After passing the branch which leads to Drammen, the fjord contracts so as to resemble a river or one of our island-studded New England lakes. The alternation of bare rocky islets, red-ribbed cliffs, fir-woods, grey-green birchen groves, tracts of farm land, and red-frame cottages, rendered this part of the voyage delightful, although, as the morning advanced, we saw everything through a gauzy veil of rain. Finally, the watering-pot was turned on again, obliging even oil cloths to beat a retreat to the cabin, and so continued until we reached Christiania.

After a mild custom-house visitation, not a word being said about passports, we stepped ashore in republican Norway, and were piloted by a fellow-passenger to the Victoria Hotel, where an old friend awaited me. He who had walked with me in the colonnades of Karnak, among the sands of Kôm-Ombos, and under the palms of Philæ, was there to resume our old companionship on the bleak fjelds of Norway and on the shores of the Arctic Sea. We at once set about preparing for the journey. First, to the banker's who supplied me with a sufficient quantity of small money for the post-stations on the road to Drontheim; then to a seller of carrioles, of whom we procured three, at $36 apiece, to be resold to him for $24, at the expiration of two months; and then to supply ourselves with maps, posting-book, hammer, nails rope, gimlets, and other necessary helps in case of a breakdown. The carriole (carry-all, lucus a non lucendo, because it only carries one) is the national Norwegian vehicle, and deserves special mention. It resembles a reindeer-pulk, mounted on a pair of wheels, with long, flat, flexible ash shafts, and no springs. The seat, much like the stern of a canoe, and rather narrow for a traveller of large basis, slopes down into a trough for the feet, with a dashboard in front. Your single valise is strapped on a flat board behind, upon which your postillion sits. The whole machine resembles an American sulky in appearance, except that it is springless, and nearly the whole weight is forward of the axle. We also purchased simple and strong harness, which easily accommodates itself to any horse.

179

Christiania furnishes a remarkable example of the progress which Norway has made since its union with Sweden and the adoption of a free Constitution. In its signs of growth and improvement, the city reminds one of an American town. Its population has risen to 40,000, and though inferior to Gottenburg in its commerce, it is only surpassed by Stockholm in size. The old log houses of which it once was built have almost entirely disappeared; the streets are broad, tolerably paved, and have—what Stockholm cannot yet boast of—decent side-walks. From the little nucleus of the old town, near the water, branch off handsome new streets, where you often come suddenly from stately three-story blocks upon the rough rock and meadow land. The broad Carl-Johansgade, leading directly to the imposing white front of the Royal Palace, upon an eminence in the rear of the city, is worthy of any European capital. On the old market square a very handsome market hall of brick, in semi-Byzantine style, has recently been erected, and the only apparent point in which Christiania has not kept up with the times, is the want of piers for her shipping. A railroad, about forty miles in length, is already in operation as far as Eidsvold, at the foot of the long Miösen Lake, on which steamers ply to Lillehammer, at its head, affording an outlet for the produce of the fertile Guldbrandsdal and the adjacent country. The Norwegian Constitution is in almost all respects as free as that of any American state, and it is cheering to see what material well-being and solid progress have followed its adoption.

The environs of Christiania are remarkably beautiful. From the quiet basin of the fjord, which vanishes between blue, interlocking islands to the southward, the land rises gradually on all sides, speckled with smiling country-seats and farm-houses, which trench less and less on the dark evergreen forests as they recede, until the latter keep their old dominion and sweep in unbroken lines to the summits of the mountains on either hand. The ancient citadel of Aggershus, perched upon a rock, commands the approach to the city, fine old linden trees rising above its white walls and tiled roofs; beyond, over the trees of the palace park, in which stand the new Museum and University, towers the long palace-front, behind which commences a range of villas and gardens, stretching westward around a deep bight of the fjord, until they reach the new palace of Oscar-hall, on a peninsula facing the city. As we floated over the glassy water, in a skiff, on the afternoon following our arrival, watching the

180

scattered sun-gleams move across the lovely panorama, we found it difficult to believe that we were in the latitude of Greenland. The dark, rich green of the foliage, the balmy odours which filled the air, the deep blue of the distant hills and islands, and the soft, warm colors of the houses, all belonged to the south. Only the air, fresh without being cold, elastic, and exciting, not a delicious opiate, was wholly northern, and when I took a swim under the castle walls, I found that the water was northern too. It was the height of summer, and the showers of roses in the gardens, the strawberries and cherries in the market, show that the summer's best gifts are still enjoyed here.

The English were off the next day with their dogs, guns, fishing tackle, waterproofs, clay pipes, and native language, except one, who became home-sick and went back in the next steamer. We also prepared to set out for Ringerike, the ancient dominion of King Ring, on our way to the Dovre-fjeld and Drontheim.

CHAPTER XXI. INCIDENTS OF CARRIOLE TRAVEL.

It is rather singular that whenever you are about to start upon a new journey, you almost always fall in with some one who has just made it, and who overwhelms you with all sorts of warning and advice. This has happened to me so frequently that I have long ago ceased to regard any such communications, unless the individual from whom they come inspires me with more than usual confidence. While inspecting our carrioles at the hotel in Christiania, I was accosted by a Hamburg merchant, who had just arrived from Drontheim, by way of the Dovre Fjeld and the Miösen Lake. "Ah," said he, "those things won't last long. That oil-cloth covering for your luggage will be torn to pieces in a few days by the postillions climbing upon it. Then they hold on to your seat and rip the cloth lining with their long nails; besides, the rope reins wear the leather off your dashboard, and you will be lucky if your wheels and axles don't snap on the rough roads." Now, here was a man who had travelled much in Norway, spoke the language perfectly, and might be supposed to know something; but his face betrayed the croaker, and I knew, moreover, that of all fretfully luxurious men, merchants—and especially North-German merchants—are the worst, so I let him talk and kept my own private opinion unchanged.

At dinner he renewed the warnings. "You will have great delay in getting horses at the stations. The only way is to be rough and swaggering, and threaten the people—and even that won't always answer." Most likely, I thought.— "Of course you have a supply of provisions with you?" he continued. "No," said I, "I always adopt the diet of the country in which I travel."—"But you can't do it here!" he exclaimed in horror, "you can't do it here! They have no wine, nor no white bread, nor no fresh meat; and they don't know how to cook anything!" "I am perfectly aware of that," I answered; "but as long as I am not obliged to come down to bread made of fir-bark and barley-straw, as last winter in Lapland, I shall not complain."—"You possess the courage of a hero if you can do such a thing; but you will not start now, in this rain?" We answered by bidding him a polite adieu, for the post-horses had come, and our carrioles were at the door. As if to reward our resolution, the rain, which had been falling heavily all the morning, ceased at that moment, and the grey blanket of heaven broke and rolled up into loose masses of cloud.

I mounted into the canoe-shaped seat, drew the leathern apron over my legs, and we set out, in single file, through the streets of Christiania. The carriole, as I have already said, has usually no springs (ours had none at least), except those which it makes in bounding over the stones. We had not gone a hundred yards before I was ready to cry out—"Lord, have mercy upon me!" Such a shattering of the joints, such a vibration of the vertebræ, such a churning of the viscera, I had not felt since travelling by banghy-cart in India. Breathing went on by fits and starts, between the jolts; my teeth struck together so that I put away my pipe, lest I should bite off the stem, and the pleasant sensation of having been pounded in every limb crept on apace. Once off the paving-stones, it was a little better; beyond the hard turnpike which followed, better still; and on the gravel and sand of the first broad hill, we found the travel easy enough to allay our fears. The two skydsbonder, or postillions, who accompanied us, sat upon our portmanteaus, and were continually jumping off to lighten the ascent of the hills. The descents were achieved at full trotting speed, the horses leaning back, supporting themselves against the weight of the carrioles, and throwing out their feet very firmly, so as to avoid the danger of slipping. Thus, no matter how steep the hill, they took it with perfect assurance and boldness, never making a stumble. There was just sufficient risk left, however, to make these flying descents pleasant and exhilarating.

Our road led westward, over high hills and across deep valleys, down which we had occasional glimpses of the blue fjord and its rocky islands. The grass and grain were a rich, dark green, sweeping into a velvety blue in the distance, and against this deep ground, the bright red of the houses showed with strong effect—a contrast which was subdued and harmonised by the still darker masses of the evergreen forests, covering the mountain ranges. At the end of twelve or thirteen miles we reached the first post-station, at the foot of the mountains which bound the inland prospect from Christiania on the west. As it was not a "fast" station, we were subject to the possibility of waiting two or three hours for horses, but fortunately were accosted on the road by one of the farmers who supply the skyds, and changed at his house. The Norwegian skyds differs from the Swedish skjuts in having horses ready only at the fast stations, which are comparatively few, while at all others you must wait from one to three hours, according to the distance from which the horses must be brought. In Sweden there are always from two to four horses ready, and you are only obliged to wait after these are exhausted. There, also, the regulations are better, and likewise more strictly enforced. It is, at best, an awkward mode of travelling—very pleasant, when everything goes rightly, but very annoying when otherwise.

We now commenced climbing the mountain by a series of terribly steep ascents, every opening in the woods disclosing a wider and grander view backward over the lovely Christiania Fjord and the intermediate valleys. Beyond the crest we came upon a wild mountain plateau, a thousand feet above the sea, and entirely covered with forests of spruce and fir. It was a black and dismal region, under the lowering sky: not a house or a grain field to be seen, and thus we drove for more than two hours, to the solitary inn of Krogkleven, where we stopped for the night in order to visit the celebrated King's View in the morning. We got a tolerable supper and good beds, sent off a messenger to the station of Sundvolden, at the foot of the mountain, to order horses for us, and set out soon after sunrise, piloted by the landlord's son, Olaf. Half an hour's walk through the forest brought us to a pile of rocks on the crest of the mountain, which fell away abruptly to the westward. At our feet lay the Tyri Fjord, with its deeply indented shores and its irregular, scattered islands, shining blue and bright in the morning sun, while away beyond it stretched a great semicircle of rolling hills covered with green farms, dotted with red farm-houses, and here and there a white church glimmering like a spangle on the breast of the landscape. Behind this soft, warm, beautiful region, rose dark, wooded hills, with lofty mountain-ridges above them, until, far and faint, under and among the clouds, streaks of snow betrayed some peaks of the Nore Fjeld, sixty or seventy miles distant. This is one of the most famous views in Norway, and has been compared to that from the Righi, but without sufficient reason. The sudden change, however, from the gloomy wilderness through which you first pass to the sunlit picture of the enchanting lake, and green, inhabited hills and valleys, may well excuse the raptures of travellers. Ringerike, the realm of King Ring, is a lovely land, not only as seen from this eagle's nest, but when you have descended upon its level. I believe the monarch's real name was Halfdan the Black. So beloved was he in life that after death his body was divided into four portions, so that each province might possess some part of him. Yet the noblest fame is transitory, and nobody now knows exactly where any one of his quarters was buried.

A terrible descent, through a chasm between perpendicular cliffs some hundreds of feet in height, leads from Krogkleven to the level of the Tyri Fjord. There is no attempt here, nor indeed upon the most of the Norwegian roads we travelled, to mitigate, by well-arranged curves, the steepness of the hills. Straight down you go, no matter of how breakneck a character the declivity may be. There are no drags to the carrioles and country carts, and were not the native horses the toughest and surest-footed little animals in the world, this sort of travel would be trying to the nerves.

Our ride along the banks of the Tyri Fjord, in the clear morning sunshine, was charming. The scenery was strikingly like that on the lake of Zug, in Switzerland, and we missed the only green turf, which this year's rainless spring had left brown and withered. In all Sweden we had seen no such landscapes, not even in Norrland. There, however, the people carried off the palm. We found no farm-houses here so stately and clean as the Swedish, no such symmetrical forms and frank, friendly faces. The Norwegians are big enough, and strong enough, to be sure, but their carriage is awkward, and their faces not only plain but ugly. The countrywomen we saw were remarkable in this latter respect, but nothing could exceed their development of waist, bosom and arms. Here is the stuff of which Vikings were made, I thought, but there has been no refining or ennobling since those times. These are the rough primitive formations of the human race—the bare granite and gneiss, from which sprouts no luxuriant foliage, but at best a few simple and hardy flowers. I found much less difficulty in communicating with the Norwegians than I anticipated. The language is so similar to the Swedish that I used the latter, with a few alterations, and easily made myself understood.

The Norwegian dialect, I imagine, stands in about the same relation to pure Danish as the Scotch does to the English. To my ear, it is less musical and sonorous than the Swedish, though it is often accented in the same peculiar sing-song way.

Leaving the Tyri Fjord, we entered a rolling, well-cultivated country, with some pleasant meadow scenery. The crops did not appear to be thriving remarkably, probably on account of the dry weather. The hay crop, which the farmers were just cutting, was very scanty; rye and winter barley were coming into head, but the ears were thin and light, while spring barley and oats were not more than six inches in height. There were many fields of potatoes, however, which gave a better promise. So far as one could judge from looking over the fields, Norwegian husbandry is yet in a very imperfect state, and I suspect that the resources of the soil are not half developed. The whole country was radiant with flowers, and some fields were literally mosaics of blue, purple, pink, yellow, and crimson bloom. Clumps of wild roses fringed the road, and the air was delicious with a thousand odours. Nature was throbbing with the fullness of her short midsummer life, with that sudden and splendid rebound from the long trance of winter which she nowhere makes except in the extreme north.

At Kläkken, which is called a lilsigelse station, where horses must be specially engaged, we were obliged to wait two hours and a half, while they were sent for from a distance of four miles. The utter coolness and indifference of the people to our desire to get on faster was quite natural, and all the better for them, no doubt, but it was provoking to us. We whiled away a part of the time with breakfast, which was composed mainly of boiled eggs and an immense dish of wild strawberries, of very small size but exquisitely fragrant flavour. The next station brought us to Vasbunden, at the head of the beautiful Randsfjord, which was luckily a fast station, and the fresh horses were forthcoming in two minutes. Our road all the afternoon lay along the eastern bank of the Fjord, coursing up and down the hills through a succession of the loveliest landscape pictures. This part of Norway will bear a comparison with the softer parts of Switzerland, such as the lakes of Zurich and Thun. The hilly shores of the Fjord were covered with scattered farms, the villages being merely churches with half a dozen houses clustered about them.

At sunset we left the lake and climbed a long wooded mountain to a height of more than two thousand feet. It was a weary pull until we reached the summit, but we rolled swiftly down the other side to the inn of Teterud, our destination, which we reached about 10 P.M. It was quite light enough to read, yet every one was in bed, and the place seemed deserted, until we remembered what latitude we were in. Finally, the landlord appeared, followed by a girl, whom, on account of her size and blubber, Braisted compared to a cow-whale. She had been turned out of her bed to make room for us, and we two instantly rolled into the warm hollow she had left, my Nilotic friend occupying a separate bed in another corner. The guests' room was an immense apartment; eight sets of quadrilles might have been danced in it at one time. The walls were hung with extraordinary pictures of the Six Days of Creation, in which the Almighty was represented as an old man dressed in a long gown, with a peculiarly good-humoured leer, suggesting a wink, on his face. I have frequently seen the same series of pictures in the Swedish inns. In the morning I was aroused by Braisted exclaiming, "There she blows!" and the whale came up to the surface with a huge pot of coffee, some sugar candy, excellent cream, and musty biscuit.

It was raining when we started, and I put on a light coat, purchased in London, and recommended in the advertisement as being "light in texture, gentlemanly in appearance, and impervious to wet," with strong doubts of its power to resist a Norwegian rain. Fortunately, it was not put to a severe test; we had passing showers only, heavy, though short. The country, between the Randsfjord and the Miösen Lake was open and rolling, everywhere under cultivation, and apparently rich and prosperous. Our road was admirable, and we rolled along at the rate of one Norsk mile (seven miles) an hour, through a land in full blossom, and an atmosphere of vernal odours. At the end of the second station we struck the main road from Christiania to Drontheim. In the station-house I found translations of the works of Dickens and Captain Chamier on the table. The landlord was the most polite and attentive Norwegian we had seen; but he made us pay for it, charging one and a half marks apiece for a breakfast of boiled eggs and cheese.

Starting again in a heavy shower, we crossed the crest of a hill, and saw all at once the splendid Miösen Lake spread out before us, the lofty Island of Helge, covered with farms and forests, lying in the centre of the picture. Our road went northward along the side of the vast, sweeping slope of farm-land which bounds the lake on the west. Its rough and muddy condition showed how little land-travel there is at present, since the establishment of a daily line of steamers on the lake. At the station of Gjövik, a glass furnace, situated in a wooded little dell on the shore, I found a young Norwegian who spoke tolerable English, and who seemed astounded at our not taking the steamer in preference to our carrioles. He hardly thought it possible that we could be going all the way to Lillehammer, at the head of the lake, by the land road. When we set out, our postillion took a way leading up the hills in the rear of the place. Knowing that our course was along the shore, we asked him if we were on the road to Sveen, the next station. "Oh, yes; it's all right," said he, "this is a new road." It was, in truth, a superb highway; broad and perfectly macadamised, and leading along the brink of a deep rocky chasm, down which thundered a powerful stream. From the top of this glen we struck inland, keeping more and more to the westward. Again we asked the postillion, and again received the same answer. Finally; when we had travelled six or seven miles, and the lake had wholly disappeared, I stopped and demanded where Sveen was. "Sveen is not on this road," he answered; "we are going to Mustad!" "But," I exclaimed, "we are bound for Sveen and Lillehammer!" "Oh," said he, with infuriating coolness, "you can go there afterwards!" You may judge that the carrioles were whirled around in a hurry, and that the only answer to the fellow's remonstrances was a shaking by the neck which frightened him into silence.

We drove back to Gjövik in a drenching shower, which failed to cool our anger. On reaching the station I at once made a complaint against the postillion, and the landlord called a man who spoke good English, to settle the matter. The latter brought me a bill of $2 for going to Mustad and back. Knowing that the horses belonged to farmers, who were not to blame in the least, we had agreed to pay for their use; but I remonstrated against paying the full price when we had not gone the whole distance, and had not intended to go at all. "Why, then, did you order horses for Mustad?" he asked. "I did no such thing!" I exclaimed, in amazement. "You did!" he persisted, and an investigation ensued, which resulted in the discovery that the Norwegian who had advised us to go by steamer, had gratuitously taken upon himself to tell the landlord to send us to the Randsfjord, and had given the postillion similar directions! The latter, imagining, perhaps, that we didn't actually know our own plans, had followed his instructions. I must say that I never before received such an astonishing mark of kindness. The ill-concealed satisfaction of the people at our mishap made it all the more exasperating. The end of it was that two or three marks were taken off the account, which we then paid, and in an hour afterwards shipped ourselves and carrioles on board a steamer for Lillehammer. The Norwegian who had caused all this trouble came along just before we embarked, and heard the story with the most sublime indifference, proffering not a word of apology, regret, or explanation. Judging from this specimen, the King of Sweden and Norway has good reason to style himself King of the Goths and Vandals.

I was glad, nevertheless, that we had an opportunity of seeing the Miösen, from the deck of a steamer. Moving over the glassy pale-green water, midway between its shores, we had a far better exhibition of its beauties than from the land-road. It is a superb piece of water, sixty miles in length by from two to five in breadth, with mountain shores of picturesque and ever-varying outline. The lower slopes are farm land, dotted with the large gaards, or mansions of the farmers, many of which have a truly stately air; beyond them are forests of fir, spruce, and larch, while in the glens between, winding groves of birch, alder, and ash come down to fringe the banks of the lake. Wandering gleams of sunshine, falling through the broken clouds, touched here and there the shadowed slopes and threw belts of light upon the water—and these illuminated spots finely relieved the otherwise sombre depth of colour. Our boat was slow, and we had between two and three hours of unsurpassed scenery before reaching our destination. An immense raft of timber, gathered from the loose logs which are floated down the Lougen Elv, lay at the head of the lake, which contracts into the famous Guldbrandsdal. On the brow of a steep hill on the right lay the little town of Lillehammer, where we were ere long quartered in a very comfortable hotel.

CHAPTER XXII. GULDBRANDSDAL AND THE DOVRE FJELD.

We left Lillehammer on a heavenly Sabbath morning. There was scarcely a cloud in the sky, the air was warm and balmy, and the verdure of the valley, freshened by the previous day's rain, sparkled and glittered in the sun. The Miösen Lake lay blue and still to the south, and the bald tops of the mountains which inclose Guldbrandsdal stood sharp and clear, and almost shadowless, in the flood of light which streamed up the valley. Of Lillehammer, I can only say that it is a commonplace town of about a thousand inhabitants. It had a cathedral and bishop some six hundred years ago, no traces of either of which now remain. We drove out of it upon a splendid new road, leading up the eastern bank of the river, and just high enough on the mountain side to give the loveliest views either way. Our horses were fast and spirited, and the motion of our carrioles over the firmly macadamised road was just sufficient to keep the blood in nimble circulation. Rigid Sabbatarians may be shocked at our travelling on that day; but there were few hearts in all the churches of Christendom whose hymns of praise were more sincere and devout than ours. The Lougen roared an anthem for us from his rocky bed; the mountain streams, flashing down their hollow channels, seemed hastening to join it; the mountains themselves stood silent, with uncovered heads; and over all the pale-blue northern heaven looked lovingly and gladly down—a smile of God upon the grateful earth. There is no Sabbath worship better than the simple enjoyment of such a day.

Toward the close of the stage, our road descended to the banks of the Lougen, which here falls in a violent rapid—almost a cataract—over a barrier of rocks. Masses of water, broken or wrenched from the body of the river, are hurled intermittently high into the air, scattering as they fall, with fragments of rainbows dancing over them. In this scene I at once recognised the wild landscape by the pencil of Dahl, the Norwegian painter, which had made such an impression upon me in Copenhagen. In Guldbrandsdal, we found at once what we had missed in the scenery of Ringerike—swift, foaming streams. Here they leapt from every rift of the upper crags, brightening the gloom of the fir-woods which clothed the mountain-sides, like silver braiding upon a funeral garment. This valley is the pride of Norway, nearly as much for its richness as for its beauty and grandeur. The houses were larger and more substantial, the fields blooming, with frequent orchards of fruit-trees, and the farmers, in their Sunday attire showed in their faces a little more intelligence than the people we had seen on our way thither. Their countenances had a plain, homely stamp; and of all the large-limbed, strong-backed forms I saw, not one could be called graceful, or even symmetrical. Something awkward and uncouth stamps the country people of Norway. Honest and simple-minded they are said to be, and probably are; but of native refinement of feeling they can have little, unless all outward signs of character are false.

We changed horses at Moshûûs, and drove up a level splendid road to Holmen, along the river-bank. The highway, thus far, is entirely new, and does great credit to Norwegian enterprise. There is not a better road in all Europe; and when it shall be carried through to Drontheim, the terrors which this trip has for timid travellers will entirely disappear. It is a pity that the skyds system should not be improved in equal ratio, instead of becoming even more inconvenient than at present. Holmen, hitherto a fast station, is now no longer so; and the same retrograde change is going on at other places along the road. The waiting at the tilsigelse stations is the great drawback to travelling by skyds in Norway. You must either wait two hours or pay fast prices, which the people are not legally entitled to ask. Travellers may write complaints in the space allotted in the post-books for such things, but with very little result, if one may judge from the perfect indifference which the station-masters exhibit when you threaten to do so. I was more than once tauntingly asked whether I would not write a complaint. In Sweden, I found but one instance of inattention at the stations, during two months' travel, and expected, from the boasted honesty of the Norwegians, to meet with an equally fortunate experience. Travellers, however, and especially English, are fast teaching the people the usual arts of imposition. Oh, you hard-shelled, unplastic, insulated Englishmen! You introduce towels and fresh water, and tea, and beefsteak, wherever you go, it is true; but you teach high prices, and swindling, and insolence likewise!

A short distance beyond Holmen, the new road terminated, and we took the old track over steep spurs of the mountain, rising merely to descend and rise again. The Lougen River here forms a broad, tranquil lake, a mile in width, in which the opposite mountains were splendidly reflected. The water is pale, milky-green colour, which, under certain effects of light, has a wonderful aerial transparency. As we approached Lösnäs, after this long and tedious stage, I was startled by the appearance of a steamer on the river. It is utterly impossible for any to ascend the rapids below Moshûûs; and she must therefore have been built there. We could discover no necessity for such an undertaking in the thin scattered population and their slow, indifferent habits. Her sudden apparition in such a place was like that of an omnibus in the desert.

The magnificent vista of the valley was for a time closed by the snowy peaks of the Rundan Fjeld; but as the direction of the river changed they disappeared, the valley contracted, and its black walls, two thousand feet high, almost overhung us. Below, however, were still fresh meadows, twinkling birchen groves and comfortable farm-houses. Out of a gorge on our right, plunged a cataract from a height of eighty or ninety feet, and a little further on, high up the mountain, a gush of braided silver foam burst out of the dark woods, covered with gleaming drapery the face of a huge perpendicular crag, and disappeared in the woods again, My friend drew up his horse in wonder and rapture. "I know all Switzerland and the Tyrol," he exclaimed, "but I have never seen a cataract so wonderfully framed in the setting of a forest." In the evening, as we approached our destination, two streams on the opposite side of the valley, fell from a height of more than a thousand feet, in a series of linked plunges, resembling burnished chains hanging dangling from the tremendous parapet of rock. On the meadow before us, commanding a full view of this wild and glorious scene, stood a stately gaard, entirely deserted, its barns, out-houses and gardens utterly empty and desolate. Its aspect saddened the whole landscape.

We stopped at the station of Lillehaave, which had only been established the day before, and we were probably the first travellers who had sojourned there. Consequently the people were unspoiled, and it was quite refreshing to be courteously received, furnished with a trout supper and excellent beds, and

192

to pay therefor an honest price. The morning was lowering, and we had rain part of the day; but, thanks to our waterproofs and carriole aprons, we kept comfortably dry. During this day's journey of fifty miles, we had very grand scenery, the mountains gradually increasing in height and abruptness as we ascended the Guldbrandsdal, with still more imposing cataracts "blowing their trumpets from the steeps." At Viik, I found a complaint in the post-book, written by an Englishman who had come with us from Hull, stating that the landlord had made him pay five dollars for beating his dog off his own. The complaint was written in English, of course, and therefore useless so far as the authorities were concerned. The landlord whom I expected, from this account, to find a surly, swindling fellow, accosted us civilly, and invited us into his house to see some old weapons, principally battle-axes. There was a cross-bow, a battered, antique sword, and a buff coat, which may have been stripped from one of Sinclair's men in the pass of Kringelen. The logs of his house, or part of them, are said to have been taken from the dwelling in which the saint-king Olaf—the apostle of Christianity in the North,—was born. They are of the red Norwegian pine, which has a great durability; and the legend may be true, although this would make them eight hundred and fifty years old.

Colonel Sinclair was buried in the churchyard at Viik, and about fifteen miles further we passed the defile of Kringelen, where his band was cut to pieces. He landed in Romsdal's Fjord, on the western coast, with 900 men intending to force his way across the mountains to relieve Stockholm, which was then (1612) besieged by the Danes. Some three hundred of the peasants collected at Kringelen, gathered together rocks and trunks of trees on the brow of the cliff, and, at a concerted signal, rolled the mass down upon the Scotch, the greater part of whom were crushed to death or hurled into the river. Of the whole force only two escaped. A wooden tablet on the spot says, as near as I could make it out, that there was never such an example of courage and valour known in the world, and calls upon the people to admire this glorious deed of their fathers. "Courage and valour;" cried Braisted, indignantly; "it was a cowardly butchery! If they had so much courage, why did they allow 900 Scotchmen to get into the very heart of the country before they tried to stop them?" Well, war is full of meanness and cowardice. If it were only fair fighting on an open field, there would be less of it.

Beyond Laurgaard, Guldbrandsdal contracts to a narrow gorge, down which the Lougen roars in perpetual foam. This pass is called the Rusten; and the road here is excessively steep and difficult. The forests disappear; only hardy firs and the red pine cling to the ledges of the rocks; and mountains, black, grim, and with snow-streaked summits, tower grandly on all sides. A broad cataract, a hundred feet high, leaped down a chasm on our left, so near to the road that its sprays swept over us, and then shot under a bridge to join the seething flood in the frightful gulf beneath. I was reminded of the Valley of the Reuss, on the road to St. Gothard, like which, the pass of the Rusten leads to a cold and bleak upper valley. Here we noticed the blight of late frost on the barley fields, and were for the first time assailed by beggars. Black storm-clouds hung over the gorge, adding to the savage wildness of its scenery; but the sun came out as we drove up the Valley of Dovre, with its long stretch of grain-fields on the sunny sweep of the hill-side, sheltered by the lofty Dovre Fjeld behind them. We stopped for the night at the inn of Toftemoen, long before sunset, although it was eight o'clock, and slept in a half-daylight until morning.

The sun was riding high in the heavens when we left, and dark lowering clouds slowly rolled their masses across the mountain-tops. The Lougen was now an inconsiderable stream, and the superb Guldbrandsdal narrowed to a bare, bleak dell, like those in the high Alps. The grain-fields had a chilled, struggling appearance; the forests forsook the mountain-sides and throve only in sheltered spots at their bases; the houses were mere log cabins, many of which were slipping off their foundation-posts and tottering to their final fall; and the people, poorer than ever, came out of their huts to beg openly and shamelessly as we passed. Over the head of the valley, which here turns westward to the low water-shed dividing it from the famous Romsdal, rose two or three snow-streaked peaks of the Hurunger Fjeld; and the drifts filling the ravines of the mountains on our left descended lower and lower into the valley.

At Dombaas, a lonely station at the foot of the Dovre Fjeld, we turned northward into the heart of the mountains. My postillion, a boy of fifteen, surprised me by speaking very good English. He had learned it in the school at Drontheim. Sometimes, he said, they had a schoolmaster in the house, and sometimes one at Jerkin, twenty miles distant. Our road ascended gradually through half-cut woods of red pine, for two or three miles, after which it entered a long valley, or rather basin, belonging to the table land of the Dovre Fjeld. Stunted heath and dwarfed juniper-bushes mixed with a grey, foxy shrub-willow, covered the soil, and the pale yellow of the reindeer moss stained the rocks. Higher greyer and blacker ridges hemmed in the lifeless landscape; and above them, to the north and west, broad snow-fields shone luminous under the heavy folds of the clouds. We passed an old woman with bare legs and arms, returning from a söter, or summer châlet of the shepherds. She was a powerful but purely animal specimen of humanity,—"beef to the heel," as Braisted said. At last a cluster of log huts, with a patch of green pasture-ground about them, broke the monotony of the scene. It was Fogstuen, or next station, where we were obliged to wait half an hour until the horses had been caught and brought in. The place had a poverty stricken air; and the slovenly woman who acted as landlady seemed disappointed that we did not buy some horridly coarse and ugly woolen gloves of her own manufacture.

Our road now ran for fourteen miles along the plateau of the Dovre, more than 3000 feet above the level of the sea. This is not a plain or table land, but an undulating region, with hills, valleys, and lakes of its own; and more desolate landscapes one can scarcely find elsewhere. Everything is grey, naked, and barren, not on a scale grand enough to be imposing, nor with any picturesqueness of form to relieve its sterility. One can understand the silence and sternness of the Norwegians, when he has travelled this road. But I would not wish my worst enemy to spend more than one summer as a solitary herdsman on these hills. Let any disciple of Zimmerman try the effect of such a solitude. The statistics of insanity in Norway exhibit some of its effects, and that which is most common is most destructive. There never was a greater humbug than the praise of solitude: it is the fruitful mother of all evil, and no man covets it who has not something bad or morbid in his nature.

By noon the central ridge or comb of the Dovre Fjeld rose before us, with the six-hundred-year old station of Jerkin in a warm nook on its southern side. This is renowned as the best post-station in Norway, and is a favourite resort of English travellers and sportsmen, who come hither to climb the peak of Snæhätten, and to stalk reindeer. I did not find the place particularly inviting. The two women who had charge of it for the time were unusually silent and morose, but our dinner was cheap and well gotten up, albeit the trout were not the freshest. We admired the wonderful paintings of the landlord, which although noticed by Murray, give little promise for Norwegian art in these high latitudes. His cows, dogs, and men are all snow-white, and rejoice in an original anatomy.

The horses on this part of the road were excellent, the road admirable, and our transit was therefore thoroughly agreeable. The ascent of the dividing ridge, after leaving Jerkin, is steep and toilsome for half a mile, but with this exception the passage of the Dovre Fjeld is remarkably easy. The highest point which the road crossed is about 4600 feet above the sea, or a little higher than the Brenner Pass in the Tyrol. But there grain grows and orchards bear fruit, while here, under the parallel of 62°, nearly all vegetation ceases, and even the omnivorous northern sheep can find no pasturage. Before and behind you lie wastes of naked grey mountains, relieved only by the snow-patches on their summits. I have seen as desolate tracts of wilderness in the south made beautiful by the lovely hues which they took from the air; but Nature has no such tender fancies in the north. She is a realist of the most unpitying stamp, and gives atmospheric influences which make that which is dark and bleak still darker and bleaker. Black clouds hung low on the horizon, and dull grey sheets of rain swept now and then across the nearer heights. Snæhätten, to the westward, was partly veiled, but we could trace his blunt mound of alternate black rock and snow nearly to the apex. The peak is about 7700 feet above the sea, and was until recently considered the highest in Norway, but the Skagtolstind has been ascertained to be 160 feet higher, and Snæhätten is dethroned.

The river Driv came out of a glen on our left, and entered a deep gorge in front, down which our road lay, following the rapid descent of the foaming stream. At the station of Kongsvold, we had descended to 3000 feet again, yet no trees appeared. Beyond this, the road for ten miles has been with great

196

labour hewn out of the solid rock, at the bottom of a frightful defile, like some of those among the Alps. Formerly, it climbed high up on the mountain-side, running on the brink of almost perpendicular cliffs, and the Vaarsti, as it is called, was then reckoned one of the most difficult and dangerous roads in the country. Now it is one of the safest and most delightful. We went down the pass on a sharp trot, almost too fast to enjoy the wild scenery as it deserved. The Driv fell through the cleft in a succession of rapids, while smaller streams leaped to meet him in links of silver cataract down a thousand feet of cliff. Birch and fir now clothed the little terraces and spare corners of soil, and the huge masses of rock, hanging over our heads, were tinted with black, warm brown, and russet orange, in such a manner as to produce the most charming effects of colour. Over the cornices of the mountain-walls, hovering at least two thousand feet above, gleamed here and there the scattered snowy jötuns of the highest fjeld.

The pass gradually opened into a narrow valley, where we found a little cultivation again. Here was the post of Drivstuen, kept by a merry old lady. Our next stage descended through increasing habitation and culture to the inn of Rise, where we stopped for the night, having the Dovre Fjeld fairly behind us. The morning looked wild and threatening, but the clouds gradually hauled off to the eastward, leaving us the promise of a fine day. Our road led over hills covered with forests of fir and pine, whence we looked into a broad valley clothed with the same dark garment of forest, to which the dazzling white snows of the fjeld in the background made a striking contrast. We here left the waters of the Driv and struck upon those of the Orkla, which flow into Drontheim Fjord. At Stuen, we got a fair breakfast of eggs, milk, cheese, bread and butter. Eggs are plentiful everywhere, yet, singularly enough, we were nearly a fortnight in Norway before we either saw or heard a single fowl. Where they were kept we could not discover, and why they did not crow was a still greater mystery. Norway is really the land of silence. For an inhabited country, it is the quietest I have ever seen. No wonder that anger and mirth, when they once break through the hard ice of Norwegian life, are so furious and uncontrollable. These inconsistent extremes may always be reconciled, when we understand how nicely the moral nature of man is balanced.

Our road was over a high, undulating tract for two stages, commanding

197

wide views of a wild wooded region, which is said to abound with game. The
range of snowy peaks behind us still filled the sky, appearing so near at hand
as to deceive the eye in regard to their height. At last, we came upon the
brink of a steep descent, overlooking the deep glen of the Orkla, a singularly
picturesque valley, issuing from between the bases of the mountains, and
winding away to the northward. Down the frightful slant our horses plunged
and in three minutes we were at the bottom, with flower-sown meadows on
either hand, and the wooded sides of the glen sweeping up to a waving and
fringed outline against the sky. After crossing the stream, we had an ascent
as abrupt, on the other side; but half-way up stood the station of Bjærkager,
where we left our panting horses. The fast stations were now at an end, but
by paying fast prices we got horses with less delay. In the evening, a man
travelling on foot offered to carry förbud notices for us to the remaining
stations, if we would pay for his horse. We accepted; I wrote the orders in
my best Norsk, and on the following day we found the horses in readiness
everywhere.

The next stage was an inspiring trot through a park-like country, clothed
with the freshest turf and studded with clumps of fir, birch, and ash. The air
was soft and warm, and filled with balmy scents from the flowering grasses,
and the millions of blossoms spangling the ground. In one place, I saw half an
acre of the purest violet hue, where the pansy of our gardens grew so thickly
that only its blossoms were visible. The silver green of the birch twinkled in
the sun, and its jets of delicate foliage started up everywhere with exquisite
effect amid the dark masses of the fir. There was little cultivation as yet, but
these trees formed natural orchards, which suggested a design in their planting
and redeemed the otherwise savage character of the scenery. We dipped at last
into a hollow, down which flowed one of the tributaries of the Gûûl Elv, the
course of which we thence followed to Drontheim.

One of the stations was a lonely gaard, standing apart from the road, on
a high hill. As we drove up, a horrid old hag came out to receive us. "Can I get
three horses soon?" I asked. "No," she answered with a chuckle. "How soon?"
"In a few hours," was her indifferent reply, but the promise of paying fast
rates got them in less than one. My friend wanted a glass of wine, but the old

woman said she had nothing but milk. We were sitting on the steps with our pipes, shortly afterwards, when she said: "Why don't you go into the house?" "It smells too strongly of paint," I answered. "But you had better go in," said she, and shuffled off. When we entered, behold! there were three glasses of very good Marsala on the table. "How do you sell your milk?" I asked her. "That kind is three skillings a dram," she answered. The secret probably was that she had no license to sell wine. I was reminded of an incident which occurred to me in Maine, during the prevalence of the prohibitory law. I was staying at an hotel in a certain town, and jestingly asked the landlord: "Where is the Maine Law? I should like to see it." "Why," said he, "I have it here in the house;'" and he unlocked a back room and astonished me with the sight of a private bar, studded with full decanters.

The men folks were all away at work, and our postillion was a strapping girl of eighteen, who rode behind Braisted. She was gotten up on an immense scale, but nature had expended so much vigour on her body that none was left for her brain. She was a consummate representation of health and stupidity. At the station where we stopped for the night I could not help admiring the solid bulk of the landlady's sister. Although not over twenty four she must have weighed full two hundred. Her waist was of remarkable thickness, and her bust might be made into three average American ones. I can now understand why Mügge calls his heroine Ilda "the strong maiden."

A drive of thirty-five miles down the picturesque valley of the Gûûl brought us to Drontheim the next day—the eighth after leaving Christiania.

CHAPTER XXIII. DRONTHEIM.—VOYAGE UP THE COAST OF NORWAY.

Our first view of Drontheim (or Trondhjem, as it should properly be written) was from the top of the hill behind the town, at the termination of six miles of execrable road, and perhaps the relief springing from that circumstance heightened the agreeable impression which the scene made upon our minds. Below us, at the bottom of a crescent-shaped bay, lay Drontheim—a mass of dark red, yellow, and brown buildings, with the grey cathedral in the rear. The rich, well cultivated valley of the Nid stretched behind it, on our right, past the Lierfoss, whose column of foam was visible three miles away, until the hills, rising more high and bleak behind each other, completely enclosed it. The rock-fortress of Munkholm, in front of the city, broke the smooth surface of the fjord, whose further shores, dim with passing showers, swept away to the north-east, hiding the termination of this great sea-arm, which is some fifty miles distant. The panorama was certainly on a grand scale, and presented very diversified and picturesque features; but I can by no means agree with Dr. Clarke, who compares it to the Bay of Naples. Not only the rich colours of the Mediterranean are wanting, but those harmonic sweeps and curves of the Italian shores and hills have nothing in common with these rude, ragged, weather beaten, defiant forms.

Descending the hill between rows of neat country-houses, we passed a diminutive fortification, and entered the city. The streets are remarkably wide and roughly paved, crossing each other at right angles, with a Philadelphian regularity. The houses are all two stories high, and raised upon ample foundations, so that the doors are approached by flights of steps—probably on account of the deep snows during the winter. They are almost exclusively of wood, solid logs covered with neat clap-boards, but a recent law forbids the erection of any more wooden houses, and in the course of time, the town, like Christiania, will lose all that is peculiar and characteristic in its architecture. A cleaner place can scarcely be found, and I also noticed, what is quite rare in the North, large square fountains or wells, at the intersection of all the principal streets. The impression which Drontheim makes upon the stranger is therefore a cheerful and genial one. Small and unpretending though it be, it is full of pictures; the dark blue fjord closes the vista of half its streets; hills of grey rock, draped with the greenest turf, overlook it on either side, and the beautiful valley of the Nid, one of the loveliest nooks of Norway, lies in its rear.

We drove to the Hotel de Belle-Vue, one of the two little caravanserais of which the town boasts, and were fortunate in securing the two vacant rooms. The hotel business in Norway is far behind that of any other country, except in regard to charges, where it is far in advance. Considering what one gets for his money, this is the most expensive country in the world for foreigners. Except where the rates are fixed by law, as in posting, the natives pay much less; and here is an instance of double-dealing which does not harmonise with the renowned honesty of the Norwegians. At the Belle-Vue, we were furnished with three very meagre meals a day, at the rate of two dollars and a half. The attendance was performed by two boys of fourteen or fifteen, whose services, as may be supposed, were quite inadequate to the wants of near twenty persons. The whole business of the establishment devolved on these two fellows, the landlady, though good-humoured and corpulent, as was meet, knowing nothing about the business, and, on the whole, it was a wonder that matters were not worse. It is singular that in a pastoral country like Norway one gets nothing but rancid butter, and generally sour cream, where both should be of the finest quality. Nature is sparing of her gifts, to be sure; but what she does furnish is of the best, as it comes from her hand. Of course, one does not look for much culinary skill, and is therefore not disappointed, but the dairy is the primitive domestic art of all races, and it is rather surprising to find it in so backward a state.

My friend, who received no letters, and had no transatlantic interests to claim his time, as I had, applied himself to seeing the place, which he accomplished, with praiseworthy industry, in one day. He walked out to the falls of the Nid, three miles up the valley, and was charmed with them. He then entered the venerable cathedral, where he had the satisfaction of seeing a Protestant clergyman perform high mass in a scarlet surplice, with a gold cross on his back. The State Church of Norway, which, like that of Sweden, is Lutheran of a very antiquated type, not only preserves this ritual, but also the form of confession (in a general way, I believe, and without reference to particular sins) and of absolution. Of course, it is violently dogmatic and illiberal, and there is little vital religious activity in the whole country. Until within a very few years, no other sects were tolerated, and even yet there is simply freedom of conscience, but not equal political rights, for those of other denominations. This concession has perhaps saved the church from becoming a venerable fossil, yet one still finds persons who regret that it should have been made, not knowing that all truth, to retain its temper, must be whetted against an opposing blade. According to the new constitution of Norway, the king must be crowned in the cathedral of Drontheim. Bernadotte received the proper consecration, but Oscar, though King of Norway, has not yet seen fit to accept it. I once heard a Norwegian exclaim, with a sort of jealous satisfaction: "Oscar calls himself King of Norway, but he is a king without a crown!" I cannot see, however, that this fact lessens his authority as sovereign, in the least.

There is a weekly line of steamers, established by the Storthing (Legislative Assembly), to Hammerfest and around the North Cape. The "Nordkap," the largest and best of these boats, was to leave Drontheim on Saturday evening, the 18th of July, and we lost no time in securing berths, as another week would have made it too late for the perpetual sunshine of the northern summer. Here again, one is introduced to a knowledge of customs and regulations unknown elsewhere. The ticket merely secures you a place on board the steamer, but neither a berth nor provisions. The latter you obtain from a restaurateur on board, according to fixed rates; the former depends on the will of the captain, who can stow you where he chooses. On the "Nordkap" the state-rooms were already occupied, and there remained a single small saloon containing eight berths. Here we did very well so long as there were only English and American occupants, who at once voted to have the skylight kept open; but after two Norwegians were added to our company, we lived in a state of perpetual warfare, the latter sharing the national dread of fresh air; and yet one of them was a professor from the University of Christiania, and the other a physician, who had charge of the hospital in Bergen! With this exception, we had every reason to be satisfied with the vessel. She was very stanch and steady-going, with a spacious airy saloon on deck; no captain could have been more kind and gentlemanly, and there was quite as much harmony among the passengers as could reasonably have been expected. Our party consisted of five Americans, three English, two Germans, and one Frenchman (M. Gay, Membre de l'Academie), besides a variety of Norwegians from all parts of the country.

Leaving our carrioles and part of our baggage behind us, we rowed out to the steamer in a heavy shower. The sun was struggling with dark grey rain-clouds all the evening, and just as we hove anchor, threw a splendid triumphal iris across the bay, completely spanning the town, which, with the sheltering hills, glimmered in the rosy mist floating within the bow. Enclosed by such a dazzling frame the picture of Drontheim shone with a magical lustre, like a vision of Asgaard, beckoning to us from the tempestuous seas. But we were bound for the north, the barriers of Niflhem, the land of fog and sleet, and we disregarded the celestial token, though a second perfect rainbow overarched the first, and the two threw their curves over hill and fortress and the bosom of the rainy fjord, until they almost touched our vessel on either side. In spite of the rain, we remained on deck until a late hour, enjoying the bold scenery of the outer fjord—here, precipitous woody shores, gashed with sudden ravines; there, jet-black rocky peaks, resembling the porphyry hills of the African deserts; and now and then, encircling the sheltered coves, soft green fields glowing with misty light, and the purple outlines of snow-streaked mountains in the distance.

The morning was still dark and rainy. We were at first running between mountain-islands of bare rock and the iron coast of the mainland, after which came a stretch of open sea for two hours, and at noon we reached Björö, near the mouth of the Namsen Fjord. Here there was half a dozen red houses on a bright green slope, with a windmill out of gear crowning the rocky hill in the rear. The sky gradually cleared as we entered the Namsen Fjord, which charmed us with the wildness and nakedness of its shores, studded with little nooks and corners of tillage, which sparkled like oases of tropical greenness, in such a rough setting. Precipices of dark-red rock, streaked with foamy lines of water from the snows melting upon their crests, frowned over the narrow channels between the islands, and through their gaps and gorges we caught sight of the loftier ranges inland. Namsos, at the head of the fjord, is a red-roofed town of a few hundred inhabitants, with a pleasant background of barley-fields and birchen groves. The Namsen valley, behind it, is one of the richest in this part of Norway, and is a great resort of English salmon-fishers. There was a vessel of two hundred tons on the stocks, and a few coasting crafts lying at anchor.

We had a beautiful afternoon voyage out another arm of the fjord, and again entered the labyrinth of islands fringing the coast. Already, the days had perceptibly lengthened, and the increased coldness of the air at night indicated our approach to the Arctic Circle. I was surprised at the amount of business done at the little stations where we touched. Few of these contained a dozen houses, yet the quantity of passengers and freight which we discharged and took on board, at each, could only be explained by the fact that these stations are generally outlets for a tolerably large population, hidden in the valleys and fjords behind, which the steamer does not visit. Bleak and desolate as the coast appears, the back country has its fertile districts—its pasture-ground, its corn-land and forests, of which the voyager sees nothing, and thus might be led to form very erroneous conclusions. Before we had been twenty-four hours out from Drontheim, there was a marked change in the appearance of the people we took on board. Not even in the neighborhood of Christiania or in the rich Guldbrandsdal were the inhabitants so well-dressed, so prosperous (judging from outward signs, merely), or so intelligent. They are in every respect more agreeable and promising specimens of humanity than their brothers of Southern Norway, notwithstanding the dark and savage scenery amidst which their lot is cast.

Toward midnight, we approached the rock of Torghätten, rising 1200 feet high, in the shape of a tall-crowned, battered "wide-awake," above the low, rocky isles and reefs which surround it. This rock is famous for a natural tunnel, passing directly through its heart—the path of an arrow which the Giant Horseman (of whom I shall speak presently) shot at a disdainful maiden, equally colossal, in the old mythological times, when Odin got drunk nightly in Walhalla. We were all on the look-out for this tunnel, which, according

204

to Murray, is large enough for a ship to go through—if it were not some six hundred feet above the sea-level. We had almost passed the rock and nothing of the kind could be seen; but Capt. Riis, who was on deck, encouraged us to have a little patience, changed the steamer's course, and presently we saw a dark cavern yawning in the face of a precipice on the northern side. It was now midnight, but a sunset light tinged the northern sky, and the Torghätten yet stood in twilight. "Shall we see through it?" was the question; but while we were discussing the chances, a faint star sparkled in the midst of the cavernous gloom. "You see it because you imagine it," cried some; yet, no, it was steadfast, and grew broad and bright, until even the most sceptical recognised the pale midnight sky at the bottom of the gigantic arch.

My friend aroused me at five in the morning to see the Seven Sisters—seven majestic peaks, 4000 feet high, and seated closely side by side, with their feet in the sea. They all wore nightcaps of gray fog, and had a sullen and sleepy [Pg 277]air. I imagined they snored, but it was a damp wind driving over the rocks. They were northern beauties, hard-featured and large-boned, and I would not give a graceful southern hill, like Monte Albano or the Paphian Olympus, for the whole of them. So I turned in again, and did not awake until the sun had dried the decks, and the split, twisted and contorted forms of the islands gave promise of those remarkable figures which mark the position of the Arctic Circle. There was already a wonderful change in the scenery. The islands were high and broken, rising like towers and pyramids from the water, and grouped together in the most fantastic confusion. Between their jagged pinnacles, and through their sheer walls of naked rock, we could trace the same formation among the hills of the mainland, while in the rear, white against the sky, stretched the snowy table-land which forms a common summit for all. One is bewildered in the attempt to describe such scenery. There is no central figure, no prevailing character, no sharp contrasts, which may serve as a guide whereby to reach the imagination of the reader. All is confused, disordered, chaotic. One begins to understand the old Norse myth of these stones being thrown by the devil in a vain attempt to prevent the Lord from finishing the world. Grand as they are, singly, you are so puzzled by their numbers and by the fantastic manner in which they seem to dance around you, as the steamer threads the watery labyrinth, that you scarcely appreciate them as they deserve. Take almost any one of these hundreds, and place it inland, anywhere in Europe or America, and it will be visited, sketched and sung to distraction.

At last we saw in the west, far out at sea, the four towers of Threnen, rising perpendicularly many hundred feet from the water. Before us was the Hestmand, or Horseman, who bridles his rocky steed with the polar circle. At first, he appeared like a square turret crowning an irregular mass of island-rock, but, as we approached a colossal head rounded itself at the top, and a sweeping cloak fell from the broad shoulder, flowing backward to the horse's flanks. Still, there was no horse; but here again our captain took the steamer considerably out of her course, so that, at a distance of a mile the whole enormous figure, 1500 feet in height, lay clearly before us. A heavy beard fell from the grand, Jupitolian head; the horse, with sharp ears erect and head bent down, seemed to be plunging into the sea, which was already above his belly; the saddle had slipped forward, so that the rider sat upon his shoulders, but with his head proudly lifted, as if conscious of his fate, and taking a last look at the world. Was it not All-Father Odin, on his horse Sleipner, forsaking the new race which had ceased to worship him? The colossi of the Orient—Rameses and Brahma and Boodh—dwindle into insignificance before this sublime natural monument to the lost gods of the North.

At the little fishing-village of Anklakken, near the Horseman, a fair was being held, and a score or more of coasting craft, gay with Norwegian flags, lay at anchor. These jægts, as they are called, have a single mast, with a large square sail, precisely like those of the Japanese fishing junks, and their hulls are scarcely less heavy and clumsy. They are the Norwegian boats of a thousand years ago; all attempt to introduce a better form of ship-building having been in vain. But the romantic traveller should not suppose that he beholds the "dragons" of the Vikings, which were a very different craft, and have long since disappeared. The jægts are slow, but good seaboats, and as the article haste is not in demand anywhere in Norway, they probably answer every purpose as well as more rational vessels. Those we saw belonged to traders who cruise along the coast during the summer, attending the various fairs, which appear to be the principal recreation of the people. At any rate, they bring some life and activity into these silent solitudes. We had on board the effects of an Englishman who went on shore to see a fair and was left behind by a previous steamer. He had nothing with him but the clothes on his back, and spoke no Norsk: so the captain anxiously looked out for a melancholy, dilapidated individual at every station we touched at—but he looked in vain, for we neither saw nor heard anything of the unfortunate person.

All the afternoon, we had a continuation of the same wonderful scenery—precipices of red rock a thousand feet high, with snowy, turreted summits, and the loveliest green glens between. To the east were vast snow-fields, covering the eternal glaciers of the Alpine range. As we looked up the Salten Fjord, while crossing its mouth, the snows of Sulitelma, the highest mountain in Lappmark, 6000 feet above the sea, were visible, about fifty miles distant. Next came the little town of Bodö where we stopped for the night. It is a cluster of wooden houses, with roofs of green sod, containing about three hundred inhabitants. We found potatoes in the gardens, some currant bushes, and a few hardy vegetables, stunted ash trees and some patches of barley. The sun set a little before eleven o'clock, but left behind him a glory of colours which I have never seen surpassed. The snowy mountains of Lappmark were transmuted into pyramids of scarlet flame, beside which the most gorgeous sunset illuminations of the Alps would have been pale and tame. The sky was a sheet of saffron, amber and rose, reduplicated in the glassy sea, and the peaked island of Landegode in the west, which stood broad against the glow, became a mass of violet hue, topped with cliffs of crimson fire. I sat down on deck and tried to sketch this superb spectacle, in colours which nobody will believe to be real. Before I had finished, the sunset which had lighted one end of Landegode became sunrise at the other, and the fading Alps burned anew with the flames of morning.

CHAPTER XXIV. THE LOFODEN ISLES.

The northern summer soon teaches one fashionable habits of life. Like the man whose windows Sidney Smith darkened, and who slept all day because he thought it was night, you keep awake all night because you forget that it is not day. One's perception of time contracts in some mysterious way, and the sun, setting at eleven, seems to be no later than when he set at seven. You think you will enjoy the evening twilight an hour or two before going to bed, and lo! the morning begins to dawn. It seems absurd to turn in and sleep by daylight, but you sleep, nevertheless, until eight or nine o'clock, and get up but little refreshed with your repose. You miss the grateful covering of darkness, the sweet, welcome gloom, which shuts your senses, one after one, like the closing petals of a flower, in the restoring trance of the night. The light comes through your eyelids as you sleep, and a certain nervous life of the body that should sleep too keeps awake and active. I soon began to feel the wear and tear of perpetual daylight, in spite of its novelty and the many advantages which it presents to the traveller.

At Bodö we were in sight of the Lofoden Islands, which filled up all the northern and western horizon, rising like blue saw-teeth beyond the broad expanse of the West Fjord, which separates them from the group of the shore islands. The next morning, we threaded a perfect labyrinth of rocks, after passing Grotö, and headed across the fjord, for Balstad, on West-Vaagöe, one of the outer isles. This passage is often very rough, especially when the wind blows from the south-west, rolling the heavy swells of the Atlantic into the open mouth of the fjord. We were very much favoured by the weather, having a clear sky, with a light north wind and smooth sea. The long line of jagged peaks, stretching from Væröe in the south west to the giant ridges of Hindöe in the north east, united themselves in the distance with the Alpine chain of the mainland behind us, forming an amphitheatre of sharp, snowy summits, which embraced five-sixths of the entire circle of the horizon, and would have certainly numbered not less than two hundred. Von Buch compares the Lofodens to the jaws of a shark, and most travellers since his time have resuscitated the comparison, but I did not find it so remarkably applicable. There are shark tooth peaks here and there, it is true, but the peculiar conformation of Norway—extensive plateaus, forming the summit-level of the mountains—extends also to these islands, whose only valleys are those which open to the sea, and whose interiors are uninhabitable snowy tracts, mostly above the line of vegetation.

On approaching the islands, we had a fair view of the last outposts of the group—the solid barriers against which the utmost fury of the Atlantic dashes in vain. This side of Væröe lay the large island of Mosköe, between which and a large solitary rock in the middle of the strait dividing them, is the locality of the renowned Maelström—now, alas! almost as mythical as the kraaken or great sea snake of the Norwegian fjords. It is a great pity that the geographical illusions of our boyish days cannot retrain. You learn that the noise of Niagara can be heard 120 miles off, and that "some Indians, in their canoes, have ventured down it, with safety." Well, one could give up the Indians without much difficulty; but it is rather discouraging to step out of the Falls Depôt for the first time, within a quarter of a mile of the cataract, and hear no sound except "Cab sir?" "Hotel, sir?" So of the Maelström, denoted on my schoolboy map by a great spiral twist, which suggested to me a tremendous whirl of the ocean currents, aided by the information that "vessels cannot approach nearer than seven miles." In Olney, moreover, there was a picture of a luckless bark, half-way down the vortex. I had been warming my imagination, as we came up the coast, with Campbell's sonorous lines:

"Round the shores where runic Odin

Howls his war-song to the gale;

Round the isles where loud Lofoden

Whirls to death the roaring whale;"

and, as we looked over the smooth water towards Mosköe, felt a renewed desire to make an excursion thither on out return from the north. But, according to Captain Riis, and other modern authorities which I consulted, the Maelström has lost all its terrors and attractions. Under certain conditions of wind and tide, an eddy is formed in the strait it is true, which may be dangerous to small boats—but the place is by no means so much dreaded as the Salten Fjord, where the tide, rushing in, is caught in such a manner as to form a bore, as in the Bay of Fundy, and frequently proves destructive to the fishing craft. It is the general opinion that some of the rocks which formerly made the Maelström so terrible have been worn away, or that some submarine convulsion has taken place which has changed the action of the waters; otherwise it is impossible to account for the reputation it once possessed.

It should also be borne in mind that any accident to a boat among these islands is more likely to prove disastrous than elsewhere, since there are probably not a score out of the twenty thousand Lofoden fishermen who pass half their lives on the water, who know how to swim. The water is too cold to make bathing a luxury, and they are not sufficiently prepossessed in favour of cleanliness to make it a duty. Nevertheless, they are bold sailors, in their way, and a tougher, hardier, more athletic class of men it would be difficult to find. Handsome they are not, but quite the reverse, and the most of them have an awkward and uncouth air; but it is refreshing to look at their broad shoulders, their brawny chests, and the massive muscles of their legs and arms. During the whole voyage, I saw but one man who appeared to be diseased. Such men, I suspect, were the Vikings—rough, powerful, ugly, dirty fellows, with a few primitive virtues, and any amount of robust vices. We noticed, however, a marked change for the better in the common people, as we advanced northward. They were altogether better dressed, better mannered, and more independent and intelligent, but with a hard, keen, practical expression of face, such as one finds among the shoremen of New-England. The school system of Norway is still sadly deficient, but there is evidently no lack of natural capacity among these people. Their prevailing vice is intemperance, which here, as in all other parts of the country, is beginning to diminish since restrictions have been placed upon the manufacture and sale of spirituous liquors, simultaneously with the introduction of cheap and excellent fermented drinks. The statistics of their morality also show a better state of things than in the South. There is probably no country population in the world where licentiousness prevails to such an extent as in the districts of

Guldbrandsdal and Hedemark.

A voyage of four hours across the West Fjord brought us to the little village of Balstad, at the southern end of West-Vaagöe. The few red, sod-roofed houses were built upon a rocky point, behind which were some patches of bright green pasture, starred with buttercups, overhung by a splendid peak of dark-red rock, two thousand feet in height. It was a fine frontispiece to the Lofoden scenery which now opened before us. Running along the coast of West and East Vaagöe, we had a continual succession of the wildest and grandest pictures—thousand feet precipices, with turrets and needles of rock piercing the sky, dazzling snow-fields, leaking away in cataracts which filled the ravines with foam, and mazes of bald, sea-worn rocks, which seem to have been thrown down from the scarred peaks in some terrible convulsion of nature. Here and there were hollows, affording stony pasturage for a few sheep and cows and little wooden fisher-huts stood on the shore in the arms of sheltered coves. At the village of Svolvær, which is built upon a pile of bare stones, we took on board a number of ladies in fashionable dresses, with bonnets on the backs of their heads and a sufficiency of cumbrous petticoats to make up for the absence of hoops, which have not yet got further north than Drontheim. In seeing these unexpected apparitions emerge from such a wild corner of chaos I could not but wonder at the march of modern civilisation. Pianos in Lapland, Parisian dresses among the Lofodens, billiard-tables in Hammerfest—whither shall we turn to find the romance of the North!

We sailed, in the lovely nocturnal sunshine, through the long, river-like channel—the Rasksund, I believe, it is called—between the islands of East-Vaagöe and Hindöe, the largest of the Lofodens. For a distance of fifteen miles the strait was in no place more than a mile in breadth, while it was frequently less than a quarter. The smooth water was a perfect mirror, reflecting on one side the giant cliffs, with their gorges choked with snow, their arrowy pinnacles and white lines of falling water—on the other, hills turfed to the summit with emerald velvet, sprinkled with pale groves of birch and alder, and dotted, along their bases, with the dwellings of the fishermen. It was impossible to believe that we were floating on an arm of the Atlantic— it was some unknown river, or a lake high up among the Alpine peaks. The silence of these shores added to the impression. Now and then a white sea-gull fluttered about the cliffs, or an eider duck paddled across some glassy cove, but no sound was heard: there was no sail on the water, no human being on the shore. Emerging at last from this wild and enchanting strait, we stood across a bay, opening southward to the Atlantic, to the port of Steilo, on one of the outer islands. Here the broad front of the island, rising against the roseate sky, was one swell of the most glorious green, down to the very edge of the sea, while the hills of East-Vaagöe, across the bay, showed only naked and defiant rock, with summit-fields of purple-tinted snow. In splendour of coloring, the tropics were again surpassed, but the keen north wind obliged us to enjoy it in an overcoat.

Toward midnight, the sun was evidently above the horizon, though hidden by intervening mountains. Braisted and another American made various exertions to see it, such as climbing the foremast, but did not succeed until about one o'clock, when they were favoured by a break in the hills. Although we had daylight the whole twenty-four hours, travellers do not consider that their duty is fulfilled unless they see the sun itself, exactly at midnight. In the morning, we touched at Throndenaes, on the northern side of Hindöe, a beautiful bay with green and wooded shores, and then, leaving the Lofodens behind us, entered the archipelago of large islands which lines the coast of Finmark. Though built on the same grand and imposing scale as the Lofodens, these islands are somewhat less jagged and abrupt in their forms, and exhibit a much more luxuriant vegetation. In fact, after leaving the Namsen Fjord, near Drontheim, one sees very little timber until he reaches the parallel of 69°. The long straits between Senjen and Qvalö and the mainland are covered with forests of birch and turfy slopes greener than England has ever shown. At the same time the snow level was not more than 500 feet above the sea, and broad patches lay melting on all the lower hills. This abundance of snow seems a singular incongruity, when you look upon the warm summer sky and the dark, mellow, juicy green of the shores. One fancies that he is either sailing upon some lofty inland lake, or that the ocean-level in these latitudes must be many thousand feet higher than in the temperate zone. He cannot believe that he is on the same platform with Sicily and Ceylon.

After a trip up the magnificent Maans Fjord, and the sight of some sea-green glaciers, we approached Tromsöe, the capital of Finmark. This is a town of nearly 3000 inhabitants, on a small island in the strait between Qvalö and the mainland. It was just midnight when we dropped anchor, but, although the sun was hidden by a range of snowy hills in the north, the daylight was almost perfect. I immediately commenced making a sketch of the harbour, with its fleet of coasting vessels. Some Russian craft from Archangel, and a Norwegian cutter carrying six guns, were also at anchor before the town. Our French traveller, after amusing himself with the idea of my commencing a picture at sunset and finishing it at sunrise, started for a morning ramble over the hills. Boats swarmed around the steamer; the coal-lighters came off, our crew commenced their work, and when the sun's disc appeared, before one o'clock, there was another day inaugurated. The night had vanished mysteriously, no one could tell how.

CHAPTER XXV. FINMARK AND HAMMERFEST.

The steamer lay at Tromsöe all day, affording us an opportunity to visit an encampment of Lapps in Tromsdal, about four miles to the eastward. So far as the Lapps were concerned, I had seen enough of them, but I joined the party for the sake of the northern summer. The captain was kind enough to despatch a messenger to the Lapps, immediately on our arrival, that their herd of reindeer, pasturing on the mountains, might be driven down for our edification, and also exerted himself to procure a horse for the American lady. The horse came, in due time, but a side saddle is an article unknown in the arctic regions, and the lady was obliged to trust herself to a man's saddle and the guidance of a Norseman of the most remarkable health, strength, and stupidity.

Our path led up a deep valley, shut in by overhanging cliffs, and blocked up at the eastern end by the huge mass of the fjeld. The streams, poured down the crags from their snowy reservoirs, spread themselves over the steep side of the hill, making a succession of quagmires, over which we were obliged to spring and scramble in breakneck style. The sun was intensely hot in the enclosed valley, and we found the shade of the birchen groves very grateful. Some of the trees grew to a height of forty feet, with trunks the thickness of a man's body. There were also ash and alder trees, of smaller size, and a profusion of brilliant wild flowers. The little multeberry was in blossom; the ranunculus, the globe-flower, the purple geranium, the heath, and the blue forget-me-not spangled the ground, and on every hillock the young ferns unrolled their aromatic scrolls written with wonderful fables of the southern spring. For it was only spring here, or rather the very beginning of summer. The earth had only become warm enough to conceive and bring forth flowers, and she was now making the most of the little maternity vouchsafed to her. The air was full of winged insects, darting hither and thither in astonishment at finding themselves alive; the herbage seemed to be visibly growing under your eyes; even the wild shapes of the trees were expressive of haste, lest the winter might come on them unawares; and I noticed that the year's growth had been shot out at once, so that the young sprays might have time to harden and to protect the next year's buds. There was no lush, rollicking out-burst of foliage, no mellow, epicurean languor of the woods, no easy unfolding of leaf on leaf, as in the long security of our summers; but everywhere a feverish hurry on the part of nature to do something, even if it should only be half done. And above the valley, behind its mural ramparts, glowered the cold white snows, which had withdrawn for a little while, but lay in wait, ready to spring down as soon as the protecting sunshine should fail.

The lady had one harmless tumble into the mud, and we were all pretty well fatigued with our rough walk, when we reached the Lapp encampment. It consisted only of two families, who lived in their characteristic gammes, or huts of earth, which serve them also for winter dwellings. These burrows were thrown up on a grassy meadow, beside a rapid stream which came down from the fjeld; and at a little distance were two folds, or corrals for their reindeer, fenced with pickets slanting outward. A number of brown-haired, tailless dogs, so much resembling bear-cubs that at first sight we took them for such, were playing about the doors. A middle-aged Lapp, with two women and three or four children, were the inmates. They scented profit, and received us in a friendly way, allowing the curious strangers to go in and out at pleasure, to tease the dogs, drink the reindeer milk, inspect the children, rock the baby, and buy horn spoons to the extent of their desire. They were smaller than the Lapps of Kautokeino—or perhaps the latter appeared larger in their winter dresses—and astonishingly dirty. Their appearance is much more disgusting in summer than in winter, when the snow, to a certain extent, purifies everything. After waiting an hour or more, the herd appeared descending the fjeld, and driven toward the fold by two young Lapps, assisted by their dogs. There were about four hundred in all, nearly one-third being calves. Their hoarse bleating and the cracking noise made by their knee-joints, as they crowded together into a dense mass of grey, mossy backs, made a very peculiar sound; and this combined with their ragged look, from the process of shedding their coats of hair, did not very favourably impress those of our party who saw them for the first time. The old Lapp and his boy, a strapping fellow of fifteen, with a ruddy, olive complexion and almost Chinese features, caught a number of the cows with lassos, and proceeded to wean the young deer by anointing the mothers' dugs with cow-dung, which they carried in pails slung over their shoulders. In this delightful occupation we left them, and returned to Tromsöe.

As we crossed the mouth of the Ulvsfjord, that evening we had an open sea horizon toward the north, a clear sky, and so much sunshine at eleven o'clock that it was evident the Polar day had dawned upon us at last. The illumination of the shores was unearthly in its glory, and the wonderful effects of the orange sunlight, playing upon the dark hues of the island cliffs, can neither be told nor painted. The sun hung low between Fuglöe, rising like a double dome from the sea, and the tall mountains of Arnöe, both of which islands resembled immense masses of transparent purple glass, gradually melting into crimson fire at their bases. The glassy, leaden-coloured sea was powdered with a golden bloom, and the tremendous precipices at the mouth of the Lyngen Fjord, behind us, were steeped in a dark red, mellow flush, and touched with pencillings of pure, rose-coloured light, until their naked ribs seemed to be clothed in imperial velvet. As we turned into the Fjord and ran southward along their bases, a waterfall, struck by the sun, fell in fiery orange foam down the red walls, and the blue ice-pillars of a beautiful glacier filled up the ravine beyond it. We were all on deck, and all faces, excited by the divine splendour of the scene, and tinged by the same wonderful aureole, shone as if transfigured. In my whole life I have never seen a spectacle so unearthly beautiful.

Our course brought the sun rapidly toward the ruby cliffs of Arnöe, and it was evident that he would soon be hidden from sight. It was not yet half-past eleven, and an enthusiastic passenger begged the captain to stop the vessel until midnight. "Why," said the latter, "it is midnight now, or very near it; you have Drontheim time, which is almost forty minutes in arrears." True enough, the real time lacked but five minutes of midnight, and those of us who had sharp eyes and strong imaginations saw the sun make his last dip and rise a little, before he vanished in a blaze of glory behind Arnöe. I turned away with my eyes full of dazzling spheres of crimson and gold, which danced before me wherever I looked, and it was a long time before they were blotted out by the semi-oblivion of a daylight sleep.

The next morning found us at the entrance of the long Alten Fjord. Here the gashed, hacked, split, scarred and shattered character of the mountains ceases, and they suddenly assume a long, rolling outline, full of bold features, but less wild and fantastic. On the southern side of the fjord many of them are clothed with birch and fir to the height of a thousand feet. The valleys here are cultivated to some extent, and produce, in good seasons, tolerable crops of potatoes, barley, and buckwheat. This is above lat. 70°, or parallel with the northern part of Greenland, and consequently the highest cultivated land in the world. In the valley of the Alten River, the Scotch fir sometimes reaches a height of seventy or eighty feet. This district is called the Paradise of Finmark, and no doubt floats in the imaginations of the settlers on Mageröe and the dreary Porsanger Fjord, as Andalusia and Syria float in ours. It is well that human bliss is so relative in its character.

At Talvik, a cheerful village with a very neat, pretty church, who should come on board but Pastor Hvoslef, our Kautokeino friend of the last winter! He had been made one of a Government Commission of four, appointed to investigate and report upon the dissensions between the nomadic Lapps and those who have settled habitations. A better person could not have been chosen than this good man, who has the welfare of the Lapps truly at heart, and in whose sincerity every one in the North confides.

We had on board Mr. Thomas, the superintendent of the copper works at Kaafjord, who had just resigned his seat in the Storthing and given up his situation for the purpose of taking charge of some mines at Copiapo, in Chili. Mr. Thomas is an Englishman, who has been for twenty years past one of the leading men of Finmark, and no other man, I venture to say, has done more to improve and enlighten that neglected province. His loss will not be easily replaced. At Talvik, his wife, a pleasant, intelligent Norwegian lady, came on board; and, as we passed the rocky portals guarding the entrance to the little harbour of Kaafjord, a gun, planted on a miniature battery above the landing-place, pealed forth a salute of welcome. I could partly understand Mr. Thomas's long residence in those regions, when I saw what a wild, picturesque spot he had chosen for his home. The cavernous entrances to the copper mines yawned in the face of the cliff above the outer bay below, on the water's edge, stood the smelting works, surrounded by labourers' cottages; a graceful white church crowned a rocky headland a little further on; and beyond, above a green lawn, decked with a few scattering birches, stood a comfortable mansion, with a garden in the rear. The flag of Norway and the cross of St. George floated from separate staffs on the lawn. There were a number of houses, surrounded with potato-fields on the slope stretching around the bay, and an opening of the hills at its head gave us a glimpse of the fir forests of the inland valleys. On such a cloudless day as we had, it was a cheerful and home-like spot.

We took a friendly leave of Mr. Thomas and departed, the little battery giving us I don't know how many three-gun salutes as we moved off. A number of whales spouted on all sides of us as we crossed the head of the fjord to Bosekop, near the mouth of the Alten River. This is a little village on a bare rocky headland, which completely shuts out from view the rich valley of the Alten, about which the Finmarkers speak with so much enthusiasm. "Ah, you should see the farms on the Alten," say they; "there we have large houses, fields, meadows, cattle, and the finest timber." This is Altengaard, familiar to all the readers of Mügge's "Afraja." The gaard, however, is a single large estate, and not a name applied to the whole district, as those unfamiliar with Norsk nomenclature might suppose. Here the Catholics have established a mission— ostensibly a missionary boarding-house, for the purpose of acclimating arctic apostles; but the people, who regard it with the greatest suspicion and distrust, suspect that the ultimate object is the overthrow of their inherited, venerated, and deeply-rooted Lutheran faith. At Bosekop we lost Pastor Hvoslef, and took on board the chief of the mission, the Catholic Bishop of the Arctic Zone—for I believe his diocese includes Greenland, Spitzbergen, and Polar America. Here is a Calmuck Tartar, thought I, as a short, strongly-built man, with sallow complexion, deep-set eyes, broad nostrils, heavy mouth, pointed chin, and high cheek-bones, stepped on board; but he proved to be a Russian baron, whose conversion cost him his estates. He had a massive head, however, in which intellect predominated, and his thoroughly polished manners went far to counteract the effect of one of the most unprepossessing countenances I ever saw.

M. Gay, who had known the bishop at Paris, at once entered into conversation with him. A short time afterwards, my attention was drawn to the spot where they stood by loud and angry exclamations. Two of our Norwegian savans stood before the bishop, and one of them, with a face white with rage, was furiously vociferating: "It is not true! it is not true! Norway is a free country!" "In this respect, it is not free," answered the bishop, with more coolness than I thought he could have shown, under such circumstances: "You know very well that no one can hold office except those who belong to your State Church—neither a Catholic, nor a Methodist, nor a Quaker: whereas in France, as I have said, a Protestant may even become a minister of the Government." "But we do not believe in the Catholic faith:—we will have nothing to do with it!" screamed the Norwegian. "We are not discussing our creeds," answered the bishop: "I say that, though Norway is a free country, politically, it does not secure equal rights to all its citizens, and so far as the toleration of religious beliefs is concerned, it is behind most other countries of Europe." He thereupon retreated to the cabin, for a crowd had gathered about the disputants, and the deck-passengers pressing aft, seemed more than usually excited by what was going on. The Norwegian shaking with fury, hissed through his set teeth: "How dare he come here to insult our national feeling!" Yes, but every word was true; and the scene was only another illustration of the intense vanity of the Norwegians in regard to their country. Woe to the man who says a word against Norway, though he say nothing but what everybody knows to be true! So long as you praise everything—scenery, people, climate, institutions, and customs—or keep silent where you cannot praise, you have the most genial conversation; but drop a word of honest dissent or censure, and you will see how quickly every one draws back into his shell. There are parts of our own country where a foreigner might make the same observation. Let a Norwegian travel in the Southern States, and dare to say a word in objection to slavery!

There is nothing of interest between Alten and Hammerfest, except the old sea-margins on the cliffs and a small glacier on the island of Seiland. The coast is dismally bleak and barren. Whales were very abundant; we sometimes saw a dozen spouting at one time. They were of the hump-backed species, and of only moderate size; yet the fishery would doubtless pay very well, if the natives had enterprise enough to undertake it. I believe, however, there is no whale fishery on the whole Norwegian coast. The desolate hills of Qvalö surmounted by the pointed peak of the Tjuve Fjeld, or "Thief Mountain,"— so called because it steals so much of the winter sunshine,—announced our approach to Hammerfest, and towards nine o'clock in the evening we were at anchor in the little harbour. The summer trade had just opened, and forty Russian vessels, which had arrived from the White Sea during the previous week or two, lay crowded before the large fish warehouses built along the water. They were all three-masted schooners, the main and mizen masts set close together, and with very heavy, square hulls. Strong Muscovite faces, adorned with magnificent beards, stared at us from the decks, and a jabber of Russian, Finnish, Lapp, and Norwegian, came from the rough boats crowding about our gangways. The north wind, blowing to us off the land, was filled with the perfume of dried codfish, train oil, and burning whale-"scraps," with which, as we soon found, the whole place is thoroughly saturated.

There is one hotel in the place, containing half a dozen chambers of the size of a state-room. We secured quarters here with a great deal of difficulty, owing to slowness of comprehension on the part of an old lady who had charge of the house. The other American, who at first took rooms for himself and wife, gave them up again very prudently; for the noises of the billiard-room penetrated through the thin wooden partitions, and my bed, at least, had been slept in by one of the codfish aristocracy, for the salty odour was so pungent that it kept me awake for a long time. With our fare, we had less reason to complain. Fresh salmon, arctic ptarmigan, and reindeer's tongue were delicacies which would have delighted any palate, and the wine had really seen Bordeaux, although rainy weather had evidently prevailed during the voyage thence to Hammerfest. The town lies in a deep bight, inclosed by precipitous cliffs, on the south-western side of the island, whence the sun, by this time long past his midsummer altitude, was not visible at midnight. Those of our passengers who intended returning by the Nordkap climbed the hills to get another view of him, but unfortunately went upon the wrong summit, so that they did not see him after all. I was so fatigued, from the imperfect sleep of the sunshiny nights and the crowd of new and exciting impressions which the voyage had given me, that I went to bed; but my friend sat up until long past midnight, writing, with curtains drawn.

CHAPTER XXVI. THE MIDNIGHT SUN.

Most of the travellers who push as far north as Hammerfest content themselves with one experience of the midnight sun, and return with the same steamer to Drontheim. A few extend their journey to the North Cape, and, once a year, on an average, perhaps, some one is adventurous enough to strike across Lapland to Torneå. The steamers, nevertheless, pass the North Cape, and during the summer make weekly trips to the Varanger Fjord, the extreme eastern limit of the Norwegian territory. We were divided in opinion whether to devote our week of sunshine to the North Cape, or to make the entire trip and see something of the northern coast of Europe, but finally decided that the latter, on the whole, as being unfamiliar ground, would be most interesting. The screw-steamer Gyller (one of Odin's horses) was lying in the harbour when we arrived, and was to leave in the course of the next night; so we lost no time in securing places, as she had but a small cabin and no state-rooms. Nevertheless, we found her very comfortable, and in every respect far superior to the English vessels which ply between Hull and Christiania. Our fellow travellers were all returning to Drontheim—except three Norwegian officers on their way to make an official inspection of the fortress of Wardöhuus—and the last we saw of them was their return, an hour past midnight, from making a second attempt to see the sun from the hills. The night was somewhat obscured, and I doubt if they were successful.

When I went on deck on the morning after our departure, we were in the narrow strait between the island of Mageröe, the northern extremity of which forms the North Cape, and the mainland. On either side, the shores of bare bleak rock, spotted with patches of moss and stunted grass, rose precipitously from the water, the snow filling up their ravines from the summit to the sea. Not a tree nor a shrub, nor a sign of human habitation was visible; there was no fisher's sail on the lonely waters, and only the cries of some sea-gulls, wheeling about the cliffs, broke the silence. As the strait opened to the eastward, a boat appeared, beating into Kjelvik, on the south-eastern corner of the island; but the place itself was concealed from us by an intervening cape. This is the spot which Von Buch visited in the summer of 1807, just fifty years ago, and his description would be equally correct at the present day. Here, where the scurvy carries off half the inhabitants,—where pastors coming from Southern Norway die within a year,—where no trees grow, no vegetables come to maturity, and gales from every quarter of the Icy Sea beat the last faint life out of nature, men will still persist in living, in apparent defiance of all natural laws. Yet they have at least an excuse for it, in the miraculous provision which Providence has made for their food and fuel. The sea and fjords are alive with fish, which are not only a means of existence but of profit to them, while the wonderful Gulf Stream, which crosses 5000 miles of the Atlantic to die upon this Ultima Thule in a last struggle with the Polar Sea, casts up the spoils of tropical forests to feed their fires. Think of arctic fishers burning upon their hearths the palms of Hayti, the mahogany of Honduras, and the precious woods of the Amazon and the Orinoco!

In the spring months, there are on an average 800 vessels on the northern coast, between the North Cape and Vadsö, with a fishing population of 5000 men on board, whose average gains, even at the scanty prices they receive amount to $30 apiece, making a total yield of $150,000. It is only within a very few years that the Norwegian Government has paid any attention to this far corner of the peninsula. At present, considering the slender population, the means of communication are well kept up during eight months in the year, and the result is an increase (perceptible to an old resident, no doubt) in the activity and prosperity of the country.

On issuing from the strait, we turned southward into the great Porsanger Fjord, which stretches nearly a hundred miles into the heart of Lapland, dividing Western from Eastern Finmark. Its shores are high monotonous hills, half covered with snow, and barren of vegetation except patches of grass and moss. If once wooded, like the hills of the Alten Fjord, the trees have long since disappeared, and now nothing can be more bleak and desolate. The wind blew violently from the east, gradually lifting a veil of grey clouds from the cold pale sky, and our slow little steamer with jib and fore-topsail set, made somewhat better progress. Toward evening (if there is such a time in the arctic summer), we reached Kistrand, the principal settlement on the fjord.

222

It has eight or nine houses, scattered along a gentle slope a mile in length, and a little red church, but neither gardens, fields, nor potato patches. A strip of grazing ground before the principal house was yellow with dandelions, the slope behind showed patches of brownish green grass, and above this melancholy attempt at summer stretched the cold, grey, snow-streaked ridge of the hill. Two boats, manned by sea-Lapps, with square blue caps, and long ragged locks of yellow hair fluttering in the wind, brought off the only passenger and the mails, and we put about for the mouth of the fjord.

Running along under the eastern shore, we exchanged the dreadful monotony through which we had been sailing for more rugged and picturesque scenery. Before us rose a wall of dark cliff, from five to six hundred feet in height, gaping here and there with sharp clefts or gashes, as if it had cracked in cooling, after the primeval fires. The summit of these cliffs was the average level of the country; and this peculiarity, I found, applies to all the northern shore of Finmark, distinguishing the forms of the capes and islands from those about Alten and Hammerfest, which, again, are quite different from those of the Lofodens. "On returning from Spitzbergen," said a Hammerfest merchant to me, "I do not need to look at chart or compass, when I get sight of the coast; I know, from the formation of the cliffs, exactly where I am." There is some general resemblance to the chalk bluffs of England, especially about Beachy Head, but the rock here appears to be mica-slate, disposed in thin, vertical strata, with many violent transverse breaks.

As we approached the end of the promontory which divides the Porsanger from the Laxe Fjord, the rocks became more abrupt and violently shattered. Huge masses, fallen from the summit, lined the base of the precipice, which was hollowed into cavernous arches, the home of myriads of sea-gulls. The rock of Sværholtklub, off the point, resembled a massive fortress in ruins. Its walls of smooth masonry rested on three enormous vaults, the piers of which were buttressed with slanting piles of rocky fragments. The ramparts, crenelated in some places, had mouldered away in others, and one fancied he saw in the rents and scars of the giant pile the marks of the shot and shell which had wrought its ruin. Thousands of white gulls, gone to their nightly roost, rested on every ledge and cornice of the rock; but preparations were already made to disturb their slumbers. The steamer's cannon was directed towards the largest vault, and discharged. The fortress shook with the crashing reverberation; "then rose a shriek, as of a city sacked"—a wild, piercing, maddening, myriad-tongued cry, which still rings in my ears. With the cry, came a rushing sound, as of a tempest among the woods; a white cloud burst out of the hollow arch-way, like the smoke of an answering shot, and, in the space of a second, the air was filled with birds, thicker than autumn leaves, and rang with one universal, clanging shriek. A second shot, followed by a second outcry and an answering discharge from the other caverns, almost darkened the sky. The whirring, rustling and screaming, as the birds circled overhead, or dropped like thick scurries of snow-flakes on the water, was truly awful. There could not have been less than fifty thousand in the air at one time, while as many more clung to the face of the rock, or screamed from the depth of the vaults. Such an indignation meeting I never attended before; but, like many others I have heard of, the time for action was passed before they had decided what to do.

It was now eleven o'clock, and Sværholt glowed in fiery bronze lustre as we rounded it, the eddies of returning birds gleaming golden in the nocturnal sun, like drifts of beech leaves in the October air. Far to the north, the sun lay in a bed of saffron light over the clear horizon of the Arctic Ocean. A few bars of dazzling orange cloud floated above him, and still higher in the sky, where the saffron melted through delicate rose-colour into blue, hung light wreaths of vapour, touched with pearly, opaline flushes of pink and golden grey. The sea was a web of pale slate-colour, shot through and through with threads of orange and saffron, from the dance of a myriad shifting and twinkling ripples. The air was filled and permeated with the soft, mysterious glow, and even the very azure of the southern sky seemed to shine through a net of golden gauze. The headlands of this deeply-indented coast—the capes of the Laxe and Porsanger Fjords, and of Mageröe—lay around us, in different degrees of distance, but all with foreheads touched with supernatural glory. Far to the north-east was Nordkyn, the most northern point of the mainland of Europe, gleaming rosily and faint in the full beams of the sun, and just as our watches denoted midnight the North Cape appeared to the westward—a long line of purple bluff, presenting a vertical front of nine hundred feet in height to the Polar Sea. Midway between those two magnificent headlands stood the Midnight Sun, shining on us with subdued fires, and with the gorgeous colouring of an hour for which we have no name, since it is neither sunset nor sunrise, but the blended loveliness of both—but shining at the same moment, in the heat and splendour of noonday, on the Pacific Isles.

This was the midnight sun as I had dreamed it—as I had hoped to see it.

Within fifteen minutes after midnight, there was a perceptible increase of altitude, and in less than half an hour the whole tone of the sky had changed, the yellow brightening into orange, and the saffron melting into the pale vermilion of dawn. Yet it was neither the colours, nor the same character of light as we had had, half an hour before midnight. The difference was so slight as scarcely to be described; but it was the difference between evening and morning. The faintest transfusion of one prevailing tint into another had changed the whole expression of heaven and earth, and so imperceptibly and miraculously that a new day was already present to our consciousness. Our view of the wild cliffs of Sværholt, less than two hours before, belonged to yesterday, though we had stood on deck, in full sunshine, during all the intervening time. Had the sensation of a night slipped through our brains in the momentary winking of the eyes? Or was the old routine of consciousness so firmly stereotyped in our natures, that the view of a morning was sufficient proof to them of the preëxistence of a night? Let those explain the phenomenon who can—but I found my physical senses utterly at war with those mental perceptions wherewith they should harmonise. The eye saw but one unending day; the mind notched the twenty-four hours on its calendar, as before.

Before one o'clock we reached the entrance of the Kiöllefjord, which in the pre-diluvial times must have been a tremendous mountain gorge, like that of Gondo, on the Italian side of the Simplon. Its mouth is about half a mile in breadth, and its depth is not more than a mile and a half. It is completely walled in with sheer precipices of bare rock, from three to five hundred feet in height, except at the very head, where they subside into a stony heap, upon which some infatuated mortals have built two or three cabins. As we neared the southern headland, the face of which was touched with the purest orange light, while its yawning fissures lay in deep-blue gloom, a tall ruin, with shattered turrets and crumbling spires, detached itself from the mass, and stood alone at the foot of the precipice. This is the Finnkirka, or "Church of the Lapps," well known to all the northern coasters. At first it resembles a tall church with a massive square spire; but the two parts separate again, and you have a crag-perched castle of the middle-ages, with its watch-tower—the very counterpart of scores in Germany—and a quaint Gothic chapel on the point beyond. The vertical strata of the rock, worn into sharp points at the top and gradually broadening to the base, with numberless notched ornaments and channels fluted by the rain, make the resemblance marvellous, when seen under the proper effects of light and shade. The lustre in which we saw it had the effect of enchantment. There was a play of colours upon it, such as one sees in illuminated Moorish halls, and I am almost afraid to say how much I was enraptured by a scene which has not its equal on the whole Norwegian coast, yet of which none of us had ever heard before.

We landed a single passenger—a government surveyor apparently—on the heap of rocks beyond, and ran out under the northern headland, which again charmed us with a glory peculiarly its own. Here the colours were a part of the substance of the rock, and the sun but heightened and harmonised their tones. The huge projecting masses of pale yellow had a mellow gleam, like golden chalk; behind them were cliffs, violet in shadow; broad strata of soft red, tipped on the edges with vermilion; thinner layers, which shot up vertically to the height of four or five hundred feet, and striped the splendid sea-wall with lines of bronze, orange, brown, and dark red, while great rents and breaks interrupted these marvellous frescoes with their dashes of uncertain gloom. I have seen many wonderful aspects of nature, in many lands, but rock-painting such as this I never beheld. A part of its effect may have been owing to atmospheric conditions which must be rare, even in the North; but, without such embellishments, I think the sight of this coast will nobly repay any one for continuing his voyage beyond Hammerfest.

We lingered on deck, as point after point revealed some change in the dazzling diorama, uncertain which was finest, and whether something still grander might not be in store. But at last Nordkyn drew nigh, and at three o'clock the light became that of day, white and colourless. The north-east wind blew keenly across the Arctic Ocean, and we were both satisfied and fatigued enough to go to bed. It was the most northern point of our voyage— about 71° 20', which is further north than I ever was before, or ever wish to be again.

CHAPTER XXVII. THE VARANGER FJORD.—ARCTIC LIFE.

When we awoke, after six hours' sleep, with curtains drawn to keep out the daylight, our steamer was deep in the Tana Fjord, which receives the waters of the Tana River, the largest Lapland stream flowing into the Arctic Ocean. The greater part of the day was consumed in calling at two settlements of three houses each, and receiving and delivering mails of one letter, or less. The shores of this fjord are steep hills of bare rock, covered with patches of snow to the water's edge. The riven walls of cliff, with their wonderful configuration and marvellous colouring, were left behind us, and there was nothing of the grand or picturesque to redeem the savage desolation of the scenery. The chill wind, blowing direct from Nova Zembla, made us shiver, and even the cabin saloon was uncomfortable without a fire. After passing the most northern point of Europe, the coast falls away to the south-east, so that on the second night we were again in the latitude of Hammerfest, but still within the sphere of perpetual sunshine. Our second night of sun was not so rich in colouring as the first, yet we remained on deck long enough to see the orb rise again from his lowest dip, and change evening into morning by the same incomprehensible process. There was no golden transfiguration of the dreadful shore; a wan lustre played over the rocks—pictures of eternal death—like a settled pallor of despair on Nature's stony face.

One of the stations on this coast, named Makur, consisted of a few fishermen's huts, at the bottom of a dismal rocky bight. There was no grass to be seen, except some tufts springing from the earth with which the roofs were covered, and it was even difficult to see where so much earth had been scraped together. The background was a hopelessly barren hill, more than half enveloped in snow. And this was midsummer—and human beings passed their lives here! "Those people surely deserve to enter Paradise when they die," I remarked to my friend, "for they live in hell while upon earth." "Not for that," he answered, "but because it is impossible for them to commit sin. They cannot injure their neighbours, for they have none. They cannot steal, for there is nothing to tempt them. They cannot murder, for there are none of the usual incentives to hate and revenge. They have so hard a struggle merely to live, that they cannot fall into the indulgences of sense; so that if there is nothing recorded in their favour, there is also nothing against them, and they commence the next life with blank books."

"But what a life!" I exclaimed. "Men may be happy in poverty, in misfortune, under persecution, in life-long disease even, so that they are not wholly deprived of the genial influences of society and Nature—but what is there here?" "They know no other world," said he, "and this ignorance keeps them from being miserable. They do no more thinking than is necessary to make nets and boats, catch fish and cook them, and build their log-houses. Nature provides for their marrying and bringing up their children, and the pastor, whom they see once in a long time, gives them their religion ready made." God keep them ignorant, then! was my involuntary prayer. May they never lose their blessed stupidity, while they are chained to these rocks and icy seas! May no dreams of summer and verdure, no vision of happier social conditions, or of any higher sphere of thought and action, flash a painful light on the dumb-darkness of their lives!

The next day, we were in the Varanger Fjord, having passed the fortress of Vardöhuus and landed our military committee. The Norwegian shore was now low and tame, but no vegetation, except a little brown grass, was to be seen. The Russian shore, opposite, and some twenty-five or thirty miles distant, consisted of high, bold hills, which, through a glass, appeared to be partially wooded. The Varanger Fjord, to which so important a political interest has attached within the last few years, is about seventy miles in depth, with a general direction towards the south-west. The boundary-line between Norwegian and Russian Finmark strikes it upon the southern side, about half-way from the mouth, so that three-fourths, or more, of the waters of the fjord belong to Norway. There is, however, a wonderful boundary-line, in addition, drawn by Nature between the alien waters. That last wave of the Gulf Stream which washes the North Cape and keeps the fjords of Finmark open and unfrozen the whole year through, sweeps eastward along the coast, until it reaches the head of Varanger Fjord. Here its power is at last spent, and from this point commences that belt of solid ice which locks up the harbours of the northern coast of Russia for six months in the year. The change from open water to ice is no less abrupt than permanent. Pastor Hvoslef informed me that in crossing from Vadsö, on the northern coast, to Pasvik, the last Norwegian settlement, close upon the Russian frontier, as late as the end of May, he got out of his boat upon the ice, and drove three or four miles over the frozen sea, to reach his destination.

The little fort of Vardöhuus, on an island at the northern entrance of the fjord, is not a recent defence, meant to check Russian plans in this quarter. It was established by Christian IV. nearly two and a half centuries ago. The king himself made a voyage hither, and no doubt at that time foresaw the necessity of establishing, by military occupation, the claims of Denmark to this part of the coast. The little fortress has actually done this service; and though a single frigate might easily batter it to pieces, its existence has kept Russia from the ownership of the Varanger Fjord and the creation (as is diplomatically supposed,) of an immense naval station, which, though within the Arctic waters, would at all times of the year be ready for service. It is well known that Russia has endeavoured to obtain possession of the northern side of the fjord, as well as of the Lyngen Fjord, near Tromsöe, towards which her Lapland territory stretches out a long arm. England is particularly suspicious of these attempts, and the treaty recently concluded between the Allied Powers and Sweden had a special reference thereto. The importance of such an acquisition to Russia is too obvious to be pointed out, and the jealous watchfulness of England is, therefore, easy to understand. But it is a singular thing that the conflicting forces of Europe find a fulcrum on a little corner of this dead, desolate, God-forsaken shore.

About ten o'clock we reached Vadsö, the limit of the steamer's route. Here we had intended taking a boat, continuing our voyage to Nyborg, at the head of the fjord, crossing thence to the Tana, and descending that river in season to meet the steamer in the Tana Fjord on her return. We were behind time, however, and the wind was light; the people informed us that we could scarcely carry out the project; so we reluctantly gave it up, and went ashore to spend the day. Vadsö is a town of about 800 inhabitants, with a secure though shallow harbour, which was crowded with fishing vessels and Russian traders from the White Sea. It lies on the bleak hill-side, without a tree or bush, or a patch of grass large enough to be seen without close inspection, and its only summer perfume is that of dried fish. I saw in gardens attached to one or two houses a few courageous radishes and some fool-hardy potatoes, which had ventured above ground without the least chance of living long enough to blossom. The snow had been four feet deep in the streets in the beginning of June, and in six weeks it would begin to fall again. A few forlorn cows were hunting pasture over the hills, now and then looking with melancholy resignation at the strings of codfish heads hanging up to dry, on the broth of which they are fed during the winter. I took a walk and made a sketch during the afternoon, but the wind was so chill that I was glad to come back shivering to our quarters.

We obtained lodgings at the house of a baker, named Aas, who had learned the art of charging, and was therefore competent to conduct a hotel. In order to reach our room, we were obliged to pass successively through the family dwelling-room, kitchen, and a carpenter's workshop, but our windows commanded a full view of a grogshop across the way, where drunken Lapps were turned out with astonishing rapidity. It was the marriage month of the Lapps, and the town was full of young couples who had come down to be joined, with their relatives and friends, all in their gayest costumes. Through the intervention of the postmaster, I procured two women and a child, as subjects for a sketch. They were dressed in their best, and it was impossible not to copy the leer of gratified vanity lurking in the corners of their broad mouths. The summer dress consisted of a loose gown of bright green cloth, trimmed on the neck and sleeves with bands of scarlet and yellow, and a peculiar head-dress, shaped like a helmet, but with a broader and flatter crest, rounded in front. This, also, was covered with scarlet cloth, and trimmed with yellow and blue. They were greatly gratified with the distinction, and all the other Lapps, as in Kautokeino, would have willingly offered themselves. I found the same physical characteristics here as there—a fresh, ruddy complexion, inclining to tawny; bright blue eyes, brown hair, high cheek-bones, and mouths of enormous width. They are not strikingly below the average size, Heine says, in one of his mad songs:

"In Lapland the people are dirty,

Flat-headed, and broad-mouthed, and small

They squat round the fire while roasting

Their fishes, and chatter and squall;"

which is as good a description of them as can be packed into a stanza. On the present occasion they were all drunk, in addition. One of them lay for a long time at the door, with his legs doubled under him as he fell, the others stepping over his body as they went in and out. These poor creatures were openly and shamelessly allowed to drug themselves, as long as their money lasted. No wonder the race is becoming extinct, when the means of destruction is so freely offered.

Vadsö, although only forty miles from Vardö, at the mouth of the fjord, has a much drier and more agreeable climate, and the inhabitants are therefore loud in praise of their place. "We have no such fogs as at Vardö," say they; "our fish dry much better, and some years we can raise potatoes." For the last four or five years, however, the winters have been getting more and more severe, and now it is impossible to procure hay enough to keep their few cattle through the winter. We had on board a German who had been living there five years, and who appeared well satisfied with his lot. "I have married here," said he; "I make a good living with less trouble than in Germany, and have no wish to return." Singularly enough, there were also two Italian organ grinders on board, whom I accosted in their native language; but they seemed neither surprised nor particularly pleased. They dropped hints of having been engaged in some political conspiracy; and one of them said, with a curious mixture of Italian and Norsk words "Jeg voglio ikke ritornare." I said the same thing ("I shall not return") as I left Vadsö.

We sailed early the next morning, and in the afternoon reached Vardö, where we lay three hours. Here we took on board the three officers, who had in the meantime made their inspection. Vardöhuus is a single star-shaped fort, with six guns and a garrison of twenty-seven men. During the recent war, the garrison was increased to three hundred—an unnecessary precaution, if there was really any danger of an attack to be apprehended, so long as the defences of the place were not strengthened. One of the officers, who had gone out fishing the night previous, caught eighty-three splendid cod in the space of two hours. It was idle sport, however, for no one would take his fish as a gift, and they were thrown on the shore to rot. The difficulty is not in catching but in curing them. Owing to the dampness of the climate they cannot be hung up on poles to dry slowly, like the stock-fish of the Lofodens, but must be first salted and then laid on the rocks to dry, whence the term klip (cliff) fish, by which they are known in trade.

At the mouth of the Tana we picked up four Englishmen, who had been salmon fishing on the river. They were sunburnt, spotted with mosquito bites, and had had little luck, the river being full of nets and the fjord of seals, between which the best of the salmon are either caught or devoured; but they spoke of their experience with true English relish. "Oh, it was very jolly!" said one: "we were so awfully bitten by mosquitoes. Then our interpreter always lost everything just before we wanted it—think of his losing our frying-pan, so that we had to fry in the lids of our kettles; He had a habit of falling overboard and getting nearly drowned before we could pull him in. We had a rough time of it, but it was very jolly, I assure you!" The young fellows meant what they said; they were all the better for their roughing, and I wish the spindle-shanked youths who polk and flirt at Newport and Saratoga had manliness enough for such undertakings.

We reached Hammerfest on the last day of July, and re-occupied our old quarters. That night the sun went below the horizon for the first time in eight days, but his depth was too slight to make any darkness visible. I was quite tired of the unending daylight, and would willingly have exchanged the pomp of the arctic midnight for the starlit darkness of home. We were confused by the loss of night; we lost the perception of time. One is never sleepy, but simply tired, and after a sleep of eight hours by sunshine, wakes up as tired as ever. His sleep at last is broken and irregular; he substitutes a number of short naps, distributed through the twenty-four hours, for the one natural repose, and finally gets into a state of general uneasiness and discomfort. A Hammerfest merchant, who has made frequent voyages to Spitzbergen, told me that in the latitude of 80° he never knew certainly whether it was day or night, and the cook was the only person on board who could tell him.

At first the nocturnal sunshine strikes you as being wonderfully convenient. You lose nothing of the scenery; you can read and write as usual; you never need be in a hurry, because there is time enough for everything. It is not necessary to do your day's work in the daytime, for no night cometh. You are never belated, and somewhat of the stress of life is lifted from your shoulders; but, after a time, you would be glad of an excuse to stop seeing, and observing, and thinking, and even enjoying. There is no compulsive rest such as darkness brings—no sweet isolation, which is the best refreshment of sleep. You lie down in the broad day, and the summons, "Arise!" attends on every reopening of your eyes. I never went below and saw my fellow-passengers all asleep around me without a sudden feeling that something was wrong: they were drugged, or under some unnatural influence, that they thus slept so fast while the sunshine streamed in through the port-holes.

There are some advantages of this northern summer which have presented themselves to me in rather a grotesque light. Think what an aid and shelter is removed from crime—how many vices which can only flourish in the deceptive atmosphere of night, must be checked by the sober reality of daylight! No assassin can dog the steps of his victim; no burglar can work in sunshine; no guilty lover can hold stolen interviews by moonlight—all concealment is removed, for the sun, like the eye of God, sees everything, and the secret vices of the earth must be bold indeed, if they can bear his gaze. Morally, as well as physically, there is safety in light and danger in darkness; and yet give me the darkness and the danger! Let the patrolling sun go off his beat for awhile, and show a little confidence in my ability to behave properly, rather than worry me with his sleepless vigilance.

I have described the smells of Hammerfest, which are its principal characteristic. It seemed to me the dreariest place in the world on first landing, a week previous; but, by contrast with what we had in the meantime seen, it became rather cheerful and comfortable. I was visiting a merchant after our return, and noticed with pleasure a stunted ash about eight feet high, in an adjoining garden. "Oh!" said he, in a tone of irritated pride, "we have plenty of trees here; there is quite a forest up the valley." This forest, after some search, I found. The trees were about six feet high, and some of them might have been as thick as my wrist. In the square before the merchant's house lay a crowd of drunken Lapps, who were supplied with as much bad brandy as they wanted by a licensed grogshop. The Russian sailors made use of the same privilege, and we frequently heard them singing and wrangling on board their White Sea junks. They were unapproachably picturesque, especially after the day's work was over, when they generally engaged in hunting in the extensive forests of their beards, and exercised the law of retaliation on all the game they caught.

A long street of turf-roofed houses, whose inhabitants may be said to be under the sod even before they die, leads along the shore of the bay to a range of flakes redolent of drying codfish. Beyond this you clamber over rocks and shingles to a low grassy headland, whereon stands a pillar commemorating the measurement of a meridian line of 25° 20', from the Danube to the Polar Sea, which was accomplished by the Governments of Austria, Russia, and Sweden, between the years 1816 and 1852. The pillar marks the northern terminus of the line, and stands in lat. 70° 40' 11.3". It is a plain shaft of polished red granite, standing on a base of grey granite, and surmounted by a bronze globe, on which a map of the earth is roughly outlined.

CHAPTER XXVIII. THE RETURN TO DARKNESS.—NORWEGIAN CHARACTER.

I do not intend to trace our return, step by step, down the Norwegian coast. The splendid weather which prevailed during our upward voyage, enabled us to see all the interesting points, leaving only those parts which we missed in the few hours devoted to sleep, to give a little novelty to our return. During the whole trip we had not a drop of rain,—the rarest good fortune in these latitudes,—and were therefore twice enabled to enjoy, to the fullest extent, the sublime scenery of the Lofoden Isles and the coast of Nordland. This voyage has not its like in the world. The traveller, to whom all other lands are familiar, has here a new volume of the most wonderful originality and variety, opened to him. The days are illuminated pages, crowded with pictures, the forms and hues of which he can never forget. After I returned to the zone of darkness, and recovered from the stress and tension of three weeks of daylight, I first fully appreciated the splendours of the arctic sun. My eyes were still dazzled with the pomp of colour, and the thousand miles of coast, as I reviewed them in memory, with their chaos of island-pyramids of shattered rock, their colossal cliffs, their twisted fjords, and long fjeld-levels of eternal snow, swam in a sea of saffron and rosy light, in comparison with which the pale blue day around me seemed dull and dead. My dream of the North, in becoming a reality, has retained the magical atmosphere of dreams, and basks in the same gorgeous twilight which irradiates the Scandinavian sagas.

I was particularly struck during the return, with the rapid progress of summer—the flying leaps with which she clears her short course. Among the Lofodens, the potatoes were coming into blossom, and the rye and barley into head; the grass was already cut, in many places, and drying on poles, and the green of the woods and meadows showed the dark, rich character of southern lands. Owing to this rapidity of growth, all the more hardy varieties of vegetables may be successfully cultivated. Mr. Thomas informed me that his peas and beans at Kaafjord (lat. 70° N.) grew three inches in twenty-four hours, and, though planted six weeks later than those about Christiania, came to maturity at the same time. He has even succeeded in raising excellent cauliflowers. But very few of the farmers have vegetable gardens, and those which I saw contained only radishes and lettuce, with a few useful herbs. One finds the same passion for flowers, however, as in Northern Sweden, and the poorest are rarely without a rose or a geranium in their windows.

Pastor Hvoslef, who was again our fellow-traveller for a few hours, gave me some interesting information concerning the Lapps. They are, it seems, entitled to the right of suffrage, and to representation in the Storthing, equally with the Norwegians. The local jurisdiction repeats on a small scale what the Storthing transacts on a large one, being entirely popular in its character, except that the vogts and länsmen (whose powers are somewhat similar to those of our judges and country magistrates) are not elected. But each district chooses from among its inhabitants a committee to confer upon and arrange all ordinary local matters. These committees, in turn, choose persons to constitute a higher body, who control the reciprocal relations of the several districts, and intervene in case of difficulties between them. The system is necessarily simpler and somewhat more primitive in its character than our local organisations in America; but it appears at present to answer every purpose. The heavy responsibility resting upon judges in Norway— the severity of the checks and penalties by which their probity is insured— probably contributes to make the administration of the laws more efficacious and easy. The Lapps are not a difficult people to govern, and much of the former antagonism between them and the poorer classes of the Norwegians has passed away. There is little, if any, amalgamation of the two races, nor will there ever be, but there is probably as little conflict between them as is compatible with the difference of blood.

At Tromsöe, a tall, strong, clerical gentleman came on board, who proved to be the noted Pastor Lamers, one of the first if not the very first Clergyman in Norway, who has refused to receive the government support— or, in other words, has seceded from the Church, as a State establishment, while adhering to all its fundamental doctrines. It is the first step towards the separation of Church and State, which must sooner or later come, in Norway and in Sweden. He has a congregation of three hundred members, in Tromsöe, and is about organising a church at Gibostad, on the island of Senjen. He has some peculiar views, I believe, in relation to the baptism of children, and insists that the usual absolution dealt out by the Pastors is of no effect without full confession and the specification of particular sins—but in other respects he is entirely orthodox, retaining even the ceremonial of the Eucharist. This, in the Lutheran church of Norway, comes so near to the Roman Catholic doctrine of transubstantiation, that one cannot easily perceive any difference. Instead of bread, an unleavened wafer is administered to the communicants, the priest saying, as he gives it, "This is the true body and blood of Jesus Christ." Mr. Forrester, a devout admirer of the Church, which he thinks identical with that of England in all its essentials, says, "The Lutherans reject the Romish doctrine of transubstantiation, but they hold that of a spiritual and ineffable union of the divine nature with the elements, the substance of which remains unchanged. This is called consubstantiation." Verily, the difference between tweedledum and tweedledee—one being as absurd as the other.

No one, coming from a land where all sects stand upon an equal footing, and where every church must depend for existence on its own inherent vitality, can fail to be struck with the effete and decrepit state of religion in Sweden and Norway. It is a body of frigid mechanical forms and ceremonies, animated here and therewith a feeble spark of spiritual life, but diffusing no quickening and animating glow. I have often been particularly struck with the horror with which the omission of certain forms was regarded by persons in whom I could discover no trace of any religious principle. The Church has a few dissensions to combat; she has not been weakened by schism; but she is slowly ossifying from sheer inertia. The Reformation needs to be reformed again, and perhaps the tardy privileges granted to the Haugianer and Läsare—the northern Methodists—may result in producing a body of Dissenters large enough to excite emulation, action, and improvement. In Norway, the pastors have the best salaries and the easiest places of all government officials. Those who conscientiously discharge their duties have enough to do; but were this universally the case, one would expect to find the people less filthy, stupid, and dishonest than they are in many parts of the country. A specimen of the intelligence of one, who is now a member of the Storthing, was communicated to me by a gentleman who heard it. The clergyman advocated the establishment of telegraph lines in Norway, "not for the sake of sending news," said he, "that is of no consequence. But it is well known that no wolf can pass under a telegraph wire, and if we can get lines put up throughout the country, all the wolves will be obliged to leave!" Of course, I do not mean to assert that the Norwegian clergymen, as a body, are not sincere, zealous, well-informed men. The evil lies rather in that system which makes religion as much a branch of government service as law or diplomacy; and which, until very recently, has given one sect an exclusive monopoly of the care of human souls.

I had a strong desire to converse with Pastor Lamers in relation to the stand he has taken, but he was surrounded by a crowd of persons during his stay on board, and no opportunity presented itself. The sensation which his presence produced, showed that there are restless elements at work in the mind of the people. The stony crust is beginning to heave and split at last. Even the deck-passengers gathered into little groups and talked earnestly. Two gentlemen near me were discussing the question of an Established Church, one contending, that a variety of sects tended only to confuse, perplex, and unchristianise the uneducated, unthinking class, while the other asserted that this very class adhered most tenaciously to whatever faith had been taught them. At this moment a woman standing near us exclaimed: "There were false prophets in all times, and there are false prophets now! We must beware of them!"—the earnestness of her speech affording a good comment on the argument just produced. Whatever may be the popular opinion concerning the course of Pastor Lamers, I could not but notice the marked respect displayed by every one who approached him.

In passing Hindöe we saw two magnificent golden eagles wheeling around one of the loftiest cliffs. The wind blew strongly from the south-west, increasing until we had what sailors call a dry gale in crossing the West Fjord, but it abated the next day and by the late twilight we recrossed the arctic circle. This night there was great rejoicing on board, at the discovery of a star. We had not seen one for a month, and some of the passengers coming from Finmark had been more than two months in daylight. While we were all gazing upon it as upon some extraordinary phenomenon, a flood of yellow lamp-light suddenly streamed through the cabin skylight. The sky was still brilliant with sunset in the north, but it was dark enough to see to sleep. We could not yet cover ourselves all over, even as with a cloak; still there was a shelter and friendly covering for the helpless body. Our sleep became sound and regular, and its old power of restoration was doubly sweet, since we had known what it was to be deprived of it.

Our fellow-passengers, after leaving Carlsoe, where the young Englishmen stopped to hunt, were almost exclusively Norwegian, and this gave us further opportunities of becoming acquainted with some peculiarities of the national character. Intelligent Norwegians, especially those who have travelled, are exceedingly courteous, gentlemanly, and agreeable persons. The three officers on board were men of unusual intelligence and refinement, and we considered ourselves fortunate in having their company during the entire voyage. The landhand lare, or country merchants, and government officials of the lower ranks, exhibit more reserve, and not unfrequently a considerable amount of ignorance and prejudice. Perhaps the most general feature of the Norwegian character is an excessive national vanity, which is always on the alert, and fires up on the slightest provocation. Say everything you like, except that Norway in any respect is surpassed by any other country. One is assailed with questions about his impressions of the scenery, people, government, &c.—a very natural and pardonable curiosity, it is true, and one only demands in return that his candour be respected, and no offence taken. This, however, is rarely the case. If there is no retaliatory answer on the spot, you hear a remark days afterwards which shows how your mild censure has rankled in the mind of the hearer. My friend was asked by a passenger whether he did not think the women of Finmark very beautiful. It was impossible to answer in the affirmative: the questioner went off in high dudgeon, and did not speak to him again for several days.

In the Varanger Fjord, we had pretty freely expressed our impressions of the desolate coast. Afterwards on returning past the grand cliff scenery of Nordkyn, we were admiring some bold formation of the rocks, when a Norwegian came up and said, in a tone of angry irony: "Ah, you find a little to admire at last, do you? You find some beauty in our country, after all?" So in regard to the government. The Norwegians may be justly proud of their constitution, which is as republican in its character as our own. There is so much in the administration of the government which every one must heartily commend, that they should be less sensitive in regard to minor faults. This sensitiveness, however, is partly accounted for, when we remember that for four hundred years Norway was a Danish province, and that only forty-three years ago she leaped at once from subjection to a freedom such as no other country in Europe enjoys. The intense pride and self-glorification of the people resembles that of a youth who for the first time assumes a dress-coat and standing collar. King Oscar, on his accession to the throne, gave the country a separate national flag, and nowhere does one see such a display of flags. All over the land and all along the shores, the colours of Norway are flying.

Jealousy of Sweden and dislike of the Swedes are inherited feelings, and are kept alive by a mutual prejudice on the part of the latter people. One cannot but smile a little at the present union of Sweden and Norway, when he finds that the countries have separate currencies, neither of which will pass at its full value in the other—separate tariffs, and of course Custom-house examinations between the two, and, if the Norwegians had their way, would have separate diplomatic representatives abroad. Yet the strength of Norway is undoubtedly in her alliance with Sweden: alone, she would be but a fourth-rate power. Enough has been done to satisfy her national feeling and secure her liberties against assault, and it is now time that this unnecessary jealousy and mistrust of a kindred race should cease. The Swedes have all the honesty which the Norwegians claim for themselves, more warmth and geniality of character, and less selfish sharpness and shrewdness. Mügge tells a story of a number of Swedes who were at a dinner party in Paris, where the health of "the King of Sweden and Norway" was proposed and drunk with great enthusiasm. One glass was observed to be untouched. It belonged to a Norwegian, who, when called upon for an explanation, said: "I cannot drink such a toast as this, but I will drink the health of the King of Norway, who is also King of Sweden!"

One cannot find fault with a people for their patriotism. I have always

241

admired that love of Gamle Norge which shines through Norwegian history, song, and saga—but when it is manifested in such ridiculous extremes, one doubts the genuineness of the feeling, and suspects it of being alloyed with some degree of personal vanity. There are still evils to be eradicated,—reproaches to be removed,—reforms to be achieved, which claim all the best energies of the best men of the country, and positive harm is done by concealing or denying the true state of things.

CHAPTER XXIX. DRONTHEIM AND BERGEN.

We spent another day and a half in Drontheim, before reshipping in the steamer for Bergen. With the exception of a trip to the Lierfoss, or falls of the Nid, however, it was by no means a satisfactory sojourn. The hotel was full, and we could only get quarters in the billiard-room, through which other guests were continually passing and repassing. Two small boys were quite inadequate to the service; the table d'hote was the scantiest I ever saw, and the charges at the rate of three dollars a day. The whole of Sunday was consumed in an attempt to recover our carrioles, which we left behind us on embarking for Hammerfest. The servants neglected to get them on Saturday evening, as we had ordered, and in the morning the man who had the key of the warehouse went into the country, taking it with him. The whole day was spent in searching and waiting, and it was only by unremitting exertions that we succeeded in putting them on board in the evening. Owing to this annoyance, I was unable to attend service in the cathedral, or even to see the inside of it.

Our drive to the Lierfoss, in the evening, was an exquisite enjoyment. The valley of the Nid, behind Drontheim, is one of the most carefully cultivated spots in Norway. Our road led up the stream, overlooking rich levels of grain and hay fields, studded with large and handsome farm-houses, while the lower slopes of the hills and the mound-like knolls scattered along their bases, were framed to the very summit, steep as they were. The whole scene was like a piece of landscape gardening, full of the loveliest effects, which were enhanced by the contrast of the grey, sterile mountains by which the picture was framed. The soft, level sunshine, streaming through the rifts of broken thunder-clouds in the west, slowly wandered over the peaceful valley, here lighting up a red-roofed homestead, there a grove in full summer foliage, or a meadow of so brilliant an emerald that it seemed to shine by its own lustre. As we approached the Lierfoss, the road was barred with a great number of gates, before which waited a troop of ragged boys, who accompanied us the whole of the way, with a pertinacity equal to that of the little Swiss beggars.

The Nid here makes two falls about half a mile apart, the lower one being eighty, and the upper one ninety feet in height. The water is of a dark olive-green colour, and glassy transparency, and so deep that at the brink it makes huge curves over the masses of rock in its bed without breaking into the faintest ripple. As you stand on a giant boulder above it, and contrast the swift, silent rush with the thundering volume of amber-tinted spray which follows, you feel in its full force the strange fascination of falling water—the temptation to plunge in and join in its headlong revelry. Here, however, I must admit that the useful is not always the beautiful. The range of smoky mills driven by a sluice from the fall had better be away. The upper fall is divided in the centre by a mass of rock, and presents a broader and more imposing picture, though the impetus of the water is not so great.

The coast between Drontheim and Bergen is, on the whole, much less striking than that further north; but it has some very grand features. The outer islands are, with few exceptions, low and barren, but the coast, deeply indented with winding fjords, towers here and there into sublime headlands, and precipitous barriers of rock. Christiansund, where we touched the first afternoon, is a singularly picturesque place, built on four islands, separated by channels in the form of a cross. The bare, rounded masses of grey rock heave up on all sides behind the houses, which are built along the water's edge; here and there a tree of superb greenness shines against the colourless background, and the mountains of the mainland, with their tints of pink and purple, complete the picture. The sun was burningly hot, and the pale-green water reflected the shores in its oily gloss; but in severe storms, I was told, it is quite impossible to cross from one island to another, and the different parts of the town sometimes remain for days in a state of complete isolation. I rose very early next morning, to have a view of Molde and the enchanting scenery of the Romsdals-fjord. The prosperous-looking town, with its large square houses, its suburban cottages and gardens, on the slope of a long green hill, crowned with woods, was wholly Swiss in its appearance, but the luminous morning vapors hovering around the Alpine peaks in the east, entirely hid them from our view. In this direction lies the famous Romsdal, which many travellers consider the grandest specimen of Norwegian scenery. Unfortunately we could not have visited it without taking an entire week, and we were apprehensive lest the fine weather, which we had now enjoyed for twenty-four days, should come to an end before we were done with the Bergenstift. It is almost unexampled that travellers make the voyage from Drontheim to the Varanger Fjord and back without a cloudy day. While we had perpetual daylight, the tourists whom we left behind were drenched with continual rains.

Aalesund is another island port, smaller than Christiansund, but full as picturesque. The intense heat and clearness of the day, the splendour of the sunshine, which turned the grassy patches on the rocks into lustrous velvet, and the dark, dazzling blue of the sea belonged rather to southern Italy than to Norway. As we approached Bergen, however, the sky became gradually overcast, and the evening brought us clouds and showers. Not far from Aalesund was the castle of Rollo, the conqueror of Normandy. All this part of the coast is Viking ground: from these fjords went forth their piratical dragons, and hither they returned, laden with booty, to rest and carouse in their strongholds. They were the buccaneers of the north in their time, bold, brave, with the virtues which belong to courage and hardihood, but coarse, cruel, and brutal. The Viking of Scandinavian song is a splendid fellow; but his original, if we may judge from his descendants, was a stupid, hard-headed, lustful, and dirty giant, whom we should rather not have had for a companion. Harold Haarfager may have learnt in Constantinople to wash his face, and comb his beautiful hair, but I doubt if many of his followers imitated him. Let us hope that Ingeborg changed her dress occasionally, and that Balder's temple was not full of fleas; that Thorsten Vikingsson placed before his guests something better than fladbröd and rancid butter; and that Björn and Frithiof acted as honestly towards strangers as towards each other. The Viking chiefs, undoubtedly, must have learned the comfort of cleanliness and the delights of good living, but if such habits were general, the nation has greatly degenerated since their time.

We stayed on deck until midnight, notwithstanding the rain, to see the grand rock of Hornelen, a precipice 1200 feet high. The clouds lifted a little, and there was a dim, lurid light in the sky as our steamer swept under the awful cliff. A vast, indistinct mass, reaching apparently to the zenith, the summit crowned with a pointed tour, resembling the Cathedral of Drontheim, and the sides scarred with deep fissures, loomed over us. Now a splintered spire disengaged itself from the gloom, and stood defined against the sky; lighter streaks marked the spots where portions had slid away; but all else was dark, uncertain, and sublime. Our friendly captain had the steamer's guns discharged as we were abreast of the highest part. There were no separate echoes, but one tremendous peal of sound, prolonged like the note of an organ-pipe, and gradually dying away at the summit in humming vibrations.

Next morning, we were sailing in a narrow strait, between perpendicular cliffs, fluted like basaltic pillars. It was raining dismally, but we expected nothing else in the neighbourhood of Bergen. In this city the average number of rainy days in a year is two hundred. Bergen weather has become a by-word throughout the north, and no traveller ventures to hope for sunshine when he turns his face thither. "Is it still raining at Bergen?" ask the Dutch skippers when they meet a Norwegian captain. "Yes, blast you; is it still blowing at the Texel?" is generally the response.

We took on board four or five lepers, on their way to the hospital at Bergen. A piece of oil-cloth had been thrown over some spars to shield them from the rain, and they sat on deck, avoided by the other passengers, a melancholy picture of disease and shame. One was a boy of fourteen, upon whose face wart-like excrescences were beginning to appear; while a woman, who seemed to be his mother, was hideously swollen and disfigured. A man, crouching down with his head between his hands, endeavoured to hide the seamed and knotted mass of protruding blue flesh, which had once been a human face. The forms of leprosy, elephantiasis, and other kindred diseases, which I have seen in the East, and in tropical countries, are not nearly so horrible. For these unfortunates there was no hope. Some years, more or less, of a life which is worse than death, was all to which they could look forward. No cure has yet been discovered for this terrible disease. There are two hospitals in Bergen, one of which contains about five hundred patients; while the other, which has recently been erected for the reception of cases in the earlier stages, who may be subjected to experimental courses of treatment, has already one hundred. This form of leprosy is supposed to be produced partly by an exclusive diet of salt fish, and partly by want of personal cleanliness. The latter is the most probable cause, and one does not wonder at the result, after he has had a little experience of Norwegian filth. It is the awful curse which falls upon such beastly habits of life. I wish the Norwegians could be made Mussulmen for awhile, for the sake of learning that cleanliness is not only next to godliness, but a necessary part of it. I doubt the existence of filthy Christians, and have always believed that St. Jerome was atrociously slandered by the Italian painters. But is there no responsibility resting upon the clergymen of the country, who have so much influence over their flocks, and who are themselves clean and proper persons?

Bergen is also, as I was informed, terribly scourged by venereal diseases. Certainly, I do not remember a place, where there are so few men—tall, strong, and well-made as the people generally are—without some visible mark of disease or deformity. A physician of the city has recently endeavoured to cure syphilis in its secondary stage, by means of inoculation, having first tried the experiment upon himself; and there is now a hospital where this form of treatment is practiced upon two or three hundred patients, with the greatest success, as another physician informed me. I intended to have visited it, as well as the hospital for lepers; but the sight of a few cases, around the door of the latter establishment, so sickened me, that I had no courage to undertake the task.

Let me leave these disagreeable themes, and say that Bergen is one of the most charmingly picturesque towns in all the North. Its name, "The Mountain," denotes one of its most striking features. It is built upon two low capes, which project from the foot of a low mountain, two thousand feet high, while directly in its rear lies a lovely little lake, about three miles in circumference. On the end of the northern headland stands the fortress of Berghenhuus, with the tall square mass of Walkendorf's Tower, built upon the foundations of the former palace of King Olaf Kyrre, the founder of the city. The narrow harbour between is crowded with fishing-vessels,—during the season often numbering from six to eight hundred,—and beyond it the southern promontory, quite covered with houses, rises steeply from the water. A public grove, behind the fortress, delights the eye with its dark-green mounds of foliage; near it rise the twin towers of the German Church, which boasts an age of nearly seven hundred years, and the suburbs on the steep mountain-sides gradually vanish among gardens and country-villas, which are succeeded by farms and grazing fields, lying under the topmost ridges of the bare rock. The lake in the rear is surrounded with the country residences of the rich merchants—a succession of tasteful dwellings, each with its garden and leafy arbours, its flowers and fountains, forming a rich frame to the beautiful sheet of water. Avenues of fine old lindens thread this suburban paradise, and seats, placed at the proper points, command views of which one knows not the loveliest. Everything has an air of ancient comfort, taste, and repose. One sees yet, the footsteps of mighty Hansa, who for three centuries reigned here supreme. The northern half of Bergen is still called the "German Quarter," and there are very few citizens of education who do not speak the language.

With one or two exceptions, the streets are rough and narrow. There are no quaint peculiarities in the architecture, the houses being all of wood, painted white or some light colour. At every door stands a barrel filled with water, to be ready in case of fire. Owing to the great number of fishing-vessels and its considerable foreign trade, Bergen is a much more lively and bustling place than either Christiania or Drontheim. The streets are well populated, and the great square at the head of the harbour is always thronged with a motley concourse of fishermen, traders, and country people. Drunkenness seems to be a leading vice. I saw, at least, fifty people, more or less intoxicated, in the course of a short walk, one afternoon. The grog shops, however, are rigidly closed at six o'clock on Saturday evening, and remain so until Monday morning, any violation or evasion of the law being severely punished. The same course has been adopted here as in Sweden; the price of brandy has been doubled, by restrictions on its manufacture, and every encouragement has been afforded to breweries. The beer of Christiania is equal in flavour and purity to any in the world, and it is now in great demand all over Norway.

The day after our arrival the sky cleared again, and we were favoured with superb weather; which might well be the case, as the people told me it had previously been raining every day for a month. The gardens, groves,

248

and lawns of velvet turf, so long moistened, now blazed out with splendid effect in the hot August sunshine. "Is there such a green anywhere else in the world?" asked my friend. "If anywhere, only in England—but scarcely there," I was obliged to confess. Yet there was an acquaintance of mine in Bergen, a Hammerfest merchant, who, in this rare climax of summer beauty, looked melancholy and dissatisfied. "I want to get back to the north," said he, "I miss our Arctic summer. These dark nights are so disagreeable, that I am very tired of them. There is nothing equal to our three months of daylight, and they alone reconcile us to the winter." Who will say, after this, that anything more than the fundamental qualities of human nature are the same in all climates? But from the same foundation you may build either a Grecian temple or a Chinese pagoda.

The lions of Bergen are soon disposed of. After you have visited the fortress and admired the sturdy solidity of Walkendorf's Tower, you may walk into the German church which stands open (or did, when we were there), without a soul to prevent you from carrying off some of the queer old carved work and pictures. The latter are hideous enough to be perfectly safe, and the church, though exceedingly quaint and interesting, is not beautiful. Then you may visit the museum, which contains an excellent collection of northern fish, and some very curious old furniture. The collection of antiquities is not remarkable; but it should be remembered that the museum has been created within the last twenty years, and is entirely the result of private taste and enterprise. One of the most singular things I saw was a specimen (said to be the only one in existence) of a fish called the "herring-king," about twelve feet in length by one in thickness, and with something of the serpent in its appearance. The old Kraaken has not shown himself for a number of years, possibly frightened away by the appearance of steamers in his native waters. In spite of all the testimony which Capell Brooke has collected in favour of his existence, he is fast becoming a myth.

Bergen, we found, is antiquated in more respects than one. On sending for horses, on the morning fixed for our departure, we were coolly told that we should have to wait twenty-four hours; but after threatening to put the law in force against the skyds-skaffer, he promised to bring them by one o'clock in the afternoon. In this city of 30,000 inhabitants, no horses are kept in readiness at the post-station; but are furnished by farmers somewhere at a distance. In the matter of hotels, however, Bergen stands in the front rank of progress, rivalling Christiania and Drontheim. The fare is not so good, and the charges are equally high. There are two little inns, with five or six rooms each, and one boarding-house of the same size. We could only get one small room, into which all three were packed, at a charge of a dollar and a quarter per day; while for two wretched meals we paid a dollar and a half each. The reader may judge of our fare from the fact that one day our soup was raspberry juice and water, and another time, cold beer, flavoured with pepper and cinnamon. Add tough beafsteaks swimming in grease and rancid butter, and you have the principal ingredients. For the first time in my life I found my digestive powers unequal to the task of mastering a new national diet.

CHAPTER XXX. A TRIP TO THE VÖRING-FOSS.

After waiting only five hours, we obtained three horses and drove away from Bergen. It was a superb afternoon, spotlessly blue overhead, with still bluer water below, and hills of dark, velvety verdure throbbing and sparkling in the sunshine, and the breezes from off the fjord. We sped past the long line of suburban gardens, through the linden avenues, which, somehow or other, suggested to me the days of the Hanseatic League, past Tivoli, the Hoboken of Bergen, and on the summit of the hill beyond stopped to take a parting look at the beautiful city. She sat at the foot of her guardian mountain, across the lake, her white towers and red roofs rising in sharp relief against the purple background of the islands which protect her from the sea. In colour, form, and atmospheric effect, the picture was perfect. Norway is particularly fortunate in the position and surroundings of her three chief cities. Bergen bears away the palm, truly, but either of them has few rivals in Europe.

Our road led at first over well-cultivated hills dotted with comfortable farmhouses—a rolling, broken country enclosed by rugged and sterile groups of hills. After some miles we turned northward into a narrow valley running parallel to the coast line. The afternoon sun, shining over the shoulder of the mountain-ridge on our left, illuminated with dazzling effect the green pastures in the bosom of the valley, and the groves of twinkling birch and sombre fir on the opposite slope. I have never seen purer tints in the sunshine—never a softer transparency in the shadows. The landscape was ideal in its beauty, except the houses, whose squalor and discomfort were real. Our first station lay off the road, on a hill. A very friendly old man promised to get us horses as soon as possible, and his wife set before us the best fare the house afforded—milk, oaten shingles, and bad cheese. The house was dirty, and the aspect of the family bed, which occupied one end of the room, merely divided by boards into separate compartments for the parents, children and servants was sufficient to banish sleep. Notwithstanding the poverty of the place, the old woman set a good value upon her choice provender. The horses were soon forthcoming, and the man, whose apparent kindness increased every moment, said to me, "Have I not done well? Is it not very well that I have brought you horses so soon?" I assented cheerfully, but he still repeated the same questions, and I was stupid enough not to discover their meaning, until he added; "I have done everything so well, that you ought to give me something for it." The naïve manner of this request made it seem reasonable, and I gave him something accordingly, though a little disappointed, for I had congratulated myself on finding at last a friendly and obliging skyds-skaffer (Postmaster) in Norway.

Towards evening we reached a little village on the shore of the Osterfjord. Here the road terminated, and a water station of eighteen miles in length lay before us. The fjords on the western coast of Norway are narrow, shut in by lofty and abrupt mountains, and penetrate far into the land—frequently to the distance of a hundred miles. The general direction of the valleys is parallel to the line of the coast, intersecting the fjords at nearly a right angle, so that they, in connection with these watery defiles, divide the mountains into immense irregular blocks, with very precipitous sides and a summit table-land varying from two to four thousand feet above the sea level. For this reason there is no continuous road in all western Norway, but alternate links of land and water—boats and post-horses. The deepest fjords reach very nearly to the spinal ridge of the mountain region, and a land-road from Bergen to this line would be more difficult to construct than any of the great highways across the Alps. In proportion to her population and means, Norway has done more for roads than any country in the world. Not only her main thoroughfares, but even her by-ways, give evidence of astonishing skill, industry, and perseverance. The Storthing has recently appropriated a sum of $188,000 for the improvement of roads, in addition to the repairs which the farmers are obliged to make, and which constitute almost their only tax, as there is no assessment whatever upon landed property. There seems a singular incongruity, however, in finding such an evidence of the highest civilisation, in connection with the semi-barbaric condition of the people. Generally, the improvement of the means of communication in a country is in the ratio of its social progress.

As we were obliged to wait until morning before commencing our voyage, we set about procuring supper and lodging. Some dirty beds in a dirty upper room constituted the latter, but the former was a doubtful affair. The landlord, who persisted in calling me "Dock," made a foraging excursion among the houses, and, after some time, laid before us a salted and smoked leg of mutton, some rancid butter, hard oaten bread, and pestilential cheese. I ate as a matter of duty towards my body, but my companions were less conscientious. We deserve no credit for having risen early the next morning, neither was there any self-denial in the fact of our being content with a single cup of coffee. The boatmen, five in number, who had been engaged the evening before, took our carrioles apart and stowed them in the stern, while we three disposed ourselves very uneasily in the narrow bow. As we were about pushing off, one of the men stepped upon a stone and shouted in a loud voice, "Come and help us, fairies!"—whereat the others laughed heartily. The wind was against us, but I thought the men hugged the shore much more than was necessary. I noticed the same thing afterwards, and spoke of it, but they stated that there were strong currents in these fjords, setting towards the sea. The water, in fact, is but slightly brackish, and the ebb and flow of the tides is hardly felt.

The scenery in the Osterfjord is superb. Mountains, 2000 feet high, inclose and twist it between their interlocking bases. Cliffs of naked rock overhang it, and cataracts fall into it in long zigzag chains of foam. Here and there a little embayed dell rejoices with settlement and cultivation, and even on the wildest steeps, where it seems almost impossible for a human foot to find hold, the people scramble at the hazard of their lives, to reap a scanty harvest of grass for the winter. Goats pasture everywhere, and our boatmen took delight in making the ewes follow us along the cliffs, by imitating the bleating of kids. Towards noon we left the main body of the fjord and entered a narrow arm which lay in eternal shadow under tremendous walls of dark rock. The light and heat of noonday were tropical in their silent intensity, painting the summits far above with dashes of fierce colour, while their bases sank in blue gloom to meet the green darkness of the water. Again and again the heights enclosed us, so that there was no outlet; but they opened as if purposely to make way for us, until our keel grated the pebbly barrier of a narrow valley, where the land road was resumed. Four miles through this gap brought us to another branch of the same fjord, where we were obliged to have our carrioles taken to pieces and shipped for a short voyage.

At its extremity the fjord narrowed, and still loftier mountains overhung it. Shut in by these, like some palmy dell in the heart of the porphyry mountains of the Sahara, lay Bolstadören, a miracle of greenness and beauty. A mantle of emerald velvet, falling in the softest slopes and swells to the water's edge, was thrown upon the valley; the barley had been cut and bound to long upright poles to dry, rising like golden pillars from the shaven stubble; and, to crown all, above the landing-place stood a two-story house, with a jolly fat landlord smoking in the shade, and half-a-dozen pleasant-looking women gossiping in-doors. "Can we get anything to eat?" was the first question. "The gentlemen can have fresh salmon and potatoes, and red wine if they wish it," answered the mistress. Of course we wished it; we wished for any food clean enough to be eatable, and the promise of such fare was like the falling of manna in the desert. The salmon, fresh from the stream, was particularly fine; the fish here is so abundant that the landlord had caught 962, as he informed us, in the course of one season.

We had but two miles of land before another sheet of water intervened, and our carrioles were again taken to pieces. The postillions and boatmen along this route were great scamps, frequently asking more than the legal fare, and in one instance threatened to prevent us from going on unless we paid it. I shall not bore the reader with accounts of our various little squabbles on the road, all of which tended more and more to convince us, that unless the Norwegians were a great deal more friendly, kind, and honest a few years ago than they are now, they have been more over-praised than any people in the world. I must say, however, that they are bungling swindlers, and could only be successful with the greenest of travellers. The moment an imposition is resisted, and the stranger shows himself familiar with the true charges and methods of travel, they give up the attempt; but the desire to cheat is only less annoying to one than cheating itself. The fees for travelling by skyds are, it is true, disproportionably low, and in many instances the obligation to furnish horses is no doubt an actual loss to the farmer. Very often we would have willingly paid a small increase upon the legal rates if it had been asked for as a favour; but when it was boldly demanded as a right, and backed by a falsehood, we went not a stiver beyond the letter of the law.

Landing at Evanger, an intelligent landlord, who had four brothers in America, gave us return horses to Vossevangen, and we enjoyed the long twilight of the warm summer evening, while driving along the hills which overlook the valley connecting the lakes of Vossevangen and Evanger. It was a lovely landscape, ripe with harvest, and the air full of mellow, balmy odours from the flowers and grain. The black spire of Vossevangen church, standing dark against the dawning moonlight, was the welcome termination of our long day's journey, and not less welcome were our clean and comfortable quarters in the house of a merchant there. Here we left the main road across Norway, and made an excursion to the Vöring-Foss, which lies beyond the Hardanger Fjord, about fifty miles distant, in a south-eastern direction.

Vossevangen, in the splendour of a cloudless morning, was even more beautiful than as a moonlit haven of repose. The compact little village lay half buried in trees, clustered about the massive old church, with its black, pointed tower, and roof covered with pitched shingles, in the centre of the valley, while the mountains around shone bald and bright through floating veils of vapour which had risen from the lake. The people were all at work in the fields betimes, cutting and stacking the barley. The grass-fields, cut smooth and close, and of the softest and evenest green, seemed kept for show rather than for use. The bottom of the valley along which we drove, was filled with an unbroken pine forest, inclosing here and there a lake,

"Where Heaven itself, brought down to Earth,

Seemed fairer than above;"

while the opposite mountain rose rich with harvest fields and farmhouses. There are similar landscapes between Fribourg and Vevay, in Switzerland— finer, perhaps, except that all cultivated scenery in Norway gains wonderfully in effect from the savage environment of the barren fields. Here, cultivation is somewhat of a phenomenon, and a rich, thickly settled valley strikes one with a certain surprise. The Norwegians have been accused of neglecting agriculture; but I do not see that much more could be expected of them. The subjugation of virgin soil, as we had occasion to notice, is a serious work. At the best, the grain harvests are uncertain, while fish are almost as sure as the season; and so the surplus agricultural population either emigrates or removes to the fishing grounds on the coast. There is, undoubtedly, a considerable quantity of wild land which could be made arable, but the same means, applied to the improvement of that which is at present under cultivation, would accomplish far more beneficent results.

Leaving the valley, we drove for some time through pine forests, and here, as elsewhere, had occasion to notice the manner in which this source of wealth has been drained of late years. The trees were very straight and beautiful, but there were none of more than middle age. All the fine old timber had been cut away; all Norway, in fact, has been despoiled in like manner, and the people are but just awaking to the fact, that they are killing a goose which lays golden eggs. The government, so prudently economical that it only allows $100,000 worth of silver to be quarried annually in the mines of Kongsberg, lest the supply should be exhausted, has, I believe, adopted measures for the preservation of the forests; but I am not able to state their precise character. Except in valleys remote from the rivers and fjords, one now finds very little mature timber.

"The tallest pine,

Hewn on Norwegian hills, to be the mast

Of some great admiral,"

I have not yet seen.

We at last came upon a little lake, in a close glen with walls 1000 feet high. Not suspecting that we had ascended much above the sea-level, we were surprised to see the gorge all at once open below us, revealing a dark-blue lake, far down among the mountains. We stood on the brink of a wall, over which the stream at our side fell in a "hank" of divided cataracts. Our road was engineered with great difficulty to the bottom of the steep, whence a gentler descent took us to the hamlet of Vasenden, at the head of the lake. Beyond this there was no road for carrioles, and we accordingly gave ours in charge of a bright, active and intelligent little postmaster, twelve years old. He and his mother then rowed us across the lake to the village of Graven, whence there was a bridle-road across the mountains to a branch of the Hardanger Fjord. They demanded only twelve skillings (ten cents) for the row of three miles, and then posted off to a neighbouring farmhouse to engage horses for us.

There was a neat white dwelling on the hill, which we took to be the parsonage, but which proved to be the residence of an army captain on leave, whom we found sitting in the door, cleaning his gun, as we approached. He courteously ushered us into the house, and made his appearance soon afterwards in a clean shirt, followed by his wife, with wine and cakes upon a tray. I found him to be a man of more than ordinary intelligence, and of an earnest and reflective turn of mind, rare in men of his profession. He spoke chiefly of the passion for emigration which now possesses the Norwegian farmers, considering it not rendered necessary by their actual condition, but rather one of those contagions which spread through communities and nations, overcoming alike prudence and prejudice. He deplored it as retarding the development of Norway. Personal interest, however, is everywhere stronger than patriotism, and I see no signs of the emigration decreasing for some years to come.

After waiting a considerable time, we obtained two horses and a strapping farmer's son for guide. The fellow was delighted to find out where we came from, and was continually shouting to the people in the fields: "Here these are Americans: they were born there!" whereat the people stared, saluted, and then stared again. He shouldered our packs and marched beside the horses with the greatest ease. "You are strong," I remarked. "Yes," he replied, "I am a strong Normand," making his patriotism an excuse for his personal pride. We had a terribly tough pull up the mountain, through fine woods, to the summit level of the field. The view backwards, over the lake, was enchanting, and we lingered long on the steep, loth to lose it. Turning again, a desolate lake lay before us, heathery swells of the bleak table-land and distant peaks, touched with snow. Once upon the broad, level summit of a Norwegian field, one would never guess what lovely valleys lie under those misty breaks which separate its immense lobes—what gashes of life and beauty penetrate its stony heart. There are, in fact, two Norways: one above—a series of detached, irregular masses, bleak, snowy, wind-swept and heather-grown, inhabited by herdsmen and hunters: and one below—a ramification of narrow veins of land and water, with fields and forests, highways and villages.

So, when we had traversed the upper land for several miles, we came to a brink overlooking another branch of the lower land, and descended through thick woods to the farms of Ulvik, on the Eyfjord, an arm of the Hardanger. The shores were gloriously beautiful; slopes of dazzling turf inclosed the bright blue water, and clumps of oak, ash, and linden, in park-like groups, studded the fields. Low red farmhouses, each with its hollow square of stables and granaries, dotted the hill-sides, and the people, male and female, were everywhere out reaping the ripe barley and piling it, pillar-wise, upon tall stakes. Owing to this circumstance we were obliged to wait some time for oarsmen. There was no milk to be had, nor indeed anything to eat, notwithstanding the signs of plenty on all sides. My friend, wandering from house to house, at last discovered an old man, who brought him a bowl of mead in exchange for a cigar. Late in the afternoon two men came, put us into a shabby and leaky boat, and pulled away slowly for Vik, ten miles distant.

The fjord was shut in by lofty and abrupt mountains, often interrupted by deep lateral gorges. This is the general character of the Hardanger Fjord, a broad winding sheet of water, with many arms, but whose extent is diminished to the eye by the grandeur of its shores. Nothing can be wilder or more desolate than this scenery, especially at the junction of the two branches, where all signs of habitation are shut out of sight, and one is surrounded by mighty precipices of dark-red rock, vanishing away to the eastward in a gloomy defile. It was three hours and a half before we reached Vik, at the head of a bay on the southern side. Here, however, some English fishermen were quartered and we made sure of a supper. The landlord, of course, received their superfluous salmon, and they were not the men to spare a potato-field, so both were forthcoming, and in the satisfaction of appeased hunger, we were willing to indorse the opinion of a former English traveller in the guest's book: "This place seems to me a paradise, although very probably it is not one." The luxury of fishing, which I never could understand, has taught the Norwegians to regard travellers as their proper prey. Why should a man, they think, pay 50l. for the privilege of catching fish, which he gives away as soon as caught, unless he don't know how else to get rid of his money? Were it not that fishing in Norway includes pure air, hard fare, and healthy exercise, I should agree with somebody's definition of angling, "a rod with a fly at one end and a fool at the other;" but it is all that, and besides furnished us with a good meal more than once; wherefore I respect it.

We were now but eight miles from the Vöring-Foss, and set out betimes the next morning, taking with us a bottle of red wine, some dry bread, and Peder Halstensen as guide. I mention Peder particularly, because he is the only jolly, lively, wide-awake, open-hearted Norwegian I have ever seen. As rollicking as a Neapolitan, as chatty as an Andalusian, and as frank as a Tyrolese, he formed a remarkable contrast to the men with whom we had hitherto come in contact. He had long black hair, wicked black eyes, and a mouth which laughed even when his face was at rest. Add a capital tenor voice, a lithe, active frame, and something irresistibly odd and droll in his motions, and you have his principal points. We walked across the birch-wooded isthmus behind Vik to the Eyfjordsvand, a lake about three miles long, which completely cuts off the further valley, the mountains on either side falling to it in sheer precipices 1000 feet high.

We embarked in a crazy, leaky boat, Peder pulling vigorously and singing. "Frie dig ved lifvet" ("Life let us cherish"), with all the contentment on his face which is expressed in Mozart's immortal melody. "Peder," said I, "do you know the national song of Norway?" "I should think so," was his answer, stopping short in the midst of a wild fjeld-song, clearing his throat, and singing with a fervour and enthusiasm which rang wide over the lonely lake:—

"Minstrel, awaken the harp from its slumbers,

Strike for old Norway, the land of the free!

High and heroic, in soul-stirring numbers,

Clime of our fathers, we strike it for thee!

Old recollections awake our affections—

Hallow the name of the land of our birth;

Each heart beats its loudest, each cheek glows its proudest,

For Norway the ancient, the throne of the earth!"[D]

"Dost thou know," said he, becoming more familiar in his address, "that a lawyer (by the name of Bjerregaard) wrote this song, and the Storthing at Christiania gave him a hundred specie dollars for it. That was not too much, was it?" "No," said I, "five hundred dollars would have been little enough for such a song." "Yes, yes, that it would," was his earnest assent; and as I happened at that moment to ask whether we could see the peaks of the Halling Jökeln, he commenced a sœter-song of life on the lofty fjeld—a song of snow, and free winds, and blue sky. By this time we had reached the other end of the lake, where, in the midst of a little valley of rich alluvial soil, covered with patches of barley and potatoes, stood the hamlet of Sæbö. Here Peder procured a horse for my friend, and we entered the mouth of a sublime gorge which opened to the eastward—a mere split in the mighty ramparts of the Hardanger-Fjeld. Peder was continually shouting to the people in the fields: "Look here! These are Americans, these two, and the other one is a German! This one talks Norsk, and the others don't."

We ascended the defile by a rough footpath, at first through alder thickets, but afterwards over immense masses of rocky ruin, which had tumbled from the crags far above, and almost blocked up the valley. For silence, desolation, and awful grandeur, this defile equals any of the Alpine passes. In the spring, when the rocks, split by wedges of ice, disengage themselves from the summit, and thunder down upon the piled wrecks of ages, it must be terribly sublime. A bridge, consisting of two logs spanned across abutments of loose stones, and vibrating strongly under our tread, took us over the torrent. Our road, for some distance was now a mere staircase, scrambling up, down, under, over, and between the chaos of sundered rocks. A little further, and the defile shut in altogether, forming a cul de sac of apparently perpendicular walls, from 2000 to 3000 feet high. "How are we to get out of this?" I asked Peder. "Yonder," said he, pointing to the inaccessible summit in front. "But where does the stream come from?" "That you will soon see." Lo! all at once a clean split from top to bottom disclosed itself in the wall on our left, and in passing its mouth we had a glimpse up the monstrous chasm, whose dark-blue sides, falling sheer 3000 feet, vanished at the bottom in eternal gloom and spray.

Crossing the stream again, we commenced ascending over the débris of stony avalanches, the path becoming steeper and steeper, until the far-off summit almost hung over our heads. It was now a zigzag ladder, roughly thrown together, but very firm. The red mare which my friend rode climbed it like a cat, never hesitating, even at an angle of 50°, and never making a false step. The performance of this noble animal was almost incredible. I should never have believed a horse capable of such gymnastics, had I not seen it with my own eyes, had I not mounted her myself at the most difficult points, in order to test her powers. You, who have climbed the Mayenwand, in going from the glacier of the Rhone to the Grimsel, imagine a slant higher, steeper, and composed of loose rocks, and you will have an exact picture of our ascent. We climbed well; and yet it took us just an hour and a half to reach the summit.

We were now on the great plateau of the Hardanger Fjeld, 2500 feet above the sea. A wild region lay before us—great swells, covered with heather, sweeping into the distance and given up to solitude and silence. A few isolated peaks, streaked with snow, rose from this upper level; and a deep break on our left revealed the top of the chasm through which the torrent made its way. At its extremity, a mile or more distant, rose a light cloud of vapour, seeming close at hand in the thin mountain air. The thick, spongy soil, not more than two feet deep, rests on a solid bed of rock,—the entire Hardanger Fjeld, in fact, is but a single rock,—and is therefore always swampy. Whortleberries were abundant, as well as the multeberry (Rubus chamœmorus), which I have found growing in Newfoundland; and Peder, running off on the hunt of them, was continually leading us astray. But at last, we approached the wreath of whirling spray, and heard the hollow roar of the Vöring-Foss. The great chasm yawned before us; another step, and we stood on the brink. I seized the branch of a tough pine sapling as a support and leaned over. My head did not swim; the height was too great for that, the impression too grand and wonderful. The shelf of rock on which I stood projected far out over a gulf 1200 feet deep, whose opposite side rose in one great escarpment from the bottom to a height of 800 feet above my head. On this black wall, wet with eternal spray, was painted a splendid rainbow, forming two thirds of a circle before it melted into the gloom below. A little stream fell in one long thread of silver from the very summit, like a plumb-line dropped to measure the 2000 feet. On my right hand the river, coming down from the level of the fjeld in a torn, twisted, and boiling mass, reached the brink of the gulf at a point about 400 feet below me, whence it fell in a single sheet to the bottom, a depth of between 800 and 900 feet.

Could one view it from below, this fall would present one of the grandest spectacles in the world. In height, volume of water, and sublime surroundings it has no equal. The spectator, however, looks down upon it from a great height above its brink, whence it is so foreshortened that he can only guess its majesty and beauty. By lying upon your belly and thrusting your head out beyond the roots of the pines, you can safely peer into the dread abyss, and watch, through the vortex of whirling spray in its tortured womb, the starry coruscations which radiate from the bottom of the fall, like rockets of water incessantly exploding. But this view, sublime as it is, only whets your desire to stand below, and see the river, with its sprayey crest shining against the sky, make but one leap from heaven to hell. Some persons have succeeded, by entering the chasm at its mouth in the valley below, in getting far enough to see a portion of the fall, the remainder being concealed by a projecting rock; and the time will come, no doubt, when somebody will have energy enough to carry a path to its very foot. I envy the travellers who will then visit the Vöring-Foss.

A short distance above the fall there are a few cabins inhabited by sœters, or herdsmen, whither we repaired to procure some fresh milk. The house was rude and dirty; but the people received us in a friendly manner. The powerful housewife laid aside her hay-rake, and brought us milk which was actually sweet (a rare thing in Norway,) dirty, but not rancid butter, and tolerable cheese. When my friend asked for water, she dipped a pailful from a neighbouring stream, thick with decayed moss and vegetable mould, and handed it to him. He was nice enough to pick out a rotten root before drinking, which one of the children snatched up from the floor and ate. Yet these people did not appear to be in want; they were healthy, cheerful, and contented; and their filthy manner of living was the result of sheer indolence and slovenliness. There was nothing to prevent them from being neat and comfortable, even with their scanty means; but the good gifts of God are always spoiled and wasted in dirty hands.

When we opened our bottle of wine, an exquisite aroma diffused itself through the room—a mingled smell of vine blossoms and ripe grapes. How could the coarse vintage sent to the North, watered and chemically doctored as it is, produce such a miracle? We tasted—superb old Chateau Latour, from the sunniest hill of Bordeaux! By whatever accident it had wandered thither, it did not fall into unappreciative hands. Even Brita Halstendsdatter Höl, the strong housewife, smacked her lips over the glass which she drank after sitting to me for her portrait.

When the sketch was completed, we filled the empty bottle with milk and set out on our return.

FOOTNOTES:

[D] Latham's translation.

CHAPTER XXXI. SKETCHES FROM THE BERGENSTIFT.

Our return from the Vöring-Foss to the hamlet of Sæbö was accomplished without accident or particular incident. As we were crossing the Eyfjordsvand, the stillness of the savage glen, yet more profound in the dusk of evening, was broken by the sudden thunder of a slide in some valley to the eastward. Peder stopped in the midst of "Frie dig ved lifvet" and listened. "Ho!" said he, "the spring is the time when the rocks come down, but that sounds like a big fellow, too." Peder was not so lively on the way back, not because he was fatigued, for in showing us how they danced on the fjeld, he flung himself into the air in a marvellous manner, and turned over twice before coming down, but partly because he had broken our bottle of milk, and partly because there was something on his mind. I waited patiently, knowing that it would come out at last, as indeed it did. "You see," said he, hesitatingly, "some travellers give a drink-money to the guide. It isn't an obligation, you know; but then some give it. Now, if you should choose to give me anything, don't pay it to the landlord for me, because then I won't get it. You are not bound to do so you know but some travellers do it, and I don't know but you might also. Now, if you should, give it directly to me, and then I will have it." When we reached Vik, we called Peder aside and gave him three marks. "Oh, you must pay your bill to the landlord," said he. "But that is your drink-money," I explained. "That?" he exclaimed; "it is not possible! Frie dig ved lifvet," &c., and so he sang, cut a pigeon-wing or two, and proceeded to knot and double knot the money in a corner of his pocket-handkerchief.

"Come and take a swim!" said Peder, reappearing. "I can swim ever since I fell into the water. I tumbled off the pier, you must know, and down I went. Everything became black before my eyes; and I thought to myself, 'Peder, this is the end of you.' But I kicked and splashed nevertheless, until my eyes opened again, wide enough to see where a rope was. Well, after I found I could fall into the water without drowning, I was not afraid to swim." In fact, Peder now swam very well, and floundered about with great satisfaction in the ice cold water. A single plunge was all I could endure. After supper the landlady came in to talk to me about America. She had a son in California, and a daughter in Wisconsin, and showed me their daguerreotypes and some bits of gold with great pride. She was a stout, kindly, motherly body, and paid especial attention to our wants on finding where we came from. Indeed we were treated in the most friendly manner by these good people, and had no reason to complain of our reckoning on leaving. This experience confirms me in the belief that honesty and simplicity may still be characteristics of the Norwegians in the more remote parts of the country.

We bade a cordial farewell to Vik next morning, and set off on our return, in splendid sunshine. Peder was in the boat, rejoiced to be with us again; and we had no sooner gotten under way, than he began singing, "Frie dig ved lifvet." It was an intensely hot day, and the shores of Ulvik were perfectly dazzling. The turf had a silken gloss; the trees stood darkly and richly green, and the water was purest sapphire. "It is a beautiful bay, is it not?" said the farmer who furnished us with horses, after we had left the boat and were slowly climbing the field. I thought I had never seen a finer; but when heaven and earth are in entire harmony, when form, colour and atmosphere accord like some rich swell of music, whatever one sees is perfect. Hence I shall not say how beautiful the bay of Ulvik was to me, since under other aspects the description would not be true.

The farmer's little daughter, however, who came along to take back one of the horses, would have been a pleasant apparition at any time and in any season. She wore her Sunday dress, consisting of a scarlet boddice over a white chemise, green petticoat, and white apron, while her shining flaxen hair was plaited into one long braid with narrow strips of crimson and yellow cloth and then twisted like a garland around her head. She was not more than twelve or thirteen years old, but tall, straight as a young pine, and beautifully formed, with the promise of early maidenhood in the gentle swell of her bosom. Her complexion was lovely—pink, brightened with sunburnt gold,—and her eyes like the blossoms of the forget-me-not, in hue. In watching her firm yet graceful tread, as she easily kept pace with the horse, I could not realise that in a few more years she would probably be no more graceful and beautiful than the women at work in the fields—coarse, clumsy shapes, with frowzy hair, leathery faces, and enormous hanging breasts.

In the Bergenstift, however, one sometimes sees a pretty face; and the natural grace of the form is not always lost. About Vossevangen, for instance, the farmers' daughters are often quite handsome; but beauty, either male or female, is in Norway the rarest apparition. The grown-up women, especially after marriage, are in general remarkably plain. Except among some of the native tribes of Africa, I have nowhere seen such overgrown, loose, pendant breasts as among them. This is not the case in Sweden, where, if there are few beauties, there are at least a great many passable faces. There are marked differences in the blood of the two nations; and the greater variety of feature and complexion in Norway seems to indicate a less complete fusion of the original stocks.

We were rowed across the Graven Lake by an old farmer, who wore the costume of the last century,—a red coat, à la Frederic the Great, long waistcoat, and white knee-breeches. He demanded double the lawful fare, which, indeed, was shamefully small; and we paid him without demur. At Vasenden we found our carrioles and harness in good condition, nothing having been abstracted except a ball of twine. Horses were in waiting, apparently belonging to some well-to-do farmer; for the boys were well dressed, and took especial care of them. We reached the merchant's comfortable residence at Vossevangen before sunset, and made amends on his sumptuous fare for the privations of the past three days.

We now resumed the main road between Christiania and Bergen. The same cloudless days continued to dawn upon us. For one summer, Norway had changed climates with Spain. Our oil-cloths were burnt up and cracked by the heat, our clothes covered with dust, and our faces became as brown as those of Bedouins. For a week we had not a cloud in the sky; the superbly clear days belied the old saying of "weather-breeders."

Our road, on leaving Vossevangen, led through pine-forests, following the course of a stream up a wild valley, enclosed by lofty mountains. Some lovely cataracts fell from the steep on our left; but this is the land of cataracts and there is many a one, not even distinguished by a name, which would be renowned in Switzerland. I asked my postillion the name of the stream beside us. "Oh," said he, "it has none; it is not big enough!" He wanted to take us all the way through to Gudvangen, twenty-eight miles, on our paying double fare, predicting that we would be obliged to wait three hours for fresh horses at each intermediate station. He waited some time at Tvinde, the first station, in the hope that we would yield, but departed suddenly in a rage on seeing that the horses were already coming. At this place, a stout young fellow, who had evidently been asleep, came out of the house and stood in the door staring at us with open mouth for a full hour. The postmaster sat on the step and did likewise. It was the height of harvest-time, and the weather favourable almost to a miracle; yet most of the harvesters lay upon their backs under the trees as we passed. The women appeared to do most of the out-door, as well as the in-door work. They are certainly far more industrious than the men, who, judging from what I saw of them, are downright indolent Evidences of slow, patient, plodding toil, one sees truly; but active industry, thrift, and honest ambition, nowhere.

The scenery increased in wildness and roughness as we proceeded. The summit of Hvitnaset (White-nose) lifted its pinnacles of grey rock over the brow of the mountains on the north, and in front, pale, blue-grey peaks, 5000 feet high, appeared on either hand. The next station was a village of huts on the side of a hill. Everybody was in the fields except one woman, who remained to take charge of the station. She was a stupid creature, but had a proper sense of her duty; for she started at full speed to order horses, and we afterwards found that she must have run full three English miles in the space of half an hour. The emigration to America from this part of Bergenstift has been very great, and the people exhibited much curiosity to see and speak with us.

The scenery became at the same time more barren and more magnificent, as we approached the last station, Stalheim, which is a miserable little village at the head of the famous Naerödal. Our farmer-postillion wished to take us on to Gudvangen with the same horses, urging the same reasons as the former one. It would have been better if we had accepted his proposal; but our previous experience had made us mistrustful. The man spoke truth, however;

hour after hour passed away, and the horses came not. A few miserable people collected about us, and begged money. I sketched the oldest, ugliest and dirtiest of them, as a specimen, but regretted it afterwards, as his gratitude on receiving a trifle for sitting, obliged me to give him my hand. Hereupon another old fellow, not quite so hideous, wanted to be taken also. "Lars," said a woman to the former, "are you not ashamed to have so ugly a face as yours go to America?" "Oh," said he, "it does not look so ugly in the book." His delight on getting the money created some amusement. "Indeed," he protested, "I am poor, and want it; and you need not laugh."

The last gush of sunset was brightening the tops of the savage fjeld when the horses arrived. We had waited two hours and three quarters and I therefore wrote a complaint in the post-book in my best Norsk. From the top of a hill beyond the village, we looked down into the Naerödal. We stood on the brink of a tremendous wall about a thousand feet above the valley. On one side, the stream we had been following fell in a single cascade 400 feet; on the other, a second stream, issuing from some unseen defile, flung its several ribbons of foam from nearly an equal height. The valley, or rather gorge, disappeared in front between mountains of sheer rock, which rose to the height of 3000 feet. The road—a splendid specimen of engineering—was doubled back and forth around the edge of a spur projecting from the wall on which we stood, and so descended to the bottom. Once below, our carrioles rolled rapidly down the gorge, which was already dusky with twilight. The stream, of the most exquisite translucent azure-green colour, rolled between us; and the mountain crests towered so far above, that our necks ached as we looked upwards. I have seen but one valley which in depth and sublimity can equal the Naerödal— the pass of the Taurus, in Asia Minor, leading from Cappadocia into Cilicia. In many places the precipices were 2000 feet in perpendicular height; and the streams of the upper fjeld, falling from the summits, lost themselves in evanescent water-dust before they reached the bottom. The bed of the valley was heaped with fragments of rock; which are loosed from above with every returning spring.

It was quite dark before we reached Gudvangen, thoroughly tired and as hungry as wolves. My postillion, on hearing me complain, pulled a piece of dry mutton out of his pocket and gave it to me. He was very anxious to learn whether brandy and tobacco were as dear in America as in Norway; if so, he did not wish to emigrate. A stout girl had charge of Braisted's horse; the female postillions always fell to his lot. She complained of hard work and poor pay, and would emigrate if she had the money. At Gudvangen we had a boat journey of thirty-five miles before us, and therefore engaged two boats with eight oarsmen for the morrow. The people tried hard to make us take more, but we had more than the number actually required by law, and, as it turned out, quite as many as were necessary. Travellers generally supply themselves with brandy for the use of their boatmen, from an idea that they will be stubborn and dilatory without it. We did so in no single instance; yet our men were always steady and cheerful.

We shipped our carrioles and sent them off in the larger boat, delaying our own departure until we had fortified ourselves with a good breakfast, and laid in some hard bread and pork omelette, for the day. The Gudvangen Fjord, down which we now glided over the glassy water, is a narrow mountain avenue of glorious scenery. The unseen plateaus of the Blaa and Graa Fjelds, on either hand, spilled their streams over precipices from 1000 to 2000 feet in height, above whose cornices shot the pointed summits of bare grey rock, wreathed in shifting clouds, 4000 feet above the sea. Pine-trees feathered the less abrupt steeps, with patches of dazzling turf here and there; and wherever a gentler slope could be found in the coves, stood cottages surrounded by potato-fields and ripe barley stacked on poles. Not a breath of air rippled the dark water, which was a perfect mirror to the mountains and the strip of sky between them, while broad sheets of morning sunshine, streaming down the breaks in the line of precipices, interrupted with patches of fiery colour the deep, rich, transparent gloom of the shadows. It was an enchanted voyage until we reached the mouth of the Aurlands Fjord, divided from that of Gudvangen by a single rocky buttress 1000 feet high. Beyond this point the watery channel is much broader, and the shores diminish in grandeur as they approach the Sogne Fjord, of which this is but a lateral branch.

I was a little disappointed in the scenery of Sogne Fjord, The mountains which enclose it are masses of sterile rock, neither lofty nor bold enough in their forms to make impression, after the unrivalled scenery through which we had passed. The point of Vangnæs, a short distance to the westward, is the "Framnæs" of Frithiof's Saga, and I therefore looked towards it with some interest, for the sake of that hero and his northern lily, Ingeborg. There are many bauta-stones still standing on the shore, but one who is familiar with Tegner's poem must not expect to find his descriptions verified, either in scenery or tradition. On turning eastward, around the point of Fronningen, we were surprised by the sudden appearance of two handsome houses, with orchards and gardens, on the sunny side of the bank. The vegetation, protected in some degree from the sea-winds, was wonderfully rich and luxuriant. There were now occasional pine-woods on the southern shore, but the general aspect of this fjord is bleak and desolate. In the heat and breathless silence of noonday, the water was like solid crystal. A faint line, as if drawn with a pencil along the bases of the opposite mountains, divided them from the equally perfect and palpable mountains inverted below them. In the shadows near us, it was quite impossible to detect the boundary between the substance and its counterpart. In the afternoon we passed the mouth of the northern arms of the fjord, which strike into the heart of the wildest and grandest region of Norway; the valley of Justedal, with its tremendous glaciers, the snowy teeth of the Hurunger, and the crowning peaks of the Skagtolstind. Our course lay down the other arm, to Lærdalsören, at the head of the fjord. By five o'clock it came in sight, at the mouth of a valley opening through the barren flanks on the Fille Fjeld. We landed, after a voyage of ten hours, and found welcome signs of civilisation in a neat but exorbitant inn.

Our boatmen, with the exception of stopping half an hour for breakfast, had pulled steadily the whole time. We had no cause to be dissatisfied with them, while they were delighted with the moderate gratuity we gave them. They were tough, well-made fellows, possessing a considerable amount of endurance, but less actual strength than one would suspect. Braisted, who occasionally tried his hand at an oar, could pull them around with the greatest ease. English travellers whom I have met inform me that in almost every trial they find themselves stronger than the Norwegians. This is probably to be accounted for by their insufficient nourishment. Sour milk and oaten bread never yet fed an athlete. The proportions of their bodies would admit of fine muscular development; and if they cannot do what their Viking ancestors once did, it is because they no longer live upon the spoils of other lands, as they.

CHAPTER XXXII. HALLINGDAL—THE COUNTRY-PEOPLE OF NORWAY.

There are two roads from Lærdalsören to Christiania, the eastern one passing through the districts of Valders and Hadeland, by way of the Little Miösen Lake and the Randsfjord, while the western, after crossing the Fille Fjeld, descends the long Hallingdal to Ringerike. In point of scenery there is little difference between them; but as we intended visiting the province of Tellemark, in Southern Norway, we chose the latter. The valley of the Fille Fjeld, which we entered on leaving Lærdalsören, is enclosed by wild, barren mountains, more isolated and irregular in their forms than the Hardanger and Dovre Fjelds. There were occasional precipices and dancing waterfalls, but in general the same tameness and monotony we had found on the Sogne Fjord. Down the bed of the valley flowed a large rapid stream, clear as crystal, and of a beautiful beryl tint. The cultivation was scanty; and the potato fields, utterly ruined by disease, tainted the air with sickening effluvia. The occasional forests on the hill-sides were of fir and birch, while poplar, ash, and linden grew in the valley. The only fruit-trees I saw were some sour red cherries.

But in the splendour of the day, this unfriendly valley shone like a dell of the Apennines. Not a cloud disturbed the serenity of the sky; the brown grass and yellow moss on the mountains were painted with sunny gold, and the gloss and sparkle of the foliage equalled that of the Italian ilex and laurel. On the second stage a new and superb road carried us through the rugged defile of Saltenaaset. This pass is evidently the effect of some mighty avalanche thousands of ages ago. The valley is blocked up by tremendous masses of rock, hurled one upon the other in the wildest confusion, while the shattered peaks from which they fell still tower far above. Threading this chaos in the shadow of the rocks, we looked across the glen upon a braided chain of foam, twisted together at the end into a long white cascade, which dropped into the gulf below. In another place, a rainbow meteor suddenly flashed across the face of a dark crag, betraying the dusty spray of a fall, else invisible.

On the third stage the road, after mounting a difficult steep, descended into the valley of Borgund, in which stands most probably the most ancient church in Norway. It is a singular, fantastic structure, bristling with spiky spires and covered with a scale armour of black pitched shingles. It is certainly of no more recent date than the twelfth century, and possibly of the close of the eleventh. The architecture shows the Byzantine style in the rounded choir and the arched galleries along the sides, the Gothic in the windows and pointed gables, and the horned ornaments on the roof suggest the pagan temples of the ante-Christian period. A more grotesque affair could hardly be found in Christendom; it could only be matched among the monstrosities of Chinese art. With the exception of the church of Hitterdal, in Tellemark, a building of similar date, this is the best preserved of the few antiquities of Norway. The entire absence of feudal castles is a thing to be noticed. Serfdom never existed here, and one result of this circumstance, perhaps, is the ease with which institutions of a purely republican stamp have been introduced.

Our road still proceeded up the bottom of a rough barren valley, crossing stony headlands on either side. At the station of Haug our course turned to the south-east, climbing a slope leading to the plateau of the Fille Fjeld—a severe pull for our horses in the intense heat. The birch woods gradually diminished in size until they ceased altogether, and the naked plain stretched before us. In this upper land the air was delicious and inspiring. We were more than 3000 feet above the sea, but the summits to the right and left, with their soft gleams of pale gray, lilac and purple hues in the sunshine, and pure blue in shadow, rose to the height of 6000. The heat of the previous ten days had stripped them bare of snow, and the landscape was drear and monotonous. The summits of the Norwegian Fjelds have only the charm of wildness and bleakness. I doubt whether any mountains of equal height exhibit less grandeur in their upper regions. The most imposing features of Norwegian scenery are its deep valleys, its tremendous gorges with their cataracts, flung like banners from steeps which seem to lean against the very sky, and, most of all, its winding, labyrinthine fjords—valleys of the sea, in which the phenomena of the valleys of the land are repeated. I found no scenery in the Bergenstift of so original and impressive a character as that of the Lofoden Isles.

The day was Sunday, and we, of course, expect to see some evidence of it in the appearance of the people. Yet, during the whole day, we found but one clean person—the hostess of an inn on the summit of Fille Fjeld, where we stopped to bait our horses. She was a young fresh-faced woman, in the first year of her wifehood, and her snowy chemise and tidy petticoat made her shine like a star among the dirty and frowzy creatures in the kitchen. I should not forget a boy, who was washing his face in a brook as we passed; but he was young, and didn't know any better. Otherwise the people lounged about the houses, or sat on the rocks in the sun, filthy, and something else, to judge from certain signs. At Haug, forgetting that it was a fast station, where there is no tilsigelse (money for ordering horses) to be paid, I handed the usual sum to the landlady, saying: "This is for tilsigelse." "It is quite right," said she, pocketing the coin.

Skirting an azure lake, we crossed the highest part of the pass, nearly four thousand feet above the sea, and descended a naked valley to the inn of Bjöberg. The landlord received us very cordially; and as the inn promised tolerable accommodation, he easily persuaded us to stop there for the night. His wife wore a frightful costume, which we afterwards found to prevail throughout all Hemsedal and Hallingdal. It consisted simply of a band across the shoulders, above the breasts, passing around the arms and over the back of the neck, with an immense baggy, dangling skirt hanging therefrom to the ancles. Whether she was fat or lean, straight or crooked, symmetrical or deformed, it was impossible to discern, except when the wind blew. The only thing to be said in favour of such a costume is, that it does not impede the development and expansion of the body in any direction. Hence I would strongly recommend its adoption to the advocates of reform in feminine dress at home. There is certainly none of that weight upon the hips, of which they complain in the fashionable costume. It is far more baggy, loose, and hideous than the Bloomer, with the additional advantage of making all ages and styles of beauty equally repulsive, while on the score of health and convenience, there is still less to be said against it. Do not stop at half-way measures, oh, fair reformers!

It seems incredible that, in a pastoral country like Norway, it should be almost impossible to procure sweet milk and good butter. The cattle are of good quality, there is no better grass in the world; and the only explanation of the fact is to be found in the general want of cleanliness, especially among the inhabitants of the mountain districts, which are devoted to pasturage alone. Knowing this, one wonders the less to see no measures taken for a supply of water in the richer grain-growing valleys, where it is so easily procurable. At Bjöberg, for instance, there was a stream of delicious water flowing down the hill, close beside the inn, and four bored pine-trunks would have brought it to the very door; but, instead of that, the landlady whirled off to the stream in her revolving dress, to wash the dishes, or to bring us half a pint to wash ourselves. We found water much more abundant the previous winter in Swedish Lapland.

Leaving Bjöberg betimes, we drove rapidly down Hemsedal, enjoying the pure delicious airs of the upper fjeld. The scenery was bleak and grey; and even the soft pencil of the morning sun failed to impart any charm to it, except the nameless fascination of utter solitude and silence. The valley descends so gradually that we had driven two Norsk miles before the fir-forests in its bed began to creep up the mountain-sides. During the second stage we passed the remarkable peak of Saaten, on the opposite side of the valley—the end or cape of a long projecting ridge, terminating in a scarped cliff, from the very summit of which fell a cascade from three to four hundred feet in height. Where the water came from, it was impossible to guess, unless there were a large deposit of snow in the rear; for the mountains fell away behind Saaten, and the jagged, cleft headland rose alone above the valley. It was a strange and fantastic feature of the landscape, and, to me, a new form in the repertory of mountain aspects.

We now drove, through fir-woods balmy with warm resinous odours, to Ekre, where we had ordered breakfast by förbud. The morning air had given us a healthy appetite; but our spirits sank when the only person at the station, a stupid girl of twenty, dressed in the same bulging, hideous sack, informed us that nothing was to be had. After some persuasion she promised us coffee, cheese, and bread, which came in due time; but with the best will we found it impossible to eat anything. The butter was rather black than yellow, the cheese as detestable to the taste as to the smell, the bread made apparently of saw-dust, with a slight mixture of oat-bran, and the coffee muddy dregs, with some sour cream in a cup, and sugar-candy which appeared to have been sucked and then dropped in the ashes. The original colour of the girl's hands was barely to be distinguished through their coating of dirt; and all of us, tough old travellers as we were, sickened at the sight of her. I verily believe that the poorer classes of the Norwegians are the filthiest people in Europe. They are even worse than the Lapps, for their habits of life allow them to be clean.

After passing Ekre, our view opened down the valley, over a wild stretch of wooded hills, to the blue mountain folds of the Hallingdal, which crosses the Hemsedal almost at right angles, and receives its tributary waters. The forms of the mountains are here more gradual; and those grand sweeps and breaks which constitute the peculiar charms of the scenery of the Bergenstift are met with no longer. We had a hot ride to the next station, where we were obliged to wait nearly an hour in the kitchen, our förbud not having been forwarded from the former station as soon as the law allowed us to expect. A strapping boy of eighteen acted as station master. His trowsers reached considerably above his shoulder blades, leaving barely room for a waistcoat, six inches long, to be buttoned over his collar bone. The characteristic costumes of Norway are more quaint and picturesque in the published illustrations than in the reality, particularly those of Hemsedal. My postillion to this station was a communicative fellow, and gave me some information about the value of labour. A harvest-hand gets from one mark (twenty-one cents) to one and a half daily, with food, or two marks without. Most work is paid by the job; a strong lumber-man may make two and a half marks when the days are long, at six skillings (five cents) a tree—a plowman two marks. In the winter the usual wages of labourers are two marks a week, with board. Shoemakers, tailors, and other mechanics average about the same daily. When one considers the scarcity of good food, and the high price of all luxuries, especially tobacco and brandy, it does not seem strange that the emigration fever should be so prevalent. The Norwegians have two traits in common with a large class of Americans—rampant patriotism and love of gain; but they cannot so easily satisfy the latter without sacrificing the former.

From the village of Göl, with its dark pretty church, we descended a steep of many hundred feet, into Hallingdal, whose broad stream flashed blue in the sunshine far below us. The mountains were now wooded to their very summits; and over the less abrupt slopes, ripe oats and barley-fields made yellow spots of harvest among the dark forests. By this time we were out of smoking material, and stopped at the house of a landhandlare, or country merchant, to procure a supply. A riotous sound came from the door as we approached. Six or eight men, all more or less drunk, and one woman, were inside, singing, jumping, and howling like a pack of Bedlamites. We bought the whole stock of tobacco, consisting of two cigars, and hastened out of the den. The last station of ten miles was down the beautiful Hallingdal, through a country which seemed rich by contrast with Hemsedal and the barren fjeld. Our stopping-place was the village of Næs, which we reached in a famished condition, having eaten nothing all day. There were two landhandlare in the place, with one of whom we lodged. Here we found a few signs of Christianity, such as gardens and decent dresses; but both of the merchant's shops swarmed with rum-drinkers.

I had written, and sent off from Bjöberg, förbud tickets for every station as far as Kongsberg. By the legal regulations, the skyds-skaffer is obliged to send forward such tickets as soon as received, the traveller paying the cost thereof on his arrival. Notwithstanding we had given our förbud twelve hours' start, and had punctually paid the expense at every station, we overtook it at Næs. The postmaster came to know whether we would have it sent on by special express, or wait until some traveller bound the same way would take it for us. I ordered it to be sent immediately, astounded at such a question, until, making the acquaintance of a Scotchman and his wife, who had arrived in advance of us, the mystery was solved. They had spent the night at the first station beyond Bjöberg, where our förbud tickets were given to them, with the request that they would deliver them. They had punctually done so as far as Næs, where the people had endeavoured to prevent them from stopping for the night, insisting that they were bound to go on and carry the förbud. The cool impudence of this transaction reached the sublime. At every station that day, pay had been taken for service unperformed, and it was more than once demanded twice over.

We trusted the repeated assurance of the postmaster at Næs, that our tickets had been forwarded at once, and paid him accordingly. But at the first station next morning we found that he had not done so; and this interlinked chain of swindling lasted the whole day. We were obliged to wait an hour or two at every post, to pay for messengers who probably never went, and then to resist a demand for payment at the other end of the station. What redress was there? We might indeed have written a complaint in imperfect Norsk, which would be read by an inspector a month afterwards; or perhaps it would be crossed out as soon as we left, as we saw done in several cases. Unless a traveller is very well versed in the language and in the laws relating to the skyds system, he has no defence against imposition, and even in such a case, he can only obtain redress through delay. The system can only work equitably when the people are honest; and perhaps they were so when it was first adopted.

Here I must tell an unpleasant truth. There must have been some foundation in the beginning for the wide reputation which the Norwegians have for honest simplicity of character; but the accounts given by former travellers are undeserved praise if applied at present. The people are trading on fictitious capital. "Should I have a written contract?" I asked of a landlord, in relation to a man with whom I was making a bargain. "Oh, no," said he, "everybody is honest in Norway;" and the same man tried his best to cheat me. Said Braisted, "I once heard an old sailor say,—'when a man has a reputation for honesty, watch him!'"—and there is some knowledge of human nature in the remark. Norway was a fresh field when Laing went thither opportunities for imposition were so rare, that the faculty had not been developed; he found the people honest, and later travellers have been content with echoing his opinion. "When I first came to the country," said an Irish gentleman who for ten years past has spent his summers there, "I was advised, as I did not understand the currency, to offer a handful in payment, and let the people take what was due to them." "Would you do it now?" I asked. "No, indeed," said he, "and the man who then advised me, a Norwegian merchant, now says he would not do it either." An English salmon-fisher told me very much the same thing. "I believe they are honest in their intercourse with each other," said he; "but they do not scruple to take advantage of travellers whenever they can." For my own part, I must say that in no country of Europe, except Italy, have I experienced so many attempts at imposition. Another Englishman, who has been farming in Norway for several years, and who employs about forty labourers, has been obliged to procure Swedes, on account of the peculations of native hands. I came to Norway with the popular impression concerning the people, and would not confess myself so disagreeably undeceived, could I suppose that my own experiences were exceptional. I found, however, that they tallied with those of other travellers; and the conclusion is too flagrant to be concealed.

As a general rule, I have found the people honest in proportion as they are stupid. They are quick-witted whenever the spirit of gain is aroused; and the ease with which they pick up little arts of acquisitiveness does not suggest an integrity proof against temptation. It is but a negative virtue, rather than that stable quality rooted in the very core of a man's nature. I may, perhaps, judge a little harshly; but when one finds the love of gain so strongly developed, so keen and grasping, in combination with the four capital vices of the Norwegians—indolence, filth, drunkenness, and licentiousness,—the descent to such dishonest arts as I have described is scarcely a single step. There are, no doubt, many districts where the people are still untempted by rich tourists and sportsmen, and retain the virtues once ascribed to the whole population: but that there has been a general and rapid deterioration of character cannot be denied. The statistics of morality, for instance, show that one child out of every ten is illegitimate; and the ratio has been steadily increasing for the past fifty years. Would that the more intelligent classes would seriously set themselves to work for the good of "Gamle Norge" instead of being content with the poetical flourish of her name!

The following day, from Næs to Green, was a continuation of our journey down the Hallingdal. There was little change in the scenery,—high fir-wooded mountains on either hand, the lower slopes spotted with farms. The houses showed some slight improvement as we advanced. The people were all at work in the fields, cutting the year's satisfactory harvest. A scorching sun blazed in a cloudless sky; the earth was baked and dry, and suffocating clouds of dust rose from under our horses' hoofs. Most of the women in the fields, on account of the heat, had pulled off their body-sacks, and were working in shifts made on the same principle, which reached to the knees. Other garments they had none. A few, recognising us as strangers, hastily threw on their sacks or got behind a barley-stack until we had passed; the others were quite unconcerned. One, whose garment was exceedingly short, no sooner saw us than she commenced a fjeld dance, full of astonishing leaps and whirls to the great diversion of the other hands. "Weel done, cutty sark!" I cried; but the quotation was thrown away upon her.

Green, on the Kröder Lake, which we did not reach until long after dark, was an oasis after our previous experience. Such clean, refined, friendly people, such a neat table, such excellent fare, and such delicious beds we had certainly never seen before. Blessed be decency! blessed be humanity! was our fervent ejaculation. And when in the morning we paid an honest reckoning and received a hearty "lycksame resa!" (a lucky journey!) at parting, we vowed that the place should always be green in our memories. Thence to Kongsberg we had fast stations and civilised people; the country was open, well settled, and cultivated, the scenery pleasant and picturesque, and, except the insufferable heat and dust, we could complain of nothing.

CHAPTER XXXIII. TELLEMARK AND THE RIUKAN FOSS.

Kongsberg, where we arrived on the 26th of August, is celebrated for its extensive silver mines, which were first opened by Christian IV in 1624, and are now worked by the Government. They are doubtless interesting to mineralogists; but we did not visit them. The guide-book says, "The principal entrance to the mines is through a level nearly two English miles in length; from this level you descend by thirty-eight perpendicular ladders, of the average length of five fathoms each, a very fatiguing task, and then find yourself at the bottom of the shaft, and are rewarded by the sight of the veins of native silver"—not a bit of which, after all, are you allowed to put into your pocket. Thank you! I prefer remaining above ground, and was content with having in my possession smelted specimens of the ore, stamped with the head of Oscar I.

The goal of our journey was the Riukan Foss, which lies in Upper Tellemark, on the south-eastern edge of the great plateau of the Hardanger Fjeld. This cascade disputes with the Vöring Foss the supremacy of the thousand waterfalls of Norway. There are several ways from Kongsberg thither; and in our ignorance of the country, we suffered ourselves to be guided by the landlord of our hotel. Let no traveller follow our example! The road he recommended was almost impassable for carrioles, and miserably supplied with horses, while that through Hitterdal, by which we returned, is broad, smooth, and excellent. We left on the morning after our arrival, taking a road which led up the valley of the Lauven for some distance, and then struck westward through the hills to a little station called Moen. Here, as the place was rarely visited by travellers, the people were simple, honest, and friendly. Horses could not be had in less than two hours; and my postillion, an intelligent fellow far gone in consumption, proposed taking the same horse to the next station, fifteen miles further. He accepted my offer of increased pay; but another, who appeared to be the owner of the horses, refused, demanding more than double the usual rates. "How is it?" said I, "that you were willing to bring us to Moen for one and a half marks, and will not take us to Bolkesjö for less than five?" "It was my turn," he answered, "to furnish post-horses. I am bound by law to bring you here at the price fixed by the law; but now I can make my own bargain, and I want a price that will leave me some profit." This was reasonable enough; and we finally agreed to retain two of the horses, taking the postmaster's for a third.

The region we now traversed was almost a wilderness. There were grazing-farms in the valley, with a few fields of oats or barley; but these soon ceased, and an interminable forest enclosed us. The road, terribly rough and stony, crossed spurs of the hills, slowly climbing to a wild summit-level, whence we caught glimpses of lakes far below us, and the blue mountain-ranges in the west, with the pyramidal peak of the Gousta Fjeld crowning them. Bolkesjö, which we reached in a little more than two hours, is a small hamlet on the western slope of the mountain, overlooking a wide tract of lake and forest. Most of the inhabitants were away in the harvest-fields; but the skyds-shaffer, a tall powerful fellow, with a grin of ineffable stupidity on his face, came forward as we pulled in our horses on the turfy square between the rows of magazines. "Can we get horses at once?" "Ne-e-ey!" was his drawling answer, accompanied with a still broader grin, as if the thing were a good joke. "How soon?" "In three hours." "But if we pay fast prices?" He hesitated, scratched his head, and drawled, "In a liten stund" (a "short time"), which may mean any time from five minutes to as many hours. "Can we get fresh milk?" "Ne-e-ey!" "Can we get butter?" "Ne-e-ey!" "What can we get?" "Nothing." Fortunately we had foreseen this emergency, and had brought a meal with us from Kongsberg.

We took possession of the kitchen, a spacious and tolerably clean apartment, with ponderous benches against two sides of it, and two bedsteads, as huge and ugly as those of kings, built along the third. Enormous platters of pewter, earthen and stone ware, were ranged on shelves; while a cupboard, fantastically painted, contained the smaller crockery. There was a heavy red and green cornice above the bed, upon which the names of the host and his wife, with the date of their marriage, were painted in yellow letters. The worthy couple lay so high that several steps were necessary to enable them to reach the bed, in which process their eyes encountered words of admonition, painted upon triangular boards, introduced to strengthen the pillars at the head and foot. One of these inscriptions ran, "This is my bed: here I take my rest in the night, and when morning comes I get up cheerfully and go to work;" and the other, "When thou liest down to sleep think on thy last hour, pray that God will guard thy sleep, and be ready for thy last hour when it comes." On the bottom of the cupboard was a representation of two individuals with chalk-white faces and inky eyes, smoking their pipes and clinking glasses. The same fondness for decorations and inscriptions is seen in all the houses in Tellemark and a great part of Hallingdal. Some of them are thoroughly Chinese in gaudy colour and grotesque design.

In the course of an hour and a half we obtained three strong and spirited stallions, and continued our journey towards the Tind-Sö. During this stage of twelve or thirteen miles, the quality of our carrioles was tested in the most satisfactory manner. Up-hill and down, over stock and stone, jolted on rock and wrenched in gulley, they were whirled at a smashing rate; but the tough ash and firmly-welded iron resisted every shock. For any other than Norwegian horses and vehicles, it would have been hazardous travelling. We were anxious to retain the same animals for the remaining stage to Tinoset, at the foot of the lake; but the postillions refused, and a further delay of two hours was the consequence. It was dark when the new horses came; and ten miles of forest lay before us. We were ferried one by one across the Tind Elv, on a weak, loose raft and got our carrioles up a frightful bank on the opposite side by miraculous luck. Fortunately we struck the post-road from Hitterdal at this place; for it would have been impossible to ride over such rocky by-ways as we had left behind us. A white streak was all that was visible in the gloom of the forest. We kept in the middle of it, not knowing whether the road went up, down, or on a level, until we had gone over it. At last, however, the forest came to an end, and we saw Tind Lake lying still and black in the starlight. All were in bed at Tinoset; but we went into the common sleeping-room, and stirred the people up promiscuously until we found the housewife, who gave us the only supper the house afforded—hard oaten bread and milk. We three then made the most of two small beds.

In the morning we took a boat, with four oarsmen, for Mael, at the mouth of the Westfjord-dal, in which lies the Riukan Foss. There was no end to our wonderful weather. In rainy Norway the sky had for once forgotten its clouds. One after another dawned the bright Egyptian days, followed by nights soft, starry, and dewless. The wooded shores of the long Tind Lake were illuminated with perfect sunshine, and its mirror of translucent beryl broke into light waves under the northern breeze. Yet, with every advantage of sun and air, I found this lake undeserving of its reputation for picturesque beauty. The highest peaks rise to the height of 2000 feet, but there is nothing bold and decided in their forms, and after the splendid fjords of the western coast the scenery appears tame and commonplace. Our boatmen pulled well, and by noon brought us to Hakenaes, a distance of twenty-one miles. Here we stopped to engage horses to the Riukan Foss, as there is no post-station at Mael. While the old man put off in his boat to notify the farmers whose turn it was to supply the animals, we entered the farm-house, a substantial two-story building. The rooms were tolerably clean and well stocked with the clumsy, heavy furniture of the country, which is mostly made by the farmers themselves, every man being his own carpenter, cooper, and blacksmith. There were some odd old stools, made of segments of the trunk of a tree, the upper part hollowed out so as to receive the body, and form a support for the back. I have no doubt that this fashion of seat is as old as the time of the Vikings. The owner was evidently a man in tolerable circumstances, and we therefore cherished the hope of getting a good meal; but all that the old woman, with the best will in the world, was able to furnish, was milk, butter, oaten bread, and an egg apiece. The upper rooms were all supplied with beds, one of which displayed remarkable portraits of the Crown Prince of Denmark and his spouse, upon the head-board. In another room was a loom of primitive construction.

It was nearly two hours before the old farmer returned with the information that the horses would be at Mael as soon as we; but we lay upon the bank for some time after arriving there, watching the postillions swim them across the mouth of the Maan Elv. Leaving the boat, which was to await our return the next day, we set off up the Westfjord-dal, towards the broad cone-like mass of the Gousta-Fjeld, whose huge bulk, 6000 feet in height, loomed grandly over the valley. The houses of Mael, clustered about its little church, were scattered over the slope above the lake; and across the river, amid the fields of grass and grain, stood another village of equal size. The bed of the valley, dotted with farms and groups of farm-houses, appeared to be thickly populated; but as a farmer's residence rarely consists of less than six buildings—sometimes even eight—a stranger would naturally overrate the number of inhabitants. The production of grain, also, is much less than would be supposed from the amount of land under cultivation, owing to the heads being so light. The valley of the Maan, apparently a rich and populous region, is in reality rather the reverse. In relation to its beauty, however, there can be no two opinions. Deeply sunken between the Gousta and another bold spur of the Hardanger, its golden harvest-fields and groves of birch, ash, and pine seem doubly charming from the contrast of the savage steeps overhanging them, at first scantily feathered with fir-trees, and scarred with the tracks of cataracts and slides, then streaked only with patches of grey moss, and at last bleak and sublimely bare. The deeply-channelled cone of the Gousta, with its indented summit, rose far above us, sharp and clear in the thin ether; but its base, wrapped in forests and wet by many a waterfall—sank into the bed of blue vapour which filled the valley.

There was no Arabian, nor even Byzantine blood in our horses; and our attendants—a stout full-grown farmer and a boy of sixteen—easily kept pace with their slow rough trot. In order to reach Tinoset the next day, we had determined to push on to the Riukan Foss the same evening. Our quarters for the night were to be in the house of the old farmer, Ole Torgensen, in the village of Däl, half-way between Mael and the cataract, which we did not reach until five o'clock, when the sun was already resting his chin on the shoulder of the Gousta. On a turfy slope surrounded with groves, above the pretty little church of Däl, we found Ole's gaard. There was no one at home except the daughter, a blooming lass of twenty, whose neat dress, and graceful, friendly deportment, after the hideous feminines of Hallingdal, in their ungirdled sacks and shifts, so charmed us that if we had been younger, more sentimental, and less experienced in such matters, I should not answer for the consequences. She ushered us into the guests' room, which was neatness itself, set before us a bottle of Bavarian beer and promised to have a supper ready on our return.

There were still ten miles to the Riukan, and consequently no time to be lost. The valley contracted, squeezing the Maan between the interlocking bases of the mountains, through which, in the course of uncounted centuries, it had worn itself a deep groove, cut straight and clean into the heart of the rock. The loud, perpetual roar of the vexed waters filled the glen; the only sound except the bleating of goats clinging to the steep pastures above us. The mountain walls on either hand were now so high and precipitous, that the bed of the valley lay wholly in shadow; and on looking back, its further foldings were dimly seen through purple mist. Only the peak of the Gousta, which from this point appeared an entire and perfect pyramid, 1500 feet in perpendicular height above the mountain platform from which it rose, gleamed with a rich bronze lustre in the setting sun. The valley was now a mere ascending gorge, along the sides of which our road climbed. Before us extended a slanting shelf thrust out from the mountain, and affording room for a few cottages and fields; but all else was naked rock and ragged pine. From one of the huts we passed, a crippled, distorted form crawled out on its hands and knees to beg of us. It was a boy of sixteen, struck with another and scarcely less frightful form of leprosy. In this case, instead of hideous swellings and fungous excrescences, the limbs gradually dry up and drop off piecemeal at the joints. Well may the victims of both these forms of hopeless disease curse the hour in which they were begotten. I know of no more awful example of that visitation of the sins of the parents upon the children, which almost always attends confirmed drunkenness, filth, and licentiousness.

When we reached the little hamlet on the shelf of the mountain, the last rays of the sun were playing on the summits above. We had mounted about 2000 feet since leaving the Tind Lake, and the dusky valley yawned far beneath us, its termination invisible, as if leading downward into a lower world. Many hundreds of feet below the edge of the wild little platform on which we stood, thundered the Maan in a cleft, the bottom of which the sun has never beheld. Beyond this the path was impracticable for horses; we walked, climbed, or scrambled along the side of the dizzy steep, where, in many places, a false step would have sent us to the brink of gulfs whose mysteries we had no desire to explore. After we had advanced nearly two miles in this manner, ascending rapidly all the time, a hollow reverberation, and a glimpse of profounder abysses ahead, revealed the neighbourhood of the Riukan. All at once patches of lurid gloom appeared through the openings of the birch thicket we were threading, and we came abruptly upon the brink of the great chasm into which the river falls.

The Riukan lay before us, a miracle of sprayey splendour, an apparition of unearthly loveliness, set in a framework of darkness and terror befitting the jaws of hell. Before us, so high against the sky as to shut out the colours of sunset, rose the top of the valley—the level of the Hardanger table land, on which, a short distance further, lies the Miös-Vand, a lovely lake, in which the Maan Elv is born. The river first comes into sight a mass of boiling foam, shooting around the corner of a line of black cliffs which are rent for its passage, curves to the right as it descends, and then drops in a single fall of 500 feet in a hollow caldron of bare black rock. The water is already foam as it leaps from the summit; and the successive waves, as they are whirled into the air, and feel the gusts which for ever revolve around the abyss, drop into beaded fringes in falling, and go fluttering down like scarfs of the richest lace. It is not water, but the spirit of water. The bottom is lost in a shifting snowy film, with starry rays of foam radiating from its heart, below which, as the clouds shifts, break momentary gleams of perfect emerald light. What fairy bowers of some Northern Undine are suggested in those sudden flashes of silver and green! In that dim profound, which human eye can but partially explore, in which human foot shall never be set, what secret wonders may still lie hidden! And around this vision of perfect loveliness, rise the awful walls wet with spray which never dries, and crossed by ledges of dazzling turf, from the gulf so far below our feet, until, still further above our heads, they lift their irregular cornices against the sky.

I do not think I am extravagant when I say that the Riukan Foss is the most beautiful cataract in the world. I looked upon it with that involuntary suspension of the breath and quickening of the pulse, which is the surest recognition of beauty. The whole scene, with its breadth and grandeur of form, and its superb gloom of colouring, enshrining this one glorious flash of grace, and brightness, and loveliness, is indelibly impressed upon my mind. Not alone during that half hour of fading sunset, but day after day, and night

287

after night, the embroidered spray wreaths of the Riukan were falling before me.

We turned away reluctantly at last, when the emerald pavement of Undine's palace was no longer visible through the shooting meteors of silver foam. The depths of Westfjord-dal were filled with purple darkness: only the perfect pyramid of the Gousta, lifted upon a mountain basement more than 4000 feet in height, shone like a colossal wedge of fire against the violet sky. By the time we reached our horses we discovered that we were hungry, and, leaving the attendants to follow at their leisure, we urged the tired animals down the rocky road. The smell of fresh-cut grain and sweet mountain hay filled the cool evening air; darkness crept under the birches and pines, and we no longer met the home-going harvesters. Between nine and ten our horses took the way to a gaard standing a little off the road; but it did not appear to be Ole Torgensen's, so we kept on. In the darkness, however, we began to doubt our memory, and finally turned back again. This time there could be no mistake: it was not Ole Torgensen's. I knocked at various doors, and hallooed loudly, until a sleepy farmer made his appearance, and started us forward again. He kindly offered to accompany us, but we did not think it necessary. Terribly fatigued and hungry, we at last saw a star of promise—the light of Ole's kitchen window. There was a white cloth on the table in the guests' house, and Ole's charming daughter—the Rose of Westfjord-dalen—did not keep us long waiting. Roast mutton, tender as her own heart, potatoes plump as her cheeks, and beer sparkling as her eyes, graced the board; but emptiness, void as our own celibate lives, was there when we arose. In the upper room there were beds, with linen fresh as youth and aromatic as spring; and the peace of a full stomach and a clear conscience descended upon our sleep.

In the morning we prepared for an early return to Mael, as the boatmen were anxious to get back to their barley-fields. I found but one expression in the guests' book—that of satisfaction with Ole Torgensen, and cheerfully added our amen to the previous declarations. Ole's bill proved his honesty, no less than his worthy face. He brightened up on learning that we were Americans. "Why," said he, "there have only been two Americans here before in all my life; and you cannot be a born American, because you speak Norsk

288

so well." "Oh," said I, "I have learned the language in travelling." "Is it possible?" he exclaimed: "then you must have a powerful intellect." "By no means," said I, "it is a very easy thing; I have travelled much, and can speak six other languages." "Now, God help us!" cried he; "seven languages! It is truly wonderful how much comprehension God has given unto man, that he can keep seven languages in his head at one time. Here am I, and I am not a fool; yet I do not see how it would be possible for me to speak anything but Norsk; and when I think of you, it shows me what wonders God has done. Will you not make a mark under your name, in the book, so that I may distinguish you from the other two?" I cheerfully complied, and hereby notify future visitors why my name is italicised in Ole's book.

We bade farewell to the good old man, and rode down the valley of the Maan, through the morning shadow of the Gousta. Our boat was in readiness; and its couch of fir boughs in the stern became a pleasant divan of indolence, after our hard horses and rough roads. We reached Tinoset by one o'clock, but were obliged to wait until four for horses. The only refreshment we could obtain was oaten bread, and weak spruce beer. Off at last, we took the post-road to Hitterdal, a smooth, excellent highway, through interminable forests of fir and pine. Towards the close of the stage, glimpses of a broad, beautiful, and thickly-settled valley glimmered through the woods, and we found ourselves on the edge of a tremendous gully, apparently the bed of an extinct river. The banks on both sides were composed entirely of gravel and huge rounded pebbles, masses of which we loosened at the top, and sent down the sides, gathering as they rolled, until in a cloud of dust they crashed with a sound like thunder upon the loose shingles of the bottom 200 feet below. It was scarcely possible to account for this phenomenon by the action of spring torrents from the melted snow. The immense banks of gravel, which we found to extend for a considerable distance along the northern side of the valley, seemed rather to be the deposit of an ocean-flood.

Hitterdal, with its enclosed fields, its harvests, and groups of picturesque, substantial farm-houses, gave us promise of good quarters for the night; and when our postillions stopped at the door of a prosperous-looking establishment, we congratulated ourselves on our luck. But (—) never whistle until you are out of the woods. The people seemed decidedly not to like the idea of our remaining, but promised to give us supper and beds. They were stupid, but not unfriendly; and our causes of dissatisfaction were, first, that they were so outrageously filthy, and secondly, that they lived so miserably when their means evidently allowed them to do better. The family room, with its two cumbrous bedsteads built against the wall, and indescribably dirty beds, was given up to us, the family betaking themselves to the stable. As they issued thence in the morning, in single garments, we were involuntary observers of their degree of bodily neatness; and the impression was one we would willingly forget. Yet a great painted desk in the room contained, amid many flourishes, the names and character of the host and hostess, as follows:—"Andres Svennogsen Bamble, and Ragnil Thorkilsdatter Bamble, Which These Two Are Respectable People." Over the cupboard, studded with earthen-ware dishes, was an inscription in misspelt Latin: "Solli Deo Glorria." Our supper consisted of boiled potatoes and fried salt pork, which, having seen the respectable hosts, it required considerable courage to eat, although we had not seen the cooking. Fleas darkened the floor; and they, with the fear of something worse, prevented us from sleeping much. We did not ask for coffee in the morning, but, as soon as we could procure horses, drove away hungry and disgusted from Bamble-Kaasa and its respectable inhabitants.

The church of Hitterdal, larger than that of Borgund, dates from about the same period, probably the twelfth century. Its style is similar, although it has not the same horned ornaments upon the roof, and the Byzantine features being simpler, produce a more harmonious effect. It is a charmingly quaint and picturesque building, and the people of the valley are justly proud of it. The interior has been renovated, not in the best style.

Well, to make this very long chapter short, we passed the beautiful falls of the Tind Elv, drove for more than twenty miles over wild piny hills, and then descended to Kongsberg, where Fru Hansen comforted us with a good dinner. The next day we breakfasted in Drammen, and, in baking heat and stifling dust, traversed the civilised country between that city and Christiania. Our Norwegian travel was now at an end; and, as a snobby Englishman once said to me of the Nile, "it is a good thing to have gotten over."

290

CHAPTER XXXIV. NORWAY AND SWEDEN.

We spent four days in Christiania, after completing our Norwegian travels. The sky was still perfectly clear, and up to the day of our departure no rain fell. Out of sixty days which we had devoted to Norway, only four were rainy—a degree of good fortune which rarely falls to the lot of travellers in the North.

Christiania, from its proximity to the continent, and its character as capital of the country, is sufficiently advanced in the arts of living, to be a pleasant resting-place after the désagrémens and privations of travel in the interior. It has two or three tolerably good and very exorbitant hotels, and some bankers with less than the usual amount of conscience. One of them offered to change some Prussian thalers for my friend, at only ten per cent. less than their current value. The vognmand from whom we purchased our carrioles, endeavoured to evade his bargain, and protested that he had not money enough to repurchase them. I insisted, however, and with such good effect that he finally pulled a roll of notes, amounting to several hundred dollars out of his pocket, and paid me the amount in full. The English travellers whom I met had not fared any better; and one and all of us were obliged to recede from our preconceived ideas of Norwegian character. But enough of an unpleasant theme; I would rather praise than blame, any day, but I can neither praise nor be silent when censure is a part of the truth.

I had a long conversation with a distinguished Norwegian, on the condition of the country people. He differed with me in the opinion that the clergy were to some extent responsible for their filthy and licentious habits, asserting that, though the latter were petits seigneurs, with considerable privileges and powers, the people were jealously suspicious of any attempt to exert an influence upon their lives. But is not this a natural result of the preaching of doctrinal religion, of giving an undue value to external forms and ceremonies? "We have a stubborn people," said my informant; "their excessive self-esteem makes them difficult to manage. Besides, their morals are perhaps better than would be inferred from the statistics. Old habits have been retained, in many districts, which are certainly reprehensible, but which spring from custom rather than depravity. I wish they were less vain and sensitive, since in that case they would improve more rapidly." He stated also that the surprising number of illegitimate births is partly accounted for by the fact that there are a great number of connections which have all the character of marriage except the actual ceremony. This is an affair of considerable cost and show; and many of the poorer people, unable to afford it, live together rather than wait, hoping that a time may come when they will be able to defray the expenses, and legitimate the children who may meanwhile be born. In some cases the parties disagree, the connection is broken off, and each one seeks a new mate. Whatever palliation there may be in particular instances, the moral effect of this custom is unquestionably bad; and the volume of statistics recently published by Herr Sundt, who was appointed by the Storthing to investigate the subject, shows that there is no agricultural population in the world which stands lower in the scale of chastity, than that of Norway.

In the course of our conversation, the gentleman gave an amusing instance of the very sensitiveness which he condemned. I happened, casually, to speak of the Icelandic language. "The Icelandic language!" he exclaimed. "So you also in America call it Icelandic; but you ought to know that it is Norwegian. It is the same language spoken by the Norwegian Vikings who colonised Iceland—the old Norsk, which originated here, and was merely carried thither." "We certainly have some reason," I replied, "seeing that it now only exists in Iceland, and has not been spoken in Norway for centuries; but let me ask why you, speaking Danish, call your language Norsk." "Our language, as written and printed, is certainly pure Danish," said he; "but there is some difference of accent in speaking it." He did not add that this difference is strenuously preserved and even increased by the Norwegians, that they may not be suspected of speaking Danish, while they resist with equal zeal, any approach to the Swedish. Often, in thoughtlessly speaking of the language as Danish, I have heard the ill-humoured reply, "Our language is not Danish, but Norsk." As well might we say at home, "We speak American, not English."

292

I had the good fortune to find Professor Munck, the historian of Norway, at home, though on the eve of leaving for Italy. He is one of the few distinguished literary names the country has produced. Holberg the comedian was born in Bergen; but he is generally classed among the Danish authors. In art, however, Norway takes no mean rank, the names of her painters Dahl, Gude, and Tidemand having a European reputation. Professor Munck is about fifty years of age, and a fine specimen of the Viking stock. He speaks English fluently, and I regretted that the shortness of my stay did not allow me to make further drafts on his surplus intelligence. In the Museum of Northern Antiquities, which is small, as compared with that of Copenhagen, but admirably arranged, I made the acquaintance of Professor Keyser, the author of a very interesting work, on the "Religion of Northmen," a translation of which by Mr. Barclay Pennock, appeared in New York, some three years ago.

I was indebted to Professor Munck, for a sight of the Storthing, or National Legislative Assembly, which was then in session. The large hall of the University, a semi-circular room, something like our Senate Chamber, has been given up to its use, until an appropriate building shall be erected. The appearance and conduct of the body strikingly reminded me of one of our State Legislatures. The members were plain, practical-looking men, chosen from all classes, and without any distinguishing mark of dress. The speaker was quite a young man, with a moustache. Schweigaard the first jurist in Norway, was speaking as we entered. The hall is very badly constructed for sound, and I could not understand the drift of his speech, but was exceedingly struck by the dryness of his manner. The Norwegian Constitution has been in operation forty-three years, and its provisions, in most respects so just and liberal, have been most thoroughly and satisfactorily tested. The Swedes and a small conservative party in Norway, would willingly see the powers of the Storthing curtailed a little; but the people now know what they have got, and are further than ever from yielding any part of it. In the house of almost every Norwegian farmer, one sees the constitution, with the facsimile autographs of its signers, framed and conspicuously hung up. The reproach has been made, that it is not an original instrument—that it is merely a translation of the Spanish Constitution of 1812, a copy of the French Constitution of 1791,

&c.; but it is none the worse for that. Its framers at least had the wisdom to produce the right thing at the right time, and by their resolution and determined attitude to change a subject province into a free and independent state: for, carefully guarded as it is, the union with Sweden is only a source of strength and security.

One peculiarity of the Storthing is, that a majority of its members are, and necessarily must be, farmers; whence Norway is sometimes nicknamed the Farmer State. Naturally, they take very good care of their own interests, one of their first steps being to abolish all taxes on landed property; but in other respects I cannot learn that their rule is not as equitable as that of most legislative bodies. Mügge, in his recently published Nordisches Bilderbuch (Northern Picture Book), gives an account of a conversation which he had with a Swedish statesman on this subject. The latter was complaining of the stubbornness and ignorance of the Norwegian farmers. Mügge asked, (the remainder of the dialogue is too good to be omitted):—

"The Storthing, then, consists of a majority of coarse and ignorant people?"

Statesman. "I will not assert that. A certain practical understanding cannot be denied to most of these farmers, and they often bestow on their sons a good education before giving them the charge of the paternal fields. One, therefore, finds in the country many accomplished men: how could there be 700 students in Christiania, if there were not many farmers' sons among them?"

Author. "But does this majority of farmers in the Storthing commit absurdities? does it govern the country badly, burden it with debts or enact unjust laws?"

Statesman. "That cannot exactly be admitted, although this majority naturally gives its own interests the preference, and shapes the government accordingly. The state has no debts; on the contrary, its treasury is full, an abundance of silver, its bank-notes in demand, order everywhere, and, as you see, an increase of prosperity, with a flourishing commerce. Here lies a statement before me, according to which, in the last six months alone, more than a hundred vessels have been launched in different ports."

Author. "The Farmer-Legislature, then, as I remark, takes care of itself, but is niggardly and avaricious when its own interests are not concerned?"

Statesman. "It is a peculiar state of affairs. In very many respects this reproach cannot be made against the farmers. If anything is to be done for science, or for so-called utilitarian objects, they are always ready to give money. If a deserving man is to be assisted, if means are wanted for beneficial purposes, insane asylums, hospitals, schools, and such like institutions, the Council of State is always sure that it will encounter no opposition. On other occasions, however, these lords of the land are as hard and tough as Norwegian pines, and button up their pockets so tight that not a dollar drops out."

Author. "On what occasions?"

Statesman. "Why, you see (shrugging his shoulders), those farmers have not the least comprehension of statesmanship! As soon as there is any talk of appropriations for increasing the army, or the number of officers, or the pay of foreign ministers, or the salaries of high official persons, or anything of that sort, you can't do anything with them."

Author. (To himself.) "God keep them a long time without a comprehension of statesmanship! If I were a member of the Storthing, I would have as thick a head as the rest of them."

On the 5th of September, Braisted and I took passage for Gottenburg, my friend having already gone home by way of Kiel. We had a smooth sea and an agreeable voyage, and awoke the next morning in Sweden. On the day after our arrival, a fire broke out in the suburb of Haga, which consumed thirteen large houses, and turned more than two hundred poor people out of doors. This gave me an opportunity to see how fires are managed here. It was full half an hour after the alarm-bell was rung before the first engine began to play; the water had to be hauled from the canal, and the machine, of a very small and antiquated pattern, contributed little towards stopping the progress of the flames. The intervention of a row of gardens alone saved the whole suburb from destruction. There must have been from six to eight thousand spectators present, scattered all over the rocky knolls which surround Gottenburg. The fields were covered with piles of household furniture and clothing, yet no guard seemed to be necessary for their protection, and the owners showed no concern for their security.

There is a degree of confidence exhibited towards strangers in Sweden, especially in hotels, at post-stations, and on board the inland steamers, which tells well for the general honesty of the people. We went on board the steamer Werner on the morning of the 8th, but first paid our passage two days afterwards, just before reaching Carlstad. An account book hangs up in the cabin, in which each passenger enters the number of meals or other refreshments he has had, makes his own bill and hands over the amount to the stewardess. In posting, the skjutsbonder very often do not know the rates, and take implicitly what the traveller gives them. I have yet to experience the first attempt at imposition in Sweden. The only instances I heard of were related to me by Swedes themselves, a large class of whom make a point of depreciating their own country and character. This habit of detraction is carried to quite as great an extreme as the vanity of the Norwegians, and is the less pardonable vice of the two.

It was a pleasant thing to hear again the musical Swedish tongue, and to exchange the indifference and reserve of Norway for the friendly, genial, courteous manner of Sweden. What I have said about the formality and affectation of manners, and the rigidity of social etiquette, in the chapters relating to Stockholm, was meant to apply especially to the capital. Far be it from me to censure that natural and spontaneous courtesy which is a characteristic of the whole people. The more I see of the Swedes, the more I am convinced that there is no kinder, simpler, and honester people in the world. With a liberal common school system, a fairer representation, and release from the burden of a state church, they would develop rapidly and nobly.

Our voyage from Gottenburg to Carlstad, on the Wener Lake, had but one noteworthy point—the Falls of Trollhätten. Even had I not been fresh from the Riukan-Foss, which was still flashing in my memory, I should have been disappointed in this renowned cataract. It is not a single fall, but four successive descents, within the distance of half a mile, none of them being over twenty feet in perpendicular height. The Toppö Fall is the only one which at all impressed me, and that principally through its remarkable form. The huge mass of the Gotha River, squeezed between two rocks, slides down a plane with an inclination of about 50°, strikes a projecting rock at the bottom, and takes an upward curve, flinging tremendous volumes of spray, or rather broken water, into the air. The bright emerald face of the watery plane is covered with a network of silver threads of shifting spray, and gleams of pale blue and purple light play among the shadows of the rising globes of foam below.

CHAPTER XXXV. A TRAMP THROUGH WERMELAND AND DALECARLIA.

On leaving Carlstad our route lay northward up the valley of the Klar Elv, in the province of Wermeland, and thence over the hills, by way of Westerdal, in Dalecarlia, to the head of the Siljan Lake. The greater part of this region is almost unknown to travellers, and belongs to the poorest and wildest parts of Sweden. We made choice of it for this reason, that we might become acquainted with the people in their true character, and compare them with the same class in Norway. Our heavy luggage had all been sent on to Stockholm, in the charge of an Irish friend, and we retained no more than could be carried easily in two packs, as we anticipated being obliged to perform part of the journey on foot.

It rained in torrents during the day we spent in Carlstad, and some lumber merchants of Gottenburg, who were on their way to Fryxendal, to superintend the getting down of their rafts, predicted that the deluge would last an entire month. There was always a month of rainy weather at this season they said, and we had better give up our proposed journey. We trusted to our combined good luck however, and were not deceived, for, with the exception of two days, we had charming weather during the remainder of our stay in Sweden. Having engaged a two-horse cart for the first post-station, we left Carlstad on the morning of the 11th of September. The clouds were still heavy, but gradually rolled into compacter masses, giving promise of breaking away. The city is built upon a little island at the head of the lake, whence we crossed to the mainland by a strong old bridge. Our road led eastward through a slightly undulating country, where broad woods of fir and birch divided the large, well cultivated farms. The gårds, or mansions, which we passed, with their gardens and ornamental shrubbery, gave evidence of comfort and competence. The people were in the harvest-fields, cutting oats, which they piled upon stakes to dry. Every one we met saluted us courteously, with a cheerful and friendly air, which was all the more agreeable by contrast with the Norwegian reserve.

At the station, Prestegård, we procured a good breakfast of ham, eggs, and potatoes, and engaged two carts to take us further. We now turned northward over a lovely rolling country, watered with frequent streams,—a land of soft outlines, of woods and swelling knolls, to which the stately old houses gave an expression of contentment and household happiness. At Deye we left our carts, shouldered our packs, and trudged off on foot up the valley of the Klar Elv, which is here a broad lazy stream, filled with tens of thousands of pine-logs, waiting to be carried down to the Wener by the first freshet. The scenery charmed us by its rich and quiet beauty; it was without grand or striking features, but gently undulating, peaceful, and home-like. We found walking very fatiguing in the hot sun, which blazed upon us all the afternoon with a summer heat. The handsome residences and gardens, which we occasionally passed, gave evidence of taste and refinement in their possessors, and there was a pleasant grace in the courteous greetings of the country people whom we met. Towards evening we reached a post-station, and were tired enough to take horses again. It was after dark before we drew up at Ohlsäter, in the heart of Wermeland. Here we found a neat, comfortable room, with clean beds, and procured a supper of superb potatoes. The landlord was a tall, handsome fellow, whose friendly manners, and frank face, breathing honesty and kindness in every lineament, quite won my heart. Were there more such persons in the world, it would be a pleasanter place of residence.

We took horses and bone-shattering carts in the morning, for a distance of thirteen miles up the valley of the Klar Elv. The country was very picturesque and beautiful, well cultivated, and quite thickly settled. The wood in the sheltered bed of the valley was of remarkably fine growth; the birch trees were the largest I ever saw, some of them being over one hundred feet in height. Comfortable residences, with orchards and well-kept gardens attached, were quite frequent, and large sawmills along the river, which in some places was entirely concealed by floating rafts of lumber, gave an air of industry and animation to the landscape. In one place the road was spanned, for a considerable distance, with triumphal arches of foliage. I inquired the meaning of this display of the boy who accompanied us. "Why," said he, "there was a wedding a week ago, at the herregård (gentleman's residence); the young Herr got married, and these arches were put up for him and his bride." The herregård, which we passed soon afterwards, was an imposing mansion, upon an eminence overlooking the valley. Beside it was a jernbruk, or iron-works, from which a tramway, some miles in length, led to the mines.

Resuming our knapsacks, we walked on up the valley. The hills on either side increased in height, and gloomed darkly under a threatening sky. The aspect of the country gradually became wilder, though, wherever there was cultivation, it bore the same evidence of thrift and prosperity. After a steady walk of four hours, we reached the village of Råda, where our road left the beautiful Klar Elv, and struck northwards towards Westerdal, in Dalecarlia. We procured a dinner of potatoes and bacon, with excellent ale, enjoying, meanwhile, a lovely view over a lake to the eastward, which stretched away for ten miles between the wooded hills. The evening was cold and raw: we drove through pine-woods, around the head of the lake, and by six o'clock reached Asplund, a miserable little hamlet on a dreary hill. The post-station was a forlorn cottage with a single room, not of the most inviting appearance. I asked if we could get quarters for the night. "If you will stay, of course you can," said the occupant, an old woman; "but there is no bed, and I can get you horses directly to go on." It was a distance of thirteen miles to the next station, but we yielded to the old woman's hint, and set forward. The road led through woods, which seemed interminable. We were jammed together into a little two-wheeled cart, with the boy between our knees. He seemed much disinclined to hurry the horse, but soon fell asleep, and one of us held him by the collar to prevent his tumbling out, while the other took the lines, and urged on our slow beast. The night was so dark that we had great difficulty in keeping the road, but towards eleven o'clock we emerged from the woods, and found, by shaking the boy, that we were approaching the station at last. This was a little place called Laggasen, on the northern frontier of Wermeland.

Everybody had gone to bed in the hut at which we stopped. We entered the kitchen, which was at the same time the bedroom, and aroused the inmates, who consisted of a lonely woman, with two or three children. She got up in a very scanty chemise, lit a wooden splinter, and inspected us, and, in answer to our demand for a bed, informed us that we would have to lie upon the floor. We were about to do this, when she said we could get good quarters at the Nore, on the top of the hill. Her earnestness in persuading us to go made me suspect that she merely wanted to get rid of us, and I insisted that she should accompany us to show the way. After some hesitation she consented, and we set out. We first crossed a broad swamp, on a road made of loose logs, then climbed a hill, and trudged for some distance across stubble-fields, until my patience was quite worn out, and Braisted made use of some powerful maritime expressions. Finally, we reached a house, which we entered without more ado. The close, stifling atmosphere, and the sound of hard breathing on all sides, showed us that a whole family had been for some hours asleep there. Our guide thumped on the door, and hailed, and at length somebody awoke. "Can you give two travellers a bed?" she asked. "No," was the comfortable reply, followed by the yell of an aroused baby and the noises of the older children. We retreated at once, and opened a battery of reproaches on the old woman for having brought us on a fool's errand. "There is Ohlsen's," she replied, very quietly, "I think I can get you a bed there." Whereupon we entered another house in the same unceremonious manner, but with a better result. A plump, good-natured housewife jumped out of bed, went to an opposite door, and thumped upon it. "Lars!" she cried, "come out of that this minute!" As we entered, with a torch of dry fir, Lars, who proved to be a middle-aged man, got out of bed sleepily, picked up his clothes and marched off. The hostess then brought clean sheets and pillow-cases, and by midnight we were sweetly and blissfully stowed away together in the place vacated by poor Lars.

Nothing could exceed the kindness and courtesy of the good people in the morning. The hostess brought us coffee, and her son went off to get us a horse and cart. She would make no charge, as we had had so little, she said, and was quite grateful for the moderate sum I gave her. We had a wild road over hills, covered with pine forests, through the breaks in which we now and then caught a glimpse of a long lake to the westward, shining with a steel-blue gleam in the morning sun. There were but few clearings along the road, and miles frequently intervened without a sign of human habitation. We met, however, with great numbers of travellers, mostly farmers, with laden hay-carts. It was Sunday morning, and I could not help contrasting these people with those we had seen on the same day three weeks previous whilst crossing the Fille Fjeld. Here, every one had evidently been washed and combed: the men wore clean shirts and stockings, and the women chemises of snowy whiteness under their gay boddices. They were mostly Dalecarlians, in the picturesque costume of the province. We entered Dalecarlia on this stage, and the frank fresh faces of these people, their unmistakable expression of honesty and integrity, and the hearty cordiality of their greetings, welcomed us delightfully to the storied ground of Sweden.

Towards noon we reached the village of Tyngsjö, a little settlement buried in the heart of the wild woods. A mile or two of the southern slope of a hill had been cleared away, and over this a number of dark wooden farmhouses were scattered, with oats and potato-fields around them. An odd little church stood in midst, and the rich swell of a hymn, sung by sweet Swedish voices, floated to us over the fields as we drove up to the post-station. The master, a tall, slender man, with yellow locks falling upon his shoulders, and a face which might be trusted with millions, welcomed us with a fine antique courtesy, and at once sent off for horses. In a little while three farmers came, saluting us gracefully, and standing bareheaded while they spoke to us. One of them, who wore a dark brown jacket and knee-breeches, with a clean white shirt and stockings, had a strikingly beautiful head. The face was a perfect oval, the eyes large and dark, and the jet-black hair, parted on the forehead, fell in silky waves upon his shoulders. He was as handsome and graceful as one of Vandyk's cavaliers, and showed the born gentleman in his demeanour. He proposed that we should take one horse, as it could be gotten without delay, while two (which the law obliged us to take and pay for, if the farmers chose), would have detained us an hour. As the women were in church, the postmaster himself cooked us some freshly-dug potatoes, which, with excellent butter, he set before us. "I have a kind of ale," said he, "which is called porter; if you will try it, perhaps you will like it." It was, in reality, so good, that we took a second bottle with us for refreshment on the road. When I asked how much we should pay, he said: "I don't think you should pay anything, there was so little." "Well," said I, "It is worth at least half a rigsdaler." "Oh, but that may be too much," he answered, hesitatingly.

Our postillion was a fine handsome fellow, so rosy and robust that it made one feel stronger and healthier to sit beside him. He did not spare the horse, which was a big, capable animal, and we rolled along through endless forests of fir and pine as rapidly as the sandy road would allow. After we had gone about eight miles he left us, taking a shorter footpath through the woods. We guessed at our proper direction, sometimes taking the wrong road, but finally, after two hours or more, emerged from the woods into Westerdal, one of the two great valleys from which Dalecarlia (Dalarne, or The Dales) takes its name. The day was magnificent, clear, and with a cold north-east wind, resembling the latter part of October at home. The broad, level valley, with its fields and clustered villages, lay before us in the pale, cold autumnal sunshine, with low blue hills bounding it in the distance. We met many parties in carts, either returning from church, or on their way to visit neighbours. All were in brilliant Sunday costume, the men in blue jackets and knee-breeches, with vests of red or some other brilliant colour, and the women with gay embroidered boddices, white sleeves, and striped petticoats of blue, red, brown, and purple, and scarlet stockings. Some of them wore, in addition, an outer jacket of snowy sheepskin, with elaborate ornamental stitch-work on the back. Their faces were as frank and cheerful as their dresses were tidy, and they all greeted us with that spontaneous goodness of heart which recognises a brother in every man. We had again taken a wrong road, and a merry party carefully set us right again, one old lady even proposing to leave her friends and accompany us, for fear we should go astray again.

We crossed the Westerdal by a floating bridge, and towards sunset reached the inn of Rågsveden, our destination. It was a farmer's gård, standing a little distance off the road. An entrance through one of the buildings, closed with double doors, admitted us into the courtyard, a hollow square, surrounded with two story wooden dwellings, painted dark red. There seemed to be no one at home, but after knocking and calling for a time an old man made his appearance. He was in his second childhood, but knew enough to usher us into the kitchen and ask us to wait for the landlord's arrival. After half an hour our postillion arrived with four or five men in their gayest and trimmest costume, the landlord among them. They immediately asked who and what we were, and we were then obliged to give them an account of all our travels. Their questions were shrewd and intelligent, and their manner of asking, coupled as it was with their native courtesy, showed an earnest desire for information, which we were most willing to gratify. By and by the hostess came, and we were ushered into a very pleasant room, with two beds, and furnished with a supper of fresh meat, potatoes, and mead. The landlord and two or three of the neighbours sat with us before the fire until we were too sleepy to answer any more questions. A more naturally independent and manly bearing I have never seen than that of our host. He was a tall, powerful man, of middle age, with very handsome features, which were softened but not weakened in expression by his long blond hair, parted on his forehead. He had the proper pride which belongs to the consciousness of worth, and has no kinship with empty vanity. "We have come to Dalecarlia to see the descendants of the people who gave Gustavus Vasa his throne," said I, curious to see whether he would betray any signs of flattered pride. His blue eye flashed a little, as he sat with his hands clasped over one knee, gazing at the fire, a light flush ran over his temples—but he said nothing. Some time ago a proposition was made to place a portrait of Gustavus Vasa in the church at Mora. "No," said the Dalecarlians, "we will not have it: we do not need any picture to remind us of what our fathers have done."

The landlady was a little woman, who confessed to being forty-nine years old, although she did not appear to be more than forty. "I have had a great deal of headache," said she, "and I look much older than I am." Her teeth were superb, as were those of all the women we saw. I do not suppose a tooth-brush is known in the valley; yet the teeth one sees are perfect pearls. The use of so much sour milk is said to preserve them. There was a younger person in the house, whom we took to be a girl of sixteen, but who proved to be the son's wife, a woman of twenty-six, and the mother of two or three children. The Dalecarlians marry young when they are able, but even in opposite cases they rarely commit any violation of the laws of morality. Instances are frequent, I was told, where a man and woman, unable to defray the expense of marriage, live together for years in a state of mutual chastity, until they have saved a sum sufficient to enable them to assume the responsibilities of married life. I know there is no honester, and I doubt whether there is a purer, people on the earth than these Dalecarlians.

We awoke to another glorious autumnal day. The valley was white with

304

frost in the morning, and the air deliciously keen and cold; but after sunrise heavy white vapours arose from the spangled grass, and the day gradually grew milder. I was amused at the naïve curiosity of the landlady and her daughter-in-law, who came into our room very early, that they might see the make of our garments and our manner of dressing. As they did not appear to be conscious of any impropriety, we did not think it necessary to feel embarrassed. Our Lapland journey had taught us habits of self-possession under such trying circumstances. We had coffee, paid an absurdly small sum for our entertainment, and took a cordial leave of the good people. A boy of fifteen, whose eyes, teeth and complexion kept my admiration on the stretch during the whole stage, drove us through unbroken woods to Skamhed, ten miles further down the valley. Here the inn was a little one story hut, miserable to behold externally, but containing a neat guest's room and moreover, as we discovered in the course of time—a good breakfast. While we were waiting there, a man came up who greeted us in the name of our Lord Jesus Christ, on learning that we came from America. "Are you not afraid to travel so far from home?" he asked: "how could you cross the great sea?" "Oh," I answered, "there is no more danger in one part of the world than another." "Yes," said he, "God is as near on the water as on the land"—unconsciously repeating the last words of Sir Humphrey Gilbert: "Christ walked upon the waves and quieted them, and he walks yet, for them that believe in Him." Hereupon he began repeating some hymns, mingled with texts of Scripture, which process he continued until we became heartily tired. I took him at a venture, for an over-enthusiastic Läsare, or "Reader," the name given to the Swedish dissenters.

We had a station of twenty three miles before us, to the village of Landbobyn, which lies in the wooded wilderness between Osterdal and Westerdal. Our postillion, a fine young fellow of twenty-two, over six feet in height, put on his best blue jacket and knee-breeches, with a leather apron reaching from his shoulders to below his knees. This is an article worn by almost all Dalecarlians for the purpose of saving their clothes while at work, and gives them an awkward and ungraceful air. This fellow, in spite of a little fear at the bare idea, expressed his willingness to go with us all over the world, but the spirit of wandering was evidently so easy to be kindled in him, that I rather discouraged him. We had a monotonous journey of five hours through a forest of pine, fir, and birch, in which deer and elk are frequently met with; while the wolf and the bear haunt its remoter valleys. The ground was but slightly undulating, and the scenery in general was as tame as it was savage.

Landbobyn was a wretched hamlet on the banks of a stream, with a few cleared fields about it. As the sun had not yet set, we determined to push on to Kettbo, eight or ten miles further, and engaged a boy to pilot us through the woods. The post-station was a miserable place, where we found it impossible to get anything to eat. I sat down and talked with the family while our guide recruited himself with a large dish of thick sour milk. "Why do you travel about the earth?" asked his mother: "is it that you may spy out the poverty of the people and see how miserably they live?" "No," said I, "it is that I may become acquainted with the people, whether they are poor or not." "But," she continued, "did you ever see a people poorer than we?" "Often," said I; "because you are contented, and no one can be entirely poor who does not complain." She shook her head with a sad smile and said nothing.

Our guide poled us across the river in a rickety boat, and then plunged into the woods. He was a tall, well grown boy of fifteen or sixteen, with a beautiful oval face, long fair hair parted in the middle and hanging upon his shoulders, and a fine, manly, resolute expression. With his jacket, girdle, knee-breeches, and the high crowned and broad brimmed felt hat he wore, he reminded me strongly of the picture of Gustavus Vasa in his Dalecarlian disguise, in the cathedral of Upsala. He was a splendid walker, and quite put me, old pedestrian as I am, out of countenance. The footpath we followed was terribly rough; we stumbled over stock and stone, leaped fallen trees, crossed swamps on tussocks of spongy moss, and climbed over heaps of granite boulders: yet, while we were panting and exhausted with our exertions to keep pace with him, he walked onward as quietly and easily as if the smoothest meadow turf were under his feet. I was quite puzzled by the speed he kept up on such a hard path, without seeming to put forth any extra strength. At sunset he pointed out some clearings on a hill side over the tree tops, a mile or two ahead, as our destination. Dusk was gathering as we came upon a pretty lake, with a village scattered along its hilly shore. The post-station, however, was beyond it, and after some delay the boy procured a boat and rowed us across. Telling us to go up the hill and we should find the inn, he bade us good bye and set out on his return.

We soon reached a gård, the owner whereof, after satisfying his curiosity concerning us by numerous questions, informed us that the inn was still further. After groping about in the dark for awhile, we found it. The landlord and his wife were sitting before the fire, and seemed, I thought, considerably embarrassed by our arrival. There was no bed, they said, and they had nothing that we could eat; their house was beyond the lake, and they only came over to take charge of the post-station when their turn arrived. We were devoured with hunger and thirst, and told them we should be satisfied with potatoes and a place on the floor. The wife's brother, who came in soon afterwards, was thereupon despatched across the lake to bring coffee for us, and the pleasant good-wife put our potatoes upon the fire to boil. We lit our pipes, meanwhile, and sat before the fire, talking with our host and some neighbours who came in. They had much to ask about America, none of them having ever before seen a native of that country. Their questions related principally to the cost of living, to the value of labour, the price of grain, the climate and productions, and the character of our laws. They informed me that the usual wages in Dalecarlia were 24 skillings (13 cents) a day, and that one tunne (about 480 lbs.) of rye cost 32 rigsdaler ($8.37-1/2). "No doubt you write descriptions of your travels?" asked the landlord. I assented. "And then, perhaps, you make books of them?" he continued: whereupon one of the neighbours asked, "But do you get any money for your books?"

The potatoes were finally done, and they, with some delicious milk, constituted our supper. By this time the brother had returned, bringing with him coffee, a pillow, and a large coverlet made entirely of cat-skins. A deep bed of hay was spread upon the floor, a coarse linen sheet thrown over it, and, with the soft fur covering, we had a sumptuous bed. About midnight we were awakened by an arrival. Two tailors, one of them hump-backed, on their way to Wermeland, came in, with a tall, strong woman as postillion. The fire was rekindled, and every thing which the landlord had extracted from us was repeated to the new comers, together with a very genial criticism upon our personal appearance and character. After an hour or two, more hay was brought in and the two tailors and the postillioness lay down side by side. We had barely got to sleep again, when there was another arrival. "I am the post-girl," said a female voice. Hereupon everybody woke up, and the story of the two foreign travellers was told over again. In the course of the conversation I learned that the girl carried the post twenty English miles once a week, for which she received 24 rigs ($6.25) annually. "It is a hard business," said the hump-backed tailor. "Yes; but I am obliged to do it," answered the girl. After her departure we were not again disturbed, and managed to get some sleep at last.

We all completed our toilettes in the same room, without the least embarrassment; and, with a traveller's curiosity, I may be pardoned for noticing the general bodily cleanliness of my various bed-fellows, especially as the city Swedes are in the habit of saying that the country people are shockingly dirty. We had coffee, and made arrangements with the girl who had brought the tailors to take us back in her cart. Our host would make no charge for the bed, and next to nothing for our fare, so I put a bank-note in the hand of little Pehr, his only child, telling him to take care of it, and spend it wisely when he grew up. The delight of the good people knew no bounds. Pehr must hold up his little mouth to be kissed, again and again; the mother shook us warmly by the hand, and the father harnessed his horse and started with us. May the blessing of God be upon all poor, honest, and contented people!

Our road led between wooded hills to the Siljan-Forss, a large iron-foundry upon a stream which flows into the Siljan Lake. It was a lovely morning, and our postillion who was a woman of good sense and some intelligence, chatted with me the whole way. She was delighted to find that we could so easily make ourselves understood. "When I saw you first in the night," said she, "I thought you must certainly be Swedes. All the foreigners I saw in Stockholm had something dark and cloudy in their countenances, but both of you have shining faces." She questioned me a great deal about the sacred localities of Palestine, and about the state of religion in America. She evidently belonged to the Läsare, who, she stated, were very numerous in Dalecarlia. "It is a shame," said she, "that we poor people are obliged to pay so much for the support of the Church, whether we belong to it or not. Our taxes amount to 40 rigs yearly, ten of which, in Mora parish, go to the priest. They say he has an income of half a rigs every hour of his life. King Oscar wishes to make religion free, and so it ought to be, but the clergy are all against him, and the clergy control the Bondestånd (House of Peasants), and so he can do nothing." The woman was thirty-one years old, and worn with hard labour. I asked her if she was married. "No," she answered, with a deep sigh, looking at the betrothal-ring on her finger. "Ah," she continued, "we are all poor, Sweden is a poor country; we have only iron and timber, not grain, and cotton, and silk, and sugar, like other countries."

As we descended towards the post-station of Vik we caught a glimpse of the Siljan Lake to the south, and the tall tower of Mora Church, far to the eastward. At Vik, where we found the same simple and honest race of people, we parted with the postillioness and with our host of Kettbo, who thanked us again in Pehr's name, as he shook hands for the last time. We now had fast horses, and a fine road over a long wooded hill, which was quite covered with the lingon, or Swedish cranberry. From the further slope we at last looked down upon Mora, at the head of the Siljan Lake, in the midst of a broad and fertile valley. Ten miles to the eastward arose the spire of Orsa, and southward, on an island in the lake, the tall church of Sollerön. "You can see three churches at once," said our postillion with great pride. So we could, and also the large, stately inn of Mora—a most welcome sight to us, after five days on potato diet.

CHAPTER XXXVI. LAST DAYS IN THE NORTH.

Mora, in Dalecarlia, is classic ground. It was here that Gustavus Vasa first harangued the people, and kindled that spark of revolution, which in the end swept the Danes from Sweden. In the cellar of a house which was pointed out to us, on the southern shore of the Siljan Lake, he lay hidden three days; in the barn of Ivan Elfssen he threshed corn, disguised as a peasant; and on the road by which we had travelled from Kettbo, in descending to the lake, we had seen the mounds of stone, heaped over the Danes, who were slain in his first victorious engagement. This district is considered, also, one of the most beautiful in Sweden. It has, indeed, a quiet, tranquil beauty, which gradually grows upon the eye, so that if one is not particularly aroused on first acquaintance, he at least carries away a delightful picture in his memory. But in order to enjoy properly any Swedish landscape whatsoever, one should not be too fresh from Norway.

After dinner we called at the "Parsonage of Mora," which has given Miss Fredrika Bremer the materials for one of her stories of Swedish life.

The Prost, Herr Kjelström, was not at home, but his wife received us with great cordiality, and insisted upon our remaining to tea. The magister——, who called at the same time, gave us some information concerning the porphyry quarries at Elfdal, which we were debating whether we should visit. Very little is doing at present, not more than ten men in all being employed, and in his opinion we would hardly be repaid for the journey thither; so we determined to turn southward again, and gradually make our way to Stockholm. Fru Kjelström was one of the few Swedes I met, who was really an enthusiastic admirer of Tegner; she knew by heart the greater part of his "Frithiof's Saga."

The morning after our arrival in Mora dawned dark and cloudy, with a wailing wind and dashes of rain. There were threats of the equinoctial storm, and we remembered the prediction of the lumber merchants in Carlstad. During the night, however, a little steamer belonging to an iron company arrived, offering us the chance of a passage down the lake to Leksand. While we were waiting on the shore, the magister, who had come to see us depart, gave me some information about the Läsare. He admitted that there were many in Dalecarlia, and said that the policy of persecution, which was practiced against them in the beginning, was now dropped. They were, in general, ignored by the clerical authorities. He looked upon the movement rather as a transient hallucination than as a permanent secession from the Established Church, and seemed to think that it would gradually disappear, if left to itself. He admitted that the king was in favour of religious liberty, but was so guarded in speaking of the subject that I did not ascertain his own views.

We had on board about sixty passengers, mostly peasants from Upper Elfdal, bound on a peddling excursion through Sweden, with packs of articles which they manufacture at home. Their stock consisted mostly of pocketbooks, purses, boxes, and various small articles of ornament and use. The little steamer was so well laden with their solid forms that she settled into the mud, and the crew had hard poling to get her off. There was service in Mora Church, and the sound of the organ and choir was heard along the lake. Many friends and relatives of the wandering Elfdalians were on the little wooden pier to bid them adieu. "God's peace be with thee!" was a parting salutation which I heard many times repeated. At last we got fairly clear and paddled off through the sepia-coloured water, watching the softly undulating shores, which soon sank low enough to show the blue, irregular hills in the distant background. Mora spire was the central point in the landscape, and remained visible until we had nearly reached the other end of the lake. The Siljan has a length of about twenty-five miles, with a breadth of from six to ten. The shores are hilly, but only moderately high, except in the neighborhood of Rättvik, where they were bold and beautiful. The soft slopes on either hand were covered with the yellow pillars of the ripe oats, bound to upright stakes to dry. From every village rose a tall midsummer pole, yet laden with the withered garlands of Sweden's fairest festival, and bearing aloft its patriotic symbol, the crossed arrows of Dalecarlia. The threatened storm broke and dispersed as we left Mora, and strong sun-bursts between the clouds flashed across these pastoral pictures.

Soon after we left, a number of the men and women collected together on the after-deck, and commenced singing hymns, which occupation they kept up with untiring fervour during the whole voyage. The young girls were remarkable for weight and solidity of figure, ugliness of face, and sweetness of voice. The clear, ringing tones, with a bell-like purity and delicious timbre, issued without effort from between their thick, beefy lips, and there was such a contrast between sound and substance, that they attracted my attention more than I should have thought possible. Some of the men, who had heard what we were, entered into conversation with us. I soon discovered that they were all Läsare, and one of them, who seemed to exercise a kind of leadership, and who was a man of considerable intelligence, gave me a good deal of information about the sect. They met together privately, he said, to read the New Testament, trusting entirely to its inspired pages for the means of enlightenment as to what was necessary for the salvation of their souls. The clergy stood between them and the Voice of God, who had spoken not to a particular class, but to all mankind. They were liable to a fine of 200 rigs ($52) every time they thus met together, my informant had once been obliged to pay it himself. Nevertheless, he said they were not interfered with so much at present, except that they were obliged to pay tithes, as before. "The king is a good man," he continued, "he means well, and would do us justice if he had the power; but the clergy are all against him, and his own authority is limited. Now they are going to bring the question of religious freedom before the Diet, but we have not the least hope that anything will be done." He also stated—what, indeed, must be evident to every observing traveller—that the doctrines of the Läsare had spread very rapidly, and that their numbers were continually increasing.

The creation of such a powerful dissenting body is a thing that might have been expected. The Church, in Sweden, had become a system of forms and ceremonies. The pure spiritualism of Swedenborg, in the last century, was a natural and gigantic rebound to the opposite extreme, but, from its lofty intellectuality, was unfitted to be the nucleus of a popular protest. Meanwhile, the souls of the people starved on the dry husks which were portioned out to them. They needed genuine nourishment. They are an earnest, reflective race, and the religious element is deeply implanted in their nature. The present movement, so much like Methodism in many particulars, owes its success to the same genial and all-embracing doctrine of an impartial visitation of Divine grace, bringing man into nearer and tenderer relations to his Maker. In a word, it is the democratic, opposed to the aristocratic principle in religion. It is fashionable in Sweden to sneer at the Läsare; their numbers, character, and sincerity are very generally under-estimated. No doubt there is much that is absurd and grotesque in their services; no doubt they run into violent and unchristian extremes, and often merely substitute fanaticism for spiritual apathy; but I believe they will in the end be the instrument of bestowing religious liberty upon Sweden.

There was no end to the desire of these people for knowledge. They overwhelmed us with questions about our country, its government, laws, climate, productions and geographical extent. Next to America, they seemed most interested in Palestine, and considered me as specially favoured by Providence in having beheld Jerusalem. They all complained of the burdens which fall upon a poor man in Sweden, in the shape of government taxes, tithes, and the obligation of supporting a portion of the army, who are distributed through the provinces. Thus Dalecarlia, they informed me, with a population of 132,000, is obliged to maintain 1200 troops. The tax on land corresponded very nearly with the statement made by my female postillion the previous day. Dalecarlia, its mines excepted, is one of the poorest of the Swedish provinces. Many of its inhabitants are obliged to wander forth every summer, either to take service elsewhere, or to dispose of the articles they fabricate at home, in order, after some years of this irregular life, to possess enough to enable them to pass the rest of their days humbly at home. Our fellow-passengers told me of several who had emigrated to America, where they had spent five or six years. They grew home-sick at last, and returned to their chilly hills. But it was not the bleak fir-woods, the oat-fields, or the wooden huts which they missed; it was the truth, the honesty, the manliness, and the loving tenderness which dwell in Dalecarlian hearts.

We had a strong wind abeam, but our little steamer made good progress down the lake. The shores contracted, and the white church of Leksand rose over the dark woods, and between two and three o'clock in the afternoon, we were moored in the Dal River, where it issues from the Siljan. The Elfdal peddlers shouldered their immense packs and set out, bidding us a friendly adieu as we parted. After establishing ourselves in the little inn, where we procured a tolerable dinner, we called upon the Domprost Hvasser, to whom I had a letter from a countryman who made a pedestrian journey through Dalecarlia five years ago. The parsonage was a spacious building near the church, standing upon the brink of a lofty bank overlooking the outflow of the Dal. The Domprost, a hale, stout old man, with something irresistibly hearty and cheering in his manner, gave us both his hands and drew us into the room, on seeing that we were strangers. He then proceeded to read the letter. "Ho!" he exclaimed, "to think that he has remembered me all this time! And he has not forgotten that it was just midsummer when he was here!" Presently he went out, and soon returned with a basket in one hand and some plates in the other, which he placed before us and heaped with fine ripe cherries. "Now it is autumn," said he; "it is no longer midsummer, but we have a little of the summer's fruit left." He presented us to his sister and daughter, and to two handsome young magisters, who assisted him in his parochial duties.

We walked in the garden, which was laid out with some taste along the brow of the hill. A superb drooping birch, eighty feet in height, was the crowning glory of the place. The birch is the characteristic tree of Sweden, as the fir is of Norway, the beech of Denmark, the oak of England and Germany, the chestnut of Italy, and the palm of Esrypt. Of northern trees, there is none more graceful in outline, but in the cold, silvery hue of its foliage, summer can never find her best expression. The parson had a neat little bowling-alley, in a grove of pine, on a projecting spur of the hill. He did not disdain secular recreations; his religion was cheerful and jubilant; he had found something else in the Bible than the Lamentations of Jeremiah. There are so many Christians who—to judge from the settled expression of their faces—suffer under their belief, that it is a comfort to find those who see nothing heretical in the fullest and freest enjoyment of life. There was an apple-tree in the garden which was just bursting into blossoms for the second time. I called the Domprost's attention to it, remarking, in a line from Frithiof's Saga:—"Hösten bjuder sin thron til varen" (Autumn offers his

314

throne to the spring). "What!" he exclaimed in joyful surprise, "do you know Tegner?" and immediately continued the quotation.

There was no resisting the hospitable persuasions of the family; we were obliged to take supper and spend the evening with them. The daughter and the two magisters sang for us all the characteristic songs of Wermeland and Dalecarlia which they could remember, and I was more than ever charmed with the wild, simple, original character of the native melodies of Sweden. They are mostly in the minor key, and some of them might almost be called monotonous; yet it is monotony, or rather simplicity, in the notation, which sticks to the memory. The longings, the regrets, the fidelity, and the tenderness of the people, find an echo in these airs, which have all the character of improvisations, and rekindle in the heart of the hearer the passions they were intended to relieve.

We at last took leave of the good old man and his friendly household. The night was dark and rainy, and the magisters accompanied us to the inn. In the morning it was raining dismally,—a slow, cold, driving rain, which is the climax of bad weather. We determined, however, to push onward as far as Fahlun, the capital of Dalecarlia, about four Swedish miles distant. Our road was down the valley of the Dal Elv, which we crossed twice on floating bridges, through a very rich, beautiful, and thickly settled country. The hills were here higher and bolder than in Westerdal, dark with forests of fir and pine, and swept south-eastward in long ranges, leaving a broad, open valley for the river to wander in. This valley, from three to five miles in width, was almost entirely covered with enclosed fields, owing to which the road was barred with gates, and our progress was much delayed thereby. The houses were neat and substantial, many of them with gardens and orchards attached, while the unusual number of the barns and granaries gave evidence of a more prosperous state of agriculture than we had seen since leaving the neighborhood of Carlstad. We pressed forward in the rain and raw wind, and reached Fahlun towards evening, just in time to avoid a drenching storm.

Of the celebrated copper-mines of Fahlun, some of which have been worked for 600 years, we saw nothing. We took their magnitude and richness for granted, on the strength of the immense heaps of dross through which we drove on approaching the town, and the desolate appearance of the surrounding country, whose vegetation has been for the most part destroyed by the fumes from the smelting works. In our sore and sodden condition, we were in no humour to go sight seeing, and so sat comfortably by the stove, while the rain beat against the windows, and the darkness fell. The next morning brought us a renewal of the same weather, but we set out bravely in our open cart, and jolted over the muddy roads with such perseverance, that we reached Hedemora at night. The hills diminished in height as we proceeded southward, but the scenery retained its lovely pastoral character. My most prominent recollection of the day's travel, however, is of the number of gates our numb and blue-faced boy-postillions were obliged to jump down and open.

From Hedemora, a journey of two days through the provinces of Westerås and Uppland, brought us to Upsala. After leaving Dalecarlia and crossing the Dal River for the fifth and last time, the country gradually sank into those long, slightly rolling plains, which we had traversed last winter, between Stockholm and Gefle. Here villages were more frequent, but the houses had not the same air of thrift and comfort as in Dalecarlia. The population also changed in character, the faces we now saw being less bright, cheerful, and kindly, and the forms less tall and strongly knit.

We had very fair accommodations, at all the post-stations along the road, and found the people everywhere honest and obliging. Still, I missed the noble simplicity which I had admired so much in the natives of Westerdal, and on the frontier of Wermeland,—the unaffected kindness of heart, which made me look upon every man as a friend.

The large town of Sala, where we spent a night, was filled with fugitives from Upsala, where the cholera was making great ravages. The violence of the disease was over by the time we arrived; but the students, all of whom had left, had not yet returned, and the fine old place had a melancholy air. The first thing we saw on approaching it, was a funeral. Professor Bergfalk, who had remained at his post, and to whom I had letters, most kindly gave me an entire day of his time. I saw the famous Codex argenteus, in the library, the original manuscript of Frithiof's Saga, the journals of Swedenborg and Linnæus, the Botanical Garden, and the tombs of Gustavus Vasa and John III. in the cathedral. But most interesting of all was our drive to Old Upsala, where we climbed upon the mound of Odin, and drank mead out of the silver-mounted drinking horn, from which Bernadotte, Oscar, and the whole royal family of Sweden, are in the habit of drinking when they make a pilgrimage to the burial place of the Scandinavian gods.

A cold, pale, yellow light lay upon the landscape; the towers of Upsala Cathedral, and the massive front of the palace, rose dark against the sky, in the south-west; a chill autumnal wind blew over the plains, and the yellowing foliage of the birch drifted across the mysterious mounds, like those few golden leaves of poetry, which the modern bards of the North have cast upon the grave of the grand, muscular religion of the earlier race. There was no melodious wailing in the wind, like that which proclaimed "Pan is dead!" through the groves of Greece and Ionia; but a cold rustling hiss, as if the serpent of Midgard were exulting over the ruin of Walhalla. But in the stinging, aromatic flood of the amber-coloured mead, I drank to Odin, to Balder, and to Freja.

We reached Stockholm on the 22nd of September, in the midst of a furious gale, accompanied with heavy squalls of snow—the same in which the Russian line-of-battle ship "Lefort," foundered in the Gulf of Finland. In the mild, calm, sunny, autumn days which followed, the beautiful city charmed us more than ever, and I felt half inclined to take back all I had said against the place, during the dismal weather of last spring. The trees in the Djurgård and in the islands of Mälar, were still in full foliage; the Dalecarlian boatwomen plied their crafts in the outer harbour; the little garden under the Norrbro was gay with music and lamps every evening; and the brief and jovial summer life of the Swedes, so near its close, clung to the flying sunshine, that not a moment might be suffered to pass by unenjoyed.

In another week we were standing on the deck of the Prussian steamer "Nagler," threading the rocky archipelago between Stockholm and the open Baltic on our way to Stettin. In leaving the North, after ten months of winter and summer wanderings, and with scarce a hope of returning again, I found myself repeating, over and over again, the farewell of Frithiof:—

317

"Farväl, J fjällar,

Der äran bor;

J runohällar,

För väldig Thor;

J blåa sjöar,

Jag känt så väl;

J skär och öar,

Farväl, farväl"

THE END.

VIEWS A-FOOT

"Jog on, jog on, the foot-path way,

And merrily hent the stile-a;

A merry heart goes all the day,

Your sad tires in a mile-a."

Winter's Tale.

PREFACE.

BY N.P. WILLIS.

The book which follows, requires little or no introduction. It tells its own story, and tells it well. The interest in it, which induces the writer of this preface to be its usher to the public, is simply that of his having chanced to be among the first appreciators of the author's talent—an appreciation that has since been so more than justified, that the writer is proud to call the author of this book his friend, and bespeak attention to the peculiar energies he has displayed in travel and authorship. Mr. Taylor's poetical productions while he was still a printer's apprentice, made a strong impression on the writer's mind, and he gave them their due of praise accordingly in the newspaper of which he was then Editor. Some correspondence ensued, and other fine pieces of writing strengthened the admiration thus awakened, and when the young poet-mechanic came to the city, and modestly announced the bold determination of visiting foreign lands—with means, if they could be got, but with reliance on manual labor if they could not—the writer, understanding the man, and seeing how capable he was of carrying out his manly and enthusiastic scheme, and that it would work uncorruptingly for the improvement of his mind and character, counselled him to go. He went—his book tells how successfully for all his purposes. He has returned, after two years' absence, with large knowledge of the world, of men and of manners, with a pure, invigorated and healthy mind, having passed all this time abroad, and seen and accomplished more than most travelers, *at the cost of only $500, and this sum earned on the road.* This, in the writer's opinion, is a fine instance of character and energy. The book, which records the difficulties and struggles of a printer's apprentice achieving this, must be interesting to Americans. The pride of the country is in its self-made men.

What Mr. Taylor is, or what he is yet to become, cannot well be touched upon here, but that it will yet be written, and on a bright page, is, of course, his own confident hope and the writer's confident expectation. The book, which is the record of his progress thus far, is now cordially commended to the public, and it will be read, perhaps, more understandingly after a perusal of the following outline sketch of the difficulties the author had to contend with—a letter written in reply to a note from the writer asking for some of the particulars of his start and progress:

To. Mr. Willis,—

MY DEAR SIR:—

Nearly three years ago (in the beginning of 1844) the time for accomplishing my long cherished desire of visiting Europe, seemed to arrive. A cousin, who had long intended going abroad, was to leave in a few months, and although I was then surrounded by the most unfavorable circumstances, I determined to accompany him, at whatever hazard. I had still two years of my apprenticeship to serve out; I was entirely without means, and my project was strongly opposed by my friends, as something too visionary to be practicable. A short time before, Mr. Griswold advised me to publish a small volume of youthful effusions, a few of which had appeared in Graham's Magazine, which he then edited; the idea struck me, that by so doing, I might, if they should be favorably noticed, obtain a newspaper correspondence which would enable me to make the start.

The volume was published; a sufficient number was sold among my friends to defray all expenses, and it was charitably noticed by the Philadelphia press. Some literary friends, to whom I confided my design, promised to aid me with their influence. Trusting to this, I made arrangements for leaving the printing-office, which I succeeded in doing, by making a certain compensation for the remainder of my time. I was now fully confident of success, feeling satisfied, that a strong will would always make itself a way. After many applications to different editors and as many disappointments, I finally succeeded, about two weeks before our departure, in making a partial engagement. Mr. Chandler of the United States Gazette and Mr. Patterson of the Saturday Evening Post, paid me fifty dollars, each, in advance for twelve letters, to be sent from Europe, with the probability of accepting more, if these should be satisfactory. This, with a sum which I received from Mr. Graham for poems published in his Magazine, put me in possession of about a hundred and forty dollars, with which I determined to start, trusting to future remuneration for letters, or if that should fail, to my skill as a compositor, for I supposed I could at the worst, work my way through Europe, like the German hand werker. Thus, with another companion, we left home, an enthusiastic and hopeful trio.

I need not trace our wanderings at length. After eight months of suspense, during which time my small means were entirely exhausted, I received a letter from Mr. Patterson, continuing the engagement for the remainder of my stay, with a remittance of one hundred dollars from himself and Mr. Graham. Other remittances, received from time to time, enabled me to stay abroad two years, during which I traveled on foot upwards of three thousand miles in Germany,

327

Switzerland, Italy and France. I was obliged, however, to use the strictest economy—to live on pilgrim fare, and do penance in rain and cold. My means several times entirely failed; but I was always relieved from serious difficulty through unlooked-for friends, or some unexpected turn of fortune. At Rome, owing to the expenses and embarrassments of traveling in Italy, I was obliged to give up my original design of proceeding on foot to Naples and across the peninsula to Otranto, sailing thence to Corfu and making a pedestrian journey through Albania and Greece. But the main object of my pilgrimage is accomplished; I visited the principal places of interest in Europe, enjoyed her grandest scenery and the marvels of ancient and modern art, became familiar with other languages, other customs and other institutions, and returned home, after two years' absence, willing now, with satisfied curiosity, to resume life in America.

Yours, most sincerely,

J. BAYARD TAYLOR.

TO

FRANK TAYLOR,

THESE RECORDS OF THE PILGRIMAGE,

WHOSE TOILS AND ENJOYMENTS WE HAVE SHARED
TOGETHER,

ARE

AFFECTIONATELY INSCRIBED,

BY

HIS RELATIVE AND FRIEND.

PART I.

CHAPTER I. — THE VOYAGE.

An enthusiastic desire of visiting the Old World haunted me from early childhood. I cherished a presentiment, amounting almost to belief, that I should one day behold the scenes, among which my fancy had so long wandered. The want of means was for a time a serious check to my anticipations; but I could not content myself to wait until I had slowly accumulated so large a sum as tourists usually spend on their travels. It seemed to me that a more humble method of seeing the world would place within the power of almost every one, what has hitherto been deemed the privilege of the wealthy few. Such a journey, too, offered advantages for becoming acquainted with people as well as places—for observing more intimately, the effect of government and education, and more than all, for the study of human nature, in every condition of life. At length I became possessed of a small sum, to be earned by letters descriptive of things abroad, and on the 1st of July, 1844, set sail for Liverpool, with a relative and friend, whose circumstances were somewhat similar to mine. How far the success of the experiment and the object of our long pilgrimage were attained, these pages will show.

LAND AND SEA.

There are springs that rise in the greenwood's heart,

Where its leafy glooms are cast,

And the branches droop in the solemn air,

Unstirred by the sweeping blast.

There are hills that lie in the noontide calm,

On the lap of the quiet earth;

And, crown'd with gold by the ripened grain,

Surround my place of birth.

Dearer are these to my pining heart,

Than the beauty of the deep,

When the moonlight falls in a bolt of gold

On the waves that heave in sleep.

The rustling talk of the clustered leaves

That shade a well-known door,

Is sweeter far than the booming sound

Of the breaking wave before.

When night on the ocean sinks calmly down,

I climb the vessel's prow,

Where the foam-wreath glows with its phosphor light,

Like a crown on a sea-nymph's brow.

Above, through the lattice of rope and spar,

The stars in their beauty burn;

And the spirit longs to ride their beams,

And back to the loved return.

They say that the sunset is brighter far

When it sinks behind the sea;

That the stars shine out with a softer fire—

Not thus they seem to me.

Dearer the flush of the crimson west

Through trees that my childhood knew.

When the star of love with its silver lamp,

Lights the homes of the tried and true!

Could one live on the sense of beauty alone, exempt from the necessity of "creature comforts," a sea-voyage would be delightful. To the landsman there is sublimity in the wild and ever-varied forms of the ocean; they fill his mind with living images of a glory he had only dreamed of before. But we would have been willing to forego all this and get back the comforts of the shore. At New York we took passage in the second cabin of the Oxford, which, as usual in the Liverpool packets, consisted of a small space amid-ships, fitted up with rough, temporary berths. The communication with the deck is by an open hatchway, which in storms is closed down. As the passengers in this cabin furnish their own provisions, we made ourselves acquainted with the contents of certain storehouses on Pine St. wharf, and purchased a large box of provisions, which was stowed away under our narrow berth. The cook, for a small compensation, took on himself the charge of preparing them, and we made ourselves as comfortable as the close, dark dwelling would admit.

As we approached the Banks of Newfoundland, a gale arose, which for two days and nights carried us on, careering Mazeppa-like, up hill and down. The sea looked truly magnificent, although the sailors told us it was nothing at all in comparison with the storms of winter. But we were not permitted to pass the Banks, without experiencing one of the calms, for which that neighborhood is noted. For three days we lay almost motionless on the glassy water, sometimes surrounded by large flocks of sea-gulls. The weed brought by the gulf stream, floated around—some branches we fished up, were full of beautiful little shells. Once a large school of black-fish came around the vessel, and the carpenter climbed down on the fore-chains, with a harpoon to strike one. Scarcely had he taken his position, when they all darted off in a straight line, through the water, and were soon out of sight. He said they smelt the harpoon.

We congratulated ourselves on having reached the Banks in seven days, as it is considered the longest third-part of the passage. But the hopes of reaching Liverpool in twenty days, were soon overthrown. A succession of southerly winds drove the vessel as far north as lat. 55 deg., without bringing us much nearer our destination. It was extremely cold, for we were but five degrees south of the latitude of Greenland, and the long northern twilights came on. The last glow of the evening twilight had scarcely faded, before the first glimmering of dawn appeared. I found it extremely easy to read, at 10 P.M., on the deck.

We had much diversion on board from a company of Iowa Indians, under the celebrated chief "White Cloud," who are on a visit to England. They are truly a wild enough looking company, and helped not a little to relieve the tedium of the passage. The chief was a very grave and dignified person, but some of the braves were merry enough. One day we had a war-dance on deck, which was a most ludicrous scene. The chief and two braves sat upon the deck, beating violently a small drum and howling forth their war-song, while the others in full dress, painted in a grotesque style, leaped about, brandishing tomahawks and spears, and terminating each dance with a terrific yell. Some of the men are very fine-looking, but the squaws are all ugly. They occupied part of the second cabin, separated only by a board partition from our room. This proximity was any thing but agreeable. They kept us awake more than half the night, by singing and howling in the most dolorous manner, with the accompaniment of slapping their hands violently on their bare breasts. We tried an opposition, and a young German student, who was returning home after two years' travel in America, made our room ring with the chorus from Der Freischütz—but in vain. They would howl and beat their breasts, and the pappoose would squall. Any loss of temper is therefore not to be wondered at, when I state that I could scarcely turn in my berth, much less stretch myself out; my cramped limbs alone drove off half the night's slumber.

It was a pleasure, at least, to gaze on their strong athletic frames. Their massive chests and powerful limbs put to shame our dwindled proportions. One old man, in particular, who seemed the patriarch of the band, used to stand for hours on the quarter deck, sublime and motionless as a statue of

Jupiter. An interesting incident occurred during the calm of which I spoke. They began to be fearful we were doomed to remain there forever, unless the spirits were invoked for a favorable wind. Accordingly the prophet lit his pipe and smoked with great deliberation, muttering all the while in a low voice. Then, having obtained a bottle of beer from the captain, he poured it solemnly over the stern of the vessel into the sea. There were some indications of wind at the time, and accordingly the next morning we had a fine breeze, which the Iowas attributed solely to the Prophet's incantation and Eolus' love of beer.

After a succession of calms and adverse winds, on the 25th we were off the Hebrides, and though not within sight of land, the southern winds came to us strongly freighted with the "meadow freshness" of the Irish bogs, so we could at least smell it. That day the wind became more favorable, and the next morning we were all roused out of our berths by sunrise, at the long wished-for cry of "land!" Just under the golden flood of light that streamed through the morning clouds, lay afar-off and indistinct the crags of an island, with the top of a light-house visible at one extremity. To the south of it, and barely distinguishable, so completely was it blended in hue with the veiling cloud, loomed up a lofty mountain. I shall never forget the sight! As we drew nearer, the dim and soft outline it first wore, was broken into a range of crags, with lofty precipices jutting out to the sea, and sloping off inland. The white wall of the light-house shone in the morning's light, and the foam of the breakers dashed up at the foot of the airy cliffs. It was worth all the troubles of a long voyage, to feel the glorious excitement which this herald of new scenes and new adventures created. The light-house was on Tory Island, on the north-western coast of Ireland. The Captain decided on taking the North Channel, for, although rarely done, it was in our case nearer, and is certainly more interesting than the usual route.

We passed the Island of Ennistrahul, near the entrance of Londonderry harbor, and at sunset saw in the distance the islands of Islay and Jura, off the Scottish coast. Next morning we were close to the promontory of Fairhead, a bold, precipitous headland, like some of the Palisades on the Hudson; the highlands of the Mull of Cantire were on the opposite side of the Channel, and the wind being ahead, we tacked from shore to shore, running so near the Irish coast, that we could see the little thatched huts, stacks of peat, and even rows of potatoes in the fields. It was a panorama: the view extended for miles inland, and the fields of different colored grain were spread out before us, a brilliant mosaic. Towards evening we passed Ailsa Crag, the sea-bird's home, within sight, though about twenty miles distant.

On Sunday, the 28th, we passed the lofty headland of the Mull of Galloway and entered the Irish Sea. Here there was an occurrence of an impressive nature. A woman, belonging to the steerage, who had been ill the whole passage, died the morning before. She appeared to be of a very avaricious disposition, though this might indeed have been the result of self-denial, practised through filial affection. In the morning she was speechless, and while they were endeavoring to persuade her to give up her keys to the captain, died. In her pocket were found two parcels, containing forty sovereigns, sewed up with the most miserly care. It was ascertained she had a widowed mother in the north of Ireland, and judging her money could be better applied than to paying for a funeral on shore, the captain gave orders for committing the body to the waves. It rained drearily as her corpse, covered with starred bunting, was held at the gangway while the captain read the funeral service; then one plunge was heard, and a white object, flashed up through the dark waters, as the ship passed on.

In the afternoon we passed the Isle of Man, having a beautiful view of the Calf, with a white stream tumbling down the rocks into the sea; and at night saw the sun set behind the mountains of Wales. About midnight, the pilot came on board, and soon after sunrise I saw the distant spires of Liverpool. The Welsh coast was studded with windmills, all in motion, and the harbor spotted with buoys, bells and floating lights. How delightful it was to behold the green trees on the banks of the Mersey, and to know that in a few hours we should be on land! About 11 o'clock we came to anchor in the channel of the Mersey, near the docks, and after much noise, bustle and confusion, were transferred, with our baggage, to a small steamboat, giving a parting cheer to the Iowas, who remained on board. On landing, I stood a moment to observe the scene. The baggage-wagons, drawn by horses, mules and donkeys, were extraordinary; men were going about crying "the celebrated Tralorum gingerbread!" which they carried in baskets; and a boy in the University dress, with long blue gown and yellow knee-breeches, was running to the wharf to look at the Indians.

At last the carts were all loaded, the word was given to start, and then, what a scene ensued! Away went the mules, the horses and the donkeys; away ran men and women and children, carrying chairs and trunks, and boxes and bedding. The wind was blowing, and the dust whirled up as they dashed helter-skelter through the gate and started off on a hot race, down the dock to the depot. Two wagons came together, one of which was overturned, scattering the broken boxes of a Scotch family over the pavement; but while the poor woman was crying over her loss, the tide swept on, scarcely taking time to glance at the mishap.

Our luggage was "passed" with little trouble; the officer merely opening the trunks and pressing his hands on the top. Even some American reprints of English works which my companion carried, and feared would be taken from him, were passed over without a word. I was agreeably surprised at this, as from the accounts of some travellers, I had been led to fear horrible things of custom-houses. This over, we took a stroll about the city. I was first struck by seeing so many people walking in the middle of the streets, and so many gentlemen going about with pinks stuck in their button-holes. Then, the houses being all built of brown granite or dark brick, gives the town a sombre appearance, which the sunshine (when there is any) cannot dispel. Of Liverpool we saw little. Before the twilight had wholly faded, we were again tossing on the rough waves of the Irish Sea.

CHAPTER II. — A DAY IN IRELAND.

On calling at the steamboat office in Liverpool, to take passage to Port Rush, we found that the fare in the fore cabin was but two shillings and a half, while in the chief cabin it was six times as much. As I had started to make the tour of all Europe with a sum little higher than is sometimes given for the mere passage to and fro, there was no alternative—the twenty-four hours' discomfort could be more easily endured than the expense, and as I expected to encounter many hardships, it was best to make a beginning. I had crossed the ocean with tolerable comfort for twenty-four dollars, and was determined to try whether England, where I had been told it was almost impossible to breathe without expense, might not also be seen by one of limited means.

The fore cabin was merely a bare room, with a bench along one side, which was occupied by half a dozen Irishmen in knee-breeches and heavy brogans. As we passed out of the Clarence Dock at 10 P.M., I went below and managed to get a seat on one end of the bench, where I spent the night in sleepless misery. The Irish bestowed themselves about the floor as they best could, for there was no light, and very soon the Morphean deepness of their breathing gave token of blissful unconsciousness.

The next morning was misty and rainy, but I preferred walking the deck and drying myself occasionally beside the chimney, to sitting in the dismal room below. We passed the Isle of Man, and through the whole forenoon were tossed about very disagreeably in the North Channel. In the afternoon we stopped at Larne, a little antiquated village, not far from Belfast, at the head of a crooked arm of the sea. There is an old ivy-grown tower near, and high green mountains rise up around. After leaving it, we had a beautiful panoramic view of the northern coast. Many of the precipices are of the same formation as the Causeway; Fairhead, a promontory of this kind, is grand in the extreme. The perpendicular face of fluted rock is about three hundred feet in height, and towering up sublimely from the water, seemed almost to overhang our heads.

My companion compared it to Niagara Falls petrified; and I think the simile very striking. It is like a cataract falling in huge waves, in some places leaping out from a projecting rock, in others descending in an unbroken sheet.

We passed the Giant's Causeway after dark, and about eleven o'clock reached the harbor of Port Rush, where, after stumbling up a strange old street, in the dark, we found a little inn, and soon forgot the Irish Coast and everything else.

In the morning when we arose it was raining, with little prospect of fair weather, but having expected nothing better, we set out on foot for the Causeway. The rain, however, soon came down in torrents, and we were obliged to take shelter in a cabin by the road-side. The whole house consisted of one room, with bare walls and roof, and earthen floor, while a window of three or four panes supplied the light. A fire of peat was burning on the hearth, and their breakfast, of potatoes alone, stood on the table. The occupants received us with rude but genuine hospitality, giving us the only seats in the room to sit upon; except a rickety bedstead that stood in one corner and a small table, there was no other furniture in the house. The man appeared rather intelligent, and although he complained of the hardness of their lot, had no sympathy with O'Connell or the Repeal movement.

We left this miserable hut, as soon as it ceased raining—and, though there were many cabins along the road, few were better than this. At length, after passing the walls of an old church, in the midst of older tombs, we saw the roofless towers of Dunluce Castle, on the sea-shore. It stands on an isolated rook, rising perpendicularly two hundred feet above the sea, and connected with the cliffs of the mainland by a narrow arch of masonry. On the summit of the cliffs were the remains of the buildings where the ancient lords kept their vassals. An old man, who takes care of it for Lord Antrim, on whose property it is situated, showed us the way down to the castle. We walked across the narrow arch, entered the ruined hall, and looked down on the roaring sea below. It still rained, the wind swept furiously through the decaying arches of the banqueting hall and waved the long grass on the desolate battlements. Far below, the sea foamed white on the breakers and sent up an unceasing boom. It was the most mournful and desolate picture I ever beheld. There were some low dungeons yet entire, and rude stairways, where, by stooping down, I could ascend nearly to the top of one of the towers, and look out on the wild scenery of the coast.

Going back, I found a way down the cliff, to the mouth of a cavern in the rock, which extends under the whole castle to the sea. Sliding down a heap of sand and stones, I stood under an arch eighty feet high; in front the breakers dashed into the entrance, flinging the spray half-way to the roof, while the sound rang up through the arches like thunder. It seemed to me the haunt of the old Norsemen's sea-gods!

We left the road near Dunluce and walked along the smooth beach to the cliffs that surround the Causeway. Here we obtained a guide, and descended to one of the caves which can be entered from the shore. Opposite the entrance a bare rock called Sea Gull Isle, rises out of the sea like a church steeple. The roof at first was low, but we shortly came to a branch that opened on the sea, where the arch was forty-six feet in height. The breakers dashed far into the cave, and flocks of sea-birds circled round its mouth. The sound of a gun was like a deafening peal of thunder, crashing from arch to arch till it rolled out of the cavern.

On the top of the hill a splendid hotel is erected for visitors to the Causeway; after passing this we descended to the base of the cliffs, which are here upwards of four hundred feet high, and soon began to find, in the columnar formation of the rocks, indications of our approach. The guide pointed out some columns which appeared to have been melted and run together, from which Sir Humphrey Davy attributed the formation of the Causeway to the action of fire. Near this is the Giant's Well, a spring of the purest water, the bottom formed by three perfect hexagons, and the sides of regular columns. One of us observing that no giant had ever drunk from it, the old man answered—"Perhaps not: but it was made by a giant—God Almighty!"

From the well, the Causeway commences—a mass of columns, from triangular to octagonal, lying in compact forms, and extending into the sea. I was somewhat disappointed at first, having supposed the Causeway to be of great height, but I found the Giant's Loom, which is the highest part of it, to be but about fifty feet from the water. The singular appearance of the columns and the many strange forms which they assume, render it nevertheless, an object of the greatest interest. Walking out on the rocks we came to the Ladies' Chair, the seat, back, sides and footstool, being all regularly formed by the broken columns. The guide said that any lady who would take three drinks from the Giant's Well, then sit in this chair and think of any gentleman for whom she had a preference, would be married before a twelvemonth. I asked him if it would answer as well for gentlemen, for by a wonderful coincidence we had each drank three times at the well! He said it would, and thought he was confirming his statement.

A cluster of columns about half-way up the cliff is called the Giant's Organ—from its very striking resemblance to that instrument, and a single rock, worn by the waves into the shape of a rude seat, is his chair. A mile or two further along the coast, two cliffs project from the range, leaving a vast semicircular space between, which, from its resemblance to the old Roman theatres, was appropriated for that purpose by the Giant. Halfway down the crags are two or three pinnacles of rock, called the Chimneys, and the stumps of several others can be seen, which, it is said, were shot off by a vessel belonging to the Spanish Armada, in mistake for the towers of Dunluce Castle. The vessel was afterwards wrecked in the bay below, which has ever since been called Spanish Bay, and in calm weather the wreck may be still seen. Many of the columns of the Causeway have been carried off and sold as pillars for mantels—and though a notice is put up threatening any one with the rigor of the law, depredations are occasionally made.

Returning, we left the road at Dunluce, and took a path which led along the summit of the cliffs. The twilight was gathering, and the wind blew with perfect fury, which, combined with the black and stormy sky, gave the coast an air of extreme wildness. All at once, as we followed the winding path, the crags appeared to open before us, disclosing a yawning chasm, down which a large stream, falling in an unbroken sheet, was lost in the gloom below. Witnessed in a calm day, there may perhaps be nothing striking about it, but coming upon us at once, through the gloom of twilight, with the sea thundering below and a scowling sky above, it was absolutely startling.

The path at last wound, with many a steep and slippery bend, down the almost perpendicular crags, to the shore, at the foot of a giant isolated rock, having a natural arch through it, eighty feet in height. We followed the narrow strip of beach, having the bare crags on one side and a line of foaming breakers on the other. It soon grew dark; a furious storm came up and swept like a hurricane along the shore. I then understood what Horne means by "the lengthening javelins of the blast," for every drop seemed to strike with the force of an arrow, and our clothes were soon pierced in every part.

Then we went up among the sand hills, and lost each other in the darkness, when, after stumbling about among the gullies for half an hour, shouting for my companions, I found the road and heard my call answered; but it happened to be two Irishmen, who came up and said—"And is it another gintleman ye're callin' for? we heard some one cryin', and didn't know but somebody might be kilt."

Finally, about eleven o'clock we all arrived at the inn, dripping with rain, and before a warm fire concluded the adventures of our day in Ireland.

CHAPTER III. — BEN LOMOND AND THE HIGHLAND LAKES.

The steamboat Londonderry called the next day at Port Rush, and we left in her for Greenock. We ran down the Irish coast, past Dunluce Castle and the Causeway; the Giant's organ was very plainly visible, and the winds were strong enough to have sounded a storm-song upon it. Farther on we had a distant view of Carrick-a-Rede, a precipitous rock, separated by a yawning chasm from the shore, frequented by the catchers of sea-birds. A narrow swinging bridge, which is only passable in calm weather, crosses this chasm, 200 feet above the water.

The deck of the steamer was crowded with Irish, and certainly gave no very favorable impression of the condition of the peasantry of Ireland. On many of their countenances there was scarcely a mark of intelligence—they were a most brutalized and degraded company of beings. Many of them were in a beastly state of intoxication, which, from the contents of some of their pockets, was not likely to decrease. As evening drew on, two or three began singing and the others collected in groups around them. One of them who sang with great spirit, was loudly applauded, and poured forth song after song, of the most rude and unrefined character.

We took a deck passage for three shillings, in preference to paying twenty for the cabin, and having secured a vacant place near the chimney, kept it during the whole passage. The waves were as rough in the Channel as I ever saw them in the Atlantic, and our boat was tossed about like a plaything. By keeping still we escaped sickness, but we could not avoid the sight of the miserable beings who filled the deck. Many of them spoke in the Irish tongue, and our German friend (the student whom I have already mentioned) noticed in many of the words a resemblance to his mother tongue. I procured a bowl of soup from the steward, but as I was not able to eat it, I gave it to an old man whose hungry look and wistful eyes convinced me it would not be lost on him. He swallowed it with ravenous avidity, together with a crust of bread, which was all I had to give him, and seemed for the time as happy and cheerful as if all his earthly wants were satisfied.

We passed by the foot of Goat Fell, a lofty mountain on the island of Arran, and sped on through the darkness past the hills of Bute, till we entered the Clyde. We arrived at Greenock at one o'clock at night, and walking at random through its silent streets, met a policeman, whom we asked to show us where we might find lodgings. He took my cousin and myself to the house of a poor widow, who had a spare bed which she let to strangers, and then conducted our comrade and the German to another lodging-place.

An Irish strolling musician, who was on board the Dumbarton boat, commenced playing soon after we left Greenock, and, to my surprise, struck at once into "Hail Columbia." Then he gave "the Exile of Erin," with the most touching sweetness; and I noticed that always after playing any air that was desired of him, he would invariably return to the sad lament, which I never heard executed with more feeling. It might have been the mild, soft air of the morning, or some peculiar mood of mind that influenced me, but I have been far less affected by music which would be considered immeasurably superior to his. I had been thinking of America, and going up to the old man, I quietly bade him play "Home." It thrilled with a painful delight that almost brought tears to my eyes. My companion started as the sweet melody arose, and turned towards me, his face kindling with emotion.

Dumbarton Rock rose higher and higher as we went up the Clyde, and before we arrived at the town I hailed the dim outline of Ben Lomond, rising far off among the highlands. The town is at the head of a small inlet, a short distance from the rock, which was once surrounded by water. We went immediately to the Castle. The rock is nearly 500 feet high, and from its position and great strength as a fortress, has been called the Gibraltar of Scotland. The top is surrounded with battlements, and the armory and barracks stand in a cleft between the two peaks. We passed down a green lane, around the rock, and entered the castle on the south side. A soldier conducted us through a narrow cleft, overhung with crags, to the summit. Here, from the remains of a round building, called Wallace's Tower, from its having been used as a look-out station by that chieftain, we had a beautiful view of the whole of Leven Vale to Loch Lomond, Ben Lomond and the Highlands, and on the other hand, the Clyde and the Isle of Bute. In the soft and still balminess of the morning, it was a lovely picture. In the armory, I lifted the sword of Wallace, a two-handed weapon, five feet in length. We were also shown a Lochaber battle-axe, from Bannockburn, and several ancient claymores.

We lingered long upon the summit before we forsook the stern fortress for the sweet vale spread out before us. It was indeed a glorious walk, from Dumbarton to Loch Lomond, through this enchanting valley. The air was mild and clear; a few light clouds occasionally crossing the sun, chequered the hills with sun and shade. I have as yet seen nothing that in pastoral beauty can compare with its glassy winding stream, its mossy old woods, and guarding hills—and the ivy-grown, castellated towers embosomed in its forests, or standing on the banks of the Leven—the purest of rivers. At a little village called Renton, is a monument to Smollett, but the inhabitants seem to neglect his memory, as one of the tablets on the pedestal is broken and half fallen away. Further up the vale a farmer showed us an old mansion in the midst of a group of trees on the bank of the Leven, which he said belonged to Smollett—or Roderick Random, as he called him. Two or three old pear trees were still standing where the garden had formerly been, under which he was accustomed to play in his childhood.

At the head of Leven Vale, we set off in the steamer "Water Witch" over the crystal waters of Loch Lomond, passing Inch Murrin, the deer-park of the Duke of Montrose, and Inch Caillach,

> ——*"where gray pines wave*
>
> *Their shadows o'er Clan Alpine's grave."*

Under the clear sky and golden light of the declining sun, we entered the Highlands, and heard on every side names we had learned long ago in the lays of Scott. Here were Glen Fruin and Bannochar, Ross Dhu and the pass of Beal-ma-na. Further still, we passed Rob Roy's rock, where the lake is locked in by lofty mountains. The cone-like peak of Ben Lomond rises far above on the right, Ben Voirlich stands in front, and the jagged crest of Ben Arthur looks over the shoulders of the western hills. A Scotchman on board pointed out to us the remarkable places, and related many interesting legends. Above

Inversnaid, where there is a beautiful waterfall, leaping over the rock and glancing out from the overhanging birches, we passed McFarland's Island, concerning the origin of which name, he gave a history. A nephew of one of the old Earls of Lennox, the ruins of whose castle we saw on Inch Murrin, having murdered his uncle's cook in a quarrel, was obliged to flee for his life. Returning after many years, he built a castle upon this island, which was always after named, on account of his exile, Far-land. On a precipitous point above Inversnaid, are two caves in the rock; one near the water is called Rob Roy's, though the guides generally call it Bruce's also, to avoid trouble, as the real Bruce's Cave is high up the hill. It is so called, because Bruce hid there one night, from the pursuit of his enemies. It is related that a mountain goat, who used this probably for a sleeping place, entered, trod on his mantle, and aroused him. Thinking his enemies were upon him, he sprang up, and saw the silly animal before him. In token of gratitude for this agreeable surprise, when he became king, a law was passed, declaring goats free throughout all Scotland—unpunishable for whatever trespass they might commit, and the legend further says, that not having been repealed, it continues in force at the present day.

On the opposite shore of the lake is a large rock, called "Bull's Rock," having a door in the side, with a stairway cut through the interior to a pulpit on the top, from which the pastor at Arroquhar preaches a monthly discourse. The Gaelic legend of the rock is, that it once stood near the summit of the mountain above, and was very nearly balanced on the edge of a precipice. Two wild bulls, fighting violently, dashed with great force against the rock, which, being thrown from its balance, was tumbled down the side of the mountain, till it reached its present position. The Scot was speaking with great bitterness of the betrayal of Wallace, when I asked him if it was still considered an insult to turn a loaf of bread bottom upwards in the presence of a Montieth. "Indeed it is, sir," said he, "I have often done it myself."

Until last May, travellers were taken no higher up the lake than Rob Roy's Cave, but another boat having commenced running, they can now go beyond Loch Lomond, two miles up Glen Falloch, to the Inn of Inverarnan, thereby visiting some of the finest scenery in that part of the Highlands. It was ludicrous, however, to see the steamboat on a river scarcely wider than herself, in a little valley, hemmed in completely with lofty mountains. She went on, however, pushing aside the thickets which lined both banks, and I almost began to think she was going to take the shore for it, when we came to a place widened out for her to be turned around in; here we jumped ashore in a green meadow, on which the cool mist was beginning to descend.

When we arose in the morning, at 4 o'clock, to return with the boat, the sun was already shining upon the westward hills, scarcely a cloud was in the sky, and the air was pure and cool. To our great delight Ben Lomond was unshrouded, and we were told that a more favorable day for the ascent had not occurred for two months. We left the boat at Rowardennan, an inn at the southern base of Ben Lomond. After breakfasting on Loch Lomond trout, I stole out to the shore while my companions were preparing for the ascent, and made a hasty sketch of the lake.

We purposed descending on the northern side and crossing the Highlands to Loch Katrine; though it was represented as difficult and dangerous by the guide who wished to accompany us, we determined to run the risk of being enveloped in a cloud on the summit, and so set out alone, the path appearing plain before us. We had no difficulty in following it up the lesser heights, around the base. It wound on, over rock and bog, among the heather and broom with which the mountain is covered, sometimes running up a steep acclivity, and then winding zigzag round a rocky ascent. The rains two days before, had made the bogs damp and muddy, but with this exception, we had little trouble for some time. Ben Lomond is a doubly formed mountain. For about three-fourths of the way there is a continued ascent, when it is suddenly terminated by a large barren plain, from one end of which the summit shoots up abruptly, forming at the north side, a precipice 500 feet high. As we approached the summit of the first part of the mountain, the way became very steep and toilsome; but the prospect, which had before been only on the south side, began to open on the east, and we saw suddenly spread out below us, the vale of Menteith, with "far Loch Ard and Aberfoil" in the centre, and the huge front of Benvenue filling up the picture. Taking courage from this, we hurried on. The heather had become stunted and dwarfish, and the ground was covered with short brown grass. The mountain sheep, which we saw looking at us from the rock above, had worn so many paths along the side, that we could not tell which to take, but pushed on in the direction of the summit, till thinking it must be near at hand, we found a mile and a half of plain before us, with the top of Ben Lomond at the farther end. The plain was full of wet moss, crossed in all directions by deep ravines or gullies worn in it by the mountain rains, and the wind swept across with a tempest-like force.

I met, near the base, a young gentleman from Edinburgh, who had left Rowardennan before us, and we commenced ascending together. It was hard work, but neither liked to stop, so we climbed up to the first resting place, and found the path leading along the brink of a precipice. We soon attained the summit, and climbing up a little mound of earth and stones, I saw the half of Scotland at a glance. The clouds hung just above the mountain tops, which rose all around like the waves of a mighty sea. On every side—near and far—stood their misty summits, but Ben Lomond was the monarch of them all. Loch Lomond lay unrolled under my feet like a beautiful map, and just opposite, Loch Long thrust its head from between the feet of the crowded hills, to catch a glimpse of the giant. We could see from Ben Nevis to Ayr—from Edinburgh to Staffa. Stirling and Edinburgh Castles would have been visible, but that the clouds hung low in the valley of the Forth and hid them from our sight.

The view from Ben Lomond is nearly twice as extensive as that from Catskill, being uninterrupted on every side, but it wants the glorious forest scenery, clear, blue sky, and active, rejoicing character of the latter. We stayed about two hours upon the summit, taking refuge behind the cairn, when the wind blew strong. I found the smallest of flowers under a rock, and brought it away as a memento. In the middle of the precipice there is a narrow ravine or rather cleft in the rock, to the bottom, from whence the mountain slopes regularly but steeply down to the valley. At the bottom we stopped to awake the echoes, which were repeated four times; our German companion sang the Hunter's Chorus, which resounded magnificently through this Highland hall. We drank from the river Forth, which starts from a spring at the foot of the rock, and then commenced descending. This was also toilsome enough. The mountain was quite wet and covered with loose stones, which, dislodged by our feet, went rattling down the side, oftentimes to the danger of the foremost ones; and when we had run or rather slid down the three miles, to the bottom, our knees trembled so as scarcely to support us.

Here, at a cottage on the farm of Coman, we procured some oat cakes and milk for dinner, from an old Scotch woman, who pointed out the direction of Loch Katrine, six miles distant; there was no road, nor indeed a solitary dwelling between. The hills were bare of trees, covered with scraggy bushes and rough heath, which in some places was so thick we could scarcely drag our feet through. Added to this, the ground was covered with a kind of moss that retained the moisture like a sponge, so that our boots ere long became thoroughly soaked. Several considerable streams were rushing down the side, and many of the wild breed of black Highland cattle were grazing around. After climbing up and down one or two heights, occasionally startling the moorcock and ptarmigan from their heathery coverts, we saw the valley of Loch Con; while in the middle of the plain on the top of the mountain we had ascended, was a sheet of water which we took to be Loch Ackill. Two or three wild fowl swimming on its surface were the only living things in sight. The peaks around shut it out from all view of the world; a single decayed tree leaned over it from a mossy rock, which gave the whole scene an air of the most desolate wildness. I forget the name of the lake; but we learned afterwards that the Highlanders consider it the abode of the fairies, or "men of peace," and that it is still superstitiously shunned by them after nightfall.

From the next mountain we saw Loch Ackill and Loch Katrine below, but a wet and weary descent had yet to be made. I was about throwing off my knapsack on a rock, to take a sketch of Loch Katrine, which appeared very beautiful from this point, when we discerned a cavalcade of ponies winding along the path from Inversnaid, to the head of the lake, and hastened down to take the boat when they should arrive. Our haste turned out to be unnecessary, however, for they had to wait for their luggage, which was long in coming. Two boatmen then offered to take us for two shillings and sixpence each, with the privilege of stopping at Ellen's Isle; the regular fare being two shillings.

We got in, when, after exchanging a few words in Gaelic, one of them called to the travellers, of whom there were a number, to come and take passage at two shillings—then at one and sixpence, and finally concluded by requesting them all to step on board the shilling boat! At length, having secured nine at this reduced price, we pushed off; one of the passengers took the helm, and the boat glided merrily over the clear water.

It appears there is some opposition among the boatmen this summer, which is all the better for travelers. They are a bold race, and still preserve many of the characteristics of the clan from which they sprung. One of ours, who had a chieftain-like look, was a MacGregor, related to Rob Roy. The fourth descendant in a direct line, now inhabits the Rob Roy mansion, at Glengyle, a valley at the head of the lake. A small steamboat was put upon Loch Katrine a short time ago, but the boatmen, jealous of this new invasion of their privilege, one night towed her out to the middle of the lake and there sunk her.

Near the point of Brianchoil is a very small island with a few trees upon it, of which the boatman related a story that was new to me. He said an eccentric individual, many years ago, built his house upon it—but it was soon beaten down by the winds and waves. Having built it up with like fortune several times, he at last desisted, saying, "bought wisdom was the best;" since when it has been called the Island of Wisdom. On the shore below, the boatman showed us his cottage. The whole family were out at the door to witness our progress; he hoisted a flag, and when we came opposite, they exchanged shouts in Gaelic. As our men resumed their oars again, we assisted in giving three cheers, which made the echoes of Benvenue ring again. Some one observed his dog, looking after us from a projecting rock, when he called out to him, "go home, you brute!" We asked him why he did not speak Gaelic also to his dog.

"Very few dogs, indeed," said he, "understand Gaelic, but they all understand English. And we therefore all use English when speaking to our dogs; indeed, I know some persons, who know nothing of English, that speak it to their dogs!"

They then sang, in a rude manner, a Gaelic song. The only word I could distinguish was Inch Caillach, the burying place of Clan Alpine. They told us it was the answer of a Highland girl to a foreign lord, who wished to make her his bride. Perhaps, like the American Indian, she would not leave the graves of her fathers. As we drew near the eastern end of the lake, the scenery became far more beautiful. The Trosachs opened before us. Ben Ledi looked down over the "forehead bare" of Ben An, and, as we turned a rocky point, Ellen's Isle rose up in front. It is a beautiful little turquoise in the silver setting of Loch Katrine. The northern side alone is accessible, all the others being rocky and perpendicular, and thickly grown with trees. We rounded the island to the little bay, bordered by the silver strand, above which is the rock from which Fitz-James wound his horn, and shot under an ancient oak which flung its long grey arms over the water; we here found a flight of rocky steps, leading to the top, where stood the bower erected by Lady Willoughby D'Eresby, to correspond with Scott's description. Two or three blackened beams are all that remain of it, having been burned down some years ago, by the carelessness of a traveler.

The mountains stand all around, like giants, to "sentinel this enchanted land." On leaving the island, we saw the Goblin's Cave, in the side of Benvenue, called by the Gaels, "Coirnan-Uriskin." Near it is Beal-nam-bo, the pass of cattle, overhung with grey weeping birch trees. Here the boatmen stopped to let us hear the fine echo, and the names of "Rob Roy," and "Roderick Dhu," were sent back to us apparently as loud as they were given. The description of Scott is wonderfully exact, though the forest that feathered o'er the sides of Benvenue, has since been cut down and sold by the Duke of Montrose. When we reached the end of the lake it commenced raining, and we hastened on through the pass of Beal-an-Duine, scarcely taking time to glance at the scenery, till Loch Achray appeared through the trees, and on its banks the ivy-grown front of the inn of Ardcheancrochan, with its unpronounceable name.

CHAPTER IV. — THE BURNS FESTIVAL.

We passed a glorious summer morning on the banks of Loch Katrine. The air was pure, fresh and balmy, and the warm sunshine glowed upon forest and lake, upon dark crag and purple mountain-top. The lake was a scene in fairy-land. Returning over the rugged battle-plain in the jaws of the Trosachs, we passed the wild, lonely valley of Glenfinlas and Lanric Mead, at the head of Loch Vennachar, rounding the foot of Ben Ledi to Coilantogle Ford. We saw the desolate hills of Uam-var over which the stag fled from his lair in Glenartney, and keeping on through Callander, stopped for the night at a little inn on the banks of the Teith. The next day we walked through Doune, over the lowlands to Stirling. Crossing Allan Water and the Forth, we climbed Stirling Castle and looked on the purple peaks of the Ochill Mountains, the far Grampians, and the battle-fields of Bannockburn and Sheriff Muir. Our German comrade, feeling little interest in the memory of the poet-ploughman, left in the steamboat for Edinburg; we mounted an English coach and rode to Falkirk, where we took the cars for Glasgow in order to attend the Burns Festival, on the 6th of August.

This was a great day for Scotland—the assembling of all classes to do honor to the memory of her peasant-bard. And right fitting was it, too, that such a meeting should be hold on the banks of the Doon, the stream of which he has sung so sweetly, within sight of the cot where he was born, the beautiful monument erected by his countrymen, and more than all, beside "Alloway's witch-haunted wall!" One would think old Albyn would rise up at the call, and that from the wild hunters of the northern hills to the shepherds of the Cheviots, half her honest yeomanry would be there, to render gratitude to the memory of the sweet bard who was one of them, and who gave their wants and their woes such eloquent utterance.

For months before had the proposition been made to hold a meeting on the Doon, similar to the Shakspeare Festival on the Avon, and the 10th of July was first appointed for the day, but owing to the necessity of further time for preparation, it was postponed until the 6th of August. The Earl of Eglintoun was chosen Chairman, and Professor Wilson Vice-Chairman; in addition to this, all the most eminent British authors were invited to attend. A pavilion, capable of containing two thousand persons, had been erected near the monument, in a large field, which was thrown open to the public. Other preparations were made and the meeting was expected to be of the most interesting character.

When we arose it was raining, and I feared that the weather might dampen somewhat the pleasures of the day, as it had done to the celebrated tournament at Eglintoun Castle. We reached the station in time for the first train, and sped in the face of the wind over the plains of Ayrshire, which, under such a gloomy sky, looked most desolate. We ran some distance along the coast, having a view of the Hills of Arran, and reached Ayr about nine o'clock. We came first to the New Bridge, which had a triumphal arch in the middle, and the lines, from the "Twa Brigs of Ayr:"

> "Will your poor narrow foot-path of a street,
>
> Where twa wheel-barrows tremble when they meet,
>
> Your ruin'd, formless bulk o' stane and lime,
>
> Compare wi' bonnie brigs o' modern time?"

While on the arch of the 'old brig' was the reply:

> "I'll be a brig when ye're a shapeless stane."

As we advanced into the town, the decorations became more frequent. The streets were crowded with people carrying banners and wreaths, many of the houses were adorned with green boughs and the vessels in the harbor hung out all their flags. We saw the Wallace Tower, a high Gothic building, having in front a statue of Wallace leaning on his sword, by Thom, a native of Ayr, and on our way to the green, where the procession was to assemble, passed under the triumphal arch thrown across the street opposite the inn where Tarn O'Shanter caroused so long with Souter Johnny. Leaving the companies to form on the long meadow bordering the shore, we set out for the Doon, three miles distant. Beggars were seated at regular distances along the road, uttering the most dolorous whinings. Both bridges were decorated in the same manner, with miserable looking objects, keeping up, during the whole day, a continual lamentation. Persons are prohibited from begging in England and Scotland, but I suppose, this being an extraordinary day, license was given them as a favor, to beg free. I noticed that the women, with their usual kindness of heart, bestowed nearly all the alms which these unfortunate objects received. The night before, as I was walking through the streets of Glasgow, a young man of the poorer class, very scantily dressed, stepped up to me and begged me to listen to him for a moment. He spoke hurriedly, and agitatedly, begging me, in God's name, to give him something, however little. I gave him what few pence I had with me, when he grasped my hand with a quick motion, saying: "Sir, you little think how much you have done for me." I was about to inquire more particularly into his situation, but he had disappeared among the crowd.

We passed the "cairn where hunters found the murdered bairn," along a pleasant road to the Burns cottage, where it was spanned by a magnificent triumphal arch of evergreens and flowers. To the disgrace of Scotland, this neat little thatched cot, where Burns passed the first seven years of his life, is now occupied by somebody, who has stuck up a sign over the door, "licensed to retail spirits, to be drunk on the premises;" and accordingly the rooms were crowded full of people, all drinking. There was a fine original portrait of Burns in one room, and in the old fashioned kitchen we saw the recess where he was born. The hostess looked towards us as if to inquire what we would drink, and I hastened away—there was profanity in the thought. But by this time, the bell of Old Alloway, which still hangs in its accustomed place, though the walls only are left, began tolling, and we obeyed the call. The attachment of the people for this bell, is so great, that a short time ago, when it was ordered to be removed, the inhabitants rose en masse, and prevented it. The ruin, which is close by the road, stands in the middle of the church-yard, and the first thing I saw, on going in the gate, was the tomb of the father of Burns. I looked in the old window, but the interior was filled with rank weeds, and overshadowed by a young tree, which had grown nearly to the eaves.

The crowd was now fast gathering in the large field, in the midst of

354

which the pavilion was situated. We went down by the beautiful monument to Burns, to the "Auld Brig o' Doon," which was spanned by an arch of evergreens, containing a representation of Tam O'Shanter and his grey mare, pursued by the witches. It had been arranged that the procession was to pass over the old and new bridges, and from thence by a temporary bridge over the hedge into the field. At this latter place a stand was erected for the sons of Burns, the officers of the day, and distinguished guests. Here was a beautiful specimen of English exclusiveness. The space adjoining the pavilion was fenced around, and admittance denied at first to any, except those who had tickets for the dinner, which, the price being fifteen shillings, entirely prevented the humble laborers, who, more than all, should participate on the occasion, from witnessing the review of the procession by the sons of Burns, and hearing the eloquent speeches of Professor Wilson and Lord Eglintoun. Thus, of the many thousands who were in the field, but a few hundred who were crowded between the bridge and the railing around the pavilion, enjoyed the interesting spectacle. By good fortune, I obtained a stand, where I had an excellent view of the scene. The sons of Burns were in the middle of the platform, with Eglintoun on the right, and Wilson on their left. Mrs. Begg, sister of the Poet, with her daughters, stood by the Countess of Eglintoun. She was a plain, benevolent looking woman, dressed in black, and appearing still active and vigorous, though she is upwards of eighty years old. She bears some likeness, especially in the expression of her eye, to the Poet. Robert Burns, the oldest son, appeared to me to have a strong resemblance of his father, and it is said he is the only one who remembers his face. He has for a long time had an office under Government, in London. The others have but lately returned from a residence of twenty years in India. Professor Wilson appeared to enter into the spirit of the scene better than any of them. He shouted and waved his hat, and, with his fine, broad forehead, his long brown locks already mixed with gray, streaming over his shoulders, and that eagle eye glancing over the vast assemblage, seemed a real Christopher North, yet full of the fire and vigor of youth—"a gray-haired, happy boy!"

About half of the procession consisted of lodges of masons, all of whom turned out on the occasion, as Burns was one of the fraternity. I was most interested in several companies of shepherds, from the hills, with their crooks and plaids; a body of archers in Lincoln green, with a handsome chief at their head, and some Highlanders in their most picturesque of costumes. As one of the companies, which carried a mammoth thistle in a box, came near the platform, Wilson snatched a branch, regardless of its pricks, and placed it on his coat. After this pageant, which could not have been much less than three miles long, had passed, a band was stationed on the platform in the centre of the field, around which it formed in a circle, and the whole company sang, "Ye Banks and Braes o' Bonnie Doon." Just at this time, a person dressed to represent Tam O'Shanter, mounted on a gray mare, issued from a field near the Burns Monument and rode along towards Alloway Kirk, from which, when he approached it, a whole legion of witches sallied out and commenced a hot pursuit. They turned back, however, at the keystone of the bridge, the witch with the "cutty sark" holding up in triumph the abstracted tail of Maggie. Soon after this the company entered the pavilion, and the thousands outside were entertained, as an especial favor, by the band of the 87th Regiment, while from the many liquor booths around the field, they could enjoy themselves in another way.

We went up to the Monument, which was of more particular interest to us, from the relics within, but admission was denied to all. Many persons were collected around the gate, some of whom, having come from a great distance, were anxious to see it; but the keeper only said, such were the orders and he could not disobey them. Among the crowd, a grandson of the original Tam O'Shanter was shown to us. He was a raw-looking boy of nineteen or twenty, wearing a shepherd's cap and jacket, and muttered his disapprobation very decidedly, at not being able to visit the Monument.

There were one or two showers during the day, and the sky, all the time, was dark and lowering, which was unfavorable for the celebration; but all were glad enough that the rain kept aloof till the ceremonies were nearly over. The speeches delivered at the dinner, which appeared in the papers next morning, are undoubtedly very eloquent. I noticed in the remarks of Robert Burns, in reply to Professor Wilson, an acknowledgment which the other speakers forgot. He said, "The Sons of Burns have grateful hearts, and to the last hour of their existence, they will remember the honor that has been paid them this day, by the noble, the lovely and the talented, of their native land—by men of genius and kindred spirit from our sister land—and lastly, they owe their thanks to the inhabitants of the far distant west, a country of a great, free, and kindred people! (loud cheers.)" In connexion with this subject, I saw an anecdote of the Poet, yesterday, which is not generally known. During his connexion with the Excise, he was one day at a party, where the health of Pitt, then minister, was proposed, as "his master and theirs." He immediately turned down his glass and said, "I will give you the health of a far greater and better man—GEORGE WASHINGTON!"

We left the field early and went back through the muddy streets of Ayr. The street before the railway office was crowded, and there was so dense a mass of people on the steps, that it seemed almost impossible to get near. Seeing no other chance, I managed to take my stand on the lowest steps, where the pressure of the crowd behind and the working of the throng on the steps, raised me off my feet, and in about a quarter of an hour carried me, compressed into the smallest possible space, up the steps to the door, where the crowd burst in by fits, like water rushing out of a bottle. We esteemed ourselves fortunate in getting room to stand in an open car, where, after a two hours' ride through the wind and pelting rain, we arrived at Glasgow.

CHAPTER V. — WALK FROM EDINBURG OVER THE BORDER AND ARRIVAL AT LONDON.

We left Glasgow on the morning after returning from the Burns Festival, taking passage in the open cars for Edinburg, for six shillings. On leaving the depot, we plunged into the heart of the hill on which Glasgow Cathedral stands and were whisked through darkness and sulphury smoke to daylight again. The cars bore us past a spur of the Highlands, through a beautiful country where women were at work in the fields, to Linlithgow, the birth-place of Queen Mary. The majestic ruins of its once-proud palace, stand on a green meadow behind the town. In another hour we were walking through Edinburg, admiring its palace-like edifices, and stopping every few minutes to gaze up at some lofty monument. Really, thought I, we call Baltimore the "Monumental City" for its two marble columns, and here is Edinburg with one at every street-corner! These, too, not in the midst of glaring red buildings, where they seem to have been accidentally dropped, but framed in by lofty granite mansions, whose long vistas make an appropriate background to the picture.

We looked from Calton Hill on Salisbury Crags and over the Firth of Forth, then descended to dark old Holyrood, where the memory of lovely Mary lingers like a stray sunbeam in her cold halls, and the fair, boyish face of Rizzio looks down from the canvass on the armor of his murderer. We threaded the Canongate and climbed to the Castle; and finally, after a day and a half's sojourn, buckled on our knapsacks and marched out of the Northern Athens. In a short time the tall spire of Dalkeith appeared above the green wood, and we saw to the right, perched on the steep banks of the Esk, the picturesque cottage of Hawthornden, where Drummond once lived in poetic solitude. We made haste to cross the dreary waste of the Muirfoot Hills before nightfall, from the highest summit of which we took a last view of Edinburg Castle and the Salisbury Crags, then blue in the distance. Far to the east were the hills of Lammermuir and the country of Mid-Lothian lay before us. It was all Scott-land. The inn of Torsonce, beside the Gala Water, was our resting-place for the night. As we approached Galashiels the next morning, where the bed of the silver Gala is nearly emptied by a number of dingy manufactories, the hills opened, disclosing the sweet vale of the Tweed, guarded by the triple peak of the Eildon, at whose base lay nestled the village of Melrose.

I stopped at a bookstore to purchase a view of the Abbey; to my surprise nearly half the works were by American authors. There wore Bryant, Longfellow, Channing, Emerson, Dana, Ware and many others. The bookseller told me he had sold more of Ware's Letters than any other book in his store, "and also," to use his own words, "an immense number of the great Dr. Channing." I have seen English editions of Percival, Willis, Whittier and Mrs. Sigourney, but Bancroft and Prescott are classed among the "standard British historians."

Crossing the Gala we ascended a hill on the road to Selkirk, and behold! the Tweed ran below, and opposite, in the midst of embowering trees planted by the hand of Scott, rose the grey halls of Abbotsford. We went down a lane to the banks of the swift stream, but finding no ferry, B—— and I, as it looked very shallow, thought we might save a long walk by wading across. F—— preferred hunting for a boat; we two set out together, with our knapsacks on our backs, and our boots in our hands. The current was ice-cold and very swift, and as the bed was covered with loose stones, it required the greatest care to stand upright. Looking at the bottom, through the rapid water, made my head so giddy, I was forced to stop and shut my eyes; my friend, who had firmer nerves, went plunging on to a deeper and swifter part, where the strength of the current made him stagger very unpleasantly. I called to him to return; the next thing I saw, he gave a plunge and went down to the shoulder in the cold flood. While he was struggling with a frightened expression of face to recover his footing, I leaned on my staff and laughed till I was on the point of falling also. To crown our mortification, F—— had found a ferry a few yards higher up and was on the opposite shore, watching us wade back again, my friend with dripping clothes and boots full of water. I could not forgive the pretty Scotch damsel who rowed us across, the mischievous lurking smile which told that she too had witnessed the adventure.

We found a foot-path on the other side, which led through a young forest to Abbotsford. Rude pieces of sculpture, taken from Melrose Abbey, were scattered around the gate, some half buried in the earth and overgrown with weeds. The niches in the walls were filled with pieces of sculpture, and an antique marble greyhound reposed in the middle of the court yard. We rang the bell in an outer vestibule, ornamented with several pairs of antlers, when a lady appeared, who, from her appearance, I have no doubt was Mrs. Ormand, the "Duenna of Abbotsford," so humorously described by D'Arlincourt, in his "Three Kingdoms." She ushered us into the entrance hall, which has a magnificent ceiling of carved oak and is lighted by lofty stained windows. An effigy of a knight in armor stood at either end, one holding a huge two-handed sword found on Bosworth Field; the walls were covered with helmets and breastplates of the olden time.

Among the curiosities in the Armory are Napoleon's pistols, the blunderbuss of Hofer, Rob Roy's purse and gun, and the offering box of Queen Mary. Through the folding doors between the dining-room, drawing-room and library, is a fine vista, terminated by a niche, in which stands Chantrey's bust of Scott. The ceilings are of carved Scottish oak and the doors of American cedar. Adjoining the library is his study, the walls of which are covered with books; the doors and windows are double, to render it quiet and undisturbed. His books and inkstand are on the table and his writing-chair stands before it, as if he had left them but a moment before. In a little closet adjoining, where he kept his private manuscripts, are the clothes he last wore, his cane and belt, to which a hammer and small axe are attached, and his sword. A narrow staircase led from the study to his sleeping room above, by which he could come down at night and work while his family slept. The silence about the place is solemn and breathless, as if it waited to be broken by his returning footstep. I felt an awe in treading these lonely halls, like that which impressed me before the grave of Washington—a feeling that hallowed the spot, as if there yet lingered a low vibration of the lyre, though the minstrel had departed forever!

Plucking a wild rose that grew near the walls, I left Abbotsford, embosomed among the trees, and turned into a green lane that led down to Melrose. We went immediately to the Abbey, in the lower part of the village, near the Tweed. As I approached the gate, the porteress came out, and having scrutinized me rather sharply, asked my name. I told her;—"well," she added, "there is a prospect here for you." Thinking she alluded to the ruin, I replied: "Yes, the view is certainly very fine." "Oh! I don't mean that," she replied, "a young gentleman left a prospect here for you!"—whereupon she brought out a spy-glass, which I recognized us one that our German comrade had given to me. He had gone on, and hoped to meet us at Jedburgh.

Melrose is the finest remaining specimen of Gothic architecture in Scotland. Some of the sculptured flowers in the cloister arches are remarkably beautiful and delicate, and the two windows—the south and east oriels—are of a lightness and grace of execution really surprising. We saw the tomb of Michael Scott, of King Alexander II, and that of the Douglas, marked with a sword. The heart of Bruce is supposed to have been buried beneath the high altar. The chancel is all open to the sky, and rooks build their nests among the wild ivy that climbs over the crumbling arches. One of these came tamely down and perched upon the hand of our fair guide. By a winding stair in one of the towers we mounted to the top of the arch and looked down on the grassy floor. I sat on the broken pillar, which Scott always used for a seat when he visited the Abbey, and read the disinterring of the magic book, in the "Lay of the Last Minstrel." I never comprehended its full beauty till then: the memory of Melrose will give it a thrilling interest, in the future. When we left, I was willing to say, with the Minstrel:

"Was never scene so sad and fair!"

After seeing the home and favorite haunt of Scott, we felt a wish to stand by his grave, but we had Ancrum Moor to pass before night, and the Tweed was between us and Dryburgh Abbey. We did not wish to try another watery adventure, and therefore walked on to the village of Ancrum, where a gate-keeper on the road gave us lodging and good fare, for a moderate price. Many of this class practise this double employment, and the economical traveller, who looks more to comfort than luxury, will not fail to patronize them.

Next morning we took a foot-path over the hills to Jedburgh. From the summit there was a lovely view of the valley of the Teviot, with the blue

Cheviots in the distance. I thought of Pringle's beautiful farewell:

> "Our native land, our native vale,
>
> A long, a last adieu,
>
> farewell to bonny Teviot-dale,
>
> And Cheviot's mountains blue!"

The poet was born in the valley below, and one that looks upon its beauty cannot wonder how his heart clung to the scenes he was leaving. We saw Jedburgh and its majestic old Abbey, and ascended the valley of the Jed towards the Cheviots. The hills, covered with woods of a richness and even gorgeous beauty of foliage, shut out this lovely glen completely from the world. I found myself continually coveting the lonely dwellings that were perched on the rocky heights, or nestled, like a fairy pavilion, in the lap of a grove. These forests formerly furnished the wood for the celebrated Jedwood axe, used in the Border forays.

As we continued ascending, the prospect behind us widened, till we reached the summit of the Carter Fell, whence there is a view of great extent and beauty. The Eildon Hills, though twenty-five miles distant, seemed in the foreground of the picture. With a glass, Edinburgh Castle might be seen over the dim outline of the Muirfoot Hills. After crossing the border, we passed the scene of the encounter between Percy and Douglass, celebrated in "Chevy Chase," and at the lonely inn of Whitelee, in the valley below, took up our quarters for the night.

Travellers have described the Cheviots as being bleak and uninteresting. Although they are bare and brown, to me the scenery was of a character of beauty entirely original. They are not rugged and broken like the Highlands, but lift their round backs gracefully from the plain, while the more distant ranges are clad in many an airy hue. Willis quaintly and truly remarks, that travellers only tell you the picture produced in their own brain by what they see, otherwise the world would be like a pawnbroker's shop, where each traveller wears the cast-off clothes of others. Therefore let no one, of a gloomy temperament, journeying over the Cheviots in dull November, arraign me for having falsely praised their beauty.

I was somewhat amused with seeing a splendid carriage with footmen and outriders, crossing the mountain, the glorious landscape full in view, containing a richly dressed lady, fast asleep! It is no uncommon thing to meet carriages in the Highlands, in which the occupants are comfortably reading, while being whirled through the finest scenery. And apropos of this subject, my German friend related to me an incident. His brother was travelling on the Rhine, and when in the midst of the grandest scenes, met a carriage containing an English gentleman and lady, both asleep, while on the seat behind was stationed an artist, sketching away with all his might. He asked the latter the reason of his industry, when he answered, "Oh! my lord wishes to see every night what he has passed during the day, and so I sketch as we go along!"

The hills, particularly on the English side, are covered with flocks of sheep, and lazy shepherds lay basking in the sun, among the purple heather, with their shaggy black dogs beside them. On many of the hills are landmarks, by which, when the snow has covered all the trucks, they can direct their way. After walking many miles through green valleys, down which flowed the Red Water, its very name telling of the conflicts which had crimsoned its tide, we came to the moors, and ten miles of blacker, drearier waste I never saw. Before entering them we passed the pretty little village of Otterburn, near the scene of the battle. I brought away a wild flower that grew on soil enriched by the blood of the Percys. On the village inn, is their ancient coat of arms, a lion rampant, on a field of gold, with the motto, "Esperance en Dieu." Scarcely a house or a tree enlivened the black waste, and even the road was marked on each side by high poles, to direct the traveller in winter. We were glad when at length the green fields came again in sight, and the little village of Whelpington Knowes, with its old ivy-grown church tower, welcomed us after the lonely walk.

As one specimen of the intelligence of this part of England, we saw a board conspicuously posted at the commencement of a private road, declaring that "all persons travelling this way will be persecuted." As it led to a church, however, there may have been a design in the expression.

On the fifth day after leaving Edinburgh, we reached a hill, overlooking the valley of the Tyne and the German Ocean, as sunset was reddening in the west. A cloud of coal-smoke made us aware of the vicinity of Newcastle. On the summit of the hill a large cattle fair was being held, and crowds of people were gathered in and around a camp of gaudily decorated tents. Fires were kindled here and there, and drinking, carousing and horse-racing were flourishing in full vigor.

We set out one morning to hunt the Roman Wall. Passing the fine buildings in the centre of the city and the lofty monument to Earl Grey, we went towards the western gate and soon came to the ruins of a building, about whose origin there could be no doubt. It stood there, blackened by the rust of ages, a remnant of power passed away. There was no mistaking the massive round tower, with its projecting ornaments, such as are often seen in the ruder works of the Romans. On each side a fragment of wall remained standing, and there appeared to be a chamber in the interior, which was choked up with rubbish. There is another tower, much higher, in a public square in another part of the city, a portion of which is fitted up as a dwelling for the family which takes care of it; but there was such a ridiculous contrast between the ivy-grown top, and the handsome modern windows and doors of the lower story, that it did not impress me half as much as the other, with all its neglect. These are the farthest limits of that power whose mighty works I hope hereafter to view at the seat of her grandeur and glory.

I witnessed a scene at Newcastle that cannot soon be forgotten; as it showed more plainly than I had before an opportunity of observing, the state to which the laboring classes of England are reduced. Hearing singing in the street, under my window, one morning, I looked out and saw a body of men, apparently of the lower class, but decent and sober looking, who were singing in a rude and plaintive strain some ballad, the purport of which I could not understand. On making inquiry, I discovered it was part of a body of miners, who, about eighteen weeks before, in consequence of not being able to support their families with the small pittance allowed them, had "struck" for higher wages. This their employers refused to give them, and sent to Wales, where they obtained workmen at the former price. The houses these laborers had occupied were all taken from them, and for eighteen weeks they had no other means of subsistence than the casual charity given them for singing the story of their wrongs. It made my blood boil to bear those tones, wrung from the heart of poverty by the hand of tyranny. The ignorance, permitted by the government, causes an unheard amount of misery and degradation. We heard afterwards in the streets, another company who played on musical instruments. Beneath the proud swell of England's martial airs, there sounded to my ears a tone whose gathering murmur will make itself heard ere long by the dull cars of Power.

At last at the appointed time, we found ourselves on board the "London Merchant," in the muddy Tyne, waiting for the tide to rise high enough to permit us to descend the river. There is great competition among the steamboats this summer, and the price of passage to London is reduced to five and ten shillings. The second cabin, however, is a place of tolerable comfort, and as the steward had promised to keep berths for us, we engaged passage. Following the windings of the narrow river, we passed Sunderland and Tynemouth, where it expands into the German Ocean. The water was barely stirred by a gentle wind, and little resembled the stormy sea I expected to find it. We glided over the smooth surface, watching the blue line of the distant shore till dark, when I went below expecting to enjoy a few hours' oblivion. But the faithless steward had given up the promised berth to another, and it was only with difficulty that I secured a seat by the cabin table, where I dozed half the night with my head on my arms. It grew at last too close and wearisome; I went up on deck and lay down on the windlass, taking care to balance myself well before going to sleep. The earliest light of dawn awoke me to a consciousness of damp clothes and bruised limbs. We were in sight of the low shore the whole day, sometimes seeing the dim outline of a church, or group of trees over the downs or flat beds of sand, which border the eastern coast of England. About dark, the red light of the Nore was seen, and we hoped before many hours to be in London. The lights of Gravesend were passed, but about ten o'clock, as we entered the narrow channel of the Thames, we struck another steamboat in the darkness, and were obliged to cast anchor for some time. When I went on deck in the gray light of morning again, we were gliding up a narrow, muddy river, between rows of gloomy buildings, with many vessels lying at anchor. It grew lighter, till, as we turned a point, right before, me lay a vast crowd of vessels, and in the distance, above the wilderness of buildings, stood a dim, gigantic dome in the sky; what a bound my heart gave at the sight! And the tall pillar that stood near it—I did not need a second glance to recognize the Monument. I knew the majestic bridge that spanned the river above; but on the right bank stood a cluster of massive buildings, crowned with many a turret, that attracted my eye. A crowd of old associations pressed bewilderingly upon the mind, to see standing there, grim and dark with many a bloody page of England's history—the Tower of London! The morning sky was as yet but faintly obscured by the coal-smoke, and in the misty light of coming sunrise, all objects seemed grander than their wont. In spite of the thrilling interest of the scene, I could not help thinking of Byron's ludicrous but most expressive description:

> "A mighty mass of brick and smoke and shipping,
>
> Dirty and dusky, but as wide as eye
>
> Can reach; with here and there a sail just skipping
>
> In sight, then lost amidst the forestry
>
> Of masts; a wilderness of steeples peeping
>
> On tiptoe through their sea-coal canopy;
>
> A huge dun cupola, like a fool's-cap crown
>
> On a fool's head,—and there is London town."

366

CHAPTER VI. — SOME OF THE "SIGHTS" OF LONDON.

In the course of time we came to anchor in the stream; skiffs from the shore pulled alongside, and after some little quarrelling, we were safely deposited in one, with a party who desired to be landed at the Tower Stairs. The dark walls frowned above us as we mounted from the water and passed into an open square on the outside of the moat. The laborers were about commencing work, the fashionable day having just closed, but there was still noise and bustle enough in the streets, particularly when we reached Whitechapel, part of the great thoroughfare, extending through the heart of London to Westminster Abbey and the Parliament buildings. Further on, through Leadenhall street and Fleet street—what a world! Here come the ever-thronging, ever-rolling waves of life, pressing and whirling on in their tumultuous career. Here day and night pours the stream of human beings, seeming amid the roar and din and clatter of the passing vehicles, like the tide of some great combat. How lonely it makes one to stand still and feel that of all the mighty throng which divides itself around him, not a being knows or cares for him! What knows he too of the thousands who pass him by? How many who bear the impress of godlike virtue, or hide beneath a goodly countenance a heart black with crime? How many fiery spirits, all glowing with hope for the yet unclouded future, or brooding over a darkened and desolate past in the agony of despair? There is a sublimity in this human Niagara that makes one look on his own race with something of awe.

We walked down the Thames, through the narrow streets of Wapping, Over the mouth of the Tunnel is a large circular building, with a dome to light the entrance below. Paying the fee of a penny, we descended by a winding staircase to the bottom, which is seventy-three feet below the surface. The carriage-way, still unfinished, will extend further into the city. From the bottom the view of the two arches of the Tunnel, brilliantly lighted with gas, is very fine; it has a much less heavy and gloomy appearance than I expected. As we walked along under the bed of the river, two or three girls at one end began playing on the French horn and bugle, and the echoes, when not too deep to confuse the melody, were remarkably beautiful. Between the arches of the division separating the two passages, are shops, occupied by venders of fancy articles, views of the Tunnel, engravings, &c. In the middle is a small printing press, where, a sheet containing a description of the whole work is printed for those who desire it. As I was no stranger to this art, I requested the boy to let me print one myself, but he had such a bad roller I did not succeed in getting a good impression. The air within is somewhat damp, but fresh and agreeably cool, and one can scarcely realize in walking along the light passage, that a river is rolling above his head. The immense solidity and compactness of the structure precludes the danger of accident, each of the sides being arched outwards, so that the heaviest pressure only strengthens the whole. It will long remain a noble monument of human daring and ingenuity.

St. Paul's is on a scale of grandeur excelling every thing I have yet seen. The dome seems to stand in the sky, as you look up to it; the distance from which you view it, combined with the atmosphere of London, give it a dim, shadowy appearance, that perfectly startles one with its immensity. The roof from which the dome springs is itself as high as the spires of most other churches—blackened for two hundred years with the coal-smoke of London, it stands like a relic of the giant architecture of the early world. The interior is what one would expect to behold, after viewing the outside. A maze of grand arches on every side, encompasses the dome, which you gaze up at, as at the sky; and from every pillar and wall look down the marble forms of the dead. There is scarcely a vacant niche left in all this mighty hall, so many are the statues that meet one on every side. With the exceptions of John Howard, Sir Astley Cooper and Wren, whose monument is the church itself, they are all to military men. I thought if they had all been removed except Howard's, it would better have suited such a temple, and the great soul it commemorated.

I never was more impressed with the grandeur of human invention, than when ascending the dome. I could with difficulty conceive the means by which such a mighty edifice had been lifted into the air. That small frame of Sir Christopher Wren must have contained a mind capable of vast conceptions. The dome is like the summit of a mountain; so wide is the prospect, and so great the pile upon which you stand. London lay beneath us, like an ant-hill, with the black insects swarming to and fro in their long avenues, the sound of their employments coming up like the roar of the sea. A cloud of coal-smoke hung over it, through which many a pointed spire was thrust up; sometimes the wind would blow it aside for a moment, and the thousands of red roofs would shine out clearer. The bridged Thames, covered with craft of all sizes, wound beneath us like a ringed and spotted serpent. The scene was like an immense circular picture in the blue frame of the hills around.

Continuing our way up Fleet street, which, notwithstanding the gaiety of its shops and its constant bustle, has an antique appearance, we came to the Temple Bar, the western boundary of the ancient city. In the inside of the middle arch, the old gates are still standing. From this point we entered the new portion of the city, which wore an air of increasing splendor as we advanced. The appearance of the Strand and Trafalgar Square is truly magnificent. Fancy every house in Broadway a store, all built of light granite, the Park stripped of all its trees and paved with granite, and a lofty column in the centre, double the crowd and the tumult of business, and you will have some idea of the view.

It was a relief to get into St. James's Park, among the trees and flowers again. Here, beautiful winding walks led around little lakes, in which were hundreds of water-fowl, swimming. Groups of merry children were sporting on the green lawn, enjoying their privilege of roaming every where at will, while the older bipeds were confined to the regular walks. At the western end stood Buckingham Palace, looking over the trees towards St. Paul's; through the grove on the eminence above, the towers of St. James's could be seen. But there was a dim building, with two lofty square towers, decorated with a profusion of pointed Gothic pinnacles, that I looked at with more interest than these appendages of royalty. I could not linger long in its vicinity, but going back again by the Horse Guards, took the road to Westminster Abbey.

We approached by the general entrance, Poet's Corner. I hardly stopped to look at the elaborate exterior of Henry VIIth's Chapel, but passed on to the door. On entering, the first thing that met my eyes were the words, "OH RARE BEN JONSON," under his bust. Near by stood the monuments of Spenser and Gay, and a few paces further looked down the sublime countenance of Milton. Never was a spot so full of intense interest. The light was just dim enough to give it a solemn, religious appearance, making the marble forms of poets and philosophers so shadowy and impressive, that I felt as if standing in their living presence. Every step called up some mind linked with the associations of my childhood. There was the gentle feminine countenance of Thompson, and the majestic head of Dryden; Addison with his classic features, and Gray, full of the fire of lofty thought. In another chamber, I paused long before the ashes of Shakspeare; and while looking at the monument of Garrick, started to find that I stood upon his grave. What a glorious galaxy of genius is here collected—what a constellation of stars whose light is immortal! The mind is completely fettered by their spirit. Everything is forgotten but the mighty dead, who still "rule us from their urns."

The Chapel of Henry VII., which we next entered, is one of the most elaborate specimens of Gothic workmanship in the world. If the first idea of the Gothic arch sprung from observing the forms of trees, this chapel must resemble the first conceptions of that order, for the fluted columns rise up like tall trees, branching out at the top into spreading capitals covered with leaves, and supporting arches of the ceiling resembling a leafy roof.

The side-chapels are filled with tombs of knightly families, the husband and wife lying on their backs on the tombs, with their hands clasped, while their children, about the size of dolls, are kneeling around. Numberless are the Barons and Earls and Dukes, whose grim effigies stare from their tombs. In opposite chapels are the tombs of Mary and Elizabeth, and near the former that of Darnley. After having visited many of the scenes of her life, it was with no ordinary emotion that I stood by the sepulchre of Mary. How differently one looks upon it and upon that of the proud Elizabeth!

We descended to the Chapel of Edward the Confessor, within the splendid shrine of which repose his ashes. Here we were shown the chair on which the English monarchs have been crowned for several hundred years, Under the seat is the stone, brought from the Abbey of Scone, whereon the Kings of Scotland were crowned. The chair is of oak, carved and hacked over with names, and on the bottom some one has recorded his name with the fact that, he once slept in it. We sat down and rested in it without ceremony.

Passing along an aisle leading to the grand hall, we saw the tomb of Aymer de Valence, a knight of the Crusades. Near here is the hall where the Knights of the order of Bath met. Over each seat their dusty banners are still hanging, each with its crest, and their armor is rusting upon the wall. It seemed like a banqueting hall of the olden time, where the knights had left their seats for a moment vacant. Entering the nave, we were lost in the wilderness of sculpture. Here stood the forms of Pitt, Fox, Burke, Sheridan and Watts, from the chisels of Chantry, Bacon and Westmacott. Further down were Sir Isaac Newton and Sir Godfrey Kneller—opposite Andre, and Paoli, the Italian, who died here in exile. How can I convey an idea of the scene? Notwithstanding all the descriptions I had read, I was totally unprepared for the reality, nor could I have anticipated the hushed and breathless interest with which I paced the dim aisles, gazing, at every step, on the last resting place of some great and familiar name. A place so sacred to all who inherit the English tongue, is worthy of a special pilgrimage across the deep. To those who are unable to visit it, a description may be interesting; but so far does it fall short of the scene itself, that if I thought it would induce a few of our wealthy idlers, or even those who, like myself, must travel with toil and privation to come hither, I would write till the pen dropped from my hand.

More than twenty grand halls of the British Museum are devoted to antiquities, and include the Elgin Marbles—the spoils of the Parthenon—the Fellows Marbles, brought from the ancient city of Xanthus, and Sir William Hamilton's collection of Italian antiquities. It was painful to see the friezes of the Parthenon, broken and defaced as they are, in such a place. Rather let them moulder to dust on the ruin from which they were torn, shining through the blue veil of the Grecian atmosphere, from the summit of the Acropolis!

The National Gallery, on Trafalgar Square, is open four days in the week, to the public. The "Raising of Lazarus," by Sebastian del Piombo, is considered the gem of the collection, but my unschooled eyes could not view it as such. It is also remarkable for having been transferred from wood to canvass, without injury. This delicate operation was accomplished by gluing the panel on which it was painted, flat on a smooth table, and planing the wood gradually away till the coat of hardened paint alone remained. A proper canvass was then prepared, covered with a strong cement, and laid on the back of the picture, which adhered firmly to it. The owner's nerves must have had a severe trial, if he had courage to watch the operation. I was enraptured with Murillo's pictures of St. John and the Holy Family. St. John is represented as a boy in the woods, fondling a lamb. It is a glorious head. The dark curls cluster around his fair brow, and his eyes seem already glowing with the fire of future inspiration. There is an innocence, a childish sweetness of expression in the countenance, which makes one love to gaze upon it. Both of these paintings wore constantly surrounded by ladies, and they certainly deserved the preference. In the rooms devoted to English artists, there are many of the finest works of West, Reynolds, Hogarth and Wilkie.

We spent a day in visiting the lungs of London, as the two grand parks have been called. From the Strand through the Regent Circus, the centre of the fashionable part of the city, we passed to Piccadilly, culling on our way to see our old friends, the Iowas. They were at the Egyptian Hall, in connexion with Catlin's Indian collection. The old braves knew us at once, particularly Blister Feet, who used often to walk a linweon deck with me, at sea. Further along Piccadilly is Wellington's mansion of Apsley House, and nearly opposite it, in the corner of Hyde Park, stands the colossal statue of Achilles, cast from cannon taken at Salamanca and Vittoria. The Park resembles an open common, with here and there a grove of trees, intersected by carriage roads, it is like getting into the country again to be out on its broad, green field, with the city seen dimly around through the smoky atmosphere. We walked for a mile or two along the shady avenues and over the lawns, having a view of the princely terraces and gardens on one hand, and the gentle outline of Primrose Hill on the other. Regent's Park itself covers a space of nearly four hundred acres!

But if London is unsurpassed in splendor, it has also its corresponding share of crime. Notwithstanding the large and efficient body of police, who do much towards the control of vice, one sees enough of degradation and brutality in a short time, to make his heart sick. Even the public thorough fares are thronged at night with characters of the lowest description, and it is not expedient to go through many of the narrow bye-haunts of the old city in the day-time. The police, who are ever on the watch, immediately seize and carry off any offender, but from the statements of persons who have had an opportunity of observing, as well as from my own slight experience, I am convinced that there is an untold amount of misery and crime. London is one of the wonders of the world, but there is reason to believe it is one of the curses of the world also; though, in fact, nothing but an active and unceasing philanthropy can prevent any city from becoming so.

Aug. 22.—I have now been six days in London, and by making good use of my feet and eyes, have managed to become familiar with almost every object of interest within its precincts. Having a plan mapped out for the day, I started from my humble lodgings at the Aldgate Coffee House, where I slept off fatigue for a shilling a night, and walked up Cheapside or down Whitechapel, as the case might be, hunting out my way to churches, halls and theatres. In this way, at a trifling expense, I have perhaps seen as much as many who spend here double the time and ten times the money. Our whole tour from Liverpool hither, by way of Ireland and Scotland, cost us but twenty-five dollars each! although, except in one or two cases, we denied ourselves no necessary comfort. This shows that the glorious privilege of looking on the scenes of the old world need not be confined to people of wealth and leisure. It may be enjoyed by all who can occasionally forego a little bodily comfort for the sake of mental and spiritual gain. We leave this afternoon for Dover. Tomorrow I shall dine in Belgium!

CHAPTER VII. — FLIGHT THROUGH BELGIUM.

Bruges.—On the Continent at last! How strangely look the century-old towers, antique monuments, and quaint, narrow streets of the Flemish cities! It is an agreeable and yet a painful sense of novelty to stand for the first time in the midst of a people whose language and manners are different from one's own. The old buildings around, linked with many a stirring association of past history, gratify the glowing anticipations with which one has looked forward to seeing them, and the fancy is busy at work reconciling the real scene with the ideal; but the want of a communication with the living world about, walls one up with a sense of loneliness he could not before have conceived. I envy the children in the streets of Bruges their childish language.

Yesterday afternoon we came from London through the green wooded lawns and vales of England, to Dover, which we reached at sunset, passing by a long tunnel through the lofty Shakspeare Cliff. We had barely time before it grew dark to ascend the cliff. The glorious coast view looked still wilder in the gathering twilight, which soon hid from our sight the dim hills of France. On the cliff opposite frowned the massive battlements of the Castle, guarding the town, which lay in a nook of the rocks below. As the Ostend boat was to leave at four in the morning, my cousin aroused us at three, and we felt our way down stairs in the dark. But the landlord was reluctant to part with us; we stamped and shouted and rang bells, till the whole house was in an uproar, for the door was double-locked, and the steamboat bell began to sound. At last he could stand it no longer; we gave a quick utterance to our overflowing wrath, and rushed down to the boat but a second or two before it left.

The water of the Channel was smooth as glass and as the sun rose, the far chalky cliffs gleamed along the horizon, a belt of fire. I waved a good-bye to Old England and then turned to see the spires of Dunkirk, which were visible in the distance before us. On the low Belgian coast we could see trees and steeples, resembling a mirage over the level surface of the sea; at length, about ten o'clock, the square tower of Ostend came in sight. The boat passed into a long muddy basin, in which many unwieldy, red-sailed Dutch craft were lying, and stopped beside a high pier. Here amid the confusion of three languages, an officer came on board and took charge of our passports and luggage. As we could not get the former for two or three hours, we did not hurry the passing of the latter, and went on shore quite unincumbered, for a stroll about the city, disregarding the cries of the hackney-coachmen on the pier, "Hotel d'Angleterre," "Hotel des Bains!" and another who called out in English, "I recommend you to the Royal Hotel, sir!"

There is little to be seen in Ostend. We wandered through long rows of plain yellow houses, trying to read the French and low Dutch signs, and at last came out on the wall near the sea. A soldier motioned us back as we attempted to ascend it, and muttering some unintelligible words, pointed to a narrow street near. Following this out of curiosity, we crossed the moat and found ourselves on the great bathing beach. To get out of the hands of the servants who immediately surrounded us, we jumped into one of the little wagons and were driven out into the surf.

To be certain of fulfilling the railroad regulations, we took our seats quarter of an hour before the time. The dark walls of Ostend soon vanished and we were whirled rapidly over a country perfectly level, but highly fertile and well cultivated. Occasionally there was a ditch or row of trees, but otherwise there was no division between the fields, and the plain stretched unbroken away into the distance. The twenty miles to Bruges we made in forty minutes. The streets of this antique city are narrow and crooked, and the pointed, ornamented gables of the houses, produce a novel impression on one who has been accustomed to the green American forests. Then there was the endless sound of wooden shoes clattering over the rough pavements, and people talking in that most unmusical of all languages, low Dutch. Walking at random through the streets, we came by chance upon the Cathedral of Notre Dame. I shall long remember my first impression of the scene within. The lofty gothic ceiling arched far above my head and through the stained windows the light came but dimly—it was all still, solemn and religious. A few worshippers were kneeling in silence before some of the shrines and the echo of my tread seemed like a profaning sound. On every side were pictures, saints gilded shrines. A few steps removed one from the bustle and din of the crowd to the stillness and solemnity of the holy retreat.

We learned from the guide, whom we had engaged because he spoke a few words of English, that there was still a treckshuyt line on the canals, and that one boat leaves to-night at ten o'clock for Ghent. Wishing to try this old Dutch method of travelling, he took us about half a mile along the Ghent road to the canal, where a moderate sized boat was lying. Our baggage deposited in the plainly furnished cabin, I ran back to Bruges, although it was beginning to grow dark, to get a sight of the belfry; for Longfellow's lines had been running through my head all day:

"In the market place of Bruges, stands the belfry old and brown, Thrice consumed and thrice rebuilded, still it watches o'er the town."

And having found the square, brown tower in one corner of the open market square, we waited to hear the chimes, which are said to be the finest in Europe. They rang out at last with a clear silvery tone, most beautifully musical indeed. We then returned to the boat in the twilight. We were to leave in about an hour, according to the arrangement, but as yet there was no sound to be heard, and we were the only tenants. However, trusting to Dutch regularity, we went to sleep in the full confidence of awakening in Ghent.

I awoke once in the night and saw the dark branches of trees passing before the window, but there was no perceptible sound nor motion; the boat glided along like a dream, and we were awakened next morning by its striking against the pier at Ghent. After paying three francs for the whole night journey, the captain gave us a guide to the railroad station, and as we had nearly an hour before the train left, I went to see the Cathedral of St. Bavon. After leaving Ghent, the road passes through a beautiful country, cultivated like a garden. The Dutch passion for flowers is displayed in the gardens around the cottages; even every vacant foot of ground along the railway is planted with roses and dahlias. At Ghent, the morning being fair, we took seats in the open cars. About noon it commenced raining and our situation was soon anything but comfortable. My cousin had fortunately a water-proof Indian blanket with him, which he had purchased in the "Far West," and by wrapping this around all three of us, we kept partly dry. I was much amused at the plight of a party of young Englishmen, who were in the same car; one of them held a little parasol which just covered his hat, and sent the water in streams down on his back and shoulders.

We had a misty view of Liege, through the torrents of rain, and then dashed away into the wild, mountain scenery of the Meuse. Steep, rocky hills, covered with pine and crowned with ruined towers, hemmed in the winding and swollen river, and the wet, cloudy sky seemed to rest like a canopy on their summits. Instead of threading their mazy defiles, we plunged directly into the mountain's heart, flew over the narrow valley on lofty and light-sprung arches, and went again into the darkness. At Verviers, our baggage was weighed, examined and transferred, with ourselves, to a Prussian train. There was a great deal of disputing on the occasion. A lady, who had a dog in a large willow basket, was not allowed to retain it, nor would they take it as baggage. The matter was finally compromised by their sending the basket, obliging her to carry the dog, which was none of the smallest, in her arms! The next station bore the sign of the black eagle, and here our passports were obliged to be given up. Advancing through long ranges of wooded hills, we saw at length, in the dull twilight of a rainy day, the old kingly city of Aix la Chapelle on a plain below us. After a scene at the custom-house, where our baggage was reclaimed with tickets given at Verviers, we drove to the Hotel du Rhin, and while warming our shivering limbs and drying our damp garments, felt tempted to exclaim with the old Italian author: "O! holy and miraculous tavern!"

The Cathedral with its lofty Gothic tower, was built by the emperor Otho in the tenth century. It seems at present to be undergoing repairs, for a large scaffold shut out the dome. The long hall was dim with incense smoke as we entered, and the organ sounded through the high arches with an effect that startled me. The windows glowed with the forms of kings and saints, and the dusty and mouldering shrines which rose around were colored with the light that came through. The music pealed out like a triumphal march, sinking at times into a mournful strain, as if it celebrated and lamented the heroes who slept below. In the stone pavement nearly under my feet was a large square marble slab, with words "CAROLO MAGNO." It was like a dream, to stand there on the tomb of the mighty warrior, with the lofty arches of the Cathedral above, filled with the sound of the divine anthem. I mused above his ashes till the music ceased and then left the Cathedral, that nothing might break the romantic spell associated with that crumbling pile and the dead it covered. I have always revered the memory of Charlemagne. He lived in a stern age, but he was in mind and heart a man, and like Napoleon, who placed the iron crown which had lain with him centuries in the tomb, upon his own brow, he had an Alpine grandeur of mind, which the world was forced to acknowledge.

At noon we took the chars-à-banc, or second-class carriages, for fear of rain, and continued our journey over a plain dotted with villages and old chateaux. Two or three miles from Cologne we saw the spires of the different churches, conspicuous among which were the unfinished towers of the Cathedral, with the enormous crane standing as it did when they left off building, two hundred years ago or more. On arriving, we drove to the Bonn railway, where finding the last train did not leave for four hours, we left our baggage and set out for the Cathedral. Of all Gothic buildings, the plan of this is certainly the most stupendous; even ruin as it is, it cannot fail to excite surprise and admiration. The King of Prussia has undertaken to complete it according to the original plan, which was lately found in the possession of a poor man, of whom it was purchased for 40,000 florins, but he has not yet finished repairing what is already built. The legend concerning this plan may not be known to every one. It is related of the inventor of it, that in despair of finding any sufficiently great, he was walking one day by the river, sketching with his stick upon the sand, when he finally hit upon one which pleased him so much that he exclaimed: "This shall be the plan!" "I will show you a better one than that!" said a voice suddenly behind him, and a certain black gentleman who figures in all German legends stood by him, and pulled from his pocket a roll containing the present plan of the Cathedral. The architect, amazed at its grandeur, asked an explanation of every part. As he knew his soul was to be the price of it, he occupied himself while the devil was explaining, in committing its proportions carefully to memory. Having done this, he remarked that it did not please him and he would not take it.

The devil, seeing through the cheat, exclaimed in his rage: "You may build your Cathedral according to this plan, but you shall never finish it!" This prediction seems likely to be verified, for though it was commenced in 1248, and built for 250 years, only the choir and nave and one tower to half its original height, are finished.

We visited the chapel of the eleven thousand virgins, the walls of which are full of curious grated cells, containing their bones, and then threaded the narrow streets of Cologne, which are quite dirty enough to justify Coleridge's lines:

> "The river Rhine, it is well known
>
> Doth wash the city of Cologne;
>
> But tell me nymphs, what power divine
>
> Shall henceforth wash the river Rhine!"

CHAPTER VIII. — THE RHINE TO HEIDELBERG.

HEIDELBERG, August 30. Here at last! and a most glorious place it is. This is our first morning in our new rooms, and the sun streams warmly in the eastern windows, as I write, while the old castle rises through the blue vapor on the side of the Kaiser-stuhl. The Neckar rushes on below; and the Odenwald, before, me, rejoices with its vineyards in the morning light. The bells of the old chapel near us are sounding most musically, and a confused sound of voices and the rolling of vehicles comes up from the street. It is a place to live in!

I must go back five or six days and take up the record of our journeyings at Bonn. We had been looking over Murray's infallible "Handbook," and observed that he recommended the "Star" hotel in that city, as "the most moderate in its prices of any on the Rhine;" so when the train from Cologne arrived and we were surrounded, in the darkness and confusion, by porters and valets, I sung out: "Hotel de l'Etoile d'or!" our baggage and ourselves were transferred to a stylish omnibus, and in five minutes we stopped under a brilliantly-lighted archway, where Mr. Joseph Schmidt received us with the usual number of smiles and bows bestowed upon untitled guests. We were furnished with neat rooms in the summit of the house, and then descended to the salle à manger. I found a folded note by my plate, which I opened— it contained an engraving of the front of the hotel, a plan of the city and catalogue of its lions, together with a list of the titled personages who have, from time to time, honored the "Golden Star" with their custom. Among this number were "Their Royal Highnesses the Duke and Duchess of Cambridge, Prince Albert," etc. Had it not been for fatigue, I should have spent an uneasy night, thinking of the heavy bill which was to be presented on the morrow. We escaped, however, for seven francs apiece, three of which were undoubtedly for the honor of breathing an aristocratic atmosphere.

I was glad when we were really in motion on the swift Rhine, the next morning, and nearing the chain of mountains that rose up before us. We passed Godesberg on the right, while on our left was the group of the seven mountains which extend back from the Drachenfels to the Wolkenberg, or Castle of the Clouds. Here we begin to enter the enchanted land. The Rhine sweeps around the foot of the Drachenfels, while opposite the precipitous rock of Rolandseek, crowned with the castle of the faithful knight, looks down upon the beautiful Island of Nonnenwerth, the white walls of the convent still gleaming through the trees, as they did when the warrior's weary eyes looked upon them for the last time. I shall never forget the enthusiasm with which I saw this scene in the bright, warm sunlight, the rough crags softened in the haze which filled the atmosphere, and the wild mountains springing up in the midst of vineyards, and crowned with crumbling towers, filled with the memories of a thousand years.

After passing Andernach, we saw in the distance the highlands of the middle Rhine, which rise above Coblentz, guarding the entrance to its wild scenery, and the mountains of the Moselle. They parted as we approached; from the foot shot up the spires of Coblentz, and the battlements of Ehrenbreitstein crowning the mountain opposite, grew larger and broader. The air was slightly hazy, and the clouds seemed laboring among the distant mountains to raise a storm. As we came opposite the mouth of the Moselle and under the shadow of the mighty fortress, I gazed up with awe at its massive walls. Apart from its magnitude and almost impregnable situation on a perpendicular rock, it is filled with the recollections of history and hallowed by the voice of poetry. The scene went past like a panorama, the bridge of boats opened, the city glided behind us and we entered the highlands again.

Above Coblentz almost every mountain has a ruin and a legend. One feels everywhere the spirit of the past, and its stirring recollections come back upon the mind with irresistible force. I sat upon the deck the whole afternoon, as mountains, towns and castles passed by on either side, watching them with a feeling of the most enthusiastic enjoyment. Every place was familiar to me in memory, and they seemed like friends I had long communed with in spirit and now met face to face. The English tourists, with whom the deck was covered, seemed interested too, but in a different manner. With Murray's Handbook open in their hands, they sat and read about the very towns and towers they were passing, scarcely lifting their eyes to the real scenes, except now and then, to observe that it was "very nice."

As we passed Boppart, I sought out the Inn of the "Star," mentioned in "Hyperion"; there was a maiden sitting on the steps who might have been Paul Flemming's fair boat-woman. The clouds which had here gathered among the hills, now came over the river, and the rain cleared the deck of its crowd of admiring tourists. As we were approaching Lurlei Berg, I did not go below, and so enjoyed some of the finest scenery on the Rhine alone. The mountains approach each other at this point, and the Lurlei Rock rises up for six hundred feet from the water. This is the haunt of the water nymph, Lurlei, whose song charmed the ear of the boatman while his barque was dashed to pieces on the rocks below. It is also celebrated for its remarkable echo. As we passed between the rocks, a guard, who has a little house built on the road-side, blew a flourish on his bugle, which was instantly answered by a blast from the rocky battlements of Lurlei. The German students have a witty trick with this echo: they call out, "Who is the Burgomaster of Oberwesel?" a town just above. The echo answers with the last syllable "Esel!" which is the German for ass.

The sun came out of the cloud as we passed Oberwesel, with its tall round tower, and the light shining through the ruined arches of Schonberg castle, made broad bars of light and shade in the still misty air. A rainbow sprang up out of the Rhine, and lay brightly on the mountain side, coloring vineyard and crag, in the most singular beauty, while its second reflection faintly arched like a glory above the high summits. In the bed of the river were the seven countesses of Schonberg, turned into seven rocks for their cruelty and hard-heartedness towards the knights whom their beauty had made captive. In front, at a little distance was the castle of Pfalz, in the middle of the river, and from the heights above Caub frowned the crumbling citadel of Gutenfels. Imagine all this, and tell me if it is not a picture whose memory should last a life-time!

We came at last to Bingen, the southern gate of the Highlands. Here, on an island in the middle of the stream, is the old Mouse tower where Bishop Hatto of Mayence was eaten up by the rats for his wicked deeds.

Passing Rudesheim and Geissenheim, celebrated for their wines, at sunset, we watched the varied shore in the growing darkness, till like a line of stars across the water, we saw before us the bridge of Mayence.

The next morning I parted from my friends, who were going to Heidelberg by way of Mannheim, and set out alone for Frankfort. The cars passed through Hochheim, whose wines are celebrated all over the world; there is little to interest the traveler till he arrives at Frankfort, whose spires are seen rising from groves of trees as he approaches. I left the cars, unchallenged for my passport, greatly to my surprise, as it had cost me a long walk and five shillings in London, to get the signature of the Frankfort Consul. I learned afterwards it was not at all necessary. Before leaving America, N.P. Willis had kindly given me a letter to his brother, Richard S. Willis, who is now cultivating a naturally fine taste for music in Frankfort, and my first care was to find the American Consul, in order to learn his residence. I discovered at last, from a gentleman who spoke a little French, that the Consul's office was in the street Bellevue, which street I not only looked for through the city, but crossed over the bridge to the suburb of Sachsenhausen, and traversed its narrow, dirty alleys three several times, but in vain. I was about giving up the search, when I stumbled upon the office accidentally. The name of the street had been given to me in French and very naturally it was not to be found. Willis received me very kindly and introduced me to the amiable German family with whom he resides.

After spending a delightful evening with my newly-found friends, I left the next morning in the omnibus for Heidelberg. We passed through Sachsenhausen and ascended a long hill to the watch-tower, whence there is a beautiful view of the Main valley. Four hours' driving over the monotonous plain, brought me to Darmstadt. The city wore a gay look, left by the recent fêtes. The monument of the old Duke Ludwig had just been erected in the centre of the great square, and the festival attendant upon the unveiling of it, which lasted three days, had just closed. The city was hung with garlands, and the square filled with the pavilions of the royal family and the musicians, of whom there were a thousand present, while everywhere were seen red and white flags—the colors of Darmstadt. We met wagons decorated with garlands, full of pleasant girls, in the odd dress which they have worn for three hundred years.

After leaving Darmstadt we entered upon the Bergstrasse, or Mountain-way, leading along the foot of the mountain chain which extends all the way to Heidelberg on the left, while on the right stretches far away the Rhine-plain, across which we saw the dim outline of the Donnersberg, in France. The hills are crowned with castles and their sides loaded with vines; along the road the rich green foliage of the walnut trees arched and nearly met above us. The sun shone warm and bright, and every body appeared busy and contented and happy. All we met had smiling countenances. In some places we saw whole families sitting under the trees shelling the nuts they had beaten down, while others were returning from the vineyards, laden with baskets of purple and white grapes. The scene seemed to realize all I had read of the happiness of the German peasantry, and the pastoral beauty of the German plains.

With the passengers in the omnibus I could hold little conversation. One, who knew about as much French as I did, asked me where I came from, and I shall not soon forget his expression of incredulity, as I mentioned America. "Why," said he, "you are white—the Americans are all black!"

We passed the ruined castles of Auerback and Starkenburg, and Burg Windeck, on the summit of a mountain near Weinheim, formerly one of the royal residences of Charlemagne, and finally came to the Heiligenberg or Holy Mountain, guarding the entrance into the Odenwald by the valley of the Neckar. As we wound around its base to the river, the Kaiserstuhl rose before us, with the mighty castle hanging upon its side and Heidelberg at its feet. It was a most strikingly beautiful scene, and for a moment I felt inclined to assent to the remark of my bad-French acquaintance—"America is not beautiful—Heidelberg is beautiful!" The sun had just set as we turned the corner of the Holy Mountain and drove up the bank of the Neckar; all the chimes of Heidelberg began suddenly to ring and a cannon by the riverside was fired off every minute—the sound echoing five times distinctly from mountain back to mountain, and finally crashing far off, along the distant hills of the Odenwald. It was the birthday of the Grand Duke of Baden, and these rejoicings were for the closing fête.

CHAPTER IX. — SCENES IN AND AROUND HEIDELBERG.

Sept. 30.—There is so much to be seen around this beautiful place, that I scarcely know where to begin a description of it. I have been wandering among the wild paths that lead up and down the mountain side, or away into the forests and lonely meadows in the lap of the Odenwald. My mind is filled with images of the romantic German scenery, whose real beauty is beginning to displace the imaginary picture which I had painted with the enthusiastic words of Howitt. I seem to stand now upon the Kaiser-stuhl, which rises above Heidelberg, with that magnificent landscape around me, from the Black Forest and Strasburg to Mainz, and from the Vosges in France to the hills of Spessart in Bavaria. What a glorious panorama! and not less rich in associations than in its natural beauty. Below me had moved the barbarian hordes of old, the triumphant followers of Arminius, and the Cohorts of Rome; and later, full many a warlike host bearing the banners of the red cross to the Holy Land,—many a knight returning with his vassals from the field, to lay at the feet of his lady-love the scarf he had worn in a hundred battles and claim the reward of his constancy and devotion. But brighter spirits had also toiled below. That plain had witnessed the presence of Luther, and a host who strove with him to free the world from the chains of a corrupt and oppressive religion. There had also trodden the master spirits of German song—the giant twain, with their scarcely less harmonious brethren: they, too, had gathered inspiration from those scenes—more fervent worship of nature and a deeper love for their beautiful fatherland! Oh! what waves of crime and bloodshed have swept like the waves of a deluge down the valley of the Rhine! War has laid his mailed hand on those desolate towers and ruthlessly torn down what time has spared, yet he could not mar the beauty of the shore, nor could Time himself hurl down the mountains that guard it. And what if I feel a new inspiration on beholding the scene? Now that those ages have swept by, like the red waves of a tide of blood, we see not the darkened earth, but the golden sands which the flood has left behind. Besides, I have come from a new world, where the spirit of man is untrammeled by the mouldering shackles of the past, but in its youthful and joyous freedom, goes on to make itself a noble memory for the ages that are to come!

Then there is the Wolfsbrunnen, which one reaches by a beautiful walk up the bank of the Neckar, to a quiet dell in the side of the mountain. Through this the roads lead up by rustic mills, always in motion, and orchards laden with ripening fruit, to the commencement of the forest, where a quaint stone fountain stands, commemorating the abode of a sorceress of the olden time, who was torn in pieces by a wolf. There is a handsome rustic inn here, where every Sunday afternoon a band plays in the portico, while hundreds of people are scattered around in the cool shadow of the trees, or feeding the splendid trout in the basin formed by the little stream. They generally return to the city by another walk leading along the mountain side, to the eastern terrace of the castle, where they have fine views of the great Rhine plain, terminated by the Alsatian hills, stretching along the western horizon like the long crested swells on the ocean. We can even see these from the windows of our room on the bank of the Neckar; and I often look with interest on one sharp peak, for on its side stands the Castle of Trifels, where Coeur de Lion was imprisoned by the Duke of Austria, and where Blondel, his faithful minstrel, sang the ballad which discovered the retreat of the noble captive.

The people of Heidelberg are rich in places of pleasure and amusement. From the Carl Platz, an open square at the upper end of the city, two paths lead directly up to the castle. By the first walk we ascend a flight of steps to the western gate, passing through which, we enter a delightful garden, between the outer walls of the Castle, and the huge moat which surrounds it. Great linden, oak and beech trees shadow the walk, and in secluded nooks, little mountain streams spring from the side of the wall into stone basins. There is a tower over the moat on the south side, next the mountain, where the portcullis still hangs with its sharp teeth as it was last drawn up; on each side stand two grim knights guarding the entrance. In one of the wooded walks is an old tree brought from America in the year 1618. It is of the kind called arbor vitæ, and uncommonly tall and slender for one of this species; yet it does not seem to thrive well in a foreign soil. I noticed that persons had cut many slips off the lower branches, and I would have been tempted to do the same myself if there had been any I could reach. In the curve of the mountain is a handsome pavilion, surrounded with beds of flowers and fountains; here all classes meet together in the afternoon to sit with their refreshments in the shade, while frequently a fine band of music gives them their invariable recreation. All this, with the scenery around them, leaves nothing unfinished to their present enjoyment. The Germans enjoy life under all circumstances, and in this way they make themselves much happier than we, who have far greater means of being so.

At the end of the terrace built for the princess Elizabeth, of England, is one of the round towers, which was split in twain by the French. Half has fallen entirely away, and the other semicircular shell which joins the terrace and part of the Castle buildings, clings firmly together, although part of its foundation is gone, so that its outer ends actually hang in the air. Some idea of the strength of the castle may be obtained when I state that the walls of this tower are twenty-two feet thick, and that a staircase has been made through them to the top, where one can sit under the lindens growing upon it, or look down from the end on the city below with the pleasant consciousness that the great mass upon which he stands is only prevented from crashing down with him by the solidity of its masonry. On one side, joining the garden, the statue of the Archduke Louis, in his breastplate and flowing beard, looks out from among the ivy.

There is little to be seen about the Castle except the walls themselves. The guide conducted us through passages, in which were heaped many of the enormous cannon balls which it had received in sieges, to some chambers in the foundation. This was the oldest part of the Castle, built in the thirteenth century. We also visited the chapel, which is in a tolerable state of preservation. A kind of narrow bridge crosses it, over which we walked, looking down on the empty pulpit and deserted shrines. We then went into the cellar to see the celebrated Tun. In a large vault are kept several enormous hogsheads, one of which is three hundred years old, but they are nothing in comparison with the tun, which itself fills a whole vault. It is as high as a common two story house; on the top is a platform upon which the people used to dance after it was filled, to which one ascends by two flights of steps. I forgot exactly how many casks it holds, but I believe eight hundred. It has been empty for fifty years.

We are very pleasantly situated here. My friends, who arrived a day before me, hired three rooms (with the assistance of a courier) in a large house on the banks of the Neckar. We pay for them, with attendance, thirty florins—about twelve dollars—a month, and Frau Dr. Grosch, our polite and talkative landlady, gives us a student's breakfast—coffee and biscuit—for about seven cents apiece. We are often much amused to hear her endeavors to make us understand. As if to convey her meaning plainer, she raises both thumbs and forefingers to her mouth and pulls out the words like a long string; her tongue goes so fast that it keeps my mind always on a painful stretch to comprehend an idea here and there. Dr. S——, from whom we take lessons in German, has kindly consented to our dining with his family for the sake of practice in speaking. We have taken several long walks with them along the banks of the Neckar, but I should be puzzled to repeat any of the conversations that took place. The language, however, is fast growing more familiar, since women are the principal teachers.

Opposite my window rises the Heiligenberg, on the other side of the Neckar. The lower part of it is rich with vineyards, and many cottages stand embosomed in shrubbery among them. Sometimes we see groups of maidens standing under the grape arbors, and every morning the peasant women go toiling up the steep paths with baskets on their heads, to labor among the vines. On the Neckar below us, the fishermen glide about in their boats, sink their square nets fastened to a long pole, and haul them up with the glittering fish, of which the stream is full. I often lean out of the window late at night, when the mountains above are wrapped in dusky obscurity, and listen to the low, musical ripple of the river. It tells to my excited fancy a knightly legend of the old German time. Then comes the bell, rung for closing the inns, breaking the spell with its deep clang, which vibrates far away on the night air, till it has roused all the echoes of the Odenwald. I then shut the window, turn into the narrow box which the Germans call a bed, and in a few minutes am wandering in America. Half way up the Heiligenberg runs a beautiful walk, dividing the vineyards from the forest above. This is called the

Philosopher's Way, because it was the favorite ramble of the old Professors of the University. It can be reached by a toilsome, winding path among the vines, called the Snake-way, and when one has ascended to it he is well rewarded by the lovely view. In the evening, when the sun has got behind the mountain, it is delightful to sit on the stone steps and watch the golden light creeping up the side of the Kaiser-stuhl, till at last twilight begins to darken in the valley and a mantle of mist gathers above the Neckar.

We ascended the mountain a few days ago. There is a path which leads up through the forest, but we took the shortest way, directly up the side, though it was at an angle of nearly fifty degrees. It was hard enough work, scrambling through the thick broom and heather, and over stumps and stones. In one of the stone-heaps I dislodged a large orange-colored salamander, seven or eight inches long. They are sometimes found on these mountains, as well as a very large kind of lizard, called the eidechse, which the Germans say is perfectly harmless, and if one whistles or plays a pipe, will come and play around him. The view from the top reminded me of that from Catskill Mountain House, but is on a smaller scale. The mountains stretch off sideways, confining the view to but half the horizon, and in the middle of the picture the Hudson is well represented by the lengthened windings of the "abounding Rhine." Nestled at the base below us, was the little village of Handschuhheim, one of the oldest in this part of Germany. The castle of its former lords has nearly all fallen down, but the massive solidity of the walls which yet stand, proves its antiquity. A few years ago, a part of the outer walls which was remarked to have a hollow sound, was taken down, when there fell from a deep niche built therein, a skeleton, clad in a suit of the old German armor. We followed a road through the woods to the peak on which stand the ruins of St. Michael's chapel, which was built in the tenth century and inhabited for a long time by a sect of white monks. There is now but a single tower remaining, and all around is grown over with tall bushes and weeds. It had a wild and romantic look, and I sat on a rock and sketched at it, till it grew dark, when we got down the mountain the best way we could.

We lately visited the great University Library. You walk through one hall after another, filled with books of all kinds, from the monkish manuscript of the middle ages, to the most elegant print of the present day. There is something to me more impressive in a library like this than a solemn Cathedral. I think involuntarily of the hundreds of mighty spirits who speak from these three hundred thousand volumes—of the toils and privations with which genius has ever struggled, and of his glorious reward. As in a church, one feels as it were, the presence of God; not because the place has been hallowed by his worship, but because all around stand the inspirations of his spirit, breathed through the mind of genius, to men. And if the mortal remains of saints and heroes do not repose within its walls, the great and good of the whole earth are there, speaking their counsels to the searcher for truth, with voices whose last reverberation will die away only when the globe falls into ruin.

A few nights ago there was a wedding of peasants across the river. In order to celebrate it particularly, the guests went to the house where it was given, by torchlight. The night was quite dark, and the bright red torches glowed on the surface of the Neckar, as the two couriers galloped along the banks to the bridegroom's house. Here, after much shouting and confusion, the procession was arranged, the two riders started back again with their torches, and the wagons containing the guests followed after with their flickering lights glancing on the water, till they disappeared around the foot of the mountain. The choosing of Conscripts also took place lately. The law requires one person out of every hundred to become a soldier, and this, in the city of Heidelberg, amounts to nearly 150. It was a sad spectacle. The young men, or rather boys, who were chosen, went about the city with cockades fastened on their hats, shouting and singing, many of them quite intoxicated. I could not help pitying them because of the dismal, mechanical life they are doomed to follow. Many were rough, ignorant peasants, to whom nearly any kind of life would be agreeable; but there were some whose countenances spoke otherwise, and I thought involuntarily, that their drunken gaiety was only affected to conceal their real feelings with regard to the lot which had fallen upon them.

We are gradually becoming accustomed to the German style of living, which is very different from our own. Their cookery is new to us, but is, nevertheless, good. We have every day a different kind of soup, so I have

390

supposed they keep a regular list of three hundred and sixty-five, one for every day in the year! Then we have potatoes "done up" in oil and vinegar, veal flavored with orange peel, barley pudding, and all sorts of pancakes, boiled artichokes, and always rye bread, in loaves a yard long! Nevertheless, we thrive on such diet, and I have rarely enjoyed more sound and refreshing sleep than in their narrow and coffin-like beds, uncomfortable as they seem. Many of the German customs are amusing. We never see oxen working here, but always cows, sometimes a single one in a cart, and sometimes two fastened together by a yoke across their horns. The women labor constantly in the fields; from our window we can hear the nut-brown maidens singing their cheerful songs among the vineyards on the mountain side. Their costume, too, is odd enough. Below the light-fitting vest they wear such a number of short skirts, one above another, that it reminds one of an animated hogshead, with a head and shoulders starting out from the top. I have heard it gravely asserted that the wealth of a German damsel may be known by counting the number of her "kirtles." An acquaintance of mine remarked, that it would be an excellent costume for falling down a precipice!

We have just returned from a second visit to Frankfort, where the great annual fair filled the streets with noise and bustle. On our way back, we stopped at the village of Zwingenberg, which lies at the foot of the Melibochus, for the purpose of visiting some of the scenery of the Odenwald. Passing the night at the inn there, we slept with one bed under and two above, and started early in the morning to climb up the side of the Melibochus. After a long walk through the forests, which were beginning to change their summer foliage for a brighter garment, we reached the summit and ascended the stone tower which stands upon it. This view gives one a better idea of the Odenwald, than that from the Kaiser-stuhl at Heidelberg. In the soft autumn atmosphere it looked even more beautiful. After an hour in that heaven of uplifted thought, into which we step from the mountain-top, our minds went with the path downward to earth, and we descended the eastern side into the wild region which contains the Felsenmeer, or Sea of Rocks.

We met on the way a student from Fulda—a fine specimen of that free-spirited class, and a man whose smothered aspiration was betrayed in the flashing of his eye, as he spoke of the present painful and oppressed condition of Germany. We talked so busily together that without noticing the path, which had been bringing us on, up hill and down, through forest and over rock, we came at last to a halt in a valley among the mountains. Making inquiries there, we found we had gone wrong, and must ascend by a different path the mountain we had just come down. Near the summit of this, in a wild pine wood, was the Felsenmeer—a great collection of rocks heaped together like pebbles on the sea shore, and worn and rounded as if by the action of water: so much do they resemble waves, that one standing at the bottom and looking up, cannot resist the idea, that they will flow down upon him. It must have been a mighty tide whose receding waves left these masses piled up together! The same formation continues at intervals, to the foot, of the mountains. It reminded me of a glacier of rocks instead of ice. A little higher up, lies a massive block of granite called the "Giant's Column." It is thirty-two feet long and three to four feet in diameter, and still bears the mark of the chisel. When or by whom it was made, remains a mystery. Some have supposed it was intended to be erected for the worship of the Sun, by the wild Teutonic tribes who inhabited this forest; it is more probably the work of the Romans. A project was once started, to erect it as a monument on the battle-field of Leipsic, but it was found too difficult to carry into execution.

After dining at the little village of Reichelsdorf in the valley below, where the merry landlord charged my friend two kreutzers less than myself because he was not so tall, we visited the Castle of Schönberg, and joined the Bergstrasse again. We walked the rest of the way here; long before we arrived, the moon shone down on us over the mountains, and when we turned around the foot of the Heiligenberg, the mist descending in the valley of the Neckar, rested like a light cloud on the church spires.

CHAPTER X. — A WALK THROUGH THE ODENWALD.

B—— and I are now comfortably settled in Frankfort, having, with Mr. Willis's kind assistance, obtained lodgings with the amiable family, with whom he has resided for more than two years. My cousin remains in Heidelberg to attend the winter course of lectures at the University.

Having forwarded our baggage by the omnibus, we came hither on foot, through the heart of the Odenwald, a region full of interest, yet little visited by travellers. Dr. S—— and his family walked with us three or four miles of the way, and on a hill above Ziegelhausen, with a splendid view behind us, through the mountain-door, out of which the Neckar enters on the Rhine-plain, we parted. This was a first, and I must confess, a somewhat embarrassing experience in German leave-taking. After bidding adieu three or four times, we started to go up the mountain and they down it, but at every second step we had to turn around to acknowledge the waving of hands and handkerchiefs, which continued so long that I was glad when we were out of sight of each other. We descended on the other side into a wild and romantic valley, whose meadows were of the brightest green; a little brook which wound through them, put now and then its "silvery shoulder" to the wheel of a rustic mill. By the road-side two or three wild-looking gipsies sat around a fire, with some goats feeding near them.

Passing through this valley and the little village of Schönau, we commenced ascending one of the loftiest ranges of the Odenwald. The side of the mountain was covered with a thick pine forest. There was no wind to wake its solemn anthem; all was calm and majestic, and even awful. The trees rose all around like the pillars of a vast Cathedral, whose long arched aisles vanished far below in the deepening gloom.

"Nature with folded hands seemed there,

Kneeling at her evening prayer,"

for twilight had already begun to gather. We went on and up and ever higher, like the youth in "Excelsior;" the beech and dwarf oak took the place of the pine, and at last we arrived at a cleared summit whose long brown grass waved desolately in the dim light of evening. A faint glow still lingered over the forest-hills, but down in the valley the dusky shades hid every vestige of life, though its sounds came up softened through the long space. When we reached the top a bright planet stood like a diamond over the brow of the eastern hill, and the sound of a twilight bell came up clearly and sonorously on the cool damp air. The white veil of mist slowly descended down the mountain side, but the peaks rose above it like the wrecks of a world, floating in space. We made our way in the dusk down the long path, to the rude little dorf of Elsbach. I asked at the first inn for lodging, where we were ushered into a great room, in which a number of girls who had been at work in the fields, were assembled. They were all dressed in men's jackets, and short gowns, and some had their hair streaming down their back. The landlord's daughter, however, was a beautiful girl, whose modest, delicate features contrasted greatly with the coarse faces of the others. I thought of Uhland's beautiful little poem of "The Landlady's Daughter," as I looked on her. In the room hung two or three pair of antlers, and they told us deer were still plenty in the forests.

When we left the village the next morning, we again commenced ascending. Over the whole valley and halfway up the mountain, lay a thick white frost, almost like snow, which contrasted with the green trees and bushes scattered over the meadows, produced the most singular effect. We plucked blackberries ready iced from the bushes by the road-side, and went on in the cold, for the sun shone only on the top of the opposite mountain, into another valley, down which rushed the rapid Ulver. At a little village which bears the beautiful name Anteschönmattenwag, we took a foot-path directly over a steep mountain to the village of Finkenbach. Near the top I found two wild-looking children, cutting grass with knives, both of whom I prevailed upon for a few kreutzers to stand and let me sketch them. From the summit the view on the other side was very striking. The hills were nearly every one covered with wood, and not a dwelling in sight. It reminded me of our forest scenery at home. The principal difference is, that our trees are two or three times the size of theirs.

At length, after scaling another mountain, we reached a wide, elevated plain, in the middle of which stood the old dorf of Beerfelden. It was then crowded with people, on account of a great cattle-fair being held there. All the farmers of the neighborhood were assembled, clad in the ancient country costume—broad cocked hats and blue frocks. An orchard near the town was filled with cattle and horses, and near by, in the shade, a number of pedlars had arranged their wares. The cheerful looking country people touched their hats to us as we passed. This custom of greeting travellers, universal in Germany, is very expressive of their social, friendly manners. Among the mountains, we frequently met groups of children, who sang together their simple ballads as we passed by.

From Beerfelden we passed down the valley of the Mimling to Erbach, the principal city in the Odenwald, and there stopped a short time to view the Rittersaal in the old family castle of the Counts of Erbach. An officer, who stood at the gates, conducted us to the door, where we were received by a noble-looking, gray-headed steward. He took us into the Rittersaal at once, which was like stepping back three hundred years. The stained windows of the lofty Gothic hall, let in a subdued light which fell on the forms of kings and knights, clad in the armor they wore during life. On the left as we entered, were mail-covered figures of John and Cosmo do Medici; further on stood the Emperor Maximilian, and by his side the celebrated dwarf who was served up in a pie at one of the imperial feasts. His armor was most delicate and beautiful, but small as it was, General Thumb would have had room in it. Gustavus Adolphus and Wallenstein looked down from the neighboring pedestals, while at the other end stood Goetz von Berlichingen and Albert of Brunswick. Guarding the door were Hans, the robber-knight of Nuremberg, and another from the Thüringian forest. The steward told me that the iron hand of Goetz was in possession of the family, but not shown to strangers; he pointed out, however, the buckles on the armor, by which it was fastened. Adjoining the hall is an antique chapel, filled with rude old tombs, and containing the sarcophagus of Count Eginhard of Denmark, who lived about the tenth century. There were also monkish garments five hundred years old hanging up in it.

The collection of antiquities is large and interesting; but it is said that the old Count obtained some of them in rather a questionable manner. Among other incidents, they say that when in Rome he visited the Pope, taking with him an old servant who accompanied him in all his travels, and was the accomplice in most of his antiquarian thefts. In one of the outer halls, among the curiosities, was an antique shield of great value. The servant was left in this hall while the Count had his audience, and in a short time this shield was missed. The servant who wore a long cloak, was missed also; orders were given to close the gates and search every body, but it was too late—the thief was gone.

Leaving Erbach we found out the direction of Snellert, the Castle of the Wild Huntsman, and took a road that led us for two or three hours along the top of a mountain ridge. Through the openings in the pine and larch forests, we had glimpses of the hills of Spessart, beyond the Main. When we finally left the by-road we had chosen it was quite dark, and we missed the way altogether among the lanes and meadows. We came at last to a full stop at the house of a farmer, who guided us by a foot path over the fields to a small village. On entering the only inn, kept by the Burgomaster, the people finding we were Americans, regarded us with a curiosity quite uncomfortable. They crowded around the door, watching every motion, and gazed in through the windows. The wild huntsman himself could scarcely have made a greater sensation. The news of our arrival seemed to have spread very fast, for the next morning when we stopped at a prune orchard some distance from the village to buy some fruit, the farmer cried out from a tree, "they are the Americans; give them as many as they want for nothing!"

With the Burgomaster's little son for a guide, we went back a mile or two of our route to Snellert, which we had passed the night before, and after losing ourselves two or three times in the woods, arrived at last at the top of the mountain, where the ruins of the castle stand. The walls are nearly level with the ground. The interest of a visit rests entirely on the romantic legend, and the wild view over the hills around, particularly that in front, where on the opposite mountain are the ruins of Rodenstein, to which the wild Huntsman was wont to ride at midnight—where he now rides no more. The echoes of Rodenstein are no longer awakened by the sound of his bugle, and the hoofs of his demon steed clanging on the battlements. But the hills around are wild enough, and the roar of the pine forests deep enough to have inspired the simple peasants with the romantic tradition.

Stopping for dinner at the town of Rheinheim, we met an old man, who, on learning we were Americans, walked with us as far as the next village. He had a daughter in America and was highly gratified to meet any one from the country of her adoption. He made me promise to visit her, if I ever should go to St. Louis, and say that I had walked with her father from Rheinheim to Zwangenburg. To satisfy his fears that I might forget it, I took down his name and that of his daughter. He shook me warmly by the hand at parting, and was evidently made happier for that day.

We reached Darmstadt just in time to take a seat in the omnibus for Frankfort. Among the passengers were a Bavarian family, on their way to Bremen, to ship from thence to Texas. I endeavored to discourage the man from choosing such a country as his home, by telling him of its heats and pestilences, but he was too full of hope to be shaken in his purpose. I would have added that it was a slave-land, but I thought on our own country's curse, and was silent. The wife was not so sanguine; she seemed to mourn in secret at leaving her beautiful fatherland. It was saddening to think how lonely they would feel in that far home, and how they would long, with true German devotion, to look again on the green vintage-hills of their forsaken country. As night drew on, the little girl crept over to her father for his accustomed evening kiss, and then sank back to sleep in a corner of the wagon. The boy, in the artless confidence of childhood, laid his head on my breast, weary with the day's travel, and soon slept also. Thus we drove on in the dark, till at length the lights of Frankfort glimmered on the breast of the rapid Main, as we passed over the bridge, and when we stopped near the Cathedral, I delivered up my little charge and sent my sympathy with the wanderers on their lonely way.

CHAPTER XI. — SCENES IN FRANKFORT—AN AMERICAN COMPOSER— THE POET FREILIGRATH.

Dec. 4.—This is a genuine old German city. Founded by Charlemagne, afterwards a rallying point of the Crusaders, and for a long time the capital of the German empire, it has no lack of interesting historical recollections, and notwithstanding it is fast becoming modernized, one is every where reminded of the Past. The Cathedral, old as the days of Peter the Hermit, the grotesque street of the Jews, the many quaint, antiquated dwellings and the mouldering watch-towers on the hills around, give it a more interesting character than any German city I have yet seen. The house we dwell in, on the Markt Platz, is more than two hundred years old; directly opposite is a great castellated building, gloomy with the weight of six centuries, and a few steps to the left brings me to the square of the Roemerberg, where the Emperors were crowned, in a corner of which is a curiously ornamented house, formerly the residence of Luther. There are legends innumerable connected with all these buildings, and even yet discoveries are frequently made in old houses, of secret chambers and staircases. When you add to all this, the German love of ghost stories, and, indeed, their general belief in spirits, the lover of romance could not desire a more agreeable residence.

I often look out on the singular scene below my window. On both sides of the street, leaving barely room to enter the houses, sit the market women, with their baskets of vegetables and fruit. The middle of the street is filled with women buying, and every cart or carriage that comes along, has to force its way through the crowd, sometimes rolling against and overturning the baskets on the side, when for a few minutes there is a Babel of unintelligible sounds. The country women in their jackets and short gowns go backwards and forwards with great loads on their heads, sometimes nearly as high as themselves. It is a most singular scene, and so varied that one never tires of looking upon it. These women sit here from sunrise till sunset, day after day, for years. They have little furnaces for cooking and for warmth in winter, and when it rains they sit in large wooden boxes. One or two policemen are generally on the ground in the morning to prevent disputing about their places, which often gives rise to interesting scenes. Perhaps this kind of life in the open air is conducive to longevity; for certainly there is no country on earth that has as many old women. Many of them look like walking machines made of leather; and to judge from what I see in the streets here, I should think they work till they die.

On the 21st of October a most interesting fete took place. The magnificent monument of Goethe, modelled by the sculptor Schwanthaler, at Munich, and cast in bronze, was unveiled. It arrived a few days before, and was received with much ceremony and erected in the destined spot, an open square in the western part of the city, planted with acacia trees. I went there at ten o'clock, and found the square already full of people. Seats had been erected around the monument for ladies, the singers and musicians. A company of soldiers was stationed to keep an entrance for the procession, which at length arrived with music and banners, and entered the enclosure. A song for the occasion was sung by the choir; it swelled up gradually, and with such perfect harmony and unity, that it seemed like some glorious instrument touched by a single hand. Then a poetical address was delivered; after which four young men took their stand at the corners of the monument; the drums and trumpets gave a flourish, and the mantle fell. The noble figure seemed to rise out of the earth, and thus amid shoutings and the triumphal peal of the band, the form of Goethe greeted the city of his birth. He is represented as leaning on the trunk of a tree, holding in his right hand a roll of parchment, and in his left a wreath. The pedestal, which is also of bronze, contains bas reliefs, representing scenes from Faust, Wilhelm Meister and Egmont. In the evening Goethe's house, in a street near, was illuminated by arches of lamps between the windows, and hung with wreaths of flowers. Four pillars of colored lamps lighted the statue. At nine o'clock the choir of singers came again in a procession, with colored lanterns, on poles, and after singing two or three songs, the statue was exhibited in the red glare of the Bengal light. The trees and houses around the square were covered with the glow, which streamed in broad sheets up against the dark sky.

Within the walls the greater part of Frankfort is built in the old German

399

style—the houses six or seven stones high, and every story projecting out over the other, so that those living in the upper part can nearly shake hands out of the windows. At the corners figures of men are often seen, holding up the story above on their shoulders and making horrible faces at the weight. When I state that in all these narrow streets which constitute the greater part of the city, there are no sidewalks, the windows of the lower stories with an iron grating extending a foot or so into the street, which is only wide enough for one cart to pass along, you can have some idea of the facility of walking through them, to say nothing of the piles of wood, and market-women with baskets of vegetables which one is continually stumbling over. Even in the wider streets, I have always to look before and behind to keep out of the way of the fiacres; the people here get so accustomed to it, that they leave barely room for them to pass, and the carriages go dashing by at a nearness which sometimes makes me shudder.

As I walked across the Main, and looked down at the swift stream on its way from the distant Thuringian forest to join the Rhine, I thought of the time when Schiller stood there in the days of his early struggles, an exile from his native land, and looking over the bridge, said in the loneliness of his heart, "That water flows not so deep as my sufferings!" In the middle, on an iron ornament, stands the golden cock at which Goethe used to marvel when a boy. Perhaps you have not heard the legend connected with this. The bridge was built several hundred years ago, with such strength and solidity that it will stand many hundred yet. The architect had contracted to build it within a certain time, but as it drew near, without any prospect of fulfilment, the devil appeared to him and promised to finish it, on condition of having the first soul that passed over it. This was agreed upon end the devil performed his part of the bargain. The artist, however, on the day appointed, drove a cook across before he suffered any one to pass over it. His majesty stationed himself under the middle arch of the bridge, awaiting his prey; but enraged at the cheat, he tore the unfortunate fowl in pieces and broke two holes in the arch, saying they should never be built up again. The golden cock was erected on the bridge as a token of the event, but the devil has perhaps lost some of his power in these latter days, for the holes were filled up about thirty years ago.

From the hills on the Darmstadt road, I had a view of the country around—the fields were white and bare, and the dark Tannus, with the broad patches of snow on his sides, looked grim and shadowy through the dim atmosphere. It was like the landscape of a dream—dark, strange and silent. The whole of last month we saw the sun but two or three days, the sky being almost continually covered with a gloomy fog. England and Germany seem to have exchanged climates this year, for in the former country we had delightfully clear weather.

I have seen the banker Rothschild several times driving about the city. This one—Anselmo, the most celebrated of the brothers—holds a mortgage on the city of Jerusalem. He rides about in style, with officers attending his carriage. He is a little bald-headed man, with marked Jewish features, and is said not to deceive his looks. At any rate, his reputation is none of the best, either with Jews or Christians. A caricature was published some time ago, in which he is represented as giving a beggar woman by the way-side, a kreutzer—the smallest German coin. She is made to exclaim, "God reward you, a thousand fold!" He immediately replies, after reckoning up in his head: "How much have I then?—sixteen florins and forty kreutzers!"

I have lately heard one of the most perfectly beautiful creations that ever emanated from the soul of genius—the opera of Fidelio. I have caught faint glimpses of that rich world of fancy and feeling, to which music is the golden door. Surrendering myself to the grasp of Beethoven's powerful conception, I read in sounds far more expressive than words, the almost despairing agony of the strong-hearted, but still tender and womanly Fidelio—the ecstatic joy of the wasted prisoner, when he rose from his hard couch in the dungeon, seeming to fuel, in his maniac brain, the presentiment of a bright being who would come to unbind his chains—and. the sobbing and wailing, almost-human, which came from the orchestra, when they dug his grave, by the dim lantern's light. When it was done, the murderer stole into the dungeon, to gloat on the agonies of his victim, ere he gave the death-blow. Then, while the prisoner is waked to reason by that sight, and Fidelio throws herself before the uplifted dagger, rescuing her husband with the courage which love gives to a woman's heart, the storm of feeling which has been gathering in the music, swells to a height beyond which it seemed impossible for the soul to pass.

My nerves were thrilled till I could bear no more. A mist seemed to come before my eyes and I scarcely knew what followed, till the rescued kneeled together and poured forth in the closing hymn the painful fullness of their joy. I dreaded the sound of voices after the close, and the walk home amid the harsh rattling of vehicles on the rough streets. For days afterwards my brain was filled with a mingled and confused sense of melody, like the half-remembered music of a dream.

Why should such magnificent creations of art be denied the new world? There is certainly enthusiasm and refinement of feeling enough at home to appreciate them, were the proper direction given to the popular taste. What country possesses more advantages to foster the growth of such an art, than ours? Why should not the composer gain mighty conceptions from the grandeur of our mountain scenery, from the howling of the storm through our giant forests, from the eternal thunder of Niagara? All these collateral influences, which more or less tend to the development and expansion of genius, are characteristics of our country; and a taste for musical compositions of a refined and lofty character, would soon give birth to creators.

Fortunately for our country, this missing star in the crown of her growing glory, will probably soon be replaced. Richard S. Willis, with whom we have lived in delightful companionship, since coming here, has been for more than two years studying and preparing himself for the higher branches of composition. The musical talent he displayed while at college, and the success following the publication of a set of beautiful waltzes he there composed, led him to choose this most difficult but lofty path; the result justifies his early promise and gives the most sanguine anticipations for the future. He studied the first two years here under Schnyder von Wartensee, a distinguished Swiss composer; and his exercises have met with the warmest approval from Mendelsohn, at present the first German composer, and Rinck, the celebrated organist. The enormous labor and application required to go through the preparatory studies alone, would make it seem almost impossible for one with the restless energy of the American character, to undertake it; but as this very energy gives genius its greatest power, we may now trust with confidence that Willis, since he has nearly completed his studies, will win himself and his country honor in the difficult path he has chosen.

One evening, after sunset, we took a stroll around the promenades. The swans were still floating on the little lake, and the American poplar beside it, was in its full autumn livery. As we made the circuit of the walks, guns were firing far and near, celebrating the opening of the vintage the next day, and rockets went glittering and sparkling up into the dark air. Notwithstanding the late hour and lowering sky, the walks were full of people and we strolled about with them till it grew quite dark, watching the fire-works which arose from the gardens around.

The next day, we went into the Frankfort wood. Willis and his brother-in-law, Charles F. Dennett, of Boston, Dr. Dix and another young gentleman from the same city, formed the party—six Americans in all; we walked over the Main and through the dirty suburbs of Sachsenhausen, where we met many peasants laden with the first day's vintage, and crowds of people coming down from the vineyards. As we ascended the hill, the sound of firing was heard in every direction, and from many vineyards arose the smoke of fires where groups of merry children were collecting and burning the rubbish. We became lost among the winding paths of the pine forest, so that by the time we came out upon the eminence overlooking the valley of the Main, it was quite dark. From every side, far and near, rockets of all sizes and colors darted high up into the sky. Sometimes a flight of the most brilliant crimson and gold lights rushed up together, then again by some farm-house in the meadow, the vintagers would burn a Roman candle, throwing its powerful white light on the gardens and fields around. We stopped under a garden wall, by which a laughing company were assembled in the smoke and red blaze, and watched several comets go hissing and glancing far above us. The cracking of ammunition still continued, and when we came again upon the bridge, the city opposite was lighted as if illuminated. The full moon had just risen, softening and mellowing the beautiful scene, while beyond, over the tower of Frankfort, rose and fell the meteors that heralded the vintage.

Since I have been in Frankfort, an event has occurred, which shows very distinctly the principles at work in Germany, and gives us some foreboding of the future. Ferdinand Freiligrath, the first living poet with the exception of Uhland, has within a few weeks published a volume of poems entitled, "My Confession of Faith, or Poems for the Times." It contains some thrilling appeals to the free spirit of the German people, setting forth the injustice under which they labor, in simple but powerful language, and with the most forcible illustrations, adapted to the comprehension of everyone. Viewed as a work of genius alone, it is strikingly powerful and original: but when we consider the effect it is producing among the people—the strength it will add to the rising tide of opposition to every form of tyranny, it has a still higher interest. Freiligrath had three or four years before, received a pension of three hundred thalers from the King of Prussia, soon after his accession to the throne: he ceased to draw this about a year ago, stating in the preface to his volume that it was accepted in the belief the King would adhere to his promise of giving the people a new constitution, but that now since free spirit which characterises these men, who come from among the people, shows plainly the tendency of the times; and it is only the great strength with which tyranny here has environed himself, and the almost lethargic slowness of the Germans, which has prevented a change ere this.

In this volume of Freiligrath's, among other things, is a translation of Bryant's magnificent poem "The Winds," and Burns's "A man's a man for a' that;" and I have translated one of his, as a specimen of the spirit in which they are written:

FREEDOM AND RIGHT.

Oh! think not she rests in the grave's chilly slumber

Nor sheds o'er the present her glorious light,

Since Tyranny's shackles the free soul incumber

And traitors accusing, deny to us Right!

No: whether to exile the sworn ones are wending,

Or weary of power that crushed them unending,

In dungeons have perished, their veins madly rending,[*]

Yet Freedom still liveth, and with her, the Right!

Freedom and Right!

A single defeat can confuse us no longer:

It adds to the combat's last gathering might,

It bids us but doubly to struggle, and stronger

To raise up our battle-cry—"Freedom and Right!"

For the Twain know a union forever abiding,

Together in Truth and in majesty striding;

Where Right is, already the free are residing

And ever, where dwell the free, governeth Right!

Freedom and Right!

And this is a trust: never made, us at present,

The glad pair from battle to battle their flight;

Never breathed through the soul of the down-trodden peasant,

Their spirit so deeply its promptings of light!

They sweep o'er the earth with a tempest-like token;

From strand unto strand words of thunder are spoken:

Already the serf finds his manacles broken,

And those of the negro are falling from sight

Freedom and Right!

Yes, every where wide is their war-banner waving.

On the armies of Wrong their revenge to requite;

The strength of Oppression they boldly are braving

And at last they will conquer, resistless in might!

Oh, God! what a glorious wreath then appearing

Will blend every leaf in the banner they're bearing—The

olive of Greece and the shamrock of Erin,

   And the oak-bough of Germany, greenest in light!

         Freedom and Right!

And many who suffered, are now calmly sleeping,

   The slumber of freemen, borne down by the fight;

While the Twain o'er their graves still a bright watch are keeping,

   Whom we bless for their memories—Freedom and Right!

Meanwhile lift your glasses! to those who have striven!

And striving with bold hearts, to misery were driven!

Who fought for the Right and but Wrong then were given!

   To Right, the immortal—to Freedom through Right!

         Freedom through Right!

* [This allusion is to Weidig, who, imprisoned for years at Darmstadt on account of his political principles, finally committed suicide by cutting his throat with the glass of his prison-window.]

CHAPTER XII. – A WEEK AMONG THE STUDENTS.

Receiving a letter from my cousin one bright December morning, the idea of visiting him struck me, and so, within an hour, B—— and I were on our way to Heidelberg. It was delightful weather; the air was mild as the early days of spring, the pine forests around wore a softer green, and though the sun was but a hand's breadth high, even at noon, it was quite warm on the open road. We stopped for the night at Bensheim; the next morning was as dark as a cloudy day in the north can be, wearing a heavy gloom I never saw elsewhere. The wind blew the snow down from the summits upon us, but being warm from walking, we did not heed it. The mountains looked higher than in summer, and the old castles more grim and frowning. From the hard roads and freezing wind, my feet became very sore, and after limping along in excruciating pain for a league or two, I filled my boots with brandy, which deadened the wounds so much, that I was enabled to go on in a kind of trot, which I kept up, only stopping ten minutes to dinner, till we reached Heidelberg.

The same evening there was to be a general commers, or meeting of the societies among the students, and I determined not to omit witnessing one of the most interesting and characteristic features of student-life. So borrowing a cap and coat, I looked the student well enough to pass for one of them, though the former article was somewhat of the Philister form. Baader, a young poet of some note, and president of the "Palatia" Society, having promised to take us there, we met at eight o'clock at an inn frequented by the students, and went to the rendezvous, near the Markt Platz.

A confused sound of voices came from the inn, as we drew near; groups of students were standing around the door. In the entry we saw the Red Fisherman, one of the most conspicuous characters about the University. He is a small, stout man, with bare neck and breast, red hair, whence his name, and a strange mixture of roughness and benevolence in his countenance. He has saved many persons at the risk of his own life, from drowning in the

Neckar, and on that account is leniently dealt with by the faculty whenever he is arrested for assisting the students in any of their unlawful proceedings. Entering the room I could scarcely see at first, on account of the smoke that ascended from a hundred pipes. All was noise and confusion. Near the door sat some half dozen musicians who were getting their instruments ready for action, and the long room was filled with tables, all of which seemed to be full and the students were still pressing in. The tables were covered with great stone jugs and long beer glasses; the students were talking and shouting and drinking.—One who appeared to have the arrangement of the meeting, found seats for us together, and having made a slight acquaintance with those sitting next us, we felt more at liberty to witness their proceedings. They were all talking in a sociable, friendly way, and I saw no one who appeared to be intoxicated. The beer was a weak mixture, which I should think would make one fall over from its weight before it would intoxicate him. Those sitting near me drank but little, and that principally to make or return compliments. One or two at the other end of the table were more boisterous, and more than one glass was overturned on the legs below it. Leaves containing the songs for the evening lay at each seat, and at the head, where the President sat, were two swords crossed, with which he occasionally struck upon the table to preserve order. Our President was a fine, romantic-looking young man, dressed in the old German costume, which is far handsomer than the modern. I never saw in any company of young men, so many handsome, manly countenances. If their faces were any index of their characters, there were many noble, free souls among them. Nearly opposite to me sat a young poet, whose dark eyes flashed with feeling as he spoke to those near him. After some time passed in talking and drinking together, varied by an occasional air from the musicians, the President beat order with the sword, and the whole company joined in one of their glorious songs, to a melody at the same time joyous and solemn. Swelled by so many manly voices it rose up like a hymn of triumph—all other sounds were stilled. Three times during the singing all rose up, clashed their glasses together around the tables and drank to their Fatherland, a health and blessing to the patriot, and honor to those who struggle in the cause of freedom, at the close thundering out their motto:

"Fearless in strife, to the banner still true!"

After this song the same order as before was continued, except that students from the different societies made short speeches, accompanied by some toast or sentiment. One spoke of Germany—predicting that all her dissensions would be overcome, and she would rise up at last, like a phoenix among the nations of Europe; and at the close gave 'strong, united, regenerated Germany!' Instantly all sprang to their feet, and clashing the glasses together, gave a thundering "hoch!" This enthusiasm for their country is one of the strongest characteristics of the German students; they have ever been first in the field for her freedom, and on them mainly depends her future redemption.

Cloths were passed around, the tables wiped off, and preparations made to sing the "Landsfather" or consecration song. This is one of the most important and solemn of their ceremonies, since by performing it the new students are made burschen, and the bands of brotherhood continually kept fresh and sacred. All became still a moment, then they commenced the lofty song:

"Silent bending, each one lending

To the solemn tones his ear,

Hark, the song of songs is sounding—

Back from joyful choir resounding,

Hear it, German brothers, hear!

"German proudly, raise it loudly,

Singing of your fatherland—

Fatherland! thou land of story,

To the altars of thy glory

Consecrate us, sword in hand!

"Take the beaker, pleasure seeker,

With thy country's drink brimmed o'er!

In thy left the sword is blinking.

Pierce it through the cap, while drinking

To thy Fatherland once more!"

With the first line of the last stanza, the Presidents sitting at the head of the table, take their glasses in their right hands, and at the third line, the sword in their left, at the end striking their glasses together and drinking.

"In left hand gleaming, thou art beaming,

Sword from all dishonour free!

Thus I pierce the cap, while swearing,

It in honor ever wearing,

I a valiant Bursch will be!"

They clash their swords together till the third line is sung, when each takes his cap, and piercing the point of the sword through the crown, draws it down to the guard. Leaving their caps on the swords, the Presidents stand behind the two next students, who go through the same ceremony, receiving the swords at the appropriate time, and giving it back loaded with their caps also. This ceremony is going on at every table at the same time. These two stanzas are repeated for every pair of students, till all have gone through with it, and the Presidents have arrived at the bottom of the table, with their swords strung full of caps. Here they exchange swords, while all sing:

"Come thou bright sword, now made holy,

Of free men the weapon free;

Bring it solemnly and slowly,

Heavy with pierced caps, to me!

From its burden now divest it;

Brothers be ye covered all,

And till our next festival,

Hallowed and unspotted rest it!

"Up, ye feast companions! ever

Honor ye our holy band!

And with heart and soul endeavor

E'er as high-souled men to stand!

Up to feast, ye men united!

Worthy be your fathers' fame,

And the sword may no one claim,

Who to honor is not plighted!"

Then each President, taking a cap of his sword, reached it to the student opposite, and they crossed their swords, the ends resting on the two students' heads, while they sang the next stanza:

"So take it back; thy head I now will cover

And stretch the bright sword over.

Live also then this Bursche, hoch!

Wherever we may meet him,

Will we, as Brother greet him—

Live also this, our Brother, hoch!"

This ceremony was repeated till all the caps were given back, and they then concluded with the following:

"Rest, the Bursehen-feast is over,

Hallowed sword and thou art free!

Each one strive a valiant lover

Of his fatherland to be!

Hail to him, who, glory-haunted,

Follows still his fathers bold;

And the sword may no one hold

But the noble and undaunted!"

The Landsfather being over, the students were less orderly; the smoking and drinking began again and we left, as it was already eleven o'clock, glad to breathe the pure cold air.

In the University I heard Gervinus, who was formerly professor in Göttingen, but was obliged to leave on account of his liberal principles. He is much liked by the students and his lectures are very well attended. They had this winter a torchlight procession in honor of him. He is a stout, round-faced man, speaks very fast, and makes them laugh continually with his witty remarks. In the room I saw a son of Rückert, the poet, with a face strikingly like his father's. The next evening I went to hear Schlosser, the great historian. Among his pupils are the two princes of Baden, who are now at the University. He came hurriedly in, threw down his portfolio and began instantly to speak. He is an old, gray-headed man, but still active and full of energy. The Germans find him exceedingly difficult to understand, as he is said to use the English construction almost entirely; for this reason, perhaps, I understood him quite easily. He lectures on the French Revolution, but is engaged in writing a Universal History, the first numbers of which are published.

Two or three days after, we heard that a duel was to take place at Neuenheim, on the opposite side of the Neckur, where the students have a house hired for that purpose. In order to witness the spectacle, we started immediately with two or three students. Along the road were stationed old women, at intervals, as guards, to give notice of the approach of the police, and from these we learned that one duel had already been fought, and they were preparing for the other. The Red Fisherman was busy in an outer room grinding the swords, which are made as sharp as razors. In the large room some forty or fifty students were walking about, while the parties were preparing. This was done by taking off the coat and vest and binding a great thick leather garment on, which reached from the breast to the knees, completely protecting the body. They then put on a leather glove reaching nearly to the shoulder, tied a thick cravat around the throat, and drew on a cap with a large vizor. This done, they were walked about the room a short time, the seconds holding out their arms to strengthen them; their faces all this time betrayed considerable anxiety.

All being ready, the seconds took their stations immediately behind them, each armed with a sword, and gave the words: "ready—bind your weapons—loose!" They instantly sprang at each other, exchanged two or three blows, when the seconds cried "halt!" and struck their swords up. Twenty-four rounds of this kind ended the duel, without either being hurt, though the cap of one of them was cut through and his forehead grazed. All their duels do not end so fortunately, however, as the frightful scars on the faces of many of those present, testified. It is a gratification to know that but a small portion of the students keep up this barbarous custom. The great body is opposed to it; in Heidelberg, four societies, comprising more than one half the students, have been formed against it. A strong desire for such a reform seems to prevail, and the custom will probably be totally discontinued in a short time.

This view of the student-life was very interesting to me; it appeared in a much better light than I had been accustomed to view it. Their peculiar customs, except duelling and drinking, of course, may be the better tolerated when we consider their effect on the liberty of Germany. It is principally through them that a free spirit is kept alive; they have ever been foremost to rise up for their Fatherland, and bravest in its defence. And though many of their customs have so often been held up to ridicule, among no other class can one find warmer, truer or braver hearts.

CHAPTER XIII. — CHRISTMAS AND NEW YEAR IN GERMANY.

Jan. 2, 1845.—I have lately been computing how much my travels have cost me up to the present time, and how long I can remain abroad to continue the pilgrimage, with my present expectations. The result has been most encouraging to my plan. Before leaving home, I wrote to several gentlemen who had visited Europe, requesting the probable expense of travel and residence abroad. They sent different accounts; E. Joy Morris said I must calculate to spend at least $1500 a year; another suggested $1000, and the most moderate of all, said that it was impossible to live in Europe a year on less than $500. Now, six months have elapsed since I left home—six months of greater pleasure and profit than any year of my former life—and my expenses, in full, amount to $130! This, however, nearly exhausts the limited sum with which I started, but through the kindness of the editorial friends who have been publishing my sketches of travel, I trust to receive a remittance shortly. Printing is a business attended with so little profit here, as there are already so many workmen, that it is almost useless for a stranger to apply. Besides, after a tough grapple, I am just beginning to master the language, and it seems so necessary to devote every minute to study, that I would rather undergo some privation, than neglect turning these fleeting hours into gold, for the miser Memory to stow away in the treasure-vaults of the mind.

We have lately witnessed the most beautiful and interesting of all German festivals—Christmas. This is here peculiarly celebrated. About the commencement of December, the Christmarkt or fair, was opened in the Roemerberg, and has continued to the present time. The booths, decorated with green boughs, were filled with toys of various kinds, among which during the first days the figure of St. Nicholas was conspicuous. There were bunches of wax candles to illuminate the Christmas tree, gingerbread with printed mottos in poetry, beautiful little earthenware, basket-work, and a wilderness of playthings. The 5th of December, being Nicholas evening, the booths were lighted up, and the square was filled with boys, running from one stand to another, all shouting and talking together in the most joyous confusion. Nurses were going around, carrying the smaller children in their arms, and parents bought presents decorated with sprigs of pine and carried them away. Some of the shops had beautiful toys, as for instance, a whole grocery store in miniature, with barrels, boxes and drawers, all filled with sweetmeats, a kitchen with a stove and all suitable utensils, which could really be used, and sets of dishes of the most diminutive patterns. All was a scene of activity and joyous feeling.

Many of the tables had bundles of rods with gilded bands, which were to be used that evening by the persons who represented St. Nicholas. In the family with whom we reside, one of our German friends dressed himself very comically, with a mask, fur robe and long tapering cap. He came in with a bunch of rods and a sack, and a broom for a sceptre. After we all had received our share of the beating, he threw the contents of his bag on the table, and while we were scrambling for the nuts and apples, gave us many smart raps over the fingers. In many families the children are made to say, "I thank you, Herr Nicolaus," and the rods are hung up in the room till Christmas to keep them in good behavior. This was only a forerunner of the Christ-kindchen's coming. The Nicolaus is the punishing spirit, the Christ-kindchen the rewarding one.

When this time was over, we all began preparing secretly our presents for Christmas. Every day there were consultations about the things which should be obtained. It was so arranged that all should interchange presents, but nobody must know beforehand what he would receive. What pleasure there was in all these secret purchases and preparations! Scarcely anything was thought or spoken of but Christmas, and every day the consultations became more numerous and secret. The trees were bought sometime beforehand, but as we were to witness the festival for the first time, we were not allowed to see them prepared, in order that the effect might be as great as possible. The market in the Roeinerberg Square grew constantly larger and more brilliant. Every night it was lit up with lamps and thronged with people. Quite a forest sprang up in the street before our door. The old stone house opposite, with the traces of so many centuries on its dark face, seemed to stand in the midst of a garden. It was a pleasure to go out every evening and see the children rushing to and fro, shouting and seeking out toys from the booths, and talking all the time of the Christmas that was so near. The poor people went by with their little presents hid under their cloaks, lest their children might see them; every heart was glad and every countenance wore a smile of secret pleasure.

Finally the day before Christmas arrived. The streets were so full I could scarce make my way through, and the sale of trees went on more rapidly than ever. These wore commonly branches of pine or fir, set upright in a little miniature garden of moss. When the lamps were lighted at night, our street had the appearance of an illuminated garden. We were prohibited from entering the rooms up stairs in which the grand ceremony was to take place, being obliged to take our seats in those arranged for the guests, and wait with impatience the hour when Christ-kindchen should call. Several relations of the family came, and what was more agreeable, they brought with them five or six children. I was anxious to see how they would view the ceremony. Finally, in the middle of an interesting conversation, we heard the bell ringing up stairs. We all started up, and made for the door. I ran up the steps with the children at my heels, and at the top met a blaze of light coming from the open door, that dazzled me. In each room stood a great table, on which the presents were arranged, amid flowers and wreaths. From the centre, rose the beautiful Christmas tree covered with wax tapers to the very top, which made it nearly as light as day, while every bough was hung with sweetmeats and gilded nuts. The children ran shouting around the table, hunting their presents, while the older persons had theirs pointed out to them. I had qui'e a little library of German authors as my share; and many of the others received quite valuable gifts.

But how beautiful was the heart-felt joy that shone on every countenance! As each one discovered he embraced the givers, and all was a scene of the purest feelings. It is a glorious feast, this Christmas time! What a chorus from happy hearts went up on that evening to Heaven! Full of poetry and feeling and glad associations, it is here anticipated with joy, and leaves a pleasant memory behind it. We may laugh at such simple festivals at home, and prefer to shake ourselves loose from every shackle that bears the rust of the Past, but we would certainly be happier if some of these beautiful old customs were

416

better honored. They renew the bond of feeling between families and friends, and strengthen their kindly sympathy; even life-long friends require occasions of this kind to freshen the wreath that binds them together.

New Year's Eve is also favored with a peculiar celebration in Germany. Every body remains up and makes himself merry till midnight. The Christmas trees are again lighted, and while the tapers are burning down, the family play for articles which they have purchased and hung on the boughs. It is so arranged that each one shall win as much as he gives, which change of articles makes much amusement. One of the ladies rejoiced in the possession of a red silk handkerchief and a cake of soap, while a cup and saucer and a pair of scissors fell to my lot! As midnight drew near, it was louder in the streets, and companies of people, some of them singing in chorus, passed by on their way to the Zeil. Finally three-quarters struck, the windows were opened and every one waited anxiously for the clock to strike. At the first sound, such a cry arose as one may imagine, when thirty or forty thousand persons all set their lungs going at once. Every body in the house, in the street, over the whole city, shouted, "Prosst Neu Jahr?" In families, all the members embrace each other, with wishes of happiness for the new year. Then the windows are thrown open, and they cry to their neighbors or those passing by.

After we had exchanged congratulations, Dennett, B—— and I set out for the Zeil. The streets were full of people, shouting to one another and to those standing at the open windows. We failed not to cry, "Prosst Neu Jahr!" wherever we saw a damsel at the window, and the words came back to us more musically than we sent them. Along the Zeil the spectacle was most singular. The great wide street was filled with companies of men, marching up and down, while from the mass rang up one deafening, unending shout, that seemed to pierce the black sky above. The whole scene looked stranger and wilder from the flickering light of the swinging lamps, and I could not help thinking it must resemble a night in Paris during the French Revolution. We joined the crowd and used our lungs as well as any of them. For some time after we returned home, companies passed by, singing "with us 'tis ever so!" but at three o'clock all was again silent.

CHAPTER XIV. — WINTER IN FRANKFORT—A FAIR, AN INUNDATION AND A FIRE.

After New Year, the Main, just above the city, and the lakes in the promenades, were frozen over. The ice was tried by the police, and having been found of sufficient thickness, to the great joy of the schoolboys, permission was given to skate. The lakes were soon covered with merry skaters, and every afternoon the banks were crowded with spectators. It was a lively sight to see two or three hundred persons darting about, turning and crossing like a flock of crows, while, by means of arm-chairs mounted on runners, the ladies were enabled to join in the sport, and whirl around among them. Some of the broad meadows near the city, which were covered with water, were the resort of the schools. I went there often in my walks, and always found two or three schools, with the teachers, all skating together, and playing their winter games on the ice. I have often seen them on the meadows along the Main; the teachers generally made quite as much noise as the scholars in their sports.

In the Art Institute I saw the picture of "Huss before the Council of Constance," by the painter Lessing. It contains upwards of twenty figures. The artist has shown the greatest skill in the expression and grouping of these. Bishops and Cardinals in their splendid robes are seated around a table, covered with parchment folios, and before them stands Huss alone. His face, pale and thin with long imprisonment, he has lain one hand on his breast, while with the other he has grasped one of the volumes on the table; there is an air of majesty, of heavenly serenity on his lofty forehead and calm eye. One feels instinctively that he has truth on his side. There can be no deception, no falsehood in those noble features. The three Italian cardinals before him appear to be full of passionate rage; the bishop in front, who holds the imperial pass given to Huss, looks on with an expression of scorn, and the priests around have an air of mingled curiosity and hatred. There is one, however, in whose mild features and tearful eye is expressed sympathy and pity for the prisoner. It is said this picture has had a great effect upon Catholics who have seen it, in softening the bigotry with which they regarded the early reformers; and if so, it is a triumphant proof how much art can effect in the cause of truth and humanity. I was much interested in a cast of the statue of St. George, by the old Italian sculptor Donatello. It is a figure full of youth and energy, with a countenance that seems to breathe. Donatello was the teacher of Michael Angelo, and when the young sculptor was about setting off for Rome, he showed him the statue, his favorite work. Michael gazed at it long and intensely, and at length, on parting, said to Donatello, "It wants but one thing." The artist pondered long over this expression, for he could not imagine in what could fail the matchless figure. At length, after many years, Michael Angelo, in the noon of his renown, visited the deathbed of his old master. Donatello begged to know, before he died, what was wanting to his St. George. Angelo answered, "the gift of speech!" and a smile of triumph lighted the old man's face, as he closed his eyes forever.

The Eschernheim Tower, at the entrance of one of the city gates, is universally admired by strangers, on account of its picturesque appearance, overgrown with ivy and terminated by the little pointed turrets, which one sees so often in Germany, on buildings three or four centuries old. There are five other watch towers of similar form, which stand on different sides of the city, at the distance of a mile or two, and generally upon an eminence overlooking the country. They were erected several centuries ago, to discern from afar the approach of an enemy, and protect the caravans of merchants, which at that time travelled from city to city, from the attacks of robbers. The Eschernheim Tower is interesting from another circumstance, which, whether true or not, is universally believed. When Frankfort was under the sway of a prince, a Swiss hunter, for some civil offence, was condemned to die. He begged his life from the prince, who granted it only on condition that he should fire the figure 9 with his rifle through the vane of this tower. He agreed, and did it; and at the present time, one can distinguish a rude 9 on the vane, as if cut with bullets, while two or three marks at the side appear to be from shots that failed.

The promise of spring which lately visited us, was not destined for fulfilment. Shortly afterwards it grew cold again, with a succession of snows and sharp northerly winds. Such weather at the commencement of spring is not uncommon at home; but here they say there has not been such a winter known for 150 years. In the north of Prussia many persons have been starved to death on account of provisions becoming scarce. Among the Hartz also, the suffering is very great. We saw something of the misery even here. It was painful to walk through the streets and see so many faces bearing plainly the marks of want, so many pale, hollow-eyed creatures, with suffering written on every feature. We were assailed with petitions for help which could not be relieved, though it pained and saddened the heart to deny. The women, too, labor like brutes, day after day. Many of them appear cheerful and contented, and are no doubt, tolerably happy, for the Germans have all true, warm hearts, and are faithful to one another, as far as poverty will permit; but one cannot see old, gray-headed women, carrying loads on their heads as heavy as themselves, exposed to all kinds of weather and working from morning till night, without pity and indignation.

So unusually severe has been the weather, that the deer and hares in the mountains near, came nearly starved and tamed down by hunger, into the villages to hunt food. The people fed them everyday, and also carried grain into the fields for the partridges and pheasants, who flew up to them like domestic fowls. The poor ravens made me really sorry; some lay dead in the fields and many came into the city perfectly tame, flying along the Main with wings hardly strong enough to boar up their skeleton bodies. The storks came at the usual time, but went back again. I hope the year's blessing has not departed with them, according to the old German superstition.

March 26.—We have hopes of spring at last. Three days ago the rain began and has continued with little intermission till now. The air is warm, the snow goes fast, and every thing seems to announce that the long winter is breaking up. The Main rises fast, and goes by the city like an arrow, whirling large masses of ice upon the banks. The hills around are coming out from under the snow, and the lilac-buds in the promenades begin to expand for the second time.

The Fair has now commenced in earnest, and it is a most singular and interesting sight. The open squares are filled with booths, leaving narrow streets between them, across which canvas is spread. Every booth is open and filled with a dazzling display of wares of all kinds. Merchants assemble from all parts of Europe. The Bohemians come with their gorgeous crystal ware; the Nuremborgers with their toys, quaint and fanciful as the old city itself; men from the Thuringian forest, with minerals and canes, and traders from Berlin, Vienna, Paris and Switzerland, with dry goods and wares of all kinds. Near the Exchange are two or three companies of Tyrolese, who attract much of my attention. Their costume is exceedingly picturesque. The men have all splendid manly figures, and honor and bravery are written on their countenances. One of the girls is a really handsome mountain maiden, and with her pointed, broad-brimmed black hat, as romantic looking as one could desire. The musicians have arrived, and we are entertained the whole day long by wandering bands, some of whom play finely. The best, which is also the favorite company, is from Saxony, called "The Mountain Boys." They are now playing in our street, and while I write, one of the beautiful choruses from Norma comes up through the din of the crowd. In fact, music is heard over the whole city, and the throngs that fill every street with all sorts of faces and dresses, somewhat relieve the monotony that was beginning to make Frankfort tiresome.

We have an ever-varied and interesting scene from our window. Besides the motley crowd of passers-by, there are booths and tables stationed thick below. One man in particular is busily engaged in selling his store of blacking in the auction style, in a manner that would do credit to a real Down-caster. He has flaming certificates exhibited, and prefaces his calls to buy with a high-sounding description of his wonderful qualities. He has a bench in front, where he tests on the shoes of his customers, or if none of those are disposed to try it, he rubs it on his own, which shine like mirrors. So he rattles on with amazing fluency in French, German and Italian, and this, with his black beard and moustache and his polite, graceful manner, keeps a crowd of customers around him, so that the wonderful blacking goes off as fast as he can supply it.

April 6.—Old Winter's gales are shut close behind us, and the sun looks down with his summer countenance. The air, after the long cold rain, is like that of Paradise. All things are gay and bright, and everybody is in motion.

421

Spring commenced with yesterday in earnest, and lo! before night the roads were all dry and fine as if there had been no rain for a month; and the gardeners dug and planted in ground which, eight days before, was covered with snow!

After having lived through the longest winter here, for one hundred and fifty years, we were destined to witness the greatest flood for sixty, and little lower than any within the last three hundred years. On the 28th of March, the river overflooded the high pier along the Main, and rising higher and higher, began to come into the gates and alleys. Before night the whole bank was covered and the water intruded into some of the booths in the Römerberg. When I went there the next morning, it was a sorrowful sight. Persons were inside the gate with boats; so rapidly had it risen, that many of the merchants had no time to move their wares, and must suffer great damage. They were busy rescuing what property could bo seized in the haste, and constructing passages into the houses which were surrounded. No one seemed to think of buying or selling, but only on the best method to escape the danger. Along the Main it was still worse. From the measure, it had risen seventeen feet above its usual level, and the arches of the bridge were filled nearly to the top. At the Upper-Main gate, every thing was flooded—houses, gardens, workshops, &c.; the water had even overrun the meadows above and attacked the city from behind, so that a part of the beautiful promenades lay deep under water. On the other side, we could see houses standing in it up to the roof. It came up through the sewers into the middle of Frankfort; a large body of men were kept at work constructing slight bridges to walk on, and transporting boats to places where they were needed. This was all done at the expense of the city; the greatest readiness was everywhere manifested to render all possible assistance. In the Fischergasse, I saw them taking provisions to the people in boats; one man even fastened a loaf of bread to the end of a broomstick and reached it across the narrow street from an upper story window, to the neighbor opposite. News came that Hausen, a village towards the Taunus, about two miles distant, was quite under water, and that the people clung to the roofs and cried for help; but it was fortunately false. About noon, cannon shots were heard, and twenty boats were sent out from the city.

In the afternoon I ascended the tower of the Cathedral, which commands a wide view of the valley, up and down. Just above the city the whole plain was like a small lake—between two and three miles wide. A row of new-built houses stretched into it like a long promontory, and in the middle, like an island, stood a country-seat with large out-buildings. The river sent a long arm out below, that reached up through the meadows behind the city, as if to clasp it all and bear it away together. A heavy storm was raging along the whole extent of the Taunus; but a rainbow stood in the eastern sky. I thought of its promise, and hoped, for the sake of the hundreds of poor people who were suffering by the waters, that it might herald their fall.

We afterwards went over to Sachsenhausen, which was, if possible, in a still more unfortunate condition. The water had penetrated the passages and sewers, and from these leaped and rushed up into the streets, as out of a fountain. The houses next to the Main, which were first filled, poured torrents out of the doors and windows into the street below. These people were nearly all poor, and could ill afford the loss of time and damage of property it occasioned them. The stream was filled with wood and boards, and even whole roofs, with the tiles on, went floating down. The bridge was crowded with people; one saw everywhere mournful countenances, and heard lamentations over the catastrophe. After sunset, a great cloud, filling half the sky, hung above; the reflection of its glowing crimson tint, joined to the brown hue of the water, made it seem like a river of fire.

What a difference a little sunshine makes! I could have forgotten the season the next day, but for the bare trees and swelling Main, as I threaded my way through the hundreds of people who thronged its banks. It was that soft warmth that comes with the first spring days, relaxing the body and casting a dreamy hue over the mind. I leaned over the bridge in the full enjoyment of it, and listening to the roaring of the water under the arches, forgot every thing else for a time. It was amusing to walk up and down the pier and look at the countenances passing by, while the phantasy was ever ready, weaving a tale for all. My favorite Tyrolese were there, and I saw a Greek leaning over the stone balustrade, wearing the red cap and white frock, and with the long dark hair and fiery eye of the Orient. I could not but wonder, as he looked at the dim hills of the Odenwald, along the eastern horizon, whether they called up in his mind the purple isles of his native Archipelago.

The general character of a nation is plainly stamped on the countenances of its people. One who notices the faces in the streets, can soon distinguish, by the glance he gives in going by, the Englishman or the Frenchman from the German, and the Christian from the Jew. Not less striking is the difference of expression between the Germans themselves; and in places where all classes of people are drawn together, it is interesting to observe how accurately these distinctions are drawn. The boys have generally handsome, intelligent faces, and like all boys, they are full of life and spirit, for they know nothing of the laws by which their country is chained down, and would not care for them, if they did. But with the exception of the students, who talk, at least, of Liberty and Right, the young men lose this spirit and at last settle down into the calm, cautious, lethargic citizen. One distinguishes an Englishman and I should think an American, also, in this respect, very easily; the former, moreover, by a certain cold stateliness and reserve. There is something, however, about a Jew, whether English or German, which marks him from all others. However different their faces, there is a family character which runs through the whole of them. It lays principally in their high cheek-bones, prominent nose and thin, compressed lips; which, especially in elderly men, gives a peculiar miserly expression that is unmistakeable. I regret to say, one looks almost in vain, in Germany, for a handsome female countenance. Here and there, perhaps, is a woman with regular features, but that intellectual expression, which gives such a charm to the most common face, is wanting. I have seen more beautiful women in one night, in a public assembly in America, than during the seven months I have been on the Continent. Some of the young Jewesses, in Frankfort, are considered handsome, but their features soon become too strongly marked. In a public walk the number of positively ugly faces is really astonishing.

About ten o'clock that night, I heard a noise of persons running in the street, and going to the Römerberg, found the water had risen, all at once, much higher, and was still rapidly increasing. People were setting up torches and lengthening the rafts, which had been already formed. The lower part of the city was a real Venice—the streets were full of boats and people

424

could even row about in their own houses; though it was not quite so bad as the flood in Georgia, where they went up stairs to bed in boats! I went to the bridge. Persons were calling around—"The water! the water! it rises continually!" The river rushed through the arches, foaming and dashing with a noise like thunder, and the red light of the torches along the shore cost a flickering glare on the troubled waves. It was then twenty-one feet above its usual level. Men were busy all around, carrying boats and ladders to the places most threatened, or emptying cellars into which it was penetrating. The sudden swelling was occasioned by the coming down of the floods from the mountains of Spessart.

Part of the upper quay cracked next morning and threatened to fall in, and one of the projecting piers of the bridge sunk away from the main body three or four inches. In Sachsenhausen the desolation occasioned by the flood is absolutely frightful; several houses have fallen into total ruin. All business was stopped for the day; the Exchange was even shut up. As the city depends almost entirely on pumps for its supply of water, and these were filled with the flood, we have been drinking the muddy current of the Main ever since. The damage to goods is very great. The fair was stopped at once, and the loss in this respect alone, must be several millions of florins. The water began to fall on the 1st, and has now sunk about ten feet, so that most of the houses are again released, though in a bad condition.

Yesterday afternoon, as I was sitting in my room, writing, I heard all at once an explosion like a cannon in the street, followed by loud and continued screams. Looking out the window, I saw the people rushing by with goods in their arms, some wringing their hands and crying, others running in all directions. Imagining that it was nothing less than the tumbling down of one of the old houses, we ran down and saw a store a few doors distant in flames. The windows were bursting and flying out, and the mingled mass of smoke and red flame reached half way across the street. We learned afterwards it was occasioned by the explosion of a jar of naphtha, which instantly enveloped the whole room in fire, the people barely escaping in time. The persons who had booths near were standing still in despair, while the flames were beginning to touch their property. A few butchers who first came up, did almost everything. A fire engine arrived soon, but it was ten minutes before it began to play, and by that time the flames were coming out of the upper stories. Then the supply of water soon failed, and though another engine came up shortly after, it was sometime before it could be put in order, so that by the time they got fairly to work, the fire had made its way nearly through the house. The water was first brought in barrels drawn by horses, till some officer came and opened the fire plug. The police were busy at work seizing those who came by and setting them to work; and as the alarm had drawn a great many together, they at last began to effect something. All the military are obliged to bo out, and the officers appeared eager to use their authority while they could, for every one was ordering and commanding, till all was a scene of perfect confusion and uproar. I could not help laughing heartily, so ludicrous did the scene appear. There were little, miserable engines, not much bigger than a hand-cart, and looking as if they had not been used for half a century, the horses running backwards and forwards, dragging barrels which were emptied into tubs, after which the water was finally dipped up in buckets, and emptied into the engines! These machines can only play into the second or third story, after which the hose was taken up in the houses on the opposite side of the street, and made to play across. After four hours the fire was overcome, the house being thoroughly burnt out; it happened to have double fire walls, which prevented those adjoining from catching easily.

CHAPTER XV. – THE DEAD AND THE DEAF–MENDELSSOHN THE COMPOSER.

It is now a luxury to breathe. These spring days are the perfection of delightful weather. Imagine the delicious temperature of our Indian summer joined to the life and freshness of spring, add to this a sky of the purest azure, and a breeze filled with the odor of violets,—the most exquisite of all perfumes—and you have some idea of it. The meadows are beginning to bloom, and I have already heard the larks singing high up in the sky. Those sacred birds, the storks, have returned and taken possession of their old nests on the chimney-tops; they are sometimes seen walking about in the fields, with a very grave and serious air, as if conscious of the estimation in which they are held. Everybody is out in the open air; the woods, although they still look wintry, are filled with people, and the boatmen on the Main are busy ferrying gay parties across. The spring has been so long in coming, that all are determined to enjoy it well, while it lasts.

We visited the cemetery a few days ago. The dead-house, where corpses are placed in the hope of resuscitation, is an appendage to cemeteries found only in Germany. We were shown into a narrow chamber, on each side of which were six cells, into which one could distinctly see, by means of a large plate of glass. In each of these is a bier for the body, directly above which hangs a cord, having on the end ten thimbles, which are put upon the fingers of the corpse, so that the slightest motion strikes a bell in the watchman's room. Lamps are lighted at night, and in winter the rooms are warmed. In the watchman's chamber stands a clock with a dial-plate of twenty-four hours, and opposite every hour is a little plate, which can only be moved two minutes before it strikes. If then the watchman has slept or neglected his duty at that time, he cannot move it afterwards, and his neglect, is seen by the superintendent. In such a case, he is severely lined, and for the second or third offence, dismissed. There are other rooms adjoining, containing beds, baths, galvanic battery, &c. Nevertheless, they say there has been no resuscitation during the fifteen years it has been established.

We afterwards went to the end of the cemetery to see the bas-reliefs of Thorwaldsen, in the vault of the Bethmann family. They are three in number, representing the death of a son of the present banker, Moritz von Bethmann, who was drowned in the Arno about fourteen years ago. The middle one represents the young man drooping in his chair, the beautiful Greek Angel of Death standing at his back, with one arm over his shoulder, while his younger brother is sustaining him, and receiving the wreath that drops from his sinking hand. The young woman who showed us these, told us of Thorwaldsen's visit to Frankfort, about three years ago. She described him as a beautiful and venerable old man, with long white locks hanging over his shoulders, still vigorous and active for his years. There seems to have been much resemblance between him and Dannecker—not only in personal appearance and character, but, in the simple and classical beauty of their works.

The cemetery contains many other monuments; with the exception of one or two by Launitz, and an exquisite Death Angel in sandstone, from a young Frankfort sculptor, they are not remarkable. The common tombstone is a white wooden cross; opposite the entrance is a perfect forest of them, involuntarily reminding one of a company of ghosts, with outstretched arms. These contain the names of the deceased with mottoes, some of which are beautiful and touching, as for instance: "Through darkness unto light;" "Weep not for her; she is not dead, but sleepeth" "Slumber sweet!" etc. The graves are neatly bordered with grass, and planted with flowers, and many of the crosses have withered wreathes hanging upon them. In summer it is a beautiful place; in fact, the very name of cemetery in German—Friedhuf or Court of Peace—takes away the idea of death; the beautiful figure of the youth, with his inverted torch, makes one think of the grave only us a place of repose.

On our way back we stopped at the Institute for the Deaf; for by the new method of teaching they are no longer dumb. It is a handsome building in the gardens skirting the city. We applied, and on learning we were strangers, they gave us permission to enter. On finding we were Americans, the instructress immediately spoke of Dr. Howe, who had visited the Institute a year or two before, and was much pleased to find that Mr. Dennett was acquainted with him. She took us into a room where about fifteen small children were assembled, and addressing one of the girls, said in a distinct tone: "These gentlemen are from America; the deaf children there speak with their fingers—canst thou speak so?" To which the child answered distinctly, but with some effort: "No, we speak with our mouths." She then spoke to several others with the same success; one of the boys in particular, articulated with astonishing success. It was interesting to watch their countenances, which were alive with eager attention, and to see the apparent efforts they made to utter the words. They spoke in a monotonous tone, slowly and deliberately, but their voices had a strange, sepulchral sound, which was at first unpleasant to the ear. I put one or two questions to a little boy, which he answered quite readily; as I was a foreigner, this was the best test that could be given of the success of the method. We conversed afterwards with the director, who received us kindly, and appointed a day for us to come and witness the system more fully. He spoke of Dr. Howe and Horace Mann, of Boston, and seemed to take a great interest in the introduction of his system in America.

We went again at the appointed time, and as their drawing teacher was there, we had an opportunity of looking over their sketches, which were excellent. The director showed us the manner of teaching them, with a looking-glass, in which they were shown the different positions of the organs of the mouth, and afterwards made to feel the vibrations of the throat and breast, produced by the sound. He took one of the youngest scholars, covered her eyes, and placing her hand upon his throat, articulated the second sound of A. She followed him, making the sound softer or louder as he did. All the consonants were made distinctly, by placing her hand before his mouth. Their exercises in reading, speaking with one another, and writing from dictation, succeeded perfectly. He treated them all like his own children, and sought by jesting and playing, to make the exercise appear as sport. They call him father and appear to be much attached to him.

One of the pupils, about fourteen years old, interested me through his history. lie and his sister were found in Sachsenhausen, by a Frankfort merchant, in a horrible condition. Their mother had died about two years and a half before, and during all that time their father had neglected them till they were near dead through privation and filth. The boy was placed in this Institute, and the girl in that of the Orphans. He soon began to show a talent for modelling figures, and for some time he has been taking lessons of the sculptor Launitz. I saw a beautiful copy of a bas-relief of Thorwaldsen which he made, as well as an original, very interesting, from its illustration of his history. It was in two parts; the first represented himself and his sister, kneeling in misery before a ruined family altar, by which an angel was standing, who took him by one hand, while with the other he pointed to his benefactor, standing near. The other represented the two kneeling in gratitude before a restored altar, on which was the anchor of Hope. From above streamed down a light, where two angels were rejoicing over their happiness. For a boy of fourteen, deprived of one of the most valuable senses, and taken from such a horrible condition of life, it is a surprising work and gives brilliant hopes for his future.

We went lately into the Roemerberg, to see the Kaisersaal and the other rooms formerly used by the old Emperors of Germany, and their Senates. The former is now in the process of restoration. The ceiling is in the gorgeous illuminated style of the middle ages; along each side arc rows of niches for the portraits of the Emperors, which have been painted by the best artists in Berlin, Dresden, Vienna and Munich. It is remarkable that the number of the old niches in the hall should exactly correspond with the number of the German Emperors, so that the portrait of the Emperor Francis of Austria, who was the last, will close the long rank coming down from Charlemagne. The pictures, or at least such of them as are already finished, are kept in another room; they give one a good idea of the changing styles of royal costumes, from the steel shirt and helmet to the jewelled diadem and velvet robe. I looked with interest on a painting of Frederic Barbarossa, by Leasing, and mused over the popular tradition that he sits with his paladins in a mountain cave under the Castle of Kyffhäuser, ready to come forth and assist his Fatherland in the hour of need. There was the sturdy form of Maximilian; the martial Conrad; and Ottos, Siegfrieds and Sigismunds in plenty—many of whom moved a nation in their day, but are now dust and forgotten.

I yesterday visited Mendelssohn, the celebrated composer. Having heard rame of his music this winter, particularly that magnificent creation, the "Walpurgisnacht," I wished to obtain his autograph before leaving, and sent a note for that purpose. He sent a kind note in answer, adding a chorus out of the Walpurgisnacht from his own hand. After this, I could not repress the desire of speaking with him. lie received me with true German cordiality, and on learning I was an American, spoke of having been invited to attend a musical festival in New York. He invited me to call on him if he happened to bo in Leipsic or Dresden when we should pass through, and spoke particularly of the fine music there. I have rarely seen a man whose countenance bears so plainly the stamp of genius. He has a glorious dark eye, and Byron's expression of a "dome of thought," could never be more appropriately applied than to his lofty and intellectual forehead, the marble whiteness and polish of which arc heightened by the raven hue of his hair. He is about forty years of age, in the noon of his fame and the full maturity of his genius. Already as a boy of fourteen he composed an opera, which was played with much success at Berlin; he is now the first living composer of Germany. Moses Mendelssohn, the celebrated Jewish philosopher, was his grandfather; and his father, now living, is accustomed to say that in his youth he was spoken of as the son of the great Mendelssohn; now he is known as the father of the great Mendelssohn!

CHAPTER XVI. — JOURNEY ON FOOT FROM FRANKFORT TO CASSEL.

The day for leaving Frankfort came at last, and I bade adieu to the gloomy, antique, but still quaint and pleasant city. I felt like leaving a second home, so much had the memories of many delightful hours spent there attached me to it: I shall long retain the recollection of its dark old streets, its massive, devil-haunted bridge and the ponderous cathedral, telling of the times of the Crusaders. I toiled up the long hill on the road to Friedberg, and from the tower at the top took a last look at the distant city, with a heart heavier than the knapsack whose unaccustomed weight rested uneasily on my shoulders. Being alone—starting out into the wide world, where us yet I know no one,—I felt much deeper what it was to find friends in a strange land. But such is the wanderer's lot.

We had determined on making the complete tour of Germany on foot, and in order to vary it somewhat, my friend and I proposed taking different routes from Frankfort to Leipsic. He choose a circuitous course, by way of Nuremberg and the Thuringian forests; while I, whose fancy had been running wild with Goethe's witches, preferred looking on the gloom and grandeur of the rugged Hartz. We both left Frankfort on the 23d of April, each bearing a letter of introduction to the same person in Leipsic, where we agreed to meet in fourteen days. As we were obliged to travel as cheaply as possible, I started with but seventynine florins, (a florin is forty cents American) well knowing that if I took more, I should, in all probability, spend proportionally more also. Thus, armed with my passport, properly visèd, a knapsack weighing fifteen pounds and a cane from the Kentucky Mammoth Cave, I began my lonely walk through Northern Germany. The warm weather of the week before had brought out the foliage of the willows and other early trees—violets and cowslips were springing up in the meadows. Keeping along the foot of the Taunus, I passed over great, broad hills, which were brown with the spring ploughing, and by sunset reached Friedberg—a, largo city, on the summit of a hill. The next morning, after sketching its old, baronial castle, I crossed the meadows to Nauheim, to see the salt springs there. They are fifteen in number; the water, which is very warm, rushes up with such force as to leap several feet above the earth. The buildings made for evaporation are nearly two miles in length; a walk along the top gives a delightful view of the surrounding valleys. After reaching the chaussée again, I was hailed by a wandering journeyman, or handwerker, as they are called, who wanted company. As I had concluded to accept all offers of this kind, we trudged along together very pleasantly, He was from Holstein, on the borders of Denmark and was just returning home, after an absence of six years, having escaped from Switzerland after the late battle of Luzerne, which he had witnessed. He had his knapsack and tools fastened on two wheels, which he drew after him quite conveniently. I could not help laughing at the adroit manner in which he begged his way along, through every village. He would ask me to go on and wait for him at the other end; after a few minutes he followed, with a handful of small copper money, which he said he had fought for,—the handworker's term for begged.

We passed over long ranges of hills, with an occasional view of the Vogelsgebirge, or Bird's Mountains, far to the cast. I knew at length, by the pointed summits of the hills, that we were approaching Giessen and the valley of the Lahn. Finally, two sharp peaks appeared in the distance, each crowned with a picturesque fortress, while the spires of Giessen rose from the valley below. Parting from my companion, I passed through the city without stopping, for it was the time of the university vacation, and Dr. Liebeg, the world-renowned chemist, whom I desired to see, was absent.

Crossing a hill or two, I came down into the valley of the Lahn, which flows through meadows of the brightest green, with redroofed cottages nestled among gardens and orchards upon its banks. The women here wear a remarkable costume, consisting of a red boddice with white sleeves, and a dozen skirts, one above another, reaching only to the knees. I slept again at a little village among the hills, and started early for Marburg. The meadows were of the purest emerald, through which the stream wound its way, with even borders, covered to the water's edge with grass so smooth and velvety, that a fairy might have danced along on it for miles without stumbling over an uneven tuft. This valley is one of the finest districts in Germany. I thought, as I saw the peaceful inhabitants at work in their fields, I had most probably, on the battle-field of Brandywine, walked over the bones of some of their ancestors, whom a despotic prince had torn from their happy homes, to die in a distant land, fighting against the cause of freedom.

I now entered directly into the heart of Hesse Cassel. The country resembled a collection of hills thrown together in confusion—sometimes a wide plain left between them, sometimes a clustre of wooded peaks, and here and there a single pointed summit rising above the rest. The vallies were green as ever, the hill-sides freshly ploughed and the forests beginning to be colored by the tender foliage of the larch and birch. I walked two or three hours at a "stretch," and then, when I could find a dry, shady bank, I would rest for half an hour and finish some hastily sketched landscape, or lay at full length, with my head on my knapsack, and peruse the countenances of those passing by. The observation which every traveller excites, soon ceases to be embarrassing. It was at first extremely unpleasant; but I am now so hardened, that the strange, magnetic influence of the human eye, which we cannot avoid feeling, passes by me as harmlessly as if turned aside by invisible mail.

During the day several showers came by, but as none of them penetrated further than my blouse, I kept on, and reached about sunset a little village in the valley. I chose a small inn, which had an air of neatness about it, and on going in, the tidy landlady's "be you welcome," as she brought a pair of slippers for my swollen feet, made me feel quite at home. After being furnished with eggs, milk, butter and bread, for supper, which I ate while listening to an animated discussion between the village schoolmaster and some farmers, I was ushered into a clean, sanded bedroom, and soon forgot all fatigue. For this, with breakfast in the morning, the bill was six and a half groschen—about sixteen cents! Tin air was freshened by the rain and I journeyed over the hills at a rapid rate. Stopping for dinner at the large village of Wabern, a boy at the inn asked me if I was going to America? I said no, I came from there. He then asked me many silly questions, after which he ran out and told the people of the village. When I set out again, the children pointed at me and cried: "see there! he is from America!" and the men took off their hats and bowed!

The sky was stormy, which added to the gloom of the hills around, though some of the distant ranges lay in mingled light and shade—the softest alternation of purple and brown. There were many isolated, rocky hills, two of which interested me, through their attendant legends. One is said to have been the scene of a battle between the Romans and Germans, where, after a long conflict the rock opened and swallowed up the former. The other, which is crowned with a rocky wall, so like a ruined fortress, as at a distance to be universally mistaken for one, tradition says is the death-place of Charlemagne, who still walks around its summit every night, clad in complete armor. On ascending a hill late in the afternoon, I saw at a great distance the statue of Hercules, which stands on the Wilhelmshöhe, near Cassel. Night set in with a dreary rain, and I stopped at an inn about five miles short of the city. While tea was preparing a company of students came in and asked for a separate room. Seeing I was alone, they invited me up with them. They seemed much interested in America, and leaving the table gradually, formed a ring around me, where I had enough to do to talk with them all at once. When the omnibus came along, the most of them went with it to Cassel; but five remained and persuaded me to set out with them on foot. They insisted on carrying my knapsack the whole way, through the rain and darkness, and when I had passed the city gate with them, unchallenged, conducted me to the comfortable hotel, "Zur Krone."

It is a pleasant thing to wake up in the morning in a strange city. Every thing is new; you walk around it for the first time in the full enjoyment of the novelty, or the not less agreeable feeling of surprise, if it is different from your anticipations. Two of my friends of the previous night called for me in the morning, to show me around the city, and the first impression, made in such agreeable company, prepossessed me very favorably. I shall not, however, take up time in describing its many sights, particularly the Frederick's Platz, where the statue of Frederick the Second, who sold ten thousand of his subjects to England, has been re-erected, after having lain for years in a stable where it was thrown by the French.

I was much interested in young Carl K——, one of my new acquaintances. His generous and unceasing kindness first won my esteem, and I found on nearer acquaintance, the qualities of his mind equal those of his heart. I saw many beautiful poems of his which were of remarkable merit, considering his youth, and thought I could read in his dark, dreamy eye, the unconscious presentiment of a power he does not yet possess. He seemed as one I had known for years.

He, with a brother student, accompanied me in the afternoon, to Wilhelmshöhe, the summer residence of the Prince, on the side of a range of mountains three miles west of the city. The road leads in a direct line to the summit of the mountain, which is thirteen hundred feet in height, surmounted by a great structure, called the Giant's Castle, on the summit of which is a pyramid ninety-six feet high, supporting a statue of Hercules, copied after the Farnese, and thirty-one feet in height. By a gradual ascent through beautiful woods, we reached the princely residence, a magnificent mansion standing on a natural terrace of the mountain. Near it is a little theatre built by Jerome Buonaparte, in which he himself used to play. We looked into the green house in passing, where the floral splendor of every zone was combined. There were lofty halls, with glass roofs, where the orange grew to a great tree, and one could sit in myrtle bowers, with the brilliant bloom of the tropics around him. It was the only thing there I was guilty of coveting.

The greatest curiosity is the water-works, which are perhaps unequalled in the world. The Giant's Castle on the summit contains an immense tank in which water is kept for the purpose; but unfortunately, at the time I was there, the pipes, which had been frozen through the winter, were not in condition to play. From the summit an inclined plane of masonry descends the mountain nine hundred feet, broken every one hundred and fifty feet by perpendicular descents. These are the Cascades, down which the water first rushes from the tank. After being again collected in a great basin at the bottom, it passes into an aqueduct, built like a Roman ruin, and goes over beautiful arches through the forest, where it falls in one sheet down a deep precipice. When it has descended several other beautiful falls, made in exact imitation of nature, it is finally collected and forms the great fountain, which rises twelve inches in diameter from the middle of a lake to the height of one hundred and ninety feet! We descended by lovely walks through the forest to the Löwenburg, built as the ruin of a knightly castle, and fitted out in every respect to correspond with descriptions of a fortress in the olden time, with moat, drawbridge, chapel and garden of pyramidal trees. Farther below, are a few small houses, inhabited by the descendants of the Hessians who fell in America, supported here at the Prince's expense!

CHAPTER XVII. — ADVENTURES AMONG THE HARTZ.

On taking leave of Carl at the gate over the Göttingen road, I felt tempted to bestow a malediction upon traveling, from its merciless breaking of all links, as soon as formed. It was painful to think we should meet no more. The tears started into his eyes, and feeling a mist gathering over mine, I gave his hand a parting pressure, turned my back upon Cassel and started up the long mountain, at a desperate rate. On the summit I passed out of Hesse into Hanover, and began to descend the remaining six miles. The road went down by many windings, but I shortened the way considerably by a footpath through a mossy old forest. The hills bordering the Weser are covered with wood, through which I saw the little red-roofed city of Münden, at the bottom. I stopped there for the night, and next morning walked around the place. It is one of the old German cities that have not yet felt the effect of the changing spirit of the age. It is still walled, though the towers are falling to ruin. The streets are narrow, crooked, and full of ugly old houses, and to stand in the little square before the public buildings, one would think himself born in the sixteenth century. Just below the city the Werra and Fulda unito and form the Weser. The triangular point has been made into a public walk, and the little steamboat was lying at anchor near, waiting to start for Bremen.

In the afternoon I got into the omnibus for Göttingen. The ride over the wild, dreary, monotonous hills was not at all interesting. There were two other passengers inside, one of whom, a grave, elderly man, took a great interest in America, but the conversation was principally on his side, for I had been taken with a fever in Münden. I lay crouched up in the corner of the vehicle, trying to keep off the chills which constantly came over me, and wishing only for Göttingen, that I might obtain medicine and a bed. We reached it at last, and I got out with my knapsack and walked wearily through half a dozen streets till I saw an inn. But on entering, I found it so dark and dirty and unfriendly, that I immediately went out again and hired the first pleasant looking boy I met, to take me to a good hotel. He conducted me to the first one in the city. I felt a trepidation of pocket, but my throbbing head plead more powerfully, so I ordered a comfortable room and a physician. The host, Herr Wilhelm, sent for Professor Trefurt, of the University, who told me I had over-exerted myself in walking. He made a second call the next day, when, as he was retiring, I inquired the amount of his fee. He begged to be excused and politely bowed himself out. I inquired the meaning of this of Herr Wilhelm, who said it was customary for travellers to leave what they chose for the physician, as there was no regular fee. He added, moreover, that twenty groschen, or about sixty cents, was sufficient for the two visits!

I stayed in Göttingen two dull, dreary, miserable days, without getting much better. I took but one short walk through the city, in which I saw the outsides of a few old churches and got a hard fall on the pavement. Thinking that the cause of my illness might perhaps become its cure, I resolved to go on rather than remain in the melancholy—in spite of its black-eyed maidens, melancholy—Göttingen. On the afternoon of the second day, I took the post to Nordheim, about twelve miles distant. The Göttingen valley, down which we drove, is green and beautiful, and the trees seem to have come out all at once. we were not within sight of the Hartz, but the mountains along the Weser were visible on the left. The roads were extremely muddy from the late rains, so that I proceeded but slowly.

A blue range along the horizon told me of the Hartz, as I passed; although there were some fine side-glimpses through the hills, I did not see much of them till I reached Osterode, about twelve miles further. Here the country begins to assume a different aspect. The city lies in a narrow valley, and as the road goes down a steep hill towards it, one sees on each side many quarries of gypsum, and in front the gloomy pine mountains are piled one above another in real Alpine style. But alas! the city, though it looks exceedingly romantic from above, is one of the dirtiest I ever saw. I stopped at Herzberg, six miles farther, for the night. The scenery was very striking; and its effect was much heightened by a sky full of black clouds, which sent down a hail-storm as they passed over. The hills are covered with pine, fir and larch. The latter tree, in its first foliage, is most delicate and beautiful. Every bough is like a long ostrich plume, and when one of them stands among the dark pines, it seems so light and airy that the wind might carry it away. Just opposite Herzberg, the Hartz

439

stands in its gloomy and mysterious grandeur, and I went to sleep with the pleasant thought that an hour's walk on the morrow would shut me up in its deep recesses.

The next morning I entered them. The road led up a narrow mountain valley, down which a stream was rushing—on all sides were magnificent forests of pine. It was glorious to look down their long aisles, dim and silent, with a floor of thick green moss. There was just room enough for the road and the wild stream which wound its way zigzag between the hills, affording the most beautiful mountain-view along the whole route. As I ascended, the mountains became rougher and wilder, and in the shady hollows were still drifts of snow. Enjoying every thing very much, I walked on without taking notice of the road, and on reaching a wild, rocky chasm called the "Schlucht," was obliged to turn aside and take a footpath over a high mountain to Andreasberg, a town built on a summit two thousand feet above the sea. It is inhabited almost entirely by the workmen in the mines.

The way from Andreasberg to the Brocken leads along the Rehberger Graben, which carry water about six miles for the oreworks. After going through a thick pine wood, I came out on the mountain-side, where rough crags overhung the way above, and through the tops of the trees I had glimpses into the gorge below. It was scenery of the wildest character. Directly opposite rose a mountain wall, dark and stern through the gloomy sky; far below the little stream of the Oder foamed over the rocks with a continual roar, and one or two white cloud-wreaths were curling up from the forests.

I followed the water-ditch around every projection of the mountain, still ascending higher amid the same wild scenery, till at length I reached the Oderteich, a great dam, in a kind of valley formed by some mountain peaks on the side of the Brocken. It has a breastwork of granite, very firm, and furnishes a continual supply of water for the works. It began to rain soon, and I took a foot-path which went winding up through the pine wood. The storm still increased, till everything was cloud and rain, so I was obliged to stop about five o'clock at Oderbruch, a toll-house and tavern on the side of the Brocken, on the boundary between Brunswick and Hanover—the second highest inhabited house in the Hartz. The Brocken was invisible through the storm and the weather forboded a difficult ascent. The night was cold, but by a warm fire I let the winds howl and the rain beat. When I awoke the next morning, we were in clouds. They were thick on every side, hiding what little view there was through the openings of the forest. After breakfast, however, they were somewhat thinner, and I concluded to start for the Brocken. It is not the usual way for travellers who ascend, being not only a bad road but difficult to find, as I soon discovered. The clouds gathered around again after I set out, and I was obliged to walk in a storm of mingled rain and snow. The snow lay several feet deep in the forests, and the path was, in many places, quite drifted over. The white cloud-masses were whirled past by the wind, continually enveloping me and shutting out every view. During the winter the path had become, in ninny places, the bed of a mountain torrent, so that I was obliged sometimes to wade kneedeep in snow, and sometimes to walk over the wet, spongy moss, crawling under the long, dripping branches of the stunted pines. After a long time of such dreary travelling, I came to two rocks called the Stag Horns, standing on a little peak. The storm, now all snow, blew more violently than ever, and the path became lost under the deep drifts.

Comforting myself with the assurance that if I could not find it, I could at least make my way back, I began searching, and after some time, came upon it again. Here the forest ceased; the way led on large stones over a marshy ascending plain, but what was above, or on either side, I could not see. It was solitude of the most awful kind. There was nothing but the storm, which had already wet me through, and the bleak gray waste of rocks. It grew sleeper and steeper; I could barely trace the path by the rocks which were worn, and the snow threatened soon to cover these. Added to this, although the walking and fresh mountain air had removed my illness, I was still weak from the effects of it, and the consequences of a much longer exposure to the storm were greatly to be feared. I was wondering if the wind increased at the same rate, how much longer it would be before I should be carried off, when suddenly something loomed up above me through the storm. A few steps more and I stood beside the Brocken House, on the very summit of the mountain! The mariner, who has been floating for days on a wreck at sea, could scarcely be more rejoiced at a friendly sail, than I was on entering the low building. Two large Alpine dogs in the passage, as I walked in, dripping with wet, gave notice to the inmates, and I was soon ushered into a warm room, where I changed my soaked garments for dry ones, and sat down by the fire with feelings of comfort not easily imagined. The old landlord was quite surprised, on hearing the path by which I came, that I found the way at all. The summit was wrapped in the thickest cloud, and he gave me no hope for several hours of any prospect at all, so I sat down and looked over the Stranger's Album.

I saw but two names from the United States—B.F. Atkins, of Boston, and C.A. Hay, from York, Pa. There were a great many long-winded German poems—among them, one by Schelling, the philosopher. Some of them spoke of having seen the "Spectre of the Brocken." I inquired of the landlord about the phenomenon; he says in winter it is frequently seen, in summer more seldom. The cause is very simple. It is always seen at sunrise, when the eastern side of the Brocken is free from clouds, and at the same time, the mist rises from the valley on the opposite side. The shadow of every thing on the Brocken is then thrown in grand proportions upon the mist, and is seen surrounded with a luminous halo. It is somewhat singular that such a spectacle can be seen upon the Brocken alone, but this is probably accounted for by the formation of the mountain, which collects the mist at just such a distance from the summit as to render the shadow visible.

Soon after dinner the storm subsided and the clouds separated a little. I could see down through the rifts on the plains of Brunswick, and sometimes, when they opened a little more, the mountains below us to the east and the adjoining plains, as far as Magdeburg. It was like looking on the earth from another planet, or from some point in the air which had no connection, with it; our station was completely surrounded by clouds, rolling in great masses around us, now and then giving glimpses through their openings of the blue plains, dotted with cities and villages, far below. At one time when they were tolerably well separated, I ascended the tower, fifty feet high, standing near the Brocken House. The view on three sides was quite clear, and I can easily imagine what a magnificent prospect it must be in fine weather. The Brocken is only about four thousand feet high, nearly the same as the loftiest peak of the Catskill, but being the highest mountain in Northern Germany, it commands a more extensive prospect. Imagine a circle described with a radius of a hundred miles, comprising thirty cities, two or three hundred villages and one whole mountain district! We could see Brunswick and Magdeburg, and beyond them the great plain which extends to the North Sea in one direction and to Berlin in the other, while directly below us lay the dark mountains of the Hartz, with little villages in their sequestered valleys. It was but a few moments I could look on this scene—in an instant the clouds swept together again and completely hid it. In accordance with a custom of the mountain, one of the girls made me a "Brocken nosegay," of heather, lichens and moss. I gave her a few pfennings and stowed it away carefully in a corner of my knapsack.

I now began descending the east side, by a good road over fields of bare rock and through large forests of pine. Two or three bare brown peaks rose opposite with an air of the wildest sublimity, and in many places through the forest towered lofty crags. This is the way by which Goethe brings Faust up the Brocken, and the scenery is graphically described in that part of the poem. At the foot of the mountain is the little village of Schiercke, the highest in the Hartz. Here I took a narrow path through the woods, and after following a tediously long road over the hills, reached Elbingerode, where I spent the night, and left the next morning for Blankenburg. I happened to take the wrong road, however, and went through Rubeland, a little village in the valley of the Bode. There are many iron works here, and two celebrated caves, called "Baumann's Höhle," and "Biel's Höhle." I kept on through the gray, rocky hills to Huttenrode, where I inquired the way to the Rosstrappe, but was directed wrong, and after walking nearly two hours in a heavy rain, arrived at Ludwigshütte, on the Bode, in one of the wildest and loneliest corners of the Hartz. I dried my wet clothes at a little inn, ate a dinner of bread and milk, and learning that I was just as far from the Rosstrappe as ever, and that the way was impossible to find alone, I hunted up a guide.

We went over the mountains through a fine old forest, for about two hours, and came out on the brow of a hill near the end of the Hartz, with a beautiful view of the country below and around. Passing the little inn, the path led through thick bushes along the summit, over a narrow ledge of rocks that seemed to stretch out into the air, for on either side the foot of the precipice vanished in the depth below.

Arrived at last at the end, I looked around me. What a spectacle! I was standing on the end of a line of precipice which ran out from the mountain like a wall for several hundred feet—the hills around rising up perpendicularly from the gorge below, where the Bode pressed into a narrow channel foamed its way through. Sharp masses of gray rock rose up in many places from the main body like pillars, with trees clinging to the clefts, and although the defile was near seven hundred feet deep, the summits, in one place, were very near to one another. Near the point at which I stood, which was secured by a railing, was an impression in the rock like the hoof of a giant horse, from which the place takes its name. It is very distinct and perfect, and nearly two feet in length.

I went back to the little inn and sat down to rest and chat awhile with the talkative landlady. Notwithstanding her horrible Prussian dialect, I was much amused with the budget of wonders, which she keeps for the information of travelers. Among other things, she related to me the legend of the Rosstrappe, which I give in her own words: "A great many hundred years ago, when there were plenty of giants through the world, there was a certain beautiful princess, who was very much loved by one of them. Now, although the parents of this princess were afraid of the giant, and wanted her to marry him, she herself hated him, because she was in love with a brave knight. But, you see, the brave knight could do nothing against the great giant, and so a day was appointed for the wedding of the princess. When they were married, the giant had a great feast and he and all his servants got drunk. So the princess mounted his black horse and rode away over the mountains, till she reached this valley. She stood on that square rock which you see there opposite to us, and when she saw her knight on this side, where we are, she danced for joy, and the rock is called the Tanzplatz, to this very day. But when the giant found she had gone, he followed her as fast as he might; then a holy bishop, who saw the princess, blessed the feet of her horse, and she jumped on it across to this side, where his fore feet made two marks in the rock, though there is only one left now. You should not laugh at this, for if there were giants then, there must have

444

been very big horses too, as one can see from the hoofmark, and the valley was narrower then than it is now. My dear man, who is very old now, (you see him through the bushes, there, digging,) says it was so when he was a child, and that the old people living then, told him there were once four just such hoof-tracks, on the Tanzplatz, where the horse stood before he jumped over. And we cannot doubt the words of the good old people, for there were many strange things then, we all know, which the dear Lord does not let happen now. But I must tell you, lieber Herr, that the giant tried to jump after her and fell away down into the valley, where they say he lives yet in the shape of a big black dog, guarding the crown of the princess, which fell off as she was going over. But this part of the story is perhaps not true, as nobody, that I ever heard of, has seen either the black dog or the crown!"

After listening to similar gossip for a while, I descended the mountainside, a short distance to the Bülowshöhe. This is a rocky shaft that shoots, upward from the mountain, having from its top a glorious view through the door which the Bode makes in passing out of the Hartz. I could see at a great distance the towers of Magdeburg, and further, the vast plain stretching away like a sea towards Berlin. From Thale, the village below, where the air was warmer than in the Hartz and the fruit-trees already in blossom, it was four hours' walk to Halberstadt, by a most tiresome road over long ranges of hills, all ploughed and planted, and extending as far as the eye could reach, without a single fence or hedge. It is pleasant to look over scenes where nature is so free and unshackled; but the people, alas! wear the fetters. The setting sun, which lighted up the old Brocken and his snowy top, showed me also Halberstadt, the end of my Hartz journey; but its deceitful towers fled as I approached, and I was half dead with fatigue on arriving there.

The ghostly, dark and echoing castle of an inn (the Black Eagle) where I stopped, was enough to inspire a lonely traveller, like myself, with unpleasant fancies. It looked heavy and massive enough to have been a stout baron's stronghold in some former century; the taciturn landlord and his wife, who, with a solemn servant girl, were the only tenants, had grown into perfect keeping with its gloomy character. When I groped my way under the heavy, arched portal into the guests' room—a large, lofty, cheerless hall—all was dark, and I could barely perceive, by the little light which came through two deep-set windows, the inmates of the house, sitting on opposite sides of the room. After some delay, the hostess brought a light. I entreated her to bring me something instantly for supper, and in half an hour she placed a mixture on the table, the like of which I never wish to taste again. She called it beer-soup! I found, on examination, it was beer, boiled with meat, and seasoned strongly with pepper and salt! My hunger disappeared, and pleading fatigue as an excuse for want of appetite, I left the table. When I was ready to retire, the landlady, who had been sitting silently in a dark corner, called the solemn servant girl, who took up a dim lamp, and bade me follow her to the "sleeping chamber." Taking up my knapsack and staff, I stumbled down the steps into the arched gateway; before me was a long, damp, deserted court-yard, across which the girl took her way. I followed her with some astonishment, imagining where the sleeping chamber could be, when she stopped at a small, one-story building, standing alone in the yard. Opening the door with a rusty key, she led me into a bare room, a few feet square, opening into another, equally bare, with the exception of a rough bed. "Certainly," said I, "I am not to sleep here!" "Yes," she answered, "this is the sleeping chamber," at the same time setting down the light and disappearing. I examined the place—it smelt mouldy, and the walls were cold and damp; there had been a window at the head of the bed, but it was walled up, and that at the foot was also closed to within a few inches of the top. The bed was course and dirty; and on turning down the ragged covers, I saw with horror, a dark brown stain near the pillow, like that of blood! For a moment I hesitated whether to steal out of the inn, and seek another lodging, late as it was; at last, overcoming my fears, I threw my clothes into a heap, and lay down, placing my heavy staff at the head of the bed. Persons passed up and down the courtyard several times, the light of their lamps streaming through the narrow aperture up against the ceiling, and I distinctly heard voices, which seemed to be near the door. Twice did I sit up in bed, breathless, with my hand on the cane, in the most intense anxiety; but fatigue finally overcame suspicion, and I sank into a deep sleep, from which I was gladly awakened by daylight. In reality, there may have been no cause for my fears—I may have wronged the lonely innkeepers by them; but certainly no place or circumstances ever seemed to me more appropriate to a deed of robbery or crime. I left immediately, and when a turn in the street hid the ill-omened front of the inn, I began to breathe with my usual freedom.

CHAPTER XVIII. — NOTES IN LEIPSIC AND DRESDEN.

Leipsic, May 8.—I have now been nearly two days in this wide-famed city, and the more I see of it the better I like it. It is a pleasant, friendly town, old enough to be interesting, and new enough to be comfortable. There in much active business life, through which it is fast increasing in size and beauty. Its publishing establishments are the largest in the world, and its annual fairs attended by people from all parts of Europe. This is much for a city to accomplish, situated alone in the middle of a great plain, with no natural charms of scenery or treasures of art to attract strangers. The energy and enterprise of its merchants have accomplished all this, and it now stands, in importance, among the first cities of Europe.

The bad weather obliged me to take the railroad at Halberstadt, to keep the appointment with my friend, in this city. I left at six for Magdeburg, and after two hours' ride over a dull, tiresome plain, rode along under the mounds and fortifications by the side of the Elbe, and entered the old town. It was very cold, and the streets were muddy, so I contented myself with looking at the Broadway, (der breite Weg,) the Cathedral and one or two curious old churches, and in walking along the parapet leading to the fortress, which has a view of the winding Elbe. The Citadel was interesting from having been the prison in which Baron Trenck was confined, whose narrative I read years ago, when quite a child.

We were soon on the road to Leipsic. The way was over one great, uninterrupted plain—a more monotonous country, even, than Belgium. Two of the passengers in the car with me were much annoyed at being taken by the railway agents for Poles. Their movements were strictly watched by the gens d'arme at every station we passed, and they were not even allowed to sit together! At Kothen a branch track went off to Berlin. We passed by Halle without being able to see anything of it or its University, and arrived here in four hours after leaving Magdeburg.

On my first walk around the city, yesterday morning, I passed the

Augustus Platz—a broad green lawn, on which front the University and several other public buildings. A chain of beautiful promenades encircles the city, on the site of its old fortifications. Following their course through walks shaded by large trees and bordered with flowering shrubs, I passed a small but chaste monument to Sebastian Bach, the composer, which was erected almost entirely at the private cost of Mendelssohn, and stands opposite the building in which Bach once directed the choirs. As I was standing beside it, a glorious choral, swelled by a hundred voices, came through the open windows, like a tribute to the genius of the great master.

Having found my friend we went together to the Stern Warte, or Observatory, which gives a fine view of the country around the city, and in particular the battle field. The Castellan who is stationed there, is well acquainted with the localities, and pointed out the position of the hostile armies. It was one of the most bloody and hard-fought battles which history records. The army of Napoleon stretched like a semicircle around the southern and eastern sides of the city, and the plain beyond was occupied by the allies, whose forces met together here. Schwarzenberg, with his Austrians, came from Dresden; Blucher, from Halle, with the Emperor Alexander. Their forces amounted to three hundred thousand, while those of Napoleon ranked at one hundred and ninety-two thousand men. It must have been a terrific scene. Four days raged the battle, and the meeting of half a million of men in deadly conflict was accompanied by the thunder of sixteen hundred cannon. The small rivers which flow through Leipsic were swollen with blood, and the vast plain was strewed with more than fifty thousand dead. It is difficult to conceive of such slaughter, while looking at the quiet and tranquil landscape below. It seemed more like a legend of past ages, when ignorance and passion led men to murder and destroy, than an event which the last half century witnessed. For the sake of humanity it is to be hoped that the world will never see such another.

There are some lovely walks around Leipsic. We went yesterday afternoon with a few friends to the Rosenthal, a beautiful meadow, bordered by forests of the German oak, very few of whose Druid trunks have been left standing. There are Swiss cottages embowered in the foliage, where every afternoon the social citizens assemble to drink their coffee enjoy a few hours' escape from the noisy and dusty streets, One can walk for miles along these lovely paths by the side of the velvet meadows, or the banks of some shaded stream. We visited the little village of Golis, a short distance off, where, in the second story of a little white house, hangs the sign: "Schiller's Room." Some of the Leipsic literati have built a stone arch over the entrance, with the inscription above: "Here dwelt Schiller in 1795, and wrote his Hymn to Joy." Every where through Germany the remembrances of Schiller are sacred. In every city where he lived, they show his dwelling. They know and reverence the mighty spirit who has been among them. The little room where he conceived that sublime poem is hallowed as if by the presence of unseen spirits.

I was anxious to see the spot where Poniatowsky fell. We returned over the plain to the city and passed in at the gate by which the Cossacks entered, pursuing the flying French. Crossing the lower part, we came to the little river Elster, in whose waves the gallant prince sank. The stone bridge by which we crossed was blown up by the French, to cut off pursuit. Napoleon had given orders that it should not be blown up till the Poles had all passed over, as the river, though narrow, is quite deep, and the banks are steep. Nevertheless, his officers did not wait, and the Poles, thus exposed to the fire of the enemy, were obliged to plunge into the stream to join the French army, which had begun the retreat towards Frankfort. Poniatowsky, severely wounded, made his way through a garden near and escaped on horseback into the water. He became entangled among the fugitives and sank. By walking a little distance along the road towards Frankfort, we could see the spot where his body was taken out of the river; it is now marked by a square stone, covered with the names of his countrymen who have visited it. We returned through the narrow arched way, by which Napoleon fled when the battle was lost.

Another interesting place in Leipsic is Auerback's Cellar, which, it is said, contains an old manuscript history of Faust, from which Goethe derived the first idea of his poem. He used to frequent this cellar, and one of his scenes in "Faust" is laid in it. We looked down the arched passage; not wishing to purchase any wine, we could find no pretence for entering. The streets are full of book stores and one half the business of the inhabitants appears to consist in printing, paper-making and binding. The publishers have a handsome Exchange of their own, and during the Fairs, the amount of business transacted is enormous. The establishment of Brockhaus is contained in an immense building, adjoining which stands his dwelling, in the midst of magnificent gardens. That of Tauchnitz is not less celebrated. His edition of the classics, in particular, are the best that have ever been made; and he has lately commenced publishing a number of English works, in a cheap form. Otto Wigand, who has also a large establishment, has begun to issue translations of American works. He has already published Prescott and Bancroft, and I believe intends giving out shortly, translations from some of our poets and novelists. I became acquainted at the Museum, with a young German author who had been some time in America, and was well versed in our literature. He is now engaged in translating American works, one of which—Hoffman's "Wild Scenes of the Forest and Prairie"—will soon appear. In no place in Germany have I found more knowledge of our country, her men and her institutions, than in Leipsic, and as yet I have seen few that would be preferable as a place of residence. Its attractions lie not in its scenery, but in the social and intellectual character of its inhabitants.

May 11.—At last in this "Florence of the Elbe," as the Saxons have christened it. Exclusive of its glorious galleries of art, which are scarcely surpassed by any in Europe, Dresden charms one by the natural beauty of its environs. It stands in a curve of the Elbe, in the midst of green meadows, gardens and fine old woods, with the hills of Saxony sweeping around like an amphitheatre, and the craggy peaks of the Highlands looking at it from afar. The domes and spires at a distance give it a rich Italian look, which is heightened by the white villas, embowered in trees, gleaming on the hills around. In the streets there is no bustle of business—nothing of the din and confusion of traffic which mark most cities; it seems like a place for study and quiet enjoyment.

The railroad brought us in three hours from Leipsic, over the eighty miles of plain that intervene. We came from the station through the Neustadt, passing the Japanese Palace and the equestrian statue of Augustus the Strong, The magnificent bridge over the Elbe was so much injured by the late inundation as to be impassable; we worn obliged to go some distance up the river bank and cross on a bridge of boats. Next morning my first search was for the picture gallery. We set off at random, and after passing the Church of Our Lady, with its lofty dome of solid stone, which withstood the heaviest bombs during the war with Frederick the Great, came to an open square, one side of which was occupied by an old, brown, red-roofed building, which I at once recognized, from pictures, as the object of our search.

I have just taken a last look at the gallery this morning, and left it with real regret; for, during the two visits, Raphael's heavenly picture of the Madonna and child had so grown into my love and admiration, that it was painful to think I should never see it again. There are many more which clung so strongly to my imagination, gratifying in the highest degree the love for the Beautiful, that I left them with sadness, and the thought that I would now only have the memory. I can see the inspired eye and god-like brow of the Jesus-child, as if I were still standing before the picture, and the sweet, holy countenance of the Madonna still looks upon me. Yet, though this picture is a miracle of art, the first glance filled me with disappointment. It has somewhat faded, during the three hundred years that have rolled away since the hand of Raphael worked on the canvass, and the glass with which it is covered for better preservation, injures the effect. After I had gazed on it awhile, every thought of this vanished. The figure of the virgin seemed to soar in the air, and it was difficult to think the clouds were not in motion. An aerial lightness clothes her form, and it is perfectly natural for such a figure to stand among the clouds. Two divine cherubs look up from below, and in her arms sits the sacred child. Those two faces beam from the picture like those of angels. The wild, prophetic eye and lofty brow of the young Jesus chains one like a spell. There is something more than mortal in its expression—something in the infant face which indicates a power mightier than the proudest manhood. There is no glory around the head; but the spirit which shines from those features, marks his divinity. In the sweet face of the mother there speaks a sorrowful foreboding mixed with its tenderness, as if she knew the world into which the Saviour was born, and foresaw the path in which he was to tread. It is a picture which one can scarce look upon without tears.

There are in the same room six pictures by Correggio, which are said to

451

be among his best works; one of them his celebrated Magdalen. There is also Correggio's "Holy Night," or the virgin with the shepherds in the manger, in which all the light comes from the body of the child. The surprise of the shepherds is most beautifully expressed. In one of the halls there is a picture by Van der Werff, in which the touching story of Hagar is told more feelingly than words could do it. The young Ishmael is represented full of grief at parting with Isaac, who, in childish unconsciousness of what has taken place, draws in sport the corner of his mother's mantle around him, and smiles at the tears of his lost playmate. Nothing can come nearer real flesh and blood than the two portraits of Raphael Mengs, painted by himself when quite young. You almost think the artist has in sport crept behind the frame, and wishes to make you believe he is a picture. It would be impossible to speak of half the gems of art contained in this unrivalled collection. There are twelve large halls, containing in all nearly two thousand pictures.

The plain, south of Dresden, was the scene of the hard-fought battle between Napoleon and the allied armies, in 1813. On the heights above the little village of Räcknitz, Moreau was shot on the second day of the battle. We took a foot-path through the meadows, shaded by cherry trees in bloom, and reached the spot after an hour's walk. The monument is simple—a square block of granite, surmounted by a helmet and sword, with the inscription: "The hero Moreau fell here by the side of Alexander, August 17th, 1813." I gathered, as a memorial, a few leaves of the oak which shades it.

By applying an hour before the appointed time, we obtained admission to the Royal Library. It contains three hundred thousand volumes—among them the most complete collection of historical works in existence. Each hall is devoted to a history of a separate country, and one large room is filled with that of Saxony alone. There is a large number of rare and curious manuscripts, among which are old Greek works of the seventh and eighth centuries; a Koran which once belonged to the Sultan Bajazet; the handwriting of Luther and Melancthon; a manuscript volume with pen and ink sketches, by Albert Durer, and the earliest works after the invention of printing. Among these latter was a book published by Faust and Schaeffer, at Mayence, in 1457. There were also Mexican manuscripts, written on the Aloe leaf, and many illuminated monkish volumes of the middle ages.

We were fortunate in seeing the Grüne Gewölbe, or Green Gallery, a collection of jewels and costly articles, unsurpassed in Europe. The entrance is only granted to six persons at a time, who pay a fee of two thalers. The customary way is to employ a Lohnbedienter, who goes around from one hotel to another, till he has collected the number, when he brings them together and conducts them to the person in the palace, who has charge of the treasures. As our visit happened to be during the Pentecost holidays, when every body in Dresden goes to the mountains, there was some difficulty in effecting this, but after two mornings spent in hunting up curious travelers, the servant finally conducted us in triumph to the palace. The first hall into which we were ushered, contained works in bronze. They were all small, and chosen with regard to their artistical value. Some by John of Bologna were exceedingly fine, as was also a group in iron, cut out of a single block; perhaps the only successful attempt in this branch. The next room contained statues, and vases covered with reliefs, in ivory. The most remarkable work was the fall of Lucifer and his angels, containing ninety-two figures in all, carved out of a single piece of ivory sixteen inches high! It was the work of an Italian monk, and cost him many years of hard labor. There were two tables of mosaic-work, that would not be out of place in the fabled halls of the eastern genii, so much did they exceed my former ideas of human skill. The tops were of jasper, and each had a border of fruit and flowers, in which every color was represented by some precious stone, all with the utmost delicacy and truth to nature! It is impossible to conceive the splendid effect it produced. Besides some fine pictures on gold by Raphael Mengs, there was a Madonna, the largest specimen of enamel painting in existence.

However costly the contents of these halls, they were only an introduction to those which followed. Each one exceeded the other in splendor and costliness. The walls were covered to the ceiling with rows of goblets, vases, &c., of polished jasper, agate and lapiz lazuli. Splendid mosaic tables stood around, with caskets of the most exquisite silver and gold work upon them, and vessels of solid silver, some of them weighing six hundred pounds were placed at the foot of the columns. We were shown two goblets,

453

each prized at six thousand thalers, made of gold and precious stones; also the great pearl called the Spanish Dwarf, nearly as large as a pullet's egg; globes and vases cut entirely out of the mountain crystal; magnificent Nuremberg watches and clocks, and a great number of figures, made ingeniously of rough pearls and diamonds. The officer showed us a hen's egg of silver. There was apparently nothing remarkable about it, but by unscrewing, it came apart, and disclosed the yelk of gold. This again opened and a golden chicken was seen; by touching a spring, a little diamond crown came from the inside, and the crown being again taken apart, out dropped a valuable diamond ring! The seventh hall contains the coronation robes of Augustus II., of Poland, and many costly specimens of carving in wood, A cherry stone is shown in a glass case, which has one hundred and twenty-five faces, all perfectly finished, carved upon it! The next room we entered sent back a glare of splendor that perfectly dazzled us. It was all gold, diamond, ruby and sapphire! Every case sent out such a glow and glitter that it seemed like a cage of imprisoned lightnings. Wherever the eye turned it was met by a blaze of broken rainbows. They were there by hundreds, and every gem was a fortune. Whole cases of swords, with hilts and scabbards of solid gold, studded with gems; the great two-handed coronation sword of the German emperors; daggers covered with brilliants and rubies; diamond buttons, chains and orders, necklaces and bracelets of pearl and emerald, and the order of the Golden Fleece made in gems of every kind. We were also shown the largest known onyx, nearly seven inches long and four inches broad! One of the most remarkable works is the throne and court of Aurungzebe, the Indian king, by Dinglinger, a celebrated goldsmith of the last century. It contains one hundred and thirty-two figures, all of enamelled gold, and each one most perfectly and elaborately finished. It was purchased by Prince Augustus for fifty-eight thousand thalers,[**] which was not a high sum, considering that the making of it occupied Dinglinger and thirteen workmen for seven years!

It is almost impossible to estimate the value of the treasures these halls contain. That of the gold and jewels alone must bo many millions of dollars, and the amount of labor expended on these toys of royalty is incredible. As monuments of patient and untiring toil, they are interesting: but it is sad to think how much labor and skill and energy have been wasted, in producing things which are useless to the world, and only of secondary importance as works of art. Perhaps, however, if men could be diverted by such play-things from more dangerous games, it would be all the better.

** [A Prussian or Saxon thaler is about 70 cts.]

CHAPTER XIX. — RAMBLES IN THE SAXON SWITZERLAND.

After four days' sojourn in Dresden we shouldered our knapsacks, not to be laid down again till we reached Prague. We were elated with the prospect of getting among the hills again, and we heeded not the frequent showers which had dampened the enjoyment of the Pentecost holidays, to the good citizens of Dresden, and might spoil our own. So we trudged gaily along the road to Pillnitz and waved an adieu to the domes behind us as the forest shut them out from view. After two hours' walk the road led down to the Elbe, where we crossed in a ferry-boat to Pillnitz, the seat of a handsome palace and gardens, belonging to the King of Saxony. He happened to be there at the time, on an afternoon excursion from Dresden; as we had seen him before, in the latter place, we passed directly on, only pausing to admire the flower-beds in the palace court. The King is a tall, benevolent looking man, and is apparently much liked by his people. As far as I have yet seen, Saxony is a prosperous and happy country. The people are noted all over Germany for their honest, social character, which is written on their cheerful, open countenances. On our entrance into the Saxon Switzerland, at Pillnitz, we were delighted with the neatness and home-like appearance of every thing. Every body greeted us; if we asked for information, they gave it cheerfully. The villages were all pleasant and clean and the meadows fresh and blooming. I felt half tempted to say, in the words of an old ballad, which I believe Longfellow has translated:

> "The fairest kingdom on this earth,
>
> It is the Saxon land!"

Going along the left bank of the Elbe, we passed over meadows purple with the tri-colored violet, which we have at home in gardens, and every little bank was bright with cowslips. At length the path led down into a cleft or ravine filled with trees, whose tops were on a level with the country around. This is a peculiar feature of Saxon scenery. The country contains many of these clefts, some of which are several hundred feet deep, having walls of perpendicular rock, in whose crevices the mountain pine roots itself and grows to a tolerable height without any apparent soil to keep it alive. We descended by a foot-path into this ravine, called the Liebethaler Grund. It is wider than many of the others, having room enough for a considerable stream and several mills. The sides are of sandstone rock, quite perpendicular. As we proceeded, it grew narrower and deeper, while the trees covering its sides and edges nearly shut out the sky. An hour's walk brought us to the end, where we ascended gradually to the upper level again.

After passing the night at the little village of Uttewalde, a short distance further, we set out early in the morning for the Bastei, a lofty precipice on the Elbe. The way led us directly through the Uttewalder Grund, the most remarkable of all these chasms. We went down by steps into its depths, which in the early morning were very cold. Water dripped from the rocks, which but a few feet apart, rose far above us, and a little rill made its way along the bottom, into which the sun has never shone. Heavy masses of rock, which had tumbled down from the sides lay in the way, and tall pine trees sprung from every cleft. In one place the defile is only four feet wide, and a large mass of rock, fallen from above, has lodged near the bottom, making an arch across, under which the traveller has to creep. After going under two or three arches of this kind, the defile widened and an arrow cut upon a rock directed us to a side path, which branched off from this into a mountain. Here the stone masses immediately assumed another form. They projected out like shelves sometimes as much as twenty feet from the straight side, and hung over the way, looking as if they might break off every moment. I felt glad when we had passed under them. Then as we ascended higher, we saw pillars of rock separated entirely from the side and rising a hundred feet in height, with trees growing on their summits. They stood there gray and limeworn, like the ruins of a Titan temple.

The path finally led us out into the forest and through the clustering pine trees, to the summit of the Bastei. An inn has been erected in the woods and an iron balustrade placed around the rock. Protected by this, we advanced to the end of the precipice and looked down to the swift Elbe, more than seven hundred feet below! Opposite through the blue mists of morning, rose Königstein, crowned with an impregnable fortress, and the crags of Lilienstein, with a fine forest around their base, frowned from the left bank. On both sides were horrible precipices of gray rock, with rugged trees hanging from the crevices. A hill rising up from one side of the Bastei, terminates suddenly a short distance from it, in on abrupt precipice. In the intervening space stand three or four of those rock-columns, several hundred feet high, with their tops nearly on a level with the Bastei. A wooden bridge has been made across from one to the other, over which the traveller passes, looking on the trees and rocks far below him, to the mountain, where a steep zigzag path takes him to the Elbe below.

We crossed the Elbe for the fourth time at the foot of the Bastei, and walked along its right bank towards Königstein. The injury caused by the inundation was everywhere apparent. The receding flood had left a deposit of sand, in many places several feet deep on the rich meadows, so that the labor of years will be requisite to remove it and restore the land to an arable condition. Even the farm-houses on the hillside, some distance from the river, had been reached, and the long grass hung in the highest branches of the fruit trees. The people wore at work trying to repair their injuries, but it will fall heavily upon the poorer classes.

The mountain of Königstein is twelve hundred feet high. A precipice, varying from one to three hundred feet in height, runs entirely around the summit, which is flat, and a mile and a half in circumference. This has been turned into a fortress, whose natural advantages make it entirely impregnable. During the Thirty Years' War and the late war with Napoleon, it was the only place in Saxony unoccupied by the enemy. Hence is it used as a depository for the archives and royal treasures, in times of danger. By giving up our passports at the door, we received permission to enter; the officer called a guide to take us around the battlements. There is quite a little village on the summit, with gardens, fields, and a wood of considerable size. The only entrance is by a road cut through the rock, which is strongly guarded. A well seven hundred feet deep supplies the fortress with water, and there are storehouses sufficient to hold supplies for many years. The view from the ramparts is glorious—it takes in the whole of the Saxon Highlands, as far as the lofty Schneeberg in Bohemia. On the other side the eye follows the windings of the Elbe, as far as the spires of Dresden. Lilienstein, a mountain of exactly similar formation, but somewhat higher, stands directly opposite. On walking around, the guide pointed out a little square tower standing on the brink of a precipice, with a ledge, about two feet wide, running around it, just below the windows. He said during the reign of Augustus the Strong, a baron attached to his court, rose in his sleep after a night of revelry, and stepping out the window, stretched himself at full length along the ledge. A guard fortunately observed his situation and informed Augustus of it, who had him bound and secured with cords, and then awakened by music. It was a good lesson, and one which no doubt sobered him for the future.

Passing through the little city of Königstein, we walked on to Schandau, the capital of the Saxon Switzerland, situated on the left bank. It had sustained great damage from the flood, the whole place having been literally under water. Here we turned up a narrow valley which led to the Kuhstall, some eight miles distant. The sides, as usual, were of steep gray rock, but wide enough apart to give room to some lovely meadows, with here and there a rustic cottage. The mountain maidens, in their bright red dresses, with a fanciful scarf bound around the head, made a romantic addition to the scene. There were some quiet secluded nooks, where the light of day stole in dimly through the thick foliage above and the wild stream rushed less boisterously over the rocks. We sat down to rest in one of these cool retreats, and made the glen ring with a cheer for America. The echoes repeated the name as if they had heard it for the first time, and I gave them a strict injunction to give it back to the next countryman who should pass by.

As we advanced further into the hills the way became darker and wilder. We heard the sound of falling water in a little dell on one side, and going nearer, saw a picturesque fall of about fifteen feet. Great masses of black rock were piled together, over which the mountain-stream fell in a snowy sheet. The pines above and around grew so thick and close, that not a sunbeam could enter, and a kind of mysterious twilight pervaded the spot. In Greece it would have been chosen for an oracle. I have seen, somewhere, a picture of the Spirit of Poetry, sitting beside just such a cataract, and truly the nymph could choose no more appropriate dwelling. But alas for sentiment! while we were admiring its picturesque beauty, we did not notice a man who came from a hut near by and went up behind the rocks. All at once there was a roar of water, and a real torrent came pouring down. I looked up, and lo! there he stood, with a gate in his hand which had held the water imprisoned, looking down at us to observe the effect, I motioned him to shut it up again, and he ran down to us, lest he should lose his fee for the "sight!"

Our road now left the valley and ascended through a forest to the Kuhstall, which we came upon at once. It is a remarkable natural arch, through a rocky wall or rampart, one hundred and fifty feet thick. Going through, we came at the other end to the edge of a very deep precipice, while the rock towered precipitously far above. Below lay a deep circular valley, two miles in diameter, and surrounded on every side by ranges of crags, such as we saw on the Bastei. It was entirely covered with a pine forest, and there only appeared to be two or three narrow defiles which gave it a communication with the world. The top of the Kuhstall can be reached by a path which runs up through a split in the rock, directly to the summit. It is just wide enough for one person to squeeze himself through; pieces of wood have been fastened in as steps, and the rocks in many places close completely above. The place derives its name from having been used by the mountaineers as a hiding-place for their cattle in time of war.

Next morning we descended by another crevice in the rock to the lonely valley, which we crossed, and climbed the Little Winterberg on the opposite side. There is a wide and rugged view from a little tower on a precipitous rock near the summit, erected to commemorate the escape of Prince Augustus of Saxony, who, being pursued by a mad stag, rescued himself on the very brink, by a lucky blow. Among the many wild valleys that lay between the hills, we saw scarcely one without the peculiar rocky formation which gives to Saxon scenery its most interesting character. They resemble the remains of some mighty work of art, rather than one of the thousand varied forms in which Nature delights to clothe herself.

The Great Winterberg, which is reached by another hour's walk along an elevated ridge, is the highest of the mountains, celebrated for the grand view from its summit. We found the handsome Swiss hotel recently built there, full of tourists who had come to enjoy the scone, but the morning clouds hid every thing. We ascended the tower, and looking between them as they rolled by, caught glimpses of the broad landscape below. The Giant's Mountains in Silesia were hidden by the mist, but sometimes when the wind freshened, we could see beyond the Elbe into Bohemian Switzerland, where the long Schneeberg rose conspicuous above the smaller mountains. Leaving the other travellers to wait at their leisure for clearer weather, we set off for the Prebisehthor, in company with two or three students from the Polytechnic School in Dresden. An hour's walk over high hills, whose forest clothing had been swept off by fire a few years before, brought us to it.

The Prebisehthor is a natural arch, ninety feet high, in a wall of rock which projects at right angles from the precipitous side of the mountain. A narrow path leads over the top of the arch to the end of the rock, where, protected by a railing, the traveller seems to hang in the air. The valley is far below him—mountains rise up on either side—and only the narrow bridge connects him with the earth. We descended by a wooden staircase to the bottom of the arch, near which a rustic inn is built against the rock, and thence into the valley below, which we followed through rude lonely scenery, to Hirnischkretschen (!) on the Elbe.

Crossing the river again for the sixth and last time, we followed the right bank to Neidergrund, the first Austrian village. Here our passports were visèd for Prague, and we were allowed to proceed without any examination of baggage. I noticed a manifest change in our fellow travelers the moment we crossed the border. They appeared anxious and careful; if we happened to speak of the state of the country, they always looked around to see if anybody was near, and if we even passed a workman on the road, quickly changed to some other subject. They spoke much of the jealous strictness of the government, and from what I heard from Austrians themselves, there may have been ground for their cautiousness.

We walked seven or eight miles along the bank of the Elbe, to Tetschen, there left our companions and took the road to Teplitz. The scenery was very picturesque; it must be delightful to float down the swift current in a boat, as we saw several merry companies do. The river is just small enough and the banks near enough together, to render such a mode of travelling delightful, and the strength of the current would carry one to Dresden in a day.

I was pleasantly disappointed on entering Bohemia. Instead of a dull, uninteresting country, as I expected, it is a land full of the most lovely scenery. There is every thing which can gratify the eye—high blue mountains, valleys of the sweetest pastoral look and romantic old ruins. The very name of Bohemia is associated with wild and wonderful legends, of the rude barbaric ages. Even the chivalric tales of the feudal times of Germany grow tame beside these earlier and darker histories. The fallen fortresses of the Rhine, or the robber-castles of the Odenwald had not for me so exciting an interest as the shapeless ruins cumbering these lonely mountains. The civilized Saxon race was left behind; I saw around me the features and heard the language of one of those rude Sclavonic tribes, whose original home was on the vast steppes of Central Asia. I have rarely enjoyed traveling more than our first two days' journey towards Prague. The range of the Erzgebirge ran along on our right; the snow still lay in patches upon it, but the valleys between, with their little clusters of white cottages, were green and beautiful. About six miles before reaching Teplitz, we passed Kulm, the great battle-field, which in a measure decided the fate of Napoleon. He sent Vandamme with 40,000 men to attack the allies before they could unite their forces, and thus effect their complete destruction. Only the almost despairing bravery of the Russian guards under Ostermann, who held him in check till the allied troops united, prevented Napoleon's design. At the junction of the roads, where the fighting was hottest, the Austrians have erected a monument to one of their generals. Not far from it is that of Prussia, simple and tasteful. A woody hill near, with the little village of Kulm at its foot, was the station occupied by Vandamme at the commencement of the battle. There is now a beautiful chapel on its summit, which can be seen far and wide. A little distance further, the Emperor of Russia has erected a third monument to the memory of the Russians who fell. Four lions rest on the base of the pedestal, and on the top of the shaft, forty-five feet high, Victory is represented as engraving the date, "Aug. 30, 1813," on a shield. The dark, pine-covered mountains on the right, overlook the whole field and the valley of Teplitz; Napoleon rode along their crests several days after the battle, to witness the scene of his defeat.

Teplitz lies in a lovely valley, several miles wide, bounded by the Bohemian mountains on one side, and the Erzgebirge on the other. One straggling peak near is crowned with a picturesque ruin, at whose foot the spacious bath-buildings lie half hidden in foliage. As we went down the principal street, I noticed nearly every house was a hotel; we learned afterwards that in summer the usual average of visitors is five thousand. The waters resemble those of the celebrated Carlsbad; they are warm and particularly efficacious in rheumatism and diseases of like character. After leaving Teplitz, the road turned to the east, towards a lofty mountain, which we had seen the morning before. The peasants as they passed by, saluted us with "Christ greet you!"

We stopped for the night at the foot of the peak called the Milleschauer, and must have ascended nearly 2,000 feet, for we had a wide view the next morning, although the mists and clouds hid the half of it. The weather being so unfavorable, we concluded not to ascend, and taking leave of the Jena student who came there for that purpose, descended through green fields and orchards snowy with blossoms, to Lobositz, on the Elbe. Here we reached the plains again, where every thing wore the luxuriance of summer; it was a pleasant change from the dark and rough scenery we left. The road passed through Theresienstadt, the fortress of Northern Bohemia. The little city is surrounded by a double wall and moat, which can be filled with water, rendering it almost impossible to be taken. In the morning we were ferried over the Moldau, and after journeying nearly all day across barren, elevated plains, saw late in the afternoon the sixty-seven spires of Prague below us! The dark clouds which hung over the hills, gave us little time to look upon the singular scene; and we were soon comfortably settled in the half-barbaric, half-Asiatic city, with a pleasant prospect of seeing its wonders on the morrow.

463

CHAPTER XX. — SCENES IN PRAGUE.

Prague.—I feel as if out of the world, in this strange, fantastic, yet beautiful old city. We have been rambling all morning through its winding streets, stopping sometimes at a church to see the dusty tombs and shrines, or to hear the fine music which accompanies the morning mass. I have seen no city yet that so forcibly reminds one of the past, and makes him forget everything but the associations connected with the scenes around him. The language adds to the illusion. Three-fourths of the people in the streets speak Bohemian and many of the signs are written in the same tongue, which is not at all like German. The palace of the Bohemian kings still looks down on the city from the western heights, and their tombs stand in the Cathedral of the holy Johannes. When one has climbed up the stone steps lending to the fortress, there is a glorious prospect before him. Prague, with its spires and towers, lies in the valley below, through which curves the Moldau with its green islands, disappearing among the hills which enclose the city on every side. The fantastic Byzantine architecture of many of the churches and towers, gives the city a peculiar oriental appearance; it seems to have been transported from the hills of Syria. Its streets are full of palaces, fallen and dwelt in now by the poorer classes. Its famous University, which once boasted forty thousand students, has long since ceased to exist. In a word, it is, like Venice, a fallen city; though as in Venice, the improving spirit of the age is beginning to give it a little life, and to send a quicker stream through its narrow and winding arteries. The railroad, which, joining that to Brünn, shall bring it in connection with Vienna, will be finished this year; in anticipation of the increased business which will arise from this, speculators are building enormous hotels in the suburbs and tearing down the old buildings to give place to more splendid edifices. These operations, and the chain bridge which spans the Moldau towards the southern end of the city, are the only things which look modern—every thing else is old, strange and solemn.

Having found out first a few of the locations, we hunted our way with difficulty through its labyrinths, seeking out every place of note or interest.

Reaching the bridge at last, we concluded to cross over and ascend to the Hradschin—the palace of the Bohemian kings. The bridge was commenced in 1357, and was one hundred and fifty years in building. That was the way the old Germans did their work, and they made a structure which will last a thousand years longer. Every pier is surmounted with groups of saints and martyrs, all so worn and time-beaten, that there is little left of their beauty, if they ever had any. The most important of them, at least to Bohemians, is that of the holy "Johannes of Nepomuck," now considered as the patron-saint of the land. He was a priest many centuries ago, whom one of the kings threw from the bridge into the Moldau, because he refused to reveal to him what the queen confessed. The legend says the body swam for some time on the river, with five stars around its head. The 16th of May, the day before we arrived, was that set apart for his particular honor; the statue on the bridge was covered with an arch of green boughs and flowers, and the shrine lighted with burning tapers. A railing was erected around it, near which numbers of the believers were kneeling, and a priest stood in the inside. The bridge was covered with passers-by, who all took their hats off till they had passed. Had it been a place of public worship, the act would have been natural and appropriate, but to uncover before a statue seemed to us too much like idolatry, and we ventured over without doing it. A few years ago it might have been dangerous, but now we only met with scowling looks. There are many such shrines and statues through the city, and I noticed that the people always took off their hats and crossed themselves in passing. On the hill above the western end of the city, stands a chapel on the spot where the Bavarians put an end to Protestantism in Bohemia by the sword, and the deluded peasantry of the land make pilgrimages to this spot, as if it were rendered holy by an act over which Religion weeps!

Ascending the broad flight of steps to the Hradschin, I paused a moment to look at the scene below. A slight blue haze hung over the clustering towers, and the city looked dim through it, like a city seen in a dream. It was well that it should so appear, for not less dim and misty are the memories that haunt its walls. There was no need of a magician's wand to bid that light cloud shadow forth the forms of other times. They came uncalled for, even by fancy. Far, far back in the past, I saw the warrior-princess who founded

465

the kingly city—the renowned Libussa, whose prowess and talent inspired the women of Bohemia to rise at her death and storm the land that their sex might rule where it obeyed before. On the mountain opposite once stood the palace of the bloody Wlaska, who reigned with her Amazon band for seven years over half Bohemia. Those streets below had echoed with the fiery words of Huss, and the castle of his follower—the blind Ziska, who met and defeated the armies of the German Empire—moulders on the mountain above. Many a year of war and tempest has passed over the scene. The hills around have borne the armies of Wallenstein and Frederic the Great; the war-cry of Bavaria, Sweden and Poland has echoed in the valley, and the red glare of the midnight cannon or the flames of burning palaces have often gleamed along the "blood-dyed waters" of the Moldau!

But this was a day-dream. The throng of people coming up the steps waked me out of it. We turned and followed them through several spacious courts, till we arrived at the Cathedral, which is magnificent in the extreme. The dark Gothic pillars, whose arches unite high above, are surrounded with gilded monuments and shrines, and the side chapels are rich in elaborate decorations. A priest was speaking from a pulpit in the centre, in the Bohemian language, which not being the most intelligible, I went to the other end to see the shrine of the holy Johannes of Nepomuck. It stands at the end of one of the side aisles and is composed of a mass of gorgeous silver ornaments. At a little distance, on each side, hang four massive lamps of silver, constantly burning. The pyramid of statues, of the same precious metal, has at each corner a richly carved urn, three feet high, with a crimson lamp burning at the top. Above, four silver angels, the size of life, are suspended in the air, holding up the corners of a splendid drapery of crimson and gold. If these figures were melted down and distributed among the poor and miserable people who inhabit Bohemia, they would then be angels indeed, bringing happiness and blessing to many a ruined home- altar. In the same chapel is the splendid burial-place of the Bohemian kings, of gilded marble and alabaster. Numberless tombs, covered with elaborate ornamental work, fill the edifice. It gives one a singular feeling to stand at one end and look down the lofty hall, dim with incense smoke and dark with the weight of many centuries.

On the way down again, we stepped into the St. Nicholas Church, which was built by the Jesuits. The interior has a rich effect, being all of brown and gold. The massive pillars are made to resemble reddish-brown marble, with gilded capitals, and the statues at the base are profusely ornamented in the same style. The music chained me there a long time. There was a grand organ, assisted by a full orchestra and large choir of singers. It was placed above, and at every sound of the priest's bell, the flourish of trumpets and deep roll of the drums filled the dome with a burst of quivering sound, while the giant pipes of the organ breathed out their full harmony and the very air shook under the peal. It was like a triumphal strain; the soul became filled with thoughts of power and glory—every sense was changed into one dim, indistinct emotion of rapture, which held the spirit as if spell-bound. I could almost forgive the Jesuits the superstition and bigotry they have planted in the minds of men, for the indescribable enjoyment that music gave. When it ceased, we went out to the world again, and the recollection of it seems now like a dream—but a dream whose influence will last longer than many a more palpable reality.

Not far from this place is the palace of Wallenstein, in the same condition as when he inhabited it, and still in the possession of his descendants. It is a plain, large building, having beautiful gardens attached to it, which are open to the public. We went through the courtyard, threaded a passage with a roof of rough stalactitic rock, and entered the garden where a revolving fountain was casting up its glittering arches. Among the flowers at the other end of the garden there is a remarkable fountain. It is but a single jet of water which rises from the middle of a broad basin of woven wire, but by some means it sustains a hollow gilded ball, sometimes for many minutes at a time. When the ball drops, the sloping sides of the basin convey it directly to the fountain again, and it is carried up to dance a while longer on the top of the jet. I watched it once, thus supported on the water, for full fifteen minutes.

There is another part of Prague which is not less interesting, though much less poetical—the Jews' City. In our rambles we got into it before we were aware, but hurried immediately out of it again, perfectly satisfied with one visit. We came first into a dark, narrow street, whose sides were lined with booths of old clothes and second-hand articles. A sharp featured old woman thrust a coat before my face, exclaiming, "Herr, buy a fine coat!" Instantly a man assailed me on the other side, "Here are vests! pantaloons! shirts!" I broke loose from them and ran on, but it only became worse. One seized me by the arm, crying, "Lieber Herr, buy some stockings!" and another grasped my coat: "Hats, Herr! hats! buy something, or sell me something!" I rushed desperately on, shouting "no! no!" with all my might, and finally got safe through. My friend having escaped their clutches also, we hunted the way to the old Jewish cemetery. This stands in the middle of the city, and has not been used for a hundred years. We could find no entrance, but by climbing upon the ruins of an old house near, I could look over the wall. A cold shudder crept over me, to think that warm, joyous Life, as I then felt it, should grow chill and pass back to clay in such a foul charnel-house. Large mounds of earth, covered with black, decaying grave-stones, which were almost hidden under the weeds and rank grass, filled the inclosure. A few dark, crooked alder-trees grew among the crumbling tombs, and gave the scene an air of gloom and desolation, almost fearful. The dust of many a generation lies under these mouldering stones; they now scarcely occupy a thought in the minds of the living; and yet the present race toils and seeks for wealth alone, that it may pass away and leave nothing behind—not even a memory for that which will follow it!

CHAPTER XXI. — JOURNEY THROUGH EASTERN BOHEMIA AND MORAVIA TO THE DANUBE.

Our road the first two days after leaving Prague led across broad, elevated plains, across which a cold wind came direct from the summits of the Riesengebirge, far to our left. Were it not for the pleasant view we had of the rich valley of the Upper Elbe, which afforded a delightful relief to the monotony of the hills around us, the journey would have been exceedingly tiresome. The snow still glistened on the distant mountains; but when the sun shone out, the broad valley below, clad in the luxuriance of summer, and extending for at least fifty miles with its woods, meadows and white villages, looked like a real Paradise. The long ridges over which we travelled extend for nearly a hundred and fifty miles—from the Elbe almost to the Danube. The soil is not fertile, the inhabitants are exceedingly poor, and from our own experience, the climate must be unhealthy. In winter the country is exposed to the full sweep of the northern winds, and in summer the sun shines down on it with unbroken force. There are few streams running through it, and the highest part, which divides the waters of the Baltic from those of the Black Sea is filled for a long distance with marshes and standing pools, whose exhalations must inevitably subject the inhabitants to disease. This was perceptible in their sallow, sickly countenances; many of the women are afflicted with the goitre, or swelling of the throat; I noticed that towards evening they always carefully muffled up their faces. According to their own statements, the people suffer much from the cold in winter, as the few forests the country affords are in possession of the noblemen to whom the land belongs, and they are not willing to let them be cut down. The dominions of these petty despots are marked along the road with as much precision as the boundaries of an empire; we saw sometimes their stately castles at a distance, forming quite a contrast to the poor scattering villages of the peasants.

At Kollin, the road, which had been running eastward in the direction of Olmutz, turned to the south, and we took leave of the Elbe, after tracing back his course from Magdeburg nearly to his home in the mountains of

Silesia. The country was barren and monotonous, but a bright sunshine made it look somewhat cheerful. We passed, every few paces, some shrine or statue by the roadside. This had struck me, immediately on crossing the border, in the Saxon Switzerland—it seemed as if the boundary of Saxony was that of Protestantism. But here in the heart of Bohemia, the extent to which this image worship is carried, exceeds anything I had imagined. There is something pleasing as well as poetical in the idea of a shrine by the wayside, where the weary traveller can rest, and raise his heart in thankfulness to the Power that protects him; it was no doubt a pious spirit that placed them there; but the people appear to pay the reverence to the picture which they should give to its spiritual image, and the pictures themselves are so shocking and ghastly, they seem better calculated to excite horror than reverence. It was really repulsive to look on images of the Saviour covered with blood, and generally with swords sticking in different parts of the body. The Almighty is represented as an old man, wearing a Bishop's mitre, and the image of the Virgin is always drest in a gay silk robe, with beads and other ornaments. From the miserable painting, the faces often had an expression that would have been exceedingly ludicrous, if the shock given to our feelings of reverence were not predominant. The poor, degraded peasants always uncovered or crossed themselves when passing by these shrines, but it appeared to be rather the effect of habit than any good impulse, for the Bohemians are noted all over Germany for their dishonesty; we learned by experience they deserve it. It is not to be wondered at either; for a people so poor and miserable and oppressed will soon learn to take advantage of all who appear better off than themselves. They had one custom which was touching and beautiful. At the sound of the church bell, as it rung the morning, noon and evening chimes, every one uncovered, and repeated to himself a prayer. Often, as we rested at noon on a bank by the roadside, that voice spoke out from the house of worship and every one heeded its tone. Would that to this innate spirit of reverence were added the light of Knowledge, which a tyrannical government denies them!

The third night of our journey we stopped at the little village of Stecken, and the next morning, after three hours' walk over the ridgy heights, reached the old Moravian city of Iglau, built on a hill. It happened to be Corpus

470

Christi day, and the peasants of the neighborhood were hastening there in their gayest dresses. The young women wore a crimson scarf around the head, with long fringed and embroidered ends hanging over the shoulders, or falling in one smooth fold from the back of the head. They were attired in black velvet vests, with full white sleeves and skirts of some gay color, which were short enough to show to advantage their red stockings and polished shoe-buckles. Many of them were not deficient in personal beauty—there was a gipsy-like wildness in their eyes, that combined with their rich hair and graceful costume, reminded me of the Italian maidens. The towns too, with their open squares and arched passages, have quite a southern look; but the damp, gloomy weather was enough to dispel any illusion of this kind.

In the neighborhood of Iglau, and, in fact, through the whole of Bohemia, we saw some of the strangest teams that could well be imagined. I thought the Frankfort milkwomen with their donkeys and hearse-like carts, were comical objects enough, but they bear no comparison with these Bohemian turn-outs. Dogs—for economy's sake, perhaps—generally supply the place of oxen or horses, and it is no uncommon thing to see three large mastiffs abreast, harnessed to a country-cart. A donkey and a cow together, are sometimes met with, and one man, going to the festival at Iglau, had his wife and children in a little wagon, drawn by a dog and a donkey. These two, however, did not work well together; the dog would bite his lazy companion, and the man's time was constantly employed in whipping him off the donkey, and in whipping the donkey away from the side of the road. Once I saw a wagon drawn by a dog, with a woman pushing behind, while a man, doubtless her lord and master, sat comfortably within, smoking his pipe with the greatest complacency! The very climax of all was a woman and a dog harnessed together, taking a load of country produce to market! I hope, for the honor of the country, it was not emblematic of woman's condition there. But as we saw hundreds of them breaking stone along the road, and occupied at other laborious and not less menial labor, there is too much reason to fear that it is so.

As we approached Iglau, we heard cannon firing; the crowd increased, and following the road, we came to an open square, where a large number were already assembled; shrines were erected around it, hung with pictures and pine boughs, and a long procession of children was passing down the side as we entered. We went towards the middle, where Neptune and his Tritons poured the water from their urns into two fountains, and stopped to observe the scene. The procession came on, headed by a large body of priests, in white robes, with banners and crosses. They stopped before the principal shrine, in front of the Rathhaus, and began a solemn religious ceremony. The whole crowd of not less than ten thousand persons, stood silent and uncovered, and the deep voice of the officiating priest was heard over the whole square. At times the multitude sang responses, and I could mark the sound, swelling and rolling up like a mighty wave, till it broke and slowly sank down again to the deepest stillness. The effect was marred by the rough voice of the officers commanding the soldiery, and the volleys of musquetry which were occasionally discharged. It degraded the solemnity of the pageant to the level of a military parade.

In the afternoon we were overtaken by a travelling handwerker, on his way to Vienna, who joined company with us. We walked several miles together, talking on various matters, without his having the least suspicion we were not Germans. He had been at Trieste, and at length began speaking of the great beauty of the American vessels there. "Yes," said I, "our vessels are admired all over the world." He stared at me without comprehending;—"your vessels?" "Our country's," I replied; "we are Americans!" I can see still his look of incredulous astonishment and hear the amazed tone with which he cried: "You Americans—it is impossible!" We convinced him nevertheless, to his great joy, for all through Germany there is a curiosity to see our countrymen and a kindly feeling towards them. "I shall write down in my book," said he, "so that I shall never forget it, that I once travelled with two Americans!" We stopped together for the night at the only inn in a large, beggarly village, where we obtained a frugal supper with difficulty, for a regiment of Polish lancers was quartered there for the night, and the pretty Kellnerin was so busy in waiting on the officers that she had no eye for wandering journeymen, as she took us to be. She even told us the beds were all occupied and we must sleep on the floor. Just then the landlord came by. "Is it possible, Herr Landlord," asked our new companion, "that there is no bed here for us? Have the goodness to look again, for we are not in the habit of sleeping on the floor,

472

like dogs!" This speech had its effect, for the Kellnerin was commanded to find us beds. She came back unwillingly after a time and reported that two, only, were vacant. As a German bed is only a yard wide, we pushed these two together, but they were still too small for three persons, and I had a severe cold in the morning, from sleeping crouched up against the damp wall.

The next day we passed the dividing ridge which separates the waters of the Elbe from the Danube, and in the evening arrived at Znaim, the capital of Moravia. It is built on a steep hill looking down on the valley of the Thaya, whose waters mingle with the Danube near Pressburg. The old castle on the height near, was formerly the residence of the Moravian monarchs, and traces of the ancient walls and battlements of the city are still to be seen. The handwerker took us to the inn frequented by his craft—the leather-curriers— and we conversed together till bed-time. While telling me of the oppressive laws of Austria, the degrading vassalage of the peasants and the horrors of the conscription system, he paused as in deep thought, and looking at me with a suppressed sigh, said: "Is it not true, America is free?" I told him of our country and her institutions, adding that though we were not yet as free as we hoped and wished to be, we enjoyed far more liberty than any country in the world. "Ah!" said he, "it is hard to leave one's fatherland oppressed as it is, but I wish I could go to America!"

We left next morning at eight o'clock, after having done full justice to the beds of the "Golden Stag," and taken leave of Florian Francke, the honest and hearty old landlord. Znaim appears to great advantage from the Vienna road; the wind which blew with fury against our backs, would not permit us to look long at it, but pushed us on towards the Austrian border. In the course of three hours we were obliged to stop at a little village; it blew a perfect hurricane and the rain began to soak through our garments. Here we stayed three hours among the wagoners who stopped on account of the weather. One miserable, drunken wretch, whom one would not wish to look at more than once, distinguished himself by insulting those around him, and devouring like a beast, large quantities of food. When the reckoning was given him, he declared he had already paid, and the waiter denying it, he said, "Stop, I will show you something!" pulled out his passport and pointed to the name—"Baron von Reitzenstein." It availed nothing; he had fallen so low that his title inspired no respect, and when we left the inn they were still endeavoring to get their money and threatening him with a summary proceeding if the demand was not complied with.

Next morning the sky was clear and a glorious day opened before us. The country became more beautiful as we approached the Danube; the hills were covered with vineyards, just in the tender green of their first leaves, and the rich valleys lay in Sabbath stillness in the warm sunshine. Sometimes from an eminence we could see far and wide over the garden-like slopes, where little white villages shone among the blossoming fruit-trees. A chain of blue hills rose in front, which I knew almost instinctively stood by the Danube; when we climbed to the last height and began to descend to the valley, where the river was still hidden by luxuriant groves, I saw far to the southwest, a range of faint, silvery summits, rising through the dim ether like an airy vision. There was no mistaking those snowy mountains. My heart bounded with a sudden thrill of rapturous excitement at this first view of the Alps! They were at a great distance, and their outline was almost blended with the blue drapery of air which clothed them. I gazed till my vision became dim and I could no longer trace their airy lines. They called up images blended with the grandest events in the world's history. I thought of the glorious spirits who have looked upon them and trodden their rugged sides—of the storms in which they veil their countenances, and the avalanches they hurl thundering to the valleys—of the voices of great deeds, which have echoed from their crags over the wide earth—and of the ages which have broken, like the waves of a mighty sea, upon their everlasting summits!

As we descended, the hills and forests shut out this sublime vision, and I looked to the wood-clothed mountains opposite and tried to catch a glimpse of the current that rolled at their feet. We here entered upon a rich plain, about ten miles in diameter, which lay between a backward sweep of the hills and a curve of the Danube. It was covered with the richest grain; every thing wore the luxuriance of summer, and we seemed to have changed seasons since leaving the dreary hills of Bohemia. Continuing over the plain, we had on our left the fields of Wagram and Essling, the scene of two of Napoleon's blood-

474

bought victories. The outposts of the Carpathians skirted the horizon—that great mountain range which stretches through Hungary to the borders of Russia.

At length the road came to the river's side, and we crossed on wooden bridges over two or three arms of the Danube, all of which together were little wider than the Schuylkill at Philadelphia. When we crossed the last bridge, we came to a kind of island covered with groves of the silver ash. Crowds of people filled the cool walks; booths of refreshment stood by the roadside, and music was everywhere heard. The road finally terminated in a circle, where beautiful alleys radiated into the groves; from the opposite side a broad street lined with stately buildings extended into the heart of the city, and through this avenue, filled with crowds of carriages and people on their way to those delightful walks, we entered Vienna!

CHAPTER XXII. — VIENNA.

May 31.—I have at last seen the thousand wonders of this great capital—this German Paris—this connecting link between the civilization of Europe and the barbaric magnificence of the East. It looks familiar to be in a city again, whose streets are thronged with people, and resound with the din and bustle of business. It reminds me of the never-ending crowds of London, or the life and tumult of our scarcely less active New York. Although the end may be sordid for which so many are laboring, yet the very sight of so much activity is gratifying. It is peculiarly so to an American. After residing in a foreign land for some time, the peculiarities of our nation are more easily noticed; I find in my countrymen abroad a vein of restless energy—a love for exciting action—which to many of our good German friends is perfectly incomprehensible. It might have been this which gave at once a favorable impression of Vienna.

The morning of our arrival we sallied out from our lodgings in the Leopoldstadt, to explore the world before us. Entering the broad Praterstrasse, we passed down to the little arm of the Danube, which separates this part of the new city from the old. A row of magnificent coffee-houses occupy the bank, and numbers of persons were taking their breakfasts in the shady porticoes. The Ferdinand's Bridge, which crosses the stream, was filled with people; in the motley crowd we saw the dark-eyed Greek, and Turks in their turbans and flowing robes. Little brown Hungarian boys were going around, selling bunches of lilies, and Italians with baskets of oranges stood by the side-walk. The throng became greater as we penetrated into the old city. The streets were filled with carts and carriages, and as there are no side-pavements, it required constant attention to keep out of their way. Splendid shops, fitted up with great taste, occupied the whole of the lower stories, and goods of all kinds hung beneath the canvass awnings in front of them. Almost every store or shop was dedicated to some particular person or place, which was represented on a large panel by the door. The number of these paintings added much to the splendor of the scene; I was gratified to find, among the images of kings and dukes, one dedicated "to the American," with an Indian chief in full costume.

The Altstadt, or old city, which contains about sixty thousand inhabitants, is completely separated from the suburbs, whose population, taking the whole extent within the outer barrier, numbers nearly half a million. It is situated on a small arm of the Danube, and encompassed by a series of public promenades, gardens and walks, varying from a quarter to half a mile in length, called the Glacis. This formerly belonged to the fortifications of the city, but as the suburbs grew up so rapidly on all sides, it was changed appropriately to a public walk. The city is still surrounded with a massive wall and a deep wide moat; but since it was taken by Napoleon in 1809, the moat has been changed into a garden, with a beautiful carriage road along the bottom, around the whole city. It is a beautiful sight, to stand on the summit of the wall and look over the broad Glacis, with its shady roads branching in every direction, and filled with inexhaustible streams of people. The Vorstaedte, or new cities, stretch in a circle around, beyond this; all the finest buildings front on the Glacis, among which the splendid Vienna Theatre and the church of San Carlo Borromeo are conspicuous. The mountains of the Vienna Forest bound the view, with here and there a stately castle on their woody summits. I was reminded of London as seen from Regent's Park, and truly this part of Vienna can well compare with it. On penetrating into the suburbs, the resemblance is at an end. Many of the public thoroughfares are still unpaved, and in dry weather one is almost choked by the clouds of fine dust. A furious wind blows from the mountains, sweeping the streets almost constantly and filling the eyes and ears with it, making the city an unhealthy residence for strangers.

There is no lack of places for pleasure or amusement. Beside the numberless walks of the Glacis, there are the Imperial Gardens, with their cool shades and flowers and fountains; the Augarten, laid out and opened to the public by the Emperor Joseph: and the Prater, the largest and most beautiful of all. It lies on an island formed by the arms of the Danube, and is between two and three miles square. From the circle at the end of the Praterstrasse, broad carriage-ways extend through its forests of oak and silver ash, and over its verdant lawns to the principal stream, which bounds it on the north. These roads are lined with stately horse chesnuts, whose branches unite and form a dense canopy, completely shutting out the sun. Every afternoon the beauty and nobility of Vienna whirl through the cool groves in their gay equipages, while the sidewalks are thronged with pedestrians, and the numberless tables and seats with which every house of refreshment is surrounded, are filled with merry guests. Here, on Sundays and holidays, the people repair in thousands. The woods are full of tame deer, which run perfectly free over the whole Prater. I saw several in one of the lawns, lying down in the grass, with a number of children playing around or sitting beside them. It is delightful to walk there in the cool of the evening, when the paths are crowded, and everybody is enjoying the release from the dusty city. It is this free, social life which renders Vienna so attractive to foreigners and draws yearly thousands of visitors from all parts of Europe.

St. Stephen's Cathedral, in the centre of the old city, is one of the finest specimens of Gothic architecture in Germany. Its unrivalled tower, which rises to the height of four hundred and twenty-eight feet, is visible from every part of Vienna. It is entirely of stone, most elaborately ornamented, and is supposed to be the strongest in Europe. If the tower was finished, it might rival any church in Europe in richness and brilliancy of appearance. The inside is solemn and grand; but the effect is injured by the number of small chapels and shrines. In one of these rests, the remains of Prince Eugene of Savoy, "der edle Ritter," known in a ballad to every man, woman and child in Germany.

The Belvidere Gallery fills thirty-five halls, and contains three thousand pictures! It is absolutely bewildering to walk through such vast collections; you can do no more than glance at each painting, and hurry by face after face, and figure after figure, on which you would willingly gaze for hours and inhale the atmosphere of beauty that surrounds them. Then after you leave, the brain is filled with their forms—radiant spirit-faces look upon you, and you see constantly, in fancy, the calm brow of a Madonna, the sweet young face of a child, or the blending of divine with mortal beauty in an angel's countenance. I endeavor, if possible, always to make several visits—to study those pictures which cling first to the memory, and pass over those which make little or no impression. It is better to have a few images fresh and enduring, than a confused and indistinct memory of many.

From the number of Madonnas in every European gallery, it would almost seem that the old artists painted nothing else. The subject is one which requires the highest genius to do it justice, and it is therefore unpleasant to see so many still, inexpressive faces of the virgin and child, particularly by the Dutch artists, who clothe their figures sometimes in the stiff costume of their own time. Raphael and Murillo appear to me to be almost the only painters who have expressed what, perhaps, was above the power of other masters—the combined love and reverence of the mother, and the divine expression in the face of the child, prophetic of his mission and godlike power.

There were many glorious old paintings in the second story, which is entirely taken up with pictures; two or three of the halls were devoted to selected works from modern artists. Two of these I would give every thing I have to possess. One of them is a winter scene, representing the portico of an old Gothic church. At the base of one of the pillars a woman is seated in the snow, half-benumbed, clasping an infant to her breast, while immediately in front stands a boy of perhaps seven or eight years, his little hands folded in prayer, while the chill wind tosses the long curls from his forehead. There is something so pure and holy in the expression of his childish countenance, so much feeling in the lip and sorrowful eye, that it moves one almost to tears to look upon it. I turned back half a dozen times from the other pictures to view it again, and blessed the artist in my heart for the lesson he gave. The other is by a young Italian painter, whose name I have forgotten, but who, if he never painted anything else, is worthy a high place among the artists of his country. It represents some scene from the history of Venice. On an open piazza, a noble prisoner, wasted and pale from long confinement, has just had an interview with his children. He reaches his arm toward them as if for the last time, while a savage keeper drags him away. A lovely little girl kneels at the feet of the Doge, but there is no compassion in his stern features, and it is easy to see that her father is doomed.

The Lower Belvidere, separated from the Upper by a large garden, laid out in the style of that at Versailles, contains the celebrated Ambraser

Sammlung, a collection of armor. In the first hall I noticed the complete armor of the Emperor Maximilian, for man and horse—the armor of Charles V., and Prince Moritz of Saxony, while the walls were filled with figures of German nobles and knights, in the suits they wore in life. There is also the armor of the great "Baver of Trient," trabant of the Archduke Ferdinand. He was nearly nine feet in stature, and his spear, though not equal to Satan's, in Paradise Lost, would still make a tree of tolerable dimensions.

In the second hall we saw weapons taken from the Turkish army who besieged Vienna, with the horse-tail standards of the Grand Vizier, Kara Mustapha. The most interesting article was the battle-axe of the unfortunate Montezuma, which was probably given to the Emperor Charles V., by Cortez. It is a plain instrument of dark colored stone, about three feet long.

We also visited the Bürgerliche Zeughaus, a collection of arms and weapons, belonging to the citizens of Vienna. It contains sixteen thousand weapons and suits of armor, including those plundered from the Turks, when John Sobieski conquered them and relieved Vienna from the siege. Besides a great number of sabres, lances and horsetails, there is the blood-red banner of the Grand Vizier, as well as his skull and shroud, which is covered with sentences from the Koran. On his return to Belgrade, after the defeat at Vienna, the Sultan sent him a bow-string, and he was accordingly strangled. The Austrians having taken Belgrade some time after, they opened his grave and carried off his skull and shroud, as well as the bow-string, as relics. Another large and richly embroidered banner, which hung in a broad sheet from the ceiling, was far more interesting to me. It had once waved from the vessels of the Knights of Malta, and had, perhaps, on the prow of the Grand Master's ship, led that romantic band to battle against the Infidel.

A large number of peasants and common soldiers were admitted to view the armory at the same time. The grave custode who showed us the curiosities, explaining every thing in phrases known by heart for years and making the same starts of admiration whenever he came to any thing peculiarly remarkable, singled us out as the two persons most worthy of attention. Accordingly his remarks were directed entirely to us, and his humble countrymen might as well have been invisible, for the notice he took of them. On passing out, we gave him a coin worth about fifteen cents, which happened to be so much more than the others gave him, that, bowing graciously, he invited us to write our names in the album for strangers. While we were doing this, a poor handwerker lingered behind, apparently for the same object, whom he scornfully dismissed, shaking the fifteen cent piece in his hand, and saying: "The album is not for such as you—it is for noble gentlemen!"

On our way through the city, we often noticed a house on the southern side of St. Stephen's Platz, dedicated to "the Iron Stick." In a niche by the window, stood what appeared to be the limb of a tree, completely filled with nails, which were driven in so thick that no part of the original wood is visible. We learned afterwards the legend concerning it. The Vienna Forest is said to have extended, several hundred years ago, to this place. A locksmith's apprentice was enabled, by the devil's help, to make the iron bars and padlock which confine the limb in its place; every locksmith's apprentice who came to Vienna after that, drove a nail into it, till finally there was room for no more. It is a singular legend, and whoever may have placed the limb there originally, there it has remained for two or three hundred years at least.

We spent two or three hours delightfully one evening in listening to Strauss's band. We went about sunset to the Odeon, a new building in the Leopoldstadt. It has a refreshment hall nearly five hundred feet long, with a handsome fresco ceiling and glass doors opening into a garden walk of the same length. Both the hall and garden were filled with tables, where the people seated themselves as they came, and conversed sociably over their coffee and wine. The orchestra was placed in a little ornamental temple in the garden, in front of which I stationed myself, for I was anxious to see the world's waltz-king, whose magic tones can set the heels of half Christendom in motion. After the band had finished tuning their instruments, a middle-sized, handsome man stepped forward with long strides, with a violin in one hand and bow in the other, and began waving the latter up and down, like a magician summoning his spirits. As if he had waved the sound out of his bow, the tones leaped forth from the instruments, and guided by his eye and hand, fell into a merry measure. The accuracy with which every instrument performed its part, was truly marvellous. He could not have struck the measure or the harmony more certainly from the keys of his own piano, than from that large band. The sounds struggled forth, so perfect and distinct, that one almost expected to see them embodied, whirling in wild dance around him. Sometimes the air was so exquisitely light and bounding, the feet could scarcely keep on the earth; then it sank into a mournful lament, with a sobbing tremulousness, and died away in a long-breathed sigh. Strauss seemed to feel the music in every limb. He would wave his fiddle-bow awhile, then commence playing with desperate energy, moving his whole body to the measure, till the sweat rolled from his brow. A book was lying on the stand before him, but he made no use of it. He often glanced around with a kind of half-triumphant smile at the restless crowd, whose feet could scarcely be restrained from bounding to the magic measure. It was the horn of Oberon realized. The composition of the music displayed great talent, but its charm consisted more in the exquisite combination of the different instruments, and the perfect, the wonderful exactness with which each performed its part—a piece of art of the most elaborate and refined character.

The company, which consisted of several hundred, appeared to be full of enjoyment. They sat under the trees in the calm, cool twilight, with the stars twinkling above, and talked and laughed sociably together between the pauses of the music, or strolled up and down the lighted alleys. We walked up and down with them, and thought how much we should enjoy such a scene at home, where the faces around us would be those of friends, and the language our mother tongue!

We went a long way through the suburbs one bright afternoon, to a little cemetery about a mile from the city, to find the grave of Beethoven. On ringing at the gate a girl admitted us into the grounds, in which are many monuments of noble families who have vaults there. I passed up the narrow walk, reading the inscriptions, till I came to the tomb of Franz Clement, a young composer, who died two or three years ago. On turning again, my eye fell instantly on the word "BEETHOVEN," in golden letters, on a tombstone of gray marble. A simple gilded lyre decorated the pedestal, above which was a serpent encircling a butterfly—the emblem of resurrection to eternal life. Here then, mouldered the remains of that restless spirit, who seemed to

482

have strayed to earth from another clime, from such a height did he draw his glorious conceptions. The perfection he sought for here in vain, he has now attained in a world where the soul is freed from the bars which bind it in this. There were no flowers planted around the tomb by those who revered his genius; only one wreath, withered and dead, lay among the grass, as if left long ago by some solitary pilgrim, and a few wild buttercups hung with their bright blossoms over the slab. It might have been wrong, but I could not resist the temptation to steal one or two, while the old grave-digger was busy preparing a new tenement. I thought that other buds would open in a few days, but those I took would be treasured many a year as sacred relics. A few paces off is the grave of Schubert, the composer, whose beautiful songs are heard all over Germany.

It would employ one a week to visit all the rich collections of art in Vienna. They are all open to the public on certain days of the week, and we have been kept constantly in motion, running from one part of the city to another, in order to arrive at some gallery at the appointed time. Tickets, which have to be procured often in quite different parts of the city, are necessary for admittance to many; on applying after much trouble and search, we frequently found we came at the wrong hour, and must leave without effecting our object. We employed no guide, but preferred finding every thing ourselves. We made a list every morning, of the collections open during the day, and employed the rest of the time in visiting the churches and public gardens, or rambling through the suburbs.

We visited the Imperial Library a day or two ago. The hall is 245 feet long, with a magnificent dome in the centre, under which stands the statue of Charles V., of Carrara marble, surrounded by twelve other monarchs of the house of Hapsburg. The walls are of variegated marble, richly ornamented with gold, and the ceiling and dome are covered with brilliant fresco paintings. The library numbers 300,000 volumes, and 16,000 manuscripts, which are kept in walnut cases, gilded and adorned with medallions. The rich and harmonious effect of the whole cannot easily be imagined. It is exceedingly appropriate that a hall of such splendor, should be used to hold a library. The pomp of a palace may seem hollow and vain, for it is but the dwelling of a man; but no building can be too magnificent for the hundreds of great and immortal spirits to dwell in, who have visited earth during thirty centuries.

Among other curiosities preserved in the collection, we were shown a brass plate, containing one of the records of the Roman Senate, made 180 years before Christ, Greek manuscripts of the fifth and sixth centuries, and a volume of Psalms, printed on parchment, in the year 1457, by Faust and Schaeffer, the inventors of printing. There were also Mexican manuscripts, presented by Cortez; the prayer-book of Hildegard, wife of Charlemagne, in letters of gold; the signature of San Carlo Borromeo, and a Greek testament of the thirteenth century, which had been used by Erasmus in making his translation and contains notes in his own hand. The most interesting article was the "Jerusalem Delivered" of Tasso, in the poet's own hand, with his erasions and corrections.

We also visited the Cabinet of Natural History, which is open twice a week "to all respectably dressed persons," as the notice at the door says. But Heaven forbid that I should attempt to describe what we saw there. The Mineral Cabinet had a greater interest to me, inasmuch as it called up the recollections of many a school-boy ramble over the hills and into all kinds of quarries, far and near. It is said to be the most perfect collection in existence. I was pleased to find many old acquaintances there, from the mines of Pennsylvania; Massachusetts and New York were also very well represented. I had no idea before, that the mineral wealth of Austria was so great. Besides the iron and lead mines among the hills of Styria and the quicksilver of Idria, there is no small amount of gold and silver found, and the Carpathian mountains are rich in jasper, opal and lapiz lazuli. The largest opal ever found, was in this collection. It weighs thirty-four ounces and looks like a condensed rainbow.

In passing the palace, we saw several persons entering the basement story under the Library, and had the curiosity to follow them. By so doing, we saw the splendid equipages of the house of Austria. There must have been near a hundred carriages and sleds, of every shape and style, from the heavy, square vehicle of the last century to the most light and elegant conveyance of the present day. One clumsy, but magnificent machine, of crimson and gold, was pointed out as being a hundred and fifty years old. The misery we witnessed in starving Bohemia, formed a striking contrast to all this splendor.

Beside the Imperial Picture Gallery, there are several belonging to princes and noblemen in Vienna, which are scarcely less valuable. The most important of these is that of Prince Liechtenstein, which we visited yesterday. We applied to the porter's lodge for admittance to the gallery, but he refused to open it for two persons; as we did not wish a long walk for nothing, we concluded to wait for other visitors. Presently a gentleman and lady came and inquired if the gallery was open. We told him it would probably be opened now, although the porter required a larger number, and he went to ask. After a short time he returned, saying: "He will come immediately; I thought best to put the number a little higher, and so I told him there were six of us!" Having little artistic knowledge of paintings, I judge of them according to the effect they produce upon me—in proportion as they gratify the innate love for the beautiful and the true. I have been therefore disappointed in some painters whose names are widely known, and surprised again to find works of great beauty by others of smaller fame. Judging by such a standard, I should say that "Cupid sleeping in the lap of Venus," by Correggio, is the glory of this collection. The beautiful limbs of the boy-god droop in the repose of slumber, as his head rests on his mother's knee, and there is a smile lingering around his half-parted lips, as if he was dreaming new triumphs. The face is not that of the wicked, mischief-loving child, but rather a sweet cherub, bringing a blessing to all he visits. The figure of the goddess is exquisite. Her countenance, unearthly in its loveliness, expresses the tenderness of a young mother, as she sits with one finger pressed on her rosy lip, watching his slumber. It is a picture which "stings the brain with beauty."

The chapel of St. Augustine contains one of the best works of Canova— the monument of the Grand Duchess, Maria Christina, of Sachsen-Teschen. It is a pyramid of gray marble, twenty-eight feet high, with an opening in the side, representing the entrance to a sepulchre. A female figure personating Virtue bears in an urn to the grave, the ashes of the departed, attended by two children with torches. The figure of Compassion follows, leading an aged beggar to the tomb of his benefactor, and a little child with its hands folded.

On the lower step rests a mourning Genius beside a sleeping lion, and a bas-relief on the pyramid above represents an angel carrying Christina's image, surrounded with the emblem of eternity, to Heaven. A spirit of deep sorrow, which is touchingly portrayed in the countenance of the old man, pervades the whole group. While we looked at it, the organ breathed out a slow, mournful strain, which harmonized so fully with the expression of the figures, that we seemed to be listening to the requiem of the one they mourned. The combined effect of music and sculpture, thus united in their deep pathos, was such, that I could have sat down and wept. It was not from sadness at the death of a benevolent though unknown individual,—but the feeling of grief, of perfect, unmingled sorrow, so powerfully represented, came to the heart like an echo of its own emotion, and carried it away with irresistible influence. Travellers have described the same feeling while listening to the Miserere in the Sistine Chapel, at Rome. Canova could not have chiseled the monument without tears.

One of the most interesting objects in Vienna, is the Imperial Armory. We were admitted through tickets previously procured from the Armory Direction; as there was already one large company within, we were told to wait in the court till our turn came. Around the wall on the inside, is suspended the enormous chain which the Turks stretched across the Danube at Buda, in the year 1529, to obstruct the navigation. It has eight thousand links and is nearly a mile in length. The court is filled with cannon of all shapes and sizes, many of which were conquered from other nations. I saw a great many which were cast during the French Revolution, with the words "Liberté! Egalité!" upon them, and a number of others bearing the simple letter "N."

Finally the first company came down and the forty or fifty persons who had collected during the interval, were admitted. The Armory runs around a hollow square, and must be at least a quarter of a mile in length. We were all taken into a circular hall, made entirely of weapons, to represent the four quarters of the globe. Here the crusty old guide who admitted us, rapped with his stick on the shield of an old knight who stood near, to keep silence, and then addressed us: "When I speak every one must be silent. No one can write or draw anything. No one shall touch anything, or go to look at anything else, before I have done speaking. Otherwise, they shall be taken immediately into the street again!" Thus in every hall he rapped and scolded, driving the women to one side with his stick and the men to the other, till we were nearly through, when the thought of the coming fee made him a little more polite. He had a regular set of descriptions by heart, which he went through with a great flourish, pointing particularly to the common military caps of the late Emperors of Prussia and Austria, as "treasures beyond all price to the nation!" Whereupon, the crowd of common people gazed reverently on the shabby beavers, and I verily believe, would have devoutly kissed them, had the glass covering been removed. I happened to be next to a tall, dignified young man, who looked on all this with a displeasure almost amounting to contempt. Seeing I was a foreigner, he spoke, in a low tone, bitterly of the Austrian government. "You are not then an Austrian?" I asked. "No, thank God!" was the reply: "but I have seen enough of Austrian tyranny. I am a Pole!"

The first wing contains banners used in the French Revolution, and liberty trees with the red cap; the armor of Rudolph of Hapsburg, Maximilian I., the Emperor Charles V., and the hat, sword and order of Marshal Schwarzenberg. Some of the halls represent a fortification, with walls, ditches and embankments, made of muskets and swords. A long room in the second wing contains an encampment, in which twelve or fifteen large tents are formed in like manner. Along the sides are grouped old Austrian banners, standards taken from the French, and horsetails and flags captured from the Turks. "They make a great boast," said the Pole, "of a half dozen French colors, but let them go to the Hospital des Invalides, in Paris, and they will find hundreds of the best banners of Austria!" They also exhibited the armor of a dwarf king of Bohemia and Hungary, who died, a gray-headed old man, in his twentieth year; the sword of Marlborough; the coat of Gustavus Adolphus, pierced in the breast and back with the bullet which killed him at Lützen; the armor of the old Bohemian princess Libussa, and that of the amazon Wlaska, with a steel visor made to fit the features of her face. The last wing was the most remarkable. Here we saw the helm and breastplate of Attila, king of the Huns, which once glanced at the head of his myriads of wild hordes, before the walls of Rome; the armor of Count Stahremberg, who commanded Vienna during the Turkish siege in 1529, and the holy banner of

Mahomet, taken at that time from the Grand Vizier, together with the steel harness of John Sobieski of Poland, who rescued Vienna from the Turkish troops under Kara Mustapha; the hat, sword and breastplate of Godfrey of Bouillon, the Crusader-king of Jerusalem, with the banners of the cross the Crusaders had borne to Palestine, and the standard they captured from the Turks on the walls of the Holy City! I felt all my boyish enthusiasm for the romantic age of the Crusaders revive, as I looked on the torn and mouldering banners which once waved on the hills of Judea, or perhaps followed the sword of the Lion Heart through the fight on the field of Ascalon! What tales could they not tell, those old standards, cut and shivered by spear and lance! What brave hands have carried them through the storm of battle, what dying eyes have looked upwards to the cross on their folds, as the last prayer was breathed for the rescue of the Holy Sepulchre!

I must now close the catalogue. This morning we shall look upon Vienna for the last time. Our knapsacks are repacked, and the passports (precious documents!) visèd for Munich. The getting of this visè, however, caused a comical scene at the Police Office, yesterday. We entered the Inspector's Hall and took our stand quietly among the crowd of persons who were gathered around a railing which separated them from the main office. One of the clerks came up, scowling at us, and asked in a rough tone, "What do you want here?" We handed him our tickets of sojourn (for when a traveler spends more than twenty-four hours in a German city, he must take out a permission and pay for it) with the request that he would give us our passports. He glanced over the tickets, came back and with constrained politeness asked us to step within the railing. Here we were introduced to the Chief Inspector. "Desire Herr—— to come here," said he to a servant; then turning to us, "I am happy to see the gentlemen in Vienna." An officer immediately came up, who addressed us in fluent English. "You may speak in your native tongue," said the Inspector:—"excuse our neglect; from the facility with which you speak German, we supposed you were natives of Austria!" Our passports were signed at once and given us with a gracious bow, accompanied by the hope that we would visit Vienna again before long. All this, of course, was perfectly unintelligible to the wondering crowd outside the railing. Seeing however, the honors we were receiving, they crowded back and respectfully made room

488

for us to pass out. I kept a grave face till we reached the bottom of the stairs, when I gave way to restrained laughter in a manner that shocked the dignity of the guard, who looked savagely at me over his forest of moustache. I would nevertheless have felt grateful for the attention we received as Americans, were it not for our uncourteous reception as suspected Austrians.

We have just been exercising the risible muscles again, though from a very different cause, and one which, according to common custom, ought to draw forth symptoms of a lachrymose nature. This morning B—— suggested an examination of our funds, for we had neglected keeping a strict account, and what with being cheated in Bohemia and tempted by the amusements of Vienna, there was an apparent dwindling away. So we emptied our pockets and purses, counted up the contents, and found we had just ten florins, or four dollars apiece. The thought of our situation, away in the heart of Austria, five hundred miles from our Frankfort home, seems irresistibly laughable. By allowing twenty days for the journey, we shall have half a florin a day, to travel on. This is a homoeopathic allowance, indeed, but we have concluded to try it. So now adieu, Vienna! In two hours we shall be among the hills again.

CHAPTER XXIII. — UP THE DANUBE.

We passed out of Vienna in the face of one of the strongest winds it was ever my lot to encounter. It swept across the plain with such force that it was almost impossible to advance till we got under the lee of a range of hills. About two miles from the barrier we passed Schoenbrunn, the Austrian Versailles. It was built by the Empress Maria Theresa, and was the residence of Napoleon in 1809, when Vienna was in the hands of the French. Later, in 1832, the Duke of Reichstadt died in the same room which his father once occupied. Behind the palace is a magnificent garden, at the foot of a hill covered with rich forests and crowned with an open pillared hall, 300 feet long, called the Gloriette. The colossal eagle which surmounts it, can be seen a great distance.

The lovely valley in which Schoenbrunn lies, follows the course of the little river Vienna into the heart of that mountain region lying between the Styrian Alps and the Danube, and called the Vienna Forest. Into this our road led, between hills covered with wood, with here and there a lovely green meadow, where herds of cattle were grazing. The third day we came to the Danube again at Melk, a little city built under the edge of a steep hill, on whose summit stands the palace-like abbey of the Benedictine Monks. The old friars must have had a merry life of it, for the wine-cellar of the abbey furnished the French army 50,000 measures for several days in succession. The shores of the Danube here are extremely beautiful. The valley where it spreads out, is filled with groves, but where the hills approach the stream, its banks are rocky and precipitous, like the Rhine. Although not so picturesque as the latter river, the scenery of the Danube is on a grander scale. On the south side the mountains bend down to it with a majestic sweep, and there must be delightful glances into the valleys that lie between, in passing down the current.

But we soon left the river, and journeyed on through the enchanting inland vales. To give an idea of the glorious enjoyment of traveling through such scenes, let me copy a leaf out of my journal, written as we rested at noon on the top of a lofty hill:—"Here, while the delightful mountain breeze that comes fresh from the Alps cools my forehead, and the pines around are sighing their eternal anthem, I seize a few moments to tell what a paradise is around me. I have felt an elevation of mind and spirit, a perfect rapture from morning till night, since we left Vienna. It is the brightest and balmiest June weather; an ever fresh breeze sings through the trees and waves the ripening grain on the verdant meadows and hill-slopes. The air is filled with bird-music. The larks sing above us out of sight, the bullfinch wakes his notes in the grove, and at eve the nightingale pours forth her thrilling strain. The meadows are literally covered with flowers—beautiful purple salvias, pinks such as we have at home in our gardens and glowing buttercups, color the banks of every stream. I never saw richer or more luxuriant foliage. Magnificent forests clothe the hills, and the villages are imbedded in fruit trees, shrubbery and flowers. Sometimes we go for miles through some enchanting valley, lying like a paradise between the mountains, while the distant, white Alps look on it from afar; sometimes over swelling ranges of hills, where we can see to the right the valley of the Danube, threaded by his silver current and dotted with white cottages and glittering spires, and farther beyond, the blue mountains of the Bohemian Forest. To the left, the range of the Styrian Alps stretches along the sky, summit above summit, the farther ones robed in perpetual snow. I could never tire gazing on those glorious hills. They fill the soul with a conception of sublimity, such as one feels when listening to triumphal music. They seem like the marble domes of a mighty range of temples, where earth worships her Maker with an organ-anthem of storms!

"There is a luxury in traveling here. We walk all day through such scenes, resting often in the shade of the fruit trees which line the road, or on a mossy bank by the side of some cool forest. Sometimes for enjoyment as well as variety, we make our dining-place by a clear spring instead of within a smoky tavern; and our simple meals have a relish an epicure could never attain. Away with your railroads and steamboats and mail-coaches, or keep them for those who have no eye but for the sordid interests of life! With my knapsack and pilgrim-staff, I ask not their aid. If a mind and soul full of rapture with beauty, a frame in glowing and vigorous health, and slumbers unbroken even by dreams, are blessings any one would attain, let him pedestrianize it through Lower Austria!"

I have never been so strongly and constantly reminded of America, as during this journey. Perhaps the balmy season, the same in which I last looked upon the dear scenes of home, may have its effect; but there is besides a richness in the forests and waving fields of grain, a wild luxuriance over every landscape, which I have seen nowhere else in Europe. The large farm houses, buried in orchards, scattered over the valleys, add to the effect. Everything seems to speak of happiness and prosperity.

We were met one morning by a band of wandering Bohemian gipsies— the first of the kind I ever saw. A young woman with a small child in her arms came directly up to me, and looking full in my face with her wild black eyes, said, without any preface: "Yes, he too has met with sorrow and trouble already, and will still have more. But he is not false—he is true and sincere, and will also meet with good luck!" She said she could tell me three numbers with which I should buy a lottery ticket and win a great prize. I told her I would have nothing to do with the lottery, and would buy no ticket, but she persisted, saying: "Has he a twenty kreutzer piece?—will he give it? Lay it in his hand and make a cross over it, and I will reveal the numbers!" On my refusal, she became angry, and left me, saying: "Let him take care—the third day something will happen to him!" An old, wrinkled hag made the same proposition to my companion with no better success. They reminded me strikingly of our Indians; their complexion is a dark brown, and their eyes and hair are black as night. These belonged to a small tribe who wander through the forests of Bohemia, and support themselves by cheating and stealing.

We stopped the fourth night at Enns, a small city on the river of the same name, which divides Upper from Lower Austria. After leaving the beautiful little village where we passed the night before, the road ascended one of those long ranges of hills, which stretch off from the Danube towards the Alps. We walked for miles over the broad and uneven summit, enjoying the enchanting view which opened on both sides. If we looked to the right, we could trace the windings of the Danube for twenty miles, his current filled with green, wooded islands; white cities lie at the foot of the hills, which, covered to the

492

summit with grain fields and vineyards, extended back one behind another, till the farthest were lost in the distance. I was glad we had taken the way from Vienna to Linz by land, for from the heights we had a view of the whole course of the Danube, enjoying besides, the beauty of the inland vales and the far-off Styrian Alps. From the hills we passed over we could see the snowy range as far as the Alps of Salzburg—some of them seemed robed to the very base in their white mantles. In the morning the glaciers on their summit glittered like stars; it was the first time I saw the sun reflected at a hundred miles' distance!

On descending we came into a garden-like plain, over which rose the towers of Enns, built by the ransom money paid to Austria for the deliverance of the Lion-hearted Richard. The country legends say that St. Florian was thrown into the river by the Romans in the third century, with a millstone around his neck, which, however, held him above the water like cork, until he had finished preaching them a sermon. In the villages we often saw his imago painted on the houses, in the act of pouring a pail of water on a burning building, with the inscription beneath—"Oh, holy Florian, pray for us!" This was supposed to be a charm against fire. In Upper Austria, it is customary to erect a shrine on the road, wherever an accident has happened, with a painting and description of it, and an admonition to all passers-by to pray for the soul of the unfortunate person. On one of them, for instance, was a cart with a wild ox, which a man was holding by the horns; a woman kneeling by the wheels appeared to be drawing a little girl by the feet from under it, and the inscription stated: "By calling on Jesus, Mary and Joseph, the girl was happily rescued." Many of the shrines had images which the people no doubt, in their ignorance and simplicity, considered holy, but they were to us impious and almost blasphemous.

From Enns a morning's walk brought us to Linz. The peasant girls in their broad straw hats were weeding the young wheat, looking as cheerful and contented as the larks that sung above them. A mile or two from Linz we passed one or two of the round towers belonging to the new fortifications of the city. As walls have grown out of fashion, Duke Maximilian substituted an invention of his own. The city is surrounded by thirty two towers, one to three miles distant from it, and so placed that they form a complete line of communication and defence. They are sunk in the earth, surrounded with a ditch and embankments, and each is capable of containing ten cannon and three hundred men. The pointed roofs of these towers are seen on all the hills around. We were obliged to give up our passports at the barrier, the officer telling us to call for them in three hours at the City Police Office; we spent the intervening time very agreeably in rambling through this gay, cheerful-looking town. With its gilded spires and ornamented houses, with their green lattice blinds, it reminds one strongly of Italy, or at least, of what Italy is said to be. It has now quite an active and business-like aspect, occasioned by the steamboat and railroad lines which connect it with Vienna, Prague, Ratisbon and Salzburg. Although we had not exceeded our daily allowance by more than a few kreutzers, we found that twenty days would be hardly sufficient to accomplish the journey, and our funds must therefore be replenished. Accordingly I wrote from Linz to Frankfort, directing a small sum to be forwarded to Munich, which city we hoped to reach in eight days.

We took the horse cars at Linz for Lambach, seventeen miles on the way towards Gmunden. The mountains were covered with clouds as we approached them, and the storms they had been brewing for two or three days began to march down on the plain. They had nearly reached us, when we crossed the Traun and arrived at Lambach, a small city built upon a hill. We left the next day at noon, and on ascending the hill after crossing the Traun, had an opportunity of seeing the portrait on the Traunstein, of which the old landlord told us. I saw it at the first glance—certainly it is a most remarkable freak of nature. The rough back of the mountain forms the exact profile of the human countenance, as if regularly hewn out of the rock. What is still more singular, it is said to be a correct portrait of the unfortunate Louis XVI. The landlord said it was immediately recognized by all Frenchmen. The road followed the course of the Traun, whose green waters roared at the bottom of the glen below us; we walked for several miles through a fine forest, through whose openings we caught glimpses of the mountains we longed to reach.

The river roared at last somewhat louder, and on looking down the bank, I saw rocks and rapids, and a few houses built on the edge of the stream.

Thinking it must be near the fall, we went down the path, and lo! on crossing a little wooden bridge, the whole affair burst in sight! Judge of our surprise at finding a fall of fifteen feet, after we had been led to expect a tremendous leap of forty or fifty, with all the accompaniment of rocks and precipices. Of course the whole descent of the river at the place was much greater, and there were some romantic cascades over the rocks which blocked its course. Its greatest beauty consisted in the color of the water—the brilliant green of the waves being broken into foam of the most dazzling white—and the great force with which it is thrown below.

The Traunstein grew higher as we approached, presenting the same profile till we had nearly reached Gmünden. From the green upland meadows above the town, the view of the mountain range was glorious, and I could easily conceive the effect of the Unknown Student's appeal to the people to fight for those free hills. I think it is Howitt who relates the incident—one of the most romantic in German history. Count Pappenheim led his forces here in the year 1626, to suppress a revolution of the people of the whole Salzburg region, who had risen against an invasion of their rights by the Austrian government. The battle which took place on these meadows was about being decided in favor of the oppressors, when a young man, clad as a student, suddenly appeared and addressed the people, pointing to the Alps above them and the sweet lake below, and asking if that land should not be free. The effect was electrical; they returned to the charge and drove back the troops of Pappenheim, who were about taking to flight, when the unknown leader fell, mortally wounded. This struck a sudden panic through his followers, and the Austrians turning again, gained a complete victory. But the name of the brave student is unknown, his deed unsung by his country's bards, and almost forgotten.

CHAPTER XXIV. — THE UNKNOWN STUDENT.

Ha! spears on Gmunden's meadows green,
And banners on the wood-crowned height!
Rank after rank, their helmets' sheen
Sends back the morning light!
Where late the mountain maiden sang,
The battle-trumpet's brazen clang
Vibrates along the air;
And wild dragoons wheel o'er the plain.
Trampling to earth the yellow grain,
From which no more the merry swain
His harvest sheaves shall bear.

The eagle, in his sweep at morn,
To meet the monarch-sun on high,
Heard the unwonted warrior's horn
Peal faintly up the sky!
He saw the foemen, moving slow
In serried legions, far below,
Against that peasant-band,
Who dared to break the tyrant's thrall
And by the sword of Austria fall,

Or keep the ancient Right of all,

Held by their mountain-land;

They came to meet that mail-clad host

From glen and wood and ripening field;

A brave, stout arm, each man could boast—

A soul, unused to yield!

They met: a shout, prolonged and loud,

Went hovering upward with the cloud

That closed around them dun;

Blade upon blade unceasing clashed,

Spears in the onset shivering crashed,

And the red glare of cannon flashed

Athwart the smoky sun!

The mountain warriors wavered back,

Borne down by myriads of the foe,

Like pines before the torrent's track

When spring has warmed the snow.

Shall Faith and Freedom vainly call,

And Gmunden's warrior-herdsmen fall

On the red field in vain?

No! from the throng that back retired,

A student boy sprang forth inspired,

And while his words their bosoms fired,

Led on the charge again!

"And thus your free arms would ye give
  So tamely to a tyrant's band,
And with the hearts of vassals live
  In this, your chainless land?
The emerald lake is spread below,
And tower above, the hills of snow—
  Here, field and forest lie;
This land, so glorious and so free—
Say, shall it crushed and trodden be?
Say, would ye rather bend the knee
  Than for its freedom die?

"Look! yonder stand in mid-day's glare
  The everlasting Alps of snow,
And from their peaks a purer air
  Breathes o'er the vales below!
The Traun his brow is bent in pride—
He brooks no craven on his side—
  Would ye be fettered then?
There lifts the Sonnenstein his head,
There chafes the Traun his rocky bed
And Aurach's lovely vale is spread—
  Look on them and be men!

"Let, like a trumpet's sound of fire,

These stir your souls to manhood's part—

The glory of the Alps inspire

Each yet unconquered heart!

For, through their unpolluted air

Soars fresher up the grateful prayer

From freemen, unto God;—

A blessing on those mountains old!

On to the combat, brethren bold!

Strike, that ye free the valleys hold,

Where free your fathers trod!"

And like a mighty storm that tears

The icy avalanche from its bed,

They rushed against th' opposing spears—

The student at their head!

The bands of Austria fought in vain;

A bloodier harvest heaped the plain

At every charge they made;

Each herdsman was a hero then—

The mountain hunters stood like men,

And echoed from the farthest glen

The clash of blade on blade!

The banner in the student's hand

Waved triumph from the fight before;

What terror seized the conq'ring band?—

It fell, to rise no more!

And with it died the lofty flame,

That from his lips in lightning came

And burned upon their own;

Dread Pappenheim led back the foe,

The mountain peasants yielded slow,

And plain above and lake below

Were red when evening shone!

Now many a year has passed away

Since battle's blast rolled o'er the plain,

The Alps are bright in morning's ray—

The Traunstein smiles again.

But underneath the flowery sod,

By happy peasant children trod,

A hero's ashes lay.

O'er him no grateful nation wept,

Fame, of his deed no record kept,

And dull Forgetfulness hath swept

His very name away!

In many a grave, by poets sung,

There falls to dust a lofty brow,

But he alone, the brave and young,

   Sleeps there forgotten now.

The Alps upon that field look down,

Which won his bright and brief renown,

   Beside the lake's green shore;

Still wears the land a tyrant's chain—

Still bondmen tread the battle-plain,

Culled by his glorious soul in vain

   To win their rights of yore.

CHAPTER XXV. — THE AUSTRIAN ALPS.

It was nearly dark when we came to the end of the plain and looked on the city at our feet and the lovely lake that lost itself in the mountains before us. We were early on board the steamboat next morning, with a cloudless sky above us and a snow-crested Alp beckoning on from the end of the lake. The water was of the most beautiful green hue, the morning light colored the peaks around with purple, and a misty veil rolled up the rocks of the Traunstein. We stood on the prow and enjoyed to the fullest extent the enchanting scenery. The white houses of Gmunden sank down to the water's edge like a flock of ducks; halfway we passed castle Ort, on a rock in the lake, whose summit is covered with trees.

As we neared the other extremity, the mountains became steeper and loftier; there was no path along their wild sides, nor even a fisher's hut nestled at their feet, and the snow filled the ravines more than half-way from the summit. An hour and a quarter brought us to Ebensee, at the head of the lake, where we landed and plodded on towards Ischl, following the Traun up a narrow valley, whose mountain walls shut out more than half the sky. They are covered with forests, and the country is inhabited entirely by the woodmen who fell the mountain pines and float the timber rafts down to the Danube. The steeps are marked with white lines, where the trees have been rolled, or rather thrown from the summit. Often they descend several miles over rooks and precipices, where the least deviation from the track would dash them in a thousand pieces. This generally takes place in the winter when the sides are covered with snow and ice. It must be a dangerous business, for there are many crosses by the way-side where the pictures represent persons accidentally killed by the trees; an additional painting represents them as burning in the flames of purgatory, and the pious traveler is requested to pray an Ave or a Paternoster for the repose of their souls.

On we went, up the valley of the Traun, between mountains five and six thousand feet high, through scenes constantly changing and constantly grand, for three or four hours. Finally the hills opened, disclosing a little triangular valley, whose base was formed by a mighty mountain covered with clouds. Through the two side angles came the Traun and his tributary the Ischl, while the little town of Ischl lay in the centre. Within a few years this has become a very fashionable bathing place, and the influx of rich visitors, which in the summer sometimes amounts to two thousand, has entirely destroyed the primitive simplicity the inhabitants originally possessed. From Ischl we took a road through the forests to St. Wolfgang, on the lake of the same name. The last part of the way led along the banks of the lake, disclosing some delicious views. These Alpine lakes surpass any scenery I have yet seen. The water is of the most beautiful green, like a sheet of molten beryl, and the cloud-piercing mountains that encompass them shut out the sun for nearly half the day. St. Wolfgang is a lovely village in a cool and quiet nook at the foot of the Schafberg. The houses tire built in the picturesque Swiss style, with flat, projecting roofs and ornamented balconies, and the people are the very picture of neatness and cheerfulness.

We started next morning to ascend the Schafberg, which is called the Righi of the Austrian Switzerland. It is somewhat higher than its Swiss namesake, and commands a prospect scarcely less extensive or grand. We followed a footpath through the thick forest by the side of a roaring torrent. The morning mist still covered the lake, but the white summits of the Salzburg and Noric Alps opposite us, rose above it and stood pure and bright in the upper air. We passed a little mill and one or two cottages, and then wound round one of the lesser heights into a deep ravine, down in whose dark shadow we sometimes heard the axe and saw of the mountain woodmen. Finally the path disappeared altogether under a mass of logs and rocks, which appeared to have been whirled together by a sudden flood. We deliberated what to do; the summit rose several thousand feet above us, almost precipitously steep, but we did not like to turn back, and there was still a hope of meeting with the path again. Clambering over the ruins and rubbish we pulled ourselves by the limbs of trees up a steep ascent and descended again to the stream. We here saw the ravine was closed by a wall of rock and our only chance was to cross to the west side of the mountain, where the ascent seemed somewhat easier. A couple of mountain maidens whom we fortunately met, carrying home grass for their goats, told us the mountain could be ascended on that side, by one who could climb well—laying a strong emphasis on the word. The very doubt implied in this expression was enough to decide us; so we began the work. And work it was, too! The side was very steep, the trees all leaned downwards, and we slipped at every step on the dry leaves and grass. After making a short distance this way with the greatest labor, we came to the track of an avalanche, which had swept away the trees and earth. Here the rock had been worn rough by torrents, but by using both hands and feet, we clomb directly up the side of the mountain, sometimes dragging ourselves up by the branches of trees where the rocks were smooth. After half an hour of such work we came above the forests, on the bare side of the mountain. The summit was far above us and so steep that our limbs involuntarily shrunk from the task of climbing. The side ran up at an angle of nearly sixty degrees, and the least slip threw us flat on our faces. We had to use both hand and foot, and were obliged to rest every few minutes to recover breath. Crimson-flowered moss and bright blue gentians covered the rocks, and I filled my books with blossoms for friends at home.

Up and up, for what seemed an age, we clambered. So steep was it, that the least rocky projection hid my friend from sight, as he was coming up below me. I let stones roll sometimes, which went down, down, almost like a cannonball, till I could see them no more. At length we reached the region of dwarf pines, which was even more difficult to pass through. Although the mountain was not so steep, this forest, centuries old, reached no higher than our breasts, and the trees leaned downwards, so that we were obliged to take hold of the tops of those above us, and drag ourselves up through the others. Here and there lay large patches of snow; we sat down in the glowing June sun, and bathed our hands and faces in it. Finally the sky became bluer and broader, the clouds seemed nearer, and a few more steps through the bushes brought us to the summit of the mountain, on the edge of a precipice a thousand feet deep, whose bottom stood in a vast field of snow!

We lay down on the heather, exhausted by five hours' incessant toil, and drank in like a refreshing draught, the sublimity of the scene, The green lakes of the Salzburg Alps lay far below us, and the whole southern horizon was filled with the mighty range of the Styrian and Noric Alps, their summits of never-melting snow mingling and blending with the clouds. On the other side the mountains of Salzburg lifted their ridgy backs from the plains of Bavaria and the Chiem lake lay spread out in the blue distance. A line of mist far to the north betrayed the path of the Danube, and beyond it we could barely trace the outline of the Bohemian mountains. With a glass the spires of Munich, one hundred and twenty miles distant, can be seen. It was a view whose grandeur I can never forget. In that dome of the cloud we seemed to breathe a purer air than that of earth.

After an hour or two, we began to think of descending, as the path was yet to be found. The summit, which was a mile or more in length, extended farther westward, and by climbing over the dwarf pines for some time, we saw a little wooden house above us. It stood near the highest part of the peak, and two or three men were engaged in repairing it, as a shelter for travelers. They pointed out the path which went down on the side toward St. Gilgen, and we began descending. The mountain on this side is much less steep, but the descent is fatiguing enough. The path led along the side of a glen where mountain goats were grazing, and further down we saw cattle feeding on the little spots of verdure which lay in the forest. My knees became so weak from this continued descent, that they would scarcely support me; but we were three hours, partly walking and partly running down, before we reached the bottom. Half an hour's walk around the head of the St. Wolfgang See, brought us to the little village of St. Gilgen.

The valley of St. Gilgen lies like a little paradise between the mountains. Lovely green fields and woods slope gradually from the mountain behind, to the still greener lake spread out before it, in whose bosom the white Alps are mirrored. Its picturesque cottages cluster around the neat church with its lofty spire, and the simple inhabitants have countenances as bright and cheerful as the blue sky above them. We breathed an air of poetry. The Arcadian simplicity of the people, the pastoral beauty of the fields around and the grandeur of the mountains which shut it out from the world, realized my ideas of a dwelling place, where, with a few kindred spirits, the bliss of Eden might almost be restored.

We stopped there two or three hours to relieve our hunger and fatigue. My boots had suffered severely in our mountain adventure, and I called at a shoemaker's cottage to get them repaired. I sat down and talked for half an hour with the family. The man and his wife spoke of the delightful scenery around them, and expressed themselves with correctness and even elegance. They were much pleased that I admired their village so greatly, and related every thing which they supposed could interest me. As I rose to go, my head nearly touched the ceiling, which was very low. The man exclaimed: "Ach Gott! how tall!" I told him the people were all tall in our country; he then asked where I came from, and I had no sooner said America, than he threw up his hands and uttered an ejaculation of the greatest surprise. His wife observed that "it was wonderful how far man was permitted to travel." They wished me a prosperous journey and a safe return home.

St. Gilgen was also interesting to me from that beautiful chapter in "Hyperion"—"Footsteps of Angels,"—and on passing the church on my way back to the inn, I entered the graveyard mentioned in it. The green turf grows thickly over the rows of mounds, with here and there a rose planted by the hand of affection, and the white crosses were hung with wreaths, some of which had been freshly laid on. Behind the church, under the shade of a tree, stood a small chapel,—I opened the unfastened door, and entered. The afternoon sun shone through the side window, and all was still around. A little shrine, adorned with flowers, stood at the other end, and there were two tablets on the wall, to persons who slumbered beneath, I approached these and read on one of them with feelings not easily described: "Look not mournfully into the past—it comes not again; wisely improve the present—it is thine; and go forward to meet the shadowy future, without fear, and with a manly heart!" This then was the spot where Paul Flemming came in loneliness and sorrow to muse over what he had lost, and these were the words whose truth and eloquence strengthened and consoled him, "as if the unknown tenant of the grave had opened his lips of dust and spoken those words of consolation his soul needed." I sat down and mused a long time, for there was something in the silent holiness of the spot, that impressed me more than I could well describe.

We reached a little village on the Fuschel See, the same evening, and set off the next morning for Salzburg. The day was hot and we walked slowly, so that it was not till two o'clock that we saw the castellated rocks on the side of the Gaissberg, guarding the entrance to the valley of Salzburg. A short distance further, the whole glorious panorama was spread out below us. From the height on which we stood, we looked directly on the summit of the Capuchin Mountain, which hid part of the city from sight; the double peak of the Staufen rose opposite, and a heavy storm was raging along the Alpine heights around it, while the lovely valley lay in sunshine below, threaded by the bright current of the Salza. As we descended and passed around the foot of the hill, the Untersberg came in sight, whose broad summits lift themselves seven thousand feet above the plain. The legend says that Charlemagne and his warriors sit in its subterraneous caverns in complete armor, and that they will arise and come forth again, when Germany recovers her former power and glory.

I wish I could convey in words some idea of the elevation of spirit experienced while looking on these eternal mountains. They fill the soul with a sensation of power and grandeur which frees it awhile from the cramps and fetters of common life. It rises and expands to the level of their sublimity, till its thoughts stand solemnly aloft, like their summits, piercing the free heaven. Their dazzling and imperishable beauty is to the mind an image of its own enduring existence. When I stand upon some snowy summit—the invisible apex of that mighty pyramid—there seems a majesty in my weak will which might defy the elements. This sense of power, inspired by a silent sympathy with the forms of nature, is beautifully described—as shown in the free, unconscious instincts of childhood—by the poet Uhland, in his ballad of the "Mountain Boy." I have attempted a translation.

THE MOUNTAIN BOY.

A herd-boy on the mountain's brow,

I see the castles all below.

The sunbeam here is earliest cast

And by my side it lingers last—

I am the boy of the mountain!

The mother-house of streams is here—

I drink them in their cradles clear;

From out the rock they foam below,

I spring to catch them as they go!

   I am the boy of the mountain!

To me belongs the mountain's bound,

Where gathering tempests march around;

But though from north and south they shout,

Above them still my song rings out—

   "I am the boy of the mountain!"

Below me clouds and thunders move;

I stand amid the blue above.

I shout to them with fearless breast:

"Go, leave my father's house in rest!"

   I am the boy of the mountain!

And when the loud bell shakes the spires

And flame aloft the signal-fires,

I go below and join the throng

And swing my sword and sing my song:

   "I am the boy of the mountain!"

Salzburg lies on both sides of the Salza, hemmed in on either hand by precipitous mountains. A large fortress overlooks it on the south, from the summit of a perpendicular rock, against which the houses in that part of the city arc built. The streets are narrow and crooked, but the newer part contains many open squares, adorned with handsome fountains. The variety of costume among the people, is very interesting. The inhabitants of the salt district have a peculiar dress; the women wear round fur caps, with little wings of gauze at the side. I saw other women with headdresses of gold or silver filagree, something in shape like a Roman helmet, with a projection at the back of the head, a foot long. The most interesting objects in Salzburg to us, were the house of Mozart, in which the composer was born, and the monument lately erected to him. The St. Peter's Church, near by, contains the tomb of Haydn, the great composer, and the Church of St. Sebastian, that of the renowned Paracelsus, who was also a native of Salzburg.

Two or three hours sufficed to see every thing of interest in the city. We had intended to go further through the Alps, to the beautiful vales of the Tyrol, but our time was getting short, our boots, which are the pedestrian's sole dependence, began to show symptoms of wearing out, and our expenses among the lakes and mountains of Upper Austria, left us but two florins apiece, so we reluctantly turned our backs upon the snowy hills and set out for Munich, ninety miles distant. After passing the night at Saalbruck, on the banks of the stream which separates the two kingdoms, we entered Bavaria next morning. I could not help feeling glad to leave Austria, although within her bounds I had passed scones whose beauty will long haunt me, and met with many honest friendly hearts among her people. We noticed a change as soon as we had crossed the border. The roads were neater and handsomer, and the country people greeted us in going by, with a friendly cheerfulness that made us feel half at home. The houses are built in the picturesque Swiss fashion, their balconies often ornamented with curious figures, carved in wood. Many of them, where they are situated remote from a church, have a little bell on the roof which they ring for morning and evening prayers; we often heard these simple monitors sounding from the cottages as we passed by.

The next night we stopped at the little village of Stein, famous in former times for its robber-knight, Hans von Stein. The ruins of his castle stand on the rock above, and the caverns hewn in the sides of the precipice, where he used to confine his prisoners, are still visible. Walking on through a pleasant, well-cultivated country, we came to Wasserburg, on the Inn. The situation of the city is peculiar. The Inn has gradually worn his channel deeper in the sandy soil, so that he now flows at the bottom of a glen, a hundred feet below the plains around. Wasserburg lies in a basin, formed by the change of the current, which flows around it like a horseshoe, leaving only a narrow neck of land which connects it with the country above.

We left the little village where we were quartered for the night and took a foot path which led across the country to the field of Hohenlinden, about six miles distant. The name had been familiar to me from childhood, and my love for Campbell, with the recollection of the school-exhibitions where "On Linden when the sun was low" had been so often declaimed, induced me to make the excursion to it. We traversed a large forest, belonging to the King of Bavaria, and came out on a plain covered with grain fields and bounded on the right by a semi-circle of low hills. Over the fields, about two miles distant, a tall, minaret-like spire rose from a small cluster of houses, and this was Hohenlinden! To tell the truth, I had been expecting something more. The "hills of blood-stained snow" are very small hills indeed, and the "Isar, rolling rapidly," is several miles off; it was the spot, however, and we recited Campbell's poem, of course, and brought away a few wild flowers as memorials. There is no monument or any other token of the battle, and the people seem to endeavor to forget the scene of Moreau's victory and their defeat.

From a hill twelve miles off we had our first view of the spires of Munich, looking like distant ships over the sea-like plain. They kept in sight till we arrived at eight o'clock in the evening, after a walk of more than thirty miles. We crossed the rapid Isar on three bridges, entered the magnificent Isar Gate, and were soon comfortably quartered in the heart of Munich.

Entering the city without knowing a single soul within it, we made within a few minutes an agreeable acquaintance. After we passed the Isar Gate, we began looking for a decent inn, for the day's walk was very fatiguing.

510

Presently a young man, who had been watching us for some time, came up and said, if we would allow him, he would conduct us to a good lodging-place. Finding we were strangers, he expressed the greatest regret that he had not time to go with us every day around the city. Our surprise and delight at the splendor of Munich, he said, would more than repay him for the trouble. In his anxiety to show us something, he took us some distance out of the way, (although it was growing dark and we were very tired,) to see the Palace and the Theatre, with its front of rich frescoes.

END OF PART I. —

PART II.

CHAPTER XXVI. — MUNICH.

June 14.—I thought I had seen every thing in Vienna that could excite admiration or gratify fancy; here I have my former sensations to live over again, in an augmented degree. It is well I was at first somewhat prepared by our previous travel, otherwise the glare and splendor of wealth and art in this German Athens might blind me to the beauties of the cities we shall yet visit. I have been walking in a dream where the fairy tales of boyhood were realized, and the golden and jeweled halls of the Eastern genii rose glittering around me—"a vision of the brain no more." All I had conceived of oriental magnificence, all descriptions of the splendor of kingly halls and palaces, fall far short of what I here see. Where shall I begin to describe the crowd of splendid edifices that line its streets, or how give an idea of the profusion of paintings and statues—of marble, jasper and gold?

Art has done every thing for Munich. It lies on a large, flat plain, sixteen hundred feet above the sea, and continually exposed to the cold winds from the Alps. At the beginning of the present century it was but a third-rate city, and was rarely visited by foreigners. Since that time its population and limits have been doubled, and magnificent edifices in every style of architecture erected, rendering it scarcely secondary in this respect to any capital in Europe. Every art that wealth or taste could devise, seems to have been spent in its decoration. Broad, spacious streets and squares have been laid out, churches, halls and colleges erected, and schools of painting and sculpture established, which draw artists from all parts of the world. All this was principally brought about by the taste of the present king, Ludwig I., who began twenty or thirty years ago, when he was Crown Prince, to collect the best German artists around him and form plans for the execution of his grand design. He can boast of having done more for the arts than any other living monarch, and if he had accomplished it all without oppressing his people, he would deserve an immortality of fame.

Now, if you have nothing else to do, let us take a stroll down the Ludwigstrasse. As we pass the Theatiner Church, with its dome and towers, the broad street opens before us, stretching away to the north, between rows of magnificent buildings. Just at this southern end, is the Schlusshalle, an open temple of white marble terminating the avenue. To the right of us extend the arcades, with the trees of the Royal Garden peeping above them; on the left is the spacious concert building of the Odeon, and the palace of the Duke of Leuchtenberg, son of Eugene Beauharnois. Passing through a row of palace-like private buildings, we come to the Army Department, on the right—a neat and tasteful building of white sandstone. Beside it stands the Library, which possesses the first special claim on our admiration. With its splendid front of five hundred and eighteen feet, the yellowish brown cement with which the body is covered, making an agreeable contrast with the dark red window-arches and cornices, and the statues of Homer, Hippocrates, Thucydides and Aristotle guarding the portal, is it not a worthy receptacle for the treasures of ancient and modern lore which its halls contain?

Nearly opposite stands the Institute for the Blind, a plain but large building of dark red brick, covered with cement, and further, the Ludwig's Kirche, or Church of St. Louis. How lightly the two square towers of gray marble lift their network of sculpture! And what a novel and beautiful effect is produced by uniting the Byzantine style of architecture to the form of the Latin cross! Over the arched portal stand marble statues by Schwanthaler, and the roof of brilliant tiles worked into mosaic, looks like a rich Turkey carpet covering the whole. We must enter to get an idea of the splendor of this church. Instead of the pointed arch which one would expect to see meeting above his head, the lofty pillars on each side bear an unbroken semicircular vault, which is painted a brilliant blue, and spangled with silver stars. These pillars, and the little arches above, which spring from them, are painted in an arabesque style with gold and brilliant colors, and each side-chapel is a perfect casket of richness and elegance. The windows are of silvered glass, through which the light glimmers softly on the splendor within. The whole end of the church behind the high altar, is taken up with Cornelius's celebrated fresco painting of the "Last Judgment,"—the largest painting in the world—and the circular dome in the centre of the cross contains groups of martyrs, prophets, saints and kings, painted in fresco on a ground of gold. The work of Cornelius has been greatly praised for sublimity of design and beauty of execution, by many acknowledged judges; I was disappointed in it, but the fault lay most probably in me and not in the painting. The richness and elegance of the church took me all "aback;" it was so entirely different from anything I had seen, that it was difficult to decide whether I was most charmed by its novelty or its beauty. Still, as a building designed to excite feelings of worship, it seems to me inappropriate. A vast, dim Cathedral would be far preferable; the devout, humble heart cannot feel at home amid such glare and brightness.

As we leave the church and walk further on, the street expands suddenly into a broad square. One side is formed by the new University building and the other by the Royal Seminary, both displaying in their architecture new forms of the graceful Byzantine school, which the architects of Munich have adapted in a striking manner to so many varied purposes. On each side stands a splendid colossal fountain of bronze, throwing up a great mass of water, which falls in a triple cataract to the marble basin below. A short distance beyond this square the Ludwigstrasse terminates. It is said the end will be closed by a magnificent gate, on a style to correspond with the unequalled avenue to which it will give entrance. To one standing at the southern end, it would form a proper termination to the grand vista. Before we leave, turn around and glance back, down this street, which extends for half a mile between such buildings as we have just viewed, and tell me if it is not something of which a city and a king may boast, to have created all this within less than twenty years!

We went one morning to see the collection of paintings formerly belonging to Eugene Beauharnois, who was brother-in-law to the present king of Bavaria, in the palace of his son, the Duke of Leuchtenberg. The first hall contains works principally by French artists, among which are two by Gerard—a beautiful portrait of Josephine, and the blind Belisarius carrying his dead companion. The boy's head lies on the old man's shoulder; but for

514

the livid paleness of his limbs, he would seem to be only asleep, while a deep and settled sorrow marks the venerable features of the unfortunate Emperor. In the middle of the room are six pieces of statuary, among which Canova's world-renowned group of the Graces at once attracts the eye. There is also a kneeling Magdalen, lovely in her woe, by the same sculptor, and a very touching work of Schadow, representing a shepherd boy tenderly binding his sash around a lamb which he has accidentally wounded with his arrow.

We have since seen in the St. Michael's Church, the monument to Eugene Beauharnois, from the chisel of Thorwaldsen. The noble, manly figure of the son of Josephine is represented in the Roman mantle, with his helmet and sword lying on the ground by him. On one side sits History, writing on a tablet; on the other, stand the two brother-angels, Death and Immortality. They lean lovingly together, with arms around each other, but the sweet countenance of Death has a cast of sorrow, as he stands with inverted torch and a wreath of poppies among his clustering locks. Immortality, crowned with never-fading flowers, looks upwards with a smile of triumph, and holds in one hand his blazing torch. It is a beautiful idea, and Thorwaldsen has made the marble eloquent with feeling.

The inside of the square formed by the Arcades and the New Residence, is filled with noble old trees, which in summer make a leafy roof over the pleasant walks. In the middle, stands a grotto, ornamented with rough pebbles and shells, and only needing a fountain to make it a perfect hall of Neptune. Passing through the northern Arcade, one comes into the magnificent park, called the English Garden, which extends more than four miles along the bank of the Isar, several branches of whose milky current wander through it, and form one or two pretty cascades. It is a beautiful alternation of forest and meadow, and has all the richness and garden-like luxuriance of English scenery. Winding walks lead along the Isar, or through the wood of venerable oaks, and sometimes a lawn of half a mile in length, with a picturesque temple at its further end, comes in sight through the trees. I was better pleased with this park than with the Prater in Vienna. Its paths are always filled with persons enjoying the change from the dusty streets to its quiet and cool retirement.

515

The New Residence is not only one of the wonders of Munich, but of the world. Although commenced in 1826 and carried on constantly since that time by a number of architects, sculptors and painters, it is not yet finished; if art were not inexhaustible it would be difficult to imagine what more could be added. The north side of the Max Joseph Platz is taken up by its front of four hundred and thirty feet, which was nine years in building, under the direction of the architect Klenze. The exterior is copied after the Palazzo Pitti, in Florence. The building is of light brown sandstone, and combines an elegance and even splendor, with the most chaste and classic style. The northern front, which faces on the Royal Garden, is now nearly finished. It has the enormous length of eight hundred feet; in the middle is a portico of ten Ionic columns; instead of supporting a triangular facade, each pillar stands separate and bears a marble statue from the chisel of Schwanthaler.

The interior of the building does not disappoint the promise of the outside. It is open every afternoon in the absence of the king, for the inspection of visitors; fortunately for us, his majesty is at present on a journey through his provinces on the Rhine. We went early to the waiting hall, where several travelers were already assembled, and at four o'clock, were admitted into the newer part of the palace, containing the throne hall, ballroom, etc. On entering the first hall, designed for the lackeys and royal servants, we were all obliged to thrust our feet into cloth slippers to walk over the polished mosaic floor. The walls are of scagliola marble and the ceilings ornamented brilliantly in fresco. The second hall, also for servants, gives tokens of increasing splendor in the richer decorations of the walls and the more elaborate mosaic of the floor. We next entered the receiving saloon, in which the Court Marshal receives the guests. The ceiling is of arabesque sculpture, profusely painted and gilded. Passing through a little cabinet, we entered the great dancing saloon. Its floor is the richest mosaic of wood of different colors, the sides are of polished scagliola marble, and the ceiling a dazzling mixture of sculpture, painting and gold. At one end is a gallery for the orchestra, supported by six columns of variegated marble, above which are six dancing nymphs, painted so beautifully that they appear like living creatures. Every decoration which could be devised has been used to heighten its splendor, and the artists appear to have made free use of the Arabian Nights in forming the plan.

We entered next two smaller rooms containing the portraits of beautiful women, principally from the German nobility. I gave the preference to the daughter of Marco Bozzaris, now maid of honor to the Queen of Greece. She had a wild dark eye, a beautiful proud lip, and her rich black hair rolled in glossy waves down her neck from under the red Grecian cap stuck jauntily on the side of her head. She wore a scarf and close-fitting vest embroidered with gold, and there was a free, lofty spirit in her countenance worthy the name she bore. These pictures form a gallery of beauty, whose equal cannot easily be found.

Returning to the dancing hall, we entered the dining saloon, also called the Hall of Charlemagne. Each wall has two magnificent fresco paintings of very large size, representing some event in the life of the great emperor, beginning with his anointing at St. Deny's as a boy of twelve years, and ending with his coronation by Leo III. A second dining saloon, the Hall of Barbarossa, adjoins the first. It has also eight frescoes as the former, representing the principal events in the life of Frederic Barbarossa. Then comes a third, called the Hapsburg Hall, with four grand paintings from the life of Rudolph of Hapsburg, and a triumphal procession along the frieze, showing the improvement in the arts and sciences which was accomplished under his reign. The drawing, composition and rich tone of coloring of these glorious frescoes, are scarcely excelled by any in existence.

Finally we entered the Hall of the Throne. Here the encaustic decoration, so plentifully employed in the other rooms, is dropped, and an effect even more brilliant obtained by the united use of marble and gold. Picture a long hall with a floor of polished marble, on each side twelve columns of white marble with gilded capitals, between which stand colossal statues of gold. At the other end is the throne of gold and crimson, with gorgeous hangings of crimson velvet. The twelve statues in the hall are called the "Wittlesbach Ancestors," and represent renowned members of the house of Wittlesbach from which the present family of Bavaria is descended. They were cast in bronze by Stiglmaier, after the models of Schwanthaler, and then completely covered with a coating of gold, so that they resemble solid golden statues. The value of the precious metal on each one is about $3,000, as they are nine feet in height! What would the politicians who made such an outcry about the new papering of the President's House, say to such a palace as this?

Going back to the starting point, we went to the other wing of the edifice and joined the party who came to visit the apartments of the king. Here we were led through two or three rooms, appropriated to the servants, with all the splendor of marble doors, floors of mosaic, and frescoed ceilings. From these we entered the king's dwelling. The entrance halls are decorated with paintings of the Argonauts and illustrations of the Hymns of Hesiod, after drawings by Schwanthaler. Then came the Service Hall, containing frescoes illustrating Homer, by Schnorr, and the Throne Hall, with Schwanthaler's bas-reliefs of the songs of Pindar, on a ground of gold. The throne stands under a splendid crimson canopy. The Dining Room with its floor of polished wood is filled with illustrations of the songs of Anacreon. To these follow the Dressing Room, with twenty-seven illustrations of the Comedies of Aristophanes, and the sleeping chamber with frescoes after the poems of Theocritus, and two beautiful bas-reliefs representing angels bearing children to Heaven. It is no wonder the King writes poetry, when he breathes, eats, and even sleeps in an atmosphere of it.

We were shown the rooms for the private parties of the Court, the school-room, with scenes from the life of the Ancient Greeks, and then conducted down the marble staircases to the lower story, which is to contain Schnorr's magnificent frescoes of the Nibelungen Lied—the old German Iliad. Two halls are at present finished; the first has the figure of the author, Heinrich von Ofterdingen, and those of Chriemhilde, Brunhilde, Siegfried and the other personages of the poem; and the second, called the Marriage Hall, contains the marriage of Chriemhilde and Siegfried, and the triumphal entry of Siegfried into Worms.

Adjoining the new residence on the east, is the Royal Chapel, lately finished in the Byzantine style, under the direction of Klenze. To enter it, is like stepping into a casket of jewels. The sides are formed by a double range of arches, the windows being so far back as to be almost out of sight, so that the eye falls on nothing but painting and gold. The lower row of arches is of alternate green and purple marble, beautifully polished; but the upper, as well as the small chancel behind the high altar, is entirely covered with fresco paintings on a ground of gold! The richness and splendor of the whole church is absolutely incredible. Even after one has seen the Ludwig's Kirche and the Residence itself, it excites astonishment. I was surprised, however, to find at this age, a painting on the wall behind the altar, representing the Almighty. It seems as if man's presumption has no end. The simple altar of Athens, with its inscription "to the Unknown God," was more truly reverent than this. As I sat down awhile under one of the arches, a poor woman came in, carrying a heavy basket, and going to the steps which led up to the altar, knelt down and prayed, spreading her arms out in the form of a cross. Then, after stooping and kissing the first step, she dragged herself with her knees upon it, and commenced praying again with outspread arms. This she continued till she had climbed them all, which occupied some time; then, as if she had fulfilled a vow she turned and departed. She was undoubtedly sincere in her piety, but it made me sad to look upon such deluded superstition.

We visited yesterday morning the Glyptothek, the finest collection of ancient sculpture except that in the British Museum, I have yet seen, and perhaps elsewhere unsurpassed, north of the Alps. The building which was finished by Klenze, in 1830, has an Ionic portico of white marble, with a group of allegorical figures, representing Sculpture and the kindred arts. On each side of the portico, there are three niches in the front, containing on one side, Pericles, Phidias and Vulcan; on the other, Hadrian, Prometheus and Dædalus. The whole building forms a hollow square, and is lighted entirely from the inner side. There are in all twelve halls, each containing the remains of a particular era in the art, and arranged according to time, so that, beginning with the clumsy productions of the ancient Egyptians, one passes through the different stages of Grecian art, afterwards that of Rome, and finally ends with the works of our own times—the almost Grecian perfection of Thorwaldsen and Canova. These halls are worthy to hold such treasures, and what more could be said of them? The floors are of marble mosaic, the sides of green or purple scagliola, and the vaulted ceilings covered with raised ornaments on a ground of gold. No two are alike in color and decoration, and yet there is a unity of taste and design in the whole, which renders the variety delightful.

From the Egyptian Hall, we enter one containing the oldest remains of Grecian sculpture, before the artists won power to mould the marble to their conceptions. Then follow the celebrated Egina marbles, from the temple of Jupiter Panhellenius, on the island of Egina. They formerly stood in the two porticoes, the one group representing the fight for the body of Laomedon, the other the struggle for the dead Patroclus. The parts wanting have been admirably restored by Thorwaldsen. They form almost the only existing specimens of the Eginetan school. Passing through the Apollo Hall, we enter the large hall of Bacchus, in which the progress of the art is distinctly apparent. A satyr, lying asleep on a goat-skin which he has thrown over a rock, is believed to be the work of Praxiteles. The relaxation of the figure and perfect repose of every limb, is wonderful. The countenance has traits of individuality which led me to think it might have been a portrait, perhaps of some rude country swain.

In the Hall of Niobe, which follows, is one of the most perfect works that ever grew into life under a sculptor's chisel. Mutilated as it is, without head and arms, I never saw a more expressive figure. Ilioneus, the son of Niobe, is represented as kneeling, apparently in the moment in which Apollo raises his arrow, and there is an imploring supplication in his attitude which is touching in the highest degree. His beautiful young limbs seem to shrink involuntarily from the deadly shaft; there is an expression of prayer, almost of agony, in the position of his body. It should be left untouched. No head could be added, which would equal that one pictures to himself, while gazing upon it.

The Pinacothek is a magnificent building of yellow sandstone, five hundred and thirty feet long, containing thirteen hundred pictures, selected with great care from the whole private collection of the king, which amounts to nine thousand. Above the cornice on the southern side, stand twenty-five colossal statues of celebrated painters, by Schwanthaler. As we approached, the tall bronze door was opened by a servant in the Bavarian livery, whose size harmonized so well with the giant proportions of the building, that, until I stood beside him and could mark the contrast, I did not notice his enormous frame. I saw then that he must be near eight feet high, and stout in proportion. He reminded me of the great "Baver of Trient," in Vienna. The Pinacothek contains the most complete collection of works by old German artists, anywhere to be found. There are in the hall of the Spanish masters, half a dozen of Murillo's inimitable beggar groups. It was a relief, after looking upon the distressingly stiff figures of the old German school, to view these fresh, natural countenances. One little black-eyed boy has just cut a slice out of a melon and turns with a full mouth to his companion, who is busy eating a bunch of grapes. The simple, contented expression on the faces of the beggars is admirable. I thought I detected in a beautiful child, with dark curly locks, the original of his celebrated Infant St. John. I was much interested in two small juvenile works of Raphael and his own portrait. The latter was taken most probably after he became known as a painter. The calm, serious smile which we see on his portrait as a boy, had vanished, and the thin features and sunken eye told of intense mental labor.

One of the most remarkable buildings now in the course of erection is the Basilica, or Church of St. Bonifacius. It represents another form of the Byzantine style, a kind of double edifice, a little like a North River steamboat, with a two story cabin on deck. The inside is not yet finished, although the artists have been at work on it for six years, but we heard many accounts of its splendor, which is said to exceed anything that has been yet done in Munich. We visited to-day the atelier of Sohwanthaler, which is always open to strangers. The sculptor himself was not there, but five or six of his scholars were at work in the rooms, building up clay statues after his models and working out bas-reliefs in frames. We saw here the original models of the statues on the Pinacothek, and the "Wittelsbach Ancestors" in the Throne Hall of the palace. I was glad also to find a miniature copy in plaster, of the Herrmannsschlacht, or combat of the old German hero, Herrmann, with the Romans, from the frieze of the Walhalla, at Ratisbon. It is one of Schwanthaler's best works. Herrmann, as the middle figure, is represented in fight with the Roman general; behind him the warriors are rushing on, and an old bard is striking the chords of his harp to inspire them, while women bind up the wounds of the fallen. The Roman soldiers on the other side are about turning in confusion to fly. It is a lofty and appropriate subject for the portico of a building containing the figures of the men who have labored for the glory and elevation of their Fatherland.

Our new-found friend came to visit us last evening and learn our impressions of Munich. In the course of conversation we surprised him by revealing the name of our country. His countenance brightened up and he asked us many questions about the state of society in America. In return, he told us something more about himself—his story was simple, but it interested me. His father was a merchant, who, having been ruined by unlucky transactions, died, leaving a numerous family without the means of support. His children were obliged to commence life alone and unaided, which, in a country where labor is so cheap, is difficult and disheartening. Our friend chose the profession of a machinist, which, after encountering great obstacles, he succeeded in learning, and now supports himself as a common laborer. But his position in this respect prevents him from occupying that station in society for which he is intellectually fitted. His own words, uttered with a simple pathos which I can never forget, will best describe how painful this must be to a sensitive spirit. "I tell you thus frankly my feelings," said he, "because I know you will understand me. I could not say this to any of my associates, for they would not comprehend it, and they would say I am proud, because I cannot bring my soul down to their level. I am poor and have but little to subsist upon; but the spirit has needs as well as the body, and I feel it a duty and a desire to satisfy them also. When I am with any of my common fellow-laborers, what do I gain from them? Their leisure hours are spent in drinking and idle amusement, and I cannot join them, for I have no sympathy with such things. To mingle with those above me, would be impossible. Therefore I am alone—I have no associate!"

I have gone into minute, and it may be, tiresome detail, in describing some of the edifices of Munich, because it seemed the only way in which I could give an idea of their wonderful beauty. It is true that in copying after the manner of the daguerreotype, there is danger of imitating its dullness also, but I trust to the glitter of gold and rich paintings, for a little brightness in the picture. We leave to-morrow morning, having received the sum written for, which, to our surprise, will be barely sufficient to enable us to reach Heidelberg.

CHAPTER XXVII. — THROUGH WURTEMBERG TO HEIDELBERG.

We left Munich in the morning train for Augsburg. Between the two cities extends a vast unbroken plain, exceedingly barren and monotonous. Here and there is a little scrubby woodland, and sometimes we passed over a muddy stream which came down from the Alps. The land is not more than half-cultivated, and the villages are small and poor. We saw many of the peasants at their stations, in their gay Sunday dresses; the women wore short gowns with laced boddices, of gay colors, and little caps on the top of their heads, with streamers of ribbons three feet long. After two hours' ride, we saw the tall towers of Augsburg, and alighted on the outside of the wall. The deep moat which surrounds the city, is all grown over with velvet turf, the towers and bastions are empty and desolate, and we passed unchallenged under the gloomy archway. Immediately on entering the city, signs of its ancient splendor are apparent. The houses are old, many of them with quaint, elaborately carved ornaments, and often covered with fresco paintings. These generally represent some scene from the Bible history, encircled with arabesque borders, and pious maxims in illuminated scrolls. We went into the old Rathhaus, whose golden hall still speaks of the days of Augsburg's pride. I saw in the basement a bronze eagle, weighing sixteen tons, with an inscription on the pedestal stating that it was cast in 1606, and formerly stood on the top of an old public building, since torn down. In front of the Rathhaus is a fine bronze fountain, with a number of figures of angels and tritons.

The same afternoon, we left Augsburg for Ulm. Long, low ranges of hills, running from the Danube, stretched far across the country, and between them lay many rich, green valleys. We passed, occasionally, large villages, perhaps as old as the times of the crusaders, and looking quite pastoral and romantic from the outside; but we were always glad when we had gone through them and into the clean country again. The afternoon of the second day we came in sight of the fertile plain of the Danube; far, far to the right lay the field of Blenheim, where Marlborough and the Prince Eugene conquered the united French and Bavarian forces and decided the war of the Spanish succession.

We determined to reach Ulm the same evening, although a heavy storm was raging along the distant hills of Wurtemberg. The dark mass of the mighty Cathedral rose in the distance through the twilight, a perfect mountain in comparison with the little houses clustered around its base. We reached New Ulm, finally, and passed over the heavy wooden bridge into Wurtemberg, unchallenged for passport or baggage. I thought I could feel a difference in the atmosphere when I reached the other side—it breathed of the freer spirit that ruled through the land. The Danube is here a little muddy stream, hardly as large as my native Brandywine, and a traveler who sees it at Ulm for the first time would most probably be disappointed. It is not until below Vienna, where it receives the Drave and Save, that it becomes a river of more than ordinary magnitude.

We entered Ulm, as I have already said. It was after nine o'clock, nearly dark, and beginning to rain; we had walked thirty-three miles, and being of course tired, we entered the first inn we saw. But, to our consternation, it was impossible to get a place—the fair had just commenced, and the inn was full to the roof. We must needs hunt another, and then another, and yet another, with like fate at each. It grew quite dark, the rain increased, and we were unacquainted with the city. I grew desperate, and at last, when we had stopped at the eighth inn in vain, I told the people we must have lodgings, for it was impossible we should walk around in the rain all night. Some of the guests interfering in our favor, the hostess finally sent a servant with us to the first hotel in the city. I told him on the way we were Americans, strangers in Ulm, and not accustomed to sleeping in the streets. "Well," said he, "I will go before, and recommend you to the landlord of the Golden Wheel." I knew not what magic he used, but in half an hour our weary limbs were stretched in delightful repose and we thanked Heaven more gratefully than ever before, for the blessing of a good bed.

Next morning we ran about through the booths of the fair, and gazed up from all sides at the vast Cathedral. The style is the simplest and grandest Gothic; but the tower, which, to harmonize, with the body of the church, should be 520 feet high, was left unfinished at the height of 234 feet. I could not enough admire the grandeur of proportion in the great building. It seemed singular that the little race of animals who swarmed around its base, should have the power to conceive or execute such a gigantic work.

There is an immense fortification now in progress of erection behind Ulm. It leans on the side of the hill which rises from the Danube, and must be nearly a mile in length. Hundreds of laborers are at work, and from the appearance of the foundations, many years will be required to finish it. The lofty mountain-plain which we afterwards passed over, for eight or ten miles, divides the waters of the Danube from the Rhine. From the heights above Ulm, we bade adieu to the far, misty Alps, till we shall see them again in Switzerland. Late in the afternoon, we came to a lovely green valley, sunk as it were in the earth. Around us, on all sides, stretched the bare, lofty plains; but the valley lay below, its steep sides covered with the richest forest. At the bottom flowed the Fils. Our road led directly down the side; the glen spread out broader as we advanced, and smiling villages stood beside the stream. A short distance before reaching Esslingen, we came upon the banks of the Neckar, whom we hailed as an old acquaintance, although much smaller here in his mountain home than when he sweeps the walls of Heidelberg.

Delightful Wurtemberg! Shall I ever forget thy lovely green vales, watered by the classic current of the Neckar, or thy lofty hills covered with vineyards and waving forests, and crowned with heavy ruins, that tell many a tale of Barbarossa and Duke Ulric and Goetz with the Iron Hand! No—were even the Suabian hills less beautiful—were the Suabian people less faithful and kind and true, still I would love the land for the great spirits it has produced; still would the birth-place of Frederick Schiller, of Uhland and Hauff, be sacred. I do not wonder Wurtemberg can boast such glorious poets. Its lovely landscapes seem to have been made expressly for the cradle of genius; amid no other scenes could his infant mind catch a more benign inspiration. Even the common people are deeply imbued with a poetic feeling. We saw it in their friendly greetings and open, expressive countenances; it is shown in their love for their beautiful homes and the rapture and reverence with which they speak of their country's bards. No river in the world, equal to the Neckar in size, flows for its whole course through more delightful scenery, or among kinder and happier people.

After leaving Esslingen, we followed its banks for some time, at the foot of an amphitheatre of hills, covered to the very summit, as far as the eye could reach, with vineyards. The morning was cloudy, and white mist-wreaths hung along the sides. We took a road that led over the top of a range, and on arriving at the summit, saw all at once the city of Stuttgard, lying beneath our feet. It lay in a basin encircled by mountains, with a narrow valley opening to the south-east, and running off between the hills to the Neckar. The situation of the city is one of wonderful beauty, and even after seeing Salzburg, I could not but be charmed with it.

We descended the mountain and entered it. I inquired immediately for the monument of Schiller, for there was little else in the city I cared to see. We had become tired of running about cities, hunting this or that old church or palace, which perhaps was nothing when found. Stuttgard has neither galleries, ruins, nor splendid buildings, to interest the traveler; but it has Thorwaldsen's statue of Schiller, calling up at the same time its shame and its glory. For the poet in his youth was obliged to fly from this very same city—from home and friends, to escape the persecution of the government on account of the free sentiments expressed in his early works. We found the statue, without much difficulty. It stands in the Schloss Platz, at the southern end of the city, in an unfavorable situation, surrounded by dark old buildings. It should rather be placed aloft on a mountain summit, in the pure, free air of heaven, braving the storm and the tempest. The figure is fourteen feet high and stands on a pedestal of bronze, with bas reliefs on the four sides. The head, crowned with a laurel wreath, is inclined as if in deep thought, and all the earnest soul is seen in the countenance. Thorwaldsen has copied so truly the expression of poetic reverie, that I waited, half-expecting he would raise his head and look around him.

As we passed out the eastern gate, the workmen were busy near the city, making an embankment for the new railroad to Heilbroun, and we were obliged to wade through half a mile of mud. Finally the road turned to the left over a mountain, and we walked on in the rain, regardless of the touching entreaties of an omnibus-driver, who felt a great concern for our health, especially as he had two empty seats. There is a peculiarly agreeable sensation in walking in a storm, when the winds sweep by and the rain-drops rattle through the trees, and the dark clouds roll past just above one's head. It gives a dash of sublimity to the most common scene. If the rain did not finally soak through the boots, and if one did not lose every romantic feeling in wet garments, I would prefer storm to sunshine, for visiting some kinds of scenery. You remember, we saw the North Coast of Ireland and the Giant's Causeway in stormy weather, at the expense of being completely drenched, it is true; but our recollections of that wild day's journey are as vivid as any event of our lives—and the name of the Giant's Causeway calls up a series of pictures as terribly sublime as any we would wish to behold.

The rain at last did come down a little too hard for comfort, and we were quite willing to take shelter when we reached Ludwigsburg. This is here called a new city, having been laid out with broad streets and spacious squares, about a century ago, and is now about the size of our five-year old city of Milwaukie! It is the chief military station of Wurtemberg, and has a splendid castle and gardens, belonging to the king. A few miles to the eastward is the little village where Schiller was born. It is said the house where his parents lived is still standing.

It was not the weather alone, which prevented our making a pilgrimage to it, nor was it alone a peculiar fondness for rain which induced us to persist in walking in the storm. Our feeble pockets, if they could have raised an audible jingle, would have told another tale. Our scanty allowance was dwindling rapidly away, in spite of a desperate system of economy. We left Ulm with a florin and a half apiece—about sixty cents—to walk to Heidelberg, a distance of 110 miles. It was the evening of the third day, and this was almost exhausted. As soon therefore as the rain slackened a little, we started again, although the roads were very bad. At Betigheim, where we passed the night, the people told us of a much nearer and more beautiful road, passing through the Zabergau, a region fumed for its fertility and pastoral beauty. At the inn we were charged higher than usual for a bed, so that we had but thirteen kreutzers to start with in the morning. Our fare that day was a little bread and water; we walked steadily on, but owing to the wet roads, made only thirty miles.

A more delightful region than the Zabergau I have seldom passed through. The fields were full of rich, heavy grain, and the trees had a luxuriance of foliage that reminded me of the vale of the Jed, in Scotland. Without a single hedge or fence, stood the long sweep of hills, covered with waving fields of grain, except where they were steep and rocky, and the vineyard terraces rose one above another. Sometimes a fine old forest grew along the summit, like a mane waving back from the curved neck of a steed, and white villages lay coiled in the valleys between. A line of blue mountains always closed the vista, on looking down one of these long valleys; occasionally a ruined castle with donjon tower, was seen on a mountain at the side, making the picture complete. As we lay sometimes on the hillside and looked on one of those sweet vales, we were astonished at its Arcadian beauty. The meadows were as smooth as a mirror, and there seemed to be scarcely a grass-blade out of place. The streams wound through ("snaked themselves through," is the German expression,) with a subdued ripple, as if they feared to displace a pebble, and the great ash trees which stood here and there, had lined each of their leaves as carefully with silver and turned them as gracefully to the wind, us if they were making their toilettes for the gala-day of nature.

That evening brought us into the dominions of Baden, within five hours' walk of Heidelberg. At the humblest inn in an humble village, we found a bed which we could barely pay for, leaving a kreutzer or two for breakfast. Soon after starting the next morning, the distant Kaiserstuhl suddenly emerged from the mist, with the high tower on its summit, where nearly ten months before, we sat and looked at the summits of the Vosges in France, with all the excitement one feels on entering a foreign land. Now, the scenery around that same Kaiserstuhl was nearly as familiar to us as that of our own homes. Entering the hills again, we knew by the blue mountains of the Odenwald, that we were approaching the Neckar. At length we reached the last height. The town of Neckargemünd lay before us on the steep hillside, and the mountains on either side were scarred with quarries of the rich red sandstone, so much used in building. The blocks are hewn out, high up on the mountain side, and then sent rolling and sliding down to the river, where they are laden in boats and floated down with the current to the distant cities of the Rhine.

We were rejoiced on turning around the corner of a mountain, to see

528

on the opposite side of the river, the road winding up through the forests, where last fall our Heidelberg friends accompanied us, as we set out to walk to Frankfort, through the Odenwald. Many causes combined to render it a glad scene to us. We were going to meet our comrade again, after a separation of months; we were bringing an eventful journey to its close; and finally, we were weak and worn out from fasting and the labor of walking in the rain. A little further we saw Kloster Neuburg, formerly an old convent, and remembered how we used to look at it every day from the windows of our room on the Neckar; but we shouted aloud, when we saw at last the well-known bridge spanning the river, and the glorious old castle lifting its shattered towers from the side of the mountain above us. I always felt a strong attachment to this matchless ruin, and as I beheld it again, with the warm sunshine falling through each broken arch, the wild ivy draping its desolate chambers, it seemed to smile on me like the face of a friend, and I confessed I had seen many a grander scene, but few that would cling to the memory so familiarly.

While we were in Heidelberg, a student was buried by torch-light. This is done when particular honor is shown to the memory of the departed brother. They assembled at dark in the University Square, each with a blazing pine torch three feet long, and formed into a double line. Between the files walked at short distances an officer, who, with his sword, broad lace collar, and the black and white plumes in his cap, looked like a cavalier of the olden time. Persons with torches walked on each side of the hearse, and the band played a lament so deeply mournful, that the scene, notwithstanding its singularity, was very sad and touching. The thick smoke from the torches filled the air, and a lurid, red light was cast over the hushed crowds in the streets and streamed into the dark alleys. The Hauptstrasse was filled with two lines of flame, as the procession passed down it; when they reached the extremity of the city, the hearse went on, attended with torch-bearers, to the Cemetery, some distance further, and the students turned back, running and whirling their torches in mingled confusion. The music struck up a merry march, and in the smoke and red glare, they looked like a company of mad demons. The presence of death awed them to silence for awhile, but as soon as it had left them, they turned relieved to revel again and thought no more of the lesson. It gave me a painful feeling to see them rushing so wildly and disorderly back. They assembled again in the square, and tossing their torches up into the air cast them blazing into a pile; while the flame and black smoke rose in a column into the air, they sang in solemn chorus, the song "Gaudeamus igitur," with which they close all public assemblies.

I shall neglect telling how we left Heidelberg, and walked along the Bergstrasse again, for the sixth time; how we passed the old Melibochus and through the quiet city of Darmstadt; how we watched the blue summits of the Taunus rising higher and higher over the plain, as a new land rises from the sea, and finally, how we reached at last the old watch-tower and looked down on the valley of the Main, clothed in the bloom and verdure of summer, with the houses and spires of Frankfort in the middle of the well-known panorama. We again took possession of our old rooms, and having to wait for a remittance from America, as well as a more suitable season for visiting Italy, we sat down to a month's rest and study.

CHAPTER XXVIII. — FREIBURG AND THE BLACK FOREST.

Frankfort, July 29, 1845.—It would be ingratitude towards the old city in which I have passed so many pleasant and profitable hours, to leave it, perhaps forever, without a few words of farewell. How often will the old bridge, with its view up the Main, over the houses of Oberrad to the far mountains of the Odenwald, rise freshly and distinctly in memory, when I shall have been long absent from them! How often will I hear in fancy as I now do in reality, the heavy tread of passers-by on the rough pavement below, and the deep bell of the Cathedral, chiming the swift hours, with a hollow tone that seems to warn me, rightly to employ them! Even this old room, with its bare walls, little table and chairs, which I have thought and studied in so long, that it seems difficult to think and study anywhere else, will crowd out of memory images of many a loftier scene. May I but preserve for the future the hope and trust which have cheered and sustained me here, through the sorrow of absence and the anxiety of uncertain toil! It is growing towards midnight and I think of many a night when I sat here at this hour, answering the spirit-greeting which friends sent me at sunset over the sea. All this has now an end. I must begin a new wandering, and perhaps in ten days more I shall have a better place for thought, among the mountain-chambers of the everlasting Alps. I look forward to the journey with romantic, enthusiastic anticipation, for afar in the silvery distance, stand the Coliseum and St. Peter's, Vesuvius and the lovely Naples. Farewell, friends who have so long given us a home!

Aug. 9.—The airy, basket-work tower of the Freiburg Minster rises before me over the black roofs of the houses, and behind stand the gloomy, pine-covered mountains of the Black Forest. Of our walk to Heidelberg over the oft-trodden Bergstrasse, I shall say nothing, nor how we climbed the Kaiserstuhl again, and danced around on the top of the tower for one hour, amid cloud and mist, while there was sunshine below in the valley of the Neckar. I left Heidelberg yesterday morning in the stehwagen for Carlsruhe. The engine whistled, the train started, and although I kept my eyes steadily fixed on the spire of the Hauptkirche, three minutes hid it, and all the rest of the city from sight. Carlsruhe, the capital of Baden, which we reached in an hour and a half, is unanimously pronounced by travelers to be a most dull and tiresome city. From a glance I had through one of the gates, I should think its reputation was not undeserved. Even its name, in German, signifies a place of repose.

I stopped at Kork, on the branch road leading to Strasbourg, to meet a German-American about to return to my home in Pennsylvania, where he had lived for some time. I inquired according to the direction he had sent me to Frankfort, but he was not there; however, an old man, finding who I was, said Herr Otto had directed him to go with me to Hesselhurst, a village four or five miles off, where he would meet me. So we set off immediately over the plain, and reached the village at dusk.

At the little inn, were several of the farmers of the neighborhood, who seemed to consider it as something extraordinary to see a real, live, native-born American. They overwhelmed me with questions about the state of our country, its government, etc. The hostess brought me a supper of fried eggs and wurst, while they gathered around the table and began a real category in the dialect of the country, which is difficult to understand. I gave them the best information I could about our mode of farming, the different kinds of produce raised, and the prices paid to laborers; one honest old man cried out, on my saying I had worked on a farm, "Ah! little brother, give me your hand!" which he shook most heartily. I told them also something about our government, and the militia system, so different from the conscription of Europe, when a farmer becoming quite warm in our favor, said to the others with an air of the greatest decision: "One American is better than twenty Germans!" What particularly amused me, was, that although I spoke German with them, they seemed to think I did not understand what they said among one another, and therefore commented very freely over my appearance. I suppose they had the idea that we were a rude, savage race, for I overheard one say: "One sees, nevertheless, that he has been educated!" Their honest, unsophisticated mode of expression was very interesting to me, and we talked together till a late hour.

My friend arrived at three o'clock the next morning, and after two or three hours' talk about home, and the friends whom he expected to see so much sooner than I, a young farmer drove me in his wagon to Offenburg, a small city at the foot of the Black Forest, where I took the cars for Freiburg. The scenery between the two places is grand. The broad mountains of the Black Forest rear their fronts on the east, and the blue lines of the French Vosges meet the clouds on the west. The night before, in walking over the plain, I saw distinctly the whole of the Strasbourg Minster, whose spire is the highest in Europe, being four hundred and ninety feet, or but twenty-five feet lower than the Pyramid of Cheops.

I visited the Minster of Freiburg yesterday morning. It is a grand, gloomy old pile, dating from the eleventh century—one of the few Gothic churches in Germany that have ever been completed. The tower of beautiful fretwork, rises to the height of three hundred and ninety-five feet, and the body of the church including the choir, is of the same length. The interior is solemn and majestic. Windows stained in colors that burn, let in a "dim, religious light" which accords very well with the dark old pillars and antique shrines. In two of the chapels there are some fine altar-pieces by Holbein and one of his scholars; and a very large crucifix of silver and ebony, which is kept with great care, is said to have been carried with the Crusaders to the Holy Land. This morning was the great market-day, and the peasantry of the Black Forest came down from the mountains to dispose of their produce. The square around the Minster was filled with them, and the singular costume of the women gave the scene quite a strange appearance. Many of them wore bright red head-dresses and shawls, others had high-crowned hats of yellow oil-cloth; the young girls wore their hair in long plaits, reaching nearly to their feet. They brought grain, butter and cheese and a great deal of fine fruit to sell—I bought some of the wild, aromatic plums of the country, at the rate of thirty for a cent.

The railroad has only been open to Freiburg within a few days, and is consequently an object of great curiosity to the peasants, many of whom never saw the like before. They throng around the station at the departure of the train and watch with great interest the operations of getting up the steam and starting. One of the scenes that grated most harshly on my feelings, was seeing yesterday a company of women employed on the unfinished part of the road. They were digging and shoveling away in the rain, nearly up to their knees in mud and clay!

I called at the Institute for the Blind, under the direction of Mr. Müller. He showed me some beautiful basket and woven work by his pupils; the accuracy and skill with which everything was made astonished me. They read with amazing facility from the raised type, and by means of frames are taught to write with ease and distinctness. In music, that great solace of the blind, they most excelled. They sang with an expression so true and touching, that it was a delight to listen. The system of instruction adopted appears to be most excellent, and gives to the blind nearly every advantage which their more fortunate brethren enjoy.

I am indebted to Mr. Müller, to whom I was introduced by an acquaintance with his friend, Dr. Rivinus, of West Chester, Pa., for many kind attentions. He went with us this afternoon to the Jägerhaus, on a mountain near, where we had a very fine view of the city and its great black Minster, with the plain of the Briesgau, broken only by the Kaiserstuhl, a long mountain near the Rhine, whose golden stream glittered in the distance. On climbing the Schlossberg, an eminence near the city, we met the Grand Duchess Stephanie, a natural daughter of Napoleon, as I have heard, and now generally believed to be the mother of Caspar Hauser. Through a work lately published, which has since been suppressed, the whole history has come to light. Caspar Hauser was the lineal descendant of the house of Baden, and heir to the throne. The guilt of his imprisonment and murder rests, therefore, upon the present reigning family.

A chapel on the Schönberg, the mountain opposite, was pointed out as the spot where Louis XV., if I mistake not, usually stood while his army besieged Freiburg. A German officer having sent a ball to this chapel which struck the wall just above the king's head, the latter sent word that if they did not cease firing he would point his cannons at the Minster. The citizens thought it best to spare the monarch and save the cathedral.

We attended a meeting of the Walhalla, or society of the students who visit the Freiburg University. They pleased me better than the enthusiastic but somewhat unrestrained Burschenschaft of Heidelberg. Here, they have abolished duelling; the greatest friendship prevails among the students, and they have not that contempt for every thing philister, or unconnected with their studies, which prevails in other universities. Many respectable citizens attend their meetings; to-night there was a member of the Chamber of Deputies at Carlsruhe present, who delivered two speeches, in which every third word was "freedom!" An address was delivered also by a merchant of the city, in which he made a play upon the word spear, which signifies also in a cant sense, citizen, find seemed to indicate that both would do their work in the good cause. He was loudly applauded. Their song of union was by Charles Follen, and the students were much pleased when I told them how he was honored and esteemed in America.

After two days, delightfully spent, we shouldered our knapsacks and left Freiburg. The beautiful valley, at the mouth of which the city lies, runs like an avenue for seven miles directly into the mountains, and presents in its loveliness such a contrast to the horrid defile which follows, that it almost deserves the name which has been given to a little inn at its head—the "Kingdom of Heaven." The mountains of the Black Forest enclose it on each side like walls, covered to the summit with luxuriant woods, and in some places with those forests of gloomy pine which give this region its name. After traversing its whole length, just before plunging into the mountain-depths, the traveler rarely meets with a finer picture than that which, on looking back, he sees framed between the hills at the other end. Freiburg looks around the foot of one of the heights, with the spire of her cathedral peeping above the top, while the French Vosges grew dim in the far perspective.

The road now enters a wild, narrow valley, which grows smaller as we proceed. From Himmelreich, a large rude inn by the side of the green meadows, we enter the Höllenthal—that is, from the "Kingdom of Heaven" to the "Valley of Hell!" The latter place better deserves its appellation than the former. The road winds between precipices of black rock, above which the thick foliage shuts out the brightness of day and gives a sombre hue to the scene. A torrent foams down the chasm, and in one place two mighty pillars interpose to prevent all passage. The stream, however, has worn its way through, and the road is hewn in the rock by its side. This cleft is the only entrance to a valley three or four miles long, which lies in the very heart of the mountains. It is inhabited by a few woodmen and their families, and but for the road which passes through, would be as perfect a solitude as the Happy Valley of Rasselas. At the farther end, a winding road called "The Ascent," leads up the steep mountain to an elevated region of country, thinly settled and covered with herds of cattle. The cherries which, in the Rhine-plain below, had long gone, were just ripe here. The people spoke a most barbarous dialect; they were social and friendly, for everybody greeted us, and sometimes, as we sat on a bank by the roadside, those who passed by would say "Rest thee!" or "Thrice rest!"

Passing by the Titi Lake, a small body of water which was spread out among the hills like a sheet of ink, so deep was its Stygian hue, we commenced ascending a mountain. The highest peak of the Schwarzwald, the Feldberg, rose not far off, and on arriving at the top of this mountain, we saw that a half hour's walk would bring us to its summit. This was too great a temptation for my love of climbing heights; so with a look at the descending sun to calculate how much time we could spare, we set out. There was no path, but we pressed directly up the steep side, through bushes and long grass, and in a short time reached the top, breathless from such exertion in the thin atmosphere. The pine woods shut out the view to the north and east, which is said to be magnificent, as the mountain is about five thousand feet high. The wild, black peaks of the Black Forest were spread below us, and the sun sank through golden mist towards the Alsatian hills. Afar to the south, through cloud and storm, we could just trace the white outline of the Swiss Alps. The wind swept through the pines around, and bent the long yellow grass among which we sat, with a strange, mournful sound, well suiting the gloomy and mysterious region. It soon grew cold, the golden clouds settled down towards us, and we made haste to descend to the village of Lenzkirch before dark.

Next morning we set out early, without waiting to see the trial of archery which was to take place among the mountain youths. Their booths and targets, gay with banners, stood on a green meadow beside the town. We

536

walked through the Black Forest the whole forenoon. It might be owing to the many wild stories whose scenes are laid among these hills, but with me there was a peculiar feeling of solemnity pervading the whole region. The great pine woods are of the very darkest hue of green, and down their hoary, moss-floored aisles, daylight seems never to have shone. The air was pure and clear, and the sunshine bright, but it imparted no gaiety to the scenery: except the little meadows of living emerald which lay occasionally in the lap of a dell, the landscape wore a solemn and serious air. In a storm, it must be sublime.

About noon, from the top of the last range of hills, we had a glorious view. The line of the distant Alps could be faintly traced high in the clouds, and all the heights between were plainly visible, from the Lake of Constance to the misty Jura, which flanked the Vosges of the west. From our lofty station we overlooked half Switzerland, and had the air been a little clearer, we could have seen Mont Blanc and the mountains of Savoy. I could not help envying the feelings of the Swiss, who, after long absence from their native land, first see the Alps from this road. If to the emotions with which I then looked on them were added the passionate love of home and country which a long absence creates, such excess of rapture would be almost too great to be borne.

In the afternoon we crossed the border, and took leave of Germany with regret, after near a year's residence within its bounds. Still it was pleasant to know we were in a republic once more: the first step we took made us aware of the change. There was no policeman to call for our passports or search our baggage. It was just dark when we reached the hill overlooking the Rhine, on whose steep banks is perched the antique town of Schaffhausen. It is still walled in, with towers at regular intervals; the streets are wide and spacious, and the houses rendered extremely picturesque by the quaint projecting windows. The buildings are nearly all old, as we learned by the dates above the doors. At the inn, I met with one of the free troopers who marched against Luzerne. He was full of spirit, and ready to undertake another such journey. Indeed it is the universal opinion that the present condition of things cannot last much longer.

We took a walk before breakfast to the Falls of the Rhine, about a mile and a half from Schaffhausen. I confess I was somewhat disappointed in them, after the glowing descriptions of travelers. The river at this place is little more than thirty yards wide, and the body of water, although issuing from the Lake of Constance, is not remarkably strong. For some distance above, the fall of the water is very rapid, and as it finally reaches the spot where, narrowed between rocks, it makes the grand plunge, it has acquired a great velocity. Three rocks stand in the middle of the current, which thunders against and around their bases, but cannot shake them down. These and the rocks in the bed of the stream, break the force of the fall, so that it descends to the bottom, about fifty feet below, not in one sheet, but shivered into a hundred leaps of snowy foam. The precipitous shores, and the tasteful little castle which is perched upon the steep just over the boiling spray, add much to its beauty, taken as a picture. As a specimen of the picturesque, the whole scene is perfect. I should think Trenton Falls, in New York, must excel these in wild, startling effect; but there is such a scarcity of waterfalls in this land, that the Germans go into raptures about them, and will hardly believe that Niagara itself possesses more sublimity.

CHAPTER XXIX. — PEOPLE AND PLACES IN EASTERN SWITZERLAND.

We left Schaffhausen for Zurich, in mist and rain, and walked for some time along the north bank of the Rhine. We could have enjoyed the scenery much better, had it not been for the rain, which not only hid the mountains from sight, but kept us constantly half soaked. We crossed the rapid Rhine at Eglisau, a curious antique village, and then continued our way through the forests of Canton Zurich, to Bülach, with its groves of lindens—"those tall and stately trees, with velvet down upon their shining leaves, and rustic benches placed beneath their overhanging eaves."

When we left the little village where the rain obliged us to stop for the night, it was clear and delightful. The farmers were out, busy at work, their long, straight scythes glancing through the wet grass, while the thick pines sparkled with thousands of dewy diamonds. The country was so beautiful and cheerful, that we half felt like being in America. The farm-houses were scattered over the country in real American style, and the glorious valley of the Limmat, bordered on the west by a range of woody hills, reminded me of some scenes in my native Pennsylvania. The houses were neatly and tastefully built, with little gardens around them—and the countenances of the people spoke of intelligence and independence. There was the same air of peace and prosperity which delighted us in the valleys of Upper Austria, with a look of freedom which those had not. The faces of a people are the best index to their condition. I could read on their brows a lofty self-respect, a consciousness of the liberties they enjoy, which the Germans of the laboring class never show. It could not be imagination, for the recent occurrences in Switzerland, with the many statements I heard in Germany, had prejudiced me somewhat against the land; and these marks of prosperity and freedom were as surprising as they were delightful.

As we approached Zurich, the noise of employment from mills, furnaces and factories, came to us like familiar sounds, reminding us of the bustle of our home cities. The situation of the city is lovely. It lies at the head of the lake, and on both sides of the little river Limmat, whose clear green waters carry the collected meltings of the Alps to the Rhine. Around the lake rise lofty green hills, which, sloping gently back, bear on their sides hundreds of pleasant country-houses and farms, and the snowy Alpine range extends along the southern sky. The Limmat is spanned by a number of bridges, and its swift waters turn many mills which are built above them. From these bridges one can look out over the blue lake and down the thronged streets of the city on each side, whose bright, cheerful houses remind him of Italy.

Zurich can boast of finer promenades than any other city in Switzerland. The old battlements are planted with trees and transformed into pleasant walks, which being elevated above the city, command views of its beautiful environs. A favorite place of resort is the Lindenhof, an elevated court-yard, shaded by immense trees. The fountains of water under them are always surrounded by washerwomen, and in the morning groups of merry school children may be seen tumbling over the grass. The teachers take them there in a body for exercise and recreation. The Swiss children are beautiful, bright-eyed creatures; there is scarcely one who does not exhibit the dawning of an active, energetic spirit. It may be partly attributed to the fresh, healthy climate of Switzerland, but I am partial enough to republics to believe that the influence of the Government under which they live, has also its share in producing the effect.

There is a handsome promenade on an elevated bastion which overlooks the city and lakes. While enjoying the cool morning breeze and listening to the stir of the streets below us, we were also made aware of the social and friendly politeness of the people. Those who passed by, on their walk around the rampart, greeted us, almost with the familiarity of an acquaintance. Simple as was the act, we felt grateful, for it had at least the seeming of a friendly interest and a sympathy with the loneliness which the stranger sometimes feels. A school-teacher leading her troop of merry children on their morning walk around the bastion, nodded to us pleasantly and forthwith the whole company of chubby-cheeked rogues, looking up at us with a pleasant archness, lisped a "guten morgen" that made the hearts glad within us. I know of nothing that has given me a more sweet and tender delight than the greeting of a little child, who, leaving his noisy playmates, ran across the street to me, and taking my hand, which he could barely clasp in both his soft little ones, looked up in my face with an expression so winning and affectionate, that I loved him at once. The happy, honest farmers, too, spoke to us cheerfully everywhere. We learned a lesson from all this—we felt that not a word of kindness is ever wasted, that a simple friendly glance may cheer the spirit and warm the lonely heart, and that the slightest deed, prompted by generous sympathy, becomes a living joy in the memory of the receiver, which blesses unceasingly him who bestowed it.

We left Zurich the same afternoon, to walk to Stafa, where we were told the poet Freiligrath resided. The road led along the bank of the lake, whose shores sloped gently up from the water, covered with gardens and farm-houses, which, with the bolder mountains that rose behind them, made a combination of the lovely and grand, on which the eye rested with rapture and delight. The sweetest cottages were embowered among the orchards, and the whole country bloomed like a garden. The waters of the lake are of a pale, transparent green, and so clear that we could see its bottom of white pebbles, for some distance. Here and there floated a quiet boat on its surface. The opposite hills were covered with a soft blue haze, and white villages sat along the shore, "like swans among the reeds." Behind, we saw the woody range of the Brunig Alp. The people bade us a pleasant good evening; there was a universal air of cheerfulness and content on their countenances.

Towards evening, the clouds which hung in the south the whole day, dispersed a little and we could see the Dodiberg and the Alps of Glarus. As sunset drew on, the broad summits of snow and the clouds which were rolled around them, assumed a soft rosy hue, which increased in brilliancy as the light of day faded. The rough, icy crags and snowy steeps were fused in the warm light and half blended with the bright clouds. This blaze, as it were, of the mountains at sunset, is called the Alp-glow, and exceeds all one's highest conceptions of Alpine grandeur. We watched the fading glory till it quite died away, and the summits wore a livid, ashy hue, like the mountains of a world wherein there was no life. In a few minutes more the dusk of twilight spread over the scene, the boatmen glided home over the still lake and the herdsmen drove their cattle back from pasture on the slopes and meadows.

On inquiring for Freiligrath at Stafa, we found he had removed to Rapperschwyl, some distance further. As it was already late, we waited for the steamboat which leaves Zurich every evening. It came along about eight o'clock, and a little boat carried us out through rain and darkness to meet it, as it came like a fiery-eyed monster over the water. We stepped on board the "Republican," and in half an hour were brought to the wharf at Rapperschwyl.

There are two small islands in the lake, one of which, with a little chapel rising from among its green trees, is Ufnau, the grave of Ulrich von Hutten, one of the fathers of the German Reformation. His fiery poems have been the source from which many a German bard has derived his inspiration, and Freiligrath who now lives in sight of his tomb, has published an indignant poem, because an inn with gaming tables has been established in the ruins of the castle near Creuznach, where Hutten found refuge from his enemies with Franz von Sickingen, brother-in-law of "Goetz with the iron Hand." The monks of Einsiedeln, to whom Ufnau belongs, have carefully obliterated all traces of his grave, so that the exact spot is not known, in order that even a tombstone might be denied him who once strove to overturn their order. It matters little to that bold spirit whose motto was: "The die is cast—I have dared it!"—the whole island is his monument, if he need one.

I spent the whole of the morning with Freiligrath, the poet, who was lately banished from Germany on account of the liberal principles his last volume contains. He lives in a pleasant country-house on the Meyerberg, an eminence near Rapperschwyl, overlooking a glorious prospect. On leaving Frankfort, R.S. Willis gave me a letter to him, and I was glad to meet with a man personally whom I admired so much through his writings, and whose boldness in speaking out against the tyranny which his country suffers, forms such a noble contrast to the cautious slowness of his countrymen. He received me kindly and conversed much upon American literature. He is a warm admirer of Bryant and Longfellow, and has translated many of their poems into German. He said he had received a warm invitation from a colony of Germans in Wisconsin, to join them and enjoy that freedom which his native land denies, but that his circumstances would not allow it at present. He is perhaps thirty-five years of age. His brow is high and noble, and his eyes, which are large and of a clear gray, beam with serious, saddened thought. His long chestnut hair, uniting with a handsome beard and moustache, gives a lion-like dignity to his energetic countenance. His talented wife, Ida Freiligrath, who shares his literary labors, and an amiable sister, are with him in exile, and he is happier in their faithfulness than when he enjoyed the favors of a corrupt king.

We crossed the long bridge from Rapperschwyl, and took the road over the mountain opposite, ascending for nearly two hours along the side, with glorious views of the Lake of Zurich and the mountains which enclose it. The upper and lower ends of the lake were completely hid by the storms, which, to our regret, veiled the Alps, but the part below lay spread out dim and grand, like a vast picture. It rained almost constantly, and we were obliged occasionally to take shelter in the pine forests, whenever a heavier cloud passed over. The road was lined with beggars, who dropped on their knees in the rain before us, or placed bars across the way, and then took them down again, for which they demanded money.

At length we reached the top of the pass. Many pilgrims to Einsiedeln had stopped at a little inn there, some of whom came a long distance to pay their vows, especially as the next day was the Ascension day of the Virgin, whose image there is noted for performing many miracles. Passing on, we crossed a wild torrent by an arch called the "Devil's Bridge." The lofty, elevated plains were covered with scanty patches of grain and potatoes, and the boys tended their goats on the grassy slopes, sometimes trilling or yodling an Alpine melody. An hour's walk brought us to Einsiedeln, a small town, whose only attraction is the Abbey—after Loretto, in Italy, the most celebrated resort for pilgrims in Europe.

We entered immediately into the great church. The gorgeous vaulted roof and long aisles were dim with the early evening; hundreds of worshippers sat around the sides, or kneeled in groups on the broad stone pavements, chanting over their Paternosters and Ave Marias in a shrill, monotonous tone, while the holy image near the entrance was surrounded by persons, many of whom came in the hope of being healed of some disorder under which

543

they suffered. I could not distinctly make out the image, for it was placed back within the grating, and a strong crimson lamp behind it was made to throw the light around, in the form of a glory. Many of the pilgrims came a long distance. I saw some in the costume of the Black Forest, and others who appeared to be natives of the Italian Cantons; and a group of young women wearing conical fur caps, from the forests of Bregenz, on the Lake of Constance.

I was astonished at the splendor of this church, situated in a lonely and unproductive Alpine valley. The lofty arches of the ceiling, which are covered with superb fresco paintings, rest on enormous pillars of granite, and every image and shrine is richly ornamented with gold. Some of the chapels were filled with the remains of martyrs, and these were always surrounded with throngs of believers. The choir was closed by a tall iron grating; a single lamp, which swung from the roof, enabled me to see through the darkness, that though much more rich in ornaments than the body of the church, it was less grand and impressive. The frescoes which cover the ceiling, are said to be the finest paintings of the kind in Switzerland.

In the morning our starting was delayed by the rain, and we took advantage of it to hear mass in the Abbey and enjoy the heavenly music. The latter was of the loftiest kind; there was one voice among the singers I shall not soon forget. It was like the warble of a bird who sings out of very wantonness. On and on it sounded, making its clear, radiant sweetness heard above the chant of the choir and the thunder of the orchestra. Such a rich, varied and untiring strain of melody I have rarely listened to.

When the service ceased, we took a small road leading to Schwytz. We had now fairly entered the Alpine region, and our first task was to cross a mountain. This having been done, we kept along the back of the ridge which bounds the lake of Zug on the south, terminating in the well known Rossberg. The scenery became wilder with every step. The luxuriant fields of herbage on the mountains were spotted with the picturesque chalets of the hunters and Alp-herds; cattle and goats were browsing along the declivities, their bells tinkling most musically, and the little streams fell in foam down the steeps. We here began to realize our anticipations of Swiss scenery. Just on the other side of the range, along which we traveled, lay the little lake of Egeri and valley of Morgarten, where Tell and his followers overcame the army of the German Emperor; near the lake of Lowertz, we found a chapel by the roadside, built on the spot where the house of Werner Stauffacher, one of the "three men of Grütli," formerly stood. It bears a poetical inscription in old German, and a rude painting of the Battle of Morgarten.

As we wound around the lake of Lowertz, we saw the valley lying between the Rossberg and the Righi, which latter mountain stood full in view. To our regret, and that of all other travelers, the clouds hung low upon it, as they had done for a week at least, and there was no prospect of a change. The Rossberg, from which we descended, is about four thousand feet in height; a dark brown stripe from its very summit to the valley below, shows the track of the avalanche which, in 1806, overwhelmed Goldau, and laid waste the beautiful vale of Lowertz. We could trace the masses of rock and earth as far as the foot of the Righi. Four hundred and fifty persons perished by this catastrophe, which was so sudden that in five minutes the whole lovely valley was transformed into a desolate wilderness. The shock was so great that the lake of Lowertz overflowed its banks, and part of the village of Steinen at the upper end was destroyed by the waters.

An hour's walk through a blooming Alpine vale brought us to the little town of Schwytz, the capital of the Canton. It stands at the foot of a rock-mountain, in shape not unlike Gibraltar, but double its height. The bare and rugged summits seem to hang directly over the town, but the people dwell below without fear, although the warning ruins of Goldau are full in sight. A narrow blue line at the end of the valley which stretches westward, marks the lake of the Four Cantons. Down this valley we hurried, that we might not miss the boat which plies daily, from Luzerne to Fluelen. I regretted not being able to visit Luzerne, as I had a letter to the distinguished Swiss composer, Schnyder von Wartensee, who resides there at present. The place is said to present a most desolate appearance, being avoided by travelers, and even by artisans, so that business of all kinds has almost entirely ceased.

At the little town of Brunnen, on the lake, we awaited the coming of the steamboat. The scenery around it is exceedingly grand. Looking down towards Luzerne, we could see the dark mass of Mount Pilatus on one side, and on the other the graceful outline of the Righi, still wearing his hood of clouds. We put off in a skiff to meet the boat, with two Capuchin friars in long brown mantles and cowls, carrying rosaries at their girdles.

Nearly opposite Brunnen is the meadow of Grütli, where the union of the Swiss patriots took place, and the bond was sealed that enabled them to cast off their chains. It is a little green slope on the side of the mountain, between the two Cantons of Uri and Unterwalden, surrounded on all sides by precipices. A little crystal spring in the centre is believed by the common people to have gushed up on the spot where the three "linked the hands that made them free." It is also a popular belief that they slumber in a rocky cavern near the spot, and that they will arise and come forth when the liberties of Switzerland are in danger. She stands at present greatly in need of a new triad to restore the ancient harmony.

We passed this glorious scene, almost the only green spot on the bleak mountain-side, and swept around the base of the Axenberg, at whose foot, in a rocky cave, stands the chapel of William Tell. This is built on the spot where he leaped from Gessler's boat during the storm. It sits at the base of the rock, on the water's edge, and can be seen far over the waves. The Alps, whose eternal snows are lifted dazzling to the sky, complete the grandeur of a scene so hallowed by the footsteps of freedom. The grand and lonely solemnity of the landscape impressed me with an awe, like that one feels when standing in a mighty cathedral, when the aisles are dim with twilight. And how full of interest to a citizen of young and free America is a shrine where the votaries of Liberty have turned to gather strength and courage, through the storms and convulsions of five hundred years!

We stopped at the village of Fluelen, at the head of the lake, and walked on to Altorf, a distance of half a league. Here, in the market-place, is a tower said to be built on the spot where the linden tree stood, under which the child of Tell was placed, while, about a hundred yards distant, is a fountain with Tell's statue, on the spot from whence he shot the apple. If these localities are correct, he must indeed have been master of the cross-bow. The tower is covered with rude paintings of the principal events in the history of Swiss liberty. I viewed these scenes with double interest from having read Schiller's "Wilhelm Tell," one of the most splendid tragedies ever written. The beautiful reply of his boy, when he described to him the condition of the "land where there are no mountains," was sounding in my ears during the whole day's journey:

> *"Father, I'd feel oppressed in that broad land,*
>
> *I'd rather dwell beneath the avalanche!"*

The little village of Burglen, whose spire we saw above the forest, in a glen near by, was the birth-place of Tell, and the place where his dwelling stood, is now marked by a small chapel. In the Schachen, a noisy mountain stream that comes down to join the Reuss, he was drowned, when an old man, in attempting to rescue a child who had fallen in—a death worthy of the hero! We bestowed a blessing on his memory in passing, and then followed the banks of the rapid Reuss. Twilight was gathering in the deep Alpine glen, and the mountains on each side, half-seen through the mist, looked like vast, awful phantoms. Soon they darkened to black, indistinct masses; all was silent except the deepened roar of the falling floods; dark clouds brooded above us like the outspread wings of night, and we were glad, when the little village of Amstegg was reached, and the parlor of the inn opened to us a more cheerful, if not so romantic scene.

CHAPTER XXX. – PASSAGE OF THE ST. GOTHARD AND DESCENT INTO ITALY.

Leaving Amstegg, I passed the whole day among snowy, sky-piercing Alps, torrents, chasms and clouds! The clouds appeared to be breaking up as we set out, and the white top of the Reassberg was now and then visible in the sky. Just above the village are the remains of Zwing Uri, the castle begun by the tyrant Gessler, for the complete subjugation of the canton. Following the Reuss up through a narrow valley, we passed the Bristenstock, which lifts its jagged crags nine thousand feet in the air, while on the other side stand the snowy summits which lean towards the Rhone Glacier and St. Gothard. From the deep glen where the Reuss foamed down towards the Lake of the Forest Cantons, the mountains rose with a majestic sweep so far into the sky that the brain grew almost dizzy in following their outlines. Woods, chalets and slopes of herbage covered their bases, where the mountain cattle and goats were browsing, while the herd-boys sang their native melodies or woke the ringing echoes with the loud, sweet sounds of their wooden horns; higher up, the sides were broken into crags and covered with stunted pines; then succeeded a belt of bare rock with a little snow lying in the crevices, and the summits of dazzling white looked out from the clouds nearly three-fourths the height of the zenith. Sometimes when the vale was filled with clouds, it was startling to see them parting around a solitary summit, apparently isolated in the air at an immense height, for the mountain to which it belonged was hidden to the very base!

The road passed from one side of the valley to the other, crossing the Reuss on bridges sometimes ninety feet high. After three or four hours walking, we reached a frightful pass called the Schollenen. So narrow is the defile that before reaching it, the road seemed to enter directly into the mountain. Precipices a thousand feet high tower above, and the stream roars and boils in the black depth below. The road is a wonder of art; it winds around the edge of horrible chasms or is carried on lofty arches across, with sometimes a hold apparently so frail that one involuntarily shudders. At a place called the Devil's Bridge, the Reuss leaps about seventy feet in three or four cascades, sending up continually a cloud of spray, while a wind created by the fall, blows and whirls around, with a force that nearly lifts one from his feet. Wordsworth has described the scene in the following lines:

"Plunge with the Reuss embrowned by terror's breath,

Where danger roofs the narrow walks of Death;

By floods that, thundering from their dizzy height,

Swell more gigantic on the steadfast sight,

Black, drizzling crags, that, beaten by the din,

Vibrate, us if a voice complained within,

Loose hanging rocks, the Day's blessed eye that hide,

And crosses reared to Death on every side!"

Beyond the Devil's Bridge, the mountains which nearly touched before, interlock into each other, and a tunnel three hundred and seventy-five feet long leads through the rock into the vale of Urseren, surrounded by the Upper Alps. The little town of Andermatt lies in the middle of this valley, which with the peaks around is covered with short, yellowish-brown grass. We met near Amstegg a little Italian boy walking home, from Germany, quite alone and without money, for we saw him give his last kreutzer to a blind beggar along the road. We therefore took him with us, as he was afraid to cross the St. Gothard alone.

After refreshing ourselves at Andermatt, we started, five in number, including a German student, for the St. Gothard. Behind the village of Hospiz, which stands at the bottom of the valley leading to Realp and the Furca pass, the way commences, winding backwards and forwards, higher and higher, through a valley covered with rocks, with the mighty summits of the Alps around, untenanted save by the chamois and mountain eagle. Not a tree was to be seen. The sides of the mountains were covered with loose rocks waiting for the next torrent to wash them down, and the tops were robed in

549

eternal snow. A thick cloud rolled down over us as we went on, following the diminishing brooks to their snowy source in the peak of St. Gothard. We cut off the bends of the road by footpaths up the rocks, which we ascended in single file, one of the Americans going ahead and little Pietro with his staff and bundle bringing up the rear. The rarefied air we breathed, seven thousand feet above the sea, was like exhilarating gas. We felt no fatigue, but ran and shouted and threw snowballs, in the middle of August!

After three hours' walk we reached the two clear and silent lakes which send their waters to the Adriatic and the North Sea. Here, as we looked down the Italian side, the sky became clear; we saw the top of St. Gothard many thousand feet above, and stretching to the south, the summits of the mountains which guard the vales of the Ticino and the Adda. The former monastery has been turned into an inn; there is, however, a kind of church attached, attended by a single monk. It was so cold that although late, we determined to descend to the first village. The Italian side is very steep, and the road, called the Via Trimola, is like a thread dropped down and constantly doubling back upon itself. The deep chasms were filled with snow, although exposed to the full force of the sun, and for a long distance there was scarcely a sign of vegetation.

We thought as we went down, that every step was bringing us nearer to a sunnier land—that the glories of Italy, which had so long lain in the airy background of the future, would soon spread themselves before us in their real or imagined beauty. Reaching at dusk the last height above the vale of the Ticino, we saw the little village of Airolo with its musical name, lying in a hollow of the mountains. A few minutes of leaping, sliding and rolling, took us down the grassy declivity, and we found we had descended from the top in an hour and a half, although the distance by the road is nine miles! I need not say how glad we were to relieve our trembling knees and exhausted limbs.

I have endeavored several times to give some idea of the sublimity of the Alps, but words seem almost powerless to measure these mighty mountains. No effort of the imagination could possibly equal their real grandeur. I wish also to describe the feelings inspired by being among them,—feelings which can best be expressed through the warmer medium of poetry.

SONG OF THE ALP.

I. — I sit aloft on my thunder throne,

And my voice of dread the nations own

As I speak in storm below!

The valleys quake with a breathless fear,

When I hurl in wrath my icy spear

And shake my locks of snow!

When the avalanche forth like a tiger leaps,

How the vassal-mountains quiver!

And the storm that sweeps through the airy deeps

Makes the hoary pine-wood shiver!

Above them all, in a brighter air,

I lift my forehead proud and bare,

And the lengthened sweep of my forest-robe

Trails down to the low and captured globe,

Till its borders touch the dark green wave

In whose soundless depths my feet I lave.

The winds, unprisoned, around me blow,

And terrible tempests whirl the snow;

Rocks from their caverned beds are torn,

And the blasted forest to heaven is borne;

High through the din of the stormy band,

Like misty giants the mountains stand,

And their thunder-revel o'er-sounds the woe,

That cries from the desolate vales below!

I part the clouds with my lifted crown,

Till the sun-ray slants on the glaciers down,

And trembling men, in the valleys pale,

Rejoice at the gleam of my icy mail!

II. —   I wear a crown of the sunbeam's gold,

With glacier-gems en my forehead old—

A monarch crowned by God!

What son of the servile earth may dare

Such signs of a regal power to wear,

While chained to her darkened sod?

I know of a nobler and grander lore

Than Time records on his crumbling pages,

And the soul of my solitude teaches more

Than the gathered deeds of perished ages!

For I have ruled since Time began

And wear no fetter made by man.

I scorn the coward and craven race

Who dwell around my mighty base,

For they leave the lessons I grandly gave

And bend to the yoke of the crouching slave.

I shout aloud to the chainless skies;

The stream through its falling foam replies,

And my voice, like the sound of the surging sea,

To the nations thunders: "I am free!"

I spoke to Tell when a tyrant's hand

Lay heavy and hard on his native land,

And the spirit whose glory from mine he won

Blessed the Alpine dwellers with Freedom's sun!

The student-boy on the Gmunden-plain

Heard my solemn voice, but he fought in vain;

I called from the crags of the Passeir-glen,

When the despot stood in my realm again,

And Hofer sprang at the proud command

And roused the men of the Tyrol land!

III. —   I struggle up to the dim blue heaven,

From the world, far down in whose breast are driven

The props of my pillared throne;

And the rosy fires of morning glow

Like a glorious thought, on my brow of snow,

While the vales are dark and lone!

Ere twilight summons the first faint star,

I seem to the nations who dwell afar

Like a shadowy cloud, whose every fold

The sunset dyes with its purest gold,

And the soul mounts up through that gateway fair

To try its wings in a loftier air!

The finger of God on my brow is pressed—

His spirit beats in my giant breast,

And I breathe, as the endless ages roll,

His silent words to the eager soul!

I prompt the thoughts of the mighty mind,

Who leaves his century far behind

And speaks from the Future's sun-lit snow

To the Present, that sleeps in its gloom below!

I stand, unchanged, in creation's youth—

A glorious type of Eternal Truth,

That, free and pure, from its native skies

Shines through Oppression's veil of lies,

And lights the world's long-fettered sod

With thoughts of Freedom and of God!

When, at night, I looked out of my chamber-window, the silver moon of Italy, (for we fancied that her light was softer and that the skies were already bluer) hung trembling above the fields of snow that stretched in their wintry brilliance along the mountains around. I heard the roar of the Ticino and the deepened sound of falling cascades, and thought, if I were to take those waters for my guide, to what glorious places they would lead me!

We left Airolo early the next morning, to continue our journey down the valley of the Ticino. The mists and clouds of Switzerland were exchanged for a sky of the purest blue, and we felt, for the first time in ten days, uncomfortably warm. The mountains which flank the Alps on this side, are still giants—lofty

554

and bare, and covered with snow in many places. The limit of the German dialect is on the summit of St. Gothard, and the peasants saluted us with a "buon giorno" as they passed. This, with the clearness of the skies and the warmth of the air, made us feel that Italy was growing nearer.

The mountains are covered with forests of dark pine, and many beautiful cascades come tumbling over the rocks in their haste to join the Ticino. One of these was so strangely beautiful, that I cannot pass it without a particular description. We saw it soon after leaving Airolo, on the opposite side of the valley. A stream of considerable size comes down the mountain, leaping from crag to crag till within forty or fifty feet of the bottom, where it is caught in a hollow rock, and flung upwards into the air, forming a beautiful arch as it falls out into the valley. As it is whirled up thus, feathery curls of spray are constantly driven off and seem to wave round it like the fibres on an ostrich plume. The sun shining through, gave it a sparry brilliance which was perfectly magnificent. If I were an artist, I would give much for such a new form of beauty.

On our first day's journey we passed through two terrific mountain gorges, almost equalling in grandeur the defile of the "Devil's Bridge." The Ticino, in its course to Lago Maggiore has to make a descent of nearly three thousand feet, passing through three valleys, which lie like terraces, one below the other. In its course from one to the other, it has to force its way down in twenty cataracts through a cleft in the mountains. The road, constructed with the utmost labor, threads these dark chasms, sometimes carried in a tunnel through the rock, sometimes passing on arches above the boiling flood. The precipices of bare rock rise far above and render the way difficult and dangerous. I here noticed another very beautiful effect of the water, perhaps attributable to some mineral substance it contained. The spray and foam thrown up in the dashing of the vexed current, was of a light, delicate pink, although the stream itself was a soft blue; and the contrast of these two colors was very remarkable.

As we kept on, however, there was a very perceptible change in the scenery. The gloomy pines disappeared and the mountains were covered, in their stead, with picturesque chestnut trees, with leaves of a shining green. The grass and vegetation was much more luxuriant than on the other side of the Alps, and fields of maize and mulberry orchards covered the valley. We saw the people busy at work reeling silk in the villages. Every mile we advanced made a sensible change in the vegetation. The chesnuts were larger, the maize higher, the few straggling grape-vines increased into bowers and vineyards, while the gardens were filled with plum, pear and fig-trees, and the stands of delicious fruit which we saw in the villages, gave us promise of the luxuriance that was to come.

The vineyards are much more beautiful than the German fields of stakes. The vines are not trimmed, but grow from year to year over a frame higher than the head, supported through the whole field on stone pillars. They interlace and form a complete leafy screen, while the clusters hang below. The light came dimly through the green, transparent leaves, and nothing was wanting to make them real bowers of Arcadia. Although we were still in Switzerland, the people began to have that lazy, indolent look which characterizes the Italians; most of the occupations were carried on in the open air, and brown-robed, sandalled friars were going about from house to house, collecting money and provisions for their support.

We passed Faidò and Giornico, near which last village are the remains of an old castle, supposed to have been built by the ancient Gauls, and stopped for the night at Cresciano, which being entirely Italian, we had an opportunity to put in practice the few words we had picked up from Pietro. The little fellow parted from us with regret a few hours before, at Biasco, where he had relations. The rustic landlord at Cresciano was an honest young fellow, who tried to serve us as well as he could, but we made some ludicrous mistakes through our ignorance of the language.

Three hours' walk brought us to Bellinzona, the capital of the canton. Before reaching it, our road joined that of the Splügen which comes down through the valley of Bernardino. From the bridge where the junction takes place we had a triple view, whose grandeur took me by surprise, even after coming from Switzerland. We stood at the union of three valleys—that leading to St. Gothard, terminated by the glaciers of the Bernese Oberland, that running off obliquely to the Splügen, and finally the broad vale of the

Ticino, extending to Lago Maggiore, whose purple mountains closed the vista. Each valley was perhaps two miles broad and from twenty to thirty long, and the mountains that enclosed them from five to seven thousand feet in height, so you may perhaps form some idea what a view down three such avenues in this Alpine temple would be. Bellinzona is romantically situated, on a slight eminence, with three castles to defend it, with those square turreted towers and battlements, which remind one involuntarily of the days of the Goths and Vandals.

We left Bellinzona at noon, and saw, soon after, from an eminence, the blue line of Lago Maggiore stretched across the bottom of the valley. We saw sunset fade away over the lake, but it was clouded, and did not realize my ideal of such a scene in Italy. A band of wild Italians paraded up and down the village, drawing one of their number in a hand-cart. They made a great noise with a drum and trumpet, and were received everywhere with shouts of laughter. A great jug of wine was not wanting, and the whole seemed to me a very characteristic scene.

We were early awakened at Magadino, at the head of Lago Maggiore, and after swallowing a hasty breakfast, went on board the steamboat "San Carlo," for Sesto Calende. We got under way at six o'clock, and were soon in motion over the crystal mirror. The water is of the most lovely green hue, and so transparent that we seemed to bo floating in mid-air. Another heaven arched far below us; other chains of mountains joined their bases to those which surrounded the lake, and the mirrored cascades leaped upward to meet their originals at the surface. It may be because I have seen it more recently, that the water of Lago Maggiore appears to be the most beautiful in the world. I was delighted with the Scotch lakes, and enraptured with the Traunsee and "Zurich's waters," but this last exceeds them both. I am now incapable of any stronger feeling, until I see the Egean from the Grecian Isles.

The morning was cloudy, and the white wreaths hung low on the mountains, whose rocky sides were covered every where with the rank and luxuriant growth of this climate. As we advanced further over this glorious mirror, the houses became more Italian-like; the lower stories rested on arched passages, and the windows were open, without glass, while in the gardens stood the solemn, graceful cypress, and vines, heavy with ripening grapes, hung from bough to bough through the mulberry orchards. Half-way down, in a broad bay, which receives the waters of a stream that comes down with the Simplon, are the celebrated Borromean Islands. They are four in number, and seem to float like fairy creations on the water, while the lofty hills form a background whose grandeur enhances by contrast their exquisite beauty. There was something in the scene that reminded me of Claude Melnotte's description of his home, by Bulwer, and like the lady of Lyons, I answer readily, "I like the picture."

On passing by Isola Madre, we could see the roses in its terraced gardens and the broad-leaved aloes clinging to the rocks. Isola Bella, the loveliest of them all, as its name denotes, was farther off; it rose like a pyramid from the water, terrace above terrace to the summit, and its gardens of never fading foliage, with the glorious panorama around, might make it a paradise, if life were to be dreamed away. On the northern side of the bay lies a large town (I forget its name,) with a lofty Romanesque tower, and noble mountains sweep around as if to shut out the world from such a scene. The sea was perfectly calm, and groves and gardens slept mirrored in the dark green wave, while the Alps rose afar through the dim, cloudy air. Towards the other end the hills sink lower, and slope off into the plains of Lombardy. Near Arona, on the western side, is a large monastery, overlooking the lower part of the lake. Beside it, on a hill, is a colossal statue of San Carlo Borromeo, who gave his name to the lovely islands above.

After a seven hours' passage, we ran into Sesto Calende, at the foot of the lake. Here, passengers and baggage were tumbled promiscuously on shore, the latter gathered into the office to be examined, and the former left at liberty to ramble about an hour until their passports could be signed. We employed the time in trying the flavor of the grapes and peaches of Lombardy, and looking at the groups of travelers who had come down from the Alps with the annual avalanche at this season. The custom house officers were extremely civil and obliging, as they did not think necessary to examine our knapsacks, and our passports being soon signed, we were at liberty to enter again into the dominions of His Majesty of Austria. Our companion, the German, whose feet could carry him no further, took a seat on the top of a diligence for Milan; we left Sesto Calende on foot, and plunged into the cloud of dust which was whirling towards the capital of Northern Italy.

Being now really in the "sunny land," we looked on the scenery with a deep interest. The first thing that struck me was a resemblance to America in the fields of Indian corn, and the rank growth of weeds by the roadside. The mulberry trees and hedges, too, looked quite familiar, coming as we did, from fenceless and hedgeless Germany. But here the resemblance ceased. The people were coarse, ignorant and savage-looking, the villages remarkable for nothing except the contrast between splendid churches and miserable, dirty houses, while the luxurious palaces and grounds of the rich noblemen formed a still greater contrast to the poverty of the people. I noticed also that if the latter are as lazy as they are said to be, they make their horses work for them, as in a walk of a few hours yesterday after noon, we saw two horses drawing heavy loads, drop down apparently dead, and several others seemed nearly ready to do the same.

We spent the night at the little village of Casina, about sixteen miles from Milan, and here made our first experience in the honesty of Italian inns. We had taken the precaution to inquire beforehand the price of a bed; but it seemed unnecessary and unpleasant, as well as evincing a mistrustful spirit, to do the same with every article we asked for, so we concluded to leave it to the host's conscience not to overcharge us. Imagine our astonishment, however, when at starting, a bill was presented to us, in which the smallest articles were set down at three or four times their value. We remonstrated, hut to little purpose; the fellow knew scarcely any French, and we as little Italian, so rather than lose time or temper, we paid what he demanded and went on, leaving him to laugh at the successful imposition. The experience was of value to us, however, and it may serve as a warning to some future traveler.

About noon, the road turned into a broad and beautiful avenue of poplars, down which we saw, at a distance, the triumphal arch terminating the Simplon road, which we had followed from Sesto Calende. Beyond it rose the slight and airy pinnacle of the Duomo. We passed by the exquisite structure, gave up our passports at the gates, traversed the broad Piazza d'Armi, and found ourselves at liberty to choose one of the dozen streets that led into the heart of the city.

CHAPTER XXXI. — MILAN.

Aug. 21.—While finding our way at random to the "Pension Suisse," whither we had been directed by a German gentleman, we were agreeably impressed with the gaiety and bustle of Milan. The shops and stores are all open to the street, so that the city resembles a great bazaar. It has an odd look to see blacksmiths, tailors and shoemakers working unconcernedly in the open air, with crowds continually passing before them. The streets are filled with venders of fruit, who call out the names with a long, distressing cry, like that of a person in great agony. Organ-grinders parade constantly about and snatches of songs are heard among the gay crowd, on every side.

In this lively, noisy Italian city, nearly all there is to see may be comprised in four things: the Duomo, the triumphal arch over the Simplon, La Scala and the Picture Gallery. The first alone is more interesting than many an entire city. We went there yesterday afternoon soon after reaching here. It stands in an irregular open place, closely hemmed in by houses on two sides, so that it can be seen to advantage from only one point. It is a mixture of the Gothic and Romanesque styles; the body of the structure is entirely covered with statues and richly wrought sculpture, with needle-like spires of white marble rising up from every corner. But of the exquisite, airy look of the whole mass, although so solid and vast, it is impossible to convey an idea. It appears like some fabric of frost-work which winter traces on the window-panes. There is a unity of beauty about the whole, which the eye takes in with a feeling of perfect and satisfied delight.

Ascending the marble steps which lead to the front, I lifted the folds of the heavy curtain and entered. What a glorious aisle! The mighty pillars support a magnificent arched ceiling, painted to resemble fretwork, and the little light that falls through the small windows above, enters tinged with a dim golden hue. A feeling of solemn awe comes over one as he steps with a hushed tread along the colored marble floor, and measures the massive columns till they blend with the gorgeous arches above. There are four rows of these, nearly fifty in all, and when I state that they are eight feet in diameter, and sixty or seventy in height, some idea may be formed of the grandeur of the building. Imagine the Girard College, at Philadelphia, turned into one great hall, with four rows of pillars, equal in size to those around it, reaching to its roof, and you will have a rough sketch of the interior of the Duomo.

In the centre of the cross is a light and beautiful dome; he who will stand under this, and look down the broad middle aisle to the entrance, has one of the sublimest vistas to be found in the world. The choir has three enormous windows, covered with dazzling paintings, and the ceiling is of marble and silver. There are gratings under the high altar, by looking into which, I could see a dark, lonely chamber below, where one or two feeble lamps showed a circle of praying-places. It was probably a funeral vault, which persons visited to pray for the repose of their friends' souls. The Duomo is not yet entirely finished, the workmen being still employed in various parts, but it is said, that when completed there will be four thousand statues on the different parts of it.

The design of the Duomo is said to be taken from Monte Rosa, one of the loftiest peaks of the Alps. Its hundreds of sculptured pinnacles, rising from every part of the body of the church, certainly bear a striking resemblance to the splintered ice-crags of Savoy. Thus we see how Art, mighty and endless in her forms though she be, is in every thing but the child of Nature. Her most divine conceptions are but copies of objects which we behold every day. The faultless beauty of the Corinthian capital—the springing and intermingling arches of the Gothic aisle—the pillared portico or the massive and sky-piercing pyramid—are but attempts at reproducing, by the studied regularity of Art, the ever-varied and ever-beautiful forms of mountain, rock and forest. But there is oftentimes a more thrilling sensation of enjoyment produced by the creations of man's hand and intellect than the grander effects of Nature, existing constantly before our eyes. It would seem as if man marvelled more at his own work than at the work of the Power which created him.

The streets of Milan abound with priests in their cocked hats and long black robes. They all have the same solemn air, and seem to go about like beings shut out from all communion with pleasure. No sight lately has saddened me so much as to see a bright, beautiful boy, of twelve or thirteen years, in those gloomy garments. Poor child! he little knows now what he may have to endure. A lonely, cheerless life, where every affection must be crushed as unholy, and every pleasure denied as a crime! And I knew by his fair brow and tender lip, that he had a warm and loving heart. I could not help regarding this class as victims to a mistaken idea of religious duty, and if I am not mistaken, I read on more than one countenance the traces of passions that burned within. It is mournful to see a people oppressed in the name of religion. The holiest aspirations of man's nature, instead of lifting him up to a nearer view of Christian perfection, are changed into clouds and shut out the light of heaven. Immense treasures, wrung drop by drop from the credulity of the poor and ignorant, are made use of to pamper the luxury of those who profess to be mediators between man and the Deity. The poor wretch may perish of starvation on a floor of precious mosaic, which perhaps his own pittance has helped to form, while ceilings and shrines of inlaid gold mock his dying eye with their useless splendor. Such a system of oppression, disguised under the holiest name, can only be sustained by the continuance of ignorance and blind superstition. Knowledge—Truth—Reason—these are the ramparts which Liberty throws up to guard her dominions from the usurpations of oppression and wrong.

We were last night in La Scala. Rossini's opera of William Tell was advertised, and as we had visited so lately the scene where that glorious historical drama was enacted, we went to see it represented in sound. It is a grand subject, which in the hands of a powerful composer, might be made very effective, but I must confess I was disappointed in the present case. The overture is, however, very beautiful. It begins low and mournful, like the lament of the Swiss over their fallen liberties. Occasionally a low drum is heard, as if to rouse them to action, and meanwhile the lament swells to a cry of despair. The drums now wake the land; the horn of Uri is heard pealing forth its summoning strain, and the echoes seem to come back from the distant Alps. The sound then changes for the roar of battle—the clang of trumpets, drums and cymbals. The whole orchestra did their best to represent this combat in music, which after lasting a short time, changed into the loud, victorious march of the conquerors. But the body of the opera, although it had several fine passages, was to me devoid of interest; in fact, unworthy the reputation of Rossini.

The theatre is perhaps the largest in the world. The singers are all good; in Italy it could not be otherwise, where everybody sings. As I write, a party of Italians in the house opposite have been amusing themselves with going through the whole opera of "La fille du Regiment," with the accompaniment of the piano, and they show the greatest readiness and correctness in their performance. They have now become somewhat boisterous, and appear to be improvising. One young gentleman executes trills with amazing skill, and another appears to have taken the part of a despairing lover, but the lady has a very pretty voice, and warbles on and on, like a nightingale. Occasionally a group of listeners in the street below clap them applause, for as the windows are always open, the whole neighborhood can enjoy the performance.

This forenoon I was in the Picture Gallery. It occupies a part of the Library Building, in the Palazzo Cabrera. It is not large, and many of the pictures are of no value to anybody but antiquarians; still there are some excellent paintings, which render it well worthy a visit. Among these, a marriage, by Raphael, is still in a very good state of preservation, and there are some fine pictures by Paul Veronese and the Caracci. The most admired painting, is "Abraham sending away Hagar," by Guercino. I never saw a more touching expression of grief than in the face of Hagar. Her eyes are red with weeping, and as she listens in an agony of tears to the patriarch's command, she still seems doubting the reality of her doom. The countenance of Abraham is venerable and calm, and expresses little emotion; but one can read in that of Sarah, as she turns away, a feeling of pity for her unfortunate rival.

Next to the Duomo, the most beautiful specimen of architecture in Milan is the ARCH OF PEACE, on the north side of the city, at the commencement of the Simplon Road. It was the intention of Napoleon to carry the road under this arch, across the Piazza d'Armi, and to cut a way for it directly into the heart of the city, but the fall of his dynasty prevented the execution of this magnificent design, as well as the completion of the arch itself. This has been done by the Austrian government, according to the original plan; they have inscribed upon it the name of Francis I., and changed the bas-reliefs of Lodi and Marengo into those of a few fields where their forces had gained the victory. It is even said that in many parts which were already finished, they altered the splendid Roman profile of Napoleon into the haggard and repulsive features of Francis of Austria.

The bronze statues on the top were made by an artist of Bologna, by Napoleon's order, and are said to be the finest works of modern times. In the centre is the goddess of Peace, in a triumphal car, drawn by six horses, while on the corners four angels, mounted, are starting off to convey the tidings to the four quarters of the globe. The artist has caught the spirit of motion and chained it in these moveless figures. One would hardly feel surprised if the goddess, chariot, horses and all, were to start off and roll away through the air.

With the rapidity usual to Americans we have already finished seeing Milan, and shall start to-morrow morning on a walk to Genoa.

CHAPTER XXXII. — WALK FROM MILAN TO GENOA.

It was finally decided we should leave Milan, so the next morning we arose at five o'clock for the first time since leaving Frankfort. The Italians had commenced operations at this early hour, but we made our way through the streets without attracting quite so much attention as on our arrival. Near the gate on the road to Pavia, we passed a long colonnade which was certainly as old as the times of the Romans. The pillars of marble were quite brown with age, and bound together with iron to keep them from falling to pieces. It was a striking contrast to see this relic of the past standing in the middle of a crowded thoroughfare and surrounded by all the brilliance and display of modern trade.

Once fairly out of the city we took the road to Pavia, along the banks of the canal, just as the rising sun gilded the marble spire of the Duomo. The country was a perfect level, and the canal, which was in many places higher than the land through which it passed, served also as a means of irrigation for the many rice-fields. The sky grew cloudy and dark, and before we reached Pavia gathered to a heavy storm. Torrents of rain poured down, accompanied with heavy thunder; we crept under an old gateway for shelter, as no house was near. Finally, as it cleared away, the square brown towers of the old city rose above the trees, and we entered the gate through a fine shaded avenue. Our passports were of course demanded, but we were only detained a minute or two. The only thing of interest is the University, formerly so celebrated; it has at present about eight hundred students.

We have reason to remember the city from another circumstance—the singular attention we excited. I doubt if Columbus was an object of greater curiosity to the simple natives of the new world, than we three Americans were to the good people of Pavia. I know not what part of our dress or appearance could have caused it, but we were watched like wild animals. If we happened to pause and look at anything in the street, there was soon a crowd of attentive observers, and as we passed on, every door and window was full of heads. We stopped in the marketplace to purchase some bread and fruit for dinner, which increased, if possible, the sensation. We saw eyes staring and fingers pointing at us from every door and alley. I am generally willing to contribute as much as possible to the amusement or entertainment of others, but such attention was absolutely embarrassing. There was nothing to do but to appear unconscious of it, and we went along with as much nonchalance as if the whole town belonged to us.

We crossed the Ticino, on whose banks near Pavia, was fought the first great battle between Hannibal and the Romans. On the other side our passports were demanded at the Sardinian frontier and our knapsacks searched, which having proved satisfactory, we were allowed to enter the kingdom. Late in the afternoon we reached the Po, which in winter must be quarter of a mile wide, but the summer heats had dried it up to a small stream, so that the bridge of boats rested nearly its whole length in sand. We sat on the bank in the shade, and looked at the chain of hills which rose in the south, following the course of the Po, crowned with castles and villages and shining towers. It was here that I first began to realize Italian scenery. Although the hills were bare, they lay so warm and glowing in the sunshine, and the deep blue sky spread so calmly above, that it recalled all my dreams of the fair clime we had entered.

We stopped for the night at the little village of Casteggio, which lies at the foot of the hills, and next morning resumed our pilgrimage. Here a new delight awaited us. The sky was of a heavenly blue, without even the shadow of a cloud, and full and fair in the morning sunshine we could see the whole range of the Alps, from the blue hills of Friuli, which sweep down to Venice and the Adriatic, to the lofty peaks which stretch away to Nice and Marseilles! Like a summer cloud, except that they were far more dazzling and glorious, lay to the north of us the glaciers and untrodden snow-fields of the Bernese Oberland; a little to the right we saw the double peak of St. Gothard, where six days before we shivered in the region of eternal winter, while far to the north-west rose the giant dome of Mount Blanc. Monte Rosa stood near him, not far from the Great St. Bernard, and further to the south Mont Cenis guarded the entrance from Piedmont into France. I leave you to conceive the majesty of such a scene, and you may perhaps imagine, for I cannot describe the feelings with which I gazed upon it.

At Tortona, the next post, a great market was being held; the town was filled with country people selling their produce, and with venders of wares of all kinds. Fruit was very abundant—grapes, ripe figs, peaches and melons were abundant, and for a trifle one could purchase a sumptuous banquet. On inquiring the road to Novi, the people made us understand, after much difficulty, that there was a nearer way across the country, which came into the post-road again, and we concluded to take it. After two or three hours' walking in a burning sun, where our only relief was the sight of the Alps and a view of the battle-field of Marengo, which lay just on our right, we came to a stand—the road terminated at a large stream, where workmen were busily engaged in making a bridge across. We pulled off our boots and waded through, took a refreshing bath in the clear waters, and walked on through by-lanes. The sides were lined with luxuriant vines, bending under the ripening vintage, and we often cooled our thirst with some of the rich bunches.

The large branch of the Po we crossed, came down from the mountains, which we were approaching. As we reached the post-road again, they were glowing in the last rays of the sun, and the evening vapors that settled over the plain concealed the distant Alps, although the snowy top of the Jungfrau and her companions the Wetterhorn and Schreckhorn, rose above it like the hills of another world. A castle or church of brilliant white marble glittered on the summit of one of the mountains near us, and as the sun went down without a cloud, the distant summits changed in hue to a glowing purple, amounting almost to crimson, which afterwards darkened into a deep violet. The western half of the sky was of a pale orange, and the eastern a dark red, which blended together in the blue of the zenith, that deepened as twilight came on. I know not if it was a fair specimen of an Italian sunset, but I must say, without wishing to be partial, that though certainly very soft and beautiful, there is no comparison with the splendor of such a scene in America. The day-sky of Italy better deserves its reputation. Although no clearer than our own, it is of a far brighter blue, arching above us like a dome of sapphire and seeming to sparkle all over with a kind of crystal transparency.

We stopped the second night at Arquato, a little village among the mountains, and after having bargained with the merry landlord for our lodgings, in broken Italian, took a last look at the plains of Piedmont and the Swiss Alps, in the growing twilight. We gazed out on the darkening scene till the sky was studded with stars, and went to rest with the exciting thought of seeing Genoa and the Mediterranean on the morrow. Next morning we started early, and after walking some distance made our breakfast in a grove of chestnuts, on the cool mountain side, beside a fresh stream of water. The sky shone like a polished gem, and the glossy leaves of the chestnuts gleamed in the morning sun. Here and there, on a rocky height, stood the remains of some knightly castle, telling of the Goths and Normans who descended through these mountain passes to plunder Rome.

As the sun grew high, the heat and dust became intolerable, and this, in connection with the attention we raised everywhere, made us somewhat tired of foot-traveling in Italy. I verily believe the people took us for pilgrims on account of our long white blouses, and had I a scallop shell I would certainly have stuck it into my hat to complete the appearance. We stopped once to ask a priest the road; when he had told us, he shook hands with us and gave us a parting benediction. At the common inns, where we stopped, we always met with civil treatment, though, indeed, as we only slept in them, there was little chance of practising imposition. We bought our simple meals at the baker's and grocer's, and ate them in the shade of the grape-bowers, whose rich clusters added to the repast. In this manner, we enjoyed Italy at the expense of a franc, daily. About noon, after winding about through the narrow defiles, the road began ascending. The reflected heat from the hills on each side made it like an oven; there was not a breath of air stirring; but we all felt, although no one said it, that from the summit we could see the Mediterranean, and we pushed on as if life or death depended on it. Finally, the highest point came in sight—we redoubled our exertions, and a few minutes more brought us to the top, breathless with fatigue and expectation. I glanced down the other side—there lay a real sea of mountains, all around; the farthest peaks rose up afar and dim, crowned with white towers, and between two of them which stood apart like the pillars of a gateway, we saw the broad expanse of water stretching away to the horizon—

To where the blue of heaven on bluer waves shut down!"

It would have been a thrilling sight to see any ocean, when one has rambled thousands of miles among the mountains and vales of the inland, but to behold this sea, of all others, was glorious indeed! This sea, whose waves wash the feet of Naples, Constantinople and Alexandria, and break on the hoary shores where Troy and Tyre and Carthage have mouldered away!—whose breast has been furrowed by the keels of a hundred nations through more than forty centuries—from the first rude voyage of Jason and his Argonauts, to the thunders of Navarino that heralded the second birth of Greece! You cannot wonder we grew romantic; but short space was left for sentiment in the burning sun, with Genoa to be reached before night. The mountain we crossed is called the Bochetta, one of the loftiest of the sea-Alps (or Apennines)—the road winds steeply down towards the sea, following a broad mountain rivulet, now perfectly dried up, as nearly every stream among the mountains is. It was a long way to us; the mountains seemed as if they would never unfold and let us out on the shore, and our weary limbs did penance enough for a multitude of sins. The dusk was beginning to deepen over the bay and the purple hues of sunset were dying away from its amphitheatre of hills, as we came in sight of the gorgeous city. Half the population were out to celebrate a festival, and we made our entry in the triumphal procession of some saint.

CHAPTER XXXIII. — SCENES IN GENOA, LEGHORN AND PISA.

Have you ever seen some grand painting of a city, rising with its domes and towers and palaces from the edge of a glorious bay, shut in by mountains—the whole scene clad in those deep, delicious, sunny hues which you admire so much in the picture, although they appear unrealized in Nature? If so, you can figure to yourself Genoa, as she looked to us at sunset, from the battlements west of the city. When we had passed through the gloomy gate of the fortress that guards the western promontory, the whole scene opened at once on us in all its majesty. It looked to me less like a real landscape than a mighty panoramic painting. The battlements where we were standing, and the blue mirror of the Mediterranean just below, with a few vessels moored near the shore, made up the foreground; just in front lay the queenly city, stretching out to the eastern point of the bay, like a great meteor—-this point, crowned with the towers and dome of a cathedral representing the nucleus, while the tail gradually widened out and was lost among the numberless villas that reached to the top of the mountains behind. A mole runs nearly across the mouth of the harbor, with a tall light-house at its extremity, leaving only a narrow passage for vessels. As we gazed, a purple glow lay on the bosom of the sea, while far beyond the city, the eastern half of the mountain crescent around the gulf was tinted with the loveliest hue of orange. The impressions which one derives from looking on remarkable scenery, depend, for much of their effect, on the time and weather. I have been very fortunate in this respect in two instances, and shall carry with me through life, two glorious pictures of a very different character—the wild sublimity of the Brocken in cloud and storm, and the splendor of Genoa in an Italian sunset.

Genoa has been called the "city of palaces." and it well deserves the appellation. Row above row of magnificent structures rise amid gardens along the side of the hills, and many of the streets, though narrow and crooked, are lined entirely with the splendid dwellings of the Genoese nobles. All these speak of the republic in its days of wealth and power, when it could cope successfully with Venice, and Doria could threaten to bridle the horses of St.

Mark. At present its condition is far different; although not so fallen as its rival, it is but a shadow of its former self—the life and energy it possessed as a republic, has withered away under the grasp of tyranny.

We entered Genoa, as I have already said, in a religious procession. On passing the gate we saw from the concourse of people and the many banners hanging from the windows or floating across the streets, that it was the day of a festa. Before entering the city we reached the procession itself, which was one of unusual solemnity. As it was impossible in the dense crowd, to pass it, we struggled through till we reached a good point for seeing the whole, and slowly moved on with it through the city. First went a company of boys in white robes; then followed a body of friars, dressed in long black cassocks, and with shaven crowns; then a company of soldiers with a band of music; then a body of nuns, wrapped from head to foot in blue robes, leaving only a small place to see out of—in the dusk they looked very solemn and ghost-like, and their low chant had to me something awful and sepulchral in it; then followed another company of friars, and after that a great number of priests in white and black robes, bearing the statue of the saint, with a pyramid of flowers, crosses and blazing wax tapers, while companies of soldiery, monks and music brought up the rear. Armed guards walked at intervals on each side of the procession, to keep the way clear and prevent disturbance; two or three bands played solemn airs, alternating with the deep monotonous chanting of the friars. The whole scene, dimly lighted by the wax tapers, produced in me a feeling nearly akin to fear, as if I were witnessing some ghostly, unearthly spectacle. To rites like these, however, which occur every few weeks, the people must be well accustomed.

Among the most interesting objects in Genoa, is the Doria palace, fit in its splendor for a monarch's residence. It stands in the Strada Nova, one of the three principal streets, and I believe is still in the possession of the family. There are many others through the city, scarcely less magnificent, among which that of the Durazzo family may be pointed out. The American consulate is in one of these old edifices, with a fine court-yard and ceilings covered with frescoes. Mr. Moro, the Vice Consul, did us a great kindness, which I feel bound to acknowledge, although it will require the disclosure of some private, and perhaps uninteresting circumstances. On leaving Frankfort, we converted—for the sake of convenience—the greater part of our funds into a draft on a Saxon merchant in Leghorn, reserving just enough, as we supposed, to take us thither. As in our former case, in Germany, the sum was too small, which we found to our dismay on reaching Milan. Notwithstanding we had traveled the whole ninety miles from that city to Genoa for three francs each, in the hope of having enough, left to enable one at least to visit Leghorn, the expenses for a passport in Genoa (more than twenty francs) prevented this plan. I went therefore to the Vice Consul to ascertain whether the merchant on whom the draft was drawn, had any correspondents there, who might advance a portion of it. His secretary made many inquiries, but without effect; Mr. Moro then generously offered to furnish me with means to reach Leghorn, whence I could easily remit a sufficient sum to my two comrades. This put an end to our anxiety, (for I must confess we could not help feeling some), and I therefore prepared to leave that evening in the "Virgilio."

The feelings with which I look on this lovely land, are fast changing. What with the dust and heat, and cheating landlords, and the dull plains of Lombardy, my first experience was not very prepossessing. But the joyous and romantic anticipation with which I looked forward to realizing the dream of my earliest boyhood, is now beginning to be surpassed by the exciting reality. Every breath I drew in the city of Columbus and Doria, was deeply tinctured with the magic of history and romance. It was like entering on a new existence, to look on scenes so lovely by nature and so filled with the inspiring memories of old.

> *"Italia too, Italia! looking on thee,*
>
> *Full flashes on the soul the light of ages,*
>
> *Since the fierce Carthagenian almost won thee,*
>
> *To the last halo of the chiefs and sages*
>
> *Who glorify thy consecrated pages!*
>
> *Thou wert the throne and grave of empires."*

The Virgilio was advertised to leave at six o'clock, and I accordingly went out to her in a little boat half an hour beforehand; but we were delayed much longer, and I saw sunset again fade over the glorious amphitheatre of palaces and mountains, with the same orange glow—the same purple and crimson flush, deepening into twilight—as before. An old blind man in a skiff, floated around under the bows of the boat on the glassy water, singing to the violin a plaintive air that appeared to be an evening hymn to the virgin. There was something very touching in his venerable countenance, with the sightless eyes turned upward to the sunset heaven whose glory he could never more behold.

The lamps were lit on the tower at the end of the mole as we glided out on the open sea; I stood on deck and watched the receding lights of the city, till they and the mountains above them, were blended with the darkened sky. The sea-breeze was fresh and cool, and the stars glittered with a frosty clearness, which would have made the night delicious had not a slight rolling of the waves obliged me to go below. Here, besides being half seasick, I was placed at the mercy of many voracious fleas, who obstinately stayed, persisting in keeping me company. This was the first time I had suffered from these cannibals, and such were my torments, I almost wished some blood-thirsty Italian would come and put an end to them with his stiletto.

The first ray of dawn that stole into the cabin sent me on deck. The hills of Tuscany lay in front, sharply outlined on the reddening sky; near us was the steep and rocky isle of Gorgona; and far to the south-west, like a low mist along the water, ran the shores of Corsica—the birth place of Columbus and Napoleon![***] As the dawn brightened we saw on the southern horizon a cloud-like island, also imperishably connected with the name of the latter—the prison-kingdom of Elba! North of us extended the rugged mountains of Carrara—that renowned range whence has sprung many a form of almost breathing beauty, and where yet slumber, perhaps, in the unhewn marble, the god-like shapes of an age of art, more glorious than any the world has ever yet beheld!

*** [By recent registers found in Corsica, it has been determined that this island also gave birth to the discoverer of the new world.]

The sun rose from behind the Apennines and masts and towers became

573

visible through the golden haze, as we approached the shore. On a flat space between the sea and the hills, not far from the foot of Montenero, stands Leghorn. The harbor is protected by a mole, leaving a narrow passage, through which we entered, and after waiting two hours for the visit of the health and police officers, we were permitted to go on shore. The first thing that struck me, was the fine broad streets; the second, the motley character of the population. People were hurrying about noisy and bustling—Greeks in their red caps and capotes; grave turbaned and bearded Turks; dark Moors; the Corsair-looking natives of Tripoli and Tunis, and seamen of nearly every nation. At the hotel where I stayed, we had a singular mixture of nations at dinner:—two French, two Swiss, one Genoese, one Roman, one American and one Turk—and we were waited on by a Tuscan and an Arab! We conversed together in four languages, all at once.

To the merchant, Leghorn is of more importance than to the traveler. Its extensive trade, not only in the manufactures of Tuscany, but also in the productions of the Levant, makes it important to the former, while the latter seeks in vain for fine buildings, galleries of art, or in interesting historical reminiscences. Through the kind attention of the Saxon Consul, to whom I had letters, two or three days went by delightfully.

The only place of amusement here in summer is a drive along the sea shore, called the Ardenza, which is frequented every evening by all who can raise a vehicle. I visited it twice with a German friend. We met one evening the Princess Corsini, wife of the Governor of Leghorn, on horseback—a young, but not pretty woman. The road leads out along the Mediterranean, past an old fortress, to a large establishment for the sea bathers, where it ends in a large ring, around which the carriages pass and re-pass, until sunset has gone out over the sea, when they return to the city in a mad gallop, or as fast as the lean horses can draw them.

In driving around, we met two or three carriages of Turks, in one of which I saw a woman of Tunis, with a curious gilded head-dress, eighteen inches in height.

I saw one night a Turkish funeral. It passed me in one of the outer streets, on its way to the Turkish burying ground. Those following the coffin, which was covered with a heavy black pall, wore white turbans and long white robes—the mourning color of the Turks. Torches were borne by attendants, and the whole company passed on at a quick pace. Seen thus by night, it had a strange and spectral appearance.

There is another spectacle here which was exceedingly revolting to me. The condemned criminals, chained two and two, are kept at work through the city, cleaning the streets. They are dressed in coarse garments of a dirty red color, with the name of the crime for which they were convicted, painted on the back. I shuddered to see so many marked with the words—"omicidio premeditato." All day they are thus engaged, exposed to the scorn and contumely of the crowd, and at night dragged away to be incarcerated in damp, unwholesome dungeons, excavated under the public thoroughfares.

The employment of criminals in this way is common in Italy. Two days after crossing St. Gothard, we saw a company of abject-looking creatures, eating their dinner by the road-side, near Bellinzona. One of them had a small basket of articles of cotton and linen, and as he rose up to offer them to us, I was startled by the clank of fetters. They were all employed to labor on the road.

On going down to the wharf in Leghorn, in the morning, two or three days ago, I found F—— and B—— just stepping on shore from the steamboat, tired enough of the discomforts of the voyage, yet anxious to set out for Florence as soon as possible. After we had shaken off the crowd of porters, pedlars and vetturini, and taken a hasty breakfast at the Cafe Americano, we went to the Police Office to get our passports, and had the satisfaction of paying two francs for permission to proceed to Florence. The weather had changed since the preceding day, and the sirocco-wind which blows over from the coast of Africa, filled the streets with clouds of dust, which made walking very unpleasant. The clear blue sky had vanished, and a leaden cloud hung low on the Mediterranean, hiding the shores of Corsica and the rooky isles of Gorgona and Capraja.

The country between Leghorn and Pisa, is a flat marsh, intersected in several places by canals to carry off the stagnant water which renders this district so unhealthy. It is said that the entire plain between the mountains of Carrarra and the hills back of Leghorn has been gradually formed by the deposits of the Arno and the receding of the Mediterranean, which is so shallow along the whole coast, that large vessels have to anchor several miles out. As we approached Pisa over the level marsh, I could see the dome of the Cathedral and the Leaning Tower rising above the gardens and groves which surround it.

Our baggage underwent another examination at the gate, where we were again assailed by the vetturini, one of whom hung on us like a leech till we reached a hotel, and there was finally no way of shaking him off except by engaging him to take us to Florence. The bargain having been concluded, we had still a few hours left and set off to hunt the Cathedral. We found it on an open square near the outer wall, and quite remote from the main part of the town. Emerging from the narrow and winding street, one takes in et a glance the Baptistery, the Campo Santo, the noble Cathedral and the Leaning Tower—forming altogether a view rarely surpassed in Europe for architectural effect. But the square is melancholy and deserted, and rank, untrampled grass fills the crevices of its marble pavement.

I was surprised at the beauty of the Leaning Tower. Instead of all old, black, crumbling fabric, as I always supposed, it is a light, airy, elegant structure, of white marble, and its declension, which is interesting as a work of art (or accident,) is at the same time pleasing from its novelty. There have been many conjectures as to the cause of this deviation, which is upwards of fourteen feet from the perpendicular; it is now generally believed that the earth having sunk when the building was half finished, it was continued by the architects in the same angle. The upper gallery, which is smaller than the others, shows a very perceptible inclination back towards the perpendicular, as if in some degree to counterbalance the deviation of the other part. There are eight galleries in all, supported by marble pillars, but the inside of the Tower is hollow to the very top.

We ascended by the same stairs which were trodden so often by Galileo in going up to make his astronomical observations; in climbing spirally

576

around the hollow cylinder in the dark, it was easy to tell on which side of the Tower we were, from the proportionate steepness of the staircase. There is a fine view from the top, embracing the whole plain as far as Leghorn on one side, with its gardens and grain fields spread out like a vast map. In a valley of the Carrarrese Mountains to the north, we could see the little town of Lucca, much frequented at this season on account of its baths; the blue summits of the Appenines shut in the view to the east. In walking through the city I noticed two other towers, which had nearly as great a deviation from the perpendicular. We met a person who had the key of the Baptistery, which he opened for us. Two ancient columns covered with rich sculpture form the doorway, and the dome is supported by massive pillars of the red marble of Elba. The baptismal font is of the purest Parian marble. The most remarkable thing was the celebrated musical echo. Our cicerone stationed himself at the side of the font and sang a few notes. After a moment's pause they were repeated aloft in the dome, but with a sound of divine sweetness—as clear and pure as the clang of a crystal bell. Another pause—and we heard them again, higher, fainter and sweeter, followed by a dying note, as if they were fading far away into heaven. It seemed as if an angel lingered in the temple, echoing with his melodious lips the common harmonies of earth. Even thus does the music of good deeds, hardly noted in our grosser atmosphere, awake a divine echo in the far world of spirit.

The Campo Santo, on the north side of the Cathedral, was, until lately, the cemetery of the city; the space enclosed within its marble galleries is filled to the depth of eight or ten feet, with earth from the Holy Land. The vessels which carried the knights of Tuscany to Palestine were filled at Joppa, on returning, with this earth as ballast, and on arriving at Pisa it was deposited in the Cemetery. It has the peculiar property of decomposing all human bodies, in the space of two days. A colonnade of marble encloses it, with windows of the most exquisite sculpture opening on the inside. They reminded me of the beautiful Gothic oriels of Melrose. At each end are two fine, green cypresses, which thrive remarkably in the soil of Palestine. The dust of a German emperor, among others, rests in this consecrated ground. There are other fine churches in Pisa, but the four buildings I have mentioned, are the principal objects of interest. The tower where Count Ugolino and his sons were starved to death by the citizens of Pisa, who locked them up and threw the keys into the Arno, has lately been destroyed.

An Italian gentleman having made a bargain in the meantime with our vetturino, we found every thing ready on returning to the hotel. On the outside of the town we mounted into the vehicle, a rickety-looking concern, and as it commenced raining, I was afraid we would have a bad night of it. After a great deal of bargaining, the vetturino agreed to take us to Florence that night for five francs a piece, provided one person would sit on the outside with the driver. I accordingly mounted on front, protected by a blouse and umbrella, for it was beginning to rain dismally. The miserable, bare-boned horses were fastened with rope-traces, and the vetturino having taken the rope-lines in his hand, gave a flourish with his whip; one old horse tumbled nearly to the ground, but he jerked him up again and we rattled off.

After riding ten miles in this way, it became so wet and dreary, that I was fain to give the driver two francs extra, for the privilege of an inside seat. Our Italian companion was agreeable and talkative, but as we were still ignorant of the language, I managed to hold a scanty conversation with him in French. He seemed delighted to learn that we were from America; his polite reserve gave place to a friendly familiarity and he was loud in his praises of the Americans. I asked him why it was that he and the Italians generally, were so friendly towards us. "I hardly know," he answered; "you are so different from any other nation; and then, too, you have so much sincerity!"

The Appenines were wreathed and hidden in thick mist, and the prospect over the flat cornfields bordering the road was not particularly interesting. We had made about one-third of the way as night set in, when on ascending a hill soon after dark, F—— happened to look out, and saw one of the axles bent and nearly broken off. we were obliged to get out and walk through the mud to the next village, when after two hours' delay, the vetturino came along with another carriage. Of the rest of the way to Florence, I cannot say much. Cramped up in the narrow vehicle, we jolted along in the dark, rumbling now and then through some silent village, where lamps were burning before the solitary shrines. Sometimes a blinding light crossed the road, where we saw the tile-makers sitting in the red glare of their kilns, and often the black boughs of trees were painted momentarily on the cloudy sky. If the jolting carriage had even permitted sleep, the horrid cries of the vetturino, urging on his horses, would have prevented it; and I decided, while trying to relieve my aching limbs, that three days' walking in sun and sand was preferable to one night of such travel.

Finally about four o'clock in the morning the carriage stopped; my Italian friend awoke and demanded the cause. "Signor," said the vetturino, "we are in Florence!" I blessed the man, and the city too. The good-humored officer looked at our passports and passed our baggage without examination; we gave the gatekeeper a paul and he admitted us. The carriage rolled through the dark, silent streets—passed a public square—came out on the Arno—crossed and entered the city again—and finally stopped at a hotel. The master of the "Lione Bianco" came down in an undress to receive us, and we shut the growing dawn out of our rooms to steal that repose from the day which the night had not given.

CHAPTER XXXIV. – FLORENCE AND ITS GALLERIES.

Sept. 11.—Our situation here is as agreeable as we could well desire. We have three large and handsomely furnished rooms, in the centre of the city, for which we pay Signor Lazzeri, a wealthy goldsmith, ten scudo per month—a scudo being a trifle more than an American dollar. We live at the Cafès and Trattone very conveniently for twenty-five cents a day, enjoying moreover, at our dinner in the Trattoria del Cacciatore, the company of several American artists with whom we have become acquainted. The day after our arrival we met at the table d'hote of the "Lione Bianco," Dr. Boardman of New York, through whose assistance we obtained our present lodgings. There are at present ten or twelve American artists in Florence, and we promise ourselves much pleasure and profit from their acquaintance. B—— and I are so charmed with the place and the beautiful Tuscan dialect, that we shall endeavor to spend three or four months here. F—— returns to Germany in two weeks, to attend the winter term of the University at his favorite Heidelberg.

Our first walk in Florence was to the Royal Gallery—we wished to see the "goddess living in stone" without delay. Crossing the neighboring Piazza del Granduca, we passed Michael Angelo's colossal statue of David, and an open gallery containing, besides some antiques, the master-piece of John of Bologna. The palace of the Uffizii, fronting on the Arno, extends along both sides of an avenue running back to the Palazzo Vecchio. We entered the portico which passes around under the great building, and after ascending three or four flights of steps, came into a long hall, filled with paintings and ancient statuary. Towards the end of this, a door opened into the Tribune— that celebrated room, unsurpassed by any in the world for the number and value of the gems it contains. I pushed aside a crimson curtain and stood in the presence of the Venus.

It may be considered heresy, but I confess I did not at first go into raptures, nor perceive any traces of superhuman beauty. The predominant feeling, if I may so express it, was satisfaction; the eye dwells on its faultless outline with a gratified sense, that nothing is wanting to render it perfect. It is the ideal of a woman's form—a faultless standard by which all beauty may be measured, but without striking expression, except in the modest and graceful position of the limbs. The face, though regular, is not handsome, and the body appears small, being but five feet in height, which, I think, is a little below the average stature of women. On each side, as if to heighten its elegance by contrast with rude and unrefined nature, are the statues of the Wrestlers, and the slave listening to the conspiracy of Catiline, called also The Whetter.

As if to correspond with the value of the works it holds, the Tribune is paved with precious marbles and the ceiling studded with polished mother-of-pearl. A dim and subdued light fills the hall, which throws over the mind that half-dreamy tone necessary to the full enjoyment of such objects. On each side of the Venus de Medici hangs a Venus by Titian, the size of life, and painted in that rich and gorgeous style of coloring which has been so often and vainly attempted since his time.

Here are six of Raphael's best preserved paintings. I prefer the "St. John in the Desert" to any other picture in the Tribune. His glorious form, in the fair proportions of ripening boyhood—the grace of his attitude, with the arm lifted eloquently on high—the divine inspiration which illumines his young features—chain the step irresistibly before it. It is one of those triumphs of the pencil which few but Raphael have accomplished—the painting of spirit in its loftiest and purest form. Near it hangs the Fornarina, which he seems to have painted in as deep a love as he entertained for the original. The face is modest and beautiful, and filled with an expression of ardent and tender attachment. I never tire looking upon either of these two.

Let me not forget, while we are in this peerless hall, to point out Guercino's Samian Sybil. It is a glorious work. With her hands clasped over her volume, she is looking up with a face full of deep and expressive sadness. A picturesque turban is twined around her head, and bands of pearls gleam amidst her rich, dark brown tresses. Her face bears the softness of dawning womanhood, and nearly answers my ideal of female beauty. The same artist has another fine picture here—a sleeping Endymion. The mantle has fallen from his shoulders, as he reclines asleep, with his head on his hand, and his crook beside him. The silver crescent of Dian looks over his shoulder from the sky behind, and no wonder if she should become enamored, for a lovelier shepherd has not been seen since that of King Admetus went back to drive his chariot in the heavens.

The "Drunken Bacchus" of Michael Angelo is greatly admired, and indeed it might pass for a relic of the palmiest times of Grecian art. The face, amidst its half-vacant, sensual expression, shows traces of its immortal origin, and there is still an air of dignity preserved in the swagger of his beautiful form. It is, in a word, the ancient idea of a drunken god. It may be doubted whether the artist's talents might not have been employed better than in ennobling intoxication. If he had represented Bacchus as he really is—degraded even below the level of humanity—it might be more beneficial to the mind, though less beautiful to the eye. However, this is a question on which artists and moralists cannot agree. Perhaps, too, the rich blood of the Falernian grape produced a more godlike delirium than the vulgar brandy which oversets the moderns!

At one end of the gallery is a fine copy in marble of the Laocoon, by Bandinelli, one of the rivals of Michael Angelo. When it was finished, the former boasted it was better than the original, to which Michael made the apt reply: "It is foolish for those who walk in the footsteps of others, to say they go before them!"

Let us enter the hall of Niobe. One starts back on seeing the many figures in the attitude of flight, for they seem at first about to spring from their pedestals. At the head of the room stands the afflicted mother, bending over the youngest daughter who clings to her knees, with an upturned countenance of deep and imploring agony. In vain! the shafts of Apollo fall thick, and she will soon be childless. No wonder the strength of that woe depicted on her countenance should change her into stone. One of her sons—a beautiful, boyish form,—is lying on his back, just expiring, with the chill langour of death creeping over his limbs. We seem to hear the quick whistling of the arrows, and look involuntarily into the air to see the hovering figure of the avenging god. In a chamber near is kept the head of a faun, made by Michael Angelo, at the age of fourteen, in the garden of Lorenzo de Medici, from a piece of marble given him by the workmen.

The portraits of the painters are more than usually interesting. Every countenance is full of character. There is the pale, enthusiastic face of Raphael, the stern vigor of Titian, the majesty and dignity of Leonardo da Vinci, and the fresh beauty of Angelica Kauffmann. I liked best the romantic head of Raphael Mengs. In one of the rooms there is a portrait of Alfieri, with an autograph sonnet of his own on the back of it. The house in which he lived and died, is on the north bank of the Arno, near the Ponte Caraja, and his ashes rest in Santa Croce.

Italy still remains the home of art, and it is but just she should keep these treasures, though the age that brought them forth has passed away. They are her only support now; her people are dependent for their subsistence on the glory of the past. The spirits of the old painters, living still on their canvass, earn from year to year the bread of an indigent and oppressed people. This ought to silence those utilitarians at home, who oppose the cultivation of the fine arts, on the ground of their being useless luxuries. Let them look to Italy, where a picture by Raphael or Correggio is a rich legacy for a whole city. Nothing is useless that gratifies that perception of beauty, which is at once the most delicate and the most intense of our mental sensations, binding us by an unconscious link nearer to nature and to Him, whose every thought is born of Beauty, Truth and Love. I envy not the one who looks with a cold and indifferent spirit on these immortal creations of the old masters—these poems written in marble and on the canvass. They who oppose every thing which can refine and spiritualize the nature of man, by binding him down to the cares of the work-day world alone, cheat life of half its glory.

The eighth of this month was the anniversary of the birth of the Virgin, and the celebration, if such it might be called, commenced the evening before, It is the custom, and Heaven only knows how it originated, for the people of the lower class to go through the streets in a company, blowing little penny whistles. We were walking that night in the direction of the Duomo, when we met a band of these men, blowing with all their might on the shrill whistles, so that the whole neighborhood resounded with one continual, piercing, ear-splitting shriek. They marched in a kind of quick trot through the streets, followed by a crowd of boys, and varying the noise occasionally by shouts and howls of the most horrible character. They paraded through all the principal streets of the city, which for an hour sent up such an agonizing scream that you might have fancied it an enormous monster, expiring in great torment. The people seemed to take the whole thing as a matter of course, but it was to us a novel manner of ushering in a religious festival.

The sky was clear and blue, as it always is in this Italian paradise, when we left Florence a few days ago for Fiesole. In spite of many virtuous efforts to rise early, it was nine o'clock before we left the Porta San Gallo, with its triumphal arch to the Emperor Francis, striding the road to Bologna. We passed through the public walk at this end of the city, and followed the road to Fiesole along the dried-up bed of a mountain torrent. The dwellings of the Florentine nobility occupy the whole slope, surrounded with rich and lovely gardens. The mountain and plain are both covered with luxuriant olive orchards, whose foliage of silver gray gives the scene the look of a moonlight landscape.

At the base of the mountain of Fiesole we passed one of the summer palaces of Lorenzo the Magnificent, and a little distance beyond, took a footpath overshadowed by magnificent cypresses, between whose dark trunks we looked down on the lovely Val d'Arno. But I will reserve all description of the view till we arrive at the summit.

The modern village of Fiesole occupies the site of an ancient city, generally supposed to be of Etrurian origin. Just above, on one of the peaks of the mountain, stands the Acropolis, formerly used as a fortress, but now untenanted save by a few monks. From the side of its walls, beneath the shade of a few cypresses, there is a magnificent view of the whole of Val d'Arno, with Florence—the gem of Italy—in the centre. Stand with me a moment on the height, and let us gaze on this grand panorama, around which the Apennines stretch with a majestic sweep, wrapped in a robe of purple air, through which shimmer the villas and villages on their sides! The lovely vale lies below us in its garb of olive groves, among which beautiful villas are sprinkled as plentifully as white anemones in the woods of May. Florence lies in front of us, the magnificent cupola of the Duomo crowning its clustered palaces. We see the airy tower of the Palazzo Vecchio—the new spire of Santa Croce—and the long front of the Palazzo Pitti, with the dark foliage of the Boboli Gardens behind. Beyond, far to the south, are the summits of the mountains near Siena. We can trace the sandy bed of the Arno down the valley till it disappears at the foot of the Lower Apennines, which mingle in the distance with the mountains of Carrara.

Galileo was wont to make observations "at evening from the top of Fiesole," and the square tower of the old church is still pointed out as the spot. Many a night did he ascend to its projecting terrace, and watch the stars as they rolled around through the clearest heaven to which a philosopher ever looked up.

We passed through an orchard of fig trees, and vines laden with beautiful purple and golden clusters, and in a few minutes reached the remains of an amphitheatre, in a little nook on the mountain side. This was a work of Roman construction, as its form indicates. Three or four ranges of seats alone, are laid bare, and these have only been discovered within a few years. A few steps further we came to a sort of cavern, overhung with wild fig-trees. After creeping in at the entrance, we found ourselves in an oval chamber, tall enough to admit of our standing upright, and rudely but very strongly built. This was one of the dens in which the wild beasts were kept; they were fed by a hole in the top, now closed up. This cell communicates with four or five others, by apertures broken in the walls. I stepped into one, and could see in the dim light, that it was exactly similar to the first, and opened into another beyond.

Further down the mountain we found the ancient wall of the city, without doubt of Etrurian origin. It is of immense blocks of stone, and extends more or less dilapidated around the whole brow of the mountain. In one place there stands a solitary gateway, of large stones, which looks as if it might have been one of the first attempts at using the principle of the arch. These ruins are all gray and ivied, and it startles one to think what a history Earth has lived through since their foundations were laid!

We sat all the afternoon under the cypress trees and looked down on the lovely valley, practising Italian sometimes with two young Florentines who came up to enjoy the "bell'aria" of Fiesole. Descending as sunset drew on, we reached the Porta San Gallo, as the people of Florence were issuing forth to their evening promenade.

One of my first visits was to the church of Santa Croce. This is one of the oldest in Florence, venerated alike by foreigners and citizens, for the illustrious dead whose remains it holds. It is a plain, gloomy pile, the front of which is still unfinished, though at the base, one sees that it was originally designed to be covered with black marble. On entering the door we first saw the tomb of Michael Angelo. Around the marble sarcophagus which contains his ashes are three mourning figures, representing Sculpture, Painting and Architecture, and his bust stands above—a rough, stern countenance, like a man of vast but unrefined mind. Further on are the tombs of Alfieri and Machiavelli and the colossal cenotaph lately erected to Dante. Opposite reposes Galileo. What a world of renown in these few names! It makes one venerate the majesty of his race, to stand beside the dust of such lofty spirits.

Dante's monument may be said to be only erected to his memory; he sleeps at the place of his exile,

"Like Scipio, buried by the upbraiding shore!"

It is the work of Ricci, a Florentine artist, and has been placed there within a few years. The colossal figure of Poetry weeping over the empty urn, might better express the regret of Florence in being deprived of his ashes. The figure of Dante himself, seated above, is grand and majestic; his head is inclined as if in meditation, and his features bear the expression of sublime thought. Were this figure placed there alone, on a simple and massive pedestal, it would be more in keeping with his fame than the lumbering heaviness of the present monument.

Machiavelli's tomb is adorned with a female figure representing History, bearing his portrait. The inscription, which seems to be somewhat exaggerated, is: tanto nomini nullum par elogium. Near lies Alfieri, the "prince of tragedy," as he is called by the Italians. In his life he was fond of wandering among the

586

tombs of Santa Croce, and it is said that there the first desire and presentiment of his future glory stirred within his breast. Now he slumbers among them, not the least honored name of that immortal company.

Galileo's tomb is adorned with his bust. His face is calm and dignified, and he holds appropriately in his hands, a globe and telescope. Aretino, the historian, lies on his tomb with a copy of his works clasped to his breast; above that of Lanzi, the historian of painting, there is a beautiful fresco of the angel of fame; and opposite to him is the scholar Lamio. The most beautiful monument in the church is that of a Polish princess, in the transept. She is lying on the bier, her features settled in the repose of death, and her thin, pale hands clasped across her breast. The countenance wears that half-smile, "so coldly sweet and sadly fair," which so often throws a beauty over the face of the dead, and the light pall reveals the fixed yet graceful outline of the form.

In that part of the city, which lies on the south bank of the Arno, is the palace of the Grand Duke, known by the name of the Palazzo Pitti, from a Florentine noble of that name, by whom it was first built. It is a very large, imposing pile, preserving an air of lightness in spite of the rough, heavy stones of which it is built. It is another example of a magnificent failure. The Marquis Strozzi, having built a palace which was universally admired for its beauty, (which stands yet, a model of chaste and massive elegance,) his rival, the Marquis Pitti, made the proud boast that he would build a palace, in the court-yard of which could bo placed that of Strozzi. These are actually the dimensions of the court-yard; but in building the palace, although he was liberally assisted by the Florentine people, he ruined himself, and his magnificent residence passed into other hands, while that of Strozzi is inhabited by his descendants to this very day.

The gallery of the Palazzo Pitti is one of the finest in Europe. It contains six or seven hundred paintings, selected from the best works of the Italian masters. By the praiseworthy liberality of the Duke, they are open to the public, six hours every day, and the rooms are thronged with artists of all nations.

Among Titian's works, there is his celebrated "Bella," a half-length figure of a young woman. It is a masterpiece of warm and brilliant coloring, without any decided expression. The countenance is that of vague, undefined thought, as of one who knew as yet nothing of the realities of life. In another room is his Magdalen, a large, voluptuous form, with her brown hair falling like a veil over her shoulders and breast, but in her upturned countenance one can sooner read a prayer for an absent lover than repentance for sins she has committed.

What could excel in beauty the Madonna della Sedia of Raphael? It is another of those works of that divine artist, on which we gaze and gaze with a never-tiring enjoyment of its angelic beauty. To my eye it is faultless; I could not wish a single outline of form, a single shade of color changed. Like his unrivalled Madonna in the Dresden Gallery, its beauty is spiritual as well as earthly; and while gazing on the glorious countenance of the Jesus-child, I feel an impulse I can scarcely explain—a longing to tear it from the canvas as if it were a breathing form, and clasp it to my heart in a glow of passionate love. What a sublime inspiration Raphael must have felt when he painted it! Judging from its effect on the beholder, I can conceive of no higher mental excitement than that required to create it.

Here are also some of the finest and best preserved pictures of Salvator Rosa, and his portrait—a wild head, full of spirit and genius. Besides several landscapes in his savage and stormy style, there are two large sea-views, in which the atmosphere is of a deep and exquisite softness, without impairing the strength and boldness of the composition. "A Battle Scene," is terrible. Hundreds of combatants are met in the shock and struggle of conflict. Horses, mailed knights, vassals are mixed together in wild confusion; banners are waving and lances flashing amid the dust and smoke, while the wounded and dying are trodden under foot in darkness and blood. I now first begin to comprehend the power and sublimity of his genius. From the wildness and gloom of his pictures, he might almost be called the Byron of painters.

There is a small group of the "Fates," by Michael Angelo, which is one of the best of the few pictures which remain of him. As is well known, he disliked the art, saying it was only fit for women. This picture shows, however, how much higher he might have gone, had he been so inclined. The three weird sisters are ghostly and awful—the one who stands behind, holding the distaff, almost frightful. She who stands ready to cut the thread as it is spun out, has a slight trace of pity on her fixed and unearthly lineaments. It is a faithful embodiment of the old Greek idea of the Fates. I have wondered why some artist has not attempted the subject in a different way. In the Northern Mythology they are represented as wild maidens, armed with swords and mounted on fiery coursers. Why might they not also be pictured as angels, with countenances of a sublime and mysterious beauty—one all radiant with hope and promise of glory, and one with the token of a better future mingled with the sadness with which it severs the links of life?

There are many, many other splendid works in this collection, but it is unnecessary to mention them. I have only endeavored, by taking a few of the best known, to give some idea of them as they appear to me. There are hundreds of pictures here, which, though gems in themselves, are by masters who are rarely heard of in America, and it would be of little interest to go through the Gallery, describing it in guide-book fashion. Indeed, to describe galleries, however rich and renowned they may be, is in general a work of so much difficulty, that I know not whether the writer or the reader is made most tired thereby.

This collection possesses also the celebrated statue of Venus, by Canova. She stands in the centre of a little apartment, filled with the most delicate and graceful works of painting. Although undoubtedly a figure of great beauty, it by no means struck me as possessing that exquisite and classic perfection which has been ascribed to it. The Venus de Medici far surpasses it. The head is larger in proportion to the size of the body, than that of the latter, but has not the same modest, virgin expression. The arm wrapped in the robe which she is pressing to her breast, is finely executed, but the fingers of the other hand are bad—looking, as my friend said, as if the ends were whittled off! The body is, however, of fine proportions, though, taken as a whole, the statue is inferior to many other of Canova's works.

Occupying all the hill back of the Pitti Palace, are the Boboli Gardens, three times a week the great resort of the Florentines. They are said to be the most beautiful gardens in Italy. Numberless paths, diverging from a magnificent amphitheatre in the old Roman style, opposite the court-yard, lend either in long flights of steps and terraces, or gentle windings among beds sweet with roses, to the summit. Long avenues, entirely arched and interwoven with the thick foliage of the laurel, which here grows to a tree, stretch along the slopes or wind in the woods through thickets of the fragrant bay. Parterres, rich with flowers and shrubbery, alternate with delightful groves of the Italian pine, acacia and laurel-leaved oak, and along the hillside, gleaming among the foliage, are placed statues of marble, some of which are from the chisels of Michael Angelo and Bandinelli. In one part there is a little sheet of water, with an island of orange-trees in the centre, from which a broad avenue of cypresses and statues leads to the very summit of the hill.

We often go there to watch the sun set over Florence and the vale of the Arno. The palace lies directly below, and a clump of pine-trees on the hillside, that stand out in bold relief on the glowing sky, makes the foreground to one of the loveliest pictures this side of the Atlantic. I saw one afternoon the Grand Duke and his family get into their carriage to drive out. One of the little dukes, who seemed a mischievous imp, ran out on a projection of the portico, where considerable persuasion had to be used to induce him to jump into the arms of his royal papa. I turned from these titled infants to watch a group of beautiful American children playing, for my attention was drawn to them by the sound of familiar words, and I learned afterwards they were the children of the sculptor Powers. I contrasted involuntarily the destinies of each;—one to the enjoyment and proud energy of freedom, and one to the confining and vitiating atmosphere of a court. The merry voices of the latter, as they played on the grass, came to my ears most gratefully. There is nothing so sweet as to hear one's native tongue in a foreign land from the lips of children!

CHAPTER XXXV. — A PILGRIMAGE TO VALLOMBROSA.

A pilgrimage to Vallombrosa!—in sooth it has a romantic sound. The phrase calls up images of rosaries, and crosses, and shaven-headed friars. Had we lived in the olden days, such things might verily have accompanied our journey to that holy monastery. We might then have gone barefoot, saying prayers as we toiled along the banks of the Arno and up the steep Appenines, as did Benevenuto Cellini, before he poured the melted bronze into the mould of his immortal Perseus. But we are pilgrims to the shrines of Art and Genius; the dwelling-places of great minds are our sanctuaries. The mean dwelling, in which a poet has battled down poverty with the ecstacy of his mighty conceptions, and the dungeon in which a persecuted philosopher has languished, are to us sacred; we turn aside from the palaces of kings and the battle-fields of conquerors, to visit them. The famed miracles of San Giovanni Gualberto added little, in our eyes, to the interest of Vallombrosa, but there were reverence and inspiration in the names of Dante, Milton, and Ariosto.

We left Florence early, taking the way that leads from the Porta della Croce, up the north bank of the Arno. It was a bright morning, but there was a shade of vapor on the hills, which a practised eye might have taken as a prognostic of the rain that too soon came on. Fiesole, with its tower and Acropolis, stood out brightly from the blue background, and the hill of San Miniato lay with its cypress groves in the softest morning light. The Contadini were driving into the city in their basket wagons, and there were some fair young faces among them, that made us think Italian beauty was not altogether in the imagination.

After walking three or four miles, we entered the Appenines, keeping along the side of the Arno, whose bed is more than half dried up from the long summer heats. The mountain sides were covered with vineyards, glowing with their wealth of white and purple grapes, but the summits were naked and barren. We passed through the little town of Ponte Sieve, at the entrance of a romantic valley, where our view of the Arno was made more interesting by the lofty range of the Appenines, amid whose forests we could see the white front of the monastery of Vallombrosa. But the clouds sank low and hid it from sight, and the rain came on so hard that we were obliged to take shelter occasionally in the cottages by the wayside. In one of these we made a dinner of the hard, black bread of the country, rendered palatable by the addition of mountain cheese and some chips of an antique Bologna sausage. We were much amused in conversing with the simple hosts and their shy, gipsy-like children, one of whom, a dark-eyed, curly-haired boy, bore the name of Raphael. We also became acquainted with a shoemaker and his family, who owned a little olive orchard and vineyard, which they said produced enough to support them. Wishing to know much a family of six consumed in a year, we inquired the yield of their property. They answered, twenty small barrels of wine, and ten of oil. It was nearly sunset when we reached Pellago, and the wet walk and coarse fare we were obliged to take on the road, well qualified us to enjoy the excellent supper the pleasant landlady gave us.

This little town is among the Appenines, at the foot of the magnificent mountain of Vallombrosa. What a blessing it was for Milton, that he saw its loveliness before his eyes closed on this beautiful earth, and gained from it another hue in which to dip his pencil, when he painted the bliss of Eden! I watched the hills all day as we approached them, and thought how often his eyes had rested on their outlines, and how he had carried their forms in his memory for many a sunless year. The banished Dante, too, had trodden them, flying from his ungrateful country; and many another, whose genius has made him a beacon in the dark sea of the world's history. It is one of those places where the enjoyment is all romance, and the blood thrills as we gaze upon it.

We started early next morning, crossed the ravine, and took the well-paved way to the monastery along the mountain side. The stones are worn smooth by the sleds in which ladies and provisions are conveyed up, drawn by the beautiful white Tuscan oxen. The hills are covered with luxuriant chesnut and oak trees, of those picturesque forms which they only wear in Italy: one wild dell in particular is much resorted to by painters for the ready-made foregrounds it supplies. Further on, we passed the Paterno, a rich farm belonging to the Monks. The vines which hung from tree to tree, were almost breaking beneath clusters as heavy and rich as those which the children of Israel bore on staves from the Promised Land. Of their flavor, we can say, from experience, they were worthy to have grown in Paradise. We then entered a deep dell of the mountain, where little shepherd girls were sitting on the rocks tending their sheep and spinning with their fingers from a distaff, in the same manner, doubtless, as the Roman shepherdesses two thousand years ago. Gnarled, gray olive trees, centuries old, grew upon the bare soil, and a little rill fell in many a tiny cataract down the glen. By a mill, in one of the coolest and wildest nooks I ever saw, two of us acted the part of water-spirits under one of these, to the great astonishment of four peasants, who watched us from a distance.

Beyond, our road led through forests of chestnut and oak, and a broad view of mountain and vale lay below us. We asked a peasant boy we met, how much land the Monks of Vallombrosa possessed. "All that you see!" was the reply. The dominion of the good fathers reached once even to the gates of Florence. At length, about noon, we emerged from the woods into a broad avenue leading across a lawn, at whose extremity stood the massivs buildings of the monastery. On a rock that towered above it, was the Paradisino, beyond which rose the mountain, covered with forests—

"*Shade above shade, a woody theatre.*

Of stateliest view"—

as Milton describes it. We were met at the entrance by a young monk in cowl and cassock, to whom we applied for permission to stay till the next day, which was immediately given. Brother Placido (for that was his name) then asked us if we would not have dinner. We replied that our appetites were none the worse for climbing the mountain; and in half an hour sat down to a dinner, the like of which we had not seen for a long time. Verily, thought I, it must be a pleasant thing to be a monk, after all!—that is, a monk of Vallombrosa.

In the afternoon we walked through a grand pine forest to the western brow of the mountain, where a view opened which it would require a wonderful power of the imagination for you to see in fancy, as I did in reality. From the height where we stood, the view was uninterrupted to the Mediterranean, a distance of more than seventy miles; a valley watered by a brunch of the Arno swept far to the east, to the mountains near the Luke of Thrasymene; northwestwards the hills of Carrara bordered the horizon; the space between these wide points was filled with mountains and valleys, all steeped in that soft blue mist which makes Italian landscapes more like heavenly visions than realities. Florence was visible afar off, and the current of the Arno flashed in the sun. A cool and almost chilling wind blew constantly over the mountain, although the country below basked in summer heat. We lay on the rocks, and let our souls luxuriate in the lovely scene till near sunset. Brother Placido brought us supper in the evening, with his ever-smiling countenance, and we soon after went to our beds in the neat, plain chambers, to get rid of the unpleasant coldness.

Next morning it was damp and misty, and thick clouds rolled down the forests towards the convent. I set out for the "Little Paradise," taking in my way the pretty cascade which falls some fifty feet down the rocks. The building is not now as it was when Milton lived here, having been rebuilt within a short time. I found no one there, and satisfied my curiosity by climbing over the wall and looking in at the windows. A little chapel stands in a cleft of the rock below, to mark the miraculous escape of St. John Gualberto, founder of the monastery. Being one day very closely pursued by the Devil, he took shelter under the rock, which immediately became soft and admitted him into it, while the fiend, unable to stop, was precipitated over the steep. All this is related in a Latin inscription, and we saw a large hollow in the rock near, which must have been intended for the imprint left by his sacred person.

One of the monks told us another legend, concerning a little chapel which stands alone on a wild part of the mountain, above a rough pile of crags, called the "Peak of the Devil." "In the time of San Giovanni Gualberto, the holy founder of our order," said he, "there was a young man, of a noble family in Florence, who was so moved by the words of the saintly father, that he forsook the world, wherein he had lived with great luxury and dissipation, and became monk. But, after a time, being young and tempted again by the pleasures he had renounced, he put off the sacred garments. The holy San Giovanni warned him of the terrible danger in which he stood, and at length the wicked young man returned. It was not a great while, however, before he became dissatisfied, and in spite all holy counsel, did the same thing again. But behold what happened! As he was walking along the peak where the chapel stands, thinking nothing of his great crime, the devil sprang suddenly from behind a rock, and catching the young man in his arms, before he could escape, carried him with a dreadful noise and a great red flame and smoke over the precipice, so that he was never afterwards seen."

The church attached to the monastery is small, but very solemn and venerable. I went several times to muse in its still, gloomy aisle, and hear the murmuring chant of the Monks, who went through their exercises in some of the chapels. At one time I saw them all, in long black cassocks, march in solemn order to the chapel of St. John Gualberto, where they sang a deep chant, which to me had something awful and sepulchral in it. Behind the high altar I saw their black, carved chairs of polished oak, with ponderous gilded foliants lying on the rails before them. The attendant opened one of these, that we might see the manuscript notes, three or four centuries old, from which they sung.

We were much amused in looking through two or three Italian books, which were lying in the traveler's room. One of these which our friend Mr. Tandy, of Kentucky, read, described the miracles of the patron saint with an air of the most ridiculous solemnity. The other was a description of the Monastery, its foundation, history, etc. In mentioning its great and far-spread renown, the author stated then even an English poet, by the name of Milton, had mentioned it in the following lines, which I copied verbatim from the book:

> "*Thick as autumnal scaves that strow she brooks*
>
> *In vallombrosa, whereth Etruian Jades*
>
> *Stigh over orch d'embrover!*"

In looking over the stranger's book, I found among the names of my countrymen, that of S. V. Clevenger, the talented and lamented sculptor who died at sea on his passage home. There were also the names of Mrs. Shelley and the Princess Potemkin, and I saw written on the wall, the autograph of Jean Reboul, the celebrated modern French poet. We were so delighted with the place we would have stayed another day, but for fear of trepassing too much on the lavish and unceasing hospitality of the good fathers.

So in the afternoon we shook hands with Brother Placido, and turned our backs regretfully upon one of the loneliest and loveliest spots of which earth can boast. The sky became gradually clear as we descended, and the mist raised itself from the distant mountains. We ran down through the same chesnut groves, diverging a little to go through the village of Tosi, which is very picturesque when seen from a distance, but extremely dirty to one passing through. I stopped in the ravine below to take a sketch of the mill and bridge, and as we sat, the line of golden sunlight rose higher on the mountains above. On walking down the shady side of this glen, we were enraptured with the scenery. A brilliant yet mellow glow lay over the whole opposing height, lighting up the houses of Tosi and the white cottages half seen among the olives, while the mountain of Vallombrosa stretched far heavenward like a sunny painting, with only a misty wreath floating and waving around its summit. The glossy foliage of the chesnuts was made still brighter by the warm light, and the old olives softened down into a silvery gray, whose contrast gave the landscape a character of the mellowest beauty. As we wound out of the deep glen, the broad valleys and ranges of the Appenines lay before us, forests, castles and villages steeped in the soft, vapory blue of the Italian atmosphere, and the current of the Arno flashing like a golden belt through the middle of the picture.

The sun was nearly down, and the mountains just below him were of a deep purple hue, while those that ran out to the eastward wore the most aerial shade of blue. A few scattered clouds, floating above, soon put on the sunset robe of orange and a band of the same soft color encircled the western horizon. It did not reach half way to the zenith, however; the sky above was blue, of such a depth and transparency, that to gaze upward was like looking into eternity. Then how softly and soothingly the twilight came on! How deep a hush sank on the chestnut glades, broken only by the song of the cicada, chirping its "good-night carol!" The mountains, too, how majestic they stood in their deep purple outlines! Sweet, sweet Italy! I can feel now how the soul may cling to thee, since thou canst thus gratify its insatiable thirst for the Beautiful. Even thy plainest scene is clothed in hues that seem borrowed of heaven! In the twilight, more radiant than light, and the stillness, more eloquent than music, which sink down over the sunny beauty of thy shores, there is a silent, intense poetry that stirs the soul through all its impassioned depths. With warm, blissful tears filling the eyes and a heart overflowing with its own bright fancies, I wander in the solitude and calm of such a time, and love thee as if I were a child of thy soil!

CHAPTER XXXVI. — WALK TO SIENA AND PRATOLINO—INCIDENTS IN FLORENCE.

October 16.—My cousin, being anxious to visit Rome, and reach Heidelberg before the commencement of the winter semestre, set out towards the end of September, on foot. We accompanied him as far as Siena, forty miles distant. As I shall most probably take another road to the Eternal City, the present is a good opportunity to say something of that romantic old town, so famous throughout Italy for the honesty of its inhabitants.

We dined the first day, seventeen miles from Florence, at Tavenella, where, for a meagre dinner the hostess had the assurance to ask us seven pauls. We told her we would give but four and a half, and by assuming a decided manner, with a plentiful use of the word "Signora" she was persuaded to be fully satisfied with the latter sum. From a height near, we could see the mountains coasting the Mediterranean, and shortly after, on descending a long hill, the little town of Poggibonsi lay in the warm afternoon light, on an eminence before us. It was soon passed with its dusky towers, then Stagia looking desolate in its ruined and ivied walls, and following the advice of a peasant, we stopped for the night at the inn of Querciola. As we knew something of Italian by this time, we thought it best to inquire the price of lodging, before entering. The padrone asked if we meant to take supper also. We answered in the affirmative; "then," said he, "you will pay half a paul (about five emits) apiece for a bed." We passed under the swinging bunch of boughs, which in Italy is the universal sign of an inn for the common people, and entered the bare, smoky room appropriated to travelers. A long table, with well-worn benches, were the only furniture; we threw our knapsacks on one end of it and sat down, amusing ourselves while supper was preparing, in looking at a number of grotesque charcoal drawings on the wall, which the flaring light of our tall iron lamp revealed to us. At length the hostess, a kindly-looking woman, with a white handkerchief folded gracefully around her head, brought us a dish of fried eggs, which, with the coarse black bread of the peasants and a basket full of rich grapes, made us an excellent supper.

We slept on mattresses stuffed with corn husks, placed on square iron frames, which are the bedsteads most used in Italy. A brightly-painted caricature of some saint or a rough crucifix, trimmed with bay leaves, hung at the head of each bed, and under their devout protection we enjoyed a safe and unbroken slumber.

Next morning we set out early to complete the remaining ten miles to Siena. The only thing of interest on the road, is the ruined wall and battlements of Castiglione, circling a high hill and looking as old as the days of Etruria. The towers of Siena are seen at some distance, but approaching it from this side, the traveler does not perceive its romantic situation until he arrives. It stands on a double hill, which is very steep on some sides; the hollow between the two peaks is occupied by the great public square, ten or fifteen feet lower than the rest of the city. We left our knapsacks at a café and sought the celebrated Cathedral, which stands in the highest part of the town, forming with its flat dome and lofty marble tower, an apex to the pyramidal mass of buildings.

The interior is rich and elegantly perfect. Every part is of black and white marble, in what I should call the striped style, which has a singular but agreeable effect. The inside of the dome and the vaulted ceilings of the chapels, are of blue, with golden stars; the pavement in the centre is so precious a work that it is kept covered with boards and only shown once a year. There are some pictures of great value in this Cathedral; one of "The Descent of the Dove," is worthy of the best days of Italian art. In an adjoining chamber, with frescoed walls, and a beautiful tesselated pavement, is the library, consisting of a few huge old volumes, which with their brown covers and brazen clasps, look as much like a collection of flat leather trunks as any thing else. In the centre of the room stands the mutilated group of the Grecian Graces, found in digging the foundation of the Cathedral. The figures are still beautiful and graceful, with that exquisite curve of outline which is such a charm in the antique statues. Canova has only perfected the idea in his celebrated group, which is nearly a copy of this.

We strolled through the square and then accompanied our friend to the Roman gate, where we took leave of him for six months at least. He felt lonely at the thought of walking in Italy without a companion, but was cheered by the anticipation of soon reaching Rome. We watched him awhile, walking rapidly over the hot plain towards Radicofani, and then, turning our faces with much pleasure towards Florence, we commenced the return walk. I must not forget to mention the delicious grapes which we bought, begged and stole on the way. The whole country is like one vineyard—and the people live, in a great measure, on the fruit, during this part of the year. Would you not think it highly romantic and agreeable to sit in the shade of a cypress grove, beside some old weather-beaten statues, looking out over the vales of the Appenines, with a pile of white and purple grapes beside you, the like of which can scarcely be had in America for love or money, and which had been given you by a dark-eyed peasant girl? If so, you may envy us, for such was exactly our situation on the morning before reaching Florence.

Being in the Duomo, two or three days ago, I met a German traveler, who has walked through Italy thus far, and intends continuing his journey to Rome and Naples. His name is Von Raumer. He was well acquainted with the present state of America, and I derived much pleasure from his intelligent conversation. We concluded to ascend the cupola in company. Two black-robed boys led the way; after climbing an infinite number of steps, we reached the gallery around the foot of the dome. The glorious view of that paradise, the vale of the Arno, shut in on all sides by mountains, some bare and desolate, some covered with villas, gardens, and groves, lay in soft, hazy light, with the shadows of a few light clouds moving slowly across it. They next took us to a gallery on the inside of the dome, where we first saw the immensity of its structure. Only from a distant view, or in ascending it, can one really measure its grandeur. The frescoes, which from below appear the size of life, are found to be rough and monstrous daubs; each figure being nearly as many fathoms in length as a man is feet. Continuing our ascent, we mounted between the inside and outside shells of the dome. It was indeed a bold idea for Brunelleschi to raise such a mass in air. The dome of Saint Peter's, which is scarcely as large, was not made until a century after, and this was, therefore, the first attempt at raising one on so grand a scale. It seems still as solid as if just built.

There was a small door in one of the projections of the lantern, which the sacristan told us to enter and ascend still higher. Supposing there was a fine view to be gained, two priests, who had just come up, entered it; the German followed, and I after him. After crawling in at the low door, we found ourselves in a hollow pillar, little wider than our bodies. Looking up, I saw the German's legs just above my head, while the other two were above him, ascending by means of little iron bars fastened in the marble. The priests were very much amused, and the German said:—"This is the first time I ever learned chimney-sweeping!" We emerged at length into a hollow cone, hot and dark, with a rickety ladder going up somewhere; we could not see where. The old priest, not wishing to trust himself to it, sent his younger brother up, and we shouted after him:—"What kind of a view have you?" He climbed up till the cone got so narrow he could go no further, and answered back in the darkness:—"I see nothing at all!" Shortly after he came down, covered with dust and cobwebs, and we all descended the chimney quicker than we went up. The old priest considered it a good joke, and laughed till his fat sides shook. We asked the sacristan why he sent us up, and he answered:—"To see the construction of the Church!"

I attended service in the Cathedral one dark, rainy morning, and was never before so deeply impressed with the majesty and grandeur of the mighty edifice. The thick, cloudy atmosphere darkened still more the light which came through the stained windows, and a solemn twilight reigned in the long aisles. The mighty dome sprang far aloft, as if it enclosed a part of heaven, for the light that struggled through the windows around its base, lay in broad bars on the blue, hazy air. I would not have been surprised at seeing a cloud float along within it. The lofty burst of the organ, that seemed like the pantings of a monster, boomed echoing away through dome and nave, with a chiming, metallic vibration, that shook the massive pillars which it would defy an earthquake to rend. All was wrapped in dusky obscurity, except where, in the side-chapels, crowns of tapers were burning around the images. One knows not which most to admire, the genius which could conceive, or the perseverance which could accomplish such a work, On one side of the square, the colossal statue of the architect, glorious old Brunelleschi, is most appropriately placed, looking up with pride at his performance.

The sunshine and genial airs of Italy have gone, leaving instead a cold, gloomy sky and chilling winds. The autumnal season has fairly commenced, and I suppose I must bid adieu to the brightness which made me in love with the land. The change has been no less sudden than unpleasant, and if, as they say, it will continue all winter with little variation, I shall have to seek a clearer climate. In the cold of these European winters, there is, as I observed last year in Germany, a dull, damp chill, quite different from the bracing, exhilarating frosts of America. It stagnates the vital principle and leaves the limbs dull and heavy, with a lifeless feeling which can scarcely be overcome by vigorous action. At least, such has been my experience.

We lately made an excursion to Pratolino, on the Appenines, to see the vintage and the celebrated colossus, by John of Bologna. Leaving Florence in the morning, with a cool, fresh wind blowing down from the mountains, we began ascending by the road to Bologna. We passed Fiesole with its tower and acropolis on the right, ascending slowly, with the bold peak of one of the loftiest Appenines on our left. The abundant fruit of the olive was beginning to turn brown, and the grapes were all gathered in from the vineyards, but we learned from a peasant boy that the vintage was not finished at Pratolino.

We finally arrived at an avenue shaded with sycamores, leading to the royal park. The vintagers were busy in the fields around, unloading the vines of their purple tribute, and many a laugh and jest among the merry peasants enlivened the toil. We assisted them in disposing of some fine clusters, and then sought the "Colossus of the Appenines." He stands above a little lake, at the head of a long mountain-slope, broken with clumps of magnificent trees. This remarkable figure, the work of John of Bologna, impresses one like a relic of the Titans. He is represented as half-kneeling, supporting himself with one hand, while the other is pressed upon the head of a dolphin, from which a little stream falls into the lake. The height of the figure when erect, would amount to more than sixty feet! We measured one of the feet, which is a single piece of rock, about eight feet long; from the ground to the top of one knee is nearly twenty feet. The limbs are formed of pieces of stone, joined together, and the body of stone and brick. His rough hair and eyebrows, and the beard, which reached nearly to the ground, are formed of stalactites, taken from caves, and fastened together in a dripping and crusted mass. These hung also from his limbs and body, and gave him the appearance of Winter in his mail of icicles. By climbing up the rocks at his back, we entered his body, which contains a small-sized room; it was even possible to ascend through his neck and look out at his ear! The face is in keeping with the figure—stern and grand, and the architect (one can hardly say sculptor) has given to it the majestic air and sublimity of the Appenines. But who can build up an image of the Alp?

We visited the factory on the estate, where wine and oil are made. The men had just brought in a cart load of large wooden vessels, filled with grapes, which they were mashing with heavy wooden pestles. When the grapes were pretty well reduced to pulp and juice, they emptied them into an enormous tub, which they told us would be covered air-tight, and left for three or four weeks, after which the wine would be drawn off at the bottom. They showed us also a great stone mill for grinding olives; this estate of the Grand Duke produces five hundred barrels of wine and a hundred and fifty of oil, every year. The former article is the universal beverage of the laboring classes in Italy, or I might say of all classes; it is, however, the pure blood of the grape, and although used in such quantities, one sees little drunkenness—far less than in our own land.

Tuscany enjoys at present a more liberal government than any other part of Italy, and the people are, in many respects, prosperous and happy. The Grand Duke, although enjoying almost absolute privileges, is disposed to encourage every measure which may promote the welfare of his subjects. The people are, indeed, very heavily taxed, but this is less severely felt by them, than it would be by the inhabitants of colder climes. The soil produces with little labor all that is necessary for their support; though kept constantly in a state of comparative poverty, they appear satisfied with their lot, and rarely look further than the necessities of the present. In love with the delightful climate, they cherish their country, fallen as she is, and are rarely induced to leave her. Even the wealthier classes of the Italians travel very little; they can learn the manners and habits of foreigners nearly as well in their own country as elsewhere, and they prefer their own hills of olive and vine to the icy grandeur of the Alps or the rich and garden-like beauty of England.

But, although this sweet climate, with its wealth of sunlight and balmy airs, may enchant the traveler for awhile and make him wish at times that his whole life might be spent amid such scenes, it exercises a most enervating influence on those who are born to its enjoyment. It relaxes mental and physical energy, and disposes body and mind to dreamy inactivity. The Italians, as a race, are indolent and effeminate. Of the moral dignity of man they have little conception. Those classes who are engaged in active occupation seem even destitute of common honesty, practising all kinds of deceits in the most open manner and apparently without the least shame. The state of morals is lower than in any other country of Europe; what little virtue exists is found among the peasants. Many of the most sacred obligations of society are universally violated, and as a natural consequence, the people are almost entire strangers to that domestic happiness, which constitutes the true enjoyment of life.

This dark shadow in the moral atmosphere of Italy hangs like a curse on her beautiful soil, weakening the sympathies of citizens of freer lands with her fallen condition. I often feel vividly the sentiment which Percival puts into the mouth of a Greek in slavery:

> *"The spring may here with autumn twine*
>
> *And both combined may rule the year,*
>
> *And fresh-blown flowers and racy wine*
>
> *In frosted clusters still be near—*
>
> *Dearer the wild and snowy hills*
>
> *Where hale and ruddy Freedom smiles."*

No people can ever become truly great or free, who are not virtuous. If the soul aspires for liberty—pure and perfect liberty—it also aspires for everything that is noble in Truth, everything that is holy in Virtue. It is greatly to be feared that all those nervous and impatient efforts which have been made and are still being made by the Italian people to better their condition, will be of little avail, until they set up a better standard of principle and make their private actions more conformable with their ideas of political independence.

Oct. 22.—I attended to-day the fall races at the Cascine. This is a dairy farm of the Grand Duke on the Arno, below the city; part of it, shaded with magnificent trees, has been made into a public promenade and drive, which extends for three miles down the river. Towards the lower end, on a smooth green lawn, is the race-course. To-day was the last of the season, for which the best trials had been reserved; on passing out the gate at noon, we found a number of carriages and pedestrians going the same way. It was the very perfection of autumn temperature, and I do not remember to have ever seen so blue hills, so green meadows, so fresh air and so bright sunshine combined in one scene before. All that gloom and coldness of which I lately complained has vanished.

Traveling increases very much one's capacity for admiration. Every beautiful scene appears as beautiful as if it had been the first; and although I may have seen a hundred times as lovely a combination of sky and landscape, the pleasure which it awakens is never diminished. This is one of the greatest blessings we enjoy—the freshness and glory which Nature wears to our eyes forever. It shows that the soul never grows old—that the eye of age can take in the impression of beauty with the same enthusiastic joy that leaped through the heart of childhood.

We found the crowd around the race-course but thin; half the people there, and all the horses, appeared to be English. It was a good place to observe the beauty of Florence, which however, may be done in a short time, as there is not much of it. There is beauty in Italy, undoubtedly, but it is either among the peasants or the higher class of nobility. I will tell our American women confidentially, for I know they have too much sense to be vain of it, that they surpass the rest of the world as much in beauty as they do in intelligence and virtue. I saw in one of the carriages the wife of Alexander Dumas, the French author. She is a large, fair complexioned woman, and is now, from what cause I know not, living apart from her husband.

The jockeys paced up and down the fields, preparing their beautiful animals for the approaching heat, and as the hour drew nigh the mounted dragoons busied themselves in clearing the space. It was a one-mile course, to the end of the lawn and back. At last the bugle sounded, and off went three steeds like arrows let fly. They passed us, their light limbs bounding over the turf, a beautiful dark-brown taking the lead. We leaned over the railing and watched them eagerly. The bell rang—they reached the other end—we saw them turn and come dashing back, nearer, nearer; the crowd began to shout, and in a few seconds the brown one had won it by four or five lengths. The fortunate horse was led around in triumph, and I saw an English lady, remarkable for her betting propensities, come out from the crowd and kiss it in apparent delight.

After an interval, three others took the field—all graceful, spirited creatures. This was a more exciting race than the first; they flew past us nearly abreast, and the crowd looked after them in anxiety. They cleared the course like wild deer, and in a minute or two came back, the racer of an English nobleman a short distance ahead. The jockey threw up his hand in token of triumph as he approached the goal, and the people cheered him. It was a beautiful sight to see those noble animals stretching to the utmost of their speed, as they dashed down the grassy lawn. The lucky one always showed by his proud and erect carriage, his consciousness of success.

Florence is fast becoming modernized. The introduction of gas, and the construction of the railroad to Pisa, which is nearly completed, will make sad havoc with the air of poetry which still lingers in its silent streets. There is scarcely a bridge, a tower, or a street, which is not connected with some stirring association. In the Via San Felice, Raphael used to paint when a boy; near the Ponte Santa Trinita stands Michael Angelo's house, with his pictures, clothes, and painting implements, just as he left it three centuries ago; on the south side of the Arno is the house of Galileo, and that of Machiavelli stands in an avenue near the Ducal Palace. While threading my way through some dark, crooked streets in an unfrequented part of the city, I noticed an old, untenanted house, bearing a marble tablet above the door. I drew near and read:—"In this house of the Alighieri was born the Divine Poet!" It was the birth-place of Dante!

Nov. 1.—Yesterday morning we were apprised of the safe arrival of a new scion of the royal family in the world by the ringing of the city bells. To-day, to celebrate the event, the shops were closed, and the people made a holiday of it. Merry chimes pealed out from every tower, and discharges of cannon

606

thundered up from the fortress. In the evening the dome of the Cathedral was illuminated, and the lines of cupola, lantern, and cross were traced in flame on the dark sky, like a crown of burning stars dropped from Heaven on the holy pile. I went in and walked down the aisle, listening for awhile to the grand choral, while the clustered tapers under the dome quivered and trembled, as if shaken by the waves of music which burst continually within its lofty concave.

A few days ago Prince Corsini, Prime Minister of Tuscany, died at an advanced age. I saw his body brought in solemn procession by night, with torches and tapers, to the church of Santa Trinita. Soldiers followed with reversed arms and muffled drums, the band playing a funeral march. I forced myself through the crowd into the church, which was hung with black and gold, and listened to the long drawn chanting of the priests around the bier.

We lately visited the Florentine Museum. Besides the usual collection of objects of natural history, there is an anatomical cabinet, very celebrated for its preparations in wax. All parts of the human frame are represented so wonderfully exact, that students of medicine pursue their studies here in summer with the same facility as from real "subjects." Every bone, muscle, and nerve in the body is perfectly counterfeited, the whole forming a collection as curious as it is useful. One chamber is occupied with representations of the plague of Rome, Milan, and Florence. They are executed with horrible truth to nature, but I regretted afterwards having seen them. There are enough forms of beauty and delight in the world on which to employ the eye, without making it familiar with scenes which can only be remembered with a shudder.

We derive much pleasure from the society of the American artists who are now residing in Florence. At the houses of Powers, and Brown, the painter, we spend many delightful evenings in the company of our gifted countrymen. They are drawn together by a kindred, social feeling as well as by their mutual aims, and form among themselves a society so unrestrained, American-like, that the traveler who meets them forgets his absence for a time. These noble representatives of our country, all of whom possess the true, inborn spirit of republicanism, have made the American name known and respected in Florence. Powers, especially, who is intimate with many of the principal Italian families, is universally esteemed. The Grand Duke has more than once visited his studio and expressed the highest admiration of his talents.

CHAPTER XXXVII. — AMERICAN ART IN FLORENCE.

I have seen Ibrahim Pacha, the son of old Mehemet Ali, driving in his carriage through the streets. He is hero on a visit from Lucca, where he has been spending some time on account of his health. He is a man of apparently fifty years of age; his countenance wears a stern and almost savage look, very consistent with the character he bears and the political part he has played. He is rather portly in person, the pale olive of his complexion contrasting strongly with a beard perfectly white. In common with all his attendants, he wears the high red cap, picturesque blue tunic and narrow trowsers of the Egyptians. There is scarcely a man of them whose face with its wild, oriental beauty, does not show to advantage among us civilized and prosaic Christians.

In Florence, and indeed through all Italy, there is much reason for our country to be proud of the high stand her artists are taking. The sons of our rude western clime, brought up without other resources than their own genius and energy, now fairly rival those, who from their cradle upwards have drawn inspiration and ambition from the glorious masterpieces of the old painters and sculptors. Wherever our artists are known, they never fail to create a respect for American talent, and to dissipate the false notions respecting our cultivation and refinement, which prevail in Europe. There are now eight or ten of our painters and sculptors in Florence, some of whom, I do not hesitate to say, take the very first rank among living artists.

I have been highly gratified in visiting the studio of Mr. G.L. Brown, who, as a landscape painter, is destined to take a stand second to few, since the days of Claude Lorraine. He is now without a rival in Florence, or perhaps in Italy, and has youth, genius and a plentiful stock of the true poetic enthusiasm for his art, to work for him far greater triumphs. His Italian landscapes have that golden mellowness and transparency of atmosphere which give such a charm to the real scenes, and one would think he used on his pallette, in addition to the more substantial colors, condensed air and sunlight and the liquid crystal of streams. He has wooed Nature like a lover, and she has not withheld her sympathy. She has taught him how to raise and curve her trees, load their boughs with foliage, and spread underneath them the broad, cool shadows—to pile up the shattered crag, and steep the long mountain range in the haze of alluring distance.

He has now nearly finished, a large painting of "Christ Preaching in the Wilderness," which is of surprising beauty. You look upon one of the fairest scenes of Judea. In front, the rude multitude are grouped on one side, in the edge of a magnificent forest; on the other side, towers up a rough wall of rock and foliage that stretches back into the distance, where some grand blue mountains are piled against the sky, and a beautiful stream, winding through the middle of the picture, slides away out of the foreground. Just emerging from the shade of one of the cliffs, is the benign figure of the Saviour, with the warm light which breaks from behind the trees, falling around him as he advances. There is a smaller picture of the "Shipwreck of St. Paul," in which he shows equal skill in painting a troubled sea and breaking storm. He is one of the young artists from whom we have most to hope.

I have been extremely interested in looking over a great number of sketches made by Mr. Kellogg, of Cincinnati, during a tour through Egypt, Arabia Petræa and Palestine. He visited many places out of the general route of travelers, and beside the great number of landscape views, brought away many sketches of the characters and costumes of the Orient. From some of these he has commenced paintings, which, as his genius is equal to his practice, will be of no ordinary value. Indeed, some of these must give him at once an established reputation in America. In Constantinople, where he resided several months, he enjoyed peculiar advantges for the exercise of his art, through the favor and influence of Mr. Carr, the American, and Sir Stratford Canning, the British Minister. I saw a splendid diamond cup, presented to him by Riza Pacha, the late Grand Vizier. The sketches he brought from thence and from the valleys of Phrygia and the mountain solitudes of old Olympus, are of great interest and value. Among his later paintings, I might mention an angel, whose countenance beams with a rapt and glorious beauty. A divine light shines through all the features and heightens the glow of adoration to an expression all spiritual and immortal. If Mr. Kellogg will give us a few more

610

of these heavenly conceptions, we will place him on a pedestal, little lower than that of Guido.

Greenough, who has been sometime in Germany, returned lately to Florence, where he has a colossal group in progress for the portico of the Capitol. I have seen part of it, which is nearly finished in the marble. It shows a backwoodsman just triumphing in the struggle with an Indian; another group to be added, will represent the wife and child of the former. The colossal size of the statues gives a grandeur to the action, as if it were a combat of Titans; there is a consciousness of power, an expression of lofty disdain in the expansion of the hunter's nostril and the proud curve of his lip, that might become a god. The spirit of action, of breathing, life-like exertion, so much more difficult to infuse into the marble than that of repose, is perfectly attained. I will not enter into a more particular description, as it will probably be sent to the United States in a year or two. It is a magnificent work; the best, unquestionably, that Greenough has yet made. The subject, and the grandeur he has given it in the execution, will ensure it a much more favorable reception than a false taste gave to his Washington.

Mr. C.B. Ives, a young sculptor from Connecticut, has not disappointed the high promise he gave before leaving home. I was struck with some of his busts in Philadelphia, particularly those of Mrs. Sigourney and Joseph R. Chandler, and it has been no common pleasure to visit his studio here in Florence, and look on some of his ideal works. He has lately made two models, which, when finished in marble, will be works of great beauty. They will contribute greatly to his reputation here and in America. One of these represents a child of four or five years of age, holding in his hand a dead bird, on which he is gazing, with childish grief and wonder, that it is so still and drooping. It is a beautiful thought; the boy is leaning forward as he sits, holding the lifeless playmate close in his hands, his sadness touched with a vague expression, as if he could not yet comprehend the idea of death.

The other is of equal excellence, in a different style; it is a bust of "Jephthah's daughter," when the consciousness of her doom first flashes upon her. The face and bust are beautiful with the bloom of perfect girlhood. A simple robe covers her breast, and her rich hair is gathered up behind, and bound with a slender fillet. Her head, of the pure classical mould, is bent forward, as if weighed down by the shock, and there is a heavy drooping in the mouth and eyelids, that denotes a sudden and sickening agony. It is not a violent, passionate grief, but a deep and almost paralyzing emotion—a shock from which the soul will finally rebound, strengthened to make the sacrifice.

Would it not be better for some scores of our rich merchants to lay out their money on statues and pictures, instead of balls and spendthrift sons? A few such expenditures, properly directed, would do much for the advancement of the fine arts. An occasional golden blessing, bestowed on genius, might be returned on the giver, in the fame he had assisted in creating. There seems, however, to be at present a rapid increase in refined taste, and a better appreciation of artistic talent, in our country. And as an American, nothing has made me feel prouder than this, and the steadily increasing reputation of our artists.

Of these, no one has done more within the last few years, than Powers. With a tireless and persevering energy, such as could have belonged to few but Americans, he has already gained a name in his art, that posterity will pronounce in the same breath with Phidias, Michael Angelo and Thorwaldsen. I cannot describe the enjoyment I have derived from looking at his matchless works. I should hesitate in giving my own imperfect judgment of their excellence, if I had not found it to coincide with that of many others who are better versed in the rules of art. The sensation which his "Greek Slave" produced in England, has doubtless ere this been breezed across the Atlantic, and I see by the late American papers that they are growing familiar with his fame. When I read a notice seven or eight years ago, of the young sculptor of Cincinnati, whose busts exhibited so much evidence of genius, I little dreamed I should meet him in Florence, with the experience of years of toil added to his early enthusiasm, and every day increasing his renown.

You would like to hear of his statue of Eve, which men of taste pronounce one of the finest works of modern times. A more perfect figure never filled my eye. I have seen the masterpieces of Thorwaldsen, Dannecker and Canova, and the Venus de Medici, but I have seen nothing yet that can exceed the beauty of this glorious statue. So completely did the first view excite my surprise and delight, and thrill every feeling that awakes at the sight of the Beautiful, that my mind dwelt intensely on it for days afterwards. This is the Eve of Scripture—the Eve of Milton—mother of mankind and fairest of all her race. With the full and majestic beauty of ripened womanhood, she wears the purity of a world as yet unknown to sin. With the hearing of a queen, there is in her countenance the softness and grace of a tender, loving woman;

> *"God-like erect, with native honor clad*
>
> *In naked majesty."*

She holds the fatal fruit extended in her hand, and her face expresses the struggle between conscience, dread and desire. The serpent, whose coiled length under the leaves and flowers entirely surrounds her, thus forming a beautiful allegorical symbol, is watching her decision from an ivied trunk at her side. Her form is said to be fully as perfect as the Venus de Medici, and from its greater size, has an air of conscious and ennobling dignity. The head is far superior in beauty, and soul speaks from every feature of the countenance. I add a few stanzas which the contemplation of this statue called forth. Though unworthy the subject, they may perhaps faintly shadow the sentiment which Powers has so eloquently embodied in marble:

THE "EVE" OF POWERS.

A faultless being from the marble sprung,

   She stands in beauty there!

As when the grace of Eden 'round her clung—

   Fairest, where all was fair!

Pure, as when first from God's creating hand

   She came, on man to shine;

So seems she now, in living stone to stand—

   A mortal, yet divine!

The spark the Grecian from Olympus caught,

 Left not a loftier trace;

The daring of the sculptor's hand has wrought

 A soul in that sweet face!

He won as well the sacred fire from heaven.

 God-sent, not stolen down,

And no Promethean doom for him is given,

 But ages of renown!

The soul of beauty breathes around that form

 A more enchanting spell;

There blooms each virgin grace, ere yet the storm

 On blighted Eden fell!

The first desire upon her lovely brow,

 Raised by an evil power;

Doubt, longing, dread, are in her features now—

 It is the trial-hour!

How every thought that strives within her breast,

 In that one glance is shown!

Say, can that heart of marble be at rest,

 Since spirit warms the stone?

Will not those limbs, of so divine a mould,

 Move, when her thought is o'er—

When she has yielded to the tempter's hold

And Eden blooms no more?

Art, like a Phoenix, springs from dust again—

She cannot pass away!

Bound down in gloom, she breaks apart the chain

And struggles up today!

The flame, first kindled in the ages gone,

Has never ceased to burn,

And westward now, appears the kindling dawn,

Which marks the day's return!

The "Greek Slave" is now in the possession of Mr. Grant, of London, and I only saw the clay model. Like the Eve, it is a form that one's eye tells him is perfect, unsurpassed; but it is the budding loveliness of a girl, instead of the perfected beauty of a woman. In England it has been pronounced superior to Canova's works, and indeed I have seen nothing of his, that could be placed beside it.

Powers has now nearly finished a most exquisite figure of a fisher-boy, standing on the shore, with his net and rudder in one hand, while with the other he holds a shell to his ear and listens if it murmur to him of a gathering storm. His slight, boyish limbs are full of grace and delicacy—you feel that the youthful frame could grow up into nothing less than an Apollo. Then the head—how beautiful! Slightly bent on one side, with the rim of the shell thrust under his locks, lips gently parted, and the face wrought up to the most hushed and breathless expression, he listens whether the sound be deeper than its wont. It makes you hold your breath and listen, to look at it. Mrs. Jameson somewhere remarks that repose or suspended motion, should be always chosen for a statue that shall present a perfect, unbroken impression to the mind. If this be true, the enjoyment must be much more complete where not only the motion, but almost breath and thought are suspended, and all the faculties wrought into one hushed and intense sensation. In gazing on this exquisite conception, I feel my admiration filled to the utmost, without that painful, aching impression, so often left by beautiful works. It glides into my vision like a form long missed from the gallery of beauty I am forming in my mind, and I gaze on it with an ever new and increasing delight.

Now I come to the last and fairest of all—the divine Proserpine. Not the form, for it is but a bust rising from a capital of acanthus leaves, which curve around the breast and arms and turn gracefully outward, but the face, whose modest maiden beauty can find no peer among goddesses or mortals. So looked she on the field of Ennæ—that "fairer flower," so soon to be gathered by "gloomy Dis." A slender crown of green wheatblades, showing alike her descent from Ceres and her virgin years, circles her head. Truly, if Pygmalion stole his fire to warm such a form as this, Jove should have pardoned him. Of Powers' busts it is unnecessary for me to speak. He has lately finished a very beautiful one of the Princess Demidoff, daughter of Jerome Bonaparte.

We will soon, I hope, have the "Eve" in America. Powers has generously refused many advantageous offers for it, that he might finally send it home; and his country, therefore, will possess this statue, his first ideal work. She may well be proud of the genius and native energy of her young artist, and she should repay them by a just and liberal encouragement.

CHAPTER XXXVIII. — AN ADVENTURE ON THE GREAT ST. BERNARD—WALKS AROUND FLORENCE.

Nov. 9.—A few days ago I received a letter from my cousin at Heidelberg, describing his solitary walk from Genoa over the Alps, and through the western part of Switzerland. The news of his safe arrival dissipated the anxiety we were beginning to feel, on account of his long silence, while it proved that our fears concerning the danger of such a journey were not altogether groundless. He met with a startling adventure on the Great St. Bernard, which will be best described by an extract from his own letter:

"Such were my impressions of Rome. But leaving the 'Eternal City,' I must hasten on to give you a description of an adventure I met with in crossing the Alps, omitting for the present an account of the trip from Rome to Genoa, and my lonely walk through Sardinia. When I had crossed the mountain range north of Genoa, the plains of Piedmont stretched out before me. I could see the snowy sides and summits of the Alps more than one hundred miles distant, looking like white, fleecy clouds on a summer day. It was a magnificent prospect, and I wonder not that the heart of the Swiss soldier, after years of absence in foreign service, beats with joy when he again looks on his native mountains.

"As I approached nearer, the weather changed, and dark, gloomy clouds enveloped them, so that they seemed to present an impassible barrier to the lands beyond them. At Ivrea, I entered the interesting valley of Aosta. The whole valley, fifty miles in length, is inhabited by miserable looking people, nearly one half of them being afflicted with goitre and cretinism. They looked more idiotic and disgusting than any I have ever seen, and it was really painful to behold such miserable specimens of humanity dwelling amid the grandest scenes of nature. Immediately after arriving in the town of Aosta, situated at the upper end of the valley, I began, alone, the ascent of the Great St. Bernard. It was just noon, and the clouds on the mountains indicated rain. The distance from Aosta to the monastery or hospice of St. Bernard, is about twenty English miles.

"At one o'clock it commenced raining vary hard, and to gain shelter I went into a rude hut; but it was filled with so many of those idiotic cretins, lying down on the earthy floor with the dogs and other animals, that I was glad to leave them as soon as the storm had abated in some degree. I walked rapidly for three hours, when I met a traveler and his guide descending the mountain. I asked him in Italian the distance to the hospice, and he undertook to answer me in French, but the words did not seem to flow very fluently, so I said quickly, observing then that he was an Englishman: 'Try some other language, if you please, sir!' He replied instantly in his vernacular: 'You have a d—d long walk before you, and you'll have to hurry to get to the top before night!' Thanking him, we shook hands and hurried on, he downward and I upward. About eight miles from the summit, I was directed into the wrong path by an ignorant boy who was tending sheep, and went a mile out of the course, towards Mont Blanc, before I discovered my mistake. I hurried back into the right path again, and soon overtook another boy ascending the mountain, who asked me if he might accompany me as he was alone, to which I of course answered, yes; but when we began to enter the thick clouds that covered the mountains, he became alarmed, and said he would go no farther. I tried to encourage him by saying we had only five miles more to climb, but, turning quickly, he ran down the path and was soon out of sight.

"After a long and most toilsome ascent, spurred on as I was by the storm and the approach of night, I saw at last through the clouds a little house, which I supposed might be a part of the monastery, but it turned out to be only a house of refuge, erected by the monks to take in travelers in extreme cases or extraordinary danger. The man who was staying there, told me the monastery was a mile and a half further, and thinking therefore that I could soon reach it, I started out again, although darkness was approaching. In a short time the storm began in good earnest, and the cold winds blew with the greatest fury. It grew dark very suddenly and I lost sight of the poles which are placed along the path to guide the traveler. I then ran on still higher, hoping to find them again, but without success. The rain and snow fell thick, and although I think I am tolerably courageous, I began to be alarmed, for it was impossible to know in what direction I was going. I could hear the waterfalls dashing and roaring down the mountain hollows on each side of me; in the gloom, the foam and leaping waters resembled streaming fires. I thought of turning back to find the little house of refuge again, but it seemed quite as dangerous and uncertain as to go forward. After the fatigue I had undergone since noon, it would have been dangerous to be obliged to stay, out all night in the driving storm, which was every minute increasing in coldness and intensity.

"I stopped and shouted aloud, hoping I might be somewhere near the monastery, but no answer came—no noise except the storm and the roar of the waterfalls. I climbed up the rocks nearly a quarter of a mile higher, and shouted again. I listened with anxiety for two or three minutes, but hearing no response, I concluded to find a shelter for the night under a ledge of rocks. While looking around me, I fancied I heard in the distance a noise like the trampling of hoofs over the rocks, and thinking travelers might be near, I called aloud for the third time. After wailing a moment, a voice came ringing on my ears through the clouds, like one from Heaven in response to my own. My heart beat quickly; I hurried in the direction from which the sound came, and to my joy found two men—servants of the monastery—who were driving their mules into shelter. Never in my whole life was I more glad to hear the voice of man. These men conducted me to the monastery, one-fourth of a mile higher, built by the side of a lake at the summit of the pass, while on each side, the mountains, forever covered with snow, tower some thousands of feet higher.

"Two or three of the noble St. Bernard dogs barked a welcome as we approached, which brought a young monk to the door. I addressed him in German, but to my surprise he answered in broken English. He took me into a warm room and gave me a suit of clothes, such as are worn by the monks, for my dress, as well as my package of papers, were completely saturated with rain. I sat down to supper in company with till the monks of the Hospice, I in my monkish robe looking like one of the holy order. You would have laughed to have seen me in their costume. Indeed, I felt almost satisfied to turn monk, as everything seemed so comfortable in the warm supper room, with its blazing wood fire, while outside raged the storm still more violently. But when I thought of their voluntary banishment from the world, up in that high pass of the Alps, and that the affection of woman never gladdened their hearts, I was ready to renounce my monkish dress next morning, without reluctance.

"In the address book of the monastery, I found Longfellow's 'Excelsior' written on a piece of paper and signed 'America.' You remember the stanza:

At break of clay, as heavenward,

The pious monks of St. Bernard

Uttered the oft-repeated prayer,

A voice cried through the startled air:

Excelsior!

It seemed to add a tenfold interest to the poem, to read it on old St. Bernard. In the morning I visited the house where are kept the bodies of the travelers, who perish in crossing the mountain. It is filled with corpses, ranged in rows, and looking like mummies, for the cold is so intense that they will keep for years without decaying, and are often recognized and removed by their friends.

"Of my descent to Martigny, my walk down the Rhone, and along the shores of Lake Leman, my visit to the prison of Chilian and other wanderings across Switzerland, my pleasure in seeing the old river Rhine again, and my return to Heidelberg at night, with the bright moon shining on the Neckar and the old ruined castle, I can now say no more, nor is it necessary, for are not all these things 'written in my book of Chronicles,' to be seen by you when we meet again in Paris?

Ever yours, FRANK."

Dec. 16.—I took a walk lately to the tower of Galileo. In company with three friends, I left Florence by the Porta Romana, and ascended the Poggie Imperiale. This beautiful avenue, a mile and a quarter in length, leading up a gradual ascent to a villa of the Grand Duke, is bordered with splendid cypresses and evergreen oaks, and the grass banks are always fresh and green, so that even in winter it calls up a remembrance of summer. In fact, winter does not wear the scowl here that he has at home; he is robed rather in a threadbare garment of autumn, and it is only high up on the mountain tops, out of the reach of his enemy, the sun, that he dares to throw it off, and bluster about with his storms and scatter down his snow-flakes. The roses still bud and bloom in the hedges, the emerald of the meadows is not a whit paler, the sun looks down lovingly as yet, and there are only the white helmets of some of the Appenines, with the leafless mulberries and vines, to tell us that we have changed seasons.

A quarter of an hour's walk, part of it by a path through an olive orchard, brought us to the top of a hill, which was surmounted by a square, broken, ivied tower, forming part of a storehouse for the produce of the estate. We entered, saluted by a dog, and passing through a court-yard, in which stood two or three carts full of brown olives, found our way to the rickety staircase. I spared my sentiment in going up, thinking the steps might have been renewed since Galileo's time, but the glorious landscape which opened around us when we reached the top, time could not change, and I gazed upon it with interest and emotion, as my eye took in those forms which had once been mirrored in the philosopher's. Let me endeavor to describe the features of the scene.

Fancy yourself lifted to the summit of a high hill, whose base slopes down to the valley of the Arno, and looking northward. Behind you is a confusion of hill and valley, growing gradually dimmer away to the horizon. Before and below you is a vale, with Florence and her great domes and towers in its lap, and across its breadth of five miles the mountain of Fiesole. To the west it stretches away unbroken for twenty miles, covered thickly with white villas—like a meadow of daisies, magnified. A few miles to the east the plain is rounded with mountains, between whose interlocking bases we can see the brown current of the Arno. Some of their peaks, as well as the mountain of Vallombrosa, along the eastern sky, are tipped with snow. Imagine the air filled with a thick blue mist, like a semi-transparent veil, which softens every thing into dreamy indistinctness, the sunshine falling slantingly through this in spots, touching the landscape here and there as with a sudden blaze of fire, and you will complete the picture. Does it not repay your mental flight across the Atlantic.

One evening, on coming out of the cafè, the moon was shining so brightly and clearly, that I involuntarily bent my steps towards the river; I walked along the Lung'Arno, enjoying the heavenly moonlight—"the night of cloudless climes and starry skies!" A purer silver light never kissed the brow of Endymion. The brown Arno took into his breast "the redundant glory," and rolled down his pebbly bed with a more musical ripple; opposite stretched the long mass of buildings—the deep arches that rose from the water were filled with black shadow, and the irregular fronts of the houses touched with a mellow glow. The arches of the upper bridge were in shadow, cutting their dark outline on the silvery sweep of the Appenines, far up the stream. A veil of luminous gray covered the hill of San Miniato, with its towers and cypress groves, and there was a crystal depth in the atmosphere, as if it shone with its own light. The whole scene affected me as something too glorious to be real—painful from the very intensity of its beauty. Three moons ago, at the foot of Vallombrosa, I saw the Appenines flooded with the same silvery gush, and thought also, then, that I had seen the same moon amid far dearer scenes, but never before the same dreamy and sublime glory showered down from her pale orb. Some solitary lights were burning along the river, and occasionally a few Italians passed by, wrapped in their mantles. I went home to the Piazza del Granduca as the light, pouring into the square from behind the old palace, fell over the fountain of Neptune and sheathed in silver the back of the colossal god.

Whoever looks on the valley of the Arno from San Miniato, and observes the Appenine range, of which Fiesole is one, bounding it on the north, will immediately notice to the northwest a double peak rising high above all the others. The bare, brown forehead of this, known by the name of Monte Morello, seemed so provokingly to challenge an ascent, that we determined to try it. So we started early, the day before yesterday, from the Porta San Gallo, with nothing but the frosty grass and fresh air to remind us of the middle of December. Leaving the Prato road, at the base of the mountain, we passed

Careggi, a favorite farm of Lorenzo the Magnificent, and entered a narrow glen where a little brook was brawling down its rocky channel. Here and there stood a rustic mill, near which women were busy spreading their washed clothes on the grass. Following the footpath, we ascended a long eminence to a chapel where some boys were amusing themselves with a common country game. They have a small wheel, around which they wind a rope, and, running a little distance to increase the velocity, let it off with a sudden jerk. On a level road it can be thrown upwards of a quarter of a mile.

From the chapel, a gradual ascent along the ridge of a hill brought us to the foot of the peak, which rose high before us, covered with bare rocks and stunted oaks. The wind blew coldly from a snowy range to the north, as we commenced ascending with a good will. A few shepherds were leading their flocks along the sides, to browse on the grass and withered bushes, and we started up a large hare occasionally from his leafy covert. The ascent was very toilsome; I was obliged to stop frequently on account of the painful throbbing of my heart, which made it difficult to breathe. When the summit was gained, we lay down awhile on the leeward side to recover ourselves.

We looked on the great valley of the Arno, perhaps twenty-five miles long, and five or six broad, lying like a long elliptical basin sunk among the hills. I can liken it to nothing but a vast sea; for a dense, blue mist covered the level surface, through which the domes of Florence rose up like a craggy island, while the thousands of scattered villas resembled ships, with spread sails, afloat on its surface. The sharp, cutting wind soon drove us down, with a few hundred bounds, to the path again. Three more hungry mortals did not dine at the Cacciatore that day.

The chapel of the Medici, which we visited, is of wonderful beauty. The walls are entirely encrusted with pietra dura and the most precious kinds of marble. The ceiling is covered with gorgeous frescoes by Benevenuto, a modern painter. Around the sides, in magnificent sarcophagi of marble and jasper, repose the ashes of a few Cosmos and Ferdinands. I asked the sacristan for the tomb of Lorenzo the Magnificent. "Oh!" said he, "he lived during the republic—he has no tomb; these are only for Dukes!" I could not repress a sigh at the lavish waste of labor and treasure on this one princely chapel. They might have slumbered unnoted, like Lorenzo, if they had done as much for their country and Italy.

December 19.—It is with a heavy heart, that I sit down tonight to make my closing note in this lovely city and in the journal which has recorded my thoughts and impressions since leaving America. I should find it difficult to analyze my emotions, but I know that they oppress me painfully. So much rushes at once over the mind and heart—memories of what has passed through both, since I made the first note in its pages—alternations of hope and anxiety and aspiration, but never despondency—that it resembles in a manner, the closing of a life. I seem almost to have lived through the common term of a life in this short period. Much spiritual and mental experience has crowded into a short time the sensations of years. Painful though some of it has been, it was still welcome. Difficulty and toil give the soul strength to crush, in a loftier region, the passions which draw strength only from the earth. So long as we listen to the purer promptings within us, there is a Power invisible, though not unfelt, who protects us—amid the toil and tumult and soiling struggle, there is ever an eye that watches, ever a heart that overflows with Infinite and Almighty Love! Let us trust then in that Eternal Spirit, who pours out on us his warm and boundless blessings, through the channels of so many kindred human hearts!

CHAPTER XXXIX. — WINTER TRAVELING AMONG THE APPENINES.

Valley of the Arno, Dec 22.—It is a glorious morning after our two days' walk, through rain and mud, among these stormy Appenines. The range of high peaks, among which is the celebrated monastery of Camaldoli, lie just before us, their summits dazzling with the new fallen snow. The clouds are breaking away, and a few rosy flushes announce the approach of the sun. It has rained during the night, and the fields are as green and fresh as on a morning in spring.

We left Florence on the 20th, while citizens and strangers were vainly striving to catch a glimpse of the Emperor of Russia. He is, from some cause, very shy of being seen, in his journeys from place to place, using the greatest art and diligence to prevent the time of his departure and arrival from being known. On taking leave of Powers, I found him expecting the Autocrat, as he had signified his intention of visiting his studio; it was a cause of patriotic pride to find that crowned heads know and appreciate the genius of our sculptor. The sky did not promise much, as we set out; when we had entered the Appenines and taken a last look of the lovely valley behind us, and the great dome of the city where we had spent four delightful months, it began to rain heavily. Determined to conquer the weather at the beginning, we kept on, although before many miles were passed, it became too penetrating to be agreeable. The mountains grew nearly black under the shadow of the clouds, and the storms swept drearily down their passes and defiles, till the scenery looked more like the Hartz than Italy. We were obliged to stop at Ponte Sieve and dry our saturated garments: when, as the rain slackened somewhat, we rounded the foot of the mountain of Vallombrosa, above the swollen and noisy Arno, to the little village of Cucina.

We entered the only inn in the place, followed by a crowd of wondering boys, for two such travelers had probably never been seen there. They made a blazing fire for us in the broad chimney, and after the police of the place satisfied themselves that we were not dangerous characters, they asked many questions about our country. I excited the sympathy of the women greatly in our behalf by telling them we had three thousand miles of sea between us and our homes. They exclaimed in the most sympathising tones: "Poverini! so far to go!—three thousand miles of water!"

The next morning we followed the right bank of the Arno. At Incisa, a large town on the river, the narrow pass broadens into a large and fertile plain, bordered on the north by the mountains. The snow storms were sweeping around their summits the whole day, and I thought of the desolate situation of the good monks who had so hospitably entertained us three months before. It was weary traveling; but at Levane our fatigues were soon forgotten. Two or three peasants were sitting last night beside the blazing fire, and we were amused to hear them talking about us. I overheard one asking another to converse with us awhile. "Why should I speak to them?" said he; "they are not of our profession—we are swineherds, and they do not care to talk with us." However, his curiosity prevailed at last, and we had a long conversation together. It seemed difficult for them to comprehend how there could be so much water to cross, without any land, before reaching our country. Finding we were going to Rome, I overheard one remark we were pilgrims, which seemed to be the general supposition, as there are few foot-travelers in Italy. The people said to one another as we passed along the road:—"They are making a journey of penance!" Those peasants expressed themselves very well for persons of their station, but they were remarkably ignorant of everything beyond their own olive orchards and vine fields.

Perugia, Dec. 24.—On leaving Levane, the morning gave a promise, and the sun winked at us once or twice through the broken clouds, with a watery eye; but our cup was not yet full. After crossing one or two shoulders of the range of hills, we descended to the great upland plain of Central Italy, watered by the sources of the Arno and the Tiber. The scenery is of a remarkable character. The hills appear to have been washed and swept by some mighty flood. They are worn into every shape—pyramids, castles, towers—standing desolate and brown, in long ranges, like the ruins of mountains. The plain is scarred with deep gulleys, adding to the look of decay which accords so well with the Cyclopean relics of the country.

A storm of hail which rolled away before us, disclosed the city of Arezzo, on a hill at the other end of the plain, its heavy cathedral crowning the pyramidal mass of buildings. Our first care was to find a good trattoria, for hunger spoke louder than sentiment, and then we sought the house where Petrarch was born. A young priest showed it to us on the summit of the hill. It has not been changed since he lived in it.

On leaving Florence, we determined to pursue the same plan as in Germany, of stopping at the inns frequented by the common people. They treated us here, as elsewhere, with great kindness and sympathy, and we were freed from the outrageous impositions practised at the greater hotels. They always built a large fire to dry us, after our day's walk in the rain, and placing chairs in the hearth, which was raised several feet above the floor, stationed us there, like the giants Gog and Magog, while the children, assembled below, gazed up in open-mouthed wonder at our elevated greatness. They even invited us to share their simple meals with them, and it was amusing to hear their goodhearted exclamations of pity at finding we were so far from home. We slept in the great beds (for the most of the Italian beds are calculated for a man, wife, and four children!) without fear of being assassinated, and only met with banditti in dreams.

This is a very unfavorable time of the year for foot-traveling. We were obliged to wait three or four weeks in Florence for a remittance from America, which not only prevented our leaving as soon as was desirable, but, by the additional expense of living, left us much smaller means than we required. However, through the kindness of a generous countryman, who unhesitatingly loaned us a considerable sum, we were enabled to start with thirty dollars each, which, with care and economy, will be quite sufficient to take us to Paris, by way of Rome and Naples, if these storms do not prevent us from walking. Greece and the Orient, which I so ardently hoped to visit, are now out of the question. We walked till noon to-day, over the Val di Chiana to Camuscia, the last post-station in the Tuscan dominions. On a mountain near it is the city of Cortona, still enclosed within its Cyclopean walls, built long before the foundation of Rome. Here our patience gave way, melted down by the unremitting rains, and while eating dinner we made a bargain for a vehicle to bring us to this city. We gave a little more than half of what the vetturino demanded, which was still an exorbitant price—two scudi each for a ride of thirty miles.

In a short time we were called to take our seats; I beheld with consternation a rickety, uncovered, two-wheeled vehicle, to which a single lean horse was attached. "What!" said I; "is that the carriage you promised?" "You bargained for a calesino," said he, "and there it is!" adding, moreover, that there was nothing else in the place. So we clambered up, thrust our feet among the hay, and the machine rolled off with a kind of saw-mill motion, at the rate of five miles an hour.

Soon after, in ascending the mountain of the Spelunca, a sheet of blue water was revealed below us—the Lake of Thrasymene! From the eminence around which we drove, we looked on the whole of its broad surface and the mountains which encompass it. It is a magnificent sheet of water, in size and shape somewhat like New York Bay, but the heights around it are far higher than the hills of Jersey or Staten Island. Three beautiful islands lie in it, near the eastern shore.

While our calesino was stopped at the papal custom-house, I gazed on the memorable field below us. A crescent plain, between the mountain and the lake, was the arena where two mighty empires met in combat. The place seems marked by nature for the scene of some great event. I experienced a thrilling emotion, such as no battle plain has excited, since, when a schoolboy, I rambled over the field of Brandywine. I looked through the long arcades of patriarchal olives, and tried to cover the field with the shadows of the Roman and Carthaginian myriads. I recalled the shock of meeting legions, the clash of swords and bucklers, and the waving standards amid the dust of battle, while stood on the mountain amphitheatre, trembling and invisible, the protecting deities of Rome.

"Far other scene is Thrasymene now!"

We rode over the plain, passed through the dark old town of Passignano, built on a rocky point by the lake, and dashed along the shore. A dark, stormy sky bent over us, and the roused waves broke in foam on the rocks. The winds whistled among the bare oak boughs, and shook the olives till they twinkled all over. The vetturino whipped our old horse into a gallop, and we were borne on in unison with the scene, which would have answered for one of Hoffman's wildest stories.

Ascending a long hill, we took a last look in the dusk at Thrasymene, and continued our journey among the Appenines. The vetturino was to have changed horses at Magione, thirteen miles from Perugia, but there were none to be had, and our poor beast was obliged to perform the whole journey without rest or food. It grew very dark, and a storm, with thunder and lightning, swept among the hills. The clouds were of pitchy darkness, and we could see nothing beyond the road, except the lights of peasant-cottages trembling through the gloom. Now and then a flash of lightning revealed the black masses of the mountains, on which the solid sky seemed to rest. The wind and cold rain swept wailing past us, as if an evil spirit were abroad on the darkness. Three hours of such nocturnal travel brought us here, wet and chilly, as well as our driver, but I pitied the poor horse more than him.

When we looked out the window, on awaking, the clustered house-tops of the city, and the summits of the mountains near were covered with snow. But on walking to the battlements we saw that the valleys below were green and untouched. Perugia, for its "pride of place," must endure the storms, while the humbler villages below escape them. As the rain continues, we have taken seats in a country diligence for Foligno and shall depart in a few minutes.

Dec. 28.—We left Perugia in a close but covered vehicle, and descending the mountain, crossed the muddy and rapid Tiber in the valley below. All day we rode slowly among the hills; where the ascent was steep, two or four large oxen were hitched before the horses. I saw little of the scenery, for our Italian companions would not bear the windows open. Once, when we stopped, I got out and found we were in the region of snow, at the foot of a stormy peak, which towered sublimely above. At dusk, we entered Foligno, and were driven to the "Croce Bianca"—glad to be thirty miles further on our way to Rome.

After some discussion with a vetturino, who was to leave next morning, we made a contract with him for the remainder of the journey, for the rain, which fell in torrents, forbade all thought of pedestrianism. At five o'clock we rattled out of the gate, and drove by the waning moon and morning starlight, down the vale of the Clitumnus. As the dawn stole on, I watched eagerly the features of the scene. Instead of a narrow glen, as my fancy had pictured, we were in a valley, several miles broad, covered with rich orchards and fertile fields. A glorious range of mountains bordered it on the north, looking like Alps in their winter garments. A rosy flush stole over the snow, which kindled with the growing morn, till they shone like clouds that float in the sunrise. The Clitumnus, beside us, was the purest of streams. The heavy rains which had fallen, had not soiled in the least its limpid crystal.

When it grew light enough, I looked at our companions for the three days' journey. The two other inside seats were occupied by a tradesman of Trieste, with his wife and child; an old soldier, and a young dragoon going to visit his parents after seven years' absence, occupied the front part. Persons traveling together in a carriage are not long in becoming acquainted—close companionship soon breeds familiarity. Before night, I had made a fast friend of the young soldier, learned to bear the perverse humor of the child with as much patience as its father, and even drawn looks of grim kindness from the crusty old vetturino.

Our mid-day resting place was Spoleto. As there were two hours given us, we took a ramble through the city, visited the ruins of its Roman theatre and saw the gate erected to commemorate the victory gained here over Hannibal, which stopped his triumphal march towards Rome. A great part of the afternoon was spent in ascending among the defiles of Monte Somma, the highest pass on the road between Ancona and Rome. Assisted by two yoke of oxen we slowly toiled up through the snow, the mountains on both sides covered with thickets of box and evergreen oaks, among whose leafy screens the banditti hide themselves. It is not considered dangerous at present, but as the dragoons who used to patrol this pass have been sent off to Bologna, to keep down the rebellion, the robbers will probably return to their old haunts again. We saw many suspicious looking coverts, where they might have hidden.

We slept at Terni and did not see the falls—not exactly on Wordsworth's principle of leaving Yarrow "unvisited," but because under the circumstances, it was impossible. The vetturino did not arrive there till after dark; he was to leave before dawn; the distance was five miles, and the roads very bad. Besides, we had seen falls quite as grand, which needed only a Byron to make them as renowned—we had been told that those of Tivoli, which we shall see, were equally fine. The Velino, which we crossed near Terni, was not a large stream—in short, we hunted as many reasons as we could find, why the falls need not be seen.

Leaving Terni before day, we drove up the long vale towards Narni. The roads were frozen hard; the ascent becoming more difficult, the vetturino was obliged to stop at a farm-house and get another pair of horses, with which, and a handsome young contadino as postillion, we reached Narni in a short time. In climbing the hill, we had a view of the whole valley of Terni, shut in on all sides by snow-crested Appenines, and threaded by the Nar, whose waters flow "with many windings, through the vale!"

At Otricoli, while dinner was preparing, I walked around the crumbling battlements to look down into the valley and trace the far windings of the Tiber. In rambling through the crooked streets, we saw everywhere the remains of the splendor which this place boasted in the days of Rome. Fragments of fluted pillars stood here and there in the streets; large blocks of marble covered with sculpture and inscriptions were built into the houses, defaced statues used as door-ornaments, and the steppingstone to our rude inn, worn every day by the feet of grooms and vetturini, contained some letters of an inscription which may have recorded the glory of on emperor.

Traveling with a vetturino, is unquestionably the pleasantest way of seeing Italy. The easy rate of the journey allows time for becoming well acquainted with the country, and the tourist is freed from the annoyance of quarrelling with cheating landlords. A translation of our written contract, will best explain this mode of traveling:

"CARRIAGE" FOR ROME.

"Our contract is, to be conducted to Rome for the sum of twenty

francs each, say 20f. and the buona mano, if we are well

served. We must have from the vetturino, Giuseppe Nerpiti, supper

each night, a free chamber with two beds, and fire, until we shall

arrive at Rome.

"I, Geronymo Sartarelli, steward of the Inn of the White Cross, at

Foligno, in testimony of the above contract."

Beyond Otricoli, we passed through some relics of an age anterior to Rome. A few soiled masses of masonry, black with age, stood along the brow of the mountain, on whose extremity were the ruins of a castle of the middle ages. We crossed the Tiber on a bridge built by Augustus Cæsar, and reached Borghetto as the sun was gilding with its last rays the ruined citadel above. As the carriage with its four horses was toiling slowly up the hill, we got out and walked before, to gaze on the green meadows of the Tiber.

On descending from Narni, I noticed a high, prominent mountain, whose ridgy back, somewhat like the profile of a face, reminded me of the Traunstein, in Upper Austria. As we approached, its form gradually changed, until it stood on the Campagna

"Like a long-swept wave about to break,

That on the curl hangs pausing"—

and by that token of a great bard, I recognized Monte Soracte. The dragoon took us by the arms, and away we scampered over the Campagna, with one of the loveliest sunsets before us, that ever painted itself on my retina. I cannot portray in words the glory that flooded the whole western heaven. It was like a sea of melted ruby, amethyst and topaz—deep, dazzling and of crystal transparency. The color changed in tone every few minutes, till in half an hour it sank away before the twilight to a belt of deep orange along the west.

We left Civita Castellana before daylight. The sky was red with dawn as we approached Nepi, and we got out to walk, in the clear, frosty air. A magnificent Roman aqueduct, part of it a double row of arches, still supplies the town with water. There is a deep ravine, appearing as if rent in the ground by some convulsion, on the eastern side of the city. A clear stream that steals through the arches of the aqueduct, falls in a cascade of sixty feet down into the chasm, sending up constant wreaths of spray through the evergreen foliage that clothes the rocks. In walking over the desolate Campagna, we saw many deep chambers dug in the earth, used by the charcoal burners; the air was filled with sulphureous exhalations, very offensive to the smell, which rose from the ground in many places.

Miles and miles of the dreary waste, covered only with flocks of grazing sheep, were passed,—and about noon we reached Baccano, a small post station, twenty miles from Rome. A long hill rose before us, and we sprang out of the carriage and ran ahead, to see Rome from its summit. As we approached the top, the Campagna spread far before and around us, level and blue as an ocean. I climbed up a high bank by the roadside, and the whole scene came in view. Perhaps eighteen miles distant rose the dome of St. Peter's, near the horizon—a small spot on the vast plain. Beyond it and further east, were the mountains of Albano—on our left Soracte and the Appenines, and a blue line along the west betrayed the Mediterranean. There was nothing peculiarly beautiful or sublime in the landscape, but few other scenes on earth combine in one glance such a myriad of mighty associations, or bewilder the mind with such a crowd of confused emotions.

As we approached Rome, the dragoon, with whom we had been walking all day, became anxious and impatient. He had not heard from his parents for a long time, and knew not if they were living. His desire to be at the end of his journey finally became so great, that he hailed a peasant who was driving by in a light vehicle, left our slow carriage and went out of sight in a gallop.

As we descended to the Tiber in the dusk of evening, the domes and spires of Rome came gradually into view, St. Peter's standing like a mountain in the midst of them. Crossing the yellow river by the Ponte Molle, two miles of road, straight as an arrow, lay before us, with the light of the Porta del Popolo at the end. I felt strangely excited as the old vehicle rumbled through the arch, and we entered a square with fountains and an obelisk of Egyptian granite in the centre. Delivering up our passports, we waited until the necessary examinations were made, and then went forward. Three streets branch out from the square, the middle one of which, leading directly to the Capitol, is the Corso, the Roman Broadway. Our vetturino chose that to the left, the Via della Scrofa, leading off towards the bridge of St. Angelo. I looked out the windows as we drove along, but saw nothing except butcher-shops, grocer-stores, etc.—horrible objects for a sentimental traveler!

Being emptied out on the pavement at last, our first care was to find rooms; after searching through many streets, with a coarse old Italian who spoke like an angel, we arrived at a square where the music of a fountain was heard through the dusk and an obelisk cut out some of the starlight. At the other end I saw a portico through the darkness, and my heart gave a breathless bound on recognizing the Pantheon—the matchless temple of Ancient Rome! And now while I am writing, I hear the gush of the fountain—and if I step to the window, I see the time-worn but still glorious edifice.

On returning for our baggage, we met the funeral procession of the Princess Altieri. Priests in white and gold carried flaming torches, and the coffin, covered with a magnificent golden pall, was borne in a splendid hearse, guarded by four priests. As we were settling our account with the vetturino, who demanded much more buona mano than we were willing to give, the young dragoon returned. He was greatly agitated. "I have been at home!" said he, in a voice trembling with emotion. I was about to ask him further concerning his family, but he kissed and embraced us warmly and hurriedly, saying he had only come to say "addio!" and to leave us. I stop writing to ramble through Rome. This city of all cities to me—this dream of my boyhood—giant, god-like, fallen Rome—is around me, and I revel in a glow of anticipation and exciting thought that seems to change my whole state of being.

CHAPTER XL. ROME.

Dec. 29.—One day's walk through Rome—how shall I describe it? The Capitol, the Forum, St. Peter's, the Coliseum—what few hours' ramble ever took in places so hallowed by poetry, history and art? It was a golden leaf in my calendar of life. In thinking over it now, and drawing out the threads of recollection from the varied woof of thought I have woven to-day, I almost wonder how I dared so much at once; but within reach of them all, how was it possible to wait? Let me give a sketch of our day's ramble.

Hearing that it was better to visit the ruins by evening or moonlight, (alas! there is no moon now) we started out to hunt St. Peter's. Going in the direction of the Corso, we passed the ruined front of the magnificent Temple of Antoninus, now used as the Papal Custom House. We turned to the right on entering the Corso, expecting to have a view of the city from the hill at its southern end. It is a magnificent street, lined with palaces and splendid edifices of every kind, and always filled with crowds of carriages and people. On leaving it, however, we became bewildered among the narrow streets—passed through a market of vegetables, crowded with beggars and contadini—threaded many by-ways between dark old buildings—saw one or two antique fountains and many modern churches, and finally arrived at a hill.

We ascended many steps, and then descending a little towards the other side, saw suddenly below us the Roman Forum! I knew it at once—and those three Corinthian columns that stood near us—what could they be but the remains of the temple of Jupiter Stator? We stood on the Capitoline Hill; at the foot was the Arch of Septimus Severus, brown with age and shattered; near it stood the majestic front of the Temple of Fortune, its pillars of polished granite glistening in the sun, as if they had been erected yesterday, while on the left the rank grass was waving from the arches and mighty walls of the Palace of the Cæsars! In front, ruin upon ruin lined the way for half a mile, where the Coliseum towered grandly through the blue morning mist, at the base of the Esquiline Hill!

Good heavens, what a scene! Grandeur, such as the world never saw, once rose through that blue atmosphere; splendor inconceivable, the spoils of a world, the triumphs of a thousand armies had passed over that earth; minds which for ages moved the ancient world had thought there, and words of power and glory, from the lips of immortal men, had been syllabled on that hallowed air. To call back all this on the very spot, while the wreck of what once was, rose mouldering and desolate around, aroused a sublimity of thought and feeling too powerful for words.

Returning at hazard through the streets, we came suddenly upon the column of Trajan, standing in an excavated square below the level of the city, amid a number of broken granite columns, which formed part of the Forum dedicated to him by Rome, after the conquest of Dacia. The column is one hundred and thirty-two feet high, entirely covered with bas-reliefs representing his victories, winding about it in a spiral line to the top. The number of figures is computed at two thousand five hundred, and they were of such excellence that Raphael used many of them for his models. They are now much defaced, and the column is surmounted by a statue of some saint. The inscription on the pedestal has been erased, and the name of Sixtus V. substituted. Nothing can exceed the ridiculous vanity of the old popes in thus mutilating the finest monuments of ancient art. You cannot look upon any relic of antiquity in Rome, but your eyes are assailed by the words "PONTIFEX MAXIMUS," in staring modern letters. Even the magnificent bronzes of the Pantheon were stripped to make the baldachin under the dome of St. Peter's.

Finding our way back again, we took a fresh start, happily in the right direction, and after walking some time, came out on the Tiber, at the Bridge of St. Angelo. The river rolled below in his muddy glory, and in front, on the opposite bank, stood "the pile which Hadrian retired on high"—now, the Castle of St. Angelo. Knowing that St. Peter's was to he seen from this bridge, I looked about in search of it. There was only one dome in sight, large and of beautiful proportions. I said at once, "surely that cannot be St. Peter's!" On looking again, however, I saw the top of a massive range of building near it, which corresponded so nearly with the pictures of the Vatican, that I was unwillingly forced to believe the mighty dome was really before me. I recognized it as one of those we saw from the Capitol, but it appeared so much smaller when viewed from a greater distance, that I was quite deceived. On considering we were still three-fourths of a mile from it, and that we could see its minutest parts distinctly, the illusion was explained.

Going directly down the Borgo Vecchio, towards it, it seemed a long time before we arrived at the square of St. Peter's; when at length we stood in front with the majestic colonnade sweeping around—the fountains on each side sending up their showers of silvery spray—the mighty obelisk of Egyptian granite piercing the sky—and beyond, the great front and dome of the Cathedral, I confessed my unmingled admiration. It recalled to my mind the grandeur of ancient Rome, and mighty as her edifices must have been, I doubt if there were many views more overpowering than this. The façade of St. Peter's seemed close to us, but it was a third of a mile distant, and the people ascending the steps dwindled to pigmies.

I passed the obelisk, went up the long ascent, crossed the portico, pushed aside the heavy leathern curtain at the entrance, and stood in the great nave. I need not describe my feelings at the sight, but I will tell the dimensions, and you may then fancy what they were. Before me was a marble plain six hundred feet long, and under the cross four hundred and seventeen feet wide! One hundred and fifty feet above, sprang a glorious arch, dazzling with inlaid gold, and in the centre of the cross there were four hundred feet of air between me and the top of the dome! The sunbeam, stealing through the lofty window at one end of the transept, made a bar of light on the blue air, hazy with incense, one-tenth of a mile long, before it fell on the mosaics and gilded shrines of the other extremity. The grand cupola alone, including lantern and cross, is two hundred and eighty-five feet high, or sixty feet higher than the Bunker Hill Monument, and the four immense pillars on which it rests are each one hundred and thirty-seven feet in circumference! It seems as if human art had outdone itself in producing this temple—the grandest which the world ever erected for the worship of the Living God! The awe felt in looking up at the giant arch of marble and gold, did not humble me; on

637

the contrary, I felt exalted, ennobled—beings in the form I wore planned the glorious edifice, and it seemed that in godlike power perseverance, they were indeed but "a little lower than the angels!" I felt that, if fallen, my race was still mighty and immortal.

The Vatican is only open twice a week, on days which are not festas; most fortunately, to-day happened to be one of these, and we took a run through its endless halls. The extent and magnificence of the gallery of sculpture is perfectly amazing. The halls, which are filled to overflowing with the finest works of ancient art, would, if placed side by side, make a row more than two miles in length! You enter at once into a hall of marble, with a magnificent arched ceiling, a third of a mile long; the sides are covered for a great distance with inscriptions of every kind, divided into compartments according to the era of the empire to which they refer. One which I examined, appeared to be a kind of index of the roads in Italy, with the towns on them; and we could decipher on that time-worn block, the very route I had followed from Florence hither.

Then came the statues, and here I am bewildered, how to describe them. Hundreds upon hundreds of figures—statues of citizens, generals, emperors and gods—fauns, satyrs and nymphs—children, cupids and tritons—in fact, it seemed inexhaustible. Many of them, too, were forms of matchless beauty; there were Venuses and nymphs, born of the loftiest dreams of grace; fauns on whose faces shone the very soul of humor, and heroes and divinities with an air of majesty worthy the "land of lost gods and godlike men!"

I am lost in astonishment at the perfection of art attained by the Greeks and Romans. There is scarcely a form of beauty, that has ever met my eye, which is not to be found in this gallery. I should almost despair of such another blaze of glory on the world, were it not my devout belief that what has been done may be done again, and had I not faith that the dawn in which we live will bring another day equally glorious. And why should not America, with the experience and added wisdom which three thousand years have slowly yielded to the old world, joined to the giant energy of her youth and freedom, re-bestow on the world the divine creations of art? Let Powers answer!

But let us step on to the hemicycle of the Belvidere, and view some works greater than any we have yet seen, or even imagined. The adjoining gallery is filled with masterpieces of sculpture, but we will keep our eyes unwearied and merely glance along the rows. At length we reach a circular court with a fountain flinging up its waters in the centre. Before us is an open cabinet; there is a beautiful, manly form within, but you would not for an instant take it for the Apollo. By the Gorgon head it holds aloft, we recognize Canova's Perseus—he has copied the form and attitude of the Apollo, but he could not breathe into it the same warming fire. It seemed to me particularly lifeless, and I greatly preferred his Boxers, who stand on either side of it. One, who has drawn back in the attitude of striking, looks as if he could fell an ox with a single blow of his powerful arm. The other is a more lithe and agile figure, and there is a quick fire in his countenance which might overbalance the massive strength of his opponent.

Another cabinet—this is the far-famed Antinous. A countenance of perfect Grecian beauty, with a form such as we would imagine for one of Homer's heroes. His features are in repose, and there is something in their calm, settled expression, strikingly like life.

Now we look on a scene of the deepest physical agony. Mark how every muscle of old Laocoon's body is distended to the utmost in the mighty struggle! What intensity of pain in the quivering, distorted, features! Every nerve, which despair can call into action, is excited in one giant effort, and a scream of anguish seems just to have quivered on those marble lips. The serpents have rolled their strangling coils around father and sons, but terror has taken away the strength of the latter, and they make but feeble resistance. After looking with indifference on the many casts of this group, I was the more moved by the magnificent original. It deserves all the admiration that has been heaped upon it.

I absolutely trembled on approaching the cabinet of the Apollo, I had built up in fancy a glorious ideal, drawn from all that bards have sung or artists have rhapsodized about its divine beauty. I feared disappointment—I dreaded to have my ideal displaced and my faith in the power of human genius overthrown by a form less than perfect. However, with a feeling of desperate excitement, I entered and looked upon it.

Now what shall I say of it? How make you comprehend its immortal beauty? To what shall I liken its glorious perfection of form, or the fire that imbues the cold marble with the soul of a god? Not with sculpture, for it stands alone and above all other works of art—nor with men, for it has a majesty more than human. I gazed on it, lost in wonder and joy—joy that I could, at last, take into my mind a faultless ideal of godlike, exalted manhood. The figure appears actually to possess a spirit, and I looked on it, not as on a piece of marble, but a being of loftier mould, and half expected to see him step forward when the arrow had reached its mark. I would give worlds to feel one moment the sculptor's mental triumph when his work was completed; that one exulting thrill must have repaid him for every ill he might have suffered on earth! With what divine inspiration has he wrought its faultless lines! There is a spirit in every limb which mere toil could not have given. It must have been caught in those lofty moments.

> *"When each conception was a heavenly guest—a*
>
> *ray of immortality—and stood*
>
> *star-like, around, until they gathered to a god?"*

We ran through a series of halls, roofed with golden stars on a deep blue, midnight sky, and filled with porphyry vases, black marble gods, and mummies. Some of the statues shone with the matchless polish they had received from a Theban artisan before Athens was founded, and are, apparently, as fresh and perfect as when looked upon by the vassals of Sesostris. Notwithstanding their stiff, rough-hewn limbs, there were some figures of great beauty, and they gave me a much higher idea of Egyptian sculpture. In an adjoining hall, containing colossal busts of the gods, is a vase forty-one feet in circumference, of one solid block of red porphyry.

The "Transfiguration" is truly called the first picture in the world. The same glow of inspiration which created the Belvidere, must have been required to paint the Saviour's aerial form. The three figures hover above the earth in a blaze of glory, seemingly independent of all material laws. The terrified

Apostles on the mount, and the wondering group below, correspond in the grandeur of their expression to the awe and majesty of the scene. The only blemish in the sublime perfection of the picture is the introduction of the two small figures on the left hand; who, by-the-bye, were Cardinals, inserted there by command. Some travelers say the color is all lost, but I was agreeably surprised to find it well preserved. It is, undoubtedly, somewhat imperfect in this respect, as Raphael died before it was entirely finished; but "take it all in all," you may search the world in vain to find its equal.

January 1, 1846.—New Year's Day in the Eternal City! It will be something to say in after years, that I have seen one year open in Rome— that, while my distant friends were making up for the winter without, with good cheer around the merry board, I have walked in sunshine by the ruins of the Coliseum, watched the orange groves gleaming with golden fruitage in the Farnese gardens, trodden the daisied meadow around the sepulchre of Caius Cestius, and mused by the graves of Shelley, Keats and Salvator Rosa! The Palace of the Cassars looked even more mournful in the pale, slant sunshine, and the yellow Tiber, as he flowed through the "marble wilderness," seemed sullenly counting up the long centuries during which degenerate slaves have trodden his banks. A leaden-colored haze clothed the seven hills, and heavy silence reigned among the ruins, for all work was prohibited, and the people were gathered in their churches. Rome never appeared so desolate and melancholy as to-day.

In the morning I climbed the Quirinal Hill, now called Monte Cavallo, from the colossal statues of Castor and Pollux, with their steeds, supposed to be the work of Phidias and Praxiteles. They stand on each side of an obelisk of Egyptian granite, beside which a strong stream of water gushes up into a magnificent bronze basin, found in the old Forum. The statues, entirely browned by age, are considered masterpieces of Grecian art, and whether or not from the great masters, show in all their proportions, the conceptions of lofty genius.

We kept on our way between gardens filled with orange groves, whose glowing fruit reminded me of Mignon's beautiful reminiscence—"Im dunkeln Laub die Gold Orangen glühn!" Rome, although subject to cold winds from the Appenines, enjoys so mild a climate that oranges and palm trees grow in the open air, without protection. Daisies and violets bloom the whole winter, in the meadows of never-fading green. The basilic of the Lateran equals St. Peter's in splendor, though its size is much smaller. The walls are covered with gorgeous hangings of velvet embroidered with gold, and before the high altar, which glitters with precious stones, are four pillars of gilt bronze, said to be those which Augustus made of the spars of Egyptian vessels captured at the battle of Actium.

We descended the hill to the Coliseum, and passing under the Arch of Constantine, walked along the ancient triumphal way, at the foot of the Palatine Hill, which is entirely covered with the ruins of the Cæsars' Palace. A road, rounding its southern base towards the Tiber, brought us to the Temple of Vesta—a beautiful little relic which has been singularly spared by the devastations that have overthrown so many mightier fabrics. It is of circular form, surrounded by nineteen Corinthian columns, thirty-six feet in height; a clumsy tiled roof now takes the place of the elegant cornice which once gave the crowning charm to its perfect proportions. Close at hand are the remains of the temple of Fortuna Virilis, of which some Ionic pillars alone are left, and the house of Cola di Rienzi—the last Tribune of Rome.

As we approached the walls, the sepulchre of Caius Cestius came in sight—a single solid pyramid, one hundred feet in height. The walls are built against it, and the light apex rises far above the massive gate beside it, which was erected by Belisarius. But there were other tombs at hand, for which we had more sympathy than that of the forgotten Roman, and we turned away to look for the graves of Shelley and Keats.

They lie in the Protestant burying ground, on the side of a mound that slopes gently up to the old wall of Rome, beside the pyramid of Cestius. The meadow around is still verdant and sown thick with daisies, and the soft green of the Italian pine mingles with the dark cypress above the slumberers. Huge aloes grow in the shade, and the sweet bay and bushes of rosemary make the air fresh and fragrant. There is a solemn, mournful beauty about the place, green and lonely as it is, beside the tottering walls of ancient Rome, that takes away the gloomy associations of death, and makes one wish to lie there, too, when his thread shall be spun to the end.

We found first the simple head-stone of Keats, alone, in the grassy meadow. Its inscription states that on his death-bed, in the bitterness of his heart, at the malice of his enemies, be desired these words to be written on his tombstone: "Here lies one whose name was written in water." Not far from him reposes the son of Shelley.

Shelley himself lies at the top of the shaded slope, in a lonely spot by the wall, surrounded by tall cypresses. A little hedge of rose and bay surrounds his grave, which bears the simple inscription—

"PERCY BYSSHE SHELLEY; Cor Cordium."

"Nothing of him that doth fade,

But doth suffer a sea-change

Into something rich and strange."

Glorious, but misguided Shelley! He sleeps calmly now in that silent nook, and the air around his grave is filled with sighs from those who mourn that the bright, erratic star should have been blotted out ere it reached the zenith of its mounting fame. I plucked a leaf from the fragrant bay, as a token of his fame, and a sprig of cypress from the bough that bent lowest over his grave; and passing between tombs shaded with blooming roses or covered with unwithered garlands, left the lovely spot.

Amid the excitement of continually changing scenes, I have forgotten to mention our first visit to the Coliseum. The day after our arrival we set out with two English friends, to see it by sunset. Passing by the glorious fountain of Trevi, we made our way to the Forum, and from thence took the road to the Coliseum, lined on both sides with the remains of splendid edifices. The grass-grown ruins of the Palace of the Cæsars stretched along on our right; on our left we passed in succession the granite front of the Temple of Antoninus and Faustina, the three grand arches of the Temple of Peace and the ruins of the Temple of Venus and Rome. We went under the ruined triumphal arch of Titus, with broken friezes representing the taking of Jerusalem, and the mighty walls of the Coliseum gradually rose before us. They grew in grandeur as we approached them, and when at length we stood in the centre, with the shattered arches and grassy walls rising above and beyond one another, far around us, the red light of sunset giving them a soft and melancholy beauty, I was fain to confess that another form of grandeur had entered my mind, of which I before knew not.

A majesty like that of nature clothes this wonderful edifice. Walls rise above walls, and arches above arches, from every side of the grand arena, like a sweep of craggy, pinnacled mountains around an oval lake. The two outer circles have almost entirely disappeared, torn away by the rapacious nobles of Rome, during the middle ages, to build their palaces. When entire, and filled with its hundred thousand spectators, it must have exceeded any pageant which the world can now produce. No wonder it was said—

> "While stands the Coliseum, Rome shall stand;
>
> When falls the Coliseum, Rome shall fall;
>
> And when Rome falls, the world!"

—a prediction, which time has not verified. The world is now going forward, prouder than ever, and though we thank Rome for the legacy she has left us, we would not wish the dust of her ruin to cumber our path.

While standing in the arena, impressed with the spirit of the scene around me, which grew more spectral and melancholy as the dusk of evening began to fill up the broken arches, my eye was assailed by the shrines ranged around the space, doubtless to remove the pollution of paganism. In the middle stands also a cross, with an inscription, granting an absolution of forty days to all who kiss it. Now, although a simple cross in the centre might be very appropriate, both as a token of the heroic devotion of the martyr Telemachus and the triumph of a true religion over the barbarities of the Past, this congregation of shrines and bloody pictures mars very much the unity of association so necessary to the perfect enjoyment of any such scene.

We saw the flush of sunset fade behind the Capitoline Hill, and passed homeward by the Forum, as its shattered pillars were growing solemn and

644

spectral through the twilight. I intend to visit them often again, and "meditate amongst decay." I begin already to grow attached to their lonely grandeur. A spirit, almost human, speaks from the desolation, and there is something in the voiceless oracles it utters, that strikes an answering chord in my own breast.

In the Via de' Pontefici, not far distant from the Borghese Palace, we saw the Mausoleum of Augustus. It is a large circular structure somewhat after the plan of that of Hadrian, but on a much smaller scale. The interior has been cleared out, seats erected around the walls, and the whole is now a summer theatre, for the amusement of the peasantry and tradesmen. What a commentary on greatness! Harlequin playing his pranks in the tomb of an Emperor, and the spot which nations approached with reverence, resounding with the mirth of beggars and degraded vassals!

I visited lately the studio of a young Philadelphian, Mr. W. B. Chambers, who has been here two or three years. In studying the legacies of art which the old masters left to their country, he has caught some of the genuine poetic inspiration which warmed them. But he is modest as talented, and appears to undervalue his works, so long as they do not reach his own mental ideal. He chooses principally subjects from the Italian peasant-life, which abounds with picturesque and classic beauty. His pictures of the shepherd boy of the Albruzzi, and the brown maidens of the Campagna are fine illustrations of this class, and the fidelity with which he copies nature, is an earnest of his future success.

I was in the studio of Crawford, the sculptor; he has at present nothing finished in the marble. There were many casts of his former works, which, judging from their appearance in plaster, must be of no common excellence— for the sculptor can only be justly judged in marble. I saw some fine bas-reliefs of classical subjects, and an exquisite group of Mercury and Psyche, but his masterpiece is undoubtedly the Orpheus. There is a spirit in this figure which astonished me. The face is full of the inspiration of the poet, softened by the lover's tenderness, and the whole fervor of his soul is expressed in the eagerness with which he gazes forward, on stepping past the sleeping Cerberus. Crawford is now engaged on the statue of an Indian girl, pierced by an arrow, and dying. It is a simple and touching figure, and will, I think, be one of his best works.

We are often amused with the groups in the square of the Pantheon, which we can see from our chamber-window. Shoemakers and tinkers carry on their business along the sunny side, while the venders of oranges and roasted chesnuts form a circle around the Egyptian obelisk and fountain. Across the end of an opposite street we get a glimpse of the vegetable-market, and now and then the shrill voice of a pedlar makes its nasal solo audible above the confused chorus. As the beggars choose the Corso, St. Peter's, and the ruins for their principal haunts, we are now spared the hearing of their lamentations. Every time we go out we are assailed with them. "Maladetta sia la vostra testa!"—"Curses be upon your head!"—said one whom I passed without notice. The priests are, however, the greatest beggars. In every church are kept offering boxes, for the support of the church or some unknown institution; they even go from house to house, imploring support and assistance in the name of the Virgin and all the saints, while their bloated, sensual countenances and capacious frames tell of anything but fasts and privations. Once, as I was sitting among the ruins, I was suddenly startled by a loud, rattling sound; turning my head, I saw a figure clothed in white from head to foot, with only two small holes for the eyes. He held in his hand a money-box, on which was a figure of the Virgin, which he held close to my lips, that I might kiss it. This I declined doing, but dropped a baiocco into his box, when, making the sign of the cross, he silently disappeared.

Our present lodging (Trattoria del Sole) is a good specimen of an Italian inn for mechanics and common tradesmen. Passing through the front room, which is an eating-place for the common people—with a barrel of wine in the corner, and bladders of lard hanging among orange boughs in the window—we enter a dark court-yard filled with heavy carts, and noisy with the neighing of horses and singing of grooms, for the stables occupy part of the house. An open staircase, running all around this hollow square, leads to the second, third, and fourth stories,

On the second story is the dining-room for the better class of travelers, who receive the same provisions as those below for double the price, and the additional privilege of giving the waiter two baiocchi. The sleeping apartments are in the fourth story, and are named according to the fancy of a former landlord, in mottos above each door. Thus, on arriving here, the Triester, with his wife and child, more fortunate than our first parents, took refuge in "Paradise," while we Americans were ushered into the "Chamber of Jove." We have occupied it ever since, and find a paul (ten cents) apiece cheap enough for a good bed and a window opening on the Pantheon.

Next to the Coliseum, the baths of Caracalla are the grandest remains of Rome. The building is a thousand feet square, and its massive walls look as if built by a race of giants. These Titan remains are covered with green shrubbery, and long, trailing vines sweep over the cornice, and wave down like tresses from architrave and arch. In some of its grand halls the mosaic pavement is yet entire. The excavations are still carried on; from the number of statues already found, this would seem to have been one of the most gorgeous edifices of the olden time.

I have been now several days loitering and sketching among the ruins, and I feel as if I could willingly wander for months beside these mournful relics, and draw inspiration from the lofty yet melancholy lore they teach. There is a spirit haunting them, real and undoubted. Every shattered column, every broken arch and mouldering wall, but calls up more vividly to mind the glory that has passed away. Each lonely pillar stands as proudly as if it still helped to bear up the front of a glorious temple, and the air seems scarcely to have ceased vibrating with the clarions that heralded a conqueror's triumph.

"—the old majestic trees

Stand ghost-like in the Cæsar's home,

As if their conscious roots were set

In the old graves of giant Rome,

And drew their sap all kingly yet!"

"There every mouldering stone beneath

Is broken from some mighty thought,

647

And sculptures in the dust still breathe

The fire with which their lines were wrought,

And sunder'd arch and plundered tomb

Still thunder back the echo—'Rome!'"

In Rome there is no need that the imagination be excited to call up thrilling emotion or poetic reverie—they are forced on the mind by the sublime spirit of the scene. The roused bard might here pour forth his thoughts in the wildest climaces, and I could believe he felt it all. This is like the Italy of my dreams—that golden realm whose image has been nearly chased away by the earthly reality. I expected to find a land of light and beauty, where every step crushed a flower or displaced a sunbeam—whose very air was poetic inspiration, and whose every scene filled the soul with romantic feelings. Nothing is left of my picture but the far-off mountains, robed in the sapphire veil of the Ausonian air, and these ruins, amid whose fallen glory sits triumphant the spirit of ancient song.

I have seen the flush of morn and eve rest on the Coliseum; I have seen the noon-day sky framed in its broken loopholes, like plates of polished sapphire; and last night, as the moon has grown into the zenith, I went to view it with her. Around the Forum all was silent and spectral—a sentinel challenged us at the Arch of Titus, under which we passed and along the Cæsar's wall, which lay in black shadow. Dead stillness brooded around the Coliseum; the pale, silvery lustre streamed through its arches, and over the grassy walls, giving them a look of shadowy grandeur which day could not bestow. The scene will remain fresh in my memory forever.

CHAPTER XLI. — TIVOLI AND THE ROMAN CAMPAGNA.

Jan. 9.—A few days ago we returned from an excursion to Tivoli, one of the loveliest spots in Italy. We left the Eternal City by the Gate of San Lorenzo, and twenty minutes walk brought us to the bare and bleak Campagna, which was spread around us for leagues in every direction. Here and there a shepherd-boy in his woolly coat, with his flock of browsing sheep, were the only objects that broke its desert-like monotony.

At the fourth mile we crossed the rapid Anio, the ancient Teverone, formerly the boundary between Latium and the Sabine dominions, and at the tenth, came upon some fragments of the old Tibertine way, formed of large irregular blocks of basaltic lava. A short distance further, we saw across the plain the ruins of the bath of Agrippa, built by the side of the Tartarean Lake. The wind, blowing from it, bore us an overpowering smell of sulphur; the waters of the little river Solfatara, which crosses the road, are of a milky blue color, and carry those of the lake into the Anio. A fragment of the old bridge over it still remains.

Finding the water quite warm, we determined to have a bath. So we ran down the plain, which was covered with a thick coat of sulphur, and sounded hollow to our tread, till we reached a convenient place, where we threw off our clothes, and plunged in. The warm wave was delightful to the skin, but extremely offensive to the smell, and when we came out, our mouths and throats were filled with the stifling gas.

It was growing dark as we mounted through the narrow streets of Tivoli, but we endeavored to gain some sight of the renowned beauties of the spot, before going to rest. From a platform on a brow of the hill, we looked down into the defile, at whose bottom the Anio was roaring, and caught a sideward glance of the Cascatelles, sending up their spray amid the evergreen bushes that fringe the rocks. Above the deep glen that curves into the mountain, stands the beautiful temple of the Sybil—a building of the most perfect and graceful proportion. It crests the "rocky brow" like a fairy dwelling, and looks all the lovelier for the wild caverns below. Gazing downward from the bridge, one sees the waters of the Anio tumbling into the picturesque grotto of the Sirens; around a rugged corner, a cloud of white spray whirls up continually, while the boom of a cataract rumbles down the glen. All these we marked in the deepening dusk, and then hunted an albergo.

The shrill-voiced hostess gave us a good supper and clean beds; in return we diverted the people very much by the relation of our sulphur bath. We were awakened in the night by the wind shaking the very soul out of our loose casement. I fancied I heard torrents of rain dashing against the panes, and groaned in bitterness of spirit on thinking of a walk back to Rome in such weather. When morning came, we found it was only a hurricane of wind which was strong enough to tear off pieces of the old roofs. I saw some capuchins nearly overturned in crossing the square, by the wind seizing their white robes.

I had my fingers frozen and my eyes filled with sand, in trying to draw the Sybil's temple, and therefore left it to join my companions, who had gone down into the glen to see the great cascade. The Anio bursts out of a cavern in the mountain-side, and like a prisoner giddy with recovered liberty, reels over the edge of a precipice more than two hundred feet deep. The bottom is hid in a cloud of boiling spray, that shifts from side to side, and driven by the wind, sweeps whistling down the narrow pass. It stuns the ear with a perpetual boom, giving a dash of grandeur to the enrapturing beauty of the scene. I tried a footpath that appeared to lead down to the Cascatelles, but after advancing some distance along the side of an almost perpendicular precipice, I came to a corner that looked so dangerous, especially as the wind was nearly strong enough to carry me off, that it seemed safest to return. We made another vain attempt to get down, by creeping along the bed of a torrent, filled with briars. The Cascatelles are formed by that part of the Anio, which is used in the iron works, made out of the ruins of Mecænas' villa. They gush out from under the ancient arches, and tumble more than a hundred feet down the precipice, their white waters gleaming out from the dark and feathery foliage. Not far distant are the remains of the villa of Horace.

We took the road to Frascati, and walked for miles among cane-swamps and over plains covered with sheep. The people we saw, were most degraded and ferocious-looking, and there were many I would not willingly meet alone after nightfall. Indeed it is still considered quite unsafe to venture without the walls of Rome, after dark. The women, with their yellow complexions, and the bright red blankets they wear folded around the head and shoulders, resemble Indian Squaws.

I lately spent three hours in the Museum of the Capitol, on the summit of the sacred hill. In the hall of the Gladiator I noticed an exquisite statue of Diana. There is a pure, virgin grace in the classic outlines of the figure that keeps the eye long upon it. The face is full of cold, majestic dignity, but it is the ideal of a being to be worshipped, rather than loved. The Faun of Praxiteles, in the same room, is a glorious work; it is the perfect embodiment of that wild, merry race the Grecian poets dreamed of. One looks on the Gladiator with a hushed breath and an awed spirit. He is dying; the blood flows more slowly from the deep wound in his side; his head is sinking downwards, and the arm that supports his body becomes more and more nerveless. You feel that a dull mist is coming over his vision, and almost wait to see his relaxing limbs sink suddenly on his shield. That the rude, barbarian form has a soul, may be read in his touchingly expressive countenance. It warms the sympathies like reality to look upon it. Yet how many Romans may have gazed on this work, moved nearly to tears, who have seen hundreds perish in the arena without a pitying emotion! Why is it that Art has a voice frequently more powerful than Nature?

How cold it is here! I was forced to run home to-night, nearly at full speed, from the Café delle Belle Arti through the Corso and the Piazza Colonna, to keep warm. The clear, frosty moon threw the shadow of the column of Antoninus over me as I passed, and it made me shiver to look at the thin, falling sheet of the fountain. Winter is winter everywhere, and even the sun of Italy cannot always scorch his icy wings.

Two days ago we took a ramble outside the walls. Passing the Coliseum and Caracalla's Baths, we reached the tomb of Scipio, a small sepulchral vault, near the roadside. The ashes of the warrior were scattered to the winds long ago, and his mausoleum is fast falling to decay. The old arch over the Appian

way is still standing, near the modern Porta San Sebastiano through which
we entered on the far-famed road. Here and there it is quite entire, and we
walked over the stones once worn by the feet of Virgil and Horace and Cicero.
After passing the temple of Romulus—a shapeless and ivy-grown ruin—and
walking a mile or more beyond the walls, we reached the Circus of Caracalla,
whose long and shattered walls fill the hollow of one of the little dells of the
Campagna. The original structure must have been of great size and splendor,
but those twin Vandals—Time and Avarice—have stripped away everything
but the lofty brick masses, whose nakedness the pitying ivy strives to cover.

Further, on a gentle slope, is the tomb of "the wealthiest Roman's wife,"
familiar to every one through Childe Harold's musings. It is a round, massive
tower, faced with large blocks of marble, and still bearing the name of Cecilia
Metella. One side is much ruined, and the top is overgrown with grass and
wild bushes. The wall is about thirty feet thick, so that but a small round
space is left in the interior, which is open to the rain and filled will rubbish.
The echoes pronounced hollowly after us the name of the dead for whom it
was built, but they could tell us nothing of her life's history—

> *"How lived, how loved, how died she?"*

I made a hurried drawing of it, and we then turned to the left, across the
Campagna, to seek the grotto of Egeria. Before us, across the brown plain,
extended the Sabine Mountains; in the clear air the houses of Tivoli, twenty
miles distant, were plainly visible. The giant aqueduct stretched in a long line
across the Campagna to the mountain of Albano, its broken and disjointed
arches resembling the vertebræ of some mighty monster. With the ruins of
temples and tombs strewing the plain for miles around it, it might be called
the spine to the skeleton of Rome.

We passed many ruins, made beautiful by the clinging ivy, and reached
a solemn grove of ever-green oak, overlooking a secluded valley. I was soon
in the meadow, leaping ditches, rustling through cane-brakes, and climbing
up to mossy arches to find out the fountain of Numa's nymph; while my
companion, who had less taste for the romantic, looked on complacently
from the leeward side of the hill. At length we found an arched vault in the

hill-side, overhung with wild vines, and shaded in summer by umbrageous trees that grow on the soil above. At the further end a stream of water gushed out from beneath a broken statue, and an aperture in the wall revealed a dark cavern behind. This, then, was "Egeria's grot." The ground was trampled by the feet of cattle, and the taste of the water was anything but pleasant. But it was not for Numa and his nymph alone, that I sought it so ardently. The sunbeam of another mind lingers on the spot. See how it gilds the ruined and neglected fount!

> "*The mosses of thy fountain still are sprinkled*
>
> *With thine Elysian water-drops; the face*
>
> *Of thy cave-guarded spring, with years unwrinkled,*
>
> *Reflects the meek-eyed genius of the place,*
>
> *Whose wild, green margin, now no more erase*
>
> *Art's works; no more its sparkling waters sleep,*
>
> *Prisoned in marble; bubbling from the base*
>
> *Of the cleft statue, with a gentle leap,*
>
> *The rill runs o'er, and 'round, fern, flowers and ivy creep,*
>
> *Fantastically tangled."*

I tried to creep into the grotto, but it was unpleasantly dark, and no nymph appeared to chase away the shadow with her lustrous eyes. The whole hill is pierced by subterranean chambers and passages.

I spent another Sunday morning in St. Peter's. High mass was being celebrated in one of the side Chapels, and a great number of the priesthood were present. The music was simple, solemn, and very impressive, and a fine effect was produced by the combination of the full, sonorous voices of the priests, and the divine sweetness of that band of mutilated unfortunates, who sing here. They sang with a full, clear tone, sweet as the first lispings of a child, but it was painful to hear that melody, purchased at the expense of manhood.

Near the dome is a bronze statue of St. Peter, which seems to have a peculiar atmosphere of sanctity. People say their prayers before it by hundreds, and then kiss its toe, which is nearly worn away by the application of so many thousand lips. I saw a crowd struggle most irreverently to pay their devotion to it. There was a great deal of jostling and confusion; some went so far as to thrust the faces of others against the toe as they were about to kiss it. What is more remarkable, it is an antique statue of Jupiter, taken, I believe, from the Pantheon. An English artist, showing it to a friend, just arrived in Rome, remarked very wittily that it was the statue of Jew-Peter.

I went afterwards to the Villa Borghese, outside the Porta del Popolo. The gardens occupy thirty or forty acres, and are always thronged in the afternoon with the carriages of the Roman and foreign nobility. In summer, it must be a heavenly place; even now, with its musical fountains, long avenues, and grassy slopes, crowned with the fan-like branches of the Italian pine, it reminds one of the fairy landscapes of Boccaccio. We threaded our way through the press of carriages on the Pincian hill, and saw the enormous bulk of St. Peter's loom up against the sunset sky. I counted forty domes and spires in that part of Rome that lay below us—but on what a marble glory looked that sun eighteen centuries ago! Modern Rome—it is in comparison, a den of filth, cheats and beggars!

Yesterday, while taking a random stroll through the city, I visited the church of St. Onofrio, where Tasso is buried. It is not far from St. Peter's, on the summit of a lonely hill. The building was closed, but an old monk admitted us on application. The interior is quite small, but very old, and the floor is covered with the tombs of princes and prelates of a past century. Near the end I found a small slab with the inscription:

"TORQUATI TASSI

OSSA

HIC JACENT."

That was all—but what more was needed? Who knows not the name and fame and sufferings of the glorious bard? The pomp of gold and marble are

654

not needed to deck the slumber of genius. On the wall, above, hangs an old and authentic portrait of him, very similar to the engravings in circulation. A crown of laurel encircles the lofty brow, and the eye has that wild, mournful expression, which accords so well with the mysterious tale of his love and madness.

Owing to the mountain storms, which imposed on us the expense of a carriage-journey to Rome, we shall be prevented from going further. One great cause of this is the heavy fee required for passports in Italy. In most of the Italian cities, the cost of the different visès amounts to $4 or $5; a few such visits as these reduce our funds very materially. The American Consul's fee is $2, owing to the illiberal course of our government, in withholding all salary from her Consuls in Europe. Mr. Brown, however, in whose family we spent last evening very pleasantly, on our requesting that he would deduct something from the usual fee, kindly declined accepting anything. We felt this kindness the more, as from the character which some of our late Consuls bear in Italy, we had not anticipated it. We shall remember him with deeper gratitude than many would suppose, who have never known what it was to be a foreigner.

To-morrow, therefore, we leave Rome—here is, at last, the limit of our wanderings. We have spent much toil and privation to reach here, and now, after two weeks' rambling and musing among the mighty relics of past glory, we turn our faces homeward. The thrilling hope I cherished during the whole pilgrimage—to climb Parnassus and drink from Castaly, under the blue heaven of Greece (both far easier than the steep hill and hidden fount of poesy, I worship afar off)—to sigh for fallen art, beneath the broken friezes of the Parthenon, and look with a pilgrim's eye on the isles of Homer and of Sappho—must be given up, unwillingly and sorrowfully though it be. These glorious anticipations—among the brightest that blessed my boyhood—are slowly wrung from me by stern necessity. Even Naples, the lovely Parthenope, where the Mantuan bard sleeps on the sunny shore, by the bluest of summer seas, with the disinterred Pompeii beyond, and Pæstum amid its roses on the lonely Calabrian plain—even this, almost within sight of the cross of St. Peter's, is barred from me. Farewell then, clime of "fame and eld," since it must be! A pilgrim's blessing for the lore ye have taught him!

CHAPTER XLII. —

Palo.—The sea is breaking in long swells below the window, and a glorious planet shines in the place of the sunset that has died away. This is our first resting-place since leaving Rome. We have been walking all day over the bare and dreary Campagna, and it is a relief to look at last on the broad, blue expanse of the Tyrrhene Sea.

When we emerged from the cool alleys of Rome, and began to climb up and down the long, barren swells, the sun beat down on us with an almost summer heat. On crossing a ridge near Castel Guido, we took our last look of Rome, and saw from the other side the sunshine lying like a dazzling belt on the far Mediterranean. The country is one of the most wretched that can be imagined. Miles and miles of uncultivated land, with scarcely a single habitation, extend on either side of the road, and the few shepherds who watch their flocks in the marshy hollows, look wild and savage enough for any kind of crime. It made me shudder to see every face bearing such a villainous stamp.

Civita Vecchia, Jan. 1.—We left Palo just after sunrise, and walked in the cool of the morning beside the blue Mediterranean. On the right, the low outposts of the Appenines rose, bleak and brown, the narrow plain between them and the shore resembling a desert, so destitute was it of the signs of civilized life. A low, white cloud that hung over the sea, afar off, showed us the locality of Sardinia, though the land was not visible. The sun shone down warmly, and with the blue sky and bluer sea we could easily have imagined a milder season. The barren scenery took a new interest in my eyes, when I remembered that I was spending amidst it that birth-day which removes me, in the eyes of the world, from dependant youth to responsible manhood.

In the afternoon we found a beautiful cove in a curve of the shore, and went to bathe in the cold surf. It was very refreshing, but not quite equal to the sulphur-bath on the road to Tivoli. The mountains now ran closer to the sea, and the road was bordered with thickets of myrtle. I stopped often to beat my staff into the bushes, and inhale the fragrance that arose from their crushed leaves. The hills were covered with this poetical shrub, and any acre of the ground would make the fortune of a florist at home.

The sun was sinking in a sky of orange and rose, as Civita Vecchia came in sight on a long headland before us. Beyond the sea stretched the dim hills of Corsica. We walked nearly an hour in the clear moonlight, by the sounding shore, before the gate of the city was reached. We have found a tolerable inn, and are now enjoying the pleasures of supper and rest.

Marseilles, Jan. 16.—At length we tread the shore of France—of sunny Provence—the last unvisited realm we have to roam through before returning home. It is with a feeling of more than common relief that we see around us the lively faces and hear the glib tongues of the French. It is like an earnest that the "roughing" we have undergone among Bohemian boors and Italian savages is well nigh finished, and that, henceforth, we shall find civilized sympathy and politeness, if nothing more, to make the way smoother. Perhaps the three woful days which terminated at half-past two yesterday afternoon, as we passed through the narrow strait into the beautiful harbor which Marseilles encloses in her sheltering heart, make it still pleasanter. Now, while there is time, I must describe those three days, for who could write on the wet deck of a steamboat, amid all the sights and smells which a sea voyage creates? Description does not flourish when the bones are sore with lying on planks, and the body shivering like an aspen leaf with cold.

About the old town of Civita Vecchia there is not much to be said, except that it has the same little harbor which Trajan dug for it, and is as dirty and disagreeable as a town can well be. We saw nothing except a little church, and the prison-yard, full of criminals, where the celebrated bandit, Gasparoni, has been now confined for eight years.

The Neapolitan Company's boat, Mongibello, was advertised to leave the 12th, so, after procuring our passports, we went to the office to take passage. The official, however, refused to give us tickets for the third place, because, forsooth, we were not servants or common laborers! and words were wasted in trying to convince him that it would make no difference. As the second cabin fare was nearly three times as high, and entirely too dear for us, we went to the office of the Tuscan Company, whose boat was to leave in two days. Through the influence of an Italian gentleman, secretary to Bartolini, the American Consul, whom we met, they agreed to take us for forty-five francs, on deck, the price of the Neapolitan boat being thirty.

Rather than stay two days longer in the dull town, we went again to the latter Company's office and offered them forty-five francs to go that day in their boat. This removed the former scruples, and tickets were immediately made out. After a plentiful dinner at the albergo, to prepare ourselves for the exposure, we filled our pockets with a supply of bread, cheese, and figs, for the voyage. We then engaged a boatman, who agreed to row us out to the steamer for two pauls, but after he had us on board and an oar's length from the quay, he said two pauls apiece was his bargain. I instantly refused, and, summoning the best Italian I could command, explained our agreement; but he still persisted in demanding double price. The dispute soon drew a number of persons to the quay, some of whom, being boatmen, sided with him. Finding he had us safe in his boat, his manner was exceedingly calm and polite. He contradicted me with a "pardon, Signore!" accompanying the words with a low bow and a graceful lift of his scarlet cap, and replied to my indignant accusations in the softest and most silvery-modulated Roman sentences. I found, at last, that if I was in the right, I cut the worse figure of the two, and, therefore, put an end to the dispute by desiring him to row on at his own price.

The hour of starting was two, but the boat lay quietly in the harbor till four, when we glided out on the open sea, and went northward, with the blue hills of Corsica far on our left. A gorgeous sunset faded away over the water, and the moon rose behind the low mountains of the Italian coast. Having found a warm and sheltered place near the chimney, I drew my beaver further over my eyes, to keep out the moonlight, and lay down on the deck with my knapsack under my head. It was a hard bed, indeed; and the first time I attempted to rise, I found myself glued to the floor by the pitch which was smeared along the seams of the boards! Our fellow-sufferers were a company of Swiss soldiers going home after a four years' service under the King of

Naples, but they took to their situation more easily than we.

Sleep was next to impossible, so I paced the deck occasionally, looking out on the moonlit sea and the dim shores on either side. A little after midnight we passed between Elba and Corsica. The dark crags of Elba rose on our right, and the bold headlands of Napoleon's isle stood opposite, at perhaps twenty miles' distance. There was something dreary and mysterious in the whole scene, viewed at such a time—the grandeur of his career, who was born on one and exiled to the other, gave it a strange and thrilling interest.

We made the light-house before the harbor of Leghorn at dawn, and by sunrise were anchored within the mole. I sat on the deck the whole day, watching the picturesque vessels that skimmed about with their lateen sails, and wondering how soon the sailors, on the deck of a Boston brig anchored near us, would see my distant country. Leaving at four o'clock, we dashed away, along the mountain coast of Carrara, at a rapid rate. The wind was strong and cold, but I lay down behind the boiler, and though the boards were as hard as ever, slept two or three hours. When I awoke at half-past two in the morning, after a short rest, Genoa was close at hand. We glided between the two revolving lights on the mole, into the harbor, with the amphitheatre on which the superb city sits, dark and silent around us. It began raining soon, the engine-fire sank down, and as there was no place of shelter, we were shortly wet to the skin.

How long those dreary hours seemed, till the dawn came! All was cold and rainy and dark, and we waited in a kind of torpid misery for daylight. The entire day, I passed sitting in a coil of rope under the stern of the cabin, and even the beauties of the glorious city scarce affected me. We lay opposite the Doria palace, and the constellation of villas and towers still glittered along the hills; but who, with his teeth chattering and limbs numb and damp, could feel pleasure in looking on Elysium itself?

We got under way again at three o'clock. The rain very soon hid the coast from view, and the waves pitched our boat about in a manner not at all pleasant. I soon experienced sea-sickness in all its horrors. We had accidentally made the acquaintance of one of the Neapolitan sailors, who had been in America. He was one of those rough, honest natures I like to meet with—their blunt kindness, is better than refined and oily-tongued suavity. As we were standing by the chimney, reflecting dolefully how we should pass the coming night, he came up and said; "I am in trouble about you, poor fellows! I don't think I shall sleep three hours to-night, to think of you. I shall tell all the cabin they shall give you beds, because they shall see you are gentlemen!" Whether he did so or the officers were moved by spontaneous commiseration, we knew not, but in half an hour a servant beckoned us into the cabin, and berths were given us.

I turned in with a feeling of relief not easily imagined, and forgave the fleas willingly, in the comfort of a shelter from the storm. When I awoke, it was broad day. A fresh breeze was drying the deck, and the sun was half-visible among breaking clouds. We had just passed the Isle of the Titan, one of the Isles des Hyères, and the bay of Toulon opened on our right. It was a rugged, rocky coast, but the hills of sunny Provence rose beyond. The sailor came up with a smile of satisfaction on his rough countenance, and said: "You did sleep better, I think; I did tell them all!" coupling his assertion with a round curse on the officers.

We ran along, beside the brown, bare crags till nearly noon, when we reached the eastern point of the Bay of Marseilles. A group of small islands, formed of bare rocks, rising in precipices three or four hundred feet high, guards the point; on turning into the Gulf, we saw on the left the rocky islands of Pomegues, and If, with the castle crowning the latter, in which Mirabeau was confined. The ranges of hills which rose around the great bay, were spotted and sprinkled over with thousands of the country cottages of the Marseilles merchants, called Bastides; the city itself was hidden from view. We saw apparently the whole bay, but there was no crowd of vessels, such as would befit a great sea-port; a few spires peeping over a hill, with some fortifications, were all that was visible. At length we turned suddenly aside and entered a narrow strait, between two forts. Immediately a broad harbor opened before us, locked in the very heart of the hills on which the city stands. It was covered with vessels of all nations; on leaving the boat, we rowed past the "Aristides," bearing the blue cross of Greece, and I searched eagerly and found, among the crowded masts, the starry banner of America.

I have rambled through all the principal parts of Marseilles, and am very favorably impressed with its appearance. Its cleanliness and the air of life and business which marks the streets, are the more pleasant after coming from the dirty and depopulated Italian cities. The broad avenues, lined with trees, which traverse its whole length, must be delightful in summer. I am often reminded, by its spacious and crowded thoroughfares, of our American cities. Although founded by the Phoceans, three thousand years ago, it has scarcely an edifice of greater antiquity than three or four centuries, and the tourist must content himself with wandering through the narrow streets of the old town, observing the Provençal costumes, or strolling among Turks and Moors on the Quai d'Orléans.

We have been detained here a day longer than was necessary, owing to some misunderstanding about the passports. This has not been favorable to our reduced circumstances, for we have, now but twenty francs each, left, to take us to Paris. Our boots, too, after serving us so long, begin to show signs of failing in this hour of adversity. Although we are somewhat accustomed to such circumstances, I cannot help shrinking when I think of the solitary napoleon and the five hundred miles to be passed. Perhaps, however, the coin will do as much as its great namesake, and achieve for us a Marengo in the war with fate.

CHAPTER XLIII. – PILGRIMAGE TO VAUCLUSE AND JOURNEY UP THE RHONE.

We left Marseilles about nine o'clock, on a dull, rainy morning, for Avignon and the Rhone, intending to take in our way the glen of Vaucluse. The dirty faubourgs stretch out along the road for a great distance, and we trudged through them, past foundries, furnaces and manufactories, considerably disheartened with the prospect. We wound among the bleak stony hills, continually ascending, for nearly three hours. Great numbers of cabarets, frequented by the common people, lined the roads, and we met continually trains of heavy laden wagons, drawn by large mules. The country is very wild and barren, and would have been tiresome, except for the pine groves with their beautiful green foliage. We got something to eat with difficulty at an inn, for the people spoke nothing but the Provençal dialect, and the place was so cold and cheerless we were glad to go out again into the storm. It mattered little to us, that we heard the language in which the gay troubadours of king René sung their songs of love. We thought more of our dripping clothes and numb, cold limbs, and would have been glad to hear instead, the strong, hearty German tongue, full of warmth and kindly sympathy for the stranger. The wind swept drearily among the hills; black, gusty clouds covered the sky, and the incessant rain filled the road with muddy pools. We looked at the country chateaux, so comfortable in the midst of their sheltering poplars, with a sigh, and thought of homes afar off, whose doors were never closed to us.

This was all forgotten, when we reached Aix, and the hostess of the Café d'Afrique filled her little stove with fresh coal, and hung our wet garments around it, while her daughter, a pale-faced, crippled child, smiled kindly on us and tried to talk with us in French. Putting on our damp, heavy coats again, B—— and I rambled through the streets, while our frugal supper was preparing. We saw the statue of the Bon Roi René, who held at Aix his court of shepherds and troubadours—the dark Cathedral of St. Saveur—the ancient walls and battlements, and gazed down the valley at the dark, precipitous mass of Mont St. Victor, at whose base Marius obtained a splendid victory over the barbarians.

After leaving next morning, we saw at some distance to the south, the enormous aqueduct now being erected for the canal from the Rhone to Marseilles. The shallow, elevated valleys we passed in the forenoon's walk were stony and barren, but covered with large orchards of almond trees, the fruit of which forms a considerable article of export. This district borders on the desert of the Crau, a vast plain of stones, reaching to the mouth of the Rhone and almost entirely uninhabited. We caught occasional glimpses of its sea-like waste, between the summits of the hills. At length, after threading a high ascent, we saw the valley of the Durance suddenly below us. The sun, breaking through the clouds, shone on the mountain wall, which stood on the opposite side, touching with his glow the bare and rocky precipices that frowned far above the stream. Descending to the valley, we followed its course towards the Rhone, with the ruins of feudal bourgs crowning the crags above us.

It was dusk, when we reached the village of Senas, tired with the day's march. A landlord, standing in his door, on the lookout for customers, invited us to enter, in a manner so polite and pressing, we could not choose but do so. This is a universal custom with the country innkeepers. In a little village which we passed towards evening, there was a tavern, with the sign: "The Mother of Soldiers." A portly woman, whose face beamed with kindness and cheerfulness, stood in the door and invited us to stop there for the night. "No, mother!" I answered; "we must go much further to-day." "Go, then," said she, "with good luck, my children! a pleasant journey!" On entering the inn at Senas, two or three bronzed soldiers were sitting by the table. My French vocabulary happening to give out in the middle of a consultation about eggs and onion-soup, one of them came to my assistance and addressed me in German. He was from Fulda, in Hesse Cassel, and had served fifteen years in Africa. Two other young soldiers, from the western border of Germany, came during the evening, and one of them being partly intoxicated, created such a tumult, that a quarrel arose, which ended in his being beaten and turned out of the house.

We met, every day, large numbers of recruits in companies of one or two hundred, on their way to Marseilles to embark for Algiers. They were mostly youths, from sixteen to twenty years of age, and seemed little to forebode their probable fate. In looking on their fresh, healthy faces and bounding forms, I saw also a dim and ghastly vision of bones whitening on the desert, of men perishing with heat and fever, or stricken down by the aim of the savage Bedouin.

Leaving next morning at day-break, we walked on before breakfast to Orgon, a little village in a corner of the cliffs which border the Durance, and crossed the muddy river by a suspension bridge a short distance below, to Cavaillon, where the country people were holding a great market. From this place a road led across the meadow-land to L'Isle, six miles distant. This little town is so named, because it is situated on an island formed by the crystal Sorgues, which flows from the fountains of Vaucluse. It is a very picturesque and pretty place. Great mill-wheels, turning slowly and constantly, stand at intervals in the stream, whose grassy banks are now as green as in spring-time. We walked along the Sorgues, which is quite as beautiful and worthy to be sung as the Clitumnus, to the end of the village, to take the road to Vaucluse. Beside its banks stands a dirty, modern "Hotel de Petrarque et Laure." Alas, that the names of the most romantic and impassioned lovers of all history should be desecrated to a sign-post to allure gormandizing tourists!

The bare mountain in whose heart lies the poet's solitude, now rose before us, at the foot of the lofty Mont Ventoux, whose summit of snows extended beyond. We left the river, and walked over a barren plain, across which the wind blew most drearily. The sky was rainy and dark, and completed the desolateness of the scene, which in no wise heightened our anticipations of the renowned glen. At length we rejoined the Sorgues and entered a little green valley running up into the mountain. The narrowness of the entrance entirely shut out the wind, and except the rolling of the waters over their pebbly bed, all was still and lonely and beautiful. The sides of the dell were covered with olive trees, and a narrow strip of emerald meadow lay at the bottom. It grew more hidden and sequestered as we approached the little village of Vaucluse. Here, the mountain towers far above, and precipices of grey rock, many hundred feet high, hang over the narrowing glen. On a crag over the village are the remains of a castle; the slope below this, now rugged and stony, was once graced by the cottage and garden of Petrarch. All traces of them have long since vanished, but a simple column, bearing the inscription; "À PETRARQUE," stands beside the Sorgues.

We ascended into the defile by a path among the rocks, overshadowed by olive and wild fig trees, to the celebrated fountains of Vaucluse. The glen seems as if struck into the mountain's depths by one blow of an enchanter's wand; and just at the end, where the rod might have rested in its downward sweep, is the fathomless well whose overbrimming fulness gives birth to the Sorgues. We climbed up over the mossy rocks and sat down in the grot, beside the dark, still pool. It was the most absolute solitude. The rocks towered above and over us, to the height of six hundred feet, and the gray walls of the wild glen below shut out all appearance of life. I leaned over the rock and drank of the blue crystal that grew gradually darker towards the centre, till it became a mirror, and gave back a perfect reflection of the crags above it. There was no bubbling—no gushing up from its deep bosom—but the wealth of sparkling waters continually welled over, as from a too-full goblet.

It was with actual sorrow that I turned away from the silent spot. I never visited a place to which the fancy clung more suddenly and fondly. There is something holy in its solitude, making one envy Petrarch the years of calm and unsullied enjoyment which blessed him there. As some persons, whom we pass as strangers, strike a hidden chord in our spirits, compelling a silent sympathy with them, so some landscapes have a character of beauty which harmonizes thrillingly with the mood in which we look upon them, till we forget admiration in the glow of spontaneous attachment. They seem like abodes of the Beautiful, which the soul in its wanderings long ago visited, and now recognizes and loves as the home of a forgotten dream. It was thus I felt by the fountains of Vaucluse; sadly and with weary steps I turned away, leaving its loneliness unbroken as before.

We returned over the plain in the wind, under the gloomy sky, passed L'Isle at dusk, and after walking an hour with a rain following close behind us, stopped at an auberge in Le Thor, where we rested our tired frames and broke our long day's fasting. We were greeted in the morning with a dismal rain and wet roads, as we began the march. After a time, however, it poured down in such torrents, that we were obliged to take shelter in a remise by the road, side, where a good woman, who addressed us in the unintelligible Provençal, kindled up a blazing fire. On climbing a long hill, when the storm had abated, we experienced a delightful surprise. Below us lay the broad valley of the Rhone, with its meadows looking fresh and spring-like after the rain. The clouds were breaking away; clear blue sky was visible over Avignon, and a belt of sunlight lay warmly along the mountains of Languedoc. Many villages, with their tall, picturesque towers, dotted the landscape, and the groves of green olive enlivened the barrenness of winter. Two or three hours' walk over the plain, by a road fringed with willows, brought us to the gates of Avignon.

We walked around its picturesque turreted wall, and rambled through its narrow streets, washed here and there by streams which turn the old mill-wheels lazily around. We climbed up to the massive palace, which overlooks the city from its craggy seat, attesting the splendor it enjoyed, when for thirty years the Papal Court was held there, and the gray, weather-beaten, irregular building, resembling a pile of precipitous rocks, echoed with the revels of licentious prelates. We could not enter to learn the terrible secrets of the Inquisition, here unveiled, but we looked up at the tower, from which the captive Rienzi was liberated at the intercession of Petrarch.

After leaving Avignon, we took the road up the Rhone for Lyons, turning our backs upon the rainy south. We reached the village of Sorgues by dusk, and accepted the invitation of an old dame to lodge at her inn, which proved to be a blacksmith's shop! It was nevertheless clean and comfortable, and we sat down in one corner, out of the reach of the showers of sparks, which flew hissing from a red-hot horseshoe, that the smith and his apprentice were hammering. A Piedmontese pedlar, who carried the "Song of the Holy St. Philomène" to sell among the peasants, came in directly, and bargained for a sleep on some hay, for two sous. For a bed in the loft over the shop, we were charged five sous each, which, with seven sous for supper, made our expenses for the night about eleven cents! Our circumstances demanded the greatest economy, and we began to fear whether even this spare allowance would enable us to reach Lyons. Owing to a day's delay in Marseilles, we had left that city with but fifteen francs each; the incessant storms of winter and the worn-out state of our shoes, which were no longer proof against water or mud, prolonged our journey considerably, so that by starting before dawn and walking till dark, we were only able to make thirty miles a day. We could always procure beds for five sous, and as in the country inns one is only charged for what he chooses to order, our frugal suppers cost us but little. We purchased bread and cheese in the villages, and made our breakfasts and dinners on a bank by the roadside, or climbed the rocks and sat down by the source of some trickling rill. This simple fare had an excellent relish, and although we walked in wet clothes from morning till night, often laying down on the damp, cold earth to rest, our health was never affected.

It is worth all the toil and privation we have as yet undergone, to gain, from actual experience, the blessed knowledge that man always retains a kindness and brotherly sympathy towards his fellow—that under all the weight of vice and misery which a grinding oppression of soul and body brings on the laborers of earth, there still remain many bright tokens of a better nature. Among the starving mountaineers of the Hartz—the degraded peasantry of Bohemia—the savage contadini of Central Italy, or the dwellers on the hills of Provence and beside the swift Rhone, we almost invariably found kind, honest hearts, and an aspiration for something better, betokening the consciousness that such brute-like, obedient existence was not their proper destiny. We found few so hardened as to be insensible to a kind look or a friendly word, and nothing made us forget we were among strangers so much as the many tokens of sympathy which met us when least looked for. A young Englishman, who had traveled on foot from Geneva to Rome, enduring many privations on account of his reduced circumstances, said to me, while speaking on this subject: "A single word of kindness from a stranger would make my heart warm and my spirits cheerful, for days afterwards." There is not so much evil in man as men would have us believe; and it is a happy comfort to know and feel this.

Leaving our little inn before day break next morning, we crossed the

Sorgues, grown muddy since its infancy at Vaucluse, like many a young soul, whose mountain purity goes out into the soiling world and becomes sullied forever. The road passed over broad, barren ranges of hills, and the landscape was destitute of all interest, till we approached Orange. This city is built at the foot of a rocky height, a great square projection of which seemed to stand in its midst. As we approached nearer, however, arches and lines of cornice could be discerned, and we recognized it as the celebrated amphitheatre, one of the grandest Roman relics in the south of France.

I stood at the foot of this great fabric, and gazed up at it in astonishment. The exterior wall, three hundred and thirty-four feet in length, and rising to the height of one hundred and twenty-one feet, is still in excellent, preservation, and through its rows of solid arches one looks on the broken ranges of seats within. On the crag above, and looking as if about to topple down on it, is a massive fragment of the fortress of the Princes of Orange, razed by Louis XIV. Passing through the city, we came to the beautiful Roman triumphal arch, which to my eye is a finer structure than that of Constantino at Rome. It is built of a rich yellow marble and highly ornamented with sculptured trophies. From the barbaric shields and the letters MARIO, still remaining, it has been supposed to commemorate the victory of Marius over the barbarians, near Aix. A frieze, running along the top, on each side, shows, although broken and much defaced by the weather, the life and action which once marked the struggling figures. These Roman ruins, scattered through Provence and Languedoc, though inferior in historical interest, equal in architectural beauty the greater part of those in the Eternal City itself.

The rest of the day the road was monotonous, though varied somewhat by the tall crags of Mornas and Mont-dragon, towering over the villages of the same name. Night came on as the rock of Pierrelatte, at whose foot we were to sleep, appeared in the distance, rising like a Gibraltar from the plain, and we only reached it in time to escape the rain that came down the valley of the Rhone.

Next day we passed several companies of soldiers on their way to Africa. One of them was accompanied by a young girl, apparently the wife of the recruit by whose side she was marching. She wore the tight blue jacket of

668

the troop, and a red skirt, reaching to the knees, over her soldier pantaloons; while her pretty face showed to advantage beneath a small military cap. It was a "Fille du Regiment" in real life. Near Montelimart, we lost sight of Mont Ventoux, whose gleaming white crest had been visible all the way from Vaucluse, and passed along the base of a range of hills running near to the river. So went our march, without particular incident, till we bivouacked for the night among a company of soldiers in the little village of Loriol.

Leaving at six o'clock, wakened by the trumpets which called up the soldiery to their day's march, we reached the river Drome at dawn, and from the bridge over its rapid current, gazed at the dim, ash-colored masses of the Alps of Dauphiné, piled along the sky, far up the valley. The coming of morn threw a yellow glow along their snowy sides, and lighted up, here and there, a flashing glacier. The peasantry were already up and at work, and caravans of pack-wagons rumbled along in the morning twilight We trudged on with them, and by breakfast-time had made some distance of the way to Valence. The road, which does not approach the Rhone, is devoid of interest and tiresome, though under a summer sky, when the bare vine-hills are latticed over with green, and the fruit-trees covered with blossoms and foliage, it might be a scene of great beauty.

Valence, which we reached towards noon, is a commonplace city on the Rhone; and my only reasons for traversing its dirty streets in preference to taking the road, which passes without the walls, were—to get something for dinner, and because it might have been the birth-place of Aymer de Valence, the valorous Crusader, chronicled in "Ivanhoe," whose tomb I had seen in Westminster Abbey. One of the streets which was marked "Rue Bayard," shows that my valiant namesake—the knight without fear and reproach—is still remembered in his native province. The ruins of his chateau are still standing among the Alps near Grenoble.

In the afternoon we crossed the Isère, a swift, muddy river, which rises among the Alps of Dauphiné, We saw their icy range, among which is the desert solitude of the Grand Chartreuse, far up the valley; but the thick atmosphere hid the mighty Mont Blanc, whose cloudy outline, eighty miles distant in a "bee line," is visible in fair weather. At Tain, we came upon the

Rhone again, and walked along the base of the hills which contract its current. Here, I should call it beautiful. The scenery has a wildness that approaches to that of the Rhine. Rocky, castellated heights frown over the rushing waters, which have something of the majesty of their "exulting and abounding" rival. Winding around the curving hills, the scene is constantly varied, and the little willowed islets clasped in the embrace of the stream, mingle a trait of softened beauty with its sterner character.

After passing the night at a village on its banks, we left it again at St. Vallier, the next morning. At sunset, the spires of Vienne were visible, and the lofty Mont Pilas, the snows of whose riven summits feed the springs of the Loire on its western side, stretched majestically along the opposite bank of the Rhone. In a meadow, near Vienne, stands a curious Roman obelisk, seventy-six feet in height. The base is composed of four pillars, connected by arches, and the whole structure has a barbaric air, compared with the more elegant monuments of Orange and Nismes. Vienne, which is mentioned by several of the Roman historians under its present name, was the capital of the Allobroges, and I looked upon it with a new and strange interest, on calling to mind my school-boy days, when I had become familiar with that war-like race, in toiling over the pages of Cæsar. We walked in the mud and darkness for what seemed a great distance, and finally took shelter in a little inn at the northern end of the city. Two Belgian soldiers, coming from Africa, were already quartered there, and we listened to their tales of the Arab and the desert, while supper was preparing.

The morning of the 25th was dull and rainy; the road, very muddy and unpleasant, led over the hills, avoiding the westward curve of the Rhone, directly towards Lyons. About noon, we came in sight of the broad valley in which the Rhone first clasps his Burgundian bride—the Saone, and a cloud of impenetrable coal-smoke showed us the location of Lyons. A nearer approach revealed a large flat dome, and some ranges of tall buildings near the river. We soon entered the suburb of La Guillotière, which has sprung up on the eastern bank of the Rhone. Notwithstanding our clothes were like sponges, our boots entirely worn out, and our bodies somewhat thin with nine days exposure to the wintry storms in walking two hundred and forty miles, we entered Lyons with suspense and anxiety. But one franc apiece remained out of the fifteen with which we left Marseilles. B—— wrote home some time ago, directing a remittance to be forwarded to a merchant at Paris, to whom he had a letter of introduction, and in the hope that this had arrived, he determined to enclose the letter in a note, stating our circumstances, and requesting him to forward a part of the remittance to Lyons. We had then to wait at least four days; people are suspicious and mistrustful in cities, and if no relief should come, what was to be done?

After wading through the mud of the suburbs, we chose a common-looking inn near the river, as the comfort of our stay depended wholly on the kindness of our hosts, and we hoped to find more sympathy among the laboring classes. We engaged lodgings for four or five days; after dinner the letter was dispatched, and we wandered about through the dark, dirty city until night. Our landlord, Monsieur Ferrand, was a rough, vigorous man, with a gloomy, discontented expression; his words were few and blunt; but a certain restlessness of manner, and a secret flashing of his cold, forbidding eye betrayed to me some strong hidden excitement. Madame Ferrand was kind and talkative, though passionate; but the appearance of the place gave me an unfavorable impression, which was heightened by the thought that it was now impossible to change our lodgings until relief should arrive. When bed-time came, a ladder was placed against a sort of high platform along one side of the kitchen; we mounted and found a bed, concealed from the view of those below by a dusty muslin curtain. We lay there, between heaven and earth—the dirty earth of the brick floor and the sooty heaven of the ceiling—listening until midnight to the boisterous songs, and loud, angry disputes in the room adjoining. Thus ended our first day in Lyons.

Five weary days, each of them containing a month of torturing suspense, have since passed. Our lodging-place grew so unpleasant that we preferred wandering all day through the misty, muddy, smoky streets, taking refuge in the covered bazaars when it rained heavily. The gloom of every thing around us, entirely smothered down the lightness of heart which made us laugh over our embarrassments at Vienna. When at evening, the dull, leaden hue of the clouds seemed to make the air dark and cold and heavy, we walked beside the swollen and turbid Rhone, under an avenue of leafless trees, the damp soil chilling our feet and striking a numbness through our frames, and then I knew what those must feel who have no hope in their destitution, and not a friend in all the great world, who is not wretched as themselves. I prize the lesson, though the price of it is hard.

"This morning," I said to B——, "will terminate our suspense." I felt cheerful in spite of myself; and this was like a presentiment of coming good luck. To pass the time till the mail arrived we climbed to the chapel of Fourvières, whose walls are covered with votive offerings to a miraculous picture of the Virgin. But at the precise hour we were at the Post Office. What an intensity of suspense can be felt in that minute, while the clerk is looking over the letters! And what a lightning-like shock of joy when it did come, and was opened with eager, trembling hands, revealing the relief we had almost despaired of! The city did not seem less gloomy, for that was impossible, but the faces of the crowd which had appeared cold and suspicious, were now kind and cheerful. we came home to our lodgings with changed feelings, and Madame Ferrand must have seen the joy in our faces, for she greeted us with an unusual smile.

We leave to-morrow morning for Chalons. I do not feel disposed to describe Lyons particularly, although I have become intimately acquainted with every part of it, from Presqu' isle Perrache to Croix Rousse. I know the contents of every shop in the Bazaar, and the passage of the Hotel Dieu—the title of every volume in the bookstores in the Place Belcour—and the countenance of every boot-block and apple-woman on the Quais on both sides of the river. I have walked up the Saone to Pierre Seise—down the Rhone to his muddy marriage—climbed the Heights of Fourvières, and promenaded in the Cours Napoleon! Why, men have been presented with the freedom of cities, when they have had far less cause for such an honor than this!

CHAPTER XLIV. – TRAVELING IN BURGUNDY—THE MISERIES OF A COUNTRY DILIGENCE.

Paris, Feb. 6, 1840.—Every letter of the date is traced with an emotion of joy, for our dreary journey is over. There was a magic in the name that revived us during a long journey, and now the thought that it is all over—that these walls which enclose us, stand in the heart of the gay city—seems almost too joyful to be true. Yesterday I marked with the whitest chalk, on the blackest of all tablets to make the contrast greater, for I got out of the cramped diligence at the Barrière de Charenton, and saw before me in the morning twilight, the immense groy mass of Paris. I forgot my numbed and stiffened frame, and every other of the thousand disagreeable feelings of diligence traveling, in the pleasure which that sight afforded.

We arose in the dark at Lyons, and after bidding adieu to morose Monsieur Ferrand, traversed the silent city and found our way in the mist and gloom to the steamboat landing on the Saone. The waters were swollen much above their usual level, which was favorable for the boat, as long as there was room enough left to pass under the bridges. After a great deal of bustle we got under way, and were dashing out of Lyons, against the swift current, before day-break. We passed L'Isle Barbe, once a favorite residence of Charlemagne, and now the haunt of the Lyonnaise on summer holidays, and going under the suspension bridges with levelled chimneys, entered the picturesque hills above, which are covered with vineyards nearly to the top; the villages scattered over them have those square, pointed towers, which give such a quaintness to French country scenery.

The stream being very high, the meadows on both sides were deeply overflowed. To avoid the strong current in the centre, our boat ran along the banks, pushing aside the alder thickets and poplar shoots; in passing the bridges, the pipes were always brought down flat on the deck. A little after noon, we passed the large town of Macon, the birth-place of the poet Lamartine. The valley of the Saone, no longer enclosed among the hills, spread out to several miles in width. Along the west lay in sunshine the vine-mountains of Côte d'Or, and among the dark clouds in the eastern sky, we could barely distinguish the outline of the Jura. The waters were so much swollen as to cover the plain for two or three miles. We seemed to be sailing down a lake, with rows of trees springing up out of the water, and houses and villages lying like islands on its surface. A sunset that promised better weather tinged the broad brown flood, as Chalons came in sight, looking like a city built along the shore of a lake. We squeezed through the crowd of porters and diligence men, declining their kind offers, and hunted quarters to suit ourselves.

We left Chalons on the morning of the 1st, in high spirits at the thought that there were but little more than two hundred miles between us and Paris. In walking over the cold, muddy plain, we passed a family of strolling musicians, who were sitting on a heap of stones by the roadside. An ill-dressed, ill-natured man and woman, each carrying a violin, and a thin, squalid girl, with a tamborine, composed the group. Their faces bore that unfeeling stamp, which springs from depravity and degradation. When we had walked somewhat more than a mile, we overtook a little girl, who was crying bitterly. By her features, from which the fresh beauty of childhood had not been worn, and the steel triangle which was tied to her belt, we knew she belonged to the family we had passed. Her dress was thin and ragged and a pair of wooden shoes but ill protected her feet from the sharp cold. I stopped and asked her why she cried, but she did not at first answer. However, by questioning, I found her unfeeling parents had sent her on without food; she was sobbing with hunger and cold. Our pockets were full of bread and cheese which we had bought for breakfast, and we gave her half a loaf, which stopped her tears at once. She looked up and thanked us, smiling; and sitting down on a bank, began to eat as if half famished.

The physiognomy of this region is very singular. It appears as if the country had been originally a vast elevated plain, and some great power had scooped out, as with a hand, deep circular valleys all over its surface. In winding along the high ridges, we often looked down, on either side, into such hollows, several miles in diameter, and sometimes entirely covered with vineyards. At La Rochepot, a quaint, antique village, lying in the bottom of one of these dells, we saw the finest ruin of the middle ages that I have met with in France. An American lady had spoken to me of it in Rome, and I believe Willis mentions it in his "Pencillings," but it is not described in the guide books, nor could we learn what feudal lord had ever dwelt in its halls. It covers the summit of a stately rock, at whose foot the village is crouched, and the green ivy climbs up to the very top of its gray towers.

As the road makes a wide curve around the side of the hill, we descended to the village by the nearer foot-path, and passed among its low, old houses, with their pointed gables and mossy roofs. The path led close along the foot of the rock, and we climbed up to the ruin, and stood in its grass-grown courtyard. Only the outer walls and the round towers at each corner are left remaining; the inner part has been razed to the ground, and where proud barons once marshalled their vassals, the villagers now play their holiday games. On one side, several Gothic windows are left standing, perfect, though of simple construction, and in the towers we saw many fire-places and door-ways of richly cut stone, which looked as fresh as if just erected.

We passed the night at Ivry (not the Ivry which gained Henri Quatre his kingdom) and then continued our march over roads which I can only compare to our country roads in America during the spring thaw. In addition to this, the rain commenced early in the morning and continued all day, so that we were completely wet the whole time. The plains, too high and cold to produce wine, were varied by forests of beech and oak, and the population was thinly scattered over them in small villages. Travelers generally complain very much of the monotony of this part of France, and, with such dreary weather, we could not disagree with them.

As the day wore on, the rain increased, and the sky put on that dull, gray cast, which denotes a lengthened storm. We were fain to stop at nightfall, but there was no inn near at hand—not even a hovel of a cabaret in which to shelter ourselves, and, on enquiring of the wagoners, we received the comforting assurance that there was yet a league and a half to the nearest stopping place. On, then, we went, with the pitiless storm beating in our faces and on our breasts, till there was not a dry spot left, except what our knapsacks covered. We could not have been more completely saturated if we had been dipped in the Yonne. At length, after two hours of slipping and sliding along in the mud and wet and darkness, we reached Saulieu, and, by the warm fire, thanked our stars that the day's dismal tramp was over.

By good or bad luck (I have not yet decided which) a vehicle was to start the next morning for Auxerre, distant sixty miles, and the fare being but five francs, we thought it wisest to take places. It was always with reluctance that we departed from our usual mode of traveling, but, in the present instance, the circumstances absolutely compelled it.

Next morning, at sunrise, we took our seats in a large, square vehicle on two wheels, calculated for six persons and a driver, with a single horse. But, as he was fat and round as an elephant, and started off at a brisk pace, and we were well protected from the rain, it was not so bad after all, barring the jolts and jarred vertebræ. We drove on, over the same dreary expanse of plain and forest, passing through two or three towns in the course of the day, and by evening had made somewhat more than half our journey. Owing to the slowness of our fresh horse, we were jolted about the whole night, and did not arrive at Auxerre until six o'clock in the morning. After waiting an hour in a hotel beside the rushing Yonne, a lumbering diligence was got ready, and we were given places to Paris for seven francs. As the distance is one hundred and ten miles, this would be considered cheap, but I should not want to travel it again and be paid for doing so. Twelve persons were packed into a box not large enough for a cow, and no cabinet-maker ever dove-tailed the corners of his bureaus tighter than we did our knees and nether extremities. It is my lot to be blessed with abundance of stature, and none but tall persons can appreciate the misery of sitting for hours with their joints in an immovable vice. The closeness of the atmosphere—for the passengers would not permit the windows to be opened for fear of taking cold—combined with loss of sleep, made me so drowsy that my head was continually falling on my next neighbor, who, being a heavy country lady, thrust it indignantly away. I would then try my best to keep it up awhile, but it would droop gradually, till the crash of a bonnet or a smart bump against some other head would recall me, for a moment, to consciousness.

676

We passed Joigny, on the Yonne, Sens, with its glorious old cathedral, and at dusk reached Montercau, on the Seine. This was the scene of one of Napoleon's best victories, on his return from Elba. In driving over the bridge, I looked down on the swift and swollen current, and hoped that its hue might never be darkened again so fearfully as the last sixty years have witnessed. No river in Europe has such an association connected with it. We think of the Danube, for its majesty, of the Rhine, for its wild beauty, but of the Seine— for its blood!

In coming thus to the last famed stream I shall visit in Europe, I might say, with Barry Cornwall:

"We've sailed through banks of green,

Where the wild waves fret and quiver;

And we've down the Danube been—

The dark, deep, thundering river!

We've thridded the Elbe and Rhone,

The Tiber and blood dyed Seine,

And we've been where the blue Garonne

Goes laughing to meet the main!"

All that night did we endure squeezing and suffocation, and no morn was ever more welcome than that which revealed to us Paris. With matted hair, wild, glaring eyes, and dusty and dishevelled habiliments, we entered the gay capital, and blessed every stone upon which we placed our feet, in the fulness of our joy.

In paying our fare at Auxerre, I was obliged to use a draft on the banker, Rougemont de Lowenberg. The ignorant conductor hesitated to change this, but permitted us to go, on condition of keeping it until we should arrive. Therefore, on getting out of the diligence, after forty-eight hours of sleepless and fasting misery, the facteur of the office went with me to get it paid, leaving B—— to wait for us. I knew nothing of Paris, and this merciless man

677

kept me for three hours at his heels, following him on all his errands, before he did mine, in that time traversing the whole length of the city, in order to leave a chèvre-feuille at an aristocratic residence in the Faubourg St. Germain. Yet even combined weariness and hunger could not prevent me from looking with vivid interest down a long avenue, at the Column of the place Vendôme, in passing, and gazing up in wonder at the splendid portico of the Madeleine. But of anything else I have a very faint remembrance. "You can eat breakfast, now, I think," said he, when we returned, "we have walked more than four leagues!"

I know we will be excused, that, instead of hurrying away to Notre Dame or the Louvre, we sat down quietly to a most complete breakfast. Even the most romantic must be forced to confess that admiration does not sit well on an empty stomach. Our first walk was to a bath, and then, with complexions several shades lighter, and limbs that felt us if lifted by invisible wings, we hurried away to the Post Office. I seized the welcome missives from my far home, with a beating heart, and hastening back, read till the words became indistinct in the twilight.

CHAPTER XLV. — POETICAL SCENES IN PARIS.

What a gay little world in miniature this is! I wonder not that the French, with their exuberant gaiety of spirit, should revel in its ceaseless tides of pleasure, as if it were an earthly Elysium. I feel already the influence of its cheerful atmosphere, and have rarely threaded the crowds of a stranger city, with so light a heart as I do now daily, on the thronged banks of the Seine. And yet it would be difficult to describe wherein consists this agreeable peculiarity. You can find streets as dark and crooked and dirty anywhere in Germany, and squares and gardens as gay and sunny beyond the Alps, and yet they would affect you far differently. You could not, as here, divest yourself of every particle of sad or serious thought and be content to gaze for hours on the showy scene, without an idea beyond the present moment. It must be that the spirit of the croud is magnetically contagious.

The evening of our arrival we walked out past the massive and stately Hotel de Ville, and took a promenade along the Quais. The shops facing the river presented a scene of great splendor. Several of the Quais on the north bank of the Seine are occupied almost entirely by jewellers, the windows of whose shops, arranged in a style of the greatest taste, make a dazzling display. Rows of gold watches and chains are arranged across the crystal panes, and heaped in pyramids on long glass slabs; cylindrical wheels of wire, hung with jewelled breastpins and earrings, turn slowly around by some invisible agency, displaying row after row of their glittering treasures.

From the centre of the Pont Neuf, we could see for a long distance up and down the river. The different bridges traced on either side a dozen starry lines through the dark air, and a continued blaze lighted the two shores in their whole length, revealing the outline of the Isle da la Cité. I recognized the Palaces of the Louvre and the Tuileries in the dusky mass beyond. Eastward, looming against the dark sky, I could faintly trace the black towers of Notre Dame, The rushing of the swift waters below mingled with the rattling of a thousand carts and carriages, and the confusion of a thousand voices, till it seemed like some grand nightly festival.

I first saw Notre Dame by moonlight. The shadow of its stupendous front was thrown directly towards me, hiding the innumerable lines of the ornamental sculpture which cover its tall, square towers. I walked forward until the interlacing, Moorish arches between them stood full against the moon, and the light, struggling through the quaint openings of the tracery, streamed in silver lines down into the shadow. The square before it was quite deserted, for it stands on a lonely part of the Isle de la Cité, and it looked thus far more majestic and solemn than in the glaring daylight.

The great quadrangle of the Tuileries encloses the Place du Carrousel, in the centre of which stands a triumphal arch, erected by Napoleon after his Italian victories. Standing in the middle of this arch, you look through the open passage in the central building of the palace, into the Gardens beyond. Further on, in a direct line, the middle avenue of the Gardens extends away to the Place de la Concorde, where the Obelisk of Luxor makes a perpendicular line through your vista; still further goes the broad avenue through the Elysian Fields, until afar off, the Arc de l'Etoile, two miles distant, closes this view through the palace doorway.

Let us go through it, and on, to the Place de la Concorde, reserving the Gardens for another time. What is there in Europe—nay, in the world,— equal to this? In the centre, the mighty obelisk of red granite pierces the sky,—on either hand showers of silver spray are thrown up from splendid bronze fountains—statues and pillars of gilded bronze sweep in a grand circle around the square, and on each side magnificent vistas lead the eye off, and combine the distant with the near, to complete this unparalleled view! Eastward, beyond the tall trees in the garden of the Tuileries, rises the long front of the Palace, with the tri-color floating above; westward, in front of us, is the Forest of the Elysian Fields, with the arch of triumph nearly a mile and a half distant, looking down from the end of the avenue, at the Barriere de Neuilly. To the right and left are the marble fronts of the Church of the Madeleine and the Chamber of Deputies, the latter on the other side of the Seine. Thus the groves and gardens of Paris—the palace of her kings— the proud monument of her sons' glory—and the masterpieces of modern

French architecture are all embraced in this one splendid coup d'oeil.

Following the motley multitude to the bridge, I crossed and made my way to the Hotel des Invalides. Along the esplanade, playful companies of children were running and tumbling in their sports over the green turf, which was as fresh as a meadow; while, not the least interesting feature of the scene, numbers of scarred and disabled veterans, in the livery of the Hospital, basked in the sunshine, watching with quiet satisfaction the gambols of the second generation they have seen arise. What tales could they not tell, those wrinkled and feeble old men! What visions of Marengo and Austerlitz and Borodino shift still with a fiery vividness through their fading memories! Some may have left a limb on the Lybian desert; and the sabre of the Cossack may have scarred the brows of others. They witnessed the rising and setting of that great meteor, which intoxicated France with such a blaze of power and glory, and now, when the recollection of that wonderful period seems almost like a stormy dream, they are left to guard the ashes of their ancient General, brought back from his exile to rest in the bosom of his own French people. It was to me a touching and exciting thing, to look on those whose eyes had witnessed the filling up of such a fated leaf in the world's history.

Entrance is denied to the tomb of Napoleon until it is finished, which will not be for three or four yours yet. I went, however, into the "Church of the Banners"—a large chapel, hung with two or three hundred flags taken by the armies of the Empire. The greater part of them were Austrian and Russian. It appeared to be empty when I entered, but on looking around, I saw an old gray-headed soldier kneeling at one side. His head was bowed over his hands, and he seemed perfectly absorbed in his thoughts. Perhaps the very tattered banners which hung down motionless above his head, he might have assisted in conquering. I looked a moment on those eloquent trophies, and then noiselessly withdrew.

There is at least one solemn spot near Paris; the laughing winds that come up from the merry city sink into sighs under the cypress boughs of Pere Lachaise. And yet it is not a gloomy place, but full of a serious beauty, fitting for a city of the dead. I shall never forget the sunny afternoon when I first entered its gate and walked slowly up the hill, between rows of tombs, gleaming white amid the heavy foliage, while the green turf around them was just beginning to be starred by the opening daisies, From the little chapel on its summit I looked back at the blue spires of the city, whose roar of life dwindled to a low murmur. Countless pyramids, obelisks and urns, rising far and wide above the cedars and cypresses, showed the extent of the splendid necropolis, which is inhabited by pale, shrouded emigrants from its living sister below. The only sad part of the view, was the slope of the hill alloted to the poor, where legions of plain black crosses are drawn up into solid squares on its side and stand alone gloomy—the advanced guard of the army of Death! I mused over the tombs of Molière and La Fontaine; Massena, Mortier and Lefebre; General Foy and Casimir Perier; and finally descended to the shrine where Abelard reposes by the side of his Heloise. The old sculptured tomb, brought away from the Paraclete, still covers their remains, and pious hands (of lovers, perhaps,) keep fresh the wreaths of immortelles above their marble effigies.

In the Theatre Français, I saw Rachel, the actress. She appeared in the character of "Virginia," in a tragedy of that name, by the poet Latour. Her appearance as she came upon the stage alone, convinced me she would not belie her renown. She is rather small in stature, with dark, piercing eyes and rich black hair; her lips are full, but delicately formed, and her features have a marked yet flexible outline, which conveys the minutest shades of expression. Her voice is clear, deep and thrilling, and like sonic grand strain of music, there is power and meaning in its slightest modulations. Her gestures embody the very spirit of the character; she has so perfectly attained that rare harmony of thought, sound and action, or rather, that unity of feeling which renders them harmonious, that her acting seems the unstudied, irrepressible impulse of her soul. With the first sentence she uttered, I forgot Rachel. I only saw the innocent Roman girl; I awaited in suspense and with a powerful sympathy, the developement of the oft-told tragedy. My blood grew warm with indignation when the words of Appius roused her to anger, and I could scarcely keep back my tears, when, with a voice broken by sobs, she bade farewell to the protecting gods of her father's hearth.

Among the bewildering variety of ancient ornaments and implements in the Egyptian Gallery of the Louvre, I saw an object of startling interest. A fragment of the Iliad, written nearly three thousand years ago! One may even dare to conjecture that the torn and half-mouldered slip of papyrus, upon which he gazes, may have been taken down from the lips of the immortal Chiun. The eyes look on those faded characters, and across the great gulf of Time, the soul leaps into the Past, brought into shadowy nearness by a mirage of the mind. There, as in the desert, images start up, vivid, yet of a vague and dreamy beauty. We see the olive groves of Greece—white-robed youths and maidens sit in the shade of swaying boughs—and one of them reads aloud, in words that sound like the clashing of shields, the deeds of Achilles.

As we step out the western portal of the Tuileries, a beautiful scene greets us. We look on the palace garden, fragrant with flowers and classic with bronze copies of ancient sculpture. Beyond this, broad gravel walks divide the flower-bordered lawns and ranks of marble demigods and heroes look down on the joyous crowd. Children troll their hoops along the avenues or skip the rope under the clipped lindens, whose boughs are now tinged a pale yellow by the bursting buds. The swans glide about on a pond in the centre, begging bread of the bystanders, who watch a miniature ship which the soft breeze carries steadily across. Paris is unseen, but heard, on every side; only the Column of Luxor and the Arc de Triomphe rise blue and grand above the top of the forest. What with the sound of voices, the merry laughter of the children and a host of smiling faces, the scene touches a happy chord in one's heart, and he mingles with it, lost in pleasant reverie, till the sounds fade away with the fading light.

Just below the Baths of the Louvre, there are several floating barges belonging to the washer-women, anchored at the foot of the great stone staircase leading down to the water. They stand there day after day, beating their clothes upon flat boards and rinsing them in the Seine. One day there seemed to have been a wedding or some other cause of rejoicing among them, for a large number of the youngest were talking in great glee on one of the platforms of the staircase, while a handsome, German-looking youth stood near, with a guitar slung around his neck. He struck up a lively air, and the girls fell into a droll sort of a dance. They went at it heavily and roughly enough, but made up in good humor what they lacked in grace; the older members of the craft looked up from their work with satisfaction and many shouts of applause wore sent down to them from the spectators on the Quai and the Pont Neuf. Not content with this, they seized on some luckless men who were descending the steps, and clasping them with their powerful right arms, spun them around like so many tops and sent them whizzing off at a tangent. Loud bursts of laughter greeted this performance, and the stout river maidens returned to their dance with redoubled spirit.

Yesterday, the famous procession of the "boeuf gras" took place for the second time, with great splendor. The order of march had been duly announced beforehand, and by noon all the streets and squares through which it was to pass, were crowded with waiting spectators. Mounted gens d'armes rode constantly to and fro, to direct the passage of vehicles and keep an open thoroughfare. Thousands of country peasants poured into the city, the boys of whom were seen in all directions, blowing distressingly through hollow ox-horns. Altogether, the spirit of nonsense which animated the crowd, displayed itself very amusingly.

A few mounted guards led the procession, followed by a band of music. Then appeared Roman lictors and officers of sacrifice, leading Dagobert, the famous bull of Normandy, destined to the honor of being slaughtered as the Carnival beef. He trod rather tenderly, finding, no doubt, a difference between the meadows of Caen and the pavements of Paris, and I thought he would have been willing to forego his gilded horns and flowery crown, to get back there again. His weight was said to be four thousand pounds, and the bills pompously declared that he had no rival in France, except the elephant in the Jardin des Plantes.

After him came the farmer by whom he was raised, and M. Roland, the butcher of the carnival, followed by a hundred of the same craft, dressed as cavaliers of the different ages of France. They made a very showy appearance, although the faded velvet and soiled tinsel of their mantles were rather too apparent by daylight.

After all these had gone by, came an enormous triumphal car, very profusely covered with gilding and ornamental flowers. A fellow with long woollen hair and beard, intended to represent Time, acted as driver. In the car, under a gilded canopy, reposed a number of persons, in blue silk smocks and yellow "fleshtights," said to be Venus, Apollo, the Graces, &c. but I endeavored in vain to distinguish one divinity from another. However, three children on the back seat, dressed in the same style, with the addition of long flaxy ringlets, made very passable Cupids. This closed the march; which passed onward towards the Place de la Concorde, accompanied by the sounds of music and the shouts of the mob. The broad, splendid line of Boulevards, which describe a semi-circle around the heart of the city, were crowded, and for the whole distance of three miles, it required no slight labor to make one's way. People in masks and fancy costumes were continually passing and re-passing, and I detected in more than one of the carriages, checks rather too fair to suit the slouched hunter's hats which shaded them. It seemed as if all Paris was taking a holiday, and resolved to make the most of it.

CHAPTER XLVI. — A GLIMPSE OF NORMANDY.

After a residence of five weeks, which, in spite of some few troubles, passed away quickly and delightfully, I turned my back on Paris. It was not regret I experienced on taking my seat in the cars for Versailles, but that feeling of reluctance with which we leave places whose brightness and gaiety force the mind away from serious toil. Steam, however, cuts short all sentiment, and in much less time than it takes to bid farewell to a German, we had whizzed past the Place d'Europe, through the barrier, and were watching the spires start up from the receding city, on the way to St. Cloud.

At Versailles I spent three hours in a hasty walk through the palace, which allowed but a bare glance at the gorgeous paintings of Horace Vernet. His "Taking of Constantine" has the vivid look of reality. The white houses shine in the sun, and from the bleached earth to the blue and dazzling sky, there seems to hang a heavy, scorching atmosphere. The white smoke of the artillery curls almost visibly off the canvass, and the cracked and half-sprung walls look as if about to topple down on the besiegers. One series of halls is devoted to the illustration of the knightly chronicles of France, from the days of Charlemagne to those of Bayard and Gaston de Foix. Among these pictured legends, I looked with the deepest interest on that of the noble girl of Orleans. Her countenance—the same in all these pictures and in a beautiful statue of her, which stands in one of the corridors—is said to be copied from an old and well-authenticated portrait. United to the sweetness and purity of peasant beauty, she has the lofty brow and inspired expression of a prophetess. There is a soft light in her full blue eye that does not belong to earth. I wonder not the soldiery deemed her chosen by God to lead them to successful battle; had I lived in those times I could have followed her consecrated banner to the ends of the earth. In the statue, she stands musing, with her head drooping forward, as if the weight of the breastplate oppressed her woman's heart; the melancholy soul which shines through the marble seems to forebode the fearful winding-up of her eventful destiny.

The afternoon was somewhat advanced, by the time I had seen the palace and gardens. After a hurried dinner at a restaurant, I shouldered my knapsack and took the road to St. Germain. The day was gloomy and cheerless, and I should have felt very lonely but for the thought of soon reaching England. There is no time of the year more melancholy than a cold, cloudy day in March; whatever may be the beauties of pedestrian traveling in fairer seasons, my experience dictates that during winter storms and March glooms, it had better be dispensed with. However, I pushed on to St. Germain, threaded its long streets, looked down from the height over its magnificent tract of forest and turned westward down the Seine. Owing to the scantiness of villages, I was obliged to walk an hour and a half in the wind and darkness, before I reached a solitary inn. As I opened the door and asked for lodging, the landlady inquired if I had the necessary papers. I answered in the affirmative and was admitted. While I was eating supper, they prepared their meal on the other end of the small table and sat down together. They fell into the error, so common to ignorant persons, of thinking a foreigner could not understand them, and began talking quite unconcernedly about me. "Why don't he take the railroad?" said the old man: "he must have very little money—it would be bad for us if he had none." "Oh!" remarked his son, "if he had none, he would not be sitting there so quiet and unconcerned." I thought there was some knowledge of human nature in this remark. "And besides," added the landlady, "there is no danger for us, for we have his passport." Of course I enjoyed this in secret, and mentally pardoned their suspicions, when I reflected that the high roads between Paris and London are frequented by many imposters, which makes the people naturally mistrustful. I walked all the next day through a beautiful and richly cultivated country. The early fruit trees were bursting into bloom, and the farmers led out their cattle to pasturage in the fresh meadows. The scenery must be delightful in summer— worthy of all that has been said or sung about lovely Normandy. On the morning of the third day, before reaching Rouen, I saw at a distance the remains of Chateau Galliard, the favorite castle of Richard Coeur de Lion. Rouen breathes everywhere of the ancient times of Normandy. Nothing can be more picturesque than its quaint, irregular wooden houses, and the low, mossy mills, spanning the clear streams which rush through its streets. The Cathedral, with its four towers, rises from among the clustered cottages like a giant rook, split by the lightning and worn by the rains of centuries is into a thousand fantastic shapes.

Resuming my walk in the afternoon, I climbed the heights west of the city, and after passing through a suburb four or five miles in length, entered the vale of the Cailly. This is one of the sweetest scenes in France. It lies among the woody hills like a Paradise, with its velvet meadows and villas and breathing gardens. The grass was starred with daisies and if I took a step into the oak and chestnut woods, I trampled on thousands of anemones and fragrant daffodils. The upland plain, stretching inward from the coast, wears a different character. As I ascended, towards evening, and walked over its monotonous swells, I felt almost homesick beneath its saddening influence. The sun, hazed over with dull clouds, gave out that cold and lifeless light which is more lonely than complete darkness. The wind, sweeping dismally over the fields, sent clouds of blinding dust down the road, and as it passed through the forests, the myriads of fine twigs sent up a sound as deep and grand as the roar of a roused ocean. Every chink of the Norman cottage where I slept, whistled most drearily, and as I looked out the little window of my room, the trees were swaying in the gloom, and long, black clouds scudded across the sky. Though my bed was poor and hard, it was a sublime sound that cradled me into slumber. Homer might have used it as the lullaby of Jove.

My last day on the continent came. I rose early and walked over the hills towards Dieppe. The scenery grew more bleak as I approached the sea, but the low and sheltered valleys preserved the pastoral look of the interior. In the afternoon, as I climbed a long, elevated ridge, over which a strong northwester was blowing, I was struck with a beautiful rustic church, in one of the dells below me. While admiring its neat tower I had gained unconsciously the summit of the hill, and on turning suddenly around, lo! there was the glorious old Atlantic stretching far before and around me! A shower was sweeping mistily along the horizon and I could trace the white line of the breakers that foamed at the foot of the cliffs. The scene came over me like a vivid electric shock, and I gave an involuntary shout, which might have been heard in all the valleys around. After a year and a half of wandering over the continent, that gray ocean was something to be revered and loved, for it clasped the shores of my native America.

I entered Dieppe in a heavy shower, and after finding an inn suited to my means and obtaining a permis d'embarquement from the police office, I went out to the battlements and looked again on the sea. The landlord promised to call me in time for the boat, but my anxiety waked me sooner, and mistaking the strokes of the cathedral bell, I shouldered my knapsack and went down to the wharf at one o'clock. No one was stirring on board the boat, and I was obliged to pace the silent, gloomy streets of the town for two hours. I watched the steamer glide out on the rainy channel, and turning into the topmost berth, drew the sliding curtain and strove to keep out cold and sea-sickness. But it was unavailing; a heavy storm of snow and rain rendered our passage so dreary that I did not stir until we were approaching the chain pier of Brighton.

I looked out on the foggy shores of England with a feeling of relief; my tongue would now be freed from the difficult bondage of foreign languages, and my ears be rejoiced with the music of my own. After two hours' delay at the Custom House, I took my seat in an open car for London. The day was dull and cold; the sun resembled a milky blotch in the midst of a leaden sky. I sat and shivered, as we flew onward, amid the rich, cultivated English scenery. At last the fog grew thicker; the road was carried over the tops of houses; the familiar dome of St. Paul's stood out above the spires; and I was again in London!

CHAPTER XLVII. — LOCKHART, BERNARD BARTON AND CROLY— LONDON CHIMES AND GREENWICH FAIR.

My circumstances, on arriving at London, were again very reduced. A franc and a half constituted the whole of my funds. This, joined to the knowledge of London expenses, rendered instant exertion necessary, to prevent still greater embarrassment. I called on a printer the next morning, hoping to procure work, but found, as I had no documents with me to show I had served a regular apprenticeship, this would be extremely difficult, although workmen were in great demand. Mr. Putnam, however, on whom I had previously called, gave me employment for a time in his publishing establishment, and thus I was fortunately enabled to await the arrival of a remittance from home.

Mrs. Trollope, whom I met in Florence, kindly gave me a letter to Murray, the publisher, and I visited him soon after my arrival. In his library I saw the original portraits of Byron, Moore, Campbell and the other authors who were intimate with him and his father. A day or two afterwards I had the good fortune to breakfast with Lockhart and Bernard Barton, at the house of the former. Mr. Murray, through whom the invitation was given, accompanied me there. As it was late when we arrived at Regent's Park, we found them waiting, and sat down immediately to breakfast.

I was much pleased with Lockhart's appearance and manners. He has a noble, manly countenance—in fact, the handsomest English face I ever saw—a quick, dark eye and an ample forehead, shaded by locks which show, as yet, but few threads of gray. There is a peculiar charm in his rich, soft voice; especially when reciting poetry, it has a clear, organ-like vibration, which thrills deliciously on the ear. His daughter, who sat at the head of the table, is a most lovely and amiable girl.

Bernard Burton, who is now quite an old man, is a very lively and sociable Friend. His head is gray and almost bald, but there is still plenty of fire in his eyes and life in his limbs. His many kind and amiable qualities endear him to a large circle of literary friends. He still continues writing, and within the last year has brought out a volume of simple, touching "Household Verses." A picture of cheerful and contented old age has never been more briefly and beautifully drawn, than in the following lines, which he sent me, in answer to my desire to possess one of his poems in his own hand:

STANZAS.

I feel that I am growing old,
  Nor wish to hide that truth;
Conscious my heart is not more cold
  Than in my by-gone youth.

I cannot roam the country round,
  As I was wont to do;
My feet a scantier circle bound,
  My eyes a narrower view.

But on my mental vision rise
  Bright scenes of beauty still:
Morn's splendor, evening's glowing skies,
  Valley, and grove, and hill.

Nor can infirmities o'erwhelm
  The purer pleasures brought
From the immortal spirit's realm
  Of feeling and of Thought!

My heart! let not dismay or doubt

In thee an entrance win!

Thou hast enjoyed thyself without—

Now seek thy joy within!

During breakfast he related to us a pleasant anecdote of Scott. He once wrote to the poet in behalf of a young lady, who wished to have the description of Melrose, in the "Lay of the last Minstrel," in the poet's own writing. Scott sent it, but added these lines to the conclusion:

"Then go, and muse with deepest awe

On what the writer never saw;

Who would not wander 'neath the moon

To see what he could see at noon!"

We went afterwards into Lockhart's library, which was full of interesting objects. I saw the private diary of Scott, kept until within a short time of his death. It was melancholy to trace the gradual failing of all his energies in the very wavering of the autograph. In a large volume of his correspondence, containing letters from Campbell, Wordsworth, Byron, and all the distinguished characters of the age, I saw Campbell's "Battle of the Baltic" in his own hand. I was highly interested and gratified with the whole visit; the more so, as Mr. Lockhart had invited me voluntarily, without previous acquaintance. I have since heard him spoken of in the highest terms of esteem.

I went one Sunday to the Church of St. Stephen, to hear Croly, the poet. The service, read by a drowsy clerk, was long and monotonous; I sat in a side-aisle, looking up at the dome, and listening to the rain which dashed in torrents against the windowpanes. At last, a tall, gray-haired man came down the passage. He bowed with a sad smile, so full of benevolence and resignation, that it went into my heart at once, and I gave him an involuntary tribute of sympathy. He has a heavy affliction to bear—the death of his gallant son, one of the officers who were slain in the late battle of Ferozeshaw. His whole manner betrays the tokens of subdued but constant grief.

His sermon was peculiarly finished and appropriate; the language was clear and forcible, without that splendor of thought and dazzling vividness of imagery which mark "Salathiel." Yet I could not help noticing that he delighted to dwell on the spiritualities of religion, rather than its outward observances, which he seemed inclined to hurry over as lightly as possible. His mild, gray eye and lofty forehead are more like the benevolent divine than the poet. I thought of Salathiel, and looked at the dignified, sorrowful man before me. The picture of the accursed Judean vanished, and his own solemn lines rang on my ear:

> *"The mighty grave*
>
> *Wraps lord and slave,*
>
> *Nor pride, nor poverty dares come*
>
> *Within that prison-house, that tomb!"*

Whenever I hear them, or think of them again, I shall see, in memory, Croly's calm, pale countenance.

> *"The chimes, the chimes of Mother-land,*
>
> *Of England, green and old;*
>
> *That out from thane and ivied tower*
>
> *A thousand years have tolled!"*

I often thought of Coxe's beautiful ballad, when, after a day spent in Waterloo Place, I have listened, on my way homeward, to the chimes of Mary-le-bone Chapel, sounding sweetly and clearly above all the din of the Strand. There is something in their silvery vibration, which is far more expressive than the ordinary tones of a bell. The ear becomes weary of a continued toll—the sound of some bells seems to have nothing more in it than the ordinary clang of metal—but these simple notes, following one another so melodiously, fall on the ear, stunned by the ceaseless roar of carriages or the mingled cries of the mob, as gently and gratefully as drops of dew. Whether it be morning, and they ring out louder and deeper through the mist, or midnight, when the vast ocean of being beneath them surges less noisily than its wont, they are alike full of melody and poetry. I have often paused, deep in the night, to hear those clear tones, dropping down from the darkness, thrilling, with their full, tremulous sweetness, the still air of the lighted Strand, and winding away through dark, silent lanes and solitary courts, till the ear of the care-worn watcher is scarcely stirred with their dying vibrations. They seemed like those spirit-voices, which, at such times, speak almost audibly to the heart. How delicious it must be, to those who dwell within the limits of their sound, to wake from some happy dream and hear those chimes blending in with their midnight fancies, like the musical echo of the promised bliss. I love these eloquent bells, and I think there must be many, living out a life of misery and suffering, to whom their tones come with an almost human consolation. The natures of the very cockneys, who never go without the horizon of their vibrations, is, to my mind, invested with one hue of poetry!

A few days ago, an American friend invited me to accompany him to Greenwich Fair. We took a penny steamer from Hungerford Market to London Bridge, and jumped into the cars, which go every live minutes. Twelve minutes' ride above the chimneys of London and the vegetable-fields of Rotherhithe and Deptford brought us to Greenwich, we followed the stream of people which was flowing from all parts of the city into the Park.

Here began the merriment. We heard on every side the noise of the "scratchers," or, as the venders of these articles denominated them—"the fun of the fair." By this is meant a little notched wheel, with a piece of wood fastened on it, like a miniature watchman's rattle. The "fun" consists in drawing them down the back of any one you pass, when they make a sound precisely like that of ripping cloth. The women take great delight in this, and as it is only deemed politeness to return the compliment, we soon had enough to do. Nobody seemed to take the diversion amiss, but it was so irresistibly droll to see a large crowd engaged in this singular amusement, that we both burst into hearty laughter.

As we began ascending Greenwich Hill, we were assailed with another kind of game. The ground was covered with smashed oranges, with which the people above and below were stoutly pelting each other. Half a dozen heavy ones whizzed uncomfortably near my head as I went up, and I saw several

694

persons get the full benefit of a shot on their backs and breasts. The young country lads and lasses amused themselves by running at full spend down the steep side of a hill. This was, however, a feat attended with some risk; for I saw one luckless girl describe an arc of a circle, of which her feet was the centre and her body the radius. All was noise and nonsense. They ran to and fro under the long, hoary bough of the venerable oaks that crest the summit, and clattered down the magnificent forest-avenues, whose budding foliage gave them little shelter from the passing April showers.

The view from the top is splendid. The stately Thames curves through the plain below, which loses itself afar off in the mist; Greenwich, with its massive hospital, lies just at one's feet, and in a clear day the domes of London skirt the horizon. The wood of the Park is entirely oak—the majestic, dignified, English oak—which covers, in picturesque clumps, the sides and summits of the two billowy hills. It must be a sweet place in summer, when the dark, massive foliage is heavy on every mossy arm, and the smooth and curving sward shines with thousands of field-flowers.

Owing to the showers, the streets were coated with mud, of a consistence as soft and yielding as the most fleecy Persian carpet. Near the gate, boys were holding scores of donkeys, which they offered us at threepence for a ride of two miles. We walked down towards the river, and came at last to a group of tumblers, who with muddy hands and feet were throwing somersets in the open street. I recognized them as old acquaintances of the Rue St. Antoine and the Champs Elysées; but the little boy who cried before, because he did not want to bend his head and foot into a ring, like a hoop-snake, had learned his part better by this time, so that he went through it all without whimpering and came off with only a fiery red face. The exercises of the young gentlemen were of course very graceful and classic, and the effect of their poses of strength was very much heightened by the muddy foot-marks which they left on each other's orange-colored skins.

The avenue of booths was still more diverting. Here under sheets of leaky awning, were exposed for sale rows of gilded gingerbread kings and queens, and I cannot remember how many men and women held me fast by the arms, determined to force me into buying a pound of them. We paused at the sign: "SIGNOR URBANI'S GRAND MAGICAL DISPLAY." The title was attractive, so we paid the penny admission, and walked behind the dark, mysterious curtain. Two bare brick walls, three benches and a little boy appeared to us. A sheet hung before us upon which quivered the shadow of some terrible head. At my friend's command, the boy (also a spectator) put out the light, when the awful and grinning face of a black woman became visible. While we were admiring this striking production, thus mysteriously revealed, Signor Urbani came in, and seeing no hope of any more spectators, went behind the curtain and startled our sensitive nerves with six or seven skeleton and devil apparitions, winding up the wonderful entertainment with the same black head. We signified our entire approbation by due applause and then went out to seek further novelties.

The centre of the square was occupied by swings, where some eight or ten boat-loads of persons were flying topsy-turvy into the air, making one giddy to look at them, and constant fearful shrieks arose from the lady swingers, at finding themselves in a horizontal or inverted position, high above the ground. One of the machines was like a great wheel, with four cars attached, which mounted and descended with their motley freight. We got into the boat by way of experiment. The starting motion was pleasant, but very soon it flew with a swiftness and to a height rather alarming. I began to repent having chosen such a mode of amusement, but held on as well as I could, in my uneasy place. Presently we mounted till the long beam of our boat was horizontal; at one instant, I saw three young ladies below me, with their heads downward, like a shadow in the water—the next I was turned heels up, looking at thorn as a shadow does at its original. I was fast becoming sea-sick, when, after a few minutes of such giddy soaring, the ropes were slackened and we all got out, looking somewhat pale, and feeling nervous, if nothing else.

There were also many great tents, hung with boughs and lighted with innumerable colored lamps, where the people danced their country dances in a choking cloud of dry saw-dust. Conjurors and gymnastic performers were showing off on conspicuous platforms, and a continual sound of drums, cymbals and shrill trumpets called the attention of the crowd to some "Wonderful Exhibition"—some infant phenomenon, giant, or three-headed pig. A great part of the crowd belonged evidently to the very worst part of society, but the watchfulness of the police prevented any open disorder. We came away early and in a quarter of an hour were in busy London, leaving far behind us the revel and debauch, which was prolonged through the whole night.

London has the advantage of one of the most gloomy atmospheres in the world. During this opening spring weather, no light and scarcely any warmth can penetrate the dull, yellowish-gray mist, which incessantly hangs over the city. Sometimes at noon we have for an hour or two a sickly gleam of sunshine, but it is soon swallowed up by the smoke and drizzling fog. The people carry umbrellas at all times, for the rain seems to drop spontaneously out of the very air, without wailing for the usual preparation of a gathering cloud. Professor Espy's rules would be of little avail here.

A few days ago we had a real fog—a specimen of November weather, as the people said. If November wears such a mantle, London, during that sober month, must furnish a good idea of the gloom of Hades. The streets wore wrapped in a veil of dense mist, of a dirty yellow color, as if the air had suddenly grown thick and mouldy. The houses on the opposite sides of the street were invisible, and the gas lamps, lighted in the shops, burned with a white and ghastly flame. Carriages ran together in the streets, and I was kept constantly on the look-out, lest some one should come suddenly out of the cloud around me, and we should meet with a shock like that of two knights at a tournament. As I stood in the centre of Trafalgar Square, with every object invisible around me, it reminded me, (hoping the comparison will not be accepted in every particular) of Satan resting in the middle of Chaos. The weather sometimes continues thus for whole days together.

April 26.—An hour and a half of land are still allowed us, and then we shall set foot on the back of the oak-ribbed leviathan, which will be our home until a thousand leagues of blue ocean are crossed. I shall hear the old Aldgate clock strike for the last time—I shall take a last walk through the Minories and past the Tower yard, and as we glide down the Thames, St. Pauls, half-hidden in mist and coal-smoke, will probably be my last glimpse of London.

697

CHAPTER XLVIII. — HOMEWARD BOUND——CONCLUSION.

We slid out of St. Katharine's Dock at noon on the appointed day, and with a pair of sooty steamboats hitched to our vessel, moved slowly down the Thames in mist and drizzling rain. I stayed on the wet deck all afternoon, that I might more forcibly and joyously feel we were again in motion on the waters and homeward bound! My attention was divided between the dreary views of Blackwall, Greenwich and Woolwich, and the motley throng of passengers who were to form our ocean society. An English family, going out to settle in Canada, were gathered together in great distress and anxiety, for the father had gone ashore in London at a late hour, and was left behind. When we anchored for the night at Gravesend, their fears were quieted by his arrival in a skiff from the shore, as he had immediately followed us by railroad.

My cousin and B—— had hastened on from Paris to join me, and a day before the sailing of the "Victoria," we took berths in the second cabin, for twelve pounds ten shillings each, which in the London line of packets, includes coarse but substantial fare for the whole voyage. Our funds were insufficient to pay even this; but Captain Morgan, less mistrustful than my Norman landlord, generously agreed that the remainder of the fare should be paid in America. B—— and I, with two young Englishmen, took possession of a State-room of rough boards, lighted by a bull's-eye, which in stormy weather leaked so much that our trunks swam in water. A narrow mattrass and blanket, with a knapsack for a pillow, formed a passable bed. A long entry between the rooms, lighted by a feeble swinging lamp, was filled with a board table, around which the thirty-two second cabin passengers met to discuss politics and salt pork, favorable winds and hard sea-biscuit.

We lay becalmed opposite Sheerness the whole of the second day. At dusk a sudden squall came up, which drove us foaming towards the North Foreland. When I went on deck in the morning, we had passed Dover and Brighton, and the Isle of Wight was rising dim ahead of us. The low English coast on our right was bordered by long reaches of dazzling chalky sand, which glittered along the calm blue water.

Gliding into the Bay of Portsmouth, we dropped anchor opposite the romantic town of Ryde, built on the sloping shore of the green Isle of Wight. Eight or nine vessels of the Experimental Squadron were anchored near us, and over the houses of Portsmouth, I saw the masts of the Victory—the flagship in the battle of Trafalgar, on board of which Nelson was killed. The wind was not strong enough to permit the passage of the Needles, so at midnight we succeeded in wearing back again into the channel, around the Isle of Wight. A head wind forced us to tack away towards the shore of France. We were twice in sight of the rocky coast of Brittany, near Cherbourg, but the misty promontory of Land's End was our last glimpse of the old world.

On one of our first days at sea, I caught a curlew, which came flying on weary wings towards us, and alighted on one of the boats. Two of his brethren, too much exhausted or too timid to do likewise, dropped flat on the waves and resigned themselves to their fate without a struggle. I slipped up and caught his long, lank legs, while he was resting with flagging wings and half-shut eyes. We fed him, though it was difficult to get anything down his reed-shaped bill; but he took kindly to our force-work, and when we let him loose on the deck, walked about with an air quite tame and familiar. He died, however, two days afterwards. A French pigeon, which was caught in the rigging, lived and throve during the whole of the passage.

A few days afterwards, a heavy storm came on, and we were all sleepless and sea-sick, as long as it lasted. Thanks, however, to a beautiful law of memory, the recollection of that dismal period soon lost its unpleasantness, while the grand forms of beauty the vexed ocean presented, will remain forever, as distinct and abiding images. I kept on deck as long as I could stand, watching the giant waves over which our vessel took her course. They rolled up towards us, thirty or forty feet in height—dark gray masses, changing to a beautiful vitriol tint, wherever the light struck through their countless and changing crests. It was a glorious thing to see our good ship mount slowly up the side of one of these watery lulls, till her prow was lifted high in air, then, rocking over its brow, plunge with a slight quiver downward, and plough up a briny cataract, as she struck the vale. I never before realized the terrible sublimity of the sea. And yet it was a pride to see how man—strong in his godlike will—could bid defiance to those whelming surges, and bravo their wrath unharmed.

We swung up and down on the billows, till we scarcely knew which way to stand. The most grave and sober personages suddenly found themselves reeling in a very undignified manner, and not a few measured their lengths on the slippery decks. Boxes and barrels were affected in like manner; everything danced around us. Trunks ran out from under the berths; packages leaped down from the shelves; chairs skipped across the rooms, and at table, knives, forks and mugs engaged in a general waltz and break down. One incident of this kind was rather laughable. One night, about midnight, the gale, which had been blowing violently, suddenly lulled, "as if," to use a sailor's phrase, "it had been chopped off!" Instantly the ship gave a tremendous lurch, which was the signal for a general breaking loose. Two or three others followed, so violent, that for a moment I imagined the vessel had been thrown on her beam ends. Trunks, crockery and barrels went banging down from one end of the ship to the other. The women in the steerage set up an awful scream, and the German emigrants, thinking we were in terrible danger, commenced praying with might and main. In the passage near our room stood several barrels, filled with broken dishes, which at every lurch went banging from side to side, jarring the board partition and making a horrible din. I shall not soon forget the Babel which kept our eyes open that night.

The 19th of May a calm came on. Our white wings flapped idly on the mast, and only the top-gallant sails were bent enough occasionally to lug us along at a mile an hour. A barque from Ceylon, making the most of the wind, with every rag of canvass set, passed us slowly on the way eastward. The sun went down unclouded, and a glorious starry night brooded over us. Its clearness and brightness were to me indications of America. I longed to be on shore. The forests about home were then clothed in the delicate green of their first leaves, and that bland weather embraced the sweet earth like a blessing of heaven. The gentle breath from out the west seemed made for the odor of violets, and as it came to me over the slightly-ruffled deep, I thought how much sweeter it were to feel it, while "wasting in wood-paths the voluptuous hours."

Soon afterwards a fresh wind sprung up, which increased rapidly, till every sail was bent to the full. Our vessel parted the brine with an arrowy glide, the ease and grace of which it is impossible to describe. The breeze held on steadily for two or three days, which brought us to the southern extremity of the Banks. Here the air felt so sharp and chilling, that I was afraid we might be under the lee of an iceberg, but in the evening the dull gray mass of clouds lifted themselves from the horizon, and the sun set in clear, American beauty away beyond Labrador. The next morning we were enveloped in a dense fog, and the wind which bore us onward was of a piercing coldness. A sharp look-out was kept on the bow, but as we could see but a short distance, it might have been dangerous had we met one of the Arctic squadron. At noon it cleared away again, and the bank of fog was visible a long time astern, piled along the horizon, reminding me of the Alps, as seen from the plains of Piedmont.

On the 31st, the fortunate wind which carried us from the Banks, failed us about thirty-five miles from Sandy Hook. We lay in the midst of the mackerel fishery, with small schooners anchored all around us. Fog, dense and impenetrable, weighed on the moveless ocean, like an atmosphere of wool. The only incident to break the horrid monotony of the day, was the arrival of a pilot, with one or two newspapers, detailing the account of the Mexican War. We heard in the afternoon the booming of the surf along the low beach of Long Island—hollow and faint, like the murmur of a shell. When the mist lifted a little, we saw the faint line of breakers along the shore. The Germans gathered on deck to sing their old, familiar songs, and their voices blended beautifully together in the stillness.

Next morning at sunrise we saw Sandy Hook; at nine o'clock we were telegraphed in New York by the station at Coney Island; at eleven the steamer "Hercules" met us outside the Hook; and at noon we were gliding up the Narrows, with the whole ship's company of four hundred persons on deck, gazing on the beautiful shores of Staten Island and agreeing almost universally, that it was the most delightful scene they had ever looked upon.

And now I close the story of my long wandering, as I began it—with a

701

lay written on the deep.

HOMEWARD BOUND.

Farewell to Europe! Days have come and gone

Since misty England set behind the sea.

Our ship climbs onward o'er the lifted waves,

That gather up in ridges, mountain-high,

And like a sea-god, conscious in his power,

Buffets the surges. Storm-arousing winds

That sweep, unchecked, from frozen Labrador,

Make wintry music through the creaking shrouds.

Th' horizon's ring, that clasps the dreary view,

Lays mistily upon the gray Atlantic's breast.

Shut out, at times, by bulk of sparry blue,

That, rolling near us, heaves the swaying prow

High on its shoulders, to descend again

Ploughing a thousand cascades, and around

Spreading the frothy foam. These watery gulfs,

With storm, and winds far-sweeping, hem us in,

Alone upon the waters!

Days must pass—

Many and weary—between sea and sky.

Our eyes, that long e'en now for the fresh green

Of sprouting forests, and the far blue stretch

Of regal mountains piled along the sky,

Must see, for many an eve, the level sun

Sheathe, with his latest gold, the heaving brine,

By thousand ripples shivered, or Night's pomp

Brooding in silence, ebon and profound,

Upon the murmuring darkness of the deep,

Broken by flashings, that the parted wave

Sends white and star-like throujch its bursting foam.

Yet not more dear the opening dawn of heaven

Poured on the earth in an Italian May,

When souls take wings upon the scented air

Of starry meadows, and the yearning heart

Pains with deep sweetness in the balmy time,

Than these gray morns, and days of misty blue,

And surges, never-ceasing;—for our prow

Points to the sunset like a morning ray,

And o'er the waves, and through the sweeping storms,

Through day and darkness, rushes ever on,

Westward and westward still! What joy can send

The spirit thrilling onward with the wind,

In untamed exultation, like the thought

That fills the Homeward Bound?

Country and home!

Ah! not the charm of silver-tongued romance,

Born of the feudal time, nor whatsoe'er

Of dying glory fills the golden realms

Of perished song, where heaven-descended Art

Still boasts her later triumphs, can compare

With that one thought of liberty inherited—

Of free life giv'n by fathers who were free,

And to be left to children freer still!

That pride and consciousness of manhood, caught

From boyish musings on the holy graves

Of hero-martyrs, and from every form

Which virgin Nature, mighty and unchained,

Takes in an empire not less proudly so—

Inspired in mountain airs, untainted yet

By thousand generations' breathing—felt

Like a near presence in the awful depths

Of unhewn forests, and upon the steep

Where giant rivers take their maddening plunge—

Has grown impatient of the stifling damps

Which hover close on Europe's shackled soil.

Content to tread awhile the holy steps

Of Art and Genius, sacred through all time,

The spirit breathed that dull, oppressive air—

Which, freighted with its tyrant-clouds, o'erweighs

The upward throb of many a nation's soul—

Amid those olden memories, felt the thrall.

But kept the birth-right of its freer home,

Here, on the world's blue highway, comes again

The voice of Freedom, heard amid the roar

Of sundered billows, while above the wave

Rise visions of the forest and the stream.

Like trailing robes the morning mists uproll,

Torn by the mountain pines; the flashing rills

Shout downward through the hollows of the vales;

Down the great river's bosom shining sails

Glide with a gradual motion, while from all—

Hamlet, and bowered homestead, and proud town—

Voices of joy ring up into heaven!

Yet louder, winds! Urge on our keel, ye waves,

Swift as the spirit's yearnings! We would ride

With a loud stormy motion o'er your crests,

With tempests shouting like a sudden joy—

Interpreting our triumph! 'Tis your voice,

Ye unchained elements, alone can speak

The sympathetic feeling of the free—

The arrowy impulse of the Homeward Bound!

Although the narrative of my journey, "with knapsack and staff," is now strictly finished, a few more words of explanation seem necessary, to describe more fully the method of traveling which we adopted. I add them the more willingly, as it is my belief that many, whose circumstances are similar to mine, desire to undertake the same romantic journey. Some matter-of-fact statements may be to them useful as well as interesting.

We found the pedestrian style not only by far the best way to become acquainted with the people and scenery of a country, but the pleasantest mode of traveling. To be sure, the knapsack was, at first, rather heavy, our feet were often sore and our limbs weary, but a few days walking made a great difference, and after we had traveled two weeks, this disappeared altogether. Every morning we rose as fresh and strong as if it had been the first day—even after a walk of thirty miles, we felt but little fatigue. We enjoyed slumber in its fullest luxury, and our spirits were always light and joyous. We made it a rule to pay no regard to the weather, unless it was so bad as to render walking unhealthy. Often, during the day, we rested for half an hour on the grassy bank, or sometimes, if it was warm weather, lay at full length in the shade with our knapsacks under our heads. This is a pleasure which none but the pedestrian can comprehend.

We always accepted a companion, of whatever kind, while walking— from chimney-sweeps to barons. In a strange country one can learn something from every peasant, and we neglected no opportunity, not only to obtain information, but impart it. We found everywhere great curiosity respecting America, and we were always glad to tell them all they wished to know. In Germany, we were generally taken for Germans from some part of the country where the dialect was a little different, or, if they remarked our foreign peculiarities, they supposed we were either Poles, Russians, or Swiss. The greatest ignorance in relation to America, prevails among the common people. They imagine we are a savage race, without intelligence and almost without law. Persons of education, who had some slight knowledge of our history, showed a curiosity to know something of our political condition. They are taught by the German newspapers (which are under a strict censorship in this respect) to look only at the evil in our country, and they almost invariably began by adverting to Slavery and Repudiation. While we admitted, often with shame and mortification, the existence of things so inconsistent with true republicanism, we endeavored to make them comprehend the advantages enjoyed by the free citizen—the complete equality of birth—which places America, despite her sins, far above any other nation on earth. I could plainly see, by the kindling eye and half-suppressed sigh, that they appreciated a freedom so immeasurably greater than that which they enjoyed.

In large cities we always preferred to take the second or third-rate hotels, which are generally visited by merchants and persons who travel on business; for, with the same comforts as the first rank, they are nearly twice as cheap. A traveler, with a guide-book and a good pair of eyes, can also dispense with the services of a courier, whose duty it is to conduct strangers about the city, from one lion to another. We chose rather to find out and view the "sights" at our leisure. In small villages, where we were often obliged to stop, we chose the best hotels, which, particularly in Northern Germany and in Italy, are none too good. But if it was a post, that is, a town where the post-chaise stops to change horses, we usually avoided the post-hotel, where one must pay high for having curtains before his windows and a more elegant cover on his bed. In the less splendid country inns, we always found neat, comfortable lodging, and a pleasant, friendly reception from the people. They saluted us on entering, with "Be you welcome," and on leaving, wished us a pleasant journey and good fortune. The host, when he brought us supper or breakfast, lifted his cap, and wished us a good appetite—and when he lighted us to our chambers, left us with "May you sleep well!" We generally found honest, friendly people; they delighted in telling us about the country around; what ruins there were in the neighborhood—and what strange legends were connected with them. The only part of Europe where it is unpleasant to travel in this manner, is Bohemia. We could rarely find a comfortable inn; the people all spoke an unknown language, and were not particularly celebrated for their honesty. Beside this, travelers rarely go on foot in those regions; we were frequently taken for traveling handworker, and subjected to imposition.

With regard to passports, although they were vexatious and often expensive, we found little difficulty when we had acquainted ourselves with the regulations concerning them. In France and Germany they are comparatively little trouble; in Italy they are the traveler's greatest annoyance. Americans are treated with less strictness, in this respect, than citizens of other nations, and, owing to the absence of rank among us, we also enjoy greater advantages of acquaintance and intercourse.

The expenses of traveling in England, although much greater than in our own country, may, as we learned by experience, be brought, through economy, within the same compass. Indeed, it is my belief, from observation, that, with few exceptions, throughout Europe, where a traveler enjoys the same comfort and abundance as in America, he must pay the same prices. The principal difference is, that he only pays for what he gets, so that, if he be content with the necessities of life, without its luxuries, the expense is in proportion. I have given, at times, through the foregoing chapters, the cost of travel and residence in Europe, yet a connected estimate will better show the minimum expense of a two years' pilgrimage:

Voyage to Liverpool, in the second cabin $24.00

Three weeks' travel in Ireland and Scotland 25.00

A week in London, at three shillings a day 4.50

From London to Heidelberg 15.00

A month at Heidelberg, and trip to Frankfort 20.00

Seven months in Frankfort, at $10 per month 70.00

Fuel, passports, excursions and other expenses 30.00

Tour through Cassel, the Hartz, Saxony, Austria, Bavaria, etc. 40.00

A month in Frankfort 10.00

From Frankfort through Switzerland, and over the Alps
   to Milan 15.00

From Milan to Genoa 60

Expenses from Genoa to Florence 14.00

Four months in Florence *50.00*

Eight day's journey from Florence to Rome, two weeks in

    Rome, voyage to Marseilles and journey to Paris *40.00*

Five weeks in Paris *15.00*

From Paris to London *8.00*

Six weeks in London, at three shillings a day *31.00*

Passage home *60.00*

                                    ———

                                  $472.00

The cost for places of amusement, guides' fees, and other small expenses, not included in this list, increase the sum total to $500, for which the tour may be made. Now, having, I hope, established this to the reader's satisfaction, I respectfully take leave of him.

THE END.

JOSEPH AND HIS FRIEND: A STORY OF PENNSYLVANIA

The better angel is a man right fair;

The worser spirit a woman colour'd ill.

SHAKSPEARE: *Sonnets.*

CHAPTER I. JOSEPH.

Rachel Miller was not a little surprised when her nephew Joseph came to the supper-table, not from the direction of the barn and through the kitchen, as usual, but from the back room up stairs, where he slept. His work-day dress had disappeared; he wore his best Sunday suit, put on with unusual care, and there were faint pomatum odors in the air when he sat down to the table.

Her face said—and she knew it—as plain as any words, "What in the world does this mean?" Joseph, she saw, endeavored to look as though coming down to supper in that costume were his usual habit; so she poured out the tea in silence. Her silence, however, was eloquent; a hundred interrogation-marks would not have expressed its import; and Dennis, the hired man, who sat on the other side of the table, experienced very much the same apprehension of something forthcoming, as when he had killed her favorite speckled hen by mistake.

Before the meal was over, the tension between Joseph and his aunt had so increased by reason of their mutual silence, that it was very awkward and oppressive to both; yet neither knew how to break it easily. There is always a great deal of unnecessary reticence in the intercourse of country people, and in the case of these two it had been specially strengthened by the want of every relationship except that of blood. They were quite ignorant of the fence, the easy thrust and parry of society, where talk becomes an art; silence or the bluntest utterance were their alternatives, and now the one had neutralized the other. Both felt this, and Dennis, in his dull way, felt it too. Although not a party concerned, he was uncomfortable, yet also internally conscious of a desire to laugh.

The resolution of the crisis, however, came by his aid. When the meal was finished and Joseph betook himself to the window, awkwardly drumming upon the pane, while his aunt gathered the plates and cups together, delaying to remove them as was her wont, Dennis said, with his hand on the door-knob: "Shall I saddle the horse right off?"

"I guess so," Joseph answered, after a moment's hesitation.

Rachel paused, with the two silver spoons in her hand. Joseph was still drumming upon the window, but with very irregular taps. The door closed upon Dennis.

"Well," said she, with singular calmness, "a body is not bound to dress particularly fine for watching, though I would as soon show him that much respect, if need be, as anybody else. Don't forget to ask Maria if there's anything I can do for her."

Joseph turned around with a start, a most innocent surprise on his face.

"Why, aunt, what are you talking about?"

"You are not going to Warne's to watch? They have nearer neighbors, to be sure, but when a man dies, everybody is free to offer their services. He was always strong in the faith."

Joseph knew that he was caught, without suspecting her manœuvre. A brighter color ran over his face, up to the roots of his hair. "Why, no!" he exclaimed; "I am going to Warriner's to spend the evening. There's to be a little company there,—a neighborly gathering. I believe it's been talked of this long while, but I was only invited to-day. I saw Bob, in the road-field."

Rachel endeavored to conceal from her nephew's eye the immediate impression of his words. A constrained smile passed over her face, and was instantly followed by a cheerful relief in his.

"Isn't it rather a strange time of year for evening parties?" she then asked, with a touch of severity in her voice.

"They meant to have it in cherry-time, Bob said, when Anna's visitor had come from town."

"That, indeed! I see!" Rachel exclaimed. "It's to be a sort of celebration for—what's-her-name? Blessing, I know,—but the other? Anna Warriner was there last Christmas, and I don't suppose the high notions are out of her head yet. Well, I hope it'll be some time before they take root here! Peace and quiet, peace and quiet, that's been the token of the neighborhood; but town ways are the reverse."

"All the young people are going," Joseph mildly suggested, "and so—"

"O, I don't say you shouldn't go, this time," Rachel interrupted him; "for you ought to be able to judge for yourself what's fit and proper, and what is not. I should be sorry, to be sure, to see you doing anything and going anywhere that would make your mother uneasy if she were living now. It's so hard to be conscientious, and to mind a body's bounden duty, without seeming to interfere."

She heaved a deep sigh, and just touched the corner of her apron to her eyes. The mention of his mother always softened Joseph, and in his earnest desire to live so that his life might be such as to give her joy if she could share it, a film of doubt spread itself over the smooth, pure surface of his mind. A vague consciousness of his inability to express himself clearly upon the question without seeming to slight her memory affected his thoughts.

"But, remember, Aunt Rachel," he said, at last, "I was not old enough, then, to go into society. She surely meant that I should have some independence, when the time came. I am doing no more than all the young men of the neighborhood."

"Ah, yes, I know," she replied, in a melancholy tone; "but they've got used to it by degrees, and mostly in their own homes, and with sisters to caution them; whereas you're younger according to your years, and innocent of the ways and wiles of men, and—and girls."

Joseph painfully felt that this last assertion was true. Suppressing the impulse to exclaim, "Why am I younger 'according to my years?' why am I so much more 'innocent'—which is, ignorant—than others?" he blundered out, with a little display of temper, "Well, how am I ever to learn?"

"By patience, and taking care of yourself. There's always safety in waiting. I don't mean you shouldn't go this evening, since you've promised it, and made yourself smart. But, mark my words, this is only the beginning. The season makes no difference; townspeople never seem to know that there's such things as hay-harvest and corn to be worked. They come out for merry-makings in the busy time, and want us country folks to give up everything for their pleasure. The tired plough-horses must be geared up for 'em, and the cows wait an hour or two longer to be milked while they're driving around; and the chickens killed half-grown, and the washing and baking put off when it comes in their way. They're mighty nice and friendly while it lasts; but go back to 'em in town, six months afterwards, and see whether they'll so much as ask you to take a meal's victuals!"

Joseph began to laugh. "It is not likely," he said, "that I shall ever go to the Blessings for a meal, or that this Miss Julia—as they call her—will ever interfere with our harvesting or milking."

"The airs they put on!" Rachel continued. "She'll very likely think that she's doing you a favor by so much as speaking to you. When the Bishops had boarders, two years ago, one of 'em said,—Maria told me with her own mouth,—'Why don't all the farmers follow your example? It would be so refining for them!' They may be very well in their place, but, for my part, I should like them to stay there."

"There comes the horse," said Joseph. "I must be on the way. I expect to meet Elwood Withers at the lane-end. But—about waiting, Aunt—you hardly need—"

"O, yes, I'll wait for you, of course. Ten o'clock is not so very late for me."

"It might be a little after," he suggested.

"Not much, I hope; but if it should be daybreak, wait I will! Your mother couldn't expect less of me."

When Joseph whirled into the saddle, the thought of his aunt, grimly waiting for his return, was already perched like an imp on the crupper, and clung to his sides with claws of steel. She, looking through the window, also felt that it was so; and, much relieved, went back to her household duties.

He rode very slowly down the lane, with his eyes fixed on the ground.

There was a rich orange flush of sunset on the hills across the valley; masses of burning cumuli hung, self-suspended, above the farthest woods, and such depths of purple-gray opened beyond them as are wont to rouse the slumbering fancies and hopes of a young man's heart; but the beauty and fascination, and suggestiveness of the hour could not lift his downcast, absorbed glance. At last his horse, stopping suddenly at the gate, gave a whinny of recognition, which was answered.

Elwood Withers laughed. "Can you tell me where Joseph Asten lives?" he cried,—"an old man, very much bowed and bent."

Joseph also laughed, with a blush, as he met the other's strong, friendly face. "There is plenty of time," he said, leaning over his horse's neck and lifting the latch of the gate.

"All right; but you must now wake up. You're spruce enough to make a figure to-night."

"O, no doubt!" Joseph gravely answered; "but what kind of a figure?"

"Some people, I've heard say," said Elwood, "may look into their looking-glass every day, and never know how they look. If you appeared to yourself as you appear to me, you wouldn't ask such a question as that."

"If I could only not think of myself at all, Elwood,—if I could be as unconcerned as you are—"

"But I'm not, Joseph, my boy!" Elwood interrupted, riding nearer and laying a hand on his friend's shoulder. "I tell you, it weakens my very marrow to walk into a room full o' girls, even though I know every one of 'em. They know it, too, and, shy and quiet as they seem, they're un-merciful. There they sit, all looking so different, somehow,—even a fellow's own sisters and cousins,—filling up all sides of the room, rustling a little and whispering a little, but you feel that every one of 'em has her eyes on you, and would be so glad to see you flustered. There's no help for it, though; we've got to grow case-hardened to that much, or how ever could a man get married?"

"Elwood!" Joseph asked, after a moment's silence, "were you ever in love?"

"Well,"—and Elwood pulled up his horse in surprise,—"well, you do come out plump. You take the breath out of my body. Have I been in love? Have I committed murder? One's about as deadly a secret as the other!"

The two looked each other in the face. Elwood's eyes answered the question, but Joseph's,—large, shy, and utterly innocent,—could not read the answer.

"It's easy to see you've never been," said the former, dropping his voice to a grave gentleness. "If I should say Yes, what then?"

"Then, how do you know it,—I mean, how did you first begin to find it out? What is the difference between that and the feeling you have towards any pleasant girl whom you like to be with?"

"All the difference in the world!" Elwood exclaimed with energy; then paused, and knitted his brows with a perplexed air; "but I'll be shot if I know exactly what else to say; I never thought of it before. How do I know that I am Elwood Withers? It seems just as plain as that,—and yet—well, for one thing, she's always in your mind, and you think and dream of just nothing but her; and you'd rather have the hem of her dress touch you than kiss anybody else; and you want to be near her, and to have her all to yourself, yet it's hard work to speak a sensible word to her when you come together,—but, what's the use? A fellow must feel it himself, as they say of experiencing religion; he must get converted, or he'll never know. Now, I don't suppose you've understood a word of what I've said!"

"Yes!" Joseph answered; "indeed, I think so. It's only an increase of what we all feel towards some persons. I have been hoping, latterly, that it might come to me, but—but—"

"But your time will come, like every man's," said Elwood; "and, maybe, sooner than you think. When it does, you won't need to ask anybody; though I think you're bound to tell me of it, after pumping my own secret out of me."

Joseph looked grave.

"Never mind; I wasn't obliged to let you have it. I know you're close-mouthed and honest-hearted, Joseph; but I'll never ask your confidence unless you can give it as freely as I give mine to you."

"You shall have it, Elwood, if my time ever comes. And I can't help wishing for the time, although it may not be right. You know how lonely it is on the farm, and yet it's not always easy for me to get away into company. Aunt Rachel stands in mother's place to me, and maybe it's only natural that she should be over-concerned; any way, seeing what she has done for my sake, I am hindered from opposing her wishes too stubbornly. Now, to-night, my going didn't seem right to her, and I shall not get it out of my mind that she is waiting up, and perhaps fretting, on my account."

"A young fellow of your age mustn't be so tender," Elwood said. "If you had your own father and mother, they'd allow you more of a range. Look at me, with mine! Why, I never as much as say 'by your leave.' Quite the contrary; so long as the work isn't slighted, they're rather glad than not to have me go out; and the house is twice as lively since I bring so much fresh gossip into it. But then, I've had a rougher bringing up."

"I wish I had had!" cried Joseph. "Yet, no, when I think of mother, it is wrong to say just that. What I mean is, I wish I could take things as easily as you,—make my way boldly in the world, without being held back by trifles, or getting so confused with all sorts of doubts. The more anxious I am to do right, the more embarrassed I am to know what is the right thing. I don't believe you have any such troubles."

"Well, for my part, I do about as other fellows; no worse, I guess, and likely no better. You must consider, also, that I'm a bit rougher made, besides the bringing up, and that makes a deal of difference. I don't try to make the scales balance to a grain; if there's a handful under or over, I think it's near enough. However, you'll be all right in a while. When you find the right girl and marry her, it'll put a new face on to you. There's nothing like a sharp, wide-awake wife, so they say, to set a man straight. Don't make a mountain of anxiety out of a little molehill of inexperience. I'd take all your doubts and more, I'm sure, if I could get such a two-hundred-acre farm with them."

"Do you know," cried Joseph eagerly, his blue eyes flashing through the gathering dusk, "I have often thought very nearly the same thing! If I were to love,—if I were to marry—"

"Hush!" interrupted Elwood; "I know you don't mean others to hear you. Here come two down the branch road."

The horsemen, neighboring farmers' sons, joined them. They rode together up the knoll towards the Warriner mansion, the lights of which glimmered at intervals through the trees. The gate was open, and a dozen vehicles could be seen in the enclosure between the house and barn. Bright, gliding forms were visible on the portico.

"Just see," whispered Elwood to Joseph; "what a lot of posy-colors! You may be sure they're every one watching us. No flinching, mind; straight to the charge! We'll walk up together, and it won't be half as hard for you."

CHAPTER II. MISS BLESSING.

To consider the evening party at Warriner's a scene of "dissipation"—as some of the good old people of the neighborhood undoubtedly did—was about as absurd as to call butter-milk an intoxicating beverage. Anything more simple and innocent could not well be imagined. The very awkwardness which everybody felt, and which no one exactly knew how to overcome, testified of virtuous ignorance. The occasion was no more than sufficed for the barest need of human nature. Young men and women must come together for acquaintance and the possibilities of love, and, fortunately, neither labor nor the severer discipline of their elders can prevent them.

Where social recreation thus only exists under discouraging conditions, ease and grace and self-possession cannot be expected. Had there been more form, in fact, there would have been more ease. A conventional disposition of the guests would have reduced the loose elements of the company to some sort of order; the shy country nature would have taken refuge in fixed laws, and found a sense of freedom therein. But there were no generally understood rules; the young people were brought together, delighted yet uncomfortable, craving yet shrinking from speech and jest and song, and painfully working their several isolations into a warmer common atmosphere.

On this occasion, the presence of a stranger, and that stranger a lady, and that lady a visitor from the city, was an additional restraint. The dread of a critical eye is most keenly felt by those who secretly acknowledge their own lack of social accomplishment. Anna Warriner, to be sure, had been loud in her praises of "dear Julia," and the guests were prepared to find all possible beauty and sweetness; but they expected, none the less, to be scrutinized and judged.

Bob Warriner met his friends at the gate and conducted them to the parlor, whither the young ladies, who had been watching the arrival, had retreated. They were disposed along the walls, silent and cool, except Miss Blessing, who occupied a rocking-chair in front of the mantel-piece, where her figure was in half-shadow, the lamplight only touching some roses in her hair. As the gentlemen were presented, she lifted her face and smiled upon each, graciously offering a slender hand. In manner and attitude, as in dress, she seemed a different being from the plump, ruddy, self-conscious girls on the sofas. Her dark hair fell about her neck in long, shining ringlets; the fairness of her face heightened the brilliancy of her eyes, the lids of which were slightly drooped as if kindly veiling their beams; and her lips, although thin, were very sweetly and delicately curved. Her dress, of some white, foamy texture, hung about her like a trailing cloud, and the cluster of rosebuds on her bosom lay as if tossed there.

The young men, spruce as they had imagined themselves to be, suddenly felt that their clothes were coarse and ill-fitting, and that the girls of the neighborhood, in their neat gingham and muslin dresses, were not quite so airy and charming as on former occasions. Miss Blessing, descending to them out of an unknown higher sphere, made their deficiencies unwelcomely evident; she attracted and fascinated them, yet was none the less a disturbing influence. They made haste to find seats, after which a constrained silence followed.

There could be no doubt of Miss Blessing's amiable nature. She looked about with a pleasant expression, half smiled—but deprecatingly, as if to say, "Pray, don't be offended!"—at the awkward silence, and then said, in a clear, carefully modulated voice: "It is beautiful to arrive at twilight, but how charming it must be to ride home in the moonlight; so different from our lamps!"

The guests looked at each other, but as she had seemed to address no one in particular, so each hesitated, and there was no immediate reply.

"But is it not awful, tell me, Elizabeth, when you get into the shadows of the forests? we are so apt to associate all sorts of unknown dangers with forests, you know," she continued.

The young lady thus singled out made haste to answer: "O, no! I rather like it, when I have company."

Elwood Withers laughed. "To be sure!" he exclaimed; "the shade is full

724

of opportunities."

Then there were little shrieks, and some giggling and blushing. Miss Blessing shook her fan warningly at the speaker.

"How wicked in you! I hope you will have to ride home alone to-night, after that speech. But you are all courageous, compared with us. We are really so restricted in the city, that it's a wonder we have any independence at all. In many ways, we are like children."

"O Julia, dear!" protested Anna Warriner, "and such advantages as you have! I shall never forget the day Mrs. Rockaway called—her husband's cashier of the Commercial Bank" (this was said in a parenthesis to the other guests)—"and brought you all the news direct from head-quarters, as she said."

"Yes," Miss Blessing answered, slowly, casting down her eyes, "there must be two sides to everything, of course; but how much we miss until we know the country! Really, I quite envy you."

Joseph had found himself, almost before he knew it, in a corner, beside Lucy Henderson. He felt soothed and happy, for of all the girls present he liked Lucy best. In the few meetings of the young people which he had attended, he had been drawn towards her by an instinct founded, perhaps, on his shyness and the consciousness of it; for she alone had the power, by a few kindly, simple words, to set him at ease with himself. The straightforward glance of her large brown eyes seemed to reach the self below the troubled surface. However much his ears might have tingled afterwards, as he recalled how frankly and freely he had talked with her, he could only remember the expression of an interest equally frank, upon her face. She never dropped one of those amused side-glances, or uttered one of those pert, satirical remarks, the recollection of which in other girls stung him to the quick.

Their conversation was interrupted, for when Miss Blessing spoke, the others became silent. What Elwood Withers had said of the phenomena of love, however, lingered in Joseph's mind, and he began, involuntarily, to examine the nature of his feeling for Lucy Henderson. Was she not often in his thoughts? He had never before asked himself the question, but now he suddenly became conscious that the hope of meeting her, rather than any curiosity concerning Miss Blessing, had drawn him to Warriner's. Would he rather touch the edge of her dress than kiss anybody else? That question drew his eyes to her lips, and with a soft shock of the heart, he became aware of their freshness and sweetness as never before. To touch the edge of her dress! Elwood had said nothing of the lovelier and bolder desire which brought the blood swiftly to his cheeks. He could not help it that their glances met,—a moment only, but an unmeasured time of delight and fear to him,—and then Lucy quickly turned away her head. He fancied there was a heightened color on her face, but when she spoke to him a few minutes afterwards it was gone, and she was as calm and composed as before.

In the mean time there had been other arrivals; and Joseph was presently called upon to give up his place to some ladies from the neighboring town. Many invitations had been issued, and the capacity of the parlor was soon exhausted. Then the sounds of merry chat on the portico invaded the stately constraint of the room; and Miss Blessing, rising gracefully and not too rapidly, laid her hands together and entreated Anna Warriner,—

"O, do let us go outside! I think we are well enough acquainted now to sit on the steps together."

She made a gesture, slight but irresistibly inviting, and all arose. While they were cheerfully pressing out through the hall, she seized Anna's arm and drew her back into the dusky nook under the staircase.

"Quick, Anna!" she whispered; "who is the roguish one they call Elwood? What is he?"

"A farmer; works his father's place on shares."

"Ah!" exclaimed Miss Blessing, in a peculiar tone; "and the blue-eyed, handsome one, who came in with him? He looks almost like a boy."

"Joseph Asten? Why, he's twenty-two or three. He has one of the finest properties in the neighborhood, and money besides, they say; lives alone, with an old dragon of an aunt as housekeeper. Now, Julia dear, there's a

726

chance for you!"

"Pshaw, you silly Anna!" whispered Miss Blessing, playfully pinching her ear; "you know I prefer intellect to wealth."

"As for that"—Anna began, but her friend was already dancing down the hall towards the front door, her gossamer skirts puffing and floating out until they brushed the walls on either side. She hummed to herself, "O Night! O lovely Night!" from the Désert, skimmed over the doorstep, and sank, subsiding into an ethereal heap, against one of the pillars of the portico. Her eyelids were now fully opened, and the pupils, the color of which could not be distinguished in the moonlight, seemed wonderfully clear and brilliant.

"Now, Mr. Elwood—O, excuse me, I mean Mr. Withers," she began, "you must repeat your joke for my benefit. I missed it, and I feel so foolish when I can't laugh with the rest."

Anna Warriner, standing in the door, opened her eyes very wide at what seemed to her to be the commencement of a flirtation; but before Elwood Withers could repeat his rather stupid fun, she was summoned to the kitchen by her mother, to superintend the preparation of the refreshments.

Miss Blessing made her hay while the moon shone. She so entered into the growing spirit of the scene and accommodated herself to the speech and ways of the guests, that in half an hour it seemed as if they had always known her. She laughed with their merriment, and flattered their sentiment with a tender ballad or two, given in a veiled but not unpleasant voice, and constantly appealed to their good-nature by the phrase: "Pray, don't mind me at all; I'm like a child let out of school!" She tapped Elizabeth Fogg on the shoulder, stealthily tickled Jane McNaughton's neck with a grass-blade, and took the roses from her hair to stick into the buttonholes of the young men.

"Just see Julia!" whispered Anna Warriner to her half-dozen intimates; "didn't I tell you she was the life of society?"

Joseph had quite lost his uncomfortable sense of being watched and criticized; he enjoyed the unrestraint of the hour as much as the rest. He was rather relieved to notice that Elwood Withers seemed uneasy, and almost willing to escape from the lively circle around Miss Blessing. By and by the company broke into smaller groups, and Joseph again found himself near the pale pink dress which he knew. What was it that separated him from her? What had slipped between them during the evening? Nothing, apparently; for Lucy Henderson, perceiving him, quietly moved nearer. He advanced a step, and they were side by side.

"Do you enjoy these meetings, Joseph?" she asked.

"I think I should enjoy everything," he answered, "if I were a little older, or—or—"

"Or more accustomed to society? Is not that what you meant? It is only another kind of schooling, which we must all have. You and I are in the lowest class, as we once were,—do you remember?"

"I don't know why," said he, "—but I must be a poor scholar. See Elwood, for instance!"

"Elwood!" Lucy slowly repeated; "he is another kind of nature, altogether."

There was a moment's silence. Joseph was about to speak, when something wonderfully soft touched his cheek, and a delicate, violet-like odor swept upon his senses. A low, musical laugh sounded at his very ear.

"There! Did I frighten you?" said Miss Blessing. She had stolen behind him, and, standing on tiptoe, reached a light arm over his shoulder, to fasten her last rosebud in the upper buttonhole of his coat.

"I quite overlooked you, Mr. Asten," she continued. "Please turn a little towards me. Now!—has it not a charming effect? I do like to see some kind of ornament about the gentlemen, Lucy. And since they can't wear anything in their hair,—but, tell me, wouldn't a wreath of flowers look well on Mr. Asten's head?"

"I can't very well imagine such a thing," said Lucy.

"No? Well, perhaps I am foolish: but when one has escaped from

728

the tiresome conventionalities of city life, and comes back to nature, and delightful natural society, one feels so free to talk and think! Ah, you don't know what a luxury it is, just to be one's true self!"

Joseph's eyes lighted up, and he turned towards Miss Blessing, as if eager that she should continue to speak.

"Lucy," said Elwood Withers, approaching; "you came with the McNaughtons, didn't you?"

"Yes: are they going?"

"They are talking of it now; but the hour is early, and if you don't mind riding on a pillion, you know my horse is gentle and strong—"

"That's right, Mr. Withers!" interrupted Miss Blessing. "I depend upon you to keep Lucy with us. The night is at its loveliest, and we are all just fairly enjoying each other's society. As I was saying, Mr. Asten, you cannot conceive what a new world this is to me: oh, I begin to breathe at last!"

Therewith she drew a long, soft inspiration, and gently exhaled it again, ending with a little flutter of the breath, which made it seem like a sigh. A light laugh followed.

"I know, without looking at your face, that you are smiling at me," said she. "But you have never experienced what it is to be shy and uneasy in company; to feel that you are expected to talk, and not know what to say, and when you do say something, to be startled at the sound of your voice; to stand, or walk, or sit, and imagine that everybody is watching you; to be introduced to strangers, and be as awkward as if both spoke different languages, and were unable to exchange a single thought. Here, in the country, you experience nothing of all this."

"Indeed, Miss Blessing," Joseph replied, "it is just the same to us—to me—as city society is to you."

"How glad I am!" she exclaimed, clasping her hands. "It is very selfish in me to say it, but I can't help being sincere towards the Sincere. I shall now feel ever so much more freedom in talking with you, Mr. Asten, since we have one experience in common. Don't you think, if we all knew each other's natures truly, we should be a great deal more at ease,—and consequently happier?"

She spoke the last sentence in a low, sweet, penetrating tone, lifted her face to meet his gaze a moment, the eyes large, clear, and appealing in their expression, the lips parted like those of a child, and then, without waiting for his answer, suddenly darted away, crying, "Yes, Anna dear!"

"What is it, Julia?" Anna Warriner asked.

"O, didn't you call me? Somebody surely called some Julia, and I'm the only one, am I not? I've just arranged Mr. Asten's rosebud so prettily, and now all the gentlemen are decorated. I'm afraid they think I take great liberties for a stranger, but then, you all make me forget that I am strange. Why is it that everybody is so good to me?"

She turned her face upon the others with a radiant expression. Then, there were earnest protestations from the young men, and a few impulsive hugs from the girls, which latter Miss Blessing returned with kisses.

Elwood Withers sat beside Lucy Henderson, on the steps of the portico. "Why, we owe it to you that we're here to-night, Miss Blessing!" he exclaimed. "We don't come together half often enough as it is; and what better could we do than meet again, somewhere else, while you are in the country?"

"O, how delightful! how kind!" she cried. "And while the lovely moonlight lasts! Shall I really have another evening like this?"

The proposition was heartily seconded, and the only difficulty was, how to choose between the three or four invitations which were at once proffered. There was nothing better to do than to accept all, in turn, and the young people pledged themselves to attend. The new element which they had dreaded in advance, as a restraint, had shown itself to be the reverse: they had never been so free, so cheerfully excited. Miss Blessing's unconscious ease of manner, her grace and sweetness, her quick, bright sympathy with country ways, had so warmed and fused them, that they lost the remembrance of their stubborn selves and yielded to the magnetism of the hour. Their manners, moreover, were greatly improved, simply by their forgetting that they were expected to have any.

Joseph was one of the happiest sharers in this change. He eagerly gave his word to be present at the entertainments to come: his heart beat with delight at the prospect of other such evenings. The suspicion of a tenderer feeling towards Lucy Henderson, the charm of Miss Blessing's winning frankness, took equal possession of his thoughts; and not until he had said good night did he think of his companion on the homeward road. But Elwood Withers had already left, carrying Lucy Henderson on a pillion behind him.

"Is it ten o'clock, do you think?" Joseph asked of one of the young men, as they rode out of the gate.

The other answered with a chuckle: "Ten? It's nigher morning than evening!"

The imp on the crupper struck his claws deep into Joseph's sides. He urged his horse into a gallop, crossed the long rise in the road and dashed along the valley-level, with the cool, dewy night air whistling in his locks. After entering the lane leading upward to his home, he dropped the reins and allowed the panting horse to choose his own gait. A light, sparkling through the locust-trees, pierced him with the sting of an unwelcome external conscience, in which he had no part, yet which he could not escape.

Rachel Miller looked wearily up from her knitting as he entered the room. She made a feeble attempt to smile, but the expression of her face suggested imminent tears.

"Aunt, why did you wait?" said he, speaking rapidly. "I forgot to look at my watch, and I really thought it was no more than ten—"

He paused, seeing that her eyes were fixed. She was looking at the tall old-fashioned clock. The hand pointed to half-past twelve, and every cluck of the ponderous pendulum said, distinctly, "Late! late! late!"

He lighted a candle in silence, said, "Good night, Aunt!" and went up to his room.

"Good night, Joseph!" she solemnly responded, and a deep, hollow sigh reached his ear before the door was closed.

CHAPTER III. THE PLACE AND PEOPLE.

Joseph Asten's nature was shy and sensitive, but not merely from a habit of introversion. He saw no deeper into himself, in fact, than his moods and sensations, and thus quite failed to recognize what it was that kept him apart from the society in which he should have freely moved. He felt the difference of others, and constantly probed the pain and embarrassment it gave him, but the sources wherefrom it grew were the last which he would have guessed.

A boy's life may be weakened for growth, in all its fibres, by the watchfulness of a too anxious love, and the guidance of a too exquisitely nurtured conscience. He may be so trained in the habits of goodness, and purity, and duty, that every contact with the world is like an abrasion upon the delicate surface of his soul. Every wind visits him too roughly, and he shrinks from the encounters which brace true manliness, and strengthen it for the exercise of good.

The rigid piety of Joseph's mother was warmed and softened by her tenderness towards him, and he never felt it as a yoke. His nature instinctively took the imprint of hers, and she was happy in seeing so clear a reflection of herself in his innocent young heart. She prolonged his childhood, perhaps without intending it, into the years when the unrest of approaching manhood should have led him to severer studies and lustier sports. Her death transferred his guardianship to other hands, but did not change its character. Her sister Rachel was equally good and conscientious, possibly with an equal capacity for tenderness, but her barren life had restrained the habit of its expression. Joseph could not but confess that she was guided by the strictest sense of duty, but she seemed to him cold, severe, unsympathetic. There were times when the alternative presented itself to his mind, of either allowing her absolute control of all his actions, or wounding her to the heart by asserting a moderate amount of independence.

He was called fortunate, but it was impossible for him consciously to feel his fortune. The two hundred acres of the farm, stretching back over the softly swelling hills which enclosed the valley on the east, were as excellent soil as the neighborhood knew; the stock was plentiful; the house, barn, and all the appointments of the place were in the best order, and he was the sole owner of all. The work of his own hands was not needed, but it was a mechanical exhaustion of time,—an enforced occupation of body and mind, which he followed in the vague hope that some richer development of life might come afterwards. But there were times when the fields looked very dreary,—when the trees, rooted in their places, and growing under conditions which they were powerless to choose or change, were but tiresome types of himself,—when even the beckoning heights far down the valley failed to touch his fancy with the hint of a broader world. Duty said to him, "You must be perfectly contented in your place!" but there was the miserable, ungrateful, inexplicable fact of discontent.

Furthermore, he had by this time discovered that certain tastes which he possessed were so many weaknesses—if not, indeed, matters of reproach—in the eyes of his neighbors. The delight and the torture of finer nerves—an inability to use coarse and strong phrases, and a shrinking from all display of rude manners—were peculiarities which he could not overcome, and must endeavor to conceal. There were men of sturdy intelligence in the community; but none of refined culture, through whom he might have measured and understood himself; and the very qualities, therefore, which should have been his pride, gave him only a sense of shame.

Two memories haunted him, after the evening at Warriner's; and, though so different, they were not to be disconnected. No two girls could be more unlike than Lucy Henderson and Miss Julia Blessing; he had known one for years, and the other was the partial acquaintance of an evening; yet the image of either one was swiftly followed by that of the other. When he thought of Lucy's eyes, Miss Julia's hand stole over his shoulder; when he recalled the glossy ringlets of the latter, he saw, beside them, the faintly flushed cheek and the pure, sweet mouth which had awakened in him his first daring desire.

Phantoms as they were, they seemed to have taken equal possession of the house, the garden, and the fields. While Lucy sat quietly by the window, Miss Julia skipped lightly along the adjoining hall. One lifted a fallen rose-branch on the lawn, the other snatched the reddest blossom from it. One leaned against the trunk of the old hemlock-tree, the other fluttered in and out among the clumps of shrubbery; but the lonely green was wonderfully brightened by these visions of pink and white, and Joseph enjoyed the fancy without troubling himself to think what it meant.

The house was seated upon a gentle knoll, near the head of a side-valley sunk like a dimple among the hills which enclosed the river-meadows, scarcely a quarter of a mile away. It was nearly a hundred years old, and its massive walls were faced with checkered bricks, alternately red and black, to which the ivy clung with tenacious feet wherever it was allowed to run. The gables terminated in broad double chimneys, between which a railed walk, intended for a look-out, but rarely used for that or any other purpose, rested on the peak of the roof. A low portico paved with stone extended along the front, which was further shaded by two enormous sycamore-trees as old as the house itself. The evergreens and ornamental shrubs which occupied the remainder of the little lawn denoted the taste of a later generation. To the east, an open turfy space, in the centre of which stood a superb weeping-willow, divided the house from the great stone barn with its flanking cribs and "over-shoots;" on the opposite side lay the sunny garden, with gnarled grape-vines clambering along its walls, and a double row of tall old box-bushes, each grown into a single solid mass, stretching down the centre.

The fields belonging to the property, softly rising and following the undulations of the hills, limited the landscape on three sides; but on the south there was a fair view of the valley of the larger stream, with its herd-speckled meadows, glimpses of water between the fringing trees, and farm-houses sheltered among the knees of the farther hills. It was a region of peace and repose and quiet, drowsy beauty, and there were few farms which were not the ancestral homes of the families who held them. The people were satisfied, for they lived upon a bountiful soil; and if but few were notably rich, still fewer were absolutely poor. They had a sluggish sense of content, a half-conscious feeling that their lines were cast in pleasant places; they were orderly, moral, and generally honest, and their own types were so constantly reproduced and fixed, both by intermarriage and intercourse, that any variation therein was a thing to be suppressed if possible. Any sign of an unusual taste, or a different view of life, excited their suspicion, and the most of them were incapable of discriminating between independent thought on moral and social questions, and "free-thinking" in the religious significance which they attached to the word. Political excitements, it is true, sometimes swept over the neighborhood, but in a mitigated form; and the discussions which then took place between neighbors of opposite faith were generally repetitions of the arguments furnished by their respective county papers.

To one whose twofold nature conformed to the common mould,—into whom, before his birth, no mysterious element had been infused, to be the basis of new sensations, desires, and powers,—the region was a paradise of peaceful days. Even as a boy the probable map of his life was drawn: he could behold himself as young man, as husband, father, and comfortable old man, by simply looking upon these various stages in others.

If, however, his senses were not sluggish, but keen; if his nature reached beyond the ordinary necessities, and hungered for the taste of higher things; if he longed to share in that life of the world, the least part of which was known to his native community; if, not content to accept the mechanical faith of passive minds, he dared to repeat the long struggle of the human race in his own spiritual and mental growth; then,—why, then, the region was not a paradise of peaceful days.

Rachel Miller, now that the dangerous evening was over, was shrewd enough to resume her habitual manner towards her nephew. Her curiosity to know what had been done, and how Joseph had been affected by the merry-making, rendered her careful not to frighten him from the subject by warnings or reproaches. He was frank and communicative, and Rachel found, to her surprise, that the evening at Warriner's was much, and not wholly unpleasantly, in her thoughts during her knitting-hours. The farm-work was briskly forwarded; Joseph was active in the field, and decidedly brighter in the house; and when he announced the new engagement, with an air which hinted that his attendance was a matter of course, she was only able to say:—

"I'm very much mistaken if that's the end. Get agoing once, and there's no telling where you'll fetch up. I suppose that town's girl won't stay much longer,—the farm-work of the neighborhood couldn't stand it,—and so she means to have all she can while her visit lasts."

"Indeed, Aunt," Joseph protested, "Elwood Withers first proposed it, and the others all agreed."

"And ready enough they were, I'll be bound."

"Yes, they were," Joseph replied, with a little more firmness than usual. "All of them. And there was no respectable family in the neighborhood that wasn't represented."

Rachel made an effort and kept silence. The innovation might be temporary, and in that case it were prudent to take no further notice; or it might be the beginning of a change in the ways of the young people, and if so, she needed further knowledge in order to work successfully against it in Joseph's case.

She little suspected how swiftly and closely the question would be brought to her own door.

A week afterwards the second of the evening parties was held, and was even more successful than the first. Everybody was there, bringing a cheerful memory of the former occasion, and Miss Julia Blessing, no longer dreaded as an unknown scrutinizing element, was again the life and soul of the company. It was astonishing how correctly she retained the names and characteristics of all those whom she had already met, and how intelligently she seemed to enjoy the gossip of the neighborhood. It was remarked that her dress was studiously simple, as if to conform to country ways, yet the airy, graceful freedom of her manner gave it a character of elegance which sufficiently distinguished her from the other girls.

Joseph felt that she looked to him, as by an innocent natural instinct, for a more delicate and intimate recognition than she expected to find elsewhere. Fragments of sentences, parenthetical expressions, dropped in her lively talk, were always followed by a quick glance which said to him: "We have one feeling in common; I know that you understand me." He was fascinated, but the experience was so new that it was rather bewildering. He was drawn to catch her seemingly random looks,—to wait for them, and then shrink timidly when they came, feeling all the while the desire to be in the quiet corner, outside the merry circle of talkers, where sat Lucy Henderson.

When, at last, a change in the diversions of the evening brought him to Lucy's side, she seemed to him grave and preoccupied. Her words lacked the pleasant directness and self-possession which had made her society so comfortable to him. She no longer turned her full face towards him while speaking, and he noticed that her eyes were wandering over the company with a peculiar expression, as if she were trying to listen with them. It seemed to him, also, that Elwood Withers, who was restlessly moving about the room, was watching some one, or waiting for something.

"I have it!" suddenly cried Miss Blessing, floating towards Joseph and Lucy; "it shall be you, Mr. Asten!"

"Yes," echoed Anna Warriner, following; "if it could be, how delightful!"

"Hush, Anna dear! Let us keep the matter secret!" whispered Miss Blessing, assuming a mysterious air; "we will slip away and consult; and, of course, Lucy must come with us."

"Now," she resumed, when the four found themselves alone in the old-fashioned dining-room, "we must, first of all, explain everything to Mr. Asten. The question is, where we shall meet, next week. McNaughtons are building an addition (I believe you call it) to their barn, and a child has the measles at another place, and something else is wrong somewhere else. We cannot interfere with the course of nature; but neither should we give up these charming evenings without making an effort to continue them. Our sole hope and reliance is on you, Mr. Asten."

She pronounced the words with a mock solemnity, clasping her hands, and looking into his face with bright, eager, laughing eyes.

"If it depended on myself—" Joseph began.

"O, I know the difficulty, Mr. Asten!" she exclaimed; "and really, it's unpardonable in me to propose such a thing. But isn't it possible—just possible—that Miss Miller might be persuaded by us?"

"Julia dear!" cried Anna Warriner, "I believe there's nothing you'd be afraid to undertake."

Joseph scarcely knew what to say. He looked from one to the other, coloring slightly, and ready to turn pale the next moment, as he endeavored to imagine how his aunt would receive such an astounding proposition.

"There is no reason why she should be asked," said Lucy. "It would be a great annoyance to her."

"Indeed?" said Miss Blessing; "then I should be so sorry! But I caught a glimpse of your lovely place the other day as we were driving up the valley. It was a perfect picture,—and I have such a desire to see it nearer!"

"Why will you not come, then?" Joseph eagerly asked. Lucy's words seemed to him blunt and unfriendly, although he knew they had been intended for his relief.

"It would be a great pleasure; yet, if I thought your aunt would be annoyed—"

"I am sure she will be glad to make your acquaintance," said Joseph, with a reproachful side-glance at Lucy.

Miss Blessing noticed the glance. "I am more sure," she said, playfully, "that she will be very much amused at my ignorance and inexperience. And I don't believe Lucy meant to frighten me. As for the party, we won't think of that now; but you will go with us, Lucy, won't you,—with Anna and myself, to make a neighborly afternoon call?"

Lucy felt obliged to accede to a request so amiably made, after her apparent rudeness. Yet she could not force herself to affect a hearty acquiescence, and Joseph thought her singularly cold.

He did not doubt but that Miss Blessing, whose warm, impulsive nature seemed to him very much what his own might be if he dared to show it, would fulfil her promise. Neither did he doubt that so much innocence and sweetness as she possessed would make a favorable impression upon his aunt; but he judged it best not to inform the latter of the possible visit.

CHAPTER IV. MISS BLESSING CALLS ON RACHEL MILLER.

On the following Saturday afternoon, Rachel Miller sat at the front window of the sitting-room, and arranged her light task of sewing and darning, with a feeling of unusual comfort. The household work of the week was over; the weather was fine and warm, with a brisk drying breeze for the hay on the hill-field, the last load of which Joseph expected to have in the barn before his five o'clock supper was ready. As she looked down the valley, she noticed that the mowers were still swinging their way through Hunter's grass, and that Cunningham's corn sorely needed working. There was a different state of things on the Asten place. Everything was done, and well done, up to the front of the season. The weather had been fortunate, it was true; but Joseph had urged on the work with a different spirit. It seemed to her that he had taken a new interest in the farm; he was here and there, even inspecting with his own eyes the minor duties which had been formerly intrusted to his man Dennis. How could she know that this activity was the only outlet for a restless heart?

If any evil should come of his social recreation, she had done her duty; but no evil seemed likely. She had always separated his legal from his moral independence; there was no enactment establishing the period when the latter commenced, and it could not be made manifest by documents, like the former. She would have admitted, certainly, that her guardianship must cease at some time, but the thought of making preparation for that time had never entered her head. She only understood conditions, not the adaptation of characters to them. Going back over her own life, she could recall but little difference between the girl of eighteen and the woman of thirty. There was the same place in her home, the same duties, the same subjection to the will of her parents—no exercise of independence or self-reliance anywhere, and no growth of those virtues beyond what a passive maturity brought with it.

Even now she thought very little about any question of life in connection with Joseph. Her parents had trained her in the discipline of a rigid sect, and she could not dissociate the idea of morality from that of solemn renunciation. She could not say that social pleasures were positively wrong, but they always seemed to her to be enjoyed on the outside of an open door labelled "Temptation;" and who could tell what lay beyond? Some very good people, she knew, were fond of company, and made merry in an innocent fashion; they were of mature years and settled characters, and Joseph was only a boy. The danger, however, was not so imminent: no fault could be found with his attention to duty, and a chance so easily escaped was a comfortable guaranty for the future.

In the midst of this mood (we can hardly say train of thought), she detected the top of a carriage through the bushes fringing the lane. The vehicle presently came into view: Anna Warriner was driving, and there were two other ladies on the back seat. As they drew up at the hitching-post on the green, she recognized Lucy Henderson getting out; but the airy creature who sprang after her,—the girl with dark, falling ringlets,—could it be the stranger from town? The plain, country-made gingham dress, the sober linen collar, the work-bag on her arm—could they belong to the stylish young lady whose acquaintance had turned Anna's head?

A proper spirit of hospitality required her to meet the visitors at the gate; so there was no time left for conjecture. She was a little confused, but not dissatisfied at the chance of seeing the stranger.

"We thought we could come for an hour this afternoon, without disturbing you," said Anna Warriner. "Mother has lost your receipt for pickling cherries, and Bob said you were already through with the hay-harvest; and so we brought Julia along—this is Julia Blessing."

"How do you do?" said Miss Blessing, timidly extending her hand, and slightly dropping her eyelids. She then fell behind Anna and Lucy, and spoke no more until they were all seated in the sitting-room.

"How do you like the country by this time?" Rachel asked, feeling that a little attention was necessary to a new guest.

"So well that I think I shall never like the city again," Miss Blessing answered. "This quiet, peaceful life is such a rest; and I really never before knew what order was, and industry, and economy."

She looked around the room as she spoke, and glanced at the barn through the eastern window.

"Yes, your ways in town are very different," Rachel remarked.

"It seems to me, now, that they are entirely artificial. I find myself so ignorant of the proper way of living that I should be embarrassed among you, if you were not all so very kind. But I am trying to learn a little."

"O, we don't expect too much of town's-folks," said Rachel, in a much more friendly tone, "and we're always glad to see them willing to put up with our ways. But not many are."

"Please don't count me among those!" Miss Blessing exclaimed.

"No, indeed, Miss Rachel!" said Anna Warriner; "you'd be surprised to know how Julia gets along with everything—don't she, Lucy?"

"Yes, she's very quick," Lucy Henderson replied.

Miss Blessing cast down her eyes, smiled, and shook her head.

Rachel Miller asked some questions which opened the sluices of Miss Warriner's gossip—and she had a good store of it. The ways and doings of various individuals were discussed, and Miss Blessing's occasional remarks showed a complete familiarity with them. Her manner was grave and attentive, and Rachel was surprised to find so much unobtrusive good sense in her views. The reality was so different from her previously assumed impression, that she felt bound to make some reparation. Almost before she was aware of it, her manner became wholly friendly and pleasant.

"May I look at your trees and flowers?" Miss Blessing asked, when the gossip had been pretty well exhausted.

They all arose and went out on the lawn. Rose and woodbine, phlox and verbena, passed under review, and then the long, rounded walls of box attracted Miss Blessing's eye. This was a feature of the place in which Rachel

Miller felt considerable pride, and she led the way through the garden gate. Anna Warriner, however, paused, and said:—

"Lucy, let us go down to the spring-house. We can get back again before Julia has half finished her raptures."

Lucy hesitated a moment. She looked at Miss Blessing, who laughed and said, "O, don't mind me!" as she took her place at Rachel's side.

The avenue of box ran the whole length of the garden, which sloped gently to the south. At the bottom the green walls curved outward, forming three-fourths of a circle, spacious enough to contain several seats. There was a delightful view of the valley through the opening.

"The loveliest place I ever saw!" exclaimed Miss Blessing, taking one of the rustic chairs. "How pleasant it must be, when you have all your neighbors here together!"

Rachel Miller was a little startled; but before she could reply, Miss Blessing continued:—

"There is such a difference between a company of young people here in the country, and what is called 'a party' in the city. There it is all dress and flirtation and vanity, but here it is only neighborly visiting on a larger scale. I have enjoyed the quiet company of all your folks so much the more, because I felt that it was so very innocent. Indeed, I don't see how anybody could be led into harmful ways here."

"I don't know," said Rachel: "we must learn to mistrust our own hearts."

"You are right! The best are weak—of themselves; but there is more safety where all have been brought up unacquainted with temptation. Now, you will perhaps wonder at me when I say that I could trust the young men— for instance, Mr. Asten, your nephew—as if they were my brothers. That is, I feel a positive certainty of their excellent character. What they say they mean: it is otherwise in the city. It is delightful to see them all together, like members of one family. You must enjoy it, I should think, when they meet here."

Rachel Miller's eyes opened wide, and there was both a puzzled and a searching expression in the look she gave Miss Blessing. The latter, with an air of almost infantine simplicity, her lips slightly parted, accepted the scrutiny with a quiet cheerfulness which seemed the perfection of candor.

"The truth is," said Rachel, slowly, "this is a new thing. I hope the merry-makings are as innocent as you think; but I'm afraid they unsettle the young people, after all."

"Do you, really?" exclaimed Miss Blessing. "What have you seen in them which leads you to think so? But no—never mind my question; you may have reasons which I have no right to ask. Now, I remember Mr. Asten telling Anna and Lucy and myself, how much he should like to invite his friends here, if it were not for a duty which prevented it; and a duty, he said, was more important to him than a pleasure."

"Did Joseph say that?" Rachel exclaimed.

"O, perhaps I oughtn't to have told it," said Miss Blessing, casting down her eyes and blushing in confusion: "in that case, please don't say anything about it! Perhaps it was a duty towards you, for he told me that he looked upon you as a second mother."

Rachel's eyes softened, and it was a little while before she spoke. "I've tried to do my duty by him," she faltered at last, "but it sometimes seems an unthankful business, and I can't always tell how he takes it. And so he wanted to have a company here?"

"I am so sorry I said it!" cried Miss Blessing. "I never thought you were opposed to company, on principle. Miss Chaffinch, the minister's daughter, you know, was there the last time; and, really, if you could see it—But it is presumptuous in me to say anything. Indeed, I am not a fair judge, because these little gatherings have enabled me to make such pleasant acquaintances. And the young men tell me that they work all the better after them."

"It's only on his account," said Rachel.

"Nay, I'm sure that the last thing Mr. Asten would wish would be your giving up a principle for his sake! I know, from his face, that his own character

744

is founded on principle. And, besides, here in the country, you don't keep count of hospitality, as they do in the city, and feel obliged to return as much as you receive. So, if you will try to forget what I have said—"

Rachel interrupted her. "I meant something different. Joseph knows why I objected to parties. He must not feel under obligations which I stand in the way of his repaying. If he tells me that he should like to invite his friends to this place, I will help him to entertain them."

"You are his second mother, indeed," Miss Blessing murmured, looking at her with a fond admiration. "And now I can hope that you will forgive my thoughtlessness. I should feel humiliated in his presence, if he knew that I had repeated his words. But he will not ask you, and this is the end of any harm I may have done."

"No," said Rachel, "he will not ask me; but won't I be an offence in his mind?"

"I can understand how you feel—only a woman can judge a woman's heart. Would you think me too forward if I tell you what might be done, this once?"

She stole softly up to Rachel as she spoke, and laid her hand gently upon her arm.

"Perhaps I am wrong—but if you were first to suggest to your nephew that if he wished to make some return for the hospitality of his neighbors,—or put it in whatever form you think best,—would not that remove the 'offence' (though he surely cannot look at it in that light), and make him grateful and happy?"

"Well," said Rachel, after a little reflection, "if anything is done, that would be as good a way as any."

"And, of course, you won't mention me?"

"There is no call to do it—as I can see."

"Julia, dear!" cried Anna from the gate; "come and see the last load of hay hauled into the barn!"

"I should like to see it, if you will excuse me," said Miss Blessing to Rachel; "I have taken quite an interest in farming."

As they were passing the porch, Rachel paused on the step and said to Anna: "You'll bide and get your suppers?"

"I don't know," Anna replied: "we didn't mean to; but we stayed longer than we intended—"

"Then you can easily stay longer still."

There was nothing unfriendly in Rachel's blunt manner. Anna laughed, took Miss Blessing by the arm, and started for the barn. Lucy Henderson quietly turned and entered the house, where, without any offer of services, she began to assist in arranging the table.

The two young ladies took their stand on the green, at a safe distance, as the huge fragrant load approached. The hay overhung and concealed the wheels, as well as the hind quarters of the oxen, and on the summit stood Joseph, in his shirt-sleeves and leaning on a pitch-fork. He bent forward as he saw them, answering their greetings with an eager, surprised face.

"O, take care, take care!" cried Miss Blessing, as the load entered the barn-door; but Joseph had already dropped upon his knees and bent his shoulders. Then the wagon stood upon the barn-floor; he sprang lightly upon a beam, descended the upright ladder, and the next moment was shaking hands with them.

"We have kept our promise, you see," said Miss Blessing.

"Have you been in the house yet?" Joseph asked, looking at Anna.

"O, for an hour past, and we are going to take supper with you."

"Dennis!" cried Joseph, turning towards the barn, "we will let the load stand to-night."

"How much better a man looks in shirt-sleeves than in a dress-coat!"

remarked Miss Blessing aside to Anna Warriner, but not in so low a tone as to prevent Joseph from hearing it.

"Why, Julia, you are perfectly countrified! I never saw anything like it!" Anna replied.

Joseph turned to them again, with a bright flush on his face. He caught Miss Blessing's eyes, full of admiration, before the lids fell modestly over them.

"So you've seen my home, already?" he said, as they walked slowly towards the house.

"O, not the half yet!" she answered, in a low, earnest tone. "A place so lovely and quiet as this cannot be appreciated at once. I almost wish I had not seen it: what shall I do when I must go back to the hot pavements, and the glaring bricks, and the dust, and the hollow, artificial life?" She tried to check a sigh, but only partially succeeded; then, with a sudden effort, she laughed lightly, and added: "I wonder if everybody doesn't long for something else? Now, Anna, here, would think it heavenly to change places with me."

"Such privileges as you have!" Anna protested.

"Privileges?" Miss Blessing echoed. "The privilege of hearing scandal, of being judged by your dress, of learning the forms and manners, instead of the good qualities, of men and women? No! give me an independent life."

"Alone?" suggested Miss Warriner.

Joseph looked at Miss Blessing, who made no reply. Her head was turned aside, and he could well understand that she must feel hurt at Anna's indelicacy.

In the house Rachel Miller and Lucy had, in the mean time, been occupied with domestic matters. The former, however, was so shaken out of her usual calm by the conversation in the garden, that in spite of prudent resolves to keep quiet, she could not restrain herself from asking a question or two.

"Lucy," said she, "how do you find these evening parties you've been attending?"

"They are lively and pleasant,—at least every one says so."

"Are you going to have any more?"

"It seems to be the wish," said Lucy, suddenly hesitating, as she found Rachel's eyes intently fixed upon her face.

The latter was silent for a minute, arranging the tea-service; but she presently asked again: "Do you think Joseph would like to invite the young people here?"

"She has told you!" Lucy exclaimed, in unfeigned irritation. "Miss Rachel, don't let it trouble you a moment: nobody expects it of you!"

Lucy felt, immediately, that her expression had been too frankly positive; but even the consciousness thereof did not enable her to comprehend its effect.

Rachel straightened herself a little, and said "Indeed?" in anything but an amiable tone. She went to the cupboard and returned before speaking again. "I didn't say anybody told me," she continued; "it's likely that Joseph might think of it, and I don't see why people should expect me to stand in the way of his wishes."

Lucy was so astonished that she could not immediately reply; and the entrance of Joseph and the two ladies cut off all further opportunity of clearing up what she felt to be an awkward misunderstanding.

"I must help, too!" cried Miss Blessing, skipping into the kitchen after Rachel. "That is one thing, at least, which we can learn in the city. Indeed, if it wasn't for housekeeping, I should feel terribly useless."

Rachel protested against her help, but in vain. Miss Blessing had a laugh and a lively answer for every remonstrance, and flitted about in a manner which conveyed the impression that she was doing a great deal.

Joseph could scarcely believe his eyes, when he came down from his room in fresh attire, and beheld his aunt not only so assisted, but seeming to enjoy it. Lucy, who appeared to be ill at ease, had withdrawn from the table, and was sitting silently beside the window. Recalling their conversation a few evenings before, he suspected that she might be transiently annoyed on his aunt's account; she had less confidence, perhaps, in Miss Blessing's winning, natural manners. So Lucy's silence threw no shadow upon his cheerfulness: he had never felt so happy, so free, so delighted to assume the character of a host.

After the first solemnity which followed the taking of seats at the table, the meal proceeded with less than the usual decorum. Joseph, indeed, so far forgot his duties, that his aunt was obliged to remind him of them from time to time. Miss Blessing was enthusiastic over the cream and butter and marmalade, and Rachel Miller found it exceedingly pleasant to have her handiwork appreciated. Although she always did her best, for Joseph's sake, she knew that men have very ignorant, indifferent tastes in such matters.

When the meal was over, Anna Warriner said: "We are going to take Lucy on her way as far as the cross-roads; so there will not be more than time to get home by sunset."

Before the carriage was ready, however, another vehicle drove up the lane. Elwood Withers jumped out, gave Joseph a hearty grip of his powerful hand, greeted the others rapidly, and then addressed himself specially to Lucy: "I was going to a township-meeting at the Corner," said he; "but Bob Warriner told me you were here with Anna, so I thought I could save her a roundabout drive by taking you myself."

"Thank you; but I'm sorry you should go so far out of your road," said Lucy. Her face was pale, and there was an evident constraint in the smile which accompanied the words.

"O, he'd go twice as far for company," Anna Warriner remarked. "You know I'd take you, and welcome, but Elwood has a good claim on you, now."

"I have no claim, Lucy," said Elwood, rather doggedly.

"Let us go, then," were Lucy's words.

She rose, and the four were soon seated in the two vehicles. They drove away in the low sunshine, one pair chatting and laughing merrily as long as they were within hearing, the other singularly grave and silent.

CHAPTER V. ELWOOD'S EVENING, AND JOSEPH'S.

For half a mile Elwood Withers followed the carriage containing Anna Warriner and her friend; then, at the curve of the valley, their roads parted, and Lucy and he were alone. The soft light of the delicious summer evening was around them; the air, cooled by the stream which broadened and bickered beside their way, was full of all healthy meadow odors, and every farm in the branching dells they passed was a picture of tranquil happiness. Yet Lucy had sighed before she was aware of it,—a very faint, tremulous breath, but it reached Elwood's sensitive ear.

"You don't seem quite well, Lucy," he said.

"Because I have talked so little?" she asked.

"Not just that, but—but I was almost afraid my coming for you was not welcome. I don't mean—" But here he grew confused, and did not finish the sentence.

"Indeed, it was very kind of you," said she. This was not an answer to his remark, and both felt that it was not.

Elwood struck the horse with his whip, then as suddenly drew the reins on the startled animal. "Pshaw!" he exclaimed, in a tone that was almost fierce, "what's the use o' my beating about the bush in this way?"

Lucy caught her breath, and clenched her hands under her shawl for one instant. Then she became calm, and waited for him to say more.

"Lucy!" he continued, turning towards her, "you have a right to think me a fool. I can talk to anybody else more freely than to you, and the reason is, I want to say more to you than to any other woman! There's no use in my being a coward any longer; it's a desperate venture I'm making, but it must be made. Have you never guessed how I feel towards you?"

"Yes," she answered, very quietly.

"Well, what do you say to it?" He tried to speak calmly, but his breath came thick and hard, and the words sounded hoarsely.

"I will say this, Elwood," said she, "that because I saw your heart, I have watched your ways and studied your character. I find you honest and manly in everything, and so tender and faithful that I wish I could return your affection in the same measure."

A gleam, as of lightning, passed over his face.

"O, don't misunderstand me!" she cried, her calmness forsaking her, "I esteem, I honor you, and that makes it harder for me to seem ungrateful, unfeeling,—as I must. Elwood, if I could, I would answer you as you wish, but I cannot."

"If I wait?" he whispered.

"And lose your best years in a vain hope! No, Elwood, my friend,—let me always call you so,—I have been cowardly also. I knew an explanation must come, and I shrank from the pain I should feel in giving you pain. It is hard; and better for both of us that it should not be repeated!"

"There's something wrong in this world!" he exclaimed, after a long pause. "I suppose you could no more force yourself to love me than I could force myself to love Anna Warriner or that Miss Blessing. Then what put it into my heart to love you? Was it God or the Devil!"

"Elwood!"

"How can I help myself? Can I help drawing my breath? Did I set about it of my own will? Here I see a life that belongs to my own life,—as much a part of it as my head or heart; but I can't reach it,—it draws away from me, and maybe joins itself to some one else forever! O my God!"

Lucy burst into such a violent passion of weeping, that Elwood forgot himself in his trouble for her. He had never witnessed such grief, as it seemed to him, and his honest heart was filled with self-reproach at having caused it.

"Forgive me, Lucy!" he said, very tenderly encircling her with his arm,

751

and drawing her head upon his shoulder; "I spoke rashly and wickedly, in my disappointment. I thought only of myself, and forgot that I might hurt you by my words. I'm not the only man who has this kind of trouble to bear; and perhaps if I could see clearer—but I don't know; I can only see one thing."

She grew calmer as he spoke. Lifting her head from his shoulder, she took his hand, and said: "You are a true and a noble man, Elwood. It is only a grief to me that I cannot love you as a wife should love her husband. But my will is as powerless as yours."

"I believe you, Lucy," he answered, sadly. "It's not your fault,—but, then, it isn't mine, either. You make me feel that the same rule fits both of us, leastways so far as helping the matter is concerned. You needn't tell me I may find another woman to love; the very thought of it makes me sick at heart. I'm rougher than you are, and awkward in my ways—"

"It is not that! O, believe me, it is not that!" cried Lucy, interrupting him. "Have you ever sought for reasons to account for your feeling toward me? Is it not something that does not seem to depend upon what I am,— upon any qualities that distinguish me from other women?"

"How do you know so much?" Elwood asked. "Have you—" He commenced, but did not finish the question. He leaned silently forward, urged on the horse, and Lucy could see that his face was very stern.

"They say," she began, on finding that he was not inclined to speak,— "they say that women have a natural instinct which helps them to understand many things; and I think it must be true. Why can you not spare me the demand for reasons which I have not? If I were to take time, and consider it, and try to explain, it would be of no help to you: it would not change the fact. I suppose a man feels humiliated when this trouble comes upon him. He shows his heart, and there seems to be a claim upon the woman of his choice to show hers in return. The sense of injustice is worse than humiliation, Elwood. Though I cannot, cannot do otherwise, I shall always have the feeling that I have wronged you."

"O Lucy," he murmured, in a very sad, but not reproachful voice, "every word you say, in showing me that I must give you up, only makes it more impossible to me. And it is just impossible,—that's the end of the matter! I know how people talk about trials being sent us for our good, and its being the will of God, and all that. It's a trial, that's true: whether it's for my good or not, I shall learn after a while; but I can find out God's will only by trying the strength of my own. Don't be afeared, Lucy! I've no notion of saying or doing anything from this time on to disturb you, but here you are" (striking his breast with his clenched hand), "and here you will be when the day comes, as I feel that it must and shall come, to bring us together!"

She could see the glow of his face in the gathering dusk, as he turned towards her and offered his hand. How could she help taking it? If some pulse in her own betrayed the thrill of admiring recognition of the man's powerful and tender nature, which suddenly warmed her oppressed blood, she did not fear that he would draw courage from the token. She wished to speak, but found no words which, coming after his, would not have seemed either cold and unsympathetic, or too near the verge of the hope which she would gladly have crushed.

Elwood was silent for a while, and hardly appeared to be awaiting an answer. Meanwhile the road left the valley, climbing the shoulders of its enclosing hills, where the moist meadow fragrance was left behind, and dry, warm breezes, filled with the peculiar smell of the wheat-fields, blew over them. It was but a mile farther to the Corner, near which Lucy's parents resided.

"How came you three to go to Joseph's place this afternoon?" he asked. "Wasn't it a dodge of Miss Blessing's?"

"She proposed it,—partly in play, I think; and when she afterwards insisted on our going, there seemed to be no good reason for refusing."

"O, of course not," said Elwood; "but tell me now, honestly, Lucy, what do you make out of her?"

Lucy hesitated a moment. "She is a little wilful in her ways, perhaps, but we mustn't judge too hastily. We have known her such a short time. Her manner is very amiable."

"I don't know about that," Elwood remarked. "It reminds me of one of her dresses,—so ruffled, and puckered, and stuck over with ribbons and things, that you can't rightly tell what the stuff is. I'd like to be sure whether she has an eye to Joseph."

"To him!" Lucy exclaimed.

"Him first and foremost! He's as innocent as a year-old baby. There isn't a better fellow living than Joseph Asten, but his bringing up has been fitter for a girl than a boy. He hasn't had his eye-teeth cut yet, and it's my opinion that she has."

"What do you mean by that?"

"No harm. Used to the world, as much as anything else. He don't know how to take people; he thinks th' outside color runs down to the core. So it does with him; but I can't see what that girl is, under her pleasant ways, and he won't guess that there's anything else of her. Between ourselves, Lucy,— you don't like her. I saw that when you came away, though you were kissing each other at the time."

"What a hypocrite I must be!" cried Lucy, rather fiercely.

"Not a bit of it. Women kiss as men shake hands. You don't go around, saying, 'Julia dear!' like Anna Warriner."

Lucy could not help laughing. "There," she said, "that's enough, Elwood! I'd rather you would think yourself in the right than to say anything more about her this evening."

She sighed wearily, not attempting to conceal her fatigue and depression.

"Well, well!" he replied; "I'll pester you no more with disagreeable subjects. There's the house, now, and you'll soon be rid of me. I won't tell you, Lucy, that if you ever want for friendly service, you must look to me,— because I'm afeared you won't feel free to do it; but you'll take all I can find to do without your asking."

Without waiting for an answer he drew up his horse at the gate of her home, handed her out, said "Good night!" and drove away.

Such a singular restlessness took possession of Joseph, after the departure of his guests, that the evening quiet of the farm became intolerable. He saddled his horse and set out for the village, readily inventing an errand which explained the ride to himself as well as to his aunt.

The regular movements of the animal did not banish the unquiet motions of his mind, but it relieved him by giving them a wider sweep and a more definite form. The man who walks is subject to the power of his Antæus of a body, moving forwards only by means of the weight which holds it to the earth. There is a clog upon all his thoughts, an ever-present sense of restriction and impotence. But when he is lifted above the soil, with the air under his foot-soles, swiftly moving without effort, his mind, a poising Mercury, mounts on winged heels. He feels the liberation of new and nimble powers; wider horizons stretch around his inward vision; obstacles are measured or overlooked; the brute strength under him charges his whole nature with a more vigorous electricity.

The fresh, warm, healthy vital force which filled Joseph's body to the last embranchment of every nerve and vein—the hum of those multitudinous spirits of life, which, while building their glorious abode, march as if in triumphant procession through its secret passages, and summon all the fairest phantoms of sense to their completed chambers—constituted, far more than he suspected, an element of his disturbance. This was the strong pinion on which his mind and soul hung balanced, above the close atmosphere which he seemed to ride away from, as he rode. The great joy of human life filled and thrilled him; all possibilities of action and pleasure and emotion swam before his sight; all he had read or heard of individual careers in all ages, climates, and conditions of the race—dazzling pictures of the myriad-sided earth, to be won by whosoever dared arbitrarily to seize the freedom waiting for his grasp—floated through his brain.

Hitherto a conscience not born of his own nature,—a very fair and saintly-visaged jailer of thought, but a jailer none the less,—had kept strict guard over every outward movement of his mind, gently touching hope and desire and conjecture when they reached a certain line, and saying, "No; no farther: it is prohibited." But now, with one strong, involuntary throb, he found himself beyond the line, with all the ranges ever trodden by man stretching forward to a limitless horizon. He rose in his stirrups, threw out his arms, lifted his face towards the sky, and cried, "God! I see what I am!"

It was only a glimpse,—like that of a landscape struck in golden fire by lightning, from the darkness. "What is it," he mused, "that stands between me and this vision of life? Who built a wall of imaginary law around these needs, which are in themselves inexorable laws? The World, the Flesh, and the Devil, they say in warning. Bright, boundless world, my home, my play-ground, my battle-field, my kingdom to be conquered! And this body they tell me to despise,—this perishing house of clay, which is so intimately myself that its comfort and delight cheer me to the inmost soul: it is a dwelling fit for an angel to inhabit! Shall not its hungering senses all be fed? Who shall decide for me—if not myself—on their claims?—who can judge for me what strength requires to be exercised, what pleasure to be enjoyed, what growth to be forwarded? All around me, everywhere, are the means of gratification,—I have but to reach forth my hand and grasp; but a narrow cell, built ages ago, encloses me wherever I go!"

Such was the vague substance of his thoughts. It was the old struggle between life—primitive, untamed life, as the first man may have felt it—and its many masters: assertion, and resistance, all the more fierce because so many influences laid their hands upon its forces. As he came back to his usual self, refreshed by this temporary escape, Joseph wondered whether other men shared the same longing and impatience; and this turned his musings into another channel. "Why do men so carefully conceal what is deepest and strongest in their natures? Why is so little of spiritual struggle and experience ever imparted? The convert publicly admits his sinful experience, and tries to explain the entrance of grace into his regenerated nature; the reformed drunkard seems to take a positive delight in making his former condition degraded and loathsome; but the opening of the individual life to the knowledge of power and passion and all the possibilities of the world is kept more secret than sin. Love is hidden as if it were a reproach; friendship watched, lest it express its warmth too frankly; joy and grief and doubt and anxiety repressed as much as possible. A great lid is shut down upon the human race. They must painfully stoop and creep, instead of standing erect with only God's heaven over their heads. I am lonely, but I know not how to cry for companionship; my words would not be understood, or, if they were, would not be answered. Only one gate is free to me,—that leading to the love of woman. There, at least, must be such an intense, intimate sympathy as shall make the reciprocal revelation of the lives possible!"

Full of this single certainty, which, the more he pondered upon it, seemed to be his nearest chance of help, Joseph rode slowly homewards. Rachel Miller, who had impatiently awaited his coming, remarked the abstraction of his face, and attributed it to a very different cause. She was thereby wonderfully strengthened to make her communication in regard to the evening company; nevertheless, the subject was so slowly approached and so ambiguously alluded to, that Joseph could not immediately understand it.

"That is something! That is a step!" he said to himself; then turning towards her with a genuine satisfaction in his face, added: "Aunt, do you know that I have never really felt until now that I am the owner of this property? It will be more of a home to me after I have received the neighborhood as my guests. It has always controlled me, but now it must serve me."

He laughed in great good-humor, and Rachel Miller, in her heart, thanked Miss Julia Blessing.

CHAPTER VI. IN THE GARDEN.

Rachel Miller was not a woman to do a thing by halves. As soon as the question was settled, she gave her heart and mind to the necessary preparations. There might have been a little surprise in some quarters, when the fact became known in the neighborhood through Joseph's invitation, but no expression of it reached the Asten place. Mrs. Warriner, Anna's mother, called to inquire if she could be of service, and also to suggest, indirectly, her plan of entertaining company. Rachel detected the latter purpose, and was a little more acquiescent than could have been justified to her own conscience, seeing that at the very moment when she was listening with much apparent meekness, she was mentally occupied with plans for outdoing Mrs. Warriner. Moreover, the Rev. Mr. Chaffinch had graciously signified his willingness to be present, and the stamp of strictest orthodoxy was thus set upon the entertainment. She was both assured and stimulated, as the time drew near, and even surprised Joseph by saying: "If I was better acquainted with Miss Blessing, she might help me a good deal in fixing everything just as it should be. There are times, it seems, when it's an advantage to know something of the world."

"I'll ask her!" Joseph exclaimed.

"You! And a mess you'd make of it, very likely; men think they've only to agree to invite a company, and that's all! There's a hundred things to be thought of that women must look to; you couldn't even understand 'em. As for speaking to her,—she's one of the invites, and it would never do in the world."

Joseph said no more, but he silently determined to ask Miss Blessing on her arrival; there would still be time. She, with her wonderful instinct, her power of accommodating people to each other, and the influence which she had already acquired with his aunt, would certainly see at a glance how the current was setting, and guide it in the proper direction.

But, as the day drew near, he grew so restless and uneasy that there seemed nothing better to do than to ride over to Warriner's in the hope of catching a moment's conference with her, in advance of the occasion.

He was entirely fortunate. Anna was apparently very busy with household duties, and after the first greetings left him alone with Miss Blessing. He had anticipated a little difficulty in making his message known, and was therefore much relieved when she said: "Now, Mr. Asten, I see by your face that you have something particular to say. It's about to-morrow night, isn't it? You must let me help you, if I can, because I am afraid I have been, without exactly intending it, the cause of so much trouble to you and your aunt."

Joseph opened his heart at once. All that he had meant to say came easily and naturally to his lips, because Miss Blessing seemed to feel and understand the situation, and met him half-way in her bright, cheerful acquiescence. Almost before he knew it, he had made her acquainted with what had been said and done at home. How easily she solved the absurd doubts and difficulties which had so unnecessarily tormented him! How clearly, through her fine female instinct, she grasped little peculiarities of his aunt's nature, which he, after years of close companionship, had failed to define! Miss Rachel, she said, was both shy and inexperienced, and it was only the struggle to conceal these conscious defects which made her seem—not unamiable, exactly, but irregular in her manner. Her age, and her character in the neighborhood, did not permit her to appear incompetent to any emergency; it was a very natural pride, and must be treated very delicately and tenderly.

Would Joseph trust the matter entirely to her, Miss Blessing? It was a great deal to ask, she knew, comparative stranger as she was; but she believed that a woman, when her nature had not been distorted by the conventionalities of life, had a natural talent for smoothing difficulties, and removing obstacles for others. Her friends had told her that she possessed this power; and it was a great happiness to think so. In the present case, she was sure she should make no mistake. She would endeavor not to seem to suggest anything, but merely to assist in such a way that Miss Rachel would of herself see what else was necessary to be done.

"Now," she remarked, in conclusion, "this sounds like vanity in me; but

I really hope it is not. You must remember that in the city we are obliged to know all the little social arts,—and artifices, I am afraid. It is not always to our credit, but then, the heart may be kept fresh and uncorrupted."

She sighed, and cast down her eyes. Joseph felt the increasing charm of a nature so frank and so trustful, constantly luring to the surface the maiden secrets of his own. The confidence already established between them was wholly delightful, because their sense of reciprocity increased as it deepened. He felt so free to speak that he could not measure the fitness of his words, but exclaimed, without a pause for thought:—

"Tell me, Miss Julia, did you not suggest this party to Aunt Rachel?"

"Don't give me too much credit!" she answered; "it was talked about, and I couldn't help saying Ay. I longed so much to see you—all—again before I go away."

"And Lucy Henderson objected to it?"

"Lucy, I think, wanted to save your aunt trouble. Perhaps she did not guess that the real objection was inexperience, and not want of will to entertain company. And very likely she helped to bring it about, by seeming to oppose it; so you must not be angry with Lucy,—promise me!"

She looked at him with an irresistibly entreating expression, and extended her hand, which he seized so warmly as to give her pain. But she returned the pressure, and there was a moment's silence, which Anna Warriner interrupted at the right time.

The next day, on the Asten farm, all the preparations were quietly and successfully made long in advance of the first arrivals. The Rev. Mr. Chaffinch and a few other specially chosen guests made their appearance in the afternoon. To Joseph's surprise, the Warriners and Miss Blessing speedily joined them. It was, in reality, a private arrangement which his aunt had made, in order to secure at the start the very assistance which he had been plotting to render. One half the secret of the ease and harmony which he felt was established was thus unknown to him. He looked for hints or indications of management on Miss Blessing's part, but saw none. The two women, meeting each other half-way, needed no words in order to understand each other, and Miss Rachel, gradually made secure in her part of hostess, experienced a most unaccustomed sense of triumph.

At the supper-table Mr. Chaffinch asked a blessing with fervor; a great, balmy dish of chickens stewed in cream was smoking before his nostrils, and his fourth cup of tea made Rachel Miller supremely happy. The meal was honored in silence, as is the case where there is much to eat and a proper desire and capacity to do it; only towards its close were the tongues of the guests loosened, and content made them cheerful.

"You have entertained us almost too sumptuously, Miss Miller," said the clergyman. "And now let us go out on the portico, and welcome the young people as they arrive."

"I need hardly ask you, then, Mr. Chaffinch," said she, "whether you think it right for them to come together in this way."

"Decidedly!" he answered; "that is, so long as their conversation is modest and becoming. It is easy for the vanities of the world to slip in, but we must watch,—we must watch."

Rachel Miller took a seat near him, beholding the gates of perfect enjoyment opened to her mind. Dress, the opera, the race-course, literature, stocks, politics, have their fascination for so many several classes of the human race; but to her there was nothing on this earth so delightful as to be told of temptation and backsliding and sin, and to feel that she was still secure. The fact that there was always danger added a zest to the feeling; she gave herself credit for a vigilance which had really not been exercised.

The older guests moved their chairs nearer, and listened, forgetting the sweetness of sunset which lay upon the hills down the valley. Anna Warriner laid her arm around Miss Chaffinch's waist, and drew her towards the mown field beyond the barn; and presently, by a natural chance, as it seemed, Joseph found himself beside Miss Blessing, at the bottom of the lawn.

All the western hills were covered with one cool, broad shadow. A rich orange flush touched the tops of the woods to the eastward, and brightened as the sky above them deepened into the violet-gray of coming dusk. The moist, delicious freshness which filled the bed of the valley slowly crept up the branching glen, and already tempered the air about them. Now and then a bird chirped happily from a neighboring bush, or the low of cattle was heard from the pasture-fields.

"Ah!" sighed Miss Blessing, "this is too sweet to last: I must learn to do without it."

She looked at him swiftly, and then glanced away. It seemed that there were tears in her eyes.

Joseph was about to speak, but she laid her hand on his arm. "Hush!" she said; "let us wait until the light has faded."

The glow had withdrawn to the summits of the distant hills, fringing them with a thin, wonderful radiance. But it was only momentary. The next moment it broke on the irregular topmost boughs, and then disappeared, as if blown out by a breeze which came with the sudden lifting of the sky. She turned away in silence, and they walked slowly together towards the house. At the garden gate she paused.

"That superb avenue of box!" she exclaimed; "I must see it again, if only to say farewell."

They entered the garden, and in a moment the dense green wall, breathing an odor seductive to heart and senses, had hidden them from the sight—and almost from the hearing—of the guests on the portico. Looking down through the southern opening of the avenue, they seemed alone in the evening valley.

Joseph's heart was beating fast and strong; he was conscious of a wild fear, so interfused with pleasure, that it was impossible to separate the sensations. Miss Blessing's hand was on his arm, and he fancied that it trembled.

"If life were as beautiful and peaceful as this," she whispered, at last, "we should not need to seek for truth and—and—sympathy: we should find them everywhere."

"Do you not think they are to be found?" he asked.

"O, in how few hearts! I can say it to you, and you will not misunderstand me. Until lately I was satisfied with life as I found it: I thought it meant diversion, and dress, and gossip, and common daily duties, but now—now I see that it is the union of kindred souls!"

She clasped both her hands over his arm as she spoke, and leaned slightly towards him, as if drawing away from the dreary, homeless world. Joseph felt all that the action expressed, and answered in an unsteady voice:—

"And yet—with a nature like yours—you must surely find them."

She shook her head sadly, and answered: "Ah, a woman cannot seek. I never thought I should be able to say—to any human being—that I have sought, or waited for recognition. I do not know why I should say it now. I try to be myself—my true self—with all persons; but it seems impossible: my nature shrinks from some and is drawn towards others. Why is this? What is the mystery that surrounds us?"

"Do you believe," Joseph asked, "that two souls may be so united that they shall dare to surrender all knowledge of themselves to each other, as we do, helplessly, before God?"

"O," she murmured, "it is my dream! I thought I was alone in cherishing it! Can it ever be realized?"

Joseph's brain grew hot: the release he had invoked sprang to life and urged him forward. Words came to his lips, he knew not how.

"If it is my dream and yours,—if we both have come to the faith and the hope we find in no others, and which alone will satisfy our lives, is it not a sign that the dream is over and the reality has begun?"

She hid her face in her hands. "Do not tempt me with what I had given up, unless you can teach me to believe again?" she cried.

"I do not tempt you," he answered breathlessly. "I tempt myself. I believe."

She turned suddenly, laid a hand upon his shoulder, lifted her face and looked into his eyes with an expression of passionate eagerness and joy. All her attitude breathed of the pause of the wave that only seems to hesitate an instant before throwing itself upon the waiting strand. Joseph had no defence, knew of none, dreamed of none. The pale-brown eyes, now dark, deep, and almost tearful, drew him with irresistible force: the sense of his own shy reticent self was lost, dissolved in the strength of an instinct which possessed him body and soul,—which bent him nearer to the slight form, which stretched his arms to answer its appeal, and left him, after one dizzy moment, with Miss Blessing's head upon his breast.

"I should like to die now," she murmured: "I never can be so happy again."

"No, no," said he, bending over her; "live for me!"

She raised herself, and kissed him again and again, and this frank, almost childlike betrayal of her heart seemed to claim from Joseph the full surrender of his own. He returned her caresses with equal warmth, and the twilight deepened around them as they stood, still half-embracing.

"Can I make you happy, Joseph?"

"Julia, I am already happier than I ever thought it possible to be."

With a sudden impulse she drew away from him. "Joseph!" she whispered, "will you always bear in mind what a cold, selfish, worldly life mine has been? You do not know me; you cannot understand the school in which I have been taught. I tell you, now, that I have had to learn cunning and artifice and equivocation. I am dark beside a nature so pure and good as yours! If you must ever learn to hate me, begin now! Take back your love: I have lived so long without the love of a noble human heart, that I can live so to the end!"

She again covered her face with her hands, and her frame shrank, as if dreading a mortal blow. But Joseph caught her back to his breast, touched and even humiliated by such sharp self-accusation. Presently she looked up: her eyes were wet, and she said, with a pitiful smile:—

"I believe you do love me."

"And I will not give you up," said Joseph, "though you should be full of evil as I am, myself."

She laughed, and patted his cheek: all her frank, bright, winning manner returned at once. Then commenced those reciprocal expressions of bliss, which are so inexhaustibly fresh to lovers, so endlessly monotonous to everybody else; and Joseph, lost to time, place, and circumstance, would have prolonged them far into the night, but for Miss Julia's returning self-possession.

"I hear wheels," she warned; "the evening guests are coming, and they will expect you to receive them, Joseph. And your dear, good old aunt will be looking for me. O, the world, the world! We must give ourselves up to it, and be as if we had never found each other. I shall be wild unless you set me an example of self-control. Let me look at you once,—one full, precious, perfect look, to carry in my heart through the evening!"

Then they looked in each other's faces; and looking was not enough; and their lips, without the use of words, said the temporary farewell. While Joseph hurried across the bottom of the lawn, to meet the stream of approaching guests which filled the lane, Miss Julia, at the top of the garden, plucked amaranth leaves for a wreath which would look well upon her dark hair, and sang, in a voice loud enough to be heard from the portico:—

"Ever be happy, light as thou art,

Pride of the pirate's heart!"

Everybody who had been invited—and quite a number who had not been, availing themselves of the easy habits of country society—came to the Asten farm that evening. Joseph, as host, seemed at times a little confused and flurried, but his face bloomed, his blue eyes sparkled, and even his nearest acquaintances were astonished at the courage and cordiality with which he performed his duties. The presence of Mr. Chaffinch kept the gayety of the company within decorous bounds; perhaps the number of detached groups appeared to form too many separate circles, or atmospheres of talk, but they easily dissolved, or gave to and took from each other. Rachel Miller was not inclined to act the part of a moral detective in the house which she managed; she saw nothing which the strictest sense of propriety could condemn.

Early in the evening, Joseph met Lucy Henderson in the hall. He could not see the graver change in her face; he only noticed that her manner was not so quietly attractive as usual. Yet on meeting her eyes he felt the absurd blood rushing to his cheeks and brow, and his tongue hesitated and stammered. This want of self-possession vexed him; he could not account for it; and he cut short the interview by moving abruptly away.

Lucy half turned, and looked after him, with an expression rather of surprise than of pain. As she did so she felt that there was an eye upon her, and by a strong effort entered the room without encountering the face of Elwood Withers.

When the company broke up, Miss Blessing, who was obliged to leave with the Warriners, found an opportunity to whisper to Joseph: "Come soon!" There was a long, fervent clasp of hands under her shawl, and then the carriage drove away. He could not see how the hand was transferred to that of Anna Warriner, which received from it a squeeze conveying an entire narrative to that young lady's mind.

Joseph's duties to his many guests prevented him from seeing much of Elwood during the evening; but, when the last were preparing to leave, he turned to the latter, conscious of a tenderer feeling of friendship than he had ever before felt, and begged him to stay for the night. Elwood held up the lantern, with which he had been examining the harness of a carriage that had just rolled away, and let its light fall upon Joseph's face.

"Do you really mean it?" he then asked.

"I don't understand you, Elwood."

"Perhaps I don't understand myself." But the next moment he laughed, and then added, in his usual tone: "Never mind; I'll stay."

They occupied the same room; and neither seemed inclined to sleep.

After the company had been discussed, in a way which both felt to be awkward and mechanical, Elwood said: "Do you know anything more about love, by this time?"

Joseph was silent, debating with himself whether he should confide the wonderful secret. Elwood suddenly rose up in his bed, leaned forward, and whispered: "I see,—you need not answer. But tell me this one thing: is it Lucy Henderson?"

"No; O, no!"

"Does she know of it? Your face told some sort of a tale when you met her to-night."

"Not to her,—surely not to her!" Joseph exclaimed.

"I hope not," Elwood quietly said: "I love her."

With a bound Joseph crossed the room and sat down on the edge of his friend's bed. "Elwood!" he cried; "and you are happy, too! O, now I can tell you all,—it is Julia Blessing!"

"Ha! ha!" Elwood laughed,—a short, bitter laugh, which seemed to signify anything but happiness. "Forgive me, Joseph!" he presently added, "but there's a deal of difference between a mitten and a ring. You will have one and I have the other. I did think for a little while that you stood between Lucy and me; but I suppose disappointment makes men fools."

Something in Joseph's breast seemed to stop the warm flood of his feelings. He could only stammer, after a long pause: "But I am not in your way."

"So I see,—and perhaps nobody is, except myself. We won't talk of this any more; there's many a roundabout road that comes out into the straight one at last. But you,—I can't understand the thing at all. How did she—did you come to love her?"

"I don't know; I hardly guessed it until this evening."

"Then, Joseph, go slowly, and feel your way. I'm not the one to advise, after what has happened to me; but maybe I know a little more of womankind than you. It's best to have a longer acquaintance than yours has been; a fellow can't always tell a sudden fancy from a love that has the grip of death."

"Now I might turn your own words against you, Elwood, for you tried to tell me what love is."

"I did; and before I knew the half. But come, Joseph: promise me that you won't let Miss Blessing know how much you feel until—"

"Elwood," Joseph breathlessly interrupted, "she knows it now! We were together this evening."

Elwood fell back on the pillow with a groan. "I'm a poor friend to you," he said: "I want to wish you joy, but I can't,—not to-night. The way things are fixed in this world stumps me, out and out. Nothing fits as it ought, and if I didn't take my head in my own hands and hold it towards the light by main force, I'd only see blackness, and death, and hell."

Joseph stole back to his bed, and lay there silently. There was a subtle chill in the heart of his happiness, which all the remembered glow of that tender scene in the garden could not thaw.

768

CHAPTER VII. THE BLESSING FAMILY.

Joseph's secret was not suspected by any of the company. Elwood's manner towards him next morning was warmer and kinder than ever; the chill of the past night had been forgotten, and the betrothal, which then almost seemed like a fetter upon his future, now gave him a sense of freedom and strength. He would have gone to Warriner's at once, but for the fear lest he should betray himself. Miss Blessing was to return to the city in three days more, and a single farewell call might be made with propriety; so he controlled his impatience and allowed another day to intervene.

When, at last, the hour of meeting came, Anna Warriner proved herself an efficient ally. Circumstances were against her, yet she secured the lovers a few minutes in which they could hold each other's hands, and repeat their mutual delight, with an exquisite sense of liberty in doing so. Miss Blessing suggested that nothing should be said until she had acquainted her parents with the engagement; there might be some natural difficulties to overcome; it was so unexpected, and the idea of losing her would possibly be unwelcome, at first. She would write in a few days, and then Joseph must come and make the acquaintance of her family.

"Then," she added, "I shall have no fear. When they have once seen you all difficulties will vanish. There will be no trouble with ma and sister Clementina; but pa is sometimes a little peculiar, on account of his connections. There! don't look so serious, all at once; it is my duty, you know, to secure you a loving reception. You must try to feel already that you have two homes, as I do."

Joseph waited very anxiously for the promised letter, and in ten days it came; it was brief, but satisfactory. "Would you believe it, dear Joseph," she commenced, "pa makes no difficulty! he only requires some assurances which you can very easily furnish. Ma, on the other hand, don't like the idea of giving me up. I can hardly say it without seeming to praise myself; but Clementina never took very kindly to housekeeping and managing, and even if I were only indifferent in those branches, I should be missed. It really went to my heart when ma met me at the door, and cried out, 'Now I shall have a little rest!' You may imagine how hard it was to tell her. But she is a dear, good mother, and I know she will be so happy to find a son in you—as she certainly will. Come, soon,—soon! They are all anxious to know you."

The city was not so distant as to make a trip thither an unusual event for the young farmers of the neighborhood. Joseph had frequently gone there for a day in the interest of his sales of stock and grain, and he found no difficulty in inventing a plausible reason for the journey. The train at the nearest railway station transported him in two or three hours to the commencement of the miles of hot, dusty, rattling pavements, and left him free to seek for the brick nest within which his love was sheltered.

Yet now, so near the point whence his new life was to commence, a singular unrest took possession of him. He distinctly felt the presence of two forces, acting against each other with nearly equal power, but without neutralizing their disturbing influence. He was developing faster than he guessed, yet, to a nature like his, the last knowledge that comes is the knowledge of self. Some occult instinct already whispered that his life thenceforth would be stronger, more independent, but also more disturbed; and this was what he had believed was wanting. If the consciousness of loving and being loved were not quite the same in experience as it had seemed to his ignorant fancy, it was yet a positive happiness, and wedlock would therefore be its unbroken continuance. Julia had prepared for his introduction into her family; he must learn to accept her parents and sister as his own; and now the hour and the opportunity were at hand.

What was it, then, that struck upon his breast almost like a physical pressure, and mysteriously resisted his errand? When he reached the cross-street, in which, many squares to the northward, the house was to be found, he halted for some minutes, and then, instead of turning, kept directly onward toward the river. The sight of the water, the gliding sails, the lusty life and labor along the piers, suddenly refreshed him. Men were tramping up and down the gangways of the clipper-ships; derricks were slowly swinging over the sides the bales and boxes which had been brought up from the holds; drays were clattering to and fro: wherever he turned he saw a picture of strength, courage, reality, solid work. The men that went and came took life simply as a succession of facts, and if these did not fit smoothly into each other, they either gave themselves no trouble about the rough edges, or drove them out of sight with a few sturdy blows. What Lucy Henderson had said about going to school was recalled to Joseph's mind. Here was a class where he would be apt to stand at the foot for many days. Would any of those strapping forms comprehend the disturbance of his mind?—they would probably advise him to go to the nearest apothecary-shop and purchase a few blue-pills. The longer he watched them, the more he felt the contagion of their unimaginative, face to face grapple with life; the manly element in him, checked so long, began to push a vigorous shoot towards the light.

"It is only the old cowardice, after all," he thought. "I am still shrinking from the encounter with new faces! A lover, soon to be a husband, and still so much of a green youth! It will never do. I must learn to handle my duty as that stevedore handles a barrel,—take hold with both hands, push and trundle and guide, till the weight becomes a mere plaything. There!—he starts a fresh one,—now for mine!"

Therewith he turned about, walked sternly back to the cross-street, and entered it without pausing at the corner. It was still a long walk; and the street, with its uniform brick houses, with white shutters, green interior blinds, and white marble steps, grew more silent and monotonous. There was a mixed odor of salt-fish, molasses, and decaying oranges at every corner; dark wenches lowered the nozzles of their jetting hose as he passed, and girls in draggled calico frocks turned to look at him from the entrances of gloomy tunnels leading into the back yards. A man with something in a cart uttered from time to time a piercing unintelligible cry; barefooted youngsters swore over their marbles on the sidewalk; and, at rare intervals, a marvellous moving fabric of silks and colors and glosses floated past him. But he paused for none of these. His heart beat faster, and the strange resistance seemed to increase with the increasing numbers of houses, now rapidly approaching The One— then it came!

There was an entire block of narrow three-storied dwellings, with crowded windows and flat roofs. If Joseph had been familiar with the city, he would have recognized the air of cheap gentility which exhaled from them, and which said, as plainly as if the words had been painted on their fronts, "Here we keep up appearances on a very small capital." He noticed nothing, however, except the marble steps and the front doors, all of which were alike to him until he came upon a brass plate inscribed "B. Blessing." As he looked up a mass of dark curls vanished with a start from the window. The door suddenly opened before he could touch the bell-pull, and two hands upon his own drew him into the diminutive hall.

The door instantly closed again, but softly: then two arms were flung around his neck, and his willing lips received a subdued kiss. "Hush!" she said; "it is delightful that you have arrived, though we didn't expect you so immediately. Come into the drawing-room, and let us have a minute together before I call ma."

She tripped lightly before him, and they were presently seated side by side, on the sofa.

"What could have brought me to the window just at that moment?" she whispered; "it must have been presentiment."

Joseph's face brightened with pleasure. "And I was long on the way," he answered. "What will you think of me, Julia? I was a little afraid."

"I know you were, Joseph," she said. "It is only the cold, insensible hearts that are never agitated."

Their eyes met, and he remarked, for the first time, their peculiar pale-brown, almost tawny clearness. The next instant her long lashes slowly fell and half concealed them; she drew away slightly from him, and said: "I should like to be beautiful, for your sake; I never cared about it before."

Without giving him time to reply, she rose and moved towards the door, then looked back, smiled, and disappeared.

Joseph, left alone, also rose and walked softly up and down the room. To his eyes it seemed an elegant, if rather chilly apartment. It was long and narrow, with a small, delusive fireplace of white marble (intended only for hot air) in the middle, a carpet of many glaring colors on the floor, and a paper brilliant with lilac-bunches on the walls. There was a centre-table, with some lukewarm literature cooling itself on the marble top; an étagère, with a few nondescript cups and flagons, and a cottage piano, on which lay several sheets of music by Verdi and Balfe. The furniture, not very abundant, was swathed in a nankeen summer dress. There were two pictures on the walls, portraits of a gentleman and lady, and when once Joseph had caught the fixed stare of their lustreless eyes, he found it difficult to turn away. The imperfect light which came through the bowed window-shutters revealed a florid, puffy-faced young man, whose head was held up by a high black satin stock. He was leaning against a fluted pillar, apparently constructed of putty, behind which fell a superb crimson curtain, lifted up at one corner to disclose a patch of stormy sky. The long locks, tucked in at the temples, the carefully-delineated whiskers, and the huge signet-ring on the second finger of the one exposed hand, indicated that a certain "position" in society was either possessed or claimed of right by the painted person. Joseph could hardly doubt that this was a representation of "B. Blessing," as he appeared twenty or thirty years before.

He turned to the other picture. The lady was slender, and meant to be graceful, her head being inclined so that the curls on the left side rolled in studied disorder upon her shoulder. Her face was thin and long, with well-marked and not unpleasant features. There was rather too positive a bloom upon her cheeks, and the fixed smile on the narrow mouth scarcely harmonized with the hard, serious stare of the eyes. She was royally attired in purple, and her bare white arm—much more plumply rounded than her face would have given reason to suspect—hung with a listless grace over the end of a sofa.

Joseph looked from one face to the other with a curious interest, which the painted eyes seemed also to reflect, as they followed him. They were strangers, out of a different sphere of life, yet they must become, nay, were already, a part of his own! The lady scrutinized him closely, in spite of her smile; but the indifference of the gentleman, blandly satisfied with himself, seemed less assuring to his prospects.

Footsteps in the hall interrupted his revery, and he had barely time to slip into his seat when the door opened and Julia entered, followed by the original of one of the portraits. He recognized her, although the curls had disappeared, the dark hair was sprinkled with gray, and deep lines about the mouth and eyes gave them an expression of care and discontent. In one respect she differed from her daughter: her eyes were gray.

She bent her head with a stately air as Joseph rose, walked past Julia, and extended her hand, with the words,—

"Mr. Asten, I am glad to see you. Pray be seated."

When all had taken seats, she resumed: "Excuse me if I begin by asking a question. You must consider that I have only known you through Julia, and her description could not, under the circumstances, be very clear. What is your age?"

"I shall be twenty-three next birthday," Joseph replied.

"Indeed! I am happy to hear it. You do not look more than nineteen. I have reason to dread very youthful attachments, and am therefore reassured to know that you are fully a man and competent to test your feelings. I trust that you have so tested them. Again I say, excuse me if the question seems to imply a want of confidence. A mother's anxiety, you know—"

Julia clasped her hands and bent down her head.

"I am quite sure of myself," Joseph said, "and would try to make you as sure, if I knew how to do it."

"If you were one of us,—of the city, I mean,—I should be able to judge more promptly. It is many years since I have been outside of our own select circle, and I am therefore not so competent as once to judge of men in general. While I will never, without the most sufficient reason, influence my daughters in their choice, it is my duty to tell you that Julia is exceedingly susceptible on the side of her affections. A wound there would be incurable to her. We are alike in that; I know her nature through my own."

774

Julia hid her face upon her mother's shoulder: Joseph was moved, and vainly racked his brain for some form of assurance which might remove the maternal anxiety.

"There," said Mrs. Blessing; "we will say no more about it now. Go and bring your sister!"

"There are some other points, Mr. Asten," she continued, "which have no doubt already occurred to your mind. Mr. Blessing will consult with you in relation to them. I make it a rule never to trespass upon his field of duty. As you were not positively expected to-day, he went to the Custom-House as usual; but it will soon be time for him to return. Official labors, you understand, cannot be postponed. If you have ever served in a government capacity, you will appreciate his position. I have sometimes wished that we had not become identified with political life; but, on the other hand, there are compensations."

Joseph, impressed more by Mrs. Blessing's important manner than the words she uttered, could only say, "I beg that my visit may not interfere in any way with Mr. Blessing's duties."

"Unfortunately," she replied, "they cannot be postponed. His advice is more required by the Collector than his special official services. But, as I said, he will confer with you in regard to the future of our little girl. I call her so, Mr. Asten, because she is the youngest, and I can hardly yet realize that she is old enough to leave me. Yes: the youngest, and the first to go. Had it been Clementina, I should have been better prepared for the change. But a mother should always be ready to sacrifice herself, where the happiness of a child is at stake."

Mrs. Blessing gently pressed a small handkerchief to the corner of each eye, then heaved a sigh, and resumed her usual calm dignity of manner. The door opened, and Julia re-entered, followed by her sister.

"This is Miss Blessing," said the mother.

The young lady bowed very formally, and therewith would have finished her greeting, but Joseph had already risen and extended his hand.

775

She thereupon gave him the tips of four limp fingers, which he attempted to grasp and then let go.

Clementina was nearly a head taller than her sister, and amply proportioned. She had a small, petulant mouth, small gray eyes, a low, narrow forehead, and light brown hair. Her eyelids and cheeks had the same puffy character as her father's, in his portrait on the wall; yet there was a bloom and brilliancy about her complexion which suggested beauty. A faint expression of curiosity passed over her face, on meeting Joseph, but she uttered no word of welcome. He looked at Julia, whose manner was suddenly subdued, and was quick enough to perceive a rivalry between the sisters. The stolidity of Clementina's countenance indicated that indifference which is more offensive than enmity. He disliked her from the first moment.

Julia kept modestly silent, and the conversation, in spite of her mother's capacity to carry it on, did not flourish. Clementina spoke only in monosyllables, which she let fall from time to time with a silver sweetness which startled Joseph, it seemed so at variance with her face and manner. He felt very much relieved when, after more than one significant glance had been exchanged with her mother, the two arose and left the room. At the door Mrs. Blessing said: "Of course you will stay and take a family tea with us, Mr. Asten. I will order it to be earlier served, as you are probably not accustomed to our city hours."

Julia looked up brightly after the door had closed, and exclaimed: "Now! when ma says that, you may be satisfied. Her housekeeping is like the laws of the Medes and Persians. She probably seemed rather formal to you, and it is true that a certain amount of form has become natural to her; but it always gives way when she is strongly moved. Pa is to come yet, but I am sure you will get on very well with him; men always grow acquainted in a little while. I'm afraid that Clementina did not impress you very—very genially; she is, I may confess it to you, a little peculiar."

"She is very quiet," said Joseph, "and very unlike you."

"Every one notices that. And we seem to be unlike in character, as much so as if there were no relationship between us. But I must say for Clementina,

776

that she is above personal likings and dislikings; she looks at people abstractly. You are only a future brother-in-law to her, and I don't believe she can tell whether your hair is black or the beautiful golden brown that it is."

Joseph smiled, not ill-pleased with Julia's delicate flattery. "I am all the more delighted," he said, "that you are different. I should not like you, Julia, to consider me an abstraction."

"You are very real, Joseph, and very individual," she answered, with one of her loveliest smiles.

Not ten minutes afterwards, Julia, whose eyes and ears were keenly on the alert, notwithstanding her gay, unrestrained talk, heard the click of a latch-key. She sprang up, laid her forefinger on her lips, gave Joseph a swift, significant glance, and darted into the hall. A sound of whispering followed, and there was no mistaking the deep, hoarse murmur of one of the voices.

Mr. Blessing, without the fluted pillar and the crimson curtain, was less formidable than Joseph had anticipated. The years had added to his body and taken away from his hair; yet his face, since high stocks were no longer in fashion, had lost its rigid lift, and expressed the chronic cordiality of a popular politician. There was a redness about the rims of his eyes, and a fulness of the under lid, which also denoted political habits. However, despite wrinkles, redness, and a general roughening and coarsening of the features, the resemblance to the portrait was still strong; and Joseph, feeling as if the presentation had already been made, offered his hand as soon as Mr. Blessing entered the room.

"Very happy to see you, Mr. Asten," said the latter. "An unexpected pleasure, sir."

He removed the glove from his left hand, pulled down his coat and vest, felt the tie of his cravat, twitched at his pantaloons, ran his fingers through his straggling gray locks, and then threw himself into a chair, exclaiming: "After business, pleasure, sir! My duties are over for the day. Mrs. Blessing probably informed you of my official capacity; but you can have no conception of the vigilance required to prevent evasion of the revenue laws. We are the country's watch-dogs, sir."

"I can understand," Joseph said, "that an official position carries with it much responsibility."

"Quite right, sir, and without adequate remuneration. Figuratively speaking, we handle millions, and we are paid by dimes. Were it not for the consciousness of serving and saving for the nation—but I will not pursue the subject. When we have become better acquainted, you can judge for yourself whether preferment always follows capacity. Our present business is to establish a mutual understanding,—as we say in politics, to prepare a platform,—and I think you will agree with me that the circumstances of the case require frank dealing, as between man and man."

"Certainly!" Joseph answered; "I only ask that, although I am a stranger to you, you will accept my word until you have the means of verifying it."

"I may safely do that with you, sir. My associations—duties, I may say—compel me to know many persons with whom it would not be safe. We will forget the disparity of age and experience between us. I can hardly ask you to imagine yourself placed in my situation, but perhaps we can make the case quite as clear if I state to you, without reserve, what I should be ready to do, if our present positions were reversed: Julia, will you look after the tea?"

"Yes, pa," said she, and slipped out of the drawing-room.

"If I were a young man from the country, and had won the affections of a young lady of—well, I may say it to you—of an old family, whose parents were ignorant of my descent, means, and future prospects in life, I should consider it my first duty to enlighten those parents upon all these points. I should reflect that the lady must be removed from their sphere to mine; that, while the attachment was, in itself, vitally important to her and to me, those parents would naturally desire to compare the two spheres, and assure themselves that their daughter would lose no material advantages by the transfer. You catch my meaning?"

"I came here," said Joseph, "with the single intention of satisfying you— at least, I came hoping that I shall be able to do so—in regard to myself. It

778

will be easy for you to test my statements."

"Very well. We will begin, then, with the subject of Family. Understand me, I mention this solely because, in our old communities, Family is the stamp of Character. An established name represents personal qualities, virtues. It is indifferent to me whether my original ancestor was a De Belsain (though beauty and health have always been family characteristics); but it is important that he transmitted certain traits which—which others, perhaps, can better describe. The name of Asten is not usual; it has, in fact, rather a distinguished sound; but I am not acquainted with its derivation."

Joseph restrained a temptation to smile, and replied: "My great-grandfather came from England more than a hundred years ago: that is all I positively know. I have heard it said that the family was originally Danish."

"You must look into the matter, sir: a good pedigree is a bond for good behavior. The Danes, I have been told, were of the same blood as the Normans. But we will let that pass. Julia informs me you are the owner of a handsome farm, yet I am so ignorant of values in the country,—and my official duties oblige me to measure property by such a different standard,—that, really, unless you could make the farm evident to me in figures, I—"

He paused, but Joseph was quite ready with the desired intelligence. "I have two hundred acres," he said, "and a moderate valuation of the place would be a hundred and thirty dollars an acre. There is a mortgage of five thousand dollars on the place, the term of which has not yet expired; but I have nearly an equal amount invested, so that the farm fairly represents what I own."

"H'm," mused Mr. Blessing, thrusting his thumbs into the arm-holes of his waistcoat, "that is not a great deal here in the city, but I dare say it is a handsome competence in the country. It doubtless represents a certain annual income!"

"It is a very comfortable home, in the first place," said Joseph; "the farm ought to yield, after supplying nearly all the wants of a family, an annual return of a thousand to fifteen hundred dollars, according to the season."

779

"Twenty-six thousand dollars!—and five per cent!" Mr. Blessing exclaimed. "If you had the farm in money, and knew how to operate with it, you might pocket ten—fifteen—twenty per cent. Many a man, with less than that to set him afloat, has become a millionnaire in five years' time. But it takes pluck and experience, sir!"

"More of both than I can lay claim to," Joseph remarked; "but what there is of my income is certain. If Julia were not so fond of the country, and already so familiar with our ways, I might hesitate to offer her such a plain, quiet home, but—"

"O, I know!" Mr. Blessing interrupted. "We have heard of nothing but cows and spring-houses and willow-trees since she came back. I hope, for your sake, it may last; for I see that you are determined to suit each other. I have no inclination to act the obdurate parent. You have met me like a man, sir: here's my hand; I feel sure that, as my son-in-law, you will keep up the reputation of the family!"

CHAPTER VIII. A CONSULTATION.

The family tea was served in a small dining-room in the rear. Mr. Blessing, who had become more and more cordial with Joseph after formally accepting him, led the way thither, and managed to convey a rapid signal to his wife before the family took their seats at the table. Joseph was the only one who did not perceive the silent communication of intelligence; but its consequences were such as to make him speedily feel at ease in the Blessing mansion. Even Clementina relented sufficiently to say, in her most silvery tones, "May I offer you the butter, Mr. Asten?"

The table, it is true, was very unlike the substantial suppers of the country. There was a variety of diminutive dishes, containing slices so delicate that they mocked rather than excited the appetite; yet Julia, (of course it was she!) had managed to give the repast an air of elegance which was at least agreeable to a kindred sense. Joseph took the little cup, the thin tea, the five drops of milk, and the fragment of sugar, without asking himself whether the beverage were palatable: he divided a leaf-like piece of flesh and consumed several wafers of bread, blissfully unconscious whether his stomach were satisfied. He felt that he had been received into The Family. Mr. Blessing was magnificently bland, Mrs. Blessing was maternally interested, Clementina recognized his existence, and Julia,—he needed but one look at her sparkling eyes, her softly flushed cheeks, her bewitching excitement of manner, to guess the relief of her heart. He forgot the vague distress which had preceded his coming, and the embarrassment of his first reception, in the knowledge that Julia was so happy, and through the acquiescence of her parents, in his love.

It was settled that he should pass the night there. Mrs. Blessing would take no denial; he must now consider their house as his home. She would also call him "Joseph," but not now,—not until she was entitled to name him "son." It had come suddenly upon her, but it was her duty to be glad, and in a little while she would become accustomed to the change.

All this was so simply and cordially said, that Joseph quite warmed to the stately woman, and unconsciously decided to accept his fortune, whatever features it might wear. Until the one important event, at least; after that it would be in his own hands—and Julia's.

After tea, two or three hours passed away rather slowly. Mr. Blessing sat in the pit of a back yard and smoked until dusk; then the family collected in the "drawing-room," and there was a little music, and a variety of gossip, with occasional pauses of silence, until Mrs. Blessing said: "Perhaps you had better show Mr. Asten to his room, Mr. Blessing. We may have already passed over his accustomed hour for retiring. If so, I know he will excuse us; we shall soon become familiar with each other's habits."

When Mr. Blessing returned, he first opened the rear window, drew an arm-chair near it, took off his coat, seated himself, and lit another cigar. His wife closed the front shutters, slipped the night-bolts of the door, and then seated herself beside him. Julia whirled around on her music-stool to face the coming consultation, and Clementina gracefully posed herself in the nearest corner of the sofa.

"How do you like him, Eliza?" Mr. Blessing asked, after several silent, luxurious whiffs.

"He is handsome, and seems amiable, but younger than I expected. Are you sure of his—his feelings, Julia?"

"O ma!" Julia exclaimed; "what a question! I can only judge them by my own."

Clementina curled her lip in a singular fashion, but said nothing.

"It seems like losing Julia entirely," Mrs. Blessing resumed. "I don't know how she will be able to retain her place in our circle, unless they spend a part of the winter in the city, and whether he has means enough—"

She paused, and looked inquisitively at her husband.

"You always look at the establishment," said he, "and never consider the chances. Marriage is a deal, a throw, a sort of kite-flying, in fact (except in our case, my dear), and, after all I've learned of our future son-in-law, I must say

782

that Julia hasn't a bad hand."

"I knew you'd like him, pa!" cried the delighted Julia.

Mr. Blessing looked at her steadily a moment, and then winked; but she took no notice of it.

"There is another thing," said his wife. "If the wedding comes off this fall, we have but two months to prepare; and how will you manage about the—the money? We can save afterwards, to be sure, but there will be an immediate and fearful expense. I've thought, perhaps, that a simple and private ceremony,—married in travelling-dress, you know, just before the train leaves, and no cards,—it is sometimes done in the highest circles."

"It won't do!" exclaimed Mr. Blessing, waving his right hand. "Julia's husband must have an opportunity of learning our standing in society. I will invite the Collector, and the Surveyor, and the Appraiser. The money must be raised. I should be willing to pawn—"

He looked around the room, inspecting the well-worn carpet, the nankeen-covered chairs, the old piano, and finally the two pictures.

"—Your portrait, my dear; but, unless it were a Stuart, I couldn't get ten dollars on it. We must take your set of diamonds, and Julia's rubies, and Clementina's pearls."

He leaned back, and laughed with great glee. The ladies became rigid and grave.

"It is wicked, Benjamin," Mrs. Blessing severely remarked, "to jest over our troubles at such a time as this. I see nothing else to do, but to inform Mr. Asten, frankly, of our condition. He is yet too young, I think, to be repelled by poverty."

"Ma, it would break my heart," said Julia. "I could not bear to be humiliated in his eyes."

"Decidedly the best thing to do," warbled Clementina, speaking for the first time.

"That's the way with women,—flying from one extreme to the other. If you can't have white, you turn around and say there's no other color than black. When all devices are exhausted, a man of pluck and character goes to work and constructs a new one. Upon my soul, I don't know where the money is to come from; but give me ten days, and Julia shall have her white satin. Now, girls, you had better go to bed."

Mr. Blessing smoked silently until the sound of his daughters' footsteps had ceased on the stairs; then, bringing down his hand emphatically upon his thigh, he exclaimed, "By Jove, Eliza, if I were as sharp as that girl, I'd have had the Collectorship before this!"

"What do you mean? She seems to be strongly attached to him."

"O, no doubt! But she has a wonderful talent for reading character. The young fellow is pretty green wood still; what he'll season into depends on her. Honest as the day,—there's nothing like a country life for that. But it's a pity that such a fund for operations should lie idle; he has a nest-egg that might hatch out millions!"

"I hope, Benjamin, that after all your unfortunate experience—"

"Pray don't lament in advance, and especially now, when a bit of luck comes to us. Julia has done well, and I'll trust her to improve her opportunities. Besides, this will help Clementina's chances; where there is one marriage in a family, there is generally another. Poor girl! she has waited a long while. At thirty-three, the market gets v-e-r-y flat."

"And yet Julia is thirty," said Mrs. Blessing; "and Clementina's complexion and manners have been considered superior."

"There's just her mistake. A better copy of Mrs. Halibut's airs and attitudes was never produced, and it was all very well so long as Mrs. Halibut gave the tone to society; but since she went to Europe, and Mrs. Bass has somehow crept into her place, Clementina is quite—I may say—obsolete. I don't object to her complexion, because that is a standing fashion, but she is expected to be chatty, and witty, and instead of that she stands about like a Venus of Milo. She looks like me, and she can't lack intelligence and tact.

Why couldn't she unbend a little more to Asten, whether she likes him or not?"

"You know I never seemed to manage Clementina," his wife replied; "if she were to dispute my opinion sometimes, I might, perhaps, gain a little influence over her: but she won't enter into a discussion."

"Mrs. Halibut's way. It was new, then, and, with her husband's money to back it, her 'grace' and 'composure' and 'serenity' carried all before her. Give me fifty thousand a year, and I'll put Clementina in the same place! But, come,—to the main question. I suppose we shall need five hundred dollars!"

"Three hundred, I think, will be ample," said Mrs. Blessing.

"Three or five, it's as hard to raise one sum as the other. I'll try for five, and if I have luck with the two hundred over—small, careful operations, you know, which always succeed—I may have the whole amount on hand, long before it's due."

Mrs. Blessing smiled in a melancholy, hopeless way, and the consultation came to an end.

When Joseph was left alone in his chamber, he felt no inclination to sleep. He sat at the open window, and looked down into the dim, melancholy street, the solitude of which was broken about once every quarter of an hour by a forlorn pedestrian, who approached through gloom and lamplight, was foreshortened to his hat, and then lengthened away on the other side. The new acquaintances he had just made remained all the more vividly in his thoughts from their nearness; he was still within their atmosphere. They were unlike any persons he knew, and therefore he felt that he might do them injustice by a hasty estimate of their character. Clementina, however, was excluded from this charitable resolution. Concentrating his dislike on her, he found that her parents had received him with as much consideration as a total stranger could expect. Moreover, whatever they might be, Julia was the same here, in her own home, as when she was a guest in the country. As playful, as winning, and as natural; and he began to suspect that her present life was not congenial to such a nature. If so, her happiness was all the more assured by their union.

This thought led him into a pictured labyrinth of anticipation, in which his mind wandered with delight. He was so absorbed in planning the new household, that he did not hear the sisters entering the rear room on the same floor, which was only separated by a thin partition from his own.

"White satin!" he suddenly heard Clementina say: "of course I shall have the same. It will become me better than you."

"I should think you might be satisfied with a light silk," Julia said; "the expenses will be very heavy."

"We'll see," Clementina answered shortly, pacing up and down the room.

After a long pause, he heard Julia's voice again. "Never mind," she said, "I shall soon be out of your way."

"I wonder how much he knows about you!" Clementina exclaimed. "Your arts were new there, and you played an easy game." Here she lowered her voice, and Joseph only distinguished a detached word now and then. He rose, indignant at this unsisterly assault, and wishing to hear no more; but it seemed that the movement was not noticed, for Julia replied, in smothered, excited tones, with some remark about "complexion."

"Well, there is one thing," Clementina continued,—"one thing you will keep very secret, and that is your birthday. Are you going to tell him that you are—"

Joseph had seized the back of a chair and with a sudden impulse tilted it and let it fall on the floor. Then he walked to the window, closed it, and prepared to go to rest,—all with more noise than was habitual with him. There were whispers and hushed movements in the next room, but not another audible word was spoken. Before sleeping he came to the conclusion that he was more than Julia's lover: he was her deliverer. The idea was not unwelcome: it gave a new value and significance to his life.

However curious Julia might have been to discover how much he had overheard, she made no effort to ascertain the fact. She met him next morning with a sweet unconsciousness of what she had endured, which convinced him that such painful scenes must have been frequent, or she could not have forgotten so easily. His greeting to Clementina was brief and cold, but she did not seem to notice it in the least.

It was decided, before he left, that the wedding should take place in October.

CHAPTER IX. JOSEPH AND HIS FRIEND.

The train moved slowly along through the straggling and shabby suburbs, increasing its speed as the city melted gradually into the country; and Joseph, after a vain attempt to fix his mind upon one of the volumes he had procured for his slender library at home, leaned back in his seat and took note of his fellow-travellers. Since he began to approach the usual destiny of men, they had a new interest for him. Hitherto he had looked upon strange faces very much as on a strange language, without a thought of interpreting them; but now their hieroglyphics seemed to suggest a meaning. The figures around him were so many sitting, silent histories, so many locked-up records of struggle, loss, gain, and all the other forces which give shape and color to human life. Most of them were strangers to each other, and as reticent (in their railway conventionality) as himself; yet, he reflected, the whole range of passion, pleasure, and suffering was probably illustrated in that collection of existences. His own troublesome individuality grew fainter, so much of it seemed to be merged in the common experience of men.

There was the portly gentleman of fifty, still ruddy and full of unwasted force. The keenness and coolness of his eyes, the few firmly marked lines on his face, and the color and hardness of his lips, proclaimed to everybody: "I am bold, shrewd, successful in business, scrupulous in the performance of my religious duties (on the Sabbath), voting with my party, and not likely to be fooled by any kind of sentimental nonsense." The thin, not very well-dressed man beside him, with the irregular features and uncertain expression, announced as clearly, to any who could read: "I am weak, like others, but I never consciously did any harm. I just manage to get along in the world, but if I only had a chance, I might make something better of myself." The fresh, healthy fellow, in whose lap a child was sleeping, while his wife nursed a younger one,—the man with ample mouth, large nostrils, and the hands of a mechanic,—also told his story: "On the whole, I find life a comfortable thing. I don't know much about it, but I take it as it comes, and never worry over what I can't understand."

The faces of the younger men, however, were not so easy to decipher. On them life was only beginning its plastic task, and it required an older eye to detect the delicate touches of awakening passions and hopes. But Joseph consoled himself with the thought that his own secret was as little to be discovered as any they might have. If they were still ignorant, of the sweet experience of love, he was already their superior; if they were sharers in it, though strangers, they were near to him. Had he not left the foot of the class, after all?

All at once his eye was attracted by a new face, three or four seats from his own. The stranger had shifted his position, so that he was no longer seen in profile. He was apparently a few years older than Joseph, but still bright with all the charm of early manhood. His fair complexion was bronzed from exposure, and his hands, graceful without being effeminate, were not those of the idle gentleman. His hair, golden in tint, thrust its short locks as it pleased about a smooth, frank forehead; the eyes were dark gray, and the mouth, partly hidden by a mustache, at once firm and full. He was moderately handsome, yet it was not of that which Joseph thought; he felt that there was more of developed character and a richer past history expressed in those features than in any other face there. He felt sure—and smiled at himself, notwithstanding, for the impression—that at least some of his own doubts and difficulties had found their solution in the stranger's nature. The more he studied the face, the more he was conscious of its attraction, and his instinct of reliance, though utterly without grounds, justified itself to his mind in some mysterious way.

It was not long before the unknown felt his gaze, and, turning slowly in his seat, answered it. Joseph dropped his eyes in some confusion, but not until he had caught the full, warm, intense expression of those that met them. He fancied that he read in them, in that momentary flash, what he had never before found in the eyes of strangers,—a simple, human interest, above curiosity and above mistrust. The usual reply to such a gaze is an unconscious defiance: the unknown nature is on its guard: but the look which seems to answer, "We are men, let us know each other!" is, alas! too rare in this world.

While Joseph was fighting the irresistible temptation to look again, there was a sudden thud of the car-wheels. Many of the passengers started from their seats, only to be thrown into them again by a quick succession of violent jolts. Joseph saw the stranger springing towards the bell-rope; then he and all others seemed to be whirling over each other; there was a crash, a horrible grinding and splintering sound, and the end of all was a shock, in which his consciousness left him before he could guess its violence.

After a while, out of some blank, haunted by a single lost, wandering sense of existence, he began to awaken slowly to life. Flames were still dancing in his eyeballs, and waters and whirlwinds roaring in his ears; but it was only a passive sensation, without the will to know more. Then he felt himself partly lifted and his head supported, and presently a soft warmth fell upon the region of his heart. There were noises all about him, but he did not listen to them; his effort to regain his consciousness fixed itself on that point alone, and grew stronger as the warmth calmed the confusion of his nerves.

"Dip this in water!" said a voice, and the hand (as he now knew it to be) was removed from his heart.

Something cold came over his forehead, and at the same time warm drops fell upon his cheek.

"Look out for yourself: your head is cut!" exclaimed another voice.

"Only a scratch. Take the handkerchief out of my pocket and tie it up; but first ask yon gentleman for his flask!"

Joseph opened his eyes, knew the face that bent over his, and then closed them again. Gentle and strong hands raised him, a flask was set to his lips, and he drank mechanically, but a full sense of life followed the draught. He looked wistfully in the stranger's face.

"Wait a moment," said the latter; "I must feel your bones before you try to move. Arms and legs all right,—impossible to tell about the ribs. There! now put your arm around my neck, and lean on me as much as you like, while I lift you."

Joseph did as he was bidden, but he was still weak and giddy, and after

790

a few steps, they both sat down together upon a bank. The splintered car lay near them upside down; the passengers had been extricated from it, and were now busy in aiding the few who were injured. The train had stopped and was waiting on the track above. Some were very pale and grave, feeling that Death had touched without taking them; but the greater part were concerned only about the delay to the train.

"How did it happen?" asked Joseph: "where was I? how did you find me?"

"The usual story,—a broken rail," said the stranger. "I had just caught the rope when the car went over, and was swung off my feet so luckily that I somehow escaped the hardest shock. I don't think I lost my senses for a moment. When we came to the bottom you were lying just before me; I thought you dead until I felt your heart. It is a severe shock, but I hope nothing more."

"But you,—are you not badly hurt?"

The stranger pushed up the handkerchief which was tied around his head, felt his temple, and said: "It must have been one of the splinters; I know nothing about it. But there is no harm in a little blood-letting except"—he added, smiling—"except the spots on your face."

By this time the other injured passengers had been conveyed to the train; the whistle sounded a warning of departure.

"I think we can get up the embankment now," said the stranger. "You must let me take care of you still: I am travelling alone."

When they were seated side by side, and Joseph leaned his head back on the supporting arm, while the train moved away with them, he felt that a new power, a new support, had come to his life. The face upon which he looked was no longer strange; the hand which had rested on his heart was warm with kindred blood. Involuntarily he extended his own; it was taken and held, and the dark gray, courageous eyes turned to him with a silent assurance which he felt needed no words.

"It is a rough introduction," he then said: "my name is Philip Held. I was on my way to Oakland Station; but if you are going farther—"

"Why, that is my station also!" Joseph exclaimed, giving his name in return.

"Then we should have probably met, sooner or later, in any case. I am bound for the forge and furnace at Coventry, which is for sale. If the company who employ me decide to buy it,—according to the report I shall make,—the works will be placed in my charge."

"It is but six miles from my farm," said Joseph, "and the road up the valley is the most beautiful in our neighborhood. I hope you can make a favorable report."

"It is only too much to my own interest to do so. I have been mining and geologizing in Nevada and the Rocky Mountains for three or four years, and long for a quiet, ordered life. It is a good omen that I have found a neighbor in advance of my settlement. I have often ridden fifty miles to meet a friend who cared for something else than horse-racing or monte; and your six miles,—it is but a step!"

"How much you have seen!" said Joseph. "I know very little of the world. It must be easy for you to take your own place in life."

A shade passed over Philip Held's face. "It is only easy to a certain class of men," he replied,—"a class to which I should not care to belong. I begin to think that nothing is very valuable, the light to which a man don't earn,—except human love, and that seems to come by the grace of God."

"I am younger than you are,—not yet twenty-three," Joseph remarked. "You will find that I am very ignorant."

"And I am twenty-eight, and just beginning to get my eyes open, like a nine-days' kitten. If I had been frank enough to confess my ignorance, five years ago, as you do now, it would have been better for me. But don't let us measure ourselves or our experience against each other. That is one good thing we learn in Rocky Mountain life; there is no high or low, knowledge or ignorance, except what applies to the needs of men who come together.

So there are needs which most men have, and go all their lives hungering for, because they expect them to be supplied in a particular form. There is something," Philip concluded, "deeper than that in human nature."

Joseph longed to open his heart to this man, every one of whose words struck home to something in himself. But the lassitude which the shock left behind gradually overcame him. He suffered his head to be drawn upon Philip Held's shoulder, and slept until the train reached Oakland Station. When the two got upon the platform, they found Dennis waiting for Joseph, with a light country vehicle. The news of the accident had reached the station, and his dismay was great when he saw the two bloody faces. A physician had already been summoned from the neighboring village, but they had little need of his services. A prescription of quiet and sedatives for Joseph, and a strip of plaster for his companion, were speedily furnished, and they set out together for the Asten place.

It is unnecessary to describe Rachel Miller's agitation when the party arrived; or the parting of the two men who had been so swiftly brought near to each other; or Philip Held's farther journey to the forge that evening. He resisted all entreaty to remain at the farm until morning, on the ground of an appointment made with the present proprietor of the forge. After his departure Joseph was sent to bed, where he remained for a day or two, very sore and a little feverish. He had plenty of time for thought,—not precisely of the kind which his aunt suspected, for out of pure, honest interest in his welfare, she took a step which proved to be of doubtful benefit. If he had not been so innocent,—if he had not been quite as unconscious of his inner nature as he was over-conscious of his external self,—he would have perceived that his thoughts dwelt much more on Philip Held than on Julia Blessing. His mind seemed to run through a swift, involuntary chain of reasoning, to account to himself for his feeling towards her, and her inevitable share in his future; but towards Philip his heart sprang with an instinct beyond his control. It was impossible to imagine that the latter also would not be shot, like a bright thread, through the web of his coming days.

On the third morning, when he had exchanged the bed for an arm-chair, a letter from the city was brought to him. "Dearest Joseph," it ran, "what a fright and anxiety we have had! When pa brought the paper home, last night, and I read the report of the accident, where it said, 'J. Asten, severe contusions,' my heart stopped beating for a minute, and I can only write now (as you see) with a trembling hand. My first thought was to go directly to you; but ma said we had better wait for intelligence. Unless our engagement were generally known, it would give rise to remarks,—in short, I need not repeat to you all the worldly reasons with which she opposed me; but, oh, how I longed for the right to be at your side, and assure myself that the dreadful, dreadful danger has passed! Pa was quite shaken with the news: he felt hardly able to go to the Custom-House this morning. But he sides with ma about my going, and now, when my time as a daughter with them is growing so short, I dare not disobey. I know you will understand my position, yet, dear and true as you are, you cannot guess the anxiety with which I await a line from your hand, the hand that was so nearly taken from me forever!"

Joseph read the letter twice and was about to commence it for the third time, when a visitor was announced. He had barely time to thrust the scented sheet into his pocket; and the bright eyes and flushed face with which he met the Rev. Mr. Chaffinch convinced both that gentleman and his aunt, as she ushered the latter into the room, that the visit was accepted as an honor and a joy.

On Mr. Chaffinch's face the air of authority which he had been led to believe belonged to his calling had not quite succeeded in impressing itself; but melancholy, the next best thing, was strongly marked. His dark complexion and his white cravat intensified each other; and his eyes, so long uplifted above the concerns of this world, had ceased to vary their expression materially for the sake of any human interest. All this had been expected of him, and he had simply done his best to meet the requirements of the flock over which he was placed. Any of the latter might have easily been shrewd enough to guess, in advance, very nearly what the pastor would say, upon a given occasion; but each and all of them would have been both disappointed and disturbed if he had not said it.

After appropriate and sympathetic inquiries concerning Joseph's bodily condition, he proceeded to probe him spiritually.

"It was a merciful preservation. I hope you feel that it is a solemn thing to look Death in the face."

"I am not afraid of death," Joseph replied.

"You mean the physical pang. But death includes what comes after it,—judgment. That is a very awful thought."

"It may be to evil men; but I have done nothing to make me fear it."

"You have never made an open profession of faith; yet it may be that grace has reached you," said Mr. Chaffinch. "Have you found your Saviour?"

"I believe in him with all my soul!" Joseph exclaimed; "but you mean something else by 'finding' him. I will be candid with you, Mr. Chaffinch. The last sermon I heard you preach, a month ago, was upon the nullity of all good works, all Christian deeds; you called them 'rags, dust, and ashes,' and declared that man is saved by faith alone. I have faith, but I can't accept a doctrine which denies merit to works; and you, unless I accept it, will you admit that I have 'found' Christ?"

"There is but One Truth!" exclaimed Mr. Chaffinch, very severely.

"Yes," Joseph answered, reverently, "and that is only perfectly known to God."

The clergyman was more deeply annoyed than he cared to exhibit. His experience had been confined chiefly to the encouragement of ignorant souls, willing to accept his message, if they could only be made to comprehend it, or to the conflict with downright doubt and denial. A nature so seemingly open to the influences of the Spirit, yet inflexibly closed to certain points of doctrine, was something of a problem to him. He belonged to a class now happily becoming scarce, who, having been taught to pace a reasoned theological round, can only efficiently meet those antagonists who voluntarily come inside of their own ring.

His habit of control, however, enabled him to say, with a moderately friendly manner, as he took leave: "We will talk again when you are stronger. It is my duty to give spiritual help to those who seek it."

To Rachel Miller he said: "I cannot say that he is dark. His mind is cloudy, but we find that the vanities of youth often obscure the true light for a time."

Joseph leaned back in his arm-chair, closed his eyes, and meditated earnestly for half an hour. Rachel Miller, uncertain whether to be hopeful or discouraged by Mr. Chaffinch's words, stole into the room, but went about on tiptoe, supposing him to be asleep. Joseph was fully conscious of all her movements, and at last startled her by the sudden question:—

"Aunt, why do you suppose I went to the city?"

"Goodness, Joseph! I thought you were sound asleep. I suppose to see about the fall prices for grain and cattle."

"No, aunt," said he, speaking with determination, though the foolish blood ran rosily over his face, "I went to get a wife!"

She stood pale and speechless, staring at him. But for the rosy sign on his cheeks and temples she could not have believed his words.

"Miss Blessing?" she finally uttered, almost in a whisper.

Joseph nodded his head. She dropped into the nearest chair, drew two or three long breaths, and in an indescribable tone ejaculated, "Well!"

"I knew you would be surprised," said he; "because it is almost a surprise to myself. But you and she seemed to fall so easily into each other's ways, that I hope—"

"Why, you're hardly acquainted with her!" Rachel exclaimed. "It is so hasty! And you are so young!"

"No younger than father was when he married mother; and I have learned to know her well in a short time. Isn't it so with you, too, aunt?—you certainly liked her?"

"I'll not deny that, nor say the reverse now: but a farmer's wife should be a farmer's daughter."

"But suppose, aunt, that the farmer doesn't happen to love any farmer's daughter, and does love a bright, amiable, very intelligent girl, who is delighted with country life, eager and willing to learn, and very fond of the farmer's aunt (who can teach her everything)?"

"Still, it seems to me a risk," said Rachel; but she was evidently relenting.

"There is none to you," he answered, "and I am not afraid of mine. You will be with us, for Julia couldn't do without you, if she wished. If she were a farmer's daughter, with different ideas of housekeeping, it might bring trouble to both of us. But now you will have the management in your own hands until you have taught Julia, and afterwards she will carry it on in your way."

She did not reply; but Joseph could see that she was becoming reconciled to the prospect. After awhile she came across the room, leaned over him, kissed him upon the forehead, and then silently went away.

CHAPTER X. APPROACHING FATE.

Only two months intervened until the time appointed for the marriage, and the days rolled swiftly away. A few lines came to Joseph from Philip Held, announcing that he was satisfied with the forge and furnace, and the sale would doubtless be consummated in a short time. He did not, however, expect to take charge of the works before March, and therefore gave Joseph his address in the city, with the hope that the latter would either visit or write to him.

On the Sunday after the accident Elwood Withers came to the farm. He seemed to have grown older in the short time which had elapsed since they had last met; after his first hearty rejoicing over Joseph's escape and recovery, he relapsed into a silent but not unfriendly mood. The two young men climbed the long hill behind the house and seated themselves under a noble pin-oak on the height, whence there was a lovely view of the valley for many miles to the southward.

They talked mechanically, for a while, of the season, and the crops, and the other usual subjects which farmers never get to the end of discussing; but both felt the impendence of more important themes, and, nevertheless, were slow to approach them. At last Elwood said: "Your fate is settled by this time, I suppose?"

"It is arranged, at least," Joseph replied. "But I can't yet make clear to myself that I shall be a married man in two months from now."

"Does the time seem long to you?"

"No," Joseph innocently answered; "it is very short."

Elwood turned away his head to conceal a melancholy smile; it was a few minutes before he spoke again.

"Joseph," he then said, "are you sure, quite sure, you love her?"

"I am to marry her."

"I meant nothing unfriendly," Elwood remarked, in a gentle tone. "My thought was this,—if you should ever find a still stronger love growing upon you,—something that would make the warmth you feel now seem like ice compared to it,—how would you be able to fight it? I asked the question of myself for you. I don't think I'm much different from most soft-hearted men,—except that I keep the softness so well stowed away that few persons know of it,—but if I were in your place, within two months of marriage to the girl I love, I should be miserable!"

Joseph turned towards him with wide, astonished eyes.

"Miserable from hope and fear," Elwood went on; "I should be afraid of fever, fire, murder, thunderbolts! Every hour of the day I should dread lest something might come between us; I should prowl around her house day after day, to be sure that she was alive! I should lengthen out the time into years; and all because I'm a great, disappointed, soft-hearted fool!"

The sad, yearning expression of his eyes touched Joseph to the heart. "Elwood," he said, "I see that it is not in my power to comfort you; if I give you pain unknowingly, tell me how to avoid it! I meant to ask you to stand beside me when I am married; but now you must consider your own feeling in answering, not mine. Lucy is not likely to be there."

"That would make no difference," Elwood answered. "Do you suppose it is a pain for me to see her, because she seems lost to me? No; I'm always a little encouraged when I have a chance to measure myself with her, and to guess—sometimes this and sometimes that—what it is that she needs to find in me. Force of will is of no use; as to faithfulness,—why, what it's worth can't be shown unless something turns up to try it. But you had better not ask me to be your groomsman. Neither Miss Blessing nor her sister would be overly pleased."

"Why so?" Joseph asked; "Julia and you are quite well acquainted, and she was always friendly towards you."

Elwood was silent and embarrassed. Then, reflecting that silence, at that moment, might express even more than speech, he said: "I've got the notion in my head; maybe it's foolish, but there it is. I talked a good deal with Miss Blessing, it's true, and yet I don't feel the least bit acquainted. Her manner to me was very friendly, and yet I don't think she likes me."

"Well!" exclaimed Joseph, forcing a laugh, though he was much annoyed, "I never gave you credit for such a lively imagination. Why not be candid, and admit that the dislike is on your side? I am sorry for it, since Julia will so soon be in the house there as my wife. There is no one else whom I can ask, unless it were Philip Held—"

"Held! To be sure, he took care of you. I was at Coventry the day after, and saw something of him." With these words, Elwood turned towards Joseph and looked him squarely in the face. "He'll have charge there in a few months, I hear," he then said, "and I reckon it as a piece of good luck for you. I've found that there are men, all, maybe, as honest and outspoken as they need be; yet two of 'em will talk at different marks and never fully understand each other, and other two will naturally talk right straight at the same mark and never miss. Now, Held is the sort that can hit the thing in the mind of the man they're talking to; it's a gift that comes o' being knocked about the world among all classes of people. What we learn here, always among the same folks, isn't a circumstance."

"Then you think I might ask him?" said Joseph, not fully comprehending all that Elwood meant to express.

"He's one of those men that you're safe in asking to do anything. Make him spokesman of a committee to wait on the President, arbitrator in a crooked lawsuit, overseer of a railroad gang, leader in a prayer-meeting (if he'd consent), or whatever else you choose, and he'll do the business as if he was used to it! It's enough for you that I don't know the town ways, and he does; it's considered worse, I've heard, to make a blunder in society than to commit a real sin."

He rose, and they loitered down the hill together. The subject was quietly dropped, but the minds of both were none the less busy. They felt the stir and pressure of new experiences, which had come to one through disappointment and to the other through success. Not three months had passed since they rode together through the twilight to Warriner's, and already life was opening to them,—but how differently! Joseph endeavored to make the most kindly allowance for his friend's mood, and to persuade himself that his feelings were unchanged. Elwood, however, knew that a shadow had fallen between. It was nothing beside the cloud of his greater trouble: he also knew the cost of his own justification to Joseph, and prayed that it might never come.

That evening, on taking leave, he said: "I don't know whether you meant to have the news of your engagement circulated; but I guess Anna Warriner has heard, and that amounts to—"

"To telling it to the whole neighborhood, doesn't it?" Joseph answered. "Then the mischief is already done, if it is a mischief. It is well, therefore, that the day is set: the neighborhood will have little time for gossip."

He smiled so frankly and cheerfully, that Elwood seized his hand, and with tears in his eyes, said: "Don't remember anything against me, Joseph. I've always been honestly your friend, and mean to stay so."

He went that evening to a homestead where he knew he should find Lucy Henderson. She looked pale and fatigued, he thought; possibly his presence had become a restraint. If so, she must bear his unkindness: it was the only sacrifice he could not make, for he felt sure that his intercourse with her must either terminate in hate or love. The one thing of which he was certain was, that there could be no calm, complacent friendship between them.

It was not long before one of the family asked him whether he had heard the news; it seemed that they had already discussed it, and his arrival revived the flow of expression. In spite of his determination, he found it impossible to watch Lucy while he said, as simply as possible, that Joseph Asten seemed very happy over the prospect of the marriage; that he was old enough to take a wife; and if Miss Blessing could adapt herself to country habits, they might get on very well together. But later in the evening he took a chance of saying to her: "In spite of what I said, Lucy, I don't feel quite easy about Joseph's marriage. What do you think of it?"

She smiled faintly, as she replied: "Some say that people are attracted by mutual unlikeness. This seems to me to be a case of the kind; but they are free choosers of their own fates."

"Is there no possible way of persuading him—them—to delay?"

"No!" she exclaimed, with unusual energy; "none whatever!"

Elwood sighed, and yet felt relieved.

Joseph lost no time in writing to Philip Held, announcing his approaching marriage, and begging him—with many apologies for asking such a mark of confidence on so short an acquaintance—to act the part of nearest friend, if there were no other private reasons to prevent him.

Four or five days later the following answer arrived:—

My dear Asten:—Do you remember that curious whirling, falling sensation, when the car pitched over the edge of the embankment? I felt a return of it on reading your letter; for you have surprised me beyond measure. Not by your request, for that is just what I should have expected of you; and as well now, as if we had known each other for twenty years; so the apology is the only thing objectionable—But I am tangling my sentences; I want to say how heartily I return the feeling which prompted you to ask me, and yet how embarrassed I am that I cannot unconditionally say, "Yes, with all my heart!" My great, astounding surprise is, to find you about to be married to Miss Julia Blessing,—a young lady whom I once knew. And the embarrassment is this: I knew her under circumstances (in which she was not personally concerned, however) which might possibly render my presence now, as your groomsman, unwelcome to the family: at least, it is my duty—and yours, if you still desire me to stand beside you—to let Miss Blessing and her family decide the question. The circumstances to which I refer concern them rather than myself. I think your best plan will be simply to inform them of your request and my reply, and add that I am entirely ready to accept whatever course they may prefer.

Pray don't consider that I have treated your first letter to me ungraciously. I am more grieved than you can imagine that it happens so.

You will probably come to the city a day before the wedding, and I insist that you shall share my bachelor quarters, in any case.

Always your friend,

Philip Held.

This letter threw Joseph into a new perplexity. Philip a former acquaintance of the Blessings! Formerly, but not now; and what could those mysterious "circumstances" have been, which had so seriously interrupted their intercourse? It was quite useless to conjecture; but he could not resist the feeling that another shadow hung over the aspects of his future. Perhaps he had exaggerated Elwood's unaccountable dislike to Julia, which had only been implied, not spoken; but here was a positive estrangement on the part of the man who was so suddenly near and dear to him. He never thought of suspecting Philip of blame; the candor and cheery warmth of the letter rejoiced his heart. There was evidently nothing better to do than to follow the advice contained in it, and leave the question to the decision of Julia and her parents.

Her reply did not come by the return mail, nor until nearly a week afterwards; during which time he tormented himself by imagining the wildest reasons for her silence. When the letter at last arrived, he had some difficulty in comprehending its import.

"Dearest Joseph," she said, "you must really forgive me this long trial of your patience. Your letter was so unexpected,—I mean its contents,—and it seems as if ma and pa and Clementina would never agree what was best to be done. For that matter, I cannot say that they agree now; we had no idea that you were an intimate friend of Mr. Held, (I can't think how ever you should have become acquainted!) and it seems to break open old wounds,—none of mine, fortunately, for I have none. As Mr. Held leaves the question in our hands, there is, you will understand, all the more necessity that we should be careful. Ma thinks he has said nothing to you about the unfortunate occurrence, or you would have expressed an opinion. You never can know how happy your fidelity makes me; but I felt that, the first moment we met.

"Ma says that at very private (what pa calls informal) weddings there

803

need not be bridesmaids or groomsmen. Miss Morrisey was married that way, not long ago; it is true that she is not of our circle, nor strictly a first family (this is ma's view, not mine, for I understand the hollowness of society); but we could very well do the same. Pa would be satisfied with a reception afterwards; he wants to ask the Collector, and the Surveyor, and the Appraiser. Clementina won't say anything now, but I know what she thinks, and so does ma; however, Mr. Held has so dropped out of city life that it is not important. I suppose everything must be dim in his memory now; you do not write to me much that he related. How strange that he should be your friend! They say my dress is lovely, but I am sure I should like a plain muslin just as well. I shall only breathe freely when I get back to the quiet of the country, (and your—our charming home, and dear, good Aunt Rachel!) and away from all these conventional forms. Ma says if there is one groomsman there ought to be two; either very simple, or according to custom. In a matter so delicate, perhaps, Mr. Held would be as competent to decide as we are; at least I am quite willing to leave it to his judgment. But how trifling is all this discussion, compared with the importance of the day to us! It is now drawing very near, but I have no misgivings, for I confide in you wholly and forever!"

After reading the letter with as much coolness as was then possible to him, Joseph inferred three things: that his acquaintance with Philip Held was not entirely agreeable to the Blessing family; that they would prefer the simplest style of a wedding, and this was in consonance with his own tastes; and that Julia clung to him as a deliverer from conditions with which her nature had little sympathy. Her incoherence, he fancied, arose from an agitation which he could very well understand, and his answer was intended to soothe and encourage her. It was difficult to let Philip know that his services would not be required, without implying the existence of an unfriendly feeling towards him; and Joseph, therefore, all the more readily accepted his invitation. He was assured that the mysterious difficulty did not concern Julia; even if it were so, he was not called upon to do violence, without cause, to so welcome a friendship.

The September days sped by, not with the lingering, passionate uncertainty of which Elwood Withers spoke, but almost too swiftly. In the hurry of preparation, Joseph had scarcely time to look beyond the coming event and estimate its consequences. He was too ignorant of himself to doubt: his conscience was too pure and perfect to admit the possibility of changing the course of his destiny. Whatever the gossip of the neighborhood might have been, he heard nothing of it that was not agreeable. His aunt was entirely reconciled to a wife who would not immediately, and probably not for a long time, interfere with her authority; and the shadows raised by the two men whom he loved best seemed, at last, to be accidentally thrown from clouds beyond the horizon of his life. This was the thought to which he clung, in spite of a vague, utterly formless apprehension, which he felt lurking somewhere in the very bottom of his heart.

Philip met him on his arrival in the city, and after taking him to his pleasant quarters, in a house looking on one of the leafy squares, good-naturedly sent him to the Blessing mansion, with a warning to return before the evening was quite spent. The family was in a flutter of preparation, and though he was cordially welcomed, he felt that, to all except Julia, he was subordinate in interest to the men who came every quarter of an hour, bringing bouquets, and silver spoons with cards attached, and pasteboard boxes containing frosted cakes. Even Julia's society he was only allowed to enjoy by scanty instalments; she was perpetually summoned by her mother or Clementina, to consult about some indescribable figment of dress. Mr. Blessing was occupied in the basement, with the inspection of various hampers. He came to the drawing-room to greet Joseph, whom he shook by both hands, with such incoherent phrases that Julia presently interposed. "You must not forget, pa," she said, "that the man is waiting: Joseph will excuse you, I know." She followed him to the basement, and he returned no more.

Joseph left early in the evening, cheered by Julia's words: "We can't complain of all this confusion, when it's for our sakes; but we'll be happier when it's over, won't we?"

He gave her an affirmative kiss, and returned to Philip's room. That gentleman was comfortably disposed in an arm-chair, with a book and a cigar. "Ah!" he exclaimed, "you find that a house is more agreeable any evening than that before the wedding?"

"There is one compensation," said Joseph; "it gives me two or three hours with you."

"Then take that other arm-chair, and tell me how this came to pass. You see I have the curiosity of a neighbor, already."

He listened earnestly while Joseph related the story of his love, occasionally asking a question or making a suggestive remark, but so gently that it seemed to come as an assistance. When all had been told, he rose and commenced walking slowly up and down the room. Joseph longed to ask, in turn, for an explanation of the circumstances mentioned in Philip's letter; but a doubt checked his tongue.

As if in response to his thought, Philip stopped before him and said: "I owe you my story, and you shall have it after a while, when I can tell you more. I was a young fellow of twenty when I knew the Blessings, and I don't attach the slightest importance, now, to anything that happened. Even if I did, Miss Julia had no share in it. I remember her distinctly; she was then about my age, or a year or two older; but hers is a face that would not change in a long while."

Joseph stared at his friend in silence. He recalled the latter's age, and was startled by the involuntary arithmetic which revealed Julia's to him. It was unexpected, unwelcome, yet inevitable.

"Her father had been lucky in some of his 'operations,'" Philip continued, "but I don't think he kept it long. I hardly wonder that she should come to prefer a quiet country life to such ups and downs as the family has known. Generally, a woman don't adapt herself so readily to a change of surroundings as a man: where there is love, however, everything is possible."

"There is! there is!" Joseph exclaimed, certifying the fact to himself as much as to his friend. He rose and stood beside him.

Philip looked at him with grave, tender eyes.

"What can I do?" he said.

806

"What should you do?" Joseph asked.

"This!" Philip exclaimed, laying his hands on Joseph's shoulders,—"this, Joseph! I can be nearer than a brother. I know that I am in your heart as you are in mine. There is no faith between us that need be limited, there is no truth too secret to be veiled. A man's perfect friendship is rarer than a woman's love, and most hearts are content with one or the other: not so with yours and mine! I read it in your eyes, when you opened them on my knee: I see it in your face now. Don't speak: let us clasp hands."

But Joseph could not speak.

CHAPTER XI. A CITY WEDDING.

There was not much of the happy bridegroom to be seen in Joseph's face when he arose the next morning. To Philip's eyes he appeared to have suddenly grown several years older; his features had lost their boyish softness and sweetness, which would thenceforth never wholly come back again. He spoke but little, and went about his preparation with an abstracted, mechanical air, which told how much his mind was preoccupied. Philip quietly assisted, and when all was complete, led him before the mirror.

"There!" he said; "now study the general effect; I think nothing more is wanting."

"It hardly looks like myself," Joseph remarked, after a careless inspection.

"In all the weddings I have seen," said Philip, "the bridegrooms were pale and grave, the brides flushed and trembling. You will not make an exception to the rule; but it is a solemn thing, and I—don't misunderstand me, Joseph—I almost wish you were not to be married to-day."

"Philip!" Joseph exclaimed, "let me think, now, at least,—now, at the last moment,—that it is best for me! If you knew how cramped, restricted, fettered, my life has been, and how much emancipation has already come with this—this love! Perhaps my marriage is a venture, but it is one which must be made; and no consequence of it shall ever come between us!"

"No; and I ought not to have spoken a word that might imply a doubt. It may be that your emancipation, as you rightly term it, can only come in this way. My life has been so different, that I am unconsciously putting myself in your place, instead of trying to look with your eyes. When I next go to Coventry Forge, I shall drive over and dine with you, and I hope your Julia will be as ready to receive me as a friend as I am to find one in her. There is the carriage at the door, and you had better arrive a little before the appointed hour. Take only my good wishes, my prayers for your happiness, along with you,—and now, God bless you, Joseph!"

The carriage rolled away. Joseph, in full wedding costume, was painfully conscious of the curious glances which fell upon him, and presently pulled down the curtains. Then, with an impatient self-reprimand, he pulled them up again, lowered the window, and let the air blow upon his hot cheeks. The house was speedily reached, and he was admitted by a festive waiter (hired for the occasion) before he had been exposed for more than five seconds to the gaze of curious eyes in all the windows around.

Mrs. Blessing, resplendent in purple, and so bedight that she seemed almost as young as her portrait, swept into the drawing-room. She inspected him rapidly, and approved, while advancing; otherwise he would scarcely have received the thin, dry kiss with which she favored him.

"It lacks half an hour," she said; "but you have the usual impatience of a bridegroom. I am accustomed to it. Mr. Blessing is still in his room; he has only just commenced arranging his cambric cravat, which is a work of time. He cannot forget that he was distinguished for an elegant tie in his youth. Clementina,"—as that young lady entered the room,—"is the bride completely attired?"

"All but her gloves," replied Clementina, offering three-fourths of her hand to Joseph. "And she don't know what ear-rings to wear."

"I think we might venture," Mrs. Blessing remarked, "as there seems to be no rule applicable to the case, to allow Mr. Asten a sight of his bride. Perhaps his taste might assist her in the choice."

Thereupon she conducted Joseph up stairs, and, after some preliminary whispering, he was admitted to the room. He and Julia were equally surprised at the change in each other's appearance: he older, paler, with a grave and serious bearing; she younger, brighter, rounder, fresher, and with the loveliest pink flush on her cheeks. The gloss of her hair rivalled that of the white satin which draped her form and gave grace to its outlines; her neck and shoulders were slight, but no one could have justly called them lean; and even the thinness of her lips was forgotten in the vivid coral of their color, and the nervous life which hovered about their edges. At that moment she was certainly beautiful, and a stranger would have supposed her to be young.

She looked into Joseph's face with a smile in which some appearance of maiden shyness yet lingered. A shrewder bridegroom would have understood its meaning, and would have said, "How lovely you are!" Joseph, it is true, experienced a sense of relief, but he knew not why, and could not for his life have put it into words. His eyes dwelt upon and followed her, and she seemed to be satisfied with that form of recognition. Mrs. Blessing inspected the dress with a severe critical eye, pulling out a fold here and smoothing a bit of lace there, until nothing further could be detected. Then, the adornment of the victim being completed, she sat down and wept moderately.

"O ma, try to bear up!" Julia exclaimed, with the very slightest touch of impatience in her voice; "it is all to come yet."

There was a ring at the door.

"It must be your aunt," said Mrs. Blessing, drying her eyes. "My sister," she added, turning to Joseph,—Mrs. Woollish, with Mr. Woollish and their two sons and one daughter. He's in the—the leather trade, so to speak, which has thrown her into a very different circle; but, as we have no nearer relations in the city, they will be present at the ceremony. He is said to be wealthy. I have no means of knowing; but one would scarcely think so, to judge from his wedding-gift to Julia."

"Ma, why should you mention it?"

"I wish to enlighten Mr. Asten. Six pairs of shoes!—of course all of the same pattern; and the fashion may change in another year!"

"In the country we have no fashions in shoes," Joseph suggested.

"Certainly!" said Julia. "I find Uncle Woollish's present very practical indeed."

Mrs. Blessing looked at her daughter, and said nothing.

Mr. Blessing, very red in the face, but with triumphant cambric about his throat, entered the room, endeavoring to get his fat hands into a pair of No. 9 gloves. A strong smell of turpentine or benzine entered with him.

"Eliza," said he, "you must find me some eau de cologne. The odor

810

left from my—my rheumatic remedy is still perceptible. Indeed, patchouly would be better, if it were not the scent peculiar to parvenus."

Clementina came to say that the clergyman's carriage had just reached the door, and Mr. Blessing was hurried down stairs, mopping his gloves and the collar of his coat with liquid fragrance by the way. Mrs. Blessing and Clementina presently followed.

"Julia," said Joseph when they were quite alone, "have you thought that this is for life?"

She looked up with a tender smile, but something in his face arrested it on her lips.

"I have lived ignorantly until now," he continued,—"innocently and ignorantly. From this time on I shall change more than you, and there may be, years hence, a very different Joseph Asten from the one whose name you will take to-day. If you love me with the love I claim from you,—the love that grows with and through all new knowledge and experience,—there will be no discord in our lives. We must both be liberal and considerate towards each other; it has been but a short time since we met, and we have still much to learn."

"O, Joseph!" she murmured, in a tone of gentle reproach, "I knew your nature at first sight."

"I hope you did," he answered gravely, "for then you will be able to see its needs, and help me to supply them. But, Julia, there must not the shadow of concealment come between us: nothing must be reserved. I understand no love that does not include perfect trust. I must draw nearer, and be drawn nearer to you, constantly, or—"

He paused; it was no time to utter the further sentence in his mind. Julia glided to him, clasped her arms about his waist, and laid her head against his shoulder. Although she said nothing, the act was eloquent. It expressed acquiescence, trust, fidelity, the surrender of her life to his, and no man in his situation could have understood it otherwise. A tenderness, which seemed to be the something hitherto lacking to his love, crept softly over his heart, and

811

the lurking unrest began to fade from his face.

There was a rustle on the stairs; Clementina and Miss Woollish made their appearance. "Mr. Bogue has arrived," whispered the former, "and ma thinks you should come down soon. Are you entirely ready? I don't think you need the salts, Julia; but you might carry the bottle in your left hand: brides are expected to be nervous."

She gave a light laugh, like the purl and bubble of a brook; but Joseph shrank, with an inward chill, from the sound.

"So! shall we go? Fanny and I—(I beg pardon; Mr. Asten—Miss Woollish)—will lead the way. We will stand a little in the rear, not beside you, as there are no groomsmen. Remember, the farther end of the room!"

They rustled slowly downward, in advance, and the bridal pair followed. The clergyman, Mr. Bogue, suddenly broke off in the midst of an oracular remark about the weather, and, standing in the centre of the room, awaited them. The other members of the two families were seated, and very silent.

Joseph heard the introductory remarks, the ceremony, and the final benediction, as in a dream. His lips opened mechanically, and a voice which did not exactly seem to be his own uttered the "I will!" at the proper time; yet, in recalling the experience afterwards, he was unable to decide whether any definite thought or memory or hope had passed through his mind. From his entrance into the room until his hand was violently shaken by Mr. Blessing, there was a blank.

Of course there were tears, but the beams of congratulation shone through them, and they saddened nobody. Miss Fanny Woollish assured the bridal pair, in an audible whisper, that she had never seen a sweeter wedding; and her mother, a stout, homely little body, confirmed the opinion with, "Yes, you both did beautifully!" Then the marriage certificate was produced and signed, and the company partook of wine and refreshments to strengthen them for the reception.

Until there had been half a dozen arrivals, Mrs. Blessing moved about restlessly, and her eyes wandered to the front window. Suddenly three or four carriages came rattling together up the street, and Joseph heard her whisper to her husband: "There they are! it will be a success!" It was not long before the little room was uncomfortably crowded, and the presentations followed so rapidly that Joseph soon became bewildered. Julia, however, knew and welcomed every one with the most bewitching grace, being rewarded with kisses by the gorgeous young ladies and compliments by the young men with weak mouths and retreating chins.

In the midst of the confusion Mr. Blessing, with a wave of his hand, presented "Mr. Collector Twining" and "Mr. Surveyor Knob" and "Mr. Appraiser Gerrish," all of whom greeted Joseph with a bland, almost affectionate, cordiality. The door of the dining-room was then thrown open, and the three dignitaries accompanied the bridal pair to the table. Two servants rapidly whisked the champagne-bottles from a cooling-tub in the adjoining closet, and Mr. Blessing commenced stirring and testing a huge bowl of punch. Collector Twining made a neat little speech, proposing the health of bride and bridegroom, with a pun upon the former's name, which was received with as much delight as if it had never been heard before. Therefore Mr. Surveyor Knob repeated it in giving the health of the bride's parents. The enthusiasm of the company not having diminished, Mr. Appraiser Gerrish improved the pun in a third form, in proposing "the Ladies." Then Mr. Blessing, although his feelings overcame him, and he was obliged to use a handkerchief smelling equally of benzine and eau de cologne, responded, introducing the collector's and surveyor's names with an ingenuity which was accepted as the inspiration of genius. His peroration was especially admired.

"On this happy occasion," he said, "the elements of national power and prosperity are represented. My son-in-law, Mr. Asten, is a noble specimen of the agricultural population,—the free American yeomanry; my daughter, if I may be allowed to say it in the presence of so many bright eyes and blooming cheeks, is a representative child of the city, which is the embodiment of the nation's action and enterprise. The union of the two is the movement of our life. The city gives to the country as the ocean gives the cloud to the mountain-springs: the country gives to the city as the streams flow back to the ocean. ["Admirable!" Mr. Collector Twining exclaimed.] Then we have, as our highest honor, the representatives of the political system under which city and country flourish alike. The wings of our eagle must be extended over this fortunate house to-day, for here are the strong Claws which seize and guard its treasures!"

The health of the Claws was drunk enthusiastically. Mr. Blessing was congratulated on his eloquence; the young gentlemen begged the privilege of touching their glasses to his, and every touch required that the contents be replenished; so that the bottom of the punch-bowl was nearly reached before the guests departed.

When Joseph came down in his travelling-dress, he found the drawing-room empty of the crowd; but leaves, withered flowers, crumbs of cake, and crumpled cards scattered over the carpet, indicated what had taken place. In the dining-room Mr. Blessing, with his cravat loosened, was smoking a cigar at the open window.

"Come, son-in-law!" he cried, "take another glass of punch before you start."

Joseph declined, on the plea that he was not accustomed to the beverage.

"Nothing could have gone off better!" said Mr. Blessing. "The collector was delighted: by the by, you're to go to the St. Jerome, when you get to New York this evening. He telegraphed to have the bridal-chamber reserved for you. Tell Julia: she won't forget it. That girl has a deuced sharp intellect: if you'll be guided by her in your operations—"

"Pa, what are you saying about me?" Julia, asked, hastily entering the room.

"Only that you have a deuced sharp intellect, and to-day proves it. Asten is one of us now, and I may tell him of his luck."

He winked and laughed stupidly, and Joseph understood and obeyed his wife's appealing glance. He went to his mother-in-law in the drawing-room.

Julia lightly and swiftly shut the door. "Pa," she said, in a strong, angry whisper; "if you are not able to talk coherently, you must keep your tongue

814

still. What will Joseph think of me, to hear you?"

"What he'll think anyhow, in a little while," he doggedly replied. "Julia, you have played a keen game, and played it well; but you don't know much of men yet. He'll not always be the innocent, white-nosed lamb he is now, nibbling the posies you hold out to him. Wait till he asks for stronger feed, and see whether he'll follow you!"

She was looking on the floor, pale and stern. Suddenly one of her gloves burst, across the back of the hand. "Pa," she then said, "it's very cruel to say such things to me, now when I'm leaving you."

"So it is!" he exclaimed, tearfully contrite; "I am a wretch! They flattered my speech so much,—the collector was so impressed by me,—and said so many pleasant things, that—I don't feel quite steady. Don't forget the St. Jerome; the bridal-chamber is ordered, and I'll see that Mumm writes a good account for the 'Evening Mercury.' I wish you could be here to remember my speech for me. O, I shall miss you! I shall miss you!"

With these words, and his arm lovingly about his daughter, they joined the family. The carriage was already at the door, and the coachman was busy with the travelling-trunks. There were satchels, and little packages,—an astonishing number it seemed to Joseph,—to be gathered together, and then the farewells were said.

As they rolled through the streets towards the station, Julia laid her head upon her husband's shoulder, drew a long, deep breath, and said, "Now all our obligations to society are fulfilled, and we can rest awhile. For the first time in my life I am a free woman,—and you have liberated me!"

He answered her in glad and tender words; he was equally grateful that the exciting day was over. But, as they sped away from the city through the mellow October landscapes, Philip's earnest, dark gray eyes, warm with more than brotherly love, haunted his memory, and he knew that Philip's faithful thoughts followed him.

CHAPTER XII. CLOUDS.

There are some days when the sun comes slowly up, filling the vapory air with diffused light, in advance of his coming; when the earth grows luminous in the broad, breezeless morning; when nearer objects shine and sparkle, and the distances melt into dim violet and gold; when the vane points to the southwest, and the blood of man feels neither heat nor cold, but only the freshness of that perfect temperature wherein the limits of the body are lost, and the pulses of its life beat in all the life of the world. But ere long the haze, instead of thinning into blue, gradually thickens into gray; the vane creeps southward, swinging to southeast in brief, rising flaws of the air; the horizon darkens; the enfranchised life of the spirit creeps back to its old isolation, shorn of all its rash delight, and already foreboding the despondency which comes with the east wind and the chilly rains.

Some such variation of the atmospheric influences attended Joseph Asten's wedding-travel. The mellow, magical glory of his new life diminished day by day; the blue of his sky became colder and grayer. Yet he could not say that his wife had changed: she was always ready with her smiles, her tender phrases, her longings for quiet and rest, and simple, natural life, away from the conventionalities and claims of Society. But, even as, looking into the pale, tawny-brown of her eyes, he saw no changing depth below the hard, clear surface, so it also seemed with her nature; he painfully endeavored to penetrate beyond expressions, the repetition of which it was hard not to find tiresome, and to reach some spring of character or feeling; yet he found nothing. It was useless to remember that he had been content with those expressions before marriage had given them his own eager interpretation, independent of her will and knowledge; that his duty to her remained the same, for she had not deceived him.

On the other hand, she was as tender and affectionate as he could desire. Indeed, he would often have preferred a less artless manifestation of her fondness; but she playfully insisted on his claiming the best quarters at every stopping-place, on the ground of their bridal character, and was sometimes a little petulant when she fancied that they had not been sufficiently honored. Joseph would have willingly escaped the distinction, allowing himself to be confounded with the prosaic multitude, but she would not permit him to try the experiment.

"The newly married are always detected," she would say, "and they are only laughed at when they try to seem like old couples. Why not be frank and honest, and meet half-way the sympathy which I am sure everybody has for us?"

To this he could make no reply, except that it was not agreeable to exact a special attention.

"But it is our right!" was her answer.

In every railway-car they entered she contrived, in a short time, to impress the nature of their trip upon the other travellers; yet it was done with such apparent unconsciousness, such innocent, impulsive manifestations of her happiness in him, that he could not, in his heart, charge her with having intentionally brought upon him the discomfort of being curiously observed. He could have accustomed himself to endure the latter, had it been inevitable; the suspicion that he owed it to her made it an increasing annoyance. Yet, when the day's journey was over, and they were resting together in their own private apartment, she would bring a stool to his feet, lay her head on his knee, and say: "Now we can talk as we please,—there are none watching and listening."

At such times he was puzzled to guess whether some relic of his former nervous shyness were not remaining, and had made him over-sensitive to her ways. The doubt gave him an additional power of self-control; he resolved to be more slow and cautious of judgment, and observe men and women more carefully than he had been wont to do. Julia had no suspicion of what was passing in his mind: she took it for granted that his nature was still as shallow and transparent as when she first came in contact with it.

After nearly a fortnight this flying life came to an end. They returned to the city for a day, before going home to the farm. The Blessing mansion received them with a hearty welcome; yet, in spite of it, a depressing atmosphere seemed to fill the house. Mrs. Blessing looked pinched and care-worn, Clementina discontented, and Mr. Blessing as melancholy as was possible to so bouyant a politician.

"What's the matter? I hope pa hasn't lost his place," Julia remarked in an undertone to her mother.

"Lost my place!" Mr. Blessing exclaimed aloud; "I'd like to see how the collection of customs would go on without me. But a man may keep his place, and yet lose his house and home."

Clementina vanished, Mrs. Blessing followed, with her handkerchief to her eyes, and Julia hastened after them, crying: "Ma! dear ma!"

"It's only on their account," said Mr. Blessing, pointing after them and speaking to Joseph. "A plucky man never desponds, sir; but women, you'll find, are upset by every reverse."

"May I ask what has happened?"

"A delicate regard for you," Mr. Blessing replied, "would counsel me to conceal it, but my duty as your father-in-law leaves me no alternative. Our human feelings prompt us to show only the bright side of life to those whom we love; principle, however,—conscience, commands us not to suppress the shadows. I am but one out of the many millions of victims of mistaken judgment. The case is simply this; I will omit certain legal technicalities touching the disposition of property, which may not be familiar to you, and state the facts in the most intelligible form; securities which I placed as collaterals for the loan of a sum, not a very large amount, have been very unexpectedly depreciated, but only temporarily so, as all the market knows. If I am forced to sell them at such an untoward crisis, I lose the largest part of my limited means; if I retain them, they will ultimately recover their full value."

"Then why not retain them?" Joseph asked.

"The sum advanced upon them must be repaid, and it so happens—the

818

market being very tight—that every one of my friends is short. Of course, where their own paper is on the street, I can't ask them to float mine for three months longer, which is all that is necessary. A good indorsement is the extent of my necessity; for any one who is familiar with the aspects of the market can see that there must be a great rebound before three months."

"If it were not a very large amount," Joseph began.

"Only a thousand! I know what you were going to say it is perfectly natural: I appreciate it, because, if our positions were reversed, I should have done the same thing. But, although it is a mere form, a temporary fiction, which has the force of reality, and, therefore, so far as you are concerned, I should feel entirely easy, yet it might subject me to very dishonoring suspicions! It might be said that I had availed myself of your entrance into my family to beguile you into pecuniary entanglements; the amount might be exaggerated, the circumstance misrepresented,—no, no! rather than that, let me make the sacrifice like a man! I'm no longer young, it is true; but the feeling that I stand on principle will give me strength to work."

"On the other hand, Mr. Blessing," said Joseph, "very unpleasant things might be said of me, if I should permit you to suffer so serious a loss, when my assistance would prevent it."

"I don't deny it. You have made a two-horned dilemma out of a one-sided embarrassment. Would that I had kept the secret in my own breast! The temptation is strong, I confess, for the mere use of your name for a few months is all I should require. Either the securities will rise to their legitimate value, or some of the capitalists with whom I have dealings will be in a position to accommodate me. I have frequently tided over similar snags and sand-bars in the financial current; they are familiar even to the most skilful operators,—navigators, I might say, to carry out the figure,—and this is an instance where an additional inch of water will lift me from wreck to flood-tide. The question is, should I allow what I feel to be a just principle, a natural suggestion of delicacy, to intervene between my necessity and your generous proffer of assistance?"

"Your family—" Joseph began.

"I know! I know!" Mr. Blessing cried, leaning his head upon his hand. "There is my vulnerable point,—my heel of Achilles! There would be no alternative,—better sell this house than have my paper dishonored! Then, too, I feel that this is a turning-point in my fortunes: if I can squeeze through this narrow pass, I shall find a smooth road beyond. It is not merely the sum which is at stake, but the future possibilities into which it expands. Should I crush the seed while it is germinating? Should I tear up the young tree, with an opening fruit-bud on every twig? You see the considerations that sway me: unless you withdraw your most generous proffer, what can I do but yield and accept it?"

"I have no intention of withdrawing it," Joseph answered, taking his words literally; "I made the offer freely and willingly. If my indorsement is all that is necessary now, I can give it at once."

Mr. Blessing grasped him by the hand, winked hard three or four times, and turned away his head without speaking. Then he drew a large leather pocket-book from his breast, opened it, and produced a printed promissory note.

"We will make it payable at your county bank," said he, "because your name is known there, and upon acceptance—which can be procured in two days—the money will be drawn here. Perhaps we had better say four months, in order to cover all contingencies."

He went to a small writing-desk, at the farther end of the room, and filled the blanks in the note, which Joseph then endorsed. When it was safely lodged in his breast-pocket, he said: "We will keep this entirely to ourselves. My wife, let me whisper to you, is very proud and sensitive, although the De l'Hotels (Doolittles now) were never quite the equals of the De Belsains; but women see matters in a different light. They can't understand the accommodation of a name, but fancy that it implies a kind of humiliation, as if one were soliciting charity."

He laughed and rubbed his hands. "I shall soon be in a position," he said, "to render you a favor in return. My long experience, and, I may add, my intimate knowledge of the financial field, enables me to foresee many

820

splendid opportunities. There are, just now, some movements which are not yet perceptible on the surface. Mark my words! we shall shortly have a new excitement, and a cool, well-seasoned head is a fortune at such times."

"In the country," Joseph replied, "we only learn enough to pay off our debts and invest our earnings. We are in the habit of moving slowly and cautiously. Perhaps we miss opportunities; but if we don't see them, we are just as contented as if they had not been. I have enough for comfort, and try to be satisfied."

"Inherited ideas! They belong to the community in which you live. Are you satisfied with your neighbors' ways of living and thinking? I do not mean to disparage them, but have you no desire to rise above their level? Money,— as I once said at a dinner given to a distinguished railroad man,—money is the engine which draws individuals up the steepest grades of society; it is the lubricating oil which makes the truck of life run easy; it is the safety-break which renders collision and wreck impossible! I have long been accustomed to consider it in the light of power, not of property, and I classify men according as they take one or the other view. The latter are misers; but the former, sir, are philosophers!"

Joseph scarcely knew how to answer this burst of eloquence. But there was no necessity for it; the ladies entered the room at that moment, each one, in her own way, swiftly scrutinizing the two gentlemen. Mrs. Blessing's face lost its woe-worn expression, while a gleam of malicious satisfaction passed over Clementina's.

The next day, on their journey to the country, Julia suddenly said, "I am sure, Joseph, that pa made use of your generosity; pray don't deny it!"

There was the faintest trace of hardness in her voice, which he interpreted as indicating dissatisfaction with his failure to confide the matter to her.

"I have no intention of denying anything, Julia," he answered. "I was not called upon to exercise generosity; it was simply what your father would term an 'accommodation.'"

"I understand. How much?"

"An endorsement of his note for a thousand dollars, which is little, when it will prevent him from losing valuable securities."

Julia was silent for at least ten minutes; then, turning towards him with a sternness which she vainly endeavored to conceal under a "wreathed smile," she said: "In future, Joseph, I hope you will always consult me in any pecuniary venture. I may not know much about such matters, but it is my duty to learn. I have been obliged to hear a great deal of financial talk from pa and his friends, and could not help guessing some things which I think I can apply for your benefit. We are to have no secrets from each other, you know."

His own words! After all, what she said was just and right, and he could not explain to himself why he should feel annoyed. Perhaps he missed a frank expression of delight in the assistance he had so promptly given; but why should he suspect that it was unwelcome to her? He tried to banish the feeling, to hide it under self-reproach and shame, but it clung to him most uncomfortably.

Nevertheless, he forgot everything in the pleasure of the homeward drive from the station. The sadness of late autumn lay upon the fields, but spring already said, "I am coming!" in the young wheat; the houses looked warm and cosey behind their sheltering fir-trees; cattle still grazed on the meadows, and the corn was not yet deserted by the huskers. The sun gave a bright edge to the sombre colors of the landscape, and to Joseph's eyes it was beautiful as never before. Julia leaned back in the carriage, and complained of the cold wind.

"There!" cried Joseph, as a view of the valley opened below them, with the stream flashing like steel between the leafless sycamores,—"there is home-land! Do you know where to look for our house?"

Julia made an effort, leaned forward, smiled, and pointed silently across the shoulder of a hill to the eastward. "You surely didn't suppose I could forget," she murmured.

Rachel Miller awaited them at the gate, and Julia had no sooner alighted than she flung herself into her arms. "Dear Aunt Rachel!" she cried: "you must now take my mother's place; I have so much to learn from you! It is doubly a home since you are here. I feel that we shall all be happy together!"

Then there were kisses, of which Joseph received his share, and the first evening lapsed away in perfect harmony. Everything was delightful: the room, the furniture, the meal, even the roar of the wind in the dusky trees. While Julia lay in the cushioned rocking-chair, Rachel gave her nephew an account of all that had been done on the farm; but Joseph only answered her from the surface of his mind. Under the current of his talk ran a graver thought, which said: "You wanted independence and a chance of growth for your life; you fancied they would come in this form. Lo, now! here are the conditions which you desired to establish; from this hour begins the new life of which you dreamed. Whether you have been wise or rash, you can change nothing. You are limited, as before, though within a different circle. You may pace it to its fullest extent, but all the lessons you have yet learned require you to be satisfied within it."

CHAPTER XIII. PRESENTIMENTS.

The autumn lapsed into winter, and the household on the Asten farm began to share the isolation of the season. There had been friendly visits from all the nearest neighbors and friends, followed by return visits, and invitations which Julia willingly accepted. She was very amiable, and took pains to confirm the favorable impression which she knew she had made in the summer. Everybody remarked how she had improved in appearance, how round and soft her neck and shoulders, how bright and fresh her complexion. She thanked them, with many grateful expressions to which they were not accustomed, for their friendly reception, which she looked upon as an adoption into their society; but at home, afterwards, she indulged in criticisms of their manners and habits which were not always friendly. Although these were given in a light, playful tone, and it was sometimes impossible not to be amused, Rachel Miller always felt uncomfortable when she heard them.

Then came quiet, lonely days, and Julia, weary of her idle life, undertook to master the details of the housekeeping. She went from garret to cellar, inspecting every article in closet and pantry, wondering much, censuring occasionally, and only praising a little when she found that Rachel was growing tired and irritable. Although she made no material changes, it was soon evident that she had very stubborn views of her own upon many points, and possessed a marked tendency for what the country people call "nearness." Little by little she diminished the bountiful, free-handed manner of provision which had been the habit of the house. One could not say that anything needful was lacking, and Rachel would hardly have been dissatisfied, had she not felt that the innovation was an indirect blame.

In some directions Julia seemed the reverse of "near," persuading Joseph into expenditures which the people considered very extravagant. When the snow came, his new and elegant sleigh, with the wolf-skin robe, the silver-mounted harness, and the silver-sounding bells, was the envy of all the young men, and an abomination to the old. It was a splendor which he could easily afford, and he did not grudge her the pleasure; yet it seemed to change his relation to the neighbors, and some of them were very free in hinting that they felt it so. It would be difficult to explain why they should resent this or any other slight departure from their fashions, but such had always been their custom.

In a few days the snow vanished and a tiresome season of rain and thaw succeeded. The south-eastern winds, blowing from the Atlantic across the intervening lowlands, rolled interminable gray masses of fog over the hills and blurred the scenery of the valley; dripping trees, soaked meadows, and sodden leaves were the only objects that detached themselves from the general void, and became in turn visible to those who travelled the deep, quaking roads. The social intercourse of the neighborhood ceased perforce, though the need of it were never so great: what little of the main highway down the valley was visible from the windows appeared to be deserted.

Julia, having exhausted the resources of the house, insisted on acquainting herself with the barn and everything thereto belonging. She laughingly asserted that her education as a farmer's wife was still very incomplete; she must know the amount of the crops, the price of grain, the value of the stock, the manner of work, and whatever else was necessary to her position. Although she made many pretty blunders, it was evident that her apprehension was unusually quick, and that whatever she acquired was fixed in her mind as if for some possible future use. She never wearied of the most trivial details, while Joseph, on the other hand, would often have willingly shortened his lessons. His mind was singularly disturbed between the desire to be gratified by her curiosity, and the fact that its eager and persistent character made him uncomfortable.

When an innocent, confiding nature begins to suspect that its confidence has been misplaced, the first result is a preternatural stubbornness to admit the truth. The clearest impressions are resisted, or half-consciously misinterpreted, with the last force of an illusion which already foresees its own overthrow. Joseph eagerly clung to every look and word and action which confirmed his sliding faith in his wife's sweet and simple character, and repelled—though a deeper instinct told him that a day would come when it must be admitted—the evidence of her coldness and selfishness. Yet, even while almost fiercely asserting to his own heart that he had every reason to be happy, he was consumed with a secret fever of unrest, doubt, and dread.

The horns of the growing moon were still turned downwards, and cold, dreary rains were poured upon the land. Julia's patience, in such straits, was wonderful, if the truth had been known, but she saw that some change was necessary for both of them. She therefore proposed, not what she most desired, but what her circumstances prescribed,—a visit from her sister Clementina. Joseph found the request natural enough: it was an infliction, but one which he had anticipated; and after the time had been arranged by letter, he drove to the station to meet the westward train from the city.

Clementina stepped upon the platform, so cloaked and hooded that he only recognized her by the deliberate grace of her movements. She extended her hand, giving his a cordial pressure, which was explained by the brass baggage-checks thus transferred to his charge.

"I will wait in the ladies' room," was all she said.

At the same moment Joseph's arm was grasped.

"What a lucky chance!" exclaimed Philip: then, suddenly pausing in his greeting, he lifted his hat and bowed to Clementina, who nodded slightly as she passed into the room.

"Let me look at you!" Philip resumed, laying his hands on Joseph's shoulders. Their eyes met and lingered, and Joseph felt the blood rise to his face as Philip's gaze sank more deeply into his heart and seemed to fathom its hidden trouble; but presently Philip smiled and said: "I scarcely knew, until this moment, that I had missed you so much, Joseph!"

"Have you come to stay?" Joseph asked.

"I think so. The branch railway down the valley, which you know was projected, is to be built immediately; but there are other reasons why the furnaces should be in blast. If it is possible, the work—and my settlement with it—will begin without any further delay. Is she your first family visit?"

He pointed towards the station.

"She will be with us a fortnight; but you will come, Philip?"

"To be sure!" Philip exclaimed. "I only saw her face indistinctly through the veil, but her nod said to me, 'A nearer approach is not objectionable.' Certainly, Miss Blessing; but with all the conventional forms, if you please!"

There was something of scorn and bitterness in the laugh which accompanied these words, and Joseph looked at him with a puzzled air.

"You may as well know now," Philip whispered, "that when I was a spoony youth of twenty, I very nearly imagined myself in love with Miss Clementina Blessing, and she encouraged my greenness until it spread as fast as a bamboo or a gourd-vine. Of course, I've long since congratulated myself that she cut me up, root and branch, when our family fortune was lost. The awkwardness of our intercourse is all on her side. Can she still have faith in her charms and my youth, I wonder? Ye gods! that would be a lovely conclusion of the comedy!"

Joseph could only join in the laugh as they parted. There was no time to reflect upon what had been said. Clementina, nevertheless, assumed a new interest in his eyes; and as he drove her towards the farm, he could not avoid connecting her with Philip in his thoughts. She, too, was evidently preoccupied with the meeting, for Philip's name soon floated to the surface of their conversation.

"I expect a visit from him soon," said Joseph. As she was silent, he ventured to add: "You have no objections to meeting with him, I suppose?"

"Mr. Held is still a gentleman, I believe," Clementina replied, and then changed the subject of conversation.

Julia flew at her sister with open arms, and showered on her a profusion of kisses, all of which were received with perfect serenity, Clementina merely saying, as soon as she could get breath: "Dear me, Julia, I scarcely recognize you! You are already so countrified!"

Rachel Miller, although a woman, and notwithstanding her recent experience, found herself greatly bewildered by this new apparition.

Clementina's slow, deliberate movements and her even-toned, musical utterance impressed her with a certain respect; yet the qualities of character they suggested never manifested themselves. On the contrary, the same words, in any other mouth, would have often expressed malice or heartlessness. Sometimes she heard her own homely phrases repeated, as if by the most unconscious purposeless imitation, and had Julia either smiled or appeared annoyed her suspicions might have been excited; as it was, she was constantly and sorely puzzled.

Once only, and for a moment, the two masks were slightly lifted. At dinner, Clementina, who had turned the conversation upon the subject of birthdays, suddenly said to Joseph: "By the way, Mr. Asten, has Julia told you her age?"

Julia gave a little start, but presently looked up, with an expression meant to be artless.

"I knew it before we were married," Joseph quietly answered.

Clementina bit her lip. Julia, concealing her surprise, flashed a triumphant glance at her sister, then a tender one at Joseph, and said: "We will both let the old birthdays go; we will only have one and the same anniversary from this time on!"

Joseph felt, through some natural magnetism of his nature rather than from any perceptible evidence, that Clementina was sharply and curiously watching the relation between himself and his wife. He had no fear of her detecting misgivings which were not yet acknowledged to himself, but was instinctively on his guard in her presence.

It was not many days before Philip called. Julia received him cordially, as the friend of her husband, while Clementina bowed with an impassive face, without rising from her seat. Philip, however, crossed the room and gave her his hand, saying cheerily: "We used to be old friends, Miss Blessing. You have not forgotten me?"

"We cannot forget when we have been asked to do so," she warbled.

Philip took a chair. "Eight years!" he said: "I am the only one who has changed in that time."

Julia, looked at her sister, but the latter was apparently absorbed in comparing some zephyr tints.

"The whirligig of time!" he exclaimed: "who can foresee anything? Then I was an ignorant, petted young aristocrat,—an expectant heir; now behold me, working among miners and puddlers and forgemen! It's a rough but wholesome change. Would you believe it, Mrs. Asten, I've forgotten the mazurka!"

"I wish to forget it," Julia replied: "the spring-house is as important to me as the furnace to you."

"Have you seen the Hopetons lately?" Clementina asked.

Joseph saw a shade pass over Philip's face, and he seemed to hesitate a moment before answering: "I hear they will be neighbors of mine next summer. Mr. Hopeton is interested in the new branch down the valley, and has purchased the old Calvert property for a country residence."

"Indeed? Then you will often see them."

"I hope so: they are very agreeable people. But I shall also have my own little household: my sister will probably join me."

"Not Madeline!" exclaimed Julia.

"Madeline," Philip answered. "It has long been her wish, as well as mine. You know the little cottage on the knoll, at Coventry, Joseph! I have taken it for a year."

"There will be quite a city society," murmured Clementina, in her sweetest tones. "You will need no commiseration, Julia. Unless, indeed, the country people succeed in changing you all into their own likeness. Mrs. Hopeton will certainly create a sensation. I am told that she is very extravagant, Mr. Held?"

"I have never seen her husband's bank account," said Philip, dryly.

He rose presently, and Joseph accompanied him to the lane. Philip, with the bridle-rein over his arm, delayed to mount his horse, while the mechanical commonplaces of speech, which, somehow, always absurdly come to the lips when graver interests have possession of the heart, were exchanged by the two. Joseph felt, rather than saw, that Philip was troubled. Presently the latter said: "Something is coming over both of us,—not between us. I thought I should tell you a little more, but perhaps it is too soon. If I guess rightly, neither of us is ready. Only this, Joseph, let us each think of the other as a help and a support!"

"I do, Philip!" Joseph answered. "I see there is some influence at work which I do not understand, but I am not impatient to know what it is. As for myself, I seem to know nothing at all; but you can judge,—you see all there is."

Even as he pronounced these words Joseph felt that they were not strictly sincere, and almost expected to find an expression of reproof in Philip's eyes. But no: they softened until he only saw a pitying tenderness. Then he knew that the doubts which he had resisted with all the force of his nature were clearly revealed to Philip's mind.

They shook bands, and parted in silence; and Joseph, as he looked up to the gray blank of heaven, asked himself: "Is this all? Has my life already taken the permanent imprint of its future?"

CHAPTER XIV. THE AMARANTH.

Clementina returned to the city without having made any very satisfactory discovery. Her parting was therefore conventionally tender: she even thanked Joseph for his hospitality, and endeavored to throw a little natural emphasis into her words as she expressed the hope of being allowed to renew her visit in the summer.

During her stay it seemed to Joseph that the early harmony of his household had been restored. Julia's manner had been so gentle and amiable, that, on looking back, he was inclined to believe that the loneliness of her new life was alone responsible for any change. But after Clementina's departure his doubts were reawakened in a more threatening form. He could not guess, as yet, the terrible chafing of a smiling mask; of a restraint which must not only conceal itself, but counterfeit its opposite; of the assumption by a narrow, cold, and selfish nature of virtues which it secretly despises. He could not have foreseen that the gentleness, which had nearly revived his faith in her, would so suddenly disappear. But it was gone, like a glimpse of the sun through the winter fog. The hard, watchful expression came back to Julia's face; the lowered eyelids no longer gave a fictitious depth to her shallow, tawny pupils; the soft roundness of her voice took on a frequent harshness, and the desire of asserting her own will in all things betrayed itself through her affected habits of yielding and seeking counsel.

She continued her plan of making herself acquainted with all the details of the farm business. When the roads began to improve, in the early spring, she insisted in driving to the village alone, and Joseph soon found that she made good use of these journeys in extending her knowledge of the social and pecuniary standing of all the neighboring families. She talked with farmers, mechanics, and drovers; became familiar with the fluctuations in the prices of grain and cattle; learned to a penny the wages paid for every form of service; and thus felt, from week to week, the ground growing more secure under her feet.

Joseph was not surprised to see that his aunt's participation in the direction of the household gradually diminished. Indeed, he scarcely noticed the circumstance at all, but he was at last forced to remark her increasing silence and the trouble of her face. To all appearance the domestic harmony was perfect, and if Rachel Miller felt some natural regret at being obliged to divide her sway, it was a matter, he thought, wherein he had best not interfere. One day, however, she surprised him by the request:—

"Joseph, can you take or send me to Magnolia to-morrow?"

"Certainly, Aunt!" he replied. "I suppose you want to visit Cousin Phebe; you have not seen her since last summer."

"It was that,—and something more." She paused a moment, and then added, more firmly: "She has always wished that I should make my home with her, but I couldn't think of any change so long as I was needed here. It seems to me that I am not really needed now."

"Why, Aunt Rachel!" Joseph exclaimed, "I meant this to be your home always, as much as mine! Of course you are needed,—not to do all that you have done heretofore, but as a part of the family. It is your right."

"I understand all that, Joseph. But I've heard it said that a young wife should learn to see to everything herself, and Julia, I'm sure, doesn't need either my help or my advice."

Joseph's face became very grave. "Has she—has she—?" he stammered.

"No," said Rachel, "she has not said it—in words. Different persons have different ways. She is quick, O very quick!—and capable. You know I could never sit idly by, and look on; and it's hard to be directed. I seem to belong to the place and everything connected with it; yet there's times when what a body ought to do is plain."

In endeavoring to steer a middle course between her conscience and her tender regard for her nephew's feelings Rachel only confused and troubled him. Her words conveyed something of the truth which she sought to hide under them. She was both angered and humiliated; the resistance

832

with which she had attempted to meet Julia's domestic innovations was no match for the latter's tactics; it had gone down like a barrier of reeds and been contemptuously trampled under foot. She saw herself limited, opposed, and finally set aside by a cheerful dexterity of management which evaded her grasp whenever she tried to resent it. Definite acts, whereon to base her indignation, seemed to slip from her memory, but the atmosphere of the house became fatal to her. She felt this while she spoke, and felt also that Joseph must be spared.

"Aunt Rachel," said he, "I know that Julia is very anxious to learn everything which she thinks belongs to her place,—perhaps a little more than is really necessary. She's an enthusiastic nature, you know. Maybe you are not fully acquainted yet; maybe you have misunderstood her in some things: I would like to think so."

"It is true that we are different, Joseph,—very different. I don't say, therefore, that I'm always right. It's likely, indeed, that any young wife and any old housekeeper like myself would have their various notions. But where there can be only one head, it's the wife's place to be that head. Julia has not asked it of me, but she has the right. I can't say, also, that I don't need a little rest and change, and there seems to be some call on me to oblige Phebe. Look at the matter in the true light," she continued, seeing that Joseph remained silent, "and you must feel that it's only natural."

"I hope so," he said at last, repressing a sigh; "all things are changing."

"What can we do?" Julia asked, that evening, when he had communicated to her his aunt's resolution; "it would be so delightful if she would stay, and yet I have had a presentiment that she would leave us—for a little while only, I hope. Dear, good Aunt Rachel! I couldn't help seeing how hard it was for her to allow the least change in the order of housekeeping. She would be perfectly happy if I would sit still all day and let her tire herself to death; but how can I do that, Joseph? And no two women have exactly the same ways and habits. I've tried to make everything pleasant for her: if she would only leave many little matters entirely to me, or at least not think of them,—but I fear she cannot. She manages to see the least that I do, and secretly worries about it, in the very kindness of her heart. Why can't women carry on partnerships in housekeeping as men do in business? I suppose we are too particular; perhaps I am just as much so as Aunt Rachel. I have no doubt she thinks a little hardly of me, and so it would do her good—we should really come nearer again—if she had a change. If she will go, Joseph, she must at least leave us with the feeling that our home is always hers, whenever she chooses to accept it."

Julia bent over Joseph's chair, gave him a rapid kiss, and then went off to make her peace with Aunt Rachel. When the two women came to the tea-table the latter had an uncertain, bewildered air, while the eyelids of the former were red,—either from tears or much rubbing.

A fortnight afterwards Rachel Miller left the farm and went to reside with her widowed niece, in Magnolia.

The day after her departure another surprise came to Joseph in the person of his father-in-law. Mr. Blessing arrived in a hired vehicle from the station. His face was so red and radiant from the March winds, and perhaps some private source of satisfaction, that his sudden arrival could not possibly be interpreted as an omen of ill-fortune. He shook hands with the Irish groom who had driven him over, gave him a handsome gratuity in addition to the hire of the team, extracted an elegant travelling-satchel from under the seat, and met Joseph at the gate, with a breezy burst of feeling:—

"God bless you, son-in-law! It does my heart good to see you again! And then, at last, the pleasure of beholding your ancestral seat; really, this is quite—quite manorial!"

Julia, with a loud cry of "O pa!" came rushing from the house.

"Bless me, how wild and fresh the child looks!" cried Mr. Blessing, after the embrace. "Only see the country roses on her cheeks! Almost too young and sparkling for Lady Asten, of Asten Hall, eh? As Dryden says, 'Happy, happy, happy pair!' It takes me back to the days when I was a gay young lark; but I must have a care, and not make an old fool of myself. Let us go in and subside into soberness: I am ready both to laugh and cry."

When they were seated in the comfortable front room, Mr. Blessing opened his satchel and produced a large leather-covered flask. Julia was probably accustomed to his habits, for she at once brought a glass from the sideboard.

"I am still plagued with my old cramps," her father said to Joseph, as he poured out a stout dose. "Physiologists, you know, have discovered that stimulants diminish the wear and tear of life, and I find their theories correct. You, in your pastoral isolation and pecuniary security, can form no conception of the tension under which we men of office and of the world live, Beatus ille, and so forth,—strange that the only fragment of Latin which I remember should be so appropriate! A little water, if you please, Julia."

In the evening, when Mr. Blessing, slippered, sat before the open fireplace, with a cigar in his mouth, the object of his sudden visit crept by slow degrees to the light. "Have you been dipping into oil?" he asked Joseph.

Julia made haste to reply. "Not yet, but almost everybody in the neighborhood is ready to do so now, since Clemson has realized his fifty thousand dollars in a single year. They are talking of nothing else in the village. I heard yesterday, Joseph, that Old Bishop has taken three thousand dollars' worth of stock in a new company."

"Take my advice, and don't touch 'em!" exclaimed Mr. Blessing.

"I had not intended to," said Joseph.

"There is this thing about these excitements," Mr. Blessing continued: "they never reach the rural districts until the first sure harvest is over. The sharp, intelligent operators in the large cities—the men who are ready to take up soap, thimbles, hand-organs, electricity, or hymn-books, at a moment's notice—always cut into a new thing before its value is guessed by the multitude. Then the smaller fry follow and secure their second crop, while your quiet men in the country are shaking their heads and crying 'humbug!' Finally, when it really gets to be a humbug, in a speculative sense, they just begin to believe in it, and are fair game for the bummers and camp-followers of the financial army. I respect Clemson, though I never heard of him before; as for Old Bishop, he may be a very worthy man, but he'll never see the color of his three thousand dollars again."

"Pa!" cried Julia, "how clear you do make everything. And to think that I was wishing—O, wishing so much!—that Joseph would go into oil."

She hung her head a little, looking at Joseph with an affectionate, penitent glance. A quick gleam of satisfaction passed over Mr. Blessing's face; he smiled to himself, puffed rapidly at his cigar for a minute, and then resumed: "In such a field of speculation everything depends on being initiated. There are men in the city—friends of mine—who know every foot of ground in the Alleghany Valley. They can smell oil, if it's a thousand feet deep. They never touch a thing that isn't safe,—but, then, they know what's safe. In spite of the swindling that's going on, it takes years to exhaust the good points; just so sure as your honest neighbors here will lose, just so sure will these friends of mine gain. There are millions in what they have under way, at this moment."

"What is it?" Julia breathlessly asked, while Joseph's face betrayed that his interest was somewhat aroused.

Mr. Blessing unlocked his satchel, and took from it a roll of paper, which he began to unfold upon his knee. "Here," he said, "you see this bend of the river, just about the centre of the oil region, which is represented by the yellow color. These little dots above the bend are the celebrated Fluke Wells; the other dots below are the equally celebrated Chowder Wells. The distance between the two is nearly three miles. Here is an untouched portion of the treasure,—a pocket of Pactolus waiting to be rifled. A few of us have acquired the land, and shall commence boring immediately."

"But," said Joseph, "it seems to me that either the attempt must have been made already, or that the land must command such an enormous price as to lessen the profits."

"Wisely spoken! It is the first question which would occur to any prudent mind. But what if I say that neither is the case? And you, who are familiar with the frequent eccentricities of old farmers, can understand the explanation. The owner of the land was one of your ignorant, stubborn men, who took such a dislike to the prospectors and speculators, that he refused

836

to let them come near him. Both the Fluke and Chowder Companies tried their best to buy him out, but he had a malicious pleasure in leading them on to make immense offers, and then refusing. Well, a few months ago he died, and his heirs were willing enough to let the land go; but before it could be regularly offered for sale, the Fluke and Chowder Wells began to flow less and less. Their shares fell from 270 to 95; the supposed value of the land fell with them, and finally the moment arrived when we could purchase for a very moderate sum. I see the question in your mind; why should we wish to buy when the other wells were giving out? There comes in the secret, which is our veritable success. Consider it whispered in your ears, and locked in your bosoms,—torpedoes! It was not then generally exploded (to carry out the image), so we bought at the low figure, in the very nick of time. Within a week the Fluke and Chowder Wells were torpedoed, and came back to more than their former capacity; the shares rose as rapidly as they had fallen, and the central body we hold—to which they are, as it were, the two arms—could now be sold for ten times what it cost us!"

Here Mr. Blessing paused, with his finger on the map, and a light of merited triumph in his eyes. Julia clapped her hands, sprang to her feet, and cried: "Trumps at last!"

"Ay," said he, "wealth, repose for my old days,—wealth for us all, if your husband will but take the hand I hold out to him. You now know, son-in-law, why the endorsement you gave me was of such vital importance; the note, as you are aware, will mature in another week. Why should you not charge yourself with the payment, in consideration of the transfer to you of shares of the original stock, already so immensely appreciated in value? I have delayed making any provision, for the sake of offering you the chance."

Julia was about to speak, but restrained herself with an apparent effort.

"I should like to know," Joseph said, "who are associated with you in the undertaking?"

"Well done, again! Where did you get your practical shrewdness? The best men in the city!—not only the Collector and the Surveyor, but Congressman Whaley, E. D. Stokes, of Stokes, Pirricutt and Company, and even the Reverend Doctor Lellifant. If I had not been an old friend of Kanuck, the agent who negotiated the purchase, my chance would have been impalpably small. I have all the documents with me. There has been no more splendid opportunity since oil became a power! I hesitate to advise even one so near to me in such matters; but if you knew the certainties as I know them, you would go in with all your available capital. The excitement, as you say, has reached the country communities, which are slow to rise and equally slow to subside; all oil stock will be in demand, but the Amaranth,—'The Blessing,' they wished to call it, but I was obliged to decline, for official reasons,—the Amaranth shares will be the golden apex of the market!"

Julia looked at Joseph with eager, hungry eyes. He, too, was warmed and tempted by the prospect of easy profit which the scheme held out to him; only the habit of his nature resisted, but with still diminishing force. "I might venture the thousand," he said.

"It is no venture!" Julia cried. "In all the speculations I have heard discussed by pa and his friends, there was nothing so admirably managed as this. Such a certainty of profit may never come again. If you will be advised by me, Joseph, you will take shares to the amount of five or ten thousand."

"Ten thousand is exactly the amount I hold open," Mr. Blessing gravely remarked. "That, however, does not represent the necessary payment, which can hardly amount to more than twenty-five per cent. before we begin to realize. Only ten per cent. has yet been called, so that your thousand at present will secure you an investment of ten thousand. Really, it seems like a fortunate coincidence."

He went on, heating himself with his own words, until the possibilities of the case grew so splendid that Joseph felt himself dazzled and bewildered. Mr. Blessing was a master in the art of seductive statement. Even where he was only the mouthpiece of another, a few repetitions led him to the profoundest belief. Here there could be no doubt of his sincerity, and, moreover, every movement from the very inception of the scheme, every statistical item, all collateral influences, were clear in his mind and instantly accessible. Although he began by saying, "I will make no estimate of the profits, because it is not prudent to fix our hopes on a positive sum," he was soon carried far away from this resolution, and most luxuriously engaged, pencil in hand, in figuring out results which drove Julia wild with desire, and almost took away Joseph's breath. The latter finally said, as they rose from the session, late at night:—

"It is settled that I take as much as the thousand will cover; but I would rather think over the matter quietly for a day or two before venturing further."

"You must," replied Mr. Blessing, patting him on the shoulder. "These things are so new to your experience, that they disturb and—I might almost say—alarm you. It is like bringing an increase of oxygen into your mental atmosphere. (Ha! a good figure: for the result will be, a richer, fuller life. I must remember it.) But you are a healthy organization, and therefore you are certain to see clearly: I can wait with confidence."

The next morning Joseph, without declaring his purpose, drove to Coventry Forge to consult Philip. Mr. Blessing and Julia, remaining at home, went over the shining ground again, and yet again, confirming each other in the determination to secure it. Even Joseph, as he passed up the valley in the mild March weather, taking note of the crimson and gold of the flowering spice-bushes and maple-trees, could not prevent his thoughts from dwelling on the delights of wealth,—society, books, travel, and all the mellow, fortunate expansion of life. Involuntarily, he hoped that Philip's counsel might coincide with his father-in-law's offer.

But Philip was not at home. The forge was in full activity, the cottage on the knoll was repainted and made attractive in various ways, and Philip would soon return with his sister to establish a permanent home. Joseph found the sign-spiritual of his friend in numberless little touches and changes; it seemed to him that a new soul had entered into the scenery of the place.

A mile or two farther up the valley, a company of mechanics and laborers were apparently tearing the old Calvert mansion inside out. House, barn, garden, and lawn were undergoing a complete transformation. While he paused at the entrance of the private lane, to take a survey of the operations, Mr. Clemson rode down to him from the house. The Hopetons, he said, would migrate from the city early in May: work had already commenced on the new railway, and in another year a different life would come upon the whole neighborhood.

In the course of the conversation Joseph ventured to sound Mr. Clemson in regard to the newly formed oil companies. The latter frankly confessed that he had withdrawn from further speculation, satisfied with his fortune; he preferred to give no opinion, further than that money was still to be made, if prudently placed. Tho Fluke and Chowder Wells, he said, were old, well known, and profitable. The new application of torpedoes had restored their failing flow, and the stock had recovered from its temporary depreciation. His own venture had been made in another part of the region.

The atmosphere into which Joseph entered, on returning home, took away all further power of resistance. Tempted already, and impressed by what he had learned, he did what his wife and father-in-law desired.

CHAPTER XV. A DINNER PARTY.

Having assumed the payment of Mr. Blessing's note, as the first instalment upon his stock, Joseph was compelled to prepare himself for future emergencies. A year must still elapse before the term of the mortgage upon his farm would expire, but the sums he had invested for the purpose of meeting it when due must be held ready for use. The assurance of great and certain profit in the mean time rendered this step easy; and, even at the worst, he reflected, there would be no difficulty in procuring a now mortgage whereby to liquidate the old. A notice which he received at this time, that a second assessment of ten per cent. on the Amaranth stock had been made, was both unexpected and disquieting. Mr. Blessing, however, accompanied it with a letter, making clear not only the necessity, but the admirable wisdom of a greater present outlay than had been anticipated. So the first of April—the usual business anniversary of the neighborhood—went smoothly by. Money was plenty, the Asten credit had always been sound, and Joseph tasted for the first time a pleasant sense of power in so easily receiving and transferring considerable sums.

One result of the venture was the development of a new phase in Julia's nature. She not only accepted the future profit as certain, but she had apparently calculated its exact amount and framed her plans accordingly. If she had been humiliated by the character of Joseph's first business transaction with her father, she now made amends for it. "Pa" was their good genius. "Pa" was the agency whereby they should achieve wealth and social importance. Joseph now had the clearest evidence of the difference between a man who knew the world and was of value in it, and their slow, dull-headed country neighbors. Indeed, Julia seemed to consider the Asten property as rather contemptible beside the splendor of the Blessing scheme. Her gratitude for a quiet home, her love of country life, her disparagement of the shams and exactions of "society," were given up as suddenly and coolly as if she had never affected them. She gave herself no pains to make the transition gradual, and thus lessen its shock. Perhaps she supposed that Joseph's fresh, unsuspicious nature was so plastic that it had already sufficiently taken her impress, and that he would easily forget the mask she had worn. If so, she was seriously mistaken.

He saw, with a deadly chill of the heart, the change in her manner,—a change so complete that another face confronted him at the table, even as another heart beat beside his on the dishallowed marriage-bed. He saw the gentle droop vanish from the eyelids, leaving the cold, flinty pupils unshaded; the soft appeal of the half-opened lips was lost in the rigid, almost cruel compression which now seemed habitual to them; all the slight dependent gestures, the tender airs of reference to his will or pleasure, had rapidly transformed themselves into expressions of command or obstinate resistance. But the patience of a loving man is equal to that of a loving woman: he was silent, although his silence covered an ever-increasing sense of outrage.

Once it happened, that after Julia had been unusually eloquent concerning "what pa is doing for us," and what use they should make of "pa's money, as I call it," Joseph quietly remarked:—

"You seem to forget, Julia, that without my money not much could have been done."

An angry color came into her face; but, on second thought, she bent her head, and murmured in an offended voice: "It is very mean and ungenerous in you to refer to our temporary poverty. You might forget, by this time, the help pa was compelled to ask of you."

"I did not think of that!" he exclaimed. "Besides, you did not seem entirely satisfied with my help, at the time."

"O, how you misunderstand me!" she groaned. "I only wished to know the extent of his need. He is so generous, so considerate towards us, that we only guess his misfortune at the last moment."

The possibility of being unjust silenced Joseph. There were tears in Julia's voice, and he imagined they would soon rise to her eyes. After a long, uncomfortable pause, he said, for the sake of changing the subject: "What can have become of Elwood Withers? I have not seen him for months."

"I don't think you need care to know," she remarked. "He's a rough, vulgar fellow: it's just as well if he keeps away from us."

"Julia! he is my friend, and must always be welcome to me. You were friendly enough towards him, and towards all the neighborhood, last summer: how is it that you have not a good word to say now?"

He spoke warmly and indignantly. Julia, however, looked at him with a calm, smiling face. "It is very simple," she said. "You will agree with me, in another year. A guest, as I was, must try to see only the pleasant side of people: that's our duty; and so I enjoyed—as much as I could—the rusticity, the awkwardness, the ignorance, the (now, don't be vexed, dear!)—the vulgarity of your friend. As one of the society of the neighborhood, as a resident, I am not bound by any such delicacy. I take the same right to judge and select as I should take anywhere. Unless I am to be hypocritical, I cannot—towards you, at least—conceal my real feelings. How shall I ever get you to see the difference between yourself and these people, unless I continually point it out? You are modest, and don't like to acknowledge your own superiority."

She rose from the table, laughing, and went out of the room humming a lively air, leaving Joseph to make the best of her words.

A few days after this the work on the branch railway, extending down the valley, reached a point where it could be seen from the Asten farm. Joseph, on riding over to inspect the operations, was surprised to find Elwood, who had left his father's place and become a sub-contractor. The latter showed his hearty delight at their meeting.

"I've been meaning to come up," he said, "but this is a busy time for me. It's a chance I couldn't let slip, and now that I've taken hold I must hold on. I begin to think this is the thing I was made for, Joseph."

"I never thought of it before," Joseph answered, "and yet I'm sure you are right. How did you hit upon it?"

"I didn't; it was Mr. Held."

"Philip?"

"Him. You know I've been hauling for the Forge, and so it turned up by degrees, as I may say. He's at home, and, I expect, looking for you. But how are you now, really?"

Elwood's question meant a great deal more than he knew how to say. Suddenly, in a flash of memory, their talk of the previous year returned to Joseph's mind; he saw his friend's true instincts and his own blindness as never before. But he must dissemble, if possible, with that strong, rough, kindly face before him.

"O," he said, attempting a cheerful air, "I am one of the old folks now. You must come up—"

The recollection of Julia's words cut short the invitation upon his lips. A sharp pang went through his heart, and the treacherous blood crowded to his face all the more that he tried to hold it back.

"Come, and I'll show you where we're going to make the cutting," Elwood quietly said, taking him by the arm. Joseph fancied, thenceforth, that there was a special kindness in his manner, and the suspicion seemed to rankle in his mind as if he had been slighted by his friend.

As before, to vary the tedium of his empty life, so now, to escape from the knowledge which he found himself more and more powerless to resist, he busied himself beyond all need with the work of the farm. Philip had returned with his sister, he knew, but after the meeting with Elwood he shrank with a painful dread from Philip's heart-deep, intimate eye. Julia, however, all the more made use of the soft spring weather to survey the social ground, and choose where to take her stand. Joseph scarcely knew, indeed, how extensive her operations had been, until she announced an invitation to dine with the Hopetons, who were now in possession of the renovated Calvert place. She enlarged, more than was necessary, on the distinguished city position of the family, and the importance of "cultivating" its country members. Joseph's single brief meeting with Mr. Hopeton—who was a short, solid man, in ripe middle age, of a thoroughly cosmopolitan, though not a remarkably intellectual stamp—had been agreeable, and he recognized the obligation to be neighborly. Therefore he readily accepted the invitation on his own grounds.

When the day arrived, Julia, after spending the morning over her toilet, came forth resplendent in rosy silk, bright and dazzling in complexion, and with all her former grace of languid eyelids and parted lips. The void in Joseph's heart grew wider at the sight of her; for he perceived, as never before, her consummate skill in assuming a false character. It seemed incredible that he should have been so deluded. For the first time a feeling of repulsion, which was almost disgust, came upon him as he listened to her prattle of delight in the soft weather, and the fragrant woods, and the blossoming orchards. Was not, also, this delight assumed? he asked himself: false in one thing, false in all, was the fatal logic which then and there began its torment.

The most that was possible in such a short time had been achieved on the Calvert place. The house had been brightened, surrounded by light, airy verandas, and the lawn and garden, thrown into one and given into the hands of a skilful gardener, were scarcely to be recognized. A broad, solid gravel-walk replaced the old tan-covered path; a pretty fountain tinkled before the door; thick beds of geranium in flower studded the turf, and veritable thickets of rose-trees were waiting for June. Within the house, some rooms had been thrown together, the walls richly yet harmoniously colored, and the sumptuous furniture thus received a proper setting. In contrast to the houses of even the wealthiest farmers, which expressed a nicely reckoned sufficiency of comfort, the place had an air of joyous profusion, of a wealth which delighted in itself.

Mr. Hopeton met them with the frank, offhand manner of a man of business. His wife followed, and the two guests made a rapid inspection of her as she came down the hall. Julia noticed that her crocus-colored dress was high in the neck, and plainly trimmed; that she wore no ornaments, and that the natural pallor of her complexion had not been corrected by art. Joseph remarked the simple grace of her movement, the large, dark, inscrutable eyes, the smooth bands of her black hair, and the pure though somewhat lengthened oval of her face. The gentle dignity of her manner more than refreshed, it soothed him. She was so much younger than her husband that Joseph involuntarily wondered how they should have come together.

The greetings were scarcely over before Philip and Madeline Held arrived. Julia, with the least little gush of tenderness, kissed the latter, whom Philip then presented to Joseph for the first time. She had the same wavy hair as her brother, but the golden hue was deepened nearly into brown, and her eyes were a clear hazel. It was also the same frank, firm face, but her woman's smile was so much the sweeter as her lips were lovelier than the man's. Joseph seemed to clasp an instant friendship in her offered hand.

There was but one other guest, who, somewhat to his surprise, was Lucy Henderson. Julia concealed whatever she might have felt, and made so much reference to their former meetings as might satisfy Lucy without conveying to Mrs. Hopeton the impression of any special intimacy. Lucy looked thin and worn, and her black silk dress was not of the latest fashion: she seemed to be the poor relation of the company. Joseph learned that she had taken one of the schools in the valley, for the summer. Her manner to him was as simple and friendly as ever, but he felt the presence of some new element of strength and self-reliance in her nature.

His place at dinner was beside Mrs. Hopeton, while Lucy—apparently by accident—sat upon the other side of the hostess. Philip and the host led the conversation, confining it too exclusively to the railroad and iron interests; but those finally languished, and gave way to other topics in which all could take part. Joseph felt that while the others, except Lucy and himself, were fashioned under different aspects of life, some of which they shared in common, yet that their seeming ease and freedom of communication touched, here and there, some invisible limit, which they were careful not to pass. Even Philip appeared to be beyond his reach, for the time.

The country and the people, being comparatively new to them, naturally came to be discussed.

"Mr. Held, or Mr. Asten,—either of you know both,"—Mr. Hopeton asked, "what are the principal points of difference between society in the city and in the country?"

"Indeed, I know too little of the city," said Joseph.

"And I know too little of the country,—here, at least," Philip added. "Of course the same passions and prejudices come into play everywhere. There are circles, there are jealousies, ups and downs, scandals, suppressions, and rehabilitations: it can't be otherwise."

"Are they not a little worse in the country," said Julia, "because—I may ask the question here, among us—there is less refinement of manner?"

"If the external forms are ruder," Philip resumed, "it may be an advantage, in one sense. Hypocrisy cannot be developed into an art."

Julia bit her lip, and was silent.

"But are the country people, hereabouts, so rough?" Mrs. Hopeton asked. "I confess that they don't seem so to me. What do you say, Miss Henderson?"

"Perhaps I am not an impartial witness," Lucy answered. "We care less about what is called 'manners' than the city people. We have no fixed rules for dress and behavior,—only we don't like any one to differ too much from the rest of us."

"That's it!" Mr. Hopeton cried; "the tyrannical levelling sentiment of an imperfectly developed community! Fortunately, I am beyond its reach."

Julia's eyes sparkled: she looked across the table at Joseph, with a triumphant air.

Philip suddenly raised his head. "How would you correct it? Simply by resistance?" he asked.

Mr. Hopeton laughed. "I should no doubt get myself into a hornet's-nest. No; by indifference!"

Then Madeline Held spoke. "Excuse me," she said; "but is indifference possible, even if it were right? You seem to take the levelling spirit for granted, without looking into its character and causes; there must be some natural sense of justice, no matter how imperfectly society is developed. We are members of this community,—at least, Philip and I certainly consider ourselves so,—and I am determined not to judge it without knowledge, or to offend what may be only mechanical habits of thought, unless I can see a sure advantage in doing so."

Lucy Henderson looked at the speaker with a bright, grateful face. Joseph's eyes wandered from her to Julia, who was silent and watchful.

"But I have no time for such conscientious studies," Mr. Hopeton resumed. "One can be satisfied with half a dozen neighbors, and let the mass go. Indifference, after all, is the best philosophy. What do you say, Mr. Held?"

"Indifference!" Philip echoed. A dark flush came into his face, and he was silent a moment. "Yes: our hearts are inconvenient appendages. We suffer a deal from unnecessary sympathies, and from imagining, I suppose, that others feel them as we do. These uneasy features of society are simply the effort of nature to find some occupation for brains otherwise idle—or empty. Teach the people to think, and they will disappear."

Joseph stared at Philip, feeling that a secret bitterness was hidden under his careless, mocking air. Mrs. Hopeton rose, and the company left the table. Madeline Held had a troubled expression, but there was an eager, singular brightness in Julia's eyes.

"Emily, let us have coffee on the veranda," said Mr. Hopeton, leading the way. He had already half forgotten the subject of conversation: his own expressions, in fact, had been made very much at random, for the sole purpose of keeping up the flow of talk. He had no very fixed views of any kind, beyond the sphere of his business activity.

Philip, noticing the impression he had made on Joseph, drew him to one side. "Don't seriously remember my words against me," he said; "you were sorry to hear them, I know. All I meant was, that an over-sensitive tenderness towards everybody is a fault. Besides, I was provoked to answer him in his own vein."

"But, Philip!" Joseph whispered, "such words tempt me! What if they were true?"

Philip grasped his arm with a painful force. "They never can be true to you, Joseph," he said.

Gay and pleasant as the company seemed to be, each one felt a secret sense of relief when it came to an end. As Joseph drove homewards, silently recalling what had been said, Julia interrupted his reflections with: "Well, what do you think of the Hopetons?"

"She is an interesting woman," he answered.

"But reserved; and she shows very little taste in dress. However, I suppose you hardly noticed anything of the kind. She kept Lucy Henderson beside her as a foil: Madeline Held would have been damaging."

Joseph only partly guessed her meaning; it was repugnant, and he determined to avoid its further discussion.

"Hopeton is a shrewd business man," Julia continued, "but he cannot compare with her for shrewdness—either with her or—Philip Held!"

"What do you mean?"

"I made a discovery before the dinner was over, which you—innocent, unsuspecting man that you are—might have before your eyes for years, without seeing it. Tell me now, honestly, did you notice nothing?"

"What should I notice, beyond what was said?" he asked.

"That was the least!" she cried; "but, of course, I knew you couldn't. And perhaps you won't believe me, when I tell you that Philip Held,— your particular friend, your hero, for aught I know your pattern of virtue and character, and all that is manly and noble,—that Philip Held, I say, is furiously in love with Mrs. Hopeton!"

Joseph started as if he had been shot, and turned around with an angry red on his brow. "Julia!" he said, "how dare you speak so of Philip!"

She laughed. "Because I dare to speak the truth, when I see it. I thought I should surprise you. I remembered a certain rumor I had heard before she was married,—while she was Emily Marrable,—and I watched them closer than they guessed. I'm certain of Philip: as for her, she's a deep creature, and she was on her guard; but they are near neighbors."

Joseph was thoroughly aroused and indignant. "It is your own fancy!" he exclaimed. "You hate Philip on account of that affair with Clementina; but you ought to have some respect for the woman whose hospitality you have accepted!"

"Bless me! I have any quantity of respect both for her and her furniture. By the by, Joseph, our parlor would furnish better than hers; I have been thinking of a few changes we might make, which would wonderfully improve the house. As for Philip, Clementina was a fool. She'd be glad enough to have him now, but in these matters, once gone is gone for good. Somehow, people who marry for love very often get rich afterwards,—ourselves, for instance."

It was some time before Joseph's excitement subsided. He had resented Julia's suspicion as dishonorable to Philip, yet he could not banish the conjecture of its possible truth. If Philip's affected cynicism had tempted him, Julia's unblushing assumption of the existence of a passion which was forbidden, and therefore positively guilty, seemed to stain the pure texture of his nature. The lightness with which she spoke of the matter was even more abhorrent to him than the assertion itself; the malicious satisfaction in the tones of her voice had not escaped his ear.

"Julia," he said, just before they reached home, "do not mention your fancy to another soul than me. It would reflect discredit on you."

"You are innocent," she answered. "And you are not complimentary. If I have any remarkable quality, it is tact. Whenever I speak, I shall know the effect before-hand; even pa, with all his official experience, is no match for me in this line. I see what the Hopetons are after, and I mean to show them that we were first in the field. Don't be concerned, you good, excitable creature, you are no match for such well-drilled people. Let me alone, and before the summer is over we will give the law to the neighborhood!"

CHAPTER XVI. JOSEPH'S TROUBLE, AND PHILIP'S.

The bare, repulsive, inexorable truth was revealed at last. There was no longer any foothold for doubt, any possibility of continuing his desperate self-deceit. From that day all the joy, the trust, the hope, seemed to fade out of Joseph's life. What had been lost was irretrievable: the delusion of a few months had fixed his fate forever.

His sense of outrage was so strong and keen—so burned upon his consciousness as to affect him like a dull physical pain—that a just and temperate review of his situation was impossible. False in one thing, false in all: that was the single, inevitable conclusion. Of course she had never even loved him. Her coy maiden airs, her warm abandonment to feeling, her very tears and blushes, were artfully simulated: perhaps, indeed, she had laughed in her heart, yea, sneered, at his credulous tenderness! Her assumption of rule, therefore, became an arrogance not to be borne. What right had she, guilty of a crime for which there is no name and no punishment, to reverse the secret justice of the soul, and claim to be rewarded?

So reasoned Joseph to himself, in his solitary broodings; but the spell was not so entirely broken as he imagined. Sternly as he might have resolved in advance, there was a glamour in her mask of cheerfulness and gentleness, which made his resolution seem hard and cruel. In her presence he could not clearly remember his wrongs: the past delusion had been a reality, nevertheless; and he could make no assertion which did not involve his own miserable humiliation. Thus the depth and vital force of his struggle could not be guessed by Julia. She saw only irritable moods, the natural male resistance which she had often remarked in her father,—perhaps, also, the annoyance of giving up certain "romantic" fancies, which she believed to be common to all young men, and never permanent. Even an open rupture could not have pushed them apart so rapidly as this hollow external routine of life.

Joseph took the earliest opportunity of visiting Philip, whom he found busy in forge and foundry. "This would be the life for you!" he said: "we deal only with physical forces, human and elemental: we direct and create power, yet still obey the command to put money in our purses."

"Is that one secret of your strength?" Joseph asked.

"Who told you that I had any?"

"I feel it," said Joseph; and even as he said it he remembered Julia's unworthy suspicion.

"Come up and see Madeline a moment, and the home she has made for me. We get on very well, for brother and sister—especially since her will is about as stubborn as mine."

Madeline was very bright and cheerful, and Joseph, certainly, saw no signs of a stubborn will in her fair face. She was very simply dressed, and busy with some task of needle-work, which she did not lay aside.

"You might pass already for a member of our community," he could not help saying.

"I think your most democratic farmers will accept me," she answered, "when they learn that I am Philip's housekeeper. The only dispute we have had, or are likely to have, is in relation to the salary."

"She is an inconsistent creature, Joseph," said Philip. "I was obliged to offer her as much as she earned by her music-lessons before she would come at all, and now she can't find work enough to balance it."

"How can I, Philip, when you tempt me every day with walks and rides, botany, geology, and sketching from nature?"

So much frank, affectionate confidence showed itself through the playful gossip of the two, that Joseph was at once comforted and pained. "If I had only had a sister!" he sighed to Philip, as they walked down the knoll.

The friends took the valley road, Joseph leading his horse by the bridle. The stream was full to its banks, and crystal clear: shoals of young fishes passed like drifted leaves over the pebbly ground, and the fragrant water-beetles skimmed the surface of the eddies. Overhead the vaults of the great

852

elms and sycamores were filled with the green, delicious illumination of the tender foliage. It was a scene and a season for idle happiness.

Yet the first words Philip spoke, after a long silence, were: "May I speak now?" There was infinite love and pity in his voice. He took Joseph by the hand.

"Yes," the latter whispered.

"It has come," Philip continued; "you cannot hide it from yourself any longer. My pain is that I did not dare to warn you, though at the risk of losing your friendship. There was so little time—"

"You did try to warn me, Philip! I have recalled your words, and the trouble in your face as you spoke, a thousand times. I was a fool, a blind, miserable fool, and my folly has ruined my life!"

"Strange," said Philip, musingly, "that only a perfectly good and pure nature can fall into such a wretched snare. And yet 'Virtue is its own reward,' is dinned into our ears! It is Hell for a single fault: nay, not even a fault, an innocent mistake! But let us see what can be done: is there no common ground whereon your natures can stand together? If there should be a child—"

Joseph shuddered. "Once it seemed too great, too wonderful a hope," he said, "but now, I don't dare to wish for it. Philip, I am too sorely hurt to think clearly: there is nothing to do but to wait. It is a miserable kind of comfort to me to have your sympathy, but I fear you cannot help me."

Philip saw that he could bear no more: his face was pale to the lips and his hands trembled. He led him to the bank, sat down beside him, and laid his arm about his neck. The silence and the caress were more soothing to Joseph than any words; he soon became calm, and remembered an important part of his errand, which was to acquaint Philip with the oil speculation, and to ask his advice.

They discussed the matter long and gravely. With all his questions, and the somewhat imperfect information which Joseph was able to give, Philip could not satisfy himself whether the scheme was a simple swindle or a well-considered business venture. Two or three of the names were respectable, but the chief agent, Kanuck, was unknown to him; moreover, Mr. Blessing's apparent prominence in the undertaking did not inspire him with much confidence.

"How much have you already paid on the stock?" he asked.

"Three instalments, which, Mr. Blessing thinks, is all that will be called for. However, I have the money for a fourth, should it be necessary. He writes to me that the stock has already risen a hundred per cent. in value."

"If that is so," said Philip, "let me advise you to sell half of it, at once. The sum received will cover your liabilities, and the half you retain, as a venture, will give you no further anxiety."

"I had thought of that; yet I am sure that my father-in-law will oppose such a step with all his might. You must know him, Philip; tell me, frankly, your opinion of his character."

"Blessing belongs to a class familiar enough to me," Philip answered; "yet I doubt whether you will comprehend it. He is a swaggering, amiable, magnificent adventurer; never purposely dishonest, I am sure, yet sometimes engaged in transactions that would not bear much scrutiny. His life has been one of ups and downs. After a successful speculation, he is luxurious, open-handed, and absurdly self-confident; his success is soon flung away: he then good-humoredly descends to poverty, because he never believes it can last long. He is unreliable, from his over-sanguine temperament; and yet this very temperament gives him a certain power and influence. Some of our best men are on familiar terms with him. They are on their guard against his pecuniary approaches, they laugh at his extravagant schemes, but they now and then find him useful. I heard Gray, the editor, once speak of him as a man 'filled with available enthusiasms,' and I guess that phrase hits both his strength and his weakness."

On the whole, Joseph felt rather relieved than disquieted. The heart was lighter in his breast as he mounted his horse and rode homewards.

Philip slowly walked forwards, yielding his mind to thoughts wherein

Joseph was an important but not the principal figure. Was there a positive strength, he asked himself, in a wider practical experience of life? Did such experience really strengthen the basis of character which must support a man, when some unexpected moral crisis comes upon him? He knew that he seemed strong, to Joseph; but the latter, so far, was bearing his terrible test with a patience drawn from some source of elemental power. Joseph had simply been ignorant: he had been proud, impatient, and—he now confessed to himself—weakly jealous. In both cases, a mistake had passed beyond the plastic stage where life may still be remoulded: it had hardened into an inexorable fate. What was to be the end of it all?

A light footstep interrupted his reflections. He looked up, and almost started, on finding himself face to face with Mrs. Hopeton.

Her face was flushed from her walk and the mellow warmth of the afternoon. She held a bunch of wild-flowers,—pink azaleas, delicate sigillarias, valerian, and scarlet painted-cup. She first broke the silence by asking after Madeline.

"Busy with some important sewing,—curtains, I fancy. She is becoming an inveterate housekeeper," Philip said.

"I am glad, for her sake, that she is here. And it must be very pleasant for you, after all your wanderings."

"I must look on it, I suppose," Philip answered, "as the only kind of a home I shall ever have,—while it lasts. But Madeline's life must not be mutilated because mine happens to be."

The warm color left Mrs. Hopeton's face. She strove to make her voice cold and steady, as she said: "I am sorry to see you growing so bitter, Mr. Held."

"I don't think it is my proper nature, Mrs. Hopeton. But you startled me out of a retrospect which had exhausted my capacity for self-reproach, and was about to become self-cursing. There is no bitterness quite equal to that of seeing how weakly one has thrown away an irrecoverable fortune."

She stood before him, silent and disturbed. It was impossible not to understand, yet it seemed equally impossible to answer him. She gave one glance at his earnest, dark gray eyes, his handsome manly face, and the sprinkled glosses of sunshine on his golden hair, and felt a chill strike to her heart. She moved a step, as if to end the interview.

"Only one moment, Mrs. Hopeton—Emily!" Philip cried. "We may not meet again—thus—for years. I will not needlessly recall the past. I only mean to speak of my offence,—to acknowledge it, and exonerate you from any share in the misunderstanding which—made us what we are. You cannot feel the burden of an unpardoned fault; but will you not allow me to lighten mine?"

A softer change came over her stately form. Her arm relaxed, and the wild-flowers fell upon the ground.

"I was wrong, first," Philip went on, "in not frankly confiding to you the knowledge of a boyish illusion and disappointment. I had been heartlessly treated: it was a silly affair, not worth the telling now; but the leaven of mistrust it left behind was not fully worked out of my nature. Then, too, I had private troubles, which my pride—sore, just then, from many a trifling prick, at which I should now laugh—led me to conceal. I need not go over the appearances which provoked me into a display of temper as unjust as it was unmanly,—it is enough to say that all circumstances combined to make me impatient, suspicious, fiercely jealous. I never paused to reflect that you could not know the series of aggravations which preceded our misunderstanding. I did not guess how far I was giving expression to them, and unconsciously transferring to you the offences of others. Nay, I exacted a completer surrender of your woman's pride, because a woman had already chosen to make a plaything of my green boy-love. There is no use in speaking of any of the particulars of our quarrel; for I confess to you that I was recklessly, miserably wrong. But the time has come when you can afford to be generous, when you can allow yourself to speak my forgiveness. Not for the sake of anything I might have been to you, but as a true woman, dealing with her brother-man, I ask your pardon!"

Mrs. Hopeton could not banish the memory of the old tenderness which pleaded for Philip in her heart. He had spoken no word which could offend or alarm her: they were safely divided by a gulf which might never be bridged, and perhaps it was well that a purely human reconciliation should now clarify what was turbid in the past, and reunite them by a bond pure, though eternally sad. She came slowly towards him, and gave him her hand.

"All is not only pardoned, Philip," she said, "but it is now doubly my duty to forget it. Do not suppose, however, that I have had no other than reproachful memories. My pride was as unyielding as yours, for it led me to the defiance which you could not then endure. I, too, was haughty and imperious. I recall every word I uttered, and I know that you have not forgotten them. But let there be equal and final justice between us: forget my words, if you can, and forgive me!"

Philip took her hand, and held it softly in his own. No power on earth could have prevented their eyes from meeting. Out of the far-off distance of all dead joys, over all abysses of fate, the sole power which time and will are powerless to tame, took swift possession of their natures. Philip's eyes were darkened and softened by a film of gathering tears: he cried in a broken voice:—

"Yes, pardon!—but I thought pardon might be peace. Forget? Yes, it would be easy to forget the past, if,—O Emily, we have never been parted until now!"

She had withdrawn her hand, and covered her face. He saw, by the convulsive tremor of her frame, that she was fiercely suppressing her emotion. In another moment she looked up, pale, cold, and almost defiant.

"Why should you say more?" she asked. "Mutual forgiveness is our duty, and there the duty ends. Leave me now!"

Philip knew that he had betrayed himself. Not daring to speak another word he bowed and walked rapidly away. Mrs. Hopeton stood, with her hand pressed upon her bosom, until he had disappeared among the farther trees: then she sat down, and let her withheld tears flow freely.

Presently the merry whoops and calls of children met her ear. She gathered together the fallen flowers, rose and took her way across the meadows towards a little stone schoolhouse, at the foot of the nearest hill. Lucy Henderson already advanced to meet her. There was still an hour or two of sunshine, but the mellow, languid heat of the day was over, and the breeze winnowing down the valley brought with it the smell of the blossoming vernal grass.

The two women felt themselves drawn towards each other, though neither had as yet divined the source of their affectionate instinct. Now, looking upon Lucy's pure, gently firm, and reliant face, Mrs. Hopeton, for the second or third time in her life, yielded to a sudden, powerful impulse, and said: "Lucy, I foresee that I shall need the love and the trust of a true woman: where shall I find it if not in you?"

"If mine will content you," said Lucy.

"O my dear!" Mrs. Hopeton cried; "none of us can stand alone. God has singular trials for us, sometimes, and the use and the conquest of a trouble may both become clear in the telling of it. The heart can wear itself out with its own bitterness. You see, I force my confidence upon you, but I know you are strong to receive it."

"At least," Lucy answered, gravely, "I have no claim to strength unless I am willing to have it tested."

"Then let me make the severest test at once: I shall have less courage if I delay. Can you comprehend the nature of a woman's trial, when her heart resists her duty?"

A deep blush overspread Lucy's face, but she forced herself to meet Mrs. Hopeton's gaze. The two women were silent a moment; then the latter threw her arms around Lucy's neck and kissed her.

"Let us walk!" she said. "We shall both find the words we need."

They moved away over the fragrant, shining meadows. Down the valley, at the foot of the blue cape which wooed their eyes, and perhaps suggested to their hearts that mysterious sense of hope which lies in landscape distances, Elwood Withers was directing his gang of workmen. Over the eastern hill,

Joseph Asten stood among his fields, hardly recognizing their joyous growth. The smoke of Philip's forge rose above the trees to the northward. So many disappointed hearts, so many thwarted lives! What strand stall be twisted out of the broken threads of these destinies, thus drawn so near to each other? What new forces—fatal or beneficent—shall be developed from these elements?

Mr. Hopeton, riding homewards along the highway, said to himself: "It's a pleasant country, but what slow, humdrum lives the people lead!"

CHAPTER XVII. A STORM.

"I have a plan," said Julia, a week or two later. "Can you guess it? No, I think not; yet you might! O, how lovely the light falls on your hair: it is perfect satin!"

She had one hand on his shoulder, and ran the fingers of the other lightly through his brown locks. Her face, sparkling all over with a witching fondness, was lifted towards his. It was the climax of an amiable mood which had lasted three days.

What young man can resist a playful, appealing face, a soft, caressing touch? Joseph smiled as he asked,—

"Is it that I shall wear my hair upon my shoulders, or that we shall sow plaster on the clover-field, as old Bishop advised you the other day?"

"Now you are making fun of my interest in farming; but wait another year! I am trying earnestly to understand it, but only so that ornament—beauty—what was the word in those lines you read last night?—may grow out of use. That's it—Beauty out of Use! I know I've bored you a little sometimes——just a little, now, confess it!—with all my questions; but this is something different. Can't you think of anything that would make our home, O so much more beautiful?"

"A grove of palm-trees at the top of the garden? Or a lake in front, with marble steps leading down to the water?"

"You perverse Joseph! No: something possible, something practicable, something handsome, something profitable! Or, are you so old-fashioned that you think we must drudge for thirty years, and only take our pleasure after we grow rheumatic?"

Joseph looked at her with a puzzled, yet cheerful face.

"You don't understand me yet!" she exclaimed. "And indeed, indeed, I dread to tell you, for one reason: you have such a tender regard for old associations,—not that I'd have it otherwise, if I could. I like it: I trust I have the same feeling; yet a little sentiment sometimes interferes practically with the improvement of our lives."

Joseph's curiosity was aroused. "What do you mean, Julia?" he asked.

"No!" she cried; "I will not tell you until I have read part of pa's letter, which came this afternoon. Take the arm-chair, and don't interrupt me."

She seated herself on the window-sill and opened the letter. "I saw," she said, "how uneasy you felt when the call came for the fourth instalment of ten per cent. on the Amaranth shares, especially after I had so much difficulty in persuading you not to sell the half. It surprised me, although I knew that, where pa is concerned, there's a good reason for everything. So I wrote to him the other day, and this is what he says,—you remember, Kanuck is the company's agent on the spot:—

"'Tell Joseph that in matters of finance there's often a wheel within a wheel. Blenkinsop, of the Chowder Company, managed to get a good grab of our shares through a third party, of whom we had not the slightest suspicion. I name no name at present, from motives of prudence. We only discovered the circumstance after the third party left for Europe. Looking upon the Chowder as a rival, it is our desire, of course, to extract this entering wedge before it has been thrust into our vitals, and we can only accomplish the end by still keeping secret the discovery of the torpedoes (an additional expense, I might remark), and calling for fresh instalments from all the stockholders. Blenkinsop, not being within the inside ring,—and no possibility of his getting in!—will naturally see only the blue of disappointment where we see the rose of realized expectations. Already, so Kanuck writes to me, negotiations are on foot which will relieve our Amaranth of this parasitic growth, and a few weeks—days—hours, in fact, may enable us to explode and triumph! I was offered, yesterday, by one of our shrewdest operators, who has been silently watching us, ten shares of the Sinnemahoning Hematite for eight of ours. Think of that,—the Sinnemahoning Hematite! No better stock in the market, if you remember the quotations! Explain the significance of the figures to your husband, and let him see that he has—but no, I will restrain myself and make no estimate. I will only mention, under the seal of the profoundest secrecy, that the number of shafts now sinking (or being sunk) will give an enormous flowing capacity when the electric spark fires the mine, and I should not wonder if our shares then soared high over the pinnacles of all previous speculation!'

"No, nor I!" Julia exclaimed, as she refolded the letter; "it is certain,— positively certain! I have never known the Sinnemahoning Hematite to be less than 147. What do you say, Joseph?"

"I hope it may be true," he answered. "I can't feel so certain, while an accident—the discovery of the torpedo-plan, for instance—might change the prospects of the Amaranth. It will be a great relief when the time comes to 'realize,' as your father says."

"You only feel so because it is your first experience; but for your sake I will consent that it shall be the last. We shall scarcely need any more than this will bring us; for, as pa says, a mere competence in the city is a splendid fortune in the country. You need leisure for books and travel and society, and you shall have it. Now, let us make a place for both!"

Thereupon she showed him how the parlor and rear bed-room might be thrown into one; where there were alcoves for bookcases and space for a piano; how a new veranda might be added to the western end of the house; how the plastering might be renewed, a showy cornice supplied, and an air of elegant luxury given to the new apartment. Joseph saw and listened, conscious at once of a pang at changing the ancient order of things, and a temptation to behold a more refined comfort in its place. He only asked to postpone the work; but Julia pressed him so closely, with such a multitude of unanswerable reasons, that he finally consented to let a mechanic look at the house, and make an estimate of the expense.

In such cases, the man who deliberates is lost.

His consent once reluctantly exacted, Julia insisting that she would take the whole charge of directing the work, a beginning was made without delay, and in a few days the ruin was so complete that the restoration became a matter of necessity.

Julia kept her word only too faithfully. With a lively, playful manner in the presence of the workmen, but with a cold, inflexible obstinacy when they were alone, she departed from the original plan, adding showy and expensive features, every one of which, Joseph presently saw, was devised to surpass the changes made by the Hopetons in their new residence. His remonstrances produced no effect, and he was precluded from a practical interference by the fear of the workmen guessing his domestic trouble. Thus the days dragged on, and the breach widened without an effort on either side to heal it.

The secret of her temporary fondness gave him a sense of positive disgust when it arose in his memory. He now suspected a selfish purpose in her caresses, and sought to give her no chance of repeating them, but in the company of others he was forced to endure a tenderness which, he was surprised to find, still half deceived him, as it wholly deceived his neighbors. He saw, too,—and felt himself powerless to change the impression,—that Julia's popularity increased with her knowledge of the people, while their manner towards him was a shade less frank and cordial than formerly. He knew that the changes in his home were so much needless extravagance, to them; and that Julia's oft-repeated phrase (always accompanied with a loving look), "Joseph is making the old place so beautiful for me!" increased their mistrust, while seeming to exalt him as a devoted husband.

It is not likely that she specially intended this result; while, on the other hand, he somewhat exaggerated its character. Her object was simply to retain her growing ascendency: within the limits where her peculiar faculties had been exercised she was nearly perfect; but she was indifferent to tracing the consequences of her actions beyond those limits. When she ascertained Mr. Chaffinch's want of faith in Joseph's entire piety, she became more regular in her attendance at his church, not so much to prejudice her husband by the contrast, as to avoid the suspicion which he had incurred. To Joseph, however, in the bitterness of his deception, these actions seemed either hostile or heartless; he was repelled from the clearer knowledge of a nature so foreign to his own. So utterly foreign: yet how near beyond all others it had once seemed!

It was not a jealousy of the authority she assumed which turned his heart from her: it was the revelation of a shallowness and selfishness not at all rare in the class from which she came, but which his pure, guarded youth had never permitted him to suspect in any human being. A man familiar with men and women, if he had been caught in such toils, would have soon discovered some manner of controlling her nature, for the very shrewdest and falsest have their vulnerable side. It gave Joseph, however, so much keen spiritual pain to encounter her in her true character, that such a course was simply impossible.

Meanwhile the days went by; the expense of labor and material had already doubled the estimates made by the mechanics; bills were presented for payment, and nothing was heard from the Amaranth. Money was a necessity, and there was no alternative but to obtain a temporary loan at a county town, the centre of transactions for all the debtors and creditors of the neighboring country. It was a new and disagreeable experience for Joseph to appear in the character of a borrower, and he adopted it most reluctantly; yet the reality was a greater trial than he had suspected. He found that the most preposterous stories of his extravagance were afloat. He was transforming his house into a castle: he had made, lost, and made again a large fortune in petroleum; he had married a wealthy wife and squandered her money; he drove out in a carriage with six white horses; he was becoming irregular in his habits and heretical in his religious views; in short, such marvellous powers of invention had been exercised that the Arab story-tellers were surpassed by the members of that quiet, sluggish community.

It required all his self-control to meet the suspicions of the money-agents, and convince them of the true state of his circumstances. The loan was obtained, but after such a wear and tear of flesh and spirit as made it seem a double burden.

When he reached home, in the afternoon, Julia instantly saw, by his face, that all had not gone right. A slight effort, however, enabled her to say carelessly and cheerfully,—

"Have you brought me my supplies, dear?"

"Yes," he answered curtly.

"Here is a letter from pa," she then said. "I opened it, because I knew what the subject must be. But if you're tired, pray don't read it now, for then you may be impatient. There's a little more delay."

"Then I'll not delay to know it," he said, taking the letter from her hand. A printed slip, calling upon the stockholders of the Amaranth to pay a fifth instalment, fell out of the envelope. Accompanying it there was a hasty note from B. Blessing: "Don't be alarmed, my dear son-in-law! Probably a mere form. Blenkinsop still holds on, but we think this will bring him at once. If it don't, we shall very likely have to go on with him, even if it obliges us to unite the Amaranth and the Chowder. In any case, we shall ford or bridge this little Rubicon within a fortnight. Have the money ready, if convenient, but do not forward unless I give the word. We hear, through third parties, that Clementina (who is now at Long Branch) receives much attention from Mr. Spelter, a man of immense wealth, but, I regret to say, no refinement."

Joseph smiled grimly when he finished the note. "Is there never to be an end of humbug?" he exclaimed.

"There, now!" cried Julia; "I knew you'd be impatient. You are so unaccustomed to great operations. Why, the Muchacho Land Grant—I remember it, because pa sold out just at the wrong time—hung on for seven years!"

"D——curse the Muchacho Land Grant, and the Amaranth too!"

"Aren't you ashamed!" exclaimed Julia, taking on a playful air of offence; "but you're tired and hungry, poor fellow!" Therewith she put her hands on his shoulders, and raised herself on tiptoe to kiss him.

Joseph, unable to control his sudden instinct, swiftly turned away his head.

"O you wicked husband, you deserve to be punished!" she cried, giving him what was meant to be a light tap on the cheek.

It was a light tap, certainly; but perhaps a little of the annoyance which she banished from her face had lodged, unconsciously, in her fingers. They left just sting enough to rouse Joseph's heated blood. He started back a step, and looked at her with flaming eyes.

"No more of that, Julia! I know, now, how much your arts are worth. I am getting a vile name in the neighborhood,—losing my property,—losing my own self-respect,—because I have allowed you to lead me! Will you be content with what you have done, or must you go on until my ruin is complete?"

Before he had finished speaking she had taken rapid counsel with herself, and decided. "Oh, oh! such words to me!" she groaned, hiding her face between her hands. "I never thought you could be so cruel! I had such pleasure in seeing you rich and free, in trying to make your home beautiful; and now this little delay, which no business man would think anything of, seems to change your very nature! But I will not think it's your true self: something has worried you to-day,—you have heard some foolish story—"

"It is not the worry of to-day," he interrupted, in haste to state his whole grievance, before his weak heart had time to soften again,—"it is the worry of months past! It is because I thought you true and kind-hearted, and I find you selfish and hypocritical! It is very well to lead me into serious expenses, while so much is at stake, and now likely to be lost,—it is very well to make my home beautiful, especially when you can outshine Mrs. Hopeton! It is easy to adapt yourself to the neighbors, and keep on the right side of them, no matter how much your husband's character may suffer in the process!"

"That will do!" said Julia, suddenly becoming rigid. She lifted her head, and apparently wiped the tears from her eyes. "A little more and it would be too much for even me! What do I care for 'the neighbors'? persons whose ideas and tastes and habits of life are so different from mine? I have endeavored to be friendly with them for your sake: I have taken special pains to accommodate myself to their notions, just because I intended they should justify you in choosing me! I believed—for you told me so—that there was no calculation in love, that money was dross in comparison; and how could I imagine that you would so soon put up a balance and begin to weigh the two? Am I your wife or your slave? Have I an equal share in what is yours, or am I here merely to increase it? If there is to be a question of dollars and cents between us, pray have my allowance fixed, so that I may not overstep it, and may save myself from such reproaches! I knew you would be disappointed in pa's letter: I have been anxious and uneasy since it came, through my sympathy with you, and was ready to make any sacrifice that might relieve your mind; and now you seem to be full of unkindness and injustice! What shall I do, O what shall I do?

She threw herself upon a sofa, weeping hysterically.

"Julia!" he cried, both shocked and startled by her words, "you purposely misunderstand me. Think how constantly I have yielded to you, against my own better judgment! When have you considered my wishes?"

"When?" she repeated: then, addressing the cushion with a hopeless, melancholy air, "he asks, when! How could I misunderstand you? your words were as plain as daggers. If you were not aware how sharp they were, call them back to your mind when these mad, unjust suspicions have left you! I trusted you so perfectly, I was looking forward to such a happy future, and now— now, all seems so dark! It is like a flash of lightning: I am weak and giddy: leave me,—I can bear no more!"

She covered her face, and sobbed wretchedly.

"I am satisfied that you are not as ignorant as you profess to be," was all Joseph could say, as he obeyed her command, and left the room. He was vanquished, he knew, and a little confused by his wife's unexpected way of taking his charges in flank instead of meeting them in front, as a man would have done. Could she be sincere? he asked himself. Was she really so ignorant of herself, as to believe all that she had uttered? There seemed to be not the shadow of hypocrisy in her grief and indignation. Her tears were real: then why not her smiles and caresses? Either she was horribly, incredibly false,— worse than he dared dream her to be,—or so fatally unconscious of her nature that nothing short of a miracle could ever enlighten her. One thing only was certain: there was now no confidence between them, and there might never be again.

He walked slowly forth from the house, seeing nothing, and unconscious whither his feet were leading him.

CHAPTER XVIII. ON THE RAILROAD TRACK.

Still walking, with bent head, and a brain which vainly strove to work its way to clearness through the perplexities of his heart, Joseph went on. When, wearied at last, though not consciously calmer, he paused and looked about him, it was like waking from a dream. Some instinct had guided him on the way to Philip's forge: the old road had been moved to accommodate the new branch railway, and a rapid ring of hammers came up from the embankment below. It was near the point of the hill where Lucy's schoolhouse stood, and even as he looked she came, accompanied by her scholars, to watch the operation of laying the track. Elwood Withers, hale, sunburnt, full of lusty life, walked along the sleepers directing the workmen.

"He was right,—only too right!" muttered Joseph to himself. "Why could I not see with his eyes? 'It's the bringing up,' he would say; but that is not all. I have been an innocent, confiding boy, and thought that years and acres had made me a man. O, she understood me—she understands me now; but in spite of her, God helping me, I shall yet be a man."

Elwood ran down the steep side of the embankment, greeted Lucy, and helped her to the top, the children following with whoops and cries.

"Would it have been different," Joseph further soliloquized, "if Lucy and I had loved and married? It is hardly treating Elwood fairly to suppose such a thing, yet—a year ago—I might have loved her. It is better as it is: I should have stepped upon a true man's heart. Have they drawn nearer? and if so, does he, with his sturdier nature, his surer knowledge, find no flaw in her perfections?"

A morbid curiosity to watch the two suddenly came upon him. He clambered over the fence, crossed the narrow strip of meadow, and mounted the embankment. Elwood's back was towards him, and he was just saying: "It all comes of taking an interest in what you're doing. The practical part is easy enough, when you once have the principles. I can manage the theodolite already, but I need a little showing when I come to the calculations. Somehow, I never cared much about study before, but here it's all applied as soon as you've learned it, and that fixes it, like, in your head."

Lucy was listening with an earnest, friendly interest on her face. She scarcely saw Joseph until he stood before her. After the first slight surprise, her manner towards him was quiet and composed: Elwood's eyes were bright, and there was a fresh intelligence in his appearance. The habit of command had already given him a certain dignity.

"How can I get knowledge which may be applied as soon as learned?" Joseph asked, endeavoring to assume the manner furthest from his feelings. "I'm still at the foot of the class, Lucy," he added, turning to her.

"How?" Elwood replied. "I should say by going around the world alone. That would be about the same for you as what these ten miles I'm overseeing are to me. A little goes a great way with me, for I can only pick up one thing at a time."

"What kind of knowledge are you looking for, Joseph?" Lucy gravely asked.

"Of myself," said he, and his face grew dark.

"That's a true word!" Elwood involuntarily exclaimed. He then caught Lucy's eye, and awkwardly added: "It's about what we all want, I take it."

Joseph recovered himself in a moment, and proposed looking over the work. They walked slowly along the embankment, listening to Elwood's account of what had been done and what was yet to do, when the Hopeton carriage came up the highway, near at hand. Mrs. Hopeton sat in it alone.

"I was looking for you, Lucy," she called. "If you are going towards the cutting, I will join you there."

She sent the coachman home with the carriage, and walked with them on the track. Joseph felt her presence as a relief, but Elwood confessed to himself that he was a little disturbed by the steady glance of her dark eyes. He had already overcome his regret at the interruption of his rare and welcome chance of talking with Lucy, but then Joseph knew his heart, while this stately lady looked as if she were capable of detecting what she had no right to know. Nevertheless, she was Lucy's friend, and that fact had great weight with Elwood.

"It's rather a pity to cut into the hills and bank up the meadows in this way, isn't it?" he asked.

"And to disturb my school with so much hammering," Lucy rejoined; "when the trains come I must retreat."

"None too soon," said Mrs. Hopeton. "You are not strong, Lucy, and the care of a school is too much for you."

Elwood thanked her with a look, before he knew what he was about.

"After all," said Joseph, "why shouldn't nature be cut up? I suppose everything was given up to us to use, and the more profit the better the use, seems to be the rule of the world. 'Beauty grows out of Use,' you know."

His tone was sharp and cynical, and grated unpleasantly on Lucy's sensitive ear.

"I believe it is a rule in art," said Mrs. Hopeton, "that mere ornament, for ornament's sake, is not allowed. It must always seem to answer some purpose, to have a necessity for its existence. But, on the other hand, what is necessary should be beautiful, if possible."

"A loaf of bread, for instance," suggested Elwood.

They all laughed at this illustration, and the conversation took a lighter turn. By this time they had entered the narrower part of the valley, and on passing around a sharp curve of the track found themselves face to face with Philip and Madeline Held.

If Mrs. Hopeton's heart beat more rapidly at the unexpected meeting, she preserved her cold, composed bearing. Madeline, bright and joyous, was the unconscious agent of unconstraint, in whose presence each of the others felt immediately free.

870

"Two inspecting committees at once!" cried Philip. "It is well for you, Withers, that you didn't locate the line. My sister and I have already found several unnecessary curves and culverts."

"And we have found a great deal of use and no beauty," Lucy answered.

"Beauty!" exclaimed Madeline. "What is more beautiful than to see one's groceries delivered at one's very door? Or to have the opera and the picture-gallery brought within two hours' distance? How far are we from a lemon, Philip?"

"You were a lemon, Mad, in your vegetable, pre-human state; and you are still acid and agreeable."

"Sweets to the sweet!" she gayly cried. "And what, pray, was Miss Henderson?"

"Don't spare me, Mr. Held," said Lucy, as he looked at her with a little hesitation.

"An apple."

"And Mrs. Hopeton?"

"A date-palm," said Philip, fixing his eyes upon her face.

She did not look up, but an expression which he could not interpret just touched her lips and faded.

"Now, it's your turn, Miss Held," Elwood remarked: "what were we men?"

"O, Philip a prickly pear, of course; and you, well, some kind of a nut; and Mr. Asten—"

"A cabbage," said Joseph.

"What vanity! Do you imagine that you are all head,—or that your heart is in your head? Or that you keep the morning dew longer than the rest of us?"

"It might well be," Joseph answered; and Madeline felt her arm gently pinched by Philip, from behind. She had tact enough not to lower her pitch of gayety too suddenly, but her manner towards Joseph became grave and gentle. Mrs. Hopeton said but little: she looked upon the circling hills, as if studying their summer beauty, while the one desire in her heart was to be away from the spot,—away from Philip's haunting eyes.

After a little while, Philip seemed to be conscious of her feeling. He left his place on the opposite side of the track, took Joseph's arm and led him a little aside from the group.

"Philip, I want you!" Joseph whispered; "but no, not quite yet. There is no need of coming to you in a state of confusion. In a day or two more I shall have settled a little."

"You are right," said Philip: "there is no opiate like time, be there never so little of it. I felt the fever of your head in your hand. Don't come to me, until you feel that it is the one thing which must be done! I think you know why I say so."

"I do!" Joseph exclaimed. "I am just now more of an ostrich than anything else; I should like to stick my head in the sand, and imagine myself invisible. But—Philip—here are six of us together. One other, I know, has a secret wound, perhaps two others: is it always so in life? I think I am selfish enough to be glad to know that I am not specially picked out for punishment."

Philip could not help smiling. "Upon my soul," he said, "I believe Madeline is the only one of the six who is not busy with other thoughts than those we all seem to utter. Specially picked out? There is no such thing as special picking out, in this world! Joseph, it may seem hard and schoolmaster-like in me again to say 'wait!' yet that is the only word I can say."

"Good evening, all!" cried Elwood. "I must go down to my men; but I'd be glad of such an inspection as this, a good deal oftener."

"I'll go that far with you," said Joseph.

Mrs. Hopeton took Lucy's arm with a sudden, nervous movement. "If you are not too tired, let us walk over the hill," she said; "I want to find the right point of view for sketching our house."

The company dissolved. Philip, as he walked up the track with his sister, said to himself: "Surely she was afraid of me. And what does her fear indicate? What, if not that the love she once bore for me still lives in her heart, in spite of time and separated fates? I should not, dare not think of her; I shall never again speak a word to her which her husband might not hear; but I cannot tear from me the dream of what she might be, the knowledge of what she is, false, hopeless, fatal, as it all may be!"

"Elwood," said Joseph, when they had walked a little distance in silence, "do you remember the night you spent with me, a year ago?"

"I'm not likely to forget it."

"Let me ask you one question, then. Have you come nearer to Lucy Henderson?"

"If no further off means nearer, and it almost seems so in my case,—yes!"

"And you see no difference in her,—no new features of character, which you did not guess, at first?"

"Indeed, I do!" Elwood emphatically answered. "To me she grows less and less like any other woman,—so right, so straightforward, so honest in all her ways and thoughts! If I am ever tempted to do anything—well, not exactly mean, you know, but such as a man might as well leave undone, I have only to say to myself: 'If you're not thoroughly good, my boy, you'll lose her!' and that does the business, right away. Why, Joseph, I'm proud of myself, that I mean to deserve her!"

"Ah!" A sigh, almost a groan, came from Joseph's lips. "What will you think of me?" he said. "I was about to repeat your own words,—to warn you to be cautious, and take time, and test your feelings, and not to be too sure of her perfection! What can a young man know about women? He can only discover the truth after marriage, and then—they are indifferent how it affects him—their fortunes are made!"

"I know," answered Elwood, turning his head away slightly; "but there's a difference between the women you seek, and work to get, and the women who seek, and work to get you."

"I understand you."

"Forgive me for saying it!" Elwood cried, instantly repenting his words. "I couldn't help seeing and feeling what you know now. But what man—leastways, what friend—could ha' said it to you with any chance of being believed? You were like a man alone in a boat above a waterfall; only you could bring yourself to shore. If I stood on the bank and called, and you didn't believe me, what then? The Lord knows, I'd give this right arm, strong as it is, to put you back where you were a year ago."

"I've been longing for frankness, and I ought to bear it better," said Joseph. "Put the whole subject out of your thoughts, and come and see me as of old. It is quite time I should learn to manage my own life."

He grasped Elwood's hand convulsively, sprang down the embankment, and took to the highway. Elwood looked after him a minute, then slowly shook his head and walked onward towards the men.

Meanwhile, Mrs. Hopeton and Lucy had climbed the hill, and found themselves on the brow of a rolling upland, which fell on the other side towards the old Calvert place. The day was hot. Mrs. Hopeton's knees trembled under her, and she sank on the soft grass at the foot of a tree. Lucy took a seat beside her.

"You know so much of my trouble," said the former, when the coolness and rest had soothed her, "and I trust you so perfectly, that I can tell you all, Lucy. Can you guess the man whom I loved, but must never love again?"

"I have sometimes thought—" but here Lucy hesitated.

"Speak the name in your mind, or, let me say 'Philip Held' for you! Lucy, what am I to do? he loves me still: he told me so, just now, where we were all together below there!"

Lucy turned with a start, and gazed wonderingly upon her friend's face.

"Why does he continue telling me what I must not hear? with his eyes, Lucy! in the tones of his voice, in common words which I am forced to interpret by his meaning! I had learned to bear my inevitable fate, for it is not an unhappy one; I can bear even his presence, if he were generous enough to close his heart as I do,—either that, or to avoid me; for I now dread to meet him again."

"Is it not," Lucy asked, "because the trial is new, and takes you by surprise and unprepared? May you not be fearing more than Mr. Held has expressed, or, at least, intended?"

"The speech that kills, or makes alive, needs no words. What I mean is, there is no resistance in his face. I blush for myself, I am indignant at my own pitiful weakness, but something in his look to-day made me forget everything that has passed since we were parted. While it lasted, I was under a spell,—a spell which it humiliates me to remember. Your voices sounded faint and far-off; all that I have, and hold, seemed to be slipping from me. It was only for a moment, but, Lucy, it frightened me. My will is strong, and I think I can depend upon it; yet what if some influence beyond my control were to paralyze it?"

"Then you must try to win the help of a higher will; our souls always win something of that which they wrestle and struggle to reach. Dear Mrs. Hopeton, have you never thought that we are still as children who cannot have all they cry for? Now that you know what you fear, do not dread to hold it before your mind and examine what it is: at least, I think that would be my instinct,—to face a danger at once when I found I could not escape it."

"I have no doubt you are right, Lucy," said Mrs. Hopeton; but her tone was sad, as if she acquiesced without clearly believing.

"It seems very hard," Lucy continued, "when we cannot have the one love of all others that we need, harder still when we must put it forcibly from our hearts. But I have always felt that, when we can bring ourselves to renounce cheerfully, a blessing will follow. I do not know how, but I must believe it. Might it not come at last through the love that we have, though it now seems imperfect?"

Mrs. Hopeton lifted her head from her knees, and sat erect. "Lucy," she said, "I do not believe you are a woman who would ask another to bear what is beyond your own strength. Shall I put you to the test?"

Lucy, though her face became visibly paler, replied: "I did not mean to compare my burden with yours; but weigh me, if you wish. If I am found wanting, you will show me wherein."

"Your one love above all others is lost to you. Have you conquered the desire for it?"

"I think I have. If some soreness remains, I try to believe that it is the want of the love which I know to be possible, not that of the—the person."

"Then could you be happy with what you call an imperfect love?"

Lucy blushed a little, in spite of herself. "I am still free," she answered, "and not obliged to accept it. If I were bound, I hope I should not neglect my duty."

"What if another's happiness depended on your accepting it? Lucy, my eyes have been made keen by what I have felt. I saw to-day that a man's heart follows you, and I guess that you know it. Here is no imperfect love on his part: were you his wife, could you learn to give him so much that your life might become peaceful and satisfied?"

"You do, indeed, test me!" Lucy murmured. "How can I know? What answer can I make? I have shrunk from thinking of that, and I cannot feel that my duty lies there. Yet, if it were so, if I were already bound, irrevocably, surely all my present faith must be false if happiness in some form did not come at last!"

"I believe it would, to you!" cried Mrs. Hopeton. "Why not to me? Do you think I have ever looked for love in my husband? It seems, now, that I have been content to know that he was proud of me. If I seek, perhaps I may find more than I have dreamed of; and if I find,—if indeed and truly I find,—I shall never more lack self-possession and will!"

She rose to her full height, and a flush came over the pallor of her cheeks.

"Yes," she continued, "rather than feel again the humiliation of to-day, I will trample all my nature down to the level of an imperfect love!"

"Better," said Lucy, rising also,—"better to bend only for a while to the imperfect, that you may warm and purify and elevate it, until it shall take the place of the perfect in your heart."

The two women kissed each other, and there were tears on the cheeks of both.

CHAPTER XIX. THE "WHARF-RAT."

On his way home Joseph reviewed the quarrel with a little more calmness, and, while admitting his own rashness and want of tact, felt relieved that it had occurred. Julia now knew, at least, how sorely he had been grieved by her selfishness, and she had thus an opportunity, if she really loved him, of showing whether her nature were capable of change. He determined to make no further reference to the dissension, and to avoid what might lead to a new one. He did not guess, as he approached the house, that his wife had long been watching at the front window, in an anxious, excited state, and that she only slipped back to the sofa and covered her head just before he reached the door.

For a day or two she was silent, and perhaps a little sullen; but the payment of the most pressing bills, the progress of the new embellishments, and the necessity of retaining her affectionate playfulness in the presence of the workmen, brought back her customary manner. Now and then a sharp, indirect allusion showed that she had not forgotten, and had not Joseph closed his teeth firmly upon his tongue, the household atmosphere might have been again disturbed.

Not many days elapsed before a very brief note from Mr. Blessing announced that the fifth instalment would be needed. He wrote in great haste, he said, and would explain everything by a later mail.

Joseph was hardly surprised now. He showed the note to Julia, merely saying: "I have not the money, and if I had, he could scarcely expect me to pay it without knowing the necessity. My best plan will be to go to the city at once."

"I think so, too," she answered. "You will be far better satisfied when you have seen pa, and he can also help you to raise the money temporarily, if it is really inevitable. He knows all the capitalists."

"I shall do another thing, Julia. I shall sell enough of the stock to pay the instalment; nay, I shall sell it all, if I can do so without loss."

"Are you—" she began fiercely, but, checking herself, merely added, "see pa first, that's all I stipulate."

Mr. Blessing had not returned from the Custom-House when Joseph reached the city. He had no mind to sit in the dark parlor and wait; so he plunged boldly into the labyrinth of clerks, porters, inspectors, and tide-waiters. Everybody knew Blessing, but nobody could tell where he was to be found. Finally some one, more obliging than the rest, said: "Try the Wharf-Rat!"

The Wharf-Rat proved to be a "saloon" in a narrow alley behind the Custom-House. On opening the door, a Venetian screen prevented the persons at the bar from being immediately seen, but Joseph recognized his father-in-law's voice, saying, "Straight, if you please!" Mr. Blessing was leaning against one end of the bar, with a glass in his hand, engaged with an individual of not very prepossessing appearance. He remarked to the latter, almost in a whisper (though the words reached Joseph's ears), "You understand, the collector can't be seen every day; it takes time, and—more or less capital. The doorkeeper and others expect to be fed."

As Joseph approached, he turned towards him with an angry, auspicious look, which was not changed into one of welcome so soon that a flash of uncomfortable surprise did not intervene. But the welcome once there, it deepened and mellowed, and became so warm and rich that only a cold, contracted nature could have refused to bathe in its effulgence.

"Why!" he cried, with extended hands, "I should as soon have expected to see daisies growing in this sawdust, or to find these spittoons smelling like hyacinths! Mr. Tweed, one of our rising politicians, Mr. Asten, my son-in-law! Asten, of Asten Hall, I might almost say, for I hear that your mansion is assuming quite a palatial aspect. Another glass, if you please: your throat must be full of dust, Joseph,—pulvis faucibus hæsit, if I might be allowed to change the classic phrase."

Joseph tried to decline, but was forced to compromise on a moderate glass of ale; while Mr. Blessing, whose glass was empty, poured something into it from a black bottle, nodded to Mr. Tweed, and saying, "Always straight!" drank it off.

"You would not suppose," he then said to Joseph, "that this little room, dark as it is, and not agreeably fragrant, has often witnessed the arrangement of political manœuvres which have decided the City, and through the City the State. I have seen together at that table, at midnight, Senator Slocum, and the Honorables Whitstone, Hacks, and Larruper. Why, the First Auditor of the Treasury was here no later than last week! I frequently transact some of the confidential business of the Custom-House within these precincts, as at present."

"Shall I wait for you outside?" Joseph asked.

"I think it will not be necessary. I have stated the facts, Mr. Tweed, and if you accept them, the figures can be arranged between us at any time. It is a simple case of algebra: by taking x, you work out the unknown quantity."

With a hearty laugh at his own smartness, he shook the "rising politician's" hand, and left the Wharf-Rat with Joseph.

"We can talk here as well as in the woods," he said. "Nobody ever hears anything in this crowd. But perhaps we had better not mention the Amaranth by name, as the operation has been kept so very close. Shall we say 'Paraguay' instead, or—still better—'Reading,' which is a very common stock? Well, then, I guess you have come to see me in relation to the Reading?"

Joseph, as briefly as possible, stated the embarrassment he suffered, on account of the continued calls for payment, the difficulty of raising money for the fifth instalment, and bluntly expressed his doubts of the success of the speculation. Mr. Blessing heard him patiently to the end, and then, having collected himself, answered:—

"I understand, most perfectly, your feeling in the matter. Further, I do not deny that in respect to the time of realizing from the Am—Reading, I should say—I have also been disappointed. It has cost me no little trouble to keep my own shares intact, and my stake is so much greater than yours, for it is my all! I am ready to unite with the Chowder, at once: indeed, as one of the directors, I mentioned it at our last meeting, but the proposition, I regret to say, was not favorably entertained. We are dependent, in a great measure, on Kanuck, who is on the spot superintending the Reading; he has been telegraphed to come on, and promises to do so as soon as the funds now called for are forthcoming. My faith, I hardly need intimate, is firm."

"My only resource, then," said Joseph, "will be to sell a portion of my stock, I suppose?"

"There is one drawback to that course, and I am afraid you may not quite understand my explanation. The—Reading has not been introduced in the market, and its real value could not be demonstrated without betraying the secret lever by which we intend hoisting it to a fancy height. We could only dispose of a portion of it to capitalists whom we choose to take into our confidence. The same reason would be valid against hypothecation."

"Have you paid this last instalment?" Joseph suddenly asked.

"N—no; not wholly; but I anticipate a temporary accommodation. If Mr. Spelter deprives me of Clementina, as I hear (through third parties) is daily becoming more probable, my family expenses will be so diminished that I shall have an ample margin; indeed, I shall feel like a large paper copy, with my leaves uncut!"

He rubbed his hands gleefully; but Joseph was too much disheartened to reply.

"This might be done," Mr. Blessing continued. "It is not certain that all the stockholders have yet paid. I will look over the books, and if such be the case, your delay would not be a sporadic delinquency. If otherwise, I will endeavor to gain the consent of my fellow-directors to the introduction of a new capitalist, to whom a small portion of your interest may be transferred. I trust you perceive the relevancy of this caution. We do not mean that our flower shall always blush unseen, and waste its sweetness on the oleaginous air; we only wish to guard against its being 'untimely ripped' (as Shakespeare says) from its parent stalk. I can well imagine how incomprehensible all this may appear to you. In all probability much of your conversation at home, relative to crops and the like, would be to me an unknown dialect. But I should not, therefore, doubt your intelligence and judgment in such matters."

Joseph began to grow impatient. "Do I understand you to say, Mr. Blessing," he asked, "that the call for the fifth instalment can be met by the sale of a part of my stock?"

"In an ordinary case it might not—under the peculiar circumstances of our operation—be possible. But I trust I do not exaggerate my own influence when I say that it is within my power to arrange it. If you will confide it to my hands, you understand, of course, that a slight formality is necessary,—a power of attorney?"

Joseph, in his haste and excitement, had not considered this, or any other legal point: Mr. Blessing was right.

"Then, supposing the shares to be worth only their par value," he said, "the power need not apply to more than one-tenth of my stock?"

Mr. Blessing came into collision with a gentleman passing him. Mutual wrath was aroused, followed by mutual apologies. "Let us turn into the other street," he said to Joseph; "really, our lives are hardly safe in this crowd; it is nearly three o'clock, and the banks will soon be closed."

"It would be prudent to allow a margin," he resumed, after their course had been changed: "the money market is very tight, and if a necessity were suspected, most capitalists are unprincipled enough to exact according to the urgency of the need. I do not say—nor do I at all anticipate—that it would be so in your case; still, the future is a sort of dissolving view, and my suggestion is that of the merest prudence. I have no doubt that double the amount—say one-fifth of your stock—would guard us against all contingencies. If you prefer not to intrust the matter to my hands, I will introduce you to Honeyspoon Brothers, the bankers,—the elder Honeyspoon being a director,—who will be very ready to execute your commission."

What could Joseph do? It was impossible to say to Mr. Blessing's face that he mistrusted him: yet he certainly did not trust! He was weary of plausible phrases, the import of which he was powerless to dispute, yet which were so at variance with what seemed to be the facts of the case. He felt that he was lifted aloft into a dazzling, secure atmosphere, but as often as he turned to look at the wings which upheld him, their plumage shrivelled into dust, and he fell an immense distance before his feet touched a bit of reality.

The power of attorney was given. Joseph declined Mr. Blessing's invitation to dine with him at the Universal Hotel, the Blessing table being "possibly a little lean to one accustomed to the bountiful profusion of the country," on the plea that he must return by the evening train; but such a weariness and disgust came over him that he halted at the Farmers' Tavern, and took a room for the night. He slept until long into the morning, and then, cheered in spirit through the fresh vigor of all his physical functions, started homewards.

CHAPTER XX. A CRISIS.

Joseph had made half the distance between Oakland Station and his farm, walking leisurely, when a buggy, drawn by an aged and irreproachable gray horse, came towards him. The driver was the Reverend Mr. Chaffinch. He stopped as they met.

"Will you turn back, as far as that tree?" said the clergyman, after greetings had been exchanged. "I have a message to deliver."

"Now," he continued, reining up his horse in the shade, "we can talk without interruption. I will ask you to listen to me with the spiritual, not the carnal ear. I must not be false to my high calling, and the voice of my own conscience calls me to awaken yours."

Joseph said nothing, but the flush upon his face was that of anger, not of confusion, as Mr. Chaffinch innocently supposed.

"It is hard for a young man, especially one wise in his own conceit, to see how the snares of the Adversary are closing around him. We cannot plead ignorance, however, when the Light is there, and we wilfully turn our eyes from it. You are walking on a road, Joseph Asten, it may seem smooth and fair to you, but do you know where it leads? I will tell you: to Death and Hell!"

Still Joseph was silent.

"It is not too late! Your fault, I fear, is that you attach merit to works, as if works could save you! You look to a cold, barren morality for support, and imagine that to do what is called 'right' is enough for God! You shut your eyes to the blackness of your own sinful heart, and are too proud to acknowledge the vileness and depravity of man's nature; but without this acknowledgment your morality (as you call it) is corrupt, your good works (as you suppose them to be) will avail you naught. You are outside the pale of Grace, and while you continue there, knowing the door to be open, there is no Mercy for you!"

The flush on Joseph's face faded, and he became very pale, but he still waited. "I hope," Mr. Chaffinch continued, after a pause, "that your silence is the beginning of conviction. It only needs an awakening, an opening of the eyes in them that sleep. Do you not recognize your guilt, your miserable condition of sin?"

"No!"

Mr. Chaffinch started, and an ugly, menacing expression came into his face.

"Before you speak again," said Joseph, "tell me one thing! Am I indebted for this Catechism to the order—perhaps I should say the request—of my wife?"

"I do not deny that she has expressed a Christian concern for your state; but I do not wait for a request when I see a soul in peril. If I care for the sheep that willingly obey the shepherd, how much more am I commanded to look after them which stray, and which the wolves and bears are greedy to devour!"

"Have you ever considered, Mr. Chaffinch," Joseph rejoined, lifting his head and speaking with measured clearness, "that an intelligent man may possibly be aware that he has an immortal soul,—that the health and purity and growth of that soul may possibly be his first concern in life,—that no other man can know, as he does, its imperfections its needs, its aspirations which rise directly towards God; and that the attempt of a stranger to examine and criticise, and perhaps blacken, this most sacred part of his nature, may possibly be a pious impertinence?"

"Ah, the natural depravity of the heart!" Mr. Chaffinch groaned.

"It is not the depravity, it is the only pure quality which the hucksters of doctrine, the money-changers in God's temple of Man, cannot touch! Shall I render a reckoning to you on the day when souls are judged? Are you the infallible agent of the Divine Mercy? What blasphemy!"

Mr. Chaffinch shuddered. "I wash my hands of you!" he cried. "I have had to deal with many sinners in my day, but I have found no sin which came so directly from the Devil as the pride of the mind. If you were rotten in all your members from the sins of the flesh, I might have a little hope. Verily, it shall go easier with the murderer and the adulterer on that day than with such as ye!"

He gave the horse a more than saintly stroke, and the vehicle rattled away. Joseph could not see the predominance of routine in all that Mr. Chaffinch had said. He was too excited to remember that certain phrases are transmitted, and used without a thought of their tremendous character; he applied every word personally, and felt it as an outrage in all the sensitive fibres of his soul. And who had invoked the outrage? His wife: Mr. Chaffinch had confessed it. What representations had she made?—he could only measure them by the character of the clergyman's charges. He sat down on the bank, sick at heart; it was impossible to go home and meet her in his present frame of mind.

Presently he started up, crying aloud: "I will go to Philip! He cannot help me, I know, but I must have a word of love from a friend, or I shall go mad!"

He retraced his steps, took the road up the valley, and walked rapidly towards the Forge. The tumult in his blood gradually expended its force, but it had carried him along more swiftly than he was aware. When he reached the point where, looking across the valley, now narrowed to a glen, he could see the smoke of the Forge near at hand, and even catch a glimpse of the cottage on the knoll, he stopped. Up to this moment he had felt, not reflected; and a secret instinct told him that he should not submit his trouble to Philip's riper manhood until it was made clear and coherent in his own mind. He must keep Philip's love, at all hazards; and to keep it he must not seem simply a creature of moods and sentiments, whom his friend might pity, but could not respect.

He left the road, crossed a sloping field on the left, and presently found himself on a bank overhanging the stream. Under the wood of oaks and hemlocks the laurel grew in rich, shining clumps; the current, at this point deep, full, and silent, glimmered through the leaves, twenty feet below; the

886

opposite shore was level, and green with an herbage which no summer could wither. He leaned against a hemlock bole, and tried to think, but it was not easy to review the past while his future life overhung him like a descending burden which he had not the strength to lift. Love betrayed, trust violated, aspiration misinterpreted, were the spiritual aspects; a divided household, entangling obligations, a probability of serious loss, were the material evils which accompanied them. He was so unprepared for the change that he could only rebel, not measure, analyze, and cast about for ways of relief.

It was a miserable strait in which he found himself; and the more he thought—or, rather, seemed to think—the less was he able to foresee any other than an unfortunate solution. What were his better impulses, if men persisted in finding them evil? What was life, yoked to such treachery and selfishness? Life had been to him a hope, an inspiration, a sound, enduring joy; now it might never be so again! Then what a release were death!

He walked forward to the edge of the rock. A few pebbles, dislodged by his feet, slid from the brink, and plunged with a bubble and a musical tinkle into the dark, sliding waters. One more step, and the release which seemed so fair might be attained. He felt a morbid sense of delight in playing with the thought. Gathering a handful of broken stones, he let them fall one by one, thinking, "So I hold my fate in my hand." He leaned over and saw a shifting, quivering image of himself projected against the reflected sky, and a fancy, almost as clear as a voice, said: "This is your present self: what will you do with it beyond the gulf, where only the soul superior to circumstances here receives a nobler destiny?"

He was still gazing down at the flickering figure, when a step came upon the dead leaves. He turned and saw Philip, moving stealthily towards him, pale, with outstretched hand. They looked at each other for a moment without speaking.

"I guess your thought, Philip," Joseph then said. "But the things easiest to do are sometimes the most impossible."

"The bravest man may allow a fancy to pass through his mind, Joseph, which only the coward will carry into effect."

"I am not a coward!" Joseph exclaimed.

Philip took his hand, drew him nearer, and flinging his arms around him, held him to his heart.

Then they sat down, side by side.

"I was up the stream, on the other side, trolling for trout," said Philip, "when I saw you in the road. I was welcoming your coming, in my heart: then you stopped, stood still, and at last turned away. Something in your movements gave me a sudden, terrible feeling of anxiety: I threw down my rod, came around by the bridge at the Forge, and followed you here. Do not blame me for my foolish dread."

"Dear, dear friend," Joseph cried, "I did not mean to come to you until I seemed stronger and more rational in my own eyes. If that were a vanity, it is gone now: I confess my weakness and ignorance. Tell me, if you can, why this has come upon me? Tell me why nothing that I have been taught, why no atom of the faith which I still must cling to, explains, consoles, or remedies any wrong of my life!"

"Faiths, I suspect," Philip answered, "are, like laws, adapted to the average character of the human race. You, in the confiding purity of your nature, are not an average man: you are very much above the class, and if virtue were its own reward, you would be most exceptionally happy. Then the puzzle is, what's the particular use of virtue?"

"I don't know, Philip, but I don't like to hear you ask the question. I find myself so often on the point of doubting all that was my Truth a little while ago; and yet, why should my misfortunes, as an individual, make the truth a lie? I am only one man among millions who must have faith in the efficacy of virtue. Philip, if I believed the faith to be false, I think I should still say, 'Let it be preached!'"

Joseph related to Philip the whole of his miserable story, not sparing himself, nor concealing the weakness which allowed him to be entangled to such an extent. Philip's brow grew dark as he listened, but at the close of the recital his face was calm, though stern.

"Now," said he,—"now put this aside for a little while, and give your ear (and your heart too, Joseph) to my story. Do not compare my fortune with yours, but let us apply to both the laws which seem to govern life, and see whether justice is possible."

Joseph had dismissed his wife's suspicion, after the dinner at Hopeton's, so immediately from his memory, that he had really forgotten it; and he was not only startled, but also a little shocked, by Philip's confession. Still, he saw that it was only the reverse form of his own experience, not more strange, perhaps not more to be condemned, yet equally inevitable.

"Is there no way out of this labyrinth of wrong?" Philip exclaimed. "Two natures, as far apart as Truth and Falsehood, monstrously held together in the most intimate, the holiest of bonds,—two natures destined for each other monstrously kept apart by the same bonds! Is life to be so sacrificed to habit and prejudice? I said that Faith, like Law, was fashioned for the average man: then there must be a loftier faith, a juster law, for the men—and the women—who cannot shape themselves according to the common-place pattern of society,—who were born with instincts, needs, knowledge, and rights—ay, rights!—of their own!"

"But, Philip," said Joseph, "we were both to blame: you through too little trust, I through too much. We have both been rash and impatient: I cannot forget that; and how are we to know that the punishment, terrible as it seems, is disproportioned to the offence?"

"We know this, Joseph,—and who can know it and be patient?— that the power which controls our lives is pitiless, unrelenting! There is the same punishment for an innocent mistake as for a conscious crime. A certain Nemesis follows ignorance, regardless how good and pure may be the individual nature. Had you even guessed your wife's true character just before marriage, your very integrity, your conscience, and the conscience of the world, would have compelled the union, and Nature would not have mitigated her selfishness to reward you with a tolerable life. O no! You would still have suffered as now. Shall a man with a heart feel this horrible injustice, and not rebel? Grant that I am rightly punished for my impatience, my pride, my jealousy, how have you been rewarded for your stainless youth, your innocent trust, your almost miraculous goodness? Had you known the world better, even though a part of your knowledge might have been evil, you would have escaped this fatal marriage. Nothing can be more certain; and will you simply groan and bear? What compensating fortune have you, or can you ever expect to find?"

Joseph was silent at first; but Philip could see, from the trembling of his hands, and his quick breathing, that he was profoundly agitated. "There is something within me," he said, at last, "which accepts everything you say; and yet, it alarms me. I feel a mighty temptation in your words: they could lead me to snap my chains, break violently away from my past and present life, and surrender myself to will and appetite. O Philip, if we could make our lives wholly our own! If we could find a spot—"

"I know such a spot!" Philip cried, interrupting him,—"a great valley, bounded by a hundred miles of snowy peaks; lakes in its bed; enormous hillsides, dotted with groves of ilex and pine; orchards of orange and olive; a perfect climate, where it is bliss enough just to breathe, and freedom from the distorted laws of men, for none are near enough to enforce them! If there is no legal way of escape for you, here, at least, there is no force which can drag you back, once you are there: I will go with you, and perhaps—perhaps—"

Philip's face glowed, and the vague alarm in Joseph's heart took a definite form. He guessed what words had been left unspoken.

"If we could be sure!" he said.

"Sure of what? Have I exaggerated the wrong in your case? Say we should be outlaws there, in our freedom!—here we are fettered outlaws."

"I have been trying, Philip, to discover a law superior to that under which we suffer, and I think I have found it. If it be true that ignorance is equally punished with guilt; if causes and consequences, in which there is neither pity nor justice, govern our lives,—then what keeps our souls from despair but the infinite pity and perfect justice of God? Yes, here is the difference between human and divine law! This makes obedience safer than rebellion. If you and

I, Philip, stand above the level of common natures, feeling higher needs and claiming other rights, let us shape them according to the law which is above, not that which is below us!"

Philip grew pale. "Then you mean to endure in patience, and expect me to do the same?" he asked.

"If I can. The old foundations upon which my life rested are broken up, and I am too bewildered to venture on a random path. Give me time; nay, let us both strive to wait a little. I see nothing clearly but this: there is a Divine government, on which I lean now as never before. Yes, I say again, the very wrong that has come upon us makes God necessary!"

It was Philip's turn to be agitated. There was a simple, solemn conviction in Joseph's voice which struck to his heart. He had spoken from the heat of his passion, it is true, but he had the courage to disregard the judgment of men, and make his protest a reality. Both natures shared the desire, and were enticed by the daring of his dream; but out of Joseph's deeper conscience came a whisper, against which the cry of passion was powerless.

"Yes, we will wait," said Philip, after a long pause. "You came to me, Joseph, as you said, in weakness and confusion: I have been talking of your innocence and ignorance. Let us not measure ourselves in this way. It is not experience alone which creates manhood. What will become of us I cannot tell, but I will not, I dare not, say you are wrong!"

They took each other's hands. The day was fading, the landscape was silent, and only the twitter of nesting birds was heard in the boughs above them. Each gave way to the impulse of his manly love, rarer, alas! but as tender and true as the love of woman, and they drew nearer and kissed each other. As they walked back and parted on the highway, each felt that life was not wholly unkind, and that happiness was not yet impossible.

CHAPTER XXI. UNDER THE WATER.

Joseph said nothing that evening concerning the result of his trip to the city, and Julia, who instantly detected the signs which a powerful excitement had left upon his face, thought it prudent to ask no immediate questions. She was purposely demonstrative in little arrangements for his comfort, but spared him her caresses; she did not intend to be again mistaken in choosing the time and occasion of bestowing them.

The next morning, when he felt that he could speak calmly, Joseph told her what he had done, carefully avoiding any word that might seem to express disappointment, or even doubt.

"I hope you are satisfied that pa will make it easy for you?" she ventured to say.

"He thinks so." Then Joseph could not help adding: "He depends, I imagine, upon your sister Clementina marrying a Mr. Spelter,—'a man of immense wealth, but, I regret to say, no refinement.'"

Julia bit her lip, and her eyes assumed that hard, flinty look which her husband knew so well. "If Clementina marries immense wealth," she exclaimed, with a half-concealed sneer, "she will become simply insufferable! But what difference can that make in pa's business affairs?"

The answer tingled on Joseph's tongue: "Probably he expects Mr. Spelter to indorse a promissory note"; but he held it back. "What I have resolved to do is this," he said. "In a day or two—as soon as I can arrange to leave—I shall make a journey to the oil region, and satisfy myself where and what the Amaranth is. Your own practical instincts will tell you, Julia, that this intention of mine must be kept secret, even from your father."

She leaned her head upon her hand, and appeared to reflect. When she looked up her face had a cheerful, confiding expression.

"I think you are right," she then said. "If—if things should not happen to be quite as they are represented, you can secure yourself against any risk—and pa, too—before the others know of it. You will have the inside track; that is, if there is one. On the other hand, if all is right, pa can easily manage, if some of the others are shaky in their faith, to get their stock at a bargain. I am sure he would have gone out there himself, if his official services were not so important to the government."

It was a hard task for Joseph to keep his feelings to himself.

"And now," she continued,—"now I know you will agree to a plan of mine, which I was going to propose. Lucy Henderson's school closes this week, and Mrs. Hopeton tells me she is a little overworked and ailing. It would hardly help her much to go home, where she could not properly rest, as her father is a hard, avaricious man, who can't endure idleness, except, I suppose, in a corpse (so these people seem to me). I want to ask Lucy to come here. I think you always liked her" (here Julia shot a swift, stealthy glance at Joseph), "and so she will be an agreeable guest for both of us. She shall just rest and grow strong. While you are absent, I shall not seem quite so lonely. You may be gone a week or more, and I shall find the separation very hard to bear, even with her company."

"Why has Mrs. Hopeton not invited her?" Joseph asked.

"The Hopetons are going to the sea-shore in a few days. She would take Lucy as a guest, but there is one difficulty in the way. She thinks Lucy would accept the trip and the stay there as an act of hospitality, but that she cannot (or thinks she cannot) afford the dresses that would enable her to appear in Mrs. Hopeton's circle. But it is just as well: I am sure Lucy would feel more at home here."

"Then by all means ask her!" said Joseph. "Lucy Henderson is a noble girl, for she has forced a true-hearted man to love her, without return."

"Ind-e-e-d!"

Julia's drawl denoted surprise and curiosity, but Joseph felt that once more he had spoken too quickly. He endeavored to cover his mistake by a hearty acquiescence in the plan, which was speedily arranged between them, in all its details, Lucy's consent being taken for granted.

It required, however, the extreme of Julia's powers of disguise, aided by Joseph's frank and hearty words and Mrs. Hopeton's influence, to induce Lucy to accept the invitation. Unable to explain wholly to herself, much less mention to any other, the instinct which held her back, she found herself, finally, placed in a false position, and then resolved to blindly trust that she was doing right, inasmuch as she could not make it clear that she was doing wrong. Her decision once taken, she forcibly banished all misgivings, and determined to find nothing but a cheerful and restful holiday before her.

And, indeed, the first day or two of her residence at the farm, before Joseph's departure, brought her a more agreeable experience than she had imagined. Both host and hostess were busy, the latter in the household and the former in the fields, and when they met at meals or in the evening, her presence was an element which compelled an appearance of harmony. She was surprised to find so quiet and ordered a life in two persons whom she had imagined to be miserably unfitted for each other, and began to suspect that she had been seriously mistaken.

After Joseph left, the two women were much together. Julia insisted that she should do nothing, and amiably protested at first against Lucy giving her so much of her society; but, little by little, the companionship was extended and became more frank and intimate. Lucy was in a charitable mood, and found it very easy to fancy that Julia's character had been favorably affected by the graver duties which had come with her marriage. Indeed, Julia found many indirect ways of hinting as much: she feared she had seemed flighty (perhaps a little shallow); looking back upon her past life she could see that such a charge would not be unjust. Her education had been so superficial; all city education of young women was false; they were taught to consider external appearances, and if they felt a void in their nature which these would not fill, whither could they turn for counsel or knowledge?

Her face was sad and thoughtful while she so spoke; but when, shaking her dark curls with a pretty impatience, she would lift her head and ask, with a smile: "But it is not too late, in my case, is it? I'm really an older child, you

894

know,"—Lucy could only answer: "Since you know what you need, it can never be too late. The very fact that you do know, proves that it will be easy for you."

Then Julia would shake her head again, and say, "O, you are too kind, Lucy; you judge my nature by your own."

When the friendly relation between them had developed a little further, Julia became—though still with a modest reticence—more confiding in relation to Joseph.

"He is so good, so very, very true and good," she said, one day, "that it grieves me, more than I can tell, to be the cause of a little present anxiety of his. As it is only a business matter, some exaggerated report of which you have probably heard (for I know there have been foolish stories afloat in the neighborhood), I have no hesitation about confiding it to you. Perhaps you can advise me how to atone for my error; for, if it was an error, I fear it cannot be remedied now; if not, it will be a relief to me to confess it."

Thereupon she gave a minute history of the Amaranth speculation, omitting the energy of her persuasion with Joseph, and presenting very strongly her father's views of a sure and splendid success soon to follow. "It was for Joseph's sake," she concluded, "rather than my own, that I advised the investment; though, knowing his perfect unselfishness, I fear he complied only for mine. He had guessed already, it seems to me now, that we women like beauty as well as comfort about our lives; otherwise, he would hardly have undertaken these expensive improvements of our home. But, Lucy, it terrifies me to think that pa and Joseph and I may have been deceived! The more I shut my mind against the idea the more it returns to torment me. I, who brought so little to him, to be the instrument of such a loss! O, if you were not here, how could I endure the anxiety and the absence?"

She buried her face in her handkerchief, and sobbed.

"I know Joseph to be good and true," said Lucy, "and I believe that he will bear the loss cheerfully, if it should come. But it is never good to 'borrow trouble,' as we say in the country. Neither the worst nor the best things which we imagine ever come upon us."

"You are wrong!" cried Julia, starting up and laughing gleefully; "I have the best thing, in my husband! And yet, you are right, too: no worst thing can come to me, while I keep him!"

Lucy wished to visit the Hopetons before their departure for the sea-shore, and Julia was quite ready to accompany her. Only, with the wilfulness common to all selfish natures, she determined to arrange the matter in her own way. She drove away alone the next morning to the post-office, with a letter for Joseph, but never drew rein until she had reached Coventry Forge. Philip being absent, she confided to Madeline Held her wish (and Lucy's) that they should all spend an afternoon together, on the banks of the stream,—a free society in the open air instead of a formal one within doors. Madeline entered into the plan with joyous readiness, accepting both for herself and for Philip. They all met together too rarely, she said: a lunch or a tea under the trees would be delightful: there was a little skiff which might be borrowed, and they might even catch and cook their own fish, as the most respectable people did in the Adirondacks.

Julia then drove to the Hopetons in high spirits. Mr. Hopeton found the proposed party very pleasant, and said at once to his wife: "We have still three days, my dear: we can easily spare to-morrow?"

"Mrs. Asten is very kind," she replied; "and her proposition is tempting: but I should not like to go without you, and I thought your business might—"

"O, there is nothing pressing," he interrupted. "I shall enjoy it exceedingly, especially the boat, and the chance of landing a few trout."

So it was settled. Lucy, it is true, felt a dissatisfaction which she could scarcely conceal, and possibly did not, to Julia's eyes; but it was not for her own sake. She must seem grateful for a courtesy meant to favor both herself and her friend, and a little reflection reconciled her to the plan. Mrs. Hopeton dared not avoid Philip Held, and it might be well if she carried away with her to the sea-shore a later and less alarming memory of him. Lucy's own desire for a quiet talk with the woman in whom she felt such a loving interest was of no consequence, if this was the result.

They met in the afternoon, on the eastern side of the stream, just below the Forge, where a little bay of level shore, shaded by superb trees, was left between the rocky bluffs. Stumps and a long-fallen trunk furnished them with rough tables and seats; there was a natural fireplace among some huge tumbled stones; a spring of icy crystal gushed out from the foot of the bluff; and the shimmering, murmuring water in front, with the meadows beyond burning like emerald flame in the sunshine, offered a constant delight to the senses.

All were enchanted with the spot, which Philip and Madeline claimed as their discovery. The gypsy spirit awoke in them, and while they scattered here and there, possessed with the influences of the place, and constantly stumbling upon some new charm or convenience, Lucy felt her heart grow light for her friend, and the trouble of her own life subside. For a time no one seemed to think of anything but the material arrangements. Mr. Hopeton's wine-flasks were laid in the spring to cool; Philip improvised a rustic table upon two neighboring stumps; rough seats were made comfortable, dry sticks collected for fire-wood, stores unpacked and placed in readiness, and every little preliminary of labor, insufferable in a kitchen, took on its usual fascination in that sylvan nook.

Then they rested from their work. Mr. Hopeton and Philip lighted cigars and sat to leeward, while the four ladies kept their fingers busy with bunches of maiden-hair and faint wildwood blossoms, as they talked. It really seemed as if a peace and joy from beyond their lives had fallen upon them. Madeline believed so, and Lucy hoped so: let us hope so, too, and not lift at once the veil which was folded so closely over two restless hearts!

Mr. Hopeton threw away the stump of his cigar, adjusted his fishing-tackle, and said: "If we are to have a trout supper, I must begin to troll at once."

"May I go with you?" his wife asked.

"Yes," he answered, smiling, "if you will not be nervous. But I hardly need to make that stipulation with you, Emily."

Philip assisted her into the unsteady little craft, which was fastened to a tree. Mr. Hopeton seated himself carefully, took the two light, short oars, and held himself from the shore, while Philip loosened the rope.

"I shall row up stream," he said, "and then float back to you, trolling as I come. When I see you again, I hope I can ask you to have the coals ready."

Slowly, and not very skilfully, he worked his way against the current, and passed out of sight around a bend in the stream. Philip watched Mrs. Hopeton's slender figure as she sat in the stern, listlessly trailing one hand in the water. "Does she feel that my eyes, my thoughts, are following her?" he asked; but she did not once turn her head.

"Philip!" cried Madeline, "here are three forlorn maidens, and you the only Sir Isumbras, or whoever is the proper knight! Are you looking into the stream, expecting the 'damp woman' to arise? She only rises for fishermen: she will come up and drag Mr. Hopeton down. Let me invoke the real nymph of this stream!" She sang:—

> "Sabrina fair,
>
> Listen where thou art sitting
>
> Under the glassy, cool, translucent wave,
>
> In twisted braids of lilies knitting
>
> The loose train of thy amber-dropping hair;
>
> Listen for dear honor's sake,
>
> Goddess of the silver lake,
>
> Listen and save!"

Madeline did not know what she was doing. She could not remark Philip's paleness in the dim green light where they sat, but she was struck by the startled expression of his eyes.

"One would think you really expected Sabrina to come," she laughed.

898

"Miss Henderson, too, looks as if I had frightened her. You and I, Mrs. Asten, are the only cool, unimaginative brains in the party. But perhaps it was all owing to my poor voice? Come now, confess it! I don't expect you to say,—

'Can any mortal mixture of earth's mould

Breathe such divine, enchanting ravishment?'"

"I was trying to place the song," said Lucy; "I read it once."

"If any one could evoke a spirit, Madeline," Philip replied, "it would be you. But the spirit would be no nymph; it would have little horns and hoofs, and you would be glad to get rid of it again."

They all laughed at this, and presently, at Julia's suggestion, arranged the wood they had collected, and kindled a fire. It required a little time and patience to secure a strong blaze, and in the great interest which the task called forth the Hopetons were forgotten.

At last Philip stepped back, heated and half stifled, for a breath of fresher air, and, turning, saw the boat between the trees gliding down the stream. "There they are!" he cried; "now, to know our luck!"

Tho boat was in midstream, not far from a stony strip which rose above the water. Mrs. Hopeton sat musing with her hands in her lap, while her husband, resting on his knees and one hand, leaned over the bow, watching the fly which trailed at the end of his line. He seemed to be quite unconscious that an oar, which had slowly loosened itself from the lock, was floating away behind the boat.

"You are losing your oars!" Philip cried.

Mr. Hopeton started, as from a dream of trout, dropped his line and stretched forward suddenly to grasp the oar. The skiff was too light and unbalanced to support the motion. It rocked threateningly; Mrs. Hopeton, quite forgetting herself, started to her feet, and, instantly losing her equilibrium, was thrown headlong into the deeper water. The skiff whirled back, turned over, and before Mr. Hopeton was aware of what had happened, he plunged full length, face downwards, into the shallower current.

It was all over before Madeline and Lucy reached the bank, and Philip was already in the stream. A few strokes brought him to Mrs. Hopeton, who struggled with the current as she rose to the surface, but made no outcry. No sooner had she touched Philip than she seized and locked him in her arms, and he was dragged down again with her. It was only the physical clinging to life: if some feeble recognition at that moment told her whose was the form she held and made powerless, it could not have abated an atom of her frantic, instinctive force.

Philip felt that they had drifted into water beyond his depth. With great exertion he freed his right arm and sustained himself and her a moment at the surface. Mrs. Hopeton's head was on his shoulder; her hair drifted against his face, and even the desperation of the struggle could not make him insensible to the warmth of her breast upon his own. A wild thought flashed upon and stung his brain: she was his at last—his in death, if not in life!

His arm slackened, and they sank slowly together. Heart and brain were illuminated with blinding light, and the swift succession of his thoughts compressed an age into the fragment of a second. Yes, she was his now: clasping him as he clasped, their hearts beating against each other, with ever slower pulsations, until they should freeze into one. The world, with its wrongs and prejudices, lay behind them; the past was past, and only a short and painless atonement intervened between the immortal possession of souls! Better that it should end thus: he had not sought this solution, but he would not thrust it from him.

But, even as his mind accepted it, and with a sense of perfect peace, He heard Joseph's voice, saying, "We must shape our lives according to the law which is above, not that which is below us." Through the air and the water, on the very rock which now overhung his head, he again saw Joseph bending, and himself creeping towards him with outstretched hand. Ha! who was the coward now? And again Joseph spake, and his words were: "The very wrong that has come upon us makes God necessary." God? Then how would God in his wisdom fashion their future life? Must they sweep eternally, locked in an unsevering embrace, like Paolo and Francesca, around some dreary circle of hell? Or must the manner of entering that life together be the act to separate

900

them eternally? Only the inevitable act dare ask for pardon; but here, if not will or purpose, was at least submission without resistance! Then it seemed to him that Madeline's voice came again to him, ringing like a trumpet through the waters, as she sang:—

"Listen for dear honor's sake,

Goddess of the silver lake,

Listen and save!"

He pressed his lips to Mrs. Hopeton's unconscious brow, his heart saying, "Never, never again!" released himself by a sudden, powerful effort, seized her safely, as a practised swimmer, shot into light and air, and made for the shallower side of the stream. The upturned skiff was now within reach, and all danger was over.

Who could guess that the crisis of a soul had been reached and passed in that breath of time under the surface? Julia's long, shrill scream had scarcely come to an end; Mr. Hopeton, bewildered by his fall, was trying to run towards them through water up to his waist, and Lucy and Madeline looked on, holding their breath in an agony of suspense. In another moment Philip touched bottom, and raising Mrs. Hopeton in his arms, carried her to the opposite bank.

She was faint and stunned, but not unconscious. She passively allowed Philip to support her until Mr. Hopeton, struggling through the shallows, drew near with an expression of intense terror and concern on his broad face. Then, breaking from Philip, she half fell, half flung herself into his arms, laid her head upon his shoulder, and burst into a fit of hysterical weeping.

Tears began to run down the honest man's cheeks, and Philip, turning away, busied himself with righting the boat and recovering the oars.

"O, my darling!" said Mr. Hopeton, "what should I do if I had lost you?"

"Hold me, keep me, love me!" she cried. "I must not leave you!"

He held her in his arms, he kissed her, he soothed her with endearing words. She grew calm, lifted her head, and looked in his eyes with a light which he had never yet seen in them. The man's nature was moved and stirred: his lips trembled, and the tears still slowly trickled from his eyes.

"Let me set you over!" Philip called from the stream. "The boat is wet, but then neither of us is dry. We have, fortunately, a good fire until the carriage can be brought for Mrs. Hopeton, and your wine will be needed at once."

They had no trout, nor indeed any refreshment, except the wine. Philip tried to rally the spirits of the party, but Julia was the only one who at all seconded his efforts; the others had been too profoundly agitated. Mr. and Mrs. Hopeton were grave; it seemed scarcely possible for them to speak, and yet, as Lucy remarked with amazement, the faces of both were bright and serene.

"I shall never invoke another water-nymph," said Madeline, as they were leaving the spot.

"Yes!" Philip cried, "always invoke Sabrina, and the daughter of Locrine will arise for you, as she arose to-day."

"That is, not at all?"

"No," said Philip, "she arose."

CHAPTER XXII. KANUCK.

When he set forth upon his journey, Joseph had enough of natural shrewdness to perceive that his own personal interest in the speculation were better kept secret. The position of the Amaranth property, inserted like a wedge between the Fluke and Chowder Companies, was all the geography he needed; and he determined to assume the character of a curious traveller,—at least for a day or two,—to keep his eyes and ears open, and learn as much as might be possible to one outside the concentric "rings" of oil operations.

He reached Corry without adventure, and took passage in the train to Oil City, intending to make the latter place the starting-point of his investigations. The car was crowded, and his companion on the seat was a keen, witty, red-faced man, with an astonishing diamond pin and a gold watch-chain heavy enough to lift an anchor. He was too restless, too full of "operative" energy, to travel in silence, as is the universal and most dismal American habit; and before they passed three stations he had extracted from Joseph the facts that he was a stranger, that he intended visiting the principal wells, and that he might possibly (Joseph allowing the latter point to be inferred) be tempted to invest something, if the aspects were propitious.

"You must be sure to take a look at my wells," said the stranger; "not that any of our stock is in the market,—it is never offered to the public, unless accidentally,—but they will give you an illustration of the magnitude of the business. All wells, you know, sink after a while to what some people call the normal flowing capacity (we oilers call it 'the everidge run'), and so it was reported of ourn. But since we've begun to torpedo them, it's almost equal to the first tapping, though I don't suppose it'll hold out so long."

"Are the torpedoes generally used?" Joseph asked, in some surprise.

"They're generally tried, anyhow. The cute fellow who first hit upon the idea meant to keep it dark, but the oilers, you'll find, have got their teeth skinned, and what they can't find out isn't worth finding out! Lord! I torpedoed my wells at midnight, and it wasn't a week before the Fluke was at it, bustin' and bustin' all their dry auger-holes!"

"The what!" Joseph exclaimed.

"Fluke. Queer name, isn't it? But that's nothing: we have the Crinoline, the Pipsissaway, the Mud-Lark, and the Sunburst, between us and Tideoute."

"What is the name of your company, if I may ask?"

"About as queer as any of 'em,—the Chowder."

Joseph started, in spite of himself. "It seems to me I have heard of that company," he managed to say.

"O no doubt," replied the stranger. "'T isn't often quoted in the papers, but it's known. I'm rather proud of it, for I got it up. I was boring—boss, though—at three dollars a day, two years ago, and now I have my forty thousand a year, 'free of income tax,' as the Insurance Companies say. But then, where one is lucky like the Chowder, a hundred busts."

Joseph rapidly collected himself while the man was speaking. "I should very much like to see your wells," he said. "Will you be there a day or two from now? My name is Asten,—not that you have ever heard of it before."

"Shall be glad to hear it again, though, and to see you," said the man. "My name is Blenkinsop."

Again it was all that Joseph could do to restrain his astonishment.

"I suppose you are the President of the Chowder?" he ventured to say.

"Yes," Mr. Blenkinsop answered, "since it's a company. It was all mine at the start, but I wanted capital, and I had to work 'em."

"What other important companies are there near you?"

"None of any account, except the Fluke and the Depravity. They flow tolerable now, after torpedoing. To be sure, there are kites and catches with all sorts o' names,—the Penny-royal, the Ruby, the Wallholler (whatever that is), and the Amaranth,—ha, ha!"

"I think I have heard of the Amaranth," Joseph mildly remarked.

"Lord! are you bit already?" Mr. Blenkinsop exclaimed, fixing his small, sharp eyes on Joseph's face.

"I—I really don't know what you mean."

"No offence: I thought it likely, that's all. The Amaranth is Kanuck's last dodge. He keeps mighty close, but if he don't feather his nest in a hurry, at somebody's expense, I ain't no judge o' men!"

Joseph did not dare to mention the Amaranth again. He parted with Mr. Blenkinsop at Tarr Farm, and went on to Oil City, where he spent a day in unprofitable wanderings, and then set out up the river, first to seek the Chowder wells, and afterwards to ascertain whether there was any perennial beauty in the Amaranth.

The first thing which he remarked was the peculiar topography of the region. The Chowder property was a sloping bottom, gradually rising from the river to a range of high hills a quarter of a mile in the rear. Just above this point the river made a sharp horseshoe bend, washing the foot of the hills for a considerable distance, and then curving back again, with a second tract of bottom-land beyond. On the latter, he was informed, the Fluke wells were located. The inference was therefore irresistible that the Amaranth Company must be the happy possessor of the lofty section of hills dividing the two.

"Do they get oil up there?" he asked of Blenkinsop's foreman, pointing to the ragged, barren heights.

"They may get skunk oil, or rattlesnake oil," the man answered. "Them'll do to peddle, but you can't fill tanks with 'em. I hear they've got a company for that place,—th' Amaranth, they call it,—but any place'll do for derned fools. Why, look 'ee here! We've got seven hundred feet to bore: now, jest put twelve hundred more atop o' that, and guess whether they can even pump oil, with the Chowder and Fluke both sides of 'em! But it does for green 'uns, as well as any other place."

Joseph laughed,—a most feeble, unnatural, ridiculous laugh.

"I'll walk over that way to the Fluke," he said. "I should like to see how such things are managed."

"Then be a little on your guard with Kanuck, if you meet him," the man good-naturedly advised. "Don't ask him too many questions."

It was a hot, wearisome climb to the timber-skeletons on the summit (more like gibbets than anything else), which denoted shafts to the initiated as well as the ignorant eye. There were a dozen or more, but all were deserted.

Joseph wandered from one to the other, asking himself, as he inspected each, "Is this the splendid speculation?" What was there in that miserable, shabby, stony region, a hundred acres of which would hardly pasture a cow, whence wealth should come? Verily, as stony and as barren were the natures of the men, who on this wretched basis built their cheating schemes!

A little farther on he came to a deep ravine, cleaving the hills in twain. There was another skeleton in its bed, but several shabby individuals were gathered about it,—the first sign of life or business he had yet discovered.

He hastened down the steep declivity, the warning of the Chowder foreman recurring to his mind, yet it seemed so difficult to fix his policy in advance that he decided to leave everything to chance. As he approached he saw that the men were laborer's, with the exception of a tall, lean individual, who looked like an unfortunate clergyman. He had a sallow face, lighted by small, restless, fiery eyes, which reminded Joseph, when they turned upon him, of those of a black snake. His greeting was cold and constrained, and his manner said plainly, "The sooner you leave the better I shall be satisfied."

"This is a rough country for walking," said Joseph; "how much farther is it to the Fluke wells?"

"Just a bit," said one of the workmen.

Joseph took a seat on a stone, with the air of one who needed rest. "This well, I suppose," he remarked, "belongs to the Amaranth?"

"Who told you so?" asked the lean, dark man.

"They said below, at the Chowder, that the Amaranth was up here."

"Did Blenkinsop send you this way?" the man asked again.

"Nobody sent me," Joseph replied. "I am a stranger, taking a look at the oil country. I have never before been in this part of the State."

"May I ask your name?"

"Asten," said Joseph, unthinkingly.

"Asten! I think I know where that name belongs. Let me see."

The man pulled out a large dirty envelope from his breast-pocket, ran over several papers, unfolded one, and presently asked,—

"Joseph Asten?"

"Yes." (Joseph set his teeth, and silently cursed his want of forethought.)

"Proprietor of ten thousand dollars' worth of stock in the Amaranth! Who sent you here?"

His tone, though meant to be calm, was fierce and menacing. Joseph rose, scanned the faces of the workmen, who listened with a malicious curiosity, and finally answered, with a candor which seemed to impress, while it evidently disappointed the questioner:—

"No one sent me, and no one, beyond my own family, knows that I am here. I am a farmer, not a speculator. I was induced to take the stock from representations which have not been fulfilled, and which, I am now convinced, never will be fulfilled. My habit is, when I cannot get the truth from others, to ascertain it for myself. I presume you are Mr. Kanuck?"

The man did not answer immediately, but the quick, intelligent glance of one of the workmen showed Joseph that his surmise was correct. Mr. Kanuck conversed apart with the men, apparently giving private orders, and then, said, with a constrained civility:—

"If you are bound for the Fluke, Mr. Asten, I will join you. I am also going in that direction, and we can talk on the way."

They toiled up the opposite side of the ravine in silence. When they had reached the top and taken breath, Mr. Kanuck commenced:—

"I must infer that you have little faith in anything being realized from the Amaranth. Any man, ignorant of the technicalities of boring, might be discouraged by the external appearance of things; and I shall therefore not endeavor to explain to you my grounds of hope, unless you will agree to join me for a month or two and become practically acquainted with the locality and the modes of labor."

"That is unnecessary," Joseph replied.

"You being a farmer, of course I could not expect it. On the other hand, I think I can appreciate your,—disappointment, if we must call it so, and I should be willing, under certain conditions, to save you, not from positive loss, because I do not admit the possibility of that, but from what, at present, may seem loss to you. Do I make my meaning clear?"

"Entirely," Joseph replied, "except as to the conditions."

"We are dealing on the square, I take it?"

"Of course."

"Then," said Mr. Kanuck, "I need only intimate to you how important it is that I should develop our prospects. To do this, the faith of the principal stockholders must not be disturbed, otherwise the funds without which the prospects cannot be developed may fail me at the critical moment. Your hasty and unintelligent impressions, if expressed in a reckless manner, might do much to bring about such a catastrophe. I must therefore stipulate that you keep such impressions to yourself. Let me speak to you as man to man, and ask you if your expressions, not being founded on knowledge, would be honest? So far from it, you will be bound in all fairness, in consideration of my releasing you and restoring you what you have ventured, to adopt and disseminate the views of an expert,—namely, mine."

"Let me put it into fewer words," said Joseph. "You will buy my stock, repaying me what I have disbursed, if, on my return, I say nothing of what I have seen, and express my perfect faith (adopting your views) in the success of the Amaranth?"

"You have stated the conditions a little barely, perhaps, but not incorrectly. I only ask for perfect fairness, as between man and man."

"One question first, Mr. Kanuck. Does Mr. Blessing know the real prospects of the Amaranth?"

"No man more thoroughly, I assure you, Mr. Asten. Indeed, without Mr. Blessing's enthusiastic concurrence in the enterprise, I doubt whether we could have carried the work so far towards success. His own stock, I may say to you,—since we understand each other,—was earned by his efforts. If you know him intimately, you know also that he has no visible means of support. But he has what is much more important to us,—a thorough knowledge of men and their means."

He rubbed his hands, and laughed softly. They had been walking rapidly during the conversation, and now came suddenly upon the farthest crest of the hills, where the ridge fell away to the bottom occupied by the Fluke wells. Both paused at this point.

"On the square, then!" said Mr. Kanuck, offering his hand. "Tell me where you will be to-morrow morning, and our business can be settled in five minutes. You will carry out your part of the bargain, as man to man, when you find that I carry out mine."

"Do you take me for an infernal scoundrel?" cried Joseph, boiling over with disgust and rage.

Mr. Kanuck stepped back a pace or two. His sallow face became livid, and there was murder in his eyes. He put his hand into his breast, and Joseph, facing him, involuntarily did the same. Not until long afterwards, when other experiences had taught him the significance of the movement, did he remember what it then meant.

"So! that's your game, is it?" his antagonist said, hissing the words through his teeth. "A spy, after all! Or a detective, perhaps? I was a fool to trust a milk-and-water face: but one thing I tell you,—you may get away, but come back again if you dare!"

Joseph said nothing, but gazed steadily in the man's eyes, and did not move from his position so long as he was within sight. Then, breathing deeply, as if relieved from the dread of an unknown danger, he swiftly descended the hill.

That evening, as he sat in the bar-room of a horrible shanty (called a hotel), farther up the river, he noticed a pair of eyes fixed intently upon him: they belonged to one of the workmen in the Amaranth ravine. The man made an almost imperceptible signal, and left the room. Joseph followed him.

"Hush!" whispered the former. "Don't come back to the hill; and get away from here to-morrow morning, if you can!" With these words he darted off and disappeared in the darkness.

The counsel was unnecessary. Joseph, with all his inexperience of the world, saw plainly that his only alternatives were loss—or connivance. Nothing was to be gained by following the vile business any further. He took the earliest possible train, and by the afternoon of the following day found himself again in the city.

He was conscious of no desire to meet Mr. Blessing, yet the pressure of his recent experience seemed to drive him irresistibly in that direction. When he rang the bell, it was with the hope that he should find nobody at home. Mr. Blessing, however, answered the summons, and after the first expression of surprise, ushered him into the parlor.

"I am quite alone," he said; "Mrs. Blessing is passing the evening with her sister, Mrs. Woollish, and Clementina is still at Long Branch. I believe it is as good as settled that we are to lose her; at least she has written to inquire the extent of my available funds, which, in her case, is tantamount to—very much more."

Joseph determined to avoid all digressions, and insist on the Amaranth speculation, once for all, being clearly discussed. He saw that his father-in-law became more uneasy and excited as he advanced in the story of his journey, and, when it was concluded, did not seem immediately prepared to reply. His suspicions, already aroused by Mr. Kanuck's expressions, were confirmed, and a hard, relentless feeling of hostility took possession of his heart.

"I—I really must look into this," Mr. Blessing stammered, at last. "It seems incredible: pardon me, but I would doubt the statements, did they come from other lips than yours. It is as if I had nursed a dove in my bosom, and unexpectedly found it to be a—a basilisk!"

"It can be no serious loss to you," said Joseph, "since you received your stock in return for services."

"That is true: I was not thinking of myself. The real sting of the cockatrice is, that I have innocently misled you."

"Yet I understood you to say you had ventured your all?"

"My all of hope—my all of expectation!" Mr. Blessing cried. "I dreamed I had overtaken the rainbow at last; but this—this is senna—-quassia—aloes! My nature is so confiding that I accept the possibilities of the future as present realities, and build upon them as if they were Quincy granite. And yet, with all my experience, my acknowledged sagacity, my acquaintance with the hidden labyrinths of finance, it seems impossible that I can be so deceived! There must be some hideous misunderstanding: I have calculated all the elements, prognosticated all the planetary aspects, so to speak, and have not found a whisper of failure!"

"You omitted one very important element," Joseph said.

"What is that? I might have employed a detective, it is true—"

"No!" Joseph replied. "Honesty!"

Mr. Blessing fell back in his chair, weeping bitterly.

"I deserve this!" he exclaimed. "I will not resent it. I forgive you in advance of the time when you shall recognize my sincere, my heartfelt wish to serve you! Go, go: let me not recriminate! I meant to be, and still mean to be, your friend: but spare my too confiding child!"

Without a word of good-by, Joseph took his hat and hastened from the house. At every step the abyss of dishonesty seemed to open deeper before his feet. Spare the too confiding child! Father and daughter were alike: both mean, both treacherous, both unpardonably false to him.

With such feelings he left the city next morning, and made his way homewards.

CHAPTER XXIII. JULIA'S EXPERIMENT.

In the mean time the Hopetons had left for the sea-shore, and the two women, after a drive to Magnolia, remained quietly on the farm. Julia employed the days in studying Lucy with a soft, stealthy, unremitting watchfulness which the latter could not suspect, since, in the first place, it was a faculty quite unknown to her, and, secondly, it would have seemed absurd because inexplicable. Neither could she guess with what care Julia's manner and conversation were adapted to her own. She was only surprised to find so much earnest desire to correct faults, such artless transparency of nature. Thus an interest quite friendly took the place of her former repulsion of feeling, of which she began to be sincerely ashamed.

Moreover, Julia's continual demonstration of her love for Joseph, from which Lucy at first shrank with a delicate tremor of the heart, soon ceased to affect her. Nay, it rather seemed to interpose a protecting barrier between her present and the painful memory of her past self. She began to suspect that all regret was now conquered, and rejoiced in the sense of strength which could only thus be made clear to her mind. Her feeling towards Joseph became that of a sister or a dear woman friend; there could be no harm in cherishing it; she found a comfort in speaking to Julia of his upright, unselfish character, his guilelessness and kindness of heart.

The work upon the house was nearly finished, but new and more alarming bills began to come in; and worse was in store. There was a chimney-piece, "the loveliest ivory veins through the green marble," Julia said, which she had ordered from the city; there were boxes and packages of furniture already on hand, purchased without Joseph's knowledge and with entire faith in the virtues of the Amaranth. Although she still clung to that faith with a desperate grip, the sight of the boxes did not give her the same delight as she had felt in ordering them. She saw the necessity of being prepared, in advance, for either alternative. It was not in her nature to dread any scene or circumstance of life (although she had found the appearance of timidity very available, and could assume it admirably); the question which perplexed her was, how to retain and strengthen her ascendency over Joseph?

It is needless to say that the presence of Lucy Henderson was a part of her plan, although she held a more important service in reserve. Lucy's warm, frank expressions of friendship for Joseph gave her great satisfaction, and she was exhaustless in inventing ways to call them forth.

"You look quite like another person, Lucy," she would say; "I really think the rest has done you good."

"I am sure of it," Lucy answered.

"Then you must be in no hurry to leave. We must build you up, as the doctors say; and, besides, if—if this speculation should be unfortunate—O, I don't dare to think of it!—there will be such a comfort to me, and I am sure to Joseph also, in having you here until we have learned to bear it. We should not allow our minds to dwell on it so much, you know; we should make an exertion to hide our disappointment in your presence, and that would be such a help! Now you will say I am borrowing trouble, but do, pray, make allowances for me, Lucy! Think how everything has been kept from me that I ought to have known!"

"Of course, I will stay a little while for your sake," Lucy answered; "but Joseph is a man, and most men bear bad luck easily. He would hardly thank me for condoling with him."

"O, no, no!" Julia cried; "he thinks everything of you! He was so anxious for you to come here! he said to me, 'Lucy Henderson is a noble, true-hearted girl, and you will love her at once,' as I did, Lucy, when I first saw you, but without knowing why, as I now do."

A warm color came into Lucy's face, but she only shook her head and said nothing.

The two women had just risen from the breakfast-table the next morning, when a shadow fell into the room through the front window, and a heavy step was heard on the stone pavement of the veranda. Julia gave a little start and shriek, and seized Lucy's arm. The door opened and Joseph was there. He had risen before daybreak and taken the earliest train from the city. He had scarcely slept for two nights; his face was stern and haggard, and the fatigue, instead of exhausting, had only added to his excitement.

Julia sprang forward, threw her arm around, him, and kissed him repeatedly. He stood still and passively endured the caress, without returning it; then, stepping forward, he gave his hand to Lucy. She felt that it was cold and moist; and she did not attempt to repress the quick sympathy which came into her face and voice.

Julia guessed something of the truth instantly, and nothing but the powerful necessity of continuing to play her part enabled her to conceal the bitter anger which the contrast between Joseph's greeting to her and to Lucy aroused in her heart. She stood for a moment as if paralyzed, but in reality to collect herself; then, approaching her husband, she stammered forth: "O, Joseph—I'm afraid—I don't dare to ask you what—what news you bring. You didn't write—I've been so uneasy—and now I see from your face—that something is wrong."

He did not answer.

"Don't tell me all at once, if it's very bad!" she then cried: "but, no! it's my duty to hear it, my duty to bear it,—Lucy has taught me that,—tell me all, tell me all, this moment!"

"You and your father have ruined me: that is all."

"Joseph!" The word sounded like the essence of tender protest, of heartbreaking reproach. Lucy rose quietly and moved towards the door.

"Don't leave me, Lucy!" was Julia's appeal.

"It is better that I should go," Lucy answered, in a faint voice, and left the room.

"But, Joseph," Julia resumed, with a wild, distracted air, "why do you say such terrible things? I really do not know what you mean. What have you learned? what have you seen?"

"I have seen the Amaranth!"

"Well! Is there no oil?"

"O yes, plenty of oil!" he laughed; "skunk oil and rattlesnake oil! It is one of the vilest cheats that the Devil ever put into the minds of bad men."

"O, poor pa!" Julia cried; "what a terrible blow to him!"

"'Poor pa!' Yes, my discovery of the cheat is a terrible blow to 'poor pa,'—he did not calculate on its being found out so soon. When I learned from Kanuck that all the stock he holds was given to him for services,—that is, for getting the money out of the pockets of innocents like myself,—you may judge how much pity I feel for poor pa! I told him the fact to his face, last night, and he admitted it."

"Then," said Julia, "if the others know nothing, he may be able to sell his stock to-day,—his and yours; and we may not lose much after all."

"I should have sent you to the oil region, instead of going myself," Joseph answered, with a sneer. "You and Kanuck would soon have come to terms. He offered to take my stock off my hands, provided I would go back to the city and make such a report of the speculation as he would dictate."

"And you didn't do it?" Julia's voice rose almost to a scream, as the words burst involuntarily from her lips.

The expression on Joseph's face showed her that she had been rash; but the words were said, and she could only advance, not recede.

"It is perfectly legitimate in business," she continued. "Every investment in the Amaranth was a venture,—every stockholder knew that he risked losing his money! There is not one that would not save himself in that way, if he had the chance. But you pride yourself on being so much better than other men! Mr. Chaffinch is right; you have what he calls a 'moral pride'! You—"

"Stop!" Joseph interrupted. "Who was it that professed such concern about my faith? Who sent Mr. Chaffinch to insult me?"

"Faith and business are two different things: all the churches know that.

There was Mr. Sanctus, in the city: he subscribed ten thousand dollars to the Church of the Acceptance: he couldn't pay it, and they levied on his property, and sold him out of house and home! Really, you are as ignorant of the world as a baby!"

"God keep me so, then!" he exclaimed.

"However," she resumed, after a pause, "since you insist on our bearing the loss, I shall expect of your moral pride that you bear it patiently, if not cheerfully. It is far from being ruin to us. The rise in property will very likely balance it, and you will still be worth what you were."

"That is not all," he said. "I will not mention my greatest loss, for you are incapable of understanding it; but how much else have you saddled me with? Let me have a look at it!"

He crossed the hall and entered the new apartment, Julia following. Joseph inspected the ceiling, the elaborate and overladen cornices, the marble chimney-piece, and finally peered into the boxes and packages, not trusting himself to speak while the extent of the absurd splendor to which she had committed him grew upon his mind. Finally he said, striving to make his voice calm, although it trembled in his throat: "Since you were so free to make all these purchases, perhaps you will tell me how they are to be paid for?"

"Let me manage it, then," she answered. "There is no hurry. These country mechanics are always impatient,—I should call them impertinent, and I should like to teach them a lesson. Sellers are under obligations to the buyers, and they are bound to be accommodating. They have so many bills which are never paid, that an extension of time is the least they can do. Why, they will always wait a year, two years, three years, rather than lose."

"I suppose so."

"Then," said Julia, deceived by Joseph's quiet tone, "their profits are so enormous, that it would only be fair to reduce the bills. I am sure, that if I were to mention that you were embarrassed by heavy losses, and press them hard, they would compromise with me on a moderate amount. You know they allow what is called a margin for losses,—pa told me, but I forget how much,—they always expect to lose a certain percentage; and, of course, it can make no difference by whom they lose it. You understand, don't you?"

"Yes: it is very plain."

"Pa could help me to get both a reduction and an extension of time. The bills have not all been sent, and it will be better to wait two or three months after they have come in. If the dealers are a little uneasy in advance, they will be all the readier to compromise afterwards."

Joseph walked up and down the hollow room, with his hands clasped behind his back and his eyes fixed upon the floor. Suddenly he stopped before her and said: "There is another way."

"Not a better one, I am certain."

"The furniture has not yet been unpacked, and can be returned to them uninjured. Then the bills need not be paid at all."

"And we should be the laughing-stock of the neighborhood!" she cried, her eyes flashing. "I never heard of anything so ridiculous! If the worst comes to the worst, you can sell Bishop those fifty acres over the hill, which he stands ready to take, any day. But you'd rather have a dilapidated house,—no parlor,—guests received in the dining-room and the kitchen,—the Hopetons and your friends, the Helds, sneering at us behind our backs! And what would your credit be worth? We shall not even get trusted for groceries at the village store, if you leave things as they are!"

Joseph groaned, speaking to himself rather than answering her: "Is there no way out of this? What is done is done; shall I submit to it, and try to begin anew? or—"

He did not finish the sentence. Julia turned her head, so that only the chimney-piece and the furniture could see the sparkle of triumph in her eyes. She felt that she had maintained her position; and, what was far more, she now clearly saw the course by which she could secure it.

She left the room, drawing a full breath of relief as the door closed behind

918

her. The first shock of the evil news was over, and it had not fallen quite so heavily as she had feared. There were plenty of devices in store whereby all that was lost might be recovered. Had not her life at home been an unbroken succession of devices? Was she not seasoned to all manner of ups and downs, and wherefore should this first failure disconcert her? The loss of the money was, in reality, much less important to her than the loss of her power over Joseph. Weak as she had supposed him to he, he had shown a fierce and unexpected resistance, which must be suppressed now, or it might crush her whole plan of life. It seemed to her that he was beginning to waver: should she hasten a scheme by which she meant to entrap him into submission,—a subtle and dangerous scheme, which must either wholly succeed, or, wholly failing, involve her in its failure?

Rapidly turning over the question in her mind, she entered her bed-room. Locking the door, she walked directly to the looking-glass; the curtain was drawn from the window, and a strong light fell upon her face.

"This will never do!" she said to herself. "The anxiety and excitement have made me thin again, and I seem to have no color." She unfastened her dress, bared her neck, and pushed the ringlets behind her ears. "I look pinched; a little more, and I shall look old. If I were a perfect brunette or a perfect blonde, there would be less difficulty; but I have the most provoking, unmanageable complexion! I must bring on the crisis at once, and then see if I can't fill out these hollows."

She heard the front door opening, and presently saw Joseph on the lawn. He looked about for a moment, with a heavy, bewildered air, and then slowly turned towards the garden. She withdrew from the window, hesitated a moment, murmured to herself, "I will try, there cannot be a better time!" and then, burying her face in her hands and sobbing, rushed to Lucy's room.

"O Lucy!" she cried, "help me, or I am lost! How can I tell you? it is harder than I ever dreamed!"

"Is the loss so very serious,—so much more than you feared?" Lucy asked.

"Not that—O, if that were all! But Joseph—" Here Julia's sobs became

919

almost hysterical. "He is so cruel; I did advise him, as I told you, for his sake, and now he says that pa and I have combined to cheat him! I don't think he knows how dreadful his words are. I would sooner die than hear any more of them! Go to him, Lucy; he is in the garden; perhaps he will listen to you. I am afraid, and I never thought I should be afraid of him!"

"It is very, very sad," said Lucy. "But if he is in such an excited condition he will surely resent my coming. What can I say?"

"Say only what you heard me speak! Tell him of my anxiety, my self-reproach! Tell him that even if he will believe that pa meant to deceive him, he must not believe it of me! You know, Lucy, how he wrongs me in his thoughts; if you knew how hard it is to be wronged by a husband, you would pity me!"

"I do pity you, Julia, from my very heart; and the proof of it is, that I will try to do what you ask, against my own sense of its prudence. If Joseph repels my interference, I shall not blame him."

"Heaven bless you, Lucy! He will not repel you, he cannot!" Julia sobbed. "I will lie down and try to grow calm." She rose from the bed, upon which she had flung herself, and tottered through the door. When she had reached her own room, she again looked at her image in the glass, nodded and smiled.

Lucy walked slowly along the garden paths, plucking a flower or two, and irresolute how to approach Joseph. At last, descending the avenue of box, she found him seated in the semicircular enclosure, gazing steadfastly down the valley, but (she was sure) not seeing the landscape. As he turned his head at her approach, she noticed that his eyelids were reddened and his lips compressed with an expression of intense pain.

"Sit down, Lucy; I am a grim host, to-day," he said, with a melancholy attempt at a smile.

Lucy had come to him with a little womanly indignation, for Julia's sake, in her heart; but it vanished utterly, and the tears started into her eyes. For a moment she found it impossible to speak.

"I shall not talk of my ignorance any more, as I once did," Joseph continued. "If there is a class in the school of the world, graded according to experience of human meanness and treachery and falsehood, I ought to stand at the head."

Lucy stretched out her hand in protest. "Do not speak so bitterly, Joseph; it pains me to hear you."

"How would you have me speak?"

"As a man who will not see ruin before him because a part of his property happens to slip from him,—nay, if all were lost! I always took you to be liberal, Joseph, never careful of money for money's sake, and I cannot understand how your nature should be changed now, even though you have been the victim of some dishonesty."

"'Some dishonesty'! You are thinking only of money: what term would you give to the betrayal of a heart, the ruin of a life?"

"Surely, Joseph, you do not, you cannot mean—"

"My wife, of course. It needed no guessing."

"Joseph!" Lucy cried, seizing the opportunity, "indeed you do her wrong! I know what anxiety she has suffered during your absence. She blamed herself for having advised you to risk so much in an uncertain speculation, dreaded your disappointment, resolved to atone for it, if she could! She may have been rash and thoughtless, but she never meant to deceive you. If you are disappointed in some qualities, you should not shut your eyes and refuse to see others. I know, now, that I have myself not been fair in my judgment of Julia. A nearer acquaintance has led me to conceive what disadvantages of education, for which she is not responsible, she is obliged to overcome: she sees, she admits them, and she will overcome them. You, as her husband, are bound to show her a patient kindness—"

"Enough!" Joseph interrupted; "I see that you have touched pitch, also. Lucy, your first instinct was right. The woman whom I am bound to look upon as my wife is false and selfish in every fibre of her nature; how false and selfish I only can know, for to me she takes off her mask!"

"Do you believe me, then?" Lucy's words were slightly defiant. She had not quite understood the allusion to touching pitch, and Joseph's indifference to her advocacy seemed to her unfeeling.

"I begin to fear that Philip was right," said Joseph, not heeding her question. "Life is relentless: ignorance or crime, it is all the same. And if God cares less about our individual wrongs than we flatter ourselves He does, what do we gain by further endurance? Here is Lucy Henderson, satisfied that my wife is a suffering angel; thinks my nature is changed, that I am cold-hearted and cruel, while I know Lucy to be true and noble, and deceived by the very goodness of her own heart!"

He lifted his head, looked in her face a moment, and then went on:—

"I am sick of masks; we all wear them. Do you want to know the truth, Lucy? When I look back I can see it very clearly, now. A little more than a year ago the one girl who began to live in my thoughts was you! Don't interrupt me: I am only speaking of what was. When I went to Warriner's, it was in the hope of meeting you, not Julia Blessing. It was not yet love that I felt, but I think it would have grown to that, if I had not been led away by the cunningest arts ever a woman devised. I will not speculate on what might have been: if I had loved you, perhaps there would have been no return: had there been, I should have darkened the life of a friend. But this I say; I honor and esteem you, Lucy, and the loss of your friendship, if I now lose it, is another evil service which my wife has done me."

Joseph little suspected how he was torturing Lucy. She must have been more than woman, had not a pang of wild regret for the lost fortune, and a sting of bitter resentment against the woman who had stolen it, wrung her heart. She became deadly pale, and felt that her whole body was trembling.

"Joseph," she said, "you should not, must not, speak so to me."

"I suppose not," he answered, letting his head sink wearily; "it is certainly not conventional; but it is true, for all that! I could tell you the whole story, for I can read it backwards, from now to the beginning, without misunderstanding a word. It would make no difference; she is simple, natural, artless, amiable, for all the rest of the world, while to me—"

There was such despondency in his voice and posture, that Lucy, now longing more than ever to cheer him, and yet discouraged by the failure of her first attempt, felt sorely troubled.

"You mistake me, Joseph," she said, at last, "if you think you have lost my friendship, my sincerest sympathy. I can see that your disappointment is a bitter one, and my prayer is that you will not make it bitterer by thrusting from you the hopeful and cheerful spirit you once showed. We all have our sore trials."

Lucy found her own words very mechanical, but they were the only ones, that came to her lips. Joseph did not answer; he still sat, stooping, with his elbows on his knees, and his forehead resting on his palms.

"If I am deceived in Julia," she began again, "it is better to judge too kindly than too harshly. I know you cannot change your sentence against her now, nor, perhaps, very soon. But you are bound to her for life, and you must labor—it is your sacred duty—to make that life smoother and brighter for both. I do not know how, and I have no right to condemn you if you fail. But, Joseph, make the attempt now, when the most unfortunate experience that is likely to come to you is over; make it, and it may chance that, little by little, the old confidence will return, and you will love her again."

Joseph started to his feet. "Love her!" he exclaimed, with suppressed passion,—"love her! I hate her!"

There was a hissing, rattling sound, like that of some fierce animal at bay. The thick foliage of two of the tall box-trees was violently parted. The branches snapped and gave way: Julia burst through, and stood before them.

CHAPTER XXIV. FATE.

The face that so suddenly glared upon them was that of a Gorgon. The ringlets were still pushed behind her ears and the narrowness of the brow was entirely revealed; her eyes were full of cold, steely light; the nostrils were violently drawn in, and the lips contracted, as if in a spasm, so that the teeth were laid bare. Her hands were clenched, and there was a movement in her throat as of imprisoned words or cries; but for a moment no words came.

Lucy, who had started to her feet at the first sound, felt the blood turn chill in her veins, and fell, rather than sank, upon the seat again.

Joseph was hardly surprised, and wholly reckless. This eavesdropping was nothing worse than he already knew; indeed, there was rather a comfort in perceiving that he had not overestimated her capacity for treachery. There was now no limit; anything was possible.

"There is one just law, after all," he said, "the law that punishes listeners. You have heard the truth, for once. You have snared and trapped me, but I don't take to my captor more kindly than any other animal. From this moment I choose my own path, and if you still wish to appear as my wife, you must adapt your life to mine!"

"You mean to brazen it out, do you!" Julia cried, in a strange, hoarse, unnatural voice. "That's not so easy! I have not listened to no purpose: I have a hold upon your precious 'moral pride' at last!"

Joseph laughed scornfully.

"Yes, laugh, but it is in my hands to make or break you! There is enough decent sentiment in this neighborhood to crush a married man who dares to make love to an unmarried girl! As to the girl who sits still and listens to it, I say nothing; her reputation is no concern of mine!"

Lucy uttered a faint cry of horror.

"If you choose to be so despicable," said Joseph, "you will force me to set my truth against your falsehood. Wherever you tell your story, I shall follow with mine. It will be a wretched, a degrading business; but for the sake of Lucy's good name, I have no alternative. I have borne suspicion, misrepresentation, loss of credit,—brought upon me by you,—patiently, because they affected only myself; but since I am partly responsible in bringing to this house a guest for your arts to play upon and entrap, I am doubly bound to protect her against you. But I tell you, Julia, beware! I am desperate; and it is ill meddling with a desperate man! You may sneer at my moral pride, but you dare not forget that I have another quality,—manly self-respect,—which it will be dangerous to offend."

If Julia did not recognize, in that moment, that her subject had become her master, it was because the real, unassumed rage which convulsed her did not allow her to perceive anything clearly. Her first impulse was to scream and shriek, that servant and farm-hand might hear her, and then to repeat her accusation before them; but Joseph's last words, and the threatening sternness of his voice withheld her.

"So?" she said, at last; "this is the man who was all truth, and trust, and honor! With you the proverb seems to be reversed; it's off with the new love and on with the old. You can insult and threaten me in her presence! Well—go on: play out your little love-scene: I shall not interrupt you. I have heard enough to darken my life from this day!"

She walked away from them, up the avenue. Her dress was torn, her arms scratched and bleeding. She had played her stake and failed,—miserably, hopelessly failed. Her knees threatened to give way under her at every step, but she forced herself to walk erect, and thus reached the house without once looking back.

Joseph and Lucy mechanically followed her with their eyes. Then they turned and gazed at each other a moment without speaking. Lucy was very pale, and the expression of horror had not yet left her face.

"She told me to come to you," she stammered. "She begged me, with tears, to try and soften your anger against her; and then—oh, it is monstrous!"

"Now I see the plan!" Joseph exclaimed; "and I, in my selfish recklessness, saying what there was no need to utter, have almost done as she calculated,—have exposed you to this outrage! Why should I have recalled the past at all? I was not taking off a mask, I was only showing a scar—no, not even a scar, but a bruise!—which I ought to have forgotten. Forget it, too, Lucy, and, if you can, forgive me!"

"It is easy to forgive—everything but my own blindness," Lucy answered. "But there is one thing which I must do immediately: I must leave this house!"

"I see that," said Joseph, sadly. Then, as if speaking to himself, he murmured: "Who knows what friends will come to it in the future? Well, I will hear what can be borne; and afterwards,—there is Philip's valley. A free outlaw is better than a fettered outlaw!"

Lucy feared that his mind was wandering. He straightened himself to his full height, drew a deep breath, and exclaimed: "Action is a sedative in such cases, isn't it? Dennis has gone to the mill; I will get the other horse from the field and drive you home. Or, stay! will you not go to Philip Held's cottage for a day or two? I think his sister asked you to come."

"No, no!" cried Lucy; "you must not go! I will wait for Dennis."

"No one must suspect what has happened here this morning, unless Julia compels me to make it known, and I don't think she will. It is, therefore, better that I should take you. It will put me, I hope, in a more rational frame of mind. Go quietly to your room and make your preparations. I will see Julia, and if there is no further scene now, there will be none of the kind henceforth. She is cunning when she is calm."

On reaching the house Joseph went directly to his wife's bed-room. The necessity of an immediate interview could not be avoided, since Lucy was to leave. When he opened the door, Julia, who was bending over an open drawer of her bureau, started up with a little cry of alarm. She closed the drawer hastily, and began to arrange her hair at the mirror. Her face in the glass was flushed, but its expression was sullen and defiant.

"Julia," he said, as coolly as possible, "I am going to take Lucy home. Of course you understand that she cannot stay here an hour longer. You overheard my words to her, and you know just how much they were worth. I expect now, that—for your sake as much as hers or mine—you will behave towards her at parting in such a way that the servants may find no suggestions of gossip or slander."

"And if I don't choose to obey you?"

"I am not commanding. I propose a course which your own mind must find sensible. You have 'a deuced sharp intellect,' as your father said, on our wedding-day."

Joseph bit his tongue: he felt that he might have omitted this sting. But he was so little accustomed to victory, that he did not guess how thoroughly he had already conquered.

"Pa loved me, nevertheless," she said, and burst into tears.

Her emotion seemed real, but he mistrusted it.

"What can I do?" she sobbed: "I will try. I thought I was your wife, but I am not much more than your slave."

The foolish pity again stole into Joseph's heart, although he set his teeth and clenched his hands against it. "I am going for the horse," he said, in a kinder tone. "When I come back from this drive, this afternoon, I hope I shall find you willing to discuss our situation dispassionately, as I mean to do. We have not known each other fairly before to-day, and our plan of life must be rearranged."

It was a relief to walk forth, across the silent, sunny fields; and Joseph had learned to accept a slight relief as a substitute for happiness. The feeling that the inevitable crisis was over, gave him, for the first time in months, a sense of liberation. There was still a dreary and painful task before him, and he hardly knew why he should be so cheerful; but the bright, sweet currents of his blood were again in motion, and the weight upon his heart was lifted by some impatient, joyous energy.

The tempting vision of Philip's valley, which had haunted him from time to time, faded away. The angry tumult through which he had passed appeared to him like a fever, and he rejoiced consciously in the beginning of his spiritual convalescence. If he could simply suspend Julia's active interference in his life, he might learn to endure his remaining duties. He was yet young; and how much strength and knowledge had come to him—through sharpest pain, it was true—in a single year! Would he willingly return to his boyish innocence of the world, if that year could be erased from his life? He was not quite sure. Yet his nature had not lost the basis of that innocent time, and he felt that he must still build his future years upon it.

Thus meditating, he caught the obedient horse, led him to the barn, and harnessed him to the light carriage which Julia was accustomed to use. His anxiety concerning her probable demeanor returned as he entered the house. The two servant-women were both engaged, in the hall, in some sweeping or scouring operation, and might prove to be very inconvenient witnesses. The workmen in the new parlor—fortunately, he thought—were absent that day.

Lucy Henderson, dressed for the journey, sat in the dining-room. "I think I will go to Madeline Held for a day or two," she said; "I made a half-promise to visit her after your return."

"Where is Julia?"

"In her bed-room. I have not seen her. I knocked at the door, but there was no answer."

Joseph's trouble returned. "I will see her myself," he said, sternly; "she forgets what is due to a guest."

"No, I will go again," Lucy urged, rising hastily; "perhaps she did not hear me."

She followed him into the hall. Scarcely had he set his foot upon the first step of the staircase, when the bed-room door above suddenly burst open, and Julia, with a shriek of mortal terror, tottered down to the landing. Her face was ashy, and the dark-blue rings around her sunken eyes made them seem almost like the large sockets of a skull. She leaned against the railing, breathing short and hard.

Joseph sprang up the steps, but as he approached her she put out her

928

right hand, and pushed against his breast with all her force, crying out: "Go away! You have killed me!"

The next moment She fell senseless upon the landing.

Joseph knelt and tried to lift her. "Good God! she is dead!" he exclaimed.

"No," said Lucy, after taking Julia's wrist, "it is only a fainting fit. Bring some water, Susan."

The frightened woman, who had followed them, rushed down the stairs.

"But she must be ill, very ill," Lucy continued. "This is not an ordinary swoon. Perhaps the violent excitement has brought about some internal injury. You must send for a physician as soon as possible."

"And Dennis not here! I ought not to leave her; what shall I do?"

"Go yourself, and instantly! The carriage is ready. I will stay and do all that can be done during your absence."

Joseph delayed until, under the influence of air and water, Julia began to recover consciousness. Then he understood Lucy's glance,—the women were present and she dared not speak,—that he should withdraw before Julia could recognize him.

He did not spare the horse, but the hilly road tried his patience. It was between two and three miles to the house of the nearest physician, and he only arrived, anxious and breathless, to find that the gentleman had been called away to attend another patient. Joseph was obliged to retrace part of his road, and drive some distance in the opposite direction, in order to summon a second. Here, however, he was more fortunate. The physician was just sitting down to an early dinner, which he persisted in finishing, assuring Joseph, after ascertaining such symptoms of the case as the latter was able to describe, that it was probably a nervous attack, "a modified form of hysteria." Notwithstanding he violated his own theory of digestion by eating rapidly, the minutes seemed intolerably long. Then his own horse must be harnessed to his own sulky, during which time he prepared a few doses of valerian, belladonna, and other palliatives, which he supposed might be needed.

Meanwhile, Lucy and the woman had placed Julia in her own bed, and applied such domestic restoratives as they could procure, but without any encouraging effect. Julia appeared to be conscious, but she shook her head when they spoke to her, and even, so Lucy imagined, attempted to turn it away. She refused the tea, the lavender and ginger they brought, and only drank water in long, greedy draughts. In a little while she started up, with clutchings and incoherent cries, and then slowly sank back again, insensible.

The second period of unconsciousness was longer and more difficult to overcome. Lucy began to be seriously alarmed as an hour, two hours, passed by, and Joseph did not return. Dennis was despatched in search of him, carrying also a hastily pencilled note to Madeline Held, and then Lucy, finding that she could do nothing more, took her seat by the window and watched the lane, counting the seconds, one by one, as they were ticked off by the clock in the hall.

Finally a horse's head appeared above the hedge, where it curved around the shoulder of the hill: then the top of a carriage,—Joseph at last! The physician's sulky was only a short distance in the rear. Lucy hurried down and met Joseph at the gate.

"No better,—worse, I fear," she said, answering his look.

"Dr. Hartman," he replied,—"Worrall was away from home,—thinks it is probably a nervous attack. In that case it can soon be relieved."

"I hope so, but I fancy there is danger."

The doctor now arrived, and after hearing Lucy's report, shook his head. "It is not an ordinary case of hysteria," he remarked; "let me see her at once."

When they entered the room Julia opened her eyes languidly, fixed them on Joseph, and slowly lifted her hand to her head. "What has happened to me?" she murmured, in a hardly audible whisper.

"You had a fainting fit," he answered, "and I have brought the doctor. This is Dr. Hartman; you do not know him, but he will help you; tell him how you feel, Julia!"

"Cold!" she said, "cold! Sinking down somewhere! Will he lift me up?"

The physician made a close examination, but seemed to become more perplexed as he advanced. He administered only a slight stimulant, and then withdrew from the bedside. Lucy and the servant left the room, at his request, to prepare some applications.

"There is something unusual here," he whispered, drawing Joseph aside. "She has been sinking rapidly since the first attack. The vital force is very low: it is in conflict with some secret enemy, and it cannot resist much longer, unless we discover that enemy at once. I will do my best to save her, but I do not yet see how."

He was interrupted by a noise from the bed. Julia was vainly trying to rise: her eyes were wide and glaring. "No, no!" came from her lips, "I will not die! I heard you. Joseph, I will try—to be different—but—I must live—for that!"

Then her utterance became faint and indistinct, and she relapsed into unconsciousness. The physician re-examined her with a grave, troubled face. "She need not be conscious," he said, "for the next thing I shall do. I will not interrupt this syncope at once; it may, at least, prolong the struggle. What have they been giving her?"

He picked up, one by one, the few bottles of the household pharmacy which stood upon the bureau. Last of all, he found an empty glass shoved behind one of the supports of the mirror. He looked into it, held it against the light, and was about to set it down again, when he fancied that there was a misty appearance on the bottom, as if from some delicate sediment. Stepping to the window, he saw that he had not been mistaken. He collected a few of the minute granulations on the tip of his forefinger, touched them to his tongue, and, turning quickly to Joseph, whispered:—

"She is poisoned!"

"Impossible!" Joseph exclaimed; "she could not have been so mad!"

"It is as I tell you! This form of the operation of arsenic is very unusual, and I did not suspect it; but now I remember that it is noted in the books. Repeated syncopes, utter nervous prostration, absence of the ordinary burning and vomiting, and signs of rapid dissolution; it fits the case exactly! If I had some oxy-hydrate of iron, there might still be a possibility, but I greatly fear—"

"Do all you can!" Joseph interrupted. "She must have been insane! Do not tell me that you have no antidote!"

"We must try an emetic, though it will now be very dangerous. Then oil, white of egg,"—and the doctor hastened down to the kitchen.

Joseph walked up and down the room, wringing his hands. Here was a horror beyond anything he had imagined. His only thought was to save the life which she, in the madness of passion, must have resolved to take; she must not, must not, die now; and yet she seemed to be already in some region on the very verge of darkness, some region where it was scarcely possible to reach and pull her back. What could be done? Human science was baffled; and would God, who had allowed him to be afflicted through her, now answer his prayer to continue that affliction? But, indeed, the word "affliction" was not formed in his mind; the only word which he consciously grasped was "Life! life!"

He paused by the bedside and gazed upon her livid skin, her sunken features: she seemed already dead. Then, sinking on his knees, he tried to pray, if that was prayer which was the single intense appeal of all his confused feelings. Presently he heard a faint sigh; she slightly moved; consciousness was evidently returning.

She looked at him with half-opened eyes, striving to fix upon something which evaded her mind. Then she said, in the faintest broken whisper: "I did love you—I did—and do—love you! But—you—you hate me!"

A pang sharper than a knife went through Joseph's heart. He cried, through his tears: "I did not know what I said! Give me your forgiveness, Julia! Pardon me, not because I ask it, but freely, from your heart, and I will bless you!"

She did not speak, but her eyes softened, and a phantom smile hovered upon her lips. It was no mask this time: she was sacredly frank and true. Joseph bent over her and kissed her.

"O Julia!" he said, "why did you do it? Why did you not wait until I could speak with you? Did you think you would take a burden off yourself or me?"

Her lips moved, but no voice came. He lifted her head, supported her, and bent his ear to her mouth. It was like the dream of a voice:—

"I—did—not—mean—"

There it stopped. The doctor entered the room, followed by Lucy.

"First the emetic," said the former.

"For God's sake, be silent!" Joseph cried, with his ear still at Julia's lips. The doctor stepped up softly and looked, at her. Then, seating himself on the bed beside Joseph, he laid his hand upon her heart. For several minutes there was silence in the room.

Then the doctor removed his hand, took Julia's head out of Joseph's arms, and laid it softly upon the pillow.

She was dead.

CHAPTER XXV. THE MOURNERS.

"It cannot be!" cried Joseph, looking at the doctor with an agonized face; "it is too dreadful!"

"There is no room for doubt in relation to the cause. I suspect that her nervous system has been subjected to a steady and severe tension, probably for years past. This may have induced a condition, or at least a temporary paroxysm, during which she was—you understand me—not wholly responsible for her actions. You must have noticed whether such a condition preceded this catastrophe."

Lucy looked from one to the other, and back to the livid face on the pillow, unable to ask a question, and not yet comprehending that the end had come. Joseph arose at the doctor's words.

"That is my guilt," he said. "I was excited and angry, for I had been bitterly deceived. I warned her that her life must henceforth conform to mine: my words were harsh and violent. I told her that we had at last ascertained each other's true natures, and proposed a serious discussion for the purpose of arranging our common future, this afternoon. Can she have misunderstood my meaning? It was not separation, not divorce: I only meant to avoid the miserable strife of the last few weeks. Who could imagine that this would follow?"

Even as he spoke the words Joseph remembered the tempting fancy which had passed through his own mind,—and the fear of Philip,—as he stood on the brink of the rock, above the dark, sliding water. He covered his face with his hands and sat down. What right had he to condemn her, to pronounce her mad? Grant that she had been blinded by her own unbalanced, excitable nature rather than consciously false; grant that she had really loved him, that the love survived under all her vain and masterful ambition,—and how could he doubt it after the dying words and looks?—it was then easy to guess how sorely she had been wounded, how despair should follow her fierce excitement! Her words, "Go away! you have killed me!" were now explained. He groaned in the bitterness of his self-accusation. What were all the trials he had endured to this? How light seemed the burden from which he was now free! how gladly would he bear it, if the day's words and deeds could be unsaid and undone!

Tho doctor, meanwhile, had explained the manner of Julia's death to Lucy Henderson. She, almost overcome with this last horror, could only agree with his conjecture, for her own evidence confirmed it. Joseph had forborne to mention her presence in the garden, and she saw no need of repeating his words to her; but she described Julia's convulsive excitement, and her refusal to admit her to her room, half an hour before the first attack of the poison. The case seemed entirely clear to both.

"For the present," said the doctor, "let us say nothing about the suicide. There is no necessity for a post-mortem examination: the symptoms, and the presence of arsenic in the glass, are quite sufficient to establish the cause of death. You know what a foolish idea of disgrace is attached to families here in the country when such a thing happens, and Mr. Asten is not now in a state to bear much more. At least, we must save him from painful questions until after the funeral is over. Say as little as possible to him: he is not in a condition to listen to reason: he believes himself guilty of her death."

"What shall I do?" cried Lucy: "will you not stay until the man Dennis returns? Mr. Asten's aunt must be fetched immediately."

It was not a quarter of an hour before Dennis arrived, followed by Philip and Madeline Held.

Lucy, who had already despatched Dennis, with a fresh horse, to Magnolia, took Philip and Madeline into the dining-room, and hurriedly communicated to them the intelligence of Julia's death. Philip's heart gave a single leap of joy; then he compelled himself to think of Joseph and the exigencies of the situation.

"You cannot stay here alone," he said. "Madeline must keep you company. I will go up and take care of Joseph: we must think of both the

935

living and the dead."

No face could have been half so comforting in the chamber of death as Philip's. The physician had, in the mean time, repeated to Joseph the words he had spoken to Lucy, and now Joseph said, pointing to Philip, "Tell him everything!"

Philip, startled as he was, at once comprehended the situation. He begged Dr. Hartman to leave all further arrangements to him, and to summon Mrs. Bishop, the wife of one of Joseph's near neighbors, on his way home. Then, taking Joseph by the arm, he said:—

"Now come with me. We will leave this room awhile to Lucy and Madeline; but neither must you be alone. If I am anything to you, Joseph, now is the time when my presence should be some slight comfort. We need not speak, but we will keep together."

Joseph clung the closer to his friend's arm, without speaking, and they passed out of the house. Philip led him, mechanically, towards the garden, but as they drew near the avenue of box-trees Joseph started back, crying out:—

"Not there!—O, not there!"

Philip turned in silence, conducted him past the barn into the grass-field, and mounted the hill towards the pin-oak on its summit. From this point the house was scarcely visible behind the fir-trees and the huge weeping-willow, but the fair hills around seemed happy under the tender sky, and the melting, vapory distance, seen through the southern opening of the valley, hinted of still happier landscapes beyond. As Joseph contemplated the scene, the long strain upon his nerves relaxed: he leaned upon Philip's shoulder, as they sat side by side, and wept passionately.

"If she had not died!" he murmured, at last.

Philip was hardly prepared for this exclamation, and he did not immediately answer.

"Perhaps it is better for me to talk," Joseph continued. "You do not know the whole truth, Philip. You have heard of her madness, but not of my guilt. What was it I said when we last met? I cannot recall it now: but I know that I feared to call my punishment unjust. Since then I have deserved it all, and more. If I am a child, why should I dare to handle fire? If I do not understand life, why should I dare to set death in motion?"

He began, and related everything that had passed since they parted on the banks of the stream. He repeated the words that had been spoken in the house and in the garden, and the last broken sentences that came from Julia's lips. Philip listened with breathless surprise and attention. The greater part of the narrative made itself clear to his mind; his instinctive knowledge of Julia's nature enabled him to read much further than was then possible to Joseph; but there was a mystery connected with the suicide which he could not fathom. Her rage he could easily understand; her apparent submission to Joseph's request, however,—her manifest desire to live, on overhearing the physician's fears,—her last incomplete sentence, "I—did—not—mean—" indicated no such fatal intention, but the reverse. Moreover, she was too inherently selfish, even in the fiercest paroxysm of disappointment, to take her own life, he believed. All the evidence justified him in this view of her nature, yet at the same time rendered her death more inexplicable.

It was no time to mention these doubts to Joseph. His only duty was to console and encourage.

"There is no guilt in accident," he said. "It was a crisis which must have come, and you took the only course possible to a man. If she felt that she was defeated, and her mad act was the consequence, think of your fate had she felt herself victorious!"

"It could have been no worse than it was," Joseph answered. "And she might have changed: I did not give her time. I have accused my own mistaken education, but I had no charity, no pity for hers!"

When they descended the hill Mrs. Bishop had arrived, and the startled household was reduced to a kind of dreary order. Dennis, who had driven with speed, brought Rachel Miller at dusk, and Philip and Madeline then departed, taking Lucy Henderson with them. Rachel was tearful, but composed; she said little to her nephew, but there was a quiet, considerate tenderness in her manner which soothed him more than any words.

The reaction from so much fatigue and excitement almost prostrated him. When he went to bed in his own guest-room, feeling like a stranger in a strange house, he lay for a long time between sleep and waking, haunted by all the scenes and personages of his past life. His mother's face, so faded in memory, came clear and fresh from the shadows; a boy whom he had loved in his school-days floated with fair, pale features just before his closed eyes; and around and between them there was woven a web of twilights and moonlights, and sweet sunny days, each linked to some grief or pleasure of the buried years. It was a keen, bitter joy, a fascinating torment, from which he could not escape. He was caught and helplessly ensnared by the phantoms, until, late in the night, the strong claim of nature drove them away and left him in a dead, motionless, dreamless slumber.

Philip returned in the morning, and devoted the day not less to the arrangements which must necessarily be made for the funeral than to standing between Joseph and the awkward and inquisitive sympathy of the neighbors. Joseph's continued weariness favored Philip's exertions, while at the same time it blunted the edge of his own feelings, and helped him over that cold, bewildering, dismal period, during which a corpse is lord of the mansion and controls the life of its inmates.

Towards evening Mr. and Mrs. Blessing, who had been summoned by telegraph, made their appearance. Clementina did not accompany them. They were both dressed in mourning: Mrs. Blessing was grave and rigid, Mr. Blessing flushed and lachrymose. Philip conducted them first to the chamber of the dead and then to Joseph.

"It is so sudden, so shocking!" Mrs. Blessing sobbed; "and Julia always seemed so healthy! What have you done to her, Mr. Asten, that she should be cut off in the bloom of her youth?"

"Eliza!" exclaimed her husband, with his handkerchief to his eyes; "do not say anything which might sound like a reproach to our heart-broken son! There are many foes in the citadel of life: they may be undermining our—our foundations at this very moment!"

"No," said Joseph; "you, her father and mother, must hear the truth. I would give all I have in the world if I were not obliged to tell it."

It was, at the best, a painful task; but it was made doubly so by exclamations, questions, intimations, which he was forced to hear. Finally, Mrs. Blessing asked, in a tone of alarm:—

"How many persons know of this?"

"Only the physician and three of my friends," Joseph answered.

"They must be silent! It might ruin Clementina's prospects if it were generally known. To lose one daughter and to have the life of another blasted would be too much."

"Eliza," said her husband, "we must, try to accept whatever is inevitable. It seems to me that I no more recognize Julia's usually admirable intellect in her—yes, I must steel myself to say the word!—her suicide, than I recognized her features just now! unless Decay's effacing fingers have already swept the lines where beauty lingers. I warned her of the experiment, for such I felt it to be; yet in this last trying experience I do not complain of Joseph's disappointment, and his temporary—I trust it is only temporary—suspicion. We must not forget that he has lost more than we have."

"Where is—" Joseph began, endeavoring to turn the conversation from this point.

"Clementina? I knew you would find her absence unaccountable. We instantly forwarded a telegram to Long Branch; the answer said, 'My grief is great, but it is quite impossible to come.' Why impossible she did not particularize, and we can only conjecture. When I consider her age and lost opportunities, and the importance which a single day, even a fortunate situation, may possess for her at present, it seems to remove some of the sharpness of the serpent's tooth. Neither she nor we are responsible for Julia's rash taking off; yet it is always felt as a cloud which lowers upon the family. There was a similar case among the De Belsains, during the Huguenot times, but we never mention it. For your sake silence is rigidly imposed upon us; since the preliminary—what shall I call it?—dis-harmony of views?—would probably become a part of the narrative."

"Pray do not speak of that now!" Joseph groaned.

"Pardon me; I will not do so again. Our minds naturally become discursive under the pressure of grief. It is easier for me to talk at such times than to be silent and think. My power of recuperation seems to be spiritual as well as physical; it is congenital, and therefore exposes me to misconceptions. But we can close over the great abyss of our sorrow, and hide it from view in the depth of our natures, without dancing on the platform which covers it."

Philip turned away to hide a smile, and even Mrs. Blessing exclaimed: "Really, Benjamin, you are talking heartlessly!"

"I do not mean it so," he said, melting into tears, "but so much has come upon me all at once! If I lose my buoyancy, I shall go to the bottom like a foundered ship! I was never cut out for the tragic parts of life; but there are characters who smile on the stage and weep behind the scenes. And, you know, the Lord loveth a cheerful giver."

He was so touched by the last words he spoke, that he leaned his head upon his arms and wept bitterly.

Then Mrs. Blessing, weeping also, exclaimed: "O, don't take on so, Benjamin!"

Philip put an end to the scene, which was fast becoming a torment to Joseph. But, later in the evening, Mr. Blessing again sought the latter, softly apologizing for the intrusion, but declaring that he was compelled, then and there, to make a slight explanation.

"When you called the other evening," he said, "I was worn out, and not competent to grapple with such an unexpected revelation of villainy. I had been as ignorant of Kanuck's real character as you were. All our experience of the world is sometimes at fault; but where the Reverend Dr. Lellifant was first deceived, my own case does not seem so flagrant. Your early information, however, enabled me (through third parties) to secure a partial sale of the stock held by yourself and me,—at something of a sacrifice, it is true; but I prefer not to dissociate myself entirely from the enterprise. I do not pretend to be more than the merest tyro in geology; nevertheless, as I lay awake last night,—being, of course, unable to sleep after the shock of the telegram,—I sought relief in random scientific fancies. It occurred to mo that since the main Chowder wells are 'spouting,' their source or reservoir must be considerably higher than the surface. Why might not that source be found under the hills of the Amaranth? If so, the Chowder would be tapped at the fountain-head and the flow of Pactolean grease would be ours! When I return to the city I shall need instantly—after the fearful revelations of to-day—some violently absorbing occupation; and what could be more appropriate? If anything could give repose to Julia's unhappy shade, it would be the knowledge that her faith in the Amaranth was at last justified! I do not presume to awaken your confidence: it has been too deeply shaken; all I ask is, that I may have the charge of your shares, in order—without calling upon you for the expenditure of another cent, you understand—to rig a jury-mast on the wreck, and, D. V., float safely into port!"

"Why should I refuse to trust you with what is already worthless?" said Joseph.

"I will admit even that, if you desire. 'Exitus acta probat' was Washington's motto; but I don't consider that we have yet reached the exitus! Thank you, Joseph! Your question has hardly the air of returning confidence, but I will force myself to consider it as such, and my labor will be to deserve it."

He wrung Joseph's hand, shed a few more tears, and betook himself to his wife's chamber. "Eliza, let us be calm: we never know our strength until it has been tried," he said to her, as he opened his portmanteau and took from it the wicker-covered flask.

Then came the weariest and dreariest day of all,—when the house must be thrown open to the world; when in one room the corpse must be displayed for solemn stares and whispered comments, while in another the preparation of the funeral meats absorbs all the interest of half a dozen busy women; when the nearest relatives of the dead sit together in a room up stairs, hungering only for the consolations of loneliness and silence; when all talk under their voices, and uncomfortably fulfil what they believe to be their solemn duty; and when even Nature is changed to all eyes, and the mysterious gloom of an eclipse seems to fall from the most unclouded sun.

There was a general gathering of the neighbors from far and near. The impression seemed to be—and Philip was ready to substantiate it—that Julia had died in consequence of a violent convulsive spasm, which some attributed to one cause and some to another.

The Rev. Mr. Chaffinch made his way, as by right, to the chamber of the mourners. Rachel Miller was comforted in seeing him, Mr. and Mrs. Blessing sadly courteous, and Joseph strengthened himself to endure with patience what might follow. After a few introductory words, and a long prayer, the clergyman addressed himself to each, in turn, with questions or remarks which indicated a fierce necessity of resignation.

"I feel for you, brother," he said, as he reached Joseph and bent over his chair. "It is an inscrutable visitation, but I trust you submit, in all obedience?"

Joseph bowed silently.

"He has many ways of searching the heart," Mr. Chaffinch continued. "Your one precious comfort must be that she believed, and that she is now in glory. O, if you would but resolve to follow in her footsteps! He shows His love, in that He chastens you: it is a stretching out of His hand, a visible offer of acceptance, this on one side, and the lesson of our perishing mortality on the other! Do you not feel your heart awfully and tenderly moved to approach Him?"

Joseph sat, with bowed head, listening to the smooth, unctuous, dismal voice at his ear, until the tension of his nerves became a positive physical pain. He longed to cry aloud, to spring up and rush away; his heart was moved, but not awfully and tenderly. It had been yearning towards the pure Divine Light in which all confusions of the soul are disentangled; but now some opaque foreign substance intervened, and drove him back upon himself. How long the torture lasted he did not know. He spake no word, and made no further sign.

Then Philip took him and Rachel Miller down, for the last conventional look at the stony, sunken face. He was seated here and led there; he was dimly conscious of a crowd, of murmurs and steadfast faces; he heard some one whisper, "How dreadfully pale he looks!" and wondered whether the words could possibly refer to him. Then there was the welcome air and the sunshine, and Dennis driving them slowly down the lane, following a gloomy vehicle, in which something—not surely the Julia whom he knew—was carried.

He recalled but one other such stupor of the senses: it was during the performance of the marriage ceremony.

But the longest day wears out at last; and when night came only Philip was beside him. The Blessings had been sent to Oakland Station for the evening train to the city, and Joseph's shares in the Amaranth Company were in their portmanteau.

CHAPTER XXVI. THE ACCUSATION.

For a few days it almost seemed to Joseph that the old order of his existence had been suddenly restored, and the year of his betrothal and marriage had somehow been intercalated into his life simply as a test and trial. Rachel Miller was back again, in her old capacity, and he did not yet see—what would have been plain to any other eyes—that her manner towards him was far more respectful and considerate than formerly. But, in fact, she made a wide distinction between the "boy" that he had been and the man and widower which he had come to be. At first, she had refused to see the dividing line: having crossed it, her new course soon became as natural and fixed as the old. She was the very type of a mechanically developed old maid,—inflexibly stern towards male youth, devotedly obedient to male maturity.

Joseph had been too profoundly moved to lose at once the sense of horror which the manner of Julia's death had left in his heart. He could not forgive himself for having, though never so ignorantly, driven her to madness. He was troubled, restless, unhappy; and the mention of his loss was so painful that he made every effort to avoid hearing it. Some of his neighbors, he imagined, were improperly curious in their inquiries. He felt bound, since the doctor had suggested it, since Philip and Lucy had acquiesced, and Mrs. Blessing had expressed so much alarm lest it might become known, to keep the suicide a secret; but he was driven so closely by questions and remarks that his task became more and more difficult.

Had the people taken offence at his reticence? It seemed so; for their manner towards him was certainly changed. Something in the look and voice; an indefinable uneasiness at meeting him; an awkward haste and lame excuses for it,—all these things forced themselves upon his mind. Elwood Withers, alone, met him as of old, with even a tenderer though a more delicately veiled affection; yet in Elwood's face he detected the signs of a grave trouble. It could not be possible, he thought, that Elwood had heard some surmise, or distorted echo, of his words to Lucy in the garden,—that there had been another listener besides Julia!

There were times, again, when he doubted all these signs, when he ascribed them to his own disturbed mind, and decided to banish them from his memory. He would stay quietly at home, he resolved, and grow into a healthier mood: he would avoid the society of men, until he should cease to wrong them by his suspicions.

First, however, he would see Philip; but on reaching the Forge he found Philip absent. Madeline received him with a subdued kindness in which he felt her sympathy; but it was also deeper, he acknowledged to himself, than he had any right to claim.

"You do not see much of your neighbors, I think, Mr. Asten?" she asked. The tone of her voice indicated a slight embarrassment.

"No," he answered; "I have no wish to see any but my friends."

"Lucy Henderson has just left us. Philip took her to her father's, and was intending to call at your place on his way home. I hope you will not miss him. That is," she added, while a sudden flush of color spread over her face, "I want you to see him to-day. I beg you won't take my words as intended for a dismissal."

"Not now, certainly," said Joseph. But he rose from his seat as he spoke.

Madeline looked both confused and pained. "I know that I spoke awkwardly," she said, "but indeed I was very anxious. It was also Lucy's wish. We have been talking about you this morning."

"You are very kind. And yet—I ought to wish you a more cheerful subject."

What was it in Madeline's face that haunted Joseph on his way home? The lightsome spirit was gone from her eyes, and they were troubled as if by the pressure of tears, held back by a strong effort. Her assumed calmness at parting seemed to cover a secret anxiety; he had never before seen her bright, free nature so clouded.

Philip, meanwhile, had reached the farm, where he was received by

Rachel Miller.

"I am glad to find that Joseph is not at home," he said; "there are some things which I need to discuss with you, before I see him. Can you guess what they are? Have you heard nothing,—no stories?"

Rachel's face grew pale, yet there was a strong fire of indignation in her eyes. "Dennis told me an outrageous report he had heard in the village," she said: "if you mean the same thing, you did well to see me first. You can help me to keep this insult from Joseph's knowledge."

"If I could I would, Miss Rachel. I share your feeling about it; but suppose the report were now so extended—and of course in a more exaggerated form the farther it goes—that we cannot avoid its probable consequences? This is not like a mere slander, which can be suffered to die of itself. It is equivalent to a criminal charge, and must be faced."

She clasped her hands, and stared at him in terror.

"But why," she faltered—"why does any one dare to make such a charge? And against the best, the most innocent—"

"The fact of the poisoning cannot be concealed," said Philip. "It appears, moreover, that one of the women who was in the house on the day of Julia's death heard her cry out to Joseph: 'Go away,—you have killed me!' I need not take up the reports any further; there is enough in these two circumstances to excite the suspicions of those who do not know Joseph as we do. It is better, therefore, to meet those suspicions before they come to us in a legal form."

"What can we do?" cried Rachel; "it is terrible!"

"One course is clear, if it is possible. We must try to discover not only the cause of Julia's suicide, but the place where she procured the poison, and her design in procuring it. She must have had it already in the house."

"I never thought of that. And her ways were so quiet and sly! How shall we ever find it out? O, to think that, dead and gone as she is, she can yet bring all this upon Joseph!"

"Try to be calm, Miss Rachel," said Philip. "I want your help, and you must have all your wits about you. First, you must make a very careful examination of her clothing and effects, even to the merest scrap of paper. A man's good name—a man's life, sometimes—hangs upon a thread, in the most literal sense. There is no doubt that Julia meant to keep a secret, and she must have had a strong reason; but we have a stronger one, now, to discover it. First, as to the poison; was there any arsenic in the house when Julia came?"

"Not a speck! I never kept it, even for rats."

"Then we shall begin with ascertaining where she bought it. Let us make our investigations secretly, and as speedily as possible. Joseph need not know, at present, what we have undertaken, but he must know the charge that hangs over him. Unless I tell him, he may learn it in a more violent way. I sent Elwood Withers to Magnolia yesterday, and his report leaves me no choice of action."

Rachel Miller felt, from the stern gravity of Philip's manner, that he had not exaggerated Joseph's danger. She consented to be guided by him in all things; and this point being settled, they arranged a plan of action and communication, which was tolerably complete by the time Joseph returned.

As gently as possible Philip broke the unwelcome news; but, lightly as he pretended to consider it, Joseph's instinct saw at once what might be the consequences. The circumstances were all burned upon his consciousness, and it needed no reflection to show him how completely he was entangled in them.

"There is no alternative," he said, at last. "It was a mistake to conceal the cause of her death from the public: it is easy to misunderstand her exclamation, and make my crime out of her madness. I see the whole connection! This suspicion will not stop where it is. It will go further; and therefore I must anticipate it. I must demand a legal inquiry before the law forces one upon me. If it is not my only method of defence, it is certainly my best!"

"You are right!" Philip exclaimed. "I knew this would be your decision; I said so to Madeline this morning."

Now Madeline's confused manner became intelligible to Joseph. Yet a doubt still lingered in his mind. "Did she, did Madeline question it?" he asked.

"Neither she nor Lucy Henderson. If you do this, I cannot see how it will terminate without a trial. Lucy may then happen to be an important witness."

Joseph started. "Must that be!" he cried. "Has not Lucy been already forced to endure enough for my sake? Advise me, Philip! Is there any other way than that I have proposed?"

"I see no other. But your necessity is far greater than that for Lucy's endurance. She is a friend, and there can be no sacrifice in so serving you. What are we all good for, if not to serve you in such a strait?"

"I would like to spare her, nevertheless," said Joseph, gloomily. "I meant so well towards all my friends, and my friendship seems to bring only disgrace and sorrow."

"Joseph!" Philip exclaimed, "you have saved one friend from more than disgrace and sorrow! I do not know what might have come, but you called me back from the brink of an awful, doubtful eternity! You have given me an infinite loss and an infinite gain! I only ask you, in return, to obey your first true, proud instinct of innocence, and let me, and Lucy, and Elwood be glad to take its consequences, for your sake!"

"I cannot help myself," Joseph answered. "My rash impatience and injustice will come to light, and that may be the atonement I owe. If Lucy will spare herself, and report me truly, as I must have appeared to her, she will serve me best."

"Leave that, now! The first step is what most concerns us. When will you be ready to demand a legal investigation?"

"At once!—to-morrow!"

"Then we will go together to Magnolia. I fear we cannot change the ordinary forms of procedure, and there must be bail for your appearance at the proper time."

"Already on the footing of a criminal?" Joseph murmured, with a sinking of the heart. He had hardly comprehended, up to this moment, what his position would be.

The next day they drove to the county town. The step had not been taken a moment too soon, for such representations had been made that a warrant for Joseph's arrest was in the hands of the constable, and would have been served in a few hours. Philip and Mr. Hopeton, who also happened to be in the town by a fortunate chance (though Philip knew how the chance came), offered to accept whatever amount of bail might be demanded. The matter was arranged as privately as possible, but it leaked out in some way, and Philip was seriously concerned lest the curiosity—perhaps, even, the ill-will—of a few persons might be manifested towards Joseph. He visited the offices of the county papers, and took care that the voluntary act should be stated in such a manner as to set its character properly before the people. Everything, he felt, depended on securing a fair and unprejudiced judgment of the case.

This, indeed, was far more important than even he suspected. In a country where the press is so entirely free, and where, owing to the lazy, indifferent habit of thought—or, rather, habit of no thought—of the people, the editorial views are accepted without scrutiny, a man's good name or life may depend on the coloring given to his acts by a few individual minds, it is especially necessary to keep the balance even, to offset one statement by another, and prevent a partial presentation of the case from turning the scales in advance. The same phenomena were as likely to present themselves here, before a small public, as in the large cities, where the whole population of the country become a more or less interested public. The result might hinge, not upon Joseph's personal character as his friends knew it, but upon the political party with which he was affiliated, the church to which he belonged,— nay, even upon the accordance of his personal sentiments with the public sentiment of the community in which he lived. If he had dared to defy the latter, asserting the sacred right of his own mind to the largest liberty, he was already a marked man. Philip did not understand the extent and power of the external influences which control what we complacently call "justice," but he knew something of the world, and acted in reality more prudently than he supposed.

He was calm and cheerful for Joseph's sake; yet, now that the matter was irrevocably committed to the decision of a new, uninterested tribunal, he began to feel the gravity of his friend's position.

"I almost wish," Joseph said, as they drove homewards, "that no bail had been granted. Since the court meets in October, a few weeks of seclusion would do me no harm; whereas now I am a suspected person to nearly all whom I may meet."

"It is not agreeable," Philip answered, "but the discipline may be useful. The bail terminates when the trial commences, you understand, and you will have a few nights alone, as it is,—quite enough, I imagine, to make you satisfied with liberty under suspicion. However I have one demand to make, Joseph! I have thought over all possible lines of defence; I have secured legal assistance for you, and we are agreed as to the course to be adopted. I do not think you can help us at all. If we find that you can, we will call upon you; in the mean time, wait and hope!"

"Why should I not?" Joseph asked. "I have nothing to fear, Philip."

"No!" But Philip's emphatic answer was intended to deceive. He was purposely false, knew himself to be so, and yet his conscience never troubled him less!

When they reached the farm, Philip saw by Rachel Miller's face that she had a communication to make. It required a little management to secure an interview with her without Joseph's knowledge; but some necessity for his presence at the barn favored his friend. No sooner were they alone than Rachel approached Philip hastily and said, in a hurried whisper:—

"Here! I have found something, at last! It took a mighty search: I thought I never should come upon the least bit that we could make anything of: but this was in the upper part of a box where she kept her rings and chains, and such likes! Take it,—it makes me uncomfortable to hold it in my fingers!"

She thrust a small paper into his hand.

It was folded very neatly, and there was an apothecary's label on the back. Philip read: "Ziba Linthicum's Drug store, No. 77 Main St., Magnolia." Under this printed address was written in large letters the word "Arsenic." On unfolding the paper he saw that a little white dust remained in the creases: quite enough to identify the character of the drug.

"I shall go back to-morrow!" he said. "Thank Heaven, we have got one clew to the mystery! Joseph must know nothing of this until all is explained; but while I am gone make another and more thorough search! Leave no corner unexplored: I am sure we shall find something more."

"I'd rip up her dresses!" was Rachel's emphatic reply. "That is, if it would do any good. But perhaps feeling of the lining and the hems might be enough. I'll take every drawer out, and move the furniture! But I must wait for daylight: I'm not generally afeared, but there is some things, you know, which a body would as lief not do by night, with cracks and creaks all around you, which you don't seem to hear at other times."

CHAPTER XXVII. THE LABELS.

The work at Coventry Forge was now so well organized that Philip could easily give the most of his time to Joseph's vindication. He had secured the services of an excellent country lawyer, but he also relied much upon the assistance of two persons,—his sister Madeline and Elwood Withers: Madeline, from her rapid, clear insight, her shrewd interpretation of circumstances; and Elwood as an active, untiring practical agent.

The latter, according to agreement, had ridden up from his section of the railway, and was awaiting Philip when he returned home.

Philip gave them the history of the day,—this time frankly, with all the signs and indications which he had so carefully kept from Joseph's knowledge. Both looked aghast; and Elwood bent an ivory paper-cutter so suddenly in his hands that it snapped in twain. He colored like a girl.

"It serves me right," he said. "Whenever my hands are idle, Satan finds mischief for 'em,—as the spelling-book says. But just so the people bend and twist Joseph Asten's character, and just so unexpectedly his life may snap in their hands!"

"May the omen be averted!" Madeline cried. "Put down the pieces, Mr. Withers! You frighten me."

"No, it is reversed!" said Philip. "Just so Joseph's friends will snap this chain of circumstances. If you begin to be superstitious, I must look out for other aids. The tracing of the poison is a more fortunate step than I hoped, at the start. I cannot at all guess to what it may lead, but there is a point beyond which even the most malignant fate has no further power over an innocent man. Thus far we have met nothing but hostile circumstances: there seems to be more than Chance in the game, and I have an idea that the finding of this paper will break the evil spell. Come now, Madeline, and you, Withers, give me your guesses as to what my discovery shall be to-morrow!"

After a pause, Madeline answered: "It must have been purchased—

perhaps even by Mr. Asten—for rats or mice; and she may have swallowed the drug in a fit of passion."

"I think," said Elwood, "that she bought it for the purpose of poisoning Joseph! Then, may be, the glasses were changed, as I've heard tell of a man whose wife changed his coffee-cup because there was a fly in it, giving him hers, and thereby innocently killed him when he meant to ha' killed her."

"Ha!" Philip cried; "the most incredible things, apparently, are sometimes the most natural! I had not thought of this explanation."

"O Philip!" said Madeline, "that would be a new horror! Pray, let us not think of it: indeed, indeed, we must not guess any more."

Philip strove to put the idea from his mind: he feared lest it might warp his judgment and mislead him in investigations which it required a cool, sharp intellect to prosecute. But the idea would not stay away: it haunted him precisely on account of its enormity, and he rode again to Magnolia the next day with a foreboding sense of some tragic secret about to be revealed.

But he never could have anticipated the actual revelation.

There was no difficulty in finding Ziba Linthicum's Drug store. The proprietor was a lank, thin-faced man, with projecting, near-sighted eyes, and an exceedingly prim, pursed mouth. His words, uttered in the close, wiry twang peculiar to Southern Pennsylvania, seemed to give him a positive relish: one could fancy that his mouth watered slightly as he spoke. His long, lean lips had a settled smirk at the corner, and the skin was drawn so tightly over his broad, concave chin-bone that it shone, as if polished around the edges.

He was waiting upon a little girl when Philip entered; but he looked up from his scales, bowed, smiled, and said: "In a moment, if you please."

Philip leaned upon the glass case, apparently absorbed in the contemplation of the various soaps and perfumes under his eyes, but thinking only of the paper in his pocket-book.

"Something in this line, perhaps?"

953

Mr. Linthicum, with a still broader smile, began to enumerate: "These are from the Society Hygiennick—"

"No," said Philip, "my business is especially private. I take it for granted that you have many little confidential matters intrusted to you."

"Oh, undoubtedly, sir! Quite as much so as a physician."

"You are aware also that mistakes sometimes occur in making up prescriptions, or in using them afterwards?"

"Not by me, I should hope. I keep a record of every dangerous ingredient which goes out of my hands."

"Ah!" Philip exclaimed. Then he paused, uncertain how much to confide to Mr. Linthicum's discretion. But, on mentioning his name and residence, he found that both himself and Mr. Hopeton were known—and favorably, it seemed—to the apothecary. He knew the class of men to which the latter belonged,—prim, fussy, harmlessly vain persons, yet who take as good care of their consciences as of their cravats and shirt-bosoms. He produced the paper without further delay.

"That was bought here, certainly," said Mr. Linthicum. "The word 'Arsenic' is written in my hand. The date when, and the person by whom it was purchased, must be in my register. Will you go over it with me?"

He took a volume from a drawer, and beginning at the last entry, they went slowly backward over the names, the apothecary saying: "This is confidential: I rely upon your seeing without remembering."

They had not gone back more than two or three weeks before Philip came upon a name that made his heart stand still. There was a record in a single line:—

"Miss Henderson. Arsenic."

He waited a few seconds, until he felt sure of his voice. Then he asked: "Do you happen to know Miss Henderson?"

"Not at all! A perfect stranger."

"Can you, perhaps, remember her appearance?"

"Let me see," said Mr. Linthicum, biting the end of his forefinger; "that must have been the veiled lady. The date corresponds. Yes, I feel sure of it, as all the other poison customers are known to me."

"Pray describe her then!" Philip exclaimed.

"Really, I fear that I cannot. Dressed in black, I think; but I will not be positive. A soft, agreeable voice, I am sure."

"Was she alone? Or was any one else present?"

"Now I do recall one thing," the apothecary answered. "There was an agent of a wholesale city firm—a travelling agent, you understand—trying to persuade me into an order on his house. He stepped on one side as she came to the counter, and he perhaps saw her face more distinctly, for he laughed as she left, and said something about a handsome girl putting her lovers out of their misery."

But Mr. Linthicum could remember neither the name of the agent nor that of the firm which he represented. All Philip's questioning elicited no further particulars, and he was obliged to be satisfied with the record of the day and probable hour of the purchase, and with the apothecary's promise of the strictest secrecy.

He rode immediately home, and after a hasty consultation with Madeline, remounted his horse and set out to find Lucy Henderson. He was fortunate enough to meet her on the highway, on her way to call upon a neighbor. Springing from his horse he walked beside her, and announced his discovery at once.

Lucy remembered the day when she had accompanied Julia to Magnolia, during Joseph's absence from home. The time of the day, also, corresponded to that given by the apothecary.

"Did you visit the drug-store?" Philip asked.

"No," she answered, "and I did not know that Julia had. I paid two or

955

three visits to acquaintances, while she did her shopping, as she told me."

"Then try and remember, not only the order of those visits, but the time occupied by each," said Philip. "Write to your friends, and ask them to refresh their memories. It has become an important point, for—the poison was purchased in your name!"

"Impossible!" Lucy cried. She gazed at Philip with such amazement that her innocence was then fixed in his mind, if it had not been so before.

"Yes, I say 'impossible!' too," he answered. "There is only one explanation. Julia Asten gave your name instead of her own when she purchased it."

"Oh!" Lucy's voice sounded like a hopeless personal protest against the collective falsehood and wickedness of the world.

"I have another chance to reach the truth," said Philip. "I shall find the stranger,—the travelling agent,—if it obliges me to summon every such agent of every wholesale drug-house in the city! It is at least a positive fortune that we have made this discovery now."

He looked at his watch. "I have just time to catch the evening train," he said, hurriedly, "but I should like to send a message to Elwood Withers. If you pass through that wood on the right, you will see the track just below you. It is not more than half a mile from here; and you are almost sure to find him at or near the unfinished tunnel. Tell him to see Rachel Miller, and if anything further has been found, to inform my sister Madeline at once. That is all. I make no apology for imposing the service on you: good-by, and keep up your faith, Lucy!"

He pressed her hand, sprang into the saddle, and cantered briskly away.

Lucy, infected by his haste, crossed the field, struggled through the under-growth of the wild belt of wood, and descended to the railway track, without giving herself time to think. She met a workman near the mouth of the tunnel, and not daring to venture in, sent by him a summons to Elwood. It was not many minutes before he appeared.

"Something has happened, Lucy? he exclaimed.

"Philip thinks he has made a discovery," she answered, "and I come to you as his messenger." She then repeated Philip's words.

"Is that all?" Elwood asked, scanning her face anxiously. "You do not seem quite like your real self, Lucy."

She sat down upon the hank. "I am out of breath," she said; "I must have walked faster than I thought."

"Wait a minute!" said he. He ran up the track, to where a little side-glen crossed it, sprang down among the bushes, and presently reappeared with a tin cup full of cold, pure spring water.

The draught seemed to revive her at once. "It is not all, Elwood," she said. "Joseph is not the only one, now, who is implicated by the same circumstances."

"Who else?—not Philip Held!"

"No," she answered, very quietly, "it is a woman. Her name is Lucy Henderson."

Before Elwood could speak, she told him all that she had heard from Philip. He could scarcely bring his mind to accept its truth.

"Oh, the—" he began; "but, no! I will keep the words to myself. There is something deeper in this than any of us has yet looked for! Depend upon it, Lucy, she had a plan in getting you there!"

Lucy was silent. She fancied she knew Julia's plan already.

"Did she mean to poison Joseph herself, and throw the suspicion on you? And now by her own death, after all, she accomplishes her chief end! It is a hellish tangle, whichever way I look; but they say that the truth will sooner or later put down any amount of lies, and so it must be, here. We must get at the truth, the whole truth, and nothing but the truth! Do you not say so, Lucy?"

"Yes!" she answered firmly, looking him in the face.

"Ay, though all should come to light! We can't tell what it may be necessary to say. They may go to work and unravel Joseph's life, and yours, and mine, and hold up the stuff for everybody to look at. Well, let 'em! say I. If there are dark streaks in mine, I guess they'll look tolerably fair beside that one black heart. We're here alone, Lucy; there may not be a chance to say it soon again, so I'll say now, that if need comes to publish what I said to you one night a year ago,—to publish it for Joseph's sake, or your sake,—don't keep back a single word! The worst would be, some men or women might think me conceited."

"No, Elwood!" she exclaimed: "that reproach would fall on me! You once offered me your help, and I—I fear I spurned it; but I will take it now. Nay, I beg you to offer it to me again, and I will accept it with gratitude!"

She rose, and stretched out her hand.

Elwood clasped it tenderly, held it a moment, and seemed about to speak. But although his lips parted, and there was a movement of the muscles of his throat, he did not utter a word. In another moment he turned, walked a few yards up the track, and then came back to her.

"No one could mistake you for Julia Asten," he said. "You are at least half a head taller than she was. Your voice is not at all the same: the apothecary will surely notice the difference! Then an alibi, as they call it, can be proved."

"So Philip Held thought. But if my friends should not remember the exact time,—what should I then do?"

"Lucy, don't ask yourself the question now! It seems to me that the case stands this way: one evil woman has made a trap, fallen into it herself, and taken the secret of its make away with her. There is nothing more to be invented, and so we hold all that we gain. While we are mining, where's the counter-mining to come from? Who is to lie us out of our truth? There isn't much to stand on yet, I grant; but another step—the least little thing—may give us all the ground we want!"

He spoke so firmly and cheerily that Lucy's despondent feeling was charmed away. Besides, nothing could have touched her more than Elwood's heroic self-control. After the miserable revelation which Philip had made, it was unspeakably refreshing to be brought into contact with a nature so sound and sweet and strong. When he had led her by an easier path up the hill, and they had parted at the end of the lane leading to her father's house, she felt, as never before, the comfort of relying so wholly on a faithful man friend.

Elwood took his horse and rode to the Asten farm. Joseph's face brightened at his appearance, and they talked as of old, avoiding the dark year that lay between their past intimacy and its revival. As in Philip's case, it was difficult to communicate secretly with Rachel Miller; but Elwood, with great patience, succeeded in looking his wish to speak with her, and uniting her efforts with his own. She adroitly turned the conversation upon a geological work which Joseph had been reading.

"I've been looking into the subject myself," Elwood said. "Would you let me see the book: it may be the thing I want."

"It is on the book-shelf in your bed-room, Joseph," Rachel remarked.

There was time enough for Elwood to declare his business, and for Rachel to answer: "Mr. Held said every scrap, and it is but a scrap, with half a name on it. I found it behind and mostly under the lower drawer in the same box. I'll get it before you leave, and give it to you when we shake hands. Be careful, for he may make something out of it, after all. Tell him there isn't a stitch in a dress but I've examined, and a mortal work it was!"

It was late before Elwood could leave; nevertheless, he rode to Coventry Forge. The scrap of paper had been successfully transferred, and his pressing duty was to deliver it into the hands of Madeline Held. He found her anxiously waiting, in accordance with Philip's instructions.

When they looked at the paper, it seemed, truly, to be a worthless fragment. It had the character, also, of an apothecary's label, but the only letters remaining were those forming the end of the name, apparently —ers, and a short distance under them —Sts.

"Behind and mostly under the lower drawer of her jewel-case," said Madeline, musingly. "I think I might guess how it came there. She had seen the label, which had probably been forgotten, and then, as she supposed, had snatched it away and destroyed it, without noticing that this piece, caught behind the drawer, had been torn off. But there is no evidence—and perhaps none can be had—that the paper contained poison."

"Can you make anything out of the letters?" Elwood asked.

"The 'Sts' certainly means 'Streets'—now I see! It is a corner house! This makes the place a little more easy to be identified. If Philip cannot find it, I am sure a detective can. I will write to him at once."

"Then I'll wait and ride to the office with the letter," said Elwood.

Madeline rose, and commenced walking up and down the room: she appeared to be suddenly and unusually excited.

"I have a new suspicion," she said, at last. "Perhaps I am in too much of a hurry to make conjectures, because Philip thinks I have a talent for it,—and yet, this grows upon me every minute! I hope—oh, I hope I am right!"

She spoke with so much energy that Elwood began to share her excitement without knowing its cause. She noticed the eager, waiting expression of his face.

"You must really pardon, me, Mr. Withers. I believe I was talking to myself rather than to you; I will not mention my fancy until Philip decides whether it is worth acting upon. There will be no harm if each of us finds a different clew, and follows it. Philip will hardly leave the city to-morrow. I shall not write, but go down with the first train in the morning!"

Elwood took his leave, feeling hopeful and yet very restless.

It was a long while before Madeline encountered Philip. He was busily employed in carrying out his plan of tracing the travelling agent,—not yet successful, but sanguine of success. He examined the scrap of paper which Madeline brought, listened to her reasons for the new suspicion which had crossed her mind, and compared them with the little evidence already collected.

"Do not let us depend too seriously on this," he then said; "there is about an even chance that you are right. We will keep it as an additional and independent test, but we dare not lose sight of the fact that the law will assume Joseph's guilt, and we must establish his innocence, first of all. Nay, if we can simply prove that Julia, and not Lucy, purchased the poison, we shall save both! But, at the same time, I will try to find this —ers, who lives in a corner house, and I will have a talk with old Blessing this very evening."

"Why not go now?"

"Patience, you impetuous girl! I mean to take no step without working out every possible result in advance. If I were not here in the city, I would consult with Mr. Pinkerton before proceeding further. Now I shall take you to the train: you must return to Coventry, and watch and wait there."

When Philip called at the Blessing mansion, in the evening, he found only Mrs. Blessing at home. She was rigid and dreary in her mourning, and her reception of him was almost repellant in its stiff formality.

"Mr. Blessing is absent," she explained, inviting Philip to a seat by a wave of her hand. "His own interests rendered a trip to the Oil Regions imperative; it is a mental distraction which I do not grudge him. This is a cheerless household, sir,—one daughter gone forever, and another about to leave us. How does Mr. Asten bear his loss?"

Philip thereupon, as briefly and forcibly as possible, related all that had occurred. "I wish to consult Mr. Blessing," he concluded, "in relation to the possibility of his being able to furnish any testimony on his son-in-law's side. Perhaps you, also—"

"No!" she interrupted. "I know nothing whatever! If the trial (which I think most unnecessary and shocking) gets into the city papers, it will be a terrible scandal for us. When will it come on, did you say?"

"In two or three weeks"

"There will be barely time!" she cried.

"For that reason," said he, "I wish to secure the evidence at once. All the preparations for the defence must be completed within that time."

"Clementina," Mrs. Blessing continued, without heeding his words, "will be married about the first of October. Mr. Spelter has been desirous of making a bridal tour in Europe. She did not favor the plan; but it seems to me like an inter-position of Heaven!"

Philip rose, too disgusted to speak. He bowed in silence, and left the house.

CHAPTER XXVIII. THE TRIAL.

As the day of trial drew nigh, the anxiety and activity of Joseph's friends increased, so that even the quiet atmosphere wherein he lived was disturbed by it. He could not help knowing that they were engaged in collecting evidence, but inasmuch as Philip always said, "You can do nothing!" he forced himself to wait with such patience as was possible. Rachel Miller, who had partly taken the hired man, Dennis, into her confidence, hermetically sealed the house to the gossip of the neighborhood; but her greatest triumph was in concealing her alarm, as the days rolled by and the mystery was not yet unravelled.

There was not much division of opinion in the neighborhood, however. The growing discord between husband and wife had not been generally remarked: they were looked upon as a loving and satisfied couple. Joseph's integrity of character was acknowledged, and, even had it been doubted, the people saw no motive for crime. His action in demanding a legal investigation also operated favorably upon public opinion.

The quiet and seclusion were beneficial to him. His mind became calmer and clearer; he was able to survey the past without passion, and to contemplate his own faults with a sense of wholesome bitterness rather than pain. The approaching trial was not a pleasant thing to anticipate, but the worst which he foresaw was the probability of so much of his private life being laid bare to the world. Here, again, his own words returned to condemn him. Had he not said to Lucy, on the morning of that fatal day, "I am sick of masks!" Had he not threatened to follow Julia with his own miserable story? The system of checks which restrain impulse, and the whirl of currents and counter-currents which govern a man's movement through life, began to arrange themselves in his mind. True wisdom, he now felt, lay in understanding these, and so employing them as to reach individual liberty of action through law, and not outside of it. He had been shallow and reckless, even in his good impulses; it was now time to endure quietly for a season what their effect had been.

The day previous to the trial Philip had a long consultation with Mr. Pinkerton. He had been so far successful that the name and whereabouts of the travelling agent had been discovered: the latter had been summoned, but he could not possibly arrive before the next day. Philip had also seen Mr. Blessing, who entered with great readiness into his plans, promised his assistance in ascertaining the truth of Madeline's suspicion, and would give his testimony as soon as he could return from New York, whither he had gone to say farewell to Mrs. Clementina Spelter, before her departure for Paris on a bridal journey. These were the two principal witnesses for the defence, and it was yet uncertain what kind of testimony they would be able to give.

"We must finish the other witnesses," Mr. Pinkerton said, "(who, in spite of all we can do, will strengthen the prosecution), by the time you reach here. If Spenham gives us trouble, as I am inclined to suspect, we cannot well spare you the first day, but I suppose it cannot be helped."

"I will send a telegram to Blessing, in New York, to make sure," Philip answered. "Byle and Glanders answer for their agent, and I can try him with the photograph on the way out. If that succeeds, Blessing's failure will be of less consequence."

"If only they do not reach Linthicum in the mean time! I will prolong the impanelling of the jury, and use every other liberty of delay allowed me; yet I have to be cautious. This is Spenham's first important case, and he is ambitious to make capital."

Mr. Spenham was the prosecuting attorney, who had just been elected to his first term of service in that capacity. He had some shrewdness as a criminal lawyer, and a great deal of experience of the subterranean channels of party politics. This latter acquirement, in fact, was the secret of his election, for he was known to be coarse, unscrupulous, and offensive. Mr. Pinkerton was able to foresee his probable line of attack, and was especially anxious, for that reason, to introduce testimony which would shorten the trial.

When the hour came, and Joseph found that Philip was inevitably absent, the strength he had summoned to his heart seemed to waver for an instant. All his other friends were present, however: Lucy Henderson and

Madeline came with the Hopetons, and Elwood Withers stood by his side so boldly and proudly that he soon recovered his composure.

The court-room was crowded, not only by the idlers of the town, but also many neighbors from the country. They were grave and silent, and Joseph's appearance in the place allotted to the accused seemed to impress them painfully. The preliminaries occupied some time, and it was nearly noon before the first witness was called.

This was the physician. He stated, in a clear, business-like manner, the condition in which he found Julia, his discovery of the poison, and the unusual character of its operation, adding his opinion that the latter was owing to a long-continued nervous tension, culminating in hysterical excitement. Mr. Spenham questioned him very closely as to Joseph's demeanor, and his expressions before and after the death. The point of attack which he selected was Julia's exclamation: "Joseph, I will try to be different, but I must live for that!"

"These words," he said, "indicate a previous threat on the part of the accused. His helpless victim—"

Mr. Pinkerton protested against the epithet. But his antagonist found numberless ways of seeming to take Joseph's guilt for granted, and thus gradually to mould the pliant minds of a not very intelligent jury. The physician was subjected to a rigid cross-examination, in the course of which he was led to state that he, himself, had first advised that the fact of the poisoning should not be mentioned until after the funeral. The onus of the secrecy was thus removed from Joseph, and this was a point gained.

The next witness was the servant-woman, who had been present in the hall when Julia fell upon the landing of the staircase. She had heard the words, "Go away! you have killed me!" spoken in a shrill, excited voice. She had already guessed that something was wrong between the two. Mr. Asten came home looking quite wild and strange; he didn't seem to speak in his usual voice; he walked about in a restless way, and then went into the garden. Miss Lucy followed him, and then Mrs. Asten; but in a little while she came back, with her dress torn and her arms scratched; she, the witness, noticed this as Mrs. Asten passed through the hall, tottering as she went and with her fists shut tight.

Then Mr. Asten went up stairs to her bed-room; heard them speaking, but not the words; said to Sally, who was in the kitchen, "It's a real tiff and no mistake," and Sally remarked, "They're not used to each other yet, as they will be in a year or two."

The witness was with difficulty kept to a direct narrative. She had told the tale so often that every particular had its fixed phrases of description, and all the questioning on both sides called forth only repetitions. Joseph listened with a calm, patient air; nothing had yet occurred for which he was not prepared. The spectators, however, began to be deeply interested, and a sharp observer might have noticed that they were already taking sides.

Mr. Pinkerton soon detected that, although the woman's statements told against Joseph, she possessed no friendly feeling for Julia. He endeavored to make the most of this; but it was not much.

When Lucy Henderson's name was called, there was a stir of curiosity in the audience. They knew that the conference in the garden, from which Julia had returned in such an excited condition, must now be described. Mr. Spenham pricked up his red ears, ran his hand through his stubby hair, and prepared himself for battle; while Mr. Pinkerton, already in possession of all the facts, felt concerned only regarding the manner in which Lucy might give them. This was a case where so much depended on the impression produced by the individual!

By the time Lucy was sworn she appeared to be entirely composed; her face was slightly pale, but calm, and her voice steady. Mrs. Hopeton and Madeline Held sat near her, and Elwood Withers, leaning against a high railing, was nearly opposite.

There was profound silence as she began, and the interest increased as she approached the time of Joseph's return. She described his appearance, repeated the words she had heard, reproduced the scene in her own chamber, and so came, step by step, to the interview in the garden. The trying nature of her task now became evident. She spoke slowly, and with longer pauses; but whichever way she turned in her thought, the inexorable necessity of the whole truth stared her in the face.

"Must I repeat everything?" she asked. "I am not sure of recollecting the words precisely as they were spoken."

"You can certainly give the substance," said Mr. Spenham. "And be careful that you omit nothing: you are on your oath, and you ought to know what that means."

His words were loud and harsh. Lucy looked at the impassive face of the judge, at Elwood's earnest features, at the attentive jurymen, and went on.

When she came to Joseph's expression of the love that might have been possible, she gave also his words: "Had there been, I should have darkened the life of a friend."

"Ha!" exclaimed Mr. Spenham, "we are coming upon the motive of the murder."

Again Mr. Pinkerton protested, and was sustained by the court.

"Tell the jury," said Mr. Spenham, "whether there had been any interchange of such expressions between you and the accused previous to his marriage!"

This question was objected to, but the objection was overruled.

"None whatever!" was the answer.

Julia's sudden appearance, the accusation she made, and the manner in which Joseph met it, seemed to turn the current of sympathy the other way. Lucy's recollection of this scene was very clear and complete: had she wished it, she could not have forgotten a word or a look. In spite of Mr. Spenham's angry objections, she was allowed to go on and relate the conversation between Joseph and herself after Julia's return to the house. Mr. Pinkerton made the best use of this portion of the evidence, and it seemed that his side was strengthened, in spite of all unfavorable appearances.

"This is not all!" exclaimed the prosecuting attorney. "A married man does not make a declaration of love—"

"Of a past possible love," Mr. Pinkerton interrupted.

"A very fine hair-splitting indeed! A 'possible' love and a 'possible' return, followed by a 'possible' murder and a 'possible' remarriage! Our duty is to remove possibilities and establish facts. The question is, Was there no previous affection between the witness and the accused? This is necessary to prove a motive. I ask, then, the woman—I beg pardon, the lady—what were her sentiments towards the husband of the poisoned before his marriage, at the time of the conversation in the garden, and now?"

Lucy started, and could not answer. Mr. Pinkerton came to her aid. He protested strongly against such a question, though he felt that there was equal danger in answering it or leaving it unanswered. A portion of the spectators, sympathizing with Lucy, felt indignant at Mr. Spenham's demand; another portion, hungry for the most private and intimate knowledge of all the parties concerned, eagerly hoped that it would be acceded to.

Lucy half turned, so that she caught a glimpse of Joseph. He was calm, but his eyes expressed a sympathetic trouble. Then she felt her gaze drawn to Elwood, who had become a shade paler, and who met her eyes with a deep, inscrutable expression. Was he thinking of his recent words to her,—"If need comes to publish what I said to you, don't keep back a single word!" She felt sure of it, for all that he said was in her mind. Her decision was made: for truth's sake, and under the eye of God, she would speak. Having so resolved, she shut her mind to all else, for she needed the greatest strength of either woman or man.

The judge had decided that she was not obliged to answer the question. There was a murmur, here and there, among the spectators.

"Then I will use my freedom of choice," said Lucy, in a firm voice, "and answer it."

She kept her eyes on Elwood as she spoke, and compelled him to face her. She seemed to forget judge, jury, and the curious public, and to speak only to his ear.

"I am here to tell the whole truth, God helping me," she said. "I do not know how what I am required to say can touch the question of Joseph Asten's guilt or innocence; but I cannot pause to consider that. It is not easy for a woman to lay bare her secret heart to the world; I would like to think that every man who hears me has a wife, a sister, or a beloved girl of his choice, and that he will try to understand my heart through his knowledge of hers. I did cherish a tenderness which might have been love—I cannot tell—for Joseph Asten before his betrothal. I admit that his marriage was a grief to me at the time, for, while I had not suffered myself to feel any hope, I could not keep the feeling of disappointment out of my heart. It was both my blame and shame: I wrestled with it, and with God's help I overcame it."

There was a simple pathos in Lucy's voice, which pierced directly to the hearts of her hearers. She stood before them as pure as Godiva in her helpful nakedness. She saw on Elwood's cheek the blush which did not visit hers, and the sparkle of an unconscious tear. Joseph had hidden his face in his hands for a moment, but now looked up with a sadness which no man there could misinterpret.

Lucy had paused, as if waiting to be questioned, but the effect of her words had been so powerful and unexpected that Mr. Spenham was not quite ready. She went on:—

"When I say that I overcame it, I think I have answered everything. I went to him in the garden against my own wish, because his wife begged me with tears and sobs to intercede for her: I could not guess that he had ever thought of me otherwise than as a friend. I attributed his expressions to his disappointment in marriage, and pardoned him when he asked me to forget them—"

"O, no doubt!" Mr. Spenham interrupted, looking at the jury; "after all we have heard, they could not have been very disagreeable!"

Elwood made a rapid step forward; then, recollecting himself, resumed his position against the railing. Very few persons noticed the movement.

"They were very unwelcome," Lucy replied: "under any other circumstances, it would not have been easy to forgive them."

"And this former—'tenderness,' I think you called it," Mr. Spenham persisted, "—do you mean to say that you feel nothing of it at present?"

There was a murmur of indignation all over the room. If there is anything utterly incomprehensible to a vulgar nature, it is the natural delicacy of feeling towards women, which is rarely wanting even to the roughest and most ignorant men. The prosecution had damaged itself, and now the popular sympathy was wholly and strongly with Lucy.

"I have already answered that question," she said. "For the holy sake of truth, and of my own free-will, I have opened my heart. I did it, believing that a woman's first affection is pure, and would be respected; I did it, hoping that it might serve the cause of an innocent man; but now, since it has brought upon me doubt and insult, I shall avail myself of the liberty granted to me by the judge, and speak no word more!"

The spectators broke into applause, which the judge did not immediately check. Lucy's strength suddenly left her; she dropped into her seat and burst into tears.

"I have no further question to ask the witness," said Mr. Pinkerton.

Mr. Spenham inwardly cursed himself for his blunder,—not for his vulgarity, for of that he was sublimely unconscious,—and was only too ready to be relieved from Lucy's presence.

She rose to leave the court, Mrs. Hopeton accompanying her; but Elwood Withers was already at her side, and she leaned upon his arm as they passed through the crowd. The people fell back to make a way, and not a few whispered some honest word of encouragement. Elwood breathed heavily, and the veins on his forehead were swollen.

Not a word was spoken until they reached the hotel. Then Lucy, taking Elwood's hand, said: "Thank you, true, dear friend! I can say no more now. Go back, for Joseph's sake, and when the day is over come here and tell me, if

970

you can, that I have not injured him in trying to help him."

When Elwood returned to the court-room, Rachel Miller was on the witness stand. Her testimony confirmed the interpretation of Julia's character which had been suggested by Lucy Henderson's. The sweet, amiable, suffering wife began to recede into the background, and the cold, false, selfish wife to take her place.

All Mr. Spenham's cross-examination failed to give the prosecution any support until he asked the question:—

"Have you discovered nothing whatever, since your return to the house, which will throw any light upon Mrs. Asten's death?"

Mr. Pinkerton, Elwood, and Madeline all felt that the critical moment had come. Philip's absence threatened to be a serious misfortune.

"Yes," Rachel Miller answered.

"Ah!" exclaimed the prosecuting attorney, rubbing his hair; "what was it?"

"The paper in which the arsenic was put up."

"Will you produce that paper?" he eagerly asked.

"I cannot now," said Rachel; "I gave it to Mr. Philip Held, so that he might find out something more."

Joseph listened with a keen, undisguised interest. After the first feeling of surprise that such an important event had been kept from his knowledge, his confidence in Philip's judgment reassured him.

"Has Mr. Philip Held destroyed that paper?" Mr. Spenham asked.

"He retains it, and will produce it before this court to-morrow," Mr. Pinkerton replied.

"Was there any mark, or label, upon it, which indicated the place where the poison had been procured?"

"Yes," said Rachel Miller.

"State what it was."

"Ziba Linthicum's Drug store, No. 77 Main Street, Magnolia," she replied, as if the label were before her eyes.

"Let Ziba Linthicum be summoned at once!" Mr. Spenham cried.

Mr. Pinkerton, however, arose and stated that the apothecary's testimony required that of another person who was present when the poison was purchased. This other person had been absent in a distant part of the country, but had been summoned, and would arrive, in company with Mr. Philip Held, on the following morning. He begged that Mr. Linthicum's evidence might be postponed until then, when he believed that the mystery attending the poisoning would be wholly explained.

Mr. Spenham violently objected, but he again made the mistake of speaking for nearly half an hour on the subject,—an indiscretion into which he was led by his confirmed political habits. By the time the question was decided, and in favor of the defence, the afternoon was well advanced, and the court adjourned until the next day.

CHAPTER XXIX. NEW EVIDENCE.

Elwood accompanied Joseph to the prison where he was obliged to spend the night, and was allowed to remain with him until Mr. Pinkerton (who was endeavoring to reach Philip by telegraph) should arrive.

Owing to Rachel Miller's forethought, the bare room was sufficiently furnished. There was a clean bed, a chair or two, and a table, upon which stood a basket of provisions.

"I suppose I must eat," said Joseph, "as a matter of duty. If you will sit down and join me, Elwood, I will try."

"If I could have that fellow Spenham by the throat for a minute," Elwood growled, "it would give me a good appetite. But I will take my share, as it is: I never can think rightly when I'm hungry. Why, there is enough for a picnic! sandwiches, cold chicken, pickles, cakes, cheese, and two bottles of coffee, as I live! Just think that we're in a hotel, Joseph! It's all in one's notion, leastways for a single night; for you can go where you like to-morrow!"

"I hope so," said Joseph, as he took his seat. Elwood set the provisions before him, but he did not touch them. After a moment of hesitation he stretched out his hand and laid it on Elwood's shoulder.

"Now, old boy!" Elwood cried: "I know it. What you mean is unnecessary, and I won't have it!"

"Let me speak!"

"I don't see why I should, Joseph. It's no more than I guessed. She didn't love me: you were tolerably near together once, and if you should now come nearer—"

But he could not finish the sentence; the words stuck in his throat.

"Great Heaven!" Joseph exclaimed, starting to his feet; "what are you thinking of? Don't you see that Lucy Henderson and I are parted forever by what has happened to-day? Didn't you hear her say that she overcame the tenderness which might have become love, as I overcame mine for her? Neither of us can recall that first feeling, any more than we can set our lives again in the past. I shall worship her as one of the purest and noblest souls that breathe; but love her? make her my wife? It could never, never be! No, Elwood! I was wondering whether you could pardon me the rashness which has exposed her to to-day's trial."

Elwood began to laugh strangely. "You are foolish, Joseph," he said. "Pshaw! I can't hold my knife. These sudden downs and then ups are too much for a fellow! Pardon you? Yes, on one condition—that you empty your plate before you speak another word to me!"

They were both cheerful after this, and the narrow little room seemed freer and brighter to their eyes. It was late before Mr. Pinkerton arrived: he had waited in vain for an answer from Philip. Elwood's presence was a relief to him, for he did not wish to excite Joseph by a statement of what he expected to prove unless the two witnesses had been really secured. He adroitly managed, however, to say very little while seeming to say a great deal, and Joseph was then left to such rest as his busy memory might allow him.

Next morning there was an even greater crowd in the court-room. All Joseph's friends were there, with the exception of Lucy Henderson, who, by Mr. Pinkerton's advice, remained at the hotel. Philip had not arrived, but had sent a message saying that all was well, and he would come in the morning train.

Mr. Spenham, the evening before, had ascertained the nature of Mr. Linthicum's evidence. The apothecary, however, was only able to inform him of Philip's desire to discover the travelling agent, without knowing his purpose. In the name recorded as that of the purchaser of the poison Mr. Spenham saw a weapon which would enable him to repay Lucy for his discomfiture, and to indicate, if not prove, a complicity of crime, in which Philip Held also, he suspected, might be concerned.

The court opened at nine o'clock, and Philip could not be on hand before ten. Mr. Pinkerton endeavored to procure the examination of Dennis, and another subordinate witness, before the apothecary; but he only succeeded in gaining fifteen minutes' time by the discussion. Mr. Ziba Linthicum was then called and sworn. He carried a volume under his arm.

As Philip possessed the label, Mr. Linthicum could only testify to the fact that a veiled lady had purchased so many grains of arsenic of him on a certain day; that he kept a record of all sales of dangerous drugs; and that the lady's name was recorded in the book which he had brought with him. He then read the entry:—

"Miss Henderson. Arsenic."

Although Mr. Pinkerton had whispered to Joseph, "Do not be startled when he reads the name!" it was all the latter could do to suppress an exclamation. There was a murmur and movement through the whole court.

"We have now both the motive and the co-agent of the crime," said Mr. Spenham, rising triumphantly. "After the evidence which was elicited yesterday, it will not be difficult to connect the two. If the case deepens in enormity as it advances, we may be shocked, but we have no reason to be surprised. The growth of free-love sentiments, among those who tear themselves loose from the guidance of religious influences, naturally leads to crime; and the extent to which this evil has been secretly developed is not suspected by the public. Testimony can be adduced to show that the accused, Joseph Asten, has openly expressed his infidelity; that he repelled with threats and defiance a worthy minister of the Gospel, whom his own pious murdered wife had commissioned to lead him into the true path. The very expression which the woman Lucy Henderson testified to his having used in the garden,—'I am sick of masks,'—what does it mean? What but unrestrained freedom of the passions,—the very foundation upon which the free-lovers build up their pernicious theories? The accused cannot complain if the law lifts the mask from his countenance, and shows his nature in all its hideous deformity. But another mask, also, must be raised: I demand the arrest of the woman Lucy Henderson!"

Mr. Pinkerton sprang to his feet. In a measured, solemn voice, which contrasted strongly with the loud, sharp tones of the prosecuting attorney, he stated that Mr. Linthicum's evidence was already known to him; that it required an explanation which would now be given in a few minutes, and which would completely exonerate Miss Henderson from the suspicion of having purchased the poison, or even having any knowledge of its purchase. He demanded that no conclusion should be drawn from evidence which would mislead the minds of the jury: he charged the prosecuting attorney with most unjustly assailing the characters of both Joseph Asten and Lucy Henderson, and invoked, in the name of impartial justice, the protection of the court.

He spoke both eloquently and earnestly; but the spectators noticed that he looked at his watch from minute to minute. Mr. Spenham interrupted him, but he continued to repeat his statements, until there came a sudden movement in the crowd, near the outer door of the hall. Then he sat down.

Philip led the way, pressing the crowd to right and left in his eagerness. He was followed by a tall young man, with a dark moustache and an abundance of jewelry, while Mr. Benjamin Blessing, flushed and perspiring, brought up the rear. The spectators were almost breathless in their hushed, excited interest.

Philip seized Joseph's hand, and, bending nearer, whispered, "You are free!" His eyes sparkled and his face glowed.

Room was made for the three witnesses, and after a brief whispered consultation between Philip and Mr. Pinkerton, Elwood was despatched to bring Lucy Henderson to the court.

"May it please the Court," said Mr. Pinkerton, "I am now able to fulfil that promise which I this moment made. The evidence which was necessary to set forth the manner of Mrs. Asten's death, and which will release the court from any further consideration of the present case, is in my hands. I therefore ask leave to introduce this evidence without any further delay."

After a little discussion the permission was granted, and Philip Held was placed upon the stand.

He first described Joseph's genuine sorrow at his wife's death, and his self-accusation of having hastened it by his harsh words to her in the morning. He related the interview at which Joseph, on learning of the reports concerning him, had immediately decided to ask for a legal investigation, and in a simple, straightforward way, narrated all that had been done up to the time of consulting Ziba Linthicum's poison record.

"As I knew it to be quite impossible that Miss Lucy Henderson could have been the purchaser," he began—

Mr. Spenham instantly objected, and the expression was ruled out by the Court.

"Then," Philip resumed, "I determined to ascertain who had purchased the arsenic. Mr. Linthicum's description of the lady was too vague to be recognized. It was necessary to identify the travelling agent who was present; for this purpose I went to the city, ascertained the names and addresses of all the travelling agents of all the wholesale drug firms, and after much time and correspondence discovered the man,—Mr. Case, who is here present. He was in Persepolis, Iowa, when the summons reached him, and would have been here yesterday but for an accident on the Erie Railway.

"In the mean time I had received the small fragment of another label, and by the clew which the few letters gave me I finally identified the place as the drug-store of Wallis and Erkers, at the corner of Fifth and Persimmon Streets. There was nothing left by which the nature of the drug could be ascertained, and therefore this movement led to nothing which could be offered as evidence in this court,—that is, by the druggists themselves, and they have not been summoned. It happened, however, by a coincidence which only came to light this morning, that—"

Here Philip was again interrupted. His further testimony was of less consequence. He was sharply cross-examined by Mr. Spenham as to his relations with Joseph, and his object in devoting so much time to procuring evidence for the defence; but he took occasion, in replying, to express his appreciation of Joseph's character so emphatically, that the prosecution lost rather than gained. Then the plan of attack was changed. He was asked whether he believed in the Bible, in future rewards and punishments, in the views of the so-called free-lovers, in facile divorce and polygamy. He was too shrewd, however, to lay himself open to the least misrepresentation, and the moral and mental torture which our jurisprudence has substituted for the rack, thumb-screws, and Spanish boots of the Middle Ages finally came to an end.

Then the tall young man, conscious of his own elegance, took his place. He gave his name and occupation as Augustus Fitzwilliam Case, commercial traveller for the house of Byle and Glanders, wholesale druggists.

"State whether you were in the drug-store of Ziba Linthicum, No. 77 Main Street, in this town, on the day of the entry in Mr. Linthicum's book."

"I was."

"Did you notice the person who called for arsenic?"

"I did."

"What led you specially to notice her?"

"It is my habit," said the witness. "I am impressible to beauty, and I saw at once that the lady had what I call—style. I recollect thinking, 'More style than could be expected in these little places.'"

"Keep your thoughts to yourself!" cried Mr. Spenham.

"Describe the lady as correctly as you can," said Mr. Pinkerton.

"Something under the medium size; a little thin, but not bad lines,— what I should call jimp, natty, or 'lissome,' in the Scotch dialect. A well-trained voice; no uncertainty about it,—altogether about as keen and wide-awake a woman as you'll find in a day's travel."

"You guessed all this from her figure?" Mr. Spenham asked, with a sneer.

"Not entirely. I saw her face. I suppose something in my appearance or attitude attracted her attention. While Mr. Linthicum was weighing the arsenic she leaned over the counter, let her veil fall forward slightly, and gave me a quick side-look. I bent a little at the same time, as if to examine the soaps, and saw her face in a three-quarter position, as the photographers say."

978

"Can you remember her features distinctly?"

"Quite so. In fact, it is difficult for me to forget a female face. Hers was just verging on the sharp, but still tolerably handsome. Hair quite dark, and worn in ringlets; eyebrows clean and straight; mouth a little too thin for my fancy; and eyes—well, I couldn't undertake to say exactly what color they were, for she seemed to have the trick—very common in the city—of letting the lids droop over them."

"Were you able to judge of her age?"

"Tolerably, I should say. There is a certain air of preservation which enables a practised eye to distinguish an old girl from a young one. She was certainly not to be called young,—somewhere between twenty-eight and thirty-five."

"You heard the name she gave Mr. Linthicum?"

"Distinctly. Mr. Linthicum politely stated that it was his custom to register the names of all those to whom he furnished either poisons or prescriptions requiring care in being administered. She said, 'You are very particular, sir;' and, a moment afterward, 'Pardon me, perhaps it is necessary.'—'What name, then?' he asked. I thought she hesitated a moment, but this I will not say positively; whether or not, the answer was, 'Miss Henderson.' She went out of the store with a light, brisk step."

"You are sure you would be able to recognize the lady?" Mr. Pinkerton asked.

"Quite sure." And Mr. Augustus Fitzwilliam Case smiled patronizingly, as if the question were superfluous.

Mr. Pinkerton made a sign to Lucy, and she arose.

"Look upon this lady!" he said to the witness.

The latter made a slight, graceful inclination of his head, as much as to say, "Pardon me, I am compelled to stare." Lucy quietly endured his gaze.

"Consider her well," said the lawyer, "and then tell the jury whether she is the person."

"No considerment is necessary. This lady has not the slightest resemblance to Miss Henderson. She is younger, taller, and modelled upon a wholly different style."

"Will you now look at this photograph?"

"Ah!" the witness exclaimed; "you can yourself judge of the correctness of my memory! Here is Miss Henderson herself, and in three-quarter face, as I saw her!"

"That," said Mr. Pinkerton, addressing the judge and jury, "that is the photograph of Mrs. Julia Asten."

The spectators were astounded, and Mr. Spenham taken completely aback by this revelation. Joseph and Elwood both felt that a great weight had been lifted from their hearts. The testimony established Julia's falsehood at the same time, and there was such an instant and complete revulsion of opinion that many persons present at once suspected her of a design to poison Joseph.

"Before calling upon Mr. Benjamin Blessing, the father of the late Mrs. Asten, for his testimony," said Mr. Pinkerton,—"and I believe he will be the last witness necessary,—I wish to show that, although Miss Lucy Henderson accompanied Mrs. Asten to Magnolia, she could not have visited Mr. Linthicum's Drug store at the time indicated; nor, indeed, at any time during that day. She made several calls upon friends, each of whom is now in attendance, and their joint evidence will account for every minute of her stay in the place. The base attempt to blacken her fair name imperatively imposes this duty upon me."

No objection was made, and the witnesses were briefly examined in succession. Their testimony was complete.

"One mystery still remains to be cleared up," the lawyer continued; "the purpose of Mrs. Asten in purchasing the poison, and the probable explanation of her death. I say 'probable,' because absolute certainty is impossible. But I will not anticipate the evidence. Mr. Benjamin Blessing, step forward, if you please!"

980

CHAPTER XXX. MR. BLESSING'S TESTIMONY.

On entering the court-room Mr. Blessing had gone to Joseph, given his hand a long, significant grasp, and looked in his face with an expression of triumph, almost of exultation. The action was not lost upon the spectators or the jury, and even Joseph felt that it was intended to express the strongest faith in his innocence.

When the name was called there was a movement in the crowd, and a temporary crush in some quarters, as the people thrust forward their heads to see and listen. Mr. Blessing, bland, dignified, serene, feeling that he was the central point of interest, waited until quiet had been restored, slightly turning his head to either side, as if to summon special attention to what he should say.

After being sworn, and stating his name, he thus described his occupation:—

"I hold a position under government; nominally, it is a Deputy Inspectorship in the Custom-House, yet it possesses a confidential—I might say, if modesty did not prevent, an advisory—character."

"In other words, a Ward Politician!" said Mr. Spenham.

"I must ask the prosecuting attorney," Mr. Blessing blandly suggested, "not to define my place according to his own political experiences."

There was a general smile at these words; and a very audible chuckle from spectators belonging to the opposite party.

"You are the father of the late Mrs. Julia Asten?"

"I am—her unhappy father, whom nothing but the imperious commands of justice, and the knowledge of her husband's innocence of the crime with which he stands charged, could have compelled to appear here, and reveal the painful secrets of a family, which—"

Here Mr. Spenham interrupted him.

"I merely wish to observe," Mr. Blessing continued, with a stately wave of his hand towards the judge and jury, "that the De Belsains and their descendants may have been frequently unfortunate, but were never dishonorable. I act in their spirit when I hold duty to the innocent living higher than consideration for the unfortunate dead."

Here he drew forth a handkerchief, and held it for a moment to his eyes.

"Did you know of any domestic discords between your daughter and her husband?"

"I foresaw that such might be, and took occasion to warn my daughter, on her wedding-day, not to be too sure of her influence. There was too much disparity of age, character, and experience. It could not be called crabbed age and rosy youth, but there was difference enough to justify Shakespeare's doubts. I am aware that the court requires ocular—or auricular—evidence. The only such I have to offer is my son-in-law's own account of the discord which preceded my daughter's death."

"Did this discord sufficiently explain to you the cause and manner of her death?"

"My daughter's nature—I do not mean to digress, but am accustomed to state my views clearly—my daughter's nature was impulsive. She inherited my own intellect, but modified by the peculiar character of the feminine nervous system. Hence she might succumb to a depression which I should resist. She appeared to be sure of her control over my son-in-law's nature, and of success in an enterprise, in which—I regret to say—my son-in-law lost confidence. I assumed, at the time, that her usually capable mind was unbalanced by the double disappointment, and that she had rushed, unaneled, to her last account. This, I say, was the conclusion forced upon me; yet I cannot admit that it was satisfactory. It seemed to disparage my daughter's intellectual power: it was not the act which I should have anticipated in any possible emergency."

"Had you no suspicion that her husband might have been instrumental?"

982

Mr. Spenham asked.

"He? he is simply incapable of that, or any crime!"

"We don't want assertions," said Mr. Spenham, sternly.

"I beg pardon of the court," remarked Mr. Blessing; "it was a spontaneous expression. The touch of nature cannot always be avoided."

"Go on, sir!"

"I need not describe the shock and sorrow following my daughter's death," Mr. Blessing continued, again applying his handkerchief. "In order to dissipate it, I obtained a leave of absence from my post,—the exigencies of the government fortunately admitting of it,—and made a journey to the Oil Regions, in the interest of myself and my son-in-law. While there I received a letter from Mr. Philip Held, the contents of which—"

"Will you produce the letter?" Mr. Spenham exclaimed.

"It can be produced, if necessary. I will state nothing further, since I perceive that this would not be admissible evidence. It is enough to say that I returned to the city without delay, in order to meet Mr. Philip Held. The requirements of justice were more potent with me than the suggestions of personal interest. Mr. Held had already, as you will have noticed from his testimony, identified the fragment of paper as having emanated from the drug-store of Wallis and Erkers, corner of Fifth and Persimmon Streets. I accompanied him to that drug-store, heard the statements of the proprietors, in answer to Mr. Held's questions,—statements which, I confess, surprised me immeasurably (but I could not reject the natural deductions to be drawn from them), and was compelled, although it overwhelmed me with a sense of unmerited shame, to acknowledge that there was plausibility in Mr. Held's conjectures. Since they pointed to my elder daughter, Clementina, now Mrs. Spelter, and at this moment tossing upon the ocean-wave, I saw that Mr. Held might possess a discernment superior to my own. But for a lamentable cataclysm, he might have been my son-in-law, and I need not say that I prefer that refinement of character which comes of good blood to the possession of millions—"

Here Mr. Blessing was again interrupted, and ordered to confine himself to the simple statement of the necessary facts.

"I acknowledge the justice of the rebuke," he said. "But the sentiment of the mens conscia recti will sometimes obtrude through the rigid formula of Themis. In short, Mr. Philip Held's representations—"

"State those representations at once, and be done with them!" Mr. Spenham cried.

"I am coming to them presently. The Honorable Court understands, I am convinced, that a coherent narrative, although moderately prolix, is preferable to a disjointed narrative, even if the latter were terse as Tacitus. Mr. Held's representations, I repeat, satisfied me that an interview with my daughter Clementina was imperative. There was no time to be lost, for the passage of the nuptial pair had already been taken in the Ville de Paris. I started at once, sending a telegram in advance, and in the same evening arrived at their palatial residence in Fifth Avenue. Clementina's nature, I must explain to the Honorable Court, is very different from that of her sister,— the reappearance, I suspect, of some lateral strain of blood. She is reticent, undemonstrative,—in short, frequently inscrutable. I suspected that a direct question might defeat my object; therefore, when I was alone with her the next morning,—my son-in-law, Mr. Spelter, being called to a meeting of Erie of which he is one of the directors,—I said to her: 'My child, you are perfectly blooming! Your complexion was always admirable, but now it seems to me incomparable!'"

"This is irrelevant!" cried Mr. Spenham.

"By no means! It is the very corpus delicti,—the foot of Hercules,—the milk (powder would be more appropriate) in the cocoa-nut!" Clementina smiled in her serene way, and made no reply. 'How do you keep it up now?' I asked, tapping her cheek; 'you must be careful, here: all persons are not so discreet as Wallis and Erkers.' She was astounded, stupefied, I might say, but I saw that I had reached the core of truth. 'Did you suppose I was ignorant of it?' I said, still very friendly and playfully. 'Then it was Julia who told you!' she exclaimed. 'And if she did,' I answered, 'what was the harm? I have no doubt that Julia did the same thing.' 'She was always foolish,' Clementina then said; 'she envied me my complexion, and she watched me until she found out. I told her that it would not do for any except blondes, like myself, and her complexion was neither one thing nor the other. And I couldn't see that it improved much, afterwards.'"

Mr. Pinkerton saw that the jurymen were puzzled, and requested Mr. Blessing to explain the conversation to them.

"It is my painful duty to obey; yet a father's feelings may be pardoned if he shrinks from presenting the facts at once in their naked—unpleasantness. However, since the use of arsenic as a cosmetic is so general in our city, especially among blondes, as Wallis and Erkers assure me, my own family is not an isolated case. Julia commenced using the drug, so Clementina informed me, after her engagement with Mr. Asten, and only a short time before her marriage. To what extent she used it, after that event, I have no means of knowing; but, I suspect, less frequently, unless she feared that the disparity of age between her and her husband was becoming more apparent. I cannot excuse her duplicity in giving Miss Henderson's name instead of her own at Mr. Linthicum's Drug store, since the result might have been so fearfully fatal; yet I entreat you to believe that there may have been no inimical animus in the act. I attribute her death entirely to an over-dose of the drug, voluntarily taken, but taken in a moment of strong excitement."

The feeling of relief from suspense, not only among Joseph's friends, but throughout the crowded court-room, was clearly manifested: all present seemed to breathe a lighter and fresher atmosphere.

Mr. Blessing wiped his forehead and his fat cheeks, and looked benignly around. "There are a hundred little additional details," he said, "which will substantiate my evidence; but I have surely said sufficient for the ends of justice. The heavens will not fall because I have been forced to carve the emblems of criminal vanity upon the sepulchre of an unfortunate child,—but the judgment of an earthly tribunal may well be satisfied. However, I am ready," he added, turning towards Mr. Spenham; "apply all the engines of technical procedure, and I shall not wince."

The manner of the prosecuting attorney was completely changed. He answered respectfully and courteously, and his brief cross-examination was calculated rather to confirm the evidence for the defence than to invalidate it.

Mr. Pinkerton then rose and stated that he should call no other witnesses. The fact had been established that Mrs. Asten had been in the habit of taking arsenic to improve her complexion; also that she had purchased much more than enough of the drug to cause death, at the store of Mr. Ziba Linthicum, only a few days before her demise, and under circumstances which indicated a desire to conceal the purchase. There were two ways in which the manner of her death might be explained; either she had ignorantly taken an over-dose, or, having mixed the usual quantity before descending to the garden to overhear the conversation between Mr. Asten and Lucy Henderson, had forgotten the fact in the great excitement which followed, and thoughtlessly added as much more of the poison. Her last words to her husband, which could not be introduced as evidence, but might now be repeated, showed that her death was the result of accident, and not of design. She was thus absolved of the guilt of suicide, even as her husband of the charge of murder.

Mr. Spenham, somewhat to the surprise of those who were unacquainted with his true character, also stated that he should call no further witness for the prosecution. The testimonies of Mr. Augustus Fitzwilliam Case and Mr. Benjamin Blessing—although the latter was unnecessarily ostentatious and discursive—were sufficient to convince him that the prosecution could not make out a case. He had no doubt whatever of Mr. Joseph Asten's innocence. Lest the expressions which he had been compelled to use, in the performance of his duty, might be misunderstood, he wished to say that he had the highest respect for the characters of Mr. Asten and also of Miss Lucy Henderson. He believed the latter to be a refined and virtuous lady, an ornament to the community in which she resided. His language towards her had been professional,—by no means personal. It was in accordance with the usage of the most eminent lights of the bar; the ends of justice required the most searching examination, and the more a character was criminated the more brightly it would shine forth to the world after the test had been successfully endured. He was simply the agent of the law, and all respect of persons was prohibited to him while in the exercise of his functions.

The judge informed the jurymen that he did not find it necessary to give them any instructions. If they were already agreed upon their verdict, even the formality of retiring might be dispensed with.

There was a minute's whispering back and forth among the men, and the foreman then rose and stated that they were agreed.

The words "Not Guilty!" spoken loudly and emphatically, were the signal for a stormy burst of applause from the audience. In vain the court-crier, aided by the constables, endeavored to preserve order. Joseph's friends gathered around him with their congratulations; while Mr. Blessing, feeling that some recognition of the popular sentiment was required, rose and bowed repeatedly to the crowd. Philip led the way to the open air, and the others followed, but few words were spoken until they found themselves in the large parlor of the hotel.

Mr. Blessing had exchanged some mysterious whispers with the clerk, on arriving; and presently two negro waiters entered the room, bearing wine, ice, and other refreshments. When the glasses had been filled, Mr. Blessing lifted his with an air which imposed silence on the company, and thus spake: "'Out of the abundance of the heart the mouth speaketh.' There may be occasions when silence is golden, but to-day we are content with the baser metal. A man in whom we all confide, whom we all love, has been rescued from the labyrinth of circumstances; he comes to us as a new Theseus, saved from the Minotaur of the Law! Although Mr. Held, with the assistance of his fair sister, was the Ariadne who found the clew, it has been my happy lot to assist in unrolling it; and now we all stand together, like our classic models on the free soil of Crete, to chant a pæan of deliverance. While I propose the health and happiness and good-fortune of Joseph Asten, I beg him to believe that my words come ab imo pectore,—from my inmost heart: if any veil of mistrust, engendered by circumstances which I will not now recall, still hangs between him and myself, I entreat him to rend that veil, even as David rent his garments, and believe in my sincerity, if he cannot in my discretion!"

Philip was the only one, besides Joseph, who understood the last allusion.

He caught hold of Mr. Blessing's hand and exclaimed: "Spoken like a man!"

Joseph stepped instantly forward. "I have again been unjust," he said, "and I thank you for making me feel it. You have done me an infinite service, sacrificing your own feelings, bearing no malice against me for my hasty and unpardonable words, and showing a confidence in my character which—after what has passed between us—puts me to shame. I am both penitent and grateful: henceforth I shall know you and esteem you!"

Mr. Blessing took the offered hand, held it a moment, and then stammered, while the tears started from his eyes: "Enough! Bury the past a thousand fathoms deep! I can still say: foi de Belsain!"

"One more toast!" cried Philip. "Happiness and worldly fortune to the man whom misfortunes have bent but cannot break,—who has been often deceived, but who never purposely deceived in turn,—whose sentiment of honor has been to-day so nobly manifested,—Benjamin Blessing!"

While the happy company were pouring out but not exhausting their feelings, Lucy Henderson stole forth upon the upper balcony of the hotel. There was a secret trouble in her heart, which grew from minute to minute. She leaned upon the railing, and looked down the dusty street, passing in review the events of the two pregnant days, and striving to guess in what manner they would affect her coming life. She felt that she had done her simple duty: she had spoken no word which she was not ready to repeat; yet in her words there seemed to be the seeds of change.

After a while the hostler brought a light carriage from the stable, and Elwood Withers stepped into the street below her. He was about to take the reins, when he looked up, saw her, and remained standing. She noticed the intensely wistful expression of his face.

"Are you going, Elwood,—and alone?" she asked.

"Yes," he said eagerly; and waited.

"Then I will go with you,—that is, if you will take me." She tried to speak lightly and playfully.

In a few minutes they were out of town, passing between the tawny fields and under the russet woods. A sweet west wind fanned them with nutty and spicy odors, and made a crisp, cheerful music among the fallen leaves.

"What a delicious change!" said Lucy, "after that stifling, dreadful room."

"Ay, Lucy—and think how Joseph will feel it! And how near, by the chance of a hair, we came of missing the truth!"

"Elwood!" she exclaimed, "while I was giving my testimony, and I found your eyes fixed on me, were you thinking of the counsel you gave me, three weeks ago, when we met at the tunnel?"

"I was!"

"I knew it, and I obeyed. Do you now say that I did right?"

"Not for that reason," he answered. "It was your own heart that told you what to do. I did not mean to bend or influence you in any way: I have no right."

"You have the right of a friend," she whispered.

"Yes," said he, "I sometimes take more upon myself than I ought. But it's hard, in my case, to hit a very fine line."

"O, you are now unjust to yourself, Elwood. You are both strong and generous."

"I am not strong! I am this minute spoiling my good luck. It was a luck from Heaven to me, Lucy, when you offered to ride home with me, and it is, now—if I could only swallow the words that are rising into my mouth!"

She whispered again: "Why should you swallow them?"

"You are cruel! when you have forbidden me to speak, and I have promised to obey!"

"After all you have heard?" she asked.

"All the more for what I have heard."

She took his hand, and cried, in a trembling voice: "I have been cruel, in remaining blind to your nature. I resisted what would have been—what will be, if you do not turn away—my one happiness in this life! Do not speak—let me break the prohibition! Elwood, dear, true, noble heart,—Elwood, I love you!"

"Lucy!"

And she lay upon his bosom.

CHAPTER XXXI. BEGINNING ANOTHER LIFE.

IT was hard for the company of rejoicing friends, at the hotel in Magnolia, to part from each other. Mr. Blessing had tact enough to decline Joseph's invitation, but he was sorely tempted by Philip's, in which Madeline heartily joined. Nevertheless, he only wavered for a moment; a mysterious resolution strengthened him, and taking Philip to one side, he whispered:—

"Will you allow me to postpone, not relinquish, the pleasure? Thanks! A grave duty beckons,—a task, in short, without which the triumph of to-day would be dramatically incomplete. I must speak in riddles, because this is a case in which a whisper might start the overhanging avalanche; but I am sure you will trust me."

"Of course I will!" Philip cried, offering his hand.

"Foi de Belsain!" was Mr. Blessing's proud answer, as he hurried away to reach the train for the city.

Joseph looked at Philip, as the horses were brought from the stable, and then at Rachel Miller, who, wrapped in her great crape shawl, was quietly waiting for him.

"We must not separate all at once," said Philip, stepping forward. "Miss Miller, will you invite my sister and myself to take tea with you this evening?"

Philip had become one of Rachel's heroes; she was sure that Mr. Blessing's testimony and Joseph's triumphant acquittal were owing to his exertions. The Asten farm could produce nothing good enough for his entertainment,—that was her only trouble.

"Do tell me the time o' day," she said to Joseph, as he drove out of town, closely followed by Philip's light carriage. "It's three days in one to me, and a deal more like day after to-morrow morning than this afternoon. Now, a telegraph would be a convenience; I could send word and have chickens killed and picked, against we got there."

Joseph answered her by driving as rapidly as the rough country roads permitted, without endangering horse and vehicle. It was impossible for him to think coherently, impossible to thrust back the single overwhelming prospect of relief and release which had burst upon his life. He dared to admit the fortune which had come to him through death, now that his own innocence of any indirect incitement thereto had been established. The future was again clear before him; and even the miserable discord of the past year began to recede and form only an indistinct background to the infinite pity of the death-scene. Mr. Blessing's testimony enabled him to look back and truly interpret the last appealing looks, the last broken words; his heart banished the remembrance of its accusations, and retained only—so long as it should beat among living men—a deep and tender commiseration. As for the danger he had escaped, the slander which had been heaped upon him, his thoughts were above the level of life which they touched. He was nearer than he suspected to that only true independence of soul which releases a man from the yoke of circumstances.

Rachel Miller humored his silence as long as she thought proper, and then suddenly and awkwardly interrupted it. "Yes," she exclaimed; "there's a little of the old currant wine in the cellar-closet! Town's-folks generally like it, and we used to think it good to stay a body's stomach for a late meal,—as it'll be apt to be. But I've not asked you how you relished the supper, though Elwood, to be sure, allowed that all was tolerable nice. And I see the Lord's hand in it, as I hope you do, Joseph; for the righteous is never forsaken. We can't help rejoice, where we ought to be humbly returning thanks, and owning our unworthiness; but Philip Held is a friend, if there ever was one; and the white hen's brood, though they are new-fashioned fowls, are plump enough by this time. I disremember whether I asked Elwood to stop—"

"There he is!" Joseph interrupted; "turning the corner of the wood before us! Lucy is with him,—and they must both come!"

He drove on rapidly, and soon overtook Elwood's lagging team. The horse, indeed, had had his own way, and the sound of approaching wheels awoke Elwood from a trance of incredible happiness. Before answering Joseph, he whispered to Lucy:—

"What shall we say? It'll be the heaviest favor I've ever been called upon to do a friend."

"Do it, then!" she said: "The day is too blessed to be kept for ourselves alone."

How fair the valley shone, as they came into it out of the long glen between the hills! What cheer there was, even in the fading leaves; what happy promise in the mellow autumn sky! The gate to the lane stood open; Dennis, with a glowing face, waited for the horse. He wanted to say something, but not knowing how, shook hands with Joseph, and then pretended to be concerned with the harness. Rachel, on entering the kitchen, found her neighbor, Mrs. Bishop, embarked on a full tide of preparation. Two plump fowls, scalded and plucked, lay upon the table!

This was too much for Rachel Miller. She had borne up bravely through the trying days, concealing her anxiety lest it might be misinterpreted, hiding even her grateful emotion, to make her faith in Joseph's innocence seem the stronger; and now Mrs. Bishop's thoughtfulness was the slight touch under which she gave way. She sat down and cried.

Mrs. Bishop, with a stew-pan in one hand, while she wiped her sympathetic eyes with the other, explained that her husband had come home an hour before, with the news; and that she just guessed help would be wanted, or leastways company, and so she had made bold to begin; for, though the truth had been made manifest, and the right had been proved, as anybody might know it would be, still it was a trial, and people needed to eat more and better under trials than at any other time. "You may not feel inclined for victuals; but there's the danger! A body's body must be supported, whether or no."

Meanwhile, Joseph and his guests sat on the veranda, in the still, mild air. He drew his chair near to Philip's, their hands closed upon each other, and they were entirely happy in the tender and perfect manly love which united them. Madeline sat in front, with a nimbus of sunshine around her hair, feeling also the embarrassment of speech at such a moment, yet bravely endeavoring to gossip with Lucy on other matters. But Elwood's face, so bright

993

that it became almost beautiful, caught her eye: she glanced at Philip, who answered with a smile; then at Lucy, whose cheek bloomed with the loveliest color; and, rising without a word, she went to the latter and embraced her.

Then, stretching her hand to Elwood, she said: "Forgive me, both of you, for showing how glad I am!"

"Philip!" Joseph cried, as the truth flashed upon him; "life is not always unjust! It is we who are impatient."

They both arose and gave hands of congratulation; and Elwood, though so deeply moved that he scarcely trusted himself to speak, was so frankly proud and happy,—so purely and honestly man in such a sacred moment,—that Lucy's heart swelled with an equally proud recognition of his feeling. Their eyes met, and no memory of a mistaken Past could ever again come like a cloud across the light of their mutual faith.

"The day was blessed already," said Philip; "but this makes it perfect."

No one knew how the time went by, or could afterwards recall much that was said. Rachel Miller, with many apologies, summoned them to a sumptuous meal; and when the moon hung chill and clear above the creeping mists of the valley, they parted.

The next evening, Joseph went to Philip at the Forge. It was well that he should breathe another atmosphere, and dwell, for a little while, within walls where no ghosts of his former life wandered. Madeline, the most hospitably observant of hostesses, seemed to have planned the arrangements solely for his and Philip's intercourse. The short evening of the country was not half over, before she sent them to Philip's room, where a genial wood-fire prattled and flickered on the hearth, with two easy-chairs before it.

Philip lighted a pipe and they sat down. "Now, Joseph," said he, "I'll answer 'Yes!' to the question in your mind."

"You have been talking with Bishop, Philip?"

"No; but I won't mystify you. As I rode up the valley, I saw you two standing on the hill, and could easily guess the rest. A large estate in this country is only an imaginary fortune. You are not so much of a farmer, Joseph, that it will cut you to the heart and make you dream of ruin to part with a few fields; if you were, I should say get that weakness out of you at once! A man should possess his property, not be possessed by it."

"You are right," Joseph answered; "I have been fighting against an inherited feeling."

"The only question is, will the sale of those fifty acres relieve you of all present embarrassments?"

"So far, Philip, that a new mortgage of about half the amount will cover what remains."

"Bravo!" cried Philip. "This is better than I thought. Mr. Hopeton is looking for sure, steady investments, and will furnish whatever you need. So there is no danger of foreclosure."

"Things seem to shape themselves almost too easily now," Joseph answered. "I see the old, mechanical routine of my life coming back: it should be enough for me, but it is not; can you tell me why, Philip?"

"Yes: it never was enough. The most of our neighbors are cases of arrested development. Their intellectual nature only takes so many marks, like a horse's teeth; there is a point early in their lives, where its form becomes fixed. There is neither the external influence, nor the inward necessity, to drive them a step further. They find the Sphinx dangerous, and keep out of her way. Of course, as soon as they passively begin, to accept what is, all that was fluent or plastic in them soon hardens into the old moulds. Now, I am not very wise, but this appears to me to be truth; that life is a grand centrifugal force, forever growing from a wider circle towards one that is still wider. Your stationary men may be necessary, and even serviceable; but to me—and to you, Joseph—there is neither joy nor peace except in some kind of growth."

"If we could be always sure of the direction!" Joseph sighed.

"That's the point!" Philip eagerly continued. "If we stop to consider danger in advance, we should never venture a step. A movement is always clear after it has been made, not often before. It is enough to test one's intention; unless we are tolerably bad, something guides us, and adjusts the consequences of our acts. Why, we are like spiders, in the midst of a million gossamer threads, which we are all the time spinning without knowing it! Who are to measure our lives for us? Not other men with other necessities! and so we come back to the same point again, where I started. Looking back now, can you see no gain in your mistake?"

"Yes, a gain I can never lose. I begin to think that haste and weakness also are vices, and deserve to be punished. It was a dainty, effeminate soul you found, Philip,—a moral and spiritual Sybarite, I should say now. I must have expected to lie on rose-leaves, and it was right that I should find thorns."

"I think," said Philip, "the world needs a new code of ethics. We must cure the unfortunate tendencies of some qualities that seem good, and extract the good from others that seem evil. But it would need more than a Luther for such a Reformation. I confess I am puzzled, when I attempt to study moral causes and consequences in men's lives. It is nothing but a tangle, when I take them collectively. What if each of us were, as I half suspect, as independent as a planet, yet all held together in one immense system? Then the central force must be our close dependence on God, as I have learned to feel it through you."

"Through me!" Joseph exclaimed.

"Do you suppose we can be so near each other without giving and taking? Let us not try to get upon a common ground of faith or action: it is a thousand times more delightful to discover that we now and then reach the same point by different paths. This reminds me, Joseph, that our paths ought to separate now, for a while. It is you who should leave,—but only to come back again, 'in the fulness of time.' Heaven knows, I am merciless to myself in recommending it."

"You are right to try me. It is time that I should know something of the world. But to leave, now—so immediately—"

"It will make no difference," said Philip. "Whether you go or stay, there will be stories afloat. The bolder plan is the better."

The subject was renewed the next morning at breakfast. Madeline heartily seconded Philip's counsel, and took a lively part in the discussion.

"We were in Europe as children," she said to Joseph, "and I have very clear and delightful memories of the travel."

"I was not thinking especially of Europe," he answered. "I am hardly prepared for such a journey. What I should wish is, not to look idly at sights and shows, but to have some active interest or employment, which would bring me into contact with men. Philip knows my purpose."

"Then," said Madeline, "why not hunt on Philip's trail? I have no doubt you can track him from Texas to the Pacific by the traditions of his wild pranks and adventures! How I should enjoy getting hold of a few chapters of his history!"

"Madeline, you are a genius!" Philip cried. "How could I have forgotten Wilder's letter, a fortnight ago, you remember? One need not be a practical geologist to make the business report he wants; but Joseph has read enough to take hold, with the aid of the books I can give him! If it is not too late!"

"I was not thinking of that, Philip," Madeline answered. "Did you not say that the place was—"

She hesitated. "Dangerous?" said Philip. "Yes. But if Joseph goes there, he will come back to us again."

"O, don't invoke misfortune in that way!"

"Neither do I," he gravely replied; "but I can see the shadow of Joseph's life thrown ahead, as I can see my own."

"I think I should like to be sent into danger," said Joseph.

Philip smiled: "As if you had not just escaped the greatest! Well,—it was Madeline's guess which most helped to avert it, and now it is her chance word which will probably send you into another one."

Joseph looked up in astonishment. "I don't understand you, Philip," he said.

"O Philip!" cried Madeline.

"I had really forgotten," he answered, "that you knew nothing of the course by which we reached your defence. Madeline first suggested to me that the poison was sometimes used as a cosmetic, and on this hint, with Mr. Blessing's help, the truth was discovered."

"And I did not know how much I owe to you!" Joseph, exclaimed, turning towards her.

"Do not thank me," she said, "for Philip thinks the fortunate guess may be balanced by an evil one."

"No, no!" Joseph protested, noticing the slight tremble in her voice; "I will take it as a good omen. Now I know that danger will pass me by, if it comes!"

"If your experience should be anything like mine," said Philip, "you will only recognize the danger when you can turn and look back at it. But, come! Madeline has less superstition in her nature than she would have us believe. Wilder's offer is just the thing; I have his letter on file, and will write to him at once. Let us go down to my office at the Forge!"

The letter was from a capitalist who had an interest in several mines in Arizona and Nevada. He was not satisfied with the returns, and wished to send a private, confidential agent to those regions, to examine the prospects and operations of the companies and report thereupon. With the aid of a map the probable course of travel was marked out, and Joseph rejoiced at the broad field of activity and adventure which it opened to him.

He stayed with Philip a day or two longer, and every evening the fire made a cheery accompaniment to the deepest and sweetest confidences of their hearts, now pausing as if to listen, now rapidly murmuring some happy, inarticulate secret of its own. As each gradually acquired full possession of the other's past, the circles of their lives, as Philip said, were reciprocally widened; but as the horizon spread, it seemed to meet a clearer sky. Their eyes were no longer fixed on the single point of time wherein they breathed. Whatever pain remained, melted before them and behind them into atmospheres of resignation and wiser patience. One gave his courage and experience, the other his pure instinct, his faith and aspiration; and a new harmony came from the closer interfusion of sweetness and strength.

When Joseph returned home, he at once set about putting his affairs in order, and making arrangements for an absence of a year or more. It was necessary that he should come in contact with most of his neighbors, and he was made aware of their good will without knowing that it was, in many cases, a reaction from suspicion and slanderous gossip. Mr. Chaffinch had even preached a sermon, in which no name was mentioned, but everybody understood the allusion. This was considered to be perfectly right, so long as the prejudices of the people were with him, and Julia was supposed to be the pious and innocent victim of a crime. When, however, the truth had been established, many who had kept silent now denounced the sermon, and another on the deceitfulness of appearances, which Mr. Chaffinch gave on the following Sabbath, was accepted as the nearest approach to an apology consistent with his clerical dignity.

Joseph was really ignorant of these proceedings, and the quiet, self-possessed, neighborly way in which he met the people gave them a new impression of his character. Moreover, he spoke of his circumstances, when it was necessary, with a frankness unusual among them; and the natural result was that his credit was soon established on as sound a basis as ever. When, through Philip's persistence, the mission to the Pacific coast was secured, but little further time was needed to complete the arrangements. By the sacrifice of one-fourth of his land, the rest was saved, and intrusted to good hands during his absence. Philip, in the mean time, had fortified him with as many hints and instructions as possible, and he was ready, with a light heart and a full head, to set out upon the long and uncertain journey.

CHAPTER XXXII. LETTERS.

I. Joseph to Philip.

Camp ——, Arizona, October 19, 1868.

Since I wrote to you from Prescott, dear Philip, three months have passed, and I have had no certain means of sending you another letter. There was, first, Mr. Wilder's interest at ——, the place hard to reach, and the business difficult to investigate. It was not so easy, even with the help of your notes, to connect the geology of books with the geology of nature; these rough hills don't at all resemble the clean drawings of strata. However, I have learned all the more rapidly by not assuming to know much, and the report I sent contained a great deal more than my own personal experience. The duty was irksome enough, at times; I have been tempted by the evil spirits of ignorance, indolence, and weariness, and I verily believe that the fear of failing to make good your guaranty for my capacity was the spur which kept me from giving way. Now, habit is beginning to help me, and, moreover, my own ambition has something to stand on.

I had scarcely finished and forwarded my first superficial account of the business as it appeared to me, when a chance suddenly offered of joining a party of prospectors, some of whom I had already met: as you know, we get acquainted in little time, and with no introductions in these parts. They were bound, first, for some little-known regions in Eastern Nevada, and then, passing a point which Mr. Wilder wished me to visit (and which I could not have reached so directly from any other quarter), they meant to finish the journey at Austin. It was an opportunity I could not let go, though I will admit to you, Philip, that I also hoped to overtake the adventures, which had seemed to recede from me, rainbow-fashion, as I went on.

Some of the party were old Rocky Mountain men, as wary as courageous; yet we passed through one or two straits which tested all their endurance and invention. I won't say how I stood the test; perhaps I ought to be satisfied that I came through to the end, and am now alive and cheerful. To be sure, there are many other ways of measuring our strength. This experience wouldn't help me the least in a discussion of principles, or in organizing any of the machinery of society. It is rather like going back to the first ages of mankind, and being tried in the struggle for existence. To me, that is a great deal. I feel as if I had been taken out of civilization and set back towards the beginning, in order to work my way up again.

But what is the practical result of this journey? you will ask. I can hardly tell, at present: if I were to state that I have been acting on your system of life rather than my own,—that is, making ventures without any certainty of the consequences,—I think you would shake your head. Nevertheless, in these ten months of absence I have come out of my old skin and am a livelier snake than you ever knew me to be. No, I am wrong; it is hardly a venture after all, and my self-glorification is out of place. I have the prospect of winning a great deal where a very little has been staked, and the most timid man in the world might readily go that far. Again you will shake your head; you remember "The Amaranth." How I should like to hear what has become of that fearful and wonderful speculation!

Pray give me news of Mr. Blessing. All those matters seem to lie so far behind me, that they look differently to my eyes. Somehow, I can't keep the old impressions; I even begin to forget them. You said, Philip, that he was not intentionally dishonest, and something tells me you are right. We learn men's characters rapidly in this rough school, because we cannot get away from the close, rough, naked contact. What surprises me is that the knowledge is not only good for present and future use, but that I can take it with me into my past life. One weakness is left, and you will understand it. I blush to myself,—I am ashamed of my early innocence and ignorance. This is wrong; yet, Philip, I seem to have been so unmanly,—at least so unmasculine! I looked for love, and fidelity, and all the virtues, on the surface of life; believed that a gentle tongue was the sign of a tender heart; felt a wound when some strong and positive, yet differently moulded being approached me! Now, here are fellows prickly as a cactus, with something at the core as true and tender as you will find in a woman's heart. They would stake their lives for me sooner than some persons (whom we know) would lend me a hundred dollars, without security! Even your speculator, whom I have met in every form, is by no means the purely mercenary and dangerous man I had supposed.

In short, Philip, I am on very good terms with human nature; the other nature does not suit me so well. It is a grand thing to look down into the cañon of the Colorado, or to see a range of perfectly clear and shining snow-peaks across the dry sage-plains; but oh, for one acre of our green meadows! I dreamed of them, and the clover-fields, and the woods and running streams, through the terrific heat of the Nevada deserts, until the tears came. It is nearly a year since I left home: I should think it fifty years!

With this mail goes another report to Mr. Wilder. In three or four months my task will be at an end, and I shall then be free to return. Will you welcome the brown-faced, full bearded man, broad in cheeks and shoulders, as you would the—but how did I use to look, Philip? It was a younger brother you know; but he has bequeathed all of his love, and more, to the older.

II. Philip To Joseph.

Coventry Forge; Christmas Day.

When Madeline hung a wreath of holly around your photograph this morning, I said to it as I say now: "A merry Christmas, Joseph, wherever you are!" It is a calm sunny day, and my view, as you know, reaches much further through the leafless trees; but only the meadow on the right is green. You, on the contrary, are enjoying something as near to Paradise in color, and atmosphere, and temperature (if you are, as I guess, in Southern California), as you will ever be likely to see.

Yes, I will welcome the new man, although I shall see more of the old one in him than you perhaps think,—nor would I have it otherwise.

We don't change the bases of our lives, after all: the forces are differently combined, otherwise developed, but they hang, I fancy, to the same roots. Nay, I'll leave preaching until I have you again at the old fireside. You want news from home, and no miserable little particular is unimportant. I've been there, and know what kind of letters are welcome.

The neighborhood (I like to hover around a while, before alighting) is still a land where all things always seem the same. The trains run up and down our valley, carrying a little of the world boxed up in shabby cars, but leaving no mark behind. In another year the people will begin to visit the city more frequently; in still another, the city people will find their way to us; in five years, population will increase and property will rise in value. This is my estimate, based on a plentiful experience.

Last week, Madeline and I attended the wedding of Elwood Withers. It was at the Hopeton's, and had been postponed a week or two, on account of the birth of a son to our good old business-friend. There are two events for you! Elwood, who has developed, as I knew he would, into an excellent director of men and material undertakings, has an important contract on the new road to the coal regions. He showed me the plans and figures the other day, and I see the beginning of wealth in them. Lucy, who is a born lady, will save him socially and intellectually. I have never seen a more justifiable marriage. He was pale and happy, she sweetly serene and confident; and the few words he said at the breakfast, in answer to the health which Hopeton gave in his choice Vin d'Aï, made the unmarried ladies envy the bride. Really and sincerely, I came away from the house more of a Christian than I went.

You know all, dearest friend: was it not a test of my heart to see that she was intimately, fondly happy? It was hardly any more the face I once knew. I felt the change in the touch of her hand. I heard it in the first word she spoke. I did not dare to look into my heart to see if something there were really dead, for the look would have called the dead to life. I made one heroic effort, heaved a stone over the place, and sealed it down forever. Then I felt your arm on my shoulder, your hand on my breast. I was strong and joyous; Lucy, I imagined, looked at me from time to time, but with a bright face, as if she divined what I had done. Can she have ever suspected the truth?

Time is a specific administered to us for all spiritual shocks; but change of habit is better. Why may I not change in quiet as you in action? It seams to me, sometimes, as I sit alone before the fire, with the pipe-stem between my teeth, that each of us is going backward through the other's experience. You will thus prove my results as I prove yours. Then, parted as we are, I see our souls lie open to each other in equal light and warmth, and feel that the way to God lies through the love of man.

Two years ago, how all our lives were tangled! Now, with so little agency of our own, how they are flowing into smoothness and grace! Yours and mine are not yet complete, but they are no longer distorted. One disturbing, yet most pitiable, nature has been removed; Elwood, Lucy, the Hopetons, are happy; you and I are healed of our impatience. Yes, there is something outside of our own wills that works for or against us, as we may decide. If I once forgot this, it is all the clearer now.

I have forgotten one other,—Mr. Blessing. The other day I visited him in the city. I found him five blocks nearer the fashionable quarter, in a larger house. He was elegantly dressed, and wore a diamond on his bosom. He came to meet me with an open letter in his hand.

"From Mrs. Spelter, my daughter," he said, waving it with a grand air,—"an account of her presentation to the Emperor Napoleon. The dress was—let me see—blue moiré and Chantilly lace; Eugénie was quite struck with her figure and complexion."

"The world seems to treat you well," I suggested.

"Another turn of the wheel. However, it showed me what I am capable of achieving, when a strong spur is applied. In this case the spur was, as you probably guess, Mr. Held,—honor. Sir, I prevented a cataclysm! You of course know the present quotations of the Amaranth stock, but you can hardly be aware of my agency in the matter. When I went to the Oil Region with the available remnant of funds, Kanuck had fled. Although the merest tyro in geology, I selected a spot back of the river-bluffs, in a hollow of the undulating table-land, sunk a shaft, and—succeeded! It was what somebody calls an inspired guess. I telegraphed instantly to a friend, and succeeded in purchasing a moderate portion of the stock—not so much as I desired—before its value was known. As for the result, si monumentum quaris, circumspice!"

I wish I could give you an idea of the air with which he said this, standing before me with his feet in position, and his arms thrown out in the attitude of Ajax defying the lightning.

I ventured to inquire after your interest. "The shares are here, sir, and safe," he said, "worth not a cent less than twenty-five thousand dollars."

I urged him to sell them and deposit the money to your credit, but this he refused to do without your authority. There was no possibility of depreciation, he said: very well, if so, this is your time to sell. Now, as I write, it occurs to me that the telegraph may reach you. I close this, therefore, at once, and post over to the office at Oakland.

Madeline says: "A merry Christmas from me!" It is fixed in her head that you are still exposed to some mysterious danger. Come back, shame her superstition, and make happy your

PHILIP.

III. JOSEPH TO PHILIP.

SAN FRANCISCO, June 3, 1869.

Philip, Philip, I have found your valley!

After my trip to Oregon, in March, I went southward, along the western base of the Sierra Nevada, intending at first to cross the range; but falling in with an old friend of yours, a man of the mountains and the sea, of books and men, I kept company with him, on and on, until the great wedges of snow lay behind us, and only a long, low, winding pass divided us from the sands of the Colorado Desert. From the mouth of this pass I looked on a hundred miles of mountains; there were lakes glimmering below; there were groves of ilex on the hillsides, an orchard of oranges, olives, and vines in the hollow, millions of flowers hiding the earth, pure winds, fresh waters, and remoteness from all conventional society. I have never seen a landscape so broad, so bright, so beautiful!

Yes, but we will only go there on one of these idle epicurean journeys of which we dream, and then to enjoy the wit and wisdom of our generous friend, not to seek a refuge from the perversions of the world! For I have learned another thing, Philip: the freedom we craved is not a thing to be found in this or that place. Unless we bring it with us, we shall not find it.

The news of the decline of the Amaranth stock, in your last, does not surprise me. How fortunate that my telegraphic order arrived in season! It was in Mr. Blessing's nature to hold on; but he will surely have something left. I mean to invest half of the sum in his wife's name, in any case; for the "prospecting" of which I wrote you, last fall, was a piece of more than, ordinary luck. You must have heard of White Pine, by this time. We were the discoverers, and reaped a portion of the first harvest, which is never equal to the second; but this way of getting wealth is so incredible to me, even after I have it, that I almost fear the gold will turn into leaves or pebbles, as in the fairy tales. I shall not tell you what my share is: let me keep one secret,—nay, two,—to carry home!

More incredible than anything else is now the circumstance that we are within a week of each other. This letter, I hope, will only precede me by a fortnight. I have one or two last arrangements to make, and then the locomotive will cross the continent too slowly for my eager haste. Why should I deny it? I am homesick, body and soul. Verily, if I were to meet Mr. Chaffinch in Montgomery Street, I should fling myself upon his neck, before coming to my sober senses. Even he is no longer an antipathy: I was absurd to make one of him. I have but one left; and Eugénie's admiration of her figure and complexion does not soften it in the least.

How happy Madeline's letter made me! After I wrote to her, I would have recalled mine, at any price; for I had obeyed an impulse, and I feared foolishly. What you said of her "superstition" might have been just, I thought. But I believe that a true-hearted woman always values impulses, because she is never at a loss to understand them. So now I obey another, in sending the enclosed. Do you know that her face is as clear in my memory as yours? and as—but why should I write, when I shall so soon be with you?

CHAPTER XXXIII. ALL ARE HAPPY.

Three weeks after the date of Joseph's last letter Philip met him at the railroad station in the city. Brown, bearded, fresh, and full of joyous life after his seven days' journey across the continent, he sprang down from the platform to be caught in his friend's arms.

The next morning they went together to Mr. Blessing's residence. That gentleman still wore a crimson velvet dressing-gown, and the odor of the cigar, which he puffed in a rear room, called the library (the books were mostly Patent Office and Agricultural Reports, with Faublas and the Decamerone), breathed plainly of the Vuelte Abajo.

"My dear boy!" he cried, jumping up and extending his arms, "Asten of Asten Hall! After all your moving accidents by flood and field; back again! This is—is—what shall I say? compensation for many a blow of fate! And my brave Knight with the Iron Hand, sit down, though it be in Carthage, and let me refresh my eyes with your faces!"

"Not Carthage yet, I hope," said Joseph.

"Not quite, if I adhere strictly to facts," Mr. Blessing replied; "although it threatens to be my Third Punic War.

"There is even a slight upward tendency in the Amaranth shares, and if the company were in my hands, we should soon float upon the topmost wave. But what can I do? The Honorable Whaley and the Reverend Dr. Lellifant were retained on account of their names; Whaley made president, and I—being absent at the time developing the enterprise, not only pars magna but totus teres atque rotundus, ha! ha!—I was put off with a director's place. Now I must stand by, and see the work of my hands overthrown. But 'tis ever thus!"

He heaved a deep sigh. Philip, most heroically repressing a tendency to shriek with laughter, drew him on to state the particulars, and soon discovered, as he had already suspected, that Mr. Blessing's sanguine temperament was the real difficulty; it was still possible for him to withdraw, and secure a moderate success.

When this had been made clear, Joseph interposed.

"Mr. Blessing," said he, "I cannot forget how recklessly, in my disappointment, I charged you with dishonesty. I know also that you have not forgotten it. Will you give me an opportunity of atoning for my injustice?—not that you require it, but that I may, henceforth, have less cause for self-reproach."

"Your words are enough!" Mr. Blessing exclaimed. "I excused you long ago. You, in your pastoral seclusion—"

"But I have not been secluded for eighteen months past," said Joseph, smiling. "It is the better knowledge of men which has opened my eyes. Besides, you have no right to refuse me; it is Mrs. Blessing whom I shall have to consult."

He laid the papers on the table, explaining that half the amount realized from his shares of the Amaranth had been invested, on trust, for the benefit of Mrs. Eliza Blessing.

"You have conquered—vincisti!" cried Mr. Blessing, shedding tears. "What can I do? Generosity is so rare a virtue in the world, that it would be a crime to suppress it!"

Philip took advantage of the milder mood, and plied his arguments so skilfully that at last the exuberant pride of the De Belsain blood gave way.

"What shall I do, without an object,—a hope, a faith in possibilities?" Mr. Blessing cried. "The amount you have estimated, with Joseph's princely provision, is a competence for my old days; but how shall I fill out those days? The sword that is never drawn from the scabbard rusts."

"But," said Philip, gravely, "you forget the field for which you were destined by nature. These operations in stocks require only a low order of intellect; you were meant to lead and control multitudes of men. With your fluency of speech, your happy faculty of illustration, your power of presenting facts and probabilities, you should confine yourself exclusively to the higher arena of politics. Begin as an Alderman; then, a Member of the Assembly; then, the State Senate; then—"

"Member of Congress!" cried Mr. Blessing, rising, with flushed face and flashing eyes. "You are right! I have allowed the necessity of the moment to pull me down from my proper destiny! You are doubly right! My creature comforts once secured, I can give my time, my abilities, my power of swaying the minds of men,—come, let us withdraw, realize, consolidate, invest, at once!"

They took him at his word, and before night a future, free from want, was secured to him. While Philip and Joseph were on their way to the country by a late train, Mr. Blessing was making a speech of an hour and a half at one of the primary political meetings.

There was welcome through the valley when Joseph's arrival was known. For two or three days the neighbors flocked to the farm to see the man whose adventures, in a very marvellous form, had been circulating among them for a year past. Even Mr. Chaffinch called, and was so conciliated by his friendly reception, that he, thenceforth, placed Joseph in the ranks of those "impracticable" men, who might be nearer the truth than they seemed: it was not for us to judge.

Every evening, however, Joseph took his saddle-horse and rode up the valley to Philip's Forge. It was not only the inexpressible charm of the verdure to which he had so long been a stranger,—not only the richness of the sunset on the hills, the exquisite fragrance of the meadow-grasses in the cool air,— nay, not entirely the dear companionship of Philip which drew him thither. A sentiment so deep and powerful that it was yet unrecognized,—a hope so faint that it had not yet taken form,—was already in his heart. Philip saw, and was silent.

But, one night, when the moon hung over the landscape, edging with sparkling silver the summits of the trees below them, when the air was still and sweet and warm, and filled with the diffused murmurs of the stream, and Joseph and Madeline stood side by side, on the curving shoulder of the knoll, Philip, watching them from the open window, said to himself: "They are swiftly coming to the knowledge of each other; will it take Joseph further from my heart, or bring him nearer? It ought to fill me with perfect joy, yet there is a little sting of pain somewhere. My life had settled down so peacefully into what seemed a permanent form; with Madeline to make a home and brighten it for me, and Joseph to give me the precious intimacy of a man's love, so different from woman's, yet so pure and perfect! They have destroyed my life, although they do not guess it. Well, I must be vicariously happy, warmed in my lonely sphere by the far radiation of their nuptial bliss, seeing a faint reflection of some parts of myself in their children, nay, claiming and making them mine as well, if it is meant that my own blood should not beat in other hearts. But will this be sufficient? No! either sex is incomplete alone, and a man's full life shall be mine! Ah, you unconscious lovers, you simple-souled children, that know not what you are doing, I shall be even with you in the end! The world is a failure, God's wonderful system is imperfect, if there is not now living a noble woman to bless me with her love, strengthen me with her self-sacrifice, purify me with her sweeter and clearer faith! I will wait: but I shall find her!"

THE END.

About Author

Bayard Taylor (January 11, 1825 – December 19, 1878) was an American poet, literary critic, translator, travel author, and diplomat.

Life and work

Taylor was born on January 11, 1825, in Kennett Square in Chester County, Pennsylvania. He was the fourth son, the first to survive to maturity, of the Quaker couple, Joseph and Rebecca (née Way) Taylor. His father was a wealthy farmer. Bayard received his early instruction in an academy at West Chester, Pennsylvania, and later at nearby Unionville. At the age of seventeen, he was apprenticed to a printer in West Chester. The influential critic and editor Rufus Wilmot Griswold encouraged him to write poetry. The volume that resulted, Ximena, or the Battle of the Sierra Morena, and other Poems, was published in 1844 and dedicated to Griswold.

Using the money from his poetry and an advance for travel articles, he visited parts of England, France, Germany and Italy, making largely pedestrian tours for almost two years. He sent accounts of his travels to the Tribune, The Saturday Evening Post, and Gazette of the United States.

In 1846, a collection of his articles was published in two volumes as Views Afoot, or Europe seen with Knapsack and Staff. That publication resulted in an invitation to serve as an editorial assistant for Graham's Magazine for a few months in 1848. That same year, Horace Greeley, editor of the New York Tribune, hired Taylor and sent him to California to report on the gold rush. He returned by way of Mexico and published another two-volume collection of travel essays, El Dorado; or, Adventures in the Path of Empire (1850). Within two weeks of release, the books sold 10,000 copies in the U.S. and 30,000 in Great Britain.

In 1849 Taylor married Mary Agnew, who died of tuberculosis the next year. That same year, Taylor won a popular competition sponsored by P. T. Barnum to write an ode for the "Swedish Nightingale", singer Jenny Lind. His poem "Greetings to America" was set to music by Julius Benedict and performed by the singer at numerous concerts on her tour of the United States.

In 1851 he traveled to Egypt, where he followed the Nile River as far as 12° 30' N. He also traveled in Palestine and Mediterranean countries, writing poetry based on his experiences. Toward the end of 1852, he sailed from England to Calcutta, and then to China, where he joined the expedition of Commodore Matthew Calbraith Perry to Japan. The results of these journeys were published as A Journey to Central Africa; or, Life and Landscapes from Egypt to the Negro Kingdoms of the White Nile (1854); The Lands of the Saracen; or, Pictures of Palestine, Asia Minor, Sicily and Spain (1854); and A Visit to India, China and Japan in the Year 1853 (1855).

He returned to the U.S. on December 20, 1853, and undertook a successful public lecturer tour that extended from Maine to Wisconsin. After two years, he went to northern Europe to study Swedish life, language and literature. The trip inspired his long narrative poem Lars. His series of articles Swedish Letters to the Tribune were republished as Northern Travel: Summer and Winter Pictures (1857).

In Berlin in 1856, Taylor met the great German scientist Alexander von Humboldt, hoping to interview him for the New York Tribune. Humboldt was welcoming, and inquired whether they should speak English or German. Taylor planned to go to central Asia, where Humboldt had traveled in 1829. Taylor informed Humboldt of Washington Irving's death; Humboldt had met him in Paris. Taylor saw Humboldt again in 1857 at Potsdam.

In October 1857, he married Maria Hansen, the daughter of the Danish/German astronomer Peter Hansen. The couple spent the following winter in Greece. In 1859 Taylor returned to the American West and lectured at San Francisco.

In 1862, he was appointed to the U.S. diplomatic service as secretary of legation at St. Petersburg, and acting minister to Russia for a time during 1862-3 after the resignation of Ambassador Simon Cameron.

He published his first novel Hannah Thurston in 1863. The newspaper

The New York Times first praised him for "break new ground with such assured success". A second much longer appreciation in the same newspaper was thoroughly negative, describing "one pointless, aimless situation leading to another of the same stamp, and so on in maddening succession". It concluded: "The platitudes and puerilities which might otherwise only raise a smile, when confronted with such pompous pretensions, excite the contempt of every man who has in him the feeblest instincts of common honesty in literature." It proved successful enough for his publisher to announce another novel from him the next year.

In 1864 Taylor and his wife Maria returned to the U.S. In 1866, Taylor traveled to Colorado and made a large loop through the northern mountains on horseback with a group that included William Byers, editor of the newspaper Rocky Mountain News. His letters describing this adventure were later compiled and published as Colorado: A Summer Trip.

His late novel, Joseph and His Friend: A Story of Pennsylvania (1870), first serialized in the magazine The Atlantic, was described as a story of young man in rural Pennsylvania and "the troubles which arise from the want of a broader education and higher culture". It is believed to be based on the poets Fitz-Greene Halleck and Joseph Rodman Drake, and since the late 20th-century has been called America's first gay novel. Taylor spoke at the dedication of a monument to Halleck in his native town, Guilford, Connecticut. He said that in establishing this monument to an American poet "we symbolize the intellectual growth of the American people.... The life of the poet who sleeps here represents the long period of transition between the appearance of American poetry and the creation of an appreciative and sympathetic audience for it."

Taylor imitated and parodied the writings of various poets in Diversions of the Echo Club (London, 1873; Boston, 1876).In 1874 Taylor traveled to Iceland to report for the Tribune on the one thousandth anniversary of the first European settlement there.

During March 1878, the U.S. Senate confirmed his appointment as United States Minister to Prussia. Mark Twain, who traveled to Europe on the same ship, was envious of Taylor's command of German.

Taylor's travel writings were widely quoted by congressmen seeking to defend racial discrimination. Richard Townshend quoted passages from Taylor such as "the Chinese are morally, the most debased people on the face of the earth" and "A Chinese city is the greatest of all abominations."

A few months after arriving in Berlin, Taylor died there on December 19, 1878. His body was returned to the U.S. and buried in Kennett Square, Pennsylvania. The New York Times published his obituary on its front page, referring to him as "a great traveler, both on land and paper". Shortly after his death, Henry Wadsworth Longfellow wrote a memorial poem in Taylor's memory, at the urging of Oliver Wendell Holmes, Sr.

Legacy and honors

Cedarcroft, Taylor's home from 1859 to 1874, which he built near Kennett Square, is preserved as a National Historic Landmark.

The Bayard Taylor School was added to the National Register of Historic Places in 1988.

The Bayard Taylor Memorial Library is in Kennett Square.

Evaluations

Though he wanted to be known most as a poet, Taylor was mostly recognized as a travel writer during his lifetime. Modern critics have generally accepted him as technically skilled in verse, but lacking imagination and, ultimately, consider his work as a conventional example of 19th-century sentimentalism.

His translation of Faust, however, was recognized for its scholarly skill and remained in print through 1969. According to the 1920 edition of Encyclopedia Americana:

> It is by his translation of Faust, one of the finest attempts of the kind in any literature, that Taylor is generally known; yet as an original poet he stands well up in the second rank of Americans. His Poems of the Orient and his Pennsylvania ballads comprise his best work. His verse is finished and sonorous, but at times over-rhetorical.

According to the 1911 edition of Encyclopædia Britannica:

> Taylor's most ambitious productions in poetry— his Masque of the Gods (Boston, 1872), Prince Deukalion; a lyrical drama (Boston, 1878), The Picture of St John (Boston, 1866), Lars; a Pastoral of Norway (Boston, 1873), and The Prophet; a tragedy (Boston, 1874)— are marred by a ceaseless effort to overstrain his power. But he will be remembered by his poetic and excellent translation of Goethe's Faust (2 vols, Boston, 1870-71) in the original metres.

Taylor felt, in all truth, the torment and the ecstasy of verse; but, as a critical friend has written of him, his nature was so ardent, so full-blooded, that slight and common sensations intoxicated him, and he estimated their effect, and his power to transmit it to others, beyond the true value. He had, from the earliest period at which he began to compose, a distinct lyrical faculty: so keen indeed was his ear that he became too insistently haunted by the music of others, pre-eminently of Tennyson. But he had often a true and fine note of his own. His best short poems are The Metempsychosis of the Pine and the well-known Bedouin love-song.

In his critical essays Bayard Taylor had himself in no inconsiderable degree what he wrote of as that pure poetic insight which is the vital spirit of criticism. The most valuable of these prose dissertations are the Studies in German Literature (New York, 1879).

In Appletons' Cyclopædia of American Biography of 1889, Edmund Clarence Stedman gives the following critique:

> His poetry is striking for qualities that appeal to the ear and eye, finished, sonorous in diction and rhythm, at times too rhetorical, but rich in sound, color, and metrical effects. His early models were Byron and Shelley, and his more ambitious lyrics and dramas exhibit the latter's peculiar, often vague, spirituality. Lars, somewhat after the manner of Tennyson, is his longest and most attractive narrative poem. Prince Deukalion was designed for a masterpiece; its blank verse and choric

interludes are noble in spirit and mould. Some of Taylor's songs, oriental idyls, and the true and tender Pennsylvanian ballads, have passed into lasting favor, and show the native quality of his poetic gift. His fame rests securely upon his unequalled rendering of Faust in the original metres, of which the first and second parts appeared in 1870 and 1871. His commentary upon Part II for the first time interpreted the motive and allegory of that unique structure. (source: wikipedia)

NOTABLE WORKS

Ximena, or the Battle of the Sierra Morena, and other Poems (1844)

Views Afoot, or Europe seen with Knapsack and Staff (1846)

Rhymes of Travel: Ballads and Poems (1849)

El Dorado; or, Adventures in the Path of Empire (1850)

Romances, Lyrics, and Songs (1852)

Journey to Central Africa; or, Life and Landscapes from Egypt to the Negro Kingdoms of the White Nile, A (1854)

Lands of the Saracen; or, Pictures of Palestine, Asia Minor, Sicily and Spain, The (1854)

A visit to India, China, and Japan in the year 1853 (1855)

Lands of the Saracen; or, Pictures of Palestine, Asia Minor, Sicily and Spain, The (1855)

Poems of the Orient (Boston: Ticknor and Fields, 1855)

Poems of Home and Travel (1856)

Cyclopedia of Modern Travel (1856)

Northern Travel: Summer and Winter Pictures (1857)

View A-Foot, or Europe Seen with Knapsack and Staff (1859)

Life, Travels And Books Of Alexander Von Humboldt, The (1859)

At Home and Abroad, First Series: A Sketch-book of Life, Scenery, and Men (1859)

Cyclopaedia of Modern Travel Vol I (1861)

Prose Writings: India, China, and Japan (1862)

Travels in Greece and Russia, with an Excursion to Crete (1859)

Poet's Journal (1863)

Hanna Thurston (1863)

John Godfrey's Fortunes Related by Himself: A story of American Life (1864)

"Cruise On Lake Ladoga, A" (1864)

"The Poems of Bayard Taylor" (1865)

John Godrey's Fortunes Related By Himself - A story of American Life (1865)

The Story of Kennett (1866)

Visit To The Balearic Islands, Complete in Two Parts, A (1867)

Picture of St. John, The (1867)

Colorado: A Summer Trip (1867)

"Little Land Of Appenzell, The" (1867)

"Island of Maddalena with a Distant View of Caprera, The" (1868)

"Land Of Paoli, The" (1868)

"Catalonian Bridle-Roads" (1868)

"Kyffhauser And Its Legend, The" (1868)

By-Ways Of Europe (1869)

Joseph and His Friend: A Story of Pennsylvania (1870)

Ballad of Abraham Lincoln, The (1870)

"Sights In And Around Yedo" (1871)

Northern Travel (1871)

Japan in Our Day (1872)

Masque of the Gods, The (1872)

"Heart Of Arabia, The" (1872)

Travels in South Africa (1872)

At Home and Abroad: A Sketch-Book of Life, Scenery and Men (1872)

Diversions of the Echo Club (1873)

Lars: A Pastoral of Norway (1873)

Wonders of the Yellowstone - The Illustrated Library of Travel, Exploration and Adventure (with James Richardson) (1873)

Northern Travel: Summer and Winter Pictures - Sweden, Denmark and Lapland (1873).

Lake Regions of Central Africa (1873)

Prophet: A Tragedy, The. (1874)

Home Pastorals Ballads & Lyrics (1875)

Egypt And Iceland In The Year 1874 (1875)

Boys of Other Countries: Stories for American Boys (1876)

Echo Club and Other Literary Diversions (1876)

Picturesque Europe Part Thirty-Six (1877)

National Ode: The Memorial Freedom Poem, The (1877)

Bismarck: His Authentic Biography (1877)

"Assyrian Night-Song" (August 1877)

Prince Deukalion (1878)

Picturesque Europe (1878)

Studies in German Literature (1879)

Faust: A Tragedy translated in the Original Metres (1890)

Travels in Arabia (1892).

A school history of Germany (1882).

EDITIONS

Collected editions of his Poetical Works and his Dramatic Works were published at Boston in 1888; his Life and Letters (Boston, 2 vols., 1884) were edited by his wife and Horace Scudder.

Marie Hansen Taylor translated into German Bayard's Greece (Leipzig, 1858), Hannah Thurston (Hamburg, 1863), Story of Kennett (Gotha, 1868), Tales of Home (Berlin, 1879), Studies in German Literature (Leipzig, 1880), and notes to Faust, both parts (Leipzig, 1881). After her husband's death, she edited, with notes, his Dramatic Works (1880), and in the same year his Poems in a "Household Edition", and brought together his Critical Essays and Literary Notes. In 1885 she prepared a school edition of Lars, with notes and a sketch of its author's life.